THE WINDS OF WAR

THE BLADEBORN SAGA, BOOK FOUR

T. C. EDGE

COPYRIGHT

First edition: May 2022
Cover Design by Polar Engine

Previous book in the series:

The Song of the First Blade (Book 1)
Ghost of the Shadowfort (Book 2)
An Echo of Titans (Book 3)

CONTENTS

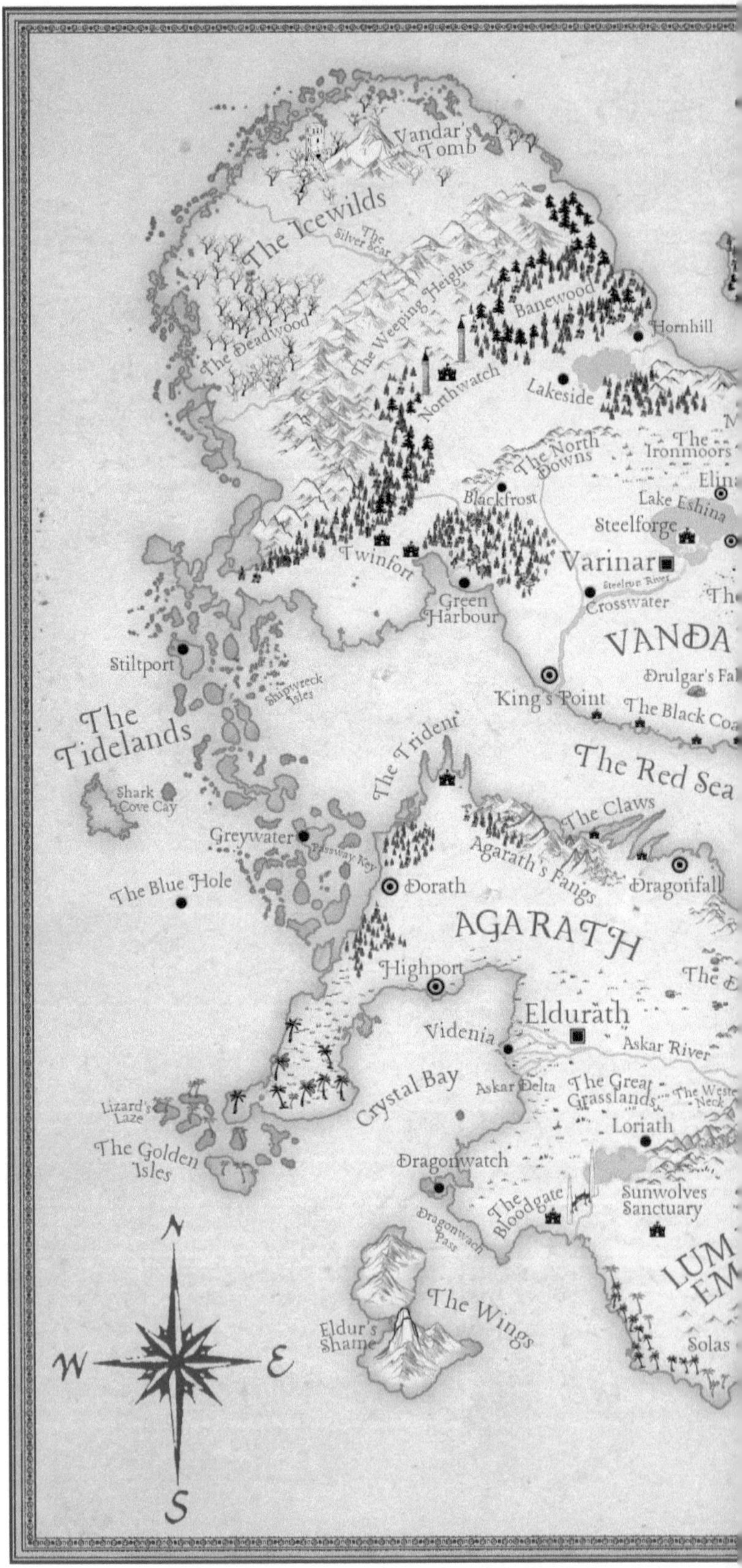

Vandar's Tomb
The Icewilds
The Silver Scar
The Deadwood
The Weeping Heights
Banewood
Hornhill
Northwatch
Lakeside
The North Downs
The Ironmoors
Blackfrost
Lake Eshina
Steelforge
Twinfort
Varinar
Steelrun River
Green Harbour
Crosswater
Stiltport
Shipwreck Isles
King's Point
Drulgar's Fa
The Black Co
The Tidelands
The Trident
The Red Sea
Shark Cove Cay
The Claws
Greywater
Passway Key
Agarath's Fangs
The Blue Hole
Dorath
Dragonfall
AGARATH
Highport
Elduråth
Videnia
Askar River
Crystal Bay
Askar Delta
The Great Grasslands
Lizard's Laze
Loriath
The Golden Isles
Dragonwatch
The Bloodgate
Sunwolves Sanctuary
Dragonwach Pass
The Wings
Eldur's Shame
Solas
N
W
E
S

100 miles
g Expanse
The Lonely Isle
The Tower of Rasalan
The Grey Keep
The Highplains
Holashan
Daari
Azure Isles
Falana
Blackhearth
Vandar's Mercy
Thalan
Bleakrock
Stormhold
Ethior
Steelport
Snowmelt Mountains
TUKOR
Rockfall
Oakshore
Northgate Castle
The Three Peaks
Broadway
RASALAN
Tulla
Tish
Windwake Islands
Gustas
The Stonehills
Ilithor
The Lowplains
Harrowmoor
The Stormy Sea
The Crescent Coast
Calmwater
Shellcrest
Whaler's Bay
Doublebay Harbour
The Links
Krarl
Eastwatch
Tukor's Pass
Redwater Bay
Lakeheart
Bhoun
Galaphan's Grounding
Horn of Aramatia
The Four Sisters
Celaph's Mire
Burning Rock
Mudport
Eagle's Perch
Dragon's Bane
Bay of Mourning
Death's Passage
Moonbear Mountain
Bloodmarsh Isles
Blademelt
The Everwood
Cloaklake
Skyloft Fort
ARAMATIA
Matia
The Aramatian Plains
Kolash
The Islands of Tellesh
Starcat Keep
Aram
PISEK
Solapian Channel
Miren
The Pisek Desert
Coast of Plenty
SOLAPIA (Sunrise Isle)
The Twin Suns
Sutrek
MARA
Sunrise Sea
Bay of Stars
The Tower of Tears
Lumara's Teardrop
Arore
Islands of the Moon

PROLOGUE

Ilith looked at the shimmering black door at the rear of the fort, cursing his mortality. "For thousands of years I have lived, Hamlyn," he said, in a voice so weak it could scarcely reach his friend's ears, "and yet there is so much I haven't done."

"You have done more than anyone who has ever lived, Ilith," Hamlyn assured him. "This world we live in was built by *you*. Your legacy will last forever."

Ilith smiled wanly. "You helped, my friend. I could not take all the credit, nor done it without you." He had another look at the door, his latest creation, and most troublesome to complete. It had taken long years of work, years he no longer had. *My body falters,* he thought, blinking. *I see the light dimming, even now.* "Take me back to my chair, Hamlyn," he said. "I must rest."

"Yes, my lord."

They turned away from the glistening door and moved through the vastness of his refuge, built high up in the northern heights of the Hammersong Mountains. Hamlyn lent Ilith his arm for support, helping him along. *I cannot even walk by myself,* Ilith thought, as they tottered through the cavernous halls, past the warm glow of firelight, burning mournfully on the walls. His decline had been swift these last years, and swifter still these last months, leaving him to lament these projects unfinished. *I was meant to connect all the north, bring us closer together than ever.* Alas, he had no time for that now. *Time,* he thought. *Once a blessing, now a curse. And mine is running so thin.*

They came to the library, its shelves stacked high with leather-bound books. Though the refuge was largely unfurnished and unfinished, Ilith had made it a priority to complete this particular room first. It had more of a lived-in feel, and that smell of leather and parchment was most comforting to him. He smiled as Hamlyn helped him to his chair, a worn old thing he'd had brought from Ilithor. "Thank you, my friend. Join me. Sit. Smoke. You know how I like the smell."

Hamlyn gave a polite smile. Long years he'd served at Ilith's side, one of the first to join him after the fall of the gods. There was no one more loyal and faithful, no one more skilled in the magical arts. "I shall fetch my pipe, my lord. It is in my bedchamber, I believe."

Ilith awaited his return with a book in his lap, idly turning pages, taking little in. After several minutes he heard footsteps and raised his eyes. It wasn't Hamlyn, unless the man had grown a long head of golden-grey hair and decided to don a dress. Through rheumy eyes he blinked at her. "Thala?"

"King Ilith." The Queen of Rasalan stepped into the library, still radiant in her dotage. She wore blue and gold as was her habit, and clasped at her chest a book.

Ilith peered at it. "Another for my library?"

She shook her head, silent. "For another," she told him. She moved to a table and set the book aside. Thala had always confounded him with her riddles and yet he would not have it any other way. She took his withered hand. "You look well, Ilith."

"And you lie, Thala." He smiled up at her through wrinkled lips. "I know how I look, and *well* is not the word I would use. I suppose you being here confirms it. I am to die, then?"

She could not answer that, he knew, but her silence told him all he needed to know.

"Well…it's not unexpected." He squeezed her fingers. "It's good to see you, one last time. Can you tell me at least how long I have?"

"Not long," she whispered, squeezing back. "You should call upon your sons and loved ones. You should not be alone at this time."

"I'm not alone, Thala. Hamlyn is here, and others." He withdrew his hand from hers. "Please, sit with me. Have a cup of wine."

She stood and moved to a side table. "Would you like one?"

"Will it be my last chance?" He chuckled before she might answer. Ilith knew well enough that Thala didn't like to discuss what she glimpsed in her master's eye. He'd sensed she knew how and when and where he would die for decades, and yet not once would she tell him. *And her coming here is telling*, he thought. *Though perhaps it isn't just for me…*

He looked at the book once more as Thala passed him his cup. "That doesn't look like light reading, Thala," he observed. The book was large and bound in dark brown leather, many hundreds of pages thick, with ornate silver claspings. "A diary, is it? Only a woman who's lived as long as you could possibly fill such pages."

She settled into an upholstered armchair, sitting as regally as ever. "Do not trouble yourself about the book, Ilith," she said. "I would sooner hear of your latest work. This door to Ilithor you've been building. That is magic beyond anything you've done before."

"Magic enough to kill me," Ilith said blithely, sipping his drink. There was truth in that as well. "It took much out of me, Thala, completing the passage. I only wish I could have done more."

"You've done enough. More than enough."

"There is always more than more than enough." Ilith smiled, then sighed. "When one reaches the end, he wonders whether his life was all it could have been. Tukor blessed me with power, and his Hammer. Have I done all I could with it? Might another have done more?"

"Ilith…"

"I know." He raised a withered hand in apology. "I grow morose, and too reflective. I ought to rejoice of a life well lived."

"A hundred lives well lived," Thala corrected. "A hundred full lives, bursting with creation. Without you this world of ours would be a graveyard compared to what it has become. You have made it grand, filled it with great cities and monuments, and still your magic surprises me. So please, let's hear less of this doubt and melancholy. Speak to me of things that are good, Ilith. Let us share in our stories, as we once did."

And so they did, telling of tidings from their kingdoms and nations, speaking of the good that was being done, reminiscing on ages long since passed and the famed friends who'd passed on with them. They drank all the while, drank and laughed, as they used to when they were younger. Time passed with as much alacrity as Ilith had come to expect these last years, flitting by far too fast. Only after several hours did he realise that Hamlyn had never returned with his pipe.

"I saw him on the way here," Thala admitted. "Told him to leave us alone, for a time." She smiled, but it was a smile tinged with sadness and grief. *This will be the last time we see one another,* Ilith knew then. *This is our last goodbye.*

The wine eventually took its toll, as Ilith settled down into his comfortable old threadbare chair, listening to the Queen of Rasalan sing. She had always been in possession of an ethereally beautiful voice. For an hour more she sang of love and glory and duty and loss, songs both happy and sad, heroic and hopeful. In different tongues she sang, moving between dialects spoken across the north, some low and brooding, others high and harmonious, all beautiful when rendered from her lips.

Ilith sat there, listening, as she took him away into other worlds. Once or twice he felt tears running down his cheeks, so sweet were some of her melodies, and once or twice he drifted away into his dreams, but each time he awoke again, there she was, still singing.

Until the last time, when his eyes broke open, and he saw Thala standing across the room, with Hamlyn.

All was silent but for their whispered voices. He saw a frown etched onto his dear friend's face, as Thala handed him the book she'd brought, and knew that she was asking something of him, something Hamlyn did not understand.

"....your task, and your purpose, Hamlyn," Ilith heard her say. "It will not be easy, nor pleasant, but I trust only you to see it done."

"Yes, Queen Thala." Hamlyn made to open the book, but Thala reached out a hand to stop him.

"No, not yet," she whispered. "The time has not yet come."

Ilith watched through the crack between his eyelids, as Hamlyn dropped his head into a bow. "I shall do as you command, my queen."

"Good." She touched his cheek, softly, with her palm. "We shall talk on this more later."

Ilith chose not to stir, not to stand, not to ask what they'd been discussing. *This is Thala*, he only thought. *Wisest of us all, the Far-Seeing Queen. I am but a humble builder and blacksmith. Who am I to question her?* So he didn't. Instead he shut his eyes once more, and slept, drifting back into his dreams.

Three days later, surrounded by friends and family, Ilith, the first

King of Tukor, passed away in his bed. He said his goodbyes to each in turn, holding hands, whispering comforts. Hamlyn stood aside, a look of great sorrow etched onto his face. When it came time for him to step forward for his final goodbye, Ilith took his hand, drawing him close. "Whatever she asked of you," he whispered, "you must do. Never question her, Hamlyn. Never ask for more than she is willing to say. There is no light in this world brighter than Thala. Let that light guide you, dear friend, as it guides us all."

And so Ilith did pass, there beneath the gaze of those he loved most. His eldest son Varyth would now take the throne, and long may he reign. A son he'd named for the old friend he'd lost long ago.

For Varin, who he would now join.

1

Jonik

3,300 Years Later…

The deck of *Invincible Iris* was a clatter of noise as the sails were furled and anchor dropped some hundred metres off the pebbly strand. Jonik stood on the quarterdeck beneath a slate grey sky, gazing out west across the turbid sea. "It's them?" he asked. "You're certain?"

Captain Gill Turner held his monocular to his right eye, his left shut tight, all crinkles and creases. He began nodding. "Aye, it's her. Can tell from that figurehead o' the naked girl on the prow. She's some three miles off, I'd say. Looks to be comin' right for us."

"Then they've seen us too." Sir Borrus Kanabar's lips split into a broad smile. "Well, what a bloody relief. I thought that storm had blown us apart for good."

Or sunk them, Jonik thought. That had been their chief concern, ever since the two ships had lost one another during a night of stormy weather five days gone. *But that figurehead…*He stared out, wrapping his fingers around the hilt of the Nightblade, his vision greatly enhanced by his blood-bond to the godly metal. It was unmistakable, the nude woman Vincent Rose had sculpted onto the front of his pristine, three-masted caravel, *One World*. The merchant was a gaudy sort and that was a gaudy figurehead, but right now, it only brought a smile to Jonik's lips. *About time,* he thought, singularly relieved. He'd missed Jack and Emeric more than he'd care to admit.

"You want the skiff lowered, lord?" Captain Turner asked him. "We could lash the ships together when they reach us, I s'pose, but the waters are choppy and that beast o' Rose's is much bigger than old Iris. She could damage us if she knocks too hard against our hull. Be safer if they drop anchor nearby and we row over to join 'em."

"*Us* row to *them*?" Sir Borrus found the idea preposterous. "Not bloody likely, Turner. The heir of House Kanabar and the bearer of the Nightblade are not to be summoned." He gave Jonik a wink. "No, *they'll* come to *us*, be sure of that."

Jonik agreed. "It's best we meet here on Iris," he said. "I want Emeric to get a measure of our new *guest*."

Borrus Kanabar grunted. "Well let's hope he counsels you wisely, and tells you to have him weighted with rocks and thrown overboard. I've told you that a hundred times already. That *Shadowmaster* of yours cannot be trusted, not for a minute. As soon as you turn your back…"

"He saved my life, Borrus," Jonik reminded him, a little tersely. The memory of it was still fresh. If Shadowmaster Gerrin hadn't turned on his two allies five nights ago, he'd have been killed for a certainty. "If he wanted me dead he could have killed me that night. I was at his mercy."

"All part of some bigger scheme," Borrus came back. "He's Janilah's catspaw, you've said. How can you trust him not to betray you later on? And with that forked-tongued snake Rose on the other ship…who's to say they're not in league together?"

It was possible, Jonik had to admit. But then, so was a great deal else. "He'll remain in chains for now. Gerrin has information I can use. But believe me, I'm never going to trust him, Borrus. You have my word on that."

"Good. Though don't forget I still have that life debt to pay…" Jonik began to protest - he'd already told Borrus that he'd not demand he pay that particular debt - but the Barrel Knight waved him off. "Yes, yes, I know. You're not going to hold it over me, but I might just go ahead and settle up anyway. I have my honour to think about, you know. It doesn't sit right that I haven't taken off someone's head for you yet. So…with all that said, maybe I'll make this a little easier for you." He looked down at his ancestral blade suggestively. "*Red Wrath* hasn't tasted Shadowmaster blood before…"

"And it won't," Jonik told him, never quite sure when the man was joking. "You're not to touch Gerrin unless I say so, Borrus. Like I say, he has information I can use." *About the mysterious Shadow King,* he thought. Only the Shadowmasters and sorcerers and senior men of the Shadowfort knew about that dark and brooding presence. And there were other matters besides that Jonik had never been privy to. *Matters Gerrin will know.* And for that alone he'd keep him alive. For now.

Turner was pulling thoughtfully at his tangled flaxen beard. "This Gerrin ain't no harm to us, not while he's chained up down in my brig, but there are *other* Shadowmasters the Barrel could slay if Red Wrath wants a taste o' their blood." He looked up at the brawny bald knight with a smile. "Plenty of chance to clear that life debt o' yours if you come with us to the Shadowfort, Sir Borrus."

"The Shadowfort is too far away," Borrus said at once. "And too damn cold by half. When we make berth at Mudport I'll be taking Sir Torvyn home to his father's castle in the Riverlands, and then adding my blade to the war."

"And if Sir Torvyn decides to come with us?" Turner probed.

Jonik watched Borrus Kanabar's reaction with interest. His holy quest to win the Shadowfort and emancipate those in chains could do with the Barrel Knight's participation, to be sure. *But I'll not ask for it,* he knew. No, the only way Sir Borrus would come with them was if his dear friend Sir Torvyn Blackshaw, whom they'd freed from the pits of Pal Palek, decided to come as well.

"Sir Torvyn is not well enough," Borrus claimed. "I'll not have him escape the dungeons of that Piseki savage only to die up there in those mountains." He turned to Jonik. "You should forget this quest of yours, boy. It'll only get you all killed."

Jonik looked the man in the eye. "You don't think I have enough men?"

"To siege a fortress?" Borrus snorted. "Typically that takes an army, and even then, it's never easy. You've got, what, a dozen?"

"Depends on whether the Sunshine Swords join us," Jonik said.

"They're the merchant's men. And sellswords besides. You can't rely on them. Whose swords have been *sworn* to you, for a certainty?"

Jonik's list was admittedly short. "There's Emeric, Big Mo, Cabel, Sir Corbray, Sir Lenard, the Silent Suncoat...all Bladeborn, all sworn to me by oath. Hopefully Rose's Bladeborn bodyguards Kazil and Harden will come as well. Neither of them like him, Harden especially, and if we summon some way to pay them…" He shrugged. That would be another challenge, because right now they were relying on Vincent Rose's patronage, and how long would that last?

"So six for sure," Borrus said. "Maybe eight if you find some coin."

"Nine," Turner said. "Don't forget Lord Jonik himself. And he counts for a small army, what with that misty black blade o' his."

Jonik went on. "If Sansullio and the Sunshine Swords join us, we'll have another dozen," he said. "They're not Bladeborn, but they're well trained and lethal, as you know."

Borrus gave that something of a begrudging nod. He didn't think much of non-Bladeborn warriors, but Sansullio and his men had proven themselves gifted when storming Pal Palek's desert fortress some weeks past.

"There's Brown Mouth too," added Turner. "And Jack, he's been getting handy with the blade."

And Devin and Soft Sid, Jonik might have said, but he was loathe to include men who weren't properly trained. Brown Mouth Braxton had fought under Taynar banners in the last war and Jack o' the Marsh had killed his first man when they'd freed the prisoners from the pits, but still…neither would last long against true Bladeborn fighters, and every assassin groomed up in the Shadowfort had Varin blood in their veins. Not always the strongest doses, no, but Bladeborn blood all the same.

Borrus seemed to have the same thought. "Forget the non-Bladeborn," he said. "They'll only get in the way. Not the Sunshine Swords - I admit they're handy - but Braxton, Jack, Sid, the rest. If you want some extra meat to distract a few of your foes, hire cheap sellswords somewhere, don't put your own friends at risk."

"I don't mean to, Borrus."

Borrus grunted, happy to be agreed with. "Then you're smarter than you look." He clapped Jonik on the shoulder. "Still, my advice stands. Give up on this folly. You'll have twenty men at best, and that's no number to take a fortress."

Not by traditional means, Jonik thought, but the Shadowfort was no traditional fortress. Accessing it with an army was almost impossible, what with the snaking paths and treacherous routes that cut and clawed their way through the mountains, and bringing siege weapons to knock down the gates even more so. If they were going to get in, it would be by subterfuge. *It'll be down to me,* Jonik knew. He was the only one who knew the way, the only one who knew the fortress, the only one who bore a Blade of Vandar. Just how he'd do it…well, that was something he was yet to figure out. And it made the sight of One World, and the imminent return of Emeric Manfrey, in particular, all the more comforting.

The ship didn't take long to reach them. Soon voices could be heard ringing out across the restless waters, passing between One World and Invincible Iris as friends old and new gathered at the gunwales in greeting. Jonik smiled as he saw Brown Mouth Braxton half way up the mainmast, shaking his fist and hollering in triumph. Emeric was at the wheel, calm as ever, Jack and young Devin side by side at the bow, arms over one another's shoulders, laughing and waving and cheering. Vincent Rose was absent; Jonik hoped he'd suffered some mishap and gone overboard during the storm, but thought it unlikely. *He's probably below decks with those Lumaran twins,* he thought bitterly, though the sourness didn't last long when he saw Sansullio's wide white smile, the tall and graceful Sunshine Sword captain waving to him fondly as he joined Emeric at the helm.

And there were others, too. Ageing Sir Corbray Walsh, with his brittle grey hair and excessively seamed face. Young Sir Lenard Borrington, eager and ever-grateful, whose father Randall was one of the most powerful lords of the North Downs of Vandar. The Silent Suncoat, standing with that intense look on his face in his tattered golden cloak. Each of them looked well restored from their long incarcerations in the pits, and more robust than Jonik had seen them last. *With luck Emeric has been training with them, honing their skills,* he thought. So long without godsteel was sure to dull a knight's edge, and it was imperative they sharpen them all up again before they reached harbour in the north.

Within minutes Rose's broad-decked caravel was resting at anchor some thirty metres to port and a rowboat was being lowered to the waters to convey a small party across. The weather was blustery, humid and warm, the skies packed hard with unbroken cloud. They'd made little progress over the last five days, fighting the winds and tides as they'd continued northward off the eastern coast of Aramatia.

The shore off which the ships had settled was not, however, the continental coastline, but one of the westernmost islands of the Telleshi Isles, and not one of the most hospitable to look at it. Rocky and rugged, it rose up beyond the pebbly beach into a formation of scarps and sparsely wooded hills, cloaked in a heavy grey fog. The Telleshis were like that, Turner had told him. Some were unsightly and uninhabitable, with high cliffs and secret coves where pirates made their dens. Others were rather more exotic, with jungles and sandy beaches fringed with palms, clean water lakes and rolling hills where settlements had been erected by the many vagrants and wanderers and lost souls who sought to leave their former lives behind.

And best we not linger here, Jonik thought, *else the men might start getting ideas.* For that reason alone, this cheerless coastline was welcome. A more appealing land might have turned a few heads.

It was Emeric Manfrey who was first to climb up from the skiff and join them on deck, arriving in his dark green cloak and fading leathers, with Braxton, Jack o' the Marsh, Harden of the Ironmoors, and Sansullio following right behind. An exchange of greetings and smiles and handshakes took place before Sansullio, moving with that long-limbed graceful gait of his, glided across the deck to go check on his men.

"No Rose?" Sir Borrus asked. He turned his eyes to Harden. "Your master didn't want to join us?"

The grim-faced sellsword snorted. "Vincent Rose is no master of mine."

"Your employer then. Let's not split hairs, man. You know what I meant."

"He's indisposed," Harden said. He was typical of the Ironmoorers, hard and mirthless, with grey hair, a grey beard, grey skin and a grey disposition. Borrus seemed to have some dislike for the men of the Ironmoors - his own Riverlanders were of a wildly different sort - though Jonik liked Harden well enough. He felt honest so far as sellswords went. "Been spending half his time in his cabin with them twins. Asked me to come on over in his stead."

Good, thought Jonik. He could do without dealing with the oily merchant today. "How are the patients?" he asked, directing the question at Emeric. The larger ship was better equipped to convey the ill and infirm, so most of those they'd freed from Pal Palek's pits had travelled under Emeric's steady care.

"Improving, mostly," the exiled lord said. "We lost one man two days ago - one of the oldest whose name we never got. He died peacefully, and in his sleep. Otherwise no losses, and the Bladeborn are beginning to spar."

As hoped, Jonik thought, nodding. "Same with Cabel and Maurice," he said, gesturing toward the pair. Cabel was watching with those wily dark eyes of his, perched like a cat on a nearby bulwark, while Maurice - who they also called Big Mo - bellowed words of greeting across to Kazil on the other ship. The two had struck up something of a friendship at Vincent Rose's manor on Goldwater Row on account of their shared Piseki heritage. It was more obvious with Kazil, with that twisting black hair that covered much of his body, but Maurice could claim some Piseki on his mother's side and could speak the language too. "I've had them practising with sparring swords the last couple of days," Jonik went on. "Both are eager to train with godsteel, but without proper armour…"

"Too dangerous," Emeric agreed. "We can talk about trying to get our hands on some godsteel armour later, but until then it's practice swords, unless running solo drills." His keen golden eyes scanned the deck. "Has Sir Torvyn been well enough to pick up a sword yet?"

"No," said Borrus at once. He was fiercely protective of his friend, and clearly had a sense that they were trying to get the old Varin Knight to join them. "He's still regaining his strength. He was in those pits for almost two decades, Manfrey. You can hardly expect him to be dancing around on deck after a few short weeks in the sun."

"Of course." Emeric rubbed his square, black-bearded jaw, the hair short and neatly trimmed. "I don't see him. Is he below?"

"In his cabin," Borrus said. "Captain Turner gave him some books to read. It helps remind him of the world he left behind. All that time in the darkness…it can leave blank spaces in a man."

"It's the same with those on One World," Jack o' the Marsh said. "The ones who were locked away longest, especially. Vincent has loads of books aboard so I've been handing them out, to get the cogs turning in the patients' heads. Lord Leyton Greymont is recovering some of his wits." Ranulf Shackton had referred to him as Lord Cluck at first, Jonik remembered, though they'd soon found out who he really was. "He doesn't make those bird noises so much anymore. And Katheryn Merrymarsh doesn't moan so much either." Ranulf's name for her had been the Moaning Maid. It was nice to hear that those nicknames were no longer so applicable.

"She likes puzzles too," Braxton put in. "I draw them out for her.

Like mazes and such. She has to find the way to the middle. And word search games as well. Helps sharpen up her mind."

It felt too nice a sentiment for anyone to make a jest. Even Turner bit his tongue. "That's sweet o' you, Brown," was all he said. "What o' that one related to King Janilah? Some older cousin or some such, was he?"

"He's still breathing, but hardly says a word," said Emeric. "Thought he might die during the storm…those seas became fairly rough…but he pulled through in the end. He's tougher than I thought."

"Do we know who he is yet?" Jonik asked. Even Ranulf hadn't been certain before he'd left them in Aram. The only reason they thought the man was a relation of Janilah's was because Pal Palek had boasted as such when he led Ranulf down into his cell.

"Jack's been trying to get him to open up," Emeric informed them, "but with little success so far. It could be Pal Palek was lying. Either way, it doesn't matter. That cloak we found him in suggests he was an Emerald Guard once, but we can't be sure, and he's far too old to offer us any help anyway. We'll see about sending him to Ilithor when we make harbour at the nearest port. But it could well be that he dies before we get there." He looked once more across the ship. "You've men missing," he realised. "Those three sellswords we found in Sutrek. Benji, Mugs, Trigger. Are they below?"

"Aye, one of them is," said Turner.

"And the other two?"

"They're below as well," Borrus said, with a devilish smirk. He gestured over the side of the gunwale. "*Far* below."

"Daarl's Domain?" asked Braxton, frowning. He rubbed the short rough bristles of his lopsided jaw. "How'd they die?"

"Not well, to look at their corpses," said Borrus. He gave Jonik a look. "Perhaps it's not my place to say."

"We share no secrets here," Jonik announced. He was done with secrets, he'd decided, and already everyone aboard Iris knew most of what had happened. "Go ahead and tell the tale, Borrus. In the meantime, I'll take Emeric below." He looked at the exile. "My lord."

With a curious frown etched upon his brow, Emeric followed Jonik toward the stairs and down through the belly of the beast. Jonik took him first to Captain Turner's cabin where they might be able to speak in private. It was there he told him the entirety of what had happened, leaving not a single detail out. The exiled lord listened in his fashion; calm, composed, showing no great surprise, and thinking all the while. "I'd like to meet him," he said once Jonik was done.

"That's why I brought you down here. I want you to get the measure of him." He looked the exile in the eye. "Borrus thinks it's all some ruse. That Gerrin slaughtered his two allies in a bid to get closer to me. He thinks he'll betray me."

"And what do you think?" asked Emeric. The firelight from a table lamp flickered in his golden eyes. "You're the only one here who knows the man, Jonik. Might he be telling the truth? Could he have truly turned from his order, as you did?"

Jonik pondered that, as he'd pondered it for the last five days. Five days during which he'd paid Gerrin only the briefest of visits, leaving him to fester and rot and weaken in the darkness, attended only by Soft Sid who brought him stale bread and hard cheese in meagre and miserly rations. A part of him - a small part, yes, but a part all the same - felt a little guilty for that. *He saved my life,* he thought. *No matter the reason, he cut off Valtho's head and put his blade through Parsivor's neck, and I've chained him to a wall with nothing but rats for company, starved of light and starved of food and starved of company too.*

Eventually, Jonik gave the only answer he could. "I don't know. Gerrin lied to me all my life. How can I know whether or not he's lying now?"

"He killed a senior Shadowknight," Emeric said, thoughtful, "and this dark mage Parsivor as well. Would that not make his life forfeit in the eyes of the order?"

"It would if they found out. But he was never serving the order, Emeric. Janilah was his true master."

Emeric nodded, tapping a finger on Turner's stained wooden desk. There was still a faint scent of pestilence in the air, from the sickness that Parsivor had spread. His nostrils flared. "This powder the sorcerer threw onto you. Have you ever heard of anything like that before?"

"Never." Jonik remembered the burning in his eyes and throat, blinding him, strangling him, making him *visible*. He remembered the colours, the little tiny motes of dust sparkling like a nebula, red and gold and silver and blue, bright and blinding as they clung to his cloak and hair and skin. *Even with the power of the Nightblade flooding through my veins, they could see me,* he thought. A cold shiver climbed up his spine. "They must have prepared it just for me," he said. "I'll know better to avoid it next time."

"A trick of Parsivor's creation, do you think?"

Jonik understood what he was meaning to say. *Can another mage make it too?* "I'm unsure," was his only answer. "It's one of many questions I hope to pose to Gerrin, though one of many answers I'll be unable to trust." His concern was clear. If they had more of that powder at the Shadowfort, it would neuter the Nightblade's magic.

Emeric studied him in that measured way of his. "The safest thing to do is to kill him, and kill him now. I know you want information, but if you cannot trust it, it's more than worthless. It's dangerous. It will confuse you at best and lead you into peril at worst. Kill him and you'll rid yourself of that choice." He paused, studying him. "But I can see already that you won't."

"And I can see you wouldn't advise it," Jonik returned.

Emeric's handsome smile broke out. "Not until I've had a chance to meet him myself, no. But so far as I can tell, there is a part of you that believes him."

Can I deny that, Jonik wondered? *Is that not the true reason I've refused to confront him? Because I know there was some truth to what he said.* Suddenly, Shadowmaster Gerrin's words from five nights past came back to him. "*I hoped to be a better father to you, Jonik,*" he had told him. "*I know you won't believe me, but I never wanted this. I was bound by service, by oath, and had no choice. There's much about my past that you do not know.*"

Much, he knew, *much and much and more.* Gerrin had spoken of being a tool of evil men, performing darkness on their behalf, bound to oaths and terms of service that had shackled him to their will. Jonik might have said all that himself for the things he'd been forced to do. *But is that all part of his ploy?* he wondered. *He knows me, he knows my weaknesses, he understands the shadows that lurk within.* Was Gerrin playing off those to win his trust, or being sincere in all he said. *How can I ever know?* he despaired. *If he cannot prove his loyalty by saving my life, how else can he do it? How?*

Emeric put his hand on Jonik's shoulder, drawing him from his thoughts. "Come, let me meet him. We can talk better of this once I've studied the man."

Jonik took a breath to steady himself, then led Emeric from the room, and down into the depths of the ship.

The heavy wooden door of the brig was fixed with a pair of iron bolts. There was a small stool outside. "Sometimes Sid likes to come down and sit on guard," Jonik told Emeric.

"To stop Gerrin getting out or stopping someone else getting in?"

"The latter. There's some…animosity toward the man, shall we say, for bringing that sickness on board. A few might want to seek retribution by breaking a bone or two."

"You've expressly ordered them not to, I assume?" Emeric asked.

"I have. And I'm sure they'd not act on it, but Sid got it into his head that he had to sit on guard, so he comes down anyway. He enjoys the duty, I think. It makes him feel important, though I'm not certain he understands the gravity of it all."

"I would imagine not. He's a sweet man Sid, but isn't going to win any prizes for his wits." Emeric reached out to take the handle of the top bolt. "Shall we?"

"After you."

The bolts were slid aside, the door pulled open to a shriek of rusted hinges. Firelight from Emeric's lamp washed into the interior, reflecting off the two inches of saltwater sloshing on the floor. A rattle of chains sounded as Gerrin stirred from his sleep. He could stand, but not quite sit, his wrists bound and chained above him to the wall. A cruel form of stress torture. *Nothing less than he deserves,* Jonik made himself think. *He did the same and worse to me, and a hundred times over…*

"Wake up, Gerrin, I've brought a friend to meet you."

The Shadowmaster blinked against the light. He looked haggard and grim, crumbs of bread caught in the bristles of his patchy greying beard. He couldn't feed himself, not chained as he was, so Sid had to do it for him. Gerrin would take that for humiliation, Jonik knew, as he would the requirement to shit and piss where he stood. A foul reek thus filled the air, and by now the rats had begun to creep. There were a couple lying dead at his feet, crushed or kicked to death as they sniffed and nibbled at him, Jonik guessed. They wouldn't be the last.

Gerrin set his grey eyes on the exile. "We've met before, my lord."

Emeric smiled, hanging the lamp on a hook on the wall. "*You've* met *me* perhaps. I only knew you as Benjy, the old Rasal sellsword. You seem rather different now, I will admit. That mage of yours was gifted."

"Parsivor had his uses."

"So I've heard." Emeric gave Jonik a glance. "This powder of his. That must have involved some complicated alchemy. The magical properties of the Blades of Vandar are not easily overcome."

"Parsivor was one of the oldest," Gerrin said. "And most corrupted. He'd darkened his soul through many experiments and that one turned out to be his last. It took the rest of his power to clothe us in our illusions, and spread the sickness he brought aboard. It was one of the reasons I waited. I needed Parsivor weakened when I made my move, else he'd not have succumbed so easily."

"So this was your plan all along?" Emeric asked. "To infiltrate our party and swear Jonik your allegiance?" He paused to judge the man, but Gerrin's eyes gave away nothing. "Why not kill Valtho and Parsivor at another time? You could have arrived at Vincent Rose's manor having already slain them. Or was it that you wanted Jonik present to see them fall?"

Gerrin wasn't going to deny it. "I hoped it might help prove my loyalty to him. Yet it gave me an opportunity to watch the boy too, see what sort of man he'd become when untethered from his chains." He turned his eyes on Jonik. "I have found myself impressed. But I understand how difficult it is to trust me, given our past. That is only natural."

I'll never trust you, Jonik thought, as the man's tortures and abuses came back to him. He could scarcely make eye contact with him still. He turned his attention to the rats on the floor. "That looks familiar," he said, gesturing. "You'll recall, won't you, Gerrin...how I was locked in a cell much smaller than this one when I was disobedient, with nothing but lice and fleas and starving rats for company."

"A standard punishment, and one every Shadowmaster inflicted on their charges. Only I let you out much sooner than the rest."

"So you say."

"So I say. And all other abuses you'll remember...each one would have been worse, much worse, with another master holding your collar."

So you say, Jonik thought again, though he gave no reply to that. The boys at the Shadowfort were not expected to become friends, but they did talk sometimes, and Jonik would see the scars, the bruises, hear of those who were having bones knitted back together, those who had even died. *I suffered, but not the worst,* he had to admit. Yet all he could whisper was, "You made my life hell."

"I did." Gerrin agreed. "I put you through years of torment, but spared you something much worse. If I'd shown too little force, or too much clemency, the others would have known. I *had* to do what I did, Jonik. Do you not see? And those times I went further…those times I pushed you harder…they were all because the council was watching. They grew suspicious of me sometimes, claimed I was being too soft. I had no choice but to become more savage to satisfy them. *No choice*, Jonik. Believe me, I suffered too."

Jonik snorted his derision. "I don't believe a word of it."

"No." Gerrin's head dropped into a slow nod. "No, and why should you? But if you'll not believe me, and you'll not trust me, why am I still alive?"

Jonik didn't answer. He turned his eyes away, as a short silence settled on that damp dim room. Emeric Manfrey ended it. "You were working for Janilah all along?" he asked. "Tell us how you came to join the Shadow Order, Sir Gerrin."

"*Sir…*" Gerrin smiled; a craggy, rare-seen thing. "I've not been called sir for many a long year, though once I was a knight, that's true. An Emerald Guard, in the service of the king, and then one of his Six after that. You know of the Six, of course. Men chosen to serve the king by unbreakable oath, sworn to do everything he bids them, no matter the cost. I was young when I entered Janilah's service, young and attracted to power and position. I did not fully understand the breadth of the man's ambition, nor his ruthlessness, until he assigned me to my task."

"To join the Shadow Order?" asked Emeric. "To watch over Jonik, train him to be Janilah's dagger in the night?"

"Yes. The Shadowfort is meant to be near impossible to find by those who don't know the way, but Janilah Lukar…he isn't just any man. He unearthed the route and told me to bring the boy there, with a dozen mountain mules for company carrying gifts of gold and jewels, armour and blades." His mouth twisted into a snarl, and he spat weakly to the side. "The Shadow Order is no ancient sect driven by balance as they claim. They are assassins and killers who bow to the highest bidder, no more, and Janilah's bids were bottomless. He became secret patron of the order, and I was inserted in as a master, with the single and express duty to train Jonik at his pleasure."

"Which you did for twenty years," Jonik snarled. "You knew what kind of man Janilah was and you still obeyed him like a beaten dog."

"I was sworn to, by oath and honour. I believed it was for a greater cause."

"A greater cause," Emeric Manfrey repeated. "Janilah used Jonik to cause unrest in the north, so he might take power. This we know. We suspect too that he wishes to gather the Five Blades. Why?"

"To combine them," Gerrin said at once. "He believes the Heart of Vandar can be restored, and with it, the world will be won. Ever has he wished to win the War Eternal. This was always his means of doing so."

Jonik scoffed. "If the blades could be combined, why haven't they before? Not even Varin held the blades as one. Or is my history wrong?"

"Not wrong, Jonik," said Emeric thoughtfully. "There is no record of Varin even wielding the Blades of Vandar as a single weapon. Not even during his famed battle with Drulgar did he do so, nor when he met Eldur and Karagar at the Ashmount. I confess I can think of no occasion when a king or First Blade or champion of Vandar has borne more than two of the blades at once."

"There has been no such occasion," Gerrin said. "Men have duel-wielded two of the blades before, yes, but none have ever been combined."

"Then how does Janilah expect to achieve this impossible feat, pray tell?" Jonik asked.

Gerrin's chains rattled as he shifted on his feet, wincing. The fetters were tight around his wrists and his ankles were still bound in hempen rope. Jonik could see welts appearing on his skin, fierce and red and painful. "That I do not know," he rasped, letting out a short throaty cough. "Janilah keeps his counsel close, and never revealed so much to me. The king likes tools that are fit for purpose, and mine was never to know the full truth of his plans. I'm not certain there is anyone who does."

Jonik scowled in thought. "A shame Ranulf left us in Aram," he grunted. "This is a field he loves to play in."

Emeric ran calloused fingers through his beard, humming pensively. "Ranulf was very tightlipped about what he'd discovered in the Book of Thala, information he seemed desperate to keep from Janilah. I wonder whether this has something to do with it." He squinted at Gerrin. "Was that your true intent, Sir Gerrin? To stalk Ranulf Shackton like a shadow, so you might learn of what he'd found?"

"My intent was as I've said. To tell you what you wish to know, and help you where I can. If you put a godsteel blade to my grasp, I will swear it on my faith."

"A worthless sentiment," Jonik dismissed, feeling his ire begin to rise. *After twenty years, he turns to my side? Why now? I cannot trust him.* "Your oaths are meaningless, Gerrin."

"My oaths are what I live by. You understand that, do you not, Lord Manfrey? They say you're a man of honour."

"All knights should be," Emeric said. "Honour is the backbone of our chivalric codes."

"Yet few knights follow those codes so stringently as you, Even in exile you have led a life of probity and justice. I would say the same of myself."

A bark of incredulous laughter burst through Jonik's lips. "You cannot be serious. Probity? Justice? *You*!"

"Such matters are often shaped by perspective," Gerrin said, quite calm. "I believed for too long that King Janilah's cause was just, no matter the consequences. I followed the orders he gave me, based on the oaths I had sworn, knowing to break them would be my life." He sighed. "I can no longer do so. You mean more to me than my honour, son."

Jonik drew his dagger. "I told you *not* to call me son."

"And I told you the truth of it. You're the closest I've ever had to one. I have *always* kept you safe, as I've *always* tried to protect you. Perhaps it didn't seem so to you, but it's true. Within the bounds of my service, I did everything I could."

"You beat me..."

"I spared you worse."

"You tortured me..."

"*And hated every moment!*"

Jonik drew back from the sudden volume of his voice, the intensity in his eyes. Gerrin seemed to stand taller for a moment, finding some strength in his legs, before his posture wilted and he slumped back down, knees buckling as he hung from the chains around his wrists.

Jonik stared. *Is this real? Is this the truth?* He'd never seen his old master like this. *I need to think,* he realised. *Really think and reflect.* He'd pushed so much of what he'd been through aside, fearing to explore that part of his past, but there was something uncomfortable tickling at the back of his head, some notion that Gerrin might be right. He *was* lenient compared to the others, even kind at times, he recalled. Jonik had always thought those moments cruel, that the rare tenderness Gerrin showed him made everything else all the worse, but perhaps he had that wrong. Maybe those moments were the only times when Gerrin could be himself, lapses in his judgement and duty before he realised his folly, remembered his oaths, and hardened up all over again.

He gave the Shadowmaster a final look, and saw nothing but an old careworn man, hanging feebly on the wall in his rusted iron fetters. He was a piteous thing, humbled and debased. Jonik could look at him no longer. "I'll visit with you again soon," he said, giving no timeframe of when that might be. Gerrin gazed up at him through weary eyes. "Sid will come soon with your rations."

With that, Jonik turned and left the room.

Emeric met him outside, shutting and bolting the door behind him. He let a moment pass before speaking. "He's weak," he then said. "These last five days have taken their toll on a man his age." He glanced back at the barred wooden door. "This stress position…the rats…is this your way of getting retribution, Jonik?"

It would be churlish to deny it. "He did worse to me."

"An eye for an eye?" Emeric said. "Justice is more complicated than that."

"I know. But it's….it's about more than that." He turned to face the exiled lord, and told him the story of that redheaded girl Leshie, how she'd insulted Gerrin when he was masquerading as old Benjy, teasing him and taunting him and getting him to snap and lash out. "She was provoking him so he might react," he finished. "I don't think she ever trusted him…she thought he was playing a role. Well, she had the right of that, Emeric, and saw straight through him when I did not. I thought that I'd try something similar by subjecting him to…to this."

Emeric nodded quietly, though he didn't entirely approve, clearly. "I see." He scratched his chin. "Well, you got a reaction, certainly. And one more honest than I'd have expected. Much of what he said…" He frowned, as though struggling to believe what he was about to say. "He spins a convincing tale, shall we say."

More convincing than I'd like. Jonik could feel himself weakening, even now. "We never asked him of the Shadow King. There are so many questions…"

"We have plenty of time." Emeric looked to the stool beside the door. "I'd suggest you have Sid increase his rations a bit, perhaps bring him some ale occasionally as well. And you might want to consider unfettering him from the wall so he might move more freely. Kindness is not weakness, Jonik. Let him feed himself with his own two hands and relieve himself in a bucket, at least. I struggle to see the merit in mistreating him like this."

Jonik felt suddenly ashamed. "As you say."

"That is not a scold, Jonik." Emeric gripped his arm, more fatherly than Gerrin ever was. *He is what Gerrin should have been,* he thought. *A true mentor, wise and just.* "I understand your reasons, but these last five days have served their purpose. Let him clean himself, feed himself, and he'll think the better of you for it. And if he's lying, no amount of torture is likely to break him. But if you want my first thoughts…" He shook his head. "I don't think he is."

Jonik nodded. He wasn't certain how to feel about that. A part of him had wanted Emeric to condemn him, see through his facade, so he might rid himself of the choice and have him thrown into the raging sea. It seemed it wouldn't be so simple as that. "Will you stay?" he asked. "I'd like you present when I speak to him next. And there's much else we need to discuss besides."

"Now that I know he's here, I shan't be going anywhere. Vincent seems to think the weather should stay fair for the time being, so we'll be able to sail close to one another. Men can be swapped between the ships as we see fit."

"I didn't realise the merchant was an augur as well," Jonik said.

"He isn't. It's the Lumaran twins who have a good nose for the weather, he says. Just don't ask me about their methods. It was enough to make even Brown Mouth blush."

"Something improper, no doubt."

"I'll leave Braxton to fill in the details."

Jonik made a mental note to ask him, though would probably fail to follow through. Matters of lust and love still made him unbearably uncomfortable. "How has he been so far? Rose?"

"Himself."

"So insufferable?"

Emeric laughed. "I'm getting used to him, in truth. He is wildly opinionated and thinks a great deal of himself, but can be amusing too, in his way. I try not to take him too seriously."

"And Sansullio and his men? Kazil. Harden. Are we likely to have them when we march on the mountains?"

"Vincent continues to assure me that we will. Do I trust him? Not particularly. But I think the sellswords will join us all the same."

That was good news, at least. "We'd still be wise to seek patronage elsewhere," Jonik said. "I want to sever ties with Rose as soon as possible."

"Difficult," returned Emeric. "We promised him we'd help protect him from Janilah, Jonik. So long as he keeps to his end of the bargain, we'll continue to do so."

Jonik grumbled something under his breath, though didn't disagree. There was just something about that soft, silk-wearing merchant that rankled him. They started down the corridor. "How's Devin? Still training every day?"

"Yes, with Jack. If you want the truth, he's been thoroughly enjoying the voyage. One World is a pleasant ship, but it's more about the company. Vincent Rose, I should say, is not possessive of the twins."

Jonik didn't need to hear more. Devin was sixteen, energetic, and hopelessly interested in the fairer sex. *I might have known Rose would offer him up one of his courtesans,* he thought. "I'm not sure I approve."

"Nor I. But what can be done? Devin is a young man and those twins, well…I've seen few so comely, and I've lived in Lumara for years."

"And Braxton? Jack? I don't suppose…"

"Only Devin. Jack is rather too pious to go in for that sort of thing and Brax is more chaste than one would think." He gave Jonik a smile. "And I'll thank you for not questioning *my* virtue, Jonik."

So soon after his beloved Brewilla's death, Jonik never would have considered it. Nor did Emeric seem the sort to indulge in loveless relations like that. "Leave that for Sir Borrus," was all he said. "As soon as he gets wind of all this, he'll be swapping ships for certain."

They laughed together as they continued up onto the main deck, where they found the men in jovial discussion. It seemed Devin had been angry about being left on One World, so had jumped into the water and swum the gap instead. He stood there, grinning and dripping wet, panting something about almost getting eaten by a shark. "Your fault for leapin' in, boy," Turner said, shaking his head. "I might have told you, there be sharks in these parts."

"There seem to be sharks everywhere in the south," complained Sir Borrus. "It's one of the many reasons I'm so bloody eager to get home."

"Aye, though I hear there're these big flying lizards that like to breathe fire about. Called dragons, I think. It's those that concern me more."

"Give me a dragon over a shark any day," Borrus came back. "Dragons I know, but sharks…" He gave a shudder and glanced over the rail.

"We all have our strengths, Sir Barrel," Turner said, grinning through the twisting hairs of his bushy lemony beard. "To me sharks are fond as friends. I am part…

"*Part Seaborn, after all,*" called Brax and Jack and Devin in unison.

Up in the crow's nest, the cackling laughter of Grim Pete broke out. The rest were soon to follow; Emeric, Borrus, Soft Sid with his great huffing honks, and Jonik, who smiled upon these men who'd become his friends, his crew, his companions. After that storm, he feared they'd never be reunited.

It's good to have them back, he thought.

2

Amara

When the chest was opened, Amara Daecar heard the faint sound of wind, blowing at the edge of hearing. "Does everyone hear that?" she asked, peering at the blade within.

"Only Bladeborn, I would think," said Sir Connor Crawfield, the gloomy captain of her guard.

That made sense. Amara wasn't trained to wield godsteel, but she had the blood of Varin in her veins all the same, and in ample quantities too. "Well, it's nice to know my Varin blood counts for *something*," she said. "I wonder if I could lift it." She reached in.

"I'd advise not, my lady," Sir Connor told her, as though she might do herself some damage. "A Blade of Vandar is heavy even for the strongest of Bladeborn knights. You might hurt yourself if you strain too hard."

"I'll satisfy myself with looking at it then." It *was* lovely to look at too, with those swirling silver mists that curled delicately around the pristine steel, puffing and whirling as they rose, and the deep-etched glowing glyphs that ran up the length of the blade. It was those particular glyphs and symbols that set the Blades of Vandar apart, engraved during their forging by Ilith over three and a half millennia ago. These were flowing in design, as curls of air and swirls of cloud and held in them the magic that enabled the bearer of the blade to soar. That was not such an easy thing, though, mastering a Blade of

Vandar. You needed the right blood, the right claim, the right will. *And Elyon has all three,* she thought.

"How does it compare, my lady?" asked the wonderful girl who'd brought it to her. Carly Flame Mane was a beautiful thing, cunning and curious as a cat and equally elastic of limb, with fiery red hair that fell in shapely tresses down her neck. She even had a few flecks of red in her eyes, if Amara saw it right, glittering amid the turquoise green.

"Compare, Carly?"

"To the other one. The Sword of Varinar. It's said the Blades of Vandar are the most beautiful godsteel blades ever forged." She looked down at the Windblade, and shrugged. "Doesn't look so different to regular godsteel to me."

Amara laughed. This was a girl after her own heart, and that was why she'd hired her to help steal the Windblade in the first place. "You're hard to please, I see. I'll admit the Sword of Varinar is rather more striking. But being big and gold does have that effect, though I always thought it rather gaudy." She took a final look at the Windblade - the swirling design of the cross-guard, the subtle curve of the steel, the silver vortex that made up the pommel - and nodded for Sir Connor to shut the lid. "Well, it's the right blade for certain. My heartfelt thanks for delivering it so soon."

"My pleasure," Carly said. "I hadn't expected to deliver it here, though, Lady Amara. Elyon told us to make for Dragon's Bane."

"Plans change. The sooner we can pair Elyon with the Windblade, the better, would you not say?"

"So he's coming here?" That seemed to excite the girl, a common enough reaction among pretty young women when Elyon Daecar was under discussion.

"We have men out looking for him now. I suppose you heard what happened to him in Ilithor?"

Carly nodded. "That big knight told me, the one who brought us here. I forget his name."

"That would be Sir Mooton Blackshaw," said Sir Connor. "This castle is his uncle's."

"So this is a castle, is it?" Carly gave a playful grin. "Seems more a woodland shack to me."

Amara chuckled. That was being a shade unfair, but she had something resembling a point. Elmhall Hold, the seat of Lord Blackshaw, was a rustic motte-and-bailey castle tucked up on the western edge of the Mistwood some fifty miles east of Ayrin's Cross. They were currently in the keep's great hall, though to call it great was a gross overstatement. The bailey at the bottom of the hill was no more impressive; a cluster of stone and timber buildings hidden behind a twelve foot stone wall, with a pair of squat square towers standing sentinel either side of the gate. As fortresses went, it was hardly impenetrable, but it didn't exactly need to be. No dragons were like to trouble them here in these woods, and they had the immense power of House Kanabar to call upon should they come under the attentions of a rival. So it served just fine, for what it was. And House Blackshaw had never been rich.

When Amara had chuckled her lot, she stepped over to a side table and poured two cups of wine, handing one to the girl. The colour of the wine was a nice match for her hair. "Tell me of your journey from Ilithor. Did you have any trouble in the mountains?"

Carly took a sip. "None," she said. "If there was any pursuit, we never heard of it. But we were quick, and I've taken that route a hundred times. I wasn't going to let us slow until we were into Vandarian lands. Not with that precious cargo there." She waved to the Windblade in its chest.

"Good girl," Amara said, though it sounded terribly condescending. "With luck Elyon will have passed just as easily."

"The big one…Sir Mooton, was it? He said Elyon left the palace only two days behind us. But from the north side."

Amara nodded. "Is that a problem?"

"Can't really say. I've never been that way." Carly drank deep of her wine, then wiped her mouth. "Should be fine, though. He's a strong boy, and he's got those other two with him, right? They'll be quick if it's just the three of them."

Amara certainly hoped so, though they'd heard no word as yet. They had scouts and outriders scouring the wood and roads in the west of the forest, and Sir Daryl Blunt was out there now with some more of the Blackshaw men. With Sir Mooton galloping straight back off with his own company after delivering Carly here, she felt confident Elyon, Lancel, and Barnibus would be found sooner rather than later.

Amara turned back to the fiery-haired sellsword. "Are you to stay with us, Carly? It might be a day or two, perhaps more, before Elyon is found. Lord Blackshaw will be happy to host you, I'm sure."

"That'd be kind, Lady Amara. My crew could do with putting

their feet up for a few days in safe surroundings. So long as Lord Blackshaw doesn't take offence to hosting a band of roguish sellswords such as us?"

"If it serves House Kanabar and by extension House Daecar, he'll be quite happy, I know." Really, Lord Blackshaw was a frail old thing and had misplaced a wit or two, so would believe anything Amara told him. He spent much of his time abed these days, up at the summit of his keep, gazing out over the tops of the trees and out into the Heartlands beyond. "I'll have the castle steward arrange accommodations for you. Sir Connor, if you'd be so kind."

"My lady." Sir Connor bowed and left, passing through the doors that opened out into the inner yard.

Beyond, Carly's crew were gathered, the wonderfully named Sally Scarlet and Crowfoot and Will Red and all the rest. Some servants were attending them, shuffling about with trays of food and refreshment, and there was a great deal of laughter going on, the sort of laughter that only comes after a job well done. The castle steward, an old whitebeard called Alberfred West, was watching on quizzically when Sir Connor tapped him on the shoulder and drew his attention. So followed a short discussion about where to house the newcomers, though Amara didn't imagine they'd much care. *So long as they have a roof over their heads and meat and mead aplenty they'll be fine.*

She turned back to their leader. "We'll host you here tonight for a feast. These woods are full of game and Lord Blackshaw's larder is never lacking in juicy boar and succulent venison. As you can probably tell, the men of the Riverlands enjoy their food as much as they do their drink." She finished the small cup of wine she'd poured. "We can celebrate properly later."

Carly got her meaning, and set her own cup aside. "I thank you for your hospitality, Lady Amara. I shall leave you to your thoughts." She smiled graciously and stepped from the hall, joining her men as old Alberfred West led them off to their lodgings, likely in some barracks in the lower yard. Amara found them a most comical lot. Every band of sellswords seemed to pick up their own unique quirks and peculiarities, and for the Flame Manes, it was the colour red. They had it in their hair and their cloaks, in the studs that dotted their boiled leather jerkins, in the tattoos that some had inked into their very skin. They'd even taken on a sigil, some screaming black skull with flaming red hair. A monstrous thing to Amara's eyes, yes, but Carly was young and fearless and a rebellious sort and for all that the standard worked well.

Sir Connor stepped back inside to join her, passing Sir Gilmoor and Sir Penrose who stood guard at the doors. Both were under the captain's command and members of the Daecar Household Guard. One might say that Lady Amara Daecar had requisitioned Elmhall Hold for herself, and they'd be absolutely right. She only had to declare the heir of House Daecar on his way and every man, woman, and child present, highborn and low, would bow to her needs.

Sir Connor looked over at the Windblade, safely stored in the trunk. "Where do you think we should put it?"

"My chambers," Amara said at once.

Sir Connor gave out a sigh. "I'd thought as much." Amara had taken for herself a set of rooms in the summit of the castle keep. It wasn't the sort of accommodation she was used to - certainly nothing like Keep Daecar or the quarters she'd been granted in Ilithor throughout the wedding festivities - but it would serve.

Sir Connor was clearly unhappy, though. "Oh come, Sir Connor, don't look so down. This is hardly the tallest fortress in the realm, is it? I'm sure you can ferry that blade up a half dozen floors."

"It's heavy, my lady."

Sir Connor did like to point out the obvious, sometimes. "Yes is it. But you were *almost* a Varin Knight, lest we forget." She clapped him on the arm. Sir Connor's never-ending gloom stemmed from his failure to make selection for the Knights of Varin in his youth. A matter Amara liked to remind him of as often as possible. "There's some mighty strong blood in you, Sir Connor Crawfield, and don't you ever forget it. Now chop chop, up the stairs. Use Sir Gilmore and Sir Penrose if you must."

Sir Connor set off to his task, grumbling as he waved the two knights from the door. *If Carly's host managed to convey it all the way here, they should have no trouble,* Amara thought. In the end, Sir Connor's complaints were unwarranted. Together, the three Bladeborn men were quite capable of lifting the chest, Windblade and all, and hauling it up the winding stairs to her chambers.

Amara followed. "Set it there, beside the bed," she said once they'd entered.

The men did so, each panting once they were done. "I'll double the guard…on your room, my lady," Sir Connor told her, wiping sweat from his brow. "We ought to guard it day and night…whether you're present or not."

"I agree." They had no enemies here, but there was no harm in being thorough. Amara heard the clang of steel beyond the window, and drifted over. Down in the training yard, Jovyn was taking Lillia through her daily routines. Some local squires had stopped in their training to gawp. The sight of a girl of thirteen training with godsteel, and a highborn beauty no less, was rare as snow in a southern summer. Even the master-at-arms, a grizzled old veteran called Sir Arnold Claw, seemed to have lost his voice for a moment. But only a moment. Then he could be heard, roaring the young squires back into position. These were Bladeborn boys, Amara knew, though none so good as to join the Varin Knights. To them, a boy like Jovyn Colborn was a hero. And he seemed to know it too, as he swished and dashed about the yard, putting Lillia through her paces.

"She's good," said Sir Connor, drawn over to watch at her side. The window of her bedchamber gave a good view of the grounds, the castle moat surrounded on all sides by elm and ash and pine, as were common in this part of the Mistwood. "She's not so far from matching him. That is most impressive, for one so callow. And a girl besides."

"I'm inclined to think a girl can become quite as skilled as a boy if given the proper training." Lillia had always claimed as such, asserting that she'd be just as good as Elyon or Aleron if permitted the opportunity. Until recently, Amron had never allowed such a thing, but times had changed and Elyon had persuaded him to yield.

Sir Connor only shrugged. "One with blood so rich as hers, perhaps." His eyes followed Jovyn for a time, judging his skill as Sir Arnold barked the other squires back to work. "The boy is better than I ever was, I'll admit." His ever-gloomy voice was gloomier than ever. "He'll have little trouble getting his spurs and joining Varin's Order, if I'm any judge. And that Strikeform of his…it's particularly advanced for a boy his age."

"And so it should be," Amara said. "Strikeform has always been Elyon's preference so it's no surprise Jovyn favours it too. And Elyon squired for Lythian in his youth, lest we forget. There's no greater proponent of the form than the Knight of the Vale, Sir Connor."

Sir Connor had sullen blue eyes to go with his sullen demeanour. "You speak of Lythian in the present, my lady. Do you believe he still lives?"

"I have hope." *As I have hope that Amron will return,* she thought. She had expected word that Amron had made his way back to Northwatch Castle by now, but alas the wait went on. In Robert Borrington's last letter to her, the Lord of Northwatch had spoken of strange tidings beyond the mountains. "Queer things have been happening of late," he'd written. "Distant earthquakes from Vandar's Tomb. Birds flocking strangely. Some of the men say they saw a distant white light, bright as the dawn, flashing beyond the peaks of the Weeping Heights. Something is happening out there, Lady Amara. I fear for Amron's safe return."

Amara had more faith. "He has Walter with him, and this ranger of yours too," she'd written back. "Keep to hope, Robert. And write me as soon as you know more."

Sir Connor turned his eyes southward beyond the bailey. "The men say there hasn't been a dragon attack for almost two weeks," he said. "I wonder if this is proof of the whispers, my lady. That there is truly unrest across the Red Sea. That the Fireborn have become divided."

Amara gave that a thoughtful nod. "King Tavash took his throne by treason, Sir Connor. That is not likely to sit well with everyone. The Fireborn of the Nest hold their honour in high regard, as we do."

"As to that...Alberfred had a crow from Southwatch. There are loose reports - and I would highlight the term *loose* - of some fracas at the Nest. Some posit that a parley took place there, among these rival Fireborn factions, and went ill. Others claim the Bondstone has been stolen, or even destroyed."

"Only a fool would make such a claim," Amara laughed. "The Bondstone is Agarath's Soul, Sir Connor. It cannot be destroyed, save by an artefact of equal power."

"Be that as it may, my lady, there have been odd occurrences of late. It's rumoured that red lightning storms have been spotted over the Wings. That the islands tremble and wake."

Tremble and wake, she thought, disquieted. It was said that Agarath's spirit rested beneath the Wings, as Vandar's did the mountain that bore his name. The very mountain she'd sent Amron to, to seek his restoration. "These are omens of war," she told the knight, hoping that's all it was. "In Renewals past these strange phenomena have been known to occur. I'd give them no mind."

"An easier thing to say than do, Lady Amara." Sir Connor's lips moved into the closest thing he had to a smile. "There is much hope among the men that the Agarathi are falling to civil discord. They believe the lack of recent dragon attacks confirms it. King Tavash has other matters to worry about, they say. Some even think him dead."

"Thinking it will not make it so. Until we have definitive, reliable word from a trusted source, it will not serve us to let this distract us." These rumours were often passed between a hundred lips before reaching anyone of note, and could scarcely be relied upon. "And have you considered that this is what Tavash wants? That this recent lull is intended to put us off our guard. The Agarathi have been testing our defences for weeks, seeking out a weakness they might exploit. Yet thus far these raids have been little more than the prod of Tavash's finger, poking here, poking here, seeking an easy way in. One day soon he may just close his hand into a fist, and put all his strength behind the blow."

Sir Connor gave that some thought. "True enough, my lady, but such an assault would require the full support of his Fireborn. Without their dragons, the Agarathi cannot hope to defeat us." He put his thumb and forefinger to his chin, rubbing at the course bristles. "One wonders about the wisdom of this invasion" he intoned. "If these rumours of infighting are true, we would do well to leave them to it. As soon as Dalton Taynar's fleet arrives to lay siege to the Trident, it will only serve to unite the Fireborn against us."

"So you would counsel caution, Sir Connor. And patience?"

"I would seek to discover the truth of what is happening in Agarath before moving forth with these plans to invade. Let them rip at each other's throats for a bit. We can march on them once they're bloodied and weak. Or not at all, should Tavash be replaced by someone more moderate. Further war might be avoided entirely."

Something told Amara that her dear sweet cousin Janilah would disagree. *He'll be smelling blood in the water,* she thought, *and will speed up his plans to invade, not slow them.* "I wish our rulers shared your temperance, Sir Connor," was all she said. "But I do fear both the Trident and Eagle's Perch will come under siege before the turn of the moon."

Sir Connor nodded. "As you say, my lady." He shifted back a step. "I shall devise a rotation, to keep watch on your rooms. Is there anything else you need from me?"

She looked out of the window again. Down in the lower bailey, the Flame Manes were filing into a barracks under the instruction of Alberfred West. A few Blackshaw soldiers were being expelled, it looked, to take up lodgings elsewhere, and seemed none too happy about it. "Go down and tell Alberfred that I'd like to host Carly and her men tonight in the hall, if you would."

"A private function, my lady?"

"By no means. All the castle are to be invited, smallfolk and large. I shall clear it with Lord Blackshaw presently, but I'm sure he'll not object."

"Very good, my lady." Sir Connor bowed and stepped away.

THE FEAST WAS HELD at the fall of dusk, Amara taking her place of honour at Lord Devyn Blackshaw's right, with Lillia sat beside her. The tables that had been stacked at the sides of the hall earlier were dusted down and set up in rows, the great hearth lit, the floor swept and banners hung. The Blackshaw standard - a black bear prowling amongst a forest of trees - was draped behind the high table, with the Daecar sigil - an armoured knight on horseback, holding a misting blade aloft - in pride of place beside it. Other knights came dressed in their own livery, some with young squires and standard-bearers of their own. Their banners were suspended from hooks on the walls and soon enough, the drab old hall had bloomed to life, bright and colourful, as the tables were filled with knights and men-at-arms, lancers and spearmen, bowmen and blacksmiths, stablehands and washerwomen, crofters and cobblers and scullions and cooks. It seemed the invite for all the castle to come had been taken up eagerly, with highborn and low rubbing shoulder to shoulder as they packed the benches full.

Lord Blackshaw looked out at the gathering through rheumy eyes, a confused expression on his face. "I've not seen my hall this full in many a long year," he croaked. "Who…who are all these people?"

"They would be *your* people, my lord," Amara told him gently. Alberfred West sat to the lord's left, Sir Connor beside him. That was the sum of the high table for the evening.

The old man seemed perplexed. "I didn't know I had so many. These…so many of these are strangers to me." Sadly, that was true. Lord Blackshaw spent little time beyond the confines of his keep and rarely visited with the commoners anymore. "Who…who are these?" He lifted a frail hand to point at the sellswords in residence at a table nearby, drinking and laughing raucously. "These peculiar red ones. These are not our colours. We Blackshaws favour brown and black, earthy tones for the forest and the hills."

His doublet was coloured as such, black on the right, umber on the left, with a black bearskin heaped on his shoulders. He'd once have filled it out, but now the fur and fabric engulfed him like a child in his father's cloak. "These are our honoured guests for the evening, my lord," Alberfred said. "I told you of them. They are sellswords in Lady Amara's service, part of her protective cohort." That wasn't quite true, but the lie was easier than explaining to the old man what had been happening with the Windblade.

"Sellswords, you say?"

"They call themselves the Flame Manes," Amara said.

A sort of snort escaped through Lord Blackshaw's nose, causing his long grey nostril hairs to flutter. "That sounds an awfully silly name."

"Very silly, I agree." In actual fact, Amara rather liked it.

"I've never liked sellswords," the old lord went on. "They lack honour, and most are middling fighters. We Blackshaws have always punched above our weight. My son was a Varin Knight, you know."

"I do, my lord. Your house is famed for siring ferocious fighters." And he'd been one himself once, not that you'd know to look at him.

Lillia gave Amara's sleeve a tug. "I thought lords were meant to hold court," she whispered. "I did, with Father away. Who deals with the common people if he's too unwell?"

"I understand Alberfred has taken on the duty of castellan, as well as steward."

"What about his children? Is his son still a Varin Knight?"

Amara shook her head and lowered her voice. "He was lost during the war. Sir Mooton is his heir now, I believe, though he isn't much one for holding court, as you know."

Lillia giggled. Sir Mooton had spent every night on the road from Ilithor drinking heavily with his men, singing songs, telling tales of his conquests and triumphs. It was all to the horror of Sir Connor, of course, who found the Riverlanders too rowdy for his tastes, but Lillia considered them a hoot, and the *Beast of Blackshaw*, as men called Sir Mooton, most of all. "No, he's much too wild," she said, grinning. "He told me he was offered a chance to join the Varin Knights, but declined. Said they were too formal and boring, that he doesn't care about Varin's Table but only wants to live while he's alive." She glanced down the table. "Con must *hate* him for that. He'd kill for an opportunity to join the order."

"Sir Connor had such an opportunity already in his youth, Lillia, and may yet get another chance, I fear." Amara spoke gravely. "Wars tend to be difficult times for Varin Knights, and when all this is said and done, there may be a vacancy or two…"

"My lady, I would ask of Lord Amron," croaked old Lord Blackshaw from his high chair. Amara turned back to him. "I heard he was maimed, in…in some monstrous attack. Alberfred, he tells me things, but I scarcely know what to believe anymore." He smiled crookedly. Some of his teeth were starting to brown, and a couple had fallen out. "Is this true? This…this terrible villainy?"

"I'm afraid so, my lord. It was a failed assassination, some half year ago."

"Oh, I…I see." He frowned, blinking, seeming to remember. "Have we…have we spoken of this already? My memory, it…well it isn't what it was."

They had, the very day she arrived. It had been one of the first things he'd asked her when Alberfred announced her arrival. For a moment he'd forgotten who she was, but as soon as he remembered, he'd asked of Amron's health.

She saw no merit in embarrassing him now, though, so just said, "No, not as yet. I will be sure to tell Amron that you asked of him, when I see him next. He always held you in high regard."

That pleased the man. "And I him, of course. I knew him from a boy, when he'd come here with his father. Lord Gideon had a fondness for the Riverlands, you know. He would visit with Wallis Kanabar frequently, staying at Eastwatch or Tallriver or one of his other castles." He smiled proudly. "But he'd always make time for me too. They would ride here together, the two greatlords, and I'd host them here in this very hall. Those were the days, my lady. Hosting the Lord of Rivers and the First Blade of Vandar in my humble castle, with our boys sparring and playing at knights. Even then…yes even then it was clear Amron was something special. We would watch them train in the yard right outside and my, how he would frustrate young Borrus." He laughed happily. "I'd never seen anyone master Blockform at such a tender age. Wallis would joke Amron had it mastered in the womb, and he didn't seem far wrong. But goodness did it vex Borrus. He'd try everything to get through young Amron's defences, but to little avail. He never did have much patience."

He reached forward and took up his cup of wine, drinking with a shaky hand. "My son Torvyn was smarter than Borrus, I always thought," he went on. "He would stand aside and watch as Borrus tried to breach Amron's guard, and take note of every move he made. He was always like that. Very watchful, very shrewd. One day he challenged Amron himself. They would spar a lot, but this was different."

"A proper duel?" Amara asked.

"A proper duel," Lord Blackshaw confirmed with a brisk nod and a wonky smile. "And he wanted everyone watching too, so half the castle came. Gideon and Wallis placed bets with some of the other men and of course everyone wagered against my son. But not me. No. I knew Torvyn, I knew what he was capable of." He took a drink of his wine, smiling all the while. "So here they come, into the training yard, and here we all are, watching from the sides. You can imagine the buzz, Amara. Gosh, Amron must have been fifteen at this point, big and broad-shouldered and already a match for the best of the Varin Knights. There were even rumours he'd bested his father back at Keep Daecar, though of course Gideon waved those away." He gave a throaty laugh. Some life was returning to the old lord as he reminisced on the past, of which his memory seemed much sharper than when discussing recent events. "My son, though…Torvyn was younger, fourteen I suppose he was, and skinny back then too. We Blackshaws breed big, my lady, but Torvyn had yet to grow into his frame. Amron was taller, bigger, older, stronger…" He smiled as though seeing it all again before his eyes. "But Torvyn bested him all the same."

"He did? Truly?" Amara had thought Lord Blackshaw would say Torvyn had managed to strike Amron once or twice, give him a good fight, but eventually be overwhelmed. But to defeat him before his very own father? No, she hadn't expected that.

"You sound surprised?" The old man had a twinkle in his deep umber eyes. Somehow they didn't look so watery anymore. "I suppose I cannot fault you for that. As a grown man Amron was almost unbeatable and he was just as imperious in his youth. But

Torvyn found a way. All those days watching Borrus crash and clamour helped him work out Amron's weaknesses. I tell you, I made a tidy profit that day, but the true profit was in seeing my son's smile. What a sight that was. I had never felt so proud."

Amara was smiling too. "A lovely tale. I shall be sure to remind Amron of it when I see him."

The old man laughed. "Ah, please do. I'm sure he recalls it fondly."

"Are you certain of that?" Amara jested. "A man such as Amron Daecar does not take kindly to being defeated."

"Not so, Lady Amara, not so. That very night, in fact, young Amron spent the entire feast at Torvyn's side, debriefing on their duel. He wanted to hear of Torvyn's process and strategy, to find out where he'd gone wrong. Amron saw his defeat as an opportunity to improve, you see. And isn't that the mark of a great champion? To see failure as a chance for greater success in the future?" He smiled a final time. "I like to think Torvyn helped him become the man he went on to be. The Slayer of Vallath. The Crippler of Kings. The Hero of the North. All with the help of my son."

Amara liked the sentiment a great deal. She reached out and gripped the man's forearm, squeezing, as she saw his smile slip away. Even twenty years on, the grief of his son's loss was still there, a wound that would never fully heal. "Torvyn would have been proud of what Amron went on to achieve." He had been lost before the end of the war, she remembered, though couldn't recall how or where. Something played about in her mind, some memory of strange circumstances, of his body never being found, but she thought better than to bring it up. So many knights had died back then and it was hard to tally them all. "I wonder…was my husband present during these visits?"

The light had faded from Lord Blackshaw's eyes. "Your husband? Oh…oh yes, Vesryn. He was there, during the later visits when he was a bit older. A pleasant boy, but shy he seemed. I don't imagine it was easy for him living in Amron's shadow."

He lives in his own shadow now, Amara thought, reflecting on her brief visit with Vesryn a week ago, accosting her in that rainstorm outside the tavern. *And where are you now, sweet husband?* she wondered. *Do you head west as well, as you said?*

"I wonder if Amron's son…the second one…I wonder if he feels the same, living in his older brother's shadow," Lord Devyn Blackshaw continued. "His name…I forget his name. The elder is Aleron, I recall." She saw some confusion in his eyes again.

He forgets that Aleron is dead, she realised. "Elyon," she said. "The younger. And heir now, my lord. Aleron, he was killed. In the final of the Song of the First Blade."

"Oh yes." He looked abashed by the slip. "My memory," he explained, fumbling a little with his words. "I have trouble retaining recent events. Short term memory loss, Alberfred calls it. And medium term, I should say. I recall the past well enough, but these last years…" He trailed off, took a small sip of wine, then placed the goblet down. A silence fell between them.

Amara felt a pang of pity for the man, as she saw him looking out over the hall, that confusion and uncertainty filling his face as he turned his eyes around, trying to place someone, anyone below whom he recognised. Men raised goblets to him as his eyes passed them by, and he gamely nodded and returned the gesture, but she could tell he did not know them. *He lives only in the past now,* she thought. *This present is so alien to him. A strange world in which he has no place.*

He battled on all the same, as noble knights and small-lords of the land stood from the benches and strode up to pay their fealty. Alberfred was on hand each time to tell him who they were. "Sir Lutherton Wane, my lord, of Pineway," he would say, and, "Sir Peter Hornmoor, of Silverkeep," and, "Lord Justin Huxley, of Wolfwood Castle."

Some he vaguely recalled, the older men whom he'd known before his decline; others were strangers to his eyes. Amara knew some of them herself, and would spare him where she could, asking of their fathers and lands, how many men they had mustered for the war, and other such smalltalk. She recalled that Lord Huxley's brother, Sir Arnald, had fought in the Song of the First Blade. "He did, my lady," the young Lord of Wolfwood confirmed. "Though did not make it far, I regret to say." He paused and then added, "I was there, for the final." His eyes flitted to Lillia. "I am most grieved by your loss. Sir Aleron would have made a storied First Blade, as his father and grandfather and great-grandfather before him, I have no doubt."

Amara agreed with a polite smile. "Kind words, my lord. We must put our faith in his younger brother now. Elyon will become a light to follow, during these dark and dangerous times."

"I wholeheartedly agree, my lady." He bowed and stepped away.

Yet through all that, the old lord sank into his shell. Eventually, once all those who wished to share words with him had come, and the feast hall rang with music and merriment, he decided to take his leave. "Well, I think…I suppose I ought to rest." The old man shivered to his feet, and the high table stood along with him. His back was so stooped by age that Amara stood an inch or two taller, where once he'd have loomed above her.

"Should I escort you to your chambers, my lord?" she asked him.

"No, no, please, don't trouble yourself, my lady. Alberfred can manage." He smiled at her and Lillia. "I bid you goodnight. It has been a pleasure, my ladies, to spend the evening with you."

"The pleasure has been ours, my lord."

With that, Alberfred took his arm and began leading him from the hall, trailed by a pair of guardsmen. Lord Devyn Blackshaw managed a cordial wave to his people, some of whom were watching him go, though most were deep in their cups and not even aware of his departure.

Sir Connor stepped over. "Will you stay long, my lady?"

Amara scanned the room. Carly and her crew were heavily invested in a drinking game with some of the Blackshaw men at the next table. By the looks of things the big woman, Sally Scarlet, was well disposed to the challenge, and Carly, dainty though she was, had quite the tolerance too. "I think I'll join our guests," she decided, "for a drink or two. Please escort Lillia to bed, Sir Connor."

"I don't want to go to bed," Lillia complained, yawning as she did so.

"You've been falling asleep in your chair for the last half hour," Amara told her. "Don't be stubborn for the sake of it."

"I'm not being stubborn," she said stubbornly. Her eyes found Jovyn and his adoring fans. "I can't go to bed *before* Jovy. If I go, he has to."

She's still such a child, Amara thought sadly. "Just go to bed, and no complaints. Sir Connor, see her to her room."

Amara didn't take long to return to her own. Her time sitting with Lord Blackshaw had drained her more than she realised, and for once she felt the pull of sleep ahead of wine. "I think I'll retire," she told Carly, after sharing a single drink with her.

Carly looked aggrieved. "But my lady, your prowess is legend. I had hoped you might help us turn the tide." The Blackshaw men were starting to get the better of them in the drinking game, but unfortunately Amara had no energy for that fight tonight.

"Another time, perhaps," she said. "Two long weeks in the saddle has driven a deep ache into my buttocks and back, I'm not ashamed to say." She sighed. "I'm getting old, Carly. You and your crew enjoy your evening. We'll talk again tomorrow."

The flame-haired girl went into a neat curtsey. "My lady. Sleep well."

Her bed was a welcome relief, and the heights of the keep muffled all sound below. She could still hear the merrymaking, but only faintly, and before long she was drifting off to sleep beneath her warm woollen blankets, more weary than she could say.

She woke to the sound of horns.

Bleary-eyed, she sat up. She had no idea how long she'd slept, yet the castle was suddenly quiet and still and it was black as pitch outside. She shifted from her bed and walked barefoot to the window, padding across the rushes, and saw them at once. *Riders*.

A knock came at the door. "Yes." She pulled a cloak over her silken nightshirt.

Sir Connor stepped in. "You heard the horns?"

She nodded, turning back to the window, rubbing sleep from her eyes. "Riders incoming," she said, her throat dry. She snatched up a half full cup of wine and took a drink. "Can you see who they are?"

The portcullis was being raised and a small host of men were riding across the drawbridge. Sir Connor stepped over, gripping his godsteel dagger. It enhanced his eyesight a little. "Sir Daryl," he said, without inflection. "And his men. They've returned from their scouting."

"No sign of Elyon?"

"I'm afraid not, my lady."

Her hope faltered a touch, though the return of Sir Daryl was comforting. *Perhaps he knows something?* Wrapping her cloak tight about herself, she descended the stone steps and headed down into the hall with Sir Connor at her side. Most of the revellers had departed yet a few still remained, lying unconscious at the benches or tucked up near the dying hearth. One had wrapped himself in a banner torn from the wall for warmth, and two grown men were spooning. There was a chill in the air, the hall draughty, the last few candles flickering as they guttered out. Outside, she could hear the thump of footsteps coming up from the lower bailey. Sir Connor marched forward and threw open the doors.

A half dozen shadows took form. "My lady," Sir Daryl Blunt said, falling to a knee.

"Arise, Sir Daryl." She had no time for courtesies. "What news? Any word of Elyon?"

A smile came and went from Sir Daryl's round face. "Yes, my lady, and good news on that account. One of Sir Mooton's scouts has reported that contact has been made. Sir Mooton is hastening to meet him now so he might escort him here. He asked that I ride here at once to relay the message."

Amara shut her eyes. *Thank the gods.* "Is he well?"

"It seems so. Unharmed and unhurt, and Sir Lancel and Sir Barnibus too."

"How long until they get here?" asked Sir Connor.

"Once they have horses, they shouldn't take long. I would expect them here within two days."

"Wonderful." Amara could think of no other word. She went so far as to give Sir Daryl a hug…and the way he was smelling after two days scouting, that said rather a lot. "Well done, Daryl, well done. I would say there is a knighthood in this for you, but you seem to have one already."

"A lordship, perhaps?" quipped Sir Connor, and goodness was that rare. But such had been the day. The Windblade delivered, Elyon found. *I should be expecting that letter from Lord Borrington next,* she thought, *to hear that Amron is safely returned.*

And then Sir Daryl spoke. "My lady, there is more."

She looked at him, and saw no mirth in the man's eyes. *But those eyes are made for mirth,* she thought, *and that mouth is made for smiling.* It wasn't smiling now. "What is it?" Suddenly her voice was a whisper.

Sir Daryl wet his lips. "Grave word from Ilithor, my lady." He drew a shaky breath. "Rylian. The prince, he…he…"

Amara Daecar stepped forward, her heart rising into her throat. She looked Sir Daryl Blunt right in the eyes. "Tell me," she said.

3

Lythian

Lythian stood alone upon a wooded hilltop, looking out through the edge of the trees. Beyond, the vast wilderness of the Western Neck stretched out to the edge of sight, sinking into a purple dusk as day ebbed into night. The skies were clogged and heavy, the scent of rain in the air. It rained a lot here, Lythian had found. And especially so since Prince Tethian had died. Tethian and Ashun Klo and Kin'rar and others too. It had rained every day since that night…that night when everything had changed.

Across the misted valleys, a shadow shifted upon a distant hill. *Neyruu,* Lythian knew at once. The dragon had remained close to them since Kin'rar's death, but for what reason he could not say. Three nights running now he had seen her out there, perched on the same hill, and before then, when they'd been on the move, they'd sighted her regularly overhead, gliding through the leaden skies, singing her song of mourning.

"I miss him too," he whispered into the gathering gloom, as the dragon furled its wings and settled once more. Kin'rar hadn't deserved to die like that, stabbed through the gut by Ashun Klo in his grief-stricken fury. He'd been trying to get Ashun to see reason, but no, the man had been driven wild by Prince Tethian's death. *And how many others died for the prince's folly?* Lythian wondered, as he gazed out into the silent night. *And mine…*

He sighed, as the last of the daylight fled, leaving darkness to blanket the land. *A darkness that will spread*, he thought solemnly. *A darkness I helped unleash.*

He drew back into the trees, quiet as he could, boots squelching on the soft mossy earth underfoot, sodden from the relentless rains. His time foraging that day had yielded scant reward. Some mushrooms, a few wild roots, little more. He'd taken Talasha's bow with him, and almost scored himself a small wild pig, but it had plunged into the undergrowth before he could get away a decent shot. Elsewise he'd seen little sign of game or wildfowl, and had to hope Pagaloth had better luck.

Unlikely, he knew. It had been three days now since they'd made a catch. Three days without meat.

Three days stuck here, as poor Mirella died…

He reached camp a half hour later, following the brook that trickled down through the woods, turning right at the boulder where the river gave way to a series of rapids, moving through the tall rangy pines and massive sentinels that took root in these parts. By the time he arrived at the cave the rains were coming down hard, showering ceaselessly through the canopy above.

He stepped beneath the broad rocky overhang that gave them shelter, escaping the deluge. The cave was shallow, yet deep enough to shield them from the elements, carved by wind and time into the base of a stumpy cliff. From its heart glowed a fire. Cevi, one of Talasha's handmaids, sat tending it, prodding at the embers, adding twigs and kindling. Her second handmaid, Mirella, lay nearby within a nest of coverlets and blankets, grimacing and mumbling in her sleep. Talasha sat beside her, dabbing her forehead with a cloth.

"Any change?" Lythian asked softly.

The princess shook her head. "She worsens, I fear." Those words caused Cevi to sniff and wipe her nose. She'd been weeping again, to judge those raw red rings around her eyes. Talasha gave her a comforting look and then asked Lythian, "Did you catch anything?"

The Knight of the Vale unslung Talasha's bow and removed the quiver of arrows from his back, placing them aside. He opened his pack and withdrew the roots and mushrooms that would serve for a stew. "Just these. I saw a wild pig, but..." He needn't explain his failing there. Talasha was better with the bow than he was, yet would not leave her handmaid, not at this time. Lythian stepped to the fire. "Cevi, would you prepare a broth?"

She nodded weakly. "I will…go and fetch water from the river."

She stood, picked up her small cooking pot, and moved out into the rains.

Talasha watched her go. "Mirella will not last much longer, I don't think," she said once Cevi was out of earshot. "Her wound, Lythian…the blight has spread to her organs. The fever is getting worse and earlier…when you were gone…" She held up another cloth, dark with blood. "She coughed this. Black blood and bile. I know what this means. I know the end is near."

Lythian moved closer; he could see the bloodstains around Mirella's mouth now, stark against the white pallor of her skin. She was a comely young girl, loyal and brave, but had taken a wound the night of Tethian's death. Not by blade or axe or bow, but by something as innocent as a jutting rock that had torn a gash in her leg. *She tried to cover it up,* Lythian thought, *so as not to slow us.* It was only when she collapsed several days later that they discovered the extent of it, the wound festering and turning septic, forcing them to stop here in this cave.

"She suffers, Talasha," he said quietly, resting a hand on her shoulder. "Perhaps…perhaps it's for the best."

The princess turned her eyes up to look at him, those warm brown eyes flecked with red. He feared a rebuke for saying that. To be called heartless and cruel. *Yet she understands*, he saw. *She knows we cannot stay here forever.* "It will destroy Cevi when she dies," is all she said. "They grew up together. They have been best friends all their lives, as close as sisters." She exhaled and looked out into the woods. "She is too soft-hearted for this life, sweet captain. She doesn't belong out here."

"None of us belong out here, Talasha." Lythian could feel her shivering in his grasp. He removed his roughspun cloak and draped it over her shoulders, kneeling beside her. "You should move closer to the fire, Princess. You need to look after yourself as well." She nodded weakly and he led her over to perch before the flames, her once glossy black hair falling unwashed down her back. Through the mouth of the cave, he could see Cevi out there, hastening back with the water. Another figure was approaching from beyond the river, Lythian saw. For a moment he feared a stranger, before spotting that rangy gait, the strong purposeful movement that signalled the return of Sir Pagaloth.

The dragonknight strode in shortly after Cevi, dripping wet, cloaked and cowled with a brace of rabbits slung over his right shoulder. He'd set traps the day before and a couple had yielded profit, it looked. "Not much meat on them," he admitted in his brooding Agarathi accent, "but they'll serve for now."

"You're a godsend, Pagaloth," Talasha told him, smilingly wanly. "Lythian had no such fortune."

Sir Pagaloth nodded as he handed the coneys to Cevi for skinning and butchering. "The woods grow scarce of game, Princess. It's these rains; they are hiding." He turned to Lythian. "A word, Captain."

They stepped aside, as Talasha took a rabbit off Cevi and helped her prepare them for the stew. "What is it?" Lythian asked him in a hushed voice. He sensed trouble in Pagaloth's eyes.

"I saw Neyruu again," the dragonknight said. "She was flying to the northeast. I think she was making for that same hilltop that…"

"She was," Lythian confirmed. "I saw her, just before I came back. She rests there every night."

The dragonknight twirled the centre braid of his beard, shimmering against the firelight. "Why do you suppose she lingers? Dragons always return to the Wings when their riders die."

"Always?" Lythian asked. He'd heard anecdotal reports to the contrary. "Some dragons bond again, I've read."

"Yes, but most do not. When their Fireborn rider is slain, they revert to a more basic state. Many become placid, it is believed. They live in mourning the rest of their days." He glanced at Talasha. "And besides, the soul-bonding of dragon and man requires the Bondstone; the Soul of Agarath. Without it the bond is only ever superficial. And the Bondstone is taken, Lythian. Taken and we do not know where."

Taken by Eldur, Lythian thought. Even now, after all these days, he struggled to fully comprehend what they'd done. *What I've done. Me…* Had he not agreed to join them in their journey to the Wings…had he not helped them navigate their way through those tunnels and passages…Eldur may never have been found. *I helped fan those flames,* he knew. *I blew on those cinders until they burst alight.*

"We know where," Lythian said eventually. "*Home*, Pagaloth. Eldur will return to the Wings…to muster all the dragons to his will. And when he does…" He thought again of his dream, of all the world burning. And he thought too of the great stone mound against which they'd found Eldur sleeping. A faint memory, thinly seen. It had been so hot down there in that great black cavern beneath the mountain, the air so thick he could hardly move. *And that mound,* he thought, shuddering. *That mound in the shape of Drulgar the Dread.* He gulped in a dry throat. "I fear he'll wake the great calamity," he finished in a whisper. "The Bondstone…it woke *him*, Pagaloth. After everything Tethian tried, all the rituals and rites, only the Bondstone could restore Eldur to life. What if…" He swallowed again, drew a shallow breath. "What if he should use it to wake the Dread as well?"

"Drulgar is dead, Lythian," Pagaloth assured him. "He was calcified, made stone, you said. He cannot be awoken."

"But Eldur…"

"Was still living. In stasis, yes, but living all the same. Sotel Dar said he was being sustained by the Breath of Agarath, by the fires beneath the tomb in which he'd come to rest. The very Soul of Agarath breathed life into him anew. But his was a vessel that could still be filled. The Dread…no. If truly gone to stone, no, he could not rise."

Lythian wasn't so sure, and behind his steadfast words knew Pagaloth wasn't either. *He tries to give me succour*, he knew. *He knows I blame myself.*

The rains were falling yet harder beyond the cave, splashing in through the gaping stone mouth. Lythian wondered what was going on out there, in the world. *Do the fires spread already? Do my countrymen rally against the coming storm?* In this vast wooded wilderness, there was no way of knowing. "We cannot stay here," he whispered, glancing across the cave. "Mirella…she will die soon. We need to decide where to go, once she's passed."

Pagaloth nodded sombrely. "We could continue south," he said. "We may find help among the communities that live on the Lumaran Saltflats. Mounts to see us safely to the coast. From there we might be able to barter passage on a ship."

"And go where?"

"Vandar," Pagaloth said at once. "Your homeland, Lythian."

"You have homes too, Pagaloth."

"None that are safe for us now. King Tavash will hunt us for our betrayals. The princess will not be safe, and I am sworn to serve you by oath. Talasha will be better protected in Vandar, under the patronage of the Knight of the Vale."

Lythian didn't doubt that, but he was inclined to believe that nowhere would be safe for any of them now. "It will take weeks to reach the coast," he said, "and weeks more to make berth in Vandar. And that is assuming all goes well." He gave their little camp a scan.

"How would we expect to pay? For these mounts. For passage to the north. We have no coin, Pagaloth."

"No, but we have other goods with which to trade." The dark-eyed man gestured to his fine dragonsteel blade. "I will sell it, if I must. And perhaps the princess will do the same with her armour."

"No," Lythian said abruptly. "I will not have her exposed." Her armour was dragonscale, forged of fine interlinking plates in purple and black and red. It was worth ten thousand head of sheep and half a fleet in itself. Lythian would not see her parted from it.

"Her bow, then. And quiver. And that necklace she wears. With my blade, that may suffice."

"It may," Lythian admitted. "But I don't think we should go to the coast, Pagaloth."

The dragonknight frowned. "Then where? There is only south, Lythian. North, east, west...they all lead deeper into Agarath."

"I know. There is danger to be faced wherever we go. But we have a responsibility too."

The dragonknight frowned, seeing something in Lythian's light hazel eyes. "The Nest," he said. "You intend to journey there through the mountains."

Lythian nodded. "The Nest contains the greatest compendium of dragonlore in the world. It may help us unravel the truth of what has happened. And Marak...Sotel Dar...they may yet be alive. We have to try."

Pagaloth's deep brown eyes flickered with doubt. "The Nest was destroyed when Eldur awoke, Lythian. When the dragons went wild, and threw the Fireborn from their backs. When they filled all the fortress in flame." He shook his head. "Marak and Sotel Dar are dead."

"We don't know that for sure."

"We do. Kin'rar told you himself that Marak stood up to Eldur. That he tried to confront him using the Fireblade. He cannot have survived that...you know it as well as I."

"Kin'rar was forced to flee before he could see what happened. He did not know for sure, and nor do we. But even so...we *must* try. This is bigger than me, you, even Talasha. We *have no choice*, Pagaloth."

When his words trailed off into the sound of falling rain, Lythian turned to find Talasha looking over at him. Cevi had overheard too, but was pretending she didn't, as she carved up the rabbits and threw the meat into the pot, sniffing all the while. Talasha stood and walked over, her slender frame enveloped within the cloak Lythian had draped about her shoulders. "You heard?" Lythian asked her.

She nodded.

"And?"

She contemplated it for a time, gazing out into the woods. "It's peaceful here," she began, her voice somehow far off, yearning for a simpler time. "I said once that we should run, didn't I, sweet captain? Do you remember? I said we should go deeper into these mountains, seek somewhere just like this. Somewhere we could live a life away from judgement and war. Where we might be together, just you and me." She smiled at Sir Pagaloth. "Well, it isn't just you and me anymore, but still…I have wondered the same thing these last days…"

Lythian stepped in. "Talasha…"

"I know, Lythian. I know that isn't possible. Wondering something…*wanting* something…it doesn't make it true, or real. No. I know we have a duty now. We brought Eldur back from the dead and we have a responsibility to put that right." She cringed to think back on that night. "He was meant to be our saviour…Cousin Tethian said so, and Sotel Dar too, and all the prophets before them. Pullio the Wise and Quarl the Blind and the Skylady of Loriath. How could they all have been so wrong?"

Lythian didn't care to debate that point. He had listened to Tethian and Sotel Dar preach and sermonise for weeks, and a part of him had even come to believe them too. *The balance,* he thought. That was how they termed it. The balance that needed to be struck to finally end the War Eternal. Eldur would rise from his tomb and control the Soul of Agarath. The heir of Varin would emerge to unite and master the Heart of Vandar. Only through their shared power could the final embers of war be stamped out for good. *Yet instead the inferno has been ignited.* And who and where this heir of Varin was, no one seemed to know.

Lythian took Talasha by the arm. "I will leave you here with Cevi," he said firmly. "Mirella…she may yet live for a day, two, three…we cannot know. You and Cevi stay, tend her. You'll be safe and hidden in these woods. Pagaloth and I will go alone."

She raised a hand to his cheek, thick with ten days of bristly growth. "Sweet noble captain, always trying to protect me." She smiled and kissed his lips. "No, you'll not leave us here. We go together or not at all."

He could see that her mind would not be changed on that, and a part of him, a large part, was happy for it too. He did not want to leave her here. To hunt and scavenge alone. To worry each night if a pack of wolves might sniff them out, or a bear, or a band of outlaws crawling through these hills. "OK, Talasha," is all he said. "We go together, or not at all."

When the rabbit stew was cooked, they gathered by the fire and ate from bowls of carved wood, listening to the sounds of the storm. There was no thunder, just rain, heavy and constant, sheeting down through the leaves and branches. Lythian hoped it would stop soon. The Nest wasn't nearly so far as the southern coast, only a hundred or so miles as the crow flies, yet the route would be fraught with danger even so and these rains wouldn't much help.

They'll stop as we get higher, he told himself. They were still in the foothills here, with the rivers bursting their banks and the slopes all garbed in green. But further to the north, where the great mountaintop fortress lay, would be harsh black scarps and treacherous passes and savage peaks crowned in snow.

He sidled over to Pagaloth, as Talasha and Cevi moved to sit with Mirella. The girl was sleeping quietly now, sweat beading on her forehead. "She fights on," Lythian said. "If she lives through the night, we'll hunt through tomorrow. Gather as many provisions as we can for the journey. Food will grow yet scarcer when we venture north."

The dragonknight nodded. "Finding the way will be difficult, Lythian. I hope you know this. Most who go to the Nest travel there on the wing. There are few ways to enter afoot."

"But there *are* ways," the Varin Knight said. "I have seen maps, diagrams, read descriptions of the fortress in books. We need to find the spiral stair at the base of the Ashway. It will lead us to the summit."

"The Ashway Stair is entered on the western side," Pagaloth mused, placing his bowl aside. "It is reachable by the Ash Road that runs alongside the Askar River from Eldurath. We will have to go around the mountains to reach it."

"We will." Lythian poured the last of his soup through his lips and lowered the bowl to his lap. "We must."

When morning came, the rains had relaxed into a gentle drizzle and the sun was pouring down in its place, casting a bright glow through the high branches of the trees and lighting puddles on the forest floor. Lythian woke to find Pagaloth sleeping, Talasha as well. Only Cevi was awake, still sitting at Mirella's side. She lifted her eyes as Lythian stirred. "She…still lives," she whispered, almost guiltily. "I am…sorry, Captain Lythian. I know you want her to let go."

"No," he breathed out at once, sitting up. "No, of course I don't…"

"I don't blame you. The world may be ending out there and you are a great knight. Only your honour compels you to remain here. But she will die, I know this now." She seemed to have accepted that overnight during her long lonely vigil. She looked down at her friend and smiled sadly. "Today, tomorrow, it doesn't matter. Not to her, anyway. But to you?" Her gaze returned to the knight. "You cannot wait any longer, I know. Maybe…maybe this is for the best." She reached out and picked up a cloth, pressing it down over Mirella's face.

Lythian sped quickly to his feet. "Cevi, no…" He hurried over, gripped her wrist, pulled her hand free and the cloth with it. The commotion caused Talasha and Pagaloth to wake.

"What is going on?" the princess demanded, scanning the scene.

Cevi's round weary eyes were all anguish and pain. "I cannot watch her suffer anymore," she wailed. "She is already dead. Dead and she just doesn't know it!" She tried to snatch the cloth back from Lythian's grasp, but he drew it away. "Give it to me. *Please!* Let me do this thing."

"This thing is killing, Cevi," Talasha told her plainly, reading between the lines. "It is a violation of the soul."

"It is *mercy*, my lady. I cannot bear to watch her die so slow…"

"*Cevi*." Talasha's voice softened. She stepped in and wrapped her into an embrace, and didn't let go. "We have no choice, sweet girl. We must follow the natural course of things. All we can do is make her as comfortable as we can."

"No. No, we should do it now." Cevi pulled back and away, retreating to the rock wall of the cave. She looked suddenly like a cornered animal, closed in by predators. "We have been here too long for her. What if she lives another three days? Another week? Like *this*." She looked down and shook her head, once, twice, thrice, hair swishing wildly. "No. She is strong. Too strong. And stubborn. She does not realise she is gone." She had a thought and looked up.

"*Command her*, my lady. She will listen to you, she will hear. Command her to die and…"

"Cevi, no! I will not do that. I *cannot* do that."

"Then you are to blame. Her pain…is on you!" Before anyone could say anything, Cevi bolted past every one of them and fled out into the woods.

Pagaloth made to follow. "I'll go after her."

Talasha breathed out. She looked more tired than ever, her golden skin losing its colour. It seemed for a moment like she would tell him no, but eventually she nodded and said, "Go, but keep a distance, Pagaloth. Watch and wait and make sure she is safe. Bring her back when she has calmed."

"Yes, Princess." Pagaloth moved from the cave.

That left them alone. Lythian's eyes went to Mirella. She looked no different from the night before, no worse and no better. There was a tension in his chest, something uncomfortable. *What if Cevi's right?* he wondered. *What if Mirella should live on like this, neither recovering nor dying, in stasis like Eldur. For days, even weeks. We cannot afford that. She…she needs to die, and soon.*

He hated that thought, but what choice did they have? His eyes met with those of the princess, the woman he had come to love. They stared at one another in silence, for five seconds, ten, how long he could not say. Yet in that silence he asked a question and saw in her eyes the answer. "Make it quick," she whispered, barely able to voice the words. She looked at Mirella one final time, a single tear trailing down her cheek.

"She won't feel a thing, I promise."

When the princess had stepped away, Lythian moved forward and knelt before the handmaid. Her mouth twitched at the corners, and there was some faint flickering about the eyes. *Mercy*, he thought, as he reached to pick up the cloth. "I am sorry you suffered so, Mirella," he whispered.

He drew the cloth to her face, he pressed down.

4

Saska

The midday sun blasted down upon the pavestones as Saska strolled through the gardens, enjoying her daily allowance of time outdoors. Her captor and host permitted her one hour beyond the confines of his palatial hilltop residence each day, but no more, and there were always guards on hand to watch her should she have a mind to try to flee.

That sunwolf is the worst, Saska thought warily, as the brawny great beast prowled along nearby, long uncut claws clacking on the stone. She'd seen some dozen sunwolves by now around the grounds, yet that one was especially mean and watchful, with broad muscular shoulders and a darker mane than most, near black against its golden fur. It was called Agarro, she'd heard, yet had no bonded rider as far as she could figure, not like the other ones. Every day when she came outside it seemed to appear from nowhere, watching with those dark narrow eyes. It made her uneasy, and more than a bit fearful. *One wrong move,* the presence of the beast said, *and you'll have Agarro's jaws around your throat, ripping.*

"You have ten more minutes, my lady," came a call behind her.

She didn't need to turn around to know who'd spoken the words; by now she knew the names and voices of every guard who escorted and attended her here. This one was called Protho, one of the nicer ones. He was young, polite, and always treated her with courtesy. She couldn't say the same for all of them.

She nodded and continued on her rounds, trying to ignore the presence of Agarro as best she could. The grounds of Lord Elio Krator's mansion in the hilly heights of Aram were ample, yet by now she knew them well. Here above the city proper, all was colourful and tranquil and sweet-smelling, with fruiting trees and flowers garnishing the gardens, fountains and statues adorning the paths, terraces and balconies and beautiful walled perches giving wondrous views over the well-ordered streets below. *A beautiful, colourful, sweet-smelling prison,* Saksa thought. *But a prison all the same.*

Joy was skulking along beside her, the cat's black, silver spotted fur glimmering beneath the baking hot sun. She always grew tense when Agarro was nearby, glancing over at the brutish sunwolf, occasionally giving out a low rumbling growl or hissing if he got too near. The wolf never responded with the same. Saska took that as a sign of superiority. He was well over twice as big as Joy, and many times heavier, and were it to come to a contest of claws and fangs, there would only be one winner.

"Ignore him," she whispered to the lithe black cat, her shoulders moving up and down as she prowled along at Saska's side. "We'll be back inside soon." She gave Joy a scratch under the chin to calm her, but it did no good. When alone in their private quarters, the starcat would stretch out and lie on her back, purring as Saska scratched and stroked at her ears and neck and belly, yet out here she was all business. *She'll defend me with her life,* Saska thought. *Not that I deserve it...*

She turned down a pathway leading away to the southwest, as the sun wheeled overhead in a glorious golden arc. Ahead, a staircase led up into a viewing platform, its white stone bannisters festooned with flowering vines. Saska climbed the two dozen steps and stopped at the railing, looking out over the city. Down the slopes of the hill, the Amedda River wended away to the northwest, its banks and bridges busy with industry, waters glimmering silver and gold as it bled away into the distant plains beyond the boundaries of her sight. Further off, looming imperiously above the buildings clustered about its base, the three-tiered pyramid palace of Aram soared, bronze at the bottom, silver in the middle, and a bright gilded gold at the summit. From its many balconies and terraces huge great banners hung down, stirring in the light breeze. They had the resemblance of feathers, invoking the great Eagle of Aramatia, Calacan, and across the city, the watchmen and city guards had cloaks shaped as feathers too, and eagle-crested halfhelms as well.

A sigh blew through Saska's lips, as she stood looking out at the view. She supposed her host would be in the palace now, holding court and hearing his people's pleas, passing his judgements and savouring the sweet taste of rule. It had been two weeks now since Saska had arrived here and still she had no word of her grandmother's return. Lord Krator refused to tell her anything in the few times he'd graced her with his presence, and Mar Malaan, the paunchy perfumed Sunrider who served at Krator's pleasure, had been vexing in his responses too. Saska had even tried to query the guards about goings-on in the city, such was her desperation, but they'd been just as tight-lipped, and the maids who attended her only ever bit their tongues or pretended not to understand if she asked them any probing questions.

She has to come soon, she thought, staring out at the palace. *She just has to...*

Saska's entire reason for journeying to Aram in the first place was to meet her grandmother and find out what she was to do. *She was meant to tell me my purpose. She was meant to show me the way.* Yet instead she'd been a fool, and in her folly, had ended up here, deaf and blind to all that went on beyond these walls. For all she knew the Grand Duchess might already have returned. *She might be down there now, and not even know I'm here.* Elio Krator had the wild notion that Saska had come to take her place as her grandmother's heir, so what would he gain to reveal her?

She sighed again. The city below was a blur of bluster and noise, ringing up from the bridges and streets and squares. From this far away it all melted together into one, a great blanket of sound at once comforting and deflating to hear. *If only I could get down there,* she thought, *maybe I could blend in.* Escape had been much in her thoughts, but it seemed impossible. At night they locked her in her rooms, and by day there were always eyes watching her. *And Agarro's...they're the worst. He longs for us to try to run.* She had that sense about the big black-maned wolf. One false move, and he'd pounce, just like that.

"You have five minutes, my lady. We should start back, else Sunrider Malaan will grow restive."

Protho again, in those courteous tones of his. This time she deigned to answer. "As you wish, Protho. Can we go back via the pools? I'd like to wet my feet, if I may. It's very hot this afternoon."

The young guardsman wore a silken cape, weaved in swirling lines of gold and bronze, and a studded leather vest, dark copper, with a gilded halfhelm crested in the likeness of a howling sunwolf above his brow. That was the sigil of House Krator, Saska had learned, adorning the back of his guardsmen's capes and the banners that hung from his gates and walls; a great howling sunwolf, dark gold and outlined in black, against a golden sun behind.

Protho gave a bow. "Of course, my lady, so long as we're quick. Come now. Time is nearly up."

The young man followed her down the steps and back along the path, moving through a maze of verdant hedges and skinny cypress trees toward the rear gardens. He had with him a much older guardsman called Hiram, grey-bearded and inky-eyed and lacking a tongue, if his refusal to speak was anything to go by. Hiram wasn't friendly like Protho or mean like Balza, he was merely silent as the grave, and rarely said a word. But he was always watching too, like Agarro. Something about that old man unsettled her.

They reached an open courtyard where a series of rectangular pools shimmered lazily beneath the cobalt skies, separated by veined marble footpaths and tinkling fountains large and small. It was a shrine of sorts, with statues of the southern gods marking the corners; Aramatia with her eagle; Pisek with his sunwolf and great double-bladed axe; Solapia and her basket of fruit and vegetables; and Lumara, mother to all, standing in flowing white robes with her staff planted at her feet before her, one side silver for the moon and the other gold for the sun.

As in the north, they'd named their nations for their gods, though Lumara was senior and matriarch among them. It was why the empires founded here - and there had been many, across the millennia - were always called the Lumaran Empire, even if one of the other nations held preeminence at the time. To gather the southern nations beneath another such banner - the Aramatian Empire, or Piseki Empire, for instance - would be a slur against the greatest of their gods, and mother to their people. Lumara the goddess had birthed the others, it was known, and her demigod followers Lumo and Sola had led her armies in war. To supersede her would be blasphemy. Yet somehow, Saska had the notion that Lord Elio Krator would not care. *And perhaps that is his true design,* she mused, looking at the statue of Aramatia, forged in such splendid detail. *To not just rule Aramatia, but the entire empire, under her name. And his own.*

She turned her eyes back over the pools. There were three of them. One was shallow and small, its bottom coloured with mosaics in copper and silver and hints of blue and green, used for dipping and paddling. A second, further on, was larger and deeper, with steps built into its edge. It was intended for relaxing and bathing, the waters reaching no more than chest height. Finally, at the back, the largest of the pools stretched out, forty metres long and fifteen wide, shallow at one end and growing ever deeper as it went on. It was used for swimming, Saska had been told, a fond pastime of her host.

As yet, Saska had only been permitted entry into the first pool. She turned to Protho. "Can I use one of the larger ones today?" she asked him. "The swimming pool? It's so hot, Protho. I'd love to swim…"

He was already shaking his head. "No time, my lady. No. You can make that request of Sunrider Malaan. Or Sunlord Krator, when you next see him."

And when will that be? she wondered, frustrated. She'd hardly seen him throughout her internment. She turned back to the largest pool, gazing at it longingly. *I could ignore him,* she thought. *Just run down there and plunge in. What exactly will he do?*

Then she saw Agarro watching from beside a nearby fountain and thought better of it. *Next time,* she decided, satisfying herself with the paddling pool instead, slipping out of her sandals and wading into the calf-high water. Shallow as it was, it wasn't so cool as the others would likely be, not with the sun heating it from dawn until dusk. Still, it was refreshing enough, and Joy came with her, splashing along at her side and occasionally dipping her head to lap up some water with that long purple tongue of hers. But all too briefly, it was done. "Come, my lady," Protho called. "It grows hot, and your time is spent. Let us retreat back into the shade."

She nodded and returned to the house.

It was a sprawling place, and half of it off-limits, its halls and corridors wide and cool, ceilings high, furnishings glorious. There must have been a hundred staff here, maids and washerwomen, scullery wenches and cooks, gardeners and pool boys and the sentries stationed at every way in and out. Others were only visitors, and technically, so was Mar Malaan. The Sunrider was of a noble line himself, a vassal to Lord Krator, with lands of his own and a smaller villa further down in the hills.

He was awaiting them in the main entrance hall, a garish place all gold and bronze, with patterned panelling on the walls depicting the great lords and ladies and famed riders of House Krator. Theirs was a storied house, an ancient house, with bloodlines rich and pure. House Krator has boasted Moonriders in its past, those who'd helped win Renewals in centuries gone by, and their Sunriders and Starriders of renown were legion. Lord Krator himself had fought bravely during the War of the Continents, it was said, leading vast hosts of men from the saddle of his own sunwolf, Braccaro. He'd even been there at the Burning Rock, and near enough to witness the battle between Amron Daecar and Vallath and Prince Dulian, if Mar Malaan told it true. The fat flowery Sunrider was happy to regale her of such matters that honoured his lord, even if current affairs in the city were to be kept from her ears.

He smiled now as he spotted her, a strong zesty scent of citrus perfume radiating from his person. "Well, there you are. A minute or two overdue, but I'll forgive it." He gave Protho a judging look. "You must be warming to her, Protho, to let her run rings around you like this."

"My apologies, Sunrider. She wanted to wet her feet in the pools. It is most warm out there today."

"I'm sure. But when you slip you're never far from falling. One or two minutes will soon become ten or fifteen. And then what? We have set rules for our guest for a reason. Keep to them in future."

"I will, Sunrider." Protho bowed low, his curled hazel hair waving a salute.

Mar Malaan waved him away. "You can go. And you, Hiram. I will escort Saska back to her rooms."

The Sunrider had his old sunwolf with him, a well-mannered beast with streaks of grey in his golden mane. His name was Taro, a word that meant *honour* in the tongue of the Islands of the Moon, from which the flowery man originally hailed. The wolf was rather more pleasant company than Agarro, it had to be said, who had slipped away as soon as they stepped foot within the residence. That one never came inside, thankfully.

"They get along better than they did," Mar Malaan noted, gesturing to Taro and Joy as they walked along side-by-side in something approaching a friendly stroll. "She has grown more relaxed these last days, I think. Can the same be said of you, Saska?"

No, she thought, *categorically no.* Instead she ignored the question and said, "Joy likes Taro well enough, but Agarro...does that wolf have to trail us around every time we walk outside? If you want us both to relax, you'd do well to start there."

"Yes," Malaan chucked, "I can see that. Agarro is a menacing beast, this is true. But alas he has the run of the gardens and goes where he pleases. I'm sure he just finds you and Joy interesting to observe, as we all do. It is curiosity that draws him to you, I think."

"Cats are curious, not wolves," Saska returned. "He'll attack Joy one of these days, I can smell it. He wants nothing more than to..."

Mar Malaan's tittering laughter broke her off. "Agarro will not attack lest he is given reason to. I have not yet told you the story of him, have I?"

"No," Saska said, brusquely. "You haven't told me *anything*."

The silken Sunrider looked aghast. Hand to mouth, he said, "Now come, this isn't true. I have told you much of House Krator and that of my own bloodline. And much of the history of our people besides. You wound me, child. Here was me thinking we got along well."

"You're my jailer. How long will you keep me hostage here?"

Malaan's smile was slimy, sunlight from a nearby window washing over his round bald head. "Where else would you like to go?" he asked her.

"You know where. The palace. I came here to see my grandmother."

"Your grandmother is not yet returned." That could still be a lie, so far as she knew. But more likely it was true. She'd been told that the Grand Duchess had gone to Lumos, the City of Light, to give war counsel to Empress Valura following the verdict of the warmoot. That seemed logical. Then again, Lord Krator had hinted during their first meeting that Safina Nemati might just happen upon some tragedy on the road home. He'd laughed it off, of course, when she'd accused him of speaking treason, but still...could he have spoken truly? *And if my grandmother should die...*

She didn't even want to think about that just yet.

"When our light and noble ruler does return you will of course be told, and brought to her," Mar Malaan was going on, in that airy lilt of his. He seemed no warrior to Saska's eyes, soft and round and delicate in his gestures as he was, yet had told her he'd fought alongside Lord Krator during the war. She found that hard to believe. "Until that time, however, you will remain here in Lord Krator's care. And care it is, child. You will not find yourself safe out there."

She wasn't believing a word he was saying. Sure, she might be vulnerable out there on the streets, but she'd sooner strike out alone with Joy than spend another moment as a prisoner here. "Your master thinks I'm here to supplant him in the line of rule," she said, scoffing. "That's why he's keeping me imprisoned. He'll sooner kill me than hand me over to the Grand Duchess."

"Oh no…no no, you have that all wrong. You are quite safe here, and you misinterpret Lord Krator's intent. The good sunlord sees something of your mother in you, child, the mother he once loved so deeply. He could never hurt you."

He sees more of my father in me, no doubt, she thought. What Elio Krator had told her the day they met had still scarcely sunk in, and half of her didn't believe it. *My father was not a slave, or a rapist,* she knew in her heart of hearts. *He was a Bladeborn of royal blood, who fell in love with a beautiful southern princess, and I was the result.*

"And Sir Ralston?" she demanded. Even to say his name brought a pang of pain and guilt and grief all at once. "Could Lord Krator hurt *him*? *Has* he? Why won't you tell me what's happened to him!"

Joy was at Saska's side in an instant as soon as her voice rose, prowling and growling and staring dark daggers at the flowery man. Taro looked as unworried as his corpulent rider. Malaan smiled a placating smile. "Sir Ralston has yet to be judged, sweet child, and remains caged for now. I know he is dear to you, and has been much in your thoughts. I can only apologise for this, truly. But we are at war now, as you know, and Sir Ralston…well…his capabilities are well known."

"He's unarmed, unarmored, imprisoned," Saska came back. "And no threat to you or anyone else here." She looked into Mar Malaan's guileful brown eyes. *He said Rolly hasn't yet been judged,* she thought, taking a pause. It was more than she'd gotten from anyone in days. "I only want to see him," she said, her voice pleading. "Please. I just want to know that he's OK."

"I'm afraid this cannot be done, lest Lord Krator permits it."

"Please, Mar, he'd never need to…"

"No." Mar Malaan turned from her, and continued walking down the hall.

She had no choice but to trail behind, clinging to some faint hope that Rolly would make it through. But faint it was now, faint and growing fainter by the day. Krator might wish to keep her hostage, but Sir Ralston? Why? He was a known hero in the north and the world was falling to war. *No, they'll make an example of him,* she knew. *I've doomed him to his death.*

Wreathed in guilt and feeling as wretched as ever, she followed forlornly until they reached the door to her chambers. A guard was stationed outside, this one called Rishan, she recalled, another youthful soldier dressed in the Krator crest and colours. At the Sunrider's command he opened the door, bowing as they passed within.

Her chambers were airy, spacious, and finely appointed. There was a writing table, comfortable chairs and cushions, rugs to warm the cool stone floor, a broad window with a generous sill on which she liked to perch, with views out over the city and harbour, and two beds. One was a large four-poster with rich gold curtains that could sleep an entire family if needed. The other was designed for starcats, roughly oval-shaped, with soft bedding and blankets as a base. Saska had heard it say that tame starcats and sunwolves commonly slept in such beds, but Joy wasn't there yet. She preferred to stretch out on the floor beside Saska's bed, and had even slept on the mattress with her once or twice when she'd heard Saska weeping at night, and had jumped up to comfort her. The cat was the only shard of sunlight cutting through the shadows of her captivity. *A captivity of my own making,* she thought, miserable. *Oh Rolly, I'm so sorry…*

Mar Malaan strode across the room, toward the grey-stone plinth positioned against the wall opposite the bed. It was one of the newer furnishings, brought in only days ago. Atop it was a skull, jaw and cheeks cracked and broken, teeth smashed and shattered. *My father,* Saska thought. Her host had been considerate enough to bring him here to keep her company. "A gruesome thing," the Sunrider said, shaking his head in sympathy. "I remember him, you know. Your father. A handsome boy. Dark curly hair. Eyes as blue as yours. Only saw him once or twice but you don't soon forget a northern slave."

"My father wasn't a slave."

"A troubling truth to confront, I am sure. Though surely you of all people can understand. You were a slave too, were you not?"

Saska said nothing to that.

The Sunrider smiled. "So you see, even those born to be great can find themselves in chains. Look at you, child. Half Lightborn, half Bladeborn, with a starcat beneath you and a godsteel blade to hand. Not many would imagine you had spent time in bondage. Yet you have." He turned and placed a hand atop the skull's cracked white dome. "Perhaps your father was the same."

The man was being more open than usual. She was loath to believe a word he said, but her curiosity was piqued. "How did he come to be in the palace?"

Mar Malaan smiled, looking down at the skull for a time. "I inquired of the very same thing, the first time I saw him. The palace steward merely said he'd been brought into port by slavers. An unpleasant practice, slavery, yet it does thrive from time to time, especially during war. You saw that yourself, I'm sure. Many southerners were taken into bondage in the north, and here in the south, the same was true. I will say, I had not expected it of Safina Nemati, however. She is a most pious and righteous woman, and not the sort to have a northern boy enslaved within her palace. Curious, I always thought. Lord Krator questioned her on that wisdom many times. Said the boy had an ill look to him...that he would do something rash. Yet she dismissed him all the same, and look what happened..." He sighed and shook his head.

Saska studied Malaan's face. "Do you believe it," she asked, sensing some doubt in the man. "That he raped her...my mother."

Mar Malaan gave out that tittering laugh. "Now of course he did. How else would the princess have gotten with child by him?"

"By willingly inviting him into her bed."

The Sunrider's smile slithered away. "Princess Leila was long betrothed to Lord Krator," he said, more curtly. "It is true she was something of a free spirit, but to bed a northern slave? No." He shook his head and folded his arms. So much about him felt contrived. "It is hard to hear, I know, but you are the product of a crime most foul, child. It would serve you to make your peace with that. To deny it will only prolong your pain."

Then I'll be in pain till the day I die, she thought, *because I'll not believe it, not once, not ever.*

Mar Malaan moved away from the plinth, inspecting the state of the room. He liked to do that every time he visited, checking in on how she was, making sure her every need was attended. Leastways those they were willing to grant. "You're being fed well?" he asked, perfunctorily looking over the trestle table, laden with fruits and nuts and sweetened breads. "And Joy?" He glanced to the starcat, who never looked especially well-fed, but that was her shape.

"She's fine," Saska grunted. "We have everything we need." *Except freedom.*

"You're sure? Wine?" He gave the flasks and flagons a swift scan. There were several grapes and vintages here, and more on offer if she wanted them. In her desolation, she'd imbibed more regularly than she'd have liked. Sometimes it was the only thing to do, when locked away in here. "I have plenty."

"Good." He tapped the shallow cleft in his flabby chin, studying the room. "Clothing? Perfumes? Oils for your bath? Are your maids treating you well?"

"Very well."

He nodded. "Lord Krator will want you bathed and washed and in a fresh dress when he next summons you. I will have a new fragrance brought. My lord's tastes are ever-changing." He smiled.

Saska frowned. "I'll see him tonight?" She'd dined with Elio Krator only twice since coming here, and those occasions had been only brief affairs, late at night when his daily business was done.

"Lord Elio has much he must attend to," the Sunrider said. "The city requires his attention, as does the war. So tonight…perhaps, though I cannot say for sure." He made for the door.

"I'd like to swim tomorrow, if I can," Saska blurted out to him, as he left. "Protho said to ask you. The main pool, the deep one. I'm fond of swimming, Sunrider Malaan, just like Lord Krator is. Perhaps I might…"

"I will have to ask him. That pool is for the lord's private use." He made to open the door, but turned back. "I never told you the story of Agarro."

"No," said Saska, utterly defeated.

"My apologies. Our discussions do tend to take tangents." He giggled, chins wobbling. "Agarro was once ridden by a Sunrider named Baldo Baralio, of a house most loyal to the Krators. Baldo… my, what a fearsome rider he was, much like the mount he would charge atop to battle. He fought at Lord Elio's side during the war, his champion and protector, deadly on claw and paw and foot alike, whether riding his wolf or with his great axe to hand. He was as the god Pisek come again, axe and wolf and man in unison, and when he charged, how people cheered. Axe swinging, wolf snapping, he was a whirlwind on the field, big and black-haired, with golden skin and a talent for death. How many did he kill? Who can say? But many…oh yes, so many, before death came instead for him at the Battle of Burning Rock."

He paused for effect, then went on. "It was your Prince Rylian Lukar who killed him, early on in the battle before he went on to slay a dragon. Baldo the Black was nothing if not bold, but in Prince Rylian he met his match and more. The Tukoran Prince cut him down from Agarro's back and with that, the battle swelled about them, swallowing all. Agarro, riderless, rudderless, slew many men in reprisal that day, maddened by his grief. He even saved Lord Krator's life, showing loyalty to him even after Baldo's death. That is rare, child, for a sunwolf or starcat to serve after their rider's fall, yet here Agarro lingers, prowling the gardens day and night, watching over the man his bonded rider had sworn his life to protect."

He reached for the door handle. "True loyalty, child, is a commodity one cannot buy. And there are many...many hundreds... many thousands who would lay down their lives for Lord Elio of House Krator. Always remember that, should you have a mind to do something reckless." He took a final glance at the skull. "Your father did, and look where that got him. Prudence, Saska, and patience. In time, you may build a life here, as Agarro did."

He smiled, opened the door, and slipped out into the hallway. Moments later, she heard the bolts go...one, two, three.

5

Elyon

"We should gather a force and return at once," said Sir Lancel Greymont, pacing side to side. His footsteps echoed off the old stone walls of the hall, the light of the hearth throwing his shadow across the floor. "We can go back the way we came. Right in through the rear of the palace. Janilah *must* pay for this. We have men enough here to strike hard and strike fast, and see this blood paid with blood!"

Elyon raised a hand to quieten him. Some men vented in a crisis and others stayed quiet, listening. He wanted to hear what those thought and Lancel had been pacing and baying for some time. "Sir Connor." He turned to the captain of the Daecar guard. "I would hear your thoughts."

The man looked surprised by the summons. Yet Elyon knew him for a deliberate and cautious knight and his counsel would be worth hearing. "I would say the palace will be well guarded," he began, in that gloomy thoughtful tone of his. "The route the sellswords took, and the one you took as well. You might get to him, but it would bear much risk to try. I would urge restraint, my lord, and counsel you to…"

"You'd counsel *cowardice*," said Sir Lancel, turning on him. "You've always taken easily to it, Sir Connor."

"Now Lancel, enough," scolded Amara. "I know you're weary from your travels, but this is no time or place for insults."

Elyon found his eyes glaring at her. *Is this your fault, Auntie, or mine?* he wondered. *We have played our part in this bloodshed. We drew Rylian into our schemes and look what has come of it…*

He closed his sword hand, squeezing his fingers tight. The hall was well stocked with knights and petty lords and it would not serve him to show weakness now. *I must lead. I must listen.* Yet for all that he wanted to rage, and thrash, and do just what Lancel was saying. *I would march right back there and take off Janilah's head. I would see him and every one of them drawn and quartered for this crime.*

He swallowed, breathed, and spoke again. "Sir Connor Crawfield is no craven, Lancel," he said, keeping his voice as steady as he could. "He has served my family dutifully for years. You'll make no such accusation again."

Lancel nodded. "My apologies, Sir Connor," he said to the man in question. "My tongue grows hot with this…this news."

"His tongue and *my* head," declared Sir Mooton Blackshaw, slamming his fist upon the table at which he sat so hard Elyon heard the wood crack. He lurched to his feet and pulled a great misting greatsword from its sheath. "I call for blood and vengeance, Sir Elyon. Greymont is right. This treason cannot be left unpaid."

Some of the other men stamped their feet and banged their fists at that. These were men of the Riverlands, Blackshaw men and their banners, who all served beneath the great power of House Kanabar. Much like their greatlord, they had no love for King Janilah Lukar. *And what will Wallis make of this?* Elyon wondered. Lord Kanabar had been part of their plotting as well, that which had paved the path to Rylian's death. *Rylian's death,* he thought again, his stomach a nest of snakes, snapping and twisting and biting at one another. He remembered the morning the prince had come for him in his cell. He remembered worrying what Janilah would do when he found out his son had betrayed him. *He told me all would be well. He told me to master the Windblade as payment for his aid.* "I'll expect to see you soon, Sir Elyon, soaring in from the skies," the prince had said. "That's the only repayment I need."

A swelling tide of guilt and shame and grief threatened to overwhelm him. *He saved my life and in doing so condemned himself to death.* The details of what had happened were vague, yet Elyon knew enough. Rylian had gone to confront his father shortly after helping him escape, Sir Daryl Blunt had reported to him when he'd arrived at Elmhall Hold barely an hour ago with Lancel, Barnibus, Sir Mooton and his men. Apparently some affray had broken out and a brace of Janilah's Six - the Hunt brothers, Sir Rees and Sir Maxwell - had been slain, with Sir Fredrick Ruxmond badly wounded. Only Sir Owen Armdall, most daring and deadly of Janilah's sworn swords, had come away without serious injury. *All were armoured in godsteel plate and mail, and Rylian nought but leather and fur, yet still he almost killed them all.* How it started, no one knew for sure, yet it wasn't hard to draw assumptions. *Janilah,* Elyon thought, as the clamour of stamping feet and banging fists and voices filled the hall. *Janilah gave the order when he found out what Rylian had done. He commanded the death of his very own son...*

"I can have fresh levies mustered from Wolfwood," called out Lord Justin Huxley over the din."My lands and castle are not far. Give me leave, Sir Elyon, and I'll ride there without delay and have a hundred fighting men for you not two days hence."

Elyon had never met the young lord, but had watched his brother Sir Arnald compete in the Song of the First Blade. *I studied his fighting patterns,* he recalled, *as I did everyone Aleron might have come up against. That was my job, to support my brother in his bid to win the contest. Yet here I stand, before knights and lords, leading in his stead...*

"Pineway is not far," rasped the gruff voice of Sir Lutherton Wane, an ageing knight with a shovel-shaped beard, brown with strands of grey. "I have three sons, all fine fighters. They'll join us if I send word."

"Your boys are barely out of their swaddling clothes," Sir Mooton said to that. "We need hardened men, killers, not whelps fresh from their mother's teat..."

Sir Lutherton didn't take that especially well. "You mention my wife's teats again and I'll serve her up your manhood on a platter."

"You'd need a big platter."

The jest had the hall erupting into laughter, though Sir Lutherton didn't look amused. Before he might have a chance to respond, Elyon turned to Carly, sitting on a table to one side with old Crowfoot and burly Sally Scarlet beside her. The rest of the Flame Manes were off in some barracks down in the bailey, or so Elyon had been told. He raised a hand to call for quiet. "You know the way back to the palace better than anyone, Carly." He looked into her cunning green eyes. "Can it be done?"

She slipped from the table and set aside the apple she'd been eating, sticking it with her dirk. Bright red hair flowed in curls down her neck. "He'll expect it," she said. "Janilah. Every way into the palace will be watched, blocked, even boobytrapped. An illusionist is only as good as his secrets. Once people learn how he performs his tricks, the magic is lost." She shrugged. "We've played our trick in getting you and the Windblade out. Won't be so easy getting back in."

"Then bugger all this sneaking," bellowed the Beast of Blackshaw. "We'll take a more direct route."

A few men laughed their derision. "What, the front gates?" snickered Sir Lutherton. "You'd need an army."

"Half the Tukoran army is sailing south to siege Eagle's Perch," said Lancel. "Might be the city is weak enough for us to..."

"To *what*?" cut in Barnibus. Both men were as dishevelled as Elyon from their long journey through the mountains and woods, and all in need of a bath and change of clothes. "Gods, Lance, have you lost your wits? You think we can take Ilithor with a few hundred men? The garrison there is in the thousands and there're half a dozen gated levels to get through."

"History proves how difficult the task is," Amara agreed. "When Galin Lukar stormed the city three centuries ago he did so with an army numbering tens of thousands. This talk is folly."

"I agree," said a willowy knight with a pointed orange beard and hooked nose whom Elyon knew to be Sir Peter Hornmoor, another vassal of House Blackshaw. "Folly is most assuredly the word, my lady. What we are discussing here is the murder of a king. A king who is allied to our own, lest we forget. To march against him would bring war and turmoil at a time when we can afford it least. Until we know for certain what happened to the prince, we cannot surely consider this course."

"Oh we know what happened, Hornmoor," grunted Sir Mooton. "A prince lies dead, and two of his father's sworn swords beside him. You bloody work it out."

"It may not be so simple as that."

Sir Mooton was having none of it. Elyon had travelled here over the past two days with him and found him very much the essence of what a Riverlander was; big, bawdy, bellicose, and given to bouts of recklessness. "It's as simple as my halfwit son," he snorted.

"Which one?" Sir Lutherton said, in vengeance for the man's earlier jest, and once more laughter gusted through the hall.

This is the way they are, Elyon had to remind himself, though he cracked nothing close to a smile of his own. The Riverlanders liked to use humour to soften tragedy, though how they could laugh at a time like this he would never know. But he'd heard enough. Enough of Sir Mooton's bellowing and enough of these ill-timed jests. *Enough laughter,* he thought. *I cannot listen to it anymore.* He raised a hand once again. "I've heard you," he called out, "and will take time to contemplate what must be done. We can gather again on the morrow, once we're all better rested. I thank you for assembling in such haste. Now return to your beds." *And I'll find one of my own…*

The men didn't take long to disperse, most of them heading for the doors and down into the lower bailey where there were a few castle taverns to accommodate them. It was well past midnight now and many had been sleeping when Elyon called to hear their counsel. It felt the right thing to do, though all he'd wanted to do was find a place to be alone, to curse himself and curse the world and curse that it had come to this. But he couldn't. He had to be decisive, as his father would have been. *A good lord and leader listens,* he could hear his father saying, though those lessons had always been for Aleron more than him. *He listens and weighs up the options before him, and then decides upon the best course.*

But what course is that? he wondered now. He had no energy to ponder the question. *By morning I will have to decide.*

The castle steward remained behind a moment as the hall began to empty. Elyon hadn't yet gotten his name. "My lord," the old man said. "I have taken the liberty of having chambers prepared for you and your companions." He gestured toward Lancel and Barnibus, who stood aside in strained discussion, still trying to get their heads around what they'd heard. It had all happened so fast. One moment they were riding across the drawbridge in Sir Mooton's company, excited to see Amara and Lillia and Jovyn again, eager for wine and the welcome embrace of a proper featherbed, and the next Sir Daryl was telling them of the foul events that accompanied their parting from the palace.

Treachery begets treachery, Elyon thought, as those snakes writhed about in his gut. To steal the Windblade was treason - a lesser treason given all that had transpired of late, but treason all the same - and yet it was the good and true and noble prince who'd paid the dearest price for what they'd done. *He should have left me in that cell. He should have let me hang.* He drew a breath and put all that aside. "That is most kind of you, Master…"

"West, my lord. Alberfred West."

"My thanks, Master West."

"I serve at your pleasure, my lord." The old man had a kind and wizened look about him. He bowed low. "And I would take this moment to apologise that Lord Blackshaw did not join here tonight. He is best left to his rest, and will speak with you tomorrow, I'm sure."

Elyon nodded. "You needn't apologise. I have heard Lord Devyn isn't in the best of health."

"Ah, of course. Sir Mooton will have told you, I'm sure." He gave a crinkly smile. "Would you like me to show you the way to your rooms?"

"Please. You will tend to Lancel and Barnibus after?"

"Of course."

"Then lead the way, Alberfred."

He followed the castle steward out of the hall and up a set of winding stairs, reaching a chamber on the fourth floor where he was to be situated during his stay. He didn't imagine it would be more than this night.

"I hope it serves, my lord."

"Very much." The room was meagre, but he cared little for that. He wanted only a bed and a flagon of wine to see him off to sleep and that was plenty. "Where does my sister sleep?"

"On the floor above us. I…I had wanted to accommodate you higher in the keep, for your status, but all of our rooms are occupied, I regret to say." He seemed ashamed to even admit it.

"It's quite all right, Alberfred. I would be happy to stay in the stables tonight so long as the straw was soft."

"Most gracious of you to say so, my lord." The man was well practiced in his courtesies. He gave an appropriate pause then asked, "Is there anything else you should need of me? I could have a bath prepared for you, if you like."

Elyon was well aware of how appallingly he reeked, but a bath would keep till morning. "Tomorrow," he said. He scanned the room. "I have everything I need. Please, do not let me keep you from your duties."

The steward bowed and prepared to withdraw. "Ah, I should say…your auntie, she asked that it be brought here for your return."

Elyon frowned. "It?"

Alberfred motioned to a trunk positioned at the end of the bed. Elyon had taken it for containing clothing or books, yet he knew immediately what lay within. "Lady Amara has had it under constant guard, to be sure of its safety. I do believe that Sir Daryl was watching it tonight, before being summoned at your arrival."

Elyon looked at the trunk through a set of dull weary eyes. "It seems my auntie has thought of everything."

"Yes, as is her way." The steward bowed again. "I shall leave you. Goodnight, my lord."

"And goodnight to you, Alberfred."

When the man was gone, Elyon walked toward the trunk and stood before it for a time, staring down at the iron-banded wood. Tiny curls of mist squeezed out between a crack near one of the hinges. In them he could hear the wind, blowing far and faint, rustling through the room. After an age he went to a knee, threw open the latches, and opened the top of the trunk. And out came the storm and the wind and the whispers, out came the fogs and silver smokes, rising and stirring and swirling up into the room. And beneath, clearing, the great silver blade, glowing with those ancient glyphs…

"Elyon." He slammed the lid shut and rose, turning. His auntie stood at the door. "I had it brought…"

"I know. Alberfred told me."

The song of storms faded into a cold and solemn silence. Elyon moved to the side table and poured a full goblet of wine. He didn't offer her one. *I'm being peevish,* he could sense, but he didn't care. He was weary…weary right down to his bones, and the wine emboldened him to speak his mind. He turned to her and came out with it. "Was it worth it, Amara?" he asked, flicking a hand at the trunk. "Was your cousin's life worth this blade?"

There were tears welling in her eyes, he saw. *Crocodile tears,* he tried to tell himself. *She puts on an act to spare herself.* "I…I never expected…" She sniffed and shook her head. "I had no idea that Rylian would…would…"

"You sent my father away," Elyon broke in. "You recklessly filled his head full of dreams and sent him away to die."

His optimism was all gone, blown off like the morning mists. He'd left the palace that day, reprieved and renewed of spirit, hopeful of a brighter dawn. *Amron Daecar still lives,* he had told himself, after being haunted for so long by King Hadrin's words and what he'd seen in the Eye of Rasalan. He'd clung to that hope through the mountains and foothills, the forests and fields, yet now…now he wasn't so sure. Rylian was gone. Aleron was gone. Lythian was likely gone too, and Borrus. *And my father,* he thought. *Perhaps he truly is dead. Great men all, warriors of rare brilliance. And now what are we left with?* He scowled in thought and looked down at the trunk. *Me, and a stolen blade.*

"Your father will return to us."

He looked back at his auntie. Even those words sounded half resigned to him. *She has begun to lose hope too.* "So you've heard nothing?" he asked.

"Not yet. I sent a crow to Lord Borrington, telling him I'm here. If he should hear anything, he will let me know."

Months, Elyon thought darkly. *It's been months and still no word.* He drew on his wine until he tasted the gritty dregs at the bottom, and filled his cup anew. He gave Amara a glance. "Will you have one?" he asked in a grunt. Her sense of shame was so palpable that he could no longer subject her to this torment. He didn't wait for an answer, pouring a full cup, marching over to hand it to her. She took it in shivering fingers.

"You're right to blame me, Elyon. My meddling is what got Rylian killed."

He sighed out heavily, still reeling from the news. "No," he felt compelled to tell her. He would likely leave on the morrow and didn't want to leave things so bitterly, no matter what he thought. "You had no idea it would come to this. You were trying to do the right thing."

She dropped her eyes to the floor and said nothing for a good long while. Elyon took himself away from her once more, walking to the window. He looked out over the darkened woods that bled away into the sprawling Heartlands, far off beyond the realms of his sight. Only then did Amara ask, "What are you going to do?"

He turned his eyes down into the bailey. He could see Carly outside her barracks, speaking with a few of her men. He wondered where they would go next. He wondered if he might summon the girl to carry out her promise. *She said she'd show me the time of my life, when next we met,* he thought, recalling the night of the wedding in Ilithor, when they'd stolen the Windblade from under Janilah's nose. *Might be I need the comfort tonight...and the distraction.* But the notion was only fleeting. What he needed was a rest and a wash. "I'll go south," he said eventually. All that in the hall earlier had been bluster, no more. Given a moment to think he knew the prudent course, and returning to the White City to enact some ill-conceived vengeance was not it.

"I'll not pay this treachery with treachery of my own. I'll not lower myself to Janilah's level." Amara was silent for a while. Elyon turned to face her. "That isn't what you want to hear? You would have me become a kingkiller too?"

She shook her head. "I would have you become a champion, Elyon."

"A *champion.*" He scoffed and looked down at the trunk at the foot of the bed. "I can scarcely even look at it, let alone think about wielding it."

"You're tired, and shaken by tragedy. By morning you will feel different."

A part of him wanted to deny her that, though in the end he knew she was right. Rylian's last wish of him had been to master the Windblade. He could hardly dishonour him by refusing to take it up.

He took another pause to gather his thoughts, looking out over the cloud-curdled skies, starless and moonless and black as pitch. *I was supposed to soar,* he thought. *Master the Windblade and master the skies and fly across the Bay of Mourning to join Rylian at Eagle's Perch.* He had been driven by that thought for two long weeks and yet now…now it all felt empty. "Who's to lead the assault?" he wondered. "Sir Mooton seems to think the siege of Eagle's Perch is to go ahead. But without Rylian…"

"Cedrik Kastor will take command," Amara said. "As far as I understand, the fleet is already under sail."

That notion appalled him. "Their prince is slain and they don't even take a moment to mourn him." He flexed his sword hand, drank his wine. "What of Prince Robbert? He is heir now. And Lillia…" All those thoughts came at once; he'd not had a moment to consider them yet. "Janilah will rescind their betrothal pact after this. Everything Rylian did will be for nought."

And everything I did, he thought, regret and shame rising high in his throat, thick and bitter. He'd prodded and poked and driven a wedge between the prince and his father. *I wanted that,* he knew. *I wanted to rip open that rift, see Rylian take his father's throne. And look where that has gotten us. Look at what my scheming has done.*

"The pact is meaningless without Rylian," Amara said. "Robbert…he is young enough to be corrupted by his grandfather. I would not want Lillia to wed him now."

Elyon agreed, yet it felt heartless to even discuss it at this time. "You'll take her west at once," he said. "I want her safe in our grandfather's care, as we agreed. Tomorrow. You'll leave tomorrow and make straight for Ilivar."

"I have already sent word to Lord Amadar to expect us," Amara confirmed. "He will send an honour guard to greet us in the Heartlands."

"Sir Mooton is sworn to escort you," Elyon said. "I'll make sure he commits to that oath, at least until you converge with my grandfather's men. He may not take well to it, though. You heard him tonight, baying for blood."

"He'll have calmed by morning, and will do as he's commanded. He may blow hot, but Sir Mooton is fiercely loyal to the Kanabars, and you have Lord Wallis' fealty. They see you as their rightful prince, Elyon. Every Riverlander is yours to command."

Prince or king, he had to wonder. For if his father didn't return...

"Then I'll tell them on the morrow what I plan to do, and hope to hear no dissent." He reflected a moment. "Lord Huxley, Sir Lutherton...both seemed eager to seek vengeance as well..."

"They offered you men if that was your decision," Amara told him. "No more than that. But as to Sir Mooton...you might want to take him with you to Dragon's Bane. He'll be wasted acting escort from here and would be better off at your side. We have Sir Connor and Sir Daryl and the rest of the guard to protect us. We should be safe when riding the Great East Road."

True as that might be, Elyon wasn't going to take any chances. "What of Carly and her men? Might they remain in your service?"

"Escorting a middle-aged woman and highborn teenage lady isn't much of an adventure for sellswords," Amara said.

"No, but I'm sure you'll pay them well. If Carly has no other contract, I'd have you hire her until you reach Ilivar."

Amara put up no fight. "I can ask."

"Good." He gulped his wine. It was helping him to think practically. "And Jovyn?" he wondered. He had thought about retaining him as his squire before all that horror unfolded in Ilithor, and hadn't expected to meet up with him again so soon. "I wonder if he might rejoin me."

Amara seemed torn. "Lillia would not take kindly to that, I don't think."

"Lillia can find some other boy to torture. Jovyn is one step away from becoming a Varin Knight, and we are at war, Amara. The realm needs him more than she does." There was something in her eyes. "What is it?" he demanded.

"I have a mind to say Lillia's feelings for the boy are starting to… evolve," she said carefully. "These last days here…the way the other boys look up to him…I think she's starting to see him differently, Elyon."

He waved that off. "Lillia's always been capricious. Last I saw her she was obsessed with Prince Robbert, and now she's developing feelings for Jovyn, you say? A childish fancy. He's a toy to her, and now that the other boys want to play with him, she wants him more. That's all it is."

"Well…if you're sure."

Her manner was frustrating him. "You disagree?" And then he saw the truth in it. "I see. You worry for how difficult Lillia will become if I take Jovyn away. You don't want to have to deal with her petulance."

"No, Elyon. I worry for her mental wellbeing. Aleron's death almost destroyed her, I'm sure you remember. It was only her training that helped bring her around. Take Jovyn away, and who knows how she'll…"

"I'm sure you can find her someone else to spar with." He was being harsh, he sensed, and perhaps not thinking entirely straight. He had men around him he could trust and would soon be with his Uncle Rikkard and Sir Killian at Dragon's Bane, learning to master a Blade of Vandar. Who needed Jovyn more? Him or his sister? He contemplated that a moment and then said, "I'll think about it, and decide tomorrow." Suddenly he was terribly tired, more than before. "Is there anything else?"

She shook her head and placed down her cup. "Nothing that can't wait."

"Then why the look on your face? What is it?"

"I can tell you later. When you're better rested."

"You'll tell me now. It's not like I haven't had enough bad news today. What is it?" he repeated, more bluntly.

"Your uncle," she said.

"Rikkard?" was his first thought. *Don't say something has befallen him too….*

"No," she told him. "Vesryn."

His eyes flattened. "What of him?" His treacherous uncle hadn't been heard from for months since disappearing with the Sword of Varinar. "Have you heard something?"

"I've *seen* something. Or more to point, I've seen *him*. He came to me a week ago."

"*What?*" His fatigue was suddenly gone. "*Where?*"

"At a tavern not far from Tukor's Pass. He accosted me outside the external privy. Gave me the fright of my life, I will say."

Elyon had to think on that for a moment, frowning. His uncle had disappeared from the siege camp outside Harrowmoor. Most thought him long gone by now, further east or south most likely. *But west?* "How did he get…"

"So deep into Tukor? He had to trade Sunsilver for passage across the Sibling Strait. Was largely on foot thereafter, he said. The bastard stole Sir Connor's horse." She huffed. "I told him not to, but he did it anyway. It's made poor Connor more gloomy than ever."

Elyon took a moment to catch up. "But he…he loved Sunsilver." It was a strange thing to think, given the circumstances, but Elyon knew how much his uncle adored his chestnut destrier.

"A necessary sacrifice, he told me. Sunsilver was too recognisable, and he had to make his way west."

"Why? What does he intend?"

"Justice," she told him. "And the restoration of House Daecar."

Elyon frowned sourly at that. "House Daecar is not yet fallen."

"No, but it is wounded."

"Wounds Vesryn himself helped inflict." He breathed out, his lip curling in anger. This was not the right time to talk of his uncle. *Rylian…I should take a moment to mourn him, drink to him, think of the man he was. I would not have this time sullied by speak of Vesryn and the treacheries he helped commit.* "House Daecar wants no help from him," was all he said, with a note of finality. "He lost that right when he helped plot to have my father killed. He lost that right the day Aleron died."

Amara gave no response, because of course it was more complicated than that. She recognised it was time to leave him be. "We can return to this in the morning."

"Or not," Elyon grunted. "If I want to hear more of Vesryn, I'll ask you. Elsewise he's dead to me."

"I understand." She began retreating toward the door. "I believe…I believe he intends to help put your father on the throne," she finished, unsolicited. "When he should return…"

Elyon snorted his scorn. "So he would kill a king, would he? Yes, of course he would. Like master, like puppet. Janilah, Hadrin, Tavash, Vesryn...they're all as bad as each other." *And Rylian, my father, Lythian, Aleron...these men were the light.*

"I'll leave you, then."

He didn't look at her as she slipped through the door and shut it tight behind her. Finally alone, he could think on what he'd done. He staggered to the window seat and looked out over the woods, taking the flagon of wine with him. Weary beyond all reckoning, he let the sorrow and remorse engulf him. *Just tonight,* he thought, as he gulped down the wine, and remembered the prince who'd saved his life and in doing so traded it for his own. Tomorrow he'd have to put his feelings aside, become the leader he needed to be. But just for tonight, he could sit, and lament.

And leave thoughts of vengeance for another day.

6

Ranulf

The palace throne room was a capacious chamber drenched in the colours of Aramatia. The floor was a polished bronze, the pillars and walls a pristine silver-grey, the lofty vaulted ceiling a burnished gold, shining with chandeliers and hanging lanterns that bathed the whole space in firelight.

"It is a little too glittery for my tastes," said Ranulf Shackton, answering the question posed to him by his good friend Sallor Sanara. "But undeniably beautiful."

Sallor smiled amiably. He was a small man, greatly smaller even than Ranulf, olive skinned and amber-eyed and dressed in a golden damask robe woven with an array of eagles in silver thread. They loved their eagles here. From the port to the palace they were in great evidence, their likeness hewn into statues and stitched onto sails, hammered onto sword-hilts and helms, inlaid into armour and decorating dresses and drapes and banners everywhere. "A shade more extravagant than you're used to in the north," the little shipwright said. "Come, let us find somewhere to sit. It will get a good deal more crowded than this."

It was already crowded enough, highborn and lowborn alike pushing and shoving their way in through the doors. A line of city guards in their eagle-crested halfhelms and feathery capes stood ahead of the stage, preventing anyone from getting too near the throne, which of course was shaped into the resemblance of an eagle too, with great outstretched wings, fierce eyes and a long hooked beak. At the sides of the hall, three tiers of seating rose up for those come to watch, and above them was a great gallery where others might spectate. The floor space before the throne was typically reserved for the supplicants. The rest were expected to move aside.

Sallor Sanara led them into the seating on the right side of the hall, somewhere near the rear where they'd have a good view of proceedings. They settled in, as the great chamber filled and hummed. "It is always this busy?" Ranulf asked, studying the hordes of people crowding in.

"It has been busier since Lord Krator took the eagle-chair. His rulings have often been straightforward and severe. The people come to witness the drama. And share in the latest tidings of war."

Ranulf looked to the throne, dispirited. He'd come to Aram to visit this very room, but had hoped to find someone else seated between those magnificent golden wings. The instructions he'd decoded in the Book of Thala had told him to seek the Grand Duchess's counsel, but she was still absent, and no one seemed certain as to when she would return. In the meanwhile, it had been left to the noble and notorious Sunlord Elio Krator to rule in her stead.

Ranulf felt a finger prodding at his side. Leshie sat beside him, her face and hair darkened by the ointment she'd made, her small nimble frame wrapped up in a colourful caftan. She had a frown on her face. "What are you talking about?" she whispered, in the common tongue of the north. Much as she could disguise herself physically here, she couldn't speak the language. When Ranulf and Sallor Sanara spoke, they did so in Aramatian, much to Leshie's frustration.

"Nothing important," he whispered back. "Now no talking, Leshie. We spoke about this."

"It's loud in here," she came back. "No one can hear us. And anyway, lots of Aramatians speak the northern tongue. I don't see the problem."

"It would look odd," he told her, glancing around. "Why would three supposed Aram natives be speaking in the tongue of the north?"

She shrugged. "Practice, maybe? We're pretending to be merchants, aren't we? Any good merchant can speak lots of languages."

That wasn't strictly true. Really it was Ranulf posing as the merchant and Leshie posing as his daughter, though he wasn't going to quibble. Either way, the deceit had worked thus far and Ranulf wanted to keep it like that. "Just be quiet, please," he pleaded. "I'll try to translate what's happening if there's anything important to say." Before she could retort, he turned back to Sallor. "When should we expect Lord Krator?" he asked, in Aramatian.

"Right now." Sallor Sanara gestured forward. More guards were emerging from the rear of the hall, causing the crowd to murmur excitedly. A moment later, Lord Krator appeared in a cloak of golden feathers, clasped at his shoulders by a pair of howling sunwolves wrought in intricate detail. Elio Krator was a man of precision; in step, in gesture, in how he spoke and what he said. He was frugal in his gait, sparing no unnecessary energy as he made right for the throne and took his place between the wings. The great hooked beak loomed above him, giving a better impression of the size of the seat. Ranulf could only imagine how small Safina Nemati must look when cradled in its embrace.

Elio Krator waved to a herald, who stepped forward to the front of the stage. "Who is first?" he called out in a ringing voice.

"Me, my lord." An old man shuffled forward from the throng, dressed in faded threadbare robes and wearing nothing but callus on his feet. He went to his knees between the cordon of city guards. The posture seemed to pain him greatly. "My lord, *great* sunlord," he croaked, "I come before you seeking justice. My son…my son was slain, my lord, in a dispute over payment of a debt. He was a good boy, a good man, much loved in our community. Yet he fell to a cruel vice. Gambling, my lord. The cruelest of all. It sent him into a spiral from which he could not…"

Lord Elio Krator raised a hand. "What is it you want from me?"

The old man spluttered. "Justice, my lord, justice, as I say." He grimaced as he shifted on his knees. "These sharks…they lent him money but continued to raise the interest. He did all he could to repay them, but could never cover the charges, let alone repay all he owed." The first sniff escaped him, echoing through the hall. "First they broke a finger…then an arm…then a leg. He worked with his hands, my lord, a carpenter he was. Once they'd maimed him he couldn't hope to keep up his contracts. I had to gather all my wealth to help him, leaving me with nothing as well, but these sharks… these *barbarians*…they kept coming, demanding more money, taking everything but the clothes on my back. And eventually... eventually..."

"They killed him," Lord Krator finished. "For not paying his debt. I understand." He pondered it a moment, stroking a single finger down his shaven cheek. "Did your son go into the terms of this loan willingly, and knowingly?"

"He...he did, my lord, but..."

"Then I cannot help you. Your son knew what he was doing, as a consenting adult, and started down the path himself. Gambling is a cruel vice, as you say. I urge you all to turn from its temptations," he called, speaking to the audience. As he did he waved the old man away. Two guards came to lead him off, and with little tenderness, Ranulf didn't fail to note.

The hall filled again with muttering and whispering as men turned to one another to share words. Some were nodding their agreement at the ruling, others seemed more ambivalent. No one looked especially outraged. "That seemed a little...callous," Ranulf said to his companion.

"Seemed, yes, but in practice..." Sallor Sanara shrugged. "The man went in with both eyes open, and the lenders hold much more power on the streets than carpenters and their grief-struck fathers. Everyone knows how brutal they can get when their debts are not paid in time, and a man with a gambling addiction...that is a pitiful thing. Lord Krator had little choice but to dismiss the case."

"I know, but..."

"But his manner was curt and cruel." Sallor nodded. "That is his way, and many praise him for it. The people want a decisive leader during wartime, my friend."

The crowd hushed as the next supplicant stepped forward. This man was much younger, straight-backed and tight of jaw, dressed in wealthy garb. He had the look of a merchant. "My lord." He went neatly to one knee. "I come before you to ask for the hand of the Lady Asherah Tamaar in marriage. She has many suitors, I know, but I, Cliffario Denlatis, will make her a most happy and wealthy woman, should you grace our union with your holy approval."

Elio Krator's lips were in a faint smile. "The Lady Asherah is wealthy enough, Denlatis. She is my cousin, I'm sure you know, and my heir. House Tamaar is rich in land and title and greatly more so than you, I should think, lowborn as you are."

"I may be born low, my lord, but I have risen high. I command a fleet of ten ships, have villas and trade shops throughout the city, and interests in Matia and Kolash as well. I am young, ambitious, and will rise higher still."

"By wedding my cousin, yes," said Elio Krator. He seemed amused by the entire thing.

"With or without I will continue the climb," declared Cliffario Denlatis proudly. "But grant me this gift and I shall grant you one in return. The use of my warships, my lord, when the northern galleons sail upon the bay."

"We are well stocked in warships, Denlatis," Lord Krator told him. "But I shall bear you in mind. Now rise, and withdraw. I commend you for your ambition but my cousin will wed a Lightborn of her station, and no lower." He honoured the young man with a smile. "I wish you luck in your future endeavours."

Cliffario Denlatis bowed respectfully and withdrew.

"He must have known that would have been the ruling," Sallor said, chuckling, as the room swelled with noise. "Ah, the boldness of youth. Another man would have been thrown from the hall for the insult, but Cliffario has always been daring. And charming. Oh yes, he is well liked around the docks."

"You know him well?"

"Well enough. He's an upstart, true, but has made great strides in recent years. He's not lying about those ten ships either. He had only two or three a couple of years ago. At this rate he'll have his own armada one day."

Ranulf put the pieces together. "You built them for him?" he asked.

"Two of them, yes. Fine carracks, swift and true, good for trading and warring both. He bought the others secondhand, cheaper vessels that had seen much use. But mine…they're the glory of his fledgling fleet." He smiled and lifted his chin.

Sallor was very proud of his work, Ranulf knew. He'd met the man over a decade ago on his first visit to Aram, bumping into him in a dockside tavern and spilling his drink right down his shirt. Amiable as the shipwright was, he'd taken the blame himself (even though it was decidedly Ranulf's fault) and bought the Rasal adventurer a cup of wine in return. That cup had turned to ten and they'd shared a hundred tales that night, becoming fast friends, and ever since then, Ranulf always spent much time in Sallor's company whenever he ventured south.

Still, he hadn't been certain the shipwright would take him in on this occasion, not with times as they were. Yet he had, and willingly. "I'll not let such a silly thing as war get in the way of a dear friendship," he'd said to Ranulf, that day he came knocking on his door with Leshie at his side. He'd embraced him as a brother and invited them both into his home. And that's where they'd spent much of the last fortnight, waiting for the Grand Duchess's return.

Ranulf looked again at the sunlord currently occupying her throne. "He enjoys this too much," he noted. "How is his support in the city?"

"As well stocked as the navy he mentioned," Sallor responded promptly. "House Krator commands the fealty of many powerful vassals, my friend. It is a poorly kept secret that he has long coveted the eagle-chair."

"Enough to commit treason?" Ranulf asked.

"A coup?" Sallor shrugged. "Safina Nemati is not without support of her own, but she is ageing, and growing senile, some say. Her reign will not last much longer, I fear."

Ranulf didn't like the sound of that. *Senile*, he thought. *I need her mind in good shape*. "And what do you say, Sallor?" he probed. "Has the Grand Duchess's wits deserted her?"

"That I cannot answer, for I have never had the pleasure of meeting Her Serenity. I know only what I hear from other tongues, and some do wag to that rumour, yes. But I would ask you this, Ranulf...would Empress Valura have requested Safina's counsel were her mind in decline? Somehow I think not. Though I am only a humble shipbuilder, and know nothing of such affairs." He smiled. "Still, senile or no, Safina is well into the twilight of her years, and has no living heir of her blood. Her only daughter Leila died many years ago, her brother Justo the Moonrider the same, and his own sons were slain during the war. There is no one to follow with the Nemati name so it is clear enough that the stewardship of Aramatia will change to a new house at her death." He gestured to the throne. "Look no further than our stand-in sunlord. He's been auditioning for the role for some weeks, and doing quite well, many would say."

Ranulf could think of a living relative of Safina Nemati's blood, though thought better than to mention her. He made no reply at all, in fact, because by the time Sallor was done speaking another petitioner was striding forward from the throng, bringing the murmuring in the galleries to a close.

This one was a woman, tall and ample-chested, and a madam she quickly confessed. She went on about brawling in her brothel and the problems a new crop of men were causing. "*Yours*, my lord," she said. "They were Patriots, of that I'm sure. Came in under the pretence of rooting out northerners, but all they were really looking for was the sweetness between my girls' legs. They took what they wanted, raping and wrangling, and were gone without so much as flicking me a coin for the trouble. I've lost custom, sunlord, and long-term clients besides, and had three of my wenches needing stitches from rough treatment. It won't do, Lord Krator. *I say it won't do*."

A murmur went out through the masses. Elio Krator was nodding solemnly. "I hear your plight, good woman, and will send men to ascertain the truth of this. If these troublemakers were indeed Patriots, as you say, they will be brought before me and appropriately punished. More likely they were no more than ruffians posing as such, and no true man of mine. Go, with a promise that you will be compensated for your trials."

The madam gave that a stiff nod, rose to her feet, and left without another word.

So followed an endless parade of beseechers and beggars, young and old, seeking restitution, restoration and reward. Elio Krator dealt with each of them in turn, dismissing some out of hand, consenting to the pleas and appeals of others, judging each dispute quickly and decisively, if not always fairly to Ranulf's mind. "He shows bias to those with money," he said to Sallor Sanara at one point. "Anyone who might support him. He's trading in favours here."

"Favours are power, my friend," Sallor intoned. "He scratches a hundred backs a day and has a hundred hands just waiting to scratch his own, at his command. But look again. It is not just the rich he favours, but the influential. Even men of poverty can wield power, and Elio Krator is shrewd enough to know this. He is a career politician. He understands how to twist men to his means."

Leshie was beginning to grow restless at Ranulf's side as the afternoon laboured on. She could understand some of what was happening by the rising and swelling of noise in the crowd, the way some of the supplicants were dragged out kicking and screaming, in the dismissive waves and gestures Elio Krator made when handling a case in which he saw no merit. But much of the detail was lost on her. "I'm bored," she complained, and more than once, tugging at

Ranulf's linen robes like a child. "Can we go? I don't even know why we came here in the first place."

She'd chosen a moment when the crowds were laughing, at least, as a pair of twin brothers argued over which one of them was the elder. Both were claiming to have been born first, and thus in line to inherit their father's farm. Even Elio Krator was smiling at the spectacle as the brothers bellowed curses at one another, and gales of mocking laughter blasted through the hall.

Ranulf's lips were in a grin too. It was rather amusing, he had to say. "We came to visit the palace," he said, "and learn a little more of its stand-in ruler. Or would you rather return to Sallor's home on the waterfront? You were getting bored there too, if you'll recall."

"Of course I was. You were keeping me cooped up in there like a hen. I need to fly, Ranulf. I've had enough of cages."

"You're not caged, Leshie, and hens don't tend to do much flying. Pal Palek's pits are long behind us now."

She snarled at the memory. "Can't we just…walk around the city? I've barely seen anything of it yet. They say it's really beautiful here. I want to *explore*. The bridges across the river. The heights to the north. There are great hilltop homes up there, as grand as palaces, Sallor says. I want to see them."

"You'd not be allowed. Those hills are reserved for the rich and powerful and only accessed by invite. And besides, you saw some of the city when we came here in Sallor's litter."

"Yeah, a bit, but not enough," she complained. "This was meant to be an *adventure*. If I'd known it would be this boring I'd have stayed with that shadowboy." She grunted and folded her arms, looking across the crowd as they guffawed all about her, then over at the stage where Elio Krator sat, one leg neatly folded over another, hands steepled in his lap. "When *is* the Grand Duchess even getting here? I thought we'd have met her by now. I want to see if there's any resemblance. With Saska, you know."

Ranulf leaned across. "You have ears as I do, Leshie. Sallor has told us Her Serenity is in Lumos several times…"

"Yeah, so why aren't *we*? You came here to meet *her*, not hang around with Sallor all day and watch him build his boats. It's dull, Ranulf. We should sail there, to Lumos. Sallor will let us use one of his ships, if we ask him."

"And if the Grand Duchess should return whilst we're at sea? It will take weeks to sail to Lumos and we'd likely pass Her Serenity on the way, and not even know about it. Then what? We'd only have to sail back again." He shook his head. "The prudent choice is to wait, and hope that she returns here soon."

"I'm not good with waiting, Ranulf." She scowled and turned away, grumpy.

The brotherly feud was ongoing, the jeering and cheering growing yet louder. By the look on Elio Krator's face, he'd seen enough, however. He raised a hand. Silence didn't take long to fall. "If your own friends and relatives cannot say which of you is the elder, I cannot be expected to do so," he proclaimed. "You both make a compelling case, so my ruling is simple. You will split your father's lands and properties and have done with it."

"But that would require we sell, sunlord," called out one of the brothers. "The farm is all we have…"

"Then run it together. You are brothers, nay twins. You came into this world together and should be able to work together too. Try. If that fails, then sell, split the proceeds, and find other vocations that suit you." He waved them off.

They departed to a tide of taunts and snickers, still squabbling as a pair of guards escorted them from the hall. Some men were hurling open abuse at them. That seemed enough to have the brothers put aside their quarrel for a time, as both turned to the abusers and gave as good as they got. When the fists started flying, Ranulf rolled his eyes. "I doubt Safina would permit this sort of thing."

Leshie looked more interested, though. "Finally, *something* I can understand." Unfortunately it didn't last long, the guards prising the combatants apart and dragging the brothers away through the door, bloody-nosed and bickering once again. Leshie's shoulders slumped. "Right, I'm going too. I don't care what you say, Ranulf…"

She made to stand but he took her wrist and pulled her right back down. "Don't be stupid."

"I know my way back to Sallor's house. I can just meet you there later."

"No. We have to stay together. The city is vast and you're likely to get lost."

"You can't get lost in a coastal city, not if you're smart. You just have to get back to the waterfront. It's simple."

She was testing him. This was just her way to speed their departure. "We can leave soon," he conceded. "I just want to see some of the prisoners first."

That was the way it worked. First the free men would come forth and make their supplications, then the prisoners would be brought before the lord, to receive judgement for their crimes. They would be men and women not deemed worthy of a court of law, their fates to be presided over by Lord Krator alone. His sanctions were said to be severe. *And that is why most people have come…to watch him swing the sword.*

The herald made the announcement. "If there is no other freeman who seeks an audience with Lord Krator, we shall move onto the felons and malefactors." He turned his eyes around the room. "Bring forth the first man."

That first was a figure so fetid and unwashed his reek could be detected even from the stands. Ranulf watched as a wave of people put their hands to their faces as the prisoner passed, the fetters about his ankles and wrists clanking and clattering on the polished bronze floor. At his side was a tall, broad-shouldered jailer who was tasked with enumerating his crimes. "Triple rape," the jailer called out in a heavy voice. "One of them a child of ten." Fury spread through the stands like an inferno and the guards had to stop several men trying to get at the man.

The herald called out for silence, though it took a little longer than normal. Clearly some of the people here had known the victims. Eventually, the hall grew quiet enough for Lord Krator to be heard. "Death by disembowelment," he declared loudly, "but first make him a eunuch." The crowd roared their approval at that. "He shall be strung up in Addonia's Square, and cut between the legs. Remove the tool he used to commit his wickedness, and make his dying slow. An hour for each woman he defiled, two for the child. I will see him suffer as he made them suffer, before his eyes go dark."

In that, if little more, Ranulf could not disagree. Yet still…"I sense Safina would have given the man a quicker end," he said to Sallor, as the hall rose up in a great pounding clangour. "I'm starting to see why Krator is so popular, however. He gives the people what they want." He watched as the rapist was drawn away, chains clinking, head low. *Blood,* he thought, *and vengeance.*

He treated the rest of the criminals no less fiercely, playing to the bloodlust of the crowd. A thief was to have his hands removed so he could never steal again. A man who'd spread a terrible slur about a noblewoman had his tongue taken out right there in the hall, torn free of his mouth with a pair of pincers. Even Leshie flinched to that. "These people are less civilised than I thought."

"War brings about the worst in people," Ranulf said gravely.

Others were condemned to die. A young stripling of a man who'd killed his best friend in a love-feud over a woman was sentenced to death by poison, for that was the method he'd used. An old crone who'd suffocated a neighbour's baby in her crib for crying too loudly was to be strangled dead by the baby's father. Elio Krator's favoured method of punishment was an eye for an eye, it seemed. He showed no mercy, brooked no interest in leniency, and relished every moment of it, Ranulf could tell.

Even a smuggler was condemned to die, he and his young mute helper. The pot-bellied man came forward nervously with the tongueless boy at his side, shivering so hard his chains rattled audibly, even as he knelt on the floor. "Smuggling fugitives," the jailer called out. He was about to say more when Elio Krator raised his hand.

"Death," he said at once. "Both will make good meat for the pits."

"My lord," called the smuggler. "Please…please no."

Elio Krator would hear no plea from him. "Take them both." The portly man was dragged right out with his poor mute helper at his side, the boy weeping all the while.

"Death for smuggling?" Leshie said, frowning. "That's *harsh.*"

"Depends who he smuggled," Ranulf said. "Fugitives could mean anything. If a person of interest, the penalty can be severe."

"Maybe it was someone dangerous…" Leshie's voice was devoured by a sudden wave of noise as the next prisoner was brought in. People started standing to get a better look, blocking Ranulf's view. He rose to his feet, as Leshie and Sallor did the same. "Gods," Leshie exclaimed, "he's *massive*!"

The biggest man in all the world, Ranulf thought, staring wide-eyed at Sir Ralston Whaleheart. He knew at once it was him. The scarred flesh, the bulging muscles, the sheer size and immensity of the man. He dwarfed every figure around him, towering a full foot and a half taller than even the broad-shouldered jailer, who'd loomed over all the other prisoners that day. A full dozen guards moved uneasily around him, stiff arms clutching at the hilts of their blades. Even dressed in rags and heavy chains they feared him, as though he'd rip free of his fetters and bludgeon them dead with nothing but his bare hands. That was the strength of Sir Ralston's legend. All across the south he was feared.

The jailer stepped forward, pulling at a length of chain attached to an iron collar at Sir Ralston's neck. He gave a sudden tug, hoping to haul the man to the floor, but the King's Wall hardly budged. A storm of laughter swept through the auditorium. The jailer didn't take that well, though when he tugged again, and harder this time, the result wasn't much different. In the end it took several of the guards to get Sir Ralston Whaleheart down to his knees.

The jailer cleared his throat, a hot flush of humiliation rising up his neck. "Attempted assassination!" he bellowed over the noise. "Against the great sunlord, Elio Krator!"

Ranulf could scarcely believe what he was hearing. *Sir Ralston is no assassin. He's too big by half and far too honourable to lower himself to such work.* Then again, there had been some rumour at the docks that the King's Wall had fled Rasalan. Some said he'd come south, though Ranulf had never expected to find him here. And there had been another with him too, the whispers said. *A girl...*

Leshie was pulling at his sleeve again. "Ranulf, that isn't..."

"The King's Wall!" someone called out from the crowd, in the northern tongue. "It is him! The Whaleheart!"

Leshie's eyes turned big as saucers. "We have to help him!"

"Shhhh." Ranulf gave her a stiff glare. She was losing control of the volume of her voice. "There's nothing we can do right now. Just watch."

Everyone was still standing, every man and every woman in every tier and gallery on their feet, straining to see. Ranulf peered through the bodies, trying to get a better look. Even on his knees, Sir Ralston looked colossal, though his head was hung low and there was something broken about him. *He's been tortured,* Ranulf realised. His body had always been a latticework of scars, but there were many fresh cuts and bruises and abrasions across the exposed flesh he could see, red and weeping.

Elio Krator stood, for the very first time that day. "This man came to our great city in a bid to slay me," he announced. "My men, in their great bravery, were able to subdue him before he could complete this awful deed, though the cost in life was dear. For that alone the King's Wall must die." He opened out his arms. "How shall it be done?"

A man in the upper terraces answered the call. "Death by fang and claw," he cried out. "Let wolf and cat feast on his living flesh."

"A hunt," called another. "The northmen love to hunt. Let us show them what it is like. A hunt, great sunlord. A hunt, a HUNT!"

The cheers began to rise.

"*All* the people should see him fall," claimed an old woman in a shrill voice. "He should be hung above the city gates for all comers and goers to look upon. Left to die slow and rot until he's carrion for the crows."

"Not crows. *Eagles*!" sang a spirited male voice. "Let them rip at him with their talons, skin and flesh and bone. Our banner is the eagle with the knight in its claws. We should bring this vision to life!"

Many agreed with that. The calls of assent grew louder. Elio Krator watched, smiling thinly, indulging them their show. *This is theatre, nothing more,* Ranulf thought. *He knows already how Sir Ralston Whaleheart will die. He just needs someone to say it.* And duly, another voice high up in the rafters obliged. "The pits, my Lord Krator, send him to the Red Pits. Let him die with the cowards who smuggled him into the city!"

Elio Krator lifted his palm. A hush fell upon the hall like a blanket, smothering out any further cries and calls. In a clean true voice he announced the ruling. "The knight will share the smuggler's fate," he said. "The Red Pits will grow yet redder still, when painted in Sir Ralston's blood."

Whether their favoured choice or not, every man, woman, and child within the audience threw up their hands and cheered. The din was deafening, a swelling tumult that had the wooden scaffold beneath them shaking. "The Red Pits," Ranulf said to Sallor. "I take it they've been active of late."

The shipwright nodded solemnly. He seemed the only man present with sympathy in his eyes. "Most active, I am sorry to say. The Patriots...they've brought many northmen there to be slaughtered before the crowds."

Ranulf was not ignorant of these pits, nor why they were so named. "Can you get us entry?"

Sallor frowned. "I fear you would not enjoy the show, my friend."

"I'm certain of it," Ranulf told him. "But one way or another, I need to speak to Sir Ralston."

Because I'm quite sure, he thought, *that he didn't come to this city alone.*

7

Saska

The sound of sliding bolts had Saska waking up in a rush. Moonlight washed in through the window, giving shape to Joy, already sat and looking at the door. Saska slid straight from the bed, her nightgown hanging loose down her frame as she hurried to the starcat's side. They were standing together when the door swung open. "Girl," said Balza, lit by the light in the hall. "You're to be washed and dressed for dinner. Lord Krator commands your company."

Saska might have complained of the hour, but she was used to these late-night calls. Instead she said nothing. Balza was the meanest of the guards tasked with watching her, all droopy sullen eyes and spiteful glances, and not one she cared to talk to if she could help it. He stepped aside to allow her maids through the door, scurrying like a mischief of mice. They held oils and balms and scented creams, scrubbing brushes and flannels to scour her skin raw. Lord Elio Krator liked her clean. She'd sooner be back in Mellio's rickety carriage, covered in a half dozen days of filth.

Balza followed behind, as the maidservants drew Saska into the washing chamber next door. He had tried that once or twice before, to get a glimpse of her being disrobed, but the maids were wise to his clumsy tricks. "No, not you," said an older woman named Yasha, shooing him away. "Wait outside. You're not to be in here."

"Lord Krator told me to stand guard."

"Yes, *outside*. Now go away. Go…go!" She started shaking her scouring brush at him, as someone might swat a fly. Eventually he scowled and withdrew. "I am sorry for him, my lady," the old woman said. Yasha was into her sixties, Saska judged, with streaks of grey in her tied-back hair, but had clearly been quite beautiful once. "No one here likes Balza. Do not worry, you are not alone in that." The other women nodded.

Saska was too weary to give much of a reply. She just smiled her thanks and waited as they went back and forth, filling the copper bath with warm water, before slipping out of her nightdress and into the tub. She sat upright and tense, hands clutched around her knees, as they set about scrubbing every inch of her clean. Then they rubbed in the oils and balms and creams, a small army of hands running all over her naked flesh, before dressing her up in the new gown of Lord Krator's own choosing. To some women this was life, a daily ritual they endured to better please their lord, and she was sure many of them even liked it. *But not me,* she thought, as they put on her shoes and silken scarf, the silver and gold bracelets Elio Krator liked to see upon her wrists. She felt like a doll being dressed up by a child. A child who might just scream and shout and rip the stuffing from her guts if she didn't play along.

"Beautiful," Yasha said once they were done, giving her an admiring smile. "Lord Elio will be very pleased, I think. Now come, let us not keep him waiting. Balza will escort you to the dining hall."

Great. Him. She had to endure the droopy-eyed stare of the witless guard as he walked her through the residence, and all without Joy for company. "The cat stays in the room," the man grunted in that lazy slur he called a voice. "Lord Krator does not like her slavering nearby when he dines."

Joy never slavers, she thought. *It's you the one that drools, you halfwit.* She didn't bother arguing, though. "What time is it?" was all she asked. She'd not yet gotten a good look at the moon, but it felt late, past midnight for a certainty. Lord Krator rarely returned to the villa until late into the night.

Balza gave a disinterested shrug of his fleshy sloping shoulders. "Does it matter? What does a rapist's bastard like you care for what time it is?"

Saska puzzled on that. She couldn't figure out why it mattered that she was a bastard, let alone a rapist's bastard at all. *Are people like me supposed to keep time differently?* she wondered. But all she said was, "I'm not a rapist's bastard."

Balza laughed like a pig. "No, you're worse. That rapist was a slave too, and northern." He spat to the side, spraying spittle on the stone wall. "You're a raping slave's bastard, that's what you are."

"Yeah, and you were probably sired in a brothel. At least my mother was a princess."

"You calling my mother a whore?" He snarled and turned on her, hand raised to lash out, but remembered himself just in time. "You're lucky Lord Krator likes you clean, or I'd mess up that pretty face of yours."

She recoiled from the reek of his breath, if not the threat. "And you're lucky I don't have my godsteel dagger with me, else I'd carve you up like a butcher's pig."

He sniggered at that and pulled back. "Mongrel," he hissed, before stamping off on his way.

Her blood was still up when the oaf pushed through the doors to the dining room. "The girl, Lord Krator," he said. "Nice and *clean* for you."

"Ah, good." Lord Elio Krator rose from his high-backed seat at the head of a rich mahogany table that could host a hundred without trouble. His cloak of fine feathers hung on a hook nearby, leaving him in a rich gold and bronze tunic. The hall was warmly lit, with candles flickering splendidly in small wall niches, and down the length of the table. The sunlord gestured her over. "Come, Saska, do join me. Balza, wait outside."

"As you wish, my lord." The guard gave Saska a dumb-faced scowl before sulking off through the door.

Saska closed a fist. Tanner Twelve Teeth had taught her how to fight dirty on the Steel Sister and oh how she wanted to put his lessons into practice. *I don't need godsteel to knock that lackwit's teeth to the back of his throat,* she thought, her mind full of bloody murder. She took her seat, glowering.

"Smile, child, it suits the dress." Elio Krator looked in good spirits this evening, a rare smile playing about his typically smile-less face. He plucked a plum tomato from his plate and popped it into his mouth, biting through the soft red flesh. "Do you like it?"

"The dress?" Saska hadn't given it a second thought. She had to look down at herself to even remember what it looked like; a samite gown the same blue as her eyes stitched with gold and silver thread in a pattern of sparkling stars. "It's beautiful."

"I had it especially made for you." Another tomato disappeared behind his slender lips. "The star patterns are to signify your Joy. I thought you might be pleased."

Why should you care if I'm pleased, she thought. *I'm your hostage.* "I am."

"You don't seem so." He moved a curl of chestnut hair from his forehead, gazing at her with those cold gold eyes.

"I'm tired," she said. "I was awoken abruptly."

"Of course." He reached across the table and picked up a chicken thigh, neatly peeling off the skin and flesh and laying it on his plate. Only once he'd completed flaying and defleshing the bones did he begin eating. "Mar Malaan tells me you want to go swimming." He looked up, with that dead-eyed stare that could chill her very blood. Then he smiled and waved to the table. "Eat, please. If you're to die in my care, it won't be by starving."

Saska had no appetite for eating, but thought it best not to offend him. "The soup looks delicious," she said, thinking it would be light. "Do you mind…"

"By all means."

She reached across and ladled a half measure into her bowl. It was thicker than she'd expected, creamy and filled with squares of potato and onion and carrot. The sunlord watched as she spooned a sip into her mouth. She hadn't gotten used to that manner of his yet, coldly studying her for long moments at a time before suddenly seeming to unthaw. And it was everything else as well. One moment he was jesting about killing her, the next he would look at her more longingly than she should like. *And he likes me clean and pretty and smelling nice too.* And in dresses, she knew, that the Princess Leila liked to wear. Old Yasha had told her that, and it had unsettled her more than she could say. *Is he trying to turn me into her? Into my mother, the woman he loved?* But he'd look at her with disdain just as often as well. And at those times she knew he was looking at her and seeing her father, the slave and rapist, he claimed, whom he'd had beaten to death right here in his halls.

"I'll permit it," he said eventually, ending the long silence between them. Saska frowned; she'd half forgotten what they'd been talking about. "The pool. You may swim in it, if you wish. But only so long as you're scrubbed clean first. I like to keep the water pristine."

Like everything else, she thought. She'd never met a man so fastidious, so particular. It bordered on the abnormal, this obsession he had with cleanliness.

"Thank you," she said, and there was something sincere in her voice for once. "I'd very much like that."

He smiled back. "I have these for you too." He reached to the side and drew up a fine leather pouch, placing it on the table. "Your things, taken from you when you first came here. I thought it time they were returned to you."

She opened the bag and looked inside. Everything was there. The quill and ink and sheets of parchment from Lancel. The pouch of coins from Barnibus. The list of lurid jokes that Bawdry Bron had written out for her. The necklace of shells and stones that sweet young Billy Bowen had made. And the coral, she saw. That little piece of pitted grey coral that had called to her from the ocean floor.

She closed the bag and looked up. "Thank you, Lord Krator. But there's still one thing missing." She added a twist to her smile. "My dagger."

Elio Krator was not amused. "That dagger is a piece of the dark god Vandar. It will be kept in my armoury until I decide what to do with it."

The armoury, Saska thought, making a mental note to find out where that was. "Of course. I wasn't being serious, my lord."

"You should do well to ignore your Bladeborn side. That is foul blood, poison in your veins. I would have you embrace the *light* in you, child, the light that was so bright in your mother. Why else do you think I allow you to keep the starcat at your side, day and night? She will strengthen that glow, and soon you'll forget the lure of godsteel, of this I have no doubt."

Saska took another sip of soup, thinking better to respond to that. *I'll embrace the mutt that I am,* she thought. *All sides of me. Lightborn, Bladeborn, Seaborn. All.*

"These items of yours, some are curious to me." Lord Krator looked at the bag, swirling a cup of dark red wine between nimble fingers. "The parchment....these are supposed to be jokes?"

Saska struggled to contain her smile, though it was a smile tinged with sadness. She'd read Bawdy Bron's jokes a dozen times over, trying to get Sir Ralston to laugh while they rode with Mellio and Pig through the plains. Now all three of them were imprisoned, maybe even dead for all she knew. "They're not to everyone's tastes."

"Not mine." Krator lifted his brow in derision. "Is this how you like to jest where you come from? With sexual innuendo and improper humour?"

"Sometimes," she admitted. "As I say, it's not to everyone's liking."

The sunlord gave a huff. "Explain to me the meaning of the rock."

The meaning of the rock, Saska thought. *Where to start?* "It's coral," she said. "I like how it feels between my fingers." She saw no merit in telling him any more than that. Somehow, Old Hob had fingered the pits and grooves and worked out that she was Bladeborn, and royal too, on her father's side. Saska was struggling to work through all that. *How can my father have been a slave and royalty at the same time?*

But then, hadn't *she* been just the same? She'd lived her entire life a servant and slave and had never known she was of royal Aramatian blood until Ranulf figured it out. *Couldn't the same be true of my father?* That mystery had eaten away at her, but she'd gotten no answers as yet. *My grandmother was supposed to tell me,* she thought. *She was supposed to fill in all the gaps.* And in that the wait went on. It was a dark tunnel with no light at the end.

"That is all?" asked Lord Krator. "You like how it *feels*?" He seemed perplexed.

She nodded. "It's a totem. I picked it up while swimming a reef, not far from Eagle's Perch."

He gave a lazy sip of his wine, disinterested. "One so pretty as you should choose a prettier rock. This grey stone is ugly and featureless." He had a look on his face, some strange smile. "But then, you seem to like ugly things. The smuggler who brought you here, and that mute boy of his. And Sir Ralston, yes, him most of all. An ugly brute, with all those scars."

Saska swallowed a sip of soup to collect her thoughts. "Mar Malaan told me you haven't judged him yet," she said. "I asked if I might see him, but…he told me to speak to you."

The smile lingered. "You'll see him again soon."

Those words might have brought her some comfort, but the look on his face did not. "Are you going to kill him?" She thought it best to ask him straight. When he gave that no response, she fell into pleading mode again. "He means no harm, I told that to Mar Malaan. You know he doesn't, Lord Krator. He only came here to escort me so that…"

"So that you might meet your grandmother, yes. This I already know. But by who's command, I wonder?" He sipped his drink. "The King's Wall took that name for his dedication to his duty, and the king in question he served. Only King Godrin could have issued such a directive to have Sir Ralston Whaleheart come so far south. I wonder why that was?"

So do I, Saska thought. *I've wondered that for months.*

Elio Krator swirled his wine. "A scheme," he went on. "That is all I can figure. A scheme to build a bridge between north and south. Yes, this seems most likely to me. King Godrin was said to be a friend to Her Serenity, did you know this? They would commune with one another, sending letters in code, and sometimes would meet as well. Some came to wonder if there was a romance between them." He laughed that off. "I never thought as such myself. No, he was always so much older, a small and feeble thing, and Safina Nemati was a wonder in her youth, as beautiful as the daughter she birthed. As beautiful as you, Saska."

He looked at her, part longing, part hateful. She shied away from his gaze and spooned more soup into her mouth.

"King Godrin sent you here to be taken under Safina's care," Lord Elio continued. "Two doves who had no love for war, hoping to hold you aloft and proclaim you the link between continents and kingdoms. How cruel that they would seek to use you such. You are no more than a pawn in a bigger game, Saska. As you have always been."

"And now you control the board," she said.

"Yes." He smiled. "Yes, well put. You are a unique piece and I have claimed you for my own. Godrin is dead and Her Serenity long leagues from here. Her health is failing and her years are numbered, but you are young and have a long life to lead. I wonder how you'll live it?" He reached out, laid a hand atop her own. "That may yet be for you to decide."

She didn't dare withdraw her fingers. "Mar Malaan told me the story of Agarro. He told me I could build a life here, in time." She wondered where she was going with this. *You have feminine wiles,* a voice inside her said. Perhaps it was Lady Marian, perhaps it was Cecilia Blakewood. Somehow it sounded like them both at once. *Use them, Saska. Lure him. Lull him. Play his games and in time, he'll drop his guard.* "Perhaps he was right," she finished, with a smile.

Something flickered in his golden eyes. *Amusement,* she realised. *He knows I'm playing tricks.* "Perhaps he was." He leaned back, slipping his hand off of hers. "The Lightborn in you belongs here. The more you bask in it, the more you'll come to see it. But so long as you have these Bladeborn ties, you will never be able to let go." He set down his cup. "When afflicted by a malady, it is best to leech the bad blood. Your Varin blood must go, Saska, and this darkness must be purged. Only then will you be able to embrace the Light."

He lifted his cup again and began tapping its base on the table. A moment later, the door opened and Balza reappeared, looking drowsy. "Yes, sunlord?"

"Summon the leecher."

Saska frowned. She had thought he was being metaphorical. "Lord Krator, I…"

He silenced her with an open palm. "You have poison in you, Saska, that needs to be drawn out. Bloodletting will help cure you."

She began shaking her head. "You don't truly believe…"

"We'll need to drain her good, sunlord," rasped Balza at the door. He grinned a brown and broken smile. "*Big* leeches to suck her clean."

"I'll leave that to Mhazem to determine." He looked back at her. "Are you done eating?"

She had no words.

"Good," he said. "Then there is no sense in wasting time." He rose to his feet. "Balza, is there a reason you linger? I gave you a command."

"Yes, my lord." The droopy-eyed guard backed out, disappearing through the door.

Saska sat stiff in her chair. "Rise," Krator told her. "The treatment is not so bad as it sounds." When she didn't move, he added a bite to his voice. "I prefer not to repeat myself. Now rise. There is nothing for you to fear."

She quivered to her feet, seeing no way she might deny him. Leeching was used in the north as well, though she'd never been subjected to it. Many physicians considered it a worthless practice there now. "It won't work," she managed to say. "You cannot suck the Varin blood out of a Bladeborn."

He studied her coldly. "But you *want* it to, do you not?"

"Want it to?"

"To work. You said as much but moments ago. That you wanted to try to build a life here." He smiled emptily. "Well this is the price.

Or…part of the price, I should say. In time we'll have you cured. Now come, follow me."

I don't need curing, she wanted to scream, but she only smiled and nodded and obeyed. *Play along,* she thought. *Play along and he'll drop his guard.* She followed as he led her from the dining hall and through the residence, into a room of horrors. She gaped about in a panic. "Oh don't look so frightened, Saska. None of these utensils will be used on you."

There were bloodstains on the floor, old and crusted, and stains of other colours besides. The walls were chipped and pitted like her coral, and there, on the left side, she saw gouges scratched into the stone, shallow and ragged and traced with blood. At the heart of the room was a slab of stone with frayed leather straps and rusted iron fetters dangling over its edges. A leather brace was fitted at its top end to lock the head into place. Beyond it, on a table, were instruments and utensils the likes of which she'd never seen, unholy tools used for cutting and scraping and crushing. Terror ran through her. She wanted to hide it, oh how she wanted to hide it, but she couldn't. "What…what are you going to do to me?" she stammered.

Elio Krator laughed. "I have told you. You're to be leeched. Now you must excuse the setting and ignore all this savagery. I might have let this happen in your room, but the blood…it may drip. And you know how I like things clean."

She tried to stay strong. "I understand," she said.

"You'll get used to it. It might take some time to draw the sickness from you. Ah…" He turned. Balza was arriving with a scrawny old man who had the bearing of a vulture. A small bald head perched atop a thin wrinkly neck, set with runny yellow eyes over bags of blackened skin. He wore a dark cloak, feathery in design, that completed the appearance. And in his spindly grasp, a stoppered jar, squirming with a hundred black-green shapes. "Mhazem, I hope you're well-rested."

"Well enough, sunlord," said the leecher. He looked anything but. A corpse had more vitality. "This is the girl?"

Elio Krator nodded gravely. "A serious case," he informed him. "Her blood is rich in dark magic. I would have it withdrawn."

The vulturous healer sniffed at her. "*Varin*. I smell it in her." He cringed away. "I'll try my best, but the scent is strong. It may take time."

"Time we have." Elio Krator looked at her again, judging her reaction. *He wants to see me afraid. He knows there is no way to remove a Bladeborn's Varin blood, no more than a Fireborn can have the blood of Eldur sucked from him or a Lightborn the blood of Lumo or Sola. This is a game, no more. He is doing this to break me.* "Are you ready, Saska?"

"I'm ready," she said.

Balza licked his lips. "I will stay, my lord. Mhazem might not be safe alone with her."

"She will be strapped and fastened," said the leecher. "My fetters will keep her restrained."

"All the same, I should stay," insisted Balza.

Elio Krator cared not. "As you wish." He made for the door, turning before he left for a final word. "I shall call upon you soon," he told her. "There is a…a particular event that I am to host, very exciting, and I should like you to accompany me. You'll be summoned when the arrangements are made." And with that he stepped away.

"Girl." Mhazem motioned her toward the stone slab. "Lie down," he commanded her. "I am going to strap you."

"Must you? I'd prefer…"

"I am going to strap you," he repeated, more firmly. "Another word and I'll let Balza do it."

The threat had her relenting. She could feel Balza's brainless expression on her as she stepped toward the table. "She'll need to undress," came his thick slurry voice. "That dress covers most of her up. You'll need to get at her skin, Mhazem."

The leecher pointed a finger at him. The nail was long and chipped, half blackened. "Do not tell me how to do my work."

"No…but I'm right."

Mhazem's bony shoulders went up and down. "So happens you are." He looked at her. "Undress."

She wore underclothes beneath her dress that were enough to cover her modesty, though her midriff and legs and much else would be exposed. "Will this do?" she asked once the blue samite dress was heaped on the floor, shining with a glitter of silver stars. *Say yes, or so help me gods, I'll kill you both right here…*

"It will serve," Mhazem said. He gave Balza a look. "It *will*," the old healer repeated to the guard. Clearly he had a reputation, and not just among the maids. "Stand by the door, Balza, and do *not* disturb us. We will be here a while."

Balza nodded, but before he stepped back, he stepped in. His rank breath filled her nostrils as Mhazem began strapping her down. "I always liked this room," he whispered, dull eyes moving lazily from wall to wall. "You see those marks over there." She looked at the gouges scratched into the wall; they looked like they'd been made by nails. "Was your father made those, when we beat him dead. You can't imagine how many bones we broke, how much blood there was." He chuckled stupidly. "You can't imagine how he screamed and pleaded and begged."

Her heart pounded in her chest, heavy and hateful. "You were…"

"There?" A slimy smile spread across his glistening wet lips. "Oh yes, I was there." He leaned so close that those lips near touched her ear. "And it was *me* that finished him off."

She craned her neck and looked right at him. *I will kill you first,* she promised herself, as he grinned horribly and then backed away, laughing. *When the time comes, when I get my chance…by Varin I'll kill you first.*

8

Cecilia

The palace training yard rang to the sound of steel, as knights in godsteel armour thrashed and clashed beneath a golden winter sun. Across the galleries was a sparse attendance. *Women and old men and cravens,* Cecilia Blakewood thought. *All the good true knights and men are away at war, and this is all that's left.* "So?" she asked, looking down at the combatants. "Your thoughts?"

Sir Owen Armdall stood beside her, tall and proudly draped in the rich, triple-coloured mantle of the Six. He had a bored look on his face. "None will serve," he said.

"*None*?" She shouldn't have been too surprised, really. As with the few spectators in the stands, these knights were the dregs at the bottom of the barrel. "You're sure, Sir Owen?" She ran her eyes across the yard. "What of Sir Bonmer?" He had been an Emerald Guard for years, she knew, and seemed skilled with blade and spear. The most worthy men remaining in Ilithor were here as part of the garrison to defend the city should it come under attack. Sir Bonmer Marsh was leading a contingent of them, charged with defending the White Shadow Gate. "He seems well fitted to the role to me."

"With a name like *Bonmer*?" The Oak of Armdall scoffed. He had an arrogance to him that had only swelled of late.

Killing a prince and famed dragon-slayer will do that, I suppose. Even though there were four of them… "You cannot count him out because of his name," she said.

He shrugged. "I don't like his face much either. And he's too old and slow. Permit me and I'll show you. I'll have him speared and gutted in two minutes sharp."

"That won't be necessary." She gave the yard another scan. "Sir Willington, then?" He was young, had a reasonably acceptable name, and was quite comely as well. "He seems to have some spirit. And I hear he went deep into the tourney at Ethior last year. Won through a few rounds in the lists and unhorsed several notable knights in the melee as well."

Sir Owen didn't think much of that. "He's too clean," he said, dismissing the option. "The Six are required to get their hands dirty from time to time, my lady. It is no place for the innocent."

And don't I know it, Cecilia thought. She rather enjoyed playing in the dirt as well. And all had become particularly filthy of late. "You have to choose someone, Sir Owen," she told him. "Your order is known as the Six for a reason, and we're two short."

"Three," said the knight, right hand resting on the pommel of his blade. Its hilt was in the likeness of the trunk of an oak tree, its pommel a twisting cluster of curved branches and leaves, all wrought in intricate detail. "Sir Fredrick may not recover. His wounds are quite severe."

Something told her Sir Owen would like that. More new faces would only serve to enhance his seniority in the Six, and gruff old Sir Fredrick Ruxmond had served longest in her father's guard. "I'm told he'll return to full health, in time."

"Time, yes, and in the meanwhile his place will need to be filled." His eyes ran over the yard, as unimpressed as a man could be. "But not by these. And speaking of time, we're wasting ours being here, my lady. I shall tell them to withdraw."

She remained on the balcony as the Oak descended the canopied stair and emerged into the yard, calling proceedings to a close. "The Lady Cecilia thanks you all for coming. Please, return to your posts and duties. We shall be in touch should we require anything further."

Several of the knights approached him, perhaps hoping for some more detailed feedback, as others muttered and marched away, resigned. Several glanced up and gave her sour looks as they left, as though wondering just why she had any say in the matter. *I can hardly blame them,* she thought. *A bastard such as I, and a woman besides.* She commanded little love here, she knew, though love was hardly something she cared for. Her father had always ruled by fear and found the notion of being loved most off-putting. She was cut from the same cloth, unlike her brother. *Oh Rylian, you sweet fool. You played with fire, and went up in flames. Just what did you think would happen?*

Sir Owen climbed back up the stairs to rejoin her. "I shall put out a call and hope for better next time," he said, pushing a hand back through his wavy brown hair. "There may yet be some worthy knights in the city willing to answer the summons."

Cecilia thought that unlikely. The war had emptied Ilithor of many a daring and dutiful knight, that was true, but it was not the only reason why so few had come. "I rather think the nobility of your order has been somewhat…tarnished of late, Sir Owen. This business with my brother…well, not everyone believes he died by his own hand."

Sir Owen huffed petulantly. "Let them bleat. It was Rylian who was first to draw his blade and Rylian who was first to swing. His death is not on our conscience. I swore an oath to protect my king and that is what I did. We should all be lauded for that, not condemned."

She smiled. "I quite agree. But be that as it may, many and more are less than convinced of the tale. As evidenced by the poor turnout at these trials." She tapped a finger on her full red lips. "It makes me wonder. Perhaps it's time to consider…modifying our strategy."

He looked down at her, eyebrows raised. "How so?"

"By handpicking men," she said, "rather than persisting with this farce. These open calls have yielded no reward thus far. Surely it would be better to offer invite to men you already know to be willing and worthy?"

The lithesome knight rubbed his cheek, shadowed with the lightest coat of afternoon stubble. "Traditionally the Six have an open policy with regards selection, my lady. All knights of the realm are welcome to compete for a place in your father's guard."

"*Traditionally*?" She laughed at that. "It was my father who formed the Six, Sir Owen. Your fledgling little order has no traditions. We can modify as we see fit. Make it the Five or the Seven if we should like."

Sir Owen frowned. "That would be for your father to decide."

"Quite. *Once* he's recovered. In the meantime, I have an idea for a fine candidate." *A fine candidate indeed,* she thought. She could work her charms on Sir Owen Armdall all she liked, but he'd always be her father's man. But a brand new shiny knight, all of her own choosing, within the sacred Six? Well, the idea held some appeal.

"And who is this candidate of yours, exactly?" Sir Owen didn't sound especially happy at the prospect.

She patted him on the arm. "No need to burden yourself with that knowledge until he has accepted the offer to join, is there?"

"*Accepted*? I rather think you're getting ahead of yourself, Lady Cecilia. Any man would need to be considered by the council first, and that's to say nothing of your father's permit..."

She cut him off with a titter. "Yes, I'm well aware." The idea of this so-called council also made her laugh. With Sir Fredrick in recovery it comprised only Sir Owen, Sir Kevyn Bolt, and Sir Edwyn Huffort, hardly the brightest bunch. *My father wanted loyal men, not clever ones,* she thought. "I only meant to say I would offer him an *opportunity* to join," she said to assuage him. "Words can be such twisty fickle things, don't you think? I mean one thing, and you hear something completely different. I apologise for the unfortunate slip."

Sir Owen regarded her cautiously, though had no talent for this game. "Well then." He rubbed his cheek again. "I will hear of this prospect later, if you insist on keeping me in the dark."

"I'll come see you this evening," she said, already taking a short step away. "I take it you'll be guarding my father again tonight?"

"All night, yes." The Six - or the Three, as they'd been for the last two weeks - split the watch of the king's chambers between them, each taking eight-hour shifts. Sir Owen was adamant he continue in the night watch, giving him time during the day to tend to other matters. It was also the king's most vulnerable time, he liked to think, and thus requiring of his most staunch and stern protector. Sir Owen Armdall was most certainly that man. He had slain the great Rylian Lukar, after all. *And in single combat, he seems to think.*

"Then I'll see you there," she told him, "when I pay him my nightly visit." Her father was still in and out of consciousness after the savage heart attack that had near killed him, though she'd been assured by his physicians that he would make a full recovery. Such assurances were hard to trust, of course, when to suggest anything else might mean one's life, but still, she believed them all the same. *Janilah Lukar is not a man to be undone by a bit of heart trouble,* she told herself. Such a storied life deserved a storied end.

She met Hog and Gerret in the corridor beyond the terrace, the pair playing dice as they awaited her return. "Game's over," she said.

"Come on." They were both men of the Blakewood lands, Bladeborn blades-for-hire whom she'd summoned to act as her bodyguards after all that foul business with her brother. Hog was more than useful with his battle-axe and Gerret was deadly with dagger and dirk, though neither had much in the way of courtly manners and civility.

"Where to next, m'lady?" Gerret asked. He was the smaller of the pair, and younger, no more than five and twenty, with prematurely receding hair, a thin, crooked nose and a missing front tooth that made an occasional whistling sound when he spoke. He liked to slide his tongue in and out through the gap; an unpleasant habit to be sure, but these were unpleasant men. "Any of those fancy knights fit the bill?"

"Not according to Sir Owen, no, but I have a man in mind who might." She began pacing down the corridor as they marched along at her flanks in the colours of her mother's house - brown and gold - with the Blakewood sigil - a charging brindle boar with gilded tusks - sewn onto their quilted jerkins and cloaks.

Hog gave out a snorting laugh. "No need to pace any further, my lady," he said. "I'm right here." He had a great curved moustache, twisted into the likeness of tusks. Cecilia had never asked for confirmation, but imagined he'd earned the nickname because of it.

She glanced over at him. "Very droll, Hog. But you have to be a knight to join the Six."

Neither of them were, and that was the point. They were bastards like she was, and just the sort of company she liked to keep. *They all look at me around here like I'm some whore to be spat on, so why not give them a couple of extra targets?*

"So this man of yours, he a knight then?" asked Gerret.

"That would be the logical assumption, yes."

"But not one of these who came for the trials?"

"Again, Gerret, your powers of deduction astonish me. Yes, he's a knight who isn't currently here right now, otherwise I wouldn't be going to find him."

"Right, right." Gerret nodded as they paced on. "So where is he?"

"At a military house in the Sentinels, I'm told." She had that from one of her informers, of which there were several scuttling about the snowy white streets of the city. "He's newly returned from escorting his dead sister home to his lands south of the Stonehills. He's to take up as part of the garrison here, I believe."

"Can't be much of a knight then," shrugged Hog. "All the best are heading for Eagle's Perch."

"Not all," Cecilia said, though the point had its merits. Cedrik Kastor had stepped into the breach left by Rylian's death, taking charge of the best part of the Tukoran army, some forty thousand swords and spears all told sailing in a great armada numbering several hundred ships. Still, the city garrison was ample, though mostly stocked with archers and crossbowmen and siege engineers manning the scorpions and great mounted crossbows that sat perched like pigeons atop the city towers and walls. This far from the coast, they had no fear of a ground attack. The only threat was from the skies.

The Sentinels was the second highest of the city levels, perched beneath the Marble Steps where the rich palatial residences and fine covered walkways of the city's upper reaches sat proudly beneath the palace. Below the Sentinels was Many Markets, and below that White Shadow, sprawling and heavily populated and the city's busiest district. Cecilia descended the steps and switchbacks as a light snow began to fall. "Careful there, my lady," said Hog. "These here steps look a little treacherous."

"I'll manage," she called back, over the breezy wind. "I've lived much of my life here, Hog. I know where to plant my feet."

Her two guards weren't quite so steady as they moved gingerly down a particularly steep stair with a plunging fall to the left and a sloping, snow-covered roof angling sharply to the right. Much of Ilithor was as such, built as it was within the mountains, with a hundred nerve-wracking bridges to navigate and great soaring towers and endless black drops equally prominent among the heights. But to Cecilia it was nothing. Her guards were used to the boar-infested woods north of the Three Peaks where the Blakewood lands were found. She was quite familiar with both, having lived her youth between them, half a Blakewood and half a Lukar, but a bastard, full and whole, as few people never let her forget.

And certainly not Rylian, she thought with a note of bitterness, as she paced recklessly down the steps, ignoring Hog's calls to slow down. Her half-brother had never respected her, nor loved her as he might have. *He looked down on me for running Father's breeding programme, but he never understood the sacrifices I made.* Unbidden, she thought of her son. The son she'd given to the darkness to be hammered and forged into a weapon. The son torn from her breast when he was nought but a newborn babe. *Jonik,* she thought, wondering where he was. She could picture him only in her mind's eye, for she'd never seen him grow. Never seen him take on his father's features, the black hair and broad shoulders, the silvery-blue eyes of the Daecars. *And mine. What of mine? Does he look like me? Does he have my nose or chin or cheekbones? Does he share a resemblance with me at all?*

She cast those thoughts aside. It did not do her any good to dwell on them. Birthing the boy and giving him away had been her purpose, the price she paid to win a place at Janilah's side. *There is no sense in regretting it now,* she told herself, as she had a thousand times before. *It was my choice, my own. Father never forced me. He never did, no…*

She reached the walled courtyard at the bottom of the steps and waited until her guards rejoined her, Hog arriving first, then Gerret some five or six steps behind. Both looked relieved to have reached safer footing. "You move like a mountain goat, as sure-footed as anything," Hog noted.

"It comes easy enough with practice."

"Practice isn't enough for everyone." Hog turned to look back up the tall steep treacherous stair. "Wasn't this where your grandsire fell?"

Cecilia gave that a nod. This particular stair had claimed the life of a king, once, tumbling from the top and all the way to the bottom and snapping both spine and neck along the way. "It happened before I was born," she said. "Some four decades ago. A blessing, many called it, though not openly. King Jeerah was not a strong man."

She turned to lead them on, passing shorter switchbacks and more gentle descents, crossing over colonnade bridges and beneath yawning arches all in marble as they made their way through the aptly named Marble Steps. The snows had come down with less intent of late, though there was still a fine fall in the air, swirling and capering on the breeze. Men worked with great shovels and brooms to brush aside the heavier drifts, clearing paths for the highborn to pass, tossing salt and grit to make the stone less slippery. At the bottom of the richest city district they came to the Marble Gate, which led down to the Sentinels. The gatehouse was a stocky thing, with squat towers either side, and to the left and right stretched a thick stone wall topped with ballistas and scorpions and crawling with bowmen at every crenel.

Sir Gerlon Rottlor had command of the gate, wearing the green and silver raiment of the Emerald Guards. "Lady Blakewood," he said upon seeing her. There was no mirth whatsoever in his voice. Sir Gerlon had served under Rylian for years and was one of those who had refused the summons to try out for the Six. "You wish to pass?"

"No, Sir Gerlon, I'm here for your sparkling company. Of course I wish to pass."

He grunted and looked at her two guards. "If you're intending to travel down to Many Markets or White Shadow, you would be wise to increase your escort. There are certain people down there who will not take kindly to seeing you."

"And why is that, pray tell?" She knew why, of course, but wanted to hear him say it.

"They think you had something to do with the prince's death," Sir Gerlon said without hesitation. "Some say you have twisted the king's mind to villainy. They call you *bad blood* and *bastard* and *sorceress* and a great deal worse. A hundred stories have arisen around you."

Gerret whistled through the gap in his teeth, twisting a cruel black dirk between his fingers. "Seems you're famous, m'lady."

Sir Gerlon Rottlor gave the mercenary a disdainful look. "If you have any wish to improve your image among the smallfolk, you might want to reconsider your choice of guards," he said.

"Well it's a good thing I have no such wish," Cecilia told him. "Now raise the gate, sir, and I'll forget this insolence ever happened..."

"*Insolence.*" The man's eyes narrowed. "You think I care to guard my tongue around the likes of *you*?"

"If you value your life, you might want to try. If I can kill a prince then *you* shouldn't be much trouble."

Sir Gerlon's eyes went wide. "You admit to your treason freely!" He reached to the hilt of his blade.

Cecilia tittered. "Goodness what a fool you are, sir. Of course I don't. Your beloved prince came to take his father's throne and lost his life because of it. But by all means, believe the mob if you'd prefer, and not the word of your own king. When I see him this evening I will be sure to tell him just how *loyal* you are."

The old knight grew as stiff as the grey whiskers on his chin. "My loyalty is without question."

"To whom? The prince who sought to betray his king father, or the king so stricken by his son's betrayal that he had a heart attack and almost died upon his own throne?" She let a moment pass. The knight said nothing. "Believe what you wish, Sir Gerlon, but the facts speak for themselves. What happened two weeks ago..." She stopped and gave a performance of mourning, shaking her head, even letting out a little sniff. "It grieves me to have been there to watch my brother die, my father come so close to the same. This is not treachery, but tragedy. Do you truly believe your king wished Rylian dead? His very own son and heir, who was to carry his battle standard into war?"

"I...well I..." He frowned and shook his head. "No, I suppose not. But something has gone amiss of late. The king...he hasn't been himself, it's said. And *you*..." He looked at her through a thin veil of scorn, but something stopped him from furthering that thought. "The prince was alone, they say, and without support. I knew him and knew him well. He would never have been so heedless as to try to stage a coup by himself."

"So you *do* deny the word of your king?" she challenged.

"No," he said at once. "No, I...well, as I say, something is amiss."

"Much has been amiss of late. This is wartime, a time of rage and greed and fear. People act recklessly, and tense words can lead to blood. *Tragedy*, Sir Gerlon, not treachery. Let me repeat that and make it plain, and perhaps you might serve your king and kingdom by helping to quash these damaging rumours."

Gerret continued to flick his dirk on her left. Hog loomed on her right, white-knuckled fingers curled about the haft of his great misting battle-axe. Sir Gerlon glanced at them in turn and gave a nod. "You are right, my lady. What's done is done, and there is no sense in dwelling on the past, not now. We ought to unite, such as we can. I served your brother for many long years, yes, but I have served your father longer. I serve him still." He smiled uncomfortably and turned to the soldiers in the gatehouse. "Raise the portcullis. The lady would like to pass."

The winces and chains groaned and rattled and up went the iron gate. "I'll return shortly," Cecilia told him. "Keep the gate up until then. There's no sense in having it down."

Sir Gerlon frowned. "I've been commanded to keep the gate shut, my lady. Watch Commander Morwood has decreed that all be kept down so that we can control the flow of people coming and going between the levels. He fears the smallfolk will try to rush into the higher districts should a dragon be sighted."

A fair concern, she had to admit. "Fine. Just watch for my return, then, and have the gate raised once you see me. I would prefer not to be kept waiting."

She had broken him, she could see. He even gave a shallow bow. "As you wish, my lady." But ever the shadow of loathing lingered.

With her men at her flanks, Cecilia Blakewood passed through the gate and into the Sentinels, a level teemed with training yards, barracks, stables, forges and armouries. Turning north, they came upon a bustling yard in which men were sparring with sword and shield beneath the late afternoon sun, all gleaming steel and flashing blades, the soft mist of godsteel rising to meet the falling snow in a sparkle of light. Elsewhere bowmen were sharpening their skills at a sprawling archery range, firing at targets shaped as dragons that were suspended on lengths of rope. A man was turning a wheel to one side, activating a series of pulleys and cogs that caused the targets to move up and down, left and right, in a vague imitation of how a dragon might fly. The bowmen were clearly well-practiced; few arrows whistled past without hitting.

Further on was a three-storey building up a set of stairs, grander and more finely made than the single-storey barracks they'd passed before. Here the more esteemed Emerald Guards made their home, each provisioned with pleasant accommodations, with communal gardens and libraries and private quads in which to train. A steward ran the military household, fetched by a servant as he saw Cecilia approach. "My lady," the steward said, emerging through the front door. "To what do we owe this pleasure?"

"A private visit. Is Sir Mallister returned?"

"This very morning, yes. He is in his chambers. I shall lead you."

"My thanks." She turned to her men. "Wait here for my return." She followed the steward inside.

Her quarry had been situated on the top floor, at the rear of the mansion overlooking the gardens. Some of the richer Emerald Guards had their own homes in the city, with staff to tend them, but for most that wasn't the case. When stationed in Ilithor they typically lived here. The steward reached the thick wooden door and knocked. "Sir Mallister, you have a visitor."

Muffled noise came from inside, the sound of footsteps, then the turn of a lock. The door swung open and the arched frame filled with the splendid form of Sir Mallister Monsort, undressed above the waist. Cecilia had rarely set eyes upon a man so beautifully made. Blond locks of hair fell easily from his head, his skin soft and creamy, eyes a bright blue, jawline sharp enough to cut diamonds. Yet for all that there was a darkness to him. A darkness Cecilia Blakewood had come here to exploit.

His eyes fell upon her. "My lady." Even struck by grief he recalled his courtesies and put his head into a bow. "This is…an unexpected pleasure."

Cecilia smiled at him then turned to the steward. "Some privacy, please."

"Of course." The man withdrew.

She looked beyond Sir Mallister and into his room. His armour and cloak had been set upon a wooden mannequin, his sword, dagger, spear and shield fastened into holdings along one wall. He wore linen breeches and nothing more, his shirt and tunic, jerkin, boots, and cloak sitting in a bundle upon a wooden chair beside his bed. "I was just catching up on some sleep," he explained. "These last weeks…I've had trouble getting proper rest."

He's vulnerable, she saw. *Good.* "I quite understand. What happened to your sister…and at the hand of a man you considered a friend." She shook her head and placed a hand on his unburdened, well-toned arm. "I am so sorry for your loss, Sir Mallister, truly."

A wrinkle of pain crossed his face. "*Elyon…*" His head began to shake. She saw him close a fist, squeezing. "What he did to her…I…I find myself struggling to believe…"

"I was there, Sir Mallister." Her voice was soft and coaxing. *It must be a potion,* she thought, *to take him under my spell.* "I saw Elyon with Melany's blood on his hands. I heard her screams before we burst in."

"But…but *why*? I just cannot figure out the *why* of it, my lady."

Because I told her that you would die, and your father would die, and everyone else she cared about would die, if she didn't. Cecilia said none of that, of course. Melany's death was suicide, not murder, but that wasn't what she'd wanted the world to believe. *No, we wanted to set Elyon up, have him caged and desperate, so he might give up the location of the Windblade.* But that was all her father's design, of course. *I am nothing but a tool for him to wield.*

"You saw Elyon taking that girl off during the wedding feast, did you not?" she said to the knight. "The girl with the red hair." She drew his eyes and saw that he had. "Well, Melany saw it too, and must have gone to confront Elyon over it. She was heard to be screaming from some way through the palace, and loud enough to draw guards to the room. It just so happened that I was nearby at the time. I suspect Elyon tried to calm her, but failing that, grew violent." She paused. "You remember what happened with Sir Griffin Kastor…"

Mallister nodded grimly. "But that was different. Sir Griffin accosted Elyon in his tent. He went there to ambush him."

Cecilia sighed "You still fail to condemn him, even now. Even after murdering your sister."

"No." The word was firm. "I would kill him for it, my lady. Should I see him again, I *shall.* We fought once over my sister's honour, the very night we first met. I would do so again, but with swords this time, not fists. And let the gods decide whether he is innocent or not."

"One day you may have that chance." She smiled and stepped past him, into his room. The balcony doors were shut. She went to open them, letting a cool wintry breeze flutter through the curtains. The smell of winter flowers and snow wafted in, cold and bracing. When she turned she found him putting on his shirt. "You don't need to dress on my account, Mallister."

"It isn't proper, my lady. I am in remiss. I ought to have dressed before I opened the door, but…well, I didn't expect *you.* We don't get many women here."

"More's the pity." She unburdened herself of her own coat, placing it on the bed. Beneath she wore a brown samite dress slashed with hues of green, hugging at the waist and bust and complimenting her womanly curves.

Sir Mallister was watching her, half cautious, half curious. "I take it you didn't come to talk about my sister. What is this about, Lady Blakewood?"

"This is about you, Sir Mallister. You have heard of course that my brother is dead?" The young knight had left the city soon after his sister's death, she knew, taking her back to her father's estate to be buried. He would have been absent the day Rylian died.

He nodded gravely. "A most tragic affair. I have heard… conflicting reports of how it happened." He raised his eyes to study her, though was not so indelicate as Sir Gerlon and his direct accusations. "I've heard it said Prince Rylian tried to remove his father from the throne. And that…that you were present, Lady Blakewood. Perhaps you might…"

"Tell you the truth of it?" she said. "The truth is…well, it's as ugly and complicated as it seems. Rylian was maddened that day, most unlike himself. To try to oust my father so openly…" She shook her head, as though trying to get her head around it still. "Once my brother struck, there really was no choice. And you know Sir Owen Armdall's reputation, I trust? He is a man who thinks a great deal of himself and something…well, I probably shouldn't say this, but I feel he wanted to prove something that day. We might have been able to subdue Rylian if it wasn't for him, make him see calm, but no, Sir Owen had an appetite for blood once Sir Rees and Sir Maxwell had been killed, and there was little stopping him then."

"I know Sir Owen a little, yes," Sir Mallister said. "He is a few years older than me, but I have come across him at tourneys and such in the past. He has a certain…swagger to him. And this you say…a desire to prove himself. Yes, that's the man I know."

Cecilia was happy to see he understood, and there was no lie in what she'd said - Sir Owen had been vocally discourteous to Rylian during that heated exchange in the throne room, and hadn't wasted a moment to engage once the fighting broke out. "The Six have become the Three," she said. "The brothers Hunt are dead. The Ram of Ruxmond in recovery. We have been holding trials, as you may have heard, but to little result. Sir Owen, Sir Kevyn, and Sir Edwyn are exhausted by their duties, at a time when the king they are sworn to protect and serve is most vulnerable." She looked at him. "I hope you know why I'm here by now, Sir Mallister. I would like to offer you a chance to join the order. You have a level head, a keen skill with blade and spear, and will be wasted as part of the garrison. The command of the city gates has been given over to older men, war-weary and tired. Sir Bonmer Marsh. Sir Gerlon Rottlor. Let these men serve beneath the Watch Commander. You are ripe for a higher calling."

She watched him, and closely. *Say yes,* she prayed. *You are perfect, Sir Mallister. Perfect, for me.* Her father's mental state was much as people claimed. Faltering. Failing. "*The king has not been himself,*" Sir Gerlon had said, and he was right. And that made Cecilia nervous. *If he should damn me for Rylian's death…what then?* She didn't delude herself into thinking her king father felt any love for her. *No, he cares for nothing and no one…except perhaps the son rotting down in the crypts. And if he feels I have manipulated him…*

The thought didn't bear thinking about. She looked at Sir Mallister again. *I must have insurance,* she thought. *I must have him.*

Eventually, he gave a nod. "I am honoured that you would think of me, my lady. Honoured and flattered. Of course, I shall consent." He gave a bow to seal it.

It was all she needed to hear. "Good," she said, hiding her relief. "Then I shall see the arrangements made."

9

Jonik

The call came first from Grim Pete, squawking about ships from the crow's nest. "Northwest, Cap'n," he cried, pointing with a cadaverous finger. "I see ten, twenty, at least. No, more, many more. It's an armada, a whole fleet! I see sails in brown and green!"

The decks soon filled as the crew manned their stations, Turner bellowing his orders from the helm. He turned them northeast and with the wind as Emeric and Borrus marched up the stairs and gathered on the aftcastle deck. Jonik was already there, gazing northwest, his black cloak flapping in the breeze. The weather had cooled dramatically as they'd headed north, the skies a shifting motley of cloud, some high and wispy, others lumpy and low, all white and grey and pacy as they sped swiftly overhead.

"Brown and green," Jonik said, confirming what Grim Pete had seen. He held the black haft of the Nightblade tight between his fingers, enhancing his sight. "There are grey sails too, and black, some white." He squinted against a sudden shaft of sunlight, breaking through the clouds. Sewn into many of the sails he saw a crossed sword and mallet, a shield behind. "I see the royal standard of Tukor," he said. "And the bear-print of Kastor on sails of black and green. Lots of them. There's the Gershan serpent, coiling around its hill. Birds against a black sky. That's House Swallow of Blackhearth. And Huffort's kneeling knight beneath a sky of falling rocks. And others…an orchard of apples, an eagle with bladed wings, three hills against a starlit sky, a bull-headed man in misting armour…"

"We get the point," said Borrus Kanabar. "Seems half the Tukoran army have come."

"Most are houses out of North Tukor," said Emeric thoughtfully. "Gershan. Swallow. Huffort. They're all Kastor bannermen. The hills and starlit sky is House Caldlow. The orchard is Gullimer."

"And that eagle?" asked Captain Turner. He glanced at the pommel of Emeric's blade, once held by his famed ancestor Sir Oswald. It was forged into the likeness of an eagle's head, the cross-guard of fine feathered wings. "I take it that isn't yours, lord?"

"No. The colours of House Manfrey are black and gold. Our sigil shows a golden eagle flanked by two black dragons. Sir Oswald took it on following his defeat of Karlog the Knight Killer and Bagazar the Brute in single combat."

"Aye, o' course. Always loved that story."

"The eagle with bladed wings is House Suffolk," Emeric went on. "They're older than House Manfrey, if less fabled. And from south of the Stonehills, not north. Either way, they're best avoided. We're carrying fugitives and southerners besides and I'd sooner keep my wrists and ankles free of fetters. Make no mistake, we'll all be in chains by day's end if they board us."

No one gave that much debate, though there was something eager about the look on Sir Borrus's face. "They'll be making for Eagle's Perch, I'll wager," he said. "Gods be good, they're really going for it."

"And taking the Aramatians unawares, it would seem." Emeric stroked his neat black beard, gazing to the far horizon. They were sailing the channel between the Horn of Aramatia and the southern coast of Rasalan, and hadn't seen an Aramatian warship in two days. The bulk of their fleet seemed to be at anchorage in Aram, or patrolling the coastline around the Port of Matia and Cloaklake. "This serves us, so long as we can slip past them unmolested," the exiled lord went on. "That many Tukoran swords and spears will leave the kingdom sparsely resourced. It'll make our travels north less bothersome, I should think."

A call came over the winds, as One World came swooping up alongside them to starboard. "Cap, you seeing all those ships out yonder?" bellowed Brown Mouth, standing at the quarterdeck gunwale. He was pointing northwest, his voice half swallowed by the wind and churning seas and caws of seabirds circling above them. "Has to be a hundred of them, maybe more. Rose thinks…" He turned to his side as Vincent Rose beckoned him into a privy discussion. A few words were shared, then Brown Mouth nodded and turned back, cupping his hands to his mouth. "Master Rose thinks we outta go around, avoid them if we can," he yelled. "I'm inclined to agree. Be no good us caught out here with these Sunshine Swords and whatnot aboard. Kazil and Big Mo and the like. We're seeing Kastor colours out there. Everyone knows how they feel about southerners. Will go ill for us, it will. Let's give 'em a wide berth!"

It will go ill for me as well, Jonik thought, as One World rolled grandly upon the waves, a third longer and taller than Invincible Iris. Jonik could see Jack o' the Marsh pulling at some rigging, Devin halfway up the mainmast reefing sails. Both had remained on Vincent Rose's ship to act as crew, though some of the other men had swapped decks of late.

Turner filled his lungs and called back. "We've had the same thought here, Brown! Why d'you think I turned us northeast? Aye, we'll head direct for Rasalan, cut back in once they've passed." He gestured down the ship in the direction they were going. The Winds favoured them, blowing northeasterly. "The island o' Bhoun isn't so far off. We'll see it soon, most like. We can hug her southern coast and turn westward into Whaler's Bay." He turned for a quieter word with the men beside him. "I know the plan was to make for Mudport, but might be best to make port at Calmwater first. We have that Lady Kathryn over on One World." The Moaning Maid, Ranulf had called her. She was sister to Humphrey Merrymarsh, most beloved to the Seaborn lord. "We can ship her to Merrymarsh's keep and offload the rest o' the Rasal patients too. Then go for Mudport after." He scanned the seas and skies, then nodded. "Aye, I've a feelin' the winds and waves'll favour that course. And with this here armada to avoid…well, it makes sense to me."

"And me," Emeric agreed. "Lord Merrymarsh exerts a great deal of control over the waters of Whaler's Bay. If we're stopped by one of his galleys we can bring out Lady Kathryn and use her for immunity. It sounds somewhat callous, I know, but we have to use every card we've been dealt. Navigating the bays during wartime won't be easy. There will be hundreds of ships patrolling the coast, we can be sure of it, and even those bearing merchant flags are likely to be stopped and searched. We'd have to get awfully lucky to completely avoid such attention."

"That helps," said Borrus, waving a great paw toward the armada on the horizon. "I'm seeing a few Rasal banners out there too. Might be they've lent a few of their ships to the fleet. Will thin the herd, so to speak. But either way, I'm not worried. We have southerners aboard, yes, and this notorious Shadowboy right here…" He gave Jonik a wink. "But we also have *me*." He puffed up his enormous barrel of a chest. "Heir to House Kanabar and future Lord of the Riverlands. There won't be many men who'd dare deny *me* passage, I'll tell you."

"*If* they recognise you, Sir Borrus," said Emeric. "You've been long away and are most likely thought dead."

"Don't you fret, Manfrey. I've slimmed down a bit, it's true, but all for the better. Just let me do the talking, OK?" He scanned his companions, on Invincible Iris and One World both. "I daresay I'm the only reputable man within this entire rabble, barring one or two of the patients, of course." He had that insufferably pompous look on his face. "You, an exile, the lad here a fugitive and feared assassin, Turner and the rest, his devious companions and crew, and a host of sellswords and cutthroats and scoundrels besides. What a lot we are! What a lot! And by the gods I've come to like you!"

"We're all flattered, I'm sure." Emeric didn't sound so flattered. "But you do have a point. Yes, you'd do well to speak for us if it comes to it, flex that lordly power of yours." He looked to the other ship. Brown Mouth Braxton was still waiting for his orders, Vincent Rose at his side in jewels and silks and satins slashed in a hundred colours; absurd dress for this sort of weather. "Vincent will do on the other, I should say. Like him or loathe him, he commands a deal of influence and has money enough to bribe every captain in the north if he must. I'm sure he can have them turn a blind eye."

"A blind eye, aye," nodded Turner, pulling on his tangly flaxen beard. "A man like Rose has his uses, schemer and snake though he is."

Braxton was starting to look a bit impatient. He held his arms out, shoulders shrugging, grinding his lopsided jaw.

"Aye, Brown, calm yourself!" bellowed Turner. "Just follow our lead, and let Master Rose do the talkin' should some warship come a-snoopin'. We're with the wind, so shouldn't be hard to outrun that lot." He gestured to the distant fleet. "And doubt they much care for us anyhow." He gave the wheel a spin, caught the handles, and they lurched over a rising swell. And that was that.

They lost sight of the fleet an hour or so later, the last of the warships fading off into the misty blue haze atop the far horizon. "Eagle's Perch, you think?" Jonik asked Sir Borrus, as the day's training got underway. The two stood aside, Emeric taking the lead, calling up Sir Corbray Walsh and Cabel to enter the duelling circle scrawled onto the forecastle deck. Sir Corbray glared at the dark youth through a set of old seamed eyes. "I'll have you this time, whelp," he said, in a growly voice. Cabel only smiled as Emeric handed him a training sword. "Just try, old man."

As the old Bladeborn knight and crafty-eyed young sellsword began their duel, Borrus gave answer. "Makes most sense," he said, over the clang of blunted steel. "Be folly to try to go much further south without taking the Perch first. If they win it, they'll have a foothold for a land *and* sea invasion. Do it quick and they could march on Aram within a moon's turn."

"Is that likely?"

"No." Borrus laughed. "The Perch is aptly named, right at the top of a surging cliff and all massive granite walls and soaring towers. You can only access it from one direction, up along the headland, and once you've set your siege lines, you can be vulnerable from the rear, as your grandfather found out twenty years ago."

"My grandfather?" Jonik repeated. He had to take a moment to think. "Lord Gideon?" It meant a great deal to him to hear Sir Borrus Kanabar include him so freely as a Daecar.

"The very one," the bald knight said. "He sieged Eagle's Perch early in the last war, and was making progress too before that Moonrider Justo Nemati came up behind him with an army of Sunriders and Starriders for company, breaking the siege."

"They fought, didn't they?" Jonik remembered now. "Justo Nemati, and my…my…"

"Your grandfather. You can say it." Borrus favoured him with a smile. "They did. Our singers say Gideon won, theirs say the opposite. The truth is it was a draw, though that part about Gideon blinding the beast in its right eye…yes, that bit's true. Either way, Lord Gideon saw the battle was lost and his men were sure to be routed, so made the only decision he could and called the retreat.

Sometimes you've got to realise when you're beat, lad. Takes strength to do that."

Jonik tried to picture it for a time as Sir Corbray and Cabel continued their bout, the men hollering and cheering around them. His grandfather Gideon with the Sword of Varinar to hand, Justo Nemati atop the famed noble moonbear Agarosh with his sparkling crystal fur and white claws as long as blades. *My grandfather,* he thought again, with a secret smile. *My grandfather, the First Blade, the war hero…*

…whose own son I crippled…whose eldest grandson I slew.

His smile withered with his shame, as he thought again of Amron, his own sire, fighting shadows in his tent. He could still feel the edge of the Nightblade cleaving through his flesh. He could still hear his bellowing grunts as he swung the Sword of Varinar back and forth, eyes narrow and trying to find him, a grimace across his face. He could smell the blood, the hot sharp bite of iron, flooding across the floor, see the great hulking frame of Amron Daecar slumping to the ground, hear the roar ripping from Elyon's throat as he sensed the commotion and came running in to find his father dying in his tent, cleaved and cut, his shoulder opened, his blood running thick and black in the dimness…

Oh, he remembered it all like it was yesterday, reliving it often in his dreams, as he did the day he'd killed Aleron. That dream came more often, in truth. When he'd crept into the tent of Amron Daecar, he'd not yet known he was his father. *But I knew Aleron was my brother,* he thought. *I knew that when I hacked through his armour and neck, when I watched his blood fountain and gush, when I stood there amid the horror of the crowd, my duty done, my soul stained forever.* Often he woke from those dreams in a cold sweat, panting and perspiring. *The closer north we get, the more I dream of it,* he thought. Was it fear that drove his nightmares? Fear of seeing Elyon again, or his father? Of facing up to what he'd done?

"I admit to being a tool of people worse than me," Gerrin had said to him, that night he'd unveiled himself. "I admit to performing horrors at the behest of evil men."

As do I, Shadowmaster, Jonik thought darkly. *But you never had to maim your own father. You never had to murder your own brother…*

A heavy clang and grunt and resulting cheer told Jonik the bout was done. He withdrew from his black musings and turned his eyes into the circle to find Sir Corbray on his back, cursing. Cabel stood over him, dark eyes shining. "Good fight, old man." He held out a hand and helped Sir Corbray to his feet. "You'll have me next time, might be." He grinned.

Sir Corbray gave that a grunt. He'd been much longer in Pal Palek's pits than Cabel and was well over twice his age to boot. It would take him time to find his feet, though Jonik was content with the progress they were making.

Next up was Sir Lenard Borrington; young, shortish of stature, and keen to please, with a wide homely face, fuzzy brown hair, and a nervous manner developed during his time as Palek's captive. Emeric looked across the group and considered his opponent. "Sir," he said, seeing the Silent Suncoat, standing still as stone in his tattered yellow cloak. The brooding man from Rasalan had not yet revealed his real name, but he'd clearly been a knight once, so Emeric just called him 'sir', courteous as ever. The intense-eyed Rasal stepped forward, slow and methodical. Men watched him uneasily, even the giant Big Mo. There was something unnerving about the Silent Suncoat, to be sure. His pale eyes seemed to blink as rarely as he spoke, and for a man without a tongue, that wasn't often.

Sir Lenard Borrington regarded him anxiously. "You…you're sure, my…my lord?" he asked Emeric. "Might I not…" He looked around for a more suitable opponent. "Might I not be paired with… with someone else."

"You do not get to choose your opponent on the battlefield, Sir Lenard," Emeric told him. "You face whom you must and are required to work out how best to defeat him." He waved a hand. "We have a range of men here, small and large, some quick, some strong, knights trained in the forms and sellswords who have adapted styles of their own. That serves us. And it will serve you to face each one of them, and often, to mature into a more rounded fighter."

Sir Lenard nodded in his jittery way. "Yes, my lord." He drew a deep bracing breath and moved into an awkward Blockform stance. The Silent Suncoat did the same, statue-still as he waited.

"Then fight," Emeric said. "And shake hands when you're done."

The bout did not last long. After a few tentative prods from Sir Lenard, his mute opponent unleashed a sudden and quite terrifying barrage of attacks. Borrus nodded appreciatively. "He has something, this one," he noted. "His skill in the forms is impressive."

"Rushform in particular," Jonik said, agreeing. That form favoured quick and powerful surges, well paired with Blockform. A strong proponent of the two would often wait and wait, holding to Blockform in defence, frustrating an opponent, before bursting out in Rushform when spotting an opening.

Sir Borrus Kanabar was a master of both, and Powerform besides. If anyone should know, it was him. "I'll want to test him myself," he said, "see what he's really got."

The bout reached a swift conclusion, Sir Lenard yielding as he was driven from the circle, a hand up in supplication. "I yield, I yield."

"Again," said Emeric.

Sir Lenard looked at him. "My lord?"

"Again," the exile repeated. "You can do better, Sir Lenard. I know you can."

His words gave the homely young man some courage. "Yes, Lord Manfrey." He stepped back into the circle for round two, though it didn't last much longer. The Silent Suncoat's attacks were swift, brutal, accurate, and he was not a man inclined to hold back. He had Sir Lenard sprawling on the floor within a swift half minute, clutching at his ribs where he'd taken a heavy thrust. The big mute loomed above him, pale eyes wide and unblinking. *Do you yield?* those eyes demanded. Sir Lenard gave answer. "I yield," he said, coughing, grimacing. "I yield, no more."

Borrus sighed and shook his head as the Silent Suncoat reached out a stiff hand and hauled Sir Lenard to his feet. "He's willing, but too jumpy," he said to Jonik, watching as Lenard Borrington withdrew gingerly from the circle, an arm cradling his stomach. "I know his father, Lord Randall, and his uncle Robert is Lord of Northwatch. Both good men, good warriors, and brave. Robert was severely burned during the war but never lost his sense of fun." He chuckled to think of the man. "A garrulous sort, unlike his older brother. Randall was never much for laughing. He was always harder, stern." He looked again at Sir Lenard, who'd spent over three years in the pits after disappearing from a brothel in Green Harbour. "Seems the darkness took its toll on the boy. You might want to consider sending him home, lad. A nervy fighter can be more burden than boon when the chaos of battle descends. Emeric knows it, that's why he's pushing him. You have to be able to rely on every man… *every man*, Jonik. You can't be having any weak links."

Jonik welcomed the advice. *At least he's done trying to convince me not to go.* "I'll keep an eye on him," he said. "We have time enough to see him improve." He looked over. "I know you'd prefer I send him home to his father, Borrus."

"His father?" Borrus laughed. "His father won't be at home, oh no. He'll be right in the thick of it somewhere, I have no doubt. Defending the western gate at the Twinfort, most likely."

"Still, I'll keep what you've said in mind. But as you say, he's eager, and willing enough to learn. I can't be casting out trained Bladeborn knights without good cause. I have too few men as it is…"

As he said those very words a figure appeared from the main deck, climbing the stairs in a faded blue cloak over ill-fitting leathers, clunky books and a swordbelt cut with brand new holes to fit around his slender waist. That waist had once been much more girthy, his shoulders broader, his chest thick and muscular. He had a sunken quality to him now, though was vastly less brittle than he'd been when they'd found him, muttering to himself down in those pits. Borrus saw him come. "Torvyn…"

"Yes, yes," Sir Torvyn Blackshaw said, raising a knobbly hand, callused and scarred. *It no longer shivers, though,* Jonik saw. *That's progress.* "I know…all this noise and clamour. You'd have me back in my bed with my books, wouldn't you, Borrus? Well, enough. It's fresh air I need and the sight of battle." A smile broke on Sir Torvyn's rumpled lips. His incarceration had aged him sorely, making him look ten years Borrus' senior, when in fact they were the same age, but there was light in the man's eyes yet. "A sight of it, and maybe a *taste.*" He had a look at the latest combatants, Emeric himself taking Maurice through his paces. Big Mo was a giant and a brute, but had no answer to Emeric's grace and skill. Sir Torvyn nodded. "Yes, that's what I need. The feel of steel between my fingers."

"No," said Borrus. "You need to rest and regain your strength, Torvyn. You can watch, but no more. Maybe in a week or two, I'll…"

"You'll what? Permit me to train?" He shook his head and muttered something unintelligible. "You mollycoddle me, old friend. Now enough of that. My eyes are open now…I'm back in the light. So stop fussing like an old maid. It's unbecoming, Borrus."

"You have become rather…overprotective," Jonik told him gently. That got a fierce look. "I'm just saying…"

"I know what you're saying. You want him training so he'll join your quest. But I won't have it. I say I won't!"

"*My* choice, Borrus. Not yours." Sir Torvyn smiled gamely, thin skin stretching over the jutting bones of his face. "Now hand me your sword, and let me have a swing."

"Not bloody likely." Borrus wrapped his meaty fist around Red Wrath's hilt and drew back. "Would you have asked Amron to hold the Sword of Varinar? I think not."

"It's hardly the same," said Jonik. "The Sword of Varinar is a Blade of Vandar. Yours is a regular godsteel sword."

"It's the ancestral blade of House Kanabar," Borrus came back, insulted.

"And still just regular godsteel," said Sir Torvyn. He looked at Jonik. "I don't suppose you'd let me hold *yours* instead?" There was a twinkle in his eye.

Gods, I might just let him if he'll swear me his oath. "You'd…struggle to bear it, right now," Jonik said, careful not to offend him.

The old knight chuckled throatily, his left eye giving a couple of rapid blinks, head jerking a little to the side. Those odd mannerisms weren't going anywhere just yet. *No doubt they'll be with him forever, scars of his long years in that subterranean hell.* "A dagger, then. Let me feel godsteel in my grip."

"It might overwhelm you," Borrus said.

"Goodness, enough." Sir Torvyn reached out a hand to Jonik. "If you would be so kind."

Jonik saw no reason not to unsheathe his dagger and set it into the man's wrinkled grasp. Borrus grumbled angrily and shook his head, muttering something about it being too early. Jonik disagreed. Godsteel was bracing, invigorating, and did wonders for a man in recovery. *He doesn't want his friend to recall its touch,* Jonik knew. *He worries where it will lead him.*

"Do you really think so little of me, old friend?" Sir Torvyn Blackshaw held the blade as though it had never left his hand. There was not a shudder, no visible difficultly in bearing its weight. *This is a man born to bear godsteel,* Jonik thought.

"I think the world of you, Torvyn. I always did, you know that."

"Then walk at my side, don't stand in my way." He took a step forward, steadier on his feet, stronger. The godsteel blew life into the dying cinders of his flame, driving away the darkness, the cold, restoring some of his warmth and light. It was a flicker only, but a start. He took a few more paces across the deck; some of the other men were watching. The bout stopped within the circle and then Emeric was watching too. Sir Torvyn seemed not to notice. He returned to Jonik, returned his blade, then turned to Emeric Manfrey, calm as anything. "My lord, is there space for another student in your class?"

Emeric gave a bow. "You would be the teacher, sir."

Sir Torvyn laughed. It sounded less ragged than before. There was a bit more power in his voice. Somehow, he seemed younger. "Oh, I rather think not. The years have stripped me of much I once knew. Still, there are a few things still rattling around back here." He gave his grey-haired head a tap. "Hand me one of those practice swords, and I'll see what I remember."

Emeric turned to Maurice. "Mo, if you would."

The scar-faced behemoth plodded over. "Here." He thrust the blunted blade into the old knight's grip.

"My thanks, friend." Sir Torvyn stepped into the circle, bowed, then put himself into a perfect Blockform stance. "Like this?" he asked, giving Borrus a little side-eyed glance.

"Just like that." Emeric smiled. "I have heard tell you were a true student of the forms, sir. Akin to a man like Lythian Lindar in your dedication and desire to improve."

Mention of the Knight of the Vale had Borrus huffing. "*I* was always better than Lythian," he muttered to Jonik. "Natural talent, lad. It's all about natural talent." He put a paw on Jonik's shoulder and watched. Jonik could feel him squeezing nervously.

"Lythian…yes, a welcome comparison," said Sir Torvyn. "Though I would never claim to match such a man as he."

"Lythian…why does everyone think Lythian so bloody good…" Borrus squeezed tighter.

"You were taken before your time," said Emeric, "and denied a chance at greatness." He pointed his blade out, moving into Strikeform.

"Gentle now," Borrus whispered under his breath. "You be bloody gentle, Manfrey." Jonik felt like his shoulder was being crushed.

"There is still time," Sir Torvyn declared proudly.

"There is always time," agreed Emeric. "And legends are forged at the anvil of war."

Borrus growled through his teeth. "Manfrey…you blasted snake. Filling his head with this poison…"

"Then let me see if I still have what it takes," said Sir Torvyn Blackshaw, shifting into Strikeform, Glideform, Rushform, Powerform, moving so splendidly from stance to stance, more neat and tidy in his motion than he had any right to be. He finished back in Block-form. "Come at me, my lord. And hard. I have always believed one sank, or he swam. I do not wish to be treated delicately."

Emeric bowed again. "As you wish." He stepped forward to engage.

10

Janilah

He was sitting on a throne of skulls and bones in a hall drenched red with blood. Bodies littered the floor, cleaved and cold and pale, dead. White maggots feasted upon them, wriggling, writhing, fat with rotting flesh. The hall seemed vast, stretching to all eternity with tall fluted pillars rising to the bleak black skies, fading away into the nothingness above.

Somewhere a voice was laughing. *Kill him,* it said, *kill him, kill your son, kill him.* Janilah opened his mouth to bellow a reply, but a choking splutter crawled out, and the laughing grew louder. *Kill him,* the voice cackled, rising, rising. *Kill him. Kill him. He's dead! Dead! DEAD!*

"No!" Janilah rose to his feet, but slipped in the blood as a tide of red washed over him. He gasped and rubbed his eyes, but it kept coming, and coming, and coming. *This is all the blood you've spilt,* said a voice. *Blood spilt for the follies of a madman.*

"Rylian..." He rubbed his eyes again, tried to stand, fell. That voice, it sounded like his son. "Rylian, no, listen to me..."

"Listen? Listen to you *now*? I'm dead, father, *dead.* You did not take me into your counsel living. Why should you now I'm gone?"

"You do not understand." More blood washed over him, splashing like waves in a raging sea. "I am trying to save the north. Win the war. I...I hold the torch, son. I light the way."

That laughing again, louder and louder, ringing all around him. It grew so loud it broke like thunder, rumbling through the skies.

Vandar, he thought. *Vandar mocks me. He has deceived me, tricked me, forsaken me. I was never meant to gather the Blades.*

He surged to his feet in a fury. "I did this for *you*!" The tide of blood beat against him, churning, boiling, filled with bits of broken bone, but he held firm. He turned his eyes up and up, searching. "I am trying to win *your* war! Trying to fulfil King Galin's promise! Why do you mock me? Tell me! *Why*!"

The only response was laughter, bellowing, shuddering, shaking through the world. A great rending tore through the air, of cracking stone, of all the earth breaking, tossing him back off his feet. He landed hard on a rough surface and wheezed into the dirt, blinking as a bright sun rose harsh and sudden, up and over the western horizon. It wheeled overhead, peaking and falling into the east, and a moment later it came up again in the west, and wheeled and fell east, and appeared again, faster each time, faster and faster, passing over him in a flash as the world began to spin…

The sun goes backward, was all he could think, confused, holding his hands to his face as the sun whirled by, each flare of yellow light a passing day, one becoming ten and ten becoming a hundred and a hundred a thousand, a thousand ten thousand, until every day of his life had seemed to pass. Then suddenly the flashing slowed and stopped as the sun came to rest above him.

He peeked out from between his fingers and looked upon a lush green garden embraced within a courtyard of pale white stone. The air was cool and bracing, the tall white towers surging skyward, enclosed all around by the black scarps of the mountains. On a path of pale cobbled stone a boy was skipping along happily, leaping between the pavestones, careful not to land on a crack. A boy no more than ten with short brown hair and greenish eyes with a head full of adventure and magic and mystery.

I remember that game, Janilah thought, watching his younger self dance through the gardens. For a time every seam and crack between every stone in the palace was off-limits to him and his siblings. *Jaylor would try to push me so I'd step on one,* he remembered, *and Myra would tut and tell him off, crossing her skinny little arms.* He smiled at the memory, and then there they were, right behind him, skipping along the stones as well, laughing. Jaylor, eight, small for his age, but keen and cunning. Myra, a mere five, always following them about. *Even then she was bossy,* he thought, though his memory of her was faint. She had died young, falling sick when she was only twelve, and never blossomed into a woman. Jaylor had died young too, killed in Agarath only five years later.

Is that what birthed my hatred for them? Janilah wondered, as he watched himself and his siblings at play. They had not been at war with the dragon-folk then, no, but his brother had fallen to their wickedness all the same. *I loved him,* he knew, *as I loved sweet Myra too. Would that they'd never been taken from me. Would that I hadn't been left alone.*

"Jan, Jay, Myra, slow down now..."

Janilah turned his eyes. From around a hedge along the garden path came his father, Jeerah Lukar, a smile upon his long bearded face. *A smile,* Janilah thought. *He would smile often, but not me.* King Jeerah had been a soft-hearted man, never strong, a peacetime ruler who'd not aspired to be anything greater. Janilah had long held him in disdain for that. *King Galin's ambition grew weaker each generation until I came along. It was I who found Ilith's ancient forge, I who learned the secret of the blades. I who held the torch. I who lit the way...*

Through the gardens came that laughter again, as a storm brewed sudden and black. Dark clouds opened and the rains came gushing down, as Janilah's father rushed up to his young children, beckoning them indoors. "Come, children, come. Out of the rains. Quick, quick."

The children giggled and splashed, leaping between the stones, Myra following Jaylor, Jaylor following Janilah, with their father right behind, chuckling as the rains came down. Janilah, the old Janilah, watched from the side, a ghost, grim and old and unseen. A mournful envy filled his eyes. An envy tinged with hate and scorn. *I could have had the same. A loving family. A brood of children. But mine was a greater purpose.* He stepped forward, following. "You never cared for Galin's promise...you never cared to win the war," he called out. "You were always *weak*, Father. You were always a shameless coward!"

His father didn't stop, or hear him, but on he went with his three young children, giggling as they ran. Janilah stopped on the path, as the rains turned suddenly red, soaking them all in blood, thick and dark and slippery. "They killed him and you did nothing," he shouted over the din. "They slew your son...*AND YOU DID NOTHING!*"

Jaylor had been just twenty summers old, a young prince setting out on his first diplomatic mission, making for Eldurath with a gleaming honour guard at his back to treat with King Tellion of Agarath. Janilah recalled how proud his younger brother had been to be given the charge. "I will return with rich tidings, Brother," he had said to him the morning he left. His instruction was to improve the flow of information between the two kingdoms, and to discuss a particular tract of land that was under dispute. "I will make Father proud, and you, Jan. I will prove myself worthy, I promise it, I will."

Prince Jaylor Lukar, secondborn of the King of Tukor, had never made it to Eldurath. Instead he had fallen in the shadow of the Ashmount, he and his guard set upon by a rogue faction at night, slaughtered as they slept, unarmoured and unarmed. Janilah recalled the day he'd learned of it. He recalled his king father's face, the pale shock as he sat his pale throne, more fear in his eyes than anger. *I knew it then, as I knew it before*, he thought. *Coward*. He had marched right up to the foot of the dais, before the knights and lords of the realm, and declared it an act of war. "We demand King Tellion find the men who did this, and bring them to us in chains, every one!" he had said to the highborn assembly. At only twenty-two he commanded their respect in a way his father never had. "Failing this, we will take his young son Dulian in recompense. And if not that, then war! We will have war!" That had got the reaction he'd wanted. Shouts and yells echoed the word, ringing through the hall. *War! War! We will have war!*

But King Jeerah Lukar had only shaken his head solemnly. "The peace must be preserved at all costs," he'd announced, in a thin and feeble voice. "We are no match for the Agarathi. We cannot risk their ire." Janilah remembered looking across the hall. He remembered the looks on the faces of the strong stout men of Tukor. The disappointment and disapproval. *This is a weak man, a weak king,* they were thinking. *A craven sits the throne.*

In the months that followed, none of the perpetrators had been delivered to their door. The boy Prince Dulian had never been handed over in restitution. No conflict had stirred, no war. *Nothing*, Janilah thought darkly. *His son was slain and he did nothing.* After that, he realised he had no choice. *This man is too weak, and Tukor needs to be strong,* he'd decided. His father had to go.

But where has it all gotten you, kingkiller? wondered a voice in his head. He blinked and found that his father had disappeared, and Myra and Jaylor too, leaving only a ten-year-old Janilah on the path alone, soaked red, alone, all alone... *You killed your own father to take his throne. You had King Horris Reynar poisoned to start a war. How many died because of that? How much blood did you spill, mad king?*

Janilah had no answer.

The voice laughed. *Now you stir another war. Now you bring the world to its knees. And for what? Those blades? To win the War Eternal?* Laughter echoed through the world. Suddenly all was still and black and cold but for that voice. *You fool, you mad old fool, look at what you've done. Look! And now your son is dead too. Your son is dead because of you.*

"No," he croaked. "I never wanted that…"

But it happened. Because of you.

"No…" He was on his knees now, all in blackness. There was a wetness on his cheeks. "No, I didn't…that wasn't…"

Because of you. Because of you. He's dead, dead, dead…because of you.

And then Janilah woke.

A voice was speaking, close to his ear. "Father…Father, they're waiting for you, Father."

He blinked against the harsh glare of sunlight spilling in through the arched windows, slanting across his bed. A dull aching pain sat heavy and hot in his chest. His eyes flickered through a sheen of moisture and saw a full face, feminine, lips red and eyes green with subtle shades of blue. She was frowning concernedly. "You're crying, Father."

Janilah Lukar grunted and lifted a hand to push her way. He shifted painfully until he was sitting up against the headboard. *I don't cry,* he thought. Yet his eyes *were* wet. He wiped his hand across them. "What do you want, Cecilia?"

"The council, Father. *Your* council," she corrected. "They await you in your audience chamber." She regarded him a moment, a sympathy in those green-blue eyes. "Perhaps I should tell them to withdraw, for today? You look paler than yesterday. Or else I could lead…"

"*You?*" The word came out a snarl. *You,* he thought. *You are all I have left.* He didn't know whether to laugh or cry to that. "No, Cecilia. It is not your place."

She dropped her head. "Of course, Father." There was a frost in her voice, though she tried to hide it. "How is your heart?"

You have no heart, laughed that voice. "Improving," he lied. Weakness was his father's curse. *I will not take on that burden. I will not be looked at like that.* "Leave me while I dress."

"You don't need help?"

"No. Leave me."

He dressed alone and with as much haste as he could, knowing she would be outside the thick oaken door, waiting. Every juddering movement hurt, every heavy step, every awkward motion. He drew on quilted breeches, shirt and jerkin, tall leather boots. His regal green cloak was clasped with silver blades, hanging off his wide shoulders. Girdling his waist was a patterned swordbelt, the leather cut with famous triumphs of his house. Those triumphs started with Galin Lukar's victory during the Siege of Ilithor and dwindled as the generations passed. He thought again of his father, the craven. *He won no triumph, no acclaim,* he scoffed. *It was mercy pushing him down those steps.*

At his hip was a fine godsteel dagger, its hilt encrusted with emeralds, its pommel in the shape of the Hammer of Tukor. He gripped the handle and felt a strength rush through him, thinking of Tyrith up in his forge. Janilah had not visited the young man in long weeks. *What is the point?* he wondered, dejected. Tyrith's entire purpose was to master the Hammer of Tukor, learn its mysteries from the scrolls and books and many parchments Ilith left behind in his forgotten forge. The boy was of Ilith's direct blood, the only one remaining, the only one capable. *For long years I've kept him up there, trapped and alone, and for what?* He had the Mistblade, and that was it. All the others had evaded him, betrayed him. *Vandar has forsaken me,* he thought, as that laughter rang through his head.

He plodded to the door, checking himself in the looking glass as he passed. His skin had a sickly look, seamed and pasty, his forehead glistening with sweat, furrowed by deep wrinkles. And that beard… tangled and twisted, growing more grey with each setting of the sun. He grunted to see himself looking so feeble, took up a cloth and wiped his forehead dry, then combed his fingers through his beard to neaten it. His council were of little importance really, with most men of power absent from the city, but still, he couldn't abide looking so frail and unhealthy.

He found Cecilia outside, preening herself as she awaited him. *She looks young and vibrant,* he noted sourly. *More so than she has for a time, or is it just me?* There was a flush to her pink cheeks, a glitter in her eyes. "Is it cold out today?" he asked her.

She seemed stumped by the question. "It's cold every day up here, isn't it?"

"Your cheeks look especially lively."

"They do? Well yes, there's a stiff breeze in the air. I suppose it brought out a bit of colour."

He huffed and began walking down the corridor, staying as upright as he could manage. The door to his audience chamber was around a corner. Outside stood Sir Mallister Monsort, raised to his Six. Cecilia assured him it was a good idea. "If Elyon ever causes us trouble again, Father, we can have Sir Mallister deal with him," she had said. "He bays for his blood for what he did to poor Melany. Or...what Mallister *thinks* he did."

"And if he should find out the truth of his sister's death?" Janilah had regarded his bastard daughter closely.

She'd given out that titter of hers, that he was finding increasingly grating. "If you don't tell him, nor will I," she promised.

I'm sure, Janilah thought. His daughter was not half so cunning as she thought she was.

Sir Mallister gave a bow, "Sire," and opened the door. Janilah passed inside and went straight to the head of the council table. It was a simple thing, not nearly so dramatic as the table within the Black Tower where he'd typically hold his war councils. It had seemed prudent to gather them here, within his privy quarters, but now he wondered how weak it made him seem.

What should I care? he told himself. *These are sheep, nothing to me*. But all the same he marched in, putting on a show of strength, and sat as straight-backed as he could in his chair. The rest of the seats were occupied by the few worthwhile voices remaining in the city. Lord Trillian Morwood, Commander of the City Watch. Lord Emmit Gershan of the Moorlands, one of Kastor's favoured lords. Young Prince Raynald was in attendance, looking grumpy and sullen. Sir Owen Armdall had no place at the table, but was standing aside, to give input if required. Then there was Cecilia, with all her spies and schemes and whispers, and old crookbacked Archibald Benton, Janilah's chief scholar, with that wine-coloured birthmark on his forehead shaped like a crow's foot.

Janilah turned his eyes around, looking across his council. "Go ahead," he said. "Begin."

Watch Commander Morwood stood promptly. "My king." He bowed. "I bring report of civil unrest, mostly down in White Shadow, but in certain parts of Many Markets as well. There have been numerous accounts of looting, brawling, rioting. Rapes and sexual crimes have been committed, and in greater abundance than I have seen in many years. It's the war, sire. It's got everyone's blood up. I have my men on regular patrol, but even so, people are still coming up dead…"

"What people?" Cecilia asked him.

Lord Morwood looked at her, confused. "*People*, my lady. Commoners. Those caught amid the violence."

"Then let's move on, shall we?"

A red shade of indignation climbed up Morwood's thick neck. He was a stocky, jowly man, with a jaw wider than the top of his head, where patches of wispy yellow hair tried desperately to cover his balding scalp. "You don't wish to hear my report?"

"Not especially, no. We all know what happens in wartime, Lord Morwood. A few dead commoners is nothing to concern a king, especially one in recovery from a near-fatal attack of the heart. There are matters more significant to cover. Or do you disagree?"

"It is my duty to report on affairs pertaining to social disturbances such as these," the watch commander said. He set his eyes on Janilah. "I had thought you were well restored, my king. But if you should prefer that I not waste your time with these…"

"I am back to full health," Janilah broke in. He could sense no one believed the lie, but on he went anyway. "My daughter speaks out of turn. She has a woman's tenderness, and would prefer that I remain abed, I am sure." He smiled in a bid to dismiss the matter of his physical condition. "As regards this civil discord, Lord Morwood, see that patrols are increased where they're needed most. Use men from the garrison, if you must. There is little threat of an attack at this time, and we have many an idle soldier in the Sentinels, with little more to do than practice on the ranges, and drink in the taverns. Set them to work, by my leave. That should see the problem solved."

Lord Morwood looked satisfied by that. "My king," he said, bowing as he sat.

Janilah turned his eyes around, that minor issue dealt with. His daughter had the right of it, in truth; he cared little for such things, but it wouldn't serve him to dismiss it out of hand. "Lord Gershan," he said. "What is the latest from Lord Kastor?"

The Master of the Moorlands was half weasel, half vulture, with a long hooked nose and a mouth made for scowling. A small man even in his youth, age had now reduced him to a truly scrawny thing, stoop-backed and sour-tempered and unerringly unpleasant to look at, listen to, and spend any length of time with. "Siege lines are up and the fortress cut off from the headland," he said, in a horrid rattle of a voice. "Lord Cedrik's wary of attack from the rear. Got two moats being dug, all full of deadly spikes, and palisade walls besides. If he had more time he might see to a stone defence." He laughed unpleasantly. "But no, should serve as is."

"Has the siege begun?" asked Prince Raynald.

"Might be, my prince," the old lord said. "Last word was two days gone. We expect another crow by today, maybe tomorrow. Right, Archie?"

Archibald Benton nodded. Old as he was, he was younger than Gershan, greatly less unpleasant though greatly more ponderous. He pulled at his long white wispy beard. "We hope for regular tidings and updates," he confirmed. "Lord Kastor has many a good crow in his company to, um, to bring word on the wing. Eagle's Perch is but eight hundred miles from here, as…as the crow flies. A strong bird can do that in a day. Some might be lost, yes, but they won't be flying over enemy lines, so we ought to have word most regularly, I…I should hope." He smiled at the young man. "We'll hear if something should befall your brother, my prince, fret not."

Raynald gave that a glum nod. The twins had lived their lives inseparable; this was the longest they'd been apart, and now the boy had to grieve his father alone. "I should be there too," he complained miserably. "I'm a prince as he is. I should be out there, fighting in our father's name."

"We cannot risk you both," Cecilia said, with a soft and tender quality to her voice. "Robbert is your grandfather's heir now, Raynald, and will see the war through, we hope. But if something *should* happen to him, we need to know that you are there to take his place. Surely you understand that?"

"I understand, Auntie. I understand that I'm nothing but a substitute, doomed to sit here and wait out the war with the old men and the women, while Robbert wins glory and acclaim. If *he's* heir, then it should be *me* out there taking the risks, not him. I want to go. I think I should go…"

"No." The word cut him right through, silencing him. Janilah linked eyes with his grandson for a short cold moment. Those curls of auburn hair, the fuzz of a rusty beard emerging from his chin, the brown eyes ringed with green. *So like his father,* he thought. *Dead, dead, dead. Dead because of you.* He took a sharp breath. "Robbert cannot be seen to be hiding here. Your father was our champion, Raynald, and that task falls now to your brother. Once you are ready, you can take up a position within the city garrison as befits your station. There is a nobility in that as well. In defending the heart of your kingdom, and your king."

"Yes, Grandfather. As you say." His voice carried a mild tone of contempt.

Janilah regarded him. "You doubt me?"

Raynald shook his head. "No, Grandfather."

There is a lot he wants to say, Janilah realised. He knew what was at the heart of it. "You still doubt the account of your father's death?" He let a moment pass, then said, "Speak truthfully, boy. If you have something to say, I would hear it."

"I have nothing to say, Grandfather. I…I mourn my father, that is all. I mourn the man he was. The man I *thought* he was."

"Your father was a great man." Cecilia reached across, put that powdered paw of hers on his forearm. "Do not think any less of him for one rash act."

Raynald nodded. "Yes, Auntie." He sighed and slumped lower into his seat.

Janilah didn't want to dwell on the death of his son, not here. He turned to Archibald Benton. "Anything further from the royal rookery, Archibald?" The old scholar had the run of the crows now, as Master of Messages, and was first to get tidings from the wing. It seemed somewhat fateful, with that crow-foot birthmark of his.

Benton reached into the folds of his airy grey cloak and withdrew a small stack of letters of interest. He began shuffling through them in his slow, ponderous way, trying to decide what to report and what to ignore. "Ah," he said eventually. "Ah yes, this one. A note from King's Point. It came some…hmmmm, two days ago now. Seems the Vandarian fleet has hauled anchor and made to sea, sire. Lady Brockenhurst writes of an armada numbering five hundred ships, though who can say how accurate that is. The Lady Brockenhurst is known to favour a certain sense of exaggeration. Even so, it would appear Prince Dalton is being quite proactive in his assault of the Trident."

Emmit Gershan gave a phlegmy grunt. "Lady Brockenhurst's turned informer, has she?"

The thought rankled. Ever since the theft of the Windblade, relations between Janilah and King Godrik Taynar had soured. "The Taynars seem disinclined to share with me what they're doing," he said. "Thankfully, we have friends who are more willing to tell us. Lady Brockenhurst is one of them, having been born of Tukor."

"It's all terribly petty," Cecilia laughed. "We are allies, and at war with a common foe. The exchange of information is critical to making sure we remain on the same page."

"A temporary rift," Janilah said. He felt confident Taynar would come around once he had proof that it was Elyon Daecar who'd stolen the Windblade, not him. *Proof that must be forthcoming,* he thought, with a bitterness that sent a stab of pain through his chest. *One day soon, we'll have reports of a knight in the skies.* "The boy Elyon," he grunted, looking at Archibald Benton again. "Any word on him?"

Benton shuffled his papers. "A sighting or two," he said. "He's been spotted heading south with Kanabar men, mostly Blackshaws. He's making for Dragon's Bane, it seems."

"We should send a party to apprehend him," spat Gershan. "The boy's a murderer, twice over. And twice he's gotten away with it."

"He's travelling Vandarian lands, those ruled by Lord Kanabar and his underlings," Janilah told him. "How would you expect to apprehend him, exactly?"

"By the rule of law."

"Laws broken in Rasalan and Tukor, not Vandar. He is out of our reach, Emmit."

"That boy…that one outside." Gershan lowered his voice, motioned with his eyes to the door. "Sir Mallister…he was brother to the Lady Melany, and now under oath to do your bidding. I say send him down to Dragon's Bane to cut Daecar's throat, same as Elyon did poor Griff. *Ten lashes,*" he snarled. "He killed Sir Griffin and only got ten lashes! Now he's butchered a highborn lady and fluttered away, free as a bird. What justice is there in that? I say have Mallister kill him."

This one is more ruthless than I realised, Janilah thought. "That would be imprudent," he said. "The East Vandarians see Elyon as their rightful prince. His murder would incite further tensions, if not open war between us, and that we can ill afford."

"But, my lord…"

"Elyon is of no consequence," he went on brusquely. He had a sudden image of the boy, brawny-shouldered and black-haired, broad smile on his face, soaring. *It should have been mine,* he thought sourly. *The Windblade, the Nightblade, the Sword of Varinar, I should have them all!* It would leave only the Frostblade, whose location remained unsolved. *But the rest…the rest…they should be mine!*

They're not yours,….and they were never going to be, returned a voice. *Another will gather them, another will hold them. One will, yes, but it won't be you…*

Janilah glowered privately. *No matter how tight my grip becomes, there is always something that slips through my fingers.* How many times had he thought that of late? How many things had gone wrong? Now his son was dead, dead by his own command. Cecilia had told him that when he'd first come around. "You…you told Sir Maxwell to…to kill him," she'd said, weeping those crocodile tears of hers. His own recollection of events had been weak, yet…there was something… something that told him he'd tried to command Sir Maxwell otherwise, but the words had got all caught in his throat. "It was the only way, Father," Cecilia had gone on. "Rylian…he knew too much. He had become a very real threat to us. A very real threat to *you*."

A threat, now eliminated, he thought dully. *Just another great man, dead or crippled by my command. My son…*

He withdrew from his dark musings, turned his eyes about the room. All had remained quiet, eyes doubtful as they regarded him. *Madness. They see the shadow of madness in me still.* He looked back at old Archibald Benton. "What of Agarathi sallies and assaults?" he asked, realigning his thoughts. *King. I must be a king still.* "Have they renewed their harries of the Black Coast?"

The scholar fiddled his papers. "Curiously…curiously no, my lord. At least…nothing from the dragons." He sifted from parchment to parchment, as though searching for something in particular."The Bloodmarsh Isles remain subject to skirmishes and such, I know. But…but otherwise, no, attacks from the wing have stopped entirely."

Cecilia yawned, evidently weary of the man's bumbling manner. "When was the last?"

Benton looked up, blinking. "The last?"

"The last attack, Archibald."

"Oh…some weeks ago, my lady. There are worries that the Agarathi are assembling for a large assault. It's thought they have tested our lines sufficiently now to know where to put their weight." He drew a shivery breath. "I will say, it's a concern, this lull. It makes me most uneasy."

Gershan shrugged his bony shoulders. "It's said the Fireborn are infighting. This business with Marak going rogue. Makes sense to me."

"Maybe they got wind of our plans," put in Raynald. He looked more eager to engage all of a sudden. Talk of dragons did stoke the excitement of a young man. *Seventeen,* Janilah thought. *Or, is he eighteen yet?* "They heard we were sending huge fleets to Eagle's Perch and the Trident, and chose to bide their time, invade while our strength is stretched." He nodded to himself, then asked, "Do you think they might attack us here? I mean, dragons aren't restricted like soldiers are, or ships. They can fly almost anywhere in the north within a day. If I were King Tavash, I'd be sending all my strongest Fireborn to one capital city after another. Burn out our hearts and watch us implode."

Foolish boy, Janilah thought. *He ought to know better.* "The chance of attack here is slim, Raynald. There is no place in the world so hard to breach as Ilithor. And what should Tavash hope to gain by doing so? Dragons can assault cities, melt them, destroy them, but they cannot hold them. You need men on the ground for that. Think of a pack of hunting wolves. How do they behave?"

The boy thought. "They chase and harry their prey until exhausted. They weaken them, before surrounding them, and closing in for the kill."

"Good," Janilah said. "But it depends on the prey, does it not? Does it take a pack to hunt a rabbit?"

"No, just one." Then he reconsidered. "One if the ambush is successful. If the rabbit bolts, two or three wolves would be better."

"Indeed. But one is sufficient, if the trap is sprung well. Now bigger prey, say a large deer, might require several to take it down. But a deer does not fight back. What if these wolves should encounter a bear?"

"The entire pack would be needed. And even then..."

"Yes, go on."

"Even then...they would be at risk. The bear is much bigger, more powerful, more dangerous. It could kill a wolf with a single swipe of its paw." He frowned, as Rylian used to frown. *Gods they look so much alike.* "But it isn't about killing a bear," he finished. "Not always. It might be about driving it away, or...or the bear might be best avoided."

"Yes." Janilah said the word emphatically. "Now this bear, best avoided, is Ilithor to the Agarathi. So is Varinar, and Thalan, though

I'll confess, the Rasal capital isn't quite so well defended as we are. These cities may become targets, in time, but first you hunt rabbits and deer. The same is true of us. Eagle's Perch, the Trident, both powerful fortresses, but not so hard to win as Eldurath or Aram. War is about calculated risk, Raynald. How many men do we need to win a fortress? How many Bladeborn men in full godsteel plate? How many bowmen, spearmen, shieldmen? How many siege engines, trebuchets and towers and ballistas and rams. But for this you need to know your enemy too. As the wolves know the rabbit and the deer and the bear, we need to know what sort of beast we're dealing with. And sometimes, Raynald, it's best to feed up before you take on that bear."

The boy smiled handsomely. "Yes, Grandfather. I think Eagle's Perch will make a good meal."

The king didn't quite laugh, but almost. *This boy...I have never seen this side of him before.* But was there any surprise in that? *You don't know him*, he told himself. *You have neglected your family for gods and glory.* "A good meal indeed," he agreed, clinging to the moment with his grandson. "Now, we must hope they make the kill quickly. That is another factor. A long hunt can drain a pack. That is where a strong alpha comes in, a leader who understands their prey..." He stopped a moment, before he might utter another word.

Then Raynald said, "My father," in a sullen voice. "He was to lead the pack."

"That duty goes to Lord Kastor now." Janilah forced a look of reassurance to his face. "It pains me more than I can say, Raynald, what happened with your father." And that was the truth, laid bare. He'd never felt an agony such as this. Not through his war wounds and losses, the deaths of his sister and brother and wife and others whom he cared for, even loved. None quite compared to this. *My first-born. My heir. My son. Rylian...*

"Lord Cedrik will do your father proud, princeling," rasped Gershan. His close-set eyes peered over his hooked beak of a nose. "He'll win that fort in your father's name, you'll see."

Raynald seemed in no way comforted by that. Lord Emmit Gershan wasn't much for inspiring solace, foul as he looked. "As you say, my lord."

"Well I do. Unless there's a Moonrider about, at least." The Moorlander gave an ugly cackle. "But Lord Cedrik's sure to have prepared for one of those."

"King Hadrin was saying something about a Moonrider before he left," put in Archibald Benton.

That caught Janilah off-guard. Hadrin had departed some time ago, taking his new queen back to Thalan while Janilah was still unconscious. *The coward crept away before I could stop him*, he thought. He wanted Amilia in Ilithor where it was safer, and had hoped Hadrin would finally see something of value in the Eye of Rasalan that might help them. All he'd moaned on about was dragons and shadows and some great fiery calamity. *But this*… "A Moonrider, Archibald?"

"Yes, when he came to collect the Book of Th…" He stopped, swallowed, looked around the room uncomfortably. "The Book, my lord."

Gershan was perplexed. "What book?"

"The Book of Thala," Janilah said, sparing poor old Archibald from having a heart attack of his own.

Gershan grinned grotesquely. "Ah, so it was you who stole it, Janilah?"

"Don't get familiar, Gershan," the king warned.

"Of course. *My king.*" The man was too old to be afraid of much. "So it was you?"

Janilah didn't take his opportunity to lie. He might have said Hadrin had it all along, and brought it to Ilithor for the wedding, but no. *A stack of lies is a stack of cards, and mine has begun to topple. I'd only be throwing bricks onto a pile of rubble.* "Yes," he said. "It was me, via a proxy." He checked Cecilia's eyes. She seemed to like where this was going. "I'd hoped to find valuable information within, though in the end, it turned into a wild goose chase." That was enough honesty for now; the city already seemed to know he was after the Blades of Vandar. *As they suspect I slew King Ellis Reynar, and had a hand in Hadrin's murder of his father as well. No wonder they doubt the account of Rylian's death. No wonder they have turned from me.*

"Well now, this I like." Emmit Gershan was a devious knave of a man, no different from the serpent on his sigil. He licked his crinkled lips with what might have been a forked tongue. "What were you hoping to find?"

"Never you mind. It was a failure, I've said." Janilah looked to Archibald. "Go on. The Moonrider."

"Yes, sire. King Hadrin, he…he made mention of seeing one in the Eye of Rasalan. It was being bonded, he seemed to think. There were…now let me think…" He began tugging gently at his beard, his old fingers running through strands of silky white hair. It went on for an inordinately long time. "Three, yes, three of them. Or…maybe it was four. I forget." He smiled uncomfortably. "Not moonbears, you understand, but people. Three or four figures, one ahead, the others behind. The one in the lead was approaching the bear in the bonding ritual, the king said."

"And the others?" Cecilia asked. "I thought these rites were sacred, man and beast only. Why were there two or three others there?"

"Who can say, my lady? Perhaps we're not so well understood of the ritual as we think?"

"Did Hadrin know when it was?" asked Raynald, increasingly invested. He was sat up now, a little forward in his chair.

"I would doubt it, Raynald," Cecilia scoffed. "As far as I understand it, your brother-in-law's mastery of the Eye of Rasalan is sorely lacking. He could just as well have dreamt the whole thing."

Raynald made a groaning sound. "*Please* don't remind me he's my brother-in-law, Auntie." The boy looked appropriately disgusted. "He's over three times my age."

"Yes, and poor Amilia, to have to lie abed with the man."

"Auntie! No."

Cecilia chuckled. "An unpleasant image, isn't it? That gawky old rat crawling over your beautiful sister."

"Enough," Janilah snapped. "Must you turn everything to depravity, Cecilia?"

"Oh, but I'm so good at it, Father."

"Yes, and not much else." He turned to Archibald. "Is there anything more to this? It seems another of Hadrin's pointless foresights where in actuality he sees very little at all."

The scholar considered that, then said, "Well, he did say the image was clearer than normal. An event soon to take place, he thought, or…or recently done so. 'Near in time', those were his words. There was a certain pride, I think, that his visions were improving in clarity."

"And yet he is no longer here." Janilah mulled on that, scowling. *If I'd been awake and aware, I'd never have permitted his departure. Never.* "What compulsion drove him to leave? And taking my granddaughter with him? Does he think they'll be safer in Thalan than they are here?"

"I suppose he wanted out of your shadow, Father. To rule as king, in his own right."

"Hadrin is no true king," Janilah said to that. *He is weak, like my father was…*

"His crown would disagree." Cecilia gave out that titter of hers, like the cat who got the cream. *She is too happy with herself by half,* Janilah thought. *She mourns Rylian not. It was she who whispered into my ear - 'he wants your throne, he wants it'* - he remembered. *Was that for me, or for herself, to rid herself of a rival?* He still did not comprehend the depths of his daughter. What he'd done…all the sinfulness and evil…it had all been in the service of a greater purpose. Yet his daughter seemed compelled by something else. *Vengeance, chaos, the sheer joy of the game?* He couldn't decide. *Might be all three.*

"She is well protected, Grandfather," said Raynald, showing some tact and understanding. "Amilia left with a strong personal guard. She will be safe in Thalan."

"Thank you, Raynald. I am sure you're right."

The boy nodded and fell silent.

The meeting felt like it had slowed to a natural stop. "Is there anything else of importance to report?" Janilah saw nothing from Gershan, Archibald, or Cecilia. He turned to Lord Morwood. "You have been silent for some time, Trillian."

"My duty is the defence of the city, sire, and its people," Morwood said, stiffly. "You have since moved beyond such things. As Lady Cecilia points out, there are more important affairs to discuss. Though much of it has seemed like visions and guesswork to me."

Janilah stared at him. "You disapprove?"

"No, sire. I only think that these troubles in White Shadow and Many Markets…the deaths of your own civilians…these are matters of significance and concern. They ought not be so easily dismissed."

"I agree. Did I not give you leave to use my garrison soldiers to restore order?"

"You did, sire." Lord Morwood fell silent.

"Yet you remain displeased."

"No, sire. I am satisfied with your ruling, certainly. It's just…"

"Yes? Come, speak plainly."

"It's just that you seem to hold your own people in disdain, sire," the watch commander blurted.

"Disdain?" The word was delivered coldly.

The man's jowls wobbled as he nodded. "Yes, sire. I have

commanded the City Watch for over a decade. More and more you seem…disinterested, shall we say, in the welfare of your people."

"Do I, Trillian? I was of the opinion that the people's welfare was my top priority. Is that not why I am trying to win this war? To secure my people's safety against these marauders from the south?"

"Yes, sire, a noble cause. But…" He swallowed. Sweat was beginning to glisten on his forehead. He seemed suddenly regretful of bringing the topic up.

But Janilah wanted to hear it. *I must listen to my subjects,* he thought. Trillian Morwood had been a leal supporter of his for many long years, if kept from his closest counsel. He had earned the right to speak his mind. "Go ahead, Trillian. No matter what you say, you will suffer no reprisal. Tell me…what is it my people are saying about me?"

"Many things, sire." He drew a ragged breath. "Many matters of…well…matters of…"

"Take a breath, old friend. Many matters, you say. Matters of negativity, I assume?"

"Yes, my lord. N-negativity. I have daily reports from the gate commanders. There is open insolence spoken against your name. Some…some call you mad. Others are inclined to believe you are being controlled by…" He glanced at Cecilia. She gave him a fierce glare in return. "By your daughter. She too is being openly insulted. You might consider…" He kept his eyes steadfastly away from her. "You might consider sending her away, back home to her ancestral lands. It would go some way to restoring your image, I feel."

"You think the king cares for his image?" Cecilia snapped at him.

Lord Morwood ignored her. "She is born of impurity, people say, my lord. A bastard. *Wrong*. Some consider her a witch, some sorceress in jewels and furs. There are even those who call for her head."

"My head?" Cecilia laughed scornfully. "This is nonsense, Father, the bleating of the simple-minded. I have served you long and true, *you know I have*. You cannot take this seriously."

Yet he was. *Her head,* he wondered. No, that was too extreme. *She is my daughter, my blood. I must take responsibility for what she has become.* But sending her away…

He thought for a long moment. *You must tread lightly, whatever you do,* he told himself. He did not delude himself into thinking his daughter wasn't dangerous. *I made her so. I ought to be proud of how she has turned out.* Yet all the same, his position had grown precarious. *The walls I've built are coming down around me.* Everywhere he looked, he saw enemies now. *And this insolence, in my own city.* His people had always respected him, feared him. *And now I become my father…mocked by the mob.*

He turned to Lord Morwood. "Can you remember the last time I walked the lower streets, Trillian? The last time I addressed the people of White Shadow, showed my face among the crowds?"

The watch commander shook his head. "I cannot, sire. It must be some years ago, now."

"Many years, yes. So many that I cannot recall the last occasion either." He mulled on that a time. "I have dwelled too long in this palace, passing the lower levels only when I come and go from the city. The people no longer know me. They hear of the rumours and whispers, the treasons. They hear of my heart attack and my health, and picture Cecilia at my side, pulling my strings." The thought of it enraged him, but he maintained his calm. "Well…it is time we shattered that image. It is time I returned to my people."

Lord Morwood nodded enthusiastically, fleshy cheeks jiggling. "Yes, sire, a most welcome thought. Once they see you, returning to health as you are, I have no doubt these rumours will stop."

"It will lift spirits," agreed Archibald. "A fine idea, my lord."

Cecilia was still staring daggers at Morwood. "Cecilia." She broke out of it, turned to her father. "I'll want you there too."

She raised her eyes. "You do?"

"Sire," started Morwood, "I would advise against…"

He raised a hand. "My daughter is no sorceress. It is best the people see that she is nothing but flesh and blood."

Morwood nodded unsurely. "Yes, sire." He thought for a time. "My lady. Perhaps we might set up some opportunities for you to speak with the commonfolk, within view of the public. You are in possession of a certain charm, I will admit. Kiss some babies. Make the children laugh. Give praise to common working men and they may soon learn to love you."

"A publicity tour," cackled Gershan. "If you ask me, this is a waste of time. I'm with the Lady Cecilia. Who cares what the people think. There are bigger concerns to worry about."

"It's decided, Emmit," Janilah told him. He didn't need the old creature sticking his oar in now. "Trillian, make the arrangements."

I will not become my father, he thought.

11

Amron

"This is where we leave one another, Lord of Daecar," said Stegra. The Snowfist had a sheen of tears in his eyes. "Our great adventure, at an end. I will remember it, always. And you. You have a place among us, my friend, should you ever wish it."

The two men stood face to face, height of a height, bonded by brotherhood and the whims of prophecy. "I shall miss you, Stegra." Amron put his hand to the Snowfist's shoulder, whose great paw came down on his own. "What shall you do, once we're gone?"

The Snowfist turned back, to where his tribesmen were gathered. "Tend the lands," he said. "For this is what the prophecy promised."

The words went through Amron Daecar's head one last time. "*In this the frost shall be taken,*" he said quietly, "*and the lands grow clear to tend.*"

Stegra smiled through the bushy white forest that was his beard. His eerie blue eyes twinkled from a face of milky skin. "And you, Steel Lord? You have the *frost* now. What do you plan to do with it?"

Amron thought on that long and hard. In the end, he could only say, "I don't yet know, my friend."

Stegra nodded. "A wise answer. Your fat friend would have said something more dramatic." He chuckled, looking to Walter Selleck, standing aside with Whitebeard. "'Win the War Eternal', he might have said. Yes, something like this. Something profound."

Amron did not doubt it. "I will do what I can to help, on that account."

"And much help you will be, with this icy blade of yours."

Amron had planted the Frostblade in the earth beside him, driving the tip ten inches deep. It shone out with an inner light, silvery-white, a deeper glow radiating from its glyphs and markings. "It will take time to master," he said.

"Not so much time, for a man like you. I have seen already the progress you have made, Lord of Daecar. The men…" He glanced back. "You have risen to a man of legend in their eyes. Just as Fat Walter sang all those times at night. Those stories and songs about you…Dauntless Daecar, the Echo of Titans, the Siege of Southwatch…no, they are not stories and songs at all, but *truths*. You stand second only to Stegra Snowfist now, as hero to my people." He grinned and thumped his chest, sending a shower of snow from the bear-head hood of his cloak.

"An honoured placing," Amron said, inclining his head.

The skies above were warmly lit, gilded blue with clusters of clouds, the sun some halfway through its daily arc. They still got a miserly allotment of sunlight each day, but nothing like the all-consuming darkness that had swallowed them some months before. *And dark had been my heart then too,* Amron reflected. *No more. Now I see the light again.* He smiled to look at the sun, casting spears of light down through the clouds. Each day it rose a little earlier than before, setting later. *Life and light breathes into me again. And now it's time to go home.*

The Snowfist's men were aligned behind him, some twenty paces back. Amron had said his goodbyes to them already, as they had Walter and Whitebeard. Svalda, the Snowfist's brawny teenage son. Kusto Crowbane, his pale face all scratches and scars. Jorgen Half-Eye, with that black patch on his right eye. Wagga the White, grey and brown-bearded and wise, in his way. And the rest. Briggor the Big, all five-foot-three of him. Arnel Hammerhand and his huge bone battle-hammer. Sigurt Seven-Sons, old and grim, who only had three of his seven sons left. Niklas. Verner. Amron would miss them all.

Further back the greatyaks waited, stacked and loaded for the tribe's onward journey. They had spent their final night here at the edge of the Weeping Heights, just south of the Silver Scar where Amron had almost drowned. His head felt a little heavy, in truth. Too much sickmilk, the aptly named grog the tribesmen liked to drink, as they'd sat around the fire on those carved wooden stools, sharing stories and songs and words of parting. They'd had Amron regale them of his story once more, of the long days in the mists, the queer experience at the river, the voice that had beckoned him on. "That voice, it was the Sea-King's," Jorgen Half-Eye had proclaimed. "It told you to follow the river, yes? It led you on, Steel Lord. It led you to the heart of the prophecy!"

Others were more interested in the battles he'd faced. They were in his mind only, he knew, but felt so startlingly real all the same. First had come Jonas the Giant, then Ronja Ironmaid, then Iceheart the legendary hunter in his mottled cloak of pelts and furs and his quiver of a thousand arrows. All fabled heroes of the Snowskins who had ventured into the mists. All fabled heroes who had never returned.

"But *you* did, Lord of Daecar," young Svaldar had said, surging to his feet, a little drunken. "You cleared the mist and fulfilled the prophecy! You have added to your legend! This is your greatest triumph!"

The men had cheered at that, toasting him for the hundredth time, and Amron had no heart to deny them. In truth he'd done little more than shamble through the wilds, fall into a trance, and wake at the coast to find the Frostblade embedded in stone.

This is bigger than me, he knew, glancing now at the great white blade. Particles of ice sparkled about its edge, catching the sunlight; a nebula of colour. His quest had been but one thread of a grander tapestry, stitched through the fabric of time. *Someone wanted me to fetch this blade*, he thought. *Someone needed me to return it to the east.* And in that he knew he would not possess it long. *I am a guardian only, that is my purpose*. It was a thought both hopeful and hurtful at once.

He turned his eyes on the Snowfist. "My friend, we should go."

"As should we." Stegra Snowfist had a smile to warm the heart, big and earthy and honest. "We must reunite with our tribe, tell them of our adventures." His smile was reshaped into a playful grin. "I look forward to seeing their faces, Lord of Daecar, when I say that the curse has been broken."

"As do I, when my people see me with this." Amron wrapped his gloved fingers around the Frostblade's ancient white hilt, and pulled it from the ice and snow. "It has been missing for over two hundred years, Stegra. Most believe it lost forever."

"They think the same of you, I am sure." A laugh moved through the big chieftain's pale lips. He put his arm to Amron's shoulder once more, saying, "*Steel and snow will meet as enemies, but part as allies and friends.* This is my favourite line of the prophecy, I think." He smiled, a gleam of moisture in his clear eyes. "Good luck to you, my good friend Amron. If you need us again, you know where we'll be."

And there they parted, as allies and friends.

Amron returned to Walter and Whitebeard, their travel packs resting on a bank of rock beside them. They were a contrasting duo; Walter short and portly and gladsome, Whitebeard tall and lean, ever-grim. "That looked a sweet exchange," Walter said, a smirk on his scraggly-bearded cheeks. "Was it just me or did I see the great Stegra Snowfist crying?"

"It wasn't just you," said Whitebeard roughly, standing straight as an arrow, all in black, hoarfrost clinging to the bristles on his face. "We ought to go, my lord. I would like to reach the foothills by nightfall."

"Oh gods," cursed Walter. "We're going to have to suffer Rogen's dreary leadership again, Amron."

"Feel free to go with the Snowskins if you'd prefer," Whitebeard growled, with that wolfish face of his, all high cheeks and hard lines and upturned amber eyes. "Your use is spent, Walter."

That seemed to hit a little close to the mark. Walter Selleck, the self-styled 'luckiest man in the world', had no riposte.

Amron knew why. "You still feel the dimming of your *light*, Walter?"

The portly man gave a reluctant nod. "I fear so, my lord. It seems my purpose is complete, my task fulfilled. Vandar has seen fit to strip me of my blessing."

Rogen frowned down at him. "I thought your purpose was to lead Amron into the mountain, so he might receive a blessing of his own?"

"The gods work in mysterious ways, Whitebeard." Walter cupped fingers around the ranger's arm in a gesture of faith. That arm was quickly withdrawn. "It seems my task was in fact to help lead him to the Frostblade."

"*Lead* him?" Rogen was in combative mood today. *Too much sick-milk,* Amron figured. *Or not enough, more likely.* "You didn't lead him anywhere, Selleck. Until we met the Snowskins, *I* was acting guide. After that, Stegra had command. And Amron went into the mist-lands alone, if you'll recall. You have been a passenger for months, nothing more. So spare me your talk of gods and their mysteries. You are not Vandar's chosen servant and never were."

"I never claimed to be," Walter came back. There was a rare truculence in his eyes. "You deny I've had my part in Amron's safe passage through these treacherous lands, and yours? You deny that I have saved *your very life* on more than one occasion?"

"I never said you did not play a role." Rogen spoke stiffly. "And I have thanked you for saving my life."

"Yes, *grudgingly*. Answer me this, Whitebeard - why do you have to be such a cold rotten bastard all the time?"

"*Bastard*?" The ranger took particular affront to the word. "Say that again, Selleck," he growled.

"Well you just might be," Walter went on, heedless. "You've told us nothing of your true parentage. There must be a reason you're so damn grouchy..."

Rogen went to speak, but Amron cut them both off. "Enough!" The word rang out, causing some of the Snowskins to turn as their party ambled forlornly away. Amron gave them a quick wave to say everything was all right. "Look, we're in the shadow of the mountains, so close to home I can taste it. I'll not spend the rest of the journey listening to the pair of you squabbling like children."

A silence followed. Then Whitebeard said, "Not so close, my lord. We're still two weeks from..."

"Yes. You know what I meant, Rogen. We're two weeks from Northwatch, I know, but the Weeping Heights...gods if they don't feel like home to me, after all these wretched weeks out here." He waved an arm out to the bleak white wilderness, endless and inhospitable. Among the Snowskins they'd lived in some measure of comfort, yet without them all was bare and grim and lifeless, and not a place he cared to revisit any time soon. "Now you said you wanted to reach the foothills by nightfall, yes?" He didn't wait for a response. "Well then, let's not stand here bickering. I have a strong yearning to get home in good time and hear tidings of my son and daughter. And all else besides. So enough. Let's go." He hauled his pack onto his shoulder and marched east in the direction of the towering black mountains, Frostblade misting icily in his grasp.

Walter hurried up next to him, as Whitebeard took the lead, marching defiantly ahead as though eager to put some distance between them. "I'll beg your forgiveness, Amron," the small man said. "I don't like to snap like that, but Whitebeard..." He sighed. "He likes to get under my skin, sometimes."

"I know. And that was tactless of him to push you like that. He ought to be more grateful to you for what you've done. And more sensitive of what you fear to lose."

"So long as you're happy with my service, my lord." Walter looked a shade off colour and brittle. Rogen's words had cut him deep.

"Most happy, and I appreciate all you've done. I am under no illusions that we'd never have made it nearly so far without you. *Mysterious ways*, Walter. The gods work as such, but so do your powers. Saving us from an avalanche or helping us avoid a landslide...well, those things are tangible and easy to credit you. But the rest, not so much. I remain convinced that much of our good fortune - and we have had plenty - has been down to you and your *light*."

Walter seemed close to tears. "It pleases me more than I can tell you to hear you say that, my lord."

"Save the tears, Walter," Amron said, not unkindly. "We've a way to go yet." He placed his spare hand on Walter's shoulder, stopping him a moment. "And for what it's worth, I still feel your light. Vandar or not, it doesn't matter. You're still a blessed man, my friend."

The next few minutes were spent in silence, as Walter took a few moments to compose himself. Ahead, Rogen Whitebeard was cutting through the snow in a fierce march, following vaguely along the southern bank of the Silver Scar as they made toward the mountains. Beyond, the flattened lands of the Icewilds gradually gave way to a sprawl of hills and wooded rises where the foothills started their surge up into the heights beyond. Snow-bearded mountains stood imperious to the east, shadowed by distance, intimidating from afar. Yet those mountains held no fear for Amron now. *We passed them once and will pass them again*, he thought. *Two weeks...just two more weeks.*

He continued to carry the Frostblade in his grasp, icy mists rising kaleidoscopically from its edge. Recomposed now, Walter turned to look at it. "Such a beautiful thing," he said, admiring the blade. "I had heard the Frostblade misted ice, though had not thought it would create such a dazzling effect. The Sword of Varinar was never so colourful, was it?"

Amron shook his head. "Its mists were gold, as with the blade. Sometimes they would be brighter, sometimes darker, but always gold and related hues, yellow and honey and such."

"The others are the same, I trust? Black shades for the Nightblade, blue for the Mistblade, silver for the Windblade?"

"Yes. The Frostblade is unique in that. I suppose is has something to do with the reflection and refraction of light through the melting ice."

"Yes, that would be my assumption too." Walter continued to admire the play of colours as they walked. "Its weight seems nothing to you, Amron. You carry it as one would carry a feather."

"I held the Sword of Varinar for twenty years, Walter, and that the heaviest of the Five Blades. I should think I am well versed in how to bear one of these weapons."

"Ah, but they're all unique. In look, in size, in weight, in magic. And one wonders…in voice as well?" Walter's attention went from the Frostblade to its bearer. His brows were in a quizzical frown, etched impishly. "Does it whisper to you, as the Sword of Varinar did?"

Amron filled his lungs. He knew this question would be levelled at him eventually. "It's taken you a while to ask."

"True. I've been biding my time for the right moment. You have had it…what, three weeks now? Or thereabouts. Seems long enough that those whispers might start creeping through."

"Your reasoning is sound, Walter. But to answer you, no, I've heard no such whispers as yet."

"I see. Common, is it? To take time to hear the voices?"

"Voice. *Singular*. Each of the Five Blades has a voice and will of its own. They are unique, as you say."

Walter brushed a bit of hoarfrost from his beard. None of them had shaved in months and were looking wildly dishevelled by now. "You've spoken of this before. A strong purpose in the bearer stays the voices. A purpose less noble, less certain…well, that can lead one ill."

"That is my understanding of it, yes. A bearer of ill intent or weak mind is more vulnerable to the blade's will. In such cases, this will is likely to manifest in its base form - the seeking of blood and death. A blade is a weapon, after all, its purpose to kill." He paced around a rock, hidden amidst the snow.

"And the Five Blades are wrought of Vandar's heart, a god most disposed to battle and war," put in Walter. "It should stand to reason that the essence of him should seek blood and chaos, if left unchecked."

"Which is why only men of stout heart and mind have ever been permitted to carry them. Men driven by a noble purpose. Men utterly assured of their right of possession. Problems arise when a man doubts his course and his claim."

Walter nodded. "Which brings me to wonder who determines the righteousness of a claim and course. A man of evil means and method, for instance, might be entirely committed to his purpose. He might consider his claim ironclad based on his own delusions. What then of this man? Would he control the blade, or the blade control him?"

"A man of such delusions would not be in his right mind," Amron said. "That would make him susceptible to the will of the blade. In such cases, historically, blood and death soon follow."

He turned his eyes to the north, to where the frozen river ran westerly along its winding course. His mind went to Aleron, slain by the bearer of the Nightblade. *My son.* He wondered, in that brief moment, where the Shadowknight's path had led him. *His purpose had been to kill me, to kill Aleron,* he mused. A path of blood and death, directed by his dark order. He had no doubt the boy would have been closely watched, yet all the same, he'd broken free of his shackles when he slew that Whisperer at the village of Russet Ridge. And since? *Where is he now, I wonder? Has the Nightblade led him on a path of destruction? Has he found some noble cause that might guide him to a better course?*

Walter's affable voice pulled him from his thoughts. "You're moving increasingly well," he noted "The leg, the arm, do they feel fully restored when you wield it?"

"Close enough, yes," Amron answered. "I should hope to have full mobility by the time we cross the mountains." He might have sheathed the blade, but didn't. This was the reason; to hold it, feel its weight, understand the nuances of its power. Even now, as they walked and talked, Amron Daecar was in training.

"No pain?" Walter asked him.

"When holding it, no, not really. The occasional pinch of discomfort, but no more."

"The healing effects are quite remarkable." Walter pursed his lips. "It's not a property of the Frostblade that is mentioned much, this physical restoration it imparts. When one thinks of it, they envisage the blade's more visually striking powers; the ability to freeze a foe, shatter him, the imperviousness to fire, and such."

"There's an obvious reason for that, Walter. The Frostblade was never wielded by a cripple such as me."

He said it in such a way to have Walter Selleck laughing. "No, no I suppose not. And in that the original intention of our quest has been completed, my lord. We came here to see you physically restored, and we have."

"Only when I am holding the blade," Amron reminded him. "When I release it, the blood-bond is broken, and the blade's power with it." That thought was sobering. *I am but a guardian…*

"Ah, of course." Walter understood the give and take, the blessing and burden that was this power. "So sleeping remains…"

"Troublesome, yes."

Sleep had been the worst of it these long months in the Icewilds, that ache in his right thigh and left shoulder a constant and ineradicable thing. Rarely had he slept more than a few hours at a time, and on waking his leg would be as hard as bone and frozen stiff, requiring massaging and movement to unthaw, all of it painful. He had come to see that this was his life now, come to see it and accept it, as he would what came next. *I will hold this blade only so long as I must,* he told himself. *When the time comes, I will give it up freely.*

The sun came down soon after, washing red and gold in the west. Its setting caused the temperature to plunge, necessitating the heaping of extra furs upon their backs as they trundled on through the twilight. Amron had not yet learned how to infuse himself with the Frostblade's power subconsciously. When mastered, he would be able to build a shield about him in an instant, a barrier against extremes of temperature, hot and cold. As yet such a thing required constant thought and effort. Weary as he was, an extra cloak was the simpler option.

They spent their first night without the Snowskins in the shadow of a wide rocky overhang, listening to the call of the wolves, the creaking and bending of the trees, the leaves whispering in their haunting way. To their left ran a sloping valley, dense with pine and sentinels and spruce. The smell of rotting needles was rich and fragrant. Amron drew deep through his nostrils, smiling wistfully. "A part of me thought I'd never smell pine again," he said, thinking of his home seat of Blackfrost where the scent was ever so rich.

"Yes, snow and rock aren't quite so aromatic," said Walter. They'd seen little else for some weeks.

Rogen grunted. "I ought to give the place a scout. Make sure we're alone."

"We're not," said Walter, setting down his pack. He gestured to the woods. The howling of the wolves seemed to be coming from there. "I suppose we ought to build a fire, keep them from sniffing around as we sleep."

"Fire is a deterrent for some things and a lure for others," Whitebeard said.

"That's not an answer, Rogen," Walter told him. "So? A fire or no?"

The ranger considered matters at length. "Not tonight," he concluded. There was something careful in his voice, something unsure in his eyes. "We'll each take a watch, two hours a man. Get the shelter up. I'll not be long." He marched off into the darkness, as ever he was wont to do.

A chill wind blew through the overhang, slicing through their furs. Walter shivered. "It does feel queer without the tribe, doesn't it?" he said, hiding his apprehension in a merry voice. "I got used to having all those eyes around, watching for danger. I suppose I came to take them for granted." He looked through the hills and the trees. "I do wish they were still here."

"As do I." Amron had to admit he felt a certain unease himself. "Something has Rogen troubled."

"He's just being himself," Walter dismissed, as he set about erecting the shelter. "He was like this every night before the Snowskins, remember? It's no great surprise he's particularly heedful the first night of our parting."

Amron nodded. The logic was sound.

"I have a mind to say he'll be worse than ever over the next fortnight," Walter went on. "You know how things can be. The closer you are to home, the further away you feel. He'll not be happy until he's delivered you to Lord Borrington's door."

"I might remind you that I don't need delivering anymore, Walter." Amron gave the Frostblade's hilt a little tap.

"Perhaps not," the man agreed. He stood up from his work, having gotten nowhere. Walter Selleck was useless when it came to manual labour. Another howl rang through the night, its distance hard to judge. A call answered, in another part of the shadowed forest. Walter gazed out into the wilds, deep in thought. "I've been meaning to ask...about...about what will happen *after*," he finally said. An air of awkwardness came over him. A rare thing. Walter Selleck was not inclined to such behaviour.

"After?" Amron repeated.

"Yes. When we get back to Northwatch." The man shifted his weight. "Where do you imagine you'll go?"

"That would depend on what Robert tells me," Amron said. "It may be all of Vandar is under siege. I will go where I'm most needed."

"Not to your daughter?"

The question caught him off guard. "Lillia will be safe in Varinar, I hope. I sincerely doubt the Agarathi have invaded so far. Most likely they've not invaded at all. Wars are like pots of water on the fire. They take time to heat up and come to the boil." He stopped, realising what the man was trying to ask. "You want to join me, Walter? Even as I march to war?"

"I do, my lord. Most assuredly, I do."

Amron frowned. He hadn't much considered what Walter would do next, in truth. Rogen Whitebeard would surely continue in his service as a Ranger of Northwatch, but Walter? "It will be dangerous," he told him. "And forgive me for saying this, but you're no soldier. Might you not prefer to return home to Lakeside?" The pretty waterfront city was only a hundred miles from Northwatch, deep in the north of Vandar and not a likely target for any southern assault. "You'd be a great deal safer there."

"My safety is not my concern, my lord." A shade of sorrow was in the man's eyes. *He thinks of the family he lost*, Amron realised. "Lakeside...I do not see it as my home anymore. It's…difficult to explain. Now that I've lost my light, I…"

"You don't know that for sure."

"I feel it, Amron. The dimming." He sighed, showing a rare vulnerability. "And a soldier…no." He managed the softest of laughs. "I am quite aware of my limitations on that front. But…but there are other functions I might serve." He thought for a moment. "I could be your scribe, perhaps? Run errands for you. Deal with your correspondence. I'd be good at that, I think."

Amron looked at him doubtfully. "After all the adventures you've taken, my friend, I daresay life as a scribe will bore you."

"No." The word came out flat with a note pleading. "No, my lord. It would please me greatly to remain in your service."

And then Amron saw the truth in it. *His light is gone, his purpose complete. The poor man has nothing else.* "Come here, then."

Walter hesitated. "My lord?"

"Come here, Walter. If you're to continue in my service, I'd have you renew your oath."

Walter shuffled over, an endearing smile beginning to open on his face. Amron removed his gloves, taking the hilt of the Frostblade in his right hand. "My lord," Walter said, seeing. "A godsteel oath? I'm no Bladeborn."

"No, but I am. And I've an oath to swear to you too, my friend." He smiled down at the man. "Take off your gloves."

Walter did as he was bidden, pulling off the quilted leather garments. "But the Frostblade, Amron. That is no normal godsteel."

Amron gave a good-natured laugh. "And this is no normal oath, Walter. All you've done for me, the help you've given…well, I think I ought to swear by a shard of Vandar's Heart, don't you?"

Walter's lips were trembling. "I don't know what to say…"

"The words of your oath, Walter," Amron told him. "But first, hear mine." He reached out, taking Walter's hand in his own, palms touching, fingers wrapping tight. Amron looked down at the smaller man, a weighty look to his hard stony face, a serious cast to his silver-blue eyes. He began, "I, Amron Daecar, Lord of Blackfrost and the North Downs, Guardian of the Frostblade and former First Blade of Vandar, do swear to you, Walter Selleck of Lakeside, that you shall have a place at my hearth, and in my home, from this day, until your last day. By my word you are bonded to me. By your service will you pay me. I swear it by godsteel, by the heart of the god in my grasp. Speak words of fealty and seal the bond." He nodded for Walter to speak.

The tears on Walter's cheeks were freezing even as they fell. He sniffed and said in a brittle voice, "I, Walter Selleck…of Lakeside, do swear to serve you, Amron Daecar…Lord of Blackfrost and the North Downs….Guardian of the Frostblade and former First Blade of Vandar…as best I can, with all loyalty and obedience, from this day, until my last day. I swear it by my honour, by my life, by the heart of the god in your grasp." He paused, and added, "And the family I miss so dear…whom I shall see again, one day."

Amron's black-bearded lips cracked into a smile, as he drew Walter forward and wrapped his arm around the man's back. *Family*, he thought, embracing him. A dozen years ago, Walter had lost his wife, his children, his parents, all destroyed in the fire that consumed his home. It had led him on this path, led him to Amron's side. *I would be dead without him*, he knew, *many times over. Never has a man saved my life so often*. And so he thought it again - *family* - and knowing that wasn't enough, spoke it out loud. "Family," he said, holding Walter by the shoulders. The man's eyes blinked up, teary. "You have become family to me, Walter. You'll always have a place at my side."

And there before him, Walter Selleck wept. He crumbled to his knees, and wept.

12

Elyon

Elyon pulled back from his uncle's embrace. "You look well, Uncle," he said, smiling broadly. "About ten years older than last I saw you, but well all the same."

Sir Rikkard Amadar gave out a bark of laughter over the clatter of noise around them; the shuffle of bodies, the ring of steel, the hubbub and hum of life in camp. His handsome face was sooted and stained, armour dappled with mud and blood, blue Varin cloaked hanging heavily at his back as though unwashed for some long days. "You might want to check your look in the mirror, young Elyon," he said. "I should say you've aged even faster than me."

"We have made some haste on the road," Elyon told him. "Sleep has come at a premium."

"You're telling me." Rikkard opened out an arm and gestured to the encampment outside the towering fortress of Dragon's Bane; an endless sprawl of tents and pavilions reaching far out across the muddied fields. The colours of the houses of East Vandar showed in particular abundance, a thousand banners fluttering in the breeze. Elyon saw the Kanabar elk with its misting, bladed antlers, the grey tower of House Fullerton and flock of starlings over a silvery lake that was Lord Shorton's sigil. He saw too the standard of Elton Rammas, the young Lord of the Marsh, with the burly knight spearing the great marshland serpent. His Uncle Rikkard's own Amadar men numbered five thousand here; he could see their pavilions arranged proudly outside the fortress walls, pink and pale blue beneath the hazy sun. And Sir Killian, heir to House Oloran, had a standing force of equal size. Their crest was simple and unfussy - a gauntleted hand, clenched in a fist, to portray the great power of the Oloran name.

Elyon took it all in at a glance, then turned back to his uncle. "A fine camp, Rikkard," he said. "It must be loud, with so many swords and armoured men, clanking and clanging all day and night."

"Loud?" Rikkard laughed. "Gods, Elyon, you miss my meaning. I'm not losing sleep on account of them! No…" His arm swept wider, beyond the camp, to where the heavy wet fogs hung over the Bloodmarsh Isles. Elyon could see the faintest movement out there, as spotters and patrols moved about in the mists. "We've had more sallies and probes than I can count," Rikkard told him. "This stretch here, this is just a part of it. Even at their narrowest point, the Bloodmarshes spread over five miles wide, and here it's several times that. The Agarathi are always searching for an easy way through."

Elyon nodded. "I take it you've led the efforts in driving them off?"

"As often as I can," Rikkard said, with a combative note. Sleek, swift, and sweetly skilled, there were few better among the Varin Knights. "The bastards seem to favour raiding after dark. I haven't had a full night's sleep in months. Ah!" He turned his eyes over Elyon's shoulder as Lancel and Barnibus stepped to join them. "I heard you three rogues were riding together."

"Sir Rikkard." Barnibus stepped in first, the two men gripping wrists. "Good to see you. You look terrible."

"So Elyon's been telling me." Rikkard Amadar ran a hand through his lengthening chestnut hair. In truth he looked just as comely as ever. The likeness with his older sister Kessia had always been strong.

Lancel followed in, shook Rikkard's wrist, gave the senior Varin Knight a scan. "You been busy this morning, Sir Rikkard? Those bloodstains look fresh."

"A few hours old," Rikkard confirmed. "We fought off another raid before dawn, a few miles west of here. They're testing our response times, seeing how well they can stretch us. One day soon we'll have a proper fight on our hands."

"Then we arrived just in time," said Lancel. "Have you had any dragon attacks?"

"Not here," Rikkard told them. "Too risky for a lone dragon. But further west...yes, there have been plenty."

"Not for some time, though," Barnibus said. "It's been weeks since the last one, so far as we've heard."

Rikkard gave that a nod. "The calm before the storm," he said, as a column of shieldmen marched past in formation. Their shields were large and rectangular, each fitted with grooves and ridges around the edges that allowed them to link together on the battlefield. When varnished with a layer of fireproof oil they made for an excellent defence against dragon attack. "We anticipate a full assault soon. The only question is when."

A bellowing call split the air behind them, as Sir Mooton Blackshaw rumbled out orders to his men. Elyon had taken Amara's advice and decided to bring the brawny Riverlander with him, along with some of the others whom he'd met at Elmhall Hold. Shovel-bearded Sir Lutherton Wane, Sir Peter Hornmoor with that pointed orange beard and hooked nose, the young Lord of Wolfwood, Justin Huxley, who had brought with him a hundred swords of his own. Wane, Hornmoor, Huxley; each of them were minor houses, lord and knightly, vassals to the Blackshaws who were but a middling house themselves, serving the great power of House Kanabar. *Yet I stand above them all,* Elyon thought, as he looked again over the encampment and thought of Amara's words. "They see you as their rightful prince, Elyon," she had told him. "Every Riverlander is yours to command."

Then this army is mine, he thought, taking no great pleasure in that notion. *I was never born to rule. That was Aleron's birthright, not mine.* Yet all the same, he felt some pull of destiny as he turned his eyes across the field of colours, the flapping banners, the grand pavilions, the great stone fortress of Dragon's Bane that loomed imperiously above it all. Even now men were recognising him, turning to look, nodding and smiling and giving gestures of salute.

"There were rumours that you were coming," Rikkard told him. "Everything that's been happening...at Harrowmoor, at Ilithor... they've not been deaf to it, Elyon."

He nodded, feeling the weight of expectation gather heavy on his shoulders. "We should talk, Uncle. Do you have space in the fortress for us?"

"Some of you," Rikkard confirmed. He glanced over Elyon's retinue. "I hadn't expected you to come with so many."

"Nor I," Elyon said. "Lord Huxley called his levies, had a hundred men join us on the road."

"And the rest?"

"Sir Mooton's men. And Sir Lutherton called on his sons. He has three, all young, but eager. He trains them every night with sword and spear. In all that's another hundred and change for the war."

"Every sword is another that can take an Agarathi life." Rikkard waved vaguely to the edge of camp, where it thinned upon the plains. "Best they all set camp together, wherever they can pitch their tents. I'll have you three accommodated in the Bane."

"And Sir Mooton? He's heir to Elmhall and the Blackshaw lands."

"I know Sir Mooton," Rikkard said, with a smile. "He'll want to stay with his men, and be close to camp. The man's half barbarian. He's not made for being confined."

"I heard that." Sir Mooton stamped over, huge beard swaying, thick neck bulking with muscle. He towered over all of them, built like a bull and just as hot-tempered.

"I hoped you would," Rikkard said. "I didn't exactly care to lower my voice, Moot."

The Beast of Blackshaw's lips parted to unleash a shuddering laugh. He slapped Rikkard's arm with a massive paw, near knocking him off his feet. "You always had a tongue on you, Amadar. Didn't you know, it's dangerous to openly insult a Blackshaw."

"Insult? You have it all wrong, my friend. I was trying to pay you a compliment."

"You called me *half* barbarian. If you wanted to compliment me, you'd have left off the 'half'." Sir Mooton's second bout of laughter was more explosive than the first. He pointed toward a quiet patch of land not far from the nearest stables and training grounds. "We'll set up there. So you'll know where to find us." He turned to Elyon. "Does that suit, my prince?"

"If it suits you, it suits me, Sir Mooton."

The big man made a fist to suggest it did. Then he turned to Rikkard and leaned down. "Next time you go out on an Agarathi hunt, you give me a call. I've been itching for a good taste of dragon-folk blood."

"I'll keep you in mind."

"You do that. And don't bloody forget."

They turned and made for the fortress, a triple-walled behemoth that made Harrowmoor look little more than a children's toy. Dragon's Bane was purpose-built to be the most monstrously impenetrable fortress in the north, the great shield that stood at the top of Death's Passage with the single imperative of preventing an Agarathi invasion through the Bloodmarshes. A hundred miles south, standing vigil at the southern edge of the marshes, the Agarathi had erected a fortress of similar magnitude; Blademelt, so named for all the northern blades melted by dragonfire across the millennia. Those very blades, Elyon had heard, had been used to decorate the fort, giving Blademelt the aspect of a gigantic black porcupine, every wall and tower spiked and studded with the swords and spears and axes of fallen northmen.

Dragon's Bane was not quite so macabre, but had taken on a certain grimness of its own. Atop each of its gargantuan towers, the skulls of dead dragons had been bolted onto poles. Even as he walked toward the massive rear gatehouse, Elyon could see them, white shapes high up upon the loftiest battlements, grim warnings to the Fireborn of what lay in wait if they dared attack.

Yet there were signs, too, of disfeaturement and damage, sobering reminders that the stronghold had been lost and overwhelmed before, that even such a brutal bastion as this could still be vulnerable when besieged. Atop the parapets, some of the crenellations had been welded together in odd distortions, fused by dragonfire and never restored. Much of the outer walls had been blackened, the stones smoothed and melted. Places where the walls had come down were obvious, with many sections patched and rebuilt over the years, giving the walls a mottled appearance in shades of grey and black.

Inside the triple walls, further evidence took shape. Some of the smaller towers had been left to ruin. Fingers of black stone reached up from the earth, turning ragged at the top, as though chewed off by some monstrous beast. Rikkard explained that those were some of the older towers, too far gone to rebuild. In their place others had sprung up, and when those had fallen still more had grown, like mushrooms in rotting wood.

"Dragon's Bane is a place of renewal," he told them. "Its position makes it an attractive target for our enemies, just as Blademelt is for us. Whoever controls both controls Death's Passage, making invasion all the easier." He looked around, craning his neck up at the soaring black towers. "This place has seen more collapse and restoration than any other fortress in the north." He gestured toward a surging tower at the south side of the fort. "The Lookout Tower," he said. "When I heard you were coming, I cleared space for you. Thought you'd enjoy a good view."

The tower was the tallest of them all, a hulking pillar of square granite rising a hundred metres high. The heart of it was a switch-back stair, cutting back and forth through the core of the tower. Torches blazed in holdings along the way, creating pools of illumination amid the dimness, though otherwise there was no natural light. Not here at the tower's heart.

Rikkard went ahead of them, climbing up step by step. "How far are we going?" Barnibus ventured.

"The top," said Rikkard, voice echoing, "or thereabouts. It's hard to appreciate how large the tower is in this stairwell. Every level has a dozen rooms. Halls. Bedchambers. Solars. Audience rooms. There's plenty of space."

They finally came to the tower's summit, exiting the stairwell and stepping into a passageway that gave circuit around the level; the stairwell on the inside, rooms on the outside. "Are the other highlords accommodated up here?" Lancel asked.

Rikkard told them no. "You've heard about the folly of putting all your eggs in one basket, Lancel? That said, my rooms *are* up here. This is one of only two of the original six great-towers here still standing. The rest have been toppled and reconstructed over the years, or left to rot entirely. But the Lookout Tower and the Golden Tower are part of the original construction, as built by Ilith three and a half millennia ago."

"Ilith," said Lancel. "Now there's a surprise."

"His magic infuses the granite," Rikkard explained. "Give it time and you might just feel it. Men can't build towers this tall anymore, Lancel. It's why the Lookout Tower and Golden Tower are the tallest, around about three hundred feet, give or take. The best men can manage these days is two hundred or so. Anything else would collapse under its own weight."

He pushed open a door that gave access to a sequence of rooms. A main hall - generously sized, with a central pinewood table and broad stone hearth - branched off into separate chambers, left and right. "Elyon, this is yours."

"Mine? *All* of it?"

"You're a prince, I hear. You deserve a princely dwelling."

"Don't mock, Uncle. I never asked for this."

"History won't care whether you asked for it or not, Elyon. Great men rise to the challenge. Do you want to be great or not?" There was a challenge in his tone.

"I've…never really thought in those terms," Elyon admitted, after a short contemplation. "The world has changed so fast."

"And yours with it," Rikkard acknowledged. He walked to the far side of the hall, footsteps echoing on stone, where a large arched window permitted a generous inflow of light. Elyon followed; the others stayed near the door, sensing they'd best leave nephew and uncle alone. Without turning, Rikkard beckoned Elyon to look out over the view.

It was magnificent.

Below, a wide yard spread from the base of the tower toward the inner wall, where the biggest gatehouse Elyon had ever set eyes on gave access out onto the plains. Beyond ranged a barren stretch of land that gradually broke up into the Bloodmarshes, a boggy archipelago of a thousand isles that made up the crossing of Death's Passage. "Our borders end here, Elyon," Rikkard intoned gravely. "The Bloodmarshes are no man's land, controlled by neither us nor them. See the mists? That is a cloak the marshes rarely take off. An army a hundred thousand strong could be out there right now, only a few miles away, and we'd never know."

"But your scouts and patrols…"

"Can only do so much. We have a hundred men out there every second of every day, but so large a stretch of land is impossible to cover entirely. We have established guard posts and communication lines so we can run messages at a moment's notice. But even then it's difficult. Men get lost in the fog, Elyon. They lose their way and never return."

"It can't always be this thick."

"It isn't, not always. The fogs come and go, thinning and thickening, but the process isn't quick. When they grow thick, they linger like that for a time, and thin only gradually. It's a curious phenomenon. No one can quite explain it."

Elyon pondered that. There were many curiosities in the world that had a certain feeling of the unnatural. He let his eyes run as far as they would go, watching a small troop of mounted men on patrol out there, no more than tiny black ants scuttling at the far edge of his vision. "The concealment works both ways, Uncle," he said. "We could just as easily march on them as they us. And Blademelt is just as close to the marshes as the Bane."

Rikkard nodded soberly. "Yes, we could use the fogs if we wanted, as we have done in the past. But now?" He pondered it with a slow shake of the head. "It wouldn't be the right time. We have Lord Kastor sieging Eagle's Perch, Sir Dalton sieging the Trident. That's a good portion of our strength. Were we to strike camp and march on Blademelt, we'd leave the north poorly defended. The prudent thing is to hold the fort. We're a defence force here, not attack. For now, at least."

Elyon didn't miss how his uncle refused to style Dalton Taynar as 'prince'. He wondered if the entire encampment was the same. "Does everyone here denounce the Taynar claim?"

"All but a few, yes. The Olorans are traditional allies of the Taynars, as you know. They find themselves…in a difficult position, shall we say."

Elyon understood. Killian was heir to House Oloran, and had always been a loyal friend to the Daecars, yet his lord father Penrith thought very different. He'd long resented House Daecar for holding the office of First Blade for so long, first Balion then Gideon then Amron assuming the role. "So these five thousand swords of Killian's," Elyon asked. "Are they his father's men, or his own?"

"A mix," Rikkard said. "Killian tells me some of his captains and commanders favour your father for the throne. Others remain loyal to their lord and traditional ally. A messy business. Though not something we need concern ourselves with quite yet."

"King Godrik might think differently, Uncle. He'll not like the idea that you're all calling me 'prince' around here."

Rikkard waved it away. "*Lord* Taynar can grumble all he likes, it isn't going to change a thing. Vandar is split. Pretty much every house here at the Bane is loyal to you, and will call you prince all they like. When you've got a man as powerful as Lord Wallis Kanabar bending the knee to you, every other house across East Vandar is going to follow."

Elyon had to smile. "How long has he been here?"

"Wallis?" Rikkard shrugged. "A fortnight? Ten days? Who can say? The days seem to blur together. But it makes no matter; he's been proclaiming House Daecar the rightful rulers of Vandar ever since he arrived. The man seems on a mission to put your father on the throne. Where he belongs, I might add."

Elyon thought of something Amara had said of Vesryn. Something about helping raise his father to the throne. The thought still cut with a bitter edge. *We don't want your help, Vesryn. House Daecar is not yours to heal…*

"I'd like to see him," Elyon said. "Lord Kanabar. There are things that happened…back in Ilithor…things I need to discuss with him."

"I could say the very same, Nephew." Rikkard's voice softened. "You've been through a lot, since we parted in Rasalan. Your Uncle Vesryn abandoning his duty. That business with Sir Griffin and the lashing you took. And…Lady Melany…*Rylian.*" His voice withered at the mention of that last. "I'd like the full story from your perspective, if you're ready to tell it."

"We can talk, Uncle," Elyon said. "And there are things…things you should know as well. About my father. And…"

"Your brother?" Rikkard asked.

Elyon frowned and drew back. "You know? About…"

"The Shadowknight." He nodded. "Wallis told me."

"Wallis?" Elyon wasn't aware that Lord Kanabar knew of Jonik's true identity. But of course he knew the reason. "Amara," he said, darkly. "She must have told him." *That bloody woman and her scheming.*

"You seem displeased to hear it?"

"The woman confounds me," Elyon grunted, wondering when he started sounding like his father. He took a moment to regard his uncle's face. The clean line of the jaw. The dusted brown stubble, a day or so old. The chestnut hair, gently curled, that had begun to grow down the sides of his neck. And those eyes. Those warm kind eyes, so full of compassion. *My mother's eyes,* Elyon thought. *My mother whom he loved so dear.* "You aren't angry," he finally said. "That my father…"

"Had a son out of wedlock? My dear Elyon, how could I be? Your father had no knowledge of it. Wallis told me everything."

Everything, Elyon thought. "Amara is too free with her tongue."

"No. You're too guarded with your secrets. I know why, of course. You're afraid your father's honour and reputation will suffer if this gets out. Well…perhaps that might once have been true, but no more." He turned his eyes out through the window. "Look at what has become of this world. Kings murdered. Princes slain. Treachery and betrayal around every corner. A man learns today that Amron Daecar sired the very assassin who crippled him, who killed his eldest son. A damning revelation, yes, until you hear the truth of it; that Amron himself was deceived, and by his own brother no less. And that shock lives only so long in a world where great prophet kings are having their throats cut by their sons, when beloved princes are being murdered at their father's command." He paused, drew a breath. "That is the world we live in, Elyon. A new treachery every day. A new tale of treason. We're all desensitised to these scandals by now."

Elyon's head went up and down in a slow thoughtful nod. "I suppose you're right, Uncle."

"When am I wrong, Nephew? Of course I'm right." And he laughed, to lighten the mood. "And don't you worry about your father. He'll not die from a bit of cold."

Elyon had to laugh. *Bloody hell, Amara.* "So she really did tell Lord Kanabar everything."

"Yes. And *he* told *me.* Secrets and lies, Elyon. They're enough to break a man's back, even one so broad as yours. Your auntie is just trying to share the load."

He saw some sense in that. "I see."

"*See*, yes. Now let me see what caused all this trouble at the wedding." Rikkard's eyes dropped to Elyon's waist. "Come on. Show it to me."

Elyon obeyed, pulling back his cloak, unveiling the silver scabbard and haft, the swirling, breezy pommel and cross-guard. Rikkard nodded approvingly. "Have you learned to harness its powers?"

Elyon could only shake his head. "We've ridden with some haste. I haven't had much time to train on the road."

"Well you're here now. I want you devoting your time to it, as much as you can spare each day. If you have one purpose here it's to master that sword."

"I'll do my best."

"You'll do better than that. Now show it to me. Properly. Come, don't be shy."

Elyon drew the Windblade from its sheath, hearing those distant whispers, the blowing winds. For a moment Rikkard's hair seemed to rustle, the candles flickering, before all went still. "You've been riding with it at your hip?"

"Every day."

Rikkard nodded. "Good. You seem well accustomed to its weight. That's good."

"In that it's little different from regular godsteel," Elyon explained to him. "As the blood-bond strengthens, the blade becomes lighter. But the rest…"

"Will come in time," Rikkard assured him. "It's a funny thing. The Sword of Varinar is always considered the greatest of the Blades of Vandar, yet in actual fact it's the easiest to master, and by far the least spectacular. Your father once told me it was the weight that was the biggest challenge. Once you can bear it, you use it as any other blade. It has no outlandish function or utility. Not like the others."

Elyon had never thought of it like that. "I'll get into my training tomorrow," he said, watching the mists billow around the blade's edge. There was a strange feature to those mists, in that spinning vortex that enrobed the blade, hilt to tip. "Have you ever seen godsteel behave as such, Rikkard?"

"This isn't godsteel, Elyon. It's more. The whirlwind pattern of the mists is part of the blade's magic, as inscribed in its glyphs. It represents the Windblade's power. The power of flight."

Elyon had read as such, he remembered. "I'll be embraced by a similar effect, once I've mastered it."

"*Once* you've mastered it," Rikkard repeated, smiling. "Some self-belief. Good."

"I'm my father's son," Elyon said. "If my half-brother can master the Nightblade, I'll be damned if I can't master this."

"A good attitude, though be careful. A selfish motivation can lead one astray. Just look at your uncle. You must have absolute conviction in your right to hold the blade. You need to be driven by selfless motive, Elyon. The defence of your kingdom, the protection of your people. That's a good one. If you try to master it only to compete with the Shadowknight - or worse, kill him - then you'll find yourself vulnerable. It may lead you astray."

"My intentions are pure, I assure you."

Rikkard studied him, searching his face. "I believe you. Yet a part of you feels guilty over how you came to possess it. You still have doubts."

"Not about taking it from the Taynars," Elyon said firmly. "It's more…Rylian." His voice fell to a whisper. "He died because of what we did."

"No, he died because his father is a madman, Elyon. All the north is starting to see that now. Don't blame yourself for Rylian. He believed in you, as I do, as we all do." He moved his hand to his shoulder, gripping. "Use that as your motivation, couple it with something bigger. A drive to protect your people, your house, your kingdom, the north. Do that and you'll control the whispers. Do that and you'll be fine."

Elyon drew a long breath, filling his lungs. He exhaled. "Since when did you become so wise, Uncle?"

"Now there's your folly, young Elyon. I was always wise. The difference is, *you're* now wise enough to see it."

"So you're saying I'm the one who's been through a change?"

"I'm saying that, yes. A distinct change, to my eyes, and others, to hear the reports of you." He gave him another challenging look. "What did I ask you when we first entered this hall?"

Elyon thought back a few minutes. "You asked whether I wanted to be a great man."

"Then I'll ask you again. Do you?"

Elyon considered it. "That would be for history to judge," he then said. "To seek greatness for greatness's sake would be a selfish motivation."

Rikkard smiled. "Well said. Now go out there, and force history to take note." He dipped his head. "My prince."

13

Ranulf

Ranulf peered through the side curtain of the litter, frowning as he gazed down the street. "It's clogged," he said. "We'll have to get out and walk."

"Just wait a few more moments, my friend," said Sallor Sanara. "It may yet clear."

"We don't have far to go." Ranulf could see the dusty arena ahead, a great blocky thing built into the side of the inner wall at the western edge of Aram. "The streets are blocked, Sallor. We'll never get through this traffic."

"A moment, Ranulf. There's one more thing we need to discuss."

The tone of the man's voice caught his attention. Ranulf slipped back inside, took a perch upon the soft cushioned seat, arranging the folds of his loose linen robe. Beside him, Leshie was waving a huge feathery fan in her face in a bid to combat the heat. So far as Ranulf could figure, it wasn't working. All she was doing was blowing the warm air around. "What is it, Sallor?"

The small olive-skinned man sat prim and proper ahead of him, dressed in his golden damask robe decorated with eagles in silver thread. They'd discussed a great many things that morning as they'd journeyed lazily through the city - the current whereabouts of the Grand Duchess (still in Lumos, it seemed), the latest rumours about the ongoing siege of Eagle's Perch, the health of the defence fleet in the harbour, and much else about Lord Elio Krator's most recent dealings besides - but apparently Sallor had saved something for last. "It's about you, my friend," the little shipwright said. "Apparently, you're a wanted man."

"Of course he is," Leshie said to that, still waving that great fan of hers. "He's northern. I'm wanted too, I'll bet."

"No, this is about something else, child. It would seem that Ranulf Shackton here has not been entirely honest with me. Or you."

Leshie huffed. "Doesn't surprise me. Ranulf likes to keep his secrets."

"Yes, I am sure, but when I agree to take a man into my home, and offer him my protection, I should like to hear the full truth of just how hunted they are."

"Hunted?" Leshie repeated. "Who's hunting him?"

"A band of sellswords known as the Bloody Traders. You may know of them, child."

Leshie shrugged. "There're loads of sellsword companies." She continued waving her fan, quite indifferent to the threat.

"Quite so. This one has been despatched by none other than Janilah Lukar, so far as I've heard. A man who goes by the name 'the Surgeon' is on the lookout for you," he said to Ranulf. "Would you care to tell me why?"

Ranulf had anticipated this might happen eventually. "I should have been more truthful with you, Sallor," he admitted. "And you, Leshie. The truth is…" He had no real option but to come out with it now. "The truth is I stole a page from the Book of Thala. A page containing information of interest, to the king in question. These sellswords must have gotten word that I was here in Aram. But there's no reason for them to suspect *you*, Sallor."

The shipwright tapped his fingers on the wooden sill beside his seat. "No. I would hope not. The Book of Thala, you say?"

"It's a long story."

"One I will hear later," the Aramatian said. "Once we have more time. In its entirety, Ranulf."

"Of course."

Leshie was frowning at him. "Why didn't you tell me that?" she demanded. "I knew you'd found *something* in the book, but…stealing a page, Ranulf? *Really*?"

"I had no choice."

"Nor did I. I had to spend a month in the darkness because of you, down in those pits, afraid I'd be raped every time I shut my eyes."

"Yes, I know. And I've...apologised for that, Leshie. I thought you understood. There are bigger things at play here than you and me."

"Like what? What was on the page?"

"A matter of great importance."

"That's it?"

"It's all I'm permitted to say."

Leshie let out a great whooshing sigh. "You're maddening, Ranulf. I don't know what I'm doing here with you."

Sallor slipped forward, the movement subtle, though enough to draw the eye. "These men who brought you to Aram," he said. "The ones who saved you from Pal Palek's pits. They didn't know..."

"I never mentioned you by name," Ranulf assured him. "I only made mention of having 'friends' in the city, whom I might call upon. And in any case, they're sure to be far from here by now. Most likely they've already made berth in the north."

"I see." Sallor thought for a time. "I wonder, then, how they knew you were here in Aram, these Bloody Traders."

Ranulf was wondering that too.

"He always spoke about coming here," Leshie said for him. "Never tried to hide that at all, but then I guess he didn't realise he was being hunted. Did you, Ranulf?" She gave him a mean stare, then snarled and said, "*Vincent.* I'll bet it was that bastard who ratted on us."

It would have sounded plausible, but for one thing. "Vincent went with Jonik," Ranulf reminded her.

"So. He might have told one of his servants to spread word of where we were going. Or maybe these Bloody Traders went to his manor in Sutrek, and tortured someone to find out?"

"Maybe," Ranulf allowed. "But I'm not so sure it matters now. No one can trace us to your home, Sallor." He gestured to his face and hair, darkened and disguised by Leshie's lotions and balms. "I'm not Ranulf Shackton here."

Sallor Sanara looked unconvinced. He had welcomed them with open arms as northerners, but this was something else. They were talking about the ire of a king. "A disguise is only so good as the person you're trying to fool," he said. "This one you wear...it works to give you the aspect of a native of these lands, yes, but isn't so effective if someone already knows you. Me, for example. I saw straight through it when you arrived at my door."

Ranulf had to allow that. Sallor had given him no more than a cursory glance before seeing the man behind the mask. *If these Bloody Traders have someone with them who knows me…*

"You're a famous man, Ranulf," Sallor went on. "I'm starting to wonder whether I should put you out on the street. These lies…I had not thought you would try to deceive me like this."

I suppose I deserve that. "For which I humbly apologise, Sallor. Of course, if you want us gone, we'll find some other accommodation. There are taverns where we can lay low until the Grand Duchess returns."

"That may not be for weeks, even months, as I have told you." Sallor sighed, shaking his head. "The things I do for friendship. Now come, we seem to have stopped entirely now. We can continue this later."

They slipped out of the litter and into the burning sun, feet crunching on the gravelly road beneath their feet. This western district was rather less ordered than other parts of the city, retaining much of its original twisting busyness after the great Aram rebuild following the war with Pisek three centuries ago. "I take it the Piseki never sieged this part of the city," Ranulf said.

"No. It is one of the oldest regions in Aram." Sallor Sanara gestured with a skinny finger to the bulky sandstone arena, huddled up against the city walls. "The Red Pits help reinforce the defences here. Make the walls thicker, stronger. The Piseki knew this. When they sieged the city, they did so from many sides, but not here. Much of this area was left untouched."

"I prefer the other streets," Leshie said, too loudly. "They're much prettier. It's too dusty here."

Ranulf hushed her with a glare of the eyes. The girl continued to forget to guard her tongue in public.

"*Yes, I know,*" she mouthed at him. "*No…northern…tongue.*" She scowled and ran a finger along her lips, as though sealing them. Ranulf wondered how long it would last this time.

The crowds were busy, pushing shoulder to shoulder down the narrow street. The air trembled with a heavy hum, that of a thousand voices all competing to be heard. Ranulf doubted anyone would hear Leshie speaking, but all the same, it paid to be careful. *The*

Bloody Traders, he mused. *This 'Surgeon' must be one of their more reliable captains, if the Warrior King is willing to hire him.*

The road was bordered by stumpy sandstone buildings, most no more than a single storey tall. Ranulf spotted people gathering on their roofs, watching the crowds as they passed. Some were women of promiscuous intent, calling down their wares, flashing their breasts to any man who took a passing interest. "Don't look, Ranulf," Sallor advised him. "They will only call out more loudly."

He kept his eyes away.

At the end of the narrow street, a bustling market opened out, erected in a square outside of the towering arena. Smells filled the air, smells heavy and pungent, light and fruity. Ranulf saw men sizzling meat on open grills, chicken and lamb and dog. Women walked about cradling oils and balms for purchase. A candlemaker had set up a stall selling scented tapers. There were stalls for fruits and vegetables, boys bustling around with baskets full of breads, entertainers and jugglers and tumblers and snake-charmers. And soldiers were in great evidence too, the men of the Aram City Guard in their shirts of copper mail and feathered cloaks. All wore eagle-crested halfhelms too, peering around the crowds through suspicious eyes, hands on the hilts of their scimitar swords.

"We should give them a wide berth," Sallor suggested, weaving through the market and toward the arena.

Ranulf offered no argument. "Where will the prisoners be kept?" he asked.

"Below. I shall take the girl to our seats. You should have no trouble finding the way on your own. Many pay extra for the privilege of visiting the prisoners before they step onto the sands. You need only follow them."

Ranulf nodded. Down in the belly of the arena right now would be murderers, rapists, child molestors and their like, all ready to face judgement before the bloodthirsty throng. Before they were taken up to the surface to die, the families and friends of those they'd wronged were permitted time to spit at them, fling filth at them, curse them and even beat them if they found a bribable guard willing to let them into the prisoner's cell. It was an old custom, Ranulf knew, long since outlawed by the Grand Duchess Safina Nemati. Yet in her absence, Lord Elio Krator had restored it. Many a northman had thus suffered debasement and humiliation down in these cells, before being executed before the crowds.

And today they shall see another, Ranulf thought sadly. He shook his head, impotent to do anything about it. The fate of Sir Ralston Whaleheart was out of his hands.

Sallor Sanara reached into his pocket and withdrew a pouch of coins. He took three out - three of particular design - and handed one to Ranulf and one to Leshie. "And this, for you, Ranulf," he said, handing the adventurer a second coin. Its engravings were different, as was its purpose. These coins were not for spending, but satisfied a single use. *Tickets*, Ranulf thought, as they joined the queue filing in through the wide arena doors. Ahead, each entrant was handing in a coin just like their own. On one side was engraved a rudimentary image of the arena, on the other a crossed sword and axe. The function of Ranulf's second coin was to permit access down to the cells, this one stamped with a series of bars to signify its specific use.

"Actually, take it all," Sallor said. He handed Ranulf the small leather purse, full of regular currency. "Should you need to bribe a guard for some…personal time with the knight."

Ranulf nodded his gratitude. "You are far too kind, Sallor."

The shipwright granted him a grin, giving his temple a tap. "I do not forget, my friend. You will owe me much after this."

The queue continued to shuffle forward, the soldiers at the door inspecting each coin before allowing passage through. Leshie tugged at Ranulf's arm. He leaned in. "What if they ask me a question?" she whispered.

"Just stay quiet. Let me and Sallor do the talking."

She glanced through the bodies. "There are men being searched, Ranulf. What if they search me?"

He didn't understand her concern, not immediately. But that look on her face… "Oh Leshie…you didn't bring it with you?"

She shrugged. "Of course I did. I'm powerless without it. I have to protect us, Ranulf."

"And at what point does your desire to protect us put us in danger?" He cursed himself for not making sure she left her godsteel blade at Sallor's waterside home. "Just stay quiet," he repeated. "You're a girl, and young. There's no reason for them to consider you a threat." He sighed and turned to Sallor. "Leshie brought her short-sword," he said, in Aramatian.

"Ah." Sallor gave a calm nod. "Not to fear, Ranulf. They would not be likely to search a girl such as her."

"That's what I told her."

Still, the news set a tension to the trio, one that might have been avoided with better foresight. *She should have known,* Ranulf thought. *There was always a chance we'd be searched. I've told her a hundred times to leave her godsteel blade at home.* He leaned down to her again, having a thought. "This isn't about Sir Ralston, is it?" Leshie had spoken these last days of trying to break him out, but of course they couldn't be so reckless. "You're not thinking of doing anything stupid, I hope."

"Me? No." She frowned at him. "Are you calling me stupid, Ranulf?"

"No. But you *are* impulsive. Just sit and be quiet," he warned her. "No matter what. Do you understand?"

"Of course I understand. What do you think I'm going to do? Stand up and throw my dagger to the King's Wall or something?" She had a look on her face as though she was contemplating just that.

"*Don't,*" Ranulf said, and firmly. "Sir Ralston's fate is not for us to decide."

"Fate? Don't talk to me about fate, Ranulf. It makes you sound like a crazy person."

And her voice was rising again. *Too loud,* he thought, withdrawing from her, glancing around. They were nearing the guards now. He turned to Sallor. "Where will we be seated?"

The little shipbuilder held up his coin for inspection. On the side showing the crossed sword and axe was printed a small letter and number combination - *S-2*. "It means south stand, tier two," Sallor explained. "Each coin is printed as such. South, north, east, and west, with tiers one through three."

"We can sit where we wish within the assigned area?"

"Yes. I shall save you a place."

"Ah, Sanara!" The voice was new, coming from the left. Ranulf whirled to find a well-dressed man moving through the crowd toward them. He remembered him from the palace. A young merchant by name of Cliffario Denlatis who had come before Lord Krator to seek the hand of his cousin, the Lady Asherah Tamaar, in marriage. A bold young man, Sallor had said of him, but much liked around the docks. He was smiling now as he approached, deep dimple lines cut into his lean, clean-shaven cheeks, a keen cast to his dark hazel eyes. He had a somewhat aquiline nose, though it did nothing to interfere with his elegant good looks. "My friend. My good friend Sallor Sanara. I had not expected to find you here."

Sallor's lips were in a smile as he looked up at the merchant. *A careful smile,* Ranulf noted. "I do not care for the sight of blood, as a rule," Sallor said. "Yet on this occasion…well, I found I could not resist."

"The King's Wall does make for a strong enticement, I agree," nodded Cliffario. He stood slender before them in a swirl of robes in gold, silver, and bronze. An extra length of golden silk had been slung over his right shoulder, a common fashion choice to signify wealth. *This is a man who enjoys attention*, Ranulf thought. "Where are you seated, my friend?"

Sallor made a quick show of checking his coin. "S-2."

"Ah, a shame. I will be on the north side, near Lord Krator." His slim lips turned up into a devious smirk. "I have a mind to press him on the issue of his cousin. I shall attempt to win entry into his royal box, and seduce him to my cause."

"Well, good luck, Cliffario. I have a sense you'll need it."

The merchant laughed blithely. "Luck, Sallor, is not so out of one's control as you might think. I like to believe one can force his own luck, if suitably determined." He turned his eyes to Ranulf, then Leshie. "And who are your companions?"

Sallor did the honours. "This is my friend Ersel San Sabar, and his daughter Ersella," the shipwright said. "They are merchants, out of Kolash. Trading in spice, mostly."

"Kolash, you say? I have dealings in Kolash myself." Cliffario Denlatis looked ready to probe further into that, but merely said, "A pleasure to meet you, Ersel." He turned to look down at Leshie, who was quite oblivious to what they were saying, "And you, Ersella. I suppose you must take after your mother." His eyes flicked playfully between false father and daughter. "You really look nothing alike."

"So I often hear," Ranulf said gamely. He noticed Cliffario's neat right eyebrow raise a little to hear him speak. Though fluent in Aramatian, Ranulf did carry a slight accent. If asked, he would always explain it as a symptom of his regular trips to the north, Rasalan in particular, where he had many dealings.

Denlatis opened his mouth to speak, but a blaring call cut him off.

"Coins! Coins at the ready!" They'd reached the front of the queue, giving Ranulf precious respite from the merchant's searching eyes. A guard was standing before them, hand held out. "Coins. Show them to me please."

Sallor went first, handing his coin in, waiting while it was inspected, then passing through. Cliffario gestured forward. "Please, Ersel, Ersella, do go ahead."

Leshie reached the guard, handed her coin in, waited, and was ushered through. Ranulf followed, with Cliffario trailing behind. They avoided being searched, much to Ranulf's relief.

"Sallor, are you going below?"

The shipwright shook his head. Through the thick stone walls of the arena, the heavy murmur of the crowds could be heard, a sense of anticipation in the air. Figures bustled past them, eager to take their seats. "No, Cliffario. I have no such interest. Ersel is, however."

Denlatis turned to him. "Oh good. I shall join you, Ersel. Will your daughter be coming?" He looked down at Leshie. "Would you like to see the brute up close, Ersella?"

Leshie had no hope of understanding that. Ranulf stepped in. "She's mute, Cliffario," he said. "A tragedy of her birth, I'm afraid."

"No tragedy at all," the man came back, whip-quick in his responses. "One who cannot speak is forced only to listen. And to listen is to be wise, do you not think?"

"A nice way of looking at it."

"There is light in all darkness, my friend. You only have to let your eyes adjust." Cliffario beckoned Ranulf down a corridor. "The viewing cells are this way. Sallor, sweet Ersella, I hope to see you again later. By then, who knows, perhaps the good Sunlord Elio will have permitted my betrothal to his lady cousin." He grinned fiendishly. "Come, Ersel. Let us see the monster up close."

I must get rid of him somehow, Ranulf thought, as he fell into step beside the lithesome merchant. Through the walls laughter broke out, rumbling through the arena. That would be the entertainers brought out to warm up the crowd. A trickle of dust fell from the ceiling above them, a dance of golden motes. Ranulf could feel Denlatis studying him as they walked, an air of playful curiosity about him. He cleared his throat to speak. "Are you interested only in the King's Wall, Ersel?" he asked. "Or is there another you wish to visit?"

"No other, Cliffario." He glanced up into the man's probing eyes. "And you?"

"Well, I cannot deny that the Whaleheart is most fascinating to me, but I have an interest in his companion as well."

"His companion?"

"Yes. The smuggler who brought him here. He lives in the Port of Matia, where I do much business. Mellio is his name. What possessed him to convey the beast to our fair capital…well, this is beyond my comprehension."

"Money?" Ranulf offered. "Isn't that what drives all smugglers?"

Cliffario Denlatis smiled. Ranulf saw that he had a golden tooth, where an old incisor had once been. And a silver one opposite, he didn't fail to miss. "Money. Yes, you're probably right. This Mellio has always been a man of low scruples." There were others moving down the corridor ahead of them, reaching a set of steps that plunged down beneath the arena. At the top of those steps a pair of guards were checking coins. "You have an access coin, yes?" Cliffario asked. Ranulf nodded, withdrawing the coin in question. They pressed on toward the guards and handed them in, before moving down the steps. "Your accent," Cliffario said. "There is a hint of something in it I cannot place." The steps were well lit, yet the merchant's face seemed hidden in shadow for a moment. "You have travelled often to the north, have you not?"

Does he recognise me? Ranulf wondered all of a sudden. He'd not been to Aram in several long years, but still…

"Many times, yes," he said. "I trade spice there, with the Rasalanians in particular."

"Ah. Well that explains it. Yes, there is a hint of Rasalanian to your accent, that's it." He mused to himself for a moment. "Perhaps we might discuss your trading contracts later, Ersel? I have a mind to expand my own operation to northern waters, once the war settles down."

"That might be a while away yet, Cliffario."

"Oh I don't doubt it. But war brings as much opportunity as it does tragedy, I'm sure you agree. I seek to take advantage where I can."

Ranulf was reminded of Vincent Rose, who'd risen so high off the same mentality, building much of his fortune during the last war. Cliffario Denlatis felt every bit as daring. *And ruthless?* he wondered. He didn't much care to find out.

At the bottom of the steps, they came upon a central hall branching into separate tunnels. Down those tunnels were the cells, iron-barred and shallow, temporary holding cells for the damned. A guard stood at the entrance to each of the tunnels, managing the flow of people, supervising the treatment of the prisoners, accepting bribes. Cliffario had a smile on his face. He drank in the sound of wailing men, the shouting and cursing, the abuses. Ranulf could hear a man being savagely beaten in one of the enclosures. Elsewhere a knot of children were throwing rotting fruit at a man cowering on the floor. Scents both sweet and foul filled the chamber, the perfumes of the rich mingled with the fetid odours of the condemned.

How many innocent northmen have had to endure this debasement before their deaths? he wondered. Sallor had told him how active the Red Pits had been of late, how northerners who'd lived peacefully in the city for years had been rounded up from their homes and herded here for execution by the thuggish Patriots of Lumara. And all by Lord Krator's command, he knew. The thought made him scowl.

"You disapprove?" He broke from his thoughts to find Cliffario Denlatis staring at him. "You think all this barbaric?"

I show my leanings, Ranulf realised. *It is written all across my face.* "I'm…not a violent man, Cliffario," he said.

"You do not need to be," Denlatis came back. "You need only be a man of justice. Down here, the families and friends of the victims are given opportunity to vent. At a glance it may seem bestial, but the truth is very different. These men and women deserve everything they get, and worse. There is great righteousness in what is done here."

"And the northmen?" Ranulf asked. He found he couldn't help himself. "Did they deserve the same treatment?"

Denlatis shrugged, indifferent. "The mob must be appeased," he said. "Lord Krator knows this, and gives them what they want. It is wartime, my friend. Examples must be made."

Ranulf saw no merit in furthering this conversation. "Perhaps," was all he said.

"*Perhaps,*" Cliffario Denlatis repeated, a tone of mocking in his voice. "This is the word of an indecisive man. You do not strike me so, Ersel San Sabar." He gave Ranulf a quizzical look, as though realising something. "Are you a relation to Manut San Sabar, perchance?"

He's testing me, Ranulf thought. *There is no man called Manut San Sabar.* "No relation," he said. He turned his eyes around, wanting rid of him. "How do we know where each prisoner is kept?"

"Ah. So you are eager to look upon the giant. Well, with that one it is easy. Look for the biggest crowd." And with that, Cliffario Denlatis slipped away, with a promise of, "I shall see you later," ringing in Ranulf's ears

Ranulf let out a breath. *I hope not,* he thought. *That man asks too many questions.* Life in Aram was growing progressively more dangerous for him and Leshie, he could sense. These Bloody Traders. The Grand Duchess so far away. And now this Denlatis sniffing about. He sighed the thought away and searched the corridors for the largest gathering. It lay almost straight ahead, where two guards were stationed to control the flow of people. It looked as though the spectators were being permitted entry via a one-in-one-out sort of rule. Ranulf marched immediately over, taking position in yet another queue. He counted three people ahead of him, waiting to be allowed through. The man at the front was complaining about the time. "Come, hurry up," he called to the guards in a sniffy voice. "The games will soon begin. I have paid good money to be here. Let me through!"

Good money. Sallor hadn't told Ranulf how much that second coin had cost him. Rather a lot, he imagined, judging by the garb of those present, the silks and jewellery they wore. *It would seem only the wealthy are permitted a chance to vent,* he thought bitterly. *This is just a means of adding more money to Krator's coffers.* He didn't delude himself into thinking the profits would be paid to the palace either. *No, Lord Krator opened these pits for a reason. Entertain the mob, yes…and get richer all the while.*

The man at the front of the queue was still causing a fuss. Eventually the guards relented, allowing him through. Ranulf stepped forward with the last two men waiting ahead of him. He peered past them, down the corridor. *So many,* he thought, seeing the mob ahead, crowding around Sir Ralston's cell. *How am I ever to speak to him in private?*

The noise was an ugly thing. They were shouting, mocking, taunting, cursing. He could see more children throwing spoiled fruit. The scent of dung wafted past and he knew worse things were being pelted at the King's Wall too. Though he couldn't see him through the bodies, he could imagine the sight. Sir Ralston, chained to the wall in his tiny little cell, head hung low as he endured this degradation. It made his blood boil just to think of it. *This is not the Aram I know. The city takes on the cruel face of its new master.*

"Go," said the lead guard. "You, yes, and you…" He let the two ahead of Ranulf through, stopping him at the front with a stiff, outheld arm. "No, not you. You must wait your turn."

"One more won't make a difference," Ranulf said. His voice came out curt. *My blood is up. I must relax.* "Please," he said, soothing his tone. "I would appreciate it greatly if you should let me pass." He looked into the guard's eyes, saw nothing but cold disdain. "Fine." He pulled out the pouch Sallor had given him. "How much?"

The cold disdain was replaced by a casual interest. "A half-sun will do." The guard shared a look with his partner. "For each." His partner nodded.

Ranulf sighed. *I'll owe Sallor more than I can repay at this rate.* In the currency of the southern nations, a half-sun was a valuable coin. He opened the purse, rummaged through the coppers and bronzes and silvers, and found what he was looking for. "Here."

The man snatched the coins up. "Go," he grunted, lowering his arm.

Ranulf shuffled through, reaching the back of the wealthy rabble. They pulsed with spiteful aggression, near every one of them laughing or mocking or hissing through the bars, flinging filth and spitting, hurling abuse. "Excuse me. Out of the way. Let me through." Ranulf pressed on, not caring to spare a thought for whom he might be shoving. A few gave him bitter looks or shoved him back, but he hardly noticed for all the jostling going on. Soon he was midway in, cutting a path to the front, getting his first glimpse of the bars and what lay beyond.

It's as I thought, as I feared. A horrid wash of pity flushed through him to see Sir Ralston Whaleheart reduced to this. The mountainous knight was dressed in the same rotting rags as he'd been wearing when Ranulf saw him in the palace almost two weeks ago. His horribly scarred flesh, bumpy and burned, was covered in fresh welts and cuts, bruises and swellings, scattered with pips and seeds and wet chunks of putrid fruit. Ranulf saw that his hands were bound in manacles chained to the wall, preventing him from turning away. All he could do was stand there and accept it.

Ranulf pushed himself right up the bars, fighting to control his own anger. A man with a drooping black moustache took umbrage at his appearance and attempted to push him away. Ranulf turned on him. "Unhand me," he said fiercely, swiping his arm from his shoulder. "This man…this man killed my brother!" he said without thinking. He turned back to the shadowed figure of Sir Ralston. "You! You killed my brother! Bastard!" he spat. "Bastard!"

The man with the drooping moustache understood. "I am sorry for your loss. This monster has slain so many."

Ranulf kept the snarl on his face, adding his voice to the ruckus of noise and slurs. *How to get his attention? How to communicate without anyone knowing?*

"You hear me, Whaleheart!" he roared, wondering if Sir Ralston even understood. *No, he cannot. The man does not speak this tongue.* But there were others, he could hear, shouting at Sir Ralston in the common tongue of the north. Ranulf decided to do the same. "You hear me!" he repeated, cloaking his Rasal accent in an Aramatian timbre. Yet leaving enough for Sir Ralston to hear. "You killed my brother, in *Rasalan*. He was a merchant, visiting those lands, and you killed him! You killed him, monster!"

To anyone else that would seem sincere, but Sir Ralston would know it to be a lie. Ranulf watched him, saw his lips flicker in a snarl. *He heard me,* he realised. So he repeated it again, shouting louder this time. And this time he saw Sir Ralston glance up…

At once Ranulf pressed his face forward, as close as he could to the bars. He widened his eyes, softened his expression, hoping the man would see him for who he was. *You know me, Sir Ralston,* he willed. *You know me. I am Ranulf Shackton, friend to your fallen king.* And in those dark eyes, he saw cognisance. *Yes, yes…he recognises me…*

Amid the tumult of heckling, he mouthed a single name. "Saska," he said silently. "Saska…did she come with you?"

Sir Ralston Whaleheart looked at him through the shadowed pits that were his eyes. Men began bellowing with more ferocity to see him lift his gaze. "Murderer! Savage! Beast!" they called, and a hundred other things in a dozen different tongues. Some were pressing forward to the bars, spitting through the iron slats. Their faces twisted in hate and spite and some were laughing from behind, laughing to see such a titan cut down to this. It swirled into one, all that scorn and ire and derision, and through it all Sir Ralston remained perfectly still, rigid as stone, his mighty chest moving up and down, slow and steady…steady and slow, up and down…

Then, with a sudden and powerful surge, he wrenched his right arm forward, tearing his chains free of the wall in a shattering rending of stone. The crowd gasped and shrieked, stumbling back. A second great grunt had the Whaleheart pulling free his left arm too, the wrist manacles and chains hanging loose as he lumbered straight toward the bars. By now half the crowd were fleeing, falling over one another in their haste to escape. The two guards at the entrance to the tunnel sped forward with their spears, ready to drive him back. Yet Ranulf stood perfectly still at the bars, waiting, as the knight reached right through them, took his neck in an enormous hand, and pulled him forward. "Saska," Ranulf said again, in a whisper this time. "Did she..."

"Krator," frowned Sir Ralston Whaleheart. "Elio Krator has her."

And then the guards were there, stabbing at him with the tips of their spears, forcing the giant to withdraw. "Back, back! Let him go! Back!"

Sir Ralston stood his ground a moment, taking the cuts as though they were nothing, clinging on to Ranulf's neck. "Save her, Shackton," he told him. "You get her out of there."

Ranulf nodded. "I will. I promise it. I will."

It seemed all the man needed to hear. He released his hold on Ranulf's neck and slumped back into the shadows, bleeding.

14

Saska

"I know this seems cruel to you, child, but you must understand my reasoning," said Lord Elio Krator from his high-backed chair, sitting beneath the shade of the awning upon the royal balcony. The stadium was loud and dusty and filled with swaying movement, the crowds on their feet as they watched the latest execution. "I take no pleasure in it, I want you to know this. But this *is* the only way. You have the leeching, yes, but that is only one part of the treatment. You must watch him fall. You must see the blood of the Whaleheart on the sand, and know that it is impure."

Saska sat beside him on a much smaller seat, wrapped up in a pale silver burnoose that showed only the slit of her eyes. She knew Elio Krator wanted to keep her hidden, and had dressed her thus as one of his private concubines, their identities not to be known in public. At her side stood a girl no older than ten, poised to translate anything Saska didn't understand. Mostly that was from the master of ceremonies, whose duty it was to announce the arrival of the prisoners and the pit-fighters who were to kill them. Though Saska was starting to understand some of the Aramatian tongue, much of what was said still eluded her. The old housemaid Yasha had been spending much time with her of late, teaching her the nuances of the language by Lord Krator's order. All part of her training and treatment. The leeching. The learning. The dismissal of her Bladeborn side and fostering of the Lightborn. *And now this,* she thought, staring wretchedly into the arena. *Now I'm to watch Sir Ralston die.*

A rising swell spread through the crowd as Mellio stumbled and fell, kicking up a cloud of dust as he tumbled heavily to the floor. He was to be the penultimate victim, the appetiser that preceded the final dish. Mellio, who'd hidden her and Rolly as they'd crossed the Aramatian Plains. Mellio, the smuggler, who never stopped smiling.

He wasn't smiling now.

"They sense his end," said the man seated on Lord Krator's other side, his voice contemptuous and thick with the guttural Piseki brogue. Krator had introduced him as Pal Palek, a Piseki moonlord and honoured guest. He fingered the twin forks of his glistening black beard, expectant. The two had conversed largely in the common tongue, partly for Saska's benefit, she imagined, and partly because Palek's Aramatian wasn't particularly refined, and nor did Lord Krator seem interested in subjecting himself to the grumbling intensity of the Piseki tongue. "He has lasted longer than I thought," Palek went on. "For that at least I must praise him." He gave a cruel laugh. "But yes, time for the main event, I think."

Saska turned back to look at Mellio. He had been given a sword and shield, but had no hope of defeating the professional pit-fighter assigned to execute him. For the last ten minutes the man had toyed with him, marching the smuggler around the sand, cutting him here and there, giving the crowd a show. Yet it was time for that show to end.

"This one likes to decapitate his victims, I hear," Pal Palek continued. "Is that true, Elio?"

Lord Krator nodded. "They all have their preferences, my pit-fighters. Decapitation can make for a spectacular end."

Saska felt numb. She'd watched over a dozen men and women suffer these execution bouts already and each had been despatched in a different, horrific way. One man had been gutted, his insides spilling out onto the sands, pink and steaming. Another's throat had been cut from ear to ear, blood flooding down his chest in thick red spurts. A great brute of an executioner had bludgeoned a woman to death with a wooden cudgel, and a second of similar size had twisted a youth's head all the way around until his face was looking the wrong way. Saska had heard the crack from up in the royal box, seen the ragged length of spine jutting viscously through the boy's neck. She tried to tell herself these prisoners were murderers and rapists, that they'd deserved it, and in some cases perhaps that was true. But not all.

Not for Mellio, she thought, as the smuggler struggled to his knees, exhausted. *Not for Pig…*

Saska swallowed past the dry lump in her throat. *Pig. Poor Pig…* The boy had been so frightened when he'd stepped out onto the sand that his bladder had evacuated, soiling his breeches. Even from up in the stands Saska could see it, that dark stain spreading, as she'd seen him trembling, his hand shivering so violently he could scarcely hold the spear they gave him. For a minute or two his executioner had toyed with him, but there was so little sport to it that the crowd had soon lost interest. Some even found pity in the sight, calling for mercy. And Lord Elio had obliged, magnanimous as he wished to appear. He'd stood and raised a hand, drawing all the attention of the crowd, then proclaimed the mute boy deserving of a quicker end. The pit-fighter had summarily stepped forward and thrust his blade through Pig's heart, and Saska had felt the tears crawling out of her eyes beneath her burnoose, warm and salty as they slid down to her lips.

"He was just a boy," she'd whispered, as Pig slumped bonelessly to the ground. "He didn't deserve to die."

"No?" Lord Elio had looked down at her, a cold hard look in those callous golden eyes. "Oh, I suppose you do not know the full tale of the boy. How he came to be in the smuggler's service?"

Saska looked at him through the slit in her hood.

"He killed his very own mother," Krator said. "Yes, it's true. He killed her and ran and thus found himself in the smuggler Mellio's service. Mute? You think that is because he had his tongue out? Or because of some impairment at his birth? No, it was shame that stopped the boy from talking. Shame for what he'd done." He sniffed. "Oh he deserved to die, Saska. And the smuggler…he is even worse."

And now he will die too, Saska thought, watching as the executioner placed the flat of his blade on Mellio's shoulder. She hadn't believed a word of that about Pig. *No, he was too sweet, too simple, too gentle to have done anything so awful. If he did kill his mother,* she told herself, *it was self-defence. That's all it could have been…*

A hush of anticipation spread through the tiers as Mellio sat back on his knees, head down, done. "He is finished," Pal Palek said. "He has not even the energy to stand."

"He knows the fight is over," Krator agreed. "Perhaps he has some courage after all? Look how he exposes his neck."

"Be brave, Mellio," Saska whispered to herself, as the executioner moved around the man's side to get a clean strike at the nape of his neck. She closed her eyes and clenched her fist. "Be brave." And then came the thin distant sound of steel slicing through flesh and bone, and the crowd erupted in a bloodthirsty roar.

"Spectacular indeed," she heard Pal Palek say. "I see now why you call these the *Red* Pits, Elio."

The men laughed together, as Saska opened her eyes and saw Mellio's headless body lying limp at the heart of the arena, blood pulsing from his severed neck and spreading out into a glistening red pool. The pit-fighter had taken his head up into his grasp, holding it aloft for the crowd to see. Cheers and applause rang out loudly as disposal men hurried out to drag Mellio's body away, the executioner following, waving to the stands as he left. The febrile intensity of Mellio's death softened into an anticipated murmuring, as the sands were swept and neatened for the final bout. Saska watched, dull-eyed behind her hood, as Mellio's lifeblood was spread and mixed with that of the dozen who'd come before. *The Red Pits,* she thought. When they'd arrived the sands had been clean and golden. No longer.

"So tell me more of this breakout at your desert stronghold, Pal," said Lord Krator, waving for wine. A boy sped from behind to fill his cup. "A most unfortunate matter. I had looked forward to returning to enjoy one of your shows."

Pal Palek had a dusky face and eyes the colour of tar. "Unfortunate would be putting it lightly, Elio. I lost every one of my beasts. *Every one.* Even those I've had for decades...gone."

"Well I'm sure your pits will be refilled, in time. We are at war, good moonlord. You shall have plenty of opportunity to restock."

"Yes, and that is part of the reason I came." Palek looked to the yawning opening that led into the belly of the arena. "This giant of yours. I had wondered whether you might give him to me instead."

A thin smile stretched across Elio Krator's neat-featured face. "You leave it late to make such a request, my friend."

"Call it a professional courtesy," said Palek. "You know how much I valued my pets, how generous I have been with them. Many times have you enjoyed the pleasure of my menagerie, Elio. Give me this beast of yours and you shall enjoy him many times too. It would be a waste to let him off so lightly."

"Lightly?" Lord Krator gave a soft huff. "He is not to go lightly, Pal. His death will be slow and severe."

"There are some fates worse than death, as you know," Palek came back. "Why should this monster get off so easily, after all the southern blood he has spilt?"

"He's *not* a monster," Saska whispered.

Both men's eyes swung down to her. Pal Palek was frowning. "This girl should not talk unless spoken to."

"Yes, I quite agree," said Krator. "She has been told as such, Pal. You will forgive her her outburst. She is troubled, as I have told you, accursed by foul blood. She struggles to control herself still, but that will change soon, I know."

Pal Palek sneered across at her. "I wonder why she is not down there as well, Elio. Clearly the devil-blood of Varin is strong in her. You should have her head and be done with it. Or better yet...give *her* to me as well, she and her guardian both."

Elio Krator did not take that kindly. "You should remember yourself, Palek Do not come here to my city and make demands. All Patriots answer to me, and you included."

"I think Lord Zon would say otherwise, Elio. The rule of the Patriots is his birthright, not yours."

Lord Krator scoffed at the concept. "Iru Zon is not even City Master of Solas. Yet here I sit, in rule of Aram, soon to be raised as Grand Duke of all of Aramatia. Zon has no authority over me."

"As you say, Lord Krator."

Saska sat quietly as the preparations were completed on the grounds below, the sands swept into shades of mixed red and gold, tidied up as Lord Krator liked it. He called for several vintages of wine for his guest to sample, as gilded trays heaped with local delights were brought forth. "The honeyed crickets are a delicacy here," he said to Saska, as a waiting boy hustled out before her. "Do try some, child."

She shook her head. "I have no appetite for eating."

"Because your guardian is about to die?"

She gave that no answer, and looked away.

"I'll not have you starve yourself, Saska." His voice carried that iron rigidity that told her he was starting to lose his temper. These long weeks in his care had been an exercise in humility for her. *I must be as pleasant as possible with him*, she would repeat to herself. *I must be amenable. I must please him, so that he might one day drop his guard.* But today…today she was struggling to maintain her sense of composure. *Pig,* she thought. *Mellio. And now…now I'm to watch Rolly die…*

"I'm not hungry," she said, more firmly. "I don't want any crickets, Elio."

He regarded her with that cold dispassion of his. The way he looked at her when he saw her father, not her mother. Saw the Bladeborn, not the Lightborn. The northern blood that ran so rich. "A good leeching this evening, I think. Yes, that will help relax you."

"It won't work," she said, inadvisably. "This leeching…it's *never* going to work."

"We shall see. Now do hush, Saska, the fun is about to begin."

The final pit-fighters were emerging into the arena now, stepping out to a chorus of cheers. Krator turned to Moonlord Palek. "I have saved the best till last," he told him over the noise. "One is almost of a size with the beast. I hope to see them wrestle a bit. Another is a woman who might undermine him. She's only small, but swift as a hare. It will be amusing to see the monster turning and trying to swat at her."

Pal Palek was laughing. "And the third?"

Krator pointed. "A grotesque," he said. "The sort you like, Palek. See the hunchback? The distorted head? He is no real fighter, in truth, but the other two will keep the beast distracted. The grotesque is just there to humiliate him." He gave Saska a look. "Show the world how weak this blood of Varin is, when a man does not hold godsteel."

"Very good," Palek chuckled, pulling at the legs of a roasted frog. He took a bite, licking the grease from his fingers. "And the beast himself? How is he to be armed, Elio?"

"With blunted sword and shield. I will not say he wasn't given a fighting chance."

"You play a risky game, my friend." Palek slurped his wine, a finger of red liquid running down his chin and into the right fork of his sharp black beard. "I have heard much of King Godrin's monster. Some say he needs no weapon with which to fight. There is even a rumour that he killed a dragon with his bare hands, strangled it to death." His laughter was mocking. "People will believe the most absurd of things."

"There is no accounting for the amount of stupidity in this world, Lord Palek."

"It is a blight, I agree." Palek tossed aside the stringy carcass of the roasted frog, waved over some sugared plums. He picked one out and took a bite, chewing noisily. "Even men of wealth can be cursed by it, this stupidity. Men who *should* know better." He grunted and turned his eyes into the crowds nearby. "That *upstart*...what was his name? He who dared ask over your cousin's hand?"

Elio Krator shrugged disinterestedly. "His name's Denlatis. A bold man, but yes, he gets ahead of himself. He asked for my cousin's hand only recently in the palace as well. I found it amusing, in truth. Yet this? No, I had not expected him to press me on it again. He risks crossing a line he will not be able to pass back over."

"He has already crossed it as far as I'm concerned. You ought to consider teaching him a lesson, Elio. Or allow me to do so."

"Already growing protective of Lady Asherah, my friend? I have not agreed to your betrothal, not yet."

"Your cousin is most dear to me, Elio. If she *is* to become my wedded wife, I will *not* have men such as this Denlatis sniffing around."

"He will give up the fight if and when your union is announced, fear not. The Lady Asherah has had many suitors, as you know. You cannot go teaching every one of them a lesson." Palek went to speak again, but Elio Krator waved him to silence. "Quiet now, my friend. The monster is about to emerge."

A drum pounded at that very instant, calling the crowd's attention to the arched opening in the arena wall. Already the three pit-fighters were circling back and forth, awaiting their kill. Saska's breath stilled as a shadow appeared within the mouth of the tunnel, a great hulking shape trudging heavily into the sun. When he emerged entirely, she felt tears sting her eyes again. These were tears of grief and rage and guilt all in one. *My Wall, my protector, my Rolly,* she thought. *So...so broken...*

Elio Krator gave an audible grunt. "They were *meant* to cover him up." He looked incensed. "The man is half dead already!"

Palek seemed to find that quietly amusing. "Perhaps the guards were taking bribes? I have heard how they allow..."

"Yes, I know what happens down there," Krator snapped. He flew out a hand. "This treatment isn't all *new*, Palek. I had him softened up on purpose, but that wasn't supposed to be *seen*." He slammed a fist onto the arm of his chair. "They were meant to cover him up! *Mar*!"

From a seat behind them, Mar Malaan came forward, a waft of sweet perfume coming with him. "Yes, my lord?" said the flowery Sunrider.

Krator didn't turn. "Find out what happened down there. Right now!"

"At once, my lord." Mar Malaan sped away in a flutter of silken robes.

Someone's going to die for this, Saska knew. She didn't care. Her eyes were on Sir Ralston, moving wearily into the centre of the arena. He was dressed in nothing but rags, his upper body unburdened. There were several fresh cuts in his torso and upper thighs, weeping blood. The rest of his body was a ruin, swollen and scarred, savaged and burned. And seeing him she couldn't help herself. She flew to her feet, ready to rip off her hood and call to him, plead for forgiveness for all she'd done. But before she could a strong hand gripped her wrist and pulled her right back down. "You sit and watch," warned Elio Krator in a low voice. "I'm *not* going to tell you again."

"I can't," she said. "Please, don't make me."

"Watch!" He threw her arm aside, glared at her, then swung his eyes to the master of ceremonies. "Begin!" he growled. "Call the start, right now!"

The man hastily stepped to the front of the box and beckoned for the crowd to listen. As he went into his address, Mar Malaan came panting back out, taking a knee at Lord Krator's side. "Well? What happened?"

"It seems Sir Ralston killed two men, my lord. There was a large crowd, I'm told, heckling him in his cell. Sir Ralston managed to break from his chains and almost strangled a man to death. Two guards forced him back with their spears, but he killed them both when they went to try to dress him." He dipped his head. "That's why he isn't in his armour, my lord. The other guards were too afraid to go near him."

"Afraid," sneered Krator. "I'll give them something to be afraid of." He dismissed the Sunrider with a wave. Mar Malaan receded back into the shadows.

Saska kept her eyes from him. *Armour,* she thought. She imagined it would be fake armour, easily cut, armour to give him the appearance of a knight. She scanned the faces in the crowd, saw the mixed confusion and disappointment. *They'd hoped for more than this,* she realised. *They wanted to see the monster, not the broken knight all dressed in rags with nothing but a blunt sword to hand.* "He doesn't have a shield," she said out loud. She glanced up at Krator. "I thought you said…"

"I know what I said. He has chosen not to use it." Elio Krator drew two long deep breaths to compose himself. "A coward," he then proclaimed. "The man refuses to fight and he will be called a coward. Yes…" He nodded. "Yes, that serves. Let all of Aram see how weak the blood of Varin is. That even this great northern brute of yours trembles before a woman and a hunchback!"

He's deranged, Saska realised. *How can he expect this to turn me to his cause? Is this all just a game to him? He cannot truly believe…*

Her thoughts broke off as the crowd began booing. Her eyes darted to the centre of the arena, where Sir Ralston was settling onto the sandy floor, crossing his legs before him, seemingly in prayer. The jeers grew swiftly louder, a deep thrumming sound peppered with voices as men and women called for the man to fight. Sir Ralston ignored them. He laid the blunt blade he'd been given on the sand and sat still and silent as stone.

Saska glanced to her right, saw Elio Krator's chest moving up and down, his eyes narrowing, nostrils flaring. *Control,* she thought. *He cannot stand to lose control.* The man grunted something under his breath, bared his teeth, shook his head, then came to a snap decision and waved the master of ceremonies over, whispering something into his ear. The announcer listened, nodded, and returned to his podium, calling out over the din. Saska leaned across to her little interpreter, who whispered into her ear what the man was saying. "If the knight wishes to die on his backside, so be it," the little girl translated. "This shames him. Shame him! Shame him!"

The crowd answered in roaring approval as the biggest of the pit-fighters stamped forward to the cross-legged giant. If Sir Ralston Whaleheart was the largest man in the world this one had good claim to be the second. *And heavier, most likely,* Saska thought. Though thick with muscle he was well endowed with fat as well, a fleshy scarred coat of mass wobbling around his trunk as he plodded across the pits. He was dressed in leather breeches cut off at the knee and a vest that left his enormous arms exposed, twisting with thick black hair. The sun shone down upon his sweaty bald dome, reflecting off the great curved khopesh he bore. In his other hand he held a round shield, well made. *And with a razor edge,* Saska saw, peering through her burnoose. The brute could just as well cut a man's head off with that shield as he could his sword.

He bellowed something, a challenge, as he stopped a pace short of the knight. Saska's interpreter leaned across to translate, but she didn't need to hear it. The crowd gave out a hectoring laugh to suggest there was mockery in the brute's words. Sir Ralston didn't stir. The brute began pacing side to side in front of him, khopesh aloft, slamming his shield hand against his chest. More taunts trumpeted through his lips, and the crowd responded, laughing, heckling.

"What if he doesn't fight?" asked Pal Palek. The man was still eating, working through a plate of dates. Every word he spoke was accompanied by loud chewing that seemed to fan at Lord Krator's ire.

"Then he'll die," the sunlord growled.

Palek deposited another date into his mouth, chewed off the flesh, spat the stone into a metal basin at his side. It made a *panging* sound.

"Do you have to eat so loudly?" Krator raged. He blew out a breath, turned his eyes back down to the arena, muttering. "The fool makes too much of it. He's not an entertainer! I pay him to kill, not make jokes."

"He's trying to goad him," Palek said, eating with a little more refinement. "The crowd seem to be enjoying it."

Something about Lord Elio Krator was snapping. *He likes things neat,* Saska thought. *He cannot stand it when things don't go his way.* She could see a thick purple vein emerging on the side of his head, throbbing out from his temple. The cords of muscle in his vascular forearms were wound tight as the skin of a drum.

"Enough of this," he said. His eyes darted to the side and the master of ceremonies was there in an instant. Word was passed on and the man returned to his podium, crying out. His words had the giant pit-fighter stopping in his pacing and turning up to face him. The brute listened, nodded, scowled, turned…

…and found Sir Ralston Whaleheart standing right behind him.

The crowd gasped.

The hulking pit-fighter stumbled back in shock.

Sir Ralston went with him, taking a sharp step forward, reaching out, gripping at forehead and chin. He twisted violently, turning the man's head sideways. The sound of his neck shattering rang out loud as any clash of steel on steel. Splinters of bone burst out in a spray of blood and torn flesh. The crowd gave out a second cry as Sir Ralston threw his carcass aside, the brute's body landing with a resounding thump and uprush of reddish dust. Calm as anything, the Wall bent down and relieved the dead man of shield and sword. He looked up into the royal box - looked at Elio Krator - and smiled.

Elio Krator was wordless. The master of ceremonies spun to him, questioning, but the sunlord gave him nothing. A shriek ripped through the air, high pitched and grating, and Saska saw the small female pit-fighter surge forward in sudden attack.

Sir Ralston saw her coming. With a swift sidestep and heave, he cleaved the woman in two, sending a shower of blood and guts across his chest as her two separate halves tumbled gorily to the ground. The crowd were screaming now, some rushing to leave the stadium. "Godsteel," she heard someone shriek. "Godsteel. He must have godsteel!"

No, he needs only his strength and training, Saska thought, *and an anger that cuts deep to his bones.*

That anger turned upon the hunchback now, standing gormless in a motley of mocking mismatched armour. He was rooted to the floor, something wet and golden tricking down the side of his leg as the Wall marched toward him. Saska wondered if he might spare him until his khopesh swung and the hunchback's malformed head toppled into the stands, some four or five rows back, to a chorus of utter dismay.

"Guards!" someone shouted. "Guards! Restrain him!" It sounded like Pal Palek but over the tide of noise it was hard to say.

All the arena was falling to chaos now, half the stadium emptying as the spectators hurried for the exits. *They fear him so,* Saska thought. *One man. One knight. One Bladeborn. And all of Aram in a panic.*

"Restrain him!" came that call again, and this time Saska saw that it was indeed Pal Palek. He moved to his feet, marching to the front of the balcony. "Take him!" Saska could see soldiers out there now, scurrying from the tunnels, city guards in their feathery cloaks and interlinking copper mail. They moved to surround the giant Bladeborn knight, but he charged and swung at them, scattering several, killing a pair more. "Take him!" blared Palek. "You have the numbers! Overwhelm him!"

Saska watched helplessly as others moved to close in. Sir Ralston was as a bear in a baiting pit, surrounded by snarling hunting dogs, swinging here, turning there, yet there was only so much he could do.

As he swiped at one man another thrust in behind him, driving the tip of his blade into the giant's flank. Sir Ralston roared, rotated, and exposed himself to another attack, the edge of a scimitar sword slicing across his thick muscular thigh, parting the meat of his leg.

"Stop!" Saska cried. She turned to Elio Krator, reached out to grip the taut muscles of his forearm. "Please…call them off. Call them off, Elio. I'll do anything. *Anything…*"

He ripped his arm away, stood, and marched to the front of the royal box to join the Piseki. "Kill him!" he bellowed.

"No!" Saska went to move but felt Mar Malaan behind her, drawing her down.

"I caution you not to interfere, my lady. It will only go ill for you."

She looked at him, then her eyes were back on Sir Ralston. He'd managed to break through the net and had limped to the side of the arena, putting his back against the wall. It was hard to make out what was happening for all the city guards pressing toward him. Several of them were dead, bodies littering the sand. Pal Palek seemed to be entreating Lord Krator to spare him. "His wounds are severe," she heard him say. "The crowd will think him dead. Give him to me, Elio. Let me take him to my pits…"

Krator gave the man a withering stare. "Enough, Palek! Enough!" He turned back to the guard. "Kill him! I say kill that man right now!"

"*You'll do no such thing,*" said a deep, resounding voice.

Krator spun. Pal Palek whirled. Saska's eyes followed to find a man marching out onto the balcony with a trail of guards at his back. He carried an air of distinguished regality, silver scalemail armour enrobing his body, a cloak of white feathers flowing behind him. A refined grey beard covered his cheeks and chin, his hair a drift of soft white snow, trim and neat, full despite his years. The wide-eyed look of rage on Elio Krator's face swept away into a frown of sudden confusion. "Lord Hasham. I thought…"

"You thought I was absent with the Grand Duchess, I know. And you were right, Lord Krator. She bid me return home." The man stepped into the sun, surveying the scene through a pair of watchful brown eyes that seemed to miss nothing. "Call off the guards, Elio. I am taking the Whaleheart into my custody."

"On whose authority?" demanded Krator.

"You know whose. Now call them off."

The sunlord snorted. "She put the rule of Aram in *my* hands,

Lord Hasham. This man…" He swung an arm at Sir Ralston. "He came to this city to assassinate me. Several of my men were lost during the attempt. And he's already dead, most likely. His wounds are sure to kill him."

"I'm sure you hope so," said Lord Hasham calmly. "A dead man can tell no tales, after all." He turned to one of his personal guards, each of them dressed in white and silver as he was, and motioned for him to make good on his orders. The man marched immediately toward the front of the balcony and called down for the city guards to pull back. As he was doing so Lord Hasham went on. "Her Serenity has heard much of what has transpired here of late. To say she regrets raising you to the station of stewardship is putting it lightly. I am here to relieve you of your command, Lord Krator. And investigate matters that the Grand Duchess finds of interest." He levelled his eyes on the man. "She had an attempt on her life, did you know this?"

Lord Elio Krator shook his head. "No. That is terrible, Lord Hasham."

"I'm sure you think so. Know that if I discover you to have had any part in it…"

"I didn't. You forget I was to wed her daughter. I have always seen Safina as a mother."

"I'm sure." Lord Hasham's eyes fell upon Pal Palek, ignoring Saska completely. *He thinks me a concubine,* she realised. *This is my chance. He is allied to my grandmother, this lord. I need only speak, tell him who I am, and…*

Joy. The thought of the starcat caused her throat to tighten. *He'll kill her for certain if I say anything.* Krator had threatened that already. "Joy will stay here today," he'd said, when they'd left his hillside estate. "Just in case you should have a mind to do something…reckless." The sight of Agarro prowling around the gardens had put an extra stamp on the point. *If I try anything, he'll set the wolf on her. I can't let that happen. I can't…*

Lord Hasham was still looking at Pal Palek, eyebrows raised. "Lord Palek," he said, recognising the moonlord. "What are you doing here in Aram?"

The Piseki looked mildly discomforted by the man's commanding presence. "I've…come to discuss certain matters with Lord Krator."

"What matters?"

"Private matters, my lord."

Lord Hasham nodded. "I can guess. The hand of Lady Asherah Tamaar?"

Pal Palek shifted on his feet.

"I might have known. The good Lord Krator was always sure to wed his cousin to one of his own. You Patriots do like to interbreed, don't you?"

Pal Palek looked ready to respond to that, but Lord Hasham had already turned from him. "As I'm sure you know, Lord Krator, the fortress of Eagle's Perch is currently under siege by a Tukoran army." He worked his eyes around the arena. "And yet here I find you, engaging in illegal butchery. These pits were closed by Her Serenity for a reason."

"I decided to reopen them. The people…"

"There is a war to fight!" roared Hasham, his eyes widening in a sudden fury. "You sit here watching men mocked and slain when a *real* army of northmen lays siege to our own lands!" Krator made to speak but Lord Hasham cut him off. "What have you done to halt the northern advance? Tell me, Lord Krator, how many men you have assembled to march on this Tukoran horde?"

Elio Krator stiffened. "An army is mustered and ready to ride," he said. "And you underestimate Eagle's Perch. It can hold out for weeks, if not months, against this army. I have been keeping abreast of it, I assure you."

"You'll lead the army yourself," Lord Hasham said.

Silence.

"My lord?"

"You heard me, Krator. Her Serenity commands it. You say the army is assembled? Good, then you will leave tomorrow. I shall take on stewardship of the city."

"Lord Hasham." Elio Krator added a gentler edge to his voice. "I have interests here that I must…"

"Interests? What interests are above the defence of your own nation? You will leave at once, Lord Krator, by holy decree of your grand duchess. And if that is not enough for you, your empress. Empress Valura is most concerned by this news of the Tukoran invasion. She wants an experienced hand on the helm, and there are few better than you for the job." He raised a rugged, callused palm."No more complaints, Elio. It is done. Break the siege and we'll talk upon your return. And you'd best hope Her Serenity decides *not* to put you in chains when you do."

He spun in a sharp turn and marched away, his guards trailing behind him in a swirl of silver and white. Down in the arena, Sir Ralston was being led away, though dragged would be a better description. Saska watched, longing to go to him. Blood ran out of him, leaving trails in the sand. For all she knew he might already be dead.

Lord Krator stood at the balcony, breathing heavily. He took a moment to himself, then turned. "Mar, get her up."

Mar Malaan swept back in, took Saska's arm. "Rise, my lady."

She rose. "Where are we going?"

"*Where*?" Krator looked at her hatefully. "You heard him. North. To Eagle's Perch."

"Me? No, I cannot…"

"You can and you will." Krator marched to her, brushed Mar Malaan aside, gripped her wrist and began pulling her toward the exit. "We can continue your treatment on the road."

"*Treatment*. My lord…Elio…isn't it time you gave up on…"

He spun, struck her with an open palm, knocking her right down to the floor. A blur spread across her vision, sparkling with spots of pale white light. "Another word and the cat is dead." She blinked, breathed, tasted blood on her lower lip. "Pick her up," Krator commanded. She felt gentle hands reaching to pull her to her feet. Mar Malaan again, the soft glove over Krator's iron fist. Her vision began to clear and she saw Lord Krator turn to his loyal Sunrider. "Take her out of the city at once, Mar. Watch for my battle standard on the road and join me in a few day's time."

Mar Malaan inclined his head. "My lord. And the Whaleheart?"

"What of him?"

"Well, he is sure to tell Lord Hasham of the girl as soon as the good Moonrider goes to speak with him. He may send men to retrieve her."

Moonrider, Saska thought, dazed. *No wonder they fear him…*

"He is sure to try, yes," dismissed Krator. "That's if the beast survives. He looked like a corpse to me."

"The Whaleheart is strong, my lord," Malaan said. "You only have to look at his scars to see that he isn't an easy man to kill."

Krator mulled on that. "I'll try to see him finished off, then. I've good men for the job. They'll see it done."

"Very good, my lord. Then we shall leave without delay." Mar

Malaan took Saska by the arm and began leading her to the exit.. "Come now, child. No more fighting. Go easy."

She stumbled alongside him, muddy-headed, as he drew her into the shadows of the corridor beyond the balcony. "Joy," she whispered. "At least…at least let me bring Joy with me."

"Of course," Mar Malaan said gently. "Lord Krator would not want you to be without your Joy. It brings out the light in you, child. If you want my advice, embrace it, and fully. Life will go a lot easier for you if you do."

"I will," Saska croaked, and that was true.

Lightborn. Bladeborn. Seaborn. I'll embrace them all.

15

Jonik

"Open the door, Sid," Jonik commanded.

The giant crewman withdrew from his daydreams - he'd been staring into empty space again - blinked a couple of times and looked up at Jonik with a puzzled face.

"Off in some other world, were you?" Jonik asked him.

The giant nodded, his lips breaking into a grin. "Other world," he said in that big breathy voice of his. "Yes, Yes. Other world."

"You can tell me all about it some other time." Jonik nodded to the door.

Sid lumbered to his feet, vacating the small stool he sat on outside the brig door, and plodded over to the bolts, pulling them aside. The sound of grinding metal disturbed the silence. All else was quiet but for the constant creaking and groaning of wood and planking, sounds all shipmen knew well. Life below decks would not be the same without them; those sounds had become a queer comfort to Jonik now.

Sid pulled open the door, and Jonik stepped past into the blackness, Emeric following behind. The light of Emeric's torch provided a welcome glow. He set it aside on the hook he always used, illuminating the old cloaked figure of Shadowmaster Gerrin within.

"What time is it?" the man croaked, sitting up on his bed, shielding his eyes. That bed had been brought down from the crewman quarters. He had a table now too, with a little oil lamp, a few books, a stack of parchment with quill pen and ink. A wooden plate sat beside his bed, nothing but a few hard crusts of bread left uneaten from his evening meal. Jonik had even permitted him a small nightly ration of beer, at Emeric's suggestion. In truth his little cell down here had taken on a measure of luxury. Even the floor had been drained of standing water, though it still looked a little damp.

"Early morning," Jonik said. He gestured to the stack of parchment. "You've been doing as we asked?"

"Just as asked," Gerrin confirmed. "Everything I know about the Shadowfort. Defences. Weaknesses. Personnel numbers. Details on all the senior Shadowmasters and knights, mages and sorcerers, and so on." He paused. "At least everything I can fit on five pages. There's a lot more up here." He gave his rutted forehead a tap. "Will need more parchment, though."

"You'll have it," Jonik said. "And the Shadow King? Have you written of him?"

Gerrin gave a half-hearted bob of the head. "Bits and pieces."

"Bits and pieces?" Jonik repeated. It wasn't a satisfactory answer. "Tell me you know more about him than bits and pieces, Gerrin."

"Depends how you define bits and pieces. There's much of the mystery about the Shadow King, Jonik. Even to me."

"Have you ever met him?" Emeric asked. "Or seen him?"

"Me? No. The demon only deals with the mages. Parsivor and his sort. Those like him."

"So he's one of them? A sorcerer like Parsivor?"

"Something like that," Gerrin said. He took up a mug from the table beside his bed and drank the dregs of his ale. "Much older, though. Five hundred years at least, though might be more. A thousand? Two? Hard to know with these creatures."

Jonik snorted. "It sounds like you're guessing. We'd hoped for something more reliable."

"Reliable? Nothing I say is going to be reliable to you, is it?" He stared at Jonik, those grey eyes hardening. "You still don't trust me, do you?"

"Of course I don't. Be thankful if ever I do. We could live to be as old as this Shadow King and still I'd have my doubts."

Gerrin laughed gutturally. "The boy's learned a bit of humour, Lord Manfrey. Is that your doing?"

"You've met the crew," Emeric said, stepping forward to pick up the papers. "Half of what they say to one another is a jape or jest of some sort."

"And some of it's rubbed off on the boy." Gerrin laughed again in that rough old voice of his and swung his feet onto the floor. "It's nice to see, Jonik. You were always so dour."

"Everyone was dour there," Jonik came back. "We were *taught* to be emotionless, Gerrin. To be friendless. To not make attachments. *You* taught me that."

Gerrin shrugged. "True enough. It warms me to see that you've overridden that conditioning, though. And you've got plenty of friends now, it seems to me. Now I wonder why that is?"

Jonik rolled his eyes. "I don't need reminding that you went easy on me. And don't try to take credit for the changes I've gone through. You've got nothing to do with it."

"Well I beg to differ, boy, but believe whatever you want. The result's the same in the end. Just nice that we can share in a sally, is all I'm saying. Now that we've both thrown off the yoke."

"You've thrown off nothing," Jonik was keen to remind him. "There was no yoke on your shoulders, Gerrin, no chains at your feet. You were there under Janilah's orders. You didn't grow up there like I did."

Gerrin shrugged. "Seems the boy's got me there, Lord Manfrey." The grim old Shadowmaster had taken on a more lighthearted manner these last weeks. He even smiled, and often, now. *Is this the real Gerrin,* Jonik had to wonder. *Is this the man he once was, before he fell under the dark spell of the Warrior King, before he bound himself to his bidding?*

Emeric was shuffling through the pages, giving each of them a swift scan, front and back, taking in the gist of what Gerrin had written. He stopped on something he found interesting, squinting to better read the old Shadowmaster's scribblings. "You've said here that the Shadow King was the one who built the order in the first place. That it was started some five hundred years ago." He looked up. "Is that true or more conjecture?"

"True, if you believe the accounts I've read. There are ancient scrolls in the Shadowfort library that deal with the formation of the order, or at least the beginnings of what it would evolve into." He glanced at Jonik. "Nothing the boy would have been permitted to read, of course, but I had access to the restricted sections on account of my rank."

"Your rank…bought by Janilah's patronage," Jonik snarled.

Gerrin gave a breezy agreement. "Just that. But there are other areas restricted to even me, and the other masters. Parts deep in the fortress…deep in the mountains. Dark places, the sort that would chill the blood of the bravest of knights. Oh yes. Only the mages would go back there."

"Why?" asked Emeric.

"Why? Well now…isn't that the question. I can't say for sure, but if you want my opinion, I think they go there to feed him. And not with *food*, mind you. Not every boy at the fort graduates to become a Shadowknight, shall we say."

Jonik felt a tide of disgust rising up through his stomach. "He eats them? These…these boys?" The thought horrified him more than he could adequately express.

"Now don't tell me you didn't notice how the odd boy would go missing, Jonik," Gerrin said.

"I did notice. I just thought…" He shook his head, thinking back. "I just thought they'd been killed during one of the trials, or…or beaten to death by their master. You were brutal, Gerrin, you and the others. You even told me that not every boy survived the training. Or were you lying about that as well?"

"No lie in that. Boys died as you say. By beatings. In training accidents. But only every once in a while. The rest…well, the mages were always watching. Some boys they would take away, and never tell us where."

"To the depths of the mountain. To their king?" Emeric was digesting this with his usual calm. "Was it the flesh of these boys that he consumed or….something else?"

Gerrin huffed. "Wolves and bears may enjoy the taste of boy-flesh, but I doubt the Shadow King hungers for anything so crude. Their blood, though? Well, that's different. Don't forget, these boys are Bladeborn, and there's something about that Varin blood…the power, the old echoes of long life in there. Seems to me the mages work their sorcery on these boys, prepare them through occult ritual, and use them to keep their master alive. But not without a price. As I've told you before, dark magic blackens the soul. Each spell leaves a scar. These mages, you might say, are cursing themselves through these rituals, reducing their own lifespans. And all for their master's sake."

"Why?" Jonik asked. "What does the Shadow King want?"

Gerrin sat back against the wall. "Now that I cannot say. To stay living, probably, just like the rest of us."

"No." That answer wasn't good enough for Jonik. "It's got to be more than that. Why even start the Shadow Order in the first place? All this talk of bringing balance to the world, of pruning at the hedges of fate. That's bullshit. Maybe it was a front all along, just some big ruse to deliver a healthy stream of Bladeborn boys to the doors of this monster." He snarled, sickened. "Is this thing killable, Gerrin?That's all I want to know. Can we kill it?"

"Everything's killable, Jonik, you know that. Kings. Demons. Even gods. Anything living can die."

"Then I'll cut the creature's head off like I did that Whisperer," he growled, thinking of that night in the village of Russet Ridge.

Emeric was more cautious, as per his custom. "Not so fast, Jonik. A wise warrior makes no such claim until he knows more about his adversary." He arched a brow in Gerrin's direction. "Do you know what powers this creature possesses?"

Gerrin's head bobbed side to side. "Not with any level of certainty, no. Might be he's barely alive, lying on a slab and waiting for the mercy of a blade. Might be the opposite. I'd say it'd be smart to go there expecting something profoundly more malevolent than any of us have faced before, and we'll find ourselves well prepared."

"*Ourselves?*" asked Jonik. "You think you're coming with us, Gerrin."

"*Yourselves*, then," Gerrin corrected. "If you don't want to use me, fine, that's your choice. Happy to be an advisor only if you'd prefer."

Emeric's eyes swept briefly to Jonik's. "Your participation is to be decided, Sir Gerrin," he said. "For now, these notes of yours are most useful." He gave the old Shadowmaster a grateful dip of the head. "A final word on the other mages, before we leave you to sleep. How many are there at the fort?"

Gerrin thrust his grizzly bearded chin at his notes. "It's all in there, for you to peruse at your leisure. There were nine, originally, before Jonik killed Ghalto and I killed Parsivor. That was the name of the Whisperer you killed in Russet Ridge, Jonik. Ghalto. Always nice to put a name to a demonic face, isn't it?"

Jonik smiled despite himself. "I guess."

"So there are seven left?" Emeric pressed.

"Seven that I know of. Might be more, but unlikely. Like Ghalto and Parsivor, most of them come and go from the Shadowfort, shadowing the men when they go out to fulfil their contracts, handling messages, supervising them, sometimes accompanying them on missions like Parsivor did with me. That usually happens when a Shadowknight breaks from the order and runs. These old sorcerers… they can be rather good at tracking a person down."

"Took you long enough to find me," Jonik said.

Gerrin grunted out a laugh. "You ran a long way, boy."

"What about the rest?" Emeric asked. "You said most come and go from the Shadowfort. That means there are others who never leave. Correct?"

"Correct. There're two who haven't stepped foot from the fort in all the years I've been there. Fhanrir and the Steward. Fhanrir's old, older even than Parsivor was I would guess. If you ask me, he's the one who does a lot of the occult ritual work, judging by his look." He laughed throatily. "You thought Parsivor was bad, Jonik, when he showed his true face. Well Fhanrir doesn't have Parsivor's skill of illusion. Shambles about in a cloak, long-nosed, empty-eyed, skin all loose and drooping, bones clicking and clacking with every step. He's a walking corpse, really; shouldn't prove too much trouble."

Jonik had never seen this creature Fhanrir, that he could recall. And by the sounds of it, he would certainly recall it if he had. Clearly, he kept himself to himself, away in the depths of the fortress, where the Shadowknights and apprentices were never permitted to tread.

"And this other one. *The Steward*?" said Emeric. "Does he have a real name?"

"If he does, I've never heard it. He's younger…or *seems* younger, anyway. With these creatures it's hard to know for sure. Oversees a lot of the day-to-day running of the fort. Jonik will have seen him around, most likely, though you'd never know he was a Whisperer unless you dealt with him directly. He's good at keeping everything running smoothly. With that voice of his…well, Jonik knows what I'm talking about."

Jonik nodded. "They have a certain…persuasion about them, the Whisperers," he told Emeric.

"I've heard." Emeric puzzled on that for a moment. "Will he prove a hurdle?"

Gerrin's shoulders did a lazy up and down movement. "Might. The Steward's use of verbal manipulation magic is strong as I've ever seen, stronger than Ghalto's was that's for certain. Who knows, Jonik.

Had it been the Steward with you in that tavern at Russet Ridge, it mightn't have gone so easy."

"Easy is not the word I would use. I had to draw on everything I had to overcome him."

"Then you have your answer. If it took all you had to overcome Ghalto, let's assume the Steward will prove a stiffer challenge."

"A challenge he'll not be facing alone, this time," put in Emeric. "Together we ought to be able to overcome what we face. And this…" He gave the handful of papers a wave. "Will prove most helpful, Sir Gerrin, as I say."

"Happy to be of aid. Get me some more parchment, and I'll keep on scribbling for you. But you ask me, I think you'd be mad to limit my support to quill and ink. You put a blade in my hand and I'll be glad to redden it with the order's blood."

"Or ours," Jonik said. "Who's to say you won't turn on us once you're safely home at your beloved fortress?"

"Beloved? Now you're just talking folly, boy, and starting to boil my blood. I never loved that place, not for a single damn second I was there. If it wasn't for Ilith's magical protections, I'd gladly see it pulled down, every cold black block of stone."

"Seems the Shadowmaster doth protest too much."

Gerrin growled and shook his head. "Vandar will surely rise from his tomb before you believe me, boy. That's your loss. I know every master, every knight, and every mage at that fortress. Every one of them I'd happily kill."

"I'm not trying to kill everyone, Gerrin," Jonik said.

"No, not the boys, not the young-uns like you. You're trying to break their chains, I know, free them like you freed yourself. That's your cause, and it's righteous I'll not deny. But you're delusional if you think any of the masters or senior knights will join you. They've been there too long. That lot…they're beyond saving."

Jonik stared at him. "I'm aware of all that."

"Good. Well that's something, then. And you be careful of any of the older ones who seem too willing to yield. They might just be trying to get beyond your guard. Don't trust them, you hear? Just take their heads and be done with it."

Jonik found the comment somewhat ironic. "Thanks for the advice, Gerrin. Perhaps I should use it on you."

"Perhaps you should. Might spare me your constant suspicions. I can see Lord Manfrey's long past those, but you? Oh no, they're too deeply embedded, aren't they?"

"Deep as the Long Abyss," Jonik said.

"Then that's something for you to figure out. But just remember…there's not a man in this crew of yours who's ever been to that fort, Jonik, and even you don't know it half so well as me. That's some big reward for a little risk, I reckon. Oh, and I almost forget. I might be the only one who can get you in."

Jonik scoffed inwardly, hating how right he was.

Emeric was frowning and rubbing his beard. "You believe you can get us entry through the gate?"

"No, my lord. I *know* I can get you entry through the gate. Now I'm sure your plan was for Jonik to go all invisible and climb the ramparts, but quite frankly, that's a lot easier said than done. The outer walls of the fortress are sheer, smooth, and most miserly in the foothold department, and beyond all that you'd have the cold and winds to contend with. Not easy. Even for you, boy. I'd say walking straight in through the front gate would be rather more simple, wouldn't you?"

"A trick," Jonik grunted. "You'd have them open the gates and then go in and betray us. You'd bring all the strength of the order down on us at once."

"Your imagination really is something. Why in Ilith's name would I ever do that?"

"Because."

"Ah, *because*. The final defence of the fool."

"You watch yourself, Gerrin. You're treading on thin ice with me here."

"Threats now, is it? I thought I taught you better than that. Use your words, your reason. As you say, I've been working all these years for Janilah, not the order. I've slain a senior Shadowknight and powerful mage. I've delayed in finding you, obfuscated the chase, and will swear by oath of godsteel, as soon as you'll allow it, that I mean only to help you, serve you, make up for what I've done. So tell me, given all that, just what could I hope to achieve by betraying you at the very gates of the order I have myself betrayed?"

Jonik had no answer. None at least that would sound witty or sensible or convincing. He could sense his own mistrust growing thin, making him seem petty and peevish and less than the leader he wanted to be. *If you are so strong in your convictions…* he told himself....*If you are so adamant that this course is righteous and just, just what do you have to fear?*

He drew a breath, cast aside his childish impulses, and looked his old master in the eye. "Can it be done?"

"You're asking whether I can get them to open the gates for me?" Gerrin said.

"That's what I'm asking, yes."

"Then it can be done. But we'd have to be careful. The order may post scouts along the passes, or otherwise have fair warning of our coming. In such a case they would be foolish to open the gates to us."

"So we need to make sure we approach unseen?" asked Emeric.

"Yes. Unseen, unheard, unknown, until we get close. At that point, depending on what has happened, we'll have options. Might be that I'll approach alone, announce my return, tell of the loss of Valtho and Parsivor and demand the gate be opened. If the rest of you are near enough, you'll be able to follow me through. If not - and this might be better - I'll enter, kill the gate-guards, and wave you in once the entrance is secure. If we do this at the right time, during dead of night, we'll be able to take them unawares."

"And the other option?" Emeric wanted to know.

"He won't like it," Gerrin said, waving at Jonik.

"What?" Jonik asked grimly, but already he knew what Gerrin would say. "Oh. I see. A hostage. You'll want to bring me to the gate as your hostage."

"It has its merits," Gerrin said. "Might be suspicious if I return alone, but with my hand round the scruff of your neck? I could say you were the one who slew Valtho and Parsivor, and no one would bat an eyelid, not after what you did to Ghalto and his men. Or else we could ignore all that, and be *particular* sneaky."

"Meaning?" said Jonik.

"Meaning we pick out two of your best men and dress them up as Valtho and Parsivor instead. It's risky, true, but from a distance, who should know? So long as I do the talking, that is. And as leader of that little crew, I often did." He turned his eyes to Emeric Manfrey. "You could throw on a cloak, couldn't you, my lord, imitate old Parsivor's crook-backed gait?"

Emeric considered it as though it was an option. "I never met the man, Sir Gerrin, not in his true form."

"No matter. I can teach you how he moved."

"I...suppose it might work. And Valtho?"

"It won't work," Jonik said.

"It might," said Gerrin. "We're talking hypotheticals at this point, that's all. And Valtho..." He pursed his old grey lips, thinking. "He was quite tall. Might be Borrus Kanabar could play him, now that he's lost that great girth of his."

"Borrus has been working hard to restore that girth, I'll have you know," Emeric said, with a whisper of a smile on his face. "And in any case, we're not sure if he's coming with us just yet. He and Sir Torvyn Blackshaw are arguing about that daily. But alas, as you say..." He glanced at the door. "This is all just hypothetical..."

It was the muted thud of footsteps outside that had caught Emeric's attention. He turned, reached to the handle, excused himself and stepped briskly out into the corridor beyond, shutting the door behind him. His voice sounded dully over the creaking of planks, the groan of water pressing on wood, the honking sound that Soft Sid made when he lurched back to his feet from his stool, standing to attention. Gerrin sat cross-legged on his bed, spinning his thumbs around one another in a manner that had the potential to drive Jonik mad.

"Would you stop that," he snapped.

Gerrin raised his eyes in innocence. "Stop what? I'm not doing any..."

"That spinning. With your thumbs. Stop it. It's irritating."

"Ok...as you wish..."

"It's irritating because this isn't the *you* I know, Gerrin. Not once in all my years at the Shadowfort did I see you do *that*. It's far too carefree. You're a grim old bastard, short-tempered and foul-spirited, and all too happy to throw fists at the slightest of provocation. I'd be more convinced if you carried on like that. All these grins and shrugged shoulders just pisses me off." He breathed out.

"Well now, boy, don't hold anything back on my account."

"And enough with this '*boy*'. You want to serve me, you'll cut that out. Or is that your entire point...to undermine me at every turn?"

Gerrin looked contrite. Somehow that annoyed Jonik too. "I didn't realise it vexed you so much."

Everything about you vexes me, he thought. And he didn't like the man he became around Gerrin either. For now, that served well enough, with his old master locked down here in the brig and out of sight. But if and when he should be allowed to interact with the crew, it would not do well for him to be dismissing Jonik with all these 'boys' all the time. "Just cut them out," he grumbled. "And when we're with the men, you'll call me 'my lord'."

Emeric re-entered at that. "Jonik, we'd best go."

"Problem?" asked Gerrin, leaning forward.

"Nothing to concern you," Jonik told him curtly, striding across the cell. "You'll have your parchment later," he added, as he passed through the door and followed Emeric outside. Sid was on hand to slide the bolts. "What's the problem?" Jonik asked. He noticed that Jack was standing at the foot of the stairs. "Jack?"

"Nothing, Ghost," said the burly Marshlander. "Just that we're nearing the harbour at Calmwater and dawn's breaking out east. Captain Turner thought it best we fetch you both. Big day ahead."

Jonik nodded and began making for the stairs. *Big day indeed*, he thought.

16

Janilah

The day was bright and crisp and cloudless, a hint of a breeze in the air but no more. The rich pine-green cloak of King Janilah Lukar billowed at his back as he walked between his honour guard down the wide cobbled steps of White Shadow, the sides of the road teeming with a sea of pale and dirty faces. Men, women, children, the young and old alike. All had come, beckoned by the news. The Warrior King was to step before the people, the heralds had been crying for days. *Come, one and all. Come and see your great king!*

"You might consider waving to them, sire," offered jowly Watch Commander Trillian Morwood, dressed in the pristine raiment of his post. "Let them know that you appreciate them coming."

Janilah obliged the man this simple request and raised his right arm to the crowds in a wave. A murmur gave out, a few cheers, but hardly what he'd hoped for. One man bellowed 'long live the king' and that seemed to lead to a chorus of laughter some way back from the street. "They seem somewhat…subdued, Trillian."

"Bear with them, sire. There is a great deal of anticipation in the air, can you not sense it? Most are just stupefied to see you, I think. The sight of you…it can serve to tie up the tongue. They'll become more animated when we reach Galin's Post and you make your public address."

Janilah peered down the broad, shallow steps, to where the wide street opened out into their intended destination. The square was the largest in the city, a great open quad that was home to theatrical performances, religious gatherings, daily markets and seasonal festivals. Today it would play host to the king, ancestor of the man who gave the square its name. When Galin Lukar sieged Ilithor and won the kingdom of Tukor three centuries ago, this great city courtyard had been the staging post for his triumphant charge up the city levels. The name had since stuck.

Janilah marched on, turning his head rigidly left and right, giving the thronging masses another generous wave. There was a little more of a reaction this time, though still it remained scattered, islands of cheers within a sea of stone-faced silence. Along the streets, the men of the City Watch were standing facing the crowds with their spears crossed between them, creating a barrier for anyone foolish enough to try to get near the king. The palace guardsmen who formed Janilah's protective escort, led by Sir Owen Armdall and Sir Kevyn Bolt, were watching them all with narrow, careful eyes. Sir Edwyn Huffort and the newly anointed Sir Mallister Monsort brought up the rear, each of them eye-catching in their triple-coloured mantles, glittery godsteel mail, and the dual blades that accompanied their rank.

Anticipation, Janilah thought, *or tension?* He had expected this, in truth, and that was the entire point of this venture. To show his face, declare his return to health, exhibit a man of sound mind and stout body. *To retain their respect and admiration*, he thought. *I will not become my father, laughed at by the mob…*

Cecilia came striding up beside him, all fur and jewels and pouty red lips. "They honour you, Father," she said. "See how quiet they are. Oh, such reverence."

"Spare me your sarcasm today, Cecilia. You know as well as I these people are far from won over."

"And who cares if they are or not? You know my mind on the mob. They're sheep and let them bleat. The lion's roar will silence them all."

"And that's what you'd have me do today? Roar to silence these rumours? I daresay Lord Morwood would advise against that, Cecilia."

"Let him." She smiled emptily across at Morwood, who was pretending not to listen. "Old Trillian has spent half his life dealing with the smallfolk, so of course he learns to think like them. That is a *lower* way of thinking, Father, if you want my opinion. Do you not have a higher calling to answer to? A war to win? Certain *blades* to gather?"

"I'll have you manage the volume of your voice," he commanded tersely. "And step back, woman, a half step behind at least. We're here to dispel these damaging rumours about you whispering into my ear. All you're doing right now is perpetuating them." He lifted his bearded chin, set a cold look of regality to his eyes, and hoped that she did as bidden.

A short silence followed before she said, "But you have it with you today, of course? You still plan to go through with it?" He could tell by her voice that she was keeping her head lower in a posture of submission.

Good, he thought, marching straight-backed and upright in a confident, kingly gait. *She knows what picture these people need to see.* "I will decide later, once I've had a chance to assess the crowd," he told her. "They may not be ready to hear the truth."

"The truth will set you free, Father," Cecilia said, halfway between a whisper and a hiss, low enough for only his ears to hear. "Look at what all this secrecy has done to you. You should speak proudly about what you are trying to achieve. Once all the world knows, then they will understand."

"Perhaps. As I say, I'll decide later."

"Yes, Father. You are the king, and know your people best." She slid back again, and out of sight behind him.

He put the thought aside, embracing the moment for what it was. *A chance for them to see me,* he thought, *and me to see them.* He searched the faces around him, sliding his gaze over the masses, never linking eyes with anyone in particular, but judging their expressions all the while. Among the blank, dull faces of the doltish and dumb, he saw many a scowl, many a frown, many a set of eyes that favoured him not. *But there is still awe, and blind reverence too.* He could see that plainly enough, the wonderstruck faces of the faithful, those who knew their place. But fear? Was there any fear in their eyes? Not that he could see. *They possess the confidence of the herd,* he mused, *one large enough in number to give them strength.* And nor did he miss the rumpled shapes of blades and blunts, dirks and daggers, hidden beneath their cloaks.

"Many have come armed," he said to Lord Morwood.

The man nodded dourly. "Yes, sire, I have noticed that as well. A sign of the times, I'm afraid to say. As I've reported to you, there have been more killings in these parts of late, more rioting and looting and other unsavoury crimes. Many have taken to carrying weapons to better defend themselves and their families."

"Or perpetrate these crimes themselves," Janilah suggested.

"Some, yes, though rarely does violence stir by daylight. It had been mostly kept to the shadier parts of the district, among the alleys and lanes. The soldiers of the garrison have been helping to keep the troubles to a minimum, but even so, it continues to break out more regularly than I would like."

"It is the fear of war, Trillian. It can stir a man to violent action, and that fear can be infectious. I will do what I can to assuage it, and suppress any further issues."

"Sire." Morwood bowed his thick red neck. "A word from you will, I'm sure, go a long way to calming the people."

Janilah lifted his right arm again, rotating it in another wave. A flutter of noise followed, no different to before. A few calls, some positive, some less so. He heard in a man's voice a tone of mocking when he yelled, "The Warrior King comes to lead our armies to war! We're saved! We're saved! Long live the Warrior King!" Then came the laughter, and this time it was louder and less localised. From both sides of the streets it hummed and crackled, men, women, children joining in.

Janilah remained calm. It was a fine line he trod here. React too sternly and he would only strengthen these rumours of his growing tyranny. React too weakly and they would soon lose all respect for him. And he thought again of his father, the weak and craven king. *I will not become him. I will not be openly mocked.* "Find out who said that," he instructed Lord Morwood.

"My lord? He was only making an innocent jest…"

"Find him. Have him beaten for his insolence. I will not tell you again."

Watch Commander Morwood dipped his eyes. "Yes, sire. At once."

The command was passed on, and Janilah sensed several guards barging through the cordon and into the crowd, barking questions. A bitter round of booing rang out at their arrival, and Janilah heard some scuffling, but soon enough they were too far gone down the street to hear.

"If I may, sire," said Lord Morwood.

Janilah turned to him. "Go on."

The stocky watch commander looked into the crowd. "If you

target every one of them who makes a joke, you'll not accomplish much today. Oughtn't you rise above it, sire? Let them have their jests. They do no harm to you."

"I beg to differ, Trillian. You heard how they laughed. That shows a lack of respect, a lack of fear, and that extends to the men under my command. If they begin to see weakness in me they will see weakness in you and your men as well. I will not let this rot persist."

The end of the street was now approaching, where it opened out into Galin's Post. The great city square was bordered by taverns and trade-shops, with a great stable to one side and grand merchant houses along another. Between them all was an empty expanse of white and grey cobbles, mottled and worn smooth by the feet of a million men, layered in a mush of melting snow. The square was crowded from one side to the other, the smallfolk pressed in, shoulder to shoulder, heaped in wools and fur and rags against the cold.

Ahead of him, the City Watch had pressed the people back to create a tunnel through which he would walk, leading toward the heart of the square where a stage had been erected. Around it more of his soldiers stood, and above it flew the banners of his kingdom, the crossed blade and mallet of Tukor, backdropped by a shield.

A silence, deep and eerie, spread upon the masses as he arrived. He could hear the shuffle of his men, the clank of metal on stone, the occasional caw of a crow, circling in the skies above. *Do they know something I do not?* he wondered, seeing the black birds wheeling and rotating above him. The sight of them filled him with a strange feeling of foreboding. The crow was a carrion bird. *They scent death in the air,* he thought.

"Sire, perhaps you might slow to speak to some of the people?" Lord Morwood offered.

They'd not discussed this. Cecilia, yes, but not him. "My daughter will take care of it. Kiss some babies. Make the children laugh. Charm the men. Isn't that what you said?"

"I did, sire, but perhaps…well it might be an opportunity for you to…"

"No. I would not want to overwhelm them."

"As you say, sire." He heard the watch commander turn to his daughter. "Lady Cecilia, are you ready to…"

"Quite ready, yes." Janilah glanced back and saw her moving to the cordon of guards, smiling warmly, greeting a young family in a manner that he never could. “Now who’s this little beauty?” she asked, leaning down to a baby clutched in swaddling clothes in her mother’s arms. “So very pretty. What is her name?”

“Amilia, m’lady,” said the woman, in a nervous stutter of a voice. “After the princess. Or…or queen, I should say. We hope she’ll turn out as beautiful, we do.”

Her husband had his arm around the woman, Janilah saw, an underfed, gangly creature, with a pair of children huddled at their legs, a girl of six or seven and little boy of about three. Judging by their looks, the baby had no hope of becoming a beauty, but all the same Cecilia said, “Well now, little Amilia is as pretty as her namesake was at the same age. I remember it like it was yesterday; such a beautiful baby. I’m sure your sweet Amilia will be just as stunning when she grows older.” She gave husband and wife a smile, touched the baby’s cheek, and pulled from her pocket a little toy soldier, carved of wood, to hand to the little boy. And with that, she moved on.

Janilah left her to it. He could never stomach dealing with the commonfolk himself, and nor was he going to endure them today. He marched straight on, as Cecilia continued down the line of peasants and labourers, tradesmen and tavern-wenches, anyone who’d managed to get themselves to the front of the queue. He heard a man chuckling, a child giggling, and a baby squeaking excitedly, and knew that Cecilia was doing her job well.

And now comes my turn.

He strode up onto the stage with Lord Trillian Morwood trailing just behind him. Sir Owen and Sir Kevyn followed, taking position several paces to his flanks. Sir Edwyn and Sir Mallister remained within the ring of guards surrounding the stage, at ground level. Janilah turned his eyes around, and for a moment he marvelled at how many had come. He couldn’t have known it when entering the square, but now he could see that the many streets leading off it were teeming as well. That children were climbing the perimeter statues and trees. That the balconies of the merchant houses and taverns were full as well. And the roofs. Those too had assumed a full complement of people in many cases, where access was possible. There were thousands, many thousands come to see him speak.

Yet still, that odd silence persisted. It was as though all the world was waiting with bated breath to see if the rumours were true. Is he mad? Will he say something crazed? Will he admit to killing kings and princes, to the foul murder of his own son? And that was the truth of it, Janilah knew. *They have come to hear me confess. They want to hear me admit to being the tyrant and monster they think me to be.*

He cleared his throat. The sound was unusually loud, given the queer stillness all about him. Down the tunnel of guards, Cecilia was still moving along, laughing in her tittering way, interacting with her audience. It was a strange pocket of life within a great barren world of silence. *Even their clothes seem drab and colourless,* Janilah thought, taking in the great mass of people. *And their faces, those most of all.* All was grey and cold and featureless to his eyes. He spanned his gaze across the ocean of blank faces, raised his voice and said in a ringing voice, "Good people of Tukor, *my* people. I have come here today to speak of...."

"*Murderer*!" someone bellowed.

Janilah swung his eyes right. A thick murmuring gave out through the people there, spreading. "Who said that?" he demanded. He could not help himself. "Who calls me murderer? Speak up! Show me who said it so I might answer him."

"*Scum*!"

This voice was left of him. His eyes spun there, searching, narrowing.

"Scum!" it said again. A woman, wide-eyed and wild-haired, a vagrant or beggar by her ragged rotten dress, was staring right up at him from a dozen rows back. "Scum!" she repeated. "*Scum, scum, scum!*"

Janilah did not need to give a command for several of the city watchmen to begin barging their way forward. Some of the crowd parted, others stood their ground and got cudgels to the head for their trouble. Several fell bleeding. The rest slinked back, though not by much, as the guards pressed through and took hold of the woman. She continued to shriek and blare, "Scum, scum, scum!" even as they laid hands on her.

Lord Morwood was at Janilah's side. "Sire, show mercy, I beg you. She is clearly a raving lunatic. Do not act rashly or we'll have a riot on our hands."

Janilah's hands were curled into fists. He could feel a vein of fury throbbing on the side of his head, his weakened, ravaged heart pumping wildly. *I will have her head off,* he thought to himself. *But later. I''ll have her tracked and taken later.* "Men, be easy with her!" his voice rang out. "She is cold and in poor health. Be gentle. Do not harm her."

Lord Morwood's advice was well judged. *He knows these people better than I,* Janilah thought, as a murmur of confused approval began to hum. They seemed surprised by his sudden show of clemency; their king was not known as a merciful man.

The woman was still shrieking, though, and trying to get others to join in. "Scum!" came that awful shrieking voice, all rotten and diseased. "King Scum and the Bastard Bitch! The Witch of Blakewood! Witch! Bitch! *Witch!*"

The woman's attention seemed to have turned to Cecilia, who was still between the cordon of guards, watching with a curious look on her face. An amused look, Janilah saw. "I do believe this woman is in need of a lie down," she declared. And then came the laughter. It started among those whom she'd already spoken to, spreading like wildfire out through the thong. Cecilia unleashed her most charming of grins. "Do take her away so we can hear the voice of our king. A soft hand over the mouth should quieten her."

One of the guards did just that, clamping his palm over the beggar's mouth, then yelping and drawing it back as she bit him. Janilah saw a flash of red, and a flash of rage, then a swinging fist and the woman was down.

"Now calm, *calm!*" bellowed Watch Commander Morwood, speeding to that side of the stage as a jostling anger began to boil. "Do not react in haste, this woman deserved it. Who here has the right to scream *scum* at a king? And such a woman as this? I ask you, who!"

"The king killed his own son!" This voice was a man's again, somewhere to the right. Janilah found him, a well-built brute of thirty-odd with the look of a labourer with little to lose. "Sounds like scum t'me!"

"A baseless charge," called out Morwood, striding stockily back across the stage, cape flowing, as the woman was dragged off and forgotten. "The rumours you have all heard spoken in tavern and square are false, vile slanders dreamt up by the king's enemies and rivals. Who here, I ask you, was there to witness how the prince died?" When no answer came, Morwood gave a victorious nod. "Now our king is not here to answer these false accusations, but to speak to you of your troubles and the latest goings-on…"

"Our troubles?" barked a woman. "Janilah Lukar ain't never cared none for our troubles!"

Agreement rumbled through the vast assemblage, and then a thousand voices seemed to call out, one after another after another.

"The king never cared for us!"

"He ain't come here in years!"

"It's his own legend what he cares for, not us!"

Janilah heard one man jest loudly about the king deigning to walk into the square, rather than 'riding in on his high horse'. Another was calling up at Sir Owen Armdall, a cadaverous pole of a creature pointing up at the knight with a shivering finger. "He slew Rylian, *that one*! The Oak o' Armdall. We demand his head for the prince's murder! Someone needs to pay!"

Sir Owen Armdall was not a man to be taunted, prideful as he was. He drew his blade at once and took two short paces across the platform. "I acted only to protect my king from a man who tried to take his throne. Anyone says otherwise will taste my steel!"

"*I* say otherwise, Oak!" screeched the old man. "Or didn't you hear me?"

Sir Owen looked set to vault off the stage before Sir Kevyn rushed over to restrain him. The noise was thickening now, the throng brimming and boiling over. Cecilia came sweeping up the short flight of stairs to the stage. "Father, this is all wrong. It feels dangerous. We should leave…"

"There she is, the Bastard Bitch of Blakewood, whispering orders in his ear!"

Janilah's patience had reached its limit. "Who said that!" He whirled, but it might have been anyone. All about him was jostling and movement and a rising, dangerous din. He caught sight of steel, flashing against the sun, blunted dull iron, hardened wooden mallets and bats. A hundred weapons seemed to have emerged from cloaks and scabbards. *A trap*, he thought. *Someone has set me up…*

"Father! We *have* to leave! They're not going to listen to…" Something red and rotten exploded against the side of Cecilia's face, pulp and pips flying. She yelped and reeled, running her hand against her cheek in shock, as a second tomato plunged itself into her chest. Janilah got the splash-back, chunks of putrid mulch flying into him. He spun in search of the culprit, bellowing for him to be taken, but just as he opened his mouth to convey the command, a volley of rotting fruit and vegetables came raining.

He swung his cloak to defend against the assault, but came away sticky and stinking all the same. There was dung in the volley, he could smell it, ripe and wet and more was coming. For a moment he could scarcely see for the sudden barrage. A small sharp stone pinged against his cheek, just missing his eye, cutting him. A hot handful of manure caught him square in the jaw, sticking to his beard. He heard laughter at that, loud and taunting, but there were panicked voices too, high-pitched wails and screaming. He reached to his eyes, wiped to clear his vision of the filth, and saw the soldiers of the City Watch surging into the crowds, commanded by the bellowing voice of Lord Morwood. At once half of those throwing fruit reached into their cloaks and pulled out weapons instead. The clash of blade and axe erupted, dirks stabbing, cudgels swinging. About the defensive cordon of guards, all shattered into a sudden and bloody maelstrom of violence.

A hand grabbed him by the arm. "Sire, we must go." Sir Mallister Monsort had climbed the stage to join him, his blade to grasp, misting. At the foot of the stage, Sir Edwyn Huffort was blaring at some men to stay back as they battled to get through the cordon. To no surprise, Sir Owen Armdall had begun carrying out his threat, carving his way through the crowd as men charged at him with blade and axe. A handful were already dead that Janilah could see, though they continued to come at him heedless, as Sir Kevyn Bolt surged to join him. "Sire!" shouted Sir Mallister. "My lord, we must…"

The young knight broke off, eyes jerking aside as he spotted a breach in the line. A cluster of armed men broke through, barging the guards aside, stabbing, shoving their way toward the stage. The first to begin scrambling up was caught in the throat by Sir Mallister's swing, his longsword slicing clean and true and toppling the man back down into his companions, blood showering from his neck. A second was killed with a swift thrust to the heart. Then Sir Mallister turned, hurried back to Janilah's side, grabbed his arm once more, leading him sharply away.

Janilah Lukar let himself be led. Above the wild chaos spreading around him he could hear something greatly more arresting; those whispers in his head. *Kill them,* the voice said, *kill them all, kill them all…*

His hand went into his cloak, taking the hilt of his blade.

Ahead he could see Cecilia between her two bastard Blackshaw guards, Hog and Gerret, the pair hauling her to safety. But already the surge of men had began to press back the cordon, breaking it apart, overwhelming the men of the watch. What had been a wide open tunnel through the square was now peppered with men, scuffling and fighting and rioting, not only commoners on guards, but commoner on commoner too, a wild crazed free-for-all that had seemed to explode from nowhere.

And through it all the voice was speaking to him, *kill them all, kill them all,* and he found that he was nodding. *I will never win them over,* he thought. *I'll be the monster, then.*

He turned and pushed Sir Mallister aside. "Go, Sir Mallister, leave me." His voice was eerily calm. "I do not need your protection."

"Sire? I am sworn to protect you by oath."

"You are sworn to obey my command. Leave me. Get Lord Morwood out of here. And my daughter. See that she is safely back to the palace."

"Sire, no, I cannot…"

Janilah turned from him, facing a sudden onrush of men, bursting through the line of guards. Already he could sense Sir Mallister being caught up in his own battles, as more men pressed forward, utterly bloodlusted. *A trap,* Janilah thought again. *These men are too well organised, too well-armed. Someone set me up to die here today.*

Yet he smiled, and slid the Mistblade from its scabbard. The Mistblade, that he'd planned to unveil to his people, along with the secrets he'd long protected. "I have been trying to gather the Five Blades," he would have declared. "I have come upon a secret, a secret to winning the war. Those blades are the key, and only I can wield them. Do you want to win the War Eternal? Do you want to make this world of ours a paradise, free of the scourge of the south?"

He had anticipated the cheers, the rising rapture, the great crashing waves of joy. To be loved, and respected, and feared all at once. *But no,* he thought now, as he faced the charging men. *It is only their fear I need.*

He lifted the Mistblade to his side, let its power rush through him, bone and body and blood all. His form rippled, fading, a shimmering blue translucence, intangible and incorporeal.

Invulnerable.

Three men reached him at once, stabbing wildly, thrusting, pouncing like beasts. But their blades had no effect. The steel of sword and dagger moved through him as though he were air, leaving wispy trails of swirling cobalt mist as they drove futilely in and out, in and out...

And Janilah waited. He stood still, Mistblade puffing soft at his side, eager for blood, eager for death, whispering. *Kill them all. Kill them all. Kill them all,* it said.

Janilah Lukar nodded. He looked into the eyes of the men around him, as their blades stilled, as they drew back, as the realisation dawned. And then he saw it, those eyes he craved to see. The abject fear. The horror. And he smiled, broad and wild, and took a slow step forward.

I'll be the monster, then, he thought, as he swung, and swung, and swung…

17

Cecilia

She peeled a small chunk of skull from her shoulder, flicking it onto the stone floor at her feet. "Water," she commanded. "I need to wash. Right now." A maid hurried off to complete the task, looking horrified at the state of her.

Understandable, Cecilia thought. She and her men were caked in blood and muck and worse, leaving filthy tracks wherever they walked following their mad dash from the square. Beyond Galin's Post, the rioting and reckless bloodshed had continued, though there the soldiers were able to drive back the maddened horde and bring horses for her and her escort to mount. She had delayed not a second in riding up the city levels, through White Shadow and Many Markets, the Sentinels and the Marble Steps, returning to the safe haven of the palace.

The maid hurried back through carrying a pail of fresh water. "Set it down there," Cecilia commanded. The girl did as ordered, then scurried off again looking pale. Even from up here, the distant din of wails and screams and frenzied fighting could be heard from far below.

Sir Mallister stepped through into the room, his triple-coloured mantle only one colour now - red. "My lady, I should return below, see what I can do to help."

Cecilia peeled out of her horribly soiled cloak. The fur was sable, hugely expensive, but there would be no recovering it now. She tossed it aside, reaching down to pick up a sponge from the bucket. "Of course, Sir Mallister. Thank you for seeing me safely home."

He nodded. "Your father ordered as such, my lady." The knight glanced to Hog and Gerret. "Can I speak freely, Lady Blakewood?"

"Of course. Never mind these two."

Sir Mallister nodded. "Your father. I was certain I saw him draw…" He paused, as though struggling to believe what he'd witnessed, but Cecilia had a sense she knew already. "He drew the Mistblade from his sheath, my lady. I saw him…shimmering, *fading*. There were men all around him, hacking and slashing but he stood there perfectly still, unharmed it looked. I was trying to get to him, to protect him, but then…but then he started…swinging, my lady. That's when I lost him in the crowd, and fought my way to you."

And so it begins, Cecilia thought, trying to picture the image. Her father, wanton and enraged, cleaving men apart. *I wonder how many he has killed by now? There will be no turning back from this…*

"My lady?" Sir Mallister's eyes had contorted into a pained frown. "Please tell me I was not seeing things. I have sworn to protect your father by oath and…to think that I failed him so soon…to think that he might be…be dead."

Dead, she thought. *We can but hope…* "You weren't seeing things," she told him. "My father has the Mistblade, yes, and well mastered. He will not be so easily overcome."

"But…" Sir Mallister filled his lungs, gave his head a swift shake. "The Mistblade has been missing for decades. Centuries. How is it that he has it?"

"I think that is rather unimportant right now, Sir Mallister. Please, don't let me keep you. Go, see to your duty. And find out what has happened to Sir Owen, Sir Kevyn, and Sir Edwyn as well. We can ill afford to lose another of the Six right now."

Sir Mallister nodded. "As you say, my lady." His mantle refused to perform its usual swish as he turned and sped off, heavy as it was with blood and grime.

Cecilia returned to her bucket, soaking the sponge, running it across her face. It came back red and brown, stinking of iron and shit and rotting fruit.

Gerret made a whistling sound through his teeth. "So…the Mistblade, huh? I didn't know your father had it, m'lady."

"Well you know now," she said.

"Aye, along with the whole city." He pulled a cloth from his leathers, and began cleaning one of his dirks - Gerret had many little knives hidden in pockets about his person, some godsteel, some not. "Sir Edwyn's dead, I reckon," he added with an air of casualness.

Cecilia turned to him sharply. "*Dead*? What do you mean, dead?"

"Dead, m'lady." The young sellsword shrugged. "Not sure how else to put it."

"*How*? I didn't see anything."

"Well, I only caught a glimpse, I'll admit, but didn't look so good from where I was standing. Men were pouring through a breach in the line of guards, surging over the top of him, stabbing and pulling him down and such." He shrugged again. "Those fancy dual blades of his didn't count for much then, did they?"

Cecilia shook her head. It was no way for a knight to die, and Sir Edwyn had always been one of the more decent of her father's Six. "That's terrible," was all she could summon. "I pray you saw wrong, Gerret."

"Beggin' your pardon, m'lady, but prayin' is for fools." He glanced up. "Who exactly do you expect to answer. All the gods are dead, or so I hear."

"It's a figure of speech," she said. "Hog, what's happening down there?"

The bigger and older of her bodyguards was at the window, staring out, his great bloody battle-axe fixed between his shoulder blades. "Smoke," he grunted. "There're fires breaking out, all across White Shadow it looks."

It didn't surprise her. Men would often start fires during riots in order to conceal what they were doing, and confuse the soldiers trying to bring everything back into order. She had no doubt that there would be a great deal of murdering and raping and looting going on in White Shadow right now. Even those who had no part in the outbreak of the violence would seek to take advantage while they could.

She heard the sound of footsteps rushing down the corridor, the scuff of leather and clank of steel. A moment later the door was being pushed open and Prince Raynald appeared, several of his personal guards behind him. "Stay here," he commanded them, stepping right in through the door. "Auntie, I heard what happened…." He rushed over to her, giving her a swift look up and down. "Gods, you're covered in blood. You're not injured, are you?"

He's a sweet boy, Cecilia thought. *Sweet and tractable.* "I'm unhurt, Raynald," she assured him. "Don't worry, it isn't my blood."

"And Grandfather?"

"He remained below," she told him. She cared not to elaborate on that until she knew more, or make mention of the Mistblade. That would reach the boy's ears soon enough.

"But he's safe?"

"I should think so, yes. He has plenty of protection. Things got a little out of hand, but it shan't take long to regain control of the streets. He'll be fine."

"I should have been there," Raynald berated himself. He marched to the window, Hog stepping dutifully aside as he came. "There's smoke down there. My gods, what are they doing, burning down their own city? It's madness!"

"We all got a bit of madness in us, young princeling," Hog said. "Men like to start burning things when they get wild."

Raynald looked up at the sellsword with a frown, as though barely aware of his presence. "You're my auntie's bodyguard, aren't you?"

"I am. Along with that skinny sapling over there with the crooked nose." He gestured to Gerret, perched on the edge of a table, dirk in hand. Even without the blood and gore on them, the pair carried a dangerous air.

Raynald gave both men a quick study. "Then I thank you for seeing her safely back to the palace. Are you men knights?"

They laughed. "Us? No, my lord."

"Well, perhaps you will be after this," Raynald declared. He turned and began making for the door.

"Where are you going?" Cecilia asked him.

"Down. I should see what's happening. They may need my voice in command. I only came to see that you were all right, Auntie."

She stepped to block him off. "Raynald, your grandfather wanted you here for a reason. It isn't safe down there."

"Safe?" Raynald looked utterly indignant. "You forget I am my father's son. Do you think he would have been worried about a few lowborn barbarians? Gods no. I'm going…"

"*Raynald.* Your father is dead, Raynald."

He stopped, turning to her, frown deeply etched on his brow. "I know, Auntie," he said. "You think I don't know that?"

I must deal with this lightly, she thought. "Your father is dead," she repeated, more tenderly. "And your grandfather…after today, who knows what state he'll be in. With the good grace of the gods, he will return to us unharmed, and continue to reign long and true, but we have to consider the other tracks that lead from this crossroad. Your grandfather is not well, Ray. Not so much as he makes out. He has suffered much, through the death of your father, through the stresses he has carried upon his back, the great weight of leading a kingdom, a continent, of juggling all these squabbling kings and lords. Understand, he has done his best. He has tried all along to do what is right. You will I'm sure have heard otherwise. Awful rumours, born of envy and greed, by those who should wish to undermine him. Ignore them, if you can. Always believe your grandfather a good man."

Raynald nodded silently. The crease between his eyes was shallowing. "What are you saying, Auntie?"

She sighed dispiritedly and shook her head. "I'm saying we cannot know what will come of the king now. He may be injured, or worse, gods forbid. Even if not, all this…this will wound him greatly. He anticipated a day of triumph and look what has happened. All has soured to tragedy. It might be enough to force your grandfather to rethink things. To step back, even, and abdicate…"

"*Abdicate*? No, he would never."

"I hope not. We *all* hope not, of course. But we must consider it a possibility, should his physical state worsen. And…and his *mental* state, Raynald. Now this is not for sharing, you understand? What I say to you, you are not to repeat."

"Of course not, Auntie."

She smiled. "Such a good boy." But that was risking crossing a line, she saw. *He does not wish to be called boy any more.* "You are growing into a wise young prince, Raynald," she told him, subtly shifting the tone of her voice. "And a fearsome swordsman, as brave and gallant as your father. These are qualities that men follow. Honesty. Probity. Duty. Honour. You possess them all. All marks of a good leader. All features of a great king."

"*King*," the boy repeated, in a whisper, and Cecilia watched his eyes, watched the soft gentle twist of his lips as they quickened into a smile and then flattened in an instant. "I cannot be king, Auntie. Even if grandfather should…" He shook his head. "Robbert is heir."

"Robbert is at war, Raynald. We cannot know what will happen to him. You must be prepared."

A silence clad the room. She saw the worry curdle in the young prince's eyes, the worry for the welfare of his twin, and yet…and yet, there was something else in there too. A knowledge that his brother's fall would raise him to heir. He pondered that for just a moment, before checking himself, and shaking his head in brisk denial. "Rob will be fine. He's a born fighter, like me. No Sunrider or Starrider will be a match for him."

Cecilia nodded her agreement. "I'm sure you're right. But it is always wise to consider all ends. It is hard for you, I know. You were born mere minutes after Robbert and yet those minutes count for so much. The notion that you might become king one day…well, I'm sure you never thought that possible. But it *is* possible, Raynald. Some might even say it is *likely* now."

The boy nodded with an air of solemn duty. "I…I suppose," he said, with a tone of mild reluctance. "But Sir Elyon…he has taken well to it, becoming heir to his father's lordship, and heir to the throne, many think. I will do the same, Auntie. I will not let anyone down, if…if the worst should happen."

Cecilia nodded. She didn't much like the mention of Elyon Daecar, though had to admit, the boy had built a certain mystique about him that had people rushing to his side. He had reached Dragon's Bane now, she'd heard, and was being proclaimed the true Prince of Vandar by the likes of Lord Kanabar and Rikkard Amadar and all the lords and knights under their wing. Even Killian Oloran was putting his word and weight behind the boy. *That will displease old King Godrik Taynar greatly*, she mused. If it came to war in Vandar, he would be hoping for Oloran support. Without it, well, his throne would be as good as lost.

She took Raynald's hand, squeezing his palm. "I'd best continue washing, sweet prince." She smiled. "If you do wish to leave the palace, take your guards with you, and go only as far as the Sentinels. The gate commanders will be able to tell you what is happening. You can await the return of your grandfather there."

The young prince nodded. "I will do that, Auntie." He turned and left the room.

Once gone, Cecilia picked up her sponge and gave herself a final wipe down, cleaning the blood from her hands. Gerret laughed behind her. "You're a devious one, m'lady. Making yourself a little king there, are we?"

"Just passing on words of advice," she said. "It pays to prepare the boy, Gerret. Denying the possibility of his kingship will not help him, should it come to that."

"Aye, and this one's all wrapped around your little finger." Gerret made that whistling sound through his missing tooth. "Now that's a powerful plaything, m'lady."

She allowed a smile, but gave no response.

"Smoke's getting thicker," grunted Hog, still at the window. "Looks like half of White Shadow is going up in flames."

Cecilia strode over to join him, tossing the filthy sponge back into the bucket. Down in the city's lower reaches plumes of thick black smoke were reaching like monstrous dead fingers to scratch at the belly of the sky. A great many highborn folk had emerged from their homes to watch from the bridges and streets of the Marble Steps. "It's worse than I thought," she said.

Cecilia was still looking out upon the rising black plumes when a shuffle of feet announced the arrival of old Archibald Benton. He had a distinctive gait, slow and ponderous. She didn't need to turn to know it was him. "Yes, Archibald?"

"My lady," he said. "I came to see how you are. The news…from below…I cannot believe it…Sir Edwyn dead? And…and Sir Bonmer Marsh as well, I've been told…such a tragedy. Awful. Just awful."

"Seems you were right about Sir Edwyn, Gerret," Cecilia said. She turned to the Master of Messages. "I didn't know about Sir Bonmer. What happened to him?"

"Disemboweled, I'm told, ripped apart by the mob." Archibald shuddered, nervously tugging at his wispy white beard. "And Sir Edwyn….another of the Six, *slain.* Do the people not realise we are at war? We need every man. *Every man*, my lady." He went so far as to stamp his foot, in a show of anger, though it was rather feebly done.

Cecilia felt obliged to cross the room and fill the old man a cup of strong spiced wine to steady him. "Here, this will settle your nerves."

He took it up gratefully, a few droplets of red inking into his beard as he drank, old hand shivering all the while. "My thanks, my lady. I feel…I feel I needed that." He looked into her cool green eyes. "Your father…I heard that…that he…that he was caught up in it all as well. You don't think…oh goodness, you don't think he could be dead too, do you?"

You'd like that, wouldn't you, old man, she thought. Archibald Benton was one of many who lived in fear of Janilah Lukar's wrath, ever since his failure to extract anything of worth from the Book of Thala.

No matter that he'd served the king for nigh on four decades, he still felt himself expendable, with an invisible noose ever around his neck. *And I know how you feel, Archibald. We all walk a fine line now, so long as the king draws breath.*

She turned from the thought, brightening her face with a smile. "My father will be fine," she made herself say. "He had the Mistblade with him, Archibald."

Benton's white eyebrows tugged together. "Oh." He seemed somewhat disappointed, it had to be said. "I say that was unwise, Lady Cecilia. Your father…we know how…how vulnerable he is becoming to its…its lure. With all these setbacks, and…" He glanced at Gerret and Hog, suddenly worried he was speaking out of turn.

Cecilia understood his concern. "You can speak freely here, Archibald. Nothing you say will go beyond this room."

"Yes, my lady. I am just…I am most concerned for your father's wellbeing, is all I mean to say. And after this…after today…the Mistblade…" He muttered a few more words, shaking his head, then looked back up into her eyes. "You don't think he would have…*used* it, do you?"

Cecilia poured a cup of wine, taking a much needed sip of the warm, spicy liquid. "I'm afraid to say he has. Sir Mallister says he saw him with it. *Swinging*, Archie. Killing."

The poor old fool looked so pitifully pained by that news. "A tragedy twice over, then," he moaned. "Soon everyone will know he has the blade. The Vandarians will demand it back. They'll…they'll condemn him for keeping it so long. Goodness me, *why*? Why would he dream of taking it with him down there? We know how unhinged he can become when near it. And on his person? That was madness, my lady. Utter madness."

"Madness has been creeping up on the king for some months, Archibald. Those of us who share his counsel know that well enough." *And now the city will see it too,* she thought to herself. *They will see him for what he is.*

She drew on her wine again, neglecting to tell the old scholar of her own part in it. That she'd been the one to persuade her father to take the Mistblade with him. That she'd urged him to unburden himself of his secrets, share the truth of his plot with the world. It said much about him that he'd agreed to go along with that. It made plain enough how desperate he was, how deluded, even, that he would think any good could come of it. *And yet I urged it,* she thought. *I have shown the world the monster's true face.*

"I saw Prince Raynald leaving from this way," Archibald went on. There was something in his eyes, something unexpectedly conspiratorial. "The boy…he is of the malleable sort, I think. Young and impressionable. Mouldable, shall we say. And…uncorrupted."

Cecilia smiled. "Careful, Archibald. One might mistake this talk for treason."

A sheen of sweat shimmered on the old man's forehead. His crow-foot birthmark looked especially red and harsh today, she thought. "No. I am merely thinking ahead, is all. And I'm sure…well I'm sure you're doing the same, my lady. Do not think I haven't seen you spending time with the boy, since his father's death."

The old creature had a backbone, it would seem. "I am but a softhearted auntie, comforting a nephew in his grief," she told him. "A nephew who, it just so happens, has seen his position elevated these last months, and may continue to do so still. I consider it my duty to help prepare him for all possible eventualities. Do not read anything more into it, Archibald. I warn you, do not."

The old scholar quailed a little, drawing back. "No, of…of course not. A softhearted auntie, offering comfort. And a wise hand, to help guide the boy. Yes, this is your intent. I know that, my lady."

Perhaps I was wrong about that backbone, she thought.

"But I…I do wonder about…well, about *others,*" the bent-backed scholar went on. "Do you not think that someone might have…have arranged what happened today?"

"And just who do you think might have arranged it, Archibald?"

He shook his head in a most hurried fashion. "Oh, I couldn't possibly say, my lady. No. It's just…well, the king has made enemies of late. I hope I am not crossing a line by…by saying that."

"I have told you already that you can speak freely here."

"Yes, my lady. I wonder then if these commoners shouting slurs…these disgraceful boors throwing fruit and dung...these armed savages…I wonder if they were planted there. By one of the king's enemies. Someone who was close with Prince Rylian, perhaps. Who still believes the awful lie that your father had something to do with his death."

"That does not narrow down the list," Cecilia said calmly. "There were many who loved Rylian, and many who have grown to hate my father. It is a list without end, Archibald."

"Yes, Lady Cecilia, I see what you're saying. Yet…would it not be wise to seek the truth of it? You have your…your *spies*. Perhaps they might help unearth the information we need. It might help us assuage your father when he returns, should we be able to hand him a culprit. Someone to…to blame."

Cecilia liked the thought of that. *Yes, very good, old man,* she thought. *Someone to blame.* "I'll send out my spiderlings," she told him, "have them skitter down my web. They're terribly good at getting lost in crowds, at listening from the shadows. If there has been some conspiracy here, they will find out for me."

The old man looked satisfied by that. He breathed out a sigh of relief, nodding, then set down his wine. "Then I shall leave you, my lady, to wash and change. I shall have word brought to you immediately should there be any news of your father."

"Please do, Archibald," she said.

And let it be bad news, she thought.

18

Jonik

"Merrymarsh, you say? Lady Kathryn Merrymarsh?" The young Suncoat looked bemused. "But she's dead, my lord. A dozen years now, if memory serves…"

"Missing, not dead," corrected Sir Borrus Kanabar. "And now found, as you can see." He gestured to the old-before-her-time figure of Lady Kathryn, furled in a large woollen cloak. From the folds of her hood a gaunt and seamed face gazed out, the shadow of mania still etched in the hollow depths of her eyes, hair withered and lank. The woman whom Ranulf Shackton had christened the 'Moaning Maid' didn't moan so much anymore, but retained something of a skittish, mumbly countenance. She had been in their care for over a month now, however, and had emerged from her shell enough to speak with an occasional cognisance.

"He says it true," she declared in a scratchy, brittle voice. "I am the…the Lady Kathryn of House Merrymarsh, beloved sister of…of the Lord Humphrey Merrymarsh of Calmwater. Returned, at last… to make my home again in my brother's halls."

"Well then, it is most wonderful to have you back, my lady." The young Suncoat didn't seem entirely convinced, but who was he to deny her word, or that of a man like Sir Borrus Kanabar? "And you as well, my lord. I find myself staggered to see you here, I will confess. You are thought to be slain. Executed in Eldurath, they say. For colluding to murder King Dulian."

"And you bloody believed that, did you?" Borrus was wearing the best leathers and furs they could find for him, and had Red Wrath at his hip, should anyone doubt who he was. "My gods, man, as if the Agarathi could kill *me*. Don't believe all you've heard, Sir Finlay. Just be a good lad, and arrange us an escort to take us to Lord Merrymarsh's keep. And these ships…" He thumbed behind him, where both Invincible Iris and One World were docked either side of a broad stone wharf. "You needn't bother searching them. We mean only to disembark a few of our companions and we'll be on our way."

"My lord. I hope you know that I have a duty to search all ships that dock here. It is war, Sir Borrus. I'm sure you understand."

"Oh I know a bit about war, Sir Finlay, believe me. And that duty of yours is decreed by Lord Merrymarsh, whom I am certain will not want the return of his beloved sister delayed by even a second. Now come, get that escort arranged. You can leave a few guards to keep watch on our ships while we're gone, if you're that worried."

The Suncoat had no option but to acquiesce. He ushered over one of his men, passed on instructions, and then turned back to Sir Borrus. "These companions of yours you wish to disembark? Who are they, exactly?"

"Rasal nationals whom we intend to see returned to their homes, same as Lady Kathryn. They were all captives of a Piseki warlord named Pal Palek. We freed them from his compound outside Sutrek."

"Sutrek?" The man sounded appropriately astonished. "What were you doing there, Sir Borrus?"

"I just told you. Freeing these poor northerners from a bloody grim fate. You may wonder why Lady Kathryn looks so frail. Well, a dozen years in a dungeon will just about do it, Sir Finlay. We have others who have suffered similarly." He raised a large palm, as Sir Finlay's mouth opened to speak. "Now enough questions. I'll have the patients disembarked and leave it to you to see them safely home. They're in your care now, Sir Finlay."

"*My* care? My lord, you cannot expect me to…"

"We'll tell you who they are, and where you're to deliver them. All you'll need to do is arrange their safe return to their own lands. It shouldn't prove difficult. Jack here has all the information you'll need." He turned his head. "Jack, come on over."

Jack o' the Marsh extracted himself from the group standing on the wharf and strode dutifully over to Sir Borrus's side. "My lord."

Borrus gave the burly Marshlander a hearty slap on the shoulder. "This amiable chap here is Jack, Sir Finlay. He'll explain everything. You have your notes, Jack?"

Jack nodded. "I do, Sir Borrus." He held them up. "Right here."

"Good. Then I'll leave you two to get acquainted."

Borrus moved back down the grey stone jetty, Invincible Iris docked on one side, One World the other. The harbour beyond wasn't so busy as they'd feared, with the Rasal fleet so spread. Some had gone south with the Tukoran armada, ferrying troops for the siege of Eagle's Perch. Others were in the Red Sea in support of the Vandarians, or at anchorage at Doublebay Harbour, which was better placed strategically to defend against a southern invasion. Many more were patrolling the coast. They'd managed to avoid any unnecessary attention during their journey through Whaler's Bay, passing Doublebay Harbour only the night before. It was a dark and cloudy evening, but even so, the great forest of masts and huge silhouettes of warships could be seen crowding the port. Mercifully, Calmwater was much less busy. Their arrival had thus been as streamlined and uneventful as Jonik could have hoped.

"Well then, that's sorted," Borrus Kanabar said to the group. "I told you it would go easy with me doing the talking, Manfrey."

Emeric smiled handsomely. "I never doubted you, Borrus. This Sir Finlay. You know him?"

"I know his father. Lord Ferry Maynard."

"The Oakenlord," said Emeric.

"The very one."

"Why's he called that?" Brown Mouth Braxton wanted to know. "He strong, is he? Strong as an oak?"

"He's strong enough," Borrus told him. "But no, it's for his seat of Oakshore, bordered by the Oakenwood to the north and south. Sir Finlay's his eldest son. I'm sure I've met him before, but…" He shrugged. "Well I'm drunk half the time, as you know. He seems to remember me, though."

"And lucky for us he recognised you, even so damn skinny as you are." Captain Turner laughed through the twisting hairs of his flax-coloured beard. His stained tan coat was flapping in the gentle breeze. "Suppose we ought to get these patients off, then. Master Rose, they're aboard your ship. Lead the way."

Vincent Rose was dressed in typically flamboyant fashion, with high red leather boots, a maroon tunic trimmed with gold, and a thick bear-fur cloak to shield him from the fierce cold. "Of course, Captain." He smiled in that thin, snide way of his and began up the ramp onto One World, Turner following along with young Devin, gangly Grim Pete, dark-eyed Cabel and grim old Harden of the Ironmoors. Jonik went with them, keen to be seen as nothing but a lowly deckhand here, dressed in sailor garb of wools and waterproofs and knitted cap to contain the long waves of his unruly black hair.

The rest of the patients were disembarked from their private rooms and the communal quarters below decks, led down the ramp in a convoy of wan and frightened faces, blinking against the harsh glare of pale sunlight. Several of them broke down, weeping uncontrollably to see the harbour walls of Calmwater again, look upon the city beyond, hear the humming sounds of a thousand northern voices as the dockworkers and deckhands, sailors and seamen went about their work.

"It makes it all worthwhile, doesn't it?" said gruff old Harden. There was a mist in his eyes. "Poor bloody souls. Bet they never thought they'd see home again."

The patients were gathered on the docks. Sir Finlay Maynard looked upon them, one after another, his face swollen with pity. Jack stood beside him, explaining to the Suncoat who each was, and where they were to be taken. Sir Finlay's doubts were now gone. He nodded solemnly, smiled soothingly, and declared to one and all that they would be returned to their homes with all the haste he could summon. After that, the patients were ushered away to be housed somewhere safe until such arrangements could be made, Jack and Braxton and others who'd helped tend them saying their goodbyes. Some had once lived here in the south of Rasalan, around the cities of Whaler's Bay or down in Galaphan's Grounding in the southeastern tip. Yet others were to endure longer journeys, their former homes far to the north in Steelport or Bleakrock or even the great city of Thalan. One had even hailed from the island of Holashan, east of the northern coast. It would be down to Sir Finlay to decide whether the waters were safe to return them by sea, or take them overland by a longer and more arduous route.

For Jonik, it was a special moment. *A cleansing moment,* he thought, *for the stains upon my soul.*

The escort for Lady Kathryn comprised a dozen city soldiers, regular men without Bladeborn blood wearing the white, grey and purple colours of House Merrymarsh. Their sigil was a kraken, emerging from a frothing white Sea. His farewells completed, Jack o' the Marsh sidled up to Jonik's flank. "Brings back memories, doesn't it?" he said, gesturing to the banners hanging from the city walls, flapping heavily in the stiff winter breeze. "The kraken. I can still scarce believe what you did that day, Ghost."

"And I can scarce remember it," Jonik said. And that was true. The kraken had caught him with a strong swinging tentacle when it had retreated to the depths, tossing him across the decks and knocking him unconscious. The whole thing wasn't much more than a blur to him now. He'd heard Jack retell the tale enough, though. *And taking liberties with the truth,* he thought. All good storytellers had a habit of exaggerating.

Emeric strode over to join them, dressed in dark leathers and his worn green cloak. "You sure you won't come with us, Jonik?"

"It's best I remain here. If anyone should recognise me, it'll only cause problems."

Emeric nodded. "As you wish. We shan't be long, I wouldn't think. Hold the fort while we're gone."

The escort began moving off, the soldiers forming an honour guard around Lady Kathryn, who had been mounted upon a beautiful white palfrey to convey her through the city. Great snorting destriers had been brought forth to carry Sir Finlay and Sir Borrus, riding either side of her. Emeric moved to the rear, following behind afoot with Braxton, who had become Lady Kathryn's unlikely carer on the voyage, and was keen to see her safely to the keep.

The rest remained behind, idly hanging around on the wharf between the ships, playing dice on deck, or otherwise staying out of sight, as was the case with Sansullio and his Sunshine Swords and the others of southern heritage. Vincent Rose declared himself interested in sampling a favourite brothel of his. "I confess, I have grown rather bored of the twins these last weeks, magnificent though they are. Who would like to join me? There's a wonderful establishment a little way down the docks. The Leaping Eel, it's called. Good drinks. Better girls. And not nearly so rancid as you'd expect from a harbourside whorehouse."

"I'll go," Devin said at once. "I just...I don't have the coin, Master Rose."

"No, but *I* do." He smiled slyly. "Who else? My treat. I think we all deserve it, don't you, after so long at sea."

That summoned a little more interest. Grim Pete crept his way forward to join them, a gleam of anticipation in his eyes, followed by Cabel and Sir Lenard Borrington. Jonik found the latter's interest curious. "Weren't you drugged and captured from a brothel, Sir Lenard?" he asked him. "That's how you ended up in Pal Palek's pits in the first place, isn't it?"

"It was, my lord, yes it was. Demons I must banish. I cannot live in fear of brothels all my life."

Jonik had never heard such a pathetic excuse, but he wasn't going to condemn these men for their interest in womanly pleasures. *I have no right,* he told himself. *They are men with needs and can do as they please.*

"How about you, Jack?" Rose's plump lips curved into a smile. "The twins weren't to your tastes, I know, but maybe we'll find someone more suitable for you here. They have plenty of variety at the Leaping Eel, as I recall. Fat, thin, young, old, big breasted and small, girls and boys. They like to playact as well, oh yes. Highborn, low, queens and princesses from far and wide. There was one who was the spit of Princess Amilia Lukar, and would dress up in fine silks and satins, all umber and jade. I've never seen such a popular whore. Men were lining up to take her, and she did *not* come cheap." He grinned unpleasantly. "Oh, I do hope she's still there. I could do with ploughing a princess today."

Jack smiled politely. "I…think I'll stay here," he said. "I've never been one for paying for a woman's comforts, Master Rose."

"Oh I can quite imagine. A man so strapping as you…why should you need to?" Vincent Rose's beady little eyes glanced to Jonik. "And you, *my lord?* Oh no, of course. You do not lower yourself to that sort of thing, do you? You prefer a celibate existence, I hear."

Jonik felt his neck growing hot. The subject still made him uncomfortable. No immediate answer came to mind and Rose saw that as some victory.

"Well then," the merchant went on. "I shall take your silence to mean you'll remain here. As you wish." He turned to his bodyguard. "Harden, come along. I'll want you guarding the door."

Harden stared at him, feet fixed to the floor. "No."

Rose raised his eyes in amused disbelief. "No?" He laughed haughtily. "You forget you're in my employ, man. Now come. Don't make me ask you again."

"And don't make me tell you again, else I'll send you to that whorehouse of yours a eunuch."

Rose looked taken aback. "You'll…what? I pay you good coin to protect me, Harden. You cannot speak to me like that."

"I can speak to you however I want. I'm done with you, Rose. *Done*. No amount of coin will force me to spend another moment at your side."

"Am I such a damnably horrible master, Harden? Goodness, if I've done something to offend you…"

"Your mere presence offends me." Harden spat to the side. Jonik knew the old sellsword misliked his master, but not to this extent. "Tell me, Rose, how many times did you visit the patients during the voyage?"

"Well, I…"

"None," growled Harden. "They were nothing but cargo to you. You never went to any one of them. Not even Lady Kathryn. Not once. You don't even know their names, do you? You're a snake, soulless, and I hope you get what's coming to you."

"Well excuse me, but these patients are only here because I had the means to…"

"Money," broke in Harden. "So it's all about money. Is there anything else to you, Rose? Anything at all beneath those jewels and furs? And gods, don't get me started on how you dress. You're an insufferable attention-seeker, and look at you! Half the docks are giving you a glance, and why, I ask, when you're so frightened of the Warrior King, are you willing to garb yourself so ridiculously." Harden waved to Jonik. "The lad here had the good sense to dress drab, but *you*? No, you couldn't help yourself, could you? And you know who that puts in danger if you're recognised by one of Janilah's men? *Me*. Your bodyguard, who has no interest…none at all…in dying for the likes of you."

Vincent Rose's face was arranged into a horrible fixed smile. "Are you quite done, Harden?"

"With you, yes. Or haven't you been listening? I'm done." Harden rubbed his old callused hands together, right in Vincent Rose's face. "*Done*."

The merchant's smile held on tight. *One of his masks*, Jonik knew. "Good. Well then…" He turned to the others. "I think I need a good bit of comforting, after that." He let out a shaky laugh, and the others smiled uncomfortably. "Come along, then. It…isn't far."

The men shared doubtful glances, but as soon as Cabel started following the merchant, the rest were soon to follow. That was Cabel, though. Nothing seemed to faze the dark-eyed youth.

"That was quite…full-on, Harden," Jack said, once they were out of earshot, Rose marching, head held high, into the crowds along the docks.

"He deserved it," Harden came back. "He doesn't speak to you the way he does me, Jack. You're not in his employ. And you're not of highborn stock either. I may be bastard born, but I'm related to Lord Styron Strand all the same. Rose hates the lot of them, every noble house in the north. And gods if I'm not an easy target. But I've had enough of it. *Enough*!"

Jack put a strong hand on his shoulder. "What will you do now?" He glanced at Jonik. "We could still use you, Harden. I doubt we'll be able to pay as well as Rose, but…well, I'm sure we could rustle something up."

Harden snorted. "He never paid me so well as he claims. That's just Vincent Rose. The man's a bloody chaos of lies and deceits and you'd do well to get rid of him as soon as damn well possible. He'll lead us all ill one of these days, that I promise."

"I'd like nothing better," Jonik said. "But Emeric seems adamant we keep our promise. And if we lose Rose we lose Sansullio and his men. And Kazil as well, most likely. That's not something we can risk."

"Risk? If you ask me, it's a risk having Sansullio and his lot here at all. It's all fine when they're hidden below decks out of sight, but what about when you head inland from Blackhearth? That's a lot of land to cover before you get to the mountains, and you'd be crossing Kastor land as well. We know what they think of southerners, don't we? Soon as anyone spots them, you'll have a big problem on your hands. Every man at the nearest garrison will be mustered to hunt you down."

Jack was looking at Jonik with his eyebrows raised. "He does have a point, Ghost. I like Sansullio as much as the next man, but he and his men do stick out around here, same as we did in the south. And you remember that. Eyes on us everywhere we went. I'm not sure it's worth it."

"We need them," Jonik said, in a tone of mild frustration. "It'll be even colder in the north of Tukor, and we'll be dressed in cloaks and cowls. And we just passed the bulk of Kastor's army, don't forget. His lands will be quiet. It's a chance I'm willing to take."

"You might get lucky, you might not," Harden said grimly. "That's a choice you've got to make. But for my money, you'll want rid of Rose all the same. I'll do it for you, if you like."

"That would be murder, Harden. No."

"Fine. But about that coin? Find me a bit, and my sword is yours. Far as I figure, if we take the Shadowfort, there'll be no safer place in the world when the dragons come swarming. No doubt Rose thinks the same. Can't figure why else he'd want to go there, to be honest."

Jonik had wondered on that as well, but it seemed as good a reason as any. Vincent Rose was a born survivor, slimily attaching himself to those he believed to be strong, making favourable alliances, buying support and influence. It was reasonable to believe he wanted to find some safe and secure sanctuary to see out the war. And Harden had the truth of it. There would be no place safer than Ilith's ancient refuge. They just had to win it first.

"Well anyway, I'll leave that with you," Harden said, his breath fogging in the cold morning air. "Might be I can help track down a few more swords for you, either way." He looked around the docks. "Could have an ask around, if you like? Merchant houses and dock-side taverns are good places to start. You often find sellswords hanging around in those, waiting for the next merchant to con into hiring him." He shrugged. "Brothels too, to be fair. I met Rose in one of those, as it happens."

Jonik considered the old sellsword's proposal. "There's no harm in you asking, I suppose. Just be careful with what you reveal, Harden. Nothing about me or the Shadowfort."

"Hard to convince a man to sell you his sword if he doesn't know what the job is, Jonik. And they'd ask about coin as well, be sure of that."

"We'll figure that out if it comes to it. I'm hoping that Borrus will be willing to back us financially, if we have need of another patron. Just ask around, Harden, but do it discreetly. If there's anyone you judge as viable, maybe I'll agree to meet them."

"Right then." The old man nodded and stalked away, gaunt-faced and ghostly pale, fading into the docks.

"You really think Sir Borrus will fund us?" Jack asked. "He's never been sold on this quest, Ghost."

"He's starting to come around to it," Jonik told him. "And for all of Rose's wealth, we forget sometimes that Borrus is ten times as rich. He could give us an army if he really wanted."

"His *father* is ten times as rich," Jack corrected. "And *he* might not be so keen to back you. Wallis Kanabar is a known ally of the Daecars...."

"Yes, and Borrus Kanabar is one of my father's oldest friends. We have moved past that, Jack. There are bigger matters at play."

"For you, yes. Not everyone will see it like that should they spot you."

"I know. Why else do you think I'm wearing this damn hat?"

"Because you've finally made a fashion choice that isn't '*wear black*'?" Jack said, with a playful smile on his broad square face. "You know, I think it suits you, Ghost." He made to reach out and shift the hat's position a little, but Jonik swatted his hand aside. Jack laughed. "We'll have you dressing up like Rose soon. How about those high red boots of his? Red and black go well together, I've always thought. It would complement the Nightblade nicely."

"Not so loud." Jonik glanced around to check that the soldiers posted by Sir Finlay hadn't heard. His voice lowered on impulse to a hiss. "You want to give me away?" He decided it best to leave the docks at that, turning sharply away and climbing the ramp up onto the main deck of Invincible Iris, wood groaning underfoot. At the forecastle, the senior figures of Sir Torvyn and Sir Corbray were engaged in a bit of sparing, blunted steel clanging, as Soft Sid watched on with that big blank expression of his. Captain Turner was there too, playing dice with the Silent Suncoat. And losing, Jonik hoped. The Silent Suncoat was not a man you wanted to aggravate.

Jonik went straight to the quarterdeck at the other end of the ship, hoping Jack wouldn't follow. But of course he did. "Cross a line, did I?"

"No." Jonik stared out over the bustling port. He could see Harden disappearing into a tavern called the Whistling Whale, huddled beneath the city walls. He tried to find the Leaping Eel, but it could have been one of several dozen stubby buildings clustered around the docks.

"You know, you can make the word '*no*' seem awfully like the word '*yes*' sometimes." Jack smiled again, but it didn't last this time. "What's eating you, Jonik? I thought you'd be more relaxed once we reached the north. I mean, we can walk the harbour without everyone staring at us or wanting to kill us now. I'm not even worried that something will happen to the others. That's good, isn't it?"

It was, when put like that. But a part of Jonik had dreaded this.

"The people didn't know me in the south. They heard the names, but they didn't really care. Here, they care." He looked out and sighed. "They hate me here, Jack. And they have every right to do so."

"They don't know you, Ghost. It doesn't matter what they think."

"Maybe," Jonik whispered.

"Definitely," Jack said. "Look at how far you've come. Look how many people follow you now. Turner, Braxton, me, Devin, Grim, Sid. Emeric Manfrey, who's about the most honourable man in the world, and isn't that saying something? And you know what says even more? The fact that Borrus Kanabar, who should by all rights loathe you… and even did at first…now looks at you and calls you friend. And how many others, who owe you their lives? The patients. The sell-swords. The grim old knights who are willing to follow you into the mountains for what you've done for them." He waved across the decks. "There are several over there right now, training. For you. So enough of this talk. Who damn well cares what strangers think. What matters is the people aboard these two ships here." He drew a breath, pausing, then went on. "And then…then there's Gerrin." He paused again, checking Jonik's eyes. "You don't fully trust him, I know, but the man might just have crossed the world for you. Doesn't that say something too?"

"Through guilt," Jonik said quietly. "He's doing this for *him*, not me."

"Perhaps. Or perhaps not. Perhaps he sees in you what we all see, Ghost. Someone special. A leader. A good man trying to make a difference in this world."

Jonik snorted softly. "Guilt," he repeated. "I'm no different from Gerrin, Jack. Maybe all I'm trying to do is purge myself of all the awful things I've done."

"You exaggerate the awful things you've done."

"I killed my own brother. I don't think you can get much more awful than that."

I need to be alone, Jonik realised. He was spiralling down that vortex of self-pity and regret and didn't want to continue the descent, not with Jack, not with anyone. He moved away from him, and Jack let him go without a word, acknowledging his need for solitude. But in truth it wasn't solitude Jonik wanted. He went instead to the cargo hold where they had made their stables for Shade. The horse stirred as he entered. "We're here, boy," Jonik said. "Rasalan." He picked up the grooming brush and began sliding it along Shade's sleek flank.

"Won't be long before we're sailing up the strait. Nearing the Rasal Highplains, Shade. You need to think about whether you want me to set you free."

The horse's big chestnut eyes gave him nothing. He could read the steed so well, but not on this.

"We can talk about that later. Just…just have a think, OK." He continued brushing, finding some comfort in the motion, as ever, in the quiet times he spent with his longest serving companion. The others had first come into his service in the Tidelands, but Shade had been with him for many months before then. The idea of seeing him go was hurtful. *But I will,* he told himself. *I've forced him to endure more than any horse should, these long months down here below decks. If he resents me for that, I'll understand. If he wants gone from me forever, I'll not deny him.*

He stopped his grooming and set the brush aside. "So, how about a ride? Emeric will be gone a while. We have plenty of time." A gentle whinny of restrained excitement signalled the horse's interest. Jonik smiled. Shade was a thoughtful and often surly sort, but there was nothing that he liked more than a gallop. "Come on, then. Let's give your legs a good stretch."

Jonik took a few minutes to saddle and bridle him, before leading him up onto the top deck and into the bracing wintry air. He descended the gangplank onto the wharf, and moved up the stone jetty. The guards there looked at him suspiciously. "My master's horse," Jonik told them. "Needs to stretch his legs. Where's good?"

"Off that way," said one of them, pointing to the west. "There's a passage that leads out into the Lowplains, below the city walls. Fields there are good for riding. Give him a good long gallop, aye. A beauty like that shouldn't be kept below decks."

Jonik agreed. "My thanks." And off they went, man and beast, exploding out into the ranging hills.

~

THEY RODE FOR HOURS, just he and Shade. No Nightblade. No friends. No men to lead or fortress to siege. No worries. No world to belong to. Just he and his horse, galloping over snow-covered hills, past wooded creeks and rutted frozen roads and the ransacked skeletons of burned out villages. Signs of the Tukoran invasion were everywhere. Razed fields dotted the land, black and ashen beneath the snow. Long dead cattle were strewn across the pastures, and corpses still hung from trees in places, rotted down to bones and rags and stripped of all wealth and worth.

"This is only the beginning," Jonik whispered, running his fingers through the long hairs of Shade's black mane as they cantered along an old farm track. The fields to the left of him were churned and destroyed, telling of the passage of a Tukoran army some months ago. He could see old wagons and wains still stuck in the mud, armoured in snow, refuse scattered across the lands like stalks of straw following the passing of a hay cart. "Soon half the world will look like this. Most people have no idea what's coming."

Yet he did. He had a sense of it, at least. He couldn't say exactly why, because the Nightblade had never whispered anything so explicit, but he knew...he just knew that the world was about to erupt into a chaos like never before. It was a feeling deep down in his bones, a gut instinct that was driving his course. Winning the Shadowfort was his purpose now, but there would be more to it than that. Something Ranulf had said that night on the ship. About giving up the Nightblade, when the time was right. "And you'll do the right thing, when the time comes," the adventurer had said. "I know in my heart you will."

The right thing, Jonik thought. *To give it up, but for who?* Ranulf had never said as much, and had left them that very night. And ever since Jonik had wondered. He'd wondered and worried on it all, for giving it up...giving it up for anyone...he wasn't so sure if he could. *I killed my own brother to keep it,* he thought. *Why should I give it up to anyone else?*

He kicked Shade into a gallop, in a bid to outrun those thoughts, but there would be no escaping them now. Suddenly he found himself anxious. *The Nightblade. I have left it on the ship.* He'd never been so far from it, not since he'd departed the Shadowfort with the blade fastened at his hip. *I must return. Something may have happened.*

He turned Shade about and galloped down the track, over the hills, past the gullies and rutted roads and scorched, abandoned villages, until he saw Calmwater rising in the distance, and he spurred Shade on, on and on and on, faster and faster, hurtling for the port.

By the time they returned the daylight was starting to recede, a biting cold breathing through the world. He could see shapes on the deck of Invincible Iris, the braziers lit. Men were coming and going up the ramps, carrying crates. Sir Lenard and Cabel, returned from the Leaping Eel. Harden, back from the taverns and merchant houses. The Silent Suncoat was helping, in his tattered yellow cloak, and Sir Corbray and Emeric, Borrus and even Sir Torvyn. Jack and Turner and Braxton and Devin were all standing on the quarterdeck, watching. Jonik couldn't figure it out. Then it dawned on him that only the Bladeborn were carrying the crates. *Just what is inside them?* he wondered.

He cantered in and dismounted, the day sinking away into a deep purple twilight. Bells were tolling out through the city, announcing the hour. All across the docks the taverns and whorehouses were doing a raucous trade, a humming din rustling through the air. Emeric was first to notice him. He took several swift paces from the others as Jonik's booted feet hit the ground. There was something approaching anger on the exiled lord's face. "Where have you been? Jack said you'd gone riding, but that was this morning. You've been gone hours, Jonik. Half of us thought you were never coming back."

"Then you don't trust me much, Emeric." Jonik didn't admit that there had been a fleeting moment when he'd wanted to continue going, all the way north, past the Lowplains and the Forks, past Thalan and the Izzun, all the way up into the heights of Rasalan where he and Shade might find some rest. But it had been no more than a moment. A wisp of smoke, swiftly devoured by the blowing storm of fate. "I suppose I must have lost track of time. Shade needed a good gallop."

"Well he got one." Emeric breathed out. "And you're back now."

Jonik nodded. His first thought was to ask whether the Nightblade was safe, but that was a thought born of paranoia, and obsession, the same thought that had driven him to gallop back with such abandon. *The Nightblade is fine,* he knew. *Safely stowed and under Big Mo's protection. If anything had happened to it, Emeric would have already told me.* He set the concern aside and looked at the crates. "What's all this? Fresh provisions?"

"In a fashion, yes. Lord Merrymarsh was overjoyed to see his sister again. You've heard the stories about him. How he was once merry by manner as well as name, but lost his smile when his dear sister went missing. Well, that smile came back today, and with long overdue interest." He opened out an arm. "The good lord saw fit to reward us."

Jonik frowned. "With what? Gold?" No, that made no sense. Only Bladeborn were carrying those crates. "Godsteel," he said, and he saw Emeric nodding. "Swords? Weapons?" He felt a sudden blaze of hope kindling inside him. "*Armour*?"

Emeric smiled. "All of the above. Lord Humphrey Merrymarsh may be a Seaborn lord, but he is obscenely wealthy and keeps a good many Bladeborn men as bodyguards. His armoury is well stocked, shall we stay. He let us fill ten full crates with whatever we wanted. Armour, plate and mail, daggers, swords, axes, spears, shields. An unimaginable gift, almost priceless." He laughed with a rare jubilance. "This could make all the difference, Jonik. We'll have breastplates for everyone, gauntlets, greaves, codpieces and halfhelms and good strong mail. It'll allow us to train with godsteel now. To grow stronger. Faster. Better." He drew forward, gripping Jonik's upper arm tight between his fingers. "This could change everything. It might just give us the edge we need."

Jonik smiled, a slow nod turning into a brisk one. "What about the others? Did you get any *regular* plate and mail for them? Not godsteel."

"We made sure to remember them," Emeric confirmed. "Leather armour, scale mail, even a bit of whaleskin. That's the sort that rich Seaborn wear. It's almost as durable as godsteel, light and extremely hard to cut."

"Did you mention why we wanted it?"

"No. Lord Merrymarsh knows Sir Borrus. But even then, he was too overwhelmed by his sister's return to pay much attention to what he was saying. I suppose he assumes it's for the war effort, for Borrus to take to Vandar."

Something in Jonik didn't like the deceit. But he put that aside. This was a victory, good and true, and wholly unexpected. "When do we plan to sail?"

"The morning tide. We'll spend the night celebrating. Vincent has kindly provisioned us with food and drink for a party aboard One World."

"No doubt he plans to poison us all."

Emeric frowned. "Now why should he want that?"

"Vengeance. Against everyone with a drop of highborn blood in their veins." He caught Emeric's questioning stare. "Harden had it out with him earlier, quit his service. Seems to think Rose has a vendetta against all the noble houses." He shrugged. "I don't really believe he'll poison us, Emeric."

"Well, we can always let Borrus sample the drinks first, just to be safe." And Emeric Manfrey laughed, loud and long. "Oh, and one more thing, Jonik. You might want to consider inviting Sir Gerrin."

"I'm sorry?"

"Oh I think you heard me just fine." He smiled. "Your choice."

"My choice," Jonik muttered, as Emeric walked away. When it came to Gerrin, he didn't want the burden of making choices, because evidently his opinion of the man was compromised. But this one was easy enough. Gerrin would spend the night in the brig, as ever. *I'll be damned if he ruins this evening.*

Jonik led Shade back along the wharf, where the final crates were being loaded. Up on deck, Cabel was opening one up, eagerly checking the contents within. He heard Emeric calling out for the rest to be opened up, so they could take inventory. Jonik spotted Harden as all that was going on, and waved him down the gangplank. The haggard old sellsword joined him on the docks beneath the purpling skies. "So?" Jonik asked. "Any luck out there today? I saw you going to the Whispering Whale earlier."

"Started there, sure," Harden acknowledged. "Then went to the Cockles and Clams, the Seaman's Sauna, the Brindle Bullshark and half a dozen more."

"And?"

"And there're plenty of willing men about, but none that'll fit your needs. Non-Bladeborn sorts, or those with barely a drop of Varin blood in them. Some looked more promising, but had those eyes you can't trust. The in-it-for the money types, you know."

"That describes all sellswords, doesn't it?"

Old Harden gave a gruff laugh. "Suppose it does. But there are degrees of it, Jonik. Nobility among sellswords is a thing, you know. It's not all about the money with us. Elsewise I'd still be in Rose's employ, wouldn't I?"

"Makes sense."

"It does, doesn't it? Glad you think so."

"So no one, then?" Jonik found he didn't much care. With this sudden boon of armour and weapons, it mightn't matter. *And perhaps even Borris will relent, if Sir Torvyn is wrapped all in plate and mail?* The thought was most promising.

"No one worthy of you and your cause, young lordling, no. But in truth I didn't expect much, not about these parts. Mudport will be more likely to yield what we need. Lots of proper fighting men coming and going from there, so might find a few good Bladeborn sellswords about."

"Mudport," Jonik repeated. The name brought a ripple of nerves. *Mudport. Vandar.* "It's only a few day's ride from Dragon's Bane, isn't it? Half the Vandarians are said to be in camp there."

"Five days at a good canter. Not sure about half the Vandarians, but lots of men and mounts there, certainly. Sir Borrus's lot mostly, Riverlanders under his father's command, and men of the lakes and marshes too. No doubt the Barrel will want to roll on over as soon as we land. I'm a man of the Ironmoors, and there's no love lost between us and those rivermen, but still…Sir Borrus…be a damn shame to lose him."

"Right." Jonik hadn't realised Lord Wallis Kanabar would be in camp at Dragon's Bane. *Perhaps Borrus will leave us after all…*The thought was rather more sobering.

"And there's one more thing too, Jonik, most interesting. Especially for you."

Jonik nodded. "Go on."

"Seems that half brother of yours is there as well. Elyon Daecar. Yes, I know he's your brother. Young Devin's not so good at keeping secrets as he thinks. All Rose had to do was give him some cheap wine and let him lay with those Lumaran twins and he was spilling all your secrets."

Jonik closed a fist. *Damn him.* Yet his anger at that news was being subdued by something else. Those nerves of his were redoubling. *Elyon, at Dragon's Bane…* The thought of meeting his half brother again, after everything…

But no, I won't. We'll disembark the Vandarian patients and leave right after, just the same as here. I won't see Elyon. I won't. But a part of him, despite it all…a part of him wanted to.

"There's a little bit more, actually," Harden went on. "About Elyon."

Jonik re-emerged from his thoughts. "Yes?"

"Seems…well it seems the two of you have more in common than you thought, Jonik, if the rumours around the docks are to be believed." He raised a single eyebrow, grey with streaks of white. "He holds a Blade of Vandar too, it's said. The Windblade. And how he got it…" He whistled. "Now there's a treacherous tale."

Jonik took the sellsword by his hard, narrow shoulder. "I'll hear that tale in full, Harden."

The old man nodded. “Then we’ll need drinks,” he said.

19

Amilia

King Hadrin rolled off her, panting exhaustedly, grinning like a fool. "Gods, Amilia…gods what a woman you are." He reached out with a spidery arm, all bone and strips of pale flaccid flesh, and took up his cup of wine, drinking deep to refresh himself.

No doubt he needs it, after all that exertion, Amilia Lukar thought, pulling the covers up over her naked body. *He almost lasted a full minute this time.*

"Would you like one, my sweet?" Her new husband smiled at her through a face that was part rat, part horse, with teeth that were too big for his mouth and a jaw that was receding to the point that it all but vanished into the wrinkly skin of his neck. He'd tried to grow a beard to strengthen the fame of his chin, but had only managed to cultivate a few sparse wisps of hoary hair that only made him look even older than his years. He was an unpleasant sight, creepy and clammy and near enough the most uncomely man she'd ever seen.

Not like my Aleron, she thought, wistful. Sometimes, when Hadrin crawled between her legs, she'd shut her eyes tight and think of her fallen knight, for all the good it would do.

"Yes," she told him, smiling as sweetly as she could. *Anything to wash the taste of your lips from my mouth.* He poured her a fine golden goblet, encrusted with sapphires and opals, and she drew on the rich wine with a liberal swallow.

"A child has taken this time, I am sure of it," King Hadrin

proclaimed. "My physicians tell me there is nothing wrong with either of us, my queen. In nine months we'll welcome a boy. A boy, yes, half Seaborn, half Bladeborn, rich with the blood of Thala and Varin both."

"A most handsome boy," she said. She thought of what her son with Aleron would have looked like. Tall, wide at the shoulder, powerful in the chest and arms. *Black hair, for his father. Green eyes, like mine. The warrior he would have been…the hearts he would have broken.* Any child by Hadrin would be sure to carry at least some of his look. Physically frail and feeble, narrow jawed and weak. The thought made her want to cry.

Hadrin's foul grin filled her vision as he went to lie atop her again. "I think I'm well recovered. One more time, before we sleep. I'm told it'll better increase our chances of conception. And isn't it such *fun* too? Oh the pleasure you give me, Amilia." His tongue approached, his breath hot and panting. "Such pleasure…"

She turned her head aside on impulse, unable to contain her disgust. "Hadrin, must we? The child…it has taken, as you say. I'm sure of it too, my king. We don't need to…"

"Oh but *I* do need to, Amilia. I have needs beyond getting you with child." He squirmed atop her, trying to prise open her legs. "I find you so….irresistible, I confess."

And I find you detestable. "I'm tired." She held her legs closed against him. It wasn't difficult; she'd never met a man so physically inadequate. "That last time…I think you wore me out." *For one full minute.* She smiled and made herself stroke the disappearing angle of his jaw, her fingers moving through the sparse hair upon his chin. The touch of it was repellent. *I hate you, Grandfather*, she thought, *for making me lay with this thing.* "Please, just let me sleep, Hadrin. Will you do that for me, sweet king?"

His horsy smile crept out, shadowed in displeasure. "Of course I will. For you? I'd do anything." He rolled off her with an awkward reluctance, flopping down to lie at her side. "Tomorrow morning," he said. "We can indulge in one another again tomorrow morning, my beauty." He leaned across and planted those thin dry lips of his on her cheek, reaching beneath the covers to fumble at her breasts a final time before turning away.

Amilia closed her eyes, silently cursing what her life had become. She could not say who she loathed more, her grandfather who'd forced her into this union or the creature she was forced to call husband. She lay there in the dimness, the hearth burning low, a few spare candles guttering out around the room, and waited.

A minute passed, then two, then ten. By then Hadrin was beginning to breathe in that horrid wheezing way of his, mumbling in his sleep as he did every night. Sometimes he would jerk suddenly awake, muttering about shadows and dragons and fire, before settling. It unnerved her more than she could say. By day Hadrin spent much of his time in solitude, gazing into the Eye of Rasalan up in his tower, obsessed with mastering it. *And he sees things,* she knew. *Terrible things. Terrifying things.* She was sure she'd heard him mumble something about Eldur once, about the world falling to darkness. "The Shadow," he would murmur. "The Shadow. The Shadow…" And one night that murmur had become a scream, and she'd had to shake him awake to stop him. He'd been shivering, a cold distant horror in his eyes, but when pressed on his nightmares he'd not remembered anything.

I want to go home, she thought miserably, holding the covers tight around herself. She was a stranger here, misliked and mistrusted, and her king husband even more so. When they'd arrived at the city upon his royal warship, sailing up the Izzun River and into the harbour, there had been no fanfare to greet their return. He had expected bunting and billowing banners, crowds teeming the streets, cheers radiating across the City of Thalan to mark the return of their king and his beautiful new queen. But barely anyone had come. And half of those who did had looked at them sourly, and at once Amilia had felt alone and unwanted.

It hadn't gotten any better since then. She missed Melany, her faithful lady-in-waiting and friend. And her father…she missed him sorely. No matter what they told her, she knew that he hadn't tried to take her grandfather's throne. Her father was too noble and honourable for that. *He was a good man,* she thought, *adored and admired, and now he's dead. And here I am, with this wretched creature for a husband, who'd killed his own father for his throne. Curse you, Grandfather, for sending me here. Curse you to the Long Abyss, bastard!*

Amilia slipped from the bed, as Hadrin mumbled and wheezed, padding silently across the room to dress. She drew on a simple silken nightdress, woollen slippers, and an overcloak for the biting cold. The candle flames stirred as she passed, flickering, and she glanced back to the bed to make sure the king was still sleeping. Satisfied he wouldn't wake, she opened the heavy wooden door with a gentle groan, and stepped out into the hall.

All was quiet outside, the palace eerily silent within the privacy of their royal residence. Amilia moved first into the adjoining chamber, opening the door and stepping into her private dressing room. She went over to her make-up table, fitted with shelves and drawers teeming with pots and powders, ointments and balms. Rummaging at the back of one of the drawers, she plucking out an ordinary glass container, cylindrical in shape, pulled off the stopper, reached inside, and drew out a second, smaller vial, hidden within.

She gave the liquid inside a swirl - dark purple, near black - removed the top, and took a small sip. The taste was most unpleasant, but she'd drink gallons of the stuff if she had to. *No child will be taking tonight,* she thought, imagining the seed of Hadrin's unborn child withering to dust within her. The thought gave her more pleasure than the rat king ever would. *I shall never bear you a son, Hadrin, or a daughter, gods forbid. Never.* She returned all the items to their correct place, shut the drawer, and left the room.

The residence was always quiet by night, though occasionally one of Hadrin's guards could be seen walking the halls. Mostly they remained outside, guarding the entrances, his King's Guard led by Sir Munroe Moore who oversaw the king's security. The palace beyond was well stocked with regular guardsmen as well. *A fortress,* she knew. *A prison.* She had not been allowed out into the city since arriving some weeks ago. "For your own safety," Sir Munroe had told her, in that stiff elegant voice of his. He had been commander of King Godrin's guard before Hadrin had taken his father's throne, and some said he'd been there when that dark treachery had been done. "The city is full of enemies, Your Majesty, and it isn't safe during war. The king made a solemn promise to your grandfather that he would keep you safe. For now, you must remain in the palace grounds." He had gone so far as to touch her arm. "Where it's safe."

Amilia felt trapped, like a bird in a cage, able to see the world beyond but never reach it. There were many balconies and terraces on the palace's western face where she could look upon Thalan, a pretty city of white and blue and yellow, with a hundred temples and holy places dedicated to their many gods and sprites and nymphs. She would find a balcony where she might be alone, and sit for hours, looking down at the bustling harbour astride the Izzun River, watch the ships come and go into port, gaze at the shimmering snaking waterway as it bled out into the distant west. And how she wanted to board a ship and leave. To depart this beautiful silent morgue of a palace and never, ever return.

She turned down a corridor, seeking out the only comfort she knew here. She had convinced her husband to let her keep some of her own men nearby, the Emerald Guards who made up her protective cohort. The king had permitted them accommodations down an unused wing of the royal residence, each given a pleasantly furnished room to match their noble station. It was a small allowance, but one that had made Amilia most happy. "Anything for you, my beautiful queen," Hadrin had said, beaming hideously. "I want you to feel safe and comfortable here. If having your men nearby accomplishes that, then of course, I shall allow it."

The fool, she thought, blind to her true intentions, as she slipped silently down a darkened corridor and came to Sir Jeremy's door. She turned the handle and entered without knocking. Sir Jeremy Gullimer was already there, awaiting her. "My queen," he said, moving straight to one knee. "You came. I prayed you would."

He was naked. Undressed but for the Emerald Guard cloak that he'd playfully left tied around his neck. A part of Amilia would prefer it be blue. *A cloak of the Varin Knights, for my Aleron,* she thought. Sir Jeremy shared a certain likeness with her erstwhile betrothed. He was tall, young, roguishly handsome, black of hair. *But not him,* she thought. *Not Aleron.*

"Rise, Sir Jeremy." She removed her cloak, unveiling the silken nightdress that did little to hide the soft curve of her frame. Her green eyes looked out, catlike, from beneath a flowing waterfall of luxuriant copper hair.

"You look stunning, my queen." And so did he, she had to admit, standing there in nothing but that cloak, generously endowed, sleekly muscled. He was the antithesis of her scraggy old husband, and a gifted lover besides.

She smiled at the sculpted sight of him, at the stiffening there between his legs. "How long were you waiting, Jeremy?"

"Time has no bearing, not when it concerns you, my queen. I would wait a lifetime if I must. To taste your sweet lips again." And his eyes moved down her body. The intent in them was clear.

She slid forward, stepping out of her slippers, and shifted the straps of the silken nightdress from her shoulders. It fell where she stood, bundling at her feet. The sight of her nude frame was far too much for Sir Jeremy Gullimer to take. He took a brisk stride forward, but she held up a palm. "Wait," she whispered, enjoying the game. "Do not move an inch, Sir Jeremy."

He fixed his feet and waited, stiffening all the while. When a minute had passed he shook his head, exhaling. "You torture me, my queen. What cruelty is this to unveil yourself before me, and deny me your touch?"

"Anticipation is part of the joy, Jeremy," she said sultrily. She broadened her red lips into a smile, turning aside, showing him a different angle of her as she stepped to the drinks counter. She filled herself a cup of spiced wine, sipped, smiled and let the wait go on. And on. And on.

"My queen…*Amilia.* I do not know how much longer I can bear this. My hunger for you…"

"You must learn to master your urges, gentle knight. You will have me, only once I allow it." She twirled the stem of her cup, wine sloshing side to side. "Oh, you'll do things to me that my husband never could. Things I would *never* permit him. But you? Oh yes. I'd let you do *anything* to me, Jeremy."

His eyes went soft with a drunken desire, mouth opening, shutting, opening again in a wordless gape. He gazed upon her smooth soft flesh. "*Anything,* my queen?"

"Oh yes, Sir Jeremy. *Anything.* But I need to know…would you do anything *for* me too?"

"*Anything,*" he breathed. "I would kill for you, die for you. Whatever you want, whatever you need. You are my queen, Amilia, and I am yours to command. Anything," he said again, dropping again to one knee. "I would do anything for you."

She knew all that already, in truth, but she liked to hear him say it. The rest of her guard were loyal to her, she sensed, but could she count on them to get their hands dirty if they had to? She wasn't certain. But Sir Jeremy…well, he was infatuated with her, she'd known that all along. The others were old seasoned knights, not the sort to forgo their vows and slide into her bed, no matter how much they might want to. But Sir Jeremy Gullimer was more easily turned.

And most handsome too, she thought, taking a step forward, seeing his eyes dilate with an unquenchable yearning to have her. And she had that yearning too, oh yes. To feel this strong young knight take her, to cast aside the latest memory of her rat-faced husband panting at her neck, pumping with those feeble thrusts that she hardly even felt. A cold thin finger ran up her spine to even think of him. Sir Jeremy brought the opposite sensation. Want. Desire. The fulfilment of her womanly needs. And those needs were powerful here. *I have nothing else but him,* she thought. *In this cold beautiful city of strangers, Sir Jeremy is my only warmth.*

And so she stepped toward him, and pushed him onto the bed, saying, "Take me, Sir Jeremy. Do to me as you please."

When they were done, Amilia lay in his arms, sweaty and satisfied, wishing he could take her away from here too. She often felt like this, after. Vulnerable, stupid, given to foolish fancies. "Would you run away with me," she whispered to him, lying with her ear against his bare chest, listening to the swift heavy pounding of his heart. "Somewhere far from here, where we don't have to worry who might see us. Home, to Tukor. Away to your father's lands."

Sir Jeremy shifted aside. She had never seen such earnest eyes. "We could leave at once, Amilia," he said, nodding briskly. "Tonight, even. I could wake the others. We could find a ship in the harbour and..."

"Shhhh, sweet knight." Her finger rested against his lips. "This is folly, we both know it. My husband would never let me leave."

"Then I would kill him, and take you anyway. I...I love you, Amilia. I don't even care to hide it. I do. I love you, my queen."

I know you do, she thought, touching his cheek, *and I'm very fond of you too.* Perhaps she could learn to love him back, in time. Gullimer was not a greathouse, no, but it was reasonably old, reasonably wealthy, and had contributed a healthy number of notable Emerald Guards across the years. Her grandfather would never approve, of course, but she cared not for him anymore. *Perhaps I should ask Sir Jeremy to slay him instead,* she thought bitterly. Janilah Lukar's death would put her younger brother Robbert on the throne. *I could return to Ilithor, then, help rule Tukor alongside him. I could even marry Sir Jeremy, if I wanted...*

"I hate that he gets to have you first," the young Emerald Guard said, frowning unhappily. "To think of that old man kissing you, making love to you. *I cannot bear it,* Amilia. Please, let me take you away. My lord father would give us safe harbour, I know it."

She kissed him on the lips, if for no other reason than to silence him. "It cannot be, my sweet noble knight. Not while my husband reigns as king. And my grandfather. Your father would never permit it. He would not risk such wrath."

"Then we run and hide. I know the north of Tukor, Amilia. I can hunt, fish, find us a place to lay low until…"

"This is folly, Jeremy. You know it cannot be."

"It can. It *can*, Amilia." His puppy eyes stared at her, so sweet and innocent, but she was still shaking her head, running her fingers across his cheek, whispering 'no'. He grunted and shook his head. "At least tell me you're taking the tonic I gave you. *Please* say you are. If *he* should get you with child…I…I cannot even bring myself to think of it."

"I take it every time," she assured him with a whisper. *As I will after this,* she thought, for getting pregnant by a man as robust and strong as Jeremy Gullimer was not an option either. No, the child would take on his characteristics, she knew, and soon enough Hadrin would work it out. "I will need some more, however. My stocks… they're running low."

"Then I will get you more, my queen. As much as you need to slay that monster's seed." He grimaced at the thought, trying not to picture it. "We have to get you away from him," he said again. "It isn't safe for you here. Half the city wants Hadrin dead for what he did. It's on everyone's tongue, I've heard it. They know he killed his father."

"I know. But the palace is well guarded, Jeremy. There's not much the mob can do."

"I'm not talking about the mob. There are rumours that Hadrin's cousins are in the city. Some are saying they're planning to march on the palace in force with their own men, demand Hadrin step down from the throne. They are united against him, and with most of the Suncoats away in the south, the king isn't so well defended as he thinks. They might have enough to overthrow him. And if they do, what do you think will happen to you? They could kill you, Amilia, or at best take you hostage."

She shook her head. "And risk my grandfather's wrath?"

"His wrath isn't what it was. People know all about his heart attack now. Some people think him dead already. Or mad. Janilah Lukar isn't a name to strike fear in people here, not anymore." He took her arm. "One way or another, we *need* to go. From Hadrin. From his cousins. If you don't want to be his queen and you don't want to bear his child, why stay? That was for your grandfather. And he's done, they say. You don't have to be afraid of him anymore."

She put her palm to his cheek again, and pressed her lips to his.

He drew back. "Why do you do that every time? You're *not listening to me*, Amilia. It isn't safe for you here! No matter which way you look at it, it isn't..."

She slapped him. "Is that better, Sir Jeremy? Would you prefer I interrupt you with a slap, or a kiss?"

He rubbed his cheek. "I'd prefer you didn't interrupt me at all."

"I am Queen of Rasalan, and Princess of Tukor. I can interrupt you all I please." She spun her lips into a grin and moved from the bed, reaching to pick up her nightdress.

"You're leaving?"

"I must. It would not do well for the king to wake to find me gone."

"It's still dead of night. We have time."

"Time for what, Sir Jeremy? To make love once more? To whisper of treason and conspiracy? We're not getting anywhere. I have to go."

She turned away, heard him lurching from the bed, pressing up behind her. "I can arrange a meeting," he said, turning her around. "The cousins. I can speak with them, see what it is they're planning. I could help them, in return for your safe passage out of here, once Hadrin has been removed from the throne."

She felt afraid at that thought. "I cannot lose you, Jeremy. I have no one else here."

"I'll be careful. Discreet. It might be the only way."

"Jeremy..."

"I'm doing it, Amilia. You must trust me. Do you trust me?"

She felt a little girl all of a sudden, standing before a noble knight, though in truth they were the same age at twenty. "I do," she whispered.

"Then let me do this for you. You don't need to walk to your grandfather's drum anymore. Neither of us do. The world...the world is changing, Amilia. We can both be free."

She leaned in and kissed him again, but not to interrupt him this time, or quieten him, but because she wanted to. *Because I care for him. Because I need him.* "I must go, Jeremy." She moved to pick up her cloak, draping it over her shoulders. "And keep this between us for now. I don't want the others knowing."

She wasn't certain if she could trust them on something like this. She had half a dozen Emerald Guards for company and more regular Lukar guardsmen besides, but any one of them might write her grandfather if they knew what she was doing. She doubted he would be happy to hear of her intentions. *I was meant to come and rule this kingdom.* "Make it a queendom," he had said. *But I never wanted that, Grandfather. And now my father is dead because of you...*

Sir Jeremy ushered her to the door, peeking out into the corridor before sending her away. She couldn't help but plant a final kiss to his lips before leaving him. *I have grown needy,* she reflected. *Since when did I so need a man to save me?* But all the same, that's who she was. A lost little princess, alone in this strange foreign city, with nothing but a boy-knight to turn to in her grief.

She backed out of the door, smiling thinly as Sir Jeremy shut it with a soft thud. Turning, she moved back through the residence, praying she didn't run into one of Hadrin's men. She made it to her dressing room, found the vial, took a second sip, and popped it back into place. Then came the final test; opening the door, returning to her royal chamber and the bed she shared with the king, hoping to find him sleeping. She'd done it a dozen times already, but tonight her nerves were frayed. All this talk of treason, of escape, of freedom…

Her hand clutched the handle, turned, and she heard the king's voice within…

She froze, but it was nothing to fear. He was speaking in his sleep, she realised, as he did most nights. She shut the door quietly, careful not to disturb him, slipped out of her clothes, and crept back beneath the sheets. The bed was damp with sweat on his side. She frowned and let her eyes adjust, and saw that her husband's eyes were open. She startled, heart skipping a beat. He was staring up at the ceiling, perspiration glistening on his forehead and neck, little droplets of dew sparkling in the sparse hairs of his chin.

"Hadrin," she whispered. Her voice was jittery. The sight of him was unnerving. "Hadrin, are you awake?"

He gave no answer. His lips were mumbling, his eyes white and wild and full of broken veins.

"Hadrin…" she reached out to give him a little shake. She couldn't sleep next to him, not like this. He looked so drawn and haggard, lost to a trance. "Hadrin, you're having a bad dream again." She touched his shoulder, preparing to shake him awake, and suddenly his voice erupted.

"Shadow! The Dread! The Dread is upon us. THE DREAD! THE DREAD!"

Amilia pulled back in fright, dragging the covers with her. The king thrashed suddenly, like a fish in a net, convulsing, and went still. Her heart hammered, blood throbbing heavily through the vein in her neck. "H-Hadrin…" She dare not touch him again. "Hadrin," she said, louder. "Hadrin, *wake up*."

He stirred, his eyes blinking, escaping the eerie trance. He rotated his head queerly and peered across at her. "Amilia, my queen." His voice was odd. *He's still half asleep,* she realised. "Is it morning?"

"No. It's still late. Go to sleep, Hadrin." *Please.*

He blinked vacantly and laid his head back down on his dampened pillow, making a smacking sound with his lips as he drifted right back off to sleep. *He won't remember this,* Amilia knew. Yet it had been the worst episode yet. Those staring white eyes, the thrashing. And the things he'd said. Shadow he said a lot. But the dread? She felt more disquieted than ever. *The dread,* she thought again. *He couldn't mean…*

She turned over, facing away from him, shifting to the edge of the bed where it was dry. For a long time she just lay there, tense, until the lure of sleep finally grew too strong, dragging her down into her dreams.

And there, nightmares awaited. Dark and dreaded dreams of shadow and fire and death. Of a world overcome by the horrors long gone. And she woke in the morning feeling more numb and fearful than ever.

I must get out of here, she knew. *One way or another, I must.*

20

Lythian

Even from a distance the fortress looked forbidding. Through the high swirling mists he could see them, the red-black towers that marked its western face, surging up beyond the mountaintop. "We're not far," he called out, over the howling gale. "If we're lucky we'll have found the Ashway Stair by nightfall."

He pulled his cloak about himself. Beneath he wore boiled leathers and roughspun wool, old stained boots and gloves. The altitude made it cold up here, though the others didn't seem to feel it, not like him. *The Agarathi have warmer blood than I*, he thought. *There is fire in their veins; mine is steel.*

"We ought to stay hidden," Sir Pagaloth said, squinting his dark eyes upward. The mists were heavy here, swirling around the mountain peaks, yet for all that it was wise to be cautious. "If anyone remains up there, they may see us. It would be best we were not spotted."

"W-what if there are…survivors?" asked Cevi in a tremulous voice.

From afar the great fortress of the Nest looked deserted, but there was no way of knowing for sure until they got there. They had seen no dragons upon the outer defences since they'd first sighted the fort two days past. Nor had they seen any flying in or out. The only dragon they'd seen these last weeks was Neyruu, but she too hadn't been sighted for some days now. *Does she fear to return?* Lythian wondered. He looked again at the high dark towers, built of black and crimson stone. *And if she does, shouldn't we?*

But they'd come too far now to turn back. "We will face that test when it comes to it, Cevi," Lythian told the handmaid. She nodded once and didn't say anything more. The weeks since Mirella's death had turned the girl quiet and thoughtful, though for all her grief, she had wept her last that day in the cave.

Pagaloth turned his eyes down the pass. The ridge on which they stood descended gradually toward a labyrinthine field of crags and shallow scarps, half hidden in mist, far below. "This way looks safe enough," he said. "Are you all ready to continue?"

He received a round of nods and wasted no time in leading them on, Talasha and Cevi falling into step behind him, Lythian bringing up the rear. They were not so high as to have to suffer snow here, making the footing mostly sure, yet here and there loose stones and scree were scattered along their path. Pagaloth continued to prove himself a good guide; he gestured to any difficult patches, calling for them to be avoided, and was not afraid to take them down circuitous routes if he was concerned about a certain section.

He had taken the lead often these last days, in fact, since they'd left behind the foothills, the rain, and Neyruu too. Now all was rock and biting winds, torpid lakes in unforested valleys where the water sat still as stone. There was an eeriness here, a quiet that only broke when the winds picked up. Occasionally they would see an eagle in the skies, or some other bird of prey, but elsewise there was no life except the sparse patches of withered shrubbery that spouted among the heights.

This place is a desolation, Lythian thought, as they descended the ridge, the sight of the fortress towers vanishing behind the thickening fogs. He reached to clutch the handle of his broadsword on instinct, to heighten his senses, but then remembered it was but regular steel, castle-forged and dinted, with spots of rust on the cross guard. He released the hilt, sighing. *Too long. I have been too long without the touch of godsteel.* And he wondered, as he often did, if he would ever see his blade again, left behind in that deep dark tomb in which they'd found Eldur. *One day,* he told himself. *One day I will return to retrieve Starslayer from that hell.*

The route soon began to flatten, the winds dropping as they climbed down into a sheltered valley. Ahead lay the labyrinth they'd sighted from above; a snarling field of rocky outcrops, jutting savagely up from the ground. Some were shallow and broad, others tall and thin, and between them lay cracks and chasms that gave no hint of an end beneath. Pagaloth took the lead once more. "I shall go first," he said. "Follow my step, and do not look down."

Talasha fixed her shoulders with a stout courage Lythian had come to expect. Cevi blinked timidly, but had some strength in her too. And on they went.

An hour passed, and progress was made. Most of the chasms were no more than a metre wide and easy enough to leap, and in places the forest of stone blocks and spires gave way to more open areas. Stopping at one of them, Lythian scrambled up a climbable outcropping to get a better view ahead. Only then did he realise how vast this place was. The field went on forever, it seemed, enclosed on either side by high black cliffs that bled away into the wet grey fogs. "It goes for some miles," he called to the others. "We could retrace our steps, try another way. If we climb back up the ridge there may be a way to avoid this place."

"No," Princess Talasha said, flexing her royal might. "We go on, Lythian. To go back would be to lose our way. It might take days to find ourselves again."

Lythian nodded and climbed back down. "As you say, Princess."

She studied the tangle of rocks that cluttered the way. Many were sharp to the touch, razor-edged and deadly. "We will need to be extra careful here. One slip and any one of us could rip a gash in our flesh, or break a bone." She fixed her jaw. "I will not have that happen, not again. I will not have a repeat of Mirella."

Mirella, Lythian thought. He preferred not to think of her. *It was a mercy*, he told himself. *Necessary. Talasha permitted it. I was only following orders.* Yet all the same, it had left something unpleasant inside him, something rotten. Lythian Lindar had killed dozens of men over the years, hundreds more likely, yet never a woman, and never like that. *The way her eyes flickered. The way she squirmed.* He'd wondered whether she might have recovered after all. *There was still fight in her, when I put my hand over her mouth. When I clamped it shut, I could feel it. She wanted to live. She wanted to, I could feel it…*

They pressed on, the winds returning, slicing through the rocks and buffeting them as they went. Lythian turned his thoughts elsewhere. *Much wickedness is done in war,* he knew. *We blacken our souls through necessity*. Still, he stayed close behind Cevi and Talasha the whole time, ready to steady them if they should stumble when passing over and between the rocks, watching all the while for tumbling stones above that might clatter down upon them. Talasha was well protected in her dragonscale armour, but not Cevi. *I'll not let anything happen to you,* he would think. *I will protect you, Cevi, as I couldn't protect your friend.*

The labyrinth grew more menacing, the rocks surging and twisting in unnatural shapes. Some seemed to take the form of dragons to Lythian's eyes. Heads and taloned limbs jutted out from the floor, roaring and clawing, and at one point a great wide arch of rock seemed wrought in the image of a dragon with wings outstretched, a gout of rigid flame pouring from its jaws.

Lythian halted there. *It warns us not to pass,* he thought, but the others went right beneath it, not seeming to see it or care. *Is it only I who sees dragons here?* He tried to veer toward more positive thoughts as he moved beneath the arch, but there was something about this place that weighed heavy on him, that turned his mind to doubt. He had felt something similar when they'd descended the mountain of Eldur's Shame, deep beneath the Wings. That growing dread, that shroud of uncertainty, the grip of fear that began to take hold, deep down in his bones. The fortress of the Nest had long been the home of the Bondstone. And much earlier, thousands of years ago, before it had even been built, Drulgar the Dread himself had made his lair up here. It was so named for that fact. For Drulgar's lair, Drulgar's nest, from which he'd perched, surveying all…

A shudder rippled through him. *This is where he once lived, up there among these peaks.* He could not say whether the others felt it as he did. *It is like the cold,* he thought. *I feel it more than they, as I do this primal unease.* It was not a fear borne of cowardice nor lack of courage, but a fear written in blood and bone. *Varin lives in my veins*, he thought. *And this is where his nightmare lurked.*

"Are you OK, sweet captain?" Talasha must have seen something in his eyes. She held back as Cevi moved past her, Pagaloth leading them on. "You do not seem yourself."

I mustn't show her my fear. "I'm fine, Talasha." He made himself smile. "I was just thinking how Borrus would have handled this. Some of these passages are so narrow I wonder if he'd have fitted through."

"In his slighter form, he may have had a chance." She studied his eyes. "You miss him, don't you? You miss having one of your own here with you. And your blade…you miss that most of all."

"I miss being the man I was." He left that vague on purpose; this wasn't a conversation he wanted to have, not here and not now. "We should keep going, or we'll risk losing them. Pagaloth sets a quick pace."

She stopped him with a hand to the chest. Those red-brown eyes of hers were unrelenting, reading him like an unrolled scroll. "This place feels wrong to you, doesn't it?" she said. "Your eyes…they have the same look as before, when we found *him* in his tomb."

Lythian wasn't going to deny it. "The Wings and the Nest are both dreaded places to my people. There is an air here…a feeling. It's hard to explain, Talasha."

She nodded quietly. "Do you think…" Her eyes went up and up, toward the mountaintop, hidden amid the clouds. "Do you think he may have returned? Eldur?"

He had no sure answer for that. "He took what he needed from here, Talasha," is all he said. "There is no reason for him to return."

She nodded in quiet thought, smiled, and kissed his cheek. "You do not need to fear, sweet captain. I will keep you safe."

Morning came and went, and afternoon passed by too. The labyrinth went on, turning them this way and that, forcing them to retreat more times than he could count, backtracking to find a safer way. Sometimes they found themselves in alleys of high stone, and lost their bearings for a time, but never for too long, for as soon as they sighted the high black cliffs to left and right they knew which way they were headed. And slowly, surely, hour by hour they edged forward, before eventually, as day began to curdle into night, the great morass of tumbled stone ended and the world opened out before them.

Lythian stepped out last, following Pagaloth, Cevi, Talasha, his eyes taking in the wonder of the view. They had come upon a high plateau, sloping away on all sides, and there before them lay the great realm of Agarath, spreading to north and west.

Pagaloth raised a finger and pointed. "There," he said, directing their eyes toward a snaking path through the mountains below. "That is it. The Ash Road. It leads directly to the Ashway Stair."

Sir Pagaloth Kadosk had never sounded so relieved. Lythian smiled to see it, squinting against the falling sun, cursing how feeble his vision was without godsteel. It was some way distant, yet reachable. "It's paved," he realised. "In cobblestone." He had imagined a more simple track.

The dragonknight nodded. "Aspiring dragonriders often use the Ash Road to reach the fortress to be tested and trained. So too the scholars, the servants, the soldiers who are assigned here. Not all are lucky enough to be brought here on the wing, Captain Lythian."

Lythian drew in a long cool breath of bracing air, drinking in the view. The cold clasping fingers that had seized him in the maze were gradually releasing their grip, yet how long that would last, he couldn't say. From their vantage he could see a hundred miles, he guessed, the high mountains diminishing into the shallower foothills beyond. Further off, the Askar River slithered away into the distant plains, splitting the Great Grasslands to the south and the Drylands to the north. Lythian recalled his journey across those lands, when he'd ridden from Dragonfall to Eldurath with Borrus and Tomos and Sir Pagaloth and his company. Somewhere out there was the sacred fire pit at which they'd stopped one night, sitting on those stones smoothed by a thousand strangers, watching as the flames flickered and danced. They'd passed around a strange liquor called *skrait*, and the Agarathi men under Pagaloth's charge, hard soldiers well seasoned by war, had wept to recall those they'd lost.

And in those flames I saw my wife, Lythian recalled. *Talia. And my infant son.* He spared a quick glance at Talasha, who shared a resemblance with her, and in that moment felt a stab of shame prodding at his heart. *I promised myself I would never love again. I promised I would live for duty, only, yet now…now…*

"Are you remembering, Captain?" came Pagaloth's voice, breaking his train of thought. "Remembering the journey we shared together?"

Lythian nodded, swallowing. He took a moment to collect himself. "I'm remembering the stones," he said, "and the fire pit. It was the night I started to understand you, I think." He glanced again at Talasha, who stood aside with Cevi, oblivious. *And not long later, I met her in the palace. Did I begin to love her, even then?*

"It feels a lifetime ago now, does it not?" Pagaloth said. He had fashioned his beard into a single braid for the last few days. He twirled it in thought and said, "I wonder what might have happened if you had never been sent here, Lythian. What paths we might both be on."

"Not the same one, I'm sure." Lythian managed a weak smile. "I have wondered that too, in truth, and often. Much might have been different." He shrugged. "Or nothing."

The dragonknight dipped his chin. "We can never know," he agreed. "I suppose it is senseless to dwell on what might have been. We need but walk the path before us, dark though it is, and hope we don't stumble." He filled his lungs. "Princess, we should continue. It would be best to reach the Ashway Stair by the fall of dark, if we can. If there are torches there, we can use them for the climb. If not, we must wait until daybreak."

The princess gave an assenting nod, and they continued on their way.

The trail that led down toward the Ash Road was generously simple to navigate, and the views a blessing following the claustrophobia of the maze. Westward, the sun began to plunge below the horizon, colouring the clouds in shades of scarlet and vermillion. "It is very pretty," Lythian heard Cevi say. There was a mournful tone to her voice. "I was born down there, Captain Lythian. A half day's walk north of the Askar River. We used to go to her banks as children, fetch water from her tributaries. I had three sisters and two brothers. Some are still there, I think."

"Are you the oldest, Cevi?" He realised how little he knew about her. *I don't even know her age,* he thought.

"I was second oldest. My older sister Milga died when I was young, so I became oldest after that. I would lead the others to the river, to get water and play, sometimes. My father did not like it if we took too long, though." She smiled at the memory. "He herded goats. And my mother would make baskets from river reeds, to sell at market in Kalin. This was the nearest village. On clear days, we could see the tip of the Ashmount, though it was far away. We would imagine the old wars. When Eldur fought Varin on the plains beyond the mountain. When Karagar died. And the newer wars too." She frowned. "What is the name you call it? When Prince Dulian fought with Amron Daecar?"

"The Echo of Titans," Lythian told her. *Nineteen, perhaps twenty*, he was thinking. He would put her age at that. Born at the end of the war, if so. No more than a child, really. "It happened north of Death's Passage, beyond the Bloodmarsh Isles. We call it the Battle of Burning Rock in Vandar."

The handmaid nodded. "You were there?"

"I was," he said. "I saw the duel myself." *Or parts of it,* he thought, *when I wasn't fighting battles of my own.*

"Have you killed a dragon as well?"

"No," he told her, wondering how she couldn't know. In the north, everyone knew who the dragonslayers were. "I fought in many battles where dragons were there," he added, "and battled some myself. But I never killed one. Not alone, anyway."

She seemed confused by that. "Then you *have* killed one."

"No..." He thought on how best to explain it. "There is a code, Cevi, one of honour between dragonriders and knights. When a Bladeborn knight calls a Fireborn rider down for a duel, he must accept or be called a coward. That is a *true* kill. To slay a dragon in single combat. That is something I have never done." *And never will now,* he thought.

They walked on in silence for a short time, cutting across a field of scree. Pagaloth and Talasha were paired ahead, some twenty metres distant now, discussing something he could not hear. Both were looking to the sunset and to the skies, perhaps keeping lookout for dragons. Yet still, there were none. *The skies are deserted,* Lythian thought. He hoped the fortress would be too.

Cevi looked skyward as well. "We would see dragons also," she said. "From our home. And when we went to the river. We would see them flying here all the time." She frowned and looked to the dusky skies. "It is so strange, that none are here. Is it true, do you think? What the princess says. Do you think that Eldur controls them all now?"

"He took the Bondstone, Cevi. He must have done it for a reason."

"But he was not himself. The princess says. He was not the *real* Eldur. The real Eldur is good-hearted, Captain. Not to you, no, but to us, yes. He fought always for our people. For *his* people. And Prince Tethian...he said that he would bring balance. And Master Dar said that too. They did not try to raise him to bring fire and blood." She bit her bottom lip, frowning. "Perhaps...perhaps he will wake. Wake properly, I mean. He had slept for so long. When he wakes, wakes fully, he will realise what he must do. Prince Tethian... he may be right, still. He said he would die for his cause, and he did. And that cause...maybe it can still be so." She looked at him in a childlike way. "Do you not think, Captain?"

He gave her the comforting smile he sensed she wanted. "I do, Cevi. I do not imagine it can have been easy for him. To open his eyes to a world so different to that he left. But yes...when he comes around, perhaps...perhaps all will be well."

She nodded, seeming satisfied, and on they went into the gathering gloom.

The sun had long departed when they reached the Ash Road, its cobblestones broken and worn and often missing after thousands of years of use. To the north, it fell away over a sharp drop; south, from the direction they'd come, were fields of broken flint and volcanic rock. Pagaloth plucked one from the side of the road and inspected it, before tossing it aside.

Cevi was watching him intently. "What is it?"

"Lava," Pagaloth answered. "Solidified to stone. There was once lots of volcanic activity across the Scales. These rocks may be thousands of years old."

"As old as the fortress?"

"Possibly older."

"How was it built? The fortress?" Cevi turned her eyes east, and up, toward the shadow of the mountains. "It would take lots of stone and tools. Did men carry it all the way up?"

Pagaloth smiled. "It was built on the back of dragons," he told the girl. "There were many great dragons back then. Large and strong, they would fly materials to the mountains, where men would forge them into towers and walls. The red you see in the rock is the result of dragonfire, used to fuse the stone together. It is why our walls here in Agarath are so strong. There is magic in the fire of dragons, Cevi."

Lythian knew that to be true. Agarathi walls were notoriously difficult to breach and would stand for tens of thousands of years before crumbling, some said. "We lace godsteel into the walls of some of our cities in the north," he told them. "It gives the same effect. Makes them durable against attack."

Cevi was still mulling on something, looking up and down the roads as it wended between great piles of rock. Further up, the road became a stair, climbing back and forward up a shallow cliff, before flattening out again, blending into the darkness. "Is the Ashway far?"

"Not far," Pagaloth said, as though he'd walked this route a hundred times before. "You see there, Cevi, where the mountain rises sheer?" The girl nodded, looking at him big-eyed. "The Ashway Stair is in there somewhere. It spirals up through the mountain's heart, all the way to the top. Some call it the *Kylash Hyndraha*. The *Stair to the Stars*," he said, translating for Lythian into the common tongue.

"There is no higher fortress in all the world. Not even Skyloft climbs so high."

Cevi's cherubic face was all wonder and awe. "How…how many steps are there? To the top?"

"Many," he told her. "Over three thousand, before you reach the Great Step. From there, there are another eight hundred and eighty eight to reach the summit."

"Eight hundred and eighty eight," Lythian repeated. The number eight was sacred to the Agarathi, he knew. Some said it was for Eldur's eight children, though most agreed it was for his eight deaths.

"Yes," Pagaloth said. "And I know what you are thinking, Knight of the Vale. That the number we so cherish here may need to be revised."

"Well…he never did die that eighth time, Pagaloth," Lythian said. Seven times Eldur had fallen during the War of the Gods, and seven times the Fire God Agarath had revived him to fight again. His eighth and final death had turned out to be a falsehood. *He was only lying in stasis*, he thought. *Lying in wait…*

"No. But he may yet, Captain."

Cevi sucked in a breath and looked at the dragonknight in horror. "*No*. You…would not want that, would you? He is our Fire Father. Our founder. His blood runs thick in Princess Talasha's veins."

"All true," Pagaloth said, quite calm. "But he is a threat as well, Cevi. A threat now to us all."

They continued the climb in silence, Cevi wondering on those words, Talasha strangely quiet. Lythian watched her closely, remembering how her eyes had gone wide and red down in those caves, how she'd fallen into a strange trance as they'd neared Eldur's tomb. *If the same happens again, might that mean he is near?* Lythian flexed his sword hand and clutched the handle of his blade. Instinct again. No wave of strength filled him, no blood-bond was ignited. Nothing. Just a leather handle beneath a leather glove. Just plain old steel and a dull dinted edge. A toy to a creature like Eldur. *I would be an ant to him, unseen and ignored, scuttling about his feet.*

Another hour passed before the mountain wall loomed before them, reaching high into the murky black skies. Banners of mist and fog swirled down through the passes, and no star could be seen, no hint of moon penetrating the roof of cloud. "Stay close to me," Pagaloth instructed. He led them over a final bridge, spanning fifty metres across a yawning chasm without bottom, across a short courtyard of stone, up a set of wide rough steps that ended in a great open arch.

Blackness awaited beyond. Blackness was all around. Lythian felt his courage wilt like a weed. The wind was so chill it froze his bones. *This is not me,* he told himself. *I am Lythian Lindar, the Knight of the Vale, the Knight of Mists, Captain of Varin's Order. I do not fear. Godsteel to grasp or no, I do not fear!*

A light bloomed within, sudden and bright, orange and red. *Fire.*

Lythian stumbled backward so abruptly he nearly fell. Cevi screamed, her voice echoing out into the night, and flew into Sir Pagaloth's arms. A form was lit, the form of a man, cloaked and cowled. *Eldur,* Lythian thought, heart thumping fiercely through his chest. He reached for his blade, drawing it with a rasping metal shriek. "Stay back!" he warned. "Stay away!"

The man stepped forward, holding the torch to one side. Behind him, Lythian glimpsed the start of the stair, spiralling up and away into the void. The hall around it was shaped circular and plain, the sconces on the walls holding unlit torches. One was missing.

"I said stay back!" Lythian surged forward, putting himself before the others. "One more step and I will strike you down!"

The man stopped. The torchlight flickered, casting his shadow across the chamber. Lythian could hear Pagaloth wrestling Cevi out of his arms, unsheathing his dragonsteel blade. A heartbeat later he was at Lythian's side, shoulder to shoulder against the darkness.

"You need not fear. I mean you no harm." The voice spoke softly from within the hall, seasoned with the accents of Agarath. "I saw you coming, from the towers. I have been sent down here to greet you."

"Who are you?" Lythian demanded of him. "Show yourself!"

The stranger dipped his head, reaching up to pull back his cowl. The face that appeared was seamed, hollow in the cheek, sharp in the nose. He wore a beard at the chin, more salt than pepper, ragged and long. There was bruising on the right side of his face, and the skin around the eye there was black as well. "Princess Talasha," he said. "It is a great pleasure to see you again."

Lythian's eyes spun back. Talasha knew the man, that was clear enough. She drifted forward, right past him, peering through the shroud of firelight. "Skymaster Nakaan? Is that you?"

"Yes, my lady. I had not expected to see you return so soon. Or at all, I will admit."

Talasha was staring at him, unblinking. "I thought you died, Sa'har. Ezukar, I saw him throw you from the saddle."

"He did, Princess. Yet I was fortunate. The fall caused nothing worse than bruising and a broken rib or two." He smiled amiably. "Come, please, let us escape these winds."

The man drew away into the hall, gesturing for them to follow. Lythian knew the name. Sa'har Nakaan had been present the day of the parley, Talasha had told them, among the escort for King Tavash under the command of Lord Vargo Ven. Lythian gripped Pagaloth's forearm as he passed, holding him back. "Can we trust him, Pagaloth?" he whispered. "What do you know of his loyalties?"

The dragonknight watched the ageing Skymaster carefully. "He was always close to Lord Marak, Lythian, that is well known. And King Dulian also. Sa'har Nakaan was Marak's wingrider during the last war, you may remember."

Lythian nodded, recalling. "He flew at Ulrik's wing when he slew King Storris and Gideon Daecar at the Burning Rock," he said.

"Yes. For this he is revered here in Agarath. Nakaan is one of the older Skymasters, and known to be wise and noble. He is to Marak what you were to Amron Daecar. A loyal captain and companion, highly skilled, widely respected."

Talasha had joined Nakaan now, Cevi nervously following behind. They approached a large iron brazier at the bottom of the steps, its outer surface etched in dragon motifs. Nakaan set about lighting it. Lythian frowned warily. "He came with Vargo Ven and Tavash to the parley," he pointed out. "His allegiance is to them now."

Pagaloth did not seem so sure. "A false allegiance, demanded of his honour," he said. "When Marak and Kin'rar colluded with you to assassinate Tavash, they acted alone. Sa'har Nakaan was not included." He glanced at Lythian. "What would you have done, Captain, if Amron Daecar had plotted a coup without your knowledge, and then fled as soon as it had failed? If another had been given the post of First Blade in his place? Would you have followed that man, as a loyal Knight of Varin, even if you misliked him?"

Lythian didn't need to think about that too long. "My honour would have compelled it of me."

"Yes. As it is with Skymaster Nakaan. Lord Marak kept him out of your plot to shield him from reprisals. Once the coup failed, he had no choice but to bend the knee to Tavash and Ven."

Lythian understood. "So you believe we can trust him?"

The dragonknight gave a single nod. "Yes, I believe that."

"Then that is good enough for me."

They stepped together through the hall, footsteps whispering on the stone, the wind hissing and howling behind them. Skymaster Nakaan had the brazier lit by now, fire and smoke swirling from the pit, casting light upon the spiralling stair above. *Kylash Hyndraha*, Lythian thought. *The Stair to the Stars.*

"Come, please, get warm," Sa'har Nakaan said. "I am sorry if I caused you alarm when I lit my torch. It was never my intention."

Lythian moved closer to the burning coals, welcoming the warming caress of the flames.

"You are Lythian Lindar, the Knight of the Vale," the man went on. He was fifty or thereabouts, short of stature and slight of build. Yet a gifted rider, Lythian remembered. Lord Ulrik Marak did not permit just any Fireborn to ride alongside him. "I have heard of your trials, Captain. Your imprisonment in Eldurath. Your escape from the Pits of Kharthar. Your time among Prince Tethian's company, and the dutiful support you did give him. You have been central to much of what has occurred here in Agarath of late." His eyes dropped to Lythian's swordbelt. "And for that you have paid a price."

He references Starslayer, Lythian realised. *He knows of my loss. Someone has told him.* "A price less dear than others, Skymaster Nakaan. Many have lost much more than I. Their lives." He paused. "And their dragons."

"Yes." Sa'har Nakaan's mild eyes dipped to the floor. There was a sadness about him, as a man who had lost a child, never to be the same again. *A sadness I understand.* "Ezukar…he abandoned me the night that the Fire Father awoke. Yet I live, at least. Not all can say the same."

"Does my brother live as well, Sa'har?" Talasha asked. *Even now, a part of her cares for him,* Lythian thought. *Despite all he's done.*

"Yes, I…I believe so, Princess. Lord Ven was able to wrest control of Malathar, and flew the king away. I am not certain how."

"Skymaster Kin'rar did the same," said Talasha. "He and Neyruu got Tethian, myself, and Ashun Klo to safety." She paused. "He…he died, Sa'har. All of them. All of them are dead."

"Oh." The Skymaster took time to digest that. It seemed to

Lythian that he'd seen as little as Talasha during the chaos of it all. "I...such tragedy. Prince Tethian, he was always such a gentle soul, and optimistic. And Kin'rar..." He shook his head. "There was no Fireborn more courteous, more noble. How did he die, pray tell?"

No one wanted to answer that, for the truth of it was too foul to voice. "We can speak on that later, Skymaster," Lythian said. He laid his gloved hand over the pommel of his blade. "You know of Starslayer, and my loss. How? Who told you?" It could only have been one of their own party, Lythian knew, and only two had failed to return from that fateful meet atop the Nest. "Does Lord Marak yet live? Or Sotel Dar, the scholar?"

Sa'har Nakaan turned his eyes upward. "Come," he said, "we have many steps to scale."

21

Elyon

Elyon landed with a thump and a splash, soaking himself in brackish brown water. He cursed under his breath and rose to his feet, dripping, pointing out with the tip of the Windblade in the direction of Lancel and Barnibus. "Don't laugh," he warned them, but too late. They were already laughing, quietly of course, but laughing all the same. "I'd like to see you do better."

"Sorry, El," chuckled Lancel, annoyingly pristine in his Varin Knight raiment of tooled leather jerkin and rich blue cloak, hair golden and washed and *not*, like Elyon's, soiled and sticky with marshland mud. "It's just…it's kinda funny, is all. You almost had it that time. That was at least four metres, I'd say. Right, Barn? Four metres?"

"At least," agreed Barnibus, who'd had the good grace to stifle his laughter as soon as Elyon had looked over. "Perhaps more."

Elyon grumbled wordlessly, shaking the silty water from his hair like a dog. "Towel," he said. Barnibus threw one over and he wiped his face down, drying himself such as he could. "Four metres. Four metres isn't exactly cruising altitude for dragons. I can leap bloody four metres!"

"It's a start," Barnibus consoled him, taking back the towel. He threw it to Lancel who bundled it into the saddlebag of his destrier, a fine beast called Monty. "You've only been training for a week, El. Be patient. The start is always the hardest."

And harder than I thought, Elyon grunted to himself. In his hubris he'd expected to unravel the mysteries of the Windblade quicker than this. *I am a Daecar. I should not be having such trouble.* But that was just stupid, he knew. No one mastered a Blade of Vandar so quickly, and it would take him weeks, if not months, to learn to fly properly.

"I'll go again," he said, looking for a good place to launch. He had taken to training out here in the marshes for two reasons. First, no one could see him. Except Lancel and Barnibus, who he only took with him for security and support. Second, the ground here was wet, soft, and made landing that much safer when he lost control and concentration and came plummeting back down to earth. When he learned the basics, and had confidence enough to fly higher, he would need to wear godsteel to protect himself should he fall, but at these low heights it wasn't so necessary.

He found firm enough footing on a small mound of mossy earth between a scattering of shallow puddles, testing their depth with a quick stab of the blade to make sure he could feel the bottom. They were about a foot deep. A good depth. If he fell - *when* he fell - he would make sure to land in one of those to cushion his landing. "OK, here goes…"

He turned his back to his friends, looking out into the empty grey mists, focusing. He was used to the sensation by now. That rhythmic flow of swirling air, moving from the blade and up his arm. The vortex spreading past elbow, to armpit, stretching and spinning around his shoulders and down his chest, torso, hips, buttocks and thighs until his entire frame was engulfed in a spiralling whirlwind of air.

That part he could do well enough; it was maintaining it that he struggled with. It required effort and concentration to generate enough force to lift him off the ground, let alone turn him in different directions or conjure any sort of speed. He knew the stories of those who'd mastered the Windblade before. How they could shoot skyward from a standing start at unimaginably explosive speeds. How they could outrun even the fleetest of dragons. How they could twist and turn and summersault through the skies, performing astonishing acrobatics that no bird or beast could hope to match.

That all seemed a long way off right now. "Four metres," he whispered to himself. "Let's get to five or six at least."

He rose gently, Windblade turned skyward, eyes looking up into the soggy grey soup above him. He could imagine his friends already laughing. The pace was truly pathetic. *I am a geriatric,* he thought. *My grandmother could go faster than this.* Still, he didn't let himself be goaded by his own self-reproach. He continued his ponderous climb, blade up, eyes up, only carefully moving the tip of the Windblade if he wanted to change direction. It must have been a comical sight. *Most people fly horizontal,* he thought. *And here I am, vertical as a pine tree…*

He held his focus a bit longer, enjoying the strange sense of calm within that spinning vortex. His friends had told him that the winds made plenty of noise from the outside, but within it was more peaceful. *I am in the eye of the storm,* he thought. *I am at the heart of the tempest…*

Once he'd climbed a few feet more, he dared a glance down and realised, with a mixed pride and alarm, that he was much higher than he'd thought. Eight, nine metres at least. Lancel and Barnibus were there, way down there, standing aside on a section of solid ground, gazing up. Their cloaks were billowing behind them, hair whipping in the breeze. Lancel had his hand up against his eyes to shield against the strong blustery winds. Barnibus looked a little concerned; a fall from this height could do him damage if he fell awkwardly in the swamp. A twisted knee or broken ankle would render him immobile for some time. *I cannot afford that,* he knew. *Enough. That's high enough, Elyon.*

The vortex was still holding well, though should he lose focus it would lose its integrity and then he'd go plummeting as he had almost every time so far. He turned his thoughts inward, narrowing his mind, focusing on the fledging blood-bond between himself and the blade. His commands were given telepathically through that bond; with enough training, they would come naturally, yet for now he had to centre his focus on a single act at a time. *Down,* he thought, giving the silent command, and the Windblade obliged him, reducing the speed of the winds, calming the tempest, permitting him a slow and gentle descent to the soft swampy earth below. Only once he'd touched the ground did the winds abate, and he could breathe out a sigh of relief.

"Yes!" exclaimed Lancel, smashing his palms together in an echoing applause. "That was awesome, Elyon. *Brilliant!*"

Is he being sarcastic? With Lancel it was often hard to tell. "It was better," Elyon allowed. In truth he was delighted. His control was much better that time. "I didn't fall, at least."

"The descent was good, very smooth." Barnibus was more reserved, as ever. The sting of the chill winds had made his plump cheeks go red. "I was concerned you might hurt yourself falling from up there. Thought I might have to rush in and try to catch you."

"Good luck with that," grinned Lancel. "A lump like him?"

Elyon strode over to join them, splashing through a few wetter sections before reaching firmer footing. "Let's call it a day," he said. "My father always told me it was good to finish on a high. It makes you more eager to train the next morning." The light was starting to fade a little too, the mists beginning to darken. He turned his eyes around, frowning. "Anyone see the fortress?"

The others began looking. They'd intentionally kept Dragon's Bane within sight for the last few hours, such as they could, though that wasn't always easy in these fogs. Only when they thinned a little, granting them a view through a pocket of cleaner air, did the fortress reveal its immensity, way off in the distance. The approach of twilight, however, had rendered it entirely unseen. The mists felt thicker too, all of a sudden, closing in tighter about them.

"No one?"

"It's that way." Lancel gestured into the fogs, though Elyon couldn't see anything out there. "That's north. I remember."

"How?" asked Barnibus. "It all looks the same out here."

Lancel made reference to a particular pattern of mossy mounds and brown-green puddles. "We passed that way. Along that raised belt between the marshy bits, right there. With the gnarled old trees on the right. I'm sure of it."

It seemed mildly familiar, though much of the marshes looked alike. There were innumerable passages between the soggy lakes and islands and those trees didn't mean so much. They were everywhere too, twisted thorny things that lurked wherever they could take root. "Fine." No one else seemed to have a better idea, so he'd have to trust Lancel's judgement. "Let's get mounted up, then."

Elyon climbed up into Snowmane's saddle - he'd been reunited with his snowy white destrier after arriving at Dragon's Bane - and began down the dry earthen bridge Lancel had pointed out. The fogs swirled and eddied about them as they passed, frogs calling out from their little watery dens. They seemed to become more animated at dusk. Even from the encampment outside the fort, they could be heard at twilight, croaking in their thousands. Elyon had never been among them when they cleared their throats and started singing, though. Usually he was long back by now, hearing them only from afar. Being amidst them he realised just how wretchedly loud they were.

"I'm not seeing anything, Lance," he called over the chorus of croaking, as the three knights trotted in the direction they thought was north. "My uncle told me people often get lost out here. I'm starting to see why."

"We should have left breadcrumbs," Barnibus said, shaking his head. "Something to follow back. It's what the patrols do. They leave markers so they know where they are."

Elyon knew there were permanent markers out here as well, stakes driven into the ground with arrows to signal where they were. And some small watchtowers had been erected too. But those were nowhere to be seen. "You're certain this is the way, Lance?"

"Yeah…absolutely."

He didn't sound certain. "If the fortress doesn't appear soon we'll have to backtrack and go another way. We'll find a marker eventually. It'll point us in the right direction."

"How little faith you have in me. We're going the right way, Elyon. I know we are."

It was twenty minutes later, with Dragon's Bane no closer to being spotted, that Lancel conceded he might have been wrong. "Those trees," he said, scratching his head. "Maybe they were on the wrong side. I thought we'd passed them on our left, so we'd have to go back with them on our right. But…maybe I got that turned around?"

"Or maybe those weren't the same trees at all," Barnibus said impatiently. "Damn it, Lancel, you've gotten us lost."

It was darker too, and the frogs were still blaring. Elyon took a moment to collect his thoughts, looking around. "It might be best to turn back around the way we came," he said. "If Lancel got things turned backward, maybe we've been going south all this time? It's safest to retrace our steps and start again. Worst comes to worst, we'll pitch our tents somewhere and make camp for the night. Find our way out in the morning. Agree?"

"You don't get a voice in this," Barnibus said to Lancel. Then, "I agree, El. It's the logical move."

"Good. Then let's go."

Retracing their steps was simpler, with each of them more watchful and aware of the route they'd taken to get here. They passed again a knot of dead trees, notable for the murder of crows gathered among the black and broken branches. There were a lot of crows here, Elyon had come to see, not so many as the frogs, but a good population all the same. *For the corpses,* he imagined. Many hundreds of Agarathi scouts and raiders had been slain in these parts over the last few months. *These marches are a buffet to them. It's just a matter of waiting for the food to be served.*

He hoped he wouldn't be on the menu. *I hold a Blade of Vandar,* he told himself. *I'm perfectly safe.* But that was his foolish hubris again. He wasn't armoured, nor were his companions, and if they came upon a strong raiding party they could find themselves in danger. Darkness and mist was a great leveller, he knew. *And so are these marshes.* Killian had told him that they often had to go out without godsteel armour, due to the softness of the ground and the weight of the godly metal. So long as they kept to the firmer roads between the bogs they were fine, but that wasn't always possible.

"I've seen men slide into the mire and never come up, Elyon," Killian had told him in that silk-soft voice of his over dinner the night they'd arrived. "The weight of our armour and blades can be a burden out here, and a fatal one at that if misused. Always make sure you know where you're stepping. Some puddles might look shallow, but they'll suck you down to your death if you're not careful. Here's a hard and fast rule we all adhere to out here…" He'd leaned across the table. "If you find yourself slipping into the waters, and you don't know where the bottom is, let go of your blade. Unsheathe it, if you don't have it to grasp already, and then *let it go.* Maybe you'll get lucky and feel firm footing a metre or so down. Fine, you can bend down and pick the blade back up. But what if the waters are ten feet deep, twenty, thirty? Some of the scholars claim the waters can reach as far down as a hundred feet in places. Even the little puddles barely wide enough to fit through. Those sinkholes can suck you down and never spit you out. So unless you feel the ground beneath you immediately, it's just not worth it. No blade is, Elyon. You just go ahead and give it up."

"And what if it's the Windblade, Killian? Do I just give that up too?"

"You give it up," he'd said, and firmly. "Unless you can fly the thing out of there, it makes no matter whether it's the Windblade or some regular godsteel dagger. Let it go, get yourself back to the surface, mark the location, and we can fish it out later. The blade will go down anyway. No sense in your drowning with it."

Elyon wasn't sure how you could fish out a blade that had sunk a hundred feet deep. You'd have to be Bladeborn and Seaborn for that. And for the life of him, he couldn't think of many of those.

"It's gone quiet," Lancel said.

Elyon had been trotting along in thought and hadn't noticed. He did now. "The frogs," he realised. "They've stopped."

The three knights came to a halt on a wide stretch of dry land, black-watered lakes spreading to their left and right. Islands of thick sedge burst from the surface in places, and stringy reeds as well, suggesting the waters weren't so deep. Elyon found that queer. How a large lake could be shallow and a tiny puddle so deep. *This place is wrong,* he thought, and not for the first time. *There's something unnatural about these marshes.*

"Do you think something has them spooked?" Lancel asked. He sounded a little spooked himself. "The frogs."

"They're animals," Barnibus told him bluntly. "Who knows what they're thinking. Maybe they just finished whatever song they were singing. Every song has to end eventually, Lance, even frog songs. You're behaving like a frightened child."

"Who says I'm frightened?"

"The tone of your voice. It's jittery."

"Yeah, well..." Lancel looked around. "It's eerie here, is all. You can play fearless all you like, Barn, I can smell the stink in your breeches from here."

Barnibus was about to respond when his horse began stamping his feet, whinnying nervously. "Hey now, Biter, come on, there's nothing to fear." He ran a hand down the horse's flank to calm him. Then Monty gave out a whinny of his own, and even Snowmane, usually so unflustered and quiet, started to snort and back away.

"We should get out of here," Lancel said. He turned left and right, peering into the mists. "Something's got them shaken and I'd rather not find out what."

"Raiders," Barny said, gripping his godsteel dagger.

Elyon knew otherwise. Somehow, he knew. "Dragon," he whispered. "There's a dragon out there."

The others turned to him, then shot their eyes to the skies. A deep beating sound *thwumped* through the air, and a black shadow passed overhead, off to their right, rippling through the cold wet fogs.

Elyon's heart stilled as he watched the shape glide effortlessly by, a single beat of its wings enough to propel it right past and away, swallowed in an instant by fog and cloud and darkness. All went quiet and still for several slow heartbeats.

Then Lancel whispered into the silence, "Do you think it saw us?" He was gripping the hilt of his blade. His knuckles were white. "We're unarmored. If it comes back…

"It's gone," Elyon said. He was watching the skies, gripping the hilt of the Windblade, hearing those winds and whispers. He could sense in the blade an uncanny stirring of excitement and unease, fading, slowly fading, as the dragon grew more distant. "It didn't see us, Lance. It must have been a scout."

"It looked big," Lancel said, swallowing. "Scouts are usually smaller than that."

"It's hard to tell through these mists." Elyon could still feel the Windblade thrumming in his grasp. There was an energy to the blade such as he'd never felt. *It is eager,* he thought. *This is the reason for its forging; to draw the blood of dragons. It wants a taste.* And yet…yet there was a fear in it all the same. A tension. Something didn't feel quite right. He cleared his mind and turned back to his friends. "Come on, let's keep going. With luck it won't come back this way."

They spurred their horses back into formation, continuing down the bridge between the lakes, watching the skies, listening for wings. Barnibus moved his big brown destrier Biter alongside Snowmane. "That was intense," he whispered. "Have you ever been that close to a dragon before?"

"Never," It was a sobering thing to admit. "You?"

"Nope. Makes you feel like you've lived a sheltered life, doesn't it?"

Elyon nodded. His heart was still beating hard from the brief sighting. The senior men had seen dragons up close, fought them, even killed them. There had always been a divide between those who'd fought in the last war, and the younger generation who'd not yet had a taste of proper battle. "We ought to report this to Lord Kanabar and the others. It might be a prelude to an attack."

Barnibus gave Lancel a stiff look. "*If* we ever find our way out of here. If it wasn't for *him* we'd never have been here in the first place."

"But perhaps it's good we were." Elyon was looking for the positives. "If this dragon is to herald an Agarathi attack, it's important we're able to warn them."

"Right. Then we have to hope Lancel is as stupid as we all think he is, and he took us in *entirely* the wrong direction earlier. If so, we should be on the right track. If not, I'm probably going to kill him."

Elyon rather hoped it wouldn't come to that, and that hope was granted a short while later when they emerged from the pall of fog to find the blazing lights of Dragon's Bane burning in the distance. "You see," Lancel said. "I was half right all along."

"*Half* right? How'd you figure that out?" Barnibus glared at him unhappily.

"Well, I was wrong the first time, and right the second time. So… half right." He spurred Monty into a gallop before Barnibus could retort.

They made straight for the fortress, passing through the bulky gatehouse, through the triple walls, and over to the thousand-horse stables where the grooms took charge of their mounts. Elyon spotted an Amadar guardsman walking past and enquired as to the whereabouts of his uncle. "In the Golden Tower, Prince Elyon," the man said. "With Lord Kanabar and some of the other lords, I believe."

The name was something of a misnomer. There was absolutely nothing golden about the Golden Tower; it was as black and bleak and uninviting as the rest of the fortress. Elyon led the way. They reached the dining chamber where they commonly held counsel, somewhere near the summit, its tall rectangular windows gifting excellent views over the marshes. Uncle Rikkard was perched at one of them, looking out into the darkness. He turned when they stepped through the high arched door, footsteps echoing through the cavernous chamber. "Ah. Thought I saw you three riding back," he said. "A little later than expected, though. Run into some trouble, did we?"

There was a spate of snickering from those seated at the table. Lord Kanabar had the head, with Killian, Lords Shorton and Fullerton and Ramas in attendance. Sir Mooton Blackshaw was there as well, which Elyon hadn't expected. There was no one else. The small gathering of men were assembled toward the far end of the large oaken table. Food had been served and eaten and wine was being drunk. "It happens to the best of us, good prince," called out Lord Kanabar. "There's no shame in getting a bit turned around in those mists."

Elyon stepped deeper into the capacious dining hall. Every tower had a dining room like this, and every one of them was dwarfed by the sprawling feast hall at the heart of the fortress. Everything about Dragon's Bane was over the top and immense, harkening back to a time of gods and monsters in an older age of the world. "Dusk closed in early," he said. "We lost sight of the Bane in the mists when they darkened. Took a while to find our way back."

"Training went well, though?" Rikkard gestured to his nephew's muddied attire. "You're getting *stuck in*, at least."

"I'm making progress. Had a bit of a breakthrough at the end, though nothing to write home about." Elyon didn't like to discuss his training if he could avoid it. It only served to put pressure on him that he could do without. He turned again to Lord Kanabar. "We saw a dragon out there, less than an hour ago. A scout, it might have been. We thought it best we warn you. They may be preparing to attack."

Sir Killian Oloran had been sitting with one leg crossed over the other, neat and dignified. He unfurled his limbs and sat forward. "None of my patrols have spotted anything, that I know of." He looked to Lord Rammas and then Rikkard. "Yours?"

Rammas shook his head.

"Not that I'm aware." Rikkard said. "How big was this dragon, Elyon?"

Elyon glanced at his friends. "We couldn't say for sure. It was shadowed by the mists."

"Just the one?" Rikkard asked.

Elyon nodded. "That we saw."

Rikkard turned to face the men seated at the table. "We'd best send out a couple of sorties, to make sure. It's a dark night out there, and the mists have thickened. That's good cover for an advance."

Lord Elton Rammas stood from the bench. "My men will see to it." Rammas was Lord of the Marshlands, and his men knew best how to scout these lands. He looked to Lord Kanabar for confirmation, got the nod he needed, and then marched muscularly from the room, quick to action and taciturn as ever.

"I like Rammas," Kanabar said once the man had left the room. "You need something done, he does it, no questions." He turned to Elyon. "If there's an Agarathi army on the march, Rammas will sniff it out. It'd be best to put the fortress on high alert, just in case."

"I'll have word spread," said Rikkard. "We've not had a dragon sighting around here for a while. It might be telling."

Elyon had thought the same. As Rikkard followed Rammas out,

Lancel moved to the table to fill them cups of wine. "You look like you need one of those, young prince," said frog-faced Fullerton, with those wide flat lips and bulging cheeks. Elyon imagined he'd feel quite at home out there in the swamp with all his croaking friends. "You're a little underdressed if you don't mind me saying."

"I prefer to dress light when I train with the Windblade, my lord. Once I've learned the basics I'll begin training in armour." Lancel handed him a cup of wine. He took a sip. "Is there any news from the Trident?"

"Not much of note," Killian told him. "Sir Dalton is trying to starve them out, last we heard. He's got the fortress cut off, but is taking the pragmatic route. I sense his lord father had ordered him not to waste too many men, if he can avoid it. He's thinking forward, Elyon. He expects a fight for his throne when all this is done, and doesn't want to be left shorthanded."

"Well that's just frankly ridiculous," Barnibus snorted. "He would save his strength for a civil war? The old fool will doom us all."

This was the last thing Elyon had wanted, the greatlords fighting over the throne. The entire intention of the two-pronged invasion of the Trident and Eagle's Perch was to take their enemies unawares before they could unite and rally. Starving them out was never an option. "What does Janilah make of this?"

"Janilah?" Lord Kanabar let out a heavy barking laugh. "Who bloody well cares what Janilah thinks? He's gone mad, haven't you heard?" And he laughed again, loudly. "The lunatic's taken to carving up his own people...and you'll never guess with what!"

Elyon knew nothing of this. "You've had word from Ilithor?"

"A crow came while you were gone," said Killian. "It seems Janilah was set upon by the mob in White Shadow, in response to Rylian's death. Another of his sworn swords was killed, along with several other knights and a whole host of soldiers from the City Watch and garrison. Janilah is said to have pulled a blue blade from his hip and started swinging." He fixed his eyes on Elyon's. "The Mistblade, Elyon. Janilah's had it all along."

Elyon digested that thoughtfully, giving no visible reaction. A part of him had suspected that for a while, in truth. The clues were all there. Janilah's growing mania. His desire to gather the Five Blades. That talk of a 'blue ghost' during the murders in Ilithor, when Janilah and Godrik Taynar had played their game of cat and mouse over the location of the Windblade. *I knew it then, if not before,* he realised. But all he said was, "I'm not surprised. Janilah has been teetering on the edge of the cliff for a while. He was always going to fall off eventually."

"And in spectacular fashion," laughed Kanabar, slapping his thigh. "The people are coming to see him for what he is, branding him monster, tyrant, madman. There are rumours he's gone into hiding. That or he went and scuttled back to the palace to live in shame and failure." The thought of Janilah's downfall clearly made Lord Wallis Kanabar a most happy man, judging by the massive smile on his wine-stained lips. "The whole north will turn against him now. And by the Steel Father it's about bloody time."

Elyon found less joy in the idea. A maddened king in possession of the Mistblade was no cause for celebration, but concern. There was no telling what he'd do now. And for all Janilah's treacheries, he was a cunning war leader and expert strategist. It was the very reason why Rylian wanted to wait until after the war before taking steps to remove him from his throne. *But now?* Elyon shook his head, sighing. "What now? Will the Tukorans take steps to overthrow him? Install Robbert as king?"

"Hard to say at this point," said Killian. "I would doubt they would do anything so rash with both Prince Robbert and Lord Kastor away at Eagle's Perch."

"Kastor," grunted Lord Kanabar. "Now there's the last man you want to be acting kingmaker. Who knows what he'll do once he gets wind of this? With Rylian dead, he might just take a knife to young Robbert's throat, march back to Ilithor and do the same to Raynald, and take the throne for himself."

"His own nephews, Wallis?" Lord Denis Shorton seemed appalled at the idea. He was tall and thin as a pole, with a huge great sweeping curve of a nose and the nasal voice to match. "Cedrik Kastor's own sister Clarris is mother to the twins. He'd never do anything so heinous."

"If you believe that, then you don't know the Kastors half as well as I do, Denis. And you don't seem to know much of history either. Most of these royal rivalries come down to blood on blood. Ambitious uncles and cruel cousins can be awfully dangerous when they start smelling weakness in the main royal line."

Elyon felt sick to even consider all that. "If Lord Kastor took that approach he'd have Vandar for an enemy," he said. "I should hope he's smart enough to realise that. His sole duty right now is to win the fortress of Eagle's Perch." He looked across the table. "Any advancements there?"

"Nothing that wasn't discussed at last council," said Killian. "He's not taking Sir Dalton's pragmatic approach, but isn't having much luck breaching the fortress either."

"He'll have an Aramatian army marching up his arse soon enough," Kanabar put in. "Unless Kastor gets his act together he'll be driven back to his ships just like your grandfather was, Elyon."

None of this news is very good, Elyon thought. And nor was his own report of the dragon sighting in the marshes. Yet still, there was something of the high spirits about the room, and from Lord Kanabar in particular, who'd been grinning and drinking with great alacrity throughout the conversation. Elyon motioned toward him with a questioning frown. There was a page of parchment on the table where he sat, laid out under his eyes. "Is that the letter from Ilithor?" he asked. "About Janilah?"

"Oh this?" Kanabar hooked it into one of his huge paws, a sparkle in his eye. "Have a read, young prince."

Elyon strode over and took the parchment between his fingers, running his eyes down the letter. It had come from Sir Finlay Maynard, a Suncoat posted over in Calmwater. Elyon knew his father, Lord Ferry the Oakenlord, and younger brother, Sir Francis, both of whom he'd gotten to know during their time in Ilithor for the wedding festivities. He read the words in Sir Finlay's graceful, flowing hand, and at once understood why Lord Wallis Kanabar was so elated. "My gods. *Borrus*..." A smile pulled up the corners of his lips. "He's alive?"

"*What*!" Lancel and Barnibus both came rushing up behind him. "What does it say!"

"That Borrus is in Calmwater. Or...or was. Apparently he's sailing here...to Mudport." He looked up. "My lord, I'm delighted for you. No wonder you're celebrating." Sir Borrus was Lord Kanabar's only son and heir. There had been rumours of a breakout at the Pits of Kharthar in Eldurath a while ago, but in truth no one expected to see him alive again. Elyon read the letter again. "It... doesn't say anything of Lythian, or Tomos." All three had gone south many moons ago, by the order of Elyon's father. He scanned the words once more, hoping he'd missed something. He hadn't. "We should send someone to Mudport at once," he said. "For when Borrus arrives."

Wallis Kanabar nodded. "That's why Mooton's here, Elyon. I though he'd be a good candidate to ride to Mudport and bring Borrus back."

"Of course. He should leave immediately."

"He wanted to make sure you were OK with it first," Lord Kanabar said. "You're his prince. He needs your consent."

Elyon felt a little embarrassed by that. "House Blackshaw are your bannermen, my lord. He answers to you, not me."

"We *all* answer to you, Elyon," Wallis Kanabar said. Then he smiled and turned to the huge, black-bearded brute at his side. "But you hear that, Mooton. You've got the go-ahead. You can ride out at first light."

"I'll do just that, my lord," rumbled Sir Mooton Blackshaw. "It'd be my honour to escort Sir Borrus back here. And to be the first to hear what the hell he's been up to…over an ale or twenty!" He laughed loudly. "Try and stop me!"

Barnibus moved in closer, reaching to take the letter from Elyon's grasp. Elyon let him have it. "So…nothing about Lythian, then? Nothing at all?"

Elyon shook his head. He'd given up any hope of seeing Lythian again a long time ago. The lack of mention of him in the letter wasn't encouraging.

Barnibus read the note. "How long is the journey to Mudport from here?"

"Five days if I ride hard," Sir Mooton told him in his blustery voice. "Borrus'll be landing about then too, if the winds are right. Be a nice welcome for him to see me there at the docks. By Varin, we're going to get *drunk*!"

Barnibus was still looking at the letter. "Sir Finlay writes that he had a boatload of companions with him. Two boatloads, in fact. That he disembarked a Lady Kathryn Merrymarsh, and some others, who'd been held captive in Pisek." He shook his head, trying to make sense of it. "Wasn't Lady Kathryn the one who went missing years ago?"

"Over a decade, if I recall," said Killian softly. "It would seem Borrus has had some adventure."

"What else does it say?" asked Lancel, peeking over Barnibus's shoulder. "Who is Borrus travelling with?"

"It doesn't mention any names."

"Borrus always had a good way of making friends," his lord

father said proudly. "Must have found some willing northmen down in the south somewhere who were happy to bring him home. And that about Lady Kathryn and the other captives? Well, beats me what's gone on there, but we'll find out soon enough. And bloody hell, Merrymarsh must be happy! He always loved that sister of his. Poor man was never the same after she went missing."

And now you have been spared that same fate, Elyon thought. He was elated by this news, yet for all that, wounded by it too. *If Lythian was with him, Sir Finlay would have said.* And much as he'd always enjoyed Sir Borrus's raucous company, there were few men in this world whom he liked more than Lythian Lindar, the noble Knight of the Vale.

He decided to leave them at that, thinking it best to wash and change and prepare should that dragon sighting augur the coming of an Agarathi army. He returned to his own quarters atop the Lookout Tower, peeled out of his filthy garb, wiped himself down and dressed himself in his wools and leathers. His armour - brought to the fortress by Lord Kanabar when he left Ilithor - had been dressed upon a mannequin, awaiting use.

Will it be tonight? he wondered, moving to the window seat of his solar, picking at a dinner of hard cheese and bread and strips of cured beef as he looked out into the thick black night. He rested the Windblade beside him, fingers wrapped loosely about its flowing hilt, strengthening the bond. The winds blew distantly, and the whispers, those too, though sometimes it was hard to tell one from the other. Elyon had taken the advice not to listen to them, not to engage or respond, yet sometimes that wasn't so easy. On occasion, he would hear the voice saying something that sent a cold shiver up his spine. It would hiss of shadow and death and a coming dread. *They will come soon,* it would say. *Soon…soon…soon…*

…soon all the skies will swarm…

The Windblade was whispering those unsettling words now, when Elyon heard the door opening and turned to find Rikkard stepping inside. His uncle must have seen the pale distant look on his face. "You're listening to the whispers," he said.

Elyon swallowed and unclasped his fingers from the haft. "Something has the Windblade spooked," he told him. "It senses an attack, I think." His eyes darted back out of the window. "Have Rammas's men found anything?"

"Not as yet." Rikkard moved into the room and shut the door.

"They've ridden a few miles into the marshes, but their messages report no sightings of an approaching army. I have the men on standby, should we hear anything."

He moved toward the window, looking out into the darkness. There were faint lights out there, blurry shapes within the fog. *Scouts and watchers,* Elyon knew. He could still hear that strange warning fluttering through his head. *Soon all the skies will swarm.* It set his heart to racing. There had been so few dragon sightings of late, almost no attacks at all. Word around camp was that the Agarathi were preparing for a massive assault, and that it was likely to be here at Dragon's Bane. *They are gathering all their strength,* the men were saying. *The hammer will fall here, hardest of all.*

Yet there were other rumours as well. Rumours of infighting among the Fireborn, of squabbling between the dragonlords, of a struggle for power and control. There were scores and scores of wild dragons at the Wings, people feared, growing restless and bold. Reports from many months ago had told of wild dragon attacks across the south coast of Lumara. Caravans were being attacked, farms raided, livestock savaged and eaten and even people too. One sailor who'd passed nearby those islands not long ago had spoken of red storms and crimson lightning and earthquakes that threw up great tidal waves across the sea.

It was hard to pick through it all, sift the truth from the hearsay and gossip. Yet Elyon was beginning to sense the stirring of a dark and baleful calamity. He was not wont to give too much credence to these rumours, yet the whispers…they were different. *They will come soon,* he thought again. *Soon all the skies will swarm.*

He turned to face his uncle. "I heard about Borrus," he said, wanting to think about something else. "And Janilah…"

Rikkard smiled. "Two quite disparate pieces of news. The return of one of our fondest heroes and the unmasking of a treacherous tyrant. For the people around here, both cause for celebration." He studied his nephew a time. "But not for you?" And he understood why. "Lythian. The note made no mention of him. You fear he is truly dead?"

"I have come to accept it, Uncle." As he had Aleron's death. And perhaps even his father's. Yet where his brother's fall had been so definitive, so final, there for all the world to see, the long absences of Lythian and his father were still weighing heavy on his mind. "It's the not knowing that's the hardest part," he said. "You end up thinking the worst."

"I understand. Expect the worst and you'll never be disappointed. Some find it easier to live that way."

"But not you? You still cling to hope?"

"Hope is important, Elyon, else you'll risk falling to despair. I try to keep a loose hold on it, at least." He turned his eyes back out of the window, spotting the return of another messenger from the scouting party. The man was riding with some haste toward the fortress. "I ought to go back down," he said. "Hear the latest report."

Elyon nodded. "I'll wait here." A part of him felt that was wrong. *I am a prince to them now, I should go down as well.* Yet another part knew different. *A prince does not rush to another man's summons. If there is any important news, someone will bring it to me.*

"As you wish." Rikkard stepped back toward the door. "I'll return if there's anything new."

Elyon found himself alone again. Alone with his thoughts and the winds and the whispers. He remained at the window, watching the lights blur at the edge of vision, listening for a rousing commotion below. *If this messenger has reported a sighting, all the fort will be stirring,* he told himself. Yet he heard nothing. No echoing calls and shouts of men. No great clattering of armour and hooves as soldiers rallied for the defence of the Bane.

All is quiet out there, he thought. Yet all the same he sat by the window for some hours more, waiting for the horns to blow and bells to toll, the beat of great war drums to signal the arrival of the Agarathi horde. He sat, and he waited, staring into the blackness.

And in that blackness he thought he saw something move; a ripple of mists, the flash of wings, a whipping tail and it was gone.

22

Amara

"Have you heard this latest from Ilithor, Amara? Goodness, such scandal. It's said he murdered women, even children. *Children*? Can you imagine it, sweet young things no older than four or five, some of the reports are saying. It's so ghastly, don't you think? I remember a time when every greatlord in the land looked up to Janilah Lukar with respect and admiration. Even those who misliked him…oh, they still respected him. But goodness me, goodness. How the mighty have fallen."

Lady Lucetia Amadar spooned a measure of chicken broth into her mouth, then took a small sip of honey-sweetened wine. For most it would be a curious breakfast meal, but Lucetia had always sworn by it, claiming chicken broth and honey-wine as being the reason for her good health. It did tend to make her rather loose-tongued and gossipy, though.

"It's troubling news, Lucy," Amara said, foregoing breakfast herself. "As if we needed more evidence that the Blades of Vandar can drive one mad, when their intentions are impure."

"It's how he had it, that's what I want to know. The Mistblade hasn't been seen for hundreds of years so far as I remember. And what a way to announce its return. Cutting up children. *Children*, Amara! For the life of me, I cannot get my head around it. What would compel Janilah to kill *children*?"

"I suppose he must have been bloodlusted," Amara offered, "not in his right mind. You know how much I have always hated my cousin, but I never took him for a child murderer." She had thought the unveiling of the monster that was her cousin would give her some pleasure, but it hadn't. *Not like this*, she thought. *I had not expected the poor people of Ilithor to suffer for his unmasking.*

"That blade *must* be taken off him at once, to prevent another catastrophe," the Lady of Ilivar announced. "We cannot have Janilah in possession of a Blade of Vandar, not if he's going to use it for such villainy. He shouldn't have had it in the first place. Those are heirlooms of Vandar, not Tukor." Lucetia took another sip of her sickly saccharine wine. "We should send someone there to demand it back."

"I'm not sure it is quite so simple as that, Lucetia. Janilah isn't likely to hand it over, no matter who demands it back. And I've heard from some sources that he's gone missing."

"Much like your husband, then. People started questioning his claim of the Sword of Varinar and look at what happened? Goodness, I never expected Janilah to do the same." She leaned in, filtering some more chicken broth through her lips, then refreshed herself with a liberal swallow of wine. "Are you not having any?"

Amara shook her head. "I am trying to cut down."

"Oh boo. Don't be boring." Lucetia clipped her fingers and a server filled a second cup.

Amara sighed. "Not the honeyed wine," she called over. If she was going to be forced to take a drink, it wasn't going to be that horrid potion that Lucetia liked to drink. "Just some watered red, please." The serving maid did as ordered and set the cup before her.

Lady Lucetia gave a triumphant nod and a smile; she didn't like to drink alone when gossiping and had no shortage of ladies here in Ilivar to call upon for that. She was sixty four now, a little weightier than she used to be, but still a handsome woman. Once, it was easy enough to see the famed beauty of her daughter Kessia in her, though now you had to look a bit harder. *But it's still there*, Amara thought. *Beneath the wrinkles and padded cheeks, the extra later of fat...she is still an attractive woman.*

"So tell me of Lillia," Lucetia said. "This boy who's always trailing her around. Jovyn, was it? Elyon's old squire. Is there something going on there?"

"Going on, Lucetia?"

"Oh come, you know what I mean. The boy's, what, fourteen,

fifteen, and Lillia's fourteenth birthday is coming up soon. It doesn't take a genius to work out what they might be doing when no one's watching."

So she's noticed it too, then. It didn't surprise her, really. They'd only been in Ilivar for a few short days, but the Lady Lucetia did not miss much of what went on under her own roof, and certainly not matters that concerned her own granddaughter. "Jovyn has always liked Lillia," Amara admitted. "It's only recently that Lillia's begun to mirror his affection."

"Well I can see why. I remember seeing the boy when we came to Varinar for the Song of the First Blade. He's grown significantly since then, leaning out into a man. You put two youngsters together for that long, have them training and dancing around all day in the yard, *sweating*. Well, it's not uncommon for sparks to fly. And you don't seem to be doing much to discourage them, Amara."

"Should I be? So far as I see it, they can do as they please now that Lillia's betrothal to Robbert Lukar had fallen through."

"But *has* it fallen through? All this with Janilah...Robbert might just be King of Tukor soon enough and Lillia his beautiful young queen. That could still happen, Amara. And this little tryst with Jovyn won't help."

"Tryst?" Amara had to chuckle at the word. "You make it sound like some sordid little love affair. Believe me, Lucy, they haven't gone further than glances and giggles so far. There's an affection there, yes, that might grow into something in time, but it's nothing to worry about as yet."

"Certainly not while they've living under my roof. Brydon would never permit it, whether this betrothal to Prince Robbert stands or not. The boy is too lowborn. Lillia will wed someone of her station."

"Is that Brydon speaking or you?"

"My voice isn't so deep as my husband's, Amara. This is *me* speaking, though Brydon and I are of the same mind on the subject. Lillia is a product of two greathouses, and her children will be as well. Colborn, as I understand it, is *not* a greathouse. If not the Lukars, we'll find someone suitable among the Kanabars, Taynars, Olorans, Pentars, or another of the Tukoran or Rasal greathouses for her."

"Well why not an Amadar, Lucetia? You seem awfully keen to 'keep it in the family'. I'm sure there's some cousin somewhere who Lillia could be wedded to."

"Oh come, Amara, don't turn that acid tongue on me. You know I give as good as I get. And since when did you become so sensitive to this? You're well aware of how this game works."

Amara didn't have much of an answer for that. Perhaps it was simply a matter of fatigue. A weariness at that horrid interbreeding game that was ripe for ending. Or maybe it was the fact that she'd not felt right since she'd found out about Rylian's death. *It was my fault,* she knew. *It was my scheming that got him killed.* She had wrestled with that knowledge ever since and couldn't seem to shift it. *And Amron,* she thought. *Amron who still hasn't returned, and may never, because of what I did.* "You sent my father away," Elyon had scolded her that night at Elmhall Hold. "You recklessly filled his head full of dreams and sent him away to die."

And perhaps that's just what I did, she reflected. *Amron and Walter both. Maybe neither will ever return, and all because of me...*

"Amara, come now, I was only having a jest..." Amara raised her eyes to find Lucetia looking at her pityingly. "You look so terribly forlorn. What *is* the matter? I know you have come to like this boy Jovyn, but he really isn't a good fit for Lillia. Does it really trouble you so to break the two apart?"

Amara shook her head and steadied her emotions. "It isn't that, Lucy, I was...my mind was elsewhere." She took a further moment to compose herself, and drew on her watered wine to help. "And Lillia's fate really isn't for me to decide. I am not her blood, Lucetia."

"Oh come, come now, don't say that." Lucetia reached over and took hold of Amara's wrist, squeezing with a plump and wrinkled hand. "You have been a mother to Lillia, and I'll never hear you say otherwise. Brydon and I...both of us are more thankful than we can say for raising her into the spirited young woman she is. Truly, Amara. Don't ever say anything so foolish again."

Amara smiled wanly. She and Lucetia had always been friendly, though grew that much closer when Kessia died and Amara was raised to the post of surrogate mother to her grandchildren. She didn't much believe that about Brydon, though. He was a stern old man and their interactions had never been warm. *And I am hardly alone in that.* Brydon Amadar, the intractable Lord of Ilivar, reminded her far too much of her sweet cousin Janilah. "That is awfully kind of you to say, Lucy," she said. "But I think you know as well as I do that Brydon has always blamed me for Lillia's capricious and impulsive nature."

Lucetia flicked a wrist. "Ignore him, Amara. Brydon forgets that Kessia was just the same at that age. But then fathers have a habit of idealising their daughters, don't they? It's sweet half the time, and rather sad the rest. Deep down Brydon knows how well you've done with Lillia. He won't ever say it, but believe me, he does."

Amara had another sip of watery wine, thinking, *I'll have to take your word for it.* She'd seen Lord Brydon just the once since arriving from across the Heartlands, and that the very morning they'd appeared at the city gates. The Lord of Ilivar had been there to greet them, hugging his granddaughter, giving Amara a frosty and perfunctory peck on the cheek, eyeing Carly Flame Mane and her band of sellswords with an upturned and disapproving eye before declaring he had business to attend to that would keep him gone for several days. That business, Amara had learned after, involved a thorough check of the city walls and defences, an accounting of its ballistas and scorpions, bowmen and soldiers. Lord Amadar was a man of meticulous war planning, and was not going to permit a single weakness in the city's fortifications at such a time. But those checks were now complete, she knew, and Lord Brydon Amadar was set to return.

They took the last of the breakfast onto the balcony of the dining hall, Amara sipping on her watered wine, Lady Lucetia moving onto a single boiled egg that she liked to consume after her chicken broth. It gave answer to the age-old question of what came first, the chicken or the egg. With Lady Lucetia, at least, it was most assuredly the chicken.

They were reclining in soft-cushioned seats, enjoying the gentle lakeside ambience and view of the sparkling waters when a household footman announced the arrival of Lucetia's husband. "Lord Amadar is approaching the castle gates, my lady. Would you like to greet him at the front door?"

"Good gracious no," Lady Lucetia huffed at the notion. "Why should we run to *his* beck and call. No, he can come here to greet *us*. Don't you agree, Amara?"

Amara didn't think it especially wise to rile the man's temper, but had no option but to laugh and say, "Oh yes, I quite agree, Lucetia," knowing that, one way or another, Lord Brydon would blame her for it, rather than his wife.

She spent the next few minutes sitting stiffly, listening to Lucetia going on about the latest scandals and gossips. This was how they'd built the foundation of their friendship, but it had all come to feel rather hollow to Amara now, a bit cheap and tawdry and so perilously unimportant given what was happening in the world. She did her bit, though, nodding, smiling, raising her eyes at the right moments, going 'ooo' and 'ahhh' when she needed. Lucetia Amadar was not a vacuous person, she was just sheltered and bored and had nothing much else to fill her time with. Amara did not begrudge her any of it. *I have been much the same,* she knew. Yet these days, the tattle had lost its savour. It just felt tasteless now.

The sound of heavy boots came thudding through the dining room behind them, as Lord Amadar's resounding voice barked out a command for a cup of water. Lord Brydon was not one for drinking. "Lucetia, you didn't want to meet me at the front entrance?" He came striding out onto the terrace, those severe hazel-green eyes of his swinging right to Amara. "Ah, *of course.* You've been drinking."

Lucetia waved up to him. "Come, darling, give me a kiss and don't be so grumpy. We were having a lovely morning before you arrived."

"I'm sure. A morning spent gossiping, no doubt." He bent down and kissed his wife's cheek with a puckered and stiff-lipped mouth. Lord Brydon was in fine fettle for his age, leaner than a man twenty years his junior, with a short grey beard over chiselled chin and cheeks and hair that was only slightly thinning. If Lucetia had added some weight to her frame that veiled her former beauty, Lord Brydon had kept a ruggedly handsome countenance deep into his sixty-seventh year. "How long have you been out here?"

His eyes looked at Amara's wine cup, stayed there a moment, and then moved away. The question within his question was, *How much have you been drinking*?

His wife gave answer. "Not long," she said, with a grin that seemed to say, *we've had a couple of cups.* "Come, Brydon, do join us. You can tell us all about your thrilling tour of the city defences." She looked over. "I could do with a morning nap, couldn't you, Amara?"

Amara didn't like how Lucetia brought her into her jests. *It makes me seem like I'm part of them,* she thought, and if she was to spend an extended time in Lord Brydon's keep, she didn't want to stir any unnecessary resentment between them. "I'm sure your lord husband's work has been most interesting," she said, trying to sound sincere, though acutely aware that Brydon Amadar was taking it as sarcasm. *Oh yes, there's that reproachful raise of the eyebrow. He hears mocking in everything I say.*

"I can tell you about it later," Brydon said bluntly. "In short, the city is watertight. We have taken every possible precaution to ensure we're well prepared. Now Lucetia, if you would please give me and Amara a moment. There's a matter I would like to discuss with her."

Oh joy.

"Something I should know about?" Lucetia asked. The joviality was gone from her voice. "You have a look on your face, Brydon."

"Lucetia, please. A moment with Amara. Alone."

His lady wife's face bunched up unhappily at that, though she seemed to know best not to argue. "Fine. Amara, you'll tell me about it right after. If he asks something unpleasant of you, come to me and we'll figure it out…"

"Gods, woman, just leave us." Lord Amadar gave her a stern look, though Lucetia merely smiled, rose, and pecked his cheek.

"So tetchy," she said, and shuffled away.

Lord Amadar stepped over to the balustrade, laying both of his gnarled old hands on the cold grey stone. He filled his lungs with a full breath of cool winter air, looking out over the vastness of the lake. He stared in a single direction for a time, eyes never seeming to move or shift or take in anything but what was ahead of his immediate line of sight. Then, eventually, he spoke. "I heard about King Janilah. That's *another* Blade of Vandar, *another* act of treachery on account of them." He shook his head; a single motion. "We never had a chance to speak about Elyon when you arrived, Amara. About this business in Ilithor. About the Windblade. Treachery," he murmured, then turned. "You stole from your very own king."

Amara remained seated. *I must appear calm,* she thought, despite the thumping in her chest. Lord Brydon Amadar was not one for pleasantries. *Straight down into it as always.* "I do not consider Godrik Taynar to be my king, Brydon."

"No matter what you think, he *is* your king by royal decree of his predecessor, our *lawful* king, and you stole from him. Worse, you had Elyon steal from him, my own grandson, and have brought dishonour upon House Amadar and House Daecar both. And now we hear this about Janilah. The Mistblade. The madness. And Vesryn, let's not forget about him. Who is to say Elyon will not follow the same path, given how he acquired the blade? Who's to say he won't be driven mad as well?"

"He won't. His path is righteous. To master the Windblade and help win the war. And Vesryn is not mad, Brydon. He has not been killing innocent children, as Janilah has."

"Your husband stole the Sword of Varinar. He abandoned his post and besmirched his name, and has not been seen since. He is your husband, and you defend him, as is your right and your duty, but do not claim he is in his right mind. The evidence speaks for itself."

She held her tongue. Amara had no intention of telling Brydon Amadar of her interaction with Vesryn a month ago, or what her husband had said.

"And where might I ask is Amron in all this?" the Lord of Ilivar blustered. "I have had word from trusted sources in the west. From the Twinfort, Green Harbour, Blackfrost and elsewhere, and every one of them reports that Amron is nowhere to be seen. I find that odd, to say the least. Aleron is dead. Vesryn a traitor. And Amron has apparently disappeared from the face of the earth. And now this with Elyon. Plotting to steal a Blade of Vandar from his lawful king and causing untold distress as a consequence." He paused and shook his head. "What has House Daecar come to? It shames us all to see it fallen so low."

"Oh spare me, Brydon. You're relishing this, admit it."

His nostrils flared. "*Relishing* it?"

"Yes, relishing it." It was inadvisable, perhaps, to speak to him like this, but on she went anyway. "You've always hated Amron. That's no secret. You're enjoying seeing him fall."

Brydon stared at her through a disbelieving squint. "You have said some things in your time, Amara, but *this*...this is truly low. This is about more than just Amron, woman. I'm talking about Elyon. I'm talking about my own *grandson*."

She stood and took a sharp step forward. "Your grandson, yes. Your grandson who your *son* bends the knee to. Rikkard is behind Elyon, like the rest of us, proclaiming him prince. Why can't you do the same?"

"Because it's not bloody lawful, that's why! When we abandon law and order, what do we have? Chaos and anarchy, every man for himself."

"So you would blindly bow to treachery? For your precious adherence to the law?"

"I would keep the peace, that is what I'd do." He stepped forward, closing the space between them. "Hold out your hand."

"What? No..."

"Hold it out, Amara." He snatched at her wrist and pulled it up. "Open your fingers."

"Why?"

"Just do it." He began prising them apart, until she relented, holding her hand up, fingers splayed.

"What are you trying to..."

He gripped her index finger, twisted it back to the point of pain. She grimaced from the sudden motion. "It hurts, doesn't it?" He bent it back a bit more. "How easy it would be to break." He let go, grabbed another finger, twisted. "And this one, oh I could break it so easily."

She cringed again, tensing. "Brydon, you're hurting me..." She jerked her hand away, and he let her fingers go, though kept hold of her wrist. Her hand instinctively closed into a defensive fist.

"*Good.* Yes, good." He pulled her hand back up, trying to dig her fingers open. She held them closed with all her strength. "See how hard it is now?" He dug some more, but to no reward. "You're prepared, fortified, defended. *United.* Your fist is the north, Amara, or how it *should* have been. That is what Janilah was trying to do, but he used the wrong damn means to do it. Now look what's happened. We're all a bunch of brittle open fingers, vulnerable to being snapped and twisted and broken. And when one falls the rest are sure to follow. You can't make a strong fist with a broken finger, Amara. One by one they'll be prised apart. One by one they'll snap." He snorted and shook his head, letting her go. She stumbled back away from him. "What you and Elyon did is but one part of a bigger problem, but you've contributed to this mess. And now I want you to help set it right."

She flexed her fingers, heart pounding. "You didn't have to be so violent, Brydon." But his point was taken. "What exactly do you want me to do?"

"Go to Varinar, speak with King Godrik, smooth out the trouble you've caused."

"No, I..."

"You're going, Amara. This rift between the Vandarian greathouses must be healed, for all our sakes. Do you have any idea what is happening at the Trident? I'm told Dalton Taynar has the fortress surrounded yet refuses to engage. To save men," he scoffed. "King Godrik is already looking ahead to civil war in Vandar and a battle for his throne. That sort of thinking makes us all vulnerable. I will not let it endure."

"And what do you expect me to do? Godrik is likely to throw me straight into the palace dungeons as soon as I arrive."

"You'll have a banner of peace with you. And my own backing. Impress upon Godrik the need to renew lines of communication between us. Give him assurances that Vandar will not descend into civil war once the south is subdued."

Amara began shaking her head. "He won't listen to a word I say. I have no authority to..."

"We have to start somewhere," Lord Amadar broke in. "I would go myself, but must remain here should we come under attack. At the least, your arrival will settle tensions. You can explain to Godrik your reasoning for stealing the Windblade. He is a rational man. He will understand."

Amara doubted that wholeheartedly. "He will want the Windblade back," she said. "You know he will, Brydon."

"Yes. And you will start that dialogue as well. As king it is Godrik's right to determine who holds the Windblade. You and Elyon should never have stolen it. If Dalton had been given the chance, he might have it mastered by now, and the Trident won, and we'd all be safer for it. But no, you had to interfere. Well enough. You're to leave at once and no more complaints. And take those damned sellswords with you. I do not want their sort polluting my city. I want them gone. Today."

Amara had never disliked the man more. "And Lillia?"

"Will stay here," he barked. "She is almost fourteen and will live with us from now on. Her father clearly has no interest in her wellbeing, and you...involving her in your sordid little schemes. You've corrupted my grandchildren enough, Amara. And you can take that boy with you as well."

Amara laughed scornfully. "You really don't know her at all, do you? She will hate you forever if you send Jovyn away."

"She is a child. She will learn to grow out of such impulses. The girl has grown far too wilful in your care. And training her? No doubt that was your idea too. It ends now."

"*No.*" Her voice took on a note of pleading. "Brydon, *don't.*

Sending Jovyn away is one thing, but denying her training…no, you can't."

"I can. And I will. She will rant and rave and throw her tantrums, I am sure, but soon she'll wear herself out and when she does, she can receive proper instruction on what it means to be the lady of a greathouse. Running around with a godsteel dagger playing at knights and assassins is not what a girl of her age and station should be doing."

"She has been learning to defend herself, for goodness sake. Elyon himself put that dagger in her hand and Amron permitted it. You have no right to go against their will."

"I have every right. I am her grandfather. And the only one who seems to have her best interests at heart, judging by what I've seen."

Amara scooped up her cup of watered wine and tossed the contents into the man's face. Pale red liquid drizzled down through his short grey bristles of his beard. He did not flinch, nor blink, not once. He merely shook his head and said, "You love the girl, I know. But we look at the world in different ways, Amara. Your time as her guardian is done. I am sorry. But it is done." He lifted his still-dripping chin, turned, and marched away across the terrace and through the dining hall.

Amara listened to his footsteps echoing away down the corridor, that purposeful stride, strong and metronomic. She could hear him barking orders for Amara's belongings to be gathered and packed. A few moments later Lucetia came hurrying back out, a ghostly look on her face. "Oh Amara, my dear, I heard what happened. Every word…I heard it."

Heard and did nothing, Amara thought.

"I'll speak to him, get this smoothed over. He gets into these moods, you know how he is, but he'll come around, he always does."

Amara turned to the Lady Lucetia, forcing a smile onto her face. "I thank you for your hospitality these last days, Lucy. You have been a kind host, as always."

Lucetia's old eyes swelled beneath a frown. "You don't truly mean to leave?"

"You heard your husband. I have a duty to attend."

"Yes, but you'll return right after? Brydon did not mean what he said. I promise you, he knows how well you have mothered Lillia. Don't listen to him, Amara, I beg you. He just needs a moment to calm down, that's all."

Amara kissed her cheek. "I'll be gone within the hour."

"Amara, come, this is madness. Wait, at least a while. You can leave tomorrow if you must. If you and Brydon speak this evening, I'm sure you'll…"

"No." Amara was too angry and upset to play this game of pleasantries anymore. "Your husband has made himself abundantly clear. I'm going, Lucetia. Thank you again for your hospitality. And be safe. These are dangerous times." She stepped past the plump old woman and strode through the hall, forcing herself to strangle her emotions. "Summon Sir Connor," she told a household servant. "I'll be in my room."

Sir Connor Crawfield arrived there a few minutes later. He took one look around, stiff-jawed and unsmiling, as ever. Her clothes and personal items were already being packed by her maids. "I'm told we're leaving, my lady."

"At once," she confirmed. "Lillia is to remain here. I will have Sir Daryl stay with her. Gods know she'll need a friendly face while we're gone."

"And the boy? Is he not to…"

"Jovyn will be coming with us. I will speak to him on the road about sending him to Dragon's Bane to return to Elyon's service, if he should wish. Elsewise I'll be happy to keep him in our company. Send word to Carly as well, have them mustered to leave. I want to be gone by midday."

"So soon?"

"Sooner."

"Then I shall see to it," Sir Connor said, bowing. "Might I ask… where exactly are we going this time?"

"Home, Sir Connor. To Varinar. It seems I have a false king I need to grovel to."

23

Cecilia

"Thank you, Sir Kevyn, you can leave me here."

The big bald knight gave a shallow bow. "I'll be waiting, my lady. You be careful on those stairs, y'hear. And on the way down in particular. Most servants who take food up never make it back."

"I am quite good on stairs, Sir Kevyn," Cecilia told him.

"I'm sure, my lady, but you've never climbed any like these, I'll wager. Just keep ahold of your godsteel dagger and stay close to the side of the cliff. If there's a sudden squall, make yourself small, or you'll find yourself blown off into the abyss."

Cecilia Blakewood had no intention of being blown off into any abyss. "Your concern is truly heartwarming, Sir Kevyn. I shan't be long." She furled her cloak about herself, stepping out of the tunnel opening and into the jagged chaos of the high Hammersongs. The wind was already blowing fiercely, snowflakes swirling in the air. A narrow chasm between tall cliff faces of frosted black rock rose up either side of her. She pressed through the gap, moving around to the right, where the left cliff shallowed and then gave way to a ranging expanse of distant peaks. To the right, Cecilia spotted the start of the stair, cut into the cliffside and disappearing into the thick white mists above her.

Well, Sir Kevyn wasn't wrong, she thought. The steps looked treacherous, cracked and broken and sprinkled with patches of ice, zigzagging back and forth up the mountain face in a frightening vertical ascent. She spared a thought for the poor servants required to make the climb. Without the bracing and strengthening effects of godsteel, she could quite imagine how many of them would slip and fall to their doom.

She strode toward the first step, tested her footing, and began the climb. A part of her doubted the sense in this, but she knew her father had made this ascent a hundred times before, and if he could do it, so could she. *And he is the reason I'm going up there,* she thought. It had been over a week since the madness at Galin's Post and Janilah Lukar was still nowhere to be found. They had searched high and low, all through the palace and city, but thus far no one had thought to venture up to Ilith's ancient forge. It was time someone rectified that. *And who better than me, his beloved daughter?* Cecilia had no real expectation of finding her father sequestered up here, of course, but even so, there was a young man kept hidden in the heights above whom she had always wanted to meet.

The way up was as hazardous as she'd imagined. The winds assailed her unrelentingly, blowing one way and then the other, pulling at her cloak and clothes, trying to dislodge her from the cliff. She took the Bull of Bolt's advice and made herself small when needed, keeping as close to the soaring mountain face as possible. Sometimes she had no choice; in places the steps had become so worn and broken as to be only a foot or so wide. *Much more narrow and I'd have to turn sideways and shimmy,* she thought, though by some mercy it never came to that. Once, these stairs had been broader, more magnificent, but had long since fallen into decay. She could see signs of the rampart that had once bordered the outer edge, the pillars that marked the turns and switchbacks. All but the stumps of a few of those remained now, the rest beaten into submission by the constant blowing winds and gales and ice. With no one to tend or restore them they had succumbed to disrepair. *These stairs are as my father,* Cecilia thought, *once magnificent, now a broken fractured thing...*

Eventually she spotted the top, where the stairs ended at the summit. *This is a place of gods,* she thought, as she climbed up onto the high plateau. *Where Ilith forged the Blades of Vandar. Where he stood upon this very step, looking out upon all the world, planning his latest marvel.*

Even now, she could hear the distant singing of his hammer, the hammer that had given these mountains their name. *Yet no,* she realised, squinting through the snows, seeing the glowing orange cave veiled amid the mists. There was a figure in there, toiling in his workshop, swinging down and down and down upon his anvil. She blinked, took a breath, as though seeing Ilith himself come back to life. Then she laughed and escaped the foolish whimsy of it all. *This is but Tyrith,* she told herself, *the demigod's last living heir. A shadow of him, no more. We are all but shadows of those who came before.*

She stepped forward, the fogs eddying and swirling around her, cloak catching and pulling in the wind. Her feet crunched upon ice and snow and the winds howled out, all the louder, as she neared. Then all of a sudden the hammering stopped, as the young blacksmith turned and saw her coming. He faced her, frowning, dressed in sweat-soiled vest and breeches, the greatest known artefact in all the world - the Hammer of Tukor - held in his grasp.

Cecilia reflected on what the histories said of Ilith. Slight of build, gold of hair with sparkling emerald eyes. He was oft described as having a silvery, soft-spoken voice, persuasive and polite. *And this young man Tyrith has much of the same about him,* she thought, as he studied her arrival with a curious smile and asked, "Who are you, my lady? You do not look like a servant."

"I'm not a servant, Tyrith." She stepped through the frigid winds and into the warmth of the cave, marvelling at the simple wooden furnishings, the ancient armour and weapons hanging on the glistening rock walls, the stacks of books and scrolls of parchment heaped upon shelves along one side.

For a moment she forgot all about the blacksmith, until he said, "Did the king send you? I have been hoping that he might come himself. It's been so long."

She turned to face him. "The king is currently indisposed, I'm afraid. He asked that I come visit you in his stead."

"Indisposed? I do hope nothing has happened to him?" The young man was modest of face, yet kind, with a certain innocence to him, Cecilia noted. *The heir of Ilith indeed.*

"Nothing to bother you, Tyrith." She saw no merit in telling him of what had gone on in the city below. *And clearly my father has not been here,* she thought. *Well, I might just stay a while anyway.* Her eyes were drawn to the hammer in the man's grasp. "The Hammer of Tukor," she said. "I have always longed to see it. Do you mind if I…"

"By all means." He placed the hammer aside on his workbench with a heavy resounding *clunk*, giving Cecilia a moment to admire it. "What do you think, my lady? Is it all you had hoped it would be?"

"Oh very much so," she said, lying. In actuality it was a disappointingly drab thing. There were etchings and markings worked into the metal that radiated a certain light, yes, but nothing so spectacular as the swirling mists that poured off the edge of a godsteel blade. It wasn't so large as she'd imagined it to be either. "I'm told you're the only man living who can wield it, Tyrith."

"Yes, that is true. Only those of Ilith's direct bloodline can bear the hammer. I am the last." He smiled with a childlike pride, then gave her a questioning look. "I am in remiss, my lady. I do not know your name."

"It is I who is in remiss, Tyrith. I forget my courtesies in the face of such wonder. The Hammer of Tukor and the heir of Ilith, here before lowly little me." She drew her eyes from the hammer and looked right at him, smiling, even managing a delicate curtsey. "My name is Cecilia Blakewood, natural born daughter of King Janilah Lukar. He may have mentioned me before."

Tyrith nodded briskly. "Lady Cecilia Blakewood, natural daughter to the king. Yes, yes of course he has mentioned you, my lady. And most often at that."

That would be a no, then, she thought, laughing inwardly at his blundering attempt to spare her. *He is sweet, this young blacksmith.* "Oh now, *this* is lovely…" She spotted a suit of armour across the forge, dressed upon a mannequin. Green godsteel plate, inlaid with gold, form-fitting and quite spectacular. She began striding over, Tyrith at her heel. "I recognise this. It's my father's armour, is it not?"

"You have a good eye, my lady. I have been working to improve it, at your father's request. He asked me to make him a suit of armour worthy of a god. And that he is, of course. Or will be, once he combines the blades, and bears the Heart of Vandar aloft."

Cecilia scoffed silently to that. *My father will never combine the blades, nor will he stand among us divine.* That ship had sailed now, and wasn't coming back. "I love the helm, Tyrith," she said. She felt no desire to distress the young man by telling him of her father's long litany of recent failures. *We'll be here all day if I do, and I have other matters to attend to.* "These are the Five Blades, I see, rising from the crest. Such beautiful work. The likenesses are perfect."

Tyrith was delighted to hear her praise, by evidence of that smile. "I have worked hard to make sure they look like the blades in question." He stepped in and picked the helm up, so she might have a closer look. "See here. The Sword of Varinar at the centre, broader and longer than the others. I have placed the Mistblade and the

Nightblade to the right, the Windblade and Frostblade to the left. These pairs are twins, as I'm sure you know. Note the subtle differences between each." He gestured excitedly toward a long countertop beneath the shelves of books and scrolls. "There are many sketches of the Blades of Vandar that have given me inspiration, and often by Ilith's own hand. I even have some of his original design ideas, before he decided upon the final forms they might take."

"Oh? That's fascinating, Tyrith."

"Yes, my lady, isn't it just? The blades as we know them might have been very different, you know. In both design and look and magic as well."

"Magic, truly?"

"Oh yes. He had many ideas. One blade was to give its bearer the power to move earth. Another to control water. He had a plan at first to endow each blade with a different elemental power. The control of earth, wind, fire, water. We ended up with the Windblade only, of course, though Ilith also forged the Fireblade as a gift for Eldur. He had planned to fashion a Waterblade for Queen Thala as well, but she told him to put his efforts elsewhere. And there were other ideas, too, even more outlandish. Mind manipulation. Magnetic control. Even the ability to teleport."

"Teleport?" she chuckled. "Now come, Tyrith, that must be a jest."

"No jest, my lady, I promise you. Ilith is famed as a blacksmith and a builder, but really, he was a wizard above all. The spells he could weave, oh my. Given time nothing seemed beyond him. During his latter years he worked hard to discover the secret to portal sorcery. He had planned to create portal doors all across the north to make travel much easier and faster. A grand vision that never came to pass unfortunately."

"A shame," Cecilia said. She imagined portal doors would make the gathering of councils and conveyance of men and munitions to war a great deal simpler. "Perhaps you might continue your ancestor's good work, Tyrith?" She smiled pleasantly. "I'm sure you've learned much of Ilith's methods from his notes and writings."

He nodded modestly. "Oh yes, Lady Cecilia. I have learned a great deal from them, though I could never claim to share his gift. There is no one in all history who can." He placed down the gold-green helm, crested with those miniature Blades of Vandar that Cecilia actually found terribly cheap, and led her over to the teeming stacks and shelves. "All of these have helped teach me how to master the Hammer of Tukor, though I still have much to learn, I will confess. The *formula* though...it does continue to vex me. I am getting closer...every day I'm getting closer...but I remain unsure of the precise method required to combine the Five Blades into one."

I wouldn't bother, she thought. *Those blades will never be combined.* "Keep working on it, Tyrith," she told him instead. "I'm sure you'll figure it out eventually."

He smiled, nodded, fidgeting with his fingers. "I wonder, my lady...has your father...has he gathered any of the others. The last time he came here he told me he would *fly* up next time, rather than climb the stairs. He said it with a smile, and I just knew he was talking about the Windblade. I would dearly like him to show it to me, if...if he does have it, that is."

Cecilia had not the heart to tell him the truth of it. *And my father, smiling?* Now that sounded most unlikely. "The king is working hard, as ever, to bring the pieces of the puzzle together," she told him, though even that was a lie. The truth would go rather differently: *The king has only the Mistblade, Tyrith, and that he has used, according to reports, to murder about a hundred men, women, and even children in a crazed and blood-lusted assault. He has since gone missing, and no one knows where. He might be hiding in some cellar somewhere, or in a long forgotten part of the palace. Or perhaps he has used the unique magical power of the Mistblade to sink down into the earth to die, entombed forever right beneath our feet with the blade eternally fixed to his grasp.*

That last theory had been gathering some momentum, in fact, and Cecilia found it rather compelling. Survivors who'd seen Janilah's frenzied onslaught had claimed he never left Galin's Post, though with all the smoke and blood and chaos of the crush who knew if that were true? Still, there was something poetic in the thought that the king had chosen to sink away into the stone and never rise again. *The blue ghost dwells here at Galin's Post,* people were starting to say. *This place is cursed and the city with it.* And on the back of all that, some had even started to leave, gathering their belongings and emptying out into the valleys and pastures beyond the mountains, away into the Stonehills and north into the moorlands and anywhere else they might go.

The world has all gone mad, Cecilia thought. And it felt like only the beginning.

"My lady?" Tyrith was gazing at her like a lost child. "Do you mean to say, your father has only the Mistblade still?"

"He is working hard," Cecilia repeated tritely. "It is not for me to say any more than that, Tyrith. I do hope you understand."

He nodded sadly.

Goodness, what a wretchedly lonely creature he must be. "Do you need a hug, Tyrith?"

He frowned at the suddenness of the question, looking abashed. "A hug, my lady? No. Oh no. Do I look like I do? Is…is it that obvious?" He laughed uncomfortably.

"It cannot be easy, living alone up here."

He swallowed. "I have my work. It is more than enough to satisfy me. Ilith was the same. He would work for weeks at a time without break, you know. And sing. Oh how he liked to sing as he worked."

"Do you sing, Tyrith?"

"Sing?" He shuffled his feet. "Well, yes, I suppose I do…on occasion. Though I would not pretend to carry a tune. Sometimes…" He had a softly endearing smile on that slim and youthful face. "Sometimes one or another of the servants will come upon me, while I'm butchering a popular tune. I say, I have embarrassed myself more than once up here. And I just know they return to their friends below to have a good long chuckle at my expense. But I don't mind, of course. A man who cannot laugh at his failings is never destined to be happy, is he?"

She liked the wisdom in that, and showed it with her smile. *My father could learn a lot from you,* she mused. *Has there ever been a man so cripplingly unable to laugh at himself as Janilah Lukar?*

She did not think he needed to worry so much about those servants, though, laughing behind his back. As Sir Kevyn had said, most slipped to their deaths on the way down, and those who survived were met with a good length of sharp steel anyway. *No, Father would never permit them knowledge of Tyrith and his ancestor's forgotten forge,* Cecilia thought. *Imagine if one of them should tell someone. No, he couldn't be risking that.* She had never asked him directly - perhaps because she didn't want to hear the answer - but she felt quite sure that every servant who tended to Tyrith's needs did so just the once. Whether they made it back down the treacherous stair or not, none of them would be allowed to live.

She had another look around the workshop. To the rear a stone passageway tunnelled away into the mountain. "What is through there?" she asked.

Tyrith followed her eyes. "Living chambers, my lady. I have a small bed and desk, some trunks for spare sets of clothes. Nothing of note. I am a man of simple pleasures."

As Ilith was, Cecilia thought. *My father has made himself a little demigod clone.* "Might I see?"

He nodded. "If you like."

The place was as unspectacular as described, meagrely furnished, small, and actually rather sad. No matter what the blacksmith said, she couldn't imagine he was happy here. "How long have you been living here, Tyrith?"

He took a few moments to think. "As long as I can remember, my lady. I was brought up here as a young boy. Your father…he wanted me learning the ways of the hammer as soon as I was able. He told me my mind was a sponge, to be soaked in knowledge and learning. I don't think he wanted me to suffer any distraction." He glanced out through the passage. "Such as you find below."

"But you've never been below, Tyrith." She found the notion strangely upsetting. "How old are you now? Twenty three? Twenty four?"

"Twenty five, my lady."

"So you've been here some twenty years?"

"Oh yes, at least."

"And you've never wanted to see more of the world? There is so much out there, Tyrith. So much that might inspire you."

But of course that wasn't his purpose, she knew. The young blacksmith was just another of her father's tools, required to master the Hammer of Tukor and combine the Five Blades, thus uniting the Heart of Vandar. Nothing else mattered to him. And without the Five Blades to unite, what was he? *A tool sitting on a workbench gathering dust and rust,* she thought. *And potentially something more dangerous too…*

The rightful King of Tukor.

She mulled on that a moment, then on she went with her probe. "Tell me of your father, Tyrith. Did you ever know him?"

To one side she spotted a clay flagon, hoping it was wine. Upon inspection it was. She found a pair of copper cups and began pouring as Tyrith said, "No, my lady. He died when I was young. But I have not missed him. Your own father has filled that breach."

She almost burst out laughing at that. *Oh, the irony. Your father did not die, you poor sweet fool,* she might have said. *He was murdered by your king. By the man who 'filled the breach'.* She could not help but shake her head at the twisted inhumanity of it all. Tyrith's father had been called Fenith, she knew, but had never been able to master the Hammer of Tukor as Janilah hoped. He had waited until Fenith sired a son before killing him, and bringing that son here. If Tyrith had been as incompetent as his father, his fate would have been just the same. Janilah would have brought him below, paired him with a suitable woman - one of Cecilia's own breeders, perhaps - and waited for a son to arrive. Once that child was old enough, and in a state of proven health, he'd have brought him to the forge, killed Tyrith, and started the cycle all over again.

And perhaps that would have been kinder, Cecilia thought. *At least he'd have had the pleasure of a woman, for a time. And some semblance of a life, before being slain.* Yet here he was instead. A lonely, rusting tool, waiting for a purpose that would never come.

She turned and handed him a cup. "Drink, Tyrith."

He nodded without hesitation and drank. *He is easily commanded,* she noted. She swirled the wine in her cup. "I do trust you understand exactly who you are, Tyrith?"

He seemed confused by the query. "Well yes, my lady. I am Tyrith, heir of Ilith, last of his blood, and Master of the Hammer of Tukor. I am here to fulfil a long-awaited destiny, and in doing so help my king fulfil his. To unite the Heart of Vandar, and thus win the War Eternal."

Cecilia smiled. "You could add another title to that list, you know."

"My lady?"

"Well, you know your line of ancestry, Tyrith. It's right there, in that fabulous list you just recited. You are Ilith's heir. You can trace your lineage back three and a half millennia to the founding father of this very kingdom. A line of kings that ruled for thousands of years until Galin Lukar marched on Tukor and slew King Neyrith three centuries ago. Neyrith was....now let me think...your great-great-grandfather's great-great-grandfather. Something like that. Suffice it to say, you are born of that ancient line. And that bestows upon you another claim." She smiled. "The King of Tukor."

Tyrith laughed uneasily. "No, my lady. I...I think you have that all wrong."

"Do I?" She sipped her wine. It wasn't the best vintage, but what would a man like Tyrith know of that, locked up here all of life. *Father could serve him spittle and swill and he'd hardly know the difference.* "The truth is in your blood, Tyrith. It gives you the right to rule."

"*Me*? Now…now come, my lady, you must be jesting. Why should I wish to rule? And why…" He looked at her curiously. "Well, now I find myself confused. Why would you be speaking of this. Your father is king, your beloved blood. Why should you seek to put this notion in my head?"

She shrugged. "No reason, Tyrith. I was only interested to see how much you knew of your heritage. You know the story, of course, of what happened to your forebears? How Galin Lukar killed King Neyrith and his sons, sparing only his eldest grandson, Kynith, to be raised beneath his wing, in secret, and Kynith's son after him, and so on and so on, until we arrive at you. You knew all of that, of course?"

"Of course," he agreed. "Yes, I knew that."

He must have, she told herself. *How else could he have come to be here?* For three hundred years King Galin and his successors had kept the line of Ilith secret, waiting for the day that the demigod's forge was found and the Hammer of Tukor with it. It seemed a rather ignoble fate for such a great line of kings, to be hidden and shackled and reduced to this. *And perhaps that's why I'm bringing it up,* she thought. *Perhaps, once the shadow of war has receded, it will be time to give Tukor back to its original, rightful rulers?*

She found herself wondering on that. There was no scheme in it, no selfish motive. She could conspire with old Archibald Benton all day long about putting Raynald on the throne, but perhaps it would be better if young Tyrith wore the crown? She mulled on it a little more, drinking her wine. *Something to consider later,* she decided. At the very least, it was nice to have options.

"Well, I suppose I ought to go."

Tyrith nodded glumly. *Oh gods, I've made him think about it all,* she thought. Or was it something else? The knowledge that, as soon as she left him, he'd be all alone again up here. "Of course, my lady. You must have…many pressing matters to attend."

She regarded him with a consoling smile. "Nothing that can't wait, Tyrith." Those words drew up his gaze. "Would you like me to stay a while longer?"

"I…well only…only if you can spare the time."

"I can." She drank down her wine, picked up the flagon, stepped out of the cramped confines of his room and started back down the tunnel to his workshop. "Perhaps you could show me some of Ilith's original works," she said on the way.

"I'd be very happy to, my lady." He sounded jubilant, the poor wretch. "Most happy to indeed."

They went over to the long wooden workbench beneath the shelves of books and scrolls. The counter teemed with heavy leather-bound tomes and worn down lengths of parchment, maps and diagrams, old and new. Some in Ilith's hand, Cecilia imagined, others in Tyrith's, and many others from kings in between. There was plenty of interesting material here, she wagered.

"Is there anything specific you'd like to look at, my lady?"

She glanced over the scattered documents and pages. To one side, she saw several of Tyrith's personal sketches and designs for her father's armour. Some were elegant, others less so, like that horrid helm he'd forged. Much of what she saw was not intelligible at a glance. Esoteric diagrams and formulas. Handwriting she couldn't read. One obviously ancient scroll was badly damaged at the bottom third. She had a closer look at that. "Ilith's," Tyrith told her. "It was this very scroll that revealed the secret of the Five Blades, my lady. That they can be combined." He pointed to the lower section. "I've been working to decipher the last paragraphs. Your father and I...we believe Ilith's formula is written within them. For uniting the blades, reforging the Heart of Vandar. Every day I get a little closer."

And every day my father gets further away. She didn't care a jot about combining those bloody blades. "What are these?" She took a couple of paces away, gesturing to a few pages of scribbled notes and a map she didn't recognise. It looked subterranean. "Is this a tunnel system?"

He nodded, following. "Yes. Accessed from somewhere in this very mountain, I have ascertained. I believe the way is found from the bottom of the steps, within the tunnel network you travel to get here. I would probably be able to find the way if I went down there. But of course, my place is here."

She wasn't fully understanding. "And where does this tunnel system lead, exactly?"

"Well now, that's the exciting part, Lady Cecilia..."

"Just Cecilia," she said. "You can leave off the lady from now on, Tyrith."

"Right, of course. *Cecilia.*" He smiled awkwardly. "Well, this tunnel…I think it has something to do with what I was telling you earlier. About the portal doors. I said that Ilith never completed the project... connecting all the north with these magical gates…but I have reason to believe he did fashion one such passage."

Cecilia was wildly skeptical. "A portal? To where?"

"His great refuge, my lady," Tyrith said. "His first priority was to secure a swift route from the capital to his sanctuary in the north, should the city ever come under attack. The fortress has had many names before." He thought a moment and then said, "I believe it is known as the Shadowfort now."

24

Saska

Yasha wiped gently at Saska's back with a pumice stone, scrubbing away the dried dirt and dead skin, scouring her clean as Lord Krator liked it. "Tell me if it hurts, sweet child," the old woman said. "I am trying to avoid the bites. They look painful today, poor dear."

"They're not," Saska assured her. She had a hundred bites on her body, little y-shaped marks left by the leeches that sucked at her daily in a mad bid to drain her of her Varin blood. Elio Krator had not been lying when he said she'd continue her treatment on the road. If anything it had gotten worse. "Mhazem tells me the leeches secrete anaesthetic when they bite. I don't feel anything. A bit lightheaded after, sometimes, but there's no pain, Yasha. You needn't worry."

The old maid puckered her face sympathetically and continued to rub at Saska's back, as she sat forward in the copper bathtub, arms around her knees. Across the large canvas pavilion, Milla was preparing the oils and balms for after, to rub into her skin, and Koya was setting out her evening clothes. The rest of the maids who'd attended Saska in Aram had been left back at Lord Krator's estate.

"OK, I think we're done. You may rise, child. Let's get you oiled."

Saska followed Yasha's instruction and rose from the bathtub, fragrant water and flower petals dripping from her golden, leech-marked flesh. A number of those petals clung to her wet skin and had to be picked off, one at a time, by Yasha or one of the other girls.

Once that was done she was to lie flat on her back upon a specially made table while the women ran their hands upon her, rubbing in the scented ointments and oils. She would get the order to turn over once they'd completed her front side, then they would do her back, buttocks, thighs and calves and the nape of her long slender neck.

It was all rote to Saska now, a simple matter of routine. *I was so prudish once,* she remembered, as she lay there nude and glistening, half a dozen hands running up and down her body. She still didn't much like it when that oaf Balza tried to get a peek of her, but otherwise she cared not to expose herself to these women.

The maids liked to talk as they worked, doing so in Aramatian. Yasha told her it would help her learn. "We will have you fluent in no time," the once-beautiful maidservant would say. Back in Aram, she'd been tutoring Saska daily, many hours at a time, though those lessons had grown less frequent now. Elio Krator was driving his army at a blistering pace along the Capital Road, riding from dawn until dusk and leaving little time for much else, and certainly not her language lessons. *No, the leeching comes first,* she thought sarcastically. *And this hour-long daily cleansing ritual. Oh, we cannot be without it.*

Still, Yasha would often steer the conversation with the other two maids in a direction Saska might understand, speaking slowly so she could listen, and learn. Right now they appeared to be discussing something about a dragon attack. One had come last night, it seemed, flying in under cover of darkness and picking off several sheep, a dog, and two young children before anyone could rally a response. Milla said these attacks had happened several times. She was young and plump, with an impish smile and cute gap between her front teeth.

Saska found herself intrigued. She propped herself up onto an oily elbow and asked, "How many times?" in Aramatian.

They all smiled at once to hear her speak their tongue. Milla gave answer. "I am not sure, my lady," she returned in the same language. "I have heard of three among the camp followers. But more elsewhere."

"Many more," agreed Koya. She was of similar age to Milla, a beauty with dark copper skin and rich black hair, tied back into a braid. "Attacks have been happening for weeks. Many since the red storm."

Saska frowned. "Red storm?" She wanted to make sure she was understanding correctly. "Where was this storm?"

"The Wings, my lady. It is said the two islands brok open like eggs, and a thousand dragons flew out. It is the end of all days."

Saska raised an eye. "*All* days? The world ending?" She felt she was getting her tenses wrong and a word or two muddled up, but they seemed to get the gist of it. "That sounds...not likely."

"No, my lady. It is very likely. It is truth. My mother told me of the legend. The red storm is a sign. It is Agarath, awakening. He will return the world to fire and ash. He will use his children."

"His children?" She had heard dragons called Agarath's children before. "The thousand dragons?" It sounded far too high a number to be real. *And too neat,* she thought. Legends always had neat numbers like that.

"Yes, my lady," said Koya.

Milla nodded. "Yes."

Saska turned to Yasha. She seemed rather more levelheaded than these others. "Folk tales and myths, child," the old woman croaked. "The red storm comes during every Renewal. Agarath stirs, yes, but he cannot wake or rise again. He has long departed these lands. Only a part of his spirit remains." She peered at Saska. "You understand?"

Saska nodded. All day every day she was surrounded by people chattering in Aramatian and such immersion had helped her immeasurably. "I understand," she confirmed. "Mostly. But…I was told always the gods were gone. Er…*dead*," she corrected, finding the right word. "They killed…killed in…fighting the…" She sighed and shook her head, unable to express herself, and went into the common tongue of the north. All her maids could speak it fluently. "I was taught the gods killed one another fighting in the War Eternal," she said.

"No, this is not true," said Yasha, shifting to Saska's northern tongue. "The gods did not die. They left."

The other girls nodded.

"Left? Where did they go?"

"Across the world," Yasha told her. "These lands we know are not all there is. There are many other lands, beyond the impassable seas. The gods made these lands we know as their arena, battlegrounds for the wars they fought. But when they tired of it, they left to make new ones. Does a child play with the same toy forever, Saska?"

Saska shook her head. "They grow bored of it eventually and look for another."

"Yes. These are the gods we know. Children, playing at a great game of war. They left parts of their spirit behind, bits of their essence in the artefacts we know. They gave them to their followers so they might continue their war. And through their essences, they live on. But only in part, you understand. The rest of them are gone, building their battlegrounds elsewhere. There are many other lands out there. And many other gods. But we will never see them."

"Then how do you know they're out there?" Saska asked. "If you can never see them."

"Because we know," said Koya, and Milla nodded.

"But…*how*?" Saska could not perceive the logic. "If no one can leave these lands, how can anyone know there's more out there?"

Yasha ran her strong wiry fingers through a knot in Saska's right shoulder. "There are many mysteries in the world, child. And many of these contrast, yes? Who can truly say who is right?"

"*We* are right," said Milla.

"Yes," agreed Koya. She scooped her finger into a jar of camomile and began rubbing at Saska's lower back. "We are right. The great eagle Calacan flew across the seas and saw these lands, everyone knows. He saw many continents. And then he flew into the Blackness Above. To the Stars of Fallen Souls, where the dead live on. He saw the heavens up there, and other places too. Worlds like this one. There are many."

"Many," said Milla. "Calacan showed us."

Yasha smiled at the two younger girls as she continued to work the knot from Saska's shoulder. "It is one tale among many," the wizened old woman said. "But there are others you may find more convincing. Tales of the great seafarers from Aramatia and Solapia voyaging away into the Peaceful Depths, and out beyond the Sunrise Sea. Most did not return, but some did, speaking wondrous tales of strange foreign lands. There are places beyond these continents, child. Some are lands like this one, where the broken parts of the gods are locked in their forever-war. Others are peaceful, it is thought. Paradise lands that the gods have left untouched. But to know for sure, you must risk it all. The seas have grown more dangerous. You have your Stormy Sea in the east that blows men to their doom. You have the Shivering Expanse in the north that is too cold for men to pass. The Peaceful Depths go on forever if you do not find the way, and the Sunset Sea can be blinding. Men who cannot see get turned around and go mad from the constant glare. And yes, to the west, beyond the Tidelands are strange phenomena that cannot be passed. All this is true and known. These are creations the gods left behind to stop people leaving. But the best and bravest still can, if they truly wish and will it. But the risk is great, oh yes. For even if you find land, you do not know what it will be. A battleground of gods and monsters, or a paradise of peace and plenty?" The old woman smiled. "One can never know."

Milla and Koya nodded reverently. "Never know," they said together.

Saska laid back down, letting the three maids complete their massaging and rubbing and stroking as she pondered all of that. The idea of there being other lands out there wasn't entirely alien to her. She had heard northern tales before, of Rasal seafarers venturing into the great unknown, and people back home in North Tukor often spoke about *the black storm that never ends*, ever-raging in the northern reaches of the Hammersongs. They said it was an ancient malice that predated the gods. That when the gods first came to these lands, they trapped the dark spirit there, shackling it beneath the mountains in great lengths of magical chain. That suggested there were other lands beyond these. Lands the gods originally hailed from. *But then who made these lands,* Saska found herself wondering, *if not the gods we know?*

She lay there for several more minutes as the maids put on her final layer of lotion, massaging the stress and strain from her muscles after another long day on the road. This was her favourite time of day. The time she had to herself in her tent, with only Yasha and Milla and Koya for company, and Joy, of course, who would find somewhere cosy on the floor to sleep. At first she'd misliked the constant bathing and cleansing but now she had come to value its benefits. *It's the only time I have away from Lord Krator and his cretins.* She rode with the sunlord all day and had to suffer him over dinner sometimes as well, when he wasn't conferring with his council. And after her ride, as soon as camp was pitched, she'd endure her leeching and bloodletting with prickly old Mhazem and pig-thick Balza always standing there watching with that lecherous look on his face.

I will kill you first, she promised herself whenever she glanced over at the man. His boast about being the one to finish off her father was never to be forgotten, always ringing in her ears whenever she set eyes on him. *I'll smash your head to pulp as you did him. I'll snap every bone in your body until you fall to your shattered knees and beg for mercy. And then I'll get to work.* She closed her fingers into a fist as she lay there on the table, thinking of poor Pig and Mellio and noble Sir Ralston who might just be dead as well. *You'll be next, Krator,* she told herself. *One day soon you'll let down your guard, and godsteel or no, I'll saw at your neck from ear to ear and carve a red smile on your throat.*

"Well, I think you are ready, child," Yasha said, as Milla and Koya stepped away and began stoppering the jars. "Give it a few minutes, as always, to let your skin drink in the oil. Then we will see you dressed."

Saska breathed out, calming herself. "Thank you, Yasha." Her eyes moved through the tent and found Joy there, stretched out on the floor, eyes flickering and nose twitching as she dreamed. *I hope they are sweet,* she thought. *Not like mine.* If one good thing had come from these long days on the Capital Road it was that Saska had had plenty of opportunity to ride atop Joy. Mar Malaan had taken the effort to fit the cat with a special lightweight saddle, plentifully cushioned in all the right places to ensure she didn't get too sore. Well, she had anyway, and all this massaging was much needed. Riding a large, lithe-bodied cat was very different to riding a horse, and Joy's long languid gait and rhythmic movement had taken some getting used to.

Her skills as a Starrider were improving, though, as she rode every day at the front of the long column, snaking down the Capital Road like a great monstrous serpent, stretching for mile upon mile along the picturesque Aramatian coast. Among the vanguard Lord Krator had a great many Sunriders and Starriders for company. But more of the wolves, Saska had noticed early on. They were greatly more abundant than starcats and easier to tame, she'd learned, and their instincts to work as a pack made them especially useful in battle. *And their size.* The sunwolves were much bigger, meaner, and more menacing than the starcats, which were better suited to night raids, using their speed and agility and night-vision to cause havoc among the enemy ranks.

Saska much preferred the Starriders too. *Perhaps because I'm becoming one?* Or perhaps it was because of their slinking beauty, prowling along darkly among the column with their shimmering black fur and spots of silver starlight. Their riders liked to wear dark attire as well, sleek black satin cloaks and sometimes shawls, to better blend in with the beast. They were quiet, she had found, and liked to keep to themselves, and many were women. Not the Sunriders, though. They talked loudly and haughtily and were almost always men, competing over the size of their sunwolves, their musculature and the length of their manes. Sometimes the animals would snap and growl at one another, or even fight at times as well. Saska had seen several such brawls break out between the beasts, when they pitched camp at night, and once several of them had teamed up and savaged a smaller wolf. It had looked dead to her eyes, but that was a part of life in these armies. "These beasts are bonded and tamed," Mar Malaan had told her, "but they still fight like men do. Sometimes these fights are fatal. We accept it, as part of war."

Saska sighed. *War*, she thought, still gazing across at Joy as she lay twitching in her sleep. She could hear the din of the encampment outside, the hum of voices, the growl of beasts, the clang and clatter of men training with sword and shield. *And I'm caught right in the middle of it.* She had been a captive of the Tukoran army at Harrowmoor, a breeder-to-be before Elyon saved her, and now here she was, a captive of the Aramatians. *My own people, all of them.* She was half northern, half southern, rich in the blood of Varin and Lumo and yet would always have enemies no matter where she went.

Maybe the open seas will have me, she wondered, because she had the blood of Thala in her too. Seaborn blood and strong at that. *I could return to the Steel Sister and Rikki Bowen and his crew. I could even accept little Billy's proposal.* She smiled at the thought, thinking of the night he'd given her that necklace of stones and shells. *We could sail the world together, maybe even try to voyage beyond these lands, beyond the impassable seas?* It was a tempting thought to her. *I am not wanted here. Perhaps somewhere else, I'll find my place.*

She was still in the throes of her wistful thoughts when she heard the swift scuff of footsteps outside the tent, and turned her eyes just in time to see Lord Elio Krator shoulder through the flaps, appearing from the hazy purple dusk in his cloak of gold, silver, and bronze feathers. He had a displeased look on his face, as ever. "Out," he barked.

"My lord..." old Yasha gaped at him. "You cannot be in here. The girl...can you not see she is still undressed? We have not yet finished her nightly routine."

Krator glared at her. "*Out*. Do not make me say it again."

Yasha hesitated a moment, then dipped her eyes. "Of course, my lord," she said, submitting. "Girls, come." Milla and Koya scurried right out of the flaps. Saska could see Balza out there, desperately trying to get a look at her with those dull witless eyes. When Yasha saw him she gave him a hissing reprimand, then turned and pulled the flaps shut.

Lord Krator took one look at her, lying naked in the middle of the tent, and averted his eyes. "Put something on."

Saska didn't need to be told twice. She slipped immediately from the oily table, padded swiftly across to her dressing stand and threw on a loose-fitting silken gown, pulling it tight to hide herself. Joy was already wide awake and on her feet, tensing at the man's rough voice. "I thought we were to have dinner tonight," she said, disturbed by his sudden arrival.

"Plans change." He stepped to the flaps, opened them back up, and called in Mar Malaan. The girthy Sunrider arrived in a billow of gold and bronze silk, a girl at his side. Saska frowned, unsure of what was happening. "Bring her over," Krator commanded.

Malaan obliged, leading the girl straight over to where Saska stood. "Stand still, Saska," the Sunrider said. "You needn't fear anything. Just stand there, nice and still."

"What's going on?" She could still speak while standing still. The question was for Lord Krator. "Who is this girl?"

"A girl," dismissed Krator. He stepped forward, looking at them both, nodding. "What do you think, Mar?"

"The likeness is good," Mar Malaan said, admiring them. "Yes, she looks very much the same, my lord. A rare beauty."

"She does," agreed Krator, and for the first time Saska took a good look at the other girl.. She had soft olive skin, long wavy auburn hair, and striking blue eyes. *She looks just like me.* "A beauty indeed. Well done, Mar. She is excellent."

The girl looked frightened. Saska had the sense that she couldn't understand what they were saying. "Who is she?" she asked again.

Krator snorted. He was rarely anything but a storm of anger these days. *Ever since he was humiliated by Lord Hasham*, Saska thought, *and ordered to lead the army to Eagle's Perch.* Hasham was a close ally to her grandmother and had taken over the stewardship of Aram in Krator's place. She had desperately hoped he would find out about her, send someone to fetch her, but so far there had been nothing. *Until now, perhaps,* she realised, putting the pieces together. *They are looking for someone who looks just like me.* "Lord Hasham's men have come, haven't they?" she said. "They've come to take me back."

Krator ignored her. He had another long look at the frightened girl. "Her hair is too long. Cut it off, Mar. Make sure the length is the same."

When Mar Malaan drew his knife the girl squealed and withdrew, stumbling away. The Sunrider smiled placatingly and held up a palm, speaking soothingly in Aramatian. "Come, child, do not be frightened. I am going to give you a little hair cut, that is all."

The girl looked close to soiling herself, such was the terror in her eyes. "Get on with it, Mar," growled Krator. "We don't have much time."

Mar stepped forward and, with that gentle touch of his, began sawing at the girl's long warm hair, tossing the severed tresses to the floor. Saska turned her eyes on Krator. "You're going to send her in my place?" she asked. "She doesn't speak a word of the common tongue, clearly. How long do you think that will deceive them, Elio?"

Krator laughed at her. "You do not understand. This girl will be going nowhere."

She didn't get his meaning. "It won't work. Whatever you're planning. Why don't you just give this up and let me go."

"Because you're mine," Krator growled. "*Mine.* Whether I want to put a child in you, or beat you dead, you are mine, Saska."

So he finally admits it, she thought. "You can't decide if I'm more my mother or my father, can you? To bed and wed or bludgeon to death." She didn't know what would be worse. *But I do,* she realised. *I'd sooner die.*

"Wed?" He huffed at the idea. "No, I will have what I need from you, and that is a child of royal blood. As I should have had from your mother. *Or* I will kill you. But I will *not* give you away." He brushed past her, as Mar Malaan finished his work. "Good. That will do. Bring her, Mar. Time is short."

"Yes, my lord." Mar Malaan drew the village girl forward. That's all Saska could imagine she was; a girl found at the nearest village or perhaps from among the camp followers, of which there were many thousands trailing the army. *Or maybe Cloaklake,* she thought. They had passed the large lakeside city only that morning, marking the half way point on their march to Eagle's Perch.

"It won't work," she said again, desperate. Joy prowled up beside her, sensing her agitation. "You can't keep me prisoner forever, Elio."

Krator turned back to face her. "After tonight, Lord Hasham will relent in his search for you," he said in a calm and measured voice. "Your grandmother will be told of your death and I will be able to do with you as I please. Now enough of this wilful resistance. Give in, Saska, and perhaps you will be resurrected in a place of prominence, as my lead concubine and mother to my children, once I have assumed control of the duchy. The alternative is death. Of you and your Joy. I urge you to think about it. Truly think about it. Submit to the light within you, and you will find me a kind and considerate partner."

He said nothing more. With that, he spun and marched out into the gathering twilight with Saska's poor doomed lookalike trailing unknowingly behind him.

25

Ranulf

Ranulf set down the bucket of water fetched from the well, letting the horses drink. The wait had been as long as usual. Almost two hours this time, though as ever he made the most of it. Waiting in line at the watering well was a wonderful place to hear of the latest gossip, after all.

He stepped over to the tent that he and Leshie shared, peering inside. "I'm back," he whispered to her. "Sorry about the wait."

"I'm used to it." She was sitting cross-legged on a blanket, sparsely garbed in a loose linen sheath dress, with a large book nestled in her lap. Leshie had been trying to learn Aramatian, with limited success; Ranulf didn't imagine the girl would ever be much of a linguist.

"How's it going?" he asked, gesturing to the book.

"Same," she said, closing it. She sounded frustrated. "I fed the horses, before you ask."

He had already spotted that; a few loose strands of hay at the ground where the horses were hobbled, beside the wagon. Sallor Sanara had kindly given them all that; a wagon with plenty of food, two strong horses to pull it, wares for them to sell to the soldiers among the army, to better fit in with the camp followers. Among the swarm of civilians trailing Lord Krator's war machine were cooks, washerwomen, nurses, prostitutes, sometimes the families of the soldiers themselves. Ranulf and Leshie had continued in the guise of merchants, as they'd been in Aram before leaving.

"Did anyone come by?" he asked. He was always worried when leaving Leshie alone, but sometimes he had no choice. Someone had to fetch water and letting Leshie go off into the sprawl of tents and wagons and rudimentary lean-tos on her own was asking for trouble.

She shrugged. "Heard a few soldiers sniffing around an hour or so ago," she told him. "Picked up a word or two, but couldn't understand the rest. Think they were wondering what was in the back of the wagon. We're going to get robbed one of these days, Ranulf, if you keep insisting I hide away in here."

"And did you?" he asked. "Keep hidden away?"

She huffed. "Of course I did. I hid away like a good little girl… from men I could easily butcher with my eyes closed." She shook her head. "I'm Bladeborn, Ranulf. I don't like having to hide from these weaklings."

Ranulf was wearying of this fight. "Until you learn to at least understand Aramatian, you have to remain in here while I'm not around," he said, for the hundredth time. Speaking the language wasn't so important, not with Leshie pretending to be mute, but understanding it was another matter.

Her eyes dipped back down to the book in her lap - another gift from Sallor Sanara - and she shook her head irritably and thrust it to the side. "I'm never going to learn," she grumbled. "I'm just going to pretend I've lost my hearing as well as my tongue. I can point and make hand gestures well enough. That's a universal language, Ranulf. I'll get by."

Ranulf sighed internally, hoping she wouldn't go through with all that, as he sat down and swung his satchel pack from his shoulder, setting it down in front of them. On the way back from the well he'd stopped to buy some fresh baked bread from a travelling baker and a few strips of roasted mutton from a butcher. Again, courtesy of his good friend Sallor who had provisioned them with coin as well. He set down a cloth between them and laid out the food for dinner. The sight of it seemed to lift Leshie's spirits. She had some appetite for a girl her size.

"So, did you hear anything at the well?" she asked, as she chewed on a strip of meat.

"I did." Ranulf gestured to the mutton in her grasp. "Apparently it's not just you who likes the taste of sheep, Leshie," he said. "There was a lot of talk about a dragon attack last night, right at the edge of camp. It took off with a brace of sheep and a couple of children as well. And a dog," he remembered. "They're growing bold to venture so near."

"Bold?" she scoffed. "What does a dragon need to fear from this rabble? It's all whores and washerwomen as far as I've seen, with swarms of kids running around their skirts. Maybe we should pitch our tent at the edge of camp tomorrow night?" She reached across and drew out her misting godsteel shortsword. "I'll give the next dragon that comes by something to think about."

"You'd do nothing but give it another meal," Ranulf came back at her. Her bravado could rankle sometimes. "And not a particularly nutritious one at that."

She laughed. "Speak for yourself. Look at you...you're all skin and bone."

That was an old insult and hardly applicable anymore. Ranulf had restored much of his physical vitality since leaving Pal Palek's pits. He tore off a bit of bread and took a bite. It was as soft and warm as he'd hoped. "You don't know much about wild dragons, do you, Leshie? They're not so brazen as people think, and tend to stay away from large gatherings if they can. It's unusual for a single beast to attack an army like this. And this isn't the first raid we've heard about either." Ranulf rubbed at the short stiff bristles on his chin, brow furrowing. It was concerning, for a certainty. Leshie could dismiss it all she liked, but there had been many strange tidings of late and none of them good. "And so far from the Wings?" he went on. "We're thousands of miles away. Wild dragons have never been known to range so far."

"Maybe it wasn't wild," she said, all nonchalant. She ripped a bit of mutton off with her teeth, chewing. "Some of the dragons are abandoning their Fireborn, aren't they? Sallor told us that. Maybe it was one of those?"

Ranulf nodded thoughtfully. That had been the most concerning rumour of all; this talk of the Bondstone being taken and the dragons behaving erratically because of it. One man had even come down from the foothills of the Western Neck, it was said, half crazed and blaring about the rise of Eldur. Sallor had heard that from one of his sources at the docks; as a shipwright he was often first to learn of rumours from a world away. This man had been part of a cult, apparently, led by the long-missing Prince Tethian, son of Dulian.

They'd been working to raise Eldur from the dead and the great Skylord Ulrik Marak had been with them, and another rogue Fireborn too, and even Lythian Lindar, the famed Knight of the Vale.

It seemed far-fetched, no more than the ravings of a lunatic, but Ranulf Shackton was more inclined to listen than most. He was a man well educated in matters esoteric and arcane and had read accounts in the past of the prophesied rise of the great and powerful Fire Father from a number of Agarathi scholars and seers. The signs were all there, certainly. *And if Eldur has truly risen?* he wondered. *If he has taken control of the Bondstone and is bending all the dragons to his will?*

He shuddered to think of it. *I must seek Her Serenity's counsel,* he thought, as he had a thousand times before. That had been King Godrin's last instruction to him in the Book of Thala; to go to the Grand Duchess Safina Nemati, share in her wisdom, yet she was still in Lumos as far as he knew and now he was here, east of Cloaklake and going further still, up and up the coast and all the way to Eagle's Perch amidst Lord Krator's great travelling horde…

"There's some commotion out there," Leshie said. Ranulf stirred from his thoughts and saw that she was clinging onto the hilt of her godsteel blade, enhancing her sense of hearing. "Another dragon attack, maybe." She shrugged and grabbed the bread, biting into the loaf. "It'd be exciting to see one up close, wouldn't it? Everyone else would be terrified, but not me. I'd call it down for a duel like the Varin Knights do. And good luck Mr Dragon, I say." She laughed through a mouthful of bread.

Ranulf turned his eyes out of the tent, trying to detect what might be happening. He could scarcely hear much over the general din of the camp. "Do you know what's going on?"

She shrugged. "Something down by the road, it sounds."

He rose to his feet. "Wait here. I'll go check it out."

"Um, yeah. Not likely." Leshie rose as well, pulling on her cloak and fixing her swordbelt and sheath. "I'm *not* leaving it here," she said, when she saw Ranulf looking at the blade disapprovingly. "Believe me, if ever we get into trouble out there you'll be thankful I have it."

If we get into any trouble, you and your little sword aren't going to make a difference, he might have said. Leshie seemed to think herself some great invulnerable knight, the match of Sir Ralston Whaleheart or Amron Daecar himself. *And we all saw what happened to Sir Ralston in the Red Pits.* Ranulf imagined the giant was probably dead by now, judging by the amount of blood that was leaking from his body when he was pulled from the arena. *But here I am,* he thought, *keeping to the promise I made him.* "Fine," he said. "Just make sure it's well hidden."

"Oh good idea, Ranulf. I had been planning to skip along with it misting in my grasp. But yeah, that's much better." She scoffed and slid the blade into its sheath, then pushed her way through the tent door.

The camp outside wasn't as cramped as it might have been given the tens of thousand travelling behind the army. They had made their home tonight in a shallow basin just north of the Capital Road, with space aplenty to accommodate everyone without them rubbing shoulder to shoulder. That wasn't always the case. Some nights the wagons and tents were lined up one after another, and they had to be extra careful to keep their voices to whispers when speaking in the northern tongue, but here there was no such need. To the north and south, east and west the camp bled away to the edge of sight, disappearing into the dusk, teeming. Away beyond the basin, south of their position, Ranulf could hear the ocean roaring distantly as it broke against the shore, and to the north the horizon was bordered by a sweep of tall black trees that made up part of the Green Cloak, the forest that stretched right around the vastness of Eagle Lake.

"It's coming from that way," Leshie said under her breath. She was still clutching her blade, keeping it well hidden beneath the folds of her cloak. "From up the road, I think. The way we came earlier. Past that Cloaklake place."

Ranulf peered westward down the Capital Road, the great paved roadway that stretched over two thousand miles along the coastline between Eagle's Perch and Solas. They had pitched their own tent some distance inland, away from the roadside rabble where many of the more ambitious sutlers and tradesmen had set up shop for the night, selling wares and services for the army. There were cobblers here, and costermongers, butchers and bakers and launderers and liquor sellers. One particularly enterprising madam had even brought along two dozen whores with her, and set up a large marquee to serve the needs of the more lustful men. No matter where they stopped each night, she commanded a great deal of trade.

"I can't see anything," Ranulf said, trying to see past all that. "This commotion you heard. Are you sure it wasn't just the noise of the market?"

Leshie shook her head. "People are looking at something," she said. "There." She pointed west; more people seemed to be gathering near the roadside that way. "There's someone coming, I think."

"Are you sure?"

She nodded. "I can hear hooves," she told him, turning her head. "I guess that's what all the buzz is about. Come on, Ranulf, let's not stand here all night."

She made an impatient noise and set off at a brisk pace toward the gathering. Ranulf followed. Within a swift half minute they were coming toward the rear of the crowds pressing up near the road. Then he saw what they were looking at; a mounted host was cantering along the Capital Road on horse and wolfback, just as Leshie had said, each of them dressed in the regal silver and white that marked them out as men of House Hasham. Ranulf felt his pulse quicken at once. He leaned immediately down to share the news with Leshie. "These are Hasham's men," he whispered into her ear.

She turned to him, brows raised. "Hasham's? You think they've come to get her?"

He nodded, a hopeful cast to his eyes. "What else could it be?"

She shrugged. "I don't know. Reinforcements, maybe?"

He shook his head. "They're too small a number for that and it's not like Lord Krator's lacking for men." He glanced around to make absolutely sure no one could hear them, though the general hum and hubbub in the air was more than sufficient to hide their voices.

"Then...well, I guess it *must* be about her." Leshie didn't seem entirely sure what to make of that. Despite her complaints Ranulf had the impression that she was enjoying this journey along the Capital Road more than she had her time in Aram, waiting for the Grand Duchess to return. It could be dull at times on the road, yes, but at least they had a mission now. A mission that Leshie was most fervently behind - rescuing their good friend Saska from the clutches of a nefarious sunlord.

But let's hope we don't have to, Ranulf thought, watching the mounted host clip-clop up the path. Ten days ago, before they'd left Aram, Ranulf had asked a final favour of his friend Sallor Sanara. "Get a message to Lord Hasham," he had said. "Tell him that the granddaughter of the Grand Duchess is being held captive by Lord Krator." Ranulf had hoped that Sir Ralston would survive his ordeal in the Red Pits to tell Lord Hasham of that himself, and perhaps he had, but either way, he wasn't going to take the chance. *I made a promise to him when I saw him in his cell,* he reflected. *I told him I would get Saska away from Krator and I will.*

Leshie was still trying to get a good look down the road. "You're certain they're the moonlord's men?"

Ranulf took in the advancing host and nodded. "The colours of House Hasham are silver and white, and that's their sigil too - the side-by-side moons. They're an old house who once hailed from Lumara. Pale colours and moon crests are popular in the raiment of the Lumaran noble houses."

"Then maybe you're getting them mixed up?"

"I'm not."

"You're certain? You get things wrong all the time, Ranulf."

He didn't dignify that with a response. Leshie was only trying to goad him, as usual. Around them, some of the crowd were turning to look the other way up the road. Ranulf sent his eyes east and spotted a second incoming host, appearing from the great forest of pavilions and tents within the main encampment. He couldn't yet see them clearly through the dim twilight but had a sense of who they were likely to be. "Seems Lord Krator had early warning that Hasham's men were coming," he said.

Leshie nodded. "And you're *sure* they're Hasham's men? Absolutely one hundred percent sure?"

"*Yes.*"

The second host began to clear as they neared, passing along the flickering torches that lined the road. The firelight gave better shape to them. "I'd not expected Lord Krator to come out himself," Ranulf whispered, surprised. But sure enough, at the head of the incoming party was the preening sunlord himself, mounted upon his great sunwolf Braccaro and with that fine cloak of feathers fluttering at his back. He had a number of others within his retinue, cantering along behind him on sunwolves and horses and camels of their own. A pair of Starriders had the rear, prowling in that graceful way of theirs, sleek and deadly.

"I think I see a girl with them," Leshie said. She was hopping on her toes to get a better look; the girl was scarcely more than five feet tall, dainty as she was dangerous. "She's sitting behind that fat Sunrider there, right next to Krator."

Ranulf spotted the figure in question. "That's Mar Malaan," he told her. He was a portly man, hardly a warrior to look at him. He favoured silks and satins in flowery colourful patterns and was well known for his liking of perfume. *Krator's right hand man,* Ranulf knew. *With a tongue as silky as his garb.* He could just about see the frame of a young woman seated behind the plump Sunrider. Hope ignited in him. "It's her," he said, though from this distance it was hard to be certain. "It has to be."

Ranulf Shackton could scarcely contain his relief. The only reason they had joined the ranks of Krator's vast horde was to liberate Saska from his custody, and for the last ten days they'd been following and watching and waiting patiently, hoping that Hasham would send men to collect her. For Ranulf that was plan A, though Leshie preferred a more direct approach. "We should rescue her ourselves," she had declared, and more than once. "We don't need Lord Hasham or anyone else. You and me, Ranulf. We can figure this out. We'll be her saviours. *You and me.*"

He had tried to think of how they might free Saska of her fetters, but for the life of him, he couldn't figure it out. There were tens of thousands in Krator's army, soldiers and spearmen and shieldmen and mounted men riding armoured horses and camels, with hundreds of Sunriders and Starriders besides. How to get Saska past all that? And even if they did, how to escape without being chased down?

Well now we don't have to worry, he thought. Hasham's men would escort Saska home and both Ranulf and Leshie could follow. *And perhaps the Grand Duchess will have returned to Aram by the time we get back, and all will be well?* Well, he could dream. For now Saska's reprieve would do.

The two parties converged, as a host of soldiers began moving into the crowds and corralling them back from the road. "My friends, I was told you were coming," Ranulf heard Lord Krator call out over the bustle and clamour. "Be welcome. I have arranged for pavilions to be prepared for you. If you would like to follow…"

"That shan't be necessary," interrupted the lead Sunrider in Hasham's host. He had a stern look to him, his armour silver scale mail, cloak a billow of glorious white wool. On its back was stitched the crest of House Hasham; two moons, side by side, one silver, one white. "We intend to ride back to Cloaklake this very night. We have only come to inquire as to the presence of a particular girl among your personal entourage. We are told she is of some import and is to be hastened back to Aram at once." The man peered down the road through narrow eyes. The dusk was deepening, the roadside lit only by firelight fringing the pavestones and shining from the torches and lanterns hanging among the market stalls. "I see a girl with you now, who matches the description I was given. Right there." He thrust his chin forward at Sunrider Malaan. "It would seem you know just why we came, Lord Krator."

"I will admit I had my suspicions." Krator opened an arm out toward Mar Malaan. "I am sure Lord Hasham understands full well why I wanted to keep the girl in my company. But I myself understand how precious she is to others, our esteemed Grand Duchess in particular. For this reason I am more than willing to pass her into your custody." He turned. "Please, Mar, help her dismount."

"Of course, my lord." Mar Malaan moved smoothly from the saddle of his sunwolf and reached up, helping Saska down. She landed tremulously, a fearful look on her face.

A confused look, Ranulf thought, as the pair began walking down the road. He peered through the bodies. *She doesn't know what's happening.* And something about the way she moved didn't look right either. The hair, yes, the shade of the skin and proportions of her figure, but that gait? Ranulf turned to look down at Leshie. Her hand was in her cloak, clinging to her dagger. "I can't get a proper look at her," he whispered. "Can you..."

"It's not her." Leshie was staring right through a gap in the crowd, eyes fixed, pupils dilated. "It's not her, Ranulf," she repeated.

Ranulf frowned, turned, gazed out onto the road. Mar Malaan and Saska - the *girl* - were some thirty or so metres away, moving past the wagons and stalls, between the flickering torches and lanterns along the route. He watched the girl move, and knew it for a certainty. *Saska had a graceful gait*, he remembered. *She moved effortlessly, and not so timidly as that.* "It's not her," he whispered under his breath, agreeing. "You're right. That's just some lookalike."

Leshie shifted her eyes left and right. "Something's going to happen." Her manner had turned circumspect all of a sudden, eyes shifty, posture tautening. "It isn't safe here, Ranulf."

He wasn't certain what to make of that. "What do you mean?"

"I mean it isn't safe. There's an *energy*, a dangerous one." She looked over the heads of those gathered in front of them. "We should back away, just a bit. It's best we don't get caught up in it when it starts."

"*Starts*? What are you..."

"Just trust me, Ranulf. I've got a sense for these things."

She grabbed his wrist and began slinking away from the mob gathered by the roadside. Ranulf felt an urge to stay, yet her grip was far too strong with godsteel to grasp and he could do nothing except stumble along behind her. She led him twenty or so paces into the sprawl of shelters and carts nearby. It was darker here, and a deal more private too. Still, Leshie had a good look around to make sure they were alone; most of those who occupied this area of the camp had been drawn toward the commotion.

And then she said, "I think they're going to kill her."

Ranulf balked. "What? No, Krator wouldn't dare. Kill her, in front of Hasham's men? That girl may not be Saska, but those men will think she is. What happens when they go back and report to their lord that Elio Krator had the granddaughter of the Grand Duchess murdered right in front of them?"

Leshie looked up at him like he was the simplest man alive. "Gods, Ranulf, you must be flustered. You're really not thinking clearly, are you."

"Well excuse me, Leshie, but I'm a little disappointed, yes. I had hoped they were coming to fetch Saska and we might be able to go home..."

"Home? Aram is *not* home, Ranulf. Once we get Saska out - the *real* Saska - and believe me, we will, *then* we can go home. Real home, I mean. The north. This trip south has been nothing but a nightmare for all of us. It's about time we said goodbye to this godsforsaken place and never came back."

Ranulf sighed. He had told Leshie that he needed to speak to Safina Nemati many times now but she continued not to hear him. *Or care, more likely,* he thought. *She doesn't grasp the gravity of all this.* "You were saying something about me not thinking clearly. So? What do you think will happen then? To this lookalike?

"Well isn't it obvious? Krator's planted men in the crowd there. I saw them, with weapons under their cloaks. They're going to start a riot and that lookalike's going to be caught up in it. There's been lots of violence at the market, hasn't there? People are scared from these dragon attacks, right, and everything else that's happening in the world. Who knows, maybe with all these people gathered around someone will think it a good opportunity to steal a loaf of bread or something. The baker will see, whop the thief on the head with his rolling pin, and right there, you have your riot. It'll start small and spread fast and Krator will call for calm and send some of his own men in to restore order…and who knows, maybe a few of them will be killed as well, to help sell the lie, but in the end he won't care, because he's a ruthless callous control-freak who's clearly obsessed with Saska because he loved her sweet dead mother and wants to keep her all to himself." She shrugged. "That's how I reckon it'll play out anyway."

Ranulf blinked. He had nothing to say. And that was rare enough, to strike the garrulous Ranulf Shackton dumb. Eventually, he managed to let out a little laugh. "Wow, you have some imagination, Leshie. I wonder, sometimes, what goes on in that funny little head of…."

And just then, at that exact moment, a heavy rumbling murmur erupted from the crowd nearby. Ranulf turned at once and watched, in something approaching awe, as Leshie's prophecy played out before his very eyes. He could not say what started it - a baker and his rolling pin or prostitute being pinched somewhere private, or perhaps the theft of a bottle of liquor from one of the many whiskey and rum stores along the route - but all the same, it *did* start and it *did* spread, and the rest…well, it was much as Leshie said.

His young companion stood beside him with a smile. "Ah well," she said, over the crash of violence and roar of voices; some of them surely coming from Krator and his men and Hasham's men as well, though it was rather impossible to tell from here. "Poor girl, but what's another casualty of war, hey? I guess we'll have to rescue Saska ourselves, then."

Ranulf watched on with a slow defeated shake of the head. *Damn that girl for being right all the time.*

26

Jonik

Jonik unhitched the Nightblade's sheath from his swordbelt and secured it within the hidden compartment in Captain Turner's quarters. He stepped out of the room, shut the door and locked it, placing the key into his pocket. The mountainous form of Big Mo was waiting outside, his enormous godsteel greatsword slung across his back. "No one goes in," Jonik told him. "Not until I get back."

Big Mo nodded that huge scarred head of his. "As you say." He'd guarded the Nightblade before at Calmwater and seemed happy enough to do so again.

"I won't be too long," Jonik said. "Do you need anything from the market?"

"Nuts," grunted the giant. "Big Mo likes nuts."

Jonik smiled. "I'd noticed." Maurice had gobbled his way through all of the nuts they had on board - almonds, pistachios, walnuts, you name it - and had been furious when their stocks had run out. It didn't seem to dawn on him that he was responsible for exhausting their supply. "I'll make sure we get some for you."

"Sacks." Big Mo nodded briskly. "Lots of sacks. Almonds especially. Those are my favourite."

Jonik had noticed that too. "I'll see it done, Mo."

He gave the man a nod, turned, and continued down the corridor, descending to the brig where Soft Sid sat sentry at Gerrin's door. "Open it up, Sid." The huge dimwitted deckhand stood, honking, and slid the bolts. Jonik stepped inside to find Gerrin sitting on his bed writing notes by lamplight. "We've stopped at Mudport," he said to the former Shadowmaster. "Emeric wants to know if you need anything while we're here."

"A taste of fresh air would be nice." Gerrin smiled that craggy old smile of his and set down his quill. "But I don't imagine you'll grant me that."

"No," Jonik said. "Once we set sail again I might consider letting you up on deck, under supervision. But here? No, Gerrin."

"Think I might try to escape?" Gerrin chuckled in that new easy-going way of his. It still infuriated Jonik, though perhaps less than it had. "Well I won't, but I see why you'd think I might."

"Good. Do you need anything?"

Gerrin pondered that for a few moments. Then he smiled wickedly and said, "Your trust. How about that?"

Jonik grumbled, exasperated. "Nothing, then." He turned to leave.

"Well now, not so fast. What exactly are you offering?"

Jonik turned back. "I'm offering to fetch you something from market, Gerrin. Something you might want or need. We're unloading the rest of the patients here and I don't plan to stop again until we reach Blackhearth. So? Is there anything you're lacking?"

Gerrin looked perplexed. "You've given me everything I need, son. I don't..." He stopped. "Sorry. I know you don't like it when I call you that."

"Then why did you?"

Gerrin shrugged. "Force of habit, I suppose." He looked over his small room. "I've got all I need, as I say. You've been generous, Jonik. I'd not want to ask anything more of you."

"Except fresh air and my trust?"

"Well, there's that."

"Nothing else?" Jonik was only here as a courtesy, and not for Gerrin. Emeric had asked him to come down and he'd oblige that man most things. "How about a bottle of whiskey? I know you used to keep a secret stash at the Shadowfort."

Gerrin raised a brow, throwing one leg up onto his bed. He leaned back against the wall. "Now how could you know that? I don't recall you ever visiting my personal chambers, Jonik."

"I didn't need to. I could smell it on your breath sometimes. You tried to cover it with mint, but that only made the smell worse."

Gerrin gave a gruff bark of laughter. "I forget sometimes how strong your blood-bond makes your senses. You've got the nose of a bloodhound, boy." He stopped again, realising his mistake. "*Boy*. Ah, another of those outlawed terms."

Jonik let this one pass. He was correcting himself now, at least. "Whiskey, then?" He permitted Gerrin a single nightly ale with his dinner, but that was all thus far.

The man nodded. "That'd be kind…my lord."

Something about that didn't feel right either. *My lord. From him?* Jonik had asked him to call him that, true, but it still felt odd. "I'll see it done." He paused before leaving. "Anything else?"

"Well, now that you're asking, maybe I could have another blanket. It's starting to get cold by night. And where we're headed, it'll only get worse."

Jonik nodded. There was truth in that. "We have spare bedding aboard. I'll have Sid bring down what you need." He judged that Gerrin might need some warmer clothing too, now that he thought about it. He'd been dressed sparsely since they'd thrown him down here a month ago and that wouldn't serve once they started sailing up the Sibling Strait. Gerrin getting pneumonia wasn't going to help anyone. "I'll have some warmer garb found for you too." *Or bought at market, more likely.* Lord Humphrey Merrymarsh had generously given them those ten trunkloads of armour and weapons, but there hadn't been much in the way of wools and furs among them.

"That'd be welcome," Gerrin said. "Oh, and a spare quill or two, if you can." He plucked his current one from the table. "This one's starting to fray. And I'm getting low on ink as well."

Jonik had a glance at the man's latest scribblings. He'd spent time poring through Gerrin's notes over the last five days at sea and found them more useful than he liked to admit. And he'd written more than those initial five pages too, many more, which were equally useful. Jonik had even started handing them out to the men so they might get a better idea of who and what they'd be facing. "What are you working on now?" he asked.

"Siege strategy," Gerrin told him. "For taking the fortress as quickly and cleanly as possible. With contingencies for each scenario."

Jonik took a step forward. "May I?" He reached out and Gerrin passed him the notes. A quick scan indicated a great deal of work had gone into them. He'd written out possible branches for each scenario, contingencies and back ups should their intended objective fail to pay off as planned. *As is likely,* Jonik thought. They would try to infiltrate the fortress unseen and unheard, but if a single man should spot them and raise the alarm before being taken out, that would rouse the entire fortress to the fight. "This is good, Gerrin," he admitted. It didn't feel good to admit that it was good, but still…it was. "Emeric will be pleased."

"They're just suggestions," Gerrin said modestly. "You can use them as you see fit, work them into your own strategy. You've got some seasoned campaigners up there, I know, who'll want their own voices heard."

But none who know the Shadowfort as you do, Jonik thought. He didn't want to openly tell the man how much they were coming to rely on him, though. "We have some forceful personalities aboard," he agreed. "But I'd best go," He handed him back the notes. "Your new provisions will be brought to you." He nodded at his former master in parting, and paced from the room.

The air was brisk above, the harbour a great bustling storm of movement and noise, much busier than it had been in Calmwater. The warships gathered bulkily in the deeper waters, their sails showing the colours and crests of their kingdoms and houses, many of them great triple-decked, four-masted monsters. Smaller cogs and carracks bobbed between them, and hundreds of troop carriers and merchant vessels were moored along the many wharves. Invincible Iris and One World had joined them. It had taken a while, but as soon as one of the port officials had rowed out on his skiff and found out that Sir Borrus Kanabar was aboard, he'd been swift to allot them a space.

Jonik joined Captain Turner on the forecastle deck. "How are things going down there, Gill?"

"Well enough, lord, seems to me. Borrus and Jack have everything in hand."

The captain was observing the docks below, where the patients were being disembarked off One World to be delivered into the care of the Mudport city soldiers. Borrus was standing with their commander, and Jack as well - trusty notes to hand - explaining who each of the poor wretched souls was, and where they were to be delivered.

"We'll have plenty o' space now," Turner went on. "You thinkin' o' takin' a single ship from here, lord?"

"We still have enough men to crew both ships, Gill. If we all bundle onto one it'll start to get crowded. I like my space."

Turner grinned, seeing the meaning behind Jonik's words. "Aye, and you don't want to sail with Vincent Rose either, do you?"

"Not particularly, no." Jonik could see the merchant now, saying his fond farewells to the patients. He had made an effort to learn their names these last days, at least, following Harden's harsh reprimand. Jonik was certain it was entirely insincere. "Did you send Braxton off to market?"

Turner nodded. "Aye. That twitchy lad Borrington went with him."

They needed to resupply their main food and water stores, and pick up some hempen rope and cloth and other bits and pieces for repairs. Their ale supply had run low as well, and required replenishing. *And more so than the water,* Jonik thought, *the way the men get through it.* "I have a few things I have to fetch myself," Jonik said. "Care to join me, Captain?"

"Need you ask?"

They descended the gangplanks, moving along the stone wharf in the direction of the market. Emeric stepped to intercept them, garbed in that worn green cloak of his over dark leathers scratched and scuffed. "Did Gerrin request anything?"

"Whiskey, quills, ink. Gill and I are going to market to fetch it. And nuts for Mo."

"Braxton's got nuts on his list, lord," Turner said.

"Best get more, just in case. Some extra almonds. He likes those."

The morning sun was streaking through the high scuttling clouds, drawing shafts of pale light across the docks. They'd spent some time in ports and harbour markets in recent months, but none so hectic as this. There were soldiers everywhere, bedecked in their house regalia, and the sight of godsteel wasn't rare. Most were out of East Vandar, men of the marshes and lakes and rivers, fiercely loyal to House Kanabar. And quite naturally, Borrus was starting to get recognised.

"We should try to leave as soon as possible," Emeric said. There was a wary note to his voice, and a careful look in his keen golden eyes. "If we stay here too long the men's heads may start to turn. They can swear their allegiance all they like, but when they get a taste of home, they might just renege on that. Best we restock and raise the sails before they can overthink things."

Jonik agreed. But he had a sense of one thing, at least. "Borrus will leave us here," he said. It gave him no joy to admit it, but there was no sense in deluding himself any longer. He'd known that ever since old Harden had told him about the army amassed at Dragon's Bane, under Lord Kanabar's rule. *And my brother's*, he thought. *My brother, the prince, and bearer of the Windblade...*

"Sir Torvyn has committed himself to you, Jonik," Emeric came back. "He is a man of honour, and will follow through."

Jonik shook his head, but before he could argue otherwise, Harden strode in, gaunt and grim and grey, and said, "So how about it, my lord? You want me to look into hiring more sellswords, then? Like we discussed in Calmwater?"

"Go ahead, Harden, but be quick," Jonik told him. "We want to leave by mid-afternoon, if we can."

Harden grunted doubtfully. "Doesn't give me much time, Jonik. A man selling his sword for a dangerous contract needs time to consider it. And you'd want to meet and get the measure of them too, no doubt."

"You won't find anyone," Emeric said. "None who are suitable anyway. We have a strong group now, well trained and well armed, and enough for the job so far as Gerrin says it. Sometimes a small tight group is better than a large loose one."

"So...that's a no, then?" Harden looked to Jonik, then back to Emeric, perhaps wondering who was really in charge. Jonik often wondered that too. Emeric Manfrey was a more natural leader than he would ever likely be. *It is only the Nightblade that gives me a right to lead*, he thought. *Without it, what am I?*

"No harm in looking," Jonik decided. "It's too late to vet anyone we don't know, but you might run into someone you do."

"Unlikely, lord, but I'll have a look anyway."

"Do that." He looked to Emeric, and saw the approval in the man's eyes. "You'll stay here?"

Emeric nodded. "I'll keep an eye on your flock, Jonik, make sure none of these sheep of yours go running off."

Jonik smiled. He couldn't ask for a better shepherd.

He stepped away with Captain Turner at that, making for the market as Harden carved a path toward the taverns and merchant houses and brothels that cluttered the sprawling port. The city beyond was much grander than its name would suggest, built of thick stone and well defenced against dragon attack. It had started out as a small backwater port, built around a muddy estuary that emptied out of the marshes and into the Bay of Mourning, yet the centuries had seen it rise up into something formidable.

"Do you know the port well, Captain?" Jonik asked, as they strolled along the busy wharves. To avoid detection, he'd dressed in sailor garb once more, and that hat he hated too. Without the Nightblade at his hip, he was just another no-name crewman amidst a heaving sea of them.

"Well enough, aye. Been here a good three, four dozen times, I should think, before I started fishin' the Tidelands. Used to run whiskey and bales of fur and such, transporting them around the bays for rich merchant sorts like Rose. The pay was never so good as I'd hoped, though, so decided to turn fisherman instead. Riskier, aye, but more rewarding too. There's something satisfying about bringing in a good catch, lord. And when you score those rare fish…there's little better."

Jonik smiled. "Do you look forward to returning to that life, when all this is done?"

Turner puzzled on the idea for a moment. "Might be a little dull now, after all the adventures we've had." He cocked a brow. "You not thinking of sending us off on our way, are you?"

"I don't want any of you hurt, Gill. When we make for the Shadowfort, you'll not be safe."

"Aye, true, but we weren't safe at sea either. We sailors and fisherfolk are brave men, lord. Every time we step on deck we know we're takin' a gamble with our lives. Not so different being in your company. But at least now there's meanin' behind what we're doin'. Saving these poor folk from them pits? Ridding the world o' this Shadow King and whatnot? Freein' them lads like you, born and raised in darkness. Aye, there's moral profit in all that, lord, that you don't get out at sea. Makes me feel good, it does, and I can say the same for the rest." He smiled fondly. "So you needn't fret about our safety. Any o' us die in your company, we'll be dyin' for a good cause."

Jonik rather hoped that none of them would die at all, but he appreciated the captain's words all the same.

The market was a typical sprawl of stalls and wagons and shouting men, calling the days catch or hollering about their latest deals and discounts. Children went among them with baskets of apples and breads and wheels of hard cheese. The air was ripe with the smell of roasting meats and nuts and fish, heavy with the noise of hawkers. "Whiskey, was it?" said Turner. "For Gerrin? Any special brand?"

"The cheapest," Jonik said.

Turner smiled. "Getting along with your old master well, then?"

"Well enough." And that was the unpleasant truth. "I'll let you do the bartering, Gill. You're much better at it than I am."

"So I should be. Been doin' it all my life."

They found a whiskey vendor and the haggling ensued, Turner fetching a decent price before they pressed on in search of ink and quills. Those were a little harder to come by, but eventually they tracked them down, a man hawking writing supplies in a quieter section of the market among the perfume-sellers and jewellers, each of whom had several burly guardsmen stationed beside them to ensure no thievery was done. A little further along, some men were sitting outside a dockside tavern, drinking ale and sharing stories. Jonik heard some mention of Janilah and lent them an ear, slipping his hand into his cloak to clutch at his godsteel dagger. He raised a brow as he listened.

"Anything interesting?" Turner asked, noticing.

"Janilah's gone missing, they're saying," Jonik told him. "Hasn't been seen for days."

Turner shrugged. They'd heard all sorts about the Warrior King's latest treacheries and treasons over in Calmwater. "Hiding away in the palace, no doubt. Come, let's fetch us those nuts for Maurice. Wouldn't want the big man going hungry, would we?"

Nuts were easier to find; several large carts were loaded with them. They lined up in one section of the market, unloading pine nuts and pecans, walnuts and hazelnuts to the soldiers passing by, selling them by the handful. Jonik spotted the cart filled with almonds and gave a sigh of relief. "Do you sell by the sack?" he asked the vendor.

The man nodded and reached behind him, picking up an empty linen bag. "How many you want?"

"Sacks?"

"That's right. How many?"

"Well…how much are they?"

"I'll take a silver clay for each."

"A silver clay!" Turner laughed incredulously, stepping over. "What do you take us for, man? A sack o' almonds ain't worth any more than a few bronze sickles and you know it."

"Once," agreed the vendor, "but we're at war now. It's simple supply and demand, friend. Supply goes down, demand goes up, prices follow. A silver clay each, as I say."

"I'm not seeing much o' a problem with supply," Turner countered, looking over the heaped wagons.

"Looks can be deceiving. These are the last of my stocks. None left once these go. So, there you have it. A silver clay for a sack or I can do you a sickle a handful, as with everyone else. Up to you." He turned to one of the soldiers waiting behind them - a man of the lakes, by his blue and green garb - and ignored any further protests.

"I'll wear him down," Turner grumbled to Jonik. He raised his eyes over the nearby crowds as a couple of oxcarts ambled their way, led by a man in stained cloak and boots. Braxton was walking beside him. His lopsided jaw broke into a smile as he spotted them. "What are you two doing here?"

"Buyin' nuts. What's it look like, Brown?"

"You told me to get nuts," Brown Mouth complained.

"Aye. Big Mo wants more, Lord Jonik says." He had a look over the carts. "You got everything we need?"

"Mostly." Braxton held up the list Turner had written out for him. "Just got nuts, a bit of good rope, and brandy left to get. None of its coming cheap, though."

"Aye. We know. This swindler's tryin' to sell us sacks for a silver clay. It's daylight bloody robbery."

The vendor turned back to them. "Fine, I'll do you a deal, but keep your voices down about it. Don't want it getting around."

"Aye?" Turner leaned in.

The vendor ran a finger between the deep bristly cleft in his chin. "A half clay and six sickles. That's the best you'll get from me and anyone else around here."

Turner looked like he wanted to drive the price down more, but seemed happy enough with that. "Fine. We'll take two o' those."

The nut merchant smiled. "Glad to do business with you, friend." He began heaping great handfuls of almonds into the linen bags under Turner's watchful eye. Jonik drew out his purse of coins and handed it over to the captain.

Then he turned to Braxton. "Where's Sir Lenard?"

Braxton gestured vaguely toward the city walls. "Ran into a knight he knew from before. Not sure who. They went off for an ale at a tavern that way."

Jonik wasn't so happy about that. "He shouldn't have left you to fetch supplies on your own."

"I'd not be so hard on the boy, my lord. He's just touched down on home soil again after all these years away. I'd not begrudge him an ale or two with an old friend. And he'd helped me gather most of this by the time he went off, to be fair to the lad."

Jonik nodded. Sir Lenard Borrington was still rather more skittish and nervy a fighter than he'd like, but he was getting more confident by the day and had never wavered in his loyalty. Still, Jonik was trying to avoid any of these interactions with old friends and acquaintances, if he could. It would only weaken their resolve and tug them in different directions. *I want everyone back on the ships,* he thought. It was far too busy here, with far too many distractions. *I want us gathered and gone as soon as possible, until we're too far north to turn back…*

Turner finished up with the almond vendor, tossing the sacks onto the carts. He set about buying some walnuts and pine nuts as well before rejoining them. "So, hemp rope and brandy, Brown? And that's it?"

Braxton checked his list once more, and nodded.

It didn't take too long to finish up, though getting those loaded oxcarts through the twisting lanes between stands and stalls wasn't always easy. Everywhere they went, children and cats seemed to be giggling and hissing and slinking underfoot, the former often chasing the latter, and in one area a wagon had turned over, causing cages filled with chickens and ducks and pheasants to shatter and smash. The birds were all rushing around chaotically, clucking and quacking, as their hapless owner tried to snatch them up with his wife and children. By the time they'd gotten the oxcarts through, most of the ducks had taken wing and a couple of sneaky thieves had made off with a pair of chickens. Another had been caught by a huge great mastiff, ripping it apart bloodily, flesh and feathers all.

Eventually, they came back in sight of the ships, to find that even more men had gathered there. Jonik didn't doubt it was about Borrus. And sure enough, he could see him there in the midst of it, bald head gleaming under the sun, regaling them of his tale. "Come on," Jonik said. "Let's get this loaded before Borrus brings all of Mudport down on us."

This attention was the last thing he wanted. And he hoped he could trust Borrus enough not to mention his name. *I want out of here, and soon,* he thought once more. Yet he still needed to get the supplies loaded and he still needed to wait for Harden to return, and Sir Lenard, and perhaps others as well. *Rose will surely have ventured off to some brothel to satisfy himself,* he thought bitterly, *and taken others with him.*

Jonik had his answer to that as soon as they pulled up beside the ships. At once Jack appeared to help with supplies, along with Emeric and Soft Sid. "Rose went off again," Jack told him. "With Devin, Cabel, and Grim."

"I'd thought as much. Did he say where? Which brothel, I mean." He wanted to know in case he had to send someone to fetch them.

"The Muddy Maiden, I think he said. Pleasant name, don't you think? Conjures a reputable image."

"No whorehouse is ever reputable."

The supplies were unloaded onto Iris, giving Jonik an opportunity to pay Shade a quick visit as the others filled the hold. He made his apologies for not taking him for a ride today. It wasn't possible here, he told him. Beyond the city was Celaph's Mire, a great open marshland that Jack knew well and used to fish in his youth before entering Turner's service. The only way through was over the plank roads that crisscrossed the bogs, and all the villages there were built on platforms of the same. The mire had its name from the ancient creature Celaph, a giant serpent-like monster that would stalk the swamps, picking off unwary travellers if ever they ventured off the road. Many still believed the creature existed; to this day, men spoke in dark and ominous tones of missing fishermen dragged to their doom, Jack had once said.

When Jonik returned to deck after giving Shade a quick groom, he found Jack, Emeric, Turner and Braxton all gathered at the gunwale, looking over onto the docks. He strode up to join them, wondering what was going on.

Below, the crowd around Borrus had given way, opening out as a man of immense black beard and belly stamped toward him. He had without a shadow of a doubt the thickest neck Jonik had ever seen, a bulking pillar of muscle throbbing with massive angry veins. And that chest of his was massive too, a great dense barrel of a thing, with legs as thick as tree trunks beneath travel-strained breeches and worn leather boots.

Only when he reached Sir Borrus was it apparent he was of similar height as well. The man was a true behemoth, not so tall as Sid or Maurice, but a great deal wider for certain. *And wild,* Jonik thought, to look at that forest of a beard and unruly black hair. The man had the aspect of a mountain barbarian, and the voice to match, a great growly ursine thing that bellowed out, "Borrus! Borrus Kanabar you old boar! I heard you'd be here!" He had a half dozen men with him, trailing behind, all heavy-bellied and bearded, though none so spectacularly as he was. "My gods, you're half the man you were! You skinny wretch! You look thin as a bloody lance!"

It was quite unusual for Borrus Kanabar to be overmatched in boisterousness, but this newcomer was doing so quite ably. "And you look half a man heavier, Mooton," he came back. "Hell, I'd not expected to see *you* here. Who told you I was coming?"

"We had it from one of the Maynard lads. He sent your father a crow at the Bane." He threw his massive arms out and hauled Borrus into a bear-hug. "By Varin I can almost get my arms all the way around you. The Barrel Knight my arse! You're hardly even a keg these days!"

Borrus's voice broke through his laughter. "My father sent you?"

"Yes, yes, your father. With Prince Elyon's consent, of course. I did sort of swear myself to the boy, you know how it goes. But I'm a Kanabar man down to my bones and wasn't going to miss this chance to come fetch the heir of Rivers!" He grabbed at Borrus's shoulders. "Gods, I can't wait to hear your story, Borrus. I had a man ride ahead of me to make sure the Singing Duck had enough ale for us. You remember that place? We used to get stinking drunk there every time we were all here together. You and me and Torvyn. Now I doubt you'll be able to keep up with me anymore in a drinking contest, not with that pathetic little gut of yours, but hey ho, you can try!"

Jonik had a sinking feeling as he watched the exchange play out. He knew who this man was now. Sir Torvyn had spoken of his younger cousin, the rumbustious Sir Mooton Blackshaw, and Borrus had made mention of him too. *He's here to bring Borrus to his father,* Jonik thought. *To Dragon's Bane, where my brother sits as prince and champion.* His last faint hope of having Borrus and Sir Torvyn remain with them was now gone.

"So these are your ships, are they?" Sir Mooton was going on. He turned his eyes over Iris and One World, giving the men assembled about the decks a passing glance. "We had no word of who you were travelling with. Well, except Lady Kathryn Merrymarsh. Now there's a tale there, I'm sure. The woman hadn't been seen for a dozen years, I'm told. And you had others with you? Captives from some southern hellhole, or something?" He waited but Borrus was oddly tongue-tied. "Well…we can get into that later, once you've got an ale or ten in you. And some meat and potato pies as well, yes, get you fattened back up a bit, Borrus." He laughed heartily. "Come. I'll have one of my men fetch your belongings from the ship." He glanced over at them. "Regnar, head up there and talk to those good fellows on deck." He pointed in the direction of Jonik and his companions. "You there, with the tan jacket and beard…you have the look of a captain to me. Is that right, Borrus? This one's captain?"

Captain Gill Turner was not the sort of man to be spoken for. "Aye, I'm captain of this here vessel, sir. Name's Gill Turner, if you're wonderin'. Gill's not my real name, though. More a nickname. I'm part Seaborn, see. Can dive some hundred metres down, no trouble, and stay under for a full quarter-hour too."

Sir Mooton Blackshaw pursed his lips. "Well, very impressive, Gill. That's a fine party trick you've…" He trailed off, eyes narrowing to squints as he stared right at Jonik.

Gods, he's recognised me. Jonik felt his chest tighten. There were enough men at the docks to make this a real problem, whether Borrus stood up to defend him or not. He felt an urge to slip back and out of sight, but suddenly he sensed a presence moving to his side and realised it wasn't him under Sir Mooton Blackshaw's gaze.

"He looks little different to when I saw him last," Sir Torvyn whispered to Jonik, stepping up next to him. "He was only young then, but still had that big belly and beard." He gave a soft laugh for Jonk's benefit, and then raised his voice and said, "You're just as blusterous as ever, Moot. I was trying to have a nap below. You woke me, you silly great oaf."

Sir Mooton's big brown eyes widened until they were near-perfect circles. "*Torvyn*? Torv, is that…is that *you*?"

"Now don't tell me your eyes have started to fail you, Mooton. You're not that old yet."

Sir Mooton's gaze swung to Borrus. "You found Torvyn, Borrus? With Merrymarsh and…and those others?"

"I was about to tell you, Mooton. We saved him from the pits of a man called Pal Palek. He's been there ever since he…"

"Come on, Borrus," broke in Sir Torvyn Blackshaw, "you've got your own tale to tell. Don't go spoiling mine. I'll have that pleasure myself, damn you."

Borrus smiled. "As you wish, Torvyn."

"*Cousin…*" Sir Mooton turned back up to look at him, utterly disbelieving. "My gods, dear cousin!" He set off at a thunderous charge, barreling along the stone wharf, up the gangplank as it gave out a storming rattle, and across the decks. Jonik drew back as the brute arrived before his shrivelled cousin, enveloping him in a huge constrictive embrace, causing poor Torvyn to wheeze for breath. "Gods, Torv, sorry! I just get overexcited, you know how I am!"

"That's quite all right, Mooton."

Sir Mooton was still beaming manically. "So? What on earth happened to you? How did you end up in these pits? And this Palek fella? Is he slain? Tell me you got sweet vengeance for what he did to you, Torvyn. Tell me elsewise I'll have these good sailors head right back south and I'll take his head myself." He swung an arm out at those standing nearby, almost hitting Jonik in the face. "Sorry, lad, sorry," Mooton said to him. "I get carried away." He reached out and grasped Jonik's shoulder, squeezing with a paw that was easily the match for Borrus's. "So, Torv? Go on, what happened? I want to hear everything. Every-bloody-thing!"

"We'll get into that later, Mooton," Sir Torvyn said calmly. He held a spindly callused hand up to his cousin's black-bearded cheek. "It's good to see you again, after all these years. Tell me, how does my father fare?"

"Well," Sir Mooton said, nodding, withdrawing his hand from Jonik's shoulder. "Well enough, anyway. His…his mind is ailing, Torvyn. He speaks of you often and fondly, to this day. And in his sleep; he calls your name in his sleep, old Alberfred tells me."

"Alberfred?" Sir Torvyn repeated, smiling reminiscently. "He still serves as steward?"

"He does. And castellan as well, since Lord Devyn's health has faltered."

Sir Torvyn raised a thin questioning brow. "Would that not be your job, Cousin? You have been my father's heir these long years I've been missing, have you not? Elmhall Hold is yours by rights."

"*Was* mine by rights, until about a minute ago. And nothing I ever wanted. But you're back now, Torv. The heir of Blackshaw, returned!" He looked to those standing nearby, grinning massively. Jonik felt obliged to smile back, as the others did the same. "And just who are you lot, then?" Sir Mooton asked them. "Heroes all, I'll say, to have brought my cousin back home. And Borrus, let's not forget him." He glanced back as Borrus arrived on deck, something wary in his eyes.

Because of me, no doubt, Jonik thought. *This is something Borrus had wanted to avoid.*

"Well? Who are these brave companions of yours, Torvyn? Some have the bearing of warriors, now that I get a good look at them." His eyes scanned from man to man, landing on Emeric in particular. "A fine blade at your hip there. Godsteel, yes? What's your name, good man?"

"This would be Lord Emeric of the noble House of Manfrey," Sir Torvyn said. "You have met Captain Turner. Beside him is his second, Braxton, who they call Brown Mouth, for reasons that become obvious when he smiles. And Jack of the Marsh, who hails from these very parts, I do believe. And finally Jonik, their leader."

Sir Mooton balked. "Leader? *You?*" His big bushy eyebrows fell into a frown, black as tar and tangled, over a heavy brow. "Well you'll have to excuse me, lad. When I hear leader I think of someone a summer or two older. And you're dressed as a deckhand…" His eyes went back to Emeric, trying to pull the pieces together. "But you're a lord? Surely you command here? And…" His frown deepened "Manfrey, was it? Like Sir Oswald?"

"As a faint shadow, Sir Mooton," Emeric said humbly. "I have Sir Oswald's name, yes, but spoken as a whisper not a cry. His blood is thin in me, I assure you."

"Lord Manfrey is rather too modest for his own good," Sir Torvyn said to that. "He is a highly-skilled fighter and very much worthy of the name."

Borrus stepped up to Sir Mooton's side, placing a hand on his shoulder. He looked as uncomfortable as Jonik had ever seen him. "Why don't we head down to that tavern you were talking about, Mooton," he suggested. "The Singing Duck, was it? Yes, I remember it fondly. Let's go share an ale." He glanced around awkwardly. "I can fill you in there."

"Not so fast, Borrus," said Sir Torvyn. "There's something we need to clear up first."

Borrus looked at him, eyes narrowing. "Don't do it, Torvyn," he warned.

"Do what?" Sir Mooton wanted to know. "I feel I'm missing something here."

"Do you have my allegiance, Cousin?" Sir Torvyn asked him directly. "And my trust?"

Sir Mooton fell sharply to one knee, the decks thudding under his weight. "*Always*, Torvyn. Your father is my lord, and you his heir. I am a Blackshaw, above all else. What is it you need of me, Cousin?"

"To swear me an oath, Mooton. That you will be there to protect me, when I step into the darkness."

"Darkness?" The beastly man looked lost. "What is it you're trying to say?"

"Your oath, Mooton."

"No," said Borrus, and firmly. "Torvyn, *don't* do this. Mooton is sworn to my father, and Prince Elyon. He has sworn to bring me to Dragon's Bane safe and unharmed. You cannot interfere."

Torvyn Blackshaw smiled at him. "I can, and I will." His eyes fell again to his cousin. The left gave a swift blink, and his right eyebrow jerked up suddenly, but elsewise he was maintaining a calm and composed facade. "So, Mooton? Is my safety paramount to you, now that I have arisen from the dead? Will you do all you can to shield me from the dangers of the dark?"

"*Anything*." Sir Mooton Blackshaw didn't hesitate. He pulled his massive battle-axe from his back, and placed it at his cousin's feet. "By godsteel I swear it, Cousin. And on my life, for what it is, I swear it on that too."

"Mooton, *no*," Borrus broke in. "House Blackshaw is sworn to serve House Kanabar. You'll bloody well do as I tell you."

"Then you can bloody well come with us," Sir Torvyn said sharply. He gave Borrus a stiff look. "I have a payment to make, Borrus, and *so do you*. That life debt the young lord has kindly deferred still hangs over your head, don't forget. Now, what is your honour worth to you, old friend? Has Jonik not earned your faith and fealty in this quest of his? Do you not owe him that, for saving your life, and mine, and those of every man and woman he emancipated from those pits?"

Borrus swallowed. "My father needs me for the war effort…" he started.

"Does he? Does he truly? One more blade is not going to help, Borrus, not in an army of them, not even one so well-honed as yours." Torvyn turned again to his cousin, who continued to look completely baffled by the exchange. "How many men are there at the Bane, Mooton?"

"I'm…not sure, exactly. Tens of thousands, Torv."

"And Varin Knights? Bladeborn? Men born to bear godsteel and bear it well?" He didn't need Sir Mooton to answer that. "Hundreds, yes hundreds, and you need not add Red Wrath to that number, Borrus. You can hurry on down to the Bane once you're done winning the fort, and who knows, perhaps we'll all come with you. But believe me when I say this, *we* need your blade more than your father does. And it's coming too, Borrus Kanabar. No more complaints, and no more quibbles, you're coming and that is that."

And he turned again to look down at his cousin. "Rise, Mooton, and join us. We sail north up the Sibling Strait on a *hunt* of great importance. I know how much you like those. And the woods and the mountains too." He smiled as Sir Mooton rose to his feet. "You're quite well suited to this task, I should think." He glanced down onto the docks. "Oh, and your men…Regnar, I recognise, and Daggart and Sir Bulmar too, if not the others at a glance. Blackshaw men," he said. "Your men…*my* men. And I think they'll come as well, so long as we have space to accommodate them?"

That question was for the others; Jonik and Emeric and Turner. The Captain of Invincible Iris gave answer. "Plenty o' room, aye," he said. "Though we might need more ale, to look at you."

As the men laughed, Sir Borrus Kanabar slipped aside and took Jonik off by the arm. He had a scowl on his face. It quickly became a wry smile. "Damn you, boy, for putting this poison in his head." Yet for all that, he gave Jonik a look of fealty and said, "You win, then, boy. Guess I'll be paying that life debt after all."

27

Amron

Robert Borrington, the voluble Lord of Northwatch, came rushing out through the crowd of watchmen and rangers, took one look at him and his ragged companions, and proceeded to unleash one of the loudest, most gratefully relieved bellows of laughter Amron Daecar had ever heard. "Well bugger me sideways and back to front!" he exclaimed. "You're bloody well back at last!"

Amron smiled through the wild salt and pepper thicket that was his beard, removed the pack from his fur-cloaked shoulders, and set it aside on the welcome grey stone of the courtyard inside the postern gate of the castle. "Surely you had forewarning of our return, Robert?" The Horn of Haldar, set at the summit of the soaring Infinity Tower, had been blowing for some time to signal their coming, booming out its thunderous song.

"I foolishly thought it was one of my rangers," Borrington said, smiling enormously. He came striding forward. "Goodness me, Amron, I thought I'd never see you again. You were gone so long!"

"But back now." The two men shared a short but hearty embrace.

Lord Borrington gave him a good look up and down, smiling and shaking his head all the while. "The famous Lord Daecar, garbed as a vagrant. Ha! Gods, Amron, I feel like I'm looking at a ghost. A horribly bedraggled and ungroomed ghost, but a ghost all the same."

"I missed you too, Robert."

Borrington laughed again. "Well I'm sure. Ah, and Whitebeard! I suppose thanks are in order, good man. Your legend grows. The men have been taking wagers on whether you'd lead Amron out, and I have to confess, the odds haven't been looking favourable of late."

The rangy figure of Rogen Whitebeard bent down into a tight bow before his lord and commander. "The men might care to have more faith in me, my lord."

"Faith only takes one so far, my friend." Borrington grinned and turned. "And Walter! Dear Walter!" The Lord of Northwatch stepped over and threw his arms around the short scruffy man. "Well my, look at you. You've aged a decade since I saw you last! And still paunchy. How is that? You ought to have returned all skin and bone!"

"You appear to have aged somewhat yourself, Lord Borrington," the luckiest man in the world - or *former* luckiest man in the world, as Walter continued to insist - said with a customary grin. "The stress of worrying for Lord Amron's return has evidently taken its toll."

"Oh my, it has, it has. *Months*. It's been months and not a word!" Lord Borrington looked across the three men, shaking his head in continued wonderment. "And I'm sure you've got a tale or two or ten to tell! Come, Walter, Rogen, get those packs off your backs. My men will take care of them." He waved a hand and several of the soldiers of Northwatch moved in to fetch up their belongings, garbed in their sombre grey. "I'll have rooms prepared for you. Nice and comfy ones. With soft featherbeds. And baths. You could all use baths, I'm sure." He took a good long sniff and nodded. "Yes, well I don't need to tell you about that. The stink is ripe, let's say. Come, come. We can share a drink in the common room. The hearth is burning well and it's plenty warm. Warmth! Now that's something I'm sure you've craved for a good long while as well." He laughed again.

Walter smiled fondly at the prospect. "I could do with a seat by the fireside," he admitted. "With a nice warm cup of mulled wine for company, perhaps?"

"Oh of course. As many as you'd like. Amron, come. All of you, come. Let's get you inside and out of the cold."

Cold, Amron thought. *This isn't cold.* Their breath was frosting, yes, and the sun was setting pretty and red in the west, ushering in a bit of a chill, but Amron had felt true cold now, that cold that bit through wool and leather and fur and went right down into the bone, and this was not it. "I'll hear first of my family, Robert," he said. He wasn't going to take another step before learning of their fate. "Are they all well?"

Robert Borrington nodded enthusiastically. "Yes, perfectly well last I heard. Lady Amara and young Lillia are in Ilivar under the stout protection of your father-in-law, I am told. She has been most concerned to hear of your return, Amron. Amara, that is. She'll surely be delighted to know that you're back."

"I shall pen her a letter as soon as I can. And what of Elyon? Has the war taken him abroad?"

"It has taken him to Harrowmoor, Ilithor, and most latterly to Dragon's Bane. But that is a story in itself. And one better regaled by the fire. Come, Amron, I shall explain inside."

Lord Borrington led the way, ushering them across the snowy courtyard and into the inner ward, where some men were engaged in archery practice, as several others clashed with sword and shield. To a man they stopped in their training and gaped to see Lord Daecar limping through their midst. "As I say, not many expected you to return after so long," Robert said. "They'll be coming up with all sorts of new names for you now. Amron the Returned. Unkillable Daecar. Lord of the Icewilds, that sort of thing. I'm not so good with the names but you get my meaning. As if you don't have enough of them already. Ha!"

His laughter echoed off the cracked stone walls of the ward as they reached the common room and pushed their way in through the heavy oaken door. The hall was fit to accommodate the entire garrison of five hundred at a push, though rarely did they all gather. As they stepped within, several groups of men could be spotted around the benches and tables, taking their dinner between duties or sharing in an ale and the latest tidings to the south and east. Some were smoking pipes, others playing cards. The hall hummed low and quiet with the voices of several dozen men, though as soon as they entered all went deathly quiet.

Lord Borrington chuckled for the dozenth time. "More gawping faces. I suppose you'll have to get used to that, Amron. Not that you aren't already." He turned toward the hearth, burning invitingly on the left side of the room. "Come, let's escape these cow-eyed fools. Two-Toe! Mulled wine and ale, and some food as well. The rest of you…no questions or disturbances. Just keep on as if we're not here."

They took seats around a table close to the fire, as the men returned to their mutterings and smoking and gambling. The man called Two-Toe hobbled over with flagons of ale and spiced wine in hand. He set them down and shuffled back off to fetch them their food. "Lost half his toes to frostbite," Robert Borrington explained. "Only has two left on the right foot so isn't much good on his feet anymore. Was a good ranger once, though. Whitebeard knows that. Now he's stuck here serving the men." He shrugged, pouring the drinks; wine for Walter and ale for the rest. "Noticed you still have that limp of yours, Amron. I take it you never made it to Vandar's Tomb, then?"

"I'll hear this about Elyon first, Robert. We'll get onto me after."

"Right you are." The Lord of Northwatch pushed the drinks across to each man. "A toast to your return first. It's damn fine to see you all again." He raised his cup and the others followed. "To the three of you, intrepid adventurers all."

They clinked cups and drank. Walter let out a long blissful sigh, shut his eyes, and indulged himself in the intense pleasure of the moment. "Well now…I don't think I've ever tasted anything quite so exquisite in all my life. It certainly beats sickmilk, doesn't it?"

"Everything beats sickmilk," Rogen Whitebeard grumbled. "I'd sooner drink my own piss."

"And sickmilk is?" Robert clearly wasn't privy to the special homebrew of the Snowskins.

"An unpleasant milky wine," Amron told him, with a certain bluntness. He didn't care to make mention of the Snowskins yet, else his friend would want to know more. "You were going to tell me of my son, Robert."

Robert Borrington took another long glug of ale, set his tankard down on the table, and wiped his mouth of the froth. "Yes…Elyon. Now where to start…"

"The beginning is usually a good place," Amron suggested.

"The beginning can be a little hard to define." Robert Borrington had terrible scarring covering a great deal of his body, courtesy of a dragon attack during the last war. Clothed, most of it was well hidden, though his right ear was hideously disfigured and his neck on that side had a mottled, leathery look to it that almost resembled scales, in a bitter irony. It glistened in the firelight. "Hmmm, how about we start at the end instead." He began refilling his tankard. "That's the most interesting part anyway."

Amron was getting the sense that his son had been up to no good. "What's he done?" he asked. "Come, Robert, out with it. I've waited months to hear news of my family and have no desire to be kept in suspense."

"No, of course." Robert had another gulp, put down his mug, wiped his lips and said, "Your son is now bearer of the Windblade, Amron, and training with it at Dragon's Bane. There's a huge bloody great army there, some thirty, forty thousand strong I've had it from a few sources, under the running of Wallis Kanabar and a few other lords and greathouse heirs, your brother-in-law Rikkard among them. But it seems to me that Elyon has risen above them all. Prince, they're calling him now. Prince of Vandar. And now that you're back...well, I suppose you'd best get used to being called king." He smiled and had another drink of ale. "There's another name for your list."

For a short while there was nothing but the murmuring at the other tables, the occasional exclamation of victory or grumble of defeat from the men playing cards, the crackle and pop of the wood in the fire. Amron could tell well enough that Walter had plenty to say, though the man was managing to hold his tongue until Amron had been given a moment to digest all that. "King," he said eventually. Amongst all the rest of it, that seemed the most pertinent of details. Elyon holding the Windblade, oh...he'd get to that. But first, he needed to dig into this other matter. "I take it that Ellis is dead, then?"

It was the only explanation. Ellis Reynar had no sons of his own and Vandar had always been a patriarchal monarchy, giving his daughter Lyriss no right to rule. As Ellis's first cousin, Amron had always known he was his closest remaining male heir and next in line to the throne.

Robert confirmed as much with a nod. "Fell from a balcony in Ilithor. The balcony in the throne room, no less. Or was thrown, I should say. Most people are saying Janilah did it himself."

Walter balked. "By Varin, why would he do a thing like that?"

"He's gone mad, they say. Mad and missing, but that's all happened recently. Oh, and he has the Mistblade. Janilah, that is. Goodness me, Amron, you've missed a lot. I should have written out a list so I didn't forget anything." He gave that a good chuckle as well; Robert Borrington had always been quick to laugh, and didn't spare his own japes the treatment.

"King," Walter hummed, pursing his lips. He was looking at Amron, nodding slowly. "Suits you, my lord. Or...I suppose we should be calling you Your Majesty now, or Your Grace or some such."

"You can keep on calling me Amron, Walter. And you, Rogen. I think you've both earned the right to call me whatever you please."

"Yes, but I should hasten to add that there's another king in all this," Robert informed them. "Godrik Taynar. It appears Ellis wrote you out of his line of succession, Amron. It's all some big conspiracy, apparently. Godrik and Janilah cooked all this up, killed Ellis, and took control of the north. Oh yes, well that reminds me. There's a new king over in Rasalan as well. Hadrin cut his own father's throat open, it's said, as the old prophet sat in his solar poring over some letters and scrolls. Horrible way to go but that Hadrin's always' been a horrible little man, so I suppose it makes some sense."

"Good grief. I'm not quite sure *horrible* covers patricide and regicide, my lord," Walter said. "That is a truly monstrous crime. I take it the Rasals have risen up in revolt against him, in outrage? Godrin was so widely loved there."

"Not as yet, no, but there's talk of a few unhappy cousins who might look to make life difficult for him. Officially, old King Godrin died of heart failure, but *officially* Ellis Reynar slipped off of that balcony drunk as a skunk, so I'm not sure the word 'official' has much meaning anymore."

"And all this by Janilah's plotting," Amron said. It wasn't a question. *He had me maimed, and my eldest son murdered, and all by the hand of my secret bastard-born boy.* There seemed nothing that Janilah Lukar would not do for power, no depths he would not plough in his desperate need for control. Amron closed a fist. *Mistblade,* he thought, as the Frostblade sat safely at his hip, concealed within the folds of his heavy black cloak. Something in him yearned for that battle. To stand face-to-face with the old Warrior King and ask him 'why', before taking his head.

"That's the talk, yes," Robert answered, leaning back in his chair. He was wearing his old Varin cloak, as always. Parts of it had been burned during the dragon attack as well, stitched and patched and sewn back together. It gave it a terribly tattered look, but like that scarring, the Lord of Northwatch had always worn it proudly. "He gave his granddaughter to Hadrin as reward for his loyalty. Lucky man. Never met Princess Amilia myself but heard tell of her bottomless beauty. There was a big wedding in Ilithor a month or so ago…that's when your Elyon stole the Windblade. He and

Amara, and a few others." He paused, frowning, scratching at his scaly neck. "Oh, and…hmmmm. Well, there's no easy way to say this, Amron, so I'll just come out with it right away. Rylian. He, er…well, he's gone as well. Dead, that is. A tragic loss, but assuaged somewhat by your return. We need our heroes at a time like this."

Rylian…dead. It took a moment for the thought to fully register. His mind flashed with memories of the man, gallant in brown and green, inspiring his men upon the battlefield. He remembered how they'd hugged after the Battle of Burning Rock, how they'd shared drinks that night and spoken of the dragons they'd killed. It was the night that both of them had come legends. The night that songs were born. *Echo of Titans. Rylian the Brave.* There was no finer warrior in all the north than Rylian Lukar, and no finer man. Amron looked Lord Borrington in the eye. "How?" he asked him. "What happened, Robert?"

The Lord of Northwatch shifted uncomfortably in his seat. "Well…that was…that was Janilah too, they say. Or his men, by his order. Accounts differ. There are some wild rumours that Rylian was making a bid for the throne, but not many are believing that. I am sorry, Amron. I know the two of you were close."

Amron nodded numbly. He could not muster words. *Rylian…gone.* The world felt suddenly less mighty and merry without him. He had to take a few moments to compose himself, as Two-Toe came hobbling back over with trenchers of hollowed-out bread full of warm chicken stew. "For you, my lords. Nice and hot from the pot."

"Thank you, Two-Toe. And more beer, if you'd be so kind."

"Aye, Lord Borrington. Right away." The man leaned across the table, fetching the empty ale flagon. He locked eyes with Amron for just a moment, and moved into a bow. "My lord. Tis an honour to serve you. And see you again."

Amron came out of his reverie, though slowly. He looked at the old crippled ranger. Up close, he realised he knew him, recognising him from a previous visit years ago. "We've met before."

The man smiled crookedly. "Aye." He had a couple of broken teeth, loose folds of skin beneath his eyes, thin grey hair swept over a balding scalp. "I was a ranger then, my lord. Had come back from a ranging only a few days before you came to visit. You wanted to hear of tidings in the Heights and beyond."

"I remember." The memory was strangely fond to him. *A better time,* he thought. *A simpler time. Rylian…* "It must have been…ten years ago now."

"You've a fine memory, my lord. Was eleven, this last winter. I lost my toes on the next ranging. And the tip of a finger or two as well." He held up a hand, showing the stumpy end of his pinky. "Been castle-bound ever since."

"And we're all the happier for it," Lord Borrington said. "Two-Toe does a mean chicken broth. Nice and thick, never thrifty with the meat. I'm not sure what we'd do without him."

The old ranger tried to smile. "Aye. I'll fetch you that ale, my lord." He shuffled back away through the smokey room, as White-beard watched him go. Amron could sense he didn't agree with a long-serving ranger being reduced to kitchen work. *And haven't people been looking at me in a similar way this last year?* he thought. *The indomitable Crippler of Kings, reduced to a cripple himself…*

He turned from that thought, looking back to the castle lord. "You said something about Janilah going missing." His appetite had gone missing too with this news of Rylian. He was struggling to move past it, but knew there was more to hear.

"Yes, that's the latest I've heard, though news can take a while to reach us here sometimes. Might be he's resurfaced by now."

"How long ago was this?"

Robert Borrington guzzled a mouthful of soup. "Ten, twelve days gone, I think. Janilah was speaking at some public address in White Shadow, hoping to calm the people's fears over the war. But since Rylian…well, he's not much loved anymore, if ever he was. People started letting him know that to his face, calling him all sorts, throwing rotting fruit and such. Well, you can imagine how a man like Janilah Lukar would react to that."

"Not especially happily?" offered Walter.

"Spot on, my friend. No, not happily at all. Now the tales do clash a bit here, but either Janilah bellowed for whoever was throwing fruit at him to be slain, and that's what started the riot, or else the people started rioting themselves for the simple joyous hell of it. Either way, a riot started, and Janilah got caught up in it."

Walter gave a bemused frown. "So the crowd carried him off somewhere? That's why he's missing? The king's been kidnapped. Or…" A cheeky grin paid a visit to his face. "King-napped, I should say." No one was particularly impressed by that. "Sorry, I couldn't resist."

"Please try to, next time," said Lord Borrington, though merrily.

Whitebeard grunted. "He won't. Selleck's full of stupid jokes like that."

"And I can imagine how trying that must have been for a man like you, Rogen. But as to Janilah being taken…no one seems to know for sure. What I can report is that he drew out the Mistblade and started swinging. Accounts vary, as I say, but some are suggesting he killed upwards of a hundred people that day. It would seem to me unlikely that anyone was able to kidnap him, if he could do *that.*"

"My gods…" Amron shook his head in dismay. "*A hundred*?"

"I'd call that an upper estimate. But even those on the lower end aren't pretty. And children among them. It's a bloody ghastly cake however you cut it. And the end result is a mad and missing king, a city in turmoil, and what might well become a fight for the crown." He hooked a hand around his ale and downed the rest of the mug, as Two-Toe shuffled back over. "But that's the world these days. None of the northern kingdoms are secure, everyone's at each other's throats, and we've got about a dozen different armies garrisoned here and there and two laying siege to the south as we speak."

Amron's ears pricked up at once, like a predator detecting prey. "*Where*?"

"The Trident and Eagle's Perch. The Tukorans are taking care of the latter, we've got the former. Though when I say we, I mean the Taynars, Olorans, Cargills and their banners. Most of your Daecar men are shielding the western gate around the Twinfort and Green Harbour. My brother Randall is there, Amron, and most others you helped muster before you went over the Weeping Heights. Then we've got Lord Pentar guarding the Black Coast, as ever, and Wallis Kanabar and the Riverlanders, Lakelanders, and Marshlanders at Dragon's Bane, as I've said, awaiting some great Agarathi invasion across Death's Passage."

"Not much happening, then," Walter said pithily. He drew liberally on his wine and had a quick pour to resupply it. "And the Rasal greathouses?"

"Defending their own coast, so far as I know, although a few are helping to bolster our southern borders. Same with the Tukorans. I heard Cedrik Kastor took most of their best to the Perch. He's having more luck down there than Dalton Taynar is, if the crows are cawing it true."

"Sir Dalton leads the siege of the Trident?" asked Amron. He mulled on that. Dalton Taynar was a miserable man, much like his father, yet a good swordsman and reasonable strategic mind. He wasn't the worst choice. *Nor the best,* Amron had to admit. *A man with more experience would be preferable.*

"Well, he's prince. Apparently," said Robert with a shrug of the shoulders. "That's what the Ironmoorers say, anyhow. And First Blade too since your brother turned deserter."

"What?" The word came out more sharply than Amron had intended. A few men looked over from a nearby table, before resuming their muttering. Amron lowered his voice. "Vesryn would never desert."

"One can never say never these days, Amron. The men around here have been saying you three would never return, and look at you, sitting right across from me at this very table. A man would be wise to scrub that word from his vocabulary. I cannot tell you how many instances of…"

"Enough, Robert. Tell me what happened to my brother."

"Well…yes, as you wish. He went missing from the siege camp outside Harrowmoor, months ago now. Took the Sword of Varinar with him." He had another scratch at the disfigured flesh of his neck, then pushed a few strands of limp grey hair from his eyes. "Was the same night they found out about Ellis's death, I think, and Godrik planting that skinny old rump of his on the godsteel throne. I've been told Dalton and Vesryn weren't getting along. Lots of undermining of your brother's claim, and such. Seems Dalton was going to strip Vesryn of his rank and blade both that night, but when they went to his pavilion to confront him, he was gone."

"So he took the Sword of Varinar and fled," Walter said, considering it. "Not so treacherous as it sounds, given the circumstances. If Sir Vesryn had some prior knowledge of this Taynar coup, perhaps he was doing the right thing, denying them that blade as well."

Amron spun his mug slowly between his fingers. "That's one way of looking at it, Walter."

"Not many agree, if I'm being brutally honest," Lord Borrington told them. "There's talk that Vesryn was beginning to misplace his marbles, same as Janilah, before he ran off."

"I wonder who your source is on all this." Amron had another sip of ale. The taste had soured. *All this damnable treachery. And what was that about Elyon? Stealing* the Windblade, Robert had said. Amron had foolishly hoped his son had been declared champion and given the blade by consent of king and council, but no, he'd sullied himself as well. He shook his head to that thought. *I don't know enough yet to judge him*, he chided, and he could smell Amara's perfumed stink all over this as well.

Robert finished off his soup, then took a bite of the softened bread. "My source? I've got plenty. But Lady Amara's been most generous with her tidings, when she sends those letters to inquire of you."

"I'm sure. She always was an awful gossip." *And far too influential to those close to her, it would seem.* Amara had been the catalyst for his journey into the Icewilds, after all, pairing him up with Walter and sending them both on their way. That she'd been instrumental in Elyon taking the Windblade would surprise him not at all. *And perhaps some good will come of that too*, he hoped, *as it did my overlong odyssey.* For that he'd have to give her credit. There was a certain lack of honour in her schemes sometimes, but they were effective, he'd give her that.

Amron was growing too hot with all this news, and the fire had warmed him sufficiently. He rose to his feet, feeling the tension in his right thigh, the striking pain in his left shoulder as he unburdened himself of his outer fur cloak, leaving him in a lighter woollen one beneath, garbed over his boiled leathers. He threw the cloak over the bench and sat back down.

"New blade, Amron?" Robert asked casually. He was staring at the now-exposed sheath, fixed at the crude leather swordbelt that Stegra and the Snowskins had fashioned for him. He'd lost his own belt and sword and dagger when he'd plunged into the Silver Scar, Whitebeard unfastening it lest he be dragged down to his doom beneath those freezing waters. But that sheath…it had been resting beside the rock from which he'd pulled the Frostblade, pale in colour, white and silver and most unusual. Not so spectacular as the blade itself, no, but plenty to draw the eye, as it had Robert Borrington's. "I recall you leaving with a broadsword of your own," the man said, "but I confess I don't recognise the sheath...and that *hilt*."

He peered closer, leaning across the table to get a better look. The Frostblade's handle was particularly eye-catching, white as bone, encrusted with tiny, diamond-like studs that gave it a sort of crystalline appearance when seen up close. The cross-guard had a similar effect, and the pommel was wrought in the image of a thousand tiny snowflakes connected to form a perfect sphere. From afar it seemed like a simple white orb, yet up close the intricate detailing was visible.

Robert whistled softly through his lips. "Well now, that is some blade, Amron. Where on earth could you have gotten it? The forgotten armouries of Vandar's Tomb, I would guess, but with that limp of yours...well, I just assumed you'd never made it to the mountain."

"We made it, Robert." Amron looked to make sure none of the other Northwatch men were taking note of their conversation. He had not wanted his possession of the Frostblade to become common knowledge just yet, and had no intention of including that tidbit in his letter to Amara either. "But no further than the outer hall. The mountain was coming down when we arrived. We had no choice but to turn back."

Lord Borrington ran thumb and forefinger up and down his broad chin. "We felt tremors here, some six, seven weeks ago. And I had reports from the rangers of dozens of snowdrifts and avalanches in the mountains."

"That sounds right," said Whitebeard, quietly nursing his ale. "Those tremors originated from the mountain."

"And you were *there*, when it happened?" Robert shook his head in awe. "Gods. How was it, being so close?"

"As if Vandar himself was rising from the earth," Walter intoned.

Robert gave another soft sigh. "I can scarcely imagine it. Well no wonder you never made it to his holy chamber, then. I don't know what to say, Amron. You went all the way, and for nothing."

"The trip was worthwhile, Robert." Amron's hand went to rest on the pommel of the Frostblade. At his touch, a soft white mist came creeping out from between blade and sheath, sparkling colourfully as it melted by the heat of the fire.

Robert Borrington gasped, open-mouthed. "No," he whispered. "That cannot be the...the..."

"I don't want it known, Robert." Amron took his fingers off the haft, and the mists settled. He drew his cloak closed. "I am still learning to master it and would prefer to be left alone while I do."

"Right...of...of course." Robert Borrington swallowed. "As you say, Amron."

"Take your time, Robert. It is something of a surprise, I know." *Though no more than what I've heard,* he thought. *Janilah holding the Mistblade. My son the Windblade. Godrik and Hadrin crowned kings. Rylian...*

"A shock would be a better description," Robert said quietly. "That blade hasn't been seen for...for centuries."

"The Mistblade was thought lost for a similar number of years,"

Walter Selleck put in. "That they should both be returned at the same time is no coincidence. There is providence here. The Five Blades, all now returned to the world. And if I have my count correct, it seems that four of them are held by Daecars."

"Three," countered Rogen Whitebeard. "Amron, his brother, his son. Three."

"*Sons*," Walter corrected. "Plural."

Amron began shaking his head. *I should never have confided that in the man*, he thought, but he had, one night out in the wilds, when Whitebeard had slinked off on one of his rangings, confessing to Walter the identity of the Shadowknight. He was half regretting it now. But only half, in all truth. *Because why should I care to hide or deny it,* he wondered, *with all the world gone to madness?*

Rogen and Robert both turned to look at him. "The Shadowknight..." Robert Borrington started.

"Is my son, yes." Amron gave Walter an unpleasant glare. "Thank you for sharing that, Walter."

"I had a concern you might continue to try to hide it, Amron. Best not. And I imagine that secret will start to get out soon, if it hasn't already."

"But he...he tried to kill you. And...Aleron, he..."

"I know, Robert. And I'd rather not discuss it." Amron took a drink of ale. In truth the boy had been creeping into his thoughts of late, ever since he'd discovered the Frostblade. "Has there been any news of him?"

"I thought you didn't want to discuss it?"

"I don't. I want to know if there has been news. That's all."

"News or rumour? I can't say anything of the Shadowknight with any great certainty. But there have been some legends spring up about him these last months. The boy seems to attract names, as you do, though none quite so noble."

Amron realised at that point that he didn't want to do this now, and not here. "You can tell me later." He glanced into the common room; more men had begun to arrive, filing in through the far door, fetching food and ale, settling around the benches. After months away from it all he'd grown used to the solitude of the wilds. The glancing, questioning eyes were something he'd not much missed. "Perhaps we ought to continue this in your solar."

Robert Borrington gave no word of argument. "As you wish." He rose to his feet.

Amron was happy to escape the growing crowd, passing back through the ward and into the Commander's Tower, at the summit of which Lord Borrington made his home. Whitebeard took his leave halfway up the stairs, asking permission to retire and catch some sleep. Though back under Lord Borrington's command, the question was for Amron. "He's your man now, it seems," Robert said, as they entered the comfortable privacy of his chambers.

Amron had scarcely seen a sight more welcome than the small flickering fire, the warm rugs and drapes, the rich wooden furniture intimately placed about the room. He moved immediately to the stone window, looking out over the mountains from whence they'd come. "We've been through a lot together," he said, staring at the shadows of distant peaks, fading with the dusk. "But he's yours again now, Robert."

"I'm not so sure." The castle lord filled more drinks, a fruity red wine this time, and handed them out. Walter moved to take a rest in a cushioned armchair, exhaling as he sank into the soft upholstery. "I should think a man like Rogen Strand is wasted here," Robert went on. "There's no war in these mountains, after all, Amron. You might consider taking him with you when you leave."

Amron turned from the window. "Strand?"

"Ah." Robert smiled easily, sampling his wine. "So Whitebeard never told you who he was, I see."

"Not for lack of trying," said Walter, disappearing into his chair. Amron had never seen a man look so unashamedly snug. "So he's a Strand, is he? A lesser branch presumably?"

"You presume wrong, Walter. Rogen is a trueborn son of Lord Styron Strand. His third, if I recall correctly. I do not believe he has much love for his father, or family at large. Something of a black sheep is Rogen."

"Truly?" quipped Walter. "I'd never have guessed." He had a drink of his wine, then gave a thoughtful frown. "Wasn't Lord Styron wed to the Lady Margery Taynar?"

"He was," confirmed Amron.

"Huh. And…just so I'm getting this right…Margery Taynar was the younger sister of Lord Godrik, yes?"

"Correct. Making Rogen nephew to a king."

"False king," Robert corrected. "Godrik Taynar is no true king around here, Amron. That'd be you."

"Yes, well half the kingdom would disagree with you, Robert."

He mulled on it for a time. *Rogen Strand.* It made sense. Lord Styron wasn't known as 'the Strong' for nothing. He'd been a formidable warrior once, and clearly Rogen had inherited his talents. *If not his look,* he thought. The Strands tended to be bigger boned than Rogen, who'd clearly taken after his mother in look. Margery Taynar had had the same hollow cheeks and grim demeanour as the rest of her house.

Amron turned back to the window, looking at the darkening skies. An odd and unexpected melancholy came upon him to gaze back to the world they'd left. *I understand Rogen's love for the wilderness now,* he thought. He found himself wondering where the Snowskins were, how Stegra and Svaldar and Kusto and Wagga and Jorgen and Arnel and all the others were doing. He wondered whether he would ever see them again. He hoped he would, should he survive the coming war. And that war. The War Eternal. The Twenty Fifth Renewal. He still had no great notion of how it was going. *We siege Eagle's Perch and the Trident, and it seems our lands are secure, but what else? Have the Agarathi rallied and joined forces with the Lumarans? Do the Fireborn swell in rank as never before, as the rumours once said.* He had a hundred questions he needed to ask and yet could find no will to ask them. *I need rest,* he knew, *and quiet, and peace. I need time to digest what I've heard.*

He turned. Walter and Robert were both looking at him patiently. "If Rogen wishes to join us, he will be welcome to," he said. "I'll leave it for him to decide."

Walter Selleck agreed with a brisk nod. "Teasing Rogen Whitebeard has become one of the great pleasures of my life. I should sorely miss it if we should part with him here."

Amron smiled faintly. "As to the rest of our tale, Robert…well, I will have to leave that to Walter to render, and more skillfully and energetically than I ever could, I'll wager. I am tired, my friend, and in desperate want of that bath. Tomorrow perhaps you will find me more talkative."

"I quite understand, Amron. Your rooms will have been prepared by now. I'll take you myself."

Walter made an effort to stand as they left the room, though Amron was quick to wave him back into his chair with an instruction to relax and enjoy himself. They descended the spiral stair, reaching a corridor a few floors down. Robert pushed through a door and into a comfortable bedchamber. "These rooms are rarely used," he said.

"Save for when men of esteem such as you come by. I hope it's to your liking, Amron."

Amron looked around. "I've stayed in this very room before," he recalled. It might have been that time eleven years ago when he'd met Two-Toe, though he couldn't be sure. "It will do nicely."

"After sleeping rough for months, I can quite imagine." Robert went to the window, pushing the shutters closed. "There's a bathing room next door. I'll have a bath filled for you. Perhaps a shave as well? Else you'd prefer to leave that for tomorrow?"

"Tomorrow," Amron said. He removed his cloak, hanging it on a hook by the door, unfastened his swordbelt and rested the sheathed Frostblade by the wall.

"Would you like me to set a guard for that, while you sleep?" Robert asked.

"Here? There are no thieves among you, are there?"

"I should hope not, no. But those blades have a lure."

"No one knows I have it, Robert, and I want to keep it that way, as I told you. Unless you or Rogen have an itch to steal it I think it's quite safe where it is." Amron walked to the shutters and pulled them back open, letting the cold night air wash in. It felt right.

"My rangers do that sometimes, after returning from long weeks away," Robert told him, watching. "You get used to the cold, they tell me. Something about those wilds changes a man, Amron." A long silence followed. "I'll see to that bath, then."

Amron remained at the window as he heard his friend depart. He could not seem to draw himself away from the cool bracing breeze, the gentle stirring of the wind as it caressed through his hair and the thick tangles of his beard. The view from this side of the tower looked over the mountains. *It was as if he knew,* he thought. And he should. Robert Borrington had commanded this castle for near on two decades and knew of the queer enchantments those mountains and wilds possessed.

And they have not seen what I have seen. The misted lands he'd cleared of the curse had been as close to a wild and rugged paradise as he could conceive. Rolling forested hills. Towering snow-capped peaks. Rivers teeming with leaping fish and woods clotted with game. A coastline of plenty, with great wide pebbly strands bordered by majestic pine and spruce. *It is the last untapped frontier,* he thought, *and the Snowskins have it all.* The thought made him smile. *I have the Frostblade, and they have their paradise.*

A fair bargain, Walter would say. But Walter would be wrong.

When the bath was filled, Amron bathed, relieving his tight hard muscles of their stresses and strains and hurts. And when he had bathed, he clothed himself in fresh hose and shirt, soft against his skin, and ambled to his bed, left shoulder pinching with pain, right thigh aching with a dull and constant throb. His eyes passed by the Frostblade, sitting enticingly against the wall. One clutch of the hilt, and his ails would be gone, his strength restored by its mystical powers of healing.

And there is a cruelty in that, he knew, as he turned away from the blade, and crept beneath the blankets. He was but a guardian of the Frostblade, as he told himself daily, and one day soon - in weeks or months or years, it made no matter - he would have to give it up.

And I will, he promised himself, as he tossed and turned on the soft featherbed and tried to find some rest. Pain ran through his thigh and shoulder and he could find no comfort here. For an hour, two, three he winced and turned and rose to stretch, trying to milk the throb from flesh and bone, but that night, as happened some nights, it would not relent or leave him.

As the hours passed by, so his temptation rose. His eyes turned back to the blade. *One quick touch*, he thought. *Ignite the blood-blond and your pain will be gone*. He took a step toward it, stopped, and turned back. *No. No, I cannot.* If he came to rely on the blade, what then? It was a path he dare not tread. *I must give it up, one day. I cannot depend on it forever.*

He moved back to the bed, took the blankets from the mattress, and threw them onto the floor. For months he'd bedded down on hard-packed earth and rock and stone with nought but a thin sheepskin bag and whatever garb he wore for cushioning. His body had grown used to it, and the featherbed was not helping. He lay down on wool and stone, calmed his racing thoughts, and let the cold winter wind comfort him.

And there on the floor next to his bed, Amron Daecar slept.

28

Lythian

Lythian stood at the top of the world, surveying the lands laid out beneath him. To the northwest, the Drylands; to northeast, the Smokeplains, provinces both parched and rugged, as much of northern Agarath was.

Amid the Smokeplains lay the great shadow of the Ashmount, that most fabled and feared of mountains, sitting imperiously upon the steppe. Lythian thought of Varin as he stared toward its faint shadow, dulled by distance, over a hundred miles away. He thought of the Steel Father's battle with Eldur and Karagar, the great dragon-son of Drulgar, at the end of the War of Fire and Steel. He thought of what had happened after. Of Eldur, creeping away to the Wings to lie in stasis, waiting. Of Varin, murdered at the parley at Death's Passage by Eldur's sons, Lori and Dor. Of Ayrin, the last living son of Varin, who took up his father's throne, and chose peace ahead of vengeance.

A wise choice, most called it. The alternative was a renewal of the war, more bloodshed and brutality, yet Ayrin elected a different path. For long years he presided over an age of peace and plenty, tutored in temperance by Queen Thala of Rasalan. Vandar flourished. The north prospered. Cities were raised and the population restored, the fields re-sown, the orchards re-planted. Yet in the end, there could be no hiding the depth of rage and resentment that had been stirred by Varin's murder. After reigning for two hundred years beneath a banner of truce, King Ayrin passed, handing his eldest son Amron the throne. And so the change in ruler brought a change in relations. King Amron sought vengeance for his grandfather's murder, and so started the Second Renewal.

The wind tugged at Lythian's cloak, as he stared north to where the plains blurred away to the edge of sight. *North. Vandar. Home.* He thought of another Amron now. His closest friend, named for that ancient king. *Do you prepare them, old friend?* he wondered. *Do you inspire them? Do you lead them as you once did?* He had heard tidings of turmoil in the northern kingdoms, of kings rising and falling, of fractured relations between the greathouses. *They can ill-afford to work against one another now,* he fretted. *If only they knew what was coming…*

He heard the sound of footsteps behind him. *Talasha,* he knew at once, as the princess came to stand at his side upon that lonely balcony. She took his hand in hers. "You are cold, sweet captain. Come back inside, where it's warm."

It was always cold up here, at the top of the *Kylash Hyndraha*, the Stair to the Stars. Around them, the peaks were capped in snow, yet far below, the plains would be sweltering. Lythian longed for the heat now. He longed to leave this mountaintop fortress behind, to start the long trek northward across the plains. *Due north,* he thought. That was the way he would go. Straight between the border where the Smokeplains met the Drylands. North, to the woods and hills that clothed the southern coast of the Red Sea, where they might find a ship to convey them to Southwatch. *Home. To Vandar. Where they know not what is coming…*

"I have to leave, Talasha," he said, after what felt like an age. "I must warn my people. I must tell them what has happened here."

She squeezed his palm tight between her fingers. "I know, sweet captain. You are dutiful, and a patriot. Yet the dangers…"

"I understand the dangers," he broke in. "But I cannot wait here any longer." His eyes shifted around him. This place had felt wrong to him from the moment he'd arrived. Every day, he felt more tense, more discomfited. *This is where Drulgar nested. This is where the Soul of Agarath lived. This is where Eldur awoke.* He could feel all that in the air, smell the ancient terrors that had long lurked here. But the others…they didn't understand. They *couldn't* understand. He breathed out, more stressed than he could say. "I know how perilous it will be down there, Talasha, but I have to try. I have to."

"I know." She clutched his hand yet tighter, to calm him. "You do not sleep well here, nor have you been eating. I understand."

You don't, he wanted to say. *Not really.* His waking hours were spent in dread. He could feel it bubbling up inside him, building, building. And when night came he saw no solace. What little sleep he got came with dreams of doom and darkness, and when he woke he felt no more rested than before. *I waste away*, he thought. *In body and mind and spirit, I fade here in his place.*

"We will leave soon, Lythian," Talasha tried to reassure him. "Once Ulrik is strong enough to travel, then…"

Lythian was already shaking his head. "I cannot wait for him," he said. He had waited too long already, down in those woods of the Western Neck, and it wasn't only Marak who was hurt. *I had to ease Mirella's passing myself*, Lythian thought bitterly. *Will I have to do the same again?*

But it wouldn't come to that, he knew. Lord Marak wasn't dying, only injured, though those injuries were enough to incapacitate him. He'd been thrown back against a wall when confronting Eldur, knocked so fiercely by the lashing tail of a raging dragon that he'd shattered his left arm and several ribs, and his scapula and clavicle too. For long weeks since he'd lain here in the fortress he'd once ruled, recuperating under the care of Sa'har Nakaan, his loyal friend and wingrider, and Sotel Dar, who'd survived the parley as well.

They were the very reason they had come; to discover the truth of their fate, and by the grace of the gods both men were alive, along with some others who had served here. Yet for all that, Lythian could not stay. *I came to find out what happened to them*, he thought, *and I have.* If he'd hoped to discover some secret to defeating Eldur, on that account he'd failed. He had read books, and scrolls, scoured the ruins of the library several times over, and spoken at length with Sotel Dar as to what might be done to combat this threat. *And nothing*, he thought. *I have found nothing.* The old scholar still had faith that Eldur was not in his right mind, that he would come around soon, that he would be the benevolent force they had hoped for, one side of the coin to bring balance to the world, with the heir of Varin still to rise. Lythian had heard enough of that. *If the heir of Varin is to rise*, he thought, *it will be to kill Eldur, not make peace with him.* His time here atop the world was done.

He turned to Talasha. "I will leave tomorrow," he said, coming to a decision he'd laboured over for days. "Ulrik will not be able to travel for weeks. And Sotel has not been able to help. Pagaloth will come with me, I'm sure. But you…" He hated what he was about to say, but he had no choice. *I've made my decision.* "You must stay as well, Talasha. I will be in great peril, crossing Agarathi lands, and will not put you in danger as well. Stay here. Stay with Ulrik and Sa'har and Sotel and the rest. Stay, and be safe. This dream of ours…" He shook his head. "It was never meant to be."

She didn't like that. "I have heard this talk before," she dismissed angrily. "We are past it, Lythian. We stay together, no matter what."

"Talasha…"

"*No*, Lythian. This is my country, my kingdom. *You* do not make decisions here." She drew her hand out of his and placed it on his chest. "This is mine as well. *Mine*, sweet captain, and I will not be parted from it. You think of your duty still, of how we cannot be. You think of your wife, I know, and the promise you made yourself to live alone, to be celibate. And do you know what I think, Lythian? I think that you think too much. I think you fret, and you worry, and you try to make everything all right. You have an instinct to protect everyone, and this is part of the reason why I love you. But enough now, sweet captain. When you leave, I shall go with you. Do *not* tell me no again."

The Knight of the Vale could only sigh. "Yes, Princess," he said. "As you wish."

"As I wish?" She shook her head, gripped his cheeks, and pulled him into a kiss. "I wish for this, and more, and often. I wish for these dark days to be done. I wish for Eldur to awaken, *fully* awaken, and become the force for good my cousin preached of. There is much I wish for, Lythian. And much that cannot be. But some things *can* be, and I will not let them go." She smiled at him. "Now come, let us escape this cold. You have been up here alone too long. Solitude will not serve you." She took his hand in hers once more and turned, leading him away.

Lythian made no objection this time. *Maybe she's right. Maybe I think too much, fret too much, show too much doubt and fear.* It was hard to help himself here. *I need to leave,* he thought, for the hundredth time. *I need to clutch godsteel again. I need to be whole and one.* He was a shadow of himself without it, and growing more anxious by the day. The thought of ranging through the Smokeplains or crossing the Drylands held no fear for him now, not compared to this place. Even now, as he crossed back through the bulky black tower that sat in the fort's northeastern corner, he could feel his head growing heavier, his limbs growing weaker. *Has any Bladeborn ever visited both the Nest and the Wings?* he wondered. *Have they had to endure these twin hells?* Somehow, he doubted it. *No, I am the only one.*

The fortress wasn't nearly so large as others Lythian had seen. In truth it wasn't a fortress at all, so much as a training academy for Fireborn. At its heart lay the Bondsquare, a large inner ward where the Bondstone had rested on its plinth. It was here that the Fireborn hopefuls would come, to be bonded to the beasts flown from the Wings. Now the plinth was destroyed, the Bondstone taken, the Bondsquare blackened and burned. The buildings around it were in ruin as well, blasted to their bones by the frenzied rage of the dragons. By luck, Sotel Dar had fled beneath a strong archway, protecting him as the ceiling of a storehouse came down around him. Sa'har Nakaan had landed safely when his dragon Ezukar had thrown him from the saddle, suffering only minor injuries. Marak, though mightiest of all of the Agarathi, had lived in large part due to the Body of Karagar armour he wore, protecting him from that dragon's lashing tail.

Yet the rest were fled or dead. Tavash and Vargo Ven had escaped upon Malathar, just as Talasha had escaped upon Neyruu. How Kin'rar and Ven had managed to control their dragons, where others could not, no one could say. Luck and happenstance seemed the most likely reasons. It had been suggested that their bonds to their beasts were stronger, forged deeper, but that could not be. Marak's bond to Garlath the Grand was as strong as godsteel, as was Sa'har Nakaan's bond to Ezukar, yet both had been abandoned. Lythian had been told that the feared Fireborn rider Kar Von Karosh had been present as well, atop his malformed dragon, Zyndrar the Unnatural. They had been a dreaded pairing in the last war, their bond as tough as teak, yet when Eldur awoke, and took hold of the Bondstone, Zyndrar the Unnatural had flown into a frenzy like most of the rest, tossing Kar Von Karosh from the saddle as the mad Fireborn fell away down the cliffside, to his doom.

And other Fireborn had fallen too. As had several of the staff who served here at the Nest, perishing in the fires and the frenzy. Only a few remained, some unharmed, others badly injured as Marak was. All now resided in the great hall, a solid stone building that had been untouched by the violence. The ceilings and walls were well decorated with etching and engravings of great Fireborn and dragons gone before, hanging with banners in red and black and gold. Here, Lord Marak once presided over the apprentice riders, guiding them, training them, instructing them on what it was to bond to one of Agarath's spawn. *And now his bonded beast has deserted him,* Lythian thought. *That is the wound that ails him. Not these broken bones and bruises. It is the darkening of half his soul; that is an ill that will never mend.*

There was a large hearth on the hall's western side, burning low as Lythian and Talasha entered. They had established their camp here, close to the fire. It was thought prudent for them to gather in one place, rather than take to separate bedchambers. The kitchens were nearby, as were the library and storerooms, to fetch food and wood and oil. Beds had been brought down from some of the chambers and laid out on the floor. Yet there was a gloom here that no fire could dispel, a cold that would not wane. *A sadness,* Lythian thought. Marak and Sa'har Nakaan, who had lost their dragons. Sotel Dar, who had lost his cause. Cevi had lost Mirella, and Talasha had lost her cousin Tethian, and everyone had lost Kin'rar, so fond to all. *This is a room of grief,* Lythian thought. *There are sorrows here that not even time can cure.*

Cevi was busying herself with a stew as they entered, stirring a pot hanging over the flames. An old cook who'd long served here at the Nest called Malgo was with her. Sa'har Nakaan sat at Marak's bedside, the pair sharing in a solemn silence. Sotel Dar was seated at a nearby table, his nose deep in a book, reading by candlelight. With him was a young librarian and scholar named Yosef, who had been stationed here to preach dragonlore to the apprentices. Lythian had spoken with him as well, in a bid to learn more of Eldur's rise, yet the man had given no answers. *They do not wish to speak against him,* he knew. Eldur was their founder, their father, their hope. Most believed he would come around. "It is like awakening from a nightmare," Sotel Dar had said. "You may thrash, at first, as you escape that dark reverie. But when you fully awaken, you will calm, and see the light. This I hope will be the case with the Fire Father. What he did here was an accident. This we must all believe."

But Lythian didn't believe that anymore. He wasn't sure if he ever had. *I should never have listened to their preaching,* he thought. *I should have slain Eldur as he slept. I should have listened to Borrus when he told me to kill him. But I didn't. And now look what I've done.*

Sir Pagaloth came striding over through the hall to join them, footsteps echoing. "You were gone a long time, Captain," he said. "Was it fresh air you sought?"

Lythian nodded. Pagaloth understood him better than most. *He knows I suffer here. He knows what a threat Eldur has become.* "I crave a wind in my face, sometimes," he said. "It can grow stuffy in here."

Talasha gave Lythian a kiss on the cheek. "I will check on the others," she told him, leaving the pair of men alone.

Pagaloth watched her go. "Has something happened?"

"I told her I'm leaving," Lythian said. "Tomorrow, I hope. If you are willing, Pagaloth, I'll have you lead me across the Drylands, as you did before."

"I am yours, by oath." Pagaloth inclined his head. It was the response Lythian had hoped for. "Which route will you intend to take?" the dragonknight asked. "It would be important to remain unseen, Lythian. We would be best advised to seek a quiet fishing village long leagues east of Dragonfall, I think. The crossing to Vandar will be shortest there. If we are lucky with the weather, a small sailboat or even skiff may do."

Lythian was grateful for his positivity. "I thought the same. The only alternative would be to try to reach Death's Passage, and cross through the Bloodmarshes. The fogs there will help conceal us if we should reach them. I know those marshes well enough."

"I am not so sure how wise that is, my friend. There is a great army amassing at Blademelt, we have heard. And the trek to the Bloodmarshes is longer."

He wasn't wrong. It was twice as far as the coast, as the crow flies, and the going would be slow on foot. "It would be best if we could find horses, no matter which road we take," Lythian said. "Do you think we might find some at a village at the base of the mountains?"

Pagaloth looked to Cevi, stirring her stew by the fire. "She will know better than me, Captain. She grew up near to here, as you know." He stopped for a thought, looking to Talasha. "Will she be coming as well?"

"She refuses not to."

Pagaloth smiled, though briefly. Lythian knew his thoughts on this. "She loves you, my friend. Many would call you blessed for that. To have captured the heart of a beautiful princess."

"Many others would call me unworthy, and all of them would be right." Lythian gave a weak smile. "She will come, against my better judgement. And Cevi as well, unless Talasha should instruct her otherwise."

"But not the others?"

"I cannot wait for Ulrik to grow stronger."

"I understand." Pagaloth glanced over at the great man, lying on his bed, stone-faced and pale. "He is…different, now. After Garlath abandoned him. Skymaster Nakaan as well. It is a curse, to bond a dragon, it seems to me. And to risk this tearing of one's soul."

"Blessings and curses are often two sides of the same coin, Pagaloth. Love is like that too, is it not?" His thoughts returned to Talasha, momentarily. "I have told you of my wife, and my son. I loved Talia fiercely, and she was taken from me. A blessing became a curse in an instant, when she died upon the birthing table. Yet we do not deny ourselves love. It is the risk we all take, when we give ourselves to another."

Pagaloth had lost more than most. His father, brothers, and uncles had all died during the last war. So wretched was her grief, his mother had taken her own life shortly after. It had made him hard, and stern. Lythian wondered whether the dragonknight would ever let himself love again. *As I tried not to*, he thought. *Until Talasha came striding into my life.*

They left the conversation there, returning to the others across the hall. It was quiet, a world of mutters and murmurs and the occasional groan of pain. A few who'd been serving at the nest lay abed, as Marak did, badly burned or injured by falling stone. One had been taken by a blood fever, and was dying slow as Mirella had. Mirella, who was still never far from Lythian's thoughts. Another victim of Tethian's doomed crusade. *Another victim of our folly.*

He went to sit with Sotel Dar and Yosef, the young librarian. "I intend to leave tomorrow, Sotel," he told the old man. "If you have anything you haven't yet told me, anything at all, please, now would be the time."

Sotel Dar looked at him through a set of confused old eyes. "What could it be that I haven't told you, my friend? Do you think I have been intentionally withholding information from you?"

"You know my thoughts on Eldur," Lythian said. "You know I don't conform to your beliefs, not anymore."

"And you think I have some secret to vanquishing our founder?" Sotel Dar shook his head. "I do not. Nor would I tell you if I did. Should Eldur be slain, the War Eternal will never end. He will bring the balance, Lythian, along with the heir of Varin. What happened here, I did not expect. Nor did Tethian, rest his good soul. Yet this setback should not lead us to abandon all hope. Eldur took the Bondstone, yes, and many of the dragons did follow him. Perhaps this was meant to be. Eldur may have gone somewhere to wrest control of Agarath's Soul, as the prophecies have foretold. Then, it will take only the heir of Varin to appear, and master the Heart of Vandar, for peace to be restored."

Lythian had heard this a hundred times before. He had lost all hope that it might be true. "Is it not possible, Sotel, that you are wrong?" *I am leaving,* he told himself. *If there's a time to speak my mind, it's now.*

"Me? Oh, it would not be me who is wrong, Captain Lythian. It would be Pullio the Wise, Quarl the Blind, and the Skylady of Loriath, who all came long before me. My learnings have come from them, as Tethian's did."

"Them, then," Lythian said, losing his patience. "Could *they* have been wrong, Sotel? Could they have misread the signs, or miscalculated, somehow? Might they themselves have been deceived?"

The old man shook his head. "No, I do not see how. Who would deceive them? And why? Has Eldur not risen, as they all foretold? We should not lose faith that the rest of their prophecies should unfold."

"And what of Agarath?" Lythian asked. "You have said yourself that the gods *are* war, Sotel. You have decried them, and often, saying that for the War Eternal to end, the last vestiges of their spirits must be controlled."

"Yes, I have. This belief is a foundational tenet of what Tethian and I have preached. And the wise masters who came before us. These relics of the gods must be controlled and commanded, for the war to end."

"And what if Eldur does not command the Bondstone? What if it's the other way around?"

The old man frowned. "So you think that Agarath works his will *through* Eldur? That he intends to *bring* war, not end it?"

Lythian had come to believe that very thing. "You were there, in the depths of Eldur's Shame. You saw the mountain against which Eldur lay sleeping. That was Drulgar, Sotel. A calamity beyond all measure." He swallowed, sensing that others were listening to them now. Marak, on his bed, and Sa'har Nakaan at his side. Talasha was with Cevi by the fire; serving out cups of soup. Pagaloth was on his rounds, checking the other infirm. All had stopped in their tasks and were watching. "I fear Eldur has returned to the Wings," Lythian went on, addressing them all. "To wake Drulgar. If the Dread should rise, what then? Eldur could never control him. We know that in the north and you know it here as well. Nor would your Fire Father seek to wake him, if he was this benevolent force you proclaim. But *Agarath* would. He would awaken his greatest weapon, to unleash chaos upon the world."

Silence followed his words, as his voice sank into the dark stone walls. It seemed that none of them wanted to confront that possible truth. *They bury their heads in the sand,* Lythian thought. *Or perhaps they think me mad, raving of terrors long dead?* He had spoken this fear to Pagaloth already, and the dragonknight had assured him that Drulgar was made stone, and could not be awoken. *Yet wasn't it possible? Wasn't it possible that was Eldur's intent? And Agarath's, working through him?*

"There is nothing in the prophecies of the old masters to say that Drulgar would ever reawaken," Sotel Dar said eventually. "I understand your fears, Captain. Yet I have said it many times now, and I will say it again. I believe, from the depths of my heart, that Eldur is seeking the path of goodness, and peace. He has stumbled, and fallen, and lost his way, yes, but all the while he seeks it. To turn down so dark a road as you suggest…." He shook his head. "No, I do not believe this is possible. If he did, perhaps you would be right. It would be the will of Agarath, not Eldur. It would be the will of destruction, death, and war."

Talasha came over to them, bearing cups of soup. "Please," she said softly. "Enough of this talk." She set the cups down on the table. "It sets us all on edge."

"You cannot ignore it, Talasha," Lythian told her. "We all must consider it a distinct poss…"

"Quiet."

Lythian's voice was cut off. He spun his eyes across the hall to where Lord Marak lay abed. The great dragonlord was shifting up, trying to stand. "Ulrik, what are you doing?" said Sa'har Nakaan.

"Quiet, Sa'har." Marak managed to get to his feet, standing unsteadily. His left arm was in a sling, face milky white and drained of blood. "My armour…" He turned his eyes around. "Where did you put it, Sa'har?"

"It is there, Ulrik." The Skymaster pointed to a chest near the door. "Why do you want to…"

"I must put it on. I can hear…someone comes."

Lythian surged straight to his feet. Pagaloth marched across the hall to where his swordbelt had been placed. He began hitching it around his waist. Lythian was already wearing his, complete with the dinted steel blade he bore. "Who is coming, Lord Marak?" he asked.

"You cannot wear your armour, Ulrik," Sa'har was saying. "You are too weak. Lay down. All of you, relax. I shall check the top of the stair."

"They are not coming from the stair," Marak said. His voice was as heavy and blunt as stone. "They come from the skies. I can hear them."

"*Them*?" Talasha asked, fearful. "Dragons, Ulrik?" She did not wait for an answer. "My brother," she said. "It…it must be Tavash… and Vargo Ven. They have returned to hunt for survivors. It can only be them."

No, Lythian thought. There was a throbbing in his chest, deep and primal. It felt like…like it had, in those depths. *It's him.*

Sa'har Nakaan was stepping briskly for the door, as Pagaloth moved to follow. Marak was lumbering heavily toward the crate containing his Body of Karagar armour. Talasha followed him, saying, "Ulrik, you are too weak. There is nothing you can do. Please, lie back down…" But the big dragonlord ignored her, reaching the chest, opening it. Swirls of steam rose out, reminding Lythian of the mists of godsteel, of Vandar's soul, yet these were different. Marak leaned down, wincing, pulling out the Fireblade with his right hand, sheathed in its special scabbard. His fist wrapped about the hilt, and at once he looked stronger. It was as godsteel to Bladeborn, a unique weapon borne only by the greatest of Agarath's champions. In it came strength, vitality, power.

"My armour," Marak said. "Princess, help me into it…"

Lythian was rushing now to the door, as Sa'har Nakaan and Sir Pagaloth stepped out. Beyond was a small antechamber, half in ruin, leading out toward the Bondsquare. As soon as the door was opened Lythian heard the beat of wings, the screech of dragons. In his youth, those sounds had stirred him. They were calls he heard only on the battlefield, where he was armoured all in godsteel, bearing Starslayer in his grasp. Now he felt nothing but fear, dread, desolation. *I am nothing to them now,* he thought. A lowly soldier, no more, bearing steel that cannot hurt them.

He stepped out all the same.

The skies were thick with dark grey clouds and lumpen bands of fog. Lythian sighted dragons perched upon the walls, their claws curled about the stone like monstrous living gargoyles. He could see five, six, seven of them, more, appearing and disappearing amidst the fog in different shapes and sizes. Some looked riderless, no saddles fixed to their backs. Sa'har Nakaan was staring up at one of them. He stumbled forward, letting out a sharp cry. "Ezukar," he called, throwing his hands forward in beseech. "Ezukar, my friend…*Ezukar*!"

Lythian saw the dragon to which he was calling, upon the western battlements. Dark brown, with patches of green, narrow in the face and long in the tail. He had seen Ezukar several times before, during the War of the Continents, riding at the wing of Garlath and Marak. A slim dragon, lithe and snakelike, he had matched Sa'har Nakaan well.

"Ezukar!" The Skymaster wailed. He stepped forward, then fell to his knees as the beast perched there, unmoved. "Please, Ezukar, please…" It was painful to watch, painful to witness. "Ezukar…why would you forsake me? Why!"

He is why, Lythian thought, standing rooted to the stone as Garlath the Grand descended. The monstrous dragon landed at the heart of the scorched square, his scales in shades of silver and blue. Lythian had ridden atop that thick broad back twice before. That back that had borne Ulrik Marak for so long. No longer. Now it bore another.

Now it bore a god.

"Eldur…Fire Father!" Sa'har Nakaan bent down before him in supplication. "Please…please give him back to me. I beg it of you, oh great one. I beg you give him back."

Eldur wore his crimson cloak, stitched with the fiery sigil of his house, his kingdom. Lythian gazed at him through the swirling mists. His hair was bone white, skin pale, eyes red. In his wizened hand he bore a tall black staff, and atop it, glowing, an orb in a shifting motley of colours in amber, red, and gold. The Bondstone.

"No," he said. Lythian recoiled from the voice, that voice of ancient thunder. Though no more than a whisper, it seemed to fill all the square, casting out all other sound. "I am sorry for your loss. But in your heart, I see the truth. You will not do what must be done."

"I will, my lord. I will. I will." Sa'har Nakaan let out a wailing sound. "I promise it, I will. Whatever it is, I will."

"You won't." The voice silenced him. "Ezukar will fly alone."

He raised his staff. It glowed brighter, shining a light upon the dragon. Lythian shielded his eyes against the glare. He could not move. He could not run. *This is the magic of gods,* he thought. "And others," the Fire Father said. "Others..." Lythian peered through the gaps in his fingers. The light illuminated another, a beast in shades of purple and black, then another, one he knew. *Zyndrar the Unnatural,* he thought. The mad dragon, malformed in body and mind. "They need no riders to steer them. They have my sight, and my will."

A chill ran up Lythian's spine, as Eldur's eyes fell to look at him. "You," he said. "You are Bladeborn." Lythian could not muster words. He could do nothing but stand and stare, paralysed. Eldur raised a finger. "Kill him."

A dragon shifted from its perch, one Lythian didn't know. It dropped to the ground, landing with a crash, took a step toward him, another, another...

This is it, Lythian thought, watching it come. *I have sealed my own doom.* He might have tried to run, he might have tried to fight. But he could do nothing but stand there, and wait. *Varin, I come. Father, I come. Talia, I come.* He shut his eyes and prepared to ascend.

The door flew open behind him. Lythian felt heat passing him by. He opened his eyes, as Lord Marak stepped out with the Fireblade to hand, Talasha and Sotel Dar following. The dragon stopped and studied them, hissing.

"Ulrik," said Eldur. He regarded him for a long moment, then raised a hand and gestured him forward. "Come. Come to me."

Marak obeyed. There was no hesitation. He stepped out into the square, his body enwrapped in his ancient dragonscale armour, Fireblade in his grasp. He moved straight into a bow, cringing against the pain in his arm, shoulder, ribs. "My Lord Eldur," he said. "I am humbled, that you know my name."

All fall to his will, Lythian thought, in horror. *In his presence, they all bend, and break.*

"Garlath has spoken of you." Eldur laid a bloodless hand upon the dragon's neck, stroking. Garlath responded, rumbling in reverence. "I see you bear my blade, Ulrik, a gift from Ilith, most fond to me. And this armour you wear..." He studied the dark scale armour that covered Marak's body. "I know these scales. This is Karagar, whom I once rode." A light burned in his eyes, sudden and frightening. The dragons perched atop the parapets shifted and screeched, spitting gouts of flame into the murky skies. "Take it off, Ulrik. Now."

Lord Marak did not hesitate. "Yes, my lord." He sheathed the Fireblade and began removing the armour, wincing through his pain, using only his right arm. Lythian watched in dismay. *He wilts so easily. Not even a question or complaint. Nothing.* The effort was hard for the dragonlord, injured as he was. Talasha hurried forward to help him, her nimble fingers moving to undo the links and chains and straps.

Eldur considered her with his unblinking red eyes. "You have my blood," he said, in that thunderous whisper. "It is strong in you. Who are you?"

Her eyes are red as well, Lythian thought. *As they were in his tomb. I am losing her.* "I am of your line of descent, my lord. My name is Talasha, Princess of Agarath, your kingdom."

That ancient face twisted into a smile. "Yes, you are. Come, child. You will come with me."

No, Lythian thought. *No…*

"Yes, my Lord Eldur." She stepped forward, and did not look back.

*No….no…*Lythian tried to move, yet he felt Pagaloth shift at his side. His voice hissed out a low warning. "Silence. Do not speak. Say nothing, Captain. *Nothing.*"

Marak was still struggling to remove his armour. Sotel Dar stepped to help him. Behind were others now, emerging from the hall; Cevi, Malgo the cook, Yosef the librarian. Those who had been lying abed had risen, as though sleepwalking, to stumble and limp outside and watch, drawn out like moths to a flame, staring up in wonder. Lythian felt in a waking nightmare. His chest thundered a beat, his limbs shivered; at any moment he felt like he might topple over and collapse. Half of him wanted to escape, to flee, back to the hall or down the steps, away, away, away from him. The other half stared at Talasha in numb despair as she began climbing up Garlath's scaly flank, to join her Fire Father atop his back. *No,* he was thinking, as tears crawled down his cheeks. Tears of loss and fear and rage. *No…*

"Where do we go, my lord?" Talasha asked.

"We go home, child. There is a king in my city, I have heard. I must visit with him. He needs my instruction."

"That king is my brother," Talasha said, smiling.

Eldur smiled back. "We shall be as one family now, warm beneath my wing."

Marak finished removing the armour with the help of Sotel Dar, the pair placing it on the ground before them. "I am sorry, Lord Eldur," the dragonlord said. "When you awoke, and I…I stood before you, with the Fireblade, I didn't…"

"Do not fear, Ulrik. You were not to know." Eldur gestured to the armour. "Bring it to me. And the blade."

"Yes, my lord." Marak cringed through his agony as he lifted the armour and stepped forward. "I will never wear it again," he said, as he placed it on the ground before Garlath, setting the Fireblade by its side. "We have learned to garb ourselves in the scales of fallen dragons to fend off the Bladeborn, my lord. Wearing Karagar's body has been a great honour. Never once was it intended as an offence."

"It is not my offence you must be wary of, Ulrik." Eldur gestured to the dragon waiting nearby, the one that had been approaching Lythian. "Child," he said to it. "You will bear Lord Marak now."

The dragon lowered its wing. Marak paused, staring up into Garlath's eyes. "I…my lord, Garlath and I…we were bonded, for decades. I could not…to ride another dragon…"

"I have broken that tether, Ulrik. In time, perhaps I will restore it. But for now, I have need of him."

Marak nodded. He looked at Garlath once more, longing, yet the dragon did not respond to him. *His eyes are red as well,* Lythian thought. All of theirs were, all of these dragons, all the beasts bewitched by their lord and leader.

"Climb, Ulrik, we must be away." Eldur raised his staff, and the dragons called out, shrieking. At once one of them flew down and grasped Marak's armour in its talons. Another followed, clutching the Fireblade, then vanished into the gloom. A third landed before Sa'har Nakaan. "Come," Eldur told the Skymaster. "Ezukar speaks well of your service, Sa'har. Join us. Serve me."

"Yes, master." Sa'har Nakaan stepped forward, as though in a daze, lost to the sorcerer's will.

Sotel Dar lurched straight after him, tumbling down onto his old aching knees. "I beg you take me with you," he cried out in a high thin voice. "You are my life's work, Lord Eldur. To raise you from your slumber. To see you command the Bondstone, and bring balance to this world!"

"Balance?" There was a curious slant to those pupil-less red eyes.

"Y-yes, my lord. The balance, to…to end the War Eternal. You and the heir of Varin…"

"*Varin*." The word was a hiss, knifing through the air. Sotel Dar recoiled. "Who is this heir of Varin?"

"I…I am not certain, my lord. It…it is foretold, that you would rise. And this heir. To put out the fires of conflict." The old scholar looked up at him, half in horror, half in wonder. "To end the…the War Eternal."

"An eternal war can never end, child. Nor does my master will it so." Eldur said something then in a tongue Lythian did not know. Something ancient and guttural, and suddenly another dragon was sweeping in from the skies, small and swift and jerky in its movements. It landed, snapping wildly at the air. "You will come with us," the demigod said. "My memory remains fragmented, and my history incomplete. Join us, child. Serve the will of Agarath. Rejoice in the spread of his Eternal Flame."

Sotel Dar stood, trembling. The dragon stalked forward, smoke gushing from its nostrils, and ducked low so he might scramble atop it. As with Marak, and Sa'har Nakaan, and Talasha, the scholar was lost to the demigod's will. In fits and starts he clambered onto the wild dragon's back, lying low, holding on.

And then Eldur saw Lythian again. "Varin," he said. "*You* are of his blood."

Lythian's mouth opened and closed. No words came out. He wanted to look away, but couldn't. *This is it,* he thought.

And then he heard her speak. "Spare him, my lord. He is of no consequence, oh great one. An ant, to be ignored. He does not even bear godsteel." Talasha laughed, eyes flashing with mirth. "Why trouble yourself with such as he? Let him live on, in shame and defeat."

Eldur looked lazily upon Lythian, then gave him not a second thought. "We fly," he said. Heavily, Garlath turned, opening out those mighty wings. The small wild beast bearing Sotel Dar flapped away into the turbid skies, screaming. Garlath required a run-up. Facing the open edge of the square where it tumbled away into the valleys, he lumbered forward, wings beating, winds howling. Paralysed, Lythian watched, staring at Talasha as the beast moved past, and away, speeding for the cliff.

A blessing becomes a curse, he could only think, as Garlath reached the edge and plunged, bearing her away from him, forever.

29

Elyon

Elyon rode through the misty swamps wearing godsteel breastplate, gauntlets, cuisses and helm, his face a fixed image of determination, his lips showing no smile despite his success. Lancel and Barnibus rode either side of him, following the trail of markers they had left. They planted those posts every time now; none wanted to get lost again, and always took precautions to direct their way out.

"That was the best day yet, Elyon," Barnibus said enthusiastically, his breath puffing with fog. It had grown cold of late, and had even snowed a little, leaving patches of snow among the soggy earthen paths through the bog. "I'd say you're ready to train in sight of the camp now if you're brave enough. You've been progressing fast these last ten days."

"Not fast enough." Elyon was not going to get carried away, despite his swift rate of improvement. That dragon sighting had driven any sense of complacency out of him, and though it hadn't augured the coming of an Agarathi horde as they'd feared, the warning had been enough to centre his thoughts and narrow his mind to a single and urgent imperative: to master the Windblade, dominate the skies, ready himself to face his fate head-on.

"We can ride north next time," Lancel said, his blond hair flung back by the winds as they cantered along a mossy wooden bridge. There were many of those too out here, set by the marshmen to make traversal easier for the scouts and patrols. "The plains up there are perfect, El. There're thousands of acres of open fields and we won't have to bother with these bogs anymore. I'm growing sick of the sight and smell of them. Wouldn't you prefer to train without worrying there's an enemy horde nearby?"

"He has a point, El," Barnibus agreed. "And speaking selfishly, it'd be nice to actually *see* you up there. You're getting too good now. We see you lift off and land, sure, but mostly we're just standing around twiddling our thumbs whilst you fly away out of sight."

"It's not a spectator sport," Elyon told them. "You're here to support me and defend me if I need you, that's all." But for all that, he understood their frustration. He could summon the winds now with some ease, rise swift from the ground, turn at sharp angles, and land without muddying himself or splashing down into some fetid bog. As soon as he'd grown comfortable doing all that in leathers and fur he began donning bits of godsteel armour, one piece at a time. It was his fourth day training in godsteel now and the first wearing a heavy breastplate. It hadn't impeded him, nor slowed him at all. If anything the gathering of plate about his person had given him the confidence he needed to thrust and swoop and glide, and even to swing with the Windblade as he soared. The long hours in training that day had seen him lose sight of his friends at least a dozen times, he guessed. And it wasn't always easy finding them again, not if he strayed too far through the fogs and clouds. "Might be you're right," he said at last. "A big open sky would be a different challenge."

"Well I'm glad you agree." Lancel cantered along happily. "We can set out at dawn, what do you say? Make a full day of it."

Every day is a full day of it, Elyon thought. He wasn't likely to master the Windblade by training casually or only when struck with inspiration, was he? No, he had to slog. To rise early and put in the work, entering the mists as dawn broke to the east and exiting as dusk fell out west. And after he got back from the marshes, it would be war council meetings and strategy sessions and long walks through the camp to show his face to the men. That had been Rikkard's advice. To be seen as often as possible, share stories with the soldiers under his charge, get to know them and let them know him. "You have always been a man of the people, Elyon," his uncle had said, "well-loved and admired. Now show them a man to respect as well. Show them a leader, and they'll follow you to the end."

And he had, walking the encampment nightly and stirring interest wherever he went. Elyon Daecar knew interest well enough -

he was the son of the Crippler of Kings and the greatest beauty of her generation, after all - but this was something else. He was a prince now, and a champion, rising high on the crest of a wave that was taking him into the heart of a war. His name was on everyone's lips. Murderer and thief and traitor to his enemies; crown prince and hero to his friends, the lionhearted knight who defied two treacherous kings.

With it came a tide of expectation he'd not experienced before, and gods was it all exhausting. When he walked through the camp, most of the men wanted to look upon the Windblade, and many would even ask if they might witness a tease of its power. Elyon tended to decline those requests. *I am a prince and champion,* he would think to himself, *not a trained monkey doing tricks.* But occasionally, if a large enough crowd had gathered, he would draw the Blade of Vandar out and summon a breeze to lift him, up and off his feet, to their rapturous applause. Sometimes, when that happened, he'd even find himself smiling. And then he'd think of how he came to have the blade, how Rylian had died so he might be here, and the smile would be stripped from his lips and the winds would settle, and he would slide the Windblade back into its rippling silver sheath and start right back toward the Bane, where he might find some peace.

Snowmane's hooves were stamping upon another wooden bridge when they emerged from the mists and the fortress came into view. It wasn't yet sunset, though the daylight was starting to fade, and a chill was deepening in the air. Away to the west, more soldiers were arriving from further along the coast, some thousands by the look of them. From this distance they seemed like ants scurrying over the hills, black beneath the waning sun.

"Reinforcement, do you think?" Barnibus said.

"Looks like it." Elyon spurred Snowmane into a gallop as they crossed the bridge onto the firmer earth beyond the marshes. As they drew nearer to camp the banners of the approaching army took form, fluttering in the breeze, showing grey and brown hills beneath a black stormy sky.

"That's House Payne," Barnibus called out. He'd always been good with house colours and crests. "I thought they were standing garrison at Kirkwell Castle up the coast?"

"They were," Elyon said. "It's possible another army took up the post, or they've left a smaller force there to defend it." Kirkwell was, in all honest truth, a castle of limited value. There were few in the war council who believed it a likely target for the Agarathi.

The count of men pouring over the hills became more apparent the closer they got. It was a strong host, five thousand to Elyon's eye, with armoured horse and mounted bowmen, shieldmen and spearmen and many knights among the company. They came to a stop upon the western edge of the encampment, trailed by a baggage train filled with provisions and weapons and packed pavilions. It looked very much like they intended to stay.

Elyon found their leader upon a sleek grey palfrey, issuing commands to her men to establish camp. There was no sign yet of Lord Kanabar, Sir Rikkard, Sir Killian, Lord Rammas or anyone else. Elyon was delighted to be the first to greet her. "Lady Payne," he said, approaching with his companions to left and right. "I had not been told you were coming."

Lady Marian Payne was as fierce as she was beautiful, though it was a masculine beauty, her features sharp where others were soft and fair, her eyes stern and steely, a cold icy blue. She sat high in the saddle of her steed, back straight, posture perfectly statuesque. The barest flicker of a smile tugged at her lips to see him. It was more than most ever got, Elyon knew. "Elyon Daecar. I hear they're calling you prince now."

"Only around here." He swung a leg across his saddle and dismounted, landing in the soft grassy earth at the western edge of camp. A boy came hurrying from the main encampment to take the reigns. "To the Bane," Elyon instructed him.

"Yes, my prince," the boy said, bowing nervously. "Right away."

Lady Marian dismounted with a grace rare-seen, landing without seeming to dent a blade of grass. There was something profoundly composed and controlled about this woman. She handed the reins of her horse to a groom.

"That's a fine animal," Elyon said, admiring the mare's sleek grey beauty. They were a match, mount and rider. Marian Payne wore the same colour; a long grey cloak over a suit of dark silver godsteel armour. Elyon had never in his life seen a woman dressed in full plate, and it was a fine suit indeed, figure-hugging, shaped to the contours of her slender, lithesome body, with long sleek scabbard at one hip for her sword and dagger positioned opposite. "What's her name?"

"Stormwind," she said. "I imagine you must like it, Sir Elyon? Storms and wind are right in your wheelhouse, I hear."

Elyon gave a laugh. Marian Payne was not without a certain dry sense of humour. "I have grown partial to them, yes."

A man stepped over from the bustle of men and mounts nearby. "You might want to style him correctly, my lady," he said in a gruff voice. Elyon recognised him from their one meeting back at Harrowmoor. Roark, his name was, a man of ageing years with deep ruts in his forehead and grey whiskers in the dark bristles of his untidy beard.

"Might I, Roark? Now why should I do that?"

Roark looked to the camp and immense fortress beyond. "They're all doing it here. Wouldn't want to upset them."

"My mere presence is sure to upset them," Lady Payne said. "These Vandarians don't like a woman in armour, Roark, less one leading five thousand men. The only women here in camp will be washerwomen and cooking wenches and whores. Yes, plenty of those, I'm sure."

"As you say, my lady. But all the same, no sense in fanning the flames."

Marian turned to face Elyon. She stood of a height with him, near the tallest woman he'd ever seen. "Does it offend you, Sir Elyon, if I don't call you 'prince'?"

He shook his head. "Not in the least. In truth I find it quite refreshing." He saw Barnibus giving him a shake of the head at that. *Of course, shouldn't admit that openly,* he thought.

"Good. Because much as I like you, *Sir* Elyon, and dislike your current king, I have no desire to position House Payne on either side of your quarrel for the crown. As I understand it, we have a rather more urgent conflict to win. And if there are civil troubles to be had, well, I need look no further than my own kingdom for that."

Elyon had heard rumours of the same. "I'm told Hadrin is hiding in his palace, too frightened to venture out into his own city, my lady. Is there any truth to that?"

"Plenty. His homecoming wasn't particularly celebratory, shall we say."

"Do you have an insider in the palace?" Elyon inquired. "One of your old spies, perhaps?"

"I am not spymaster anymore, sir."

"I said *old* for a reason, my lady. Let's put it another way. Are there any *former* spies of yours keeping tabs on the king?"

"If there were, I would not tell you."

I'll take that as a yes, Elyon thought. "You're probably wondering why I care?" he said.

"I have many things to worry about, Sir Elyon. Why you care about who sits the Rasalanian throne is not among them. But if I should hazard a guess, I would say it involves Amilia Lukar. She was to wed your brother, I know, and I suspect you feel a certain duty of care toward her."

It was a good read. "I would not want her to come to harm if there is a squabble for the crown," Elyon admitted. "And with her father's recent death…she is all alone there, my lady. And not nearly so strong as she appears. Now I may not be a prince to you, but perhaps my standing as heir to House Daecar might be enough to warrant a favour?"

Marian Payne looked at him with a face of stone. "I would have to hear of the favour first."

He stepped in, lowering his voice. "If you *do* have someone on the inside - and I'm not saying you do, but *if* you do - please try to have them check that Amilia is OK. I would want her to know that she still has friends, my lady."

Marian Payne pondered it, stiff-jawed, then gave a single nod. "I'll see what I can do."

"Wonderful. You have my thanks." Elyon looked out over the fields as the Payne men began setting up their tents and pavilions, unloading carts, digging latrines, establishing stables and spaces for training. They seemed an efficient outfit, though he knew it would take a while, and soon enough some blasted Kanabar or Amadar or Oloran would be along to give Lady Payne a welcome. He wanted more time with her first. "My lady, would you care to accompany me somewhere warm and dry, while your camp is erected?"

"I see no reason why not." She turned. "Roark, see that work continues at a good pace. And have my pavilion placed close to the front. If the Agarathi spring an attack, I want to be the first to know."

They meandered through the main encampment, passing men in training and men in their cups and men huddled around cookfires, roasting meat and sharing bawdy jokes. Elyon was much used to the attention he got now. The salutes and words of greeting were in abundant supply, and any request to present the Windblade was handled by Lancel and Barnibus, who rode behind on Monty and Biter telling the men their prince was busy. "Move along now, move along," they would call out. "The prince is in private council and not to be disturbed."

Marian walked beside him in an efficient, elegant gait. "They seem to like you, Sir Elyon," she observed.

"Only because they're told to." He smiled easily. "You had men in your service at Harrowmoor, three others aside from Roark," he said. "I do hope nothing has happened to them." Saska had spoken of them fondly, he recalled. Quilter. Braddin. Lark. He remembered it all.

"Unfortunately, they are all quite well. They'll be somewhere back there, setting up my camp. I don't expect to get rid of them until there's a proper attack. None are Bladeborn, as you know. Competent fighters, yes, but no more than fodder in a battle, really."

"And have you had any proper attacks? You were stationed at Kirkwell, weren't you?"

"We were. And it was horribly dull. No one attacks Kirkwell Castle, Sir Elyon. Frankly, why would you bother? It's a crumbly old place, half in ruin, and of no strategic importance. Oh, there were dragon attacks along the coast nearby, and we would ride out sometimes to handle those, but the beasts were always gone by the time we got there. Our efforts amounted to clean-up duty, not much else, and I'd had quite enough of it. So I decided a week ago to leave the castle to its lord and march down here instead."

Elyon liked that enormously. "You want to be in the thick of the action," he said, smiling. "I find that admirable, Lady Payne."

"Not many would agree with you." There was something bitter in her voice. "Yes, I want to contribute, and so do my men. But just as importantly, we want *not* to be left out. There's a subtle difference there, if you care to look for it. We were shipped off to Kirkwell to be kept out of the way, but I won't be having that. My men are just as capable as anyone else's. They should not have to suffer a lowly station just because they are led by a woman."

Elyon frowned. "You believe you were given the assignment because you're a woman?"

"I know I was."

"By whom?" Elyon's mind went through the likely candidates. Then it came to him. "Lord Rammas," he said. Elton Rammas was

Lord of the Marshes and it would have been his charge to assign placements.

Marian confirmed as much with a nod. "I met him when I first came here some months ago," she said. "I had expected to form a part of the standing force at Dragon's Bane, but Lord Rammas had other ideas. Nor did he care to hide his reasoning. Few Vandarians are so progressive as you, Sir Elyon, in accepting women in the vanguard, leading armies."

"I'll talk to him," Elyon said. Though he knew how that conversation would go. Rammas was a man of few words, red-blooded and blunt, and would defend his position stoutly.

The lady gave a sharp shake of the head. "Don't waste your time. What's done is done and now here I am. So long as *you* accept my coming here, that is good enough for me."

The sun was setting pink and purple when they reached their destination on the northern edge of camp. Here, Sir Mooton and his Blackshaw men had settled in, along with Lord Justin Huxley and his hundred swords, shovel-bearded Sir Lutherton Wane and his three eager sons, and Sir Peter Hornmoor, hook-nosed and scholarly. Sir Peter had brought a cook with him, along with a scribe, two squires, and an entire chestful of books. He had his great beak in one of them as they arrived, sitting on a wooden chair by the fire, humming to himself, pipe in one hand, dusty tome in the other.

"Sir Peter," Elyon said, causing the man to stir from his reading and look up. "I wonder if I might appropriate your pavilion for a few minutes."

The man stood, his pointed orange beard like a spike of flame spouting off his chin. "Of course, my prince. Take as long as you wish."

"My thanks." Elyon looked around. "It's very quiet around here, Sir Peter." He couldn't see Sir Lutherton or Lord Huxley, and half his hundred men looked to be missing as well. Out training, most like, or sampling the camp brothels. Marian hadn't been wrong about the number of whores at the Bane.

"It's been quiet for days, Prince Elyon," Sir Peter said. "Ever since Sir Mooton took off with those Blackshaw men of his." He smiled, blissful. "I've finally been able to find a bit of peace and quiet to read."

"Well, you enjoy yourself while you can, Sir Peter. We expect Sir Mooton back soon."

He slipped inside the man's tent, the floor decked with wood, the furnishings otherwise sparse. Marian came with him, leaving Lancel and Barnibus outside. "He's a strange sort of fellow," she remarked. "You don't come to a warcamp and expect peace and quiet."

"No," Elyon agreed. "But you've not met Sir Mooton Blackshaw, my lady. There's no louder man in the world, I assure you."

"I know of the Blackshaws," she said. "Wild sorts, fond of the woods and mountains. Did you send Sir Mooton off on a hunt?"

"In a fashion, yes. And the prey is Sir Borrus Kanabar."

She raised an eyebrow in demand for more.

Elyon smiled. "We had word recently that Sir Borrus has returned to the north, my lady. A long story. We sent the Beast to go fetch him from Mudport ten days ago. We have hope he'll arrive back tonight."

"Well then, I'd best not keep you too long. You'll want to celebrate the Barrel Knight's return, I'm sure."

"That is the plan, should such a thing transpire. And you'd be most welcome to join us. There's a permanent place for you in the Bane as well, if you want it, rather than staying in camp with your men."

"You know what I'll say to that, Sir Elyon. But thank you for the offer."

"Well, a seat on the council, at least? Your wisdom would be gladly received and we could always do with a Rasal perspective."

She considered that as Elyon went to a side counter and poured two cups of wine. A man as cultured as Sir Peter Hornmoor would be in possession of some fine vintages, he judged. He had a sip and knew he was right. Full-bodied and delicious. Solapian, he thought. He stepped over and handed the lady her cup. She took it, sipped, nodded approvingly, and gave answer. "I'd be happy to add my voice," she told him. "As councils go, yours is a reasonably good one. Except Rammas, perhaps, but I'll not judge the man too harshly on that. So long as I get an apology from him, I'll be satisfied." Her smile suggested she knew she wouldn't get one. "Now tell me, sir, why have you dragged me all the way out here? Is there something in particular you wanted to discuss?"

Oh, she can read me like a book, he thought, seeing that knowing expression on her face. "I can see there's no lying to you, Marian. Is it OK if I call you Marian?"

"Now that we're alone, of course."

He nodded. "Well, Marian, I suppose…well I wondered if you might have heard from Saska? Whether she has tried to get in touch with you, or…"

She raised a hand. "I'll stop your right there, Elyon, lest I let your hopes soar too high. No, I've not heard from her, nor heard anything *about* her. Reliable communication lines to the south have been cut off, as I'm sure you know. With all good luck she is in Aram in the care of her grandmother, but I could not possibly say for sure."

He nodded and took a quiet sip of his drink. "I can't say I'm surprised."

She turned her eyes around the tent, idly studying its contents. There wasn't much to look at; Sir Peter was a fussy man, neat and tidy, and kept his belongings safely stowed away in a pair of chests by his bed. "How are you coming along with your training?" she asked. She gave the Windblade a cursory look, though didn't ask him to unsheathe it. "I hear you go off into the mists every day to learn its mysteries, with those friends of yours out there. That's sensible, Elyon. To train in private, without fear of the crowd."

He was glad to hear her say so. "I worried at first that I might not learn its ways," he admitted. "I thought it best to train somewhere where my inadequacies might not be so exposed."

She smiled thinly. "And how is your training going now?"

"Well," he said, nodding. "I trained in light garb at first." He gestured to his person. "Now I wear armour, to get used to its weight. I plan to ride north on the morrow, to test myself in the open skies." He had a thought, then. "Join us, if you'd like. I should be eager for your feedback."

"*My* feedback?" She found that curious, clearly. "Now what should I know about mastering the Windblade, Sir Elyon?"

"You know *people*, my lady, and are friends with Ranulf Shackton, Saska told me. He is a known scholar of the blades. Perhaps something he said rubbed off on you?"

She moved a single strand of slick black hair from her forehead, repositioning it among the others. It was a masculine style she had as well; mid-length, oiled back behind her ears. "Not that I can think of. Ranulf Shackton speaks so much it can be hard to extract the nuggets from the nonsense. There are diamonds in there, I'm sure, but most of it is coal." She sipped her wine. "But as to your offer, I should be happy to join, if only to see your soar."

"And fall," Elyon added, with a smile. "I'm sure that would be most amusing."

"I am not easily amused, Sir Elyon. But that…yes, perhaps it might raise a smile." And there it was, her smile, full and true, and quickly gone. She recomposed herself. "You ask of Amilia, and Saska, and rely on birds to bring word on the wing. I don't know much about the mysteries of the Windblade, but I know its lore, and I have heard the stories of those who have mastered it. You'll soon have the power to check on those you care about yourself, Elyon. What do you say to that? Might you risk a flight across the Bloodmarshes, the Scales, the Aramatian Plains? Might you fly all the way to Aram and seek word of Saska yourself?"

Rylian had asked something similar of him; to fly to meet him at Eagle's Perch as he laid siege to the great southern fortress. *I'll expect to see you soon, Sir Elyon, soaring in from the skies.* It had all felt so far off back then, an impossible feat, yet now…now he was beginning to see the light at the end of that tunnel. "I'm not yet ready for long flights," he confessed. "But when I am…" He nodded, thinking of her soft skin, her smile, the touch of her flesh beneath his sheets… thinking of those long nights they'd spent alone in his tent, sharing their secrets, whispering of their dreams and fears. "I may just take that risk, yes."

"Just so long as you're not reckless, Elyon. In matters of risk, you can temper the possible dangers through good training and preparation. Aram is some six, seven hundred miles away, as the crow flies, over seas and mountains and rugged desert plains crawling with enemies. I wonder, how far have you flown thus far, in a single flight?"

Elyon felt the fool to admit it. "A half mile, maybe," he said. "I try not to venture too far from Lancel and Barnibus, when I train in the fogs, else I'll lose them."

She nodded without judgement. "And how high?"

"Hard to say. The mists make it difficult to judge. I have emerged through them and into pockets of clean air, at times, though even then, it's hard to know just how high I've gone."

She stood before him, entirely still but for the gentle movement of her thumb and forefinger, as it twirled the stem of her cup. "I'm thinking about the issue of altitude," she said. "The higher you go, the thinner the air will become. Breathing may become a problem, when you soar over mountains in particular." She raised the cup for a neat sip. "But it sounds like you're some way from that yet."

He couldn't exactly deny it, though the comment still rankled at his sense of pride. "I expect to fly some miles tomorrow," he said. "Five, ten, fifty, even. The open skies will give me a chance to spread my wings."

And Ilivar is a similar distance from here as Aram, he thought. His sister was there, and Amara, with his grandparents. *And Thalan…if I want to help Amilia, I can fly there too.* The Rasal capital wasn't much further; no more than a thousand miles away. *A thousand miles…* He had to smile. *I've flown a few hundred metres and I'm thinking of flying a thousand miles.* He was getting ahead of himself, he knew.

Lady Marian seemed to detect his doubt. "You've done the hard part, it seems to me," she said. "A man who has never walked before may take time to learn how. But soon after he will be running. And soon after that, running fast and running far. It is merely a case of strengthening your body and your bond. I do not know the Windblade, but I know godsteel, and I know how to teach people to wield it, those like Saska who never even knew they were Bladeborn at all. Above all, I have a good eye for talent. And it's clear to me, Elyon Daecar, that you were born to bear that blade."

He appreciated that more than he could say. "That means a lot, my lady, coming from you."

If there was any danger of the moment becoming too awkward, the sound of clopping hooves and voices outside drew their attention to the door. A moment later, Lancel thrust his head through the flaps. "My lady. Elyon. Sorry for the interruption."

"What it is, Lancel?"

"One of Sir Mooton's men," Lancel said. "He's back from Mudport."

Elyon frowned. "And the others?"

"He's alone, I'm not sure why. You'd best come outside, El."

Elyon turned to Lady Marian. "If you'll excuse me, my lady." He stepped outside with Lancel, to find the burly old Riverlander in question dismounting from his horse. Elyon hadn't had a chance to learn all of their names, but this one he knew as Daggart, a grumpy greybeard with a patch over his right eye.

He spotted Elyon at once. "Prince Elyon. Hadn't expected to see you here, m'lord."

"I was just stopping by," Elyon told him. He looked east, but could see no sign of other riders cantering their way beneath the darkening purply skies. "Where are the others, Daggart? Have they gone straight to the Bane?"

"No, m'lord. I was going to hand my horse to the grooms and come right over to tell you and Lord Kanabar, but since you're here…"

Elyon stepped toward him. "What happened? Are they following behind?"

"Not following at all. We met Sir Borrus at the Mudport docks sure enough, but another we'd not expected. Sir Torvyn, m'lord. Son of Lord Devyn Blackshaw. Moot's cousin, that is. Seems he was freed from the same place as that Lady Kathryn Merrymarsh."

"You're joking," exclaimed Barnibus. "Sir Torvyn Blackshaw's been missing since the war."

"No jest, sir, no. He looks an old man now and doesn't have much meat on him anymore, but it was Sir Torvyn sure as the sun sets west."

"Then where are they?" Elyon demanded. He couldn't work out what was happening. "Is Mooton escorting his cousin back to Elmhall?" He could understand that, at least. Sir Mooton had sworn him his service, true, but that all went out of the window in a case like this.

But Daggart shook his head. "Torvyn had this crew about him, m'lord. Those who freed him from them pits. I didn't get many of their names, in truth, but there was a fella called Manfrey I heard, and some lad called Jack, and a Seaborn captain or some such with a big yellow beard and tan coat. They're planning to head north, up the Sibling Strait to Blackhearth. I hardly had a chance to get the details straight before the Beast ordered me to ride back and report on what had happened."

"And what *has* happened?" Barnibus asked. He looked just as perplexed as Elyon by all that. "You're saying they're heading north, *all* of them? Sir Borrus and Sir Mooton included? And the rest of these men?"

"That's what I'm saying, aye. Moot sent me back because of my eyepatch, I think, and my age. Told me I wasn't so fit for the journey and would be best coming back here to report to you in person. With his apologies, of course. He'd never expected this, no, but what could he do? Torvyn made him swear an oath and Borrus seems to have some life debt hanging over his head like an executioner's axe. Didn't have much choice but to go with 'em."

"Go *where*?" asked Lancel. "You're not making any sense, Daggart."

"Well, I've ridden hard to get back here, m'lord, if that explains it. But this trip…well, up north, as I say, to Blackhearth for a start. Then a good long ranging across the Tukoran wilds and a trek up into the Hammersongs." He shook his head, as though disbelieving what he was about to say. "They're taking on the Shadowfort, trying to win it back from that dark order that lurks up there. Well, sounds like madness to me, but not my place to go questioning the likes of lords and knights and such as them. Was happy enough to be chosen to ride back, in truth. I don't do so well in the cold…bad on the old joints, and mine are plenty old by now."

Lancel was shaking his head. "That can't be right. The *Shadowfort*? Come on, Daggart, you're having us on."

"That's what I was told," the one-eyed soldier said. "Queer, I'll admit, but no more than the rest of it. And just as odd was this young commander of theirs. He was dressed as a deckhand, simple leathers and wools and hat and such, but I heard Sir Torvyn call him their leader. Tallish lad, about your height, Prince Elyon, black hair, pale skin. Come to think of it, he looked a bit like you, just skinnier. Heard him called John or Jonny or something."

The blood began to drain out of Elyon's cheeks. He closed a hand around the hilt of the Windblade, and heard those winds and whispers, suddenly dark. "You misheard, Daggart," he said, looking east. "His name isn't John…it's Jonik."

30

Cecilia

Cecilia Blakewood stood at the drinks counter within the council chambers of the King's Tower, lazily selecting a good vintage for the meeting. Archibald Benton stood beside her, all nerves and baggy grey robes. "I don't feel particularly good about this, Cecilia," he fretted in a low voice. "What happens if we're wrong?"

"All the evidence points toward him," Cecilia informed him evenly, pouring herself a small cup of fruity Solapian. "You said it yourself, Archibald. We need someone to blame for when my father returns. A *culprit.* That was the word you used, was it not?"

He nodded uncomfortably. "Yes, my lady, but the *real* culprit. I am not sure we have enough evidence to condemn…"

"We have plenty," she broke in, taking a taste of the wine. It was a little too plain. *Something spicier, perhaps,* she thought, *for what's about to unfold.* She placed down the cup and continued her perusal. "Prince Raynald will sit in judgement today, so we need but convince him, Archibald. I shall do the heavy lifting, fear not. Just play your part and all will be well."

The old man gave a slow unhappy sigh. "Just so long as you're sure, my lady. I really am loathe to send an innocent man to his doom."

"I'm sure," she said. "Now stop worrying and have some wine. It will help to calm you."

She made her final selection, picking out a spiced Rasalanian red from the back of the table, taking a little sip to satisfy herself of its quality, then pouring two cups. As she did so the clatter and clank of footsteps heralded the arrival of Prince Raynald and his protective guard. "Good, you're all here," she heard her young nephew say behind her. "Come, let's get right into it. Archibald, Auntie Cecilia, sit down."

She handed Archibald his cup and followed him to the table, taking the seat opposite her prince nephew, who seated himself at the head, in the high backed throne of a chair once inhabited by her father. Lord Emmit Gershan, the Master of the Moorlands, was already seated, as was Watch Commander Trillian Morwood. Sir Owen Armdall stood guard at the door, looking increasingly dishevelled by the day. He had sworn to neither shave nor cut his hair until the king was found and his beard was starting to grow out, thick and brown and gold.

Raynald looked around the assembled council. "We'll start with my grandfather," he said, looking dashing in his silver breastplate and green cloak, trimmed with gold. He had taken to wearing a circlet on his head as well, a simple golden band encrusted with tiny emeralds, to better present himself as interim ruler during his grandfather's absence, and with his twin brother abroad. "Lord Morwood, do you have anything new to report?"

Lord Trillian Morwood stood heavily. The skin beneath his eyes was black and yellow and sagging, his jowls dark from two-day stubble. He had suffered a deep gash to his right bicep during the riots that had put his arm in a sling. His left went to the table to prop himself up as he opened his mouth and said, "No news, my prince. Nothing to stir much hope, anyway. We have had several more reports of your grandfather's possible whereabouts, but upon investigation they have all turned out to be hoaxes. There is a feeling that the commoners are doing this to taunt us. After what your grandfather did, well…"

Raynald nodded sombrely. "They have every right to feel aggrieved. When my brother assumes the throne he will work to restore the good image of this house."

"Well said, princeling," croaked Lord Gershan. "And if your brother *doesn't* return, you'll do the same, I'll wager."

"I shall do my best," Raynald said. *He's beginning to like the idea,* Cecilia could tell. "What is being done about these hoaxers, Lord Morwood? Are they being suitably punished? And please, do sit down. You needn't stand on my account, my lord, not with your arm so wounded."

"My thanks, Prince Raynald." Lord Morwood took his seat, pulling a handkerchief from his pocket to wipe at his brow. "As to these hoaxers, I would advise…"

"Take their tongues," Gershan broke in. He stuck his out; a dry grey thing, as though they needed illustration. "Snip them off and they won't be hoaxing no more. That's the best way to deal with them, princeling."

"I disagree," said Lord Morwood. "Your grandfather made that very mistake during the hunt for Vesryn Daecar, and it served only to alienate the commoners. If you wish to win the love of your people, you'd do well to show them a more gentle hand, my prince."

Raynald nodded pensively. "I agree with Lord Morwood. My grandfather long ignored the needs of his people and look what happened. I must help win their trust again. For my brother, when he returns," he was quick to add. He placed his hands on the table, steepling his fingers, in a bid to look kingly. "But needless to say, these wrongdoers cannot be left unpunished. They should suffer some time in chains, at least. Or public floggings, to show that confusing the search for my grandfather will not be tolerated." He glanced around the table, and found Cecilia smiling at him in approval. That seemed to please him. "I shall ponder it some more, before deciding what to do with them. Now…what else, before we get onto this ugly business of Sir Gerlon?"

Cecilia cleared her throat. "I believe that Sir Owen has a request of you, Raynald," she said.

"Oh?" Raynald looked over at Sir Owen dispassionately. "What do you want?"

Sir Owen stepped forward from the door, hardly the epitome of chivalry he once was. *Though that was only ever a facade,* Cecilia knew. Sir Owen was classically handsome, yes, and in possession of a certain roguish charm, but he was boastful and vain and peevish for all that, and was fast becoming an irrelevance within the palace. "My prince," he said, bowing. "With your grandfather's continued disappearance, I would like to request that you permit me a place at your side. As senior among the king's sworn swords, I feel it my duty to…"

"No," Raynald said.

"No, my prince?"

"No. Of course not, no. *You*? You think I would let *you* stand guard on *me*? *You*, who slew my father, and failed to protect my grandfather when he needed you most? You are a disgrace, Sir Owen, and unfit to protect anyone." He waved him back to the door. "Stand there, where you belong. And don't say another word about joining my guard, else I'll take *your* tongue out, and a great deal more."

The Oak of Armdall withdrew, moving as stiffly as an octogenarian. His face was a white fury, scarcely contained. Cecilia's grin was equally close to bursting. Yet, she grouped her features into an expression of mild disapproval and said, "Raynald, I feel you are being unfair to Sir Owen. He has performed his duty most admirably for years. You could hope for no finer knight to protect you."

Raynald snorted. "I have plenty of wolves in my pack already, Aunt. I don't need another. And not some ragged creature like Sir Owen, either." He huffed loudly.

He is riled, Cecilia thought. *Excellent. Time to bring in Sir Gerlon…*

"Anything else, then?" Raynald said bluntly. No one ventured to speak. "Good. Then bring him in, and let's get this business done. *Guards*!"

From a separate door, two guards entered with Sir Gerlon Rottlor between them, dressed in his Emerald Guard cloak and leathers, looking wary and confused. "Prince Raynald." He stepped ahead of the two guards and put himself into a bow. "You called for me, my lord."

Raynald didn't turn to look at him. "Bring him over here." He gestured to an open space beside the table. The two guards ushered the old knight into position. "Do you know why you're here, Sir Gerlon?"

Sir Gerlon Rottlor had spent much of his life in the open, out on campaign and oft under the sun, and more latterly as Commander of the Marble Gate. It had given him a weathered face; rutted forehead and seamed cheeks and deep spiderweb wrinkles spreading from his eyes. They looked especially abundant as he stood facing them, the light spilling in from a broad frosted window across the room. "I can only imagine it's to do with your grandfather, Prince Raynald. If so, I have nothing new to report. My men are still searching for him day and night, and will continue to do so until the king is found."

Cecilia could see the first signs of discomfort infecting her princely nephew, as he drew a breath, nodded, and began fiddling with his fingers on the table. He knew Sir Gerlon well enough from the man's long years serving his father. "It…it has come to my attention, Sir Gerlon, that you…that you may have…" He swallowed, wetting his lips. Cecilia watched carefully, ready to step in. "I have been informed, Sir Gerlon, that you have had…meetings."

"Meetings, my prince?"

Raynald drew another breath. "Meetings, yes. Regarding…" He glanced down the table at Cecilia, who gave him an urging look. The prince was a mere eighteen and suddenly seemed every bit the boy he was. "Look, I'm just going to ask you straight, and I want a straight answer." He mustered the courage to look the grizzled old knight in the eye. "Was it you, Sir Gerlon? Did you plot to have my grandfather murdered?"

Sir Gerlon Rottlor's eyes shot wide open. He took a pace forward but the guards restrained him. "My prince, no! I would never…"

"We have several sources who say you met with residents of White Shadow in secret, Sir Gerlon," Cecilia came in. "You were spotted on a number of occasions, engaged in clandestine discussions with known agitators. Do you deny it?"

"Yes, I deny it!" he raged.

Cecilia looked at Archibald Benton. The crook-backed Master of Messages withdrew a rolled scroll from his sleeve and opened it out before him. "I have written accounts from several of…of your own men, Sir Gerlon," he said in that stuttering old voice of his. "They say…they say you donned cloak and cowl by night…and descended from the Sentinels to attend these secret meetings."

"Meetings intended for a single and express purpose," Cecilia added crisply. "The murder of your king."

"NO!" bellowed Rottlor. He looked at Raynald, but the prince had withdrawn, looking the other way. His eyes went instead to Lord Morwood. "Trillian, say you don't believe this? You can't! I've served the crown long and true. I would never…"

"Plot the downfall of your king," Cecilia cut in. "I disagree. You were always Rylian's man, never my father's. The prince's death left you sour and vengeful and you took steps to settle the score."

Sir Gerlon rounded on her, looking like a bull about to charge. "What score, woman! You said it to me yourself only weeks ago - the king had nothing to do with Rylian's death!"

"And you said otherwise, Sir Gerlon. You believed the wicked rumours circulating through the masses. You did nothing to stamp them out. On the contrary, you helped fan them, and look what those flames have done. A king missing and presumed dead. Hundreds of

Ilithorans slain, innocent women and children among them. Sir Bonmer Marsh dead, torn apart by the mob. Sir Edwyn Huffort gutted and defiled. Your own commander almost lost his arm." She gestured to Morwood. "Other knights and good men of the city watch will never draw breath again. And for what, Sir Gerlon? For what, I ask you?"

He looked so completely incensed by that that he couldn't even form words. Yet his silence was good as well. *No matter which way you dig, sir, you're never getting out of this hole.*

"Would you like me to innumerate the accounts?" Archibald Benton asked, playing his part. Some of those accounts were even true, and incriminating as well, Cecilia had to admit. Sir Gerlon *had* engaged in secret meetings in White Shadow, and some of the people he'd met with *had* been known troublemakers. And, by some wondrous stroke of fortune, some of those troublemakers had even been involved in the riots. It really didn't look good for the man.

"You're a hateful bitch, Cecilia," the old knight growled, eyes like burning coals. "This is you, isn't it? I'll bet all this is *you*!"

"And just what do you mean by that, Rottlor?" rasped Lord Gershan. "You accusing the good lady now, are you? Trying to move the spotlight away, huh?"

"*Good* lady?" Sir Gerlon laughed raggedly. "Excuse me, Gershan, but that scheming bitch is good for nothing but lying on her back and opening her legs. You'll have first-hand knowledge of that, no doubt. You a whoremonger, she a whore. You make a perfect match."

Cecilia smiled. *And there's your latest mistake,* she thought, delighting in the man's idiocy. A spiteful old creature like Gershan would not take kindly to being spoken to like that. "We've heard enough, Prince Raynald," the Master of the Moorlands sneered. "Save a confession we've got all we need to condemn him. Let's take his head off right now."

Sir Gerlon was breathing heavily, eyes wide and bright with fury. "A confession? You want a confession, do you?" He looked across the table, snarling. "I confess you all bloody snakes, slithering to the tune of this she-devil!" He pulled hard, freeing his arm from one of the soldiers' grasp, pointing it right at Cecilia. "You'll get yours, bastard! Oh, I was in White Shadow. Oh, I met with some unsavoury sorts. But only to see *you* done! I was going to do the whole city a favour and scrub you from existence, but no, I suppose I underestimated you. I'll give you that at least. More fool me to tangle with a bloody spider."

And I've caught you in my web, Cecilia thought, sipping her wine. "Well, thank you for your honesty, Sir Gerlon," she said. "You have saved us a lot of time, and our young prince a more troublesome decision. You are a fool indeed, and a rare one, to have so speedily sealed your own fate." She tittered, and Lord Gershan cackled, as Archibald shuffled his papers uncomfortably and Lord Morwood slowly swung his head side to side and Raynald, sweet young Raynald, looked away as though wishing he wasn't there.

But he was, and Sir Gerlon Rottlor let him know it. "I thought better of you, *boy*," he said. "Truly. Your father was a great man, and I always had high hopes for you." Still Raynald didn't stir. Rottlor sneered. "I never thought you for a craven, though. The sooner your brother returns, the better. Your father would be ashamed." For a moment Cecilia thought he might spit at the prince, but in the end, he merely smacked his lips and shook his head, looking at the boy in disgust.

And slowly, Raynald raised his eyes. "It's you, Sir Gerlon, who shames us all," he said quietly. He stared at the old knight in quiet judgement and didn't look away. "For your years of service, I'll make your end quick. You'll lose your head where my grandfather lost his." He looked to the guards. "Take him away."

Sir Gerlon struggled a bit, but was old enough to know that fighting would be helpless. Cursing them all, he was drawn back through the door, his voice still heard even as it shut. Raynald pushed himself up off his chair. "If there's nothing else?" His voice was tight, eyes sharp as razors as he looked across the room. "Then I have training to do." He flung his cloak over his shoulder as he left, stamping forcefully away through the door as his guardsmen fell into step behind him, clinking and clanking down the corridor.

Lord Morwood was next to take to his feet. "That felt wrong," he said.

"Wrong?" Gershan snickered. "He confessed, Morwood, or didn't you hear?"

"To plotting Lady Cecilia's death, not the king's."

"You think he'd admit *that*?" Gershan picked at something in his teeth. "No, that was smart of him, I say. You kill a king and you're gonna suffer. No quick death for that. But the king's natural daughter? Well, not the same, is it. He saved himself a nasty death there, clever man."

"And if he had nothing to do with the riots?"

Gershan shrugged those spindly shoulders of his. "Then we lose an old done knight who does nothing but stand at a gate all day. No loss if you ask me. And for a good gain if Janilah does come back."

"How so?" Morwood asked.

"How so, he asks?" The Master of the Moorlands cackled. "You've got a brain in that thick skull of yours, haven't you Morwood? How about you use it. How? Well I'll tell you how. Janilah comes back, finds us sitting here on our hands, guzzling wine, pining about this or that. How does that look? Not so good, I wouldn't say. But now? We've caught the baddie, Trillian. Caught him and cut him and have his head on a spike. He'd call that proactive, would Janilah. Might even put a smile on his face."

Morwood seemed in no way convinced by that. He looked at Cecilia. "Can we speak frankly here, my lady?"

"Of course, Trillian." It gave her such joy to see him defer to her. Only weeks ago, he'd urged her father to send her away to her Blakewood lands. *And now look at you, a fly in my web, hoping I don't crawl over to feed.*

"Your father," the jowly watch commander said. "How likely do we think his return is, after all this time?"

"Don't exaggerate, Morwood," Gershan hissed. "It's been weeks. Only two of them, by my count. That's not so long at all."

"It's long enough. If he was alive and well, he'd have returned by now. We've scoured the city thrice over and he's nowhere to be seen." He looked at Cecilia again. "How long before we start considering succession?"

"Not yet," Gershan said. "Another few weeks and I might start to agree with you. But not yet."

Cecilia nodded to that. "Two weeks is much too soon. We are coping fine as things stand. Raynald is just learning what it means to rule and I should hope Lord Kastor is helping to instruct Robbert in the same."

Gershan laughed at that. "Sure."

Cecilia looked at him fiercely. "No?"

"Well..." The old recreant stood from his chair and rattled over to the drinks table. "Cedrik isn't so interested in babysitting the boy," he said, as he filled himself a cup. "He's got a fortress to win, and an

Aramatian army to destroy, so we're hearing. Training up some pup isn't high on his list of priorities."

Cecilia didn't like the tone of his voice. She knew the line of succession and knew where Cedrik Kastor stood in it. *Too close,* she thought, *and Gershan is* his *lickspittle, not yours, never forget.* "I hope you and your lord aren't cooking something up, Emmit," she said.

"Cooking? Like what?"

"A plot to put Cedrik on the throne." She thought it best to put it out there, for all to sample.

"That's a spicy dish right there, Cecilia." Gershan turned from the counter. "Too spicy for my tastes. Doesn't sit well in my stomach, all that."

"I'll be watching what you're eating from now on," she told him, making the threat explicit. "I have Raynald's ear, and I'm quite sorry to tell you this, but he really doesn't like you, Emmit. One word from me and he'll cart you back off to those grim grey moors of yours. And in pieces, if I wish it."

"Now, Cecilia, there's no need for that."

"There's *every* need." She knew what Cedrik Kastor was like, and with her brother dead and father missing he'd be smelling blood. "Just be careful, Gershan, and consider your loyalties. I'll want to see all your correspondence with Lord Kastor from now on." She turned to Archibald. "Archie, see to it. I have another engagement to attend."

She left the council there, passing poor useless Sir Owen at the door, stepping out into the corridor. Hog and Gerret were waiting for her outside. "The princeling didn't look happy," Hog rumbled. "Guess it must have gone well, then?"

"Sir Gerlon will be executed at Galin's Post," Cecilia said. That was a good ruling by the boy. "It will give all the city a chance to see the man responsible for the riots die."

"Responsible?" said Gerret, grinning that gap-toothed grin. "Aye. It was all Sir Gerlon's fault, wasn't it?"

Cecilia ignored his insolence. "Did you bring Tyrith down the steps as I asked you?"

Hog gave answer, speaking through the enormous twisting bristles of his tusk-like moustache. "*I* did," he said. "Left Gerret at the bottom. Wimp was too scared to make the climb."

Gerret didn't deny it. "If I never climb them steps it'll be a lifetime too soon."

Cecilia understood his trepidation, though she'd gone up and down the stair to Tyrith's forge a handful of times now and was beginning to get the measure of them. She turned to face the bigger of her two guardsmen. "Well done, Hog. How did it go?"

"Well enough. Fixed the rope as you said, to give us something to cling onto. Should be easier going up and down now. Not sure why your father never thought of that."

Because he didn't want Tyrith coming down those steps, Cecilia thought. *A rope might have given the blacksmith the courage to make the climb.* She decided not to answer. "I'd best go check on his progress," she said, pacing off down the corridor, her men in tow.

There were no guards at the entrance to the tunnel system that led into the mountain. No one manning the gate that blocked the way in. Cecilia had learned the route from Sir Kevyn Bolt when he'd first led her to the foot of the steps, and she'd since taught it to her own men. Now Sir Kevyn wasn't needed, and Sir Mallister was best left out of this too. She had made no mention of it to Sir Owen Armdall either. *These tunnels are mine*, she thought.

It took some thirty minutes to navigate the route, passing over bottomless shafts and shimmying along narrow ledges and clambering through holes and tight tunnels to get there. As they neared the end, Cecilia began to hear the sound of distant hammering echoing through the passages. "He brought that hammer down with him," Hog told her. "Wanted to see if it would help."

"Help? How?"

"Said it might lead him," Hog said, shrugging. "Some magical pathfinding or some such. You'll have to ask him, my lady. Not my area, this sorcery stuff."

The echoing grew louder as they reached the end of the route; here, the mountain gave passage to the foot of the stair on their left, yet to their right it continued into a further series of tunnels and caves that her father hadn't bothered exploring. *No, why would he? Once he'd found the stair and forge above, what more was there to look for?* Cecilia knew her father had no knowledge of this portal and path to the Shadowfort. Tyrith had told her such. "Your father's only interest was in combining the blades, my lady," he had said. "I tried to tell him some months ago about the portal, but he didn't seem to hear me, or show any interest."

Well, I am plenty interested, Cecilia thought, as they turned a corner along the route and found Tyrith there, tapping gently upon a bare rock wall with the Hammer of Tukor in his grasp. Gerret laughed as soon as he saw him. "Sounded like you were hammering hard there, blacksmith. Then here we find you, tapping all gentle like."

Tyrith turned to them with an excited smile, hair as untidy as ever. "I had worried the ceiling might come down," he said, in his soft-spoken silvery voice. "This tunnel used to go on much further. *Much* further, my lady, right beyond this blockage." There was a light in his emerald eyes. "I think…I think this is the way, Cecilia."

Cecilia turned her eyes around, holding up her torch. The dark rocky passage looked like any other, its walls glistening, the old remains of what was once a more structured corridor spotted here and there. On one side, blocks of masonry and tool-cut stone were visible, dotted with lichen and patches of nitre. And on the ceiling above where Tyrith stood, were signs that the roof had once come down, obstructing the route ahead. "How can you be sure, Tyrith? Almost every tunnel in this system is blocked. What makes you think this is the way?"

"I can *feel* it, my lady." He pressed the Hammer of Tukor against the stone. "There is a *thrumming*, beyond. Some way down the passage. The hammer remembers the sorcery it wrought. It *remembers*, my lady."

She stepped forward, brushing past her men. She could hear the winds blowing distantly, way off down the tunnel behind them. The odd bit of dust was falling from the ceiling, a pebble or two clattering here and there. It felt unstable. "How do we get through?"

"Carefully," Tyrith said. "I have been tapping on the rock to try to gauge how deep the blockage is. It's some metres, as far as I can tell. Eight, maybe nine. I was thinking that the king could come and help. This would be no barrier to him, my lady. Not with the Mistblade."

She hadn't yet told Tyrith of her father's disappearance, preferring not to distract him. *But he deserves to know the truth,* she decided. Tyrith had developed a devotion to the king that she felt certain was one-sided. It had saddened her greatly to witness his loneliness, shackled up there in his forge, friendless and alone and brainwashed into believing his existence was somehow fated. She had spent hours with him during that first visit, more time than her father had in many years combined, she wagered, and that had angered her. It had even upset her. *They all think I have no heart, but I do. No, not always, but sometimes…sometimes I do.*

"The king has suffered some...troubles of late," she finally said. "I fear he will not come, Tyrith. He may never come again."

She watched his eyes go wide and worried. "Has something happened to him? He isn't dead, surely? He cannot be, he *cannot*. I have to combine the blades for him, Cecilia. Only he can wield them, he told me so!"

She rested a hand on his narrow shoulder. It would not do for the young man to panic and she feared his isolation had stunted his growth. *He is emotionally fragile and underdeveloped,* she thought. *I must tread carefully, lest I lose him.* "I did not mean to worry you, Tyrith. But I don't want to lie to you either. The king has gone missing, though we hope it is only temporary." She had a thought, then, one that would help to calm him. "I believe he may have gone to track down the other blades himself. As I told you when we first met, he is doing all he can to gather them. And Janilah Lukar is a proactive man. He has gone out into the world, to take what is his, I'm sure of it."

The blacksmith nodded, breathing out. "Yes...yes that must be it. It is critical he gathers those blades, my lady. He must, else all of us will fall."

"I know," she said softly. "I know. And he will. But in the meantime, let us not lose focus. We are close, Tyrith, so close. And we don't need the Mistblade to get beyond this wall." She pressed a palm to the rock. "Eight, nine metres, you say?"

"Yes, I...I think about that, yes."

Her eyes scanned the ceiling. *Unstable*, she thought again. "With time and care, good godsteel will cut through. But we'll need to take precautions, to secure the roof and walls. We cannot be having you crushed in a cave-in, Tyrith. You are far too important for that." She smiled at the young, golden-haired blacksmith.

"Yes," he agreed. "Only I can combine the blades. I should not even be here, in truth. It is dangerous. I ought to return to my forge."

Perfect, she thought. "Yes, you do that. Return to your forge and continue your good work. I will come for you when the work is complete." She turned to her men. "Hog, make sure Tyrith is safely returned up the stair. Come back here right after. Is that clear?"

"As you say, my lady." The big boar of a man waved Tyrith over. "Come along then, my lord, let's get you home."

Cecilia continued to study the blockage and surrounding walls as they left. Gerret stepped up beside her, chuckling, sliding his tongue through that missing front tooth as he liked to do. Cecilia glanced over. "I told you not to do that around me."

"Aye, you did." His tongue slid away like a snail in its shell. "Habit, my lady."

"Well break it." She looked back at the wall. "You and Hog'll be able to cut through, won't you?"

He shrugged. "Should be able to. But not until the roof's secure. I'm not being crushed for some stupid portal door."

"Stupid is not the word, Gerret. It is ancient and forgotten magic. And more complicated than your little brain could ever hope to comprehend."

"Then it's me who's stupid, not the door. All the same in the end, m'lady. I ain't getting squashed for it."

You'll get squashed if I say you'll get squashed, she thought. Gerret could be too impertinent for his own good and she liked it only half the time. Hog was much better. Dutiful, capable, and not short of wit. That was Hog. "I want you to find good men to secure the ceiling and walls with a scaffold, supports, beams, whatever it takes. There are stonemasons and labourers down in White Shadow. When Hog gets back, I want you to go and find some for me."

"The secret will get out, m'lady, soon as we bring men up here. You sure that's what you want?"

She didn't want that at all. It was her express intention to keep all knowledge of this tunnel system hidden. Having a load of masons and builders spreading word of some secret tunnel and portal door was out of the question. And all these men coming in and out might just discover the steps as well, and the forge, and Tyrith, and then what? If her father came back to learn of that he'd crucify her.

There seemed only one solution. An unpleasant one, yes, but her father had blazed that trail already, so why not follow it? "I'll have you set up living quarters as well," she said. "Nothing too extravagant. Pallet beds, tables for food, some chairs for resting. Use one of the larger caverns nearby. Any worker who comes into these tunnels isn't to leave. Do you understand me, Gerret?"

"Loud and clear, m'lady. I'll round up a few lambs for you. You know, those good for the slaughter." He began laughing - Gerret was quick to laugh at almost anything - though Cecilia wasn't finding much to be amused about here.

"You do that, Gerret. Try to find unpleasant men, if you can. Those who have been accused of beating their wives and kids or raping some poor peasant girl or something. It'd go easier on my conscience that way."

He cocked a brow at her, wondering why she cared. A part of her was wondering that too. *I'm trying to be better*, she thought. *But goodness it's a bumpy road.*

"Well, if that's what you want," the crooked-nosed sellsword said. He picked at his ear. "That about Janilah. You think that's true? That he's out there now, hunting down the other blades himself?"

Cecilia had come up with that on the spot, without giving it any thought at all. She did now. It sounded as likely as anything else they'd considered. "You know what, Gerret," she said. "He might just be mad enough to try."

31

Amara

"Have you ever visited Varinar before, Carly?" Amara Daecar asked, as they rode the last stretch of the Lakeland Pass; the road that circled around Lake Eshina at the heart of Vandar, linking the great cities along its coast.

"Not had the pleasure, my lady," Carly Flame Mane responded, looking splendid as always with that fiery hair and those pink freckly cheeks and glorious sunshine smile. Her men were riding behind them; burly Sally Scarlet and the enormously lanky Will Red and Crowfoot, the old sullen grandfather of the group. They were three of the Bladeborn in the company, though there were several more besides; Renford of the Rust and Mad Maroon Murley and Sunset Sam, who had a strange fascination with the setting of the sun and would sit solemnly and watch it descend beneath the western horizon every single night, without fail. Amara wasn't certain what she preferred, the sellswords themselves of those superbly ridiculous names. But Carly was her favourite, of that there was no doubt. "I hear it's very beautiful, my lady," the girl went on. "What with those famous ten hills and all. Your castle's built on the top of one of them, isn't it?"

"Oh yes, and in a prime location too. Not quite so prime as Palace Hill, but one cannot quibble. Many would agree that Keep Daecar stands only second to the royal residence. The views over the lake are quite wonderful from the higher balconies and terraces."

Carly turned her eyes to the right. "Seen enough of the lake, I think. And I've always preferred mountains. I like the high and low of it. Nothing so flat as a lake feels right to me."

"Well, the ten hills do give Varinar something of an up and down aspect," Amara told her. "Nothing like Ilithor, I'll grant you, but you'll like it, I hope. Once I'm done meeting with King Godrik, we can dine in Keep Daecar. Discuss what's next for you, Carly."

Amara had begun to get the sense that Carly and her men were growing restless. They'd been ambling along the Lakeland Pass as slowly as possible, stopping at the finest inns along its route and drinking in great quantity every night, but none of that was particularly exciting. Lord Brydon had instructed Amara to make haste to Varinar with the utmost speed, so of course she was going to take her time. But for these sellswords it was all rather dull, she feared. And a long stay in Varinar wasn't going to be much better.

"I have enjoyed being a part of your escort, my lady," Carly said, with grace. "You pay well, treat us with respect, and to a man and woman every one of us likes you."

"*Buuuuut?*" Amara said. "I always know when there's a 'but' coming, Carly."

"But…well, I think you probably know already."

Amara nodded. She didn't need to hear Carly say it. "You're adventurous sellswords and have spent time enough in my sour old company. I understand."

"I hope you do, Lady Amara. The last thing I'd want to do is offend you."

"You're not offending me. *Disappointing* me, perhaps, but not offending me." She smiled. "In truth, I have gotten used to having you around, Carly. Seeing Sunset Sam gaze out west every evening. Listening to Crowfoot's stories. Watching Sally Scarlet drink every man we've met under the table. You've made fine companions and it'd be a shame to part with you. And now that Lillia isn't here…" She filled her lungs and turned her eyes over the twinkling waters of the lake, steadying herself. "I feel a bit lost without her, I will admit. But that's not your burden to bear. Of course, you should go where the action is."

Carly had a hard look on her face. "What that Lord Brydon did to you…that wasn't fair, my lady. I know Lillia isn't your daughter, not by blood, but she is in all the ways that matter. My own mother never much cared about me. She was a whore, and I'm not just saying that to insult her. No, a *real* whore, bedding men for money. I was never much more than unwanted baggage to her, a ticket to a bit of coin. That's the only reason she decided to have me, I think; to squeeze some money out of my father, whoever he was, though when that didn't work she lost interest in me quickly enough and let me run amok on the streets. Those streets were my *real* mother, and raised me better than the whore ever did. I was nurtured by stone and snow and steel; blood had nothing to do with it."

Amara smiled faintly. "That's a nice sentiment, Carly."

"I'll go back and fetch her if you like," the girl went on. "Lillia. I never go to a place without learning all I can about it. And Ilivar... Lord Amadar's keep...I know those well enough after the time we spent there. Just say the word, and we'll ride on back and sneak her out for you."

Amara didn't want to give that much consideration, else she might weaken to the prospect. "Best not, Carly. Lord Brydon Amadar is not a man to tussle with."

"Oh, I don't know. I take you for a lady who'd tussle with about anyone. You stole the Windblade from Janilah Lukar after all. And King Godrik too. Got two kings with one stone there. What's Lord Amadar after that?"

One of the most powerful men in the north, she thought, *and a wrathful one at that.* "I think I'm done crossing kings and greatlords," she decided to say. "It only ever seems to get me in trouble."

They rode on for a time, passing several more fishing villages along the lake, a larger town called Duskfall that was known for its pretty multi-coloured boats, enjoying the ranging views of the Heartlands to the east, before eventually the frame of Varinar came into view, looming grandly beyond the flowing waters of the Steelrun River. At any other time the sight of her beloved city would bring a smile to Amara's lips, but not today. Today she felt a throttling sense of dread and emptiness to see the walls rise up before her, to spy those soldiers walking the walls, to see the Taynar banners flapping at the gate in their dull muted colours of grey and blue.

This is not home, she thought, *not anymore.* She shivered to think of how cold and empty Keep Daecar would be now. *Have the rooms fallen to ruin?* she wondered, ridiculously. *Has the lichen begun to spread yet, infecting the walls and halls? Will there be anyone to greet me except the spiders and the ghosts?*

She rode on through the chill morning air in morbid thought, as some of the Flame Manes began chattering excitedly behind her, pointing out this tower or that hill or remarking on the enormity of the city. And true that was. Varinar was much larger than Ilithor, Thalan, or any other city in the north, and a wonder for those who'd never seen it before. Even Carly seemed won over. "Yes, very impressive," she said, nodding appreciatively. "I see what you mean, my lady. The hills give the city some verticality."

"It's best viewed when arriving from the Great East Road," Amara admitted. "You have a higher vantage that way. Some miles out, the road summits a hill that gives a quite splendid view of the ten hills, the inner and outer walls, the towers and battlements, all of it."

"I'll take a good long look when we leave that way," Carly said.

Amara turned to her. "You plan to depart by the Great East Road?"

"I suspect we will, yes. It goes most of the way to Dragon's Bane, as I understand it. Thought we might go pay your nephew a visit, see if he has need of a few more swords. And not to be too forward, my lady, but *I* have a need of *his.* His *fleshy* sword, that is. Elyon and I, we have...unfinished business, shall we say."

"Do me a courtesy, Carly, and say no more. I can quite imagine what sort of business you're referring to."

"Elyon likes a bit of *business*, or so I've heard." Carly gave a lascivious grin. "As do I, I'll admit. Get that from my whore of a mother, I suppose." She laughed musically and glanced back to her men. "I was thinking we could take Jovyn with us, if that's what he still wants? I know you don't want him going all that way alone."

Amara didn't want that at all, not with the world so tumultuous as it was. Banditry was growing increasingly common along the Great East Road, and even a young Bladeborn as capable as Jovyn would be vulnerable to robbery and worse if he should make that journey by himself. "That might be for the best," she agreed. Jovyn had remained in her escort since leaving Ilivar, but there was no sense in him doing so anymore, not now Lillia had been stolen away from them both. "I'll talk to him about it later, see what he says. Jovyn is dutiful almost to a fault, and will stay with me if I ask him, I sense. But I know that isn't right. I can't be keeping him around any more than I can you, Carly."

They trotted on for a few more minutes, nearing the broad stone bridge that crossed the Steelrun River. Ahead, she sighted Sir Connor Crawfield returning from the city gates; she'd sent him ahead to announce her return. He wasn't alone. A half dozen mounted Taynar men were riding with him, dressed in those dull tones of solemn grey and moody blue. Their cloaks showed an armoured knight, planting his sword into the ironmoors; the crest of House Taynar. Yet not their leader, who was dressed in the livery of the Greycloaks, the protective arm of the Varin Knights sworn to guard the king: godsteel breastplate, brown leather gloves, a lightweight shiny cloak of polished silver-grey. She scowled to look at the man. "Sir Gerald Strand," she grunted. "Gods I hate that oaf."

Carly gave a sharp nod to express the same sentiment. Sir Gerald had been one of the Greycloaks present when King Ellis Reynar had been thrown from the throne room balcony in Ilithor, along with Sir Alyn Porter and Sir Nathanial Oloran. They were all widely despised for that, standing by as their king was slain, abandoning their honour and oaths.

Sir Connor hastened ahead of the others as they neared, kicking his steed into a gallop so that they might share a private word. "My lady," he said, dipping his square jaw into a nod. "Sir Gerald has come to escort you straight to the palace." He lowered his voice. "I suggest Carly and Jovyn be kept out of sight. To help…keep the peace."

Amara understood. Both Carly and Jovyn had been involved in the theft of the Windblade and it would be best to avoid any entanglements should Sir Gerald recognise them. "He's right, Carly. Draw back and join your men. My guards will take you to Keep Daecar. I'll see you there later."

Carly looked like she could care less about stirring trouble with the likes of Sir Gerald Strand, though didn't deny her lady's order. "As you wish, Lady Amara." She withdrew to the others, where Sir Gilmoor Gully and Sir Penrose Brightwood - both members of the Daecar House Guard - were riding with Amara's attendants.

Sir Connor didn't go anywhere. "I'll stay with you, my lady."

She wouldn't have it any other way.

Sir Gerald joined them a few moments later, turning his horse to ride alongside her as his men fell into escort around them. He had a glance back as Carly receded into the flow of traffic heading for the gates. "We heard about these sellswords you've been travelling with," he said, in a voice entirely without mirth. "You don't need the likes of them now. We'll take you the rest of the way."

She offered him no smile or polite expression of greeting. *I can grovel at Godrik's feet, but Sir Gerald Strand? No.* "I hope our king is happy to meet me in this state, Sir Gerald," she said. "I had expected to wash and refresh before presenting myself before his royal person."

"You'll do fine as you are." Sir Gerald was a large and doughy man, with a pockmarked face and double chin poorly hidden by his patchy beard. Where his father Lord Styron had been broad and muscular, his eldest son was just broad and fat, soft where his father was hard, weak where he was strong. *He is a farmyard pig,* Amara thought, *masquerading as a great wild boar.* "You'll have time to wash when my uncle is done with you."

"*Done* with me? Oh, how titillating. I wonder what the old creature has planned."

"That old creature is your king. You'd do well to remember your courtesies, woman."

"And you yours, Sir Gerald," Sir Connor reminded him tersely. "You are speaking to the Lady Amara of House Daecar and will treat her with due respect."

"I'll treat no thief with respect, lady or not."

"Oh? And what about a murderer?" Amara asked. "Or an oath-breaking craven? What about those, Sir Gerald? You are familiar with the sort, of course. There's one sitting on your horse right now."

"I'm no murderer," the oaf protested.

"No, perhaps not. But I find it quite instructive that you're not defending yourself against the other charges. Bravo, Sir Gerald. It is heartening to hear that you're aware of your bottomless cowardice. Everyone else is, after all."

"No one that matters," the Greycloak grunted. "Least of all a tart-tongued harridan like you."

Amara laughed. "If you think calling me a tart-tongued harridan is going to cause offence you'd best think again, sir. I have rarely heard such an apt description of myself. Well done, Sir Gerald. Credit where it's due." If she were riding close enough, she'd have reached across and given him a condescending pat on the head. As it was she satisfied herself with a smug smile, and rode on.

The gates were as busy as ever, farmers and fishermen from the lakeside villages and pasturelands meandering in and out of the city with their wagons and wains in tow. Many looked to be arriving with their families, oxcarts piled high with crates and possessions and children, who gazed up at the city in wide-eyed wonder. Sir Gerald bellowed the lot of them out of the way, gesturing for the soldiers at the gate to form a cordon so they might pass unimpeded. "Get these vermin in order!" he called out. "The king is expecting us! Make way! Move!"

"You always were a charmer, Sir Gerald," Amara remarked. "Tell me, have you had many arriving from the hinterlands of late?"

"Hinterlands?" The oaf seemed not to know the word.

"Yes, the lands that surround the city. I take it many have arrived to seek shelter from the war?"

"I suppose. My place is in the palace with the king, not out here. You'd have to talk to the gate captains."

"And I will, as soon as I get a chance." She continued to assess the numbers of arriving families as they progressed through the gate, and into the bustling yard beyond. Many seemed lost as to where to go and what to do. "You have no aid stations set up," she noticed. "No one to greet them or help them find suitable accommodations."

"They come without any place to go, that's on them," Sir Gerald Strand said.

"There are no shelters? No empty church halls or taverns to take them in? Nothing at all?"

"They'll find someplace to nest," snorted the Greycloak. "Lots of snug alleyways around the Lowers where they can settle in. They'll be fine."

"Fine? Being awoken every night by faecal runoff from the gutters, and the squeaking of rats and brawling of drunken louts is fine to you, is it? The Lowers aren't safe, Sir Gerald, especially not at this time. Many will *not* be fine. They will be raped, killed, taken into bondage. They must be housed and protected. These are our countrymen and the backbone of our kingdom. They till our fields and catch our fish, feed us, clothe us, build our homes. The least we can do is make sure they have comfortable lodgings of their own." She had a final look around, making up her mind. "I'll see to this myself, then," she decided. Amara Daecar was heavily involved in charitable causes and dealing with such issues would be nothing new to her. She turned. "Sir Connor, go straight to Keep Daecar and see what help you can rustle up. I still hold influence among the ladies of the court. See about getting word to them. Lady Bradbury, in particular. She's always been staunch in her pursuit of greater comfort for the poor."

Sir Connor looked wary. "I ought to get you safely to the palace first, my lady. And back to Keep Daecar, once you're done."

Amara laughed. "I have the mighty Sir Gerald Strand to guard me. I think I'll be quite safe, Sir Connor."

"And once you're finished?" Sir Connor looked at the man doubtfully. "Will you see her escorted back to Keep Daecar, sir?"

"No," Sir Gerald said, quite plainly. "My place is with the king."

"Yes indeed," Amara agreed, chuckling, "and you needn't trouble yourself. Just what sort of trouble do you imagine I'll get myself into, Sir Connor, between the Palace Hill and Keep Daecar? It's a short stroll and one I've walked a thousand times before. Never once have I come to harm."

Sir Connor still seemed customarily cautious all the same. "Times have changed," he said, giving Sir Gerald a sceptical glance. "It's war, Lady Amara. And we have *different* rulers now."

"Oh, I see. You believe some vengeful Taynar man is going to come lurching out from the crowds to put a dagger in my chest?"

"The thought had crossed my mind."

"Well uncross it. I'll be fine, Sir Connor, but you are sweet for worrying. Now off to Keep Daecar with you. I don't imagine I'll be with Godrik long." She looked at Sir Gerald as if he might have some insight on that, but the bloated man merely shrugged and looked away. "A slap on the wrist and I'll be right back with you, Sir Connor." She smiled to try to ease her protector's concerns, though it didn't seem to help. "Well, best be off. Wouldn't want to keep the king waiting now, would we?" She kicked her horse into a trot and set off down Maple Way.

The crowds thinned dramatically once they'd passed through the inner wall, where the Ten Hills were confined, atop which the greathouses had built their keeps. This ancient inner part of Varinar was home to the highborn and the noble, men of worth and wealth and education, a place of marble stairways lined with flowers, of grand stone squares and wide clean cobblestone streets. Beyond, between the inner and outer walls, the great vastness of the city had evolved, quadrupling its size over the millennia, giving home to a population of equal abundance. Here more hills and rises marked the land, and thus the Lowers had been named; cluttered and often dangerous districts built between the higher prominences.

As ever, Amara was struck by the sudden change in pace, the quiet and polite reserve in evidence as she rode beneath the spiked portcullis and looked upon the city's core. Where outer Varinar was ever hectic and teeming, busy with winesinks and taverns, cobblers and churches, noise and music and mirth, the older core of the city was well mannered and orderly, decidedly less populated and distinctly less fun. The noble ranks of Varinar had always been given to a certain reserve and propriety. Emotions were restrained, laughter largely absent, merriment restricted to official balls and feasts. There were taverns to drink at, yes, and pleasant public houses situated amidst the Ten Hills, but for a proper banter-filled drinking binge, one would be well advised to pass beyond the inner wall and venture a little further afield.

"It's all rather quiet, isn't it," Amara observed, looking around. "More so than I've ever seen it."

"Many are away at war," Sir Gerald said, as though she needed that explained to her.

"Yes, I am aware. So…the inner city is silent as a morgue and the outer city threatens to spill over like an overflowing cup." She tapped her lips. "Hmmm, I wonder if there might be a solution to all this…"

Sir Gerald got her meaning quickly enough. "What? Let in those field workers and labourers, with all their filthy screaming children?" He laughed loudly. "I'll let you take that up with my uncle. You'd have more chance of getting with child by that turncloak husband of yours than convincing him of *that*."

The insult stung a little, though she didn't let it show. In all truth, she found herself rather impressed by Sir Gerald's wit, cruel though it was. *A double jape,* she reflected, *attacking both my barren womb and Vesryn's long term absence. I didn't know he had it in him.* She kept her facade perfectly calm, forcing a serene smile onto her face, as they trotted toward the palace.

Sir Gerald seemed to find the lack of retort unnerving. He glanced at her several times, before muttering, "That was perhaps a little…improper of me. To refer to your inability to…to bear children. I fear I crossed a line."

She flicked a wrist. "Think nothing of it, Sir Gerald. The game of insults is one of give and take. I give with great alacrity, so must take with equal appetite. Words are my steel and you have thrust right through my defences and straight into my heart. Well done. I commend you on the killing blow."

The last few minutes were spent in silence as they climbed the gentle slope up toward the palace. When they reached the steps, they were forced to leave their saddles. Grooms from the royal stable were waiting to attend their horses. "Have her taken to Keep Daecar," Amara informed the stableboy who came forward to take the reins of Glitter, her spotted palfrey. She had never liked the name, but Vesryn had liked it less, so she'd decided to stick with it.

Sir Gerald dismounted beside her, as gracelessly as one would expect. "The king awaits you in the throne room…my lady," he said. Insulting her so gravely seemed to have reminded him of his courtesies. "I shall lead you."

"I know the way, Sir Gerald, but as you wish."

The short walk gave her a few more moments to gather herself for the inevitable. A scolding, and a harsh one, was incoming, she knew. Lord Brydon had been explicit in what he needed of her: to get down on her knees and beg forgiveness for the theft of the Windblade, help mediate its rightful return, work to mend the great pus-filled rift that had been cleaved open between the greathouses.

A simple task, then, she thought, as they summited the steps, walked through the great entrance hall, scaled staircases and crossed corridors and approached their quarry. She had time enough to take a few calming breaths before Sir Gerald Strand strode forward and pushed through the heavy double doors and the throne room opened out before them, a chamber of grandeur and gravitas and opulent beauty, high up in the palace, high up in the city, marvellous and magnificent, overlooking all. Every king since Varin had seated himself within this hallowed hall, perched upon the famous godsteel throne, ever misting upon the dais. Some great, others less so, many memorable for one reason or another. The last of Varin's direct line had been Lorin, swashbuckling and adventurous, slain by a kraken with the Nightblade to hand. After that came the Reynars; Horris and Storris who ruled through turmoil and war, Ellis who never truly ruled at all, for Amron Daecar had been the de facto king through Ellis Reynar's reign, all agreed.

And how we could do with him now, Amara thought, as she saw the wasted old figure of Godrik Taynar sitting clutched between the great arms of his newly acquired throne. *This man is not deserving of the crown. This man is a traitor by all the good laws of gods and men…*

She smiled as winningly as she could, and said, "King Godrik, Your Majesty, what a pleasure to see you again after all these long weeks apart." She brushed right past Sir Gerald Strand before he could make any formal announcement, striding into the heart of the cavernous pillar-lined chamber, footsteps echoing, silver cloak swirling. "How was your return journey from Ilithor without me? Very dull, I would wager, absent my sparkling company."

"The road is always dull, Amara," King Godrik said. His voice reminded her of the Long Abyss; lifeless, cold, entirely devoid of joy. There was much of the corpse about Godrik Taynar, in those gaunt and sunken cheeks, the bloodless wash of his skin, the eyes that seemed no more than sockets, hollow and expressionless. If the Taynars suffered the affliction of being overly dour, then the plague had its roots in the old lord of their house.

Amara continued forward, spotting a few more Greycloaks lurking in the shadows and corners. More conspicuously situated was their commander, Sir Nathaniel Oloran. *Another craven and traitor.* She favoured him with a smile. "How fares your father, Sir Nathaniel? I have heard his health is waning."

The man dipped his angular chin. He had the same golden locks as his older brother, Killian, though they were a little shorter and less impressive, as he was. "His eyesight suffers, my lady. The physicians say he may be going blind. And his lungs…he has a hacking cough that worsens by the day, I am told."

"Oh, such a pity. I do hope he recovers."

"Do you, Amara?" King Godrik scoffed. "When Penrith Oloran dies, Killian will become lord of his house. I imagine you'd like that. Rallying the Olorans to your cause."

"I have no cause, my lord, but to help seal the breach that has opened between our houses." Amara stopped as she reached the short three-step stair that gave access to the stage. *I worded that well,* she thought. *Brydon would be proud.* "Isn't that what we all desire at this dreadful time? To stand together, shoulder to shoulder, against our enemies to the south?"

"You desire no such thing," Godrik dismissed. He regarded her, looking bored. "You will lie through your teeth as always, but won't be convincing me. No, I'll not drag this out, much as I might wish to see you squirm." His eyes flicked right. "Nathaniel, take her into custody. See her confined to the dungeons in a cell to befit her station."

Amara wasn't quite comprehending the jape. She held a palm out as Sir Nathaniel advanced. "My lord," she chuckled, awkward, "I have come to parley, under Lord Brydon Amadar's protection. There is much that needs to be discussed. I have full authority to…"

"You have no authority."

She frowned up at him, growing anxious. "My lord?"

Godrik Taynar's hollow eyes stared back. "You think very highly of yourself, Amara, but in truth you are inconsequential. The only power you possess is being valuable to those who truly wield influence, and therein lies your use."

"My use?" An unpleasant tingle was beginning to crawl up her spine. She was aware that Sir Gerald was now approaching behind her. "My lord...*King* Godrik, come, do not act rashly. I have influence enough to speak for Houses Daecar and Amadar and Kanabar as well. You know that. Brydon wrote you, did he not, to tell of my coming? I am here under a banner of peace and parley and have full authority to discuss terms."

Godrik leaned forward on his throne, bones clicking. "Oh Amara, you really don't know what this is, do you? You think Brydon sent you here to parley? Poor dear, no. He sent you here to be my hostage, your life a chip with which I might bargain." He sat back up, shaking his head at her foolishness. "As I say, there are men of power who value you. Your nephew, for one, who will have no choice now but to return what you took from me. I want the Windblade back, Amara. *I* am king. It is *mine*, by rights."

Bastard., she thought. *Brydon, you foul bloody bastard!*

"Ah yes, the face of a woman who realises she's been tricked," gloated the king. "A taste of your own medicine for once. It is bitter, no?"

Amara did not answer that. Bitter was not the word. She felt sick right down to the depths of her stomach. "And if Elyon should refuse to give the Windblade up?" she managed to ask.

"Then you shall die, Amara. And rather horribly, I should think. What, did you think your crime would go unpunished? That you could plot to steal a Blade of Vandar without repercussion? Oh, sweet woman, what a fool you have been." He gave a lazy gesture of his fingers and Sir Nathanial and Sir Gerald stepped in.

"Do *not* touch me," Amara told them, when she saw their hands approach. "Come near and I'll scratch your bloody eyes out."

Sir Nathaniel raised his palms. "Go easy, my lady, and we'll need not manhandle you. So long as Sir Elyon complies, then there's no reason for you to..."

"Oh shut up, Nathaniel," Amara snapped at him. "I don't need *you* to comfort me."

The man looked mildly insulted. "Well…as you please."

"Please? It would please me to see the lot of you hanging from the gibbet. Those who conspire to murder a king are not favoured by fate, I will remind you all. Her cold grasping fingers will reach you eventually."

Godrik gave his version of a laugh. It sounded like a rattle of small bones in a pouch. "Amara, you do amuse. For twenty years Amron ruled in Ellis's stead, and when the poor witless king is finally disposed of, you all cry treason and throw up your arms. It's absurd."

Amara spun to face him. "There's a difference between ruling by proxy and murdering a king, Godrik! Amron would never have dreamed of killing Ellis."

"And where is Amron now? Missing or in hiding or dead, I've even heard. Just the same as Janilah. And where am I? Seated upon the godsteel throne at the heart of Varinar with twenty thousand loyal men guarding my gates. It would seem to me that our fortunes have switched."

"For now. Fortunes can fall just as precipitously as they can rise. You'd best remember that, Godrik. There's only one way down from that mountaintop of yours."

"Or I could just remain at the summit. If you knew anything of battle you would know that the high ground is most valuable. I have it. And have no intention of ceding it to anyone."

Amara tried to think. Her mind was racing from Lord Brydon's betrayal. *Bastard!* she thought again, near enough shouting the word out loud. *He set me up as bait.*

"I want you to send your nephew a letter, Amara, telling him of your plight," Godrik went on. "Once you have done so and he has arranged for the Windblade to be returned to me, I will release you. You have my word."

"Your word is worthless."

"It's the best you're going to get. I shall have quill and parchment brought to your cell. Do express to your nephew the urgent nature of my request. I have every intention of getting the Windblade to my son as soon as possible; any delay will go ill for you, Amara." He paused. "Do you write with your right or your left hand?"

The question disquieted her. She hesitated. "My left."

"Then we will leave that one untouched, so you can write again if needed. Your right, on the other hand, may not come away unscathed."

"*On the other hand*," chuckled Sir Gerald Strand. "Very good, my king."

"Quiet, Gerald. If I wish to hear from you I'll say so." He gave the piggish knight a sharp look. "Now, Amara, I do not wish to see you hurt, but I will if you disobey me. In all truth, you made the journey to Ilithor for the wedding more bearable. You think a great deal of yourself, that's true, but are not without wit, and can be quite entertaining when you're drinking. It is a shame you betrayed me. You have left me no choice."

Amara wished at that moment that she'd brought Sir Connor with her, though the desire was short-lived. *No, he would only try to defend me and die for it.* There was no sense in Connor Crawfield getting caught up in this. Or the others... *The others*...she thought. *Carly. Jovyn.* Her eyes went to the king once more, and she saw something in his face. *He knows. He knows they're here with me. Brydon...Brydon will have told him...*

It all came together, coalescing into one great ugly realisation. Panicking, she tried to muster some sense of composure. "I will go easy, Godrik," she said, appeasingly, "and write Elyon as you have asked me. But...do me one courtesy before I do."

He gave her a lazy look. "Yes?"

"Permit me a private word with the captain of my guard. He will only worry when I do not return to Keep Daecar. Let me explain to him what is happening, and you'll be spared any further trouble."

"The captain of your guard? Sir Connor Crawfield, is it?"

"The very one, yes."

"A man of little renown," the king dismissed. "No, you cannot see him. And do not think me blind to your true intent. You wish to send warning to your co-conspirators. Yes, I know all about them too."

Her panic was now beginning to leak out. "If you touch..."

"They will join you in the dungeons, pending your nephew's response. This flame-haired sellsword girl may not carry much meaning to him, but his squire? I'm told they are very close." He thought a moment. "What was the name, Sir Nathaniel?"

"Jovyn Colborn, sire."

"Ah yes, Colborn. An uncelebrated house, down near Green Harbour, I recall. Not one of mine, but no matter. I am king now. All houses will bend to me, in time."

"You're deluded," Amara spat. "When Amron returns..."

"Ah, so you *do* know where he is?"

Amara said nothing.

"No?" Godrik creaked forward off his throne, rattling to his feet. Over his shrivelled bony body he wore a grey doublet etched with dual sigils; that of his house over his left breast, that of the kingdom over his right. The king saw her looking at them. "They are much alike, are they not?"

They were. The Taynar sigil was the knight planting his blade into the Ironmoors. The royal sigil showed a blade embedded into the earth, with the mountain of Vandar's Tomb behind. Both were in tones of silver, grey, and blue. Some took that to mean the Taynars were always destined to rule. Godrik was one of them.

He took a pace down the steps. "*Amron*, Amara. Tell me where he is."

"I don't know." There was much truth in that too.

"I disagree." He moved down another step. "Tell me."

"I *do not know*, Godrik."

The final step of three was taken and Godrik landed at the bottom of the stage. "I see." He paused there, judging her. She did her best to meet his cold stare. "I have mulled on his absence often of late. It really is most curious, that he hasn't been seen for so long. There are rumours he travelled to Northwatch and never left. Now I wonder...did he travel beyond the mountains, perchance? Is dear Amron seeking a miracle?" He stared at her long and hard. "Nothing to say, Amara?"

She swallowed in a dry throat. "No."

"*No*. Of course not. Though, there are ways of getting you to speak, as I have indicated. That right hand of yours...so elegant and pretty with those long nimble fingers, those manicured nails." His manner darkened. "Nails that can be torn off. Fingers that can be broken. There is a great deal of pain that can be inflicted upon the hand, Amara."

He let that settle, and she could not help but think of the lesson Lord Brydon had taught her, tugging her fingers apart, speaking of the north being strong as he forced her to close a fist. *Lies*, she thought. *All lies. He only wanted me out of the picture, and Jovyn too. He only wanted Lillia for himself...*

"As I say, I'd prefer not to resort to that sort of thing...but I will, if I must. So, once more...where did Amron go?"

Her mind was full of ripped fingernails and snapped bones and flayed skin, of searing unbearable pain. But for all that, she sealed her lips and shook her head, saying nothing. It was pure defiance, nothing else. There was no great sense in hiding the truth of Amron's whereabouts anymore. *Because he is likely dead,* she thought. *It's been too long. Much too long…*

A tear was beginning to run down her cheek.

"A woman's weapon," Godrik scoffed. "It is *one* of them, at least. Your tears will not affect me, Amara."

She hardened her gaze, such as she could, and lifted a hand to wipe her cheek.

Godrik Taynar smiled. "Good. Yes, you're stronger than that." He ran thumb and forefinger together, thinking. "Such pretty hands needn't be mutilated just yet," he finally said. "No, I sense you know Amron went to Northwatch, and that he went into the Weeping Heights, but know no more than that." Without turning, he said, "Gerald," and Sir Piggy snapped to attention.

"Yes, sire."

"This is a job for you, I feel."

"Job? W…what job, sire?"

"Discovering the truth of Amron's fate. You'll find the answer at Northwatch. Take a host of your best and ride out. I'll see you separate the facts from the fiction."

"Northwatch? But that's hundreds of miles from here…"

"Then you'd best leave at once, Gerald. Take the High Way. It won't take so long if you ride long and rest little."

Amara took a shred of enjoyment from the look on the oaf's pockmarked face, but not much more. "As you command, Uncle. I'll…" He glanced enviously at Sir Nathaniel, spared the wild goose chase. "I'll leave right away, then." The man turned heavily and plodded from the hall.

Godrik watched him go, then turned to the commander of his guard. "You ought to go as well, Nathaniel. Escort Amara to her cell. I suspect her friends will already be waiting, though do make sure to situate them on different wards. I don't want them communicating."

"Of course, sire. My lady, go easy, please." Sir Nathaniel gestured for several of his men to approach, and suddenly she was surrounded. They began leading her away. Behind her she could hear King Godrik climbing back into his throne, victorious.

She turned suddenly. "At least spare the others," she pleaded. "The Flame Manes. They've got nothing to do with any of this."

Godrik settled in. "I disagree. They helped in the theft of my blade. I will keep the leader in chains should she prove of value, but the rest…no. I would not be surprised if every one of them is dead already. I had men waiting for them at Keep Daecar, with good polished godsteel to grasp."

"You loathsome monster!" she howled, pushing forward. Several hands snapped out and coiled about her wrists and arms, holding her back. She struggled, but it was no use.

Godrik watched on, impassive. "These are sellswords, Amara. Lowborn parasites. They are well rid of, so spare me your tears. I told you, I do not care for them." He flicked a single finger to dismiss her.

"Come, my lady, go easy," urged Sir Nathanial.

She ignored him. "And Connor? Please, Godrik…please, not him as well." She thought of Sir Penrose and Sir Gilmore and the other men of her household guard, but it was Connor she was closest to. And Connor's fate she feared for. "Promise me, Godrik. Promise he'll not be harmed."

The king remained unmoved. "I gave no order for Sir Connor Crawfield or your other men to be slain. But in the lust of battle, who can say. If they decided to intervene and defend these sellsword scum of yours, then that is on them."

The men continued to drag her away. Through the jumble of bodies and scrambling limbs she could see the king nonchalantly lifting an old leather-bound tome from a table beside his throne. He began reading, casually folding one spindly leg over the other, licking his finger, turning a page. The sight enraged her. The casual indifference of it. A shriek erupted from her lips. "You son of a whore, Godrik! You'll not get away with this. You know that. You won't!"

The king glanced up, looked at her with a quizzical frown, then turned his eyes back to his book. "There is nothing to get away with," he said, turning another page. "Goodness, woman, you sound the fool when you speak like that. And that mouth of yours. So unseemly." He glanced up again, though not at her. "Nathaniel, do quieten her down. I cannot abide all this bawling."

Before she knew it, the craven oathbreaker Oloran was stepping forward, drawing a knife from his swordbelt. For a moment she thought this was it, her time had come and he was going to punch that blade right through her gut and end her there and then.

But no. He spun it around between his fingers at the last moment so the pommel was facing her way. "I'm sorry about this, my lady." Then, with a good firm swipe, he cracked her on the side of the head with the handle, causing her brain to rattle in her skull. Her eyes blurred, her limbs folded, and she fell bonelessly into the arms of the men around her. She had only time to see Godrik lick his finger and turn another page, before the world closed in.

Then nothing.

Blackness.

32

Elyon

Elyon Daecar soared above the great open plains north of Dragon's Bane in the company of a flock of migratory geese. There must have been three or four dozen of them, heavy-chested birds with two-metre wingspans and long black necks, flying with effortless grace.

As I am, he thought. Windblade pointed forward, he sailed smoothly alongside the flock in a vortex of swirling air, grinning at the strange looks they gave him. "Sorry, just passing through," he called out, his words swallowed up by the rush and roar of the wind. "Don't mind me!"

The birds didn't seem so happy with his presence, honking loudly as he drew closer. He could understand their disquiet. He was not a creature they'd seen before, after all, leastways not up here. In Agarath man had conquered the skies on dragonback long ago, but the same could not be said here in the north. *I am one of a kind,* Elyon thought, as the winds whipped through his thick black hair and his Varin cloak flapped relentlessly at his back. It was more thrilling than he could say to soar these skies with such growing ease and be the only man living to do it.

The geese soon took their leave of him, gliding northward in what he assumed was a final destination of the Four Sisters; the cluster of lakes that made up the Lakelands of East Vandar. "I'll catch you later, then," he called, giddy. A couple of the birds honked out their reply. Elyon took them for words of parting, smiled, dipped his chin, and banked away south.

Far below, he could see the distant specks of his companions, standing with the horses some two or so miles away. He sped into a descent, angling his course in their direction. The plains that spread out beneath him were vast, spotted with snow from a recent fall, crisscrossed with rutted farm tracks and streams and fields and home to more wooded thickets of oak and ash and chestnut than Elyon could count. It was a picturesque place to be sure, a perfect late winter landscape. *A simple place,* he mused. They were only some eight or nine miles north of Dragon's Bane, yet even so, you'd never know there was a war on out here.

His friends cleared as he drew nearer. Barnibus and the Lady Marian were pacing together in conversation, snacking on some oatcakes and enjoying the warming smile of the pale winter sun. Lancel was sitting on a rock nearby, juggling with a few small pebbles and stones and looking bored. A large oak tree marked the land here where several fields converged; the horses stood beneath its thick gnarled branches, munching happily at the grass at its base. Only Marian's sleek grey palfrey Stormwind looked up as Elyon came in to land; Biter, Monty, and Snowmane were quite used to his flights by now.

He landed a dozen paces away, decelerating only at the last moment, swinging his legs down and landing with one knee to the ground, the other leg bent at a right angle. Lancel looked up from his rock. "Very nice," he said.

"Heroic," Barnibus agreed, nodding. "A bit showy, perhaps, but I'm sure the men will like it."

Elyon stood, dismissing the final swirls of wind. He thrust the tip of the Windblade into the frosty ground where he stood and unclasped his fingers from the hilt, letting its power drain away. He stabilised his footing, breathing deep. The sensation always left him a bit lightheaded, especially when paired with an abrupt landing. "I'm not…trying to be showy, Barny. It's just…it's a good way of landing quickly, is all."

Lady Marian studied him placidly. "Do you need to sit down for a moment, Elyon? You look a little peaky."

"It's…the landing, my lady. It can take a few moments for me to centre myself when I come down that fast." He drew a final breath, blinking to clear his vision. The feeling of nausea began to pass.

"Yes, that did seem rather more hurried than your previous landings."

"Split seconds count in battle, Marian. My father always used to tell me that." He'd been working tirelessly for weeks to improve his take-off and landing speed, should he need to join a battle quickly, or come to the aid of an ally. Not to mention his speed through the skies, his agility and acrobatics, all of which would serve him well when outmanoeuvring his leathery foes.

"So where'd you go?" Lancel asked, looking skyward. "We lost you in the glare of the sun a while back. Not even Marian could find you."

Elyon gave a gesture to the north. "There were some geese," he said, "heading for the lakes, I think. I wanted to check them out. Flew alongside them for a time. "

Barnibus swallowed a mouthful of biscuit and brushed a few crumbs from his lips. "How high did you go?"

"High. Had to be a half mile at least."

"Half a mile?" Lancel raised his eyes. "Gods, you've not gone nearly that high before. What's the view like from up there, El?"

"Astonishing, Lance. You wouldn't believe how far you can see. Seems like all the world is spread out beneath you." He spoke wistfully, enjoying the wonderment on his friends' faces. "I could see Dragon's Bane clearly to the south, Death's Passage beyond. The shimmer of the lakes to the north. The marshes to the east. All of it."

"That would make sense, from such a height," Marian said, rather less prone to awe. "From a mile high one can see a hundred miles, I have heard. How did you find the increased altitude up there? Any problems breathing? Were the winds any more fierce?"

She's all business, Elyon thought. *And isn't that why I invited her?* "No breathing issues, that I was aware of," he told her." As to the winds… well, they were a little more boisterous than normal, perhaps, but nothing I couldn't handle. Flying through thick clouds or a storm would be a different challenge, I suppose."

"Like those?" Barnibus raised a finger and pointed eastward. The skies out there were beginning to curdle with a dark grey fume that looked wholly uninviting. It had come on quickly; the day had been fair thus far. "You've got time for one final flight today, haven't you? You've done, what…five? Six? How about lucky number seven, El? Those stormclouds have your name all over them."

Elyon didn't like this mood Barnibus was in, all grins and casual goads. "I'm not sure today's the day," he said. "I'm a little tired, Barn. You know, on account of those six flights you just mentioned."

"You can't pick and choose what weather to fight in when the dragons come calling, Elyon, no more than you can pick the time," Barnibus came back. "You'll have to take up your blade and fly out to meet them whether it's sunny, snowy, stormy…morning, noon, or night."

Lancel scoffed loudly. "Nice speech from a man who's never fought a proper battle."

"Neither have you."

"I'm not the one making speeches."

"So I'm wrong, am I?"

"No. I'm just tired of listening to you prattle on."

"I'm trying to be constructive. You're just sitting there playing with rocks."

"OK, *enough*," Elyon broke in. "Loathe as I am to admit it, Barny's right. He's being a bit of an arse about it, but still…none of us will be able to choose when the enemy attacks and we'd all best prepare for the worst. That means fighting when we're tired. When we're hungry and cold and want nothing more than to sit by the fire and drown ourselves in wine. Every good warrior looks for ways to push their limits." His father had taught him that too. "You push to the point where you're feeling uncomfortable, and then stay there until you get used to it. Then you push a little further. And a little further still. That's where greatness lives."

He found Lady Marian nodding approvingly as he spoke, and was happy enough with that. Before he could second guess himself he began wrapping his fingers around the haft of the Windblade once more, turning to look to the distant skies. The clouds seemed to have redoubled their efforts to reappear foreboding, as though knowing he was coming. He paused for just a second.

"You…sure about this, El?" Lancel asked him, brow cocked in doubt. "Those clouds are getting darker by the minute."

"The darker the better." He pulled the Windblade from the hard frosty soil and pointed its tip at the storm. "My limits are out there, Lance." *Greatness*, he thought, *is hidden in those clouds.*

A soft rumble of thunder came rolling in from the east, though it might just have been the churning in his stomach. Mastering a Blade of Vandar was hard and hungry work and never failed to build an appetite. He could hear Barnibus munching on an oatcake to his side, almost smell that crunchy goodness, and that wasn't much helping either. He thought for a moment about eating something before taking off but that would defeat the purpose. *Fight hungry,* he told himself. *Fight cold and wet and weary. Be strong when you're feeling weak. Find another level, Elyon.*

He gazed east. Past those clouds that clotted the sky. East, away toward the Marshlands, away across the swamps of Celaph's Mire, out onto the great open gulf of Redwater Bay beyond. And suddenly he wondered; *are you out there now, brother? Are you sailing across the bay as we speak?* He could almost see him, furled in that black cloak of his with the Nightblade at his hip, standing on the prow of his ship as it cut through wind and wave.

His fingers tightened. *Why, Borrus? Why did you join him?* It was one of a hundred questions he'd dwelled on overnight, one of a hundred that old one-eyed Daggart hadn't been able to adequately answer. *He should be bringing us the Shadowknight's head, not bending his bloody knee to him.* And the rest of it? Sir Mooton taking off with them too, for the sake of his long-lost cousin Torvyn. This Emeric Manfrey Daggart had mentioned, who was some former lord, he'd heard, exiled by Modrik Kastor a dozen years ago, and descendent of the famed Sir Oswald.

Questions. Questions without answers. *But might I get to the truth of all this? Might I fly out there and try to find them?* It had been six days now since Sir Mooton had met Borrus at Mudport. *Six days. How far could they have gotten by now?* In good weather, they might already be crossing beneath the Links, or even snaking up the Sibling Strait for all he knew. *Could I fly that far? Several hundred miles. Could I make it? Could I confront that black-cloaked bastard again? And on level terms this time.*

He clenched his jaw, thrusting the Windblade to the skies, summoning the winds to his will. Over the swirling roar, he heard Lancel say, "So, you're going, then? You're really going to do it..."

But he gave no answer. With a loud echoing crack, he shot up and off the ground, faster than ever before, causing the horses to whinny and the oak leaves to rustle and the loose stones to rattle on the floor. He left his friends behind in an instant, angling his ascent eastward, gathering speed. The storm ahead suddenly seemed less unnerving. *I have seen my father crippled by a shadow. I have watched my brother die. I have stood before the girl I thought I loved and seen her hack through her very own neck.* The storm was nothing to him now. I *am the storm,* he thought, surging eastward. *I belong up here now. This is my domain. You keep the night, Jonik.*

I have the skies.

He could not say how long he'd flown before the world began to darken, the clouds greedily gobbling him up as he punched right through their belly. He entered an alien world. A world in shades of grey and black. A world of shifting shapes and shadows and violent, turbulent air.

I wanted a test and I have one, he thought, buffeted by the ferocious gale. It required all his focus now to hold himself steady, to keep the protective cushion of air around him from being blasted into oblivion. Should its integrity be lost he would drop into freefall, and should that happen, he'd risk losing consciousness.

Yet for all that his thoughts were still on the Shadowknight. *He could be four hundred miles from here. Or one hundred. Or two.* Finding a particular ship in the vastness of the bay was like looking for a frightened white cat in a snowstorm. There were thousands of ships down there. War galleons. Trade cogs. Fishing vessels. All dispersed through fifty thousand square miles of open sea. There was no stretch of water in the world more busy.

I might never find him, he realised. *Even if I could fly that far...could I check every ship I see?* He knew that Jonik and his makeshift band were sailing on a pair of ships. That might make it easier, but still...but still...

A thick thunderous bellow ruptured the skies, and to his immediate right came a blinding flash of light. A strange buzzing sensation crawled across his skin, sharp and prickly, and he knew he'd almost been hit.

Metal attracts lightning, something inside him warned, though that was only a myth, he knew. No, metal *conducted* lightning, it didn't attract it. All the same, he had to be careful. *If I'm hit...*Well, he didn't want to dwell on *that.*

He flew on, refusing the urge to descend and seek shelter despite the growing danger. *No, I must embrace it.* Instead he went higher, piercing the clouds like an arrow shot from a bow. He lost himself to the darkness for a time, the air thick and close about him, until a faint light appeared ahead, a shimmering paleness that opened out suddenly into a vast and open valley of air.

The sight was enough to steal his breath. To left and right, above and below, a great nebula of grey-black brume enclosed him, immense in scale and splendour. Silvery fingers of lightning flashed and faded, accompanied by their thunderous calls, and above, as the clouds rolled and blended and broke apart, thin shafts of sunlight cut down through the canopy, showing a tease of the blue heavens beyond.

This is a world between worlds, Elyon thought, awestruck. *One forbidden from man to enter. All but me.* The world of the living lay below, the Eternal Halls above. He looked up to where the sunlight pierced the clouds. *If I could just fly through one of those shafts, would I be permitted to pass? Might I see Aleron again? And Mother? And all the others I've lost?*

Then the clouds closed in and the light was shut off, and he knew he was thinking folly. *This is but a storm, no passage to the ethereal realm. You are a man still, Elyon. Only death will grant you passage.*

He flew on, rising yet higher, marvelling at the wonders around him. Lightning blazed amid the walls of black, turning night to day in an instant, bellowing like some great infernal beast and yet somehow...somehow Elyon felt no fear. Somehow it felt like home. *I am the storm,* he told himself again. *The lightning will not harm me.* He had heard tales of the Windblade being used to summon more than gales and gusts. The greatest of its bearers could even harness lightning, it was said, when the weather was right. *And I will too,* he promised himself. *I'll master it like my father did the Sword of Varinar. And my brother...he of the night.*

His mind raced back to Jonik. *Six days under sail,* he thought again. *He'll be keeping near the coast, at least until Drummond's Point. Then he'll spur them on through open water, right across the bay, directly for the Links. Six days...* He imagined the distance, the route. *Six days is plenty to be approaching the Sibling Strait, if not sailing up it. Could I make it? Could I? If I can get through this storm and come out the other side, maybe...maybe...*

The prospect excited him. He could see it now; the bastard's face stark with surprise as he came crashing down from the sky like a thunderbolt, landing on the deck of his ship, ready to fight. He would hold the tip of the Windblade in Jonik's face and say, "We meet again, Shadowknight. Only now *I* have a Blade of Vandar too."

He flew on for several more minutes, deeper and deeper into the storm, lancing through flashing stormclouds and bursts of torrential rain. His hair was slick and soaked, his Varin cloak plastered to his back. His armour sparkled and glistened each time the lightning struck. *I am the storm. I command the skies...*

Watch out...watch out...you're not alone up here...

He frowned, losing his focus a moment, dropping a few metres before steadying. *What was that?* He listened again for the whisper, blocking out the howling gale, the shattering song of the storm. Faintly, distantly, he heard it again. *He's closing on you*, the voice said. *Behind you…look behind you…*

Cold fingers crawled right up Elyon's spine at those words. He craned his neck at once, disturbed, peering into the darkness of the storm behind him, yet saw nothing to give him pause. He lost his composure for a moment, stuttering, steadying. *There's nothing there,* he thought. *It's my imagination, that's all…*

He looked around again, into the gloom and the greyness and the rain, and suddenly the storm felt an enemy, dark and forbidding. He frowned. Somewhere behind, the clouds seemed to be swirling strangely, as though something was moving through them. He squinted that way, sensing a presence in pursuit, fast approaching, a shade nearing…closing. *I need to get out of here,* he realised. *I need to get out of here right now…*

No time, came the whisper. *It's here…it's here…it's come.*

Elyon's heart was thudding frantically now. And the Windblade… the Windblade was beginning to *thrum* in his grasp, the swirling ribbons of mist that encircled it turning chaotic, frenzied, afraid and excited at once. He took a deep breath and steadied himself. He knew now what was behind him. And that was when he saw it, some two dozen metres back, a little to the right, and closing fast. A shadow and shape moving sleekly through the fog, following his scent, hunting.

Dragon.

Dive! he thought. *Dive, right now!*

He snapped his eyes straight forward and dropped into a vertical plunge, vanishing into the thick clouds beneath him. He spared a glance backward; the beast was giving chase, that monstrous shadow swooping, all scales and muscle, claws and fangs. Elyon caught sight of orange-red light, running from the beast's chest all down its throat. A great maw began to widen and inside he could see death.

He banked sharply left, just as a great spout of flame rushed past him, vaporising the mists. The air seemed to fizz and pop, the clouds parting wildly as though rushing from the creature in terror. He speared through another cloud, disappearing back into the brume. The brute was close on his heels, he could feel it, thumping the air with great powerful beats of his wide leathery wings. A horrifying screech filled the world, echoing through his very bones.

Turn, said a voice. *Turn…fight…*

He dove again, trying to outmanoeuvre it, pitching hard and sharp to the left, but the dragon was not for shifting. A second torrent of molten flame burst past him. He managed to sense it coming just in time, twisting away and down in a dizzying spiral. He righted himself, body aligned, sword arm outstretched, the other by his side. He could hear the foul terror closing once more, no more than fifteen or twenty metres back.

Turn…fight…

He thought back on all he'd learned of dragonlore. Of the accounts he'd heard from those who'd fought them. Of what he'd read in books and tomes. Of everything his father and Lythian and old Artibus had taught him. *Dragons are better going down than up*, he recalled. To gain altitude they had to use wing power; going down just required gravity.

But Elyon was not so constrained. *Fly up!* he thought. *Up! Not down!*

He shot skyward, thrusting the Windblade directly above him, surging beyond the beast's reach. *Agility,* he realised. *I have it on agility*. Through the dense stormy swamp he could see the dragon below him now, shooting straight past, snapping and shrieking in rage. It gave a thrashing beat of its wings and rose, wheeling in a wide circle, and for the first time Elyon got a proper look at his foe.

Dark brown, with mottled patches of green on its thick scale armour, it had a slim, flattened snout, curved horns jutting out from the top and sides of its head, and a long lashing tail studded with deadly, rapier-like spikes. It was not so big as he'd first thought; a brutal beast yes, but not the monstrosity he'd feared. *A scout?* he wondered. And yet…

No rider, he realised, shocked. The beast was *riderless*. There was a harness strapped about its chest, and yet the saddle itself was empty.

He had no time to consider the implications of that now. The dragon was still rising, coming back around to face him. Elyon had read that they feared the storms, yet this one…no, there was something queer about it. Even from a distance he could see that maddened red look in its eyes, glowing bright amid the murk. It gave another *thwump* of its wings and rose, shrieking that bloodcurdling shriek. Great grey banners of mist twirled and twisted away, and behind, a fizzing web of light crashed down from somewhere higher, lighting up the nebulous skies, casting the beast in all its terrible glory.

Elyon hovered in place, waiting. He spared a look up through the clouds and saw a break above. Sunlight poured through; a waterfall of pure golden light, creating a celestial glow in the gloom. *The Steel Father watches*, he thought. *He watches from the head of his Table. Along with all the great kings and champions and knights of the past.* His grandfather Gideon and great-grandfather Balion would be up there, former First Blades both. And Aleron...*Do you watch me, brother? Do you will me on?*

The beast was still screeching. So loud the hairs on Elyon's neck stood up, every sinew of him straining tight, ready. Smoke poured out from the beast's nostrils, streaming, and behind those rows of jagged teeth the furnace was burning, hotter, hotter.

Elyon stood his ground. *Five more seconds*, he thought. *Four. Three. Two...*

The dragon widened its maw and discharged its gushing flame. Elyon surged up beyond it; the dragon anticipated the move, following, yet Elyon was quicker. He shot over the top of the flame and beast and spun, banishing the cushion of air around him, dropping into freefall. The dragon swept past him, roaring in rage, moving into another wide circle. Elyon took his chance, firing up the boosters, calling the winds to his will. They gathered and grouped and spun about him, thrusting him into a chase.

Now the hunted becomes the hunter, he thought, closing in behind the beast. Its tail was whipping and lashing, fending him off like a wasp. *But my sting has a little more bite to it.* He swung with the Windblade in an attempt to sever its flesh, but the motion wasn't something he was accustomed to yet. Flying was one thing, fighting in flight another.

He lost his form, falling, tumbling down a half dozen metres in a blink. When he managed to regather himself he realised he was directly beneath the beast. *It hasn't noticed yet.* Its tail was still swinging and swiping above him. *This is my chance,* he thought, seeing the dragon's underbelly. It was weaker there; not so vulnerable as the myths made out, but less armoured than its back and flanks for sure. Dragons needed to lose weight in order to fly, he knew, and the underside paid the price. *Lucky me.* He pointed the Windblade up at where he supposed the heart to be, put all his focus into the surge, all his power, all his strength, and fired himself right at it.

*Ten metres, eight, six, four...*He closed in fast. *Three...two...*

The dragon noticed at the very last moment, turning and falling into a sharp dive, swinging its long deadly tail as it dodged and fell away. Elyon was too committed to the attack, too close to draw back. The tail struck against his breastplate with a great clanging blow, careening him sideways across the sky. For a moment his vision blurred, the storm becoming a great swirling mass of muted grey. He lost control of the winds again, falling. Spots appeared before his eyes, blinking awake like stars in the night sky, and somewhere out there, behind, beneath, above him he couldn't tell, his foe gave out a shattering roar.

Focus, Elyon! Focus, damnit!

He blinked furiously, sucked in air, filled his lungs, and tried to summon the winds. They gave no answer. *Fly or die! Fly or die!*

The world slowly came back into view, the great grey blur parting into the shapes of clouds. He was face down and falling fast. Distantly, through a gap in the thick blanket of clouds, he could see something that resembled a forest, far below. Around it was farmland, a few snaking silver scars to indicate rills and rivers. There was the suggestion of a coastline too, further off.

I couldn't have reached the coast, he thought. *No way.* The lakes were more likely, but even then, those were seventy miles away.

The Windblade gave a gentle thrum in his grasp, as though telling him he was still there. *Right.* Elyon twisted his torso and turned onto his back. From the heavy black sky above the beast was coming, plunging at him like a bird of prey, jaws gaping, taloned feet grasping. Elyon thrust the Windblade to the side and this time it answered his call, pulling him beyond the dragon's reach. Another frustrated roar shook through the air, the beast opening its wings, slowing, swooping back around.

A pang of fatigue strummed through Elyon's body. He felt heavier all of a sudden, his strength fast on the wane. *That blow took it out of me.* It had felt like being run over by a broadback. He shook away the last few cobwebs of dizziness, watched the dragon coming toward him. *It moves so freely,* he thought, momentarily struck by the fierce beauty of the thing, with those scales of mottled brown and green, the blazing red eyes, the majesty of its form. He would tire long before the dragon did, he knew that well enough. *This is a beast born to the skies. I've only been adopted by them, and recently…*

His early bravado was wilting along with his stores of energy. *I am the storm,* he thought again, mocking. *No, I'm but a passing shower at most.*

A summer squall that children go out and play in, dancing and splashing in the puddles. This beast…this beast is storm and fire and steel all in one. There was thunder in its roar, fire in its gut, steel jutting from its mouth and feet and scales. *A beast of a thousand swords, born in armour, born to kill. And what am I? What?*

A champion, came a whisper. Elyon felt the winds grow fiercer around him, felt the blade in his grasp vibrate. It was a shard of Vandar's Heart, the greatest of all the gods, a relic of formidable power, forged to slay creatures like this. He gripped tighter, knuckles whitening. A prickle ran down his fingers, up his arm, through his body.

Static, he thought. He could feel it now, feel it in the air.

A tiny spark of electricity zapped suddenly off the edge of the blade.

Then another.

Then another.

The blade works through me, he realised. *I need only let it.*

He turned his eyes toward his foe. The dragon was nearing, wings set back, sharp and deadly as a ballista bolt. Flame flowed out through its teeth, crimson and gold. Elyon narrowed his eyes and began to raise the blade to the heavens. More sparks glittered off its edge, silver and blue.

Silver and blue, he thought. *For Vandar.*

He looked the beast right in the eye as it approached. *You do not belong here, spawn of Agarath,* he thought. He gave a heave, and swung the Windblade down in a flowing arc…and at that very second, from directly above, a great torrent of lightning came fizzing from the skies as the world exploded into an earsplitting crack. Deadly fingers reached down and entangled the beast in their grip. It lurched suddenly, wings and limbs shuddering, then began falling…falling… down…down…

Elyon watched as it dropped like a stone, tumbling straight through the breach in the clouds.

He gave chase.

The world opened out below, fields and pastures, woods and rivers and that lake…yes, it *was* a lake, stretching away to the edge of his sight. He could see a farmstead nearby, a herdsman tending his flock. The man seemed not to have seen the dragon plummeting insensate to the ground. It fell faster, faster, tail trailing like a fluttering banner, wings rippling, body tumbling out of control.

Elyon followed at a distance, praying it didn't wake up. *If it does…* He had no energy left in him now, nothing but those last few scraps of strength that would see him safely to the ground. *Don't fail me now,* he thought. *Not after this…*

The pursuit went on, five seconds more, ten. The dragon began to stretch a lead, plummeting in freefall, leaving wispy trails of smoke behind as it fell. Soon Elyon was a hundred metres behind, then two. The earth was rushing up, green and brown and wet. The shepherd was close, yet still unaware of their coming. For a moment Elyon thought the beast would land right atop him, and he opened his mouth to scream out in warning, yet his voice was swallowed by the wind and rain. *Ten seconds,* he thought. *Ten and it will hit.*

It was still turning, tumbling, smouldering. Eight seconds. At the edge of hearing, Elyon could sense the sound of sheep bleating in alarm. They had noticed the airborne drama first, alerting the shepherd, who finally looked up just in time as the dragon came crashing down into his field, thudding into the earth with a great resounding thump. At once the sheep bolted like a flock of starlings frightened from a bush. The man followed, stumbling away, slipping into the mud, scrambling to his feet, slipping again…

"Halt, friend," Elyon called out. "Halt…stop!"

The earth came up to greet him sharply. He summoned the last of his reserves, pushed back with a strong gust of wind, and slowed enough to land without snapping his spine. "Stop…stop!" he called. He managed to get to one knee. "Stop…you, stop! Come back!"

Eventually, the man seemed to hear something. Still scrambling away in terror, he turned his eyes backward in a glance, continued running the other way, then came to his senses and slowed. Elyon remained on one knee, breathing heavily. Even standing at this point…no, he didn't dare try, lest he lose consciousness. "You there… come…I need you to help me with something."

The shepherd made a tentative approach. Most of his sheep had run off for cover among the nearby trees, though a few of the hardier ones had stopped as well, turning to watch. Above, the storm was beginning to pass on now, moving away west as the rains began to weaken. "That were…that were *you*?" the man said. He was old, with a short scruffy grey beard, seamed wary eyes. His garb was mud-stained and worn; breeches, boots, layered wools, with a great hood over his head and a wooden staff in his hand. "That…that were *you?*" he asked again, glancing at the fallen beast. "You killed that… that…"

Elyon nodded from his knee. "Dragon. And yes, it was me," he said. "With a little help from the storm." *Or a lot.* The man didn't seem to know what to make of that. *He's in shock. Let's keep this simple for him.* "Would you be a good man and go and check if it's still alive."

He almost fell backward again. "*Me*? Check that…that…"

"Dragon," Elyon said. "Yes. Just head on over and see if it's chest is going up and down. Look for movement at the nostrils. That'll tell you if it's still breathing." *And if it is, we're going to have a big problem,* he thought, still considering the gargantuan task of getting off his knee.

"I…I'll not go near that thing. No way, no how."

"Do you know who I am?"

The old man peered at him. "You're…you're some Varin Knight, I figure, in that armour. And cloak."

Elyon made a great effort to stand so he might look the part. His plate was spattered with filth, cloak hanging dark and heavy. He gave the hilt of the Windblade a weary tap. "I'm Elyon Daecar, called prince in these lands. Bearer of the Windblade. Champion of Vandar." He sighed deeply. "Now please, don't make me ask you again. Go check that dragon for me."

The man hesitated. "Elyon Daecar." He studied him, nodding. "Aye, seems…seems you are." He turned tremulously toward the dragon, lying in a shallow crater some thirty metres away, the earth all churned and rutted around it. "Seems dragonslayin' runs in the family." He laughed nervously. "Well I'll…I guess I'll…"

"I'll be waiting right here," Elyon told him. "I just…I need a moment." He smiled such as he could to steady the man. "It's dead, don't worry. I just want to make sure."

"Aye." The man braced himself, looking at the crater, then stepped away.

The report came back a minute or so later, after the shepherd had done his checks. That minute was one of the longest of his life. *Be dead,* he prayed. *Please be dead. Please be dead…*

"It's dead," the shepherd confirmed, and Elyon could breathe again. "Tongue lolling out its mouth and everything." He shook his head and looked up. "This the world now is it, m'lord? Bladeborn fighting dragons up in my skies?"

"Not Bladeborn. Just me." Elyon took a few short paces toward the man to test his feet. He felt too weary to walk, let alone try to fly again. "Where are we, exactly?"

The herdsman frowned. "The Lakelands, m'lord. Up near the Big Sister." He gestured north. "That's her shore over yonder. Her southern shore, I should say. Fly far, did you?"

"Far enough." Dragon's Bane was about a hundred miles away, if the old farmer was telling it true. "I need to get back to Dragon's Bane at once. I saw a farm when I was coming down. That's yours?"

"Aye, tis mine. Just around that wood there, a quarter mile or so."

"You have horses?"

"Have a few. Not one to carry a Bladeborn though if that's what you're thinking. We don't breed those big ol' destriers here."

Elyon wasn't thinking that. "I'm in no fit state to ride." Even that would take energy he didn't have. "A wagon, though, will serve. You have a sturdy wagon, don't you? And...strong workhorses or oxen to pull it?" He was struggling to get the words out now. He felt like he was going to keel over at any moment.

The man frowned worriedly, sensing his utter exhaustion. "You can't fly, I suppose?"

"No. I need to rest...I..." He glanced toward the dragon, half-hidden in that muddy hollow. *What...what just happened? How did I...?* He shook his head, and took a breath. His thoughts were scattering again. "I may be able to fly by morning...but I'd rather...rather be closer to the Bane by then."

The herdsman gave an understanding nod. "Come, then, let's get you to the farm. If we drive all night, we'll be able to shave off a good chunk of that journey by sunrise."

Elyon smiled wearily. "You have my thanks, friend." He took a final look at his fallen foe as they set off. *Elyon Daecar, dragonslayer,* he thought. Something told him it wouldn't be the last.

33

Amilia

They are almost as ugly as he is, Amilia Lukar thought, as she looked upon her king husband's cousins. There were three of them, three who had come to the secret meeting, anyway. In total Hadrin had seven cousins, so far as Amilia knew; four by his Uncle Tayrin and three by his Auntie Nula, both of whom were long dead. But not the cousins. No, all lived on, and all hated Hadrin to his bones.

"Be welcome," said the oldest of them, a man by name of Sevrin. He was roughly Hadrin's age and Tayrin's eldest son. That made him their spokesman, their leader, and Hadrin's closest heir until he sired a child of his own. "Were you followed, Princess Amilia?"

Princess, she thought. *They do not accept me as their queen.* She was fine with that. She'd never wanted to be a queen to these people. "No, my lord. I don't believe so."

"We weren't," Sir Jeremy Gullimer declared confidently. "I made sure of it, Prince Sevrin. We came by the advised route."

Sevrin nodded and took a small sip of wine. He sat in an armchair, legs crossed, exuding an authority that Hadrin didn't possess. He had much of his king cousin's look, though; sparsely bearded cheeks and chin, narrow features reminiscent of a weasel, hair that had long since withered to a few loose wisps and strands. But for all that, he was the less uncomely of the pair. It was the best Amilia could say about him. "Do take a seat," he said, gesturing Amilia to a chair by the fire.

She sat, as Sir Jeremy stood aside, trying to look gallant. The other cousins were seated as well, to either side of Prince Sevrin. Jeremy had told Amilia all about them in preparation. To Sevrin's right sat Princess Cristin, his younger sister and fourth in line to the throne after Sevrin and his two children, both of whom were absent. Cristin was into her forty-eighth year and similarly rodenty as her older brother, with crazy unbrushed hair and an eccentric style of dress, all odd blends of colours and extravagantly dagged sleeves; far too much material for a woman so small.

To Sevrin's left was Prince Garyn, the eldest son of Nula, Hadrin's long-dead aunt. He was the better looking of the three, though hardly handsome. All the same, he had a bit more stoutness, a bit more strength in his frame, and his features weren't so squirrelly. He was on the plumper side, if anything, with a potbelly and round cheeks and a scar next to his left eye. His claim to the throne was so weak to be non-existent. It would take an absolutely calamitous series of deaths for him to ascend.

And all will drop down the ladder, as soon as I have a child of my own, Amilia thought, looking at the cousins warily. For that very reason she had worried about a trap, yet Jeremy had assured her all would be well. "I have met them," he told her some days ago. "They do not mean you harm, Amilia. It is only Hadrin they want removed."

But still, it was on their minds. Princess Cristin made that clear when she looked pointedly at Amilia's belly and asked, "How is your health, sweet child? Any nausea or fatigue? Any tenderness in the breast?"

Amilia shook her head at once. "I have no intention of birthing a child by your cousin," she told them. "I hope Sir Jeremy made that clear when he came to you?"

"Oh he did. But hearing it from your pretty lips is another matter." Cristin swooned a moment, holding her hands against her chest. "And what pretty lips they are. My, you really are as they say, Amilia. Such a rare beauty. And you'll want the same for any sons or daughters you may bear, won't you? Well..." She looked at her cousin and then to her brother. "Our family isn't the comeliest, as you may have noticed, though in truth we've never cared for that. The only one of us known for her looks was Auntie Atia, and look what happened to her, dying of tuberculosis when she was so very young. Or, at least that's what people think, anyway. Others claim she died whelping a child, but I suppose it would be improper to get into that now…"

"Yes, *very* improper," said Prince Sevrin. He gave his younger sister a scolding look. "I'm sure Amilia has little interest in our old family scandals."

Amilia had always had an interest in scandal, in all truth, though this wasn't one she was aware of. She knew little of Princess Atia, the fourth and youngest child of King Astan, but for her early death by consumption and notable good looks. People called her a rose in a bush of thorns, much more comely than her siblings Godrin, Tayrin, and Nula. It was even said that King Lorin, last of the Varin kings, had taken a liking to her when he came to spend time in Thalan forty years ago, and that was saying something, because Lorin was known to like his women, as much as he did his drinking and adventuring.

Enough to get him killed, Amilia thought. It was his spirit of adventure that had him facing that fearsome kraken out on the open seas, and some people thought he was probably drunk when he did it too.

But that talk of Princess Atia dying in childbirth? That was not a rumour Amilia had heard before.

Cristin cleared her throat, yielding to her older brother's withering stare. "Anyway, as I was saying," she went on. "We aren't a family famed for our beauty, but what does that matter? Those born so high as us are paired for our blood, not for our looks. You only have to look at you and Hadrin for that." She smiled through a pair of thin purple lips. "How old are you, sweety?"

"Twenty," Amilia told her.

The woman sighed. "Ah, twenty, so very young. What a curse to be wed to that creature three decades your senior. But it seems you have taken account of yourself well enough." She narrowed her eyes. "How can you be sure you are not with child?"

Sir Jeremy spoke up. "She takes a tonic, my lady. I buy it at market and smuggle it into the palace myself."

Princess Cristin ran her eyes up and down the young Emerald Guard. "Aren't you lucky to have such a loyal knight looking out for you, Amilia," she said. "And one so *dashing* too." There was a suggestion in her voice that Amilia didn't want to address.

"I will never get with child by Hadrin," she told the cousins again. "I swear it."

"So it seems, and most profusely." Cristin grinned. "You were betrothed to Aleron Daecar not so long ago, I understand. I can quite imagine what a horror it must be for you to swap a man like that for our horrid little cousin."

"I had no choice. My grandfather commanded it of me."

"Your grandfather is missing, did you know?" said Prince Garyn. He had most of his hair still, and less of a receding chin.

Amilia gave a nod in answer. She'd heard about her grandfather's disappearance during the riots in Ilithor from several sources now.

"Did you know he had the Mistblade?" Prince Sevrin wanted to know.

"No, my lord. He was very selective with whom he shared his counsel."

"Where do you think he is, sweety?" Cristin asked.

"I don't know, my lady."

"Dead, hopefully," grunted Garyn. "That'd put your brother Robbert on the throne."

"It would, my lord."

"Would he make a good ruler?" Sevrin asked her. "I've heard he's more alike to your father than your grandfather, in spirit. Do you think I could work with him?"

Amilia's nod was brisker this time. "Robbert would be a good king, as my father would have been. He is strong, but compassionate. He will try to improve relations between our kingdoms, I am sure of it."

Sevrin mulled on that for a few moments, nursing his cup of wine. He had a deliberate way about him, in his manner and movements. It was easy enough to see why his cousins had chosen to follow him into this planned coup. As far as Amilia had heard, he was well-liked, fair, and wise in the tradition of his forebears. "They say he's the king who should have been," Sir Jeremy had told her one night in his bed, when she'd gone to purge herself of Hadrin's clammy touch. "They say the gods made a mistake by making Hadrin Godrin's only son. They say Sevrin is the son King Godrin should have had. He is respected by highborn and lowborn alike, Amilia. He will help us, if we meet with him."

I hope so, Amilia had thought, and she thought it again now as she regarded the man in question. Sevrin did not seem a cruel man, nor peevish like her husband was, and these other cousins appeared perfectly reasonable too. A bit odd, yes, but reasonable. Amilia had taken the meeting on Jeremy's word that all would go well and, so far, he had come through. The only trouble had been getting Hadrin to let her leave the palace. That had taken almost a fortnight, but eventually he'd permitted her a stroll beyond the walls, so long as her guards were with her, and only if she remained among the safer, well-watched streets higher up in the city.

From there, Jeremy set about finding the best place for them to meet. That had taken another two days, but then, just yesterday, he'd brought her the news. "I have found somewhere," he'd whispered, as they walked the palace gardens. "There's a shop near the palace, the cousins tell me, owned by one of Prince Garyn's vassals. It sells women's fineries, but there's a way, through the back, that leads to a tunnel. The passage feeds into a network of quiet alleys. Down one is a winesink. The cousins will meet us there at midday."

It had all worked out. She had the rest of her Emerald Guards with her, though they were all waiting outside the shop while she 'tried on clothes'. "Stay here," she'd commanded them. "I may be a while. Sir Jeremy, come inside with me and make sure I'm not overly harassed by the seamstresses. They can grow awfully excited by royalty, in my experience."

Thankfully, Amilia was known to enjoy these outings, and there would be nothing unusual about her spending time sampling the silks and satins within the store. And now here she was, within this dark little winesink, plotting to overthrow a king.

Prince Sevrin withdrew from his musings. "Janilah may yet return, but if he does, will Ilithor accept him?" He swirled his cup. "No, is my instinct, after what he's become. The Warrior King's goodwill among highborn and low has long since dwindled and this crazed massacre we've been hearing about will be the last straw. If he rises again he will rise a tyrant, unmasked, an enemy to all. Either way, I will not deal with him once I take my cousin's crown. But Robbert, yes, I would be happy to work with."

Cristin leaned forward in her chair, plum lips crinkling into a smile. "He'll need a steady hand to help guide him. Someone who is already a good friend to Rasalan, and will work toward our mutual interests." Her grin turned sly. "You're a good friend to Rasalan, aren't you Amilia?"

Not particularly, Amilia thought, but to admit that wouldn't serve her. "I am," she said instead. "Thalan is a most beautiful city." *A city I hate. It is not home. I want to leave and never come back.*

"We think so," agreed Cristin, holding out her cup of wine. A man appeared from the gloom behind her to refill it. Amilia looked at him warily. "Oh, don't worry about him. Everyone here can be trusted."

"When Hadrin has been removed, we will send you back to Ilithor," Sevrin told her. "In exchange for this, we hope you will advise your brother well, on our behalf. War closes in on all sides. When we escape its shadow, we hope to find Tukor an ally moving forward. We'll have treaties signed, assurances that you'll not encroach on our lands again, or interfere in our trading operations with the south. That was your grandfather's bugbear. Long did he accuse us of piracy and privateering, when all the great lords of this land have done is make use of our seafaring power, and the trading routes we have established with the southern nations. I hope Robbert will show more foresight and fairness. We have been called craven by your people for too long. It stops now."

Amilia did not argue there. *If this is the price of going home, so be it.*

"And if Janilah returns to power, what then?" asked Prince Garyn. The question was for Sevrin. "He might kill her, Cuz."

"His own granddaughter? I think not."

"He killed his own son," Garyn said to that. He looked at Amilia. "That's what we've heard. Is it true? He slew your father?"

Her throat felt tight and dry all of a sudden. She'd wept most nights for her father here, as she had for poor Melany. Much was a mystery about it all. She opened her mouth to answer, but nothing came out.

"Poor dear is stricken with grief," said Cristin. She crept forward from her chair, drawing a handkerchief from one of a hundred pockets sewn into her dress. "Here, sweety. It's clean, don't worry. I always have a handkerchief or two on hand for moments such as these."

Amilia took it gratefully, and gave her nose a wipe. "I'm sorry, my lords, my lady. The wound is still fresh."

"I can imagine." Sevrin looked at his younger cousin disapprovingly. "I think the princess has suffered quite enough to have to deal with your insensitive interrogations, Garyn."

"I only mean to prove precedent, Cuz. If Janilah killed his son, why not his granddaughter? Might be a mistake sending her back to Ilithor."

"She can come with me to my father's lands," said Sir Jeremy, far too enthusiastically. "I will keep her safe there until we're certain that King Janilah is finished."

Sevrin rubbed his narrow chin. "We can decide on that later, pending the latest tidings." He waved over a servant. "Fill the princess a cup of wine. She looks like she needs one."

Amilia took the cup gratefully. She hated how weak-spirited she'd become here. *I am a shadow of myself. I have grown timorous and uncertain.* A good gulp of wine helped fortify her somewhat. "Thank you, Prince Sevrin. I was told you were a kind man."

"Kind and fair, yes, but not afraid to be ruthless when the time calls for it. Your husband murdered his father, this you know. He thought no one would find out, that we would believe his word that Godrin died of heart failure. That having the good word of Sir Munroe Moore to back him up would be enough. Well it isn't. Hadrin will die and Sir Munroe will follow. But the timing must be right." He waved to the shadows. "Sir Karsten, bring it over."

Sir Karsten stepped over from the door. Amilia did not know him or his house, but it was obvious he was Bladeborn. Beneath his cloak he wore a glittery mail brigandine, and was well armed with broadsword and dagger. Sir Jeremy regarded him cautiously. *My sweet protector,* Amilia thought, *always sizing up the competition.*

The knight reached into his cloak and passed a small vial to his prince. Sevrin held it up. "Do you know what this is?"

Amilia did not hesitate. "Poison."

"Yes. Poison. And a rare one. We Rasals are good at distilling them, as I'm sure you're aware. We all must use the gifts the gods have given us, don't you think? Sir Karsten here was gifted with the ability to bear godsteel and bear it well, much as your Sir Jeremy was. We Seaborn have access to the bounties Rasalan hid beneath the waves, and have long used them to our advantage. Like this." He gave the vial a little shake. "We want you to kill your husband for us."

Amilia knew that was coming, but all the same, something inside her screamed a warning. "I can't," she said on instinct. "I'll be caught as soon as I…"

"The timing must be right," interrupted Prince Sevrin, choosing not to hear her. "You need but slip this into Hadrin's drink at the opportune moment, and the rest will be taken care of. The poison has a delayed effect; this is its unique function. It will linger in Hadrin's blood for two days, lying in wait. He will not know. It is tasteless, colourless. Add it to his wine or water and your job will be done. Exactly two days later, he will die suddenly and painfully. Of heart failure." He smiled. "We thought there was some poetry in that."

Cristin gave out a wicked laugh. She looked quite manic in the light of the fire with that crazed bush of wiry grey hair, shooting off her head in all directions. *There is something of the witch about this woman,* Amilia thought. "We all wanted to kill him slower than that, but Sevrin is smarter than the rest of us, and said no. Maybe that's why he'll make a good king, who knows?"

"A red smile from ear to ear," growled Garyn. "That's what he gave his father, so that's what he should get himself."

There would be some poetry in that as well, Amilia supposed, but a severed throat was hardly a slow end. "I want him to die slow as well," she said, teeth clenched. She took another gulp of wine, thinking of all those times the creature had crawled between her legs. Her excuses were growing thin now and he was starting to get more forceful. *Too forceful,* she thought, closing a fist. *'No' means nothing to him now.* "What will happen once he's dead?"

Sevrin gave answer. "We'll have our forces ready to storm the palace. As soon as Hadrin's heart gives out, most of his men will surrender quickly enough. Only those loyal to him with give any fight and we don't imagine there are many of those."

"It'll be a walkover," cackled Princess Cristin. "Hadrin was always friendless. People tolerated him for his father's sake, but after what he did....gods no. No one will quibble when he's dead, Amilia, so don't let the notion of king-killing concern you. This will be no stain on your soul, sweety. It'll be a good thing you'll do. A good thing. Remember that."

Amilia nodded. Regicide wasn't a crime she ever expected to commit, but here she was. *If it buys my freedom, so be it.* "I want him dead as much as the rest of you," she said.

"Then he must be as poor a husband as he is a man and a king," said Sevrin. "We will work with Sir Jeremy, and he'll tell you when the time is right. It would be best if Hadrin died in a public setting. It will appear natural to anyone without knowledge of our plot. We'll arrive shortly after, as I say."

Then it won't appear completely natural, Amilia thought, but didn't say. How convenient that Sevrin's host should be gathered at the palace doors the moment the king perished. She shrugged that away. *Kill him, and I'm free,* she thought. That was good enough for her.

Sir Jeremy took a step closer to them. "What about Sir Munroe?" he asked. "Will he not try to fight?"

"Sir Munroe was Captain of the King's Guard under Godrin," Prince Sevrin said, "yet he stood aside as Hadrin cut open his father's neck. He proved himself irredeemable that day. When Hadrin falls, Sir Munroe will no doubt seek to continue in his capacity of Captain of the Guard for me. He'll claim innocence over all former wrongs and seek to slide into my good graces. I may even permit him the fantasy for a time, if only to see the look in his eye when I pull the rug from under him." He drank his wine. His eyes were small and dark in that gloomy little room. "Hadrin will not die slow, regrettably, but Sir Munroe will give us a chance to put that right. I will make an example of him, for all of Rasalan to see. I want all of my kingdom to know what happens to traitors under my rule."

I like this man, Amilia realised. There had been far too much treachery of late and Sevrin, when king, would seek to draw a line under it all.

A short silence took root, long enough for Sir Jeremy to slip forward again and beckon their attention. "We ought to be leaving, my lords, my lady. The others may grow suspicious if we're absent too long."

"Then they don't know women," said the crone princess. "We can spend hours trying on clothes."

"Even so, my lady. It would be best not to risk it."

Amilia agreed, and decided to take to her feet, placing her cup aside. "The other Emerald Guards in my personal escort are not so understanding as Sir Jeremy," she informed them. "If they hear of what I've been doing, they may report it to my grandfather."

"How? If he's missing?" asked Garyn.

Amilia wasn't sure how to answer that.

"You may go, of course." Sevrin stood as well, showing his lack of height. He was very short in stature, though not in spirit. The same had always been said of his uncle, King Godrin. He stepped toward her and gave a polite bow. "At another time, with another man, you would have made us a fine queen," he told her. "Alas it isn't to be, lest I discard my lady wife for you." He teased a smile, but there was no lecherousness in the jest. Amilia even laughed, which was most rare these days. "Perhaps my son will suit you, however. Once he is prince and heir he will make an excellent match."

Amilia saw that both Cristin and Garyn were nodding. She didn't much like where this was going. *Is this another part of our bargain?* she wondered. *Must I give my hand away again to buy my passage home?*

Prince Sevrin seemed to sense her disquiet. "But of course, that will be for you to decide. I am sure the last thing you want is another old man deciding who you're to wed. That is not my place. But for what it's worth, my son does break the mould somewhat. He is not so terribly uncomely as the rest of us, if that is of importance to you."

Amilia felt shallow for admitting it to herself, but of course it did, and always had. She had always valued beauty in her bedding partners, and Sir Jeremy was merely the latest. Handsome knights and sons of lords and even charming baseborn servants had all had the pleasure of her bed. *And Hadrin believed I was a maiden,* she thought. *What a thunderous fool he is.* In truth, she could not recall how many lovers she'd had. Forty, at least, perhaps double that, and every one of them was beautiful. *So I enjoy a sculpted torso and square jaw and a man to be tall and strong. So what.*

"I would be honoured to meet him," she told Prince Sevrin. "Perhaps before I leave the city, I might have that pleasure?"

Sevrin smiled. "I shall see it arranged, once my cousin has been unseated." He looked to the door that gave passage into the alleyway, gave a nod, and Sir Karsten opened it. "We shall not see you again, Princess Amilia, not until this thing is done." He took her hand and kissed the back of her palm. "Good luck to you, and godspeed. Sir Jeremy, see her safely returned to the palace." He reached out with the vial between his fingers. "And don't forget this."

They left the way they'd come, walking through the twisting alleys, making for the secret door that gave access to the finery shop. Smoke drifted from the back of a bakery, and further off, Amilia could smell the scent of roasting meat, and the din of one of the squares, beyond the maze of lanes.

Sir Jeremy had gone quiet. "Is something wrong, Jeremy?" she asked him.

They entered a snaking passage, narrow and close. Sir Jeremy stopped suddenly and turned to her, pressing her up against the grimy wall. Without warning, his hand reached straight through her cloak, plunging down and groping.

"What are you *doing*? Jeremy, stop…" She tried to push him away.

"I want you, Amilia. There's no one here."

"No…stop…"

"I can't," he panted. "I can't resist you…"

"Jeremy, no. I said no!" She freed an arm from his fumblings and slapped him hard across the cheek, turning his head aside. "Don't you *ever* touch me without my consent. Ever!" She had to restrain her voice, but all the same, the words came out hot and fiery.

"But, I…I thought…"

"What did you think? What!"

He looked a child suddenly, a boy being reprimanded by his mother. "I…we're alone. And you were grinning. I thought you'd find it exciting."

"You think I'd find it exciting? To let you take me here in the middle of the street?"

"It's an alley, Amilia. There's no one around."

She looked at him in utter bewilderment. "What is wrong with you? We've just discussed the murder of a king and you think I want *that*."

"You always want *that*. You come to my room for it every night. And not just me."

"What does that mean?" She shoved him hard, so hard he stumbled to the opposite wall of the alley. "What!"

"It means…it means you've had lots of men. The others speak about it. Some would guard your room back in Ilithor and see you sneaking out at night. Some are even beginning to suspect *us*, Amilia."

"Well, I'd best stop coming to you, then."

"*No*," he breathed. "No, you can't." He stepped in. "I love you. I'd do anything for you."

"You don't love me, Jeremy. You mistake lust for love. You don't know what love is."

"And you do?"

"Yes. I loved Aleron."

The name seemed to spark something in him. "Why?" he said, far too loudly. "Because he was heir to a greathouse, unlike me? Is that why you'll go and marry Prince Sevrin's son as well? Because he's to be a prince and heir to a throne? Is that all you hunger for, Amilia? Power. To be worshipped and adored."

She had no idea what to make of all that. "I'm not going to marry Sevrin's son, Jeremy."

"You said you'd meet him! You said you would, just now. Why would you say that? I love you, Amilia. Can't you see how much that hurts me?"

A voice inside her called for caution. She had known men to grow obsessed with her, and Sir Jeremy Gullimer was showing those signs in great abundance. *I cannot lose him. He's all I've got.* She reached out and placed a hand on his upper arm, squeezing gently. "Jeremy…you need fear nothing," she told him. "Did you *see* Sevrin and the others? I'm not going to marry his son, believe me. I don't want anything to do with Rasalan or Seaborn lords and their heirs anymore. I want to go home. *Home*, Jeremy. I want to help my brother rule. I want to be good. I want to love and be loved and be happy, and…and…"

And suddenly she was crying, and Jeremy Gullimer's face was breaking in sympathy, and he was rushing forward and taking her into his strong protective arms and stroking her hair as he held her tight. Amilia could feel the vial of poison in his inner cloak pocket, pressing against her chest.

A woman's weapon, she thought, smiling even as she sniffed and sobbed. *Poison…*

…and tears.

34

Saska

She could see the mass of ships, huddled in a great forest of masts and sails off the eastern coast. There were hundreds, many of them great bulky galleons swaying drunkenly on the restless waters. The sails showed their colours and crests. Saska saw the Gershan snake and hill, the birds and sky of Swallow, Huffort's kneeling knight and falling rocks, the Gullimer orchard of apples, and more. All were houses she knew well, houses out of North Tukor.

And one most of all.

House Kastor's bear print, she thought, glaring at the many ships that bore the mark. She had known already that the army sieging Eagle's Perch was led by Cedrik Kastor, but all the same, seeing that sigil again brought it all back. The years of abuse and threats and humiliations. The dreaded darkness of her cell, and the hunger, and the whippings.

She tightened her grip around Joy's reins as the starcat slinked gracefully along the Capital Road. To her side rode Lord Elio Krator upon his fearsome sunwolf Braccaro, looking boldly toward the ships clotting the distant shore. *He is no better,* she thought hatefully, looking up at him through the slit in her burnoose. *Kastor…Krator…it makes no matter. I'd gladly slit open both of their bellies and watch their guts steam out.*

She glanced back down the Capital Road, at the huge great snaking column that bled away into the distance. She could not see the end of the train, vast as it was. First came Lord Krator's vanguard, the Lightborn riders on their wolves and cats and the best of the Aramatian paladins riding their great monstrous horses and camels, barded all in armour in shades of copper and silver and gold.

Behind them was the bulk of the cavalry, some thousands of them, followed by many thousands more foot soldiers and archers and spearmen, well trained and disciplined, marching ceaseless beneath the sun. After that was the baggage train, with the pavilions and provisions all packed up in carts, and the rearguard behind, comprising more men-at-arms and camelriders and cavalrymen, and plenty more foot soldiers too.

Finally, some way behind, were the camp followers, and how many of those there were Saska couldn't hope to guess. They made their camp each night nearby to the main army, looking to profit from its advance. Many were selling something - food, armour, alcohol, themselves - but many others were the families of the soldiers as well. Saska wished she could slink off and join them, lose herself amongst them perhaps, and somehow find her way back to Aram. But any time she considered it long enough, she realised how futile it would be.

I tried going on the run once, she thought. *Back when I killed Lord Quintan. I ran and ran and ran and ran and still, I got caught.*

The day was warm, despite the sea breeze, and warmer still for the garb Saska wore. Ever since that poor lookalike girl had been killed in the riot at the roadside market, Saska had been forced to travel in cloak and burnoose to hide herself. She was being presented as she had been at the Red Pits, as one of Lord Krator's concubines. And soon enough that facade would become a reality, she feared.

The coastline began to climb as they rode on, cliffs forming on their right as they progressed along the immense headland. At the end of it, Eagle's Perch could just about be sighted now, its great walls no more than a shimmering sandstone blur far off in the distance. Outside those walls, Cedrik Kastor and his army were camped, dug in and fortified and awaiting their advance. It was of a matter of great amusement to Lord Elio Krator that his rival had not managed to breach the Perch thus far. "This Kastor is weak," he had said that morning, as they'd mounted for the final march. "When he sees us coming over the horizon, he will flee, I have no doubt."

You don't know Cedrik Kastor like I do, Saska had wanted to say. He was prideful, vain, and even more in love with himself than Lord Elio was, if that was possible. To go running to his ships and return to the north empty-handed was not an option. *He will stay, and he will fight. And I'll stand by, watching, wondering which of you I want dead more.*

Gradually, the Tukoran army came into view, an immense sprawl of colour laid out in canvas just outside the fortress city. If they were planning to withdraw to their ships, they were leaving it rather late.

"It looks like they intend to stay, my lord," said Mar Malaan.

"Yes, it does." Elio Krator's voice was thick with displeasure. "So be it. I will have to crush them all. Mar, ride ahead, make sure we aren't in for any surprises. And find a good place to erect the encampment. We may be here a while."

"At once, my lord." Mar Malaan gave Taro a little tap of his heel and the sunwolf loped away, along with several more of Malaan's Sunriders.

Krator continued to stare straight forward. "Tell me of this Cedrik Kastor," he said, without deigning to give her so much as a glance. "What sort of man is he?"

Now you ask? she thought. *Oh yes, you were hoping he'd flee.* She took a moment to think of what to say. "He's…determined," she said after a time. "Cedrik Kastor has a hatred for southerners that is hard to quantify. He is well known as one of the finest swordsmen in Tukor, and the north at large. People say he was born to kill."

Krator laughed contemptuously. "I'm sure. What of his strategic mind? Is he an astute battle commander?" He gave a smug huff. "I would think not, to see his failing here. A more assertive man would have broken the Perch by now."

"Unless he wanted to draw you here," Saska offered.

Lord Krator pursed his lips. "An interesting thought. He wants the battle, you think?"

Saska didn't know what to think. She was just saying whatever came to mind, in truth. "It would weaken Aramatia substantially if you were routed. Eagle's Perch is only a foothold. If he could destroy your army, he'd be able to march to Aram all but unopposed."

"All true," Krator conceded. "But if he thinks he will rout us, he must think again. We have the high ground, so to speak. If we suffer great losses, we can call the retreat, and come again. But he is caught between my army and the fortress walls. He has nowhere to go but back to his ships."

Saska chewed on that a moment. "How many men are there? In the fortress?"

Lord Elio smiled at the question. "You wonder if they might

attack from sally ports by night? That we could push the assault from two flanks?"

"The thought occurred to me."

"And it's a good one. And sure to have occurred to this Cedrik Kastor as well. He will have the fortress well watched at all times. And he must have, for he cannot know the true strength within, can he?"

"So there are lots of soldiers there? You're trying to lure him into a trap?"

"Is it a trap if you can see it coming? No. So long as he *thinks* the fortress is well stocked with men, that is enough. It will force him to split his attention, forward and back. Eventually the stress will overwhelm him and he will either charge to his death, or flee to his ships, as we harry him all the way. Either way, the victory will be mine."

Saska had to remind herself that Elio Krator had won many victories in the last war, and was widely respected for his battle prowess. It was said that the force of Braccaro's bite could crush godsteel and his claws could scythe through gorgets like butter. *And if he and his Sunriders charge, with heavy camel and horse and a host of Starriders in support?* She was not sure who would come out top in such a fight, the Lightborn or the Bladeborn, of which Cedrik Kastor was sure to have many in his ranks; Emerald Guards and lesser household Bladeborn and sellswords and perhaps some Suncoats too.

"We shall dine together tonight," Lord Krator was going on, "once the camp has been erected, and you are bathed. I think we can forgo the leeching this evening as well." He nodded to that notion. "Yes. You have been well behaved since we passed Cloaklake. I see the light in you, Saska, more and more. Your time with Joy has brought it out, as hoped, and the leeching treatment has worked as Mhazem said it would." He looked down at her, staring through the slit in her burnoose. "Do you not think?"

She was thankful for the silken mask. "I do, my lord. Very much so."

He stared at her in that way of his, cold gold eyes unblinking. She could not read this man. *Does he believe me? Is this all some big trick and trap?* All she could do was play her part and hope he let down his guard. Eventually, he moved his eyes away, saying not a word.

The camp was to be raised several miles south of the fortress, upon a broad stretch of open, flattened grassland. To the south and west hills rose up, craggy and clothed in cypress and beech. Saska saw the old bones of villages out there, blackened and destroyed, thin fingers of smoke still swirling up from some. The Tukorans had been razing the lands south of the Perch for weeks, she knew, raiding and plundering, killing the men, raping the women.

It was the same in Rasalan, she thought. *Cedrik Kastor had let his dogs ravage the Lowplains there too.* She remembered passing several ruined villages with Lady Marian and her men, Roark and Braddin and Quilter and Lark, all rank with the scent of death. At one they'd met a sea cleric called Father Pennifor, she recalled, who let them stay the night in the rectory once they'd helped gather and cremate the bodies of the villagers. There was a boy called Mattius who'd been slung up in a tree and used for target practice. *He was only fourteen,* she thought. *And those bastards used him for sport.*

As ever, Lord Krator made sure that his own personal pavilions were erected in the finest location. "There is a suitable rise, my lord," Mar Malaan announced, as soon as he retuned from his recce. "It will serve for your command headquarters. We can build the encampment around it. I shall have men digging ditches and setting security lines at once."

"Very good, Mar. What of the Tukoran defences? Do they make any move to strike camp and leave?"

"No, my lord, they are well dug in. My best scouts have reported severe damage to the eastern wall of the Perch. These Tukorans have many siege weapons. They have brought down several towers, and the main gate has begun to falter. It will not be long before they smash their way through."

"Then we have come at the right time." Krator searched forward through the fading daylight. "You are certain of the range of their siege weapons?"

"I am, my lord. Their trebuchets shall not be able to reach us, not here. We can unpack our own over there." He pointed north, where the land rose a little higher toward the front of the planned encampment. "It should deter them from trying to shift their camp further south, toward us."

Lord Krator nodded in agreement. "I would like to meet this Cedrik Kastor," he said. "Send an envoy, Mar, so I may get the measure of him."

"At once, Sunlord Krator."

A question came to Saska's mind. "Do you follow the tradition of Battle by Champion here?" she asked.

Sunlord and Sunrider looked at her.

"It's…it's when the leaders of the opposing armies fight in single combat. The victor claims the battle and the loser…."

"Dies," broke in Elio Krator. He looked at her like she was utterly witless. "No, we do not follow this tradition here, and nor has it been practiced in the north for over a thousand years. Which you know, I am sure."

She shook her head, all innocent.

"It is a foolish practice," Krator went on, "only appealing to the weaker army with the stronger champion. A wise commander does not bet the outcome of a battle upon the swing of a blade or bite of a beast. Would I defeat this Cedrik Kastor? Most likely, yes, but it would be reckless of me to to risk it."

Craven, Saska thought. But all she said was, "I think you would too. Defeat him, I mean."

"I'm sure you do." Krator did not bother looking at her. "But either way, it will not happen. Not unless we meet on the field."

If Saska was alone, she might have put her hands together and prayed for that to happen. Just the thought of it was enough to make her exultant. She could imagine it, Cedrik Kastor all layered in misting steel, Elio Krator charging and leaping and lunging atop Braccaro, with those lethal claws and fangs. *Imagine if they killed one another.* She had to stop herself grinning openly at that thought - even behind her burnoose, Krator might see the laughter in her eyes. But there was a part of her that would be disappointed to hear of it too. *How can I kill them myself if they kill each other? I want to be the one to shut their eyes. Me. Not them. Me.*

As ever, the camp took time to pitch. Elio Krator decided to use it scouting out the enemy himself. "I would like to take a closer look at this enemy camp," he said, as his command pavilion was raised. "Mar, come along. Saska, you may wander, if you please, so long as Balza and Hiram go with you. And leave Joy with Yasha. The cat is to stay right here."

She'd expected that. *He still worries I'll try to run off.* She dismounted from Joy, handing the glittering starcat into old Yasha's care as Krator and Mar Malaan rode away upon their wolves. It was growing dusky now, the skies pretty and purple and pink. Saska wanted to get a closer look at the front; she made her way through the camp as the tents and pavilions were thrown up, the doltish moron Balza and dead-eyed Hiram going with her. Hiram was another of the guards who'd been brought from Elio Krator's Aram estate, the old one who'd made Saska most uncomfortable at first. He never spoke, and never seemed to blink either. She'd learned to just ignore him.

It was harder to ignore Balza, though. He always had a comment for her, some crude remark when he knew Lord Elio wasn't listening. He followed close behind as she wandered through the sea of working men, trying to get a sniff of her, whispering insults in her ear. "Lord Krator's going to let me have you soon, whore," he rasped. "My reward, for breaking you. You're such a good little girl now, aren't you?" She could smell his hot rancid breath as he laughed.

"Don't you ever tire of being *you*, Balza?" she asked. His threats were supposed to frighten her, but she had started to find them more amusing than anything else. *To think Krator would let that festering sack of pig-shit have me.* It was comical, really.

"I like being me," the man said, all droopy witless eyes and fleshy sloping shoulders. "I get to watch you all day. When you're leeched, I like that. But it's better when they wash you and oil you. Yes. That's the best time."

She yawned audibly. "So long as you look and don't touch." She knew he never really saw her. Yasha would never allow it.

"I do look. I look *hard*. But I'll do more than look when the sunlord gives you to me. My reward, for…"

"Breaking me, you said." She walked briskly away from him, getting a view through the rising tents and pavilions at Eagle's Perch, still some way in the distance. She couldn't see much from here but the tall thick walls and towers, the immense gate, and the great blanket of northerners encamped outside. *My people,* she thought bitterly. *My people as much as these are.*

"You're a whore."

Saska sighed deeply. The voice was right behind her, a whisper for only her to hear. "No, I'm really not."

"You are. You are of the north. Bladeborn. That is poison blood. Cursed blood. Lord Krator will never love you. *Whore*."

"He loved my mother. Why not me?"

"Because she was pure. And beautiful, more than you. You're a northern whore. That will never change."

"Lord Elio thinks it will. And he's right. The leeching is working wonderfully, Balza." She turned to him, and then swapped seamlessly from the common tongue to Aramatian. "I'm not Bladeborn anymore. I'm Lightborn, pure-blood. I will love and wed Lord Elio Krator and he will love and wed me. For a wedding gift, I will ask him...what do you think I will ask him, Balza?"

The man stared at her blankly, mouth half agape. "You can speak...you can..."

"What do you think I will ask him, Balza?" The pig knew nothing of her grasp of his tongue, clearly. "*What*?" When he gave no answer, she smiled and leaned in and said in a dark voice, "Your head," before turning away.

Balza did not approach her again as she continued her walk, looking out over the darkening plains, spotting the bones of blackened villages in the distance, burned and abandoned. She so missed the presence of godsteel at these times, enhancing her sight and hearing and touch. The world felt shrouded without it, as though her head was constantly foggy from a fall. She wondered what had become of her dagger, the one that Sir Ralston had given her, who'd been given it himself by King Godrin before he died. There was something important in that, she thought. The blade was a wonder, the steel a pale shimmering blue, the hilt and pommel inlaid with intricate symbols she couldn't translate, lit a deep silver. *Silver and blue.* Did that mean something? Might those symbols be some sort of message, or command, or instruction? She didn't know, nor had the Wall. Saska had wondered whether someone like Ranulf Shackton might be able to translate those glyphs, but he was a world away so far as she knew.

She sighed as she walked on. Sir Ralston's fate was still unknown to her, though she had started to wonder if he had survived after all. *Someone must have told Lord Hasham about me,* she thought. *Why else would he have sent men so far to find me?* Those men were gone now, though, riding back to Aram in a thunder of angry hooves. *They came to fetch me back, and only got a corpse.* That corpse belonged to the lookalike, but how were they to know? The girl looked so much like her. And now she was dead, caught up in that riot during the changeover, that she had no doubt Elio Krator had planned.

"No one will come for you, Saska," Krator had said that night, once he returned to her tent. "They think you dead, and have returned to Aram." He'd wiped a fleck of blood from his cheek. "You think they will see through the lie? No, they will not. Some of my own men died, and some of Hasham's men too. And the camp followers, yes, many of those as well. In all that death, yours will look an accident, nothing more." He'd walked over to her dresser and found her burnoose then. "You will wear this from now on, Saska. It is time for you to submit to your fate."

My fate, she thought now, kicking a stone as she walked. Her fate was not to bed Lord Krator nor bear his children. *I am meant for something else. Something greater.* She had played along all the same, submitting such as she could. Biding her time was the only way. *And now?* She had a final look over the blackened plains, and the fortress beyond, and the Tukoran camp there in between, glowing now in places as the cookfires and pit-fires and perimeter torches were lit. She wondered, for a brief moment, if she might try to sneak across. *Would it be better there, or here? Will they hear my northern voice and take me in?*

She wasn't going to delude herself of that. *If they find out who I am, it will go even worse for me there,* she did not doubt. No, the only way was back the way she'd come. *To Aram. To Lord Hasham and Sir Ralston and my grandmother, if she is there. Somehow, I have to find a way. Fate. It's my fate.*

When she got back to her pavilion, her bath was already full and steaming, the surface of the water decorated in flower petals and little sprigs of lavender. Joy got straight to her feet as she reappeared, loping straight over to nuzzle. *Two hearts, beating as one,* Saska thought. Her bond to the cat was beyond explanation now, like nothing she could have understood without experiencing it herself. It was different from her blood-bond to godsteel. That was a want, perhaps even a need. There was a drug-like quality to bearing the metal; it made you feel stronger, faster, more confident, more deadly, yet with Joy, the bond was deeper. Beyond even love, it felt like the cat was a part of her now. That if she should die, a part of Saska would die too, darkening forever. *Like losing a child of your own flesh and blood,* she knew. And that was a frightening thought.

"She grows anxious when you are gone," Yasha told her. The other girls, Milla and Koya, were still putting the furnishings into place, setting up the bed and dresser, the rugs and cushions that they would sleep on each night. "She worries something will happen, I think."

Saska rubbed Joy behind the ear. Her purr was especially loud right now, rumbling through the tent. Milla giggled from a full ten metres away. "I can feel her, vibrating in me. It tickles." Koya laughed too, though more demurely.

"She senses your agitation," Yasha went on. "Is it strange, to see your people out there?"

"They're not my people anymore." Saska walked toward the bath, removing her clothes as she went. "I'm not sure they ever were." She slipped straight into the steaming waters. Yasha followed, fetching a scourer to scrub at her skin.

"You do not believe this," the old woman said. "You are not fully northern, no, as you are not fully southern. You are more and better. Light *and* steel. You are a woman of the world."

"I'd prefer to have been one or the other," Saska admitted. She drew deep on the scent of lavender to try to relax, letting Yasha rub at her back. The water was the perfect temperature; her maids knew well enough how to manage her now. Yet for all that, and however much she liked them, she still had to be wary. Yasha and Milla and Koya were sweet and kind and seemed to have her best interests at heart, but at the end of the day, they were Krator's, not hers. *And if I reveal too much...will they tell him?* She had even wondered about asking them to help her escape, but hadn't thought on it long. *No. Even if they were to help me, it would put them in grave danger. Krator would have every one of them killed. If I'm to do this, I'll do it alone.*

Milla came over, handing Yasha a cloth. "How long do you think we'll be here, my lady?"

Saska wasn't sure how to answer. "I'm not a soldier, Milla. I don't know much about battle strategy."

"But you know the Tukorans. And you know Bladeborn. You are Bladeborn too."

"I...I was." Saska thought it best to keep her story straight on that. If she was going to lie about it all to Balza, she had to continue with her maids. "The leeching..."

"No," cut in Yasha at once. "No, this leeching does nothing. You know this really, though perhaps you are too afraid to say it. I am afraid too. Otherwise I would call Lord Elio a fool to his face, for believing it."

Milla gasped.

"Do not act surprised, Milla," Yasha reprimanded. "We all have our complaints. But here together, we speak in confidence, do we not? Nothing we say to one another is to be shared."

The dark beauty Koya agreed from across the room. "We have to trust one another. We are women. It is different."

Yasha nodded and continued to wipe at Saska's skin, moving the softer cloth across her back. "This leeching is a means of control. I do not like how Lord Elio tries to control you, Saska. It is not right. You are granddaughter to Her Serenity. She who is above us all."

Saska said nothing. *This could be a trap,* she thought. Instinct said it wasn't, but she couldn't be sure.

"I would not mind being controlled by the sunlord," grinned Milla, showing that cute gap between her teeth. "He is very handsome. And I would prefer to be the one in the bath, not outside it."

"Lord Krator is old enough to be your grandfather, Milla," Yasha scolded. She gave the girl a sharp look to shut her up, then said, "Tip your head back, Saska. I will wash your hair." As she began rubbing in the lotion, Milla took up a ladle and poured water through Saska's locks. "You *are* Bladeborn, and will be, always," Yasha went on. "As you will always be Lightborn. Lord Elio should embrace this, not condemn it. You are special. He sees it, otherwise he would not keep you. But it is the mix that makes you special. The mix of blood in you. And power."

I am Seaborn too, Saska thought, though she kept quiet once more. She still had the piece of coral that had called to her, the one Old Hob had read, though Lord Krator knew nothing of its meaning. The Seaborn was on her father's side, and the Bladeborn too, yet her father had been nothing but a servant and slave, who Lord Elio said raped her mother, seeding Saska in her womb. *He was royal as well,* she thought. *That's what Old Hob told me.* Nothing about that story added up. *And the answers…they're back in Aram.*

Saska lay back as her hair was washed, Milla pouring, Yasha massaging, Koya pottering about across the room. After a time, Milla said, "It is said the Tukoran prince is dead. The son of the Warrior King. Is this true, my lady? Did Lord Elio say anything of this?"

Saska nodded, steam rising about her face. "A scout found out from a survivor at one of those burned-out villages we passed." The man had hidden in a cubbyhole as the Tukorans raided his shack, and overheard the soldiers speaking about Prince Rylian's death. He understood enough of the common tongue of the north to hear that Rylian was slain and his father the slayer.

"He was a great warrior," Yasha said solemnly. Clearly she'd heard this as well. "This Rylian Lukar slew a dragon, girls," she said to the maids. "I think Lord Elio must be thankful he is not here. If he can kill a dragon…" She left the rest unsaid.

"It was at the big battle, this dragon-killing," said Koya. "The end battle." She seemed to be searching for the right words. "The one where Vallath was killed, by the Crippler."

"The Burning Battle at the Rock," said Milla.

"The Battle of Burning Rock," Saska corrected.

Milla blushed to have gotten it wrong.

"A simple mistranslation," Yasha said, to spare her. "We do not use this name, my lady."

Saska sat up a little in the bath, water running down her shoulders. "What do you call it?" she asked.

"Most call it the Day of Death," Yasha told her. "Aramatians, Lumarans, Piseki, Solapians…many were lost that day. Many think it the bloodiest battle that has ever been. It is why we forged the empire, after. We did not want to repeat this again. No. We wanted to live our lives in peace."

Saska nodded sadly. She'd read much about the forging of the Lumaran Empire following the War of the Continents, though it was only the latest of many empires to have arisen through the millennia. *When I shared a tent with Elyon,* she remembered. That had been another warcamp, not unlike this one, when they'd been sieging the fortress of Harrowmoor. *I was on the Tukoran side then, as a captive. And now I find myself here, a captive still.* It was a strange thought really. Her life had taken so many unexpected turns.

She pulled away from Yasha, turning to face her in her small copper bath. "Do you believe this is the Last Renewal? That the War Eternal will end…and we'll all come to a longstanding peace?"

Koya stopped in their tidying and looked over. Milla shook her head. "The Ever-War will not end," she said. "It will last until the ending of time. But there will be no more Renewals. Because there will be no one to fight them. No kingdoms and countries. People will live for themselves, and their families, and their friends, and that is all. They will fight to survive, when the monsters rise."

Koya nodded darkly. "Yes, this is how it will be. When the Wings broke open and the thousand dragons flew out, they started it. It is the Last Renewal, yes, but it will not end in peace. All the world will fall to ruin. This is foretold."

"By who?" Saska asked.

"Many," said Koya.

"Many," agreed Milla.

They did that often, agreeing with one another, though rarely did they give specifics. "How many?"

"All things are repeated when enough time has passed," Yasha said sagely. "The sun wheels overhead once every day. And every year, we see the seasons change. These things repeat. As do all things, in time. When one wise person speaks of the end of the world, another is sure to do so eventually. The stories soon blur, and get mixed up, and we are left with girls like Koya and Milla, who repeat them again. This goes on and on and on and soon enough, many people, common and famed, are known to have said this thing. But who can say if it is true, or what will really happen? Time," Yasha said with a note of finality. "Only time knows."

Time, Saska thought. The only master of time she knew was the ocean god Rasalan, and Thala, his greatest follower, whom he'd given a part of his power. She remembered how King Godrin had once described the Eye of Rasalan as a window, blurred and indistinct and hard to see through. That it showed its bearer only what it willed. She had never truly understood all that. *Was Rasalan somehow watching over them? Had he granted this power to Thala and her kin to help guide the world through the darkness, and into the light beyond?*

She sank back down into the bath and mulled upon it all. *You're exactly where you're meant to be,* she thought.

Only time would tell if King Godrin was right.

35

Ranulf

"It stinks here," Leshie complained under her breath. "I've never smelled anything so foul."

"That's death, Leshie. You'd best get used to it." Ranulf stopped the wagon at the western edge of the follower camp, where the plains stretched away into the rugged, forested hills. Around them, basic sheepskin tents and lean-tos were being thrown up, carts and wagons fixed down, horses and oxen fed and watered. It wasn't the most desirable place to pitch camp here at the edge, near the broken ruins of this village, but that's why it was perfect. "Come, let's get the tent up."

Leshie grumbled as they worked, glancing constantly at the charred skeleton of the village nearby. It looked to have been sacked a while ago, yet all the same, the reek was most unpleasant. "Did no one think to bury the bodies?" the girl groused, as she hammered a stake into the ground. Half had been burned to death, it looked, the rest cut up with blade and axe or filled with feathered shafts.

"I don't think the Tukorans cared to show them any burial rites, Leshie."

"Bastards," she spat.

"They're your people. Or have you forgotten?"

"I left Tukor behind. Or have *you* forgotten? I became a Rasalanian just like you when I swore myself to Lady Marian's service."

Ranulf decided not to engage with her for a while, to let her cool down. The girl had been growing increasingly frustrated these last long days on the Capital Road, constantly complaining that they weren't doing anything to set Saska free. "Who knows what that sunlord is doing to her, Ranulf," she would rant. "Have you *seen* Saska? How beautiful she is. We have to get her out. Now, Ranulf. Not later…now!"

She'd been like that for days, but Ranulf had his reasons for waiting. Freeing Saska on the road would be all but impossible, he'd told her. The camp was struck every morning and raised every night, and that gave them almost no time to plan. They had to wait until they reached Eagle's Perch. Only then would they have their chance.

He knew she understood all that, of course, but Leshie was not particularly good at controlling her emotions. Nor was she patient. Even now, she was hammering the stakes and raising the tent as though it was some sort of race. "Slow down, Leshie. It's better to get it right the first time, or we'll just have to start all over again."

"You do it, then." She threw the hammer to the floor, marched to the rear of the cart, found a shovel, and began striding toward the wreckage of the village.

"Where are you going?" Ranulf hissed.

"To deal with that bloody stink."

He left her to it, though kept a close enough eye, as she marched out into the gathering gloom and began digging a pit. Some of the other camp followers looked over at her with vacant eyes, yet for the most part no one seemed to care. These weren't the best stock here, out at the edge of camp. There was a hierarchy, Ranulf had come to see. The more aggressive sutlers and sellers would be first to find their spot, often riding at the front of the column that followed behind the army. They would wake earlier to make sure they had a head start, and be set up to sell their wares by the time the more idle caught up.

The families of the higher-ranked soldiers would be well situated too. As would those with any influence in the army. Madam Suchet was one of them. No matter what time she arrived, she'd have a great host of eager soldiers awaiting her. They would make sure a sought-after spot would be cleared and ready, and would even help her erect her grand pavilion so they might sooner sample her women. She had done such a roaring trade that she'd drawn other independent courtesans under her wing, taking a cut of every man she paired with them. *Riches are made in the follower camp,* Ranulf thought. *Vincent would love it here.*

Once the tent was raised and their belongings arranged, Ranulf stepped out to join Leshie. She'd made a start, though the pit would have to be large to swallow up all the bodies. "This is a good thing you're doing, Leshie," he told her. "You have a good heart."

"And a sensitive nose," she grunted. "I don't want it filled with death-stink all day and night." She looked at the dead again, scattered through the bones of the village. "I had a look at them, Ranulf. There's a child there. Only four or five years old. She was killed in her father's arms. Well, I'm guessing it was her father anyway. The sword went right through both of them as he was trying to protect her." She shook her head again, then huffed and continued digging. "I'll not see that girl rot under the sun. She deserves more than that. Same as her dad, or whoever he was. And if it helps my nose, so much the better."

A good heart, Ranulf thought again, *much as she tries to hide it.* "I have a meeting, Leshie. Will you be OK on your own?"

"I'll be fine."

He said a silent prayer of thanks. He'd feared she might want to come as well, but this pit would keep her occupied for a good long while. "If anyone comes to try to talk to you…"

"I'll pretend to be mute," she said. "I'm deaf and dumb now, remember? And who's going to come out here anyway? This is where all the dregs of the camp followers stay. We've joined the great unwashed now, Ranulf. Let's just make sure we don't stay too long."

"I'm working on that," he told her.

"Sure, these *mercenaries* of yours." She thrust the shovel into the earth and threw aside a great clod of mud. "I know you're trying, Ranulf. I just don't like having to trust anyone else. You ask me, it should be you and me, that's all. You heard the one about two many cooks spoiling the broth?"

"I did. But right now, Leshie, we're just fumbling around in the kitchen, with no idea how to make a broth at all. We need help, and you know it deep down. I'd hope you would trust *me*, at least."

She mumbled something like, "I suppose I do," under her breath, and dislodged another block of dirt from the ground.

Ranulf left her to it, returning to the tent to fetch his cloak. Across the follower encampment, lights were blinking to life as darkness fell. He set off into the sprawl, wending through wagons and wains, bypassing fire-pits and cooking pits and pissing pits and giving the nearest latrine ditches as wide a berth as possible. At the front of the camp, on the northern side, a semi-permanent market had quickly sprung up to serve the soldiers of the main encampment, where the likes of Madam Suchet and her rivals would continue to prosper. Ranulf's quarry would be a little behind all that, he suspected, and finding them would not be difficult. *Just look for the biggest marquee,* he thought. And sure enough, there it was.

He found it beside a small trickling river - upstream from the latrines, of course - with a small copse of cypress trees nearby to give shade to the horses and mules. The Butcher and the Baker liked to raise their pavilion higher than all others, and never permitted any other tent to encroach upon their space. Whether anyone else had claimed this enviable spot when they arrived didn't matter; they would have taken it anyway by force. And no one would have complained.

A clutch of men were assembled outside, drinking from an oaken barrel. They wore rough patchwork armour and cloaks, swordbelts and blades, stained leather jerkins. One had an iron pothelm on his head. Another had a silken blue scarf tied around his neck, for what reason Ranulf couldn't guess. As soon as he got anywhere near, the biggest of them looked right at him and pointed. "Stop. Turn around. Go back to wherever you came from."

"But…"

"Go back." The man turned and marched toward him, several brisk paces, drawing a dinted dagger from his belt. "One more word, and I kill you. Right here. Right now. I kill you." He stared. "So?"

Ranulf called his bluff. *Sellsword games,* he thought. "I'm here to visit the Butcher and the Baker. They're expecting me."

The men at the barrel shared looks and then started guffawing loudly, and suddenly the man with the dinted dagger was grinning from ear to ear, scooping a burly arm around Ranulf's shoulder, and laughing along with the rest. "I jest, my friend, just a jest. We like to play with men we do not know. See what sort of men they really are." He poked Ranulf's belly. "There is fight in you, little man, and courage. Have a drink with us. We have just broken open a barrel of fruit ale." He was handed a mug by one of the others and thrust it into Ranulf's face. "Drink."

If this was some sort of bizarre initiation, Ranulf wanted no part of it. Still, he favoured them by taking the cup and having a generous sip. "Delicious." He smacked his lips. "Now, are they inside?"

The sellsword smiled, nodding. "Of course. You said they are expecting you?"

"They are. I was told to come after camp was pitched by a man called Kasbar Noy."

"Kasbar Noy? The liquor seller?"

"The very one. That beer you're drinking was probably bought from him."

The man laughed. "Yes, that may be. Kasbar brews a fine ale. Well, go ahead, then. And take the cup with you. They will like you for it. Trust me."

Ranulf wasn't in the habit of trusting sellswords such as these, but he didn't have much choice, as he'd told Leshie a short while earlier. He thanked the man and pushed through the tent flaps, to find something of an orgy going on within. To left and right of him, men and women and men and men and women and women were engaged in all sorts of carnal shenanigans. He blinked, trying not to stare at any particular coupling, sprawled out on chairs and tables and heaps of cushions either side of the central aisle. There were some animals inside as well, though they weren't involved, he hoped. He saw a stumpy-legged donkey munching on hay, several chickens and ducks clucking and quacking, a brace of cats chasing after one another, and a pair of huge great wolfhounds fighting over a bone. *What in the world...*

"And who is this?" The voice was deep and sonorous and came from the far end of the room. Ranulf peered through the fuggy air, trying to ignore the lustful moans around him. There was music playing too, a harpist capering around and sinking, fully nude. Ranulf felt like he'd stepped into one of Vincent Rose's surrealist paintings. "Come closer," the voice said. "Let us see you."

Ranulf stepped down the red-carpeted aisle, moving through the swirling smog and cavorting couples. Before him cleared two men - the Butcher and the Baker, he did not doubt - sitting upon ornate lounging chairs. One was large, with a blood-coloured cloak, slashed a hundred shades of crimson and scarlet and red. He had slashes on his face and bald head as well, a dozen of them at least, some thin and long and shallow, others deep and gruesome and horribly scarred. Ranulf took this man for the Butcher.

The other man was smaller. He had knuckly hands and thick

hairy forearms but elsewise was greatly less large than his companion. Upon his broad nose was a pair of golden spectacles, which rested a little lopsided on account of his missing right ear, and his cloak was a mud-coloured brown. He looked at Ranulf with a curious frown. "Who are you?"

"My name is Ersel San Sabar, of Kolash," Ranulf said, using the name and home city he'd taken on while in Aram. He and Leshie had posed as a merchant father and daughter pair and it made sense to continue in that guise.

"Ersel San Sabar," said the Butcher. His accent was a strange mix of Aramatian spiced with notes of the north. "What do you come to us for, Ersel San Sabar?"

"Several matters," Ranulf told them. Behind him, a loud scream erupted from some woman's throat, as she climaxed in her lovemaking, causing the wolfhounds to bark. It threw him off his thoughts, somewhat.

"Pay them no mind, Ersel San Sabar," said the Butcher. "Come closer and drink your drink."

Ranulf did as bidden, stepping closer, downing his fruity ale in a single go in the hope it might impress them. It seemed to work.

"It is good, yes?" rumbled the Baker. His teeth were very white behind his lips, so bright they almost shone in the murk. These were some of the strangest sellswords Ranulf had ever met. "Have more." He waved over a naked woman, who filled his cup from a large jug. "This is Ana," the Baker said. "Very pretty, yes, Ersel? She is one of Madam Suchet's whores."

"They all are," laughed the Butcher, waving a hand into the room. "Would you like to join in, Ersel San Sabar? There are more than enough to go around."

Ranulf declined as politely as he could, though Ana was very pretty, that was true. "With thanks, no. Is there....somewhere else we might talk?"

"What is wrong with this place," demanded the Baker. "Does it make you uncomfortable, Ersel?"

"No. It's merely the noise. I can scarcely hear you."

"Then come closer. Come, come, we will not bite." The Baker turned. "Ana, leave the jug. Your presence is making Ersel embarrassed, I think."

"And stiff," chuckled the Butcher, pointing to Ranulf's groin. "He *is* a man after all, brother."

Ranulf took it all on the chin. *Bloody sellswords*, he thought. He moved a few steps nearer to the pair, as Ana placed the jug of ale upon a table and drifted back into the smoke, wordless. The Baker picked up the jug and filled his drink. "So, several matters, you say. What is the first?"

Ranulf took a sip of beer. "I was told by Kasbar Noy that you have men within the main encampment," he started. "I'm looking for a bit of information, for a start. He said you might be able to help me."

The Baker was looking at him curiously. "There is something funny about your accent, Ersel," he said. "I hear some Rasal in your voice."

"I have done much trade with the Rasalanians," Ranulf said. He'd told that lie before. This about his accent was a common query, especially for those with a good ear for them. "I sailed there often during my formative years and picked up some of their vocal quirks."

"We are the same," the Butcher said proudly. He punched his chest. Beneath that cloak of reds and scarlets he was bare-chested, and there were more slashes and scars there too, half-hidden by tangles of coarse brown hair. "The Bloody Traders have no allegiance to nation, kingdom, race or creed. All genders are equal to us, and all ages, and all beliefs. Many of our men are mutts, bastards born from north and south. The only thing we demand is fighting skill, and a thirst for blood." He smiled broadly and raised his cup. The Baker raised his too and, naturally, Ranulf felt obliged to do the same. "Down and down and down," the Butcher roared.

And they drank.

"Good, you show yourself a man who likes an ale." The Baker smiled that white smile, adjusted those golden spectacles, and gestured Ranulf forward so he might refill his mug. "Do you have fighting skill, Ersel, and a thirst for blood?"

Ranulf shook his head modestly. "I am but a humble trader."

"A humble trader who is looking for information about goings-on within the soldier camp, yes? Well, what Kasbar told you is true. We have men hired out for security and such. There are many rivalries between the Sunriders, Ersel. The Starriders not so much - no, these are quieter sorts, and better behaved - but the Sunriders are loud and envious and quarrelsome. They compete over much...the size of their wolves, their women, their possessions, and even the size of their manhoods, yes. It is said that some go so far as to pay cutthroats to cut their rivals short, down there." He laughed. "Well, not our men, but others. Our men guard their tents, however, when they are gone. They make sure no possessions are stolen, mainly. Simple contracts, but we take on many jobs, so long as the pay is right." He smiled at Ranulf and raised a brow.

"I have coin," Ranulf told him. "And goods to trade or use to pay as well. Money isn't a problem." *Thanks to Sallor Sanara,* he thought. He owed his shipwright friend a great deal.

The Butcher poked a knife into a persimmon, plucking it from a bowl beside him. He took a bite, munching loudly. Juice ran down through the scars on his chin. "Show us."

Ranulf drew out a pouch of coins, and handed it to the Baker, who peered within, nodded, and handed it back. "This will buy information. What do you want to know, Ersel?"

Ranulf Shackton wet his lips. "The location of Lord Elio Krator's headquarters, and pavilions," he said. "And the best way to reach them, without drawing attention."

The Butcher and the Baker shared a look. "Now, don't tell me that good Ersel San Sabar wants to kill the noble sunlord?" the Butcher said.

"By no means. My interest lies in another."

"Another?" The Baker leaned forward, resting those thick hairy forearms on his knees. "Who is of interest to you, Ersel of Kolash?"

"Lord Krator has in his company a concubine, whom he keeps hidden from view. She…she is my sister. I only wish to make sure she is safe."

The two sellsword captains mused on that. "There is one," the Baker said, cracking a knuckle. "She rides at the good sunlord's side most days. Though who can say if it is the same one each day. Lord Krator is known to favour many concubines, and often keeps their faces hidden in public."

"Shame," said the Butcher. "It is shame that drives him. These women of his are northern, I have heard. He hates them, and yet loves them too. Lord Elio Krator is a strange man."

"False rumours, brother," the Baker said. "There is hate in Lord Krator only, when concerns the north."

And many of these Bloody Patriots have northern blood in their veins, Ranulf thought. Their captains were often Bladeborn bastards, sired of north and south, and these two were likely no different. They had no great love for the likes of Elio Krator, Ranulf knew. But coin was coin, and here they were, following the scent of money. Ranulf hoped they'd like the smell of his. "What does Lord Krator make of your presence here?" he asked them. "Some of you have Bladeborn blood, I've heard."

"We do," confirmed the Butcher. He threw open his cloak and withdrew a misting broadsword. It had garnets at the ends of the cross-guard and a large ruby embedded into the pommel. They shone, blood-like, by the light of the braziers. "I had the jewels added myself," the captain said. The mists swirled lazily around the blade. "My brother has one too. We are brothers, did you know?"

Ranulf nodded. "Kasbar Noy mentioned it."

"I am larger, but younger," the Butcher said. He pounded his scarred chest. "And the better fighter."

The Baker ignored that. "We were sired by a Bladeborn knight from Rasalan. One of the Bucklands. They are hairy folk, these Bucklands. Lord Horus has a great black beard and looks like a bear." He smiled, and gestured to the thickets of hair on his forearms. "I am hairy all over, but I'm sure you would prefer not to see, Ersel." He looked at his brother. "Our mother was a Matian whore, who bedded our father every time he came south on trading missions. Well, he came to her twice, at least."

The Butcher laughed at that. "Or perhaps more. Maybe there is a third brother out there?"

Ranulf smiled. "Is there a Bloody Trader captain called the Candlestick Maker, perchance?"

The Butcher slapped his thigh and roared. "I like this one, yes, very much! The Butcher, the Baker, the Candlestick Maker. I have heard this rhyme!"

The Baker was smiling too. "I wonder how this Candlestick Maker would deal with those who displease him?" he mused. "My brother likes to butcher the men who dare cross him, and I like to bake them. Have you heard of the iron dragon in the Golden Square of Eldurath, Ersel? They put criminals inside this dragon and have the beasts blow fire upon it. The criminals cook to death inside. This is where I drew my inspiration." He took a sip. "We like you, Ersel, and will help you with what you need. We have men guarding the pavilions of several Sunriders in Lord Krator's trust. I will have them gather the information you seek."

"My thanks." Ranulf bowed low. He had them in high spirits with that quip about the candlestick maker, so thought it a good time to take advantage. "I had a question, if you would permit it," he said. "It involves a man I know. A friend of a friend, you might call him. I heard a rumour that there is a contract out to find him. I wondered if you might know of it."

"There are many contracts, Ersel," the Baker said. "You will have to be more specific."

I can be perfectly specific, Ranulf thought. He cleared his throat. "The man's name is Ranulf Shackton. He's a Rasalanian adventurer and scholar. A quite brilliant man, I must say. I have met him several times when trading in Thalan. It seems that the Warrior King seeks him, though for what reason I cannot say."

The Baker sat back in his chair, twisting a tuft of forearm hair between his thick, callused fingers. "The Warrior King will have to seek himself first," he said. "He has gone missing, Ersel, we have heard."

Ranulf frowned. "Missing? When?"

"Some weeks ago, in the White City. He has a Blade of Vandar, they say. The misty blue one. He used it to kill a thousand men and women and children, yes, hundreds of those. Even babies, some say. And dogs and cats and goats and horses. Whatever stood before him, he slew. And then…" He clipped his fingers. "He vanished. Just like that." He had another glug of ale. "But as to this contract…yes, I know of it. This name…Ranulf Shackton, it rings a bell. The contract was given to the Surgeon, I believe, another of our captains. A determined man, and doesn't like to leave a contract unfulfilled, but…" He paused, readjusting his spectacles. "Well, this with Janilah. The Surgeon will have heard of it, too, I am certain, and will not pursue a contract with great relish if there is a doubt he will get paid."

Ranulf nodded in relief. "Thank you. That is something of a weight off my mind." He could muse on this about Janilah later, but for now…*Yes, that sounds promising,* he thought. Sallor Sanara had warned him of this Bloody Trader captain called the Surgeon before he left Aram. It was a motivating factor in their departure, in fact, though of greater importance was rescuing Saska. *And I'd best return to that,* he told himself.

"There is one more thing I would ask of you," he said, fearing they might begin to lose interest if he lingered here too long. "It is a matter of security. I would like to hire some of your…"

The Baker held up a palm to cut him off, then stood suddenly from his seat. "Denlatis!" he shouted. "I was not aware you were here!"

"I have just arrived, my friend. I did not want to miss the fun."

Ranulf stiffened, turning. Cliffario Denlatis came striding elegantly forward down the red-carpeted aisle, an amused smile on his face as he glanced left and right at all the fornicators and farmyard animals scuttling underfoot. *Can I not escape this damnable man,* Ranulf cursed to himself. The last thing he needed was this smug young merchant nosing in. *And what on earth is he doing all the way out here anyway?*

He didn't seem to notice Ranulf until he was all but on top of him. "Oh, Ersel," he said, looking down his aquiline nose at him. "That was your name, wasn't it? Ersel. We met at the Red Pits, some weeks ago. You were with my good friend Sallor Sanara."

"I remember, Cliffario. How are you?"

"Quite well. And better now to be here." He turned a full circle, taking in the wonders of the room. "So this is how sellsword captains live, is it? I ought to change my profession." He laughed haughtily. "What brings you here, Ersel? I did not expect to find you in such a disreputable place as this."

"I…." Ranulf didn't know what to say. "Well, I could ask you the same thing, Cliffario."

"You have every right to, of course." Cliffario Denlatis smiled that lazy arrogant smile of his and gestured to the pair of captains seated before him. "I have known these two for many a year," he said. "I have excellent relations with a good many captains of the Bloody Traders."

Ranulf didn't much like the sound of that. "I see."

"Do you know why they're called the Bloody Traders, Ersel?" Denlatis went on. He wore gold and copper and silver robes, as he had in Aram, with an extra length of golden silk thrown over his shoulder. His hair was as immaculate as ever and that amused little smirk looked in fine fettle as well.

"So far as I know, they often pose as traders and merchants, during contracts."

Cliffario Denlatis's gold tooth flashed as he smiled. "Correct. I have…helped, shall we say, in this. Provided cover for their killers, for a fee. I have always found it desirable to nurture many streams of income, Ersel. I trade, I build and buy and sell ships, and I work with scoundrels like these."

Ranulf was getting a horrible feeling from this man. "Are you… working with them now?"

"These?" Denlatis shook his head.

"Any others?" Ranulf probed.

"Bloody Traders? Well, on that I cannot say. I am sworn to secrecy in these matters, Ersel. I'm sure you understand."

The Baker gestured for Ana to come over. "A drink, Denlatis?" the bespectacled captain asked. "Or are you here for Madam Suchet's pleasures instead?"

"Both. I shall take that drink, and I shall take Ana too, if she'll have me?"

"She's a whore," chortled the Butcher. "You don't need to ask."

"I always prefer to." Denlatis turned and took the girl's dainty hand. "So, my dear, will you accept me to bed, once I have completed my business with these men?"

She giggled, blushing, smitten by the man.

"I'll take that as a yes." Denlatis gave the girl a caress down the small of her back as she left, with a whispered promise of much fun to come. Then he took a cup of ale, drank it down, and said, "As to my real reason for being here, well, perhaps you might have a guess? Ersel, you saw me in Aram. Care to venture a reason for my appearance?"

Ranulf thought a moment. Then it came to him. "You seek to press Lord Krator over his cousin's hand in marriage?"

Denlatis clapped his hands together. "Just so. The Lady Asherah Tamaar remains a prize I wish to win. I hope to dazzle the good sunlord with my dogged persistence."

Ranulf had to give him that. The young merchant was unashamedly determined, to be sure.

"I have brought with me much gold and several ships to sweeten the deal as well," Cliffario went on.

"Krator has no need for your gold, Denlatis," the Butcher told him. "He's got plenty already. A hundred times what's in your coffers."

"Show me a rich man who doesn't want to be more rich, and I will show you a liar and a fool," the merchant returned. "But no, you misunderstand. This gold is not for Lord Elio, but you." He bowed to the captains. "I wish to hire every sword you have. I shall present them to the noble sunlord as more good men for his war. You have some Bladeborn here, I hope? I know the good sunlord is not so fond of northerners, but he has made use of mixed-blood Bladeborn in the past, within the ranks of his Patriots of Lumara. Just so long as their skin isn't *too* light." He laughed to himself, as though it was all so silly. "So, what do you say?"

The Butcher showed his godsteel sword in answer.

"Yes. Other than the two of you?"

"We have some," nodded the Baker. "They'll cost you a sweet star, though."

"I have many a sweet star in my chests of gold. Stars, suns, moons, all. And northern coins as well, if you'd prefer. Sickles, scythes, spears, sabres, shields, all in copper and silver and gold. I even have Rasalanian corals and shells and gemstones, many of these. Take your pick."

The two captains leaned across toward one another and conferred. This wasn't going to plan anymore, not for Ranulf Shackton. He rubbed thoughtfully at his cheek, thatched in short bristly hairs. "Something the matter, Ersel?" Cliffario Denlatis asked him, as the Butcher and the Baker shared counsel.

"Nothing, Cliffario."

"Now come, my friend, you can speak plainly to me. You have not told me yet why you are here." *I would*, thought Ranulf, *if you ever stopped talking.* The merchant smiled as though reading every thought in his head. "I heard from Sallor that you had left Aram." He shook his head and tutted. "I thought you were better than that, Ersel. The follower camp is good for the lowly trader, yes, but not for someone like you. Or did I get you wrong? I was under the impression you traded spice in large quantities?"

This man will be the death of me. "I am not here to trade."

"Oh? Well…this is confusing, I must say. What would compel you to ride with this festering rabble, if not to profit from their advance?"

Ranulf couldn't think of a suitable answer. No doubt Denlatis would learn of what he'd asked of the Butcher and the Baker already, and see right through his lies. *I must get him on side,* he thought. *But how?* The answer came to him sudden as a thunderbolt. "I can help you win her hand," he said. "The Lady Asherah Tamaar."

Cliffario Denlatis smiled easily. "You can? Truly? How so, Ersel?"

"Change is coming, Cliffario." Ranulf leaned in, conspiratorial. "We must all make sure we are on the right side."

The merchant had a twinkle in his eye that reminded Ranulf so much of Vincent Rose. He was the man's younger, more handsome, more charming southern cousin. Not yet so rich and influential, but making strides in that direction. *Cunning and cruel as well,* Ranulf thought. *He will do anything for power and profit.* "You believe that Lord Elio is the *wrong* side, do you?" the man asked.

Ranulf had made his bed now. *I must sleep in it.* "I do. This army here, Cliffario, these Tukorans. They are led by one Cedrik Kastor. Have you heard of him?"

"I have."

"Then you will know the stories. Of his cruelty toward southerners. Of his hatred for our people. Cedrik Kastor hates the south with the same passion that the Patriots of Lumara hate the north. When these armies clash - and they *will* clash - Kastor will hunt down one man, and one man only - Sunlord Elio Krator. Whether Lord Elio is leading the charge or hiding in his tent, Cedrik Kastor will find him. And kill him, I believe."

"You do?"

"I do. He is a killer, and lethal. Even atop Braccaro, Lord Krator will not be able to withstand him. Cedrik Kastor's armour is the finest godsteel, thrice beaten and forged, layered to be impenetrable. His blades are second only to the Blades of Vandar. There will be no man, no Sunrider or Starrider present among this army who will be able to stop him." He was laying it on thick. *Work*, he thought. *Please work.*

Denlatis gave the brothers a glance, though they were still conferring. "You know an *awful* lot about this Cedrik Kastor, Ersel." The man's grin was knowing.

Ranulf had to ignore it. He had to trust this man's greed would win through. *And his sense.* "I travel often to Rasalan, as I told you at the pits. You hear things there. If it was Amron Daecar leading the northerners here, or Rylian Lukar, what would you say?"

"I would rejoice. The Crippler is now a crippler himself, and Rylian the Brave feeds the worms, I have heard. I fear neither would put up much of a fight."

He has me there. "Poor choices," Ranulf admitted. "Think of them in their prime, then. What now?"

"Now I say different, of course." Denlatis ran a hand through his dark wavy hair. "It pains me to say it, but the greatest Sunrider is no match for the greatest of these Bladeborn knights. Only our Moonriders outmatch them. And there are none here, alas." He pondered it some more. "Fine. You think Lord Krator may perish here. How does that help me wed his cousin?"

"With Lord Krator gone, the Grand Duchess will be within her rights to seal the marriage pact between you."

"And why should she do that? I have no noble blood. Safina Nemati would not give me a second thought."

"Because Elio Krator currently holds her granddaughter captive," Ranulf said at once, deciding to go right into it. "*She* is why I'm here, to free her and take her back to Aram. Help me in this and I will make sure you wed the Lady Asherah. You will rise high, and higher still with the good sunlord dead. *High and higher still*, Cliffario. You'll be one of the most powerful men in Aramatia."

Cliffario Denlatis's smile was sly. Sly and greedy. *Yes, he wants this.*

"Well, Ersel, if that is your real name…you have my attention, and my ear. What is it you want from me?"

Ranulf glanced at the Butcher and the Baker as they finalised their discussion. "I was about to ask them if I could hire men before you arrived. That is all I need. Security, to help me transport Saska home."

"Saska? This is the girl?"

Ranulf nodded. *Leshie is going to kill me for this,* he thought, but he had to trust his instincts. As soon as Cliffario arrived, everything changed. *He was going to either betray me or join me. I had no choice.*

Cliffario pursed his lips and rubbed his chin. "The lost child of Leila Nemati," he murmured. "There have always been rumours…"

"Help me, Cliffario," Ranulf urged. "You need but hire me protection, that is all. You can continue to schmooze Lord Krator all you please, should my plan fail. Play both sides, I sense you're good at it. Your money and your silence, that is all I need. And I'll help make you more powerful than you ever dreamed."

"You don't know my dreams, Ersel. Sometimes I dream of being a god." He laughed aloud, even as those keen hazel eyes of his mused on it all, thinking it through. He ran a finger through the deep dimple in his left cheek, drawing a line, up, down, up, down, tapping his foot all the while. And then, after that long delay, he turned to Ranulf Shackton, reached out a long-fingered hand, and simply said, "Done."

36

Elyon

Elyon watched as the dragon was hung from the outer walls of Dragon's Bane. Chains rattled against the stone as it was winched into place, several dozen men and horses hauling at the ropes, pulling it high for all to see.

"I shouldn't have agreed to this," he said dourly. "It feels tasteless, Uncle, displaying it in this way."

Rikkard nodded. "I don't disagree with you, Elyon. But it'll inspire the men. Few have seen a dragon so close and it'll serve them well to see what they're up against. And to know what you can do."

Elyon ran his eyes over the heaving crowds. It seemed as if every man in camp had come to watch, crushing shoulder to shoulder, jeering and shouting as the dragon's carcass was raised. There were chains around its neck and abdomen, its forelimbs pulled taut and wide to display the beast with wings outstretched. It looked formidable and somehow piteous all at once, slung up like that.

"Every man, woman, and child knows what a dragon is," Elyon said. "Stringing it up isn't going to change anything." *I shouldn't have agreed,* he thought again, but he'd been outvoted in council and ended up conceding. *Still, I could have said no. I'm a prince. And this was my kill. I should have said bloody no.*

He turned, moving briskly along the wall walk, away from the grim spectacle he'd allowed. Some of those in the crowd below spotted him and began chanting out his name, calling him 'Dragonslayer' and 'Lord of Storms' and simply, 'Elyon, our prince, our prince, long live Prince Elyon Daecar!'

Rikkard followed along with him. At his urging, Elyon raised a hand in salute to the men gathered below - thousands of them, all in their house colours and arms - and heard them roar back with those names again, and several others besides. "They sprout up like weeds, these names," he complained, though why, he couldn't say. *Embrace it,* he tried to tell himself, but something didn't feel right about the praise. *It was not me who slew that dragon, but the lightning, the storm, the blade itself.* It had been instinct, luck, circumstance, whatever you wanted to call it. And yet Elyon was now a dragonslayer all the same, one of only a few men living who could say that.

He went through the names within that illustrious group. Sir Patrik Taynar, younger brother to Godrik. The Old Bull, Lord Petyr Bolt. Janilah Lukar. All old men now, all dragonkillers once upon a time. Sir Ralston Whaleheart had struck a dragon's head from its shoulders in a single cleave during the War of the Continents, and his very own father had become the most famous dragonslayer of the age when he duelled Vallath and Dulian at the Burning Rock. Prince Rylian had claimed such a title on the same day. *But he's dead now,* Elyon had to remind himself. *He's dead and I have this blade because of it.*

He wondered if Rylian would be proud. *Were you watching that day in the storm, Rylian?* Men of Tukor were not permitted a place at Varin's Table - that was reserved for the knights of his order - yet still...perhaps he was watching from the Hall of Green, where the Emerald Guards were said to go? Elyon hoped so, truly. *I have a debt to pay,* he thought. *I have a debt to pay...and one dead dragon isn't enough to pay it.*

He marched on, cloak trailing in the breeze, Rikkard trailing too. Men looked at him differently now. *They looked at me differently when I became prince to them. They looked at me differently when they saw me with the Windblade. And now they look at me differently still.* Elyon Daecar, Dragonslayer, Lord of Storms. Master of the Wind. *Elyon Daecar, fraud more like.* He huffed to himself and walked on.

"I had word from my lord father," Rikkard said behind him.

"Oh?" Elyon stopped beside one of the crenels, overlooking the plains that stretched toward the Bloodmarshes. The mists hung heavier than ever out there, a thick grey soup that never stirred or shifted. *And still no attack. Even after that dragon...still nothing...* He turned back to his uncle. "What did he say?"

Rikkard reached out and put his hand on Elyon's shoulder. "Your father, Elyon," he said, without preamble. "He's back."

"*Back*!" Elyon spluttered the word out so fast he sprayed spittle all across his uncle's face. "Oh…sorry. I just…back?" A broad smile quickened on his lips. "He's actually returned?"

Rikkard wiped the saliva away with a leather-gloved hand. "Yes, Elyon, he's back. He returned to Northwatch a week or so ago, along with the two companions he set out with. All came back healthy and hearty, it would seem."

Healthy and hearty, Elyon thought. "Did it work, then?" he blurted. "He…is he healed, Uncle? *Blessed*?"

Elyon had never agreed with the folly of his father's undertaking, but Amara had seemed convinced it was the right course for him to take. Vandar's Tomb. A blessing from a fallen god. The de-crippling of a man known as the Crippler of Kings. It seemed too far-fetched, but Elyon was done with that sort of thinking. *I flew into a storm and slew a dragon. I've no right to go doubting anything much anymore.*

Rikkard gave a shake of the head. "My father made no mention of that in his note."

Elyon frowned. It would seem the most obvious thing to make mention of. "That isn't a good sign, Rikkard."

"Perhaps not, but healed or no, the main thing is he's returned. Let's keep our focus on the positives, Elyon. Great warrior though your father always was, he has more to offer than his mastery of the forms. Insight, inspiration, leadership. A king does not need to fight in the van. He will be better placed upon the throne, where he has always belonged."

Elyon knew his uncle was right, though still…a full-strength Amron Daecar, armoured all in godsteel plate would be a fearsome prospect for their enemies. "I'd just started to hope, is all," he admitted. "Against my better judgement, I'd thought…" He sighed and trailed off. *He's back*, he told himself. *Back and well. That is all that truly matters.*

"We have you now, Elyon," his uncle told him. "People often forget that your father never bore the Sword of Varinar during the War of the Continents. He only took it up after your grandfather Gideon was slain at the Burning Rock. But you? Well, look at you, fast mastering the Windblade, slaying dragons in the skies. I daresay we don't need your father to inspire us anymore. That is your job now."

A raft of doubtful thoughts went through Elyon's mind, but he decided not to voice them. He looked over the Bloodmarshes again. A small troop of Lord Rammas's outriders were returning from a scouting, trotting back toward camp at a gentle clip. The lack of urgency made it clear they'd seen nothing of concern out there.

"This dragon..." Elyon started. "Killian seems to remember it from before. From the last war. He said it was ridden by a Fireborn called Sa'har Nakaan. Does the name ring a bell?"

Rikkard pursed his lips in thought. "A distant one, yes. When did Killian tell you this?"

"Before I joined you on the wall just now." Killian had travelled the last few days with the dragon's corpse as it was carted down from the Lakelands, and only just returned that morning. "He told me the dragon itself was called Ezukar. He'd been on the same battlefield as the beast several times, he said. It was there at the Burning Rock too, as one of Ulrik Marak's wingriders when my grandfather and King Storris were killed."

Rikkard continued to muse on that. "I ought to speak with Killian. Where is he now?"

"Went to his chambers to rest." Elyon observed him carefully. "Is there precedent for this, Uncle? For a dragon flying so far to the north without its rider?"

"Not that I've heard of. There's much oddness here, Elyon, that's clear enough. But what you said in council when you got back…I think that still holds true. The beast was somehow drawn to the Windblade, or otherwise instructed to hunt you down. By who? Well, that I don't know."

Elyon didn't know either. The obvious answer would be this Sa'har Nakaan himself, but why he wasn't atop the beast, no one could say for certain. Most likely he was dead, meaning he couldn't have issued the instruction. It was possible of course that King Tavash gave the order, or else the new Lord of Nest, Vargo Ven. But in the end it all came back to one thing: they didn't know, and weren't likely to find out either. *All that matters is that I'm a target now, with a great big 'X' on my back.*

"I suppose we should convene a council meeting," Elyon decided. He looked into his uncle's warm brown eyes. "Who else knows about this?"

"About the true identity of the dragon?" Rikkard seemed confused. "Well…Killian, you, now me…"

"No. About my father."

"Oh. Just me and you so far. Here at the Bane, anyway. I wanted you to be the first to know."

Elyon looked out over the plains. "It makes me wonder why my father hasn't written me himself. Surely he knows I'm here. Lord Borrington would have told him that as soon as he returned to Northwatch."

"That's a long way, Elyon, even for a strong-winged crow. I assume your father thought it best to write to Amara first in Ilivar, so she might pass the message on."

"Amara?" Elyon asked. He thought about that for a moment. *Of course. Father didn't write to Brydon Amadar, why would he? No, he wrote Amara.* But something wasn't adding up. "If he wrote to Amara, why exactly is it my grandfather writing you, Rikkard?"

"Because Amara isn't in Ilivar anymore," Rikkard explained.

Elyon wasn't understanding. "Why not?"

"She's gone back to Varinar, as far as I understand it. My father didn't say why. He can be very selective with what he reveals in letters, Elyon, should they fall into the wrong hands. You know what he's like."

Stubborn. Distrustful. Ruthless. Yes, Elyon knew his grandfather well enough. And something about this didn't feel right. He turned to a nearby bowman, manning the wall walk above the southward barbican. "You there." The man came marching sharply over. "Have word sent out that I want a council convened at once."

The soldier bowed. "Yes, my lord, right away."

Elyon had another look over the Bloodmarshes, placing his hands on the stone parapet. He could still hear the baying crowd away beyond the western wall of the fortress where the dragon was being strung up. His battle with the beast had taken it out of him, and more so than he'd first realised. That night, once the old shepherd had fashioned him a space to rest on the back of his sturdiest wagon, he'd fallen straight asleep and hadn't awoken until the following afternoon. When he did he felt shot to pieces, every inch of him aching, head thumping, mind abuzz with fangs and scales and fire and lightning. He'd tried to fly, but couldn't muster the energy. It had taken until dusk for him to gather himself to begin the flight back, though even then, he had to stop on multiple occasions to rest.

It was past midnight when he'd finally gotten back. At once, he'd summoned the council from their beds, where he'd proceeded to tell them what had happened, speaking of the riderless dragon, the storms, the lightning. He was adamant that he'd gotten lucky, no matter what they all said. "You killed a bloody dragon, Elyon," Lord Kanabar had announced, thrusting his cup of wine aloft. "Of course you got lucky. No man kills a dragon without a bit of luck!"

There was some kernel of truth in that, he supposed, but all the same, the kill didn't feel earned. Still, they toasted to his triumph a dozen times that night, telling him he'd secured a vaunted place at Varin's Table already. Elyon didn't want to hear it. It only made him think of Aleron. How he'd been denied a place in sight of Varin, a chance to sit among the great First Blades and kings and dragonslayers of the past. It still saddened him more than he could say to think about that. *Aleron would have killed the beast without the need of lightning and luck*, he thought. *He'd have flown somersaults around it and cut its neck or put the Windblade through its eye. He'd have killed it clean, unlike me.*

The following days had seen the story spread, and now he couldn't avoid it. Dragonslayer. Lord of Storms. Master of the Wind. Prince of the Skies. The names were springing up like mushrooms after the rains, a new one seeming to appear every day. Some men were starting to call the battle the 'Duel Above the Lakes'. Others preferred the 'Dance in the Storm'. Some jokingly referred to it as the 'Battle of Soaking Rock'. The Battle of Burning Rock had been fought nearby, after all. It was witty enough, Elyon had to admit, but only served as another reminder of his father's more famous and praiseworthy triumph.

A week on, and he was still growing used to it. A week on and he still felt weary. He could fly, train, practice, yes, but there was something deeper in his marrow that didn't feel right. Maybe time would fix it. Maybe not. Maybe he just needed more rest. But really, Elyon knew the cause. *Those eyes,* he thought. *The red manic eyes.* The dragon Ezukar…there had been something wrong about it. It seemed almost…possessed. And still he remembered the Windblade's warning…

Soon all the skies will swarm.

Council was taken in its usual place in the Golden Tower, within that spacious dining room with the tall rectangular windows that gave ranging views across the Bloodmarshes. When Elyon and Rikkard arrived, Lord Kanabar was already there, with Lords Shorton and Rammas. All three had voted to string up the dragon and were in discussion about the response. "…went well," Lord Shorton was saying, in his nasal voice. "The men seemed to enjoy the spectacle, so far as I could tell. It will help lift spirits and…" He saw Elyon enter, and trailed off. "Prince Elyon." He stood to his feet at once; Rammas did too, though Wallis Kanabar remained seated, his great red thicket of a beard resting on his belly. "We heard it was you who called this meeting, my prince."

"It was," Elyon said, striding into the hall. It was far too big for so small a council but Lord Kanabar continued to insist they meet here. He said war councils made grand decisions and needed to discuss them in grand quarters. And there was a lot of wine here, which helped. "Is Killian not yet arrived?"

"Not yet," said Lord Kanabar. "He was bathing, I think. Washing away the stink of the road. Come, good prince, have a drink with us."

Rikkard filled two cups of wine. "Did Killian tell you about the dragon?" he asked the group of lords, handing a cup to Elyon.

The question stumped them. "The one being chained up outside?" asked Lord Shorton.

"Unless Prince Elyon's killed another," put in Rammas in that deep voice of his.

Lord Kanabar chuckled. "Have you, lad?"

"No." Elyon put down his cup. He intended to train later and didn't want to drink. *I need to practice fighting while in flight,* he knew. That had been his focus the last few days. Relying on storms and lightning wasn't a good strategy. "Killian said the dragon was called Ezukar. Its rider was Sa'har Nakaan. They were wingriders to Ulrik Marak once."

Lord Kanabar nodded thoughtfully. "Killian did suspect…" he murmured. "I suppose seeing the beast up close confirmed it." He pulled at his fiery beard. "We might want to consider sending word to the other bearers. If a dragon like Ezukar was somehow drawn by the Windblade..."

"I am *not* sending word to Jonik, Wallis," Elyon interrupted firmly. "Let the bastard be hunted. See if I care."

"Borrus is with him," Lord Kanabar reminded him. "And Torvyn Blackshaw, and Mooton too. Would you like them to be hunted as well, Elyon?"

It was a gentle enough scolding, but did its job nicely. Elyon felt entirely foolish all of a sudden. "You're right," he admitted. "I spoke out of turn." He took a breath to freshen his lungs. "We can send word if you wish, Wallis, but where? They could be anywhere by now."

"They were making for Blackhearth," Lord Kanabar said. "That's what Daggart said. We can have word sent there."

"It's a nice thought," Rikkard murmured, pulling out a seat, "but pointless if you ask me. No dragon is going to fly so far north as that. And even if they did...well, forgive me for saying this, but that wouldn't be so bad. Every dragon that dies is one less for us to deal with. Borrus. Mooton. The Shadowknight. This exiled lord, Emeric Manfrey. Together they should be able to deal with whatever comes their way."

Lord Kanabar gave a loud grunt. "This talk of taking the Shadowfort is utter folly if you ask me. How Borrus got himself roped into that..." He grunted again, swigging his wine. "He should be *here* with us, defending the Bane, not heading into those bloody mountains."

They were spared any more of Wallis Kanabar's complaints by the sound of approaching footsteps. Lady Marian Payne entered, striding forward lean and graceful with the squat toadish figure of Lord Fullerton hurrying to keep pace beside her. "We got word of an urgent council," the Lord of Lakeheart said, breathless.

Elyon nodded. "Come, Lord Fullerton, Lady Marian, join us. We're discussing the idea of sending word to the other bearers."

"Bearers of the Blades of Vandar?" Lady Marian guessed.

"They need to be warned," Lord Kanabar said, still bristling a little. A few more gulps of wine did help to calm his rancour, though. He'd ranted and raved about his son many times since they'd learned of his unexpected allegiance to the Shadowknight. "My *son* needs to be warned."

"That still leaves Janilah and Vesryn," Elyon said. "Unless my information is out of date, both of them are still missing." He looked around. No one said anything to the contrary. "I fail to see how we would warn either of them."

"Or whether we'd want to," Rammas said. "Why should we give the likes of Janilah Lukar such a warning? What do we owe him?"

"The Blades of Vandar must be protected, no matter who holds them," Lady Marian said. "If one should be lost..."

"One *is* lost, my lady, or have you forgotten?" Rammas rumbled. "The Mistblade and Nightblade may have returned, but the Frostblade? No."

"Not yet," Marian said. "It may soon, my lord."

Rammas had a heavy brow. He dropped it into a frown. "Do you know something we do not?"

Elyon was wondering that too, but Marian just shook her head. "If I did, I would of course inform this fine council. No, I merely wish to point out that the other lost blades have returned of late and it would be no great surprise if the last of them did as well."

"No surprise at all," said Lord Kanabar, wiping wine from his lips. "There's been so much blasted oddness recently that we should half expect it." He pointed his cup toward her. "I'm with you, my lady. The Frostblade will turn up sooner or later, mark by bloody words, it will."

More footsteps sounded behind them at that, as Killian Oloran finally arrived, his golden hair damp and darkened from his bath. His appearance completed the central figures of the council. Sometimes other minor lords and captains would join them, but not always. "How was the road?" Rikkard asked as Killian moved to his seat.

The man sat neatly, as ever. "Fine," he said, in that whisper of a voice. "Slow and tiring. Dragons are heavy."

"So Ezukar," Rikkard went on. "You're certain, Killian?"

"Certain," he whispered in answer. "I fought him myself once, outside Skyloft. Recognised the scars my blade had left. Ezukar was a mature dragon, highly experienced, and Sa'har Nakaan an experienced rider. They had bonded long years before the War of the Continents began. Nakaan would be over fifty by now."

"He'd be a *corpse* by now," muttered Lord Kanabar. "Nakaan is dead. Why else would the dragon have flown here without him?"

Killian took a moment to fill a goblet of wine. "That's the worry. When a Fireborn rider is slain, his surviving dragon returns to the Wings, history tells us. On a rare occasion it might bond with another if their blood is strong enough, but mostly they go back to where they were born, to mourn and live in peace. They become more docile, it's said."

"But not this one," snuffled Lord Shorton.

Killian had a sip of ale. "Following the natural course of things, Ezukar *should* have returned to his birthplace, if Nakaan is indeed deceased." He looked to Elyon. "You reported Ezukar as having red eyes when you fought."

Elyon nodded. The memory was still disquieting. "Red and wild," he said. "He seemed…possessed, somehow."

"Possessed," repeated Sir Killian, so quiet one had to lean in to hear him. The hall had gone deathly silent. He frowned down at his drink. "Ezukar had golden eyes," he then said. "Golden brown eyes flecked with green, the same colour as his scales."

"Well...Elyon must have seen wrong, then," Lord Kanabar said. "There's no shame in that, lad, when in the heat of battle."

"He wasn't wrong," Killian told him. "I inspected the beast myself, and had a look behind his eyelids. The eyes *were* red, my lord. What caused it, I cannot say, but...there is something queer about it all. Something that unnerves me."

"Nothing unnerves you," Lord Kanabar said. "Borrus always said so. You're fearless, Killian."

Killian nodded quietly. "This does. Dealing with bonded dragons is one thing. If riderless dragons join in...and even rogue dragons from the Wings..." He gave an uneasy shake of the head. "We could never stand against that many."

Lord Fullerton swallowed dryly, the apple in his throat moving up and down. "H-how many are we...are we talking?"

Lord Kanabar huffed. "No one knows. Not even the Agarathi can accurately make that count. Might be over a hundred wild dragons out there on those islands, or twice that. And other foul creatures besides." He gulped his wine. "Anyway, this is all getting too morose. And falling into the realms of guesswork at best and fantasy at worst. We prepare, we train, we hold the bloody line. What else can we do? If every infernal beast with fangs and claws and a taste for blood comes crawling out of hell, we beat them back. That's our job. End of story." He wiped his hands and finished his drink, pouring another. "Now...was that all, good prince? Or was there another reason you called this council?"

Elyon nodded and looked at his uncle. Rikkard cleared his throat. "There's another matter," he confirmed. "Rather better news, I should say. Elyon's father has returned from the Icewilds. He arrived back at Northwatch Castle a week past, I'm told."

Lord Kanabar slapped his meaty hands together. A great clapping echo went around the hall. "Well, that's more like it! Finally! Borrus, now Amron. We need only Lythian to come back and we'll have the whole set." He laughed happily. "So, is he healed, Rikkard? That's why he went out there, isn't it? To sort out this left shoulder of his."

"And right leg," Elyon added.

"Yes, that too. So? Is he?"

"Unconfirmed," Rikkard told him, drawing out the note. He reached down the table and Lord Kanabar snatched it up, running those bloodshot eyes over the writing. "This is your father's hand," he observed.

Lord Fullerton was looking bewildered. "Icewilds?" he said. "I thought Amron was…"

"Quiet down, Francis, I'm trying to read." Lord Kanabar peered closer, read the note twice over, then placed it down on the table. Not everyone present knew of Amron Daecar's ill-advised expedition yet. In fact, only Killian, Rikkard, and Wallis Kanabar were aware of it. The others were looking as befuddled as poor Fullerton. "Well, doesn't say much, does it," Lord Kanabar went on. "Not even where he's headed." He frowned. "Why would Amron write your father, Rikkard? The two have never gotten along."

"He wrote Amara," Elyon informed him. "My grandfather must have read the letter in her absence, and passed on the message."

Lord Rammas scratched his muscular jaw. "I thought Lady Amara was in Ilivar?"

"She left for Varinar, Brydon writes," said Lord Kanabar, glancing again at the note. He looked a little concerned. "Now why would she do that? She must know how dangerous Varinar will be for her now."

"Perhaps Amron wrote that he'd meet her there?" offered Lord Shorton.

"Don't be stupid, Denis. Northwatch is weeks from Varinar."

"Yes, but…"

"But nothing. Or do you think Amron found a second Windblade out there in the Icewilds, and flew to meet her?" The burly lord scoffed. "I don't like this. With all those Taynars baying for blood..." He read the note again, as though trying to unearth something new from the sparse words in Lord Brydon's hand. Failing, he grunted again. "Just what was she thinking? Your auntie is a bloody force of nature, Elyon, but she needs to know when to slow down. And *stop* meddling!"

The door to the dining hall was pushed open once more. Footsteps hurried forward as the council turned. Kanabar looked up sharply. "Not now, damnit! Can you not see we're in council!"

The footman quivered to a stop. "Sorry, my lord, I…" He held out two shaking hands, one bearing an unopened letter and the other a small leather box.

"What is it?" Kanabar demanded loudly.

"I…I don't know, my lord. The box is…it's sealed, I didn't want to open it in case…"

"The letter, man! Whose bloody mark does it bear?"

The soldier looked around for help. Marian was nearest; she stood and strode toward him, fetching both letter and box.

"Well, Marian?" boomed Kanabar. "What's the seal?"

Marian was frowning. "Speak of the devil, and he shall appear," she murmured quietly. Then she looked up. "It's Godrik Taynar's. It's addressed to you, Elyon."

Something's happened, Elyon sensed at once. He stood and marched over to her, opened the letter, read the words. His face went pale. "What is it, Elyon?" asked someone. Rikkard. "What does it say?"

He ignored the question. His fingers fumbled to open the box. The interior was plain, empty, but for a single item.

His auntie's little finger, severed at the palm.

37

Amron

Amron awaited his cousin in the audience chamber of Blackfrost Castle, looking over a map of the world carved into the great pinewood table.

He'd always loved it. The intricate detailing of the cities and landmarks, the way the mountain ranges were raised to give the table a three-dimensional aspect. When he was a boy, his grandfather Balion had commissioned the carving of miniature knights and dragons and sea monsters for he and Vesryn to place about the table. They would play at war for hours, imagining how the next great Renewal might play out, where the bloodiest battles would take place, which warriors would rise as heroes and legends and who the great villains would be.

He smiled at the memory, running his hand across the table's rough uneven surface. Parts were worn by time and use, the once-sharp tips of the mountains blunted and chipped, the towers of the cities sometimes broken or missing entirely. The twin statues at Tukor's Pass had always been particularly appealing to him, and the cliff-carved statue of Drulgar at Dragonfall, and the great Eagle of Aramatia at Eagle's Perch as well. The original sculptor had even chiselled the bones of the ancient leviathan Galaphan in rich detail, marking the holy place of Galaphan's Grounding on the south-eastern tip of Rasalan.

Walter was standing there now, leaning across to get a good look.

"The detailing is extraordinary," he said. "I attended a festival at Galaphan's Grounding once, celebrating beneath the bones of the leviathan. Those were a truly memorable few days. Lots of drinking and dancing and communal prayer. The Rasals do like to celebrate their sea gods." He moved down toward the carving of Calacan, surging from the cliffs off Eagle's Perch. "Well now, this might be *even better*. The wings…goodness. Every feather and fold is so beautifully modelled." He looked up. "When was it made, my lord?"

"My ancestor Bayron Daecar had it commissioned after the Twenty First Renewal four centuries ago," Amron told him. "He was a fine warrior, though less heralded than some others of that time. Rufus Taynar took most of the plaudits back then. And Oswald Manfrey followed soon after."

"Two names every warrior-in-waiting will know well," Walter agreed. "The Twenty First Renewal," he murmured, thinking. "A bloody war, that one. And a bloody century."

"No more bloody than this one," grunted Rogen Whitebeard, brooding in his black cloak across the room. "We've had two Renewals in twenty years and if you're to be believed, Selleck, this'll be the worst of all."

"Oh it will be, Rogen," Walter said. "Isn't that why you sought to continue in Lord Amron's service in the first place? Because you know you'll be better use at his side, rather than wasting away in those mountains of yours?"

"I remained in his service because he asked me," Whitebeard came back. "And Lord Borrington all-but-insisted."

"I think the entire garrison at Northwatch insisted. Happy as they were to see Amron return, I did sense a rather opposite reaction to your own reappearance, my friend." He smiled apologetically. "I jest, Rogen, don't look at me so fierce. I honestly think that he wants to kill me sometimes, my lord."

"Can you blame him?" Amron said. True enough, Whitebeard was looking at Walter as a wolf looks at a lamb, those amber eyes glinting murderously in the gloom. "Your taunts do carry a sting, sometimes."

"So they should. If you've learned anything of my humour, it's that I like to elicit a reaction. But I exaggerate, of course. Only about four hundred and ninety-five of the garrison were disappointed to hear of your return, Rogen. The other five were most pleased, I'm sure. The blind ones." And he grinned again.

Rogen wasn't so happy about that. "I made a mistake coming with you," he growled, tightening his cloak about himself. It was cold in the audience chamber, and poorly lit besides, with a single torch burning low on each wall. "Why you keep him around remains a mystery to me, my lord."

"Mystery?" Walter gave a laugh. "You're one to talk about mystery, Rogen. How long were we out there in the Icewilds together? Months. And not once did you tell us you were a son to Lord Styron Strand."

"It wasn't relevant. Rangers put aside their family names. We give up our rights and titles. I am *not* Rogen Strand anymore." The lupine ranger got prickly whenever the subject was drawn up, though that didn't stop Walter from pressing him on it.

"Yes, but still. You're nephew to a king now. That makes you a prince of sorts."

"Godrik Taynar is no king of mine." Rogen threw open his cloak and strode across the room toward the unlit hearth, propping his hand against the stone wall, staring angrily into the ashes. He stood there, saying nothing.

"Well…something we can agree on," Walter said, after a short pause. "My king stands here before us. So…*King Amron*." He gestured to the map. "Will it be Varinar or the Twinfort? Or maybe King's Point? I trust you don't want to ride all the way to Dragon's Bane. Your princely son seems to have matters covered there."

Amron hadn't yet determined which road he would take from here. "Blackfrost," he had told Robert Borrington, when the Lord of Northwatch had inquired as to where they might go, but after that he wasn't sure. Many of the Daecar bannermen were assembled down at the Twinfort and Green Harbour, defending the western gate, Robert Borrington's lord brother Randall among them. King's Point marked a possible invasion route for the Agarathi as well, like Dragon's Bane, but Walter was right, Elyon and Lord Kanabar and the likes of Rikkard and Killian had that fortress well-defended, along with their tens of thousands of swords and spears and shields.

But Varinar? Amron turned to Walter. He understood the question within the question. "You believe I should go to Varinar and unseat Godrik Taynar from his throne?"

Walter shook his head. "*Your* throne," he corrected. "We cannot be having false kings about, not at a time like this."

"Ellis Reynar wrote me out of his line of succession, Walter. You heard what Robert said."

"Yes, but under most duplicitous conditions. Ellis was clearly being manipulated by Janilah and Godrik, as has been proven by recent events. This makes his decree void. And that makes *you* king."

Amron's eyes were on Varinar now, carved with great care and precision with the walls and towers and keeps built atop the hills. *I was king by proxy for twenty years, and now…now that I might just be king by rights, it is another who wears the crown.* There was some warped irony to that. "I can do more good elsewhere," he said, moving his eyes back toward the southern coast. He walked around the table and began pointing out the cities and strongholds Walter had mentioned, and others besides. "What good will I do sitting the steel throne if the Agarathi cross the Red Sea, or come through the Tidelands? I have my allies and Taynar has his. It doesn't matter who wears the crown."

"I disagree, my lord. You have a power of command that Godrik Taynar lacks. The ability to inspire. To lead. To…"

His words were cut off by the sudden groan of wood and the clack of a crutch through the chamber door. Light spilled in from outside. Sir Gereth Daecar came hurrying right through as fast as his maimed left leg would carry him. Over a linen shirt, he wore a brown studded tunic and vest, with a woollen cloak thrown over his shoulders. He had dressed quickly, clearly. "My lord….Amron…goodness, I am so sorry. You caught me sleeping, I'm afraid."

Amron stepped to meet him, limping a little himself. "It's the dead of night, Gereth. No need to apologise."

At Gereth's side came the castle steward, a young man by name of Quentin Snow, bearing a torch in his right hand. It had been Snow who'd admitted them when they'd arrived a short time ago, before speeding away to wake the castellan. Gereth's eyes moved to the hearth. "Quentin, why isn't the fire lit? It's freezing in here." A mild man, Gereth Daecar was never so agitated as when his lordly cousin's needs went unmet.

"I had intended to, my lord. After waking you."

"Well see to it. Quick. Quick." Gereth shuddered in his cloak, breath frosting. "I'm sorry, Amron. I should have been better prepared for you."

"You didn't expect me so late, I'm sure."

"Well no, in truth. Your letter did suggest you would be another day or so." He shook his head. "But that is no excuse. You are lord of these lands and the hearth should always be lit for you, no matter the time." He shot a glance at Quentin Snow. "Come, Quentin, quicker. You don't have the excuse of old age and a lame leg as I do. Hurry up!"

The steward was going rather slow, admittedly, but Rogen Whitebeard had something to do with that, standing stony and menacing by the hearth as he was. "Rogen, let him do his work," Amron commanded. "And come over, meet my cousin."

"Yes, yes," Gereth said enthusiastically. "The famous Rogen Whitebeard, is it?" He reached out his hand for the ranger to take. "A great pleasure, Rogen," he said, shaking briskly. "This name of yours - Whitebeard - I hear it's got something to do with the frost in your beard, from much time spent ranging in the Icewilds? Lord Borrington told me that there's no man who's spent more time out there than you."

Rogen nodded. "That is true, sir."

Sir Gereth smiled. He was not near so gaunt and angular as Whitebeard, yet no longer had that strong robustness that the Daecars were known for, his body having long since withered away due to inactivity on account of his savaged left leg, badly mauled by a sunwolf during the war. His hair was more salt than pepper and he had something of a bookish appearance now, where once he'd been stout and well built. "I would say that the name Whitebeard doesn't work quite so well, not so far south as this," the castellan said. "It gets cold here, oh yes, but not so much as you're used to, I'm sure. Though if Quentin doesn't get that fire lit soon, who knows, we'll probably all freeze to death." He gave the steward an unhappy glance and let out an exasperated breath.

Walter stepped in. "A pleasure to see you again, Sir Gereth," he said. The pair had met the day Amron departed from here, many moons ago. "As to Whitebeard's name, I've ventured the option of Blackbeard, Greybeard, or Silverbeard, seeing as he has more black, grey, and silver than white on his cheeks and chin, but he tends to just ignore my proposals."

Sir Gereth laughed. "You might want to consider shaving your face clean, Rogen, to better avoid these jests."

"He'd only come up with others," Rogen complained.

Walter nodded self-approvingly. "It's true, I would."

"Well, all jesting aside, you have my thanks, the both of you," said Sir Gereth. "I should very much like to hear your tale. Though, perhaps now isn't the time, given the hour?" He turned, as the steward finally got the fire going, the flames flickering and wood crackling, thin tendrils of smoke swirling out into the room. "Quentin, see that Rogen and Walter have bedchambers well prepared and warmed. And light the fire in Lord Amron's solar at once." The steward rose and made for the door. "And food as well. Have some warm food prepared in the kitchens."

Quentin paused. "But…the cooks and scullions are all sleeping, my lord."

"Then wake them. This castle's *true* lord has returned. He *must* be well attended."

"You really needn't trouble yourself, Gereth," Amron said. "Quentin, don't worry about the food."

Sir Gereth wasn't having it. "No, Amron, I'll hear nothing of the sort. And lord, I call you? How about *king*? You know about that, of course? Lord Borrington has kept you well abreast of the latest news?" He gave Quentin a sharp gesture and the steward scurried off.

"Robert gave us a full report the day we got back," Amron told his cousin. "It was quite overwhelming, I will say."

"Well yes, you did miss rather a lot." Gereth shambled over to a side table to pour wine. "Not too early, is it?" He filled four cups anyway for anyone who might want one. Only Walter decided to partake, with the excuse that they'd spent months in almost total darkness, so time of day had no bearing on them now.

"So, do tell me…how was it out there?" Gereth asked, sampling his wine. "You mentioned little in your note, Amron. But your injuries…well…the way you're carrying yourself. It didn't go to plan, I take it?"

Amron had had the same query from Robert Borrington. He gave the same answer, telling of their failed attempt to reach the holy chamber at Vandar's Tomb, the Snowskins, the prophecy, the blighted lands, everything. Walter chipped in with his own comments, as always, and Rogen stood by, silent and grim at the grave, still looking like he didn't want to be there.

Once he'd completed the truncated version of the tale, Amron opened his cloak and unveiled the Frostblade. Sir Gereth's blue eyes shot open in wonder. "What…the…no…that isn't the…the"

"The prophecy led me to it, Gereth," Amron told him. He let his cousin gawp at the colourful sparkle of mists, the spectacular hilt and snow-flake pommel. "This Sea-King led me to it for a reason. I'm to fulfil some purpose, of that I'm sure." He slid the blade back into the bone-white scabbard and closed his cloak. The very light in the room seemed to dim.

Gereth was still gaping. "I…I'm struggling to believe this, I have to admit."

"Robert gave a similar reaction. But I asked him to keep knowledge of it to himself for now and would have the same from you. I've had enough attention due to Ellis's death these last days, and have no want to attract anymore."

There was no lie there. Their journey down the High Way from Northwatch had not been without incident. At every town and village they'd passed, the local people had come buzzing out like bees from a hive, eager to get a good look at him and pay their respects. Word spread quickly, and before long some of the larger townships were putting up banners and bunting and planting flags alongside the roadside to welcome him. Some of those showed the Daecar sigil, others the royal crest, and others still had been halved with both. "All hail King Amron," they would shout out as they saw him ride by atop his great destrier Wolfsbane. "Long live the King of Vandar!"

"I'll…keep it secret, Amron, if that's what you want," Gereth said. He gave the folds of Amron's cloak another glance. "Though know that it won't last long. The Mistblade has been unearthed now as well, I'm sure you've heard. Janilah, he…"

"We heard all about Janilah," Amron broke in.

"Though nothing new for some days," Walter added. "Is he still missing, do you know, Sir Gereth?"

"Such that I've heard," the castellan confirmed. "News can take time to reach us here. But…" He frowned uncomfortably, as though remembering something. "Ah, well there is something you won't know as yet. Disturbing news from Varinar, involving your sister-in-law."

"Amara?" Amron puzzled on that. "Amara is in Ilivar, Gereth. I sent her a letter from Northwatch, telling of my return."

"She *was* in Ilivar," his cousin corrected. "Not anymore." He reached into one of his pockets, then another, then another, grumbling to himself. "Oh, I thought I'd brought it with me. Sorry, I must have forgotten. I did dress quite quickly."

"Forgotten what?"

"A letter, from one of your household knights," Gereth said. "He thought a moment. The son of Lady Crawfield. Sir Connor, I believe."

"Sir Connor is Captain of the Household Guard," Amron said. He was a dour man, Sir Connor Crawfield, but there was no knight more loyal or dutiful. Whatever this was, it was worrying. "What did he say?"

"Nothing good, Amron, I'm afraid to report." Gereth gave his pockets another search, speaking as he did so. "He writes of grave wounds to his person, and several others among his men. It seems there was some skirmish outside the gates of Keep Daecar between your guardsmen and a host of Taynar soldiers. Some sellswords were involved as well, who go by a name I cannot recall off the top of my head. Something about flames, or…" He sighed. "I should return to my chambers, find this letter."

Amron didn't want to wait that long. "Amara, Gereth," he pressed. "What has happened to her?"

"She's, um….well, she's been taken prisoner, such as Sir Connor writes. By Lord Taynar. Seems she went to the palace and didn't come out. He fears for her. He writes in explicit terms of a trap."

Amron's chest went up and down, steady. His eyes narrowed. "A trap?"

"Well, yes. This is all conjecture on Sir Connor's part, I should point out, but he seems to think that your own father-in-law colluded with Godrik Taynar to see Amara shackled in the dungeons. It appears Amara and Lord Amadar had a fierce argument in Ilivar over her part in the theft of the Windblade. It has caused much harm to relations between the greathouses, as you may know. Lord Amadar sent Amara to Varinar to try to build bridges with the Taynars, Sir Connor explains. But…well, as I say, he mentions a trap. Amara is worth more as a hostage than a mediator, he says, and I don't suppose he's wrong. Oh, and Elyon's squire, the boy who you came here with before…he is captured as well, Sir Connor says. And the leader of this sellsword band also. Some teenage girl, if you would believe it. It looks like Godrik has fettered everyone who had a part in the Windblade's stealing."

"Does my son know of this?" Amron demanded.

"I…I couldn't possibly say, Amron. I have only recently received word of it myself."

Amron looked over the table-map, fingers bunching into a

hammer of a fist. He took a long slow breath. "Where is Sir Connor now?"

"Recovering from his wounds in Keep Daecar. He petitioned me to send men to help him rescue the Lady Amara, but I'm rather understaffed here as it is. Most of the Daecar banners are manning the western gate. The Twinfort. Green Harbour. Even King's Point…"

As Gereth was going on, Walter moved gently to Amron's side. "My lord, don't you think we should…"

Amron raised a hand to silence them both. He could feel his blood beginning to boil. Amara had gotten herself into this mess, yes, but that made no matter to him now. "What does Godrik intend?"

"I couldn't say, Cousin. Sir Connor posits that he will use her to retrieve what he is owed. The Windblade. He wants it returned."

"Elyon will never give that up, nor should he." Amron Daecar maintained his calm, though he wanted to put his fist through this table he loved so dear. He could hear the soft whispers of the blade at his hip. The voice was different to the one that had occupied his head for near-on twenty years. It hissed softly, coldly, urgently, and often. *The blade senses the coming doom,* he thought. *The Sword of Varinar was never so vocal.* He turned back to face his cousin. "I want to see this letter, Gereth, read Sir Connor's words myself. Find it for me at once."

"Of course, Amron. I'm sure I left it in my bedchambers, on my reading table. Your coming was so swift, I…"

Amron didn't need to hear his explanation. "Lead me."

They followed Sir Gereth back through the dimness of the castle, the only sounds their scuffing footsteps and the clacking of Gereth's cane. Amron lumbered along beside him, Walter behind, Whitebeard keeping his distance at the rear. The castle was all but empty, the occasional guardsman standing at a door or performing his rounds, one or two early-bird servants already up and setting into their preparations for the morning schedule. None seemed to know that their lord and king had returned. Each looked at him with big unblinking eyes, falling to their knees or bowing as appropriate. Amron nodded back, even calling by name those he remembered. And then they were at Sir Gereth's door.

The castellan shuffled right in and over to his reading table. There were many notes and scrolls and books laid out there. The hearth was alight, to beat off the chill as he slept. Gereth moved quickly to light a taper, took it to the desk, and began searching. Amron stood in quiet contemplation all the while, but in truth this was a formality. His decision had already been made.

"Ah, here we are." Gereth plucked the scroll from a heap and handed it over. There were a few flecks of blood spattered onto the parchment, and Sir Connor's hand looked shaky. But it *was* Sir Connor's, that was plain enough.

Amron's eyes ran over his words. Just a single time was all he needed. "Please make sure our bedchambers are prepared at once," he told his cousin. "We will need to catch a few hours' rest before we set back off on the road. I'd like to leave no later than mid-morning, if I can."

Gereth looked bemused. "My lord? But Amron, you've only just arrived. I had thought that you would stay here a day or two. There is much else we need to catch up on."

"I can give you an hour in the morning, while the horses are fed and saddled," Amron said.

"An hour? Amron, you've been travelling for months. Oughtn't you rest a while? And is this not a perfect place for you to train and master that blade? And in secret, if you wish it. There is no place better…"

"I'm leaving soon after first light, Gereth," Amron cut in. "I'm sorry, but this matter is too pressing." He turned to face Walter and said, "It seems we're going to Varinar after all."

38

Saska

Balza escorted her to the tent. She wore a pale blue dress with glittering silver studs beneath her cloak and burnoose. Even moving from tent to tent, she was not permitted to be seen now. "He's in a foul mood," Balza said. "See that you don't make it worse." When they reached the tent flaps, he pushed inside. "The girl," he announced.

Krator waved him away without a glance. "Leave us."

Saska stepped inside as Balza withdrew. The pavilion was spacious, richly ornamented. Lord Krator sat at a table at its heart, a plate of food before him. It looked untouched. He took a long drink of wine as Saska stood at the door. "Remove your cloak. I want to see you." She did as he bid her, unveiling the dress that Yasha and Milla and Koya had diligently clothed her in. She wore jewellery as well, chains of gold, silver, and bronze around her neck, and a brooch etched in the image of Calacan, the Eagle of Aramatia. *He'll have me wearing feathers soon,* she thought. "You look beautiful." He gestured to the seat opposite him. "Sit."

She obeyed, taking her place before him. A plate of food had been prepared for her; chicken thighs, a greasy cut of duck, boiled vegetables and potatoes sautéed with onion. There was a soup as well, though it looked to have gone cold. Or perhaps it was meant to be eaten cold. She couldn't say. "It looks delicious, my lord."

He nodded vacantly. "Drink with me."

There were wines on the table, several different vintages. Saska served herself, and took a sip. A long silence followed as she picked at her food, drank a little. She could hear the din of camp life outside, the clang of metal, the roaring of beasts. She hated these dinners with Elio Krator. They had shared many now, and most were like this, awkward and uncomfortable with few words shared. "I heard you met with Cedrik Kastor," she said, to break the silence. She suspected his foul mood had stemmed from it. *It didn't go well,* she thought.

"*Kastor.*" He said the word like it was a curse, taking a swig of his wine. He looked a little drunk; she'd never seen him like that. *This man never loses control.* It frightened her to see him like this, his eyes dark and brooding. It reminded her of that night with Cedrik Kastor's lord father, Modrik. *The night he finally tried to rape me,* she thought. *The night he died...*

"How…how did it go?" she chanced.

He huffed and said nothing, drinking more wine. He looked down at his plate as though it was his enemy, then pushed it roughly aside. "I will kill him," he grunted to himself. "This man…this *northman*. I'll have Braccaro feast on him living."

Badly, then. Saska didn't need to hear specifics to know how the meeting would have played out. Both men held a deep-seated loathing for their counterparts and would have made that clear enough. *No doubt Cedrik made it clearer,* she thought. She imagined him there in his godsteel plate, visor up, grinning that handsome haughty grin of his. Both men were proud and vain, but Cedrik was the younger. *He would have made that clear too,* Saska knew. "Look at you, old man, you can barely hold yourself in the saddle," he might have said, laughing disdainfully. "All these long weeks on the road have been cruel to you, *Sunlord*."

Silence wrapped up the room once more. And once more Saska listened to the sounds of the camp, nursing her drink, hoping he might dismiss her. He did that, sometimes, when he grew bored of her presence or had other matters to attend to. *But tonight he only attends to his wine,* she thought, worried again. *He ordered me to dress up nicely, and is drinking heavily.* She put the pieces together and didn't like the puzzle she saw. *He will take me tonight,* she fretted. *Like Modrik Kastor did eventually. Like Lord Quintan, and Griffin Kastor too, and that ugly brutish thug of his, Borgin.* Each man who'd tried to put his hands on her had died, but that run of luck would not last forever. *I always had help, or fortune, or fate. But here, no…I'm all alone. If he tries to take me, I'll have no choice. If I fight, I'll die. If I run, I'll die. I have no choice*, she stressed.

"You are upset."

Saska met Krator's eyes. She swallowed. "My lord?"

"You look upset by something. What troubles you?"

She shook her head and smiled. "Nothing."

Those eyes of his kept staring. A moment passed, two, three, and then he said, "Balza told me you can speak Aramatian. Almost fluently, he said. Your lessons with Yasha have paid off."

"Yes, my lord. But…not fluently. That is an exaggeration."

"You do not speak it to me," he said. "Why?"

"I…I wanted to surprise you, once I had gained a better understanding of the tongue."

"You surprised Balza."

She nodded, and silence came again.

Another minute passed. Saska's heart was thumping now. *Wine*, she thought. *Just drink, it will go easier.* She was not a maiden now, no, Elyon Daecar had seen to that. *I have to be strong. Think of him, and do not struggle. You will not enjoy it, no, but maybe…maybe you can stomach it, at least.*

There seemed no other way, and something told her that Elio Krator would not be rough, not in that. *If he decides to cross that line, it means he sees in me my mother, whom he loved. He may be gentle, even. It may not be so bad.*

"I'm glad you have taken to our tongue so well," the sunlord said eventually. He reached forward and refilled his cup. "It should have been your first language. This northern tongue of yours is rough, and inelegant, and your *accent*…" He shook his head. "Speak to me in Aramatian. I would hear how it sounds."

She freshened her lungs, feeling oddly nervous. All she'd learned seemed to suddenly vanish from her head. "What…" she started, as it gradually came back to her. "What would you like…say…me to… me to say?" She smiled, abashed, and looked away. She'd messed that up, and royally.

Yet the sunlord was smiling faintly. "No, you need not feel embarrassed, Saska." His voice had turned softer. "That was…good. Your accent is much nicer when speaking our tongue."

"I have worked hard," she said. "I listen all day on the road, and Yasha…Milla…Koya…they help me much as well."

"I am pleased." He looked tired, the rugged lines about his eyes deepening. The golden hue of his skin had paled a little, it seemed to Saska. "I loved your mother." That came out of the blue. She met his eyes and saw that it was true. "I hope you know that."

"I do," she said. That was no lie.

"Her death stole all from me." He took his wine, gulped more down, staring idly down into the cup as he swirled it. "I was to rule beside her, all of Aramatia. You know this. I have not made my ambitions secret. Not to you. But…" He frowned at her, those slim eyebrows pulling in. "You understand what I'm saying? Would you prefer we return to your…*other* tongue?"

She shook her head. "I understand."

"Tell me…if you don't. I want you to know this, Saska. I want you to understand."

"Understand…what, my lord?"

"My reasons. My path. It was meant to be paved in gold, but… now the gold had faded, worn away. Your mother was to be my bride, this you know. House Nemati was to be wed to House Krator, and the product of this union…our son, or…or daughter…they would have ruled long, and true. This was always my design. Yet now…" He paused and trailed off.

Saska remained silent.

Eventually, Lord Krator went on. "My father was Lord Tullio Krator. He was a Moonrider, strong and commanding, well-loved by the people. He died during the war, swarmed upon by your Bladeborn knights. It took a dozen of them to cut him down. He slew eight before they did."

Saska wasn't sure why he was telling her this. "Did you…never wish to bond a moonbear, my lord?"

He stared down at the table. "Once. When I was young, yes. I looked at my father…I looked at how *others* looked at him. And your great uncle as well. Justo Nemati. They were great men, proud men. Men I wanted to emulate, and yet…"

You were too afraid, Saska thought.

"Yet I did not think myself worthy," Lord Elio Krator said.

Saska raised an eye. She hadn't expected that. The man she knew thought much of himself, yet this man seated before her now, reflecting on the past…this man was full of doubt.

He gave a sigh. "I have no siblings, Saska. My mother…she did not want me to risk that trial. I have often wondered if my father didn't either. Whether he put me down for that reason. He was a critical man. Nothing I did was ever good enough. His words cut me constantly, sapping my spirit, and perhaps…perhaps that was his intention…to deter me from risking myself in bonding a bear. Most die in the attempt. And had I died, my father would have lost his only heir."

He studied her eyes, perhaps wondering if she understood. When he went on, he spoke the common tongue. *He wants me to know this. He needs it,* she thought. "My mother is dead now too. And their siblings also. House Krator has never birthed big families. 'There is power in blood,' my father always told me, 'and it must not be diluted'. He believed that having many children would make each of them weaker. Yet this tradition has its risks. I am seeing that now." He glanced at her, and then away. "I have no children of my own."

Something tightened inside her. She reached for her wine and drank.

"My father had one sister, younger than him. She was beautiful, demure, yet sickly. It only fortified his thoughts on having a single child of his own. He wanted a son and he got one. He expected everything of me, more than I could give him. I shed no tears the day he died, Saska. He had not earned them, so I did not pay them." He flexed his fingers. "No, I was glad. 'It is my house now' I told myself. You need not live in his shadow anymore."

Elio Krator stood from his chair, took up his cup of wine, and moved to the brazier at the side of the room. He picked up a poker and stirred the coals. "My father's sister was Lady Sereen Krator, who wed the Moonlord Bulsho Tamaar. She died too young, worn down by her ails, yet birthed a child before she did so; my cousin, the Lady Asherah." He turned to face her. "You have heard of her, I know. She is a beautiful woman, as her mother was, yet stronger. She has many suitors, many who want her hand. Do you know why that is, Saska?"

"She's your heir," she whispered. "Until…you have a child of your own."

He nodded. "Yes," and she saw the intent in his eyes. "I have searched for the right woman to bear my children, but the pool has grown shallow. Your mother…Leila…how her death cursed me, yet you…you give me another chance, Saska. And this tradition of my house, of my father's, no…I do not believe in it, not anymore. Sons I want, and daughters. Heirs. With which to build a great legacy of my own." He stepped suddenly toward her.

Saska drew back in her chair as he approached, turning her face away as he reached for her cheek. "My lord, I..."

"Balza told me what you said." He touched her face, softly. "He is a boorish churl, yes, but his ears do not deceive."

"Elio, I..."

"You lied?" he asked, yet it didn't sound a rebuke. "This I know. You lied because Balza lusts after you. Because he sniffs at you like a dog and tries to watch you when you bathe. You hate him, this I know too. And why would you not? He is an easy man to hate. And an easy man to kill as well." He took her chin between his fingers, lifting. "Would you like me to kill him, Saska? His head, you said to him, for a wedding gift. I could give it to you in an instant."

"We could never wed. You...you said so."

"I did. And I meant it. A coupling gift instead, then. Give yourself to me, and I'll give you Balza's head."

She drew away. "No, I..."

"I need an heir, Saska. Do not force me to make one without your consent. I am not that man. But I will be, if I must."

I will never consent! she screamed in her head. *How can you ever believe I will!* She struggled to keep her features calm, to relax her cheeks and nose and mouth. "I...need more time," she managed. "The light in me...I feel it growing, every day. Maybe...maybe one day soon I will be the woman you want. Once I have mastered the Aramatian tongue and...and have a better grasp of the accent. What is the rush, Elio?"

His eyes darkened. "You delay. You make your excuses and you delay."

"I...I am afraid," she admitted. "What if you should seed a child in me and...and then the battle, with the Tukorans. What if you should..."

"Die?" He finished for her. "You believe this Cedrik Kastor will best me?"

"No, but...there are a thousand fights in every battle, and...and a hundred battles in every war." She'd read that somewhere, she remembered. "You were going to wait until after the war to wed my mother. Why can't you wait with me?"

You are not your mother, his eyes said. And suddenly she could see the thin shafts of hatred breaking back through, as sunlight through clearing clouds. *He sees my father again. He sees the north.* "I have waited enough." He reached out and gripped her arm, pulling her from the chair.

"My lord…no…"

He tugged her across the room and threw her onto the bed. The links of gold and silver and bronze rattled about her neck, the fabric of her dress tangling around her legs.

"You have forced me into this. I never wanted to…I am *not* that man."

"You're not…I know you're not…" She could hear noise outside now, near the flaps. Voices. "Elio…please. This isn't the way. You know it isn't."

"What other way is there? You are the blood of House Nemati. There is no one else." He reached for a side table and took a flagon of wine, drinking, gulping. Some of it dribbled down his chin and into his robes. *He can only do this drunk. He wants to be able to blame it on something.*

She searched for something that might give him pause. "What would my mother think?" she blurted. "The woman you loved. You would rape her daughter?"

That word made him visibly recoil. *Rape*. He snarled and threw the flagon aside, smashing it into a thousand pieces on the floor. "What do I need to do to make you submit!" he roared. "*Rape*? You would force me into *that*. That which brought you into this world. That which killed my Leila!"

"My father did not rape her!" Saska found herself shouting. "He didn't. I know he didn't!"

"You know nothing, you foolish girl! You were unborn. How could you know?"

"I just…I just *know*," she said.

"Then she betrayed me?" Elio Krator's golden eyes looked almost black in the dimness of the tent. "You think your mother a whore, who would betray me, break our oath of fidelity and betrothal, bed a northern slave behind my back?"

"He wasn't a slave," she whispered, feeble. "He was Bladeborn. Royal. Old Hob told me so."

Elio Krator shook his head in disdain. "You can believe one, not both. Either your father was a rapist or your mother a whore. Which is it, Saska? Tell me."

"I…I don't know."

He stepped forward, staring down at her. "You would side with *him*? You would curse the woman who died to bring you into this world? For *him*!"

Saska had no words. She could only sit there in silence and hope he would relent. Relent in his stare and his accusations and his rage. *Leave me alone*, she willed him, looking away. *Please, just leave me be.*

He scoffed. "You were doing so well, Saska. But I can still see much of your father in you. Mhazem will be pleased, and Balza most of all. You will continue your treatment tomorrow."

She bowed her head. That seemed the best she was going to get. "I…I understand, my lord."

A sudden rush of wind blew through the tent, accompanied by footsteps, and a voice. "My lord, you have a visitor."

Krator was still looming over her, glowering. He drew back, slowly, and turned. "I'm busy. Send them away."

"He is most determined to see you, sunlord," said the soldier. "He says he has…"

"*Gifts*," came another voice, and into the tent swept a tall dark-haired man, lithe of limb and smooth of step. He bent his back into an outrageous, swooping bow, throwing a golden sash across his shoulder. "Sunlord Krator, it is a great pleasure to see you again."

Krator stared at the intruder impassively. "Denlatis."

Saska remembered him. He was a merchant, quite young, an upstart without land or title or Lightborn blood. He had come to Lord Krator's viewing balcony at the Red Pits to petition the man over the hand of his cousin and heir.

"Indeed. *Cliffario* Denlatis," the tall merchant said, taking a step into the room. "I am glad to see you remember me."

Krator said nothing. Saska could see him squeezing his fist by his side. Denlatis smiled easily, despite the lord's obvious displeasure at the interruption. His gold tooth glinted in the firelight.

And then he saw her. "Oh, I do apologise, I did not realise you had a guest." He inclined his head at her, ignoring her drawn in shoulders, her tightly closed legs, the tension in her face. "And a very pretty guest, I might add. May I have the pleasure of an introduction, Lord Krator?"

"No. Ignore her. She is of no significance, Denlatis."

"One of your concubines, my lord?"

"She is of no significance, I said. Now, what do you want?" Krator paced away from her, as though wanting to leave something squalid behind. *He feels filthy for what he almost did*, she could tell.

The merchant's eyes lingered on her a moment. At the Red Pits, she'd been wearing her burnoose, so he'd not seen her. There was something bordering on recognition in the way those hazel eyes shone. "A *very* pretty girl," he said. "I am sorry, my lord. It is just… those blue eyes are quite mesmerising. Now I don't suppose…if not one of your concubines, I don't suppose she is….available?"

"She's no whore," Elio Krator said loudly. "Now *what* do you want? Speak and leave. I'm busy."

"Yes, I can see that." Cliffario Denlatis gave the room a cursory scan. "I won't keep you from your dinner, Lord Krator. I only mean to wish you well in the battle to come, and to do what I can to help." He clipped a finger at the soldier by the door. The man didn't much like that, but he opened the flaps all the same. "Men, for your cause," the merchant said. "Bought and paid for, by my own coin. And at some considerable cost, I will say. But worth it, I am sure. For these are formidable men."

Elio Krator looked through the opening at whoever was gathered outside. He didn't seem entirely disinterested in what he saw. "They carry godsteel," he said.

"Alas yes, these are Bladeborn men, but all are well-spiced with southern blood. I thought you could make good use of them, Lord Krator. A single Bladeborn is worth a dozen regular men in a fight, I'm told."

"That would depend on the Bladeborn. Some are worth vastly more. Some are little better than regular footsoldiers. It depends on the strength of their blood." Lord Krator looked out through the tent. "Which are these?"

"Good stock, or good enough to benefit your cause. Every little helps, my father always taught me. None are Amron Daecar, but they will cause the Tukorans some trouble, so long as you pit them against the right opponents."

"I don't need you to tell me how to run my own war, Denlatis." Krator considered things for a short time. "Where did you get them?"

"From the Bloody Traders, mostly, and a few of the other sell-sword companies. There are several independent hires sprinkled among them as well. I have ships, too, if you should wish to make use of them."

"You came by ship?"

"I did. I enjoy feeling the wind in my hair, my lord. A slow march down the Capital Road would not have suited me."

Krator took that for an insult. "We did not march slow, *merchant.* I would have sailed as well, but the risk was too great. Storms. Sea-monsters. Seaborn. All could have caused us to founder."

Cliffario Denlatis spread his hands. "I meant no offence, good sunlord."

"Your interruption is an offence," Elio Krator snapped back. "You have crossed the line into impertinence, Denlatis. I once found your boldness amusing, but not tonight. Not in my private quarters."

"I can only humbly apologise, my lord."

"I'm sure. And you hope this gift of men will appease me?" Krator raised a palm as the merchant went to speak. "I'm sure you have not brought them here from the goodness of your heart. I ask again - what do you want?"

"To drive back the heathens, Lord Krator, no more."

"No more, you say? So this is not about my cousin?"

"Well..."

"I have made myself clear on that account, Denlatis," Krator seethed. "The Lady Asherah will wed a man of *proper* standing. Moonlord Palek, most likely, who you greatly offended when you came to my royal box that day at the pits. If you think this gift of men and ships will turn my head, you are wrong, and sorely. You think I would permit someone like you to have her hand? *You*?" And he laughed. "You may wear silk, Denlatis, but you were sired in shit and squalor. Never forget it. No matter how high you stack your chests of gold, there is always going to be a ceiling you cannot breach."

Cliffario Denlatis kept his expression perfectly even. "Yes, my lord. I see your mind will not bend on this. I will not trouble you with it again."

"See that you don't. Or I'll see you short a head."

Cliffario Denlatis bowed low. "Then I will leave you, sunlord." He spared a glance at Saska. "I shall leave the gifts all the same. My men are yours to use as your please."

Elio Krator grunted. "I'm not an ungrateful man," he told the merchant. "But I know a bribe when I see one. I'll keep the men and we'll call it even. Now go. And *do not* bring this up again."

"I would dream of no such thing." The merchant fell into

another sweeping bow, then withdrew, walking briskly back through the flaps in a flow of silk and satin.

Krator took up a cup of wine. "That man…" He drank the cup dry, shaking his head. Then he looked over at Saska and waved her to stand. "You as well," he said. "Leave me. I want to be alone."

She could scarcely leave quick enough. She hurried over to the exit, fetching her cloak on the way, throwing it on. She was a pace from the flaps when Elio Krator stopped her.

"You will submit to me, Saska, and willingly," he told her. "If you don't you'll end up like Denlatis, headless. Think on that, and think hard. Deny me again, and I'll put Joy's head on a spike next to yours. Understand?"

"I understand," she said.

"Then go."

And she did, pacing swiftly out into the dark of the camp, ignoring the look on Balza's face as she shouldered straight past him and toward her own tent. There were men outside, Denlatis's sell-swords, most likely, standing around not seeming to know what to do. Saska thought for a moment about taking one of their godsteel blades and seeing Krator short a head himself, but that was folly, and she wasn't thinking straight. *No, not now. One day, but not now.*

She could smell Balza's stink behind her. "I told you not to foul up his mood," he muttered. "Heard shouting. Displease him, did you?"

She walked on, ignoring him. She could hear the oaf laughing as she moved around the side of the pavilion and crossed the yard to her own. He made no attempt to follow. *Small mercies,* she thought, as she came into sight of her refuge. She could see Joy there, waiting loyally at the flaps, though the cat wasn't alone. A man was with her, one knee on the ground, scratching the starcat under her chin. Saska frowned as she approached. The man stood, turning to face her.

"I hear your name is Saska," said Cliffario Denlatis, as he smiled and put himself into a deep, deep bow. "It is such an honour to make your acquaintance, my lady. I've never had the pleasure of meeting a *princess* before."

39

Cecilia

Cecilia looked out upon the ruin of Galin's Post, musing on the nature of the common man, how he went so easily to barbarism and looting and theft and rape and murder and such crimes most foul. Around the perimeter of the square, near every building was a twisted skeleton of blackened support beams and charred brick, a once-thriving section of the city reduced to ash and cinder by the very people who dwelt here.

"I've heard that some men set fire to their own homes in the madness of it," said Prince Raynald, who wore his little circlet of a crown atop his head, and an emerald cloak trimmed with wide borders of golden scrollwork. It was the sort of sartorial flourish that the Lukars tended to avoid, yet Raynald seemed quite happy to brush away those stifling traditions. "What sort of savage would be reduced to *that*? Burning their own homes? It's senseless, Auntie."

It's a lie, Raynald, she thought. Or at least, a fact misshaped through a thousand tellings. No man would burn down their own home or place of business unless trying to profit from some sort of insurance scam. Which was possible, she supposed. Though more likely, they were burning down a rival's business or home, and the flames simply spread on the wind. Still, she didn't see any reason to deny her nephew the curiosity of it. "There wasn't much sense employed that day, Raynald," she said. "But when a few rotten apples get into the basket, the rest can quickly go bad. That is what we saw. Good people resorting to terrible things."

Raynald nodded thoughtfully, pulling at the fuzz on his chin. "My grandfather is much to blame, I am sad to say. A city reflects its ruler, Auntie. Grandfather's mental state had taken a turn to madness, and the people followed." He looked out over the square, musing sombrely. "I shall change things," he decided. "Me…or Robbert, when he returns. No matter. He or me. I will support him if he comes back. Teach him what I've learned of ruling these last weeks."

You haven't so much as ruled your own privy chamber, sweet prince, Cecilia thought. In all truth, she'd pulled every string and banged every drum since her father's disappearance, and any decree or ruling Raynald had issued had first come from her own lips. She was rather enjoying it too, this new power she wielded. She had Raynald nicely entwined around her little finger, but Robbert? Would he be so easily spun?

She wasn't sure about that. Prince Robbert was at war, and war could easily change a man, especially one so young. A callow eighteen year-old prince could return a gallant war hero, widely loved and greatly more independent than when he left. *A man with a mind of his own,* she thought, *unlike Raynald.* In some ways, it would be so much easier if Robbert never returned at all. She hated to even think that; she had no preference between the boys and had always found them boisterous fun at feasts and festivals, but still…well, it *would* be simpler.

The square was much quieter than it had been the day of the riot, though more and more people were creeping from their hovels as the minutes passed and the clouds scuttled restlessly overhead. A breezy wind was blowing, yet even so, Cecilia could still hear the town criers and soldiers out there among the streets of White Shadow, bellowing loudly for whoever might hear that the '*conspirators and colluders are about to hang. Come, one and all, and witness their fall*'.

Cecilia had made sure that the news had been spreading for days, but had never hoped for the biggest turnout. *No, many are too afraid to come to this place now,* she thought, looking across the wide-open square at the two hundred or so who'd taken their place before the stage, atop which the gallows had been erected. On the day of the *Mad King's Massacre,* as some people were taking to calling it, there had been many times that many. Thousands, even. *But not today. No. They fear the blue ghost will come again.*

Old Archibald Benton shuffled up to Raynald's side, his layers of oversized robes trailing on the ground at his feet. *He looks like a child wearing his parent's bedsheet,* Cecilia thought. "My prince, should we not...begin proceedings?" the old Master of Messages said. "It is ill-judged to stand here too long, I feel. Being here at all is...well, it feels sinister, after what happened last time."

Raynald gave the old man a comforting smile. "Master Archibald, don't fear. We have plenty of protection and the crowds have no reason to riot again. We are perfectly safe."

Yes, and I've made sure of that too. Cecilia had spoken at length with Watch Commander Morwood about guaranteeing Raynald's safety - and by extension, her own - during the executions, and Morwood had obliged. It felt like there were five soldiers and watchmen for every local resident in the square. And they had Sir Kevyn, Sir Owen, and Sir Mallister with them as well, along with Raynald's own hand-picked troop of Emerald Guards. In all, they were perfectly safe. *But still...*

Cecilia looked out over the crowds, as more people began to arrive from the side streets and alleys and squirming passageways that webbed off the square. *Are you out there, Father?* she wondered, idly searching for cloaked men who might fit his proportions. She smiled wryly, amused by her own silly fears. "People are still coming for the show, Archibald," she said to the old scholar. "Give it a little longer. They deserve to see who is to blame for what happened. They deserve to see them die."

They waited for a few more minutes, as more people trickled into the square, before Raynald lost patience, and called for proceedings to begin. "Bring out the first ones," he commanded Watch Commander Morwood. "Sir Gerlon's co-conspirators. We'll have them swinging first."

"As you wish, my prince," Morwood said.

The men were brought out in a line, three of them, all gagged and bloodied and raggedly dressed. One was a known cutthroat who was claimed to have killed a hundred men and women, a debatable record that had nonetheless been plenty to earn him a spot here today. Another was well known as well, an agitator who often spoke at rallies and protests decrying the rule of House Lukar. Most thought him a crackpot, but he'd serve as another neck in a noose. The third and final was a large brute with thick shoulders and a bald pate, a dimwit who'd been accused many times of rape and molestation. No one would miss him.

Lord Morwood began, declaring each of the prisoners guilty of sedition and the incitement of mass rioting as the ropes were strung around their necks. He named them in turn, enumerating their other crimes as well. *Their only provable crimes,* Cecilia thought. In truth, there was no proof that any of these three were involved in the rioting, let alone its incitement and outbreak, yet the gibbet always looked better with a few more bodies lined up along it, Cecilia thought.

"For the crimes hereby mentioned," finished Watch Commander Morwood, once the men were in place, roped and ready to swing, "these three shall be hanged by the neck until dead!" The crowd gave out a muted *hummmm* of anticipation; it had grown larger now; three, four, even five hundred perhaps, and more still seemed to be coming. "Remove their gags so they might speak final words."

Fool, thought Cecilia. She'd told him not to permit that.

A soldier marched up to the cutthroat first, pulling down his gag.

"What say you?" asked Morwood. "Do you have final words before you fall into the Long Abyss?"

"I have words!" erupted the cutthroat's voice. His name was Billy 'Shank', shank being his favoured method of murdering his victims. "Words of innocence, m'lord, aye! I weren't never there, at them riots. *Never*! I tell it true. I ain't had no interest in Janilah, nor hearing what he had to say. I weren't there, I promise it!"

"Then where were you?"

Damn it, Trillian. This was not the plan!

"I was with Maggy the Marshlander. Ask her, she'll tell you!"

Morwood looked perplexed. "And who is this Maggy the Marshlander?"

"A whore, m'lord, and a well-known one." He looked into the crowds. "See faces here right now who've had her. She keeps her books, client books. Timings and payments and everything. She'll prove I weren't there, she will!"

Cecilia saw a few nodding heads in the crowd. Clearly this Maggy the Marshlander was popular. Lord Morwood finally gave her a glance, and saw her give a furtive shake of the head. "That... that isn't going to happen, I'm afraid. Whether she can prove your innocence in the matter of sedition is irrelevant. And I use the term 'prove' lightly. If you have a relationship with this woman, she may have seen fit to grant you a false alibi. A whore cannot be trusted. And we have proof of our own that says you were there, and integral to the violence…"

"No, m'lord, I weren't! I WEREN'T!"

"Silence," commanded Morwood. "You are worthy of the noose ten times over for the men you've killed alone. It's high time you met your maker." He looked to the soldier, and nodded.

Billy Shank's pleading voice was abruptly cut off as the stool was kicked from under him, the ropes tightening about his neck and throat and turning his cries into a muted splutter. He kicked, squirmed, fought for his life, and all for nothing. Within a short minute, his body had gone limp, his face had gone purple, and he was swinging gently side to side on the breeze to a gentle *creak* of wood.

"Next," bellowed Morwood. The agitator and anti-Lukarist came next, his gag removed so he might speak. Morwood looked more reluctant to permit that now, but he'd set out his stall and had to follow through. "Speak, then," he said. "Do you have words before you fall?"

The agitator was an unkempt man, all wild stringy hair and long messy beard. He looked half-starved as well, as though he'd spent much of his life begging on the street. Through a set of wide maddened eyes he looked right at Prince Raynald and said. "Words? Oh, I have words. The same words I've been shouting for years. The LUKARS ARE WRONG!" he cried out, his voice suddenly blaring so loud it rang out across the entire square. "Wrong! Wrong! Wrong! Evil! Wicked! Cruel! Tukor will judge them all! They who slew the Forgeborn lines! They who ended Ilith's blood! They are invaders and pillagers and killers and conquerors! We must free Tukor of their chains! FREE TUKOR! FREE TUKOR! FREE TUKOR!" he chanted.

Around the square, a few others took up the call. Cecilia could sense a nervousness building on the stage. She shot a look at Lord Morwood, who shot a look at his captains, who dashed off to take care of the dissenters. "Oh, gods be good, it's happening again," quailed Archibald.

"It *isn't* happening again," Cecilia snapped at him. "And you weren't even there. Grow some balls, you old fool."

She ignored the rest of Archibald's pitiful whimpering and turned to Lord Morwood once more. The agitator was still chanting, "FREE

TUKOR! FREE TUKOR!" and it felt about time he was silenced. A single nod was all that was needed; at once, Morwood marched to the man himself and swept the stool away from beneath him. His chanting ended there.

Cecilia turned to her nephew. "He's a known madman, Raynald - or *was* - don't listen to him. The Lukars have done a great deal of good for this city and this kingdom. Everyone knows it."

"Not everyone, Auntie." Raynald's voice was tight, as he watched the agitator squirm and wriggle on the rope. She knew he'd planned to make a speech today, but this lunatic had somewhat ruined that. There were still some groups calling out 'FREE TUKOR!" from the crowd, though for the most part the city watchmen were taking control of matters. A few of the chanters were attempting to escape, Cecilia could see, dashing away into the blackened border of the square, as some soldiers gave chase. Raynald looked more troubled than angry. "Do you think I should say something? I *wanted* to say something, Auntie."

"No," she said at once.

"But…some of what he said…we *are* invaders, conquerors. We did wipe out the line of Ilith. We slaughtered the Forgeborn houses…"

"No, Raynald. Galin Lukar did that, not you or your brother or anyone who might follow you. You have a chance now to cleanse the Lukar name." *And Ilith's line isn't yet broken,* she thought. *I have his direct descendent safely hidden away as we speak.*

"Do they forget my father?" Raynald frowned out at his people, shaking his head. "My grandfather may have lost his way, but Father…he was well-loved and admired. He was a hero to us all, the same as Amron Daecar. Don't they see me as the same? And Robbert? You have your spies, Auntie. What do they say about me among the streets and squares down here?"

Very little, she thought. Unfortunately, everyone was still talking about Janilah's disappearance and Rylian's death and, on occasion, what sort of king Robbert might make, but no one was talking about Raynald. If anyone ever did they would usually denounce him as the '*stand-in-king*' or '*the spare*' or sometimes simply, '*who?*'. Cecilia didn't imagine he'd like to hear that, though. So she decided to lie. "They say you'll make a fine king, if that should happen, and your brother the same. They look positively on the future you will bring to Ilithor and Tukor, Raynald." She dismissed the final hecklers with a flick of her wrist. "Forget these few rebels and dissidents, they're nothing but a vocal minority. Most are saying nothing, Raynald. They regard you with respect. Have you not seen how many admiring looks you have gotten today?"

The boy turned to her. "I have?"

"Of course you have."

"Truly? I hadn't noticed."

"And why would you? You're not meant to see. A king should be above all that."

He nodded, pondering those words, and suddenly he was Raynald the would-be king again, stiff-necked and steely, looking out upon his people with a noble clench to his jaw.

Cecilia gestured for Lord Morwood to continue proceedings, and the last of the appetisers was given a chance to speak.

She wasn't so worried about this one, lackwit that he was. "Anything to say?" the Watch Commander asked him. "Speak quickly, now. The Long Abyss awaits."

The big man started sobbing like a child. "I did nothin'. Nothin'. Not me." He snuffled loudly through his huge flat nose. "I only watched. I were there, but I watched."

"You stand accused of many counts of rape and assault," Lord Morwood said. "Do you confess to those? Do so and you will fall less burdened of sin. *Confess*," he urged.

"I couldn't help it," wailed the brute. "I got urges, I do. I can't stop it. I didn't mean nothin' by it."

"That sounds like a confession to me." Lord Morwood had heard enough. He nodded and once more the stool was kicked, and a man struggled, spluttered, and died. A few women in the crowds cheered as the brute swung and twisted on the rope. His victims, most likely, or those close to them. Then all went quiet and still for a moment before Morwood called out the main event. "Sir Gerlon Rottlor," he roared. "Bring him forward."

Sir Gerlon's days in the dungeons had not been kind to him. He was filthy with muck and stank to high heaven, stains covering his breeches at the front and rear, hair unwashed and lank, eyes hollow. His gag, Cecilia hoped, would *not* be removed. There was no knowing what Sir Gerlon might say, and she sensed Trillian Morwood knew that as well.

The Watch Commander looked most uncomfortable, however, as the old Emerald Guard was led to the gallows and forced up onto a stool, the rope bound about his neck. *No wonder. He doesn't believe that Sir Gerlon planned the riots at all.* Morwood had made his doubts clear enough the day Sir Gerlon had been brought to council and condemned, though hadn't spoken of it since. Thankfully, there was something of the coward about Watch Commander Trillian Morwood. *He wants someone to blame just as much as I do,* Cecilia thought, *should my king father return.*

The man's crimes were listed. It wasn't a particularly long list - really, Sir Gerlon had been an upstanding knight and loyal in his service to crown and country. *Except when he conspired to have me murdered.* That was his only true crime, and plenty, so far as Cecilia Blakewood thought, to have him join these other three. But did he conspire to start those riots and have his king killed, in vengeance for Prince Rylian's death, whom he had long served and admired? No, was the simple answer. No, he did not.

Still, Lord Morwood announced him guilty, as decreed by the prince. "By the order of Prince Raynald of House Lukar, standing ruler of Tukor, Sir Gerlon of House Rottlor has been condemned to die for the crime of sedition and conspiracy to commit regicide. As ringleader of these others…" He gestured to the corpses swinging on the beam… "Sir Gerlon forgoes his right to speak before his death. The crime of attempting to kill a king demands an execution to befit it. Yet in regard to his years of good service among the Emerald Guard, and by the mercy of our pure-hearted prince, he has been awarded a quicker end." He turned stockily, jowls wobbling. "Sir Gerlon Rottlor, you shall now be hanged by the neck until dead. May Tukor forgive you for…for what you have done." He turned to the soldier behind Roller and gave a reluctant nod.

And so the man did hang.

His death was worse than the others. Not because he writhed and twisted and tried to fight the rope. Not because of the purple colour that climbed his neck, or the taut muscles, or the bulging veins. No, Sir Gerlon faced his end with courage, hanging perfectly still, accepting it, even welcoming it.

Yet his eyes, Cecilia thought. They stared at her with a hatred she could scarcely fathom existed. It sent a chill through her, that look. And suddenly she was afraid, looking out toward the crowd, wondering. *Are you there? Do you watch, Father?* Every cloaked man looked like an enemy to her eyes. And there were eyes staring back at her, she didn't fail to miss. Chill eyes. Hateful eyes. Eyes that called her bitch and witch and worse. Eyes like Sir Gerlon Rottlor's. *These people want me dead,* she thought. *That will never change.*

A silence had thickened over the square. You could hear a single cough from fifty yards. Lord Morwood's voice broke it, a welcome sound, though a tad shaky. "Let this bring to a close the ugly events that have despoiled our fair city," he called. His voice echoed out into Galin's Post, and into the black wreck left by the fires beyond. "The inciters and instigators have been caught and punished and we can move forward now from here..."

"What about the king?" called a woman's voice, somewhere at the heart of the square. "Has he been found yet?"

"Not as yet," Morwood answered her. "But we are continuing the search, and will not take long to..."

"Leave him wherever he's crawled away to," shouted a man. "Let him rot." Cecilia found him in time to see him spit. He was an old man, the sort who didn't care for reprisals. "Curse him, I say. Curse him to Long Abyss along with these." He pointed a withered finger at the men hanging on the gibbet and spat again at his feet.

Several soldiers strode forward to take him, but Raynald surged forward, two sharp steps, moving to the front of the stage. "No," he called out to them. "You leave that man be. He is entitled to speak his mind. And if that's to deplore my grandfather for what he did, so be it. He's entitled to that as well."

A murmur broke out, spreading like a ripple on a pond. "You condemn your own grandfather?" someone shouted. "Your own king?"

"I do," Raynald declared. "Any sane man would, would he not?" He paused to let that question settle. "My grandfather possesses the Mistblade, this we all know, and with it he did deal terrible death. It shames me. It shames my brother who is now his heir. It shames our good name and our house. It shames Ilith, who forged those blades to be used for good, not evil. To beat back the Agarathi and their allies. To slay dragons, not children."

"How did he get it?" another voice cried.

"I don't know. None of us knows." Raynald referred to his council, standing behind him. "My grandfather hid much from his kith and kin and has paid the price with his descent into madness. And you, good people of Ilithor, of White Shadow, you have paid the price too, and more dearly. Your fathers, sons, husbands, brothers, wives and mothers and sisters and daughters. Too many were slain that day. Far too many. The Mad King's Massacre, I hear you've been calling it, and are you wrong?" He shook his head. "No, you're not. I was always taught by my father and grandfather to own up to my actions, to face them, and be accountable for them, and therefore so must he. King Janilah Lukar has to answer for this, dead or alive. Whether he returns to us or not, can we…can we let him retake the throne? Can we permit him to rule us, after what he has done and become?"

The crowd erupted now, calling out in a hundred voices. *He speaks well,* Cecilia thought. She had not expected her nephew to be so daring. Within that cacophony, however, she had a quiet word with him. "Raynald, are you sure you've thought this through?" She could hear the hissing boos now, those directed at her, no doubt, as she interfered. She ignored them. "If my father does come back…"

"If he comes back he will need to answer for his crimes," Raynald told her. And for the first time, the first true time, she thought he sounded like a king. "The people will not accept him anymore. We need new blood, Auntie. Fresh blood. *Honourable* blood." He turned back to the heaving crowds and raised a hand. "My brother Robbert is next in line to the throne," he called out to them. "Will you follow him, when he returns from the war? Will you accept him as your…"

"We'll follow *you*," a young man broke in, rallying those around him. "You're twins. Why not you, Prince Raynald? You're here, and your brother isn't. And I already see a crown on your head!"

Some laughed at that, though it didn't sound mocking. Others were cheering and throwing up their fists and suddenly it seemed like the square was as loud and busy as it had been the day of the riots. "This is but a circlet," Raynald called, raising his hand for silence once more. "My brother is the elder, and the heir. I cannot supersede him to the throne."

"Why not? You look exactly the same!" shouted someone.

"Who's for raising Prince Raynald to king?" hollered another. He swept his arms up above his head and leapt suddenly onto a crate. "Who says we call him king? King Raynald Lukar, to wash away his grandfather's sins! King Ray! All hail Raynald, King of Tukor!"

The tide was becoming overwhelming now, and Raynald's protests were being drowned out. Cecilia stole a look at old Emmit Gershan and saw that he looked none-too-pleased about this.

Archibald looked utterly lost and Lord Morwood seemed to like this turn of events, unexpected though it was.

The noise was so deafening, in fact, that at first the dragon wasn't heard or seen.

Raynald was still calling for calm and Lord Morwood was talking to his captains and Lord Gershan was creeping away with his retinue when, suddenly, someone pointed skyward and screeched out in an ear-splitting voice, "DRAGON!"

Cecilia didn't believe it at first. No dragon would fly this far north, and certainly not so low as to provoke such a reaction. But then she looked up and there it was, an immense shape in scaly purple and black, no more than fifty metres from the ground. A deep thrum of terror went right through her, and for a moment her bowels turned to water. She could feel the air being pulled by its passing, the heavy beat of its wings. Loose leaves and bits of litter swirled in its wake. And when it let out that rumbling, sky-shattering shriek that seemed to reverberate right down into her very bones, all hell broke loose.

People began screaming, running, scattering, tripping over one another as they fled. Half of Raynald's Emerald Guards rushed right forward to shield him and the other half drew their swords or raised their great long spears, readying to throw. Sir Owen Armdall leapt straight down off the stage and went charging to the heart of the square, bearded and unwashed, bellowing the dragon down for a duel. Sir Kevyn was stood on the spot, gazing upward with wide brown eyes. His dragon-killing father, the Old Bull, Lord Brayman Bolt, he was not. Sir Mallister remained to protect Cecilia. "My lady, we must go!"

Some arrows were following the dragon as it swept across the skies, and the crossbowmen stationed about the square were raising to fire as well, peppering it with quarrels and bolts. Cecilia could only watch as the beast flew one way, and then the other, arcing, wheeling, swooping, rising, ignoring the little bowmen below, and ignoring the knights and their spears and their swords, and ignoring the demand for a duel laid down by Sir Owen Armdall.

And then she saw it. "My gods, it…it has no rider." Sir Mallister Monsort had his hand around her arm, tugging her away. "Mallister, look! The beast is riderless," she shouted over the din.

He gave a glance to the skies. "I have to get you to safety, my lady."

"Didn't you hear me? It's *riderless!*"

She'd created a loyal hound in the man, clearly, because he hardly even seemed to listen to her as he hauled her away. The square was quickly emptying now, but for Sir Owen and the gallant men who had poured forth to join him. Yet for all that the dragon was not interested in them, nor was it spewing out its deadly dragon-fire, or swooping down with those great grasping talons. Only when the ballistas mounted on the nearest battlements were manned and loaded, and the huge great dragon-killing bolts shot its way, did the monster relent in its circling and climb, beating those huge leathern wings and rising, up and away into the scuttling clouds.

The men gave out a cheer, as soldiers and spearmen and shieldmen and crossbowmen all came boiling down from the Sentinels with weapons to hand. More ballistas were manned and catapults too, and all across the city, the alarm bells were ringing out as though expecting a great Agarathi horde to come pouring up through the valley.

But none of that felt likely to Cecilia. None of that felt right. As she was escorted, breathless, back to the palace, she had but a single thought running around her head.

The beast was searching for something.

And she had a feeling she knew just what.

40

Janilah

He could hear the noise from his bed. It sounded like the whole city was under siege. There was a city bell ringing somewhere directly above him, up on the battlements here in the north of White Shadow, but it was not the only one. Every time it clanged and chimed, another followed right after, further off, and he could hear others too, yet further, and others further than that.

He swung his legs to the floor, planting his feet on the cold rough stone. The basement that had become his home was an earthy damp place, a cellar hidden beneath the shack of the old woman who'd restored him to health. He'd hated her at first, wanted to kill her even, but that urge had now passed. *She strapped me down for a reason*, he told himself. *After what I did...maybe I deserved it.*

He'd had the full story from the crone when he'd finally awoken, tied up on this old bed, with only the mice and rats and spiders to attend him. There were plenty of those down here in the dimness, and worms as well, where the earth broke through the stone. At first, he'd feared the old woman would leave him to starve or be eaten alive, but no, she was kinder than that. "You killed a woman I know out there at the Post," she told him. "Never liked that bitch, though, so supposin' I'll forgive you." She had yellowy-brown teeth, though half of them were missing, bloody gums and foul breath and skin that was far too loose for her bones. "That's what poverty looks like, my king," she'd said, when she'd caught him looking at her in a mingle of horror and disgust. "When you ain't got enough to eat, you end up looking like a bag o' bones dressed in sallow skin. And you ain't much to look at yourself either. Two weeks unconscious is plenty to strip a man o' his meat."

"Two weeks?" he'd croaked. "I've been unconscious for two weeks?"

"Aye, just that. You had a second heart attack too, I figure. Seems the toil of massacrin' a hundred people has driven you over the edge."

He recalled little of that. *A hundred?* "I...I can't have," he insisted. He could remember drawing out the Mistblade, yes, and those armed men swinging at him, and he could remember swinging back at them as well, cleaving several apart, but after...no, after that all was a blur. "A hundred?" The number was hard to believe. "I couldn't have. I *wouldn't*."

"You did." The old woman had him well fastened down, his arms and legs tied with hempen rope to the legs of the bed on which he lay. She pointed to his fetters. "Had to restrain you, else you might have woken up and killed a host more. And wasn't only men, but women too. Some are sayin' children as well." She looked at him, sucking on her lower lip, her pointy jaw moving in and out. "You done a bad thing, Janilah Lukar. But there's goodness in you still, I know."

He had raged that night, trying to rip free of his ropes, but his heart and body felt so weak that he could scarcely summon the strength to shake the bed beneath him. The old woman had let him be for some hours, only returning once he'd calmed, creeping down that stair from the hovel she kept above. "You keep on shoutin', and I'll have to gag you too," she'd warned, holding up a stained piece of cloth in her crinkly old fingers. "They find out I've got you down here....well, that'll be the end for me. I may be old, but I don't want that. Not ready to feed the worms just yet, m'lord."

"Let me go!" Janilah had demanded, not listening to her. "I'm your king, you stupid wench. Let me go!"

"Aye, my king. And a madman and a monster too. You been sleepin' for two weeks, and if anyone around here learns you're down in my cellar, they'll have you sleepin' *forever*, believe me. You ain't much loved no more, Jan the Mad Man. That's what some are callin' you. But there are others, aye." She'd rattled off a few of the slanderous nicknames that had spouted since that massacre, then went on. "But I see more than they do, m'lord. I see a man who's lost his way, and needs some time to heal, so I do. So you'll stay strapped up down here until you behave. I ain't letting you loose till you're right in the head."

Janilah had barely heard any of that. "Where's my blade?" he bellowed at her through a dry and rusted throat. "The Mistblade. Where is it!"

The crone gestured to a blanket in the corner, near a few mouldy old crates. "I thought I'd best cover it up. Can't move it, much too heavy for me. Was a struggle enough gettin' *you* into that bed."

Janilah was only just beginning to catch up. "You…you found me down here?"

"Well I didn't find you out on the street, did I? Course I found you down here!" she cackled. "You must've used that Mistblade o' yours to go through the walls or some such. No signs of a break-in, so figured you needed somewhere to rest and lay low. You know, after you slaughtered all them people. That's energy sappin' work, that."

Janilah still didn't believe it. He shook his head, wordless.

"Deny it all you like," the crone said. "It happened, and things've changed for you now." She'd drawn up a stool and folded her old frame onto the seat. "What'll you do now, d'you think? The city hates you, word is, and no surprise. There's fear, aye, but hate most of all. Those people you killed had families, friends. You've lost the faith of the smallfolk, Jan."

Jan, he'd thought. No one had called him Jan since his father and brother and sister, who were all long decades dead. "I wasn't myself," he managed to rasp, pulling futilely at his ropes. He remembered the Mistblade whispering, *kill them all, kill them all, kill them all.* "They attacked me, threw fruit…dung. I was only defending myself."

"Aye, at first," nodded the crone. "Those first men you slew were well armed and baying for blood, no doubt, but after the first ten, twenty? Everyone seemed an enemy to you, man or woman or child, old or young, armed or no. You were bloodlusted, everyone says. Some crazed blue ghost, cutting everyone up to ribbons."

She pointed to the blanket under which the Mistblade was hidden. Janilah saw bloody stains on the floor there, dried into the stone and dirt. "You were covered in blood from head to toe when I found you down here. And you stank. That shit and rotting fruit, aye, that was all over you too. Thought you were dead at first, but no, only unconscious. Took me an age to clean you up and get you dressed in my husband's old rags, never mind get you into this bed. And 'why', you might ask. Well…suppose it's just in my blood and bones to want to heal people, Jan. Did that during the last war; healin' folk, that is. And for long years before then too. When I see someone who needs tendin', I have to help, no matter who they are or what they've done."

She stood. "Now, you'll have to trust me. I ain't removing those ropes until your heart is stronger, and your mind too, that most of all. I'll have you promise you won't kill me as well." She smiled, looking down at him. "Oh, you hate me now, I can see it in your eyes, but I'm doing this for your own good. You need more time before you go back into the world. And if you know what's good for you, you'll keep quiet from now on. There are men up there looking for you, and not all o' them are friends."

The next time she came to him, Janilah complained of a need to relieve himself. His bowels were a hot fury and strapped down as he was, he had no option but to soil himself lest she untie him. "Nope, not yet," she'd said, when he'd demanded just that. "You just go ahead and shit in them breeches there. Don't worry, I've seen it all."

He'd refused, threatened, and tried to cajole the crone, but she'd been resolute as a bloody rock. "Damn you, then!" he'd growled at her when his want became too fierce, letting his bowels empty out, warm and wet and reeking. "You seek to humble me? Me!" He had sworn and cursed at her, but she'd only stood there, hands on her hips, taking it all with a smile on her face.

"I've been cleaning you up for weeks, m'lord," she told him. "What difference does it make that you're awake?"

"That *is* the difference, you old bat! I'm *awake* now. And a king. You would demean me like this!"

"We all come into the world the same," she said piously, "squalling and shitting, whether king or commoner. You seem to have forgotten that. Now hold still while I wipe your royal arse and remove them breeches. Then I'll fetch you a nice fresh pair."

The utter shame of it had been almost more than he could bear, and all the while, he promised himself he would hang, draw, and quarter this wretched witch as soon as he was free. But once he was clean and dressed in fresh linen, somehow he didn't feel so enraged. *She's trying to help you,* he told himself. *If you'd woken up somewhere else, you mightn't have been so lucky. You mightn't have woken up at all.*

"Good, all better," she said when she was done. She had a long look at him. "I've been feeding you soup while you were out. Not easy, with your throat all tight, but managed to get some down to keep you goin', and water too. But now that you're awake, we need to fatten you back up. You're all skin and bone, m'lord. Won't do your heart no good to be so malnourished. It's a wonder you're still alive, really."

"I'm Bladeborn. We're not like other men."

"Aye, true. And you of that pure Lukar blood as well. Not many men who could wield the Mistblade as you did." She smiled. "Oh, I should say, there's some more on that…" It was then that she'd told him about Sir Gerlon Rottlor, who had been condemned to die for the crime of sedition and attempted regicide. "Heard someone talking about it at market. He must have gotten it from a guardsman or someone up at the palace. Seems that old Emerald Guard was behind it all along."

"A trap," Janilah whispered, remembering. He'd thought it that day in the square. The rioters were well organised and well armed and there was no coincidence there. "Someone set me up to die," he said, half to himself. Then he looked the crone in those wrinkly rheumy eyes of hers. "They're saying it was Sir Gerlon?"

"Aye, that's what I'm hearin'. Word is he was your son's man. People are sayin' he was wantin' vengeance for Rylian's death." She frowned down at him. "*Were* that you, then? Rylian? You slew your own son?" She stopped short of tutting, though the disapproval in her expression was clear enough.

"No," he rasped at her. "No, I didn't."

"What happened then? Was he tryin' to take your throne like the rumours say?"

Janilah wasn't going to talk about that with this interfering old bag. He'd merely clenched his jaw and turned away from her, imagining once again how he'd kill her when he was free.

Two days later, the upcoming execution of Sir Gerlon Rottlor was confirmed. The crone came to him once more bearing bread and soup and cheese. His desire to murder her had faded by then. "There was a crier at Galin's Post," she told him, spooning soup through his bearded lips. "Said Rottlor's gonna hang in three days, same place. By decree o' Prince Raynald. He's rulin' now in your stead, I hear."

No, Janilah thought to that. *That would be my daughter.*

He'd gone quiet for the rest of that day, falling deep in his thoughts. The crone still refused to release him from his restraints, but for all that, for all the feeding and cleaning and wiping she had to do for him, he no longer wanted to see her head parted from her shoulders. He understood her reasons for keeping him shackled and he even decided to thank her for it. The next day, he voiced that gratitude. "You were right," he simply told her, with a grunt. "To keep me here. You were right."

"Well now, my ears must be full o' wax or somethin'. Did the great Janilah Lukar just thank a fusty old bag like me?"

"Don't push it, woman," he warned. "Half the time I still want you dead."

"And there he is, *Jan the Mad Man*. What sort of thanks is that, to bless me with one hand and strike me with t'other?"

"It's the best you're going to get. Just take it for what it is. I'm trying to say thank you, woman."

She'd cocked a brow. "Truly? Wiping that royal arse o' yours n'all?" She'd cackled when he'd given no answer, and tottered over to his right ankle. Her thin dirty fingers reached out from her rags and began untying the rope.

"What are you doing?"

"What do you think? That thanks sounded sincere enough to me. So...what the hell. Seems you're ready to wipe your own arse, m'lord." She paused. "Just don't go killin' me when you're untied now. You promised, remember?"

I did, Janilah thought, though he'd been known to break promises before. Still, the woman was safe from him. "I'll not harm you," he told her. *On my honour, such as it is.*

When she'd untied all four of his limbs, he remained lying there a few moments longer. That had confused the woman. "What, all that noise you made about me letting you go, and you ain't even gonna try to stand?"

"I fear I may stumble," he admitted. "My legs...I'm still weak."

"Well let's strengthen you up then." She ambled in and gave him her arm, all bone and skinny strands of muscle. "Come on, up you get. I've helped rehabilitate men before, m'lord. I know what I'm doin'. Up."

He'd managed to stand, in the end, without falling, though his legs felt terribly weak and his head swam horribly from the effort. He did a circuit of the small cellar with the crone by his side, watchful, then another without her, before returning to his bed. "So I'm guessing you'll stay a while, then?" the old woman asked.

Janilah answered with a silent nod.

"Well, in that case I'd best fetch you a chamberpot. Got an old pail upstairs that'll serve."

Wonderful, he thought. But squatting over a bucket was better than soiling his breeches, he supposed.

It had felt good to escape his bounds, though. He spent time rubbing his wrists and ankles where the hempen rope had chaffed, and turned the stuffed staw mattress over as well, not caring to think of how much of his own filth had leaked into it. He walked the room again, back, forward, back, forward, strengthening his legs, and his heart, and his resolve. And only when he was ready, did he creep over to that blanket by those crates, bend down onto one knee, and unveil the blade beneath.

It lay on the cold grey stone, that wondrous cobalt blue, the glyphs burning bright down the length of the steel. The mists swirled lazily, rhythmically, beautifully. He reached out to take the hilt, eager to feel that familiar rush of power, but something stayed his hand. Those whispers, rustling away in the back of his head, softly, ever-so-softly saying, *kill her, kill the crone, kill them all, kill them all.*

He drew his fingers away, backing off. *No. No…I'm not ready…I'm not strong enough yet.*

He retreated to his bed. *Jan the Mad Man,* he thought. *The Mad King's Massacre. Loopy Lukar. The Child-Killer King.* They were some of the names the crone had spoken of, but not all. *I am the Warrior King no more. People forget who I once was. They forget I slew a dragon in single combat. They forget my triumphs and victories.*

And who is to blame for that? he wondered to himself. *There is no one… no one but you.*

He was still deep in his musings when the old woman returned. "See you've been gettin' reacquainted," she said, waving to the blade with a liver-spotted hand. "You sure that's wise, m'lord? Seems pointless o' me to have nursed you back to health, only for you to go off slayin' again. That ain't why I did it. I'd hoped you might change."

"I didn't touch it," he told her, growing irritated by her sanctimony. "What happened that day…it *won't* happen again. I was provoked, drawn into a trap. And this talk of dead women and children…" He shook his head. "That isn't me."

She nodded to that. "No, I believe you, m'lord. You're proud, ruthless, aye, but no killer o' innocents. I remember you when you were young. The whole city looked up to you then. The way you stood up to them dragonfolk when they slew your brother Jaylor. The way you took charge, even when your father Jeerah was king. We all wanted a stronger ruler then and you gave us that. For long years we cherished you. I should know. My husband Dickie and I would say our prayers at night, and you'd be in 'em, every time. We'd thank the good lord Tukor for sending you to us. And we'd pray for him to keep you safe. I kept that up when Dickie died and I still pray for you to this day. I know in your heart you want to be good, m'lord. And *do* good, by us all. I suppose you've just lost your way a bit, and…well…now we all know why."

Her eyes moved over to the Mistblade and her face fell into a scowl. "You want to be pointin' fingers, blaming someone, *somethin'*, you start with *that.* I'd have gotten rid of it if I could, but you'd need to be a Lukar or Daecar to be able to lift it. But keepin' it hidden… *that* I can do." She shambled across the room and threw the blanket back over it, shaking her head all the while. "If I were you, I'd leave it here when you go. It's a curse, m'lord, and has weighed heavy on you, that's clear enough. Leave it here, and I'll never speak of it. Not to a soul, I promise. You can use the stairs. Head out the alley through the back o' the house and take the passage up beside the city walls. That'll take you to the top o' White Shadow. Turn left and keep on going along the wall and you'll eventually come to the White Shadow Gate. You'll find your own men there if not before. They'll be able to get you back to the palace safe enough."

That was never going to happen, Janilah knew, but he nodded all the same, grateful for her words. "Sir Bonmer Marsh commands the White Shadow Gate."

"He did, aye. But he's dead now. He was butchered during the riots, and one o' your sworn swords too. Huffort, I think it was. One man was boastin' about that a few days later. Said he'd opened Sir Edwyn's belly and pulled his guts right out. He had a string o' sausages about his neck and was claimin' they were the man's intestines, down in some alehouse not far from here."

Janilah's mouth tightened to hear that. Sir Edwyn Huffort had been a loyal sword of his for years. It was no way to die. "What happened to this braggart?"

"Another o' your swords slew him. The Oak o' Armdall. He got wind o' the man's boasts and came bargin' in one day with a host of city watchmen at his back. Hacked him right up in front o' everyone. Don't think the man was telling the truth, myself, but hey ho, you play with fire and all that."

She told him other stories like that over the next couple of days. It seemed that the search for Janilah had been the palace's top priority for weeks, yet half the city were sending in hoaxes and false reports as to his whereabouts to confuse it. Other braggers and boasters had been slain as well, by all accounts, and Sir Owen's name seemed to crop up often in that. "He wears a beard now, and his hair's all wild and unwashed," the crone told him. "This Oak o' yours is loyal, m'lord. Word is, he won't shave till you're found. I'm just hopin' he doesn't kick in my door one o' these days. He'll have my head bouncing across the floor in a snap for keeping you here."

"I wouldn't allow that," Janilah told her. "Have they not come searching here before?"

The little woman bobbed that pencil neck of hers up and down. "Once, a few days after you'd gone missing. They had a wander around but didn't stay long. I've got an honest face, m'lord."

There was some truth in that, ugly though that face was. The cellar was accessed through a secret door in her floor, which was covered by a large rug, Janilah knew, and no one would suspect an old crone like this of harbouring the crazed King of Tukor.

And that's what I am now. Fragments of memory of the massacre were still coming back to him, and he didn't much like what he saw. Through the blood and chaos of it, he could remember cutting through the crowds without consideration or regard for who they were, utterly and entirely lost to his bloodlust. *I'll be the monster, then,* he recalled thinking, as he hacked and slashed and rained terror on that square. Yes, many hundreds of others were warring around him, but was that an excuse? Had anyone else slaughtered women, and children, and innocent men as well who were only there to see him speak?

Everyone seemed an enemy to you, the crone had told him, and she was right. Every swing of his sword was against someone who'd thrown rotting fruit and dung and swung at him with blunts and blades and axes, but that wasn't the truth. *Only some had,* he knew now. *The rest… the rest did not deserve to die.*

He'd dwelt that night in a state of dark rumination, trying to figure out where it had all gone so wrong. Everything had stacked up against him of late, the setbacks and defeats, the loss of the Nightblade and the Windblade and the Sword of Varinar too, Ranulf Shackton's theft of the page from the Book of Thala, Archibald Benton's failure to uncover the location of the Frostblade, Godrik Taynar's defiance and Elyon Daecar's escape and Rylian's death and the heart attack that had followed.

Everything, he thought. *Everything. That day in the square I was supposed to clear that away, announce my true purpose, tell them how I have held the torch, how I have lit the way, but no...it was another failure, and my worst of all, and now I am become my father, my pathetic weak-willed father, heckled and hated and mocked by the mob.*

He sat there in the basement, as the candle the crone had given him flickered and began to gutter out, wondering. Wondering where he could go from here. Wondering what was next for him now. He couldn't figure it out. Once not so long ago everything he had touched had turned to gold. Now his grasp made only ash and cinder and death.

And smiling wryly, he whispered in the darkness, "I light the torch. I light the way. It is I who is destined to combine the blades and win the war. It is I who'll fulfil King Galin's promise and win a Table of my own. Me, me, me." And down in that dank cellar, Janilah Lukar laughed to himself, at the utter fool he'd been.

When morning came, he was still sitting on his bed. The crone crept down with a fresh candle, fresh clothes, fresh food on a tray. She placed them on the table beside his bed, then took his chamberpot off for washing. "I'll be away a while, for the executions," she told him. "You'll be here when I get back?" There was something hopeful in her voice.

I have replaced her dead husband, Janilah thought. "I will."

"Aye." She smiled. "Well, I'll tell you all about it later, then. Anything in particular you want me to look out for?"

He nodded and said in a quiet voice. "Watch my daughter, closely. And my grandson, Raynald. Him too."

"As you wish, m'lord."

And now, up above him, the bells were still ringing out, chiming relentlessly throughout the city. He sat on the bed, wondering what had happened. Another riot? Have the people risen up again? He began pacing, back and forth, back and forth, as he often did. From beneath the blanket thrown over the Mistblade, he could see thin pennons of silken blue smoke curling up and out, reaching to the air like grasping fingers. He stopped, staring. Through all his long days here, the mists had been kept well hidden beneath that blanket, but no longer. *Something excites it,* he thought, stepping over. He reached to remove the cover, but a groan of wood beckoned his attention, and above he heard the creaking of floorboards and then, abruptly, the ceiling door to the cellar swung upon.

The crone peered down. She was breathing heavily, her face flush, eyes ripe with something approaching fear.

"What happened," Janilah called up to her.

She uttered a single word. "Dragon."

A moment later, Janilah Lukar had the Mistblade in his grasp, and was marching straight up those steep wooden stairs dressed in his roughspun breeches and vest and tunic. The old hag stepped aside as he emerged into her hovel for the very first time. He took one look around. The place was as small and unremarkable as expected. "Where?" he asked. She looked at him blankly. "The dragon. Where is it?"

"It…it was at the Post," she told him, swallowing.

He nodded. "Are there others? Are we under attack?"

"No, I…no, it was just the one, m'lord." She was looking at him strangely, not like she had before. "You're…you're shimmering."

He looked down the length of himself. Unbidden, he'd activated the Mistblade's power. He felt stronger for it, much stronger. "Ignore it," he said.

"Aye." Fresh fear bloomed in the old crone's watery eyes, at the sudden power in him, the intensity in his voice.

He understood well enough. "I'm not going to harm you." He could hear the whispers, but they were different, somehow. *The blade senses the dragon. It is dragon-blood it craves, not the ichor of this old crone.* He took a pace toward her, and she backed away so sharply she almost fell. "I'm *not* going to harm you," he said again, louder. "I promised it. Now this dragon. Is it still out there?" He loomed over her tiny shrunken frame. "Speak, good woman! Has it been killed? Driven away?"

"Away…" she breathed, cowering. "Aye, it…it were leaving, I think. Your Oak, Sir Owen…he were in the square, calling it for a duel, but it ignored him. And everyone else besides. It ignored 'em all."

"It didn't kill anyone? It didn't attack?" Janilah couldn't make sense of it. "Did it fly low? Was it a scout?"

The woman nodded, swallowed, and composed herself. "Low,

aye, real low. The crowd…they were proclaimin' young Raynald king, all shoutin' and hollerin', so no one seemed to notice until it were right there above us. Massive it was. Purple and black. Never felt such fear." She was trembling still, her chest rising and falling in a series of sharp breaths.

Janilah took a moment to unpack that. Raynald, king? That made no sense. Robbert was his heir now, not Raynald. He put that aside. "Purple and black," he repeated, thinking. "Did anyone recognise the beast or its rider?"

She shook her head. "Not that I heard. And it had no rider, such as I saw."

"No rider?" That made no sense either. "No dragon would fly so far north without a rider."

"That one Elyon Daecar killed had no rider."

That was new as well. "Elyon Daecar killed a dragon?" His eyes twisted into a frown. "*When*?"

"Some week or so ago…I…I thought I told you? He slew it in a storm, word is. With the Windblade. They're calling him all sorts now, as they are you. Though his names are kinder, I'll admit."

Something in Janilah darkened. *I've missed too much,* he thought, *hidden away in this damned basement.* He began moving for the door. There was a large hooded cloak there, hanging on a hook. He swept it into his grasp and threw it over his broad shoulders.

"I…that were my husband's," the woman complained piteously. "I like to leave it there to remind me of…"

"I'm sorry, but I need it." Janilah drew the hood over his head, pulled on a pair of leather boots. "You're certain the dragon is gone?" Even now, he could hear the bells beginning to fade.

"Aye, I…I think so."

He nodded and walked straight for the door.

"M'lord, you sure you're ready to…"

He could hear the pleading tone to her voice. The crone had grown used to him. *She wants me to stay.* He turned. "Tell me, woman, what is your name?" In these long days, she had been crone and hag and wench to him. But he wanted to know. He wanted to remember her.

"It's…it's Ethelda m'lord. Ethelda Rivers."

He dipped his ragged, bearded chin. "A noble name," he told her with courtesy, "for a woman of noble heart." He gave her the smile she craved. "Did you watch, as I asked you, Ethelda? My daughter, and my grandson?"

"I did, m'lord, just as you asked. The Lady Cecilia, she…she was much in charge, it looked to me. Though your grandson did make a speech. Yet, even so…the spider…Lady Cecilia, I should say…she were in his ear, whispering. She isn't much liked, I don't think. Some men even say…they say that…"

I know, Janilah thought. *I know what men say.* "I thank you again for what you've done for me, Ethelda," he cut in. And without another word, he turned, phased right through the wooden door, and left the crone and her hovel behind.

41

Elyon

The encampment outside Dragon's Bane was abuzz with noise at the news. It had only been reported to Elyon mere minutes earlier and yet already they all seemed to know, Sir Marland's report spreading like wildfire across a field of dry crop.

The Agarathi were coming.

"How soon?" demanded Lord Kanabar, who'd marched right out of the fortress to join them at the southern edge of camp, with half the council in tow.

Sir Marland was still sweating from his dash across the Bloodmarshes. "A week, my lord, ten days at most. We spotted them emptying out of Blademelt three days ago...a huge host, tens of thousands strong." He gestured to his companions. Sir Marland had left many long days ago with five other scouts, yet only he and two others had returned. "Stafford and Mesh and Pentecost...they feed the weeds now, my lord. Mesh and Stafford were killed by Agarathi quarrels and Pentecost drowned in a bog. The rest of us...we only just made it back. We left the boat half a day from here...we've been running hard since dawn."

Elyon had heard this from him already, before Lords Kanabar and Fullerton and Rammas - who was Sir Marland's own lord and cousin - had appeared. The scouting party had left afoot almost two weeks gone, with the direct instruction to take a skiff and sail south through the Bloodmarshes and watch for enemy movements. It seemed they'd made it all the way across into Agarath, keeping to the fogs and the bogs, and managed to get in sight of the fearsome fortress of Blademelt itself, where they sat witness to its emptying. Half the party had been slain in their retreat, though the rest had got back to the little boat, rowing hard for two days and nights before the skiff crashed into a submerged rock, ripping out its guts and sinking it. That forced them to continue on foot that very morning. All three were well earned of a rest.

"Dragons?" asked Lord Elton Rammas, ever to the point. "How many did you see, Cousin?"

"Many," Sir Marland told him, a worried cast to his eyes. "It was hard to be sure from where we were hidden. Seemed to be at least five or six flying about the towers. Might have been many more."

"Then we've been right all along," said Killian quietly. "The hammer will fall here, hardest of all."

"We're well prepared," Lord Kanabar said to that, defiant to the last. "Tens of thousands you say, Sir Marland? Afoot? Mounted?"

"A mix, my lord. There looked to be swarms of soldiers coming from further along the coast as well. They had a camp outside Blademelt as we do here. There might be a hundred thousand of them, in all. Or more. It's hard to say."

That got a few worried looks. Lord Fullerton took a sharp intake of air. "A...a hundred thousand?" he said, through those wide, frog-like lips. "You're...you're certain of those numbers, Sir Marland?"

"As certain as I can be, my lord. But...might be even more, as I say. There were legions of them...so many...and men were still spilling from the fortress even as we fled."

Sir Rikkard was looking toward Death's Passage, steely-eyed. "We'll need to slow their advance. We can start by smashing up every bridge we've been using to cross the larger waterways. No doubt they'll have bridge crews of their own, but we can't help that. It'll slow them at least. Then we raid them by night, flash assault and sallies. We'll use skiffs, rowboats, poleboats, barges."

"Agreed," said Lord Kanabar. "Rammas, those are your bridges Rikkard's talking about. See to sinking them at once."

"Yes, my lord." Rammas nodded, then stepped away.

Sir Marland looked like he might topple over at any moment. His two remaining scouts stood nearby, swaying. "You should return to your pavilion, Sir Marland," Elyon told him. "Rest. Unless you've got any other urgent news to report?"

The young Marshlander was little older than Elyon. He shared his lord cousin's square jaw and stocky build, though hadn't yet matured to Elton Rammas's level of rippling musculature. "Nothing I can think of, Prince Elyon."

"Then go. Rest and recover. You've done all we could have asked of you."

"My prince." The Marshland knight mustered enough energy for a bow, then dragged his weary frame away with his two outriders by his side.

Elyon turned south once more. He was dressed in his interlinking plate armour from top to toe, visor up, Windblade planted into the earth before him. He'd been training in the skies above the Bane when Sir Marland's party had been spotted, and had landed at once to take his report. Elyon Daecar was done with training in secret, done with slipping away into the misty marshes or heading north to the great lonely plains. He was a dragonkiller now, a leader and an inspiration, he was told. *Enough cowering in the shadows,* he thought, as he flexed his sword hand and said, "A week. I wish it was sooner. We've been waiting long enough."

"The waiting is often the hardest," Killian whispered. Behind them, the news was still spreading through camp in a surging conflagration. The training grounds nearby had stopped ringing with the sound of steel, and the archery ranges had gone silent. No twang of arrows sounded. No crack of bolts in wood. All was voices now, a great spreading din of voices and footfall as men passed the news from lip to lip. *The Agarathi are coming,* they said. *The Agarathi are coming.*

Rikkard continued to stare south, a tense thoughtful look on his face. "We should set traps as well," he said, hand on the pommel of his broadsword. "We can cover sinkholes, hope some of them fall in. Douse the earthen bridges with flammable unscented oils. We'll have men hidden in the bogs to light them with fire arrows when they cross. They'll grow wise to the tricks soon enough, but…"

"They know those tricks already, Rikkard," Wallis Kanabar broke in. "A hundred times the Agarathi have tried to cross here, and a hundred times some young knight like yourself has had the same bright idea. That's no reprimand. It's just the reality of it. Try to slow them all you like…they'll just keep on coming. Three days. A week. Two. Four. It makes no matter in the end. When a hundred thousand men come bursting through those mists, with a half dozen dragons in support, it'll all come down to the same thing. Blood and fire and steel." He made a fist. "I say let them come. And the sooner the bloody better."

Rikkard shook his head. "Better to slow them, and call for reinforcements. *A hundred thousand*, Wallis. That's three times our number."

Kanabar laughed in dismissal of that. "Numbers are misleading in battle. Even our weak-blooded Bladeborn are worth several of their best. Give me a man with a few drops of Varin blood against an Agarathi dragonknight any day. And we've got dozens with a great deal more than that. And how many have full godsteel plate? Ten? Fifteen?"

"Eight," said Killian. "Many more have godsteel breastplates and helms, and some have gauntlets, greaves, shirts of mail, and such, but full suits of plate armour are rare. There are probably less than a hundred across all the north. But here, eight."

Lord Kanabar grumbled at that. "Eight," he repeated, clearly thinking there were more. "Who are they, then? Me, you three. Lady Marian's got that dark silver set her lord uncle Tandrick had made for her. And Rammas. Who else?"

"Sir Charles Waynewood," Killian said.

"I know Waynewood. He's an old man now. Old enough, anyway. Solid knight, but no hero. Who's the last?"

"Garrick," Elyon told him.

Lord Kanabar balked. "*Garrick*? That bloody sellsword?"

Elyon nodded. Sam Garrick had fought in the Song of the First Blade, though hadn't progressed through the group stages. That was no great surprise, seeing as he'd been placed into a group with both Aleron and Jonik, who was masquerading as Fitzroy Ludlum at the time. "He's serving a knight called Sir Lawrence Bollingbrook," Elyon told him. "I'm guessing Bollingbrook has a good bit of coin tucked away, because I know Garrick doesn't come cheap."

"So seven, then," grunted Lord Kanabar. "Not eight. This Garrick can't be relied upon. And Bollingbrook's a glutton and a craven to boot, such as I've heard. Guess that's why he hired him. Soon as the skies fill with fang and claw and fire, both of them will tuck tail and run, believe me."

He was probably right. Sam Garrick had built his wealth and reputation on the tourney circuit, fighting as an independent swordsman, but wasn't known for his integrity. It was how he'd been able to buy his godsteel plate, Elyon knew, winning one piece here or buying another there, putting it together like a puzzle. Then he'd hired some armourer with Forgeborn blood to hammer it to his liking, which would have cost a great deal too, leaving him with a slim-fitting and stylish set.

He even had his own face etched onto the front of his visor, Elyon remembered. Garrick was vain and showy, and liked to blow kisses to the girls in the crowd. But there were no girls here to impress, no maidens to make swoon. "He'll flee, Elyon agreed. "Soon as he learns there's an army marching across the marshes, he'll turn north and head for the hills."

Kanabar seemed not to be listening. "Just seven…only seven bloody suits..." he was muttering, "and let's be honest, I'm not much for fighting these days, not at my age." He shook his head. "I thought we had twice that. What about Lancel and Barnibus?"

"Their plate is mostly godsteel," Elyon told him, "but not entirely. They have a few bits of good castle-forged steel in them, to fill in the blanks. Nowhere fatal. Greaves and sabatons, that sort of thing."

"Fine." Kanabar seemed happier with that. "That's close enough. They count."

"There are some others like that as well, if you're wanting to boost your numbers, Wallis," said Killian. "My captain, Sir Soloman Elmtree, is lacking only his right arm vambrace, but he wears a godsteel-plated shield there so it doesn't matter so much. And Sir Gereon of Greyguard is only missing a pair of poleyns."

Kanabar waved a paw. "Well, that's a full suit right there. Unless he's planning to get an arrow in his knee, he shouldn't worry about bloody *poleyns*." He nodded, pursing his bushy-bearded lips. "That sounds more promising, then. Lancel, Barnibus, Solomon, Gereon. That makes eleven in total if we forget that sellsword." He shook his head, grunting like a boar. "I only wish I'd had the foresight to have Borrus's armour carted down from the Steelforge. Lythian's too. I suppose Aleron's is there as well, is it?" He looked at Elyon.

"No. Aleron's is stored in Keep Daecar, I think."

"Right, yes, that makes sense. Either way, there are a good many suits back in Varinar and the Steelforge, sitting idle, when we could sorely use them out there. I'll bet bloody Godrik's hoarding them all for his own men, the sour old knave. Doesn't he realise our need is greater!"

Elyon's left eye flinched at the mention of the despicable Lord of Taynar. He ground his jaw from side to side, remembering the letter, remembering the severed finger in the box. It had only been two days since then, and still the urge to fly to Varinar and strike the false king's head from his shoulders was burning hot within him. *But my council advised otherwise,* he thought. *And unanimously so at that.*

"You cannot bow to his demands, Elyon," Rikkard had been the first to say, once the letter had been passed around and read, and the box placed on the table for all to see. Elyon had stood aside in a glowering fury, wanting nothing more than to march out onto the nearest balcony and take off into the northwestern skies. *I'll kill him for this,* he'd thought, raging, jaw clenched so tight he thought his teeth might just shatter. *The Windblade for my auntie's life?* That's what the letter had said. *'Give me back what you stole from me, or I'll give you back your auntie, piece by piece by piece…'*

Everyone had agreed with Rikkard, though. "You're killing dragons with that blade, lad," Lord Kanabar had told him. "You can't give it up for one old man's pride. You've got too much responsibility here."

"We all know how much you love your auntie, Elyon," Killian had added, placing a firm hand on his shoulder, "but there's nothing you can do about this letter but ignore it."

"He's bluffing," had been Lord Fullerton's best remark. "He won't follow through."

And Lord Rammas had come in with, "How do you know it's even her finger? Is there some way you can tell?"

"It looks like it," Elyon had said to that. "That's her nail paint, Lord Rammas. It's hers."

"He might have painted the nail of another woman," Kanabar suggested, taking up on Rammas's point. "There is probably some fingerless beggar down in the Lowers as we speak." He gave the letter a scan. "The bastard says he'll send more. Well, we'll see." He nodded heavily. "Fullerton's right. He's bluffing. He's trying to scare you into a reaction."

"That's exactly what he wants, Elyon," Rikkard had agreed. "A *reaction.* For you to fly to Varinar and try to rescue her. You'll only be falling into his trap. There's nothing you can do. Put this out of your mind."

He'd tried to do just that, though it wasn't easy. That night, Lancel and Barnibus had stayed close to him - under orders to watch him, he did not doubt. Any time he went to use the privy, or said he wanted to take a walk, they would shoot up out of their chairs and follow. It became uncomfortable, after a while. "Bloody hell," he raged at them, "would you let me piss in peace!" And even when he went to bed, he knew they were still there, outside the door, listening should he try to put on his armour and take up the Windblade and fly.

Well, even if he wanted to, he couldn't afford that now. *There's no leaving this fort,* he knew. *In this army, I'm the tip of the sword. And everyone is looking to me…*

The others were still in discussion when he withdrew from his musings. "…call for reinforcements from Southwatch," Rikkard was saying. "And Rustbridge and Redhelm as well. We need to gather our strength here. *Here*, where the hammer will fall hardest."

"There's more than one hammer in the south, Rikkard," Killian said to that. "They might yet cross the Red Sea, send another host north under sail. Lord Pentar will not weaken his own coast."

"They don't have the numbers," Rikkard came back. "Not if they're sending a hundred thousand here."

"They might. How do we know? It's been silence between us for years. That's why Amron sent Lythian and Borrus in the first place, to build bridges and improve communication."

"And look where that got us," grumbled Kanabar. "My son, with that damnable Shadowknight. Lythian dead, most like. Amron crippled. King Ellis only turned from him because he went against his will. If he'd only spoken to Ellis first, he might never have written him from his line. And that frosty old whoreson Godrik Taynar wouldn't be sitting the throne."

"What ifs won't help us, Wallis," Rikkard argued. "We are where we are. You said it yourself. We deal with what's ahead of us. And we *need* more men."

"We *don't,*" Kanabar shouted back, growing irate. "I've told you, man for man we're superior by far. And we have the Bane. If they try to breach its walls, they'll be in for a rude awa…"

"They have *dragons*, Wallis! Five of them, six, maybe more than that, maybe *double*. They've been quiet for weeks and now we know why. They're mustering for a full attack, as we feared they would. If they have that many dragons, we're doomed. You can forget those hundred thousand men, they won't even matter. A dozen or so dragons will rout us in a day."

"Says you, who was a squire for half the war. These are *my* lands, Rikkard Amadar, mine. They send those dragons to try to destroy this fortress and they'll discover where it gets its name." He pointed to the massive carcass of Ezukar, hanging in chains against the ancient black walls. "There, you see that. If they want to send us more dragons, let them. These walls are too dreary; they could do with the decoration."

Rikkard threw up his arms. "That blasted Kanabar bluster. You and Borrus are exactly the same. The Agarathi could send a million men and a hundred dragons and you'd probably just wave them off too."

"And why not? Confidence is critical in war, Rikkard - lose it, and you're halfway doomed already. There are over a hundred ballistas and scorpions at this fortress, every one of them well-stocked with godsteel tipped bolts. Those are dragon killers. Any Fireborn rider worth his salt knows to stay well clear of the Bane."

"Not in such numbers. In such numbers they can overwhelm us, burn us out, collapse the walls and towers."

"And risk losing half of them in the meanwhile. That's fine by me. Let them topple a tower or two…we'll be busy filling them with quarrels, and taking away their only advantage. The Agarathi are smarter than that, Rikkard. They protect their dragons. They use them to rain fire on the field and crush us in the open. That's what we have to worry about; dragons in the open. We should be so bloody lucky that they get anywhere near the Bane."

Rikkard was shaking his head in a quick side-to-side motion. "If they have three, four, maybe. But if they have a dozen…"

"They don't have a dozen…"

"If they *do* have a dozen, or ten, or just eight…then that'll be enough to cause us real problems. Our defence is stretched thin from here to the Twinfort. We need more full-armoured knights. What we have…it won't be enough."

"It *will* be enough. And it seems you're forgetting something." Wallis Kanabar turned to Elyon. "We've got a dragonslayer in our ranks, Master of the Bloody Winds, Lord of Storms, and whatever else they're calling him now. He killed one dragon, and a fierce one at that. He can kill more. That makes all the difference."

Elyon gave that a loud huff. "Are storms forecast for the coming week, my lord?" he asked, in self-mocking tones. "Best bring out the augurs and have them reading the birds and the clouds and tasting the air, or whatever the hell they do. I only killed Ezukar because of that storm. It was the *lightning* that killed him, and the blade, *not* me. I've told you that already, but no one seems to listen."

Wallis Kanabar's face was going as red as his beard. "I've had about all I can take of this." He looked to Rikkard then back at Elyon, anger boiling in his bloodshot eyes. "You two bloody naysayers." He thrust a big fleshy finger right into Elyon's breastplate, causing him to rock back a little. Men looked over. "You'd best start believing in yourself, boy. Lighting, you say. Storms? That blade? Who do you think carries it! Have some faith in yourself! You're a *Daecar*. A bloody Daecar! Act like one!" He spun and stormed away, feet throwing up clods of mud in his wake.

Elyon watched him go. He could feel the eyes of the men on him, the spearmen and squires and scribes and stewards, all looking on from nearby as they paused in their duties and watched.

"Well, I…I ought to go with him," said Lord Fullerton, most awkward. "Much to do, Prince Elyon." He smiled that toadish smile and waddled away in Wallis Kanabar's wake.

Elyon was still staring, bristling. He could feel his cheeks growing hot from the scolding. Rikkard stepped closer, as the men in camp slowly returned to their business. "Don't listen to him, Elyon," his uncle said. "He's only stressed. This matter with Borrus is still on his mind. And your auntie as well. He cares for her."

That was too much. "*He* cares for her?" Elyon spun to face him. "And what about *me*, Uncle? It's *my* half-brother that Borrus is travelling with. *Me* who's carrying the weight of expectation from every damn man in camp. He's stressed? What about me!" He didn't like how many times he said 'me' there, but his blood was up and he couldn't help it. *And the point stands,* he thought. "He has no right to speak to me like that…and in front of the men." Elyon's voice descended to a harsh whisper. "No right at all."

"We all say things we don't mean in the heat of an argument, Elyon," Rikkard said. "Let him cool off. I'm sure he'll apologise later."

Elyon was about to grumble something back when he heard Killian Oloran's whispered voice.

"We forget sometimes how young you are, Elyon," the tall knight said quietly, drawing his gaze. "Yes, of course, you have every right to feel stressed. Every man in camp does, from lowborn to high. There is pressure on you, and expectation as well, but you have the armoured shoulders to bear that weight." He turned north, to the forest of tents and pavilions lit a thousand colours by the late morning sun. "The vast majority here are regular men. They do not derive from Varin. They have no Bladeborn blood. They look to you because of that, and to me and to Rikkard and their captains and commanders as well. Whatever fear you may feel right now, whatever stress, imagine how it is for them. To step out onto that field dressed in leather and fur and rusted steel mail. With the Agarathi charging and screaming, and the dragons rushing overhead so fast and furious they hardly even see them coming.

"But they feel it. The heat, sudden and searing, and then before they know it they're on fire, and their friends are on fire too, and all the world around them is burning. That is the reality these men face. Fire and arrows and thrusts of sword and spear, any one of which could kill them. They might be trampled by their own brothers, crushed beneath an enemy charge. They may get stuck in the mud when the field churns up and be unable to wrench themselves free, just waiting for the next enemy soldier to pass by and finish them off. They could die in a hundred ways out there, by enemy actions or their own. And half the time - *most* of the time - there isn't a blind bit of difference they can make to whether they live or die.

"For these men, luck will be the biggest factor in whether they see another dawn. Not skill, or training, or their prowess with blade and shield. But luck. Did the searing river of flame from that dragon just miss them? Were they close enough to flee beneath the fire-proof shields in time? Did their brother block an attack they didn't see coming, or kill an enemy when he was about to thrust his blade through their back? Did that stray arrow fly past their ear and take another man in the neck instead? Did their commander lead them well, or make a mistake that gets them killed? Were they lucky enough to be given an easier charge, away from the thick of the fighting?" He paused. "Did *Elyon Daecar*, wrapped up in godsteel plate and impervious to harm, swoop down from the clouds in time to scatter a charge of dragonknights when they were sure to be trampled, and killed?

"Because that is how these men see you, Elyon. As someone who'll be there to save them, when they find themselves in dire need. That is what they think when they look at you. 'He can kill a dragon,' they say to themselves. 'He can fly. He wears armour that no enemy can pierce. Elyon Daecar, Prince of the Skies. He will save us all.' Right or wrong, that's what they believe, and it's what they *need* to believe, to give them strength when all else seems lost. When they squint through the flames and the smoke and the ash and see you, up there in the skies, battling dragons, saving lives.

"Yes, there is expectation. There is hope. Because without it, these men are lost. Without you, with us, without the mighty Bladeborn in our ranks. Every one of us has a burden to carry. But we carry too the chance to change things, to make a difference, as the common man cannot. Count yourself blessed in that, Elyon. And when you look into the eyes of these men, think of what it is like for them. They know who they are, and what they can do. They might kill a man, maybe two, maybe even ten if they're good. Or maybe they'll die before they even strike a blow. But no matter, they'll charge out there all the same when their captains sound the call, surging into battle with their brothers by their sides, hoping beyond reason that they might just live through it, yet never truly expecting so much. So what do they do instead? They place their expectation elsewhere. On you. On us. On the noble Varin Knights who were born for days like these."

He stepped in and gripped Elyon's steel arm. "So give it to them, Elyon. Give them that expectation, and repay them that faith. Be the man they believe you to be, *need* you to be. Wallis is right. You're a Daecar, and a dragonslayer, and a champion, and a prince. And if every man here in camp knows one thing, it's this…you were fated to bear that blade. And with it, you give us hope."

When Killian was done, a deep silence filled the air between them. For a moment there was nothing but the echo of his words. *Hope. Faith. Expectation. Fate. Give it to them, Elyon. Be the man they need you to be.* And slowly, gradually, the silence gave way to the noise of the camp; the clang of metal and the thump of wood, the stomp and squelch of feet in the mud, the whinnying and whickering of horses. Men went about their business, cleaning armour, sharpening arms, training with blade and bow. A nearby armourer was hammering on an anvil, shaping a shield. Outside, squires sat fletching arrows, placing them aside, one after another after another, in preparation for the battles to come.

Elyon looked at them all, wondering, *how many will be dead in a week, a month? How many of them will never see their mothers and wives and daughters again, their brothers and fathers and sons? How many will never see home?*

He pulled the Windblade from the earth and looked out over the encampment. *As few as possible,* he promised himself. And turning to the heir of Oloran, he said, "Thank you, Killian, for your words and your wisdom. I will be better, I swear it. I'll be the beacon of hope they need."

With that, he marched away into camp, chin high, eyes resolute, to help carry the weight of their fears.

42

Amron

Whitebeard was the first to sound the warning. "Riders," he growled, as they crested the top of the hill. "A mounted host. Ten of them."

Amron came up behind him on Wolfsbane. The riders were two or three miles away, coming down a shallow heathy hill on the other side of the valley. "Ten? You're certain?" He gripped his godsteel dagger and peered forward, eyesight sharpening. Even so, matching Rogen Whitebeard in that regard was difficult. The ranger had one of the best pairs of eyes he'd ever encountered.

"Certain, my lord. They look well armed."

Walter had no such gift of farsighted vision. He hastened to join them upon the crest, squinting against the sunlight. "Are they knights?"

"Hard to tell from here." Whitebeard turned his gaze around. "We might want to move off the road. Find cover while they come through the woods." The valley between the slopes was well blanketed in elm and ash, and the small mounted host was fast approaching the trees. "They'll take several minutes to reach the other side. That will give us time to seek shelter."

Amron waved that off at once. "These are Daecar lands, Rogen. We have nothing to fear."

They pressed on down the slope beneath skies both bright and breezy. The road was oft travelled, part of the High Way linking Varinar to Northwatch by way of Blackfrost. In this section it was mostly hard-packed earth, bedevilled by wagon ruts and the occasional cluster of old stones and cobbles from when the road was once fully paved. Walter was always quick to remark on such things. "The road isn't so well maintained here, Amron," he said. "If these are still your lands, oughtn't you see them better restored?"

"They're mine by extension of my vassals," Amron told him. "In truth these lands are under Lady Crawfield's jurisdiction. But the maintenance of the kingdom's main roads is a matter for the crown, not its lords and ladies. Ellis Reynar never had much interest in spending money on lengthy restoration projects."

"Ellis Reynar was never king," Walter said, with a blithesome smile on his face. "You were. And now you are again, by official right. Something to put on the list, for when the war is over?"

"I think restoring the roads will be less than a priority then. It will be our cities that will need rebuilding."

The sun faded off beneath a set of low lumbering clouds for a short time, dousing the world in a sulking gloom. Distantly, the clopping of hooves spread out over the valley, and a short time later came the mounted host, cantering fiercely through the thicket of elm and ash. They were close now, no more than two hundred metres away, the parties converging in the hollow between the hills. Rogen Whitebeard was quick to notice their garb. "They wear grey and darkened blue," he said. "These are Taynar men, my lord."

"Taynars?" repeated Walter, understandably surprised. "Now what are they doing all the way out here?"

Amron gave no answer to that, but he could guess. His fingers curled about the hilt of his dagger and he scanned the faces of the coming host. Their leader was a Greycloak, that became obvious at a glance, wearing those supple leather gloves that went right up to the elbow, the shining grey cloak that gave the royal guard their name. The pockmarked face was familiar too. "Sir Gerald Strand," he said, glancing over at Whitebeard as they slowed their horses to a trot. "Your brother."

The ranger was staring on darkly, his mouth set in a hard scowl. A brisk wind stirred his greying black hair. "I haven't seen him since I was a boy. I hoped never to again."

"He mightn't recognise you," Amron said. "I shall refrain from mentioning you by name."

Whitebeard said nothing to that, as the host thundered swiftly toward them, hooves clattering on the broken cobbled road. Amron quietly cursed himself for not taking Rogen's advice and avoiding them. This was a hindrance he could do without. *Though inevitable,* he thought. If not now he was sure to encounter Taynar men eventually, and many on his approach to the capital, he knew.

He called out as they neared. "Sir Gerald. I hadn't expected to see you here, so close to Blackfrost. How generous of your uncle to send us an escort."

Sir Gerald Strand could scarcely look less like his younger brother. Rogen was tall and robust, teak-tough and long-limbed, owing more to the Taynars in his appearance than the Strands. He had a closer resemblance to his cousin Dalton than he did this piggish brother of his, for Sir Gerald had always been soft and fleshy, ample in the cheek and belly and shoulder. Amron had never thought much of him. For long years he'd served under Vesryn among the Greycloaks, running his duties in the palace, and had never been suited to the rigours of life among the Varin Knights. *He rose high on the back of his name*, Amron thought. There were far too many men like that these days.

The Greycloak drew up his reins and slowed his horse to a stuttering stop. "Lord Daecar..." He seemed most surprised to see him. "I...I might say the same to you. You are thought missing by...by a great many." Sir Gerald smiled through a doughy pitted face, looking uncomfortable. "We were commanded to ride to Northwatch to seek word of you. But...here you are."

"Yes, here I am."

"Indeed. And a...a great pleasure to see you so well, my lord. You look hale and hearty, it must be said. Time has done wonders for your wounds, it would seem. This is much a boon, with war ever encroaching upon our borders." Amron gave that no response. The man was buying time with these courtesies, giving himself a moment to think. "Well...where is it you intend to go?" Sir Gerald looked back the way they had come. "We all know which way this road leads, my lord. Is Varinar your quarry, pray tell?"

Amron saw no merit in deceiving the man. "Varinar, yes. We have come upon some unpleasant news regarding my beloved sister-in-law, and seek to find the truth of it. Perhaps you can help in that regard, Sir Gerald?"

"For the Lord of House Daecar, of course." His horse was mimicking his unease, and so were his host, all of them fidgeting restlessly in their saddles. Amron, Rogen, and Walter were quite still. "What...what is it you've heard, exactly?"

Amron went straight into it. "I've heard that Amara is being held captive in the dungeons beneath the palace, by your uncle, the king."

"False king," put in Walter.

"*False* king?" Sir Gerald tried to show some affront at that, but it didn't ring true. "Well, perhaps you don't know. King Ellis decreed my uncle his direct heir before his death. He is king by rights."

"Ellis's, death," Amron said. "Of which you bore witness, I'm told." He kept his manner perfectly polite. "Is that a true telling, Sir Gerald? Were you present when Ellis fell from the balcony?"

"I…yes I was, my lord."

The winds were fierce here at the bottom of the valley, blowing hard from the south. Amron trotted Wolfsbane a little closer to better hear the man. Sir Gerald's men stiffened in response and several even reached for their blades. Amron surveyed them casually. "Tell your men to calm, Sir Gerald," he said. "They appear a little agitated."

The large Greycloak did as bidden. "Stay your hands, men. There will be no violence and crossed swords here." He spoke firmly, then turned back to Amron with a shaking head. "King Ellis's death…a most tragic accident. I have berated myself each night since for not being close enough to save him. It is the worst nightmare of any Greycloak for his king to die on his watch."

Does he think he's deceiving me? "I've been told that Janilah Lukar threw him."

Sir Gerald spluttered at that. "Goodness, no. Where did you hear that, my lord? I daresay rumours become terribly warped so far out here."

"I have heard it from a good many sources, Sir Gerald. It is widely claimed that Janilah slew Ellis in order to place your uncle on the throne and raise your cousin Dalton as First Blade. Some believe that Janilah has done this to secure the Blades of Vandar. Some have even suggested, and I whisper this quietly in present company, that your good uncle was a part of this plot." Still, his manner was light. He kept his hands visible on the reins. *Everything is fine*, that said. *I will not reach for my blade unless you do.*

"Well…as I say…much has been said of late." Despite the cold winds, Amron could see a glimmer of perspiration on the man's furrowed forehead. A shade of red was creeping up past his chins and lumpy neck. "So…who are these companions of yours, my lord?" he went on, trying to change the subject. He directed his eyes at Walter, and then Rogen, pausing a moment on the latter. "You… you seem familiar to me. Have we met before?"

Rogen Whitebeard's eyes were dangerous as daggers. He might as well have been made of stone, still as he was. "Yes. We've met."

Sir Gerald looked at him curiously. "Yes, I thought so. You have a Taynar look to you, I should say." He turned. "Who is this man, Lord Daecar?"

Amron said nothing. It was for Rogen to say, and say it he did. "I am your brother, third son of Lord Styron the Strong and the late Lady Margery Taynar, whom I *killed* to come into this world." The ranger glared through those upturned amber eyes. "Surely you remember me now, Brother?"

Sir Gerald's face gaped stupidly. "*Rogen...*" The name was a half-remembered whisper. "You were…you were sent…"

"Sent to Northwatch to become a ranger, yes. When I was but a boy. *Cast out*, for a murder I committed before I even drew breath."

"Murder?" Sir Gerald balked. "Who…who said anything about murder…" That shade of red on his meaty neck spread yet higher and darker. "My mother…*our* mother…she died in childbirth, Rogen." He shot an uncomfortable look at Amron. "How could you possibly be to blame for that?"

"He couldn't be," came in the voice of Walter Selleck. He looked angry. Rogen hadn't expressed his reasons for hating his family as yet, but now it all made sense. "No sane man would blame a newborn child for murdering their mother during their birth. It's nonsensical and utterly unconscionable."

"Oh yes, I…I quite agree." Sir Gerald nodded briskly. "I mean… *of course* I agree. Unconscionable. Yes, absolutely." His soft lips bulged into a clumsy, nervous smile. "And who are you, might I ask?"

"Walter Selleck."

"Walter Selleck," repeated the Greycloak, as though the name meant something. He looked like he wanted to spin his horse about and gallop all the way back to Varinar. "You are a friend to Lord Daecar?"

"For my part." Walter's voice was unusually mirthless. "So this is why you hate them, Rogen? Because you were blamed for your mother's death?"

Rogen Whitebeard's eyes were hard as flint. He gave a slow dark nod. "I've wondered often what I would do if I saw you again, Gerald. How I would repay you for all those years of abuse."

"Abuse?" His older brother laughed uneasily. "Come now, Rogen, we were boys. A bit of rough and tumble is perfectly normal. Whatever you imagine you remember...well, that is all long past now. Water under the bridge, no?"

"*I* was a boy," Rogen growled back. "You were five years older, five years bigger. A man." His mouth twisted into a scowl. "I have scars still, from what you did to me. Cuts. Burns. Marks that have never healed."

"I'm not...I'm not remembering any of this, I confess," the Greycloak stammered. "Now...perhaps we can talk in private, Rogen? This isn't the place to reminisce, is it? Here on the road, in front of Lord Daecar? And this wind? I can scarcely hear you. You talk so quietly. Let us put this aside, for another time, yes?"

Rogen glowered at him. Amron feared he might just pull his blade and find somewhere wet and warm in his brother's body to sheathe it, but that wouldn't serve. "Rogen," he said, drawing the ranger's eye. He gave him a look, and that was all that was needed to have him draw back, just a little.

Gerald seemed visibly relieved by that. "Thank you, my lord," be breathed out. "For a moment there, I thought..."

"I do not want your thanks, Sir Gerald," Amron bulled in. "I want to know why you're here, on my lands. I want to know why your uncle sent you to Northwatch to find me. And most of all I want to know what has happened to my sister-in-law. Now you will tell me, and in full, else I'll let Rogen seek amends for the great wrongs you once did him."

"Seek amends? *Great* wrongs? Now my lord, please be reasonable, I have ten strong swords at my back, Bladeborn knights and men-at-arms handpicked for this very mission. To seek blood would not go well for you."

"I see these men of yours," Amron told him, "and I do not quiver, Sir Gerald." He sat up straight in the saddle ignoring the pain in his shoulder and thigh. The men were armoured in breastplates beneath their cloaks but there were no full-plated knights here. "Now speak. Is my sister-in-law in good health?"

"Yes, that I know."

"That you know?"

The man swallowed. "I left, my lord, the very day she reached the city. She is being safely housed in a comfortable cell, I'm sure. My uncle…he means only to seek restitution, that is all. I'm sure you know…your son and Lady Amara stole the Windblade from him. It is his by rights to give to a champion of his choosing. You must understand, Lord Daecar…he has no want to cause Lady Amara undue harm, but…"

"But?"

"But…he will, if he must." He smiled, even as Amron's eyes narrowed. "I'm sure you…understand."

The silence that followed was long and uncomfortable, interrupted only by the gusts of wind, the soft stamp of horse hooves, the gentle clink of mail and metal as men moved uneasily in their saddles. Tension hung heavy in the air as Amron considered his next course. *If we ride with these men, they might seek to kill us in our sleep. If we ride separate from them, they might follow and do the same.* They did not have the advantage of numbers, even if they did of strength and skill. Another option was to slay them all right now, but that felt wrong and an overreaction. Sir Gerald deserved the gibbet, oh yes, but these other men were not so cursed.

He decided to seek alliance instead. "Lady Crawfield's keep is but a half day's ride from here," he said. "You shall accompany us there, Sir Gerald, in good faith that not a sword will be drawn between us. We shall remain the night in her halls, and continue on the road to Varinar on the morrow. Together, and as one, Sir Gerald." *And with many more of Lady Crawfield's men in our company*, he thought. "Does that sound acceptable to you?"

The pockfaced knight considered. "I have your full guarantee we will not come to harm? Lady Crawfield…she is no friend of House Taynar. And…" He looked at his brother. "I see murder in his eyes, my lord. You will keep him on his leash?"

Whitebeard stirred at that word - *leash* - but Amron raised a hand to calm him. "House Crawfield are my bannermen, and the good lady will do as I entreat. You can trust in my word, Sir Gerald. I continue to count my integrity in good order." *Unlike some*, he didn't say.

The portly man gave that a thought, and then nodded. "Then…I accept. My men and I will, in return, offer safe passage for you back to Varinar. I would like to write my king uncle a letter from Lady Crawfield's keep, if you would permit it, to better keep him informed of…of this latest news?"

Amron thought that a good idea. "I will read this letter before it is sent, and approve its content. Moreover, I'll add a message of my own."

"That being, my lord?"

"That being a demand that my sister-in-law be maintained in good health until we arrive. With a promise of full retaliation should she come to any harm. I would hope that this message is clear. I have been missing, Sir Gerald, but I am not dead. Those who oppose or threaten me or my kin will find me a troubling adversary, this I promise."

"I…don't doubt it, Lord Daecar," quaked the fleshy Greycloak, spineless as a worm. "Then we have an accord. Ought we shake on it? Secure it with a godsteel oath?" Amron nodded, and Sir Gerald gave his horse a little tap of his heels, urging him forward.

And just as he did so, a great scraping of steel sung out from the side, as Rogen Whitebeard ripped his sword from its scabbard. At once Sir Gerald pulled the reins with one hand, drawing back, while fumbling for his blade with the other. His men began doing the same, steel flashing out into the sunlight as it broke down through the clouds. Horses were whickering and stamping and Amron was reaching…reaching for the Frostblade.

But Whitebeard's eyes were not on his brother, or his men. They were south, and skyward, looking up into the clouds. "What…what in the name of…what are you *doing*!" demanded Sir Gerald, trying to control his horse. "I might have had your head clean off, you great fool!"

Whitebeard showed him a black-gloved palm, silencing him. He pointed his blade into the clouds, some miles off, and stared.

Sir Gerald gave a loud huff. "What are we looking at! Blast you, Rogen, you nearly gave me a heart attack." His eyes swung to Amron. "My lord, I asked you…this man *must* be controlled. You draw a blade like that and you are begging for blood. No wonder we sent him to Northwatch as a boy. I had thought he might have learned some proper behaviours as a ranger, but no, he's as wild as he always was. Still a bloody *dog*, aren't you Rogen…"

"*Shut up*, Gerald," Amron commanded, with force enough to silence the oaf's yapping. He could feel the rhythm running through the Frostblade's hilt, that thrumming beat, almost like a heart, pounding with excitement. Long years he'd held the Sword of Varinar, but not until the end of the war did he take it up. He'd never felt this sensation, yet all the same, he knew at once what it meant. "Where is it, Rogen?"

Whitebeard's amber eyes were tracing the skies, looking into a grouping of lumpen clouds coloured in white and grey. "There, my lord," he hissed softly. "Somewhere…somewhere up there."

"What…what are you talking about?" groused Sir Gerald. "What is up there, exactly, but clouds and birds, and…" He trailed off, seeing the swirl of mists, the parting of fog, the breaching in the fume as the dark winged shape burst through. "Gods…my… my gods! How…out here! What is it doing out here!"

"Hunting," Walter said from behind them.

"We flee!" Sir Gerald Strand wailed. "The trees, Lord Daecar. We'll find refuge in the trees!" He tugged at his reins so hard his horse reared up, neighing loudly, throwing the heavy-bellied Greycloak from the saddle. He landed with a thump and a crack and a groan. No one gave him a second thought as several of his men bolted for the wood a little up the hill. The braver ones stood their ground.

"What do we do, Lord Daecar?" one asked.

Amron peered southward as the dragon surged their way. "Go," he said. "All of you, go."

"I'm not going anywhere," Rogen Whitebeard told him.

"Do you serve me, Rogen?" Amron didn't wait for an answer. "Then you'll answer to my orders. You are unarmored and no match for a foe like this without plate. Take Walter into the trees. You other men, get Sir Gerald back on his horse, if you can. Ride for cover. Go."

And with that, he kicked Wolfsbane into a charge, and set off through the valley between the slopes, drawing the Frostblade as he went, letting its power infuse him, fill him. At once he felt the pain in his shoulder and thigh melt away, felt his youth and vigour return. He galloped a hundred metres from the road, as the dragon closed in. Then he pulled the reigns and drew Wolfsbane to a stop with a call of 'whoa', leaping from the saddle. "Go, run," he said, giving the horse a slap on its flank. "Seek shelter, boy. Go!"

His massive destrier snorted, white mist puffing from his nostrils, yet he obeyed. The warhorse was born for battle himself, yet without his barding would be vulnerable. The heavy thunder of hooves sounded as Wolfsbane charged away, leaving Amron alone on the field. The air sparkled about him, frosting, thickening. Particles of ice closed and condensed and welded together, hardening into a film that covered him, head to heel, in an icy shield. And thrusting the Frost-blade to the skies, he bellowed, "You! I call a duel! Fight *me*, spawn of Agarath! Feel the wrath of Amron Daecar!"

He felt the thrill thrum through him. A feeling he never thought he'd have again. His opponent issued his own challenge, shrieking out a wild ear-splitting roar that rolled out over the woods and hills. Amron narrowed his gaze to judge the beast as it approached. It was thicker at the chest than most dragons, and shorter at the wing, a stocky monstrous thing with thick armoured scales of dark green and gold and a horribly misshaped snout. Teeth sprouted from its jaws at odd angles, some bursting through the very flesh around its mouth, and its crooked tail was thick and heavy as a bat, with a great armoured club of bone mounted at the end, exploding with spikes like some nightmarish mace.

Amron recognised the beast at once. "Zyndrar," he whispered to himself, with a ripple of disquiet. The dragon had been the scourge of many a knight during the war, using that club tail to batter and scatter men in battle, fighting with a ferocity rare even among such beasts. Men feared it almost as much as Vallath and Garlath and Malathar for that. *The Unnatural*, they called it, for its odd deformities and deranged behaviour. And its rider, the unhinged Fireborn, Kar Von Karosh, was equally unpredictable, a mad-eyed lunatic who would often stand in the saddle, hurling crazed insults and slanders and slurs at his enemies as he fought.

And is that why they're here? Have beast and rider gone rogue?

Amron had only just begun to wonder on that when Zyndrar fell into a sudden dive, spiking to the ground in a sharp descent, exposing the empty saddle at his back. Buckles fluttered and waved in its wake and straps slapped against leather and scale. *No rider?* he thought. *No Kar Von Karosh?* He watched on, confused, as the dragon plummeted straight to the ground, barely slowing as it landed, crashing hard in an explosion of mud and grass.

The earth shook underfoot, yet Amron did not shift or stumble. He stood, waiting, facing his foe head-on as it emitted a bellowing scream, the very air fizzing and trembling about its jaws. Its distorted face was a twisted mess, wisps of smoke spiralling out from between jagged teeth and scarred lips and the holes in its face where its fangs had burrowed through. Beneath heavily armoured brows Amron saw eyes deep and red and raving, and in those eyes he saw cognisance.

He saw recognition. *He remembers me*, he thought. *He remembers who I am.*

"I remember you too," he shouted over the gusty winds. "I remember your master as well, Zyndrar. If he is dead, I am sorry. I understand your pain." He inclined his head, just a touch, though never let his eyes off the beast. Amron Daecar had always honoured the duel between dragon and knight.

The beast's response was to open its maws and unleash another shattering roar. This one was so loud he felt his eardrums might burst. He braced against it, sliding one foot back, the other forward into a split Blockform stance. The roar went on and on and on and then, with the sound still ringing out in his ears, Zyndrar burst forward, tearing across the field, gouging out great deep ruts with its claws as it closed the gap and turned and swung.

Amron scarcely had time to move, dashing rearward just in time to avoid the lashing tail. The club flashed low to the ground, ripping up chunks of soil with those savage spikes, and no sooner had the tail swept back around as the dragon's jaws were there to replace it, snapping and biting. A sideward shift and Amron was gone, out of reach. The Unnatural roared again, and swung again with its tail, cleaving another ditch, yet once more Amron darted rearward, and again, and again, and again that savage tail swung.

Amron leapt one swipe, managed to duck another, yet the third in the sequence struck with force enough to reduce a man to pulp. Amron went careering across the field, the shield of ice around him shattering in a nebulous burst of colours. It had taken the brunt, protecting him as godsteel would have, yet the tumble was disorienting and his breath was momentarily lost. He gasped for air, lungs shrunken, and looked up. The monster was charging, scrambling wildly across the plain. *Another swing and I'm done*, he thought. *Without my shield…*

He dropped into a squat, snatched another breath, and pressed up in a powerful leap, vaulting right over the top of the beast as it neared. By the time Amron Daecar landed behind it his shield had closed and reformed, harder than before, thicker. His time in training had started there, with that shield. Yet it wasn't his only trick.

"Come at me, Zyndrar!" he roared, lungs restored to full function. He pointed the Frostblade forward, its mists sparkling as they caught the sunlight, red and green and blue and gold, and a dozen other colours besides. *Fire and ice,* he thought. There was a purity in this battle, between dragon and Frostblade.

A manic roar trumpeted through Zyndrar the Unnatural's malformed maw, and here he came again, tearing the earth to shreds as he ran, sending great clods of earth thirty metres into the air. Amron anticipated his path. He feigned left as the monster came, zipping three metres that way, just enough to change the dragon's course. As it committed to the swing, Amron went right, flashing forward fast as lightning, upswinging against the beast's left wing. Ice spread out where the blade connected, shooting off in a spreading web of frozen veins. Zyndrar roared, stumbled, jerking wildly to the side. The wing was temporarily frozen stiff. Its thick neck twisted. Fire brewed from its barrel chest, surging suddenly up its throat and gushing out of its jaws, spraying across wing and field, and at Amron too, as he fled its path.

The ice upon its wing quickly thawed. The grass was churned and blackened and charred, and several nearby trees had caught fire, burning bright, pouring smoke. The monster spun chaotically, deep in a rage, lashing and roaring. And Amron watched. He watched and moved and prowled about it like a predator, too quick, too nimble, too smart.

He lunged again, striking at the swinging tail this time, timing his attack perfectly. Ice encased that thick heavy club, running swift up the length of the dragon's tail, freezing it. The lashings stopped and the club fell heavy to the ground. Zyndrar shrieked in fury and twisted that stumpy neck to burn the ice away, but this was no lithe dragon. *Too thick. Too slow,* Amron thought.

He struck forward as that neck craned back, slashing. There was no ice this time. By telepathic command Amron dismissed the misting frost and used the blade in its simplest form; as godsteel, and godsteel only, intended to cut and to kill. His strike caught the Unnatural at the meeting of shoulder and neck, parting the thick armoured scales there, unveiling red flesh beneath. A deep wailing roar poured out of the Unnatural's mouth and on instinct it flapped its wings and took flight. Three quick beats and it was airborne, yet its tail was not yet thawed, pulling it down like an anchor. Amron fell to his haunches and leapt. Five metres, eight, ten he went, cutting swift and true at the dragon's right wing. Flesh opened again, and blood rained, and the wing arm went limp at the elbow, its great flap of webbing folding up. Clipped and anchored, the beast toppled back down to the ground with a crash, scrambling to regain its feet, screaming all the while. It opened its maws and unleashed red flame, turning its head left, right, up, down, swirling. A great crimson-gold vortex of fire engulfed it, spreading out in all directions.

Amron had no option but to retreat. He had no idea if his icy shield would protect him. *I need godsteel,* he thought. His plate armour was fireproof against all but the most fearsome attacks and when paired with the Frostblade, would make him formidable. Standing at the edge of the fiery whirlwind, he waited for the beast to tire. The fields were a chaos of churned earth and burning trees, scorched grass and smoke. Yet through it all, he could hear movement behind him. *No,* he thought, turning. Whitebeard was running his way, blade to hand. "Rogen, stay back, I told you not to help!"

"My lord, the fire…I thought…"

"I'm all right, Rogen," Amron bellowed. "The beast's wing is clipped. It can't fly, not well. I need but wait and…"

"Amron!"

He turned. Zyndrar was bursting through the wall of flame, trailing great banners of smokey fire. "Away, Rogen!" Amron roared, rushing forward to greet the beast. They came together in a clash of teeth and flame and ice and steel, Amron dodging, ducking, swinging, swiping, as the Unnatural roared and raged. Its tail, freed of the ice, twisted and flashed like a whip, its good left wing arm reaching and grasping for him, claws stabbing like lances. It was all Amron could do to remain out of its reach. He could feel the intense heat coming off the beast, the fires still whirling in its wake. *My shield,* he thought, fighting to hold it together. Yet he could feel it melting, weakening. Colour sparkled and glittered about him as the dragon closed in, nearing…

And suddenly Zyndrar was spinning away from him, drawn to another. Amron peered through the smoke. *Rogen.* The ranger was facing it without armour, dressed in nought but leather and wool. *The madman! He'll get himself killed!* "Whitebeard, back, back!" he roared, yet the ranger was still coming, sniping forward, speeding aside, using that agility and thrust.

He's distracting it, Amron realised at once. It was folly, gallant bloody folly. But not a chance he was going to miss. Amron's eyes narrowed on that tail, swishing and flicking, its movement hard to predict. He watched, waiting, moments turning to minutes, it felt, yet really no more than a second or two had passed when he took his chance and surged in.

His strike was made a little above the club, where the tail was thinnest, enough power behind it to slice through scale and muscle and bone. The huge spiky mace went spinning through the air, landing with a dull thump in the earth, and suddenly the tail was lashing yet quicker, lessened its weight, blood spraying and showering from its severed end.

One weapon dealt with, Amron thought, though Zyndrar the Unnatural had several more. Fangs, claws, flame, strength and weight all counted in its favour. It could kill by gouging, cleaving, crushing, charring. Every dragon was a terror made to kill.

A sickening roar filled all the world. Fire poured once more from the monster's maw, soaking all about it in flame, yet it didn't last. *His energy wanes,* Amron saw, as those flames guttered out, turning to puffs of smoke. Blood was gushing now from its stump tail, and from its severed wing, and from the first slash Amron had made where shoulder met neck. Most dragons died this way, worn down, slain by a thousand cuts. To get that single killing blow was difficult. You'd need to strike through the eye and into the brain, slash with enough power and force to sever the throat, or plunge your blade deep through its chest, where its heart was encased in a basket of bone and rib.

He closed in, now, pressing on his prey. The dragon was trying to take flight, shrieking in agony as it flapped its broken wing. A great torrent of blood spewed out of its tail, painting the earth red. Amron spotted Rogen across from him, stance low and poised to run, trying to claim the beast's attention. He went in again, summoning the Frostblade's power once more. A hit to the dragon's working wing covered it once more in ice, and the monster dropped to the ground, breathing fire to free it. Amron danced around its other side, dismissing the frost, plunging the blade deep into the dragon's hindquarters at the hip. He hauled the blade out in a shower of blood, pulling back as Zyndrar coiled and lashed, then dashed back in, stabbing again, thrusting and retreating, thrusting and repeating.

And on the fight went. On and on. Smoke billowed around them on the wind, and Amron could still see Rogen moving in and out, probing distracting, sometimes slashing at the beast himself. When its wing unthawed, Zyndrar tried to take flight again, yet it could summon only enough strength for a single wing-beat before slumping. Little by little, its energy was fading as its great hulking body emptied of blood.

Give up, Zyndrar, Amron thought. *Face the inevitable. Let me ease your passing.*

A sudden shout gave out from across the field, and from the woods by the road, came the Taynar knights and men-at-arms, charging in on their horses. *The battle is won and they come to claim the spoils,* Amron thought, but that wasn't fair. *I told them to leave. They come only to help finish it.*

The men launched themselves straight from their saddles and rushed in, stabbing and slashing, dashing in and out like a pack of ravening wolves on a dying bear. One shouted out, "For King Godrik!" and another bellowed, "The Ironmoors!" yet Amron heard several shouts of, "Lord Daecar! Lord Daecar! Master of the Frostblade!" as well.

He stood aside now, watching, letting these men have their share of the kill. It was a sad sight, all told, watching them stab and stab and stab, even as Zyndrar slumped down to the earth, too weak to move or fight back. Amron had seen many dragons slain this way, yet somehow this felt different. *I am older,* he thought. He was but a young man during the war, full of bluster and bloodlust, and on the battlefield it was different. When one dragon fell it was onto another, or whatever other beast or foe awaited. You had no time to watch or ponder. But watch now he did, as Zyndrar the Unnatural gave out a piteous groan, lying prostrate and helpless as the blades hacked and slashed and cleaved and cut, stabbing in and out, in and out, on and on and on.

"Enough!" He could stand it no more. "Enough! Let me finish him."

The men stilled in their hacks and thrusts and stepped back, their godsteel breastplates soaked with blood, and faces too, and cloaks and swords. For all their work, the dragon was still alive, wheezing softly, blood seeping from a hundred wounds. Amron approached its head, where the other men had dared not go. It was the surest way to finish it off, yet the most dangerous.

"You fought well, Zyndrar," Amron said, giving the dragon the respect it had earned. For a moment that strange red eye seemed to look right at him. Then he saw it look at the white blade in his grasp. "You came for this?" he asked. He raised the Frostblade higher. The beast's eye followed it, back and forth, back and forth.

"We had word of your son, my lord," panted one of the men behind him. "They say a…a dragon hunted him…for the Windblade. Same as this. They're hunting the bearers, they say."

Amron glanced back. "My son…fought a dragon?"

"*Killed* a dragon," said another of the men, wiping blood from his eyes. "We heard last night from a traveller who passed our camp. He'd had word from…watch out, my lord!"

Amron's eyes swung back as Zyndrar gave a final flourish, heaving his neck from the ground, chomping down toward Amron's arm. He drew back just in time, the jaws clamping on nothing but air, before its horned chin plunged back into the earth, finished. "Go to your maker, Zyndrar," Amron told the beast. "Tell him Vandar is not for yielding." He thrust the Frostblade through the pupil of the dragon's red eye; a target right to its brain. And it went still.

The silence that followed was short, ending in an abrupt cheer. Amron dipped his chin at his fallen foe, then turned and joined the men as they roared and shouted. Yet not all of them had come. Only six of the ten were here, the other four cantering to join them now. Sir Gerald was with them, sitting heavy in the saddle, looking pale, and Walter as well, beaming in awe.

Rogen Whitebeard approached. "I hope you do not curse me for intervening, my lord," he said. "I thought you in grave danger. I was only intending to…"

"Help?" finished Amron. He favoured him with a smile. "It was well done, Rogen. Do not check yourself with cold counsel. I asked you to stay back, yes, and you did. Until you judged it right to join me. I could ask for nothing more from you, my friend."

Rogen Whitebeard was not one for smiling. Yet his lips did their best impression, just then. "My lord," he said, bowing his head. "I am sworn to serve and protect you, such as I can."

"And I might have perished lest you distracted the beast," Amron admitted. He looked over the body of the dragon, as blood still ran from its wounds, spreading in a great red pool beneath it. "We were ill-prepared for this. Godsteel armour, Rogen, is critical when fighting dragons."

"Your shield looked to hold up well," the tall ranger said. He had aided Amron in his training these long weeks on the road, and knew well his capabilities.

Amron agreed. "It did. But I'm not talking about me, Rogen. Yes, I shall garb myself in godsteel when I can, but you are too valiant and skilled a warrior to be left unprotected. You are wasted in leather and fur. How would you feel about fighting in full plate?"

"I…I have never considered it, my lord. Life as a ranger…well, you know how I like to dress."

"Miserably, yes." Amron smiled through his newly trim, salt and pepper beard. "Times have shifted and you must shift with it." He clapped the man on the shoulder. "We'll see you properly accoutred when we reach Varinar," he promised.

Sir Gerald and the others were arriving then. Those who'd remained in the trees got sour looks from those who'd joined the fray. One called out, "So *now* you come running," and another scoffed at their cowardice and spat to the side.

Amron gave them a light scolding for that. "Courage does not come swift to all," he said. "But that does not mean it isn't there." The men nodded. "Sir Gerald, I hope that fall did not do too much damage."

The man looked in horrible pain. "I feel…I feel I have broken my arm, Lord Daecar." He was cradling his right arm across his lap, looking like he might pass out. He blinked through a pair of droopy eyes. "The Frostblade…my lord? Where on earth did you find it?"

"A story for another time, Sir Gerald." Amron ignored the Greycloak thereafter. "Walter, is your heart rate OK?"

"I daresay it isn't," the man chuckled. "I believe I suffered several attacks while watching, my lord." He raised a quill, as though it were a sword, and to Walter it was, in a fashion. "I have the entire battle seared well into my memory. I need only put pen to parchment, so the singers will have good material to work with." He had taken well to his new role as scribe, constantly jotting down notes, recording their latest adventures to one day compile into a book. He trotted a little closer to the fallen dragon, marvelling. "Well now, that isn't something you see every day." He laughed in wonder. "Might I have time to draw a sketch or two, before we get back onto the road?"

Amron nodded. "Sir Gerald, someone best strap up that arm of yours in the meantime. Do any of your men carry roseweed oil?"

"I have some," said one of those who'd joined the fight. He looked a typical man of the Ironmoors, spare and grim, yet tough for all that. "It's in my saddlebag. I'll fetch it, my lord." He gave Amron a courteous bow, before stepping away. The others were looking at him with similar reverence now.

"Which one of you mentioned my son?" he asked them. They all looked much alike, in their matching garb. "You." He looked at the man who'd been wiping blood from his eyes. There was still a great deal of it stained on his cheeks, forehead, and chin. "You said he killed it."

"I did, my lord." The man was young, little older than Elyon himself, another Ironmoorer by his look. "A traveller passed our camp last night. We had the whole story from him."

Amron stepped toward him as Walter began his sketching. "Tell me everything," he said.

43

Amilia

They dined alone in a private chamber, dimly lit, without music or mirth. There were several attendants to serve them, yet they were rarely seen unless filling a cup of wine or serving a cut of beef. Elsewise they kept to the shadows, still as stone, waiting to be summoned.

Amilia shivered in her dark green dress; a simple thing, yet pretty. She took up her cup of wine and had a sip.

"Cold, my dear?" King Hadrin sat across from her, gnawing on a chicken leg. He'd never looked so much like the oversized rat he was. He placed the leg aside and began picking bits from his teeth.

"This room does carry a chill, dear husband." There was no hearth in here, only candles to give them warmth.

"I thought you were quite used to the cold, sweetling. Did life in Ilithor not prepare you for it?"

I hate your voice, Amilia thought. *I hate your face, and your words, and your ways.* But her expression was a mask of propriety and politeness. "I used to dress more warmly there," she said. "And there were a good many hearths in every hall."

Hadrin waved a hand. "More candles," he said, and at once the servants stirred from the shadows, filling the room with fire. "Better, my queen?"

"Oh yes," she said. "Very much." *Though now I can see your face more clearly, so no, not better at all.*

She longed for the touch of her sweet knight Sir Jeremy, despite how he'd behaved in that alleyway. She had tried to curb her nightly visits to his bedchamber since, to avoid the risk of being caught, though it hadn't been easy. Any night she didn't come, Jeremy would go sour the next morning, and give her the cold shoulder for an hour or two. *He is obsessed, lost in his lust and his love for me.* And he was jealous as well, and fiercely so. Every time he saw Hadrin so much as touch her hand or whisper something in her ear, he would stiffen and scowl, and Amilia feared he might just draw out his blade and hack the king dead right there.

But he hadn't, and after ten long days of waiting the time had finally come. "Tonight," Jeremy had whispered to her earlier, as he delivered the dress she was to wear. "Hadrin has an official function in the palace two nights from now. Put the poison in his drink at dinner, and it'll take effect then. He'll die in public as planned."

That was how Prince Sevrin had explained it. The poison had a delayed reaction and would not kill Hadrin until forty-eight hours after ingestion. It had been the news she was waiting for, and yet her nerves had spiked just then. "They'll definitely be ready? Sevrin and the others?"

Sir Jeremy had placed the vial in her palm and closed her fingers about it. "They'll be ready, my queen. There's a secret pocket, sewn into the hem of the dress. Put the vial in there. He'll never see it."

She could feel it now, against her leg, some halfway up her calf. *I need but reach for it, distract him a moment, and slip it into his drink,* she thought. Yet she'd been thinking the same all through their dinner and hadn't seen a good chance yet.

"More wine." Hadrin lifted his cup and a servant came forward to pour. They were the problem, standing in the shadows. Amilia could not say whether they would call the alarm, even if they saw her, but she could not count on them to be quiet either.

No, I need them all gone. She needed the room to herself, and her king husband well distracted, if she was to pull it off. The answer to that was obvious enough, sick as it made her to think it. "More for me as well." She waited for her cup to be poured, then drew on it with a sultry smirk. "You look very dashing this evening, husband. The candlelight dances upon you most majestically, I must say."

He gave a throaty chuckle. "Ah, so that's why you called for more light? To better appreciate your husband's good looks."

She couldn't believe that he was so delusional as to truly think that, though with this man there really was no telling. "A double benefit, to be sure. Warmth and a better view of you." She swallowed a bit of sick.

Hadrin's eyes swam a little drunkenly as he supped his wine again, gazing over at her with that grotesque lustful expression on his face. He drank most nights now, and to greater excess than at first. *Because of his dreams*, she knew. *And what he sees in the Eye of Rasalan*. Her husband had developed a nervous disposition off the back of it, worse than usual, solved only when he drank to excess, thus awakening the cruelty inside him. When sober he was mild enough, a horrid little cretin, true, but not so forceful as when drinking. But when deep in his cups he became more peevish, more bitter and paranoid, muttering of his enemies and treacherous cousins, of the great burden he carried.

"I see things, Amilia," he would confess to her by night, mostly after he'd crawled between her legs in his futile bid to get her with child. "I see things no other man does. I see dragons, so many of them, and armies, great armies too, marching and clashing in blood and steel and stone and flame. But the dragons…the dragons…there is one…one bigger than all. I see it in the skies, a shadow without end, a dread, Amilia…a dread…" Sometimes he even laughed when he spoke like that and often he wept, but never did he recall just what he'd said. "Cities will burn…thousands will die, hundreds of thousands, millions…millions, yes. And the woods will come afire and the fortresses will fall and all the foul creatures…all will come forth…"

Most of it would sound like gibberish to her, if she hadn't heard of such things herself. It was claimed now that Elyon Daecar had slain a dragon in a storm. Some beast called Ezukar who'd been ridden by a Fireborn in the last war. And only yesterday, a crow had come cawing of another dragon over Ilithor, a monstrous thing that had flown right over White Shadow, so low its belly all but shaved the cobblestones, circling several times before being driven off by ballista and bolt. Then there was this massive Aramatian army bearing in on her uncle, Lord Cedrik Kastor, down at Eagle's Perch, and the rumours of an Agarathi horde marching across the Bloodmarsh Isles as well. The commander of Hadrin's guard, Sir Munroe Moore, had told her about that only today. "Grim tidings come daily, Queen Amilia," he had said. "You ought to think yourself lucky, to be so well protected as you are here. It would be a mistake for you to try to *meddle* with that."

He had given her a stiff look that disquieted her. It made her wonder if Sir Munroe knew something of her plot with the cousins, and all that gave her pause. She hadn't mentioned it to Jeremy, though, to avoid worrying him. *No, it's nothing,* she decided, as she sat at the table, picking at her food. Sir Munroe was always like that, sneering in that conceited way of his, and hadn't liked her from day one. The feeling was mutual. *I'll enjoy watching that one die slow,* she thought, thinking of what Prince Sevrin had said. Hadrin would collapse of heart failure from the poison, but they'd be able to make Sir Munroe's end much more drawn out and painful.

The king interrupted her musings. "You've been very quiet this evening. Something on your mind, my queen?"

She smiled pleasantly. "Only how blessed I am to be here with you, with all the world becoming so dangerous."

"There are dangers everywhere, Amilia." His voice was odd, and his smile was too. "I like your dress. Have I told you that yet tonight?"

"You have…a…a couple of times, sweet husband. You do shower me with compliments so."

He raised his cup, red sloshing over the rim. "I never tire of it, and you deserve them, every one. A man could go a lifetime thinking of ways to compliment your beauty, and still be getting started when he takes his last breath on his deathbed."

"So sweet." She tittered and played at coy. "You have such a lovely tongue on you, Hadrin."

"Yes. So I do." Something about him darkened a little, as he stared at her, then threw his cup back and drank. "More." His voice was thick. "Come on, more!" A servant scuttled over to do his duty, then retreated just as swift.

Amilia stayed quiet for a short time, trying to work out how to tend him. I need him in good spirits, happy and drinking. She smiled and turned her eyes around the room. *I could order them to leave us? No, that might seem too obvious. Better to have Hadrin do it himself.* She made her decision then, and stood, chair legs scraping on stone.

The noise drew her husband's small beady eyes. "Going somewhere, Amilia?"

"Oh yes. Onto your lap." She sauntered over, feeling the vial tapping gently against her calf. The hem was slightly ruffled so as to conceal it, the dress made specially for this occasion. *A dress to kill,* she thought, taking some glee from that, as she closed in on the diminutive rodent she called husband. He looked up at her with a dumb lustful look on his face. "Make room, please, sweet king," she said, and he shifted his chair back a bit. She slid onto his feeble bony legs, feeling the jut of his hips beneath her. More vomit sought to rise up her gullet, but she forced it down, reaching to stroke at the wisps of hoary hair dangling from his chin. "Your beard is coming in nicely," she said. "It'll be a fine great thing, not long from now."

"Do you mock me?" he asked suddenly. There it was, that irritable drunken glare. "We both know I'll never grow a strong beard, Amilia."

"Never say never, sweet husband." She kissed him, sliding her tongue through his thin lips, swirling it as he liked. At once she could feel him stiffen beneath her. She moved gently in his lap, gyrating. He was as small and feeble down there as everywhere else. She drew back with a sensual smile and glanced down. "I wish we were alone," she whispered, leaning in.

"Oh yes, Amilia, so do I." He clipped his fingers. "Leave us, all of you." He did not wait for them to be gone before he stood, lifting her with great struggle and planting her on the table.

She made a girlish chuckling sound. "My, Hadrin, how strong you are." His claw-like fingers were already working to undo his breeches, tearing excitedly to free himself. Her hands came forward, gentle and calm. "Let me," she whispered. "Just close your eyes, my king. I will take care of you."

He breathed out a slow longing sigh. "Yes…do that, Amilia. Put your hands on me…how I like it." He shut his eyes.

Her expression lost its sensual glaze at once, twisting with hate. It was all she could do not to spit into that weaselly face, and plant a steak knife in his neck. *No, follow the plan,* she told herself, as she reached forward and began unlacing his breeches. She worked slow, glancing constantly to make sure his eyes were shut. When she saw one begin to flicker open, she said, "Oh no, don't peek, it'll be so much more pleasurable if you stay in the dark." With one hand untying him, she used the other to withdraw the vial from the secret pocket in her dress. It was small, half the size of her little finger, stoppered with a tiny cork. She glanced up again. Hadrin's eyes were still closed. *Now,* she told herself. *Now!*

Quick as she could, she pulled the cork from the vial with her teeth, reached back, and poured the poison into Hadrin's cup. Another glance. His eyes remained shut. "Not long now," she whispered, still untying him with her spare hand. She reached in and gave a squeeze. "You want me, don't you, my king?"

"Oh yes, Amilia," he said, voice thick and slurry. "Oh yes, so very much."

She focussed, silently spitting the cork into her hand, slipping both stopper and vial back into the pocket. *Gods be good, I did it.* Her smile was real then, the first real smile she'd ever expressed in her king husband's repellent company. She would have to suffer his pathetic little pounding now, yes, but she'd suffered that plenty by now, and it never lasted long anyway. *He's dead,* she thought, delirious. *But no…no, you have to get him to drink first.* That shouldn't be too difficult, though, given how…

"What did you put in my drink?"

She looked up sharply. Hadrin's eyes were open now. There was no smile on his face. "I…what do you mean?" *Did he see? How could he have seen!*

"I heard a little tinkle," he told her. "Some tonic, was it? To heighten the pleasure, I assume?"

She composed herself. "Yes, just that, my king. It…it was meant as a surprise. It will make the whole experience more magical than ever, I promise you." And she tittered again, reaching for his drink, ready to pass it to him.

He caught her wrist. "Surprise, Amilia? Oh no, this is no surprise. I've seen it all already."

Her heart almost stopped. "Seen it?" *In the Eye,* she thought, panicking. *He's seen it in the Eye!*

Hadrin leaned in, right past her, and picked up his cup himself. He took a sniff. "Scentless, no doubt. And tasteless as well. A gift of my cousin Sevrin, was it?"

The blood had washed right out of her face. "I don't know what you're talking about, Hadrin."

His smile was a show of horror, features warped in betrayal and hate. For a long moment he just stared at her, and she thought he might just wrestle her down and rape her right there, or kill her, that would be better...but he just withdrew and paced away. "Sir Munroe," he called out. "Sir Munroe, bring him in."

Sir Munroe Moore arrived from a side door a moment later, hauling along a man with a canvas bag covering his head, tied about the neck with string. A muffled voice came from inside that bag, and there were bloodstains at the mouth and nose. Sir Munroe swung at him with an open palm. "Quiet now, I told you. Or I'll break a few more teeth."

Hadrin stepped toward the prisoner, placing a hand on his head. "Do you know who this is, Amilia?"

Yes, she wailed inside. Tears were already crawling down her cheeks. "No," she whispered. "I don't…I don't know what this is, Hadrin."

"And yet you're weeping? Why?"

"Because…" she sniffed loudly. "Because you frighten me. When you're drunk, and…and the things you say. The things you…"

"See?" he finished for her. "I see much and more, yet most is clouded. Your betrayal…no, that was clear. I saw it coming long ago. I didn't even need the Eye of Rasalan for that." He still held in his hand the poisoned chalice. A smile crept onto his lips. "Take off the bag, Sir Munroe."

The captain of his guard obliged, ripping away the string, pulling the canvas from Sir Jeremy's head. Amilia stared at him, helpless, salt stinging her eyes. He'd been brutally beaten, his face a pulp, teeth shattered, jaw so badly broken it jutted out to one side. *My handsome knight,* Amilia thought, sobbing openly to see him like this. He was scarcely even recognisable anymore. Tufts of his hair had been torn out, that soft luxuriant hair she loved to run her fingers through. Blood wept from scalp and nose and lips alike, a bubbling red spume frothing at his mouth.

"I think our guest is in need of refreshment," King Hadrin said. He reached out with those spindly fingers and raised Sir Jeremy's chin. "Now open wide, Sir Jeremy. A sip of wine will ease your pain."

Amilia could only watch on, numb, as Hadrin poured the poisoned wine down the throat of the Emerald Guard. Tears flooded unceasingly down her cheeks and chin, dripping to the ground where she stood. "I'm…I'm sorry," she managed to whisper. She wasn't even sure what for. This had all been Jeremy's plan, yet seeing him like this…*I do love him, a little bit,* she realised. She could feel her heart rending in two. *Alone, alone…and now I'm all alone.*

Hadrin's spindly fingers gripped hard at Sir Jeremy's jaw. "My wife? My queen? You think you can bed her and get away with it!" He slapped him hard, and then once again, too feeble and weak to strike him with a fist. "Sir Munroe, another tooth. Knock out another tooth right now!"

"Yes, sire." The loathsome knight held Sir Jeremy's collar with one hand, and thrust his other right into Jeremy's mouth. His head cracked back sickeningly, rolling unconscious against his shoulders.

"Again, again!" Hadrin screamed.

And again, and again, Sir Munroe's fist struck, again and again and again.

Amilia couldn't watch. She tried to turn her eyes away, but her husband was on her at once, scrambling over, taking the back of her neck. He forced her to look. "Look!" he hissed at her. "Look at him! Your beautiful lover!" Then suddenly he was slapping her instead, thrashing, pushing her back onto the table, scattering dishes of food to the floor. Wine went tumbling, flagons crashing. He tore at her dress, scratching, ripping, forcing himself upon her. And all the while, she lay there unfeeling, a broken shattered wreck.

"Sire," Sir Munroe said, standing aside uncomfortably. "I should leave you. Take the prisoner back to his cell…"

"No, you stay!" Hadrin pulled away and took up a flagon of wine, gulping it down and down. "I need you to take her as well. A chamber with a bed, that's all she'll need." He faced her again. "And no more tonics to kill my seed! You'll be tied up, you whore of a queen! Tied up until I see your belly swell!"

"*King* Hadrin." There was something firmer in Sir Munroe's voice. "I would not advise that. Her father may be dead and grandfather too, but her brothers…they will not take kindly to her mistreatment."

"Her brothers?" Hadrin cackled, spitting wine. "Those whelps! I'll have them slain too, oh yes. I haven't forgotten how they mocked me, them and their cold dead father. At every feast they would laugh at me, dismiss me. I never forget! Everyone who has ever made mock of me will pay! Everyone!"

Amilia caught sight of Sir Munroe's hand moving to his blade. She hoped…she prayed it meant what she thought it did, but his fingers merely rested on the pommel, and he said, "Still, I would urge caution, sire. Bed her, yes, to get her with child, but tie her up? Beat her? No. That is too much, my king."

"*Too much?*" Hadrin's eyes were wide and wild now. He stormed across the room until he was a mere inch from the knight, craning his neck up to stare at him. "*I* say what is too much, Sir Munroe. Me!" he spat. "The king! Me!"

Kill him, please...please kill him, Amilia thought, as she saw Sir Munroe's sword hand twitch. He stood, saying nothing for a moment. And then came the nod. Then came the submission. "Yes, sire. You are the king."

"Remember it, Sir Munroe! I am the king. Me!" Hadrin prodded a finger into the man's chest and then stepped away. "Everything that happens to you is payment for what you've taken," he said to Amilia. "Everything!" he shrieked. "My children, Amilia! You have slain my unborn children! |

She found her strength. "You will never bear children by me! Never!" Her hand fumbled at the table for a knife. She felt a handle and lunged for him, yet Sir Munroe was too quick. He scooped her up in his arms, squeezing her wrist, dislodging the blade. And so she screamed and raged. "I'll kill you for this!" she said, looking down at Sir Jeremy, lying on the floor now, barely breathing. "I'll kill you, I promise it! You don't deserve to be king!"

"And Sevrin does? My cousin, ahead of me?"

She spat at him, spraying spittle across the room. "Yes! Sevrin carries himself as a king. You're a laughing stock, mocked and ridiculed, and rightly! Rightly, you ugly little worm! You were only ever my grandfather's puppet!"

"And where is he now? Where am I? I am king! I command the Eye. I see the darkness coming, the end. I see it, only me, only me, only meeeeeeeeee…." And suddenly he was shaking, stumbling back against the wall as though some invisible enemy was striking at him, swatting away ghosts with his hands, mumbling in abject fear.

Amilia watched in sickened horror. "Sir Munroe, *kill him*….kill him right now. Your queen commands it."

He frowned down at her, visibly unsettled. "You're not my queen."

"I am working with Prince Sevrin. Kill him now and you'll rid yourself of this lunatic. Look at him. Look! He's mad, mad!"

Hadrin was weeping now, legs curled up beneath him as he collapsed against the wall. His breeches were darkening, and she could smell the stink of piss. "I…I cannot," Sir Munroe said. "Sevrin will have me killed. I'm safe only with King Hadrin."

"Safe? How long will *he* keep you safe?" She tried to break free of his grip, but he held her tight. "Let me go! I want to go home! Let me go!" she screamed. "Let me go!"

Suddenly the door flew open, more guards rushed in, and the chance was gone. Amilia's legs gave way beneath her, and she crumbled to the floor. Men gathered around their king, lifting him, taking him off. Sir Munroe was giving instructions and outside, maids and servants were watching on in fear. Amilia recognised a face among them, a girl called Astrid who'd been kind to her. She had even said that she had a message from Elyon Daecar, to make sure she was safe. Amilia had told her 'yes' then, thinking her plot would work. *Fool, I've been a fool,* she thought. *And now I'm all alone.*

She sunk down onto the cold stone floor, to lie beside Sir Jeremy Gullimer one last time.

44

Jonik

The old man was talking dragons. He had a stringy grey beard so long it almost hit the floor, though that wasn't so hard, at his height. Jonik had never seen a man so small. He couldn't have been more than four feet tall and that was being generous.

"They're swarming, aye," he croaked, sucking on his pipe as he crouched forward at the table. He blew out a series of rings, that grew and grew as they drifted away into the smokey common room. "We got princes killin' em, that we do, and they be swirlin' about our great cities too. Ilithor, aye, one dared go there. And alone, would you believe it…no lie, I swear." He chuckled whimsically. The old man had a fondness of speaking in rhyme, they'd heard. "More are comin', oh aye, if the crows caw it true, 'cross the Red Sea, the Bloodmarshes, and the great blue too. Some even say there're dragons headed here." He grinned right at Jonik. "Maybe they're huntin' you?"

"Stop with the bloody rhyming, you old fool," grumbled the great boar that was Sir Mooton Blackshaw. "Just speak sense. What did you mean by *great blue*?"

The old man shrugged. "The sea, I suppose. Not always easy findin' the best word for a rhyme."

"Then leave off with it, damn you." Mooton slurped ale past his huge black beard, veins bulging in his massive muscular neck. "And that other bit. The lad here. You say he's being hunted?"

"Oh aye. That's the word from down south, at least. That one that chased after Elyon Daecar in the storm…was hunting him for his blade, they say."

Sir Lenard Borrington frowned at that. "What would a dragon want with a Blade of Vandar?"

The Beast of Blackshaw looked at him mockingly. "Where're your brains at, Borrington? You lose all your wits in those Piseki pits?" He made an angry face. "Blast it, now I'm rhyming too! You see what you've done, dwarf!"

Jack o' the Marsh gave a more polite response. "I think it's the bearer they want, not the blade, Sir Lenard. Kill the bearer, and someone else has to train and master it. That takes time."

"Oh yes…of course."

"Not to say a dragon can't fly off with one of them, though," rasped old Harden of the Ironmoors. "They're strong enough to carry godsteel in their talons. Imagine that. They could scatter the blades all over the world. Drop one into the ocean, hide another down some chasm. We'd never find them. Guessing that's why they get lost so often."

"Cowardly bloody dragons," grumbled Sir Mooton. "You can't go hiding a man's weapons. Where's the honour in that?"

Jonik let them rant, as he studied the tiny old man, sucking again on his pipe, shaping his lips such that a different shape spilt out of them every time he blew smoke. Now a ring, now a square, now a triangle. He could even mimic animals. A rabbit came bounding forth, then a shark swam into the room, and finally a dragon, wide-winged, drifted up and up into the air.

"You some mage?" Harden asked him, watching that dragon fade away. "Never met a man who could do that. Not without magic."

"Have you ever met a man old as me?" countered the dwarf. He gave a good-natured chuckle. "I'm a hundred and eighty years old, would you believe. A man can learn a thing or two in that time."

"Yeah, like how to rhyme badly," scoffed Sir Mooton, quaffing his ale. He waved the empty tankard above his head and the barmaid came swaggering over, a buxom woman with a tiny waist, broad hips, and an ample rear that half the men present were ogling. "Abigail, this old codger says he's a hundred and eighty," Mooton said, as the woman filled his tankard from a large wooden flagon. "That true?"

The woman laughed. "Black-Eye says lots of things. Up to you what to believe and what to ignore."

"That isn't helpful, good lady," Harden told her. "We came looking for tidings and you sent us over here. What use is it if we can't trust what he tells us?"

"And you said nothing about the bloody rhyming," complained Sir Mooton.

She took umbrage with that. "I did so. Said he's fond of a good rhyme, is Black-Eye."

"Yes, a *good* rhyme. His are bloody awful"

"I think they're rather good," put in Sir Lenard.

Mooton laughed. "But you've got sawdust in your skull, we've established that already."

Jonik was hardly listening, his thoughts on fangs and steel and gods, and his brother, him most of all. He tried to picture it. Elyon, sky-bound and soaring, slaying dragons in the storm. They'd heard rumours of that at the docks before they'd even reached the inn. It was called the Whispering Drunk, they'd been told, and there was an old dwarf there who liked to sit in the corner, sucking on his pipe, and telling anyone who happened by about tidings from across the world, so long as they had a bit of coin to pay him.

Jack shifted closer along the bench. Brawny as he was, he looked a dwarf himself next to the Beast of Blackshaw. And *he* even lacked for height, if not width, when standing next to Soft Sid or Big Mo. Jonik had some monstrous great men in his crew, that was for certain. "The old man knows you've got the Nightblade," Jack whispered under his breath. "He must do. All this talk of dragons hunting bearers, Ghost. How do you think he knows? Has he seen it at your hip, do you think?"

Jonik had tried to work that out too. "He might have spied it past my cloak," he admitted. "Or perhaps he recognises me." He gave the old man a glance. "He was looking at me strangely as soon as I arrived."

"We shouldn't be here. There's no sense in exposing ourselves like this. And we don't need to hear tidings either, no matter what Mooton says."

Mooton was something of a force of nature, though, an over-match even for Sir Borrus. Not as a swordsman, perhaps, but in bois-terousness he had no equal. As soon as they'd arrived at the Blackhearth docks that afternoon he'd announced himself in need of 'an ale or ten', and had waved along anyone who wanted to join.

"Two weeks on a ship is two weeks too long," he'd roared. "I need a flagon, a fire, and a warm fuggy common room."

Well, they had all of those. The room was smokey, there was a fire burning nearby, and he'd had a full flagon all to himself already. The others had stayed at the ships or gone off on errands of their own, as Jack, Jonik, Harden and Sir Lenard hastened to join him. It seemed that Vincent Rose was cosy with the port officials here in Blackhearth, and would see that their ships were given long term berths, safe and secure, as they headed further inland. *He has contacts everywhere*, Jonik thought. He didn't like that one bit. No matter what Emeric said, he still found it hard to trust the slippery merchant.

"We want some *proper* news," Sir Mooton was saying, shoulders bulging as he leaned forward over the table in his great wool cloak. "You hear that, dwarf. We were promised something no one else knows." He gestured to the coin beneath the old man's chin. "We paid for it, in gold. Now out with it. Dragons we know about. Prince Elyon. Yes, we've heard, everyone has. And that one in Ilithor too. What else you got?"

"Nothing that will please you, I fear. You seem a man who is hard to satisfy."

"Then you're no bloody prophet at all. Give me a good ale, a good woman, or a good fight, and I'm a happy man." His eyes wandered to Abigail, bending over to serve a group of men at another table. "There, she'd satisfy me, that I'm sure of. And I'm pleased with this ale as well. But not you, not yet." He reached forward with a thick-fingered hand, black hairs twisting from his knuckles. "Give us news no one knows or I'll take back my gold."

The dwarf chuckled and swiped the coin away. It was gone in a flash, disappearing up a sleeve.

"Quick for a man of a hundred and eighty," Harden noted.

"Aye, so I am. I like to save my energy for when it counts." He drew on his pipe again. "I have something for you, just come to me." He blew out, smoke twisting and twirling and forming into the shape of a man, cloaked, with the suggestion of a staff in his hand. "There, make of that what you will."

Mooton Blackshaw glowered. "What was that? A cloaked man with a cane? What does that damn well tell us?"

The strange little dwarf shrugged. "Just came to me, as I say. You know as much as I." He showed a crinkly, toothless smile.

"You're trying my patience, imp. Where'd you stash that coin?

Don't force me to turn you upside down and shake it out of you. I bloody will if you make me."

The old man ignored the threat. "You might prefer this, then. I've had more time to ponder it." He sucked on his pipe and blew. The smoke formed into a triple prong, though it looked like it was on fire, somehow, and there were wisps of something, birds perhaps, swooping and circling. As ever, the fume dispersed as swift as it had formed. "Can you guess on that one?"

"The Trident," said Jack o' the Marsh at once. "That was the Trident, aflame. There were dragons in the skies." He looked warily at the others. "I think that means that the Taynar army is going to be destroyed."

Black-Eye's black eye winked. His other eye was blue, but that one was black as ink. It was how he got the name, Jonik guessed. "My thinking too, Marshlander. Word will come of it any day now. The Taynar prince and his army will be scattered. And the Agarathi will cross the Red Sea, striking under sail for King's Point."

"You're bloody joking." The irritation in Sir Mooton's eyes was gone. Something more worried lurked there now. "How can you possibly know that?"

"The smoke tells me. Don't ask me how, it just does, and always has. There're lots of strange people in this world with lots of strange gifts. I s'pose I'm one of them. Lucky me." He grinned.

Sir Mooton leaned back. "I thought the Agarathi were going to cross the Bloodmarshes. That's what everyone was saying when I was there."

"Oh they are," the old dwarf said. "I thought you knew that one? A crow came just last night, though I saw it first, aye, in my smokes."

"Saw what? Speak, old man."

"A horde, of the dragonfolk kind, crawling 'cross Death's Passage. You should have stayed at Dragon's Bane," he told Sir Mooton. "You seem a strong warrior to me. They could have used you."

"I'm one of the strongest bloody warriors you've ever laid eyes on, dwarf. Across all those hundred and eighty years of yours too."

"You have no idea who I've laid eyes on," the tiny old man returned. "I've had the pleasure of sitting with kings and First Blades and champions, oh aye, all wanting a look at my smokes. Wasn't always here in the Whispering Drunk, you know. You can live a lot in a hundred eighty years, aye you can." He chuckled, eyes on Jonik. "And here, this one's stronger than you. This quiet one, with the Nightblade at his hip." He smiled mysteriously. "And who else? The Barrel Knight, the exiled lord, aye, both would best you."

Sir Mooton puffed up his chest. "*Manfrey*? Borrus maybe, he's the heir of bloody Kanabar, so no complaints, but that Manfrey…no. I'm twice his size."

"And he's twice your speed."

"Not so quick when I chop off his legs. One swing of my axe is all it would take. I can hack right through godsteel plate, imp. You ever met anyone who could do that?"

"I met Sir Ralston Whaleheart once," the dwarf said. "You're twice Lord Manfrey's size? The Wall is twice yours."

Sir Lenard Borrington chuckled quietly, getting a steely glare from the Beast of Blackshaw for his trouble. "You keep your laughter to yourself, Borrington, else I'll see you short a head."

Sir Lenard fronted up to him. He'd taken time to come out of his shell, but had grown in confidence now. The Silent Suncoat had something to do with that. At first Sir Lenard had been terrified of him; now they sparred daily, and spent much time together besides. They were a peculiar enough pairing, but this was a peculiar enough group. "You're all threats, Blackshaw," the youth said. "And no action. You see me short a head and my lord father will repay in kind, believe me."

Sir Mooton laughed. "Now there's a threat I trust. Randall Borrington's a fierce man, I know that well enough. If only he'd had a son instead of a daughter." He grinned massively at Sir Lenard, who could only huff and shake his head.

Jonik had a question for the old dwarf. "How could you know about our travelling companions?" he asked him. "Did you see them in the smoke as well?"

"That…no. I heard it elsewhere. When famous men band together, they tend to cause a stir. I caught a rumour you landed in Shellcrest, and Mudport, before you sailed up here. Word spreads easily on the wing, you know. The crows have been doing a fine trade, oh yes."

"So that's all this is," Mooton grunted. "You have spies in every rookery in town, and they whisper these tidings in your ear. You're no mage."

"I never claimed to be."

Sir Mooton lurched to his feet. "I've had all I can take of this old swindler. You keep your coin, and your lies, imp. We've got some *real* mages to kill."

When the dwarf smiled, Jonik sensed he knew about that as well. *He knows we're going to the Shadowfort. He knows what we plan to do.* That might have unsettled him once, but odd though he was, he saw no threat in this man, mage, or whatever the hell he was. He stood, and gave the old dwarf a polite bow. "We thank you for your counsel, Black-Eye," he said. "And your smoke. It has been most enlightening."

They all stood then, stepping back from the benches, making for the exit. Black-Eye gave a final word of parting as they left. "Good luck," he simply said. Then he sucked on his pipe, and blew, and out came spires and crags and peaks, and a fortress all in black.

"Creepy bloody imp," Sir Mooton complained, once they'd stepped back onto the muddied lane outside. The air was brisk, the skies leaden, snow heaped on either side of the road. Down the street, they could hear the cawing of gulls, the ringing of bells on boats, the bustle of men on the docks. Blackhearth was a busy enough harbour, but no Mudport. The big knight shook his head. "You think any of that was true, what he said?"

"Which bit?" asked Harden, grim and grey and old, though a spritely young thing compared to the dwarf.

"That about the Trident. And the Bloodmarshes. The Agarathi couldn't invade on two fronts, could they?"

"Depends how many men they've got." They began walking down the lane, every one of them cloaked against the cold. "That about the man with the staff. What was that, do you suppose?"

"Was it a staff?" asked Sir Lenard. "Or just a walking stick?"

"It was a staff," Jack confirmed, who seemed to have a good eye for those smokes. "Had an orb on top of it and everything. Looked like a wizard of some sort."

"A mage," Harden said. "Some reference to us going to the Shadowfort, maybe."

"Just an old man playing tricks, that's all," Mooton dismissed. "Damn imp," he muttered, pacing on.

They came to the end of the lane, where the docks opened out into a series of jetties and wharves. Boats bobbed on the choppy waters beyond, though there was no forest of masts here, no, more like a smallish thicket or grove. A little further down, there was a commotion going on, it looked, a crowd gathered around, all jeering and jostling. They hastened right over, Sir Mooton bulling through whoever got in the way. The rest followed in his wake. And then they saw the dead man.

He was lying on the stone floor of the harbour, his belly slashed open, guts hanging out. That hadn't killed him, though; the pinpoint puncture to the heart had seen to that. Some other men had swords drawn. They were port soldiers, some of Lord Swallow's men, bearing the birds and black sky sigil of his house in their livery of black, blue, and white. All were shouting at the individual who'd done the killing. That individual was Sansullio, who stood tall and lithe, garbed in his glittering silver scale mail, with a black mantle fastened about his neck, over the golden cloak he wore. His fine gilded sword was held aside, dripping red. Behind him, several more of his Sunshine Swords stood with swords drawn.

"What's going on here?" Sir Mooton marched right out into the middle of the crowd, standing over the dead man. "Sansullio, was this you?"

The sellsword captain moved into a graceful bow. "It was me, Sir Mooton," he said, in his warm deep voice.

Some of the Swallow men began blaring loudly. "Murderer. The filthy Lumaran murdered him without cause!"

"I doubt that," grumbled Harden, moving to Mooton's side. "Now tell it true. He was provoked, wasn't he?"

"Provoked?" One of the soldiers bristled at that. "What provocation do we need? He's southern. We're at war." He spat to the side. "We're enemies."

"We have our own war," Sansullio said. He slid forward a step. "I shall dance with anyone else who seeks quarrel. And I am a good dancer, as you have seen. Who else wishes to partner me?"

One man stepped up, a burly chested man with an axe strapped to his back. "I'll have a caper, *Lumaran*. The likes of you don't belong up here."

Sansullio turned his purple eyes over him, slow and studious. "Which style do you prefer?" he asked. "We have many dances in the south."

"The dance of death, how about that?" The soldier pulled the large axe from his back.

Sansullio grinned, teeth white against his dark skin. "My favourite." He moved elegantly into a fighting stance, limbs flowing, ready to strike.

This won't do, Jonik thought, though a part of him wanted to watch the show. "Mooton," he rasped, drawing the big knight's attention. A look was given and the Beast of Blackshaw knew what to do, marching right between the pair. "Enough," he bellowed. "There'll be no more blood spilt here." He looked to the soldier with the axe. "You, Swallow man. What's your name?"

"Gurt."

"Suits you." Big as Gurt was, Sir Mooton Blackshaw was some way bigger. "Do you know who I am?"

"No," Gurt said.

"My name is Sir Mooton Blackshaw." He waited but the man just stared at him blankly. "The Beast of Blackshaw, some men call me." He waited again. "Nothing?"

The soldier snorted. "Never heard of you."

Sir Mooton looked disgruntled by that. "Fine. You know the name of Borrus Kanabar, then?"

"Course. The Barrel Knight. Heir of Rivers."

Sir Mooton lifted a finger and pointed down the docks. "Well, look hard enough and you'll see him, somewhere down there."

"Thought the Barrel was drunk dry?" said another man from behind. "He went down south and died. Got eaten by a dragon, some say." A few others murmured in assent.

"He was dead for a time. But now he's alive again. And right here in your freezing bloody harbour, though don't ask me why, because I'm not going to tell you. Anyway…" Sir Mooton gestured to Sansullio. "This man is here under his charge. His companions as well. If his colouring offends you, suck it up or look away. We won't be in Blackhearth long."

"But he's a Lumaran," Gurt said. "They're the enemy."

The man made Soft Sid look a genius. "They're sellswords, and working for us. If they're your enemy, then so are we. You want to dance with me, little man?"

Gurt looked him up and down. "Not really."

"Good answer. I'm a terrible dancer. But I'll chop you and your friends up with my eyes closed, that I promise." He smiled toothily. "But we've got no quarrel with you. Let's put this down to a misunderstanding, how about that?"

"Yeah, but…he killed Squirrel."

Harden laughed suddenly. "With a name like that, he deserved it.

What did this Squirrel do to earn Sansullio's ire? Steal some nuts? Come on now, Tukoran, be truthful."

"Spat on him," sneered another of the soldiers. "Right in his southern face. Deserved it, he did. He's Luma…"

"Lumaran, southern, your enemy." Sir Mooton was growing bored of it. "We heard you. Seems he earned it well enough, then. Spit in a man's face and you deserve everything that comes to you. If any of you try to seek reprisal for this, there'll be a whole lot more of you bloodying the cobbles. Best leave it alone. Throw Squirrel's corpse to the sharks and be done with it." He turned at that and didn't look back.

Sansullio stepped to Jonik's side as they returned to the ship, leaving the angry mob behind, hurling curses and slurs. "I am sorry if I caused trouble, Lord Jonik. It was never my intention."

"I know, Sansullio." Jonik's voice was understanding. "What happened?"

"We only wanted to stretch our legs and get a breath of fresh air," the rangy captain explained. "It has been so long below decks, staying hidden. We will be travelling on foot and hoof now, and did not think we needed to hide any longer. Perhaps that was ill-thought. I apologise, if so."

"You needn't," Jonik said. He would forgive the man almost anything, in truth. There was something about Sansullio, some inescapable charm and light to the man, that made everyone like him. No man in Jonik's crew was so widely favoured, except maybe Jack. "I had hoped to avoid any entanglements, but I suppose they were always inevitable. Did Emeric not ask you to stay by the ships?"

"He was busy bartering a good price for horses," Sansullio said. "He and Captain Turner. I confess we slipped out without his knowing."

Emeric was still haggling when they reached Invincible Iris and One World, docked either side of a jetty. The harbour was quiet at this northern end. There were some empty cogs, a couple of merchant vessels with colourful flapping sails, and a large fishing carrack being unloaded of its catch. Jonik could see Big Mo and Cabel training on the deck of Iris, and Sir Corbray and the Silent Suncoat were engaged in a bout as well, moving about the decks of One World as some of the others watched on.

On the docks, their supplies were still being unloaded by Sir

Mooton's men: Regnar, Crasson, Norwyn, Radcliffe, and Sir Bulmar, who took charge of them when Mooton was absent. He'd had a sixth with him when they'd met at Mudport, an old greybeard named Daggart who wore a patch over his right eye, but he'd been sent back to Dragon's Bane to report to Lord Kanabar. The rest were much as Mooton was in spirit; lively, loud, and born warriors all. According to Sir Torvyn, what harm they did to your ears, they made up for when it came to battle.

As Mooton stamped off to join them, Jonik went to Brown Mouth Braxton, who was checking through some of their provisions. "How's it going?" he asked, gesturing to Emeric and Turner. "Does that horse-trader have what we need?"

Braxton scratched at his lopsided jaw. "Seems like it. They're bickering over price, so far as I can make out."

"Price isn't an issue. We can barter with some of the armour we won't use if we have to." They had so much armour and weapons from Lord Merrymarsh's armoury that they scarcely knew what to do with it all. What they needed were horses capable of bearing godsteel, and other strong mules to carry the rest of their provisions. "Where's Borrus? And Torvyn?"

"Went to pay a visit to Lord Swallow. Borrus thought he might preempt any issues of our coming here, with the southerners and such."

And me and Emeric, Jonik thought. "Sansullio killed a Swallow man." He waved down the docks, to where the crowds were distantly gathered. "Guess Borrus and Torvyn were too late."

"Huh. Wondered what that commotion was. That gonna cause a problem, do you think?"

Jonik might once have thought so. But now? His company was a fierce one, especially with the Blackshaw men in tow. "Unlikely," was all he said. "You'd be a brave man to mess with the likes of us."

Braxton gave a huff of agreement. "How was the inn?"

"Interesting," Jonik said, not wanting to get into it right now. "I'll tell you about it later, Brax, when we're on the road." He left the gruff sailor there, descending down into the belly of Invincible Iris. He found Soft Sid sitting on his stool outside the brig door, dutiful as ever. It was to be his last vigil. "You've been great, Sid," Jonik told him, "but you can go up top now. I'm going to let him out."

The giant deckhand stood from his stool and gave a disappointed honk. Sid had greatly enjoyed his time guarding the door and tending to Gerrin's needs. Jonik supposed it made him feel important. "OK," the giant said, head hanging low. "I go…upstairs."

Jonik smiled and stood aside to let him pass. Once Sid had lumbered forlornly away, he unbolted the door and pulled it open with its customary groan. He was greeted by Gerrin's smiling face. "It's time," he told him. "We're at Blackhearth."

"I'd guessed." Gerrin had kept his room tidy. Everything had its place. The parchment, in a neat pile. His quills lined up next to it. The warmer clothes he'd been given were folded and placed on a chair to one side. His oil lantern hadn't moved from its post on the table beside his bed. The former Shadowmaster reached down to the side of that bed and returned with whiskey bottle to hand. It was the one Jonik had bought for him at Mudport, along with those winter clothes and extra quills.

"You haven't finished it yet," Jonik saw.

"Was waiting for this day to come," Gerrin said. "Hoped you might finish it with me, Jonik. A toast to our arrival."

"We're only at Blackhearth. There's a long way to go yet."

"Long enough, true, but when you know the way it goes quick enough. There's a shortcut through the Darkwood, if you dare it. Or else we can take the moors."

"We'll take the moors. I'm not taking any unnecessary risks just to shave off a few days."

Gerrin nodded and uncorked the bottle. "So, how about that drink? Will you take a sip with me, Jonik?"

"I've never been much of a drinker." A short silence clad the room, though it felt harmless enough to grant the man this gesture. "But fine, if you like. I'll have a sip with you."

"Well good. A toast to our fair fortune for the battles ahead." Gerrin reached out with the bottle, brown liquid sloshing within.

Jonik refused. "No, you first."

Gerrin gave that a broad grin. "Still don't trust me?" He tipped the bottle back, guzzling it down. "There, untampered with. Now stop worrying like an old maid and relax. I'm on your side, haven't I made that clear enough?"

Jonik took the bottle, ignoring the question, and drank. The whiskey was too harsh and bitter for his tastes, but he supped it down all the same, feeling the warmth spread through his throat and stomach and settle down somewhere deep. He gave a cough and Gerrin a laugh.

"Good stuff, hey? Packs a punch, doesn't it?"

"It hits like the Beast of Blackshaw," Jonik said, hoarsely "Now come on…let's give you a drink of fresh air instead."

"Now we're talking."

They walked up together, climbing the creaking stairs and pacing the corridors below decks. Jonik felt compelled to give his old master the truth of his status as they went. "You're still my prisoner, not my companion or friend," he told him. "You'll be watched, day and night. When we make camp, I'm going to have one sentry dedicated to keeping an eye on you, and you alone. You'll take no watch yourself, or I might wake to find you've slipped away. Make any move to do so, or do anything out of the ordinary, and I'll have you tied down when we sleep, to a tree or rock or whatever we can find. Some of the men are still angry with you for spreading that blight. Yes, it was Parsivor, I know. But he's dead so they're blaming you."

"I was the one who killed him."

"Try telling them that. Big Mo still has fever dreams from that sickness, he tells me. If there's one man who mislikes you most, it's him. And if there's one man you don't want to piss off, it's him. Good luck with that."

Gerrin took it all well enough. "Any advice?"

"Feed him nuts. Big Mo likes nuts. He'll come to like you soon enough."

"You got any going spare?"

"No. You'll have to forage."

"But…you just said you'd not let me off the leash."

"So I did. And that isn't my problem."

Gerrin huffed amusedly. "You've grown cruel, Jonik."

"Then you taught me well."

It was a lighthearted exchange, though founded in truth. Some of the men had no great love for Gerrin's deceits, no matter his motives, and would be only too happy to put him in his grave if Jonik gave them the nod.

Big Mo was there waiting when they arrived on deck, extricating himself from his duel with Cabel. He was a fearsome man to look upon, with that horribly scarred face and gigantic, looming height. "So the bird is allowed out of his cage," he grumbled. "You will not fly off, will you, little bird?"

Gerrin laughed aloud. "I confess…I've never been called *little bird* before. Many things, yes, but never *that*." He breathed in deep, refreshing his lungs, gazing to the skies with a broad smile on his craggy face. "Well now, did air ever taste so good? I could sup on it forever."

"You stay in this *low* air," Maurice warned him, not taking kindly to Gerrin's relaxed manner. He took a grip of his collar. "You try to fly away, little bird, and Big Mo will clip your wings."

"I'm not going to fly anywhere, fear not. Nor will I run or take off on my horse." He looked to Jonik. "I *will* have a horse of my own, won't I? Don't tell me I'll be riding double with one of these."

"That will depend on how well Emeric's negotiations have gone," Jonik told him. He looked to the docks and saw that those negotiations were now complete. "How about you stay here, Gerrin, get to know Mo and Cabel a little better."

"I know them already," Gerrin came back. "I have a new face now, but I chatted plenty with these two when I was Benjy."

"Even so. Stay here. Maurice, if he does anything you don't like, give him a bath." He glanced overboard and stepped away.

The news on the horses was good. "We have good strong mounts capable of carrying godsteel," Emeric informed him. "A couple of destriers, some palfreys, a rouncey or two. Grade horses for the rest, good for riding. We got Grim Pete a pony. That was Turner's idea."

The ship captain smiled through his tangled flaxen beard. "Couldn't help m'self. Grim hates being on land as it is. But ridin' a little pony with the rest o' us on horses? It'll make the trip go quicker, seeing that every day. We'll get a lot o' joy outta it, lord, so we will."

The horses were soon brought out by the grooms and the money exchanged. Shade was put in charge of them and couldn't have looked any happier for it. Jonik felt the same. No longer did he have to worry for Shade's wellbeing, being stuck below decks like Sansullio and his men. For long months he'd subjected Shade to the swaying hold and the churn of the sea and frankly, he felt sick at himself for it. But ahead lay many days of hard riding out upon the open moors, through woods and valleys and over hills and rills. And then came the mountain trek, for which the Rasal thoroughbreds were so well suited. The thought of it was invigorating. *I have become a man of the sea these last months,* Jonik reflected, *but sails will never be home to me, not like the saddle is.*

As the men came down from the ships to select their mounts, Jonik spotted Vincent Rose returning, accompanied by Kazil, who'd gone along to protect him, and Devin, who probably hoped they might visit a brothel along the way. And they probably had done for all Jonik knew, the time they'd taken. He stepped to intercept them. "Did you have any trouble?" he asked the merchant stiffly.

Rose wore a rich crimson vest, light red leather boots, a bear-fur cloak beneath a mantle of gold and green, and a smug grin. It was his cold-weather garb, wool and fur rather than silk and satin, yet just as absurd and colourful. "Trouble? Now why should we have trouble, my lord?"

"We had a problem earlier, with Sansullio," Jonik said. He looked at Kazil. "No one interfered with you for being Piseki?"

The sellsword shook his head. "My skin is lighter tone, so it's harder to tell I'm from South of the Scales." He wore cloak and cowl as well, to better conceal his face. "And my beard is so bushy, all you see is hair." He laughed, which he did often and loudly. "No, no trouble for me. They dare it and they will regret it, yes." Like most of Jonik's crew, Kazil thought very highly of himself.

Jonik turned back to Rose. "You have friends here, I'm told."

"I have friends everywhere. I may have failed to win you over with my charms, young lord, but most are not so intractable as you. I fear you made a judgement of me at the beginning and have failed to let it go. That pains me. I only wish to be friends with the peerless Ghost of the Shadowfort."

"I'm sure."

"Devin is fond of me." Rose smiled across at the teen. "Isn't that right?"

"He's good company, my lord," Devin said, nodding in his bright-eyed, enthusiastic way. "And *generous*. You should give him another chance. Maybe you could ride together sometimes, on the road? You'll see what I see then...maybe?"

This felt like a set-up. Jonik wanted no part of it. "We'll see," was all he allowed. Devin had been won over by Rose's flamboyance and money and his willingness to take him to whorehouses every time they came into port. The youth wasn't yet seventeen and easy to manipulate, and Rose had been sinking his claws into him for months. *He fed him wine and fed him women, and in exchange for all that, Devin told him who I was, feeding him secrets*. That still irked Jonik, that Devin had unveiled the truth of his parentage like that. He couldn't trust him anymore, not as he could Jack or Turner or Braxton. "You took a while," he went on, ever suspicious. "Sample another brothel, did you?"

"I confess we did." Rose gave a saddened sigh. "I do miss my twins so terribly. I felt I needed some succour."

He'd left those Lumaran twins of his in Calmwater, a good long while ago, putting them up in one of his many homes. "Which one?"

"A fine establishment called Freda's Fancy. Would you like me to take you, my lord? We have time before we set off. You won't get another chance, no, not where we're going."

Jonik's skin was prickling. He could stomach no more than a few moments with this man before he needed to be away from him. "No. We'll be leaving shortly." He caught a look on Devin's face, as though he had something to say, but the youth said nothing. *I'll pursue this later,* Jonik thought. He gestured to the men and mounts down the docks. "We have purchased horses for the onward ride. Best go and pick yours, or the good ones will be gone." He sighted the return of Sir Borrus and Sir Torvyn. "If you'll excuse me."

Briskly, he walked along the docks to meet them, hoping for some good news. The look on Borrus Kanabar's face wasn't promising. "How was Lord Swallow?" he asked the pair.

"Gone," said Borrus in a huff. "He's down at Eagle's Perch with Kastor. Thought he might have stayed; Simon Swallow's no great warrior, but he went anyway and left his uncle behind to run the city in his stead."

"Sir Rupert Swallow," put in Sir Torvyn, left eye giving a quick twitch. "Brother to the late Lord Mumford Swallow, who was Simon's father. Nasty old man is Rupert. Was a close friend to Modrik Kastor."

Jonik put the pieces together. "So it didn't go well then?"

"It went bloody awfully," Borrus blustered. "I knew it was stupid going there as soon as I saw that withered little creature. Old man hates southerners with a passion, and he had the temerity to keep us waiting, too, while he met with some other guest in his audience chamber. Best we leave soon, else we'll have a great mob on our tail."

Jonik sighed. "Sansullio killed one of the Swallow men earlier. There was a standoff down the docks. Mooton broke it up, but…" He turned as Emeric stepped to join them, and here came the Beast of Blackshaw too, plodding over on those thick tree-trunk legs. "We have a problem," Jonik told them. "Seems we're not wanted here."

"We haven't been wanted anywhere we've gone for months," Emeric said to that. He wore his frayed green cloak, hand resting on the pommel of his eagle-blade. "And we anticipated this. It'll get dark soon; if we leave after nightfall and ride hard through dawn, and dusk as well, we'll put plenty of ground between us and this city. So long as we keep to farm tracks and byroads we'll be able to avoid trouble, I would hope."

"Trouble from these twittering Swallows is the least of our concern," Borrus said to the group. He drew a note from his pocket. "Had a letter from my father down at Dragon's Bane. Says we need to keep our eyes on the skies." He looked at Jonik. "There are dragons hunting you, he thinks."

Jonik had to laugh, which was a most confusing reaction to the rest of them. Except for Mooton, who laughed louder.

"Now what's so funny, I wonder?" queried Sir Torvyn, in his mild voice.

"Black-Eye," guffawed his cousin. "This old dwarf at the Whispering Drunk. Said the same thing. Apparently, that dragon was after Prince Elyon for the Windblade and now everyone with a Blade of Vandar needs to be gazing skyward all day and night. You know what I say to that? Bollocks, that's what I say."

"You believe my father is lying, Mooton?" Borrus asked, displeased. "Don't think I won't slap you around a bit if you are."

"Promise? I could do with a tickle."

Borrus stepped forward, and Emeric stepped in. "Now, come, both of you. Much as we'd all pay good money to see you two in a brawl, now isn't the time."

Mooton's big voice filled the world. "Wasn't saying anything against your father, Barrel," he explained. "Never would."

"Then what *were* you saying, Moot? Come, out with it."

"I'm saying we needn't bloody quake and quiver at the idea of one little dragon hunting the lad. I say bollocks to *that*, yes I do! You ask me, we should relish the chance to sharpen our blades. Dragon scales make for a good whetstone, I hear."

"You hear?" repeated Borrus. "Yes, you'd have to *hear*, because you've never actually fought a dragon, have you, Mooton?"

"Only in my dreams. And that happens every night." The Beast of Blackshaw raised his massive godsteel battle-axe. "I've always wanted my dreams to come true, same as everyone else."

"Settle down, Cousin," said Sir Torvyn with a soft chuckle. "You'll get that chance, I'm sure of it, but we have a few Shadowmasters and mages to take care of first."

"And on that, we should get ready to leave," said Emeric.

"Should a dragon come after us, we'll deal with it best we can, but that isn't a matter we can control. It's leaving this city safely that should concern us." He gestured to the horses gathered nearby. "Borrus, Mooton, you can fight over who gets the biggest destrier. Though save one for Maurice. He's bigger than the both of you."

~

AND SO IT was that they left their ships behind, their ships that had been so good to them, and continued away west in a fog of stamping hooves. Captain Turner turned melancholic to say farewell to Invincible Iris. "Don't know when I'll see her again," he said sadly, wiping a tear. "Been so good to us, hasn't she, lord? A good stout ship she is, my Iris."

"She is, Captain. I'll miss her too."

They wended through town without hindrance, in the end, hastening away before Sir Rupert Swallow could muster men to molest them. Emeric led the way. He knew the city well, from his years living in North Tukor, and took them through a quieter gate that led up into the moorlands. The soldiers there looked at them sourly, but made no move to stop them. And then they were free, cantering briskly along a rutted track to the northwest, quickly climbing up into the hills beyond the city under a blanket of twinkling stars.

The Darkwood soon reared its menacing face, a black blanket of trees to the north, sinister and forbidding. Grim Pete quailed to even go near it. "Heard stories about that wood," he quivered, as they rode along by torchlight. "It's evil, full of monsters and demons. Half the people who go in there never come out."

Gerrin was riding near enough to hear that. "Close," he said, "but not quite. Most of the stories about the Darkwood come from the *dreadshrooms* that grow there. They're a rare delicacy when eaten, but give off a hallucinogenic effect before they're put in the pot. It's said a man who sniffs the spores of a dreadshroom will encounter his greatest fear. So when people go in there, picking them for their soups and stews, and start seeing demons and monsters and evil things, well, mostly it's just the dreadshrooms that do it."

"Greengill," said Jonik. He knew all about those. "That's another name for them. As boys in the Shadowfort, we'd get locked into tiny cells with baskets full of them. It was meant to teach us to control our fears."

Gerrin got a few bitter looks from the others for that. "You did that to him, did you?" accused Brown Mouth Braxton. "Locked him away when he was just a nipper? With all them terrors?"

"They were only in his head, Braxton," Gerrin said. "And it wasn't my doing. The mages and senior Shadowmasters would establish the training rituals. I only followed them."

"What else did you do?" Sir Corbray Walsh wanted to know. He was a hard old man, and angry half the time. "I want to hear of these tortures."

"Well, I…it wasn't all torture. A little, yes, but…that was to harden the boys. Life in the Shadowfort was always unforgiving."

"Takes a certain sort of man to torture a boy." Sir Corbray snorted, put his heels to his horse, and rode hard up the column.

Jonik couldn't help but feel some pity for Gerrin in these exchanges. Whatever he'd done, he *was* only following orders. *And he did go easy on me.* Jonik had come to see that now. "I am who I am," he declared, to those nearby. "Torture, beatings, all of it. It made me into me." He shrugged and said with a note of finality, "Maybe that's a good thing, everything I've been through. Let's put the past behind us." He gave Gerrin a glance, and then put them all behind him, galloping hard to stretch Shade's legs in the shadow of the looming forest.

Night broke into a pretty pink dawn, and on they rode, stopping only to water the horses. Then before they knew it, the day had passed and the light was fading again, and a dusk even more pretty was painting the western skies. Some of the men and their mounts were wearying by then, so after a few more hours hard riding, they made camp, slept, shared the watch, ate, and rose and rode again.

Three days passed like that, and all the while, the men kept their eyes on the skies. Any strange movement in the clouds brought out a shout of 'dragon', and at once swords would come singing out of sheaths and the Blackshaw men would give out their battlecries and Grim Pete would whimper and bleat and all of it would be for nought. "Just a big bloody bird," someone would say, or "the clouds are just making funny shapes, is all," or, "damn it, I really thought one was coming that time!" That last would always be Sir Mooton.

"He *really* wants to fight a dragon, doesn't he," Jack remarked once, when another false alarm resulted in Sir Mooton's lament.

"Never met a man like him. Makes Borrus seem like a quiet little dormouse."

"The loudest men are rarely the greatest warriors, Jack," Jonik said. "You heard Black-Eye the other day. I don't think he was lying when he said Emeric would beat Sir Mooton. And he's hardly the loudest."

"You think? Emeric?"

Jonik looked up the column, where Emeric rode alongside Sir Torvyn and Sir Corbray. "Emeric's more than he makes out. He always dismisses himself as a faint shadow of Sir Oswald, but he's not. He's worthy of the Manfrey name."

"As you are the Daecar." Jack gave him a freckly grin. "You think you'd beat Mooton, if you weren't using the Nightblade?"

Jonik shrugged. He never saw much merit in these sorts of comparisons. "Maybe. Maybe not. I beat Dalton Taynar in the Song of the First Blade, and others too." *But not Aleron,* he thought. *No, I'd never have beaten him without cheating.* "So…maybe, like I say."

"You would, I reckon. Maybe even Borrus as well, and Emeric. You need to believe you're the best swordsman here, whether you hold the Nightblade or not. It doesn't define you, Ghost. Your power comes from within, not that blade."

"Thanks, Jack. Am I looking particularly dour today?"

Jack wasn't getting his meaning. "No, why?"

"Because clearly you thought I needed the pep talk."

On they went. More of those sorts of conversations took place. There wasn't much else to do to pass the time, though some of the men continued to spar when they made camp at night. Then it would be up again, and back on the road, ploughing through the snow. One night, a heavy fall came down, so heavy it covered the quiet farm tracks they were on with great heaps and drifts that slowed them to a crawl. They came together to debate what to do, and by Emeric's advice, decided to venture further south. "There are better roads lower in the moors," he told them, "and the snowfall may be lighter there." It went against their desire to remain off the busier tracks, but after long days of good riding they thought it worth the risk.

That turned out to be a mistake. That very day they passed farmers, travellers, and many small bands of soldiers moving through the moorlands. They'd arrived in the lands of Lord Gershan now, no great friend of southerners himself, and Kazil, Big Mo, Sansullio and his men were soon spotted. "We'd best prepare for trouble," Emeric told them all.

After that, they were watching the roads as much as the skies, though they didn't have to do that for long. The next day they heard hooves on the track behind them. It was a thunder to give pause, precipitating the arrival of a modest host. They came from the northern edge of a lake, riding two by two on the road, well armed and armoured. Jonik counted them out. "Twelve rows," he said. "Thirty six swords and shields in total."

"That all?" Sir Mooton pulled out his battle-axe, swung a leg over his horse, and walked out into the middle of the road. He had a greatsword at his hip as well, though often chose that battle-axe to look more intimidating. Borrus joined him there, taking one step ahead of him for dominance, and Big Mo followed as well, to complete the trio of Bladeborn behemoths. The rest remained on their horses, though all looked well ready for the fight. It was a bitter cold day, though there was no wind. Above them, the sun peeked out between low grey clouds that threatened more snow to come.

Jonik glanced back to make sure that Turner, Jack, and the other non-Bladeborn in the party were well away from the others. The Sunshine Swords and Kazil, who were all still technically under Vincent Rose's employ, made a protective cordon around them.

It was Borrus Kanabar who spoke first. "Hold it right there," he bellowed out, breath frosting, as the armoured host slowed and bunched, then began spreading out either side of the road. "Who are you, and why are you crossing these lands?"

Their leader trotted forward. He was an old white-haired knight, once an Emerald Guard by his green cloak and silver breastplate. His cloak was worn and breastplate scratched and that said it all. Jonik saw several different crests on the cloaks of the host behind him. Swallow. Gershan. Kastor. "We're men of North Tukor, and you are trespassing on these lands." The old knight looked toward the sell-swords at the rear, and Big Mo at the front. "You have Lumarans, Piseki, Aramatians in your party. So that begs the better question. Who are *you*, sir"

Borrus Kanabar drew Red Wrath. It glimmered against the pale sunlight, giving off a fine red mist. "You know who I am. And I know you, Sir Boleman of the Bells. We fought together at the Wailing Pass and again at the Burning Rock."

"Ah, so it's true, then." The knight remained on his horse. "Sir

Borrus Kanabar, alive and well. And deep in the moorlands of North Tukor, when a great horde marches upon the Bane. Most curious to see you here."

"But see me you do, and let us pass, you will. You're an old man, Sir Boleman. Old enough to have earned a quiet life in your keep, I should think, to while away your remaining years. You deserve that for your service. Don't be a fool and die here today."

"My life is not to end at my choosing, sir. I am a servant of House Kastor and will perish at their need."

Borrus sighed. "You were always one of the better ones, Boleman. Kastor breeds a plague of unworthy men beneath his banners, but not you. How are your sons? You have three, that I remember."

"I did, once. Now I have just one. Stanek died of the flux some years ago and Merrick fell outside the walls of Harrowmoor when Lord Cedrik charged the gate. My youngest still lives. Jesse. He fights at the Perch, along with my grandsons by Stanek and Merrick. I have five of those. All are there, under their uncle Jesse's watchful eye."

"A fine brood," said Borrus. "I'm sorry for your losses."

"There will be more to come, I'm sure." Sir Boleman seemed a tired man, the sort who'd seen much of war and yet couldn't quite give it up either. "Many will die at Eagle's Perch and my kin will likely be among them. They may be dead already. I had expected to sit in my crumbling keep and wait for news, but fate has delivered me another duty. I will die before they will, I think." He bowed his head. "I am happy with that."

"And what of these men behind you?" Borrus Kanabar looked past the old knight, and to the sides of him, where his host was spread on the snowy moors. "Half look as old as you are, Sir Boleman, and the rest...have they even been blooded yet?"

"Lord Kastor took most to war. He left us only the young and old, the unblooded and the done like me."

"And you'll let them die, same as you? Why? There's no sense in it."

"My lord gave an order."

"Which lord? Cedrik Kastor's away, so is Gershan that I know, and Simon Swallow too. Don't tell me this was his uncle's doing. Rupert Swallow is a rotten old bigot who'd let every one of you die so he can have his pound of southern flesh." Borrus breathed out heavily. "You, all of you...is that what you want? To die for your lord's intolerance?"

Jonik could see a lot of frightened eyes out there. Most would not be Bladeborn and even then those that were would be fodder for their steel. They had the numbers, and that was all. *I could probably kill every one of them myself, if I had to,* Jonik thought, feeling the cold black steel of the Nightblade in his grasp. He took no pride in that. *But if they try to kill any of my friends, they won't leave me much of a choice.*

"We have our orders, Sir Borrus," Sir Boleman of the Bells said tiredly. "We ignore them, and we'll all be hanged."

"These southerners are under our employ," Borrus told him. "They are sellswords, their services bought and paid for. House Kastor has always employed more than their fair share of southerners, as have the houses beneath their banners. This is no different."

"It is. It's wartime now, and you're not Tukoran. These are not your lands."

"No, but they're mine." Emeric Manfrey rode forward on his palfrey, his worn green cloak trailing along the spotted brown back of the steed. He always looked so noble, did Emeric Manfrey, with those keen gold eyes and trim black beard, the warrior and the wise man in one.

"And who are you?" asked Sir Boleman.

"Emeric, of House Manfrey. Once Lord of Osworth Castle and the heathlands to west of here."

"The exile," Boleman said, sourly. "We heard a rumour you'd returned." He seemed to understand their purpose now. "So that's why you're here? To reinstall this man to his castle and lands? I see. With Lord Kastor gone, you thought you'd have it easy, did you?" He drew his blade. "I'll make it a little harder, then."

Emeric Manfrey lifted a gloved hand. "No, that's not our purpose, sir…" He had to raise his voice now to be heard. More swords were coming out, catching the winter sun, gleaming. "This has nothing to do with me. I am in the service of another. Our purpose is something greater…"

"Lies and lies," called out Sir Boleman of the Bells. He seemed intent on a fight, driven by a compulsion to carry out his orders, no matter what. Jonik knew such men well enough. He thought of Gerrin, all of a sudden, and even turned to see where he was. For a second, just a second, he thought he was gone, run off during the commotion, but no. He was there, right there with Kazil and the Sunshine Swords, unarmored and not part of the fight.

"Men!" Jonik heard Sir Boleman cry, glancing to left and right.

"Hear me! These are strangers to our lands, foreigners with ill intent. If they do not surrender their arms and give themselves up for capture, we have no choice but to charge." The company behind him gave a shallow roar, though mostly it was the seasoned knights and men-at-arms who made the noise. The rest just looked scared. "Sir Borrus of House Kanabar," Boleman went on. "I give you one final chance, and one chance only. Lay down your sword and surrender. If you do not, it will be blood."

Sir Borrus Kanabar shook his head and sighed. "Then it will be blood, sir." There was nothing but sadness in his voice.

And so came the shout and the bellowing order, and the charge of the mounted host. Jonik kicked his spurs at once, and Shade dashed off from a standing start, bolting forward in a flash.

And out came the Nightblade too, black as death and misting smoke. Black was the blade and black Jonik's cloak, and black his steed and black his heart, then, too. *I do not want to do this*, he thought, even as he closed in, as he centred his eyes on his nearest target and readied himself to strike. But in a choice between his friends and these men beneath the banners of House Kastor, there was only one thing for him to do.

He killed, as he was trained to do.

As I was born to do, he thought.

45

Saska

She was strapped down on the table, garbed in nothing but a loose linen shift. The vulturous old creature Mhazem crouched over her in his feathery black cloak, gently pulling away another leech, fat with blood. The shadows played about his face, lengthening his nose, turning his runny yellow eyes to hollow black sockets. He gave the leech a sniff, cringing. "*Varin*," he hissed. A forked tongue might as well have poked out from between his lips, foul as he was.

His spindly fingers continued their work, reaching, plucking, placing the leeches into jars. It was routine to Saska now, and had been for some time. She lay there, listening to the noises of the camp outside. There was a great deal of rustling and roaring going on, more than usual. "Is something happening?" she asked.

Balza lounged repugnantly nearby, gnawing on sweetbreads and guzzling down a flagon of wine. He liked to do that while Saska was leeched, indulging himself as he watched, munching, belching, scratching and heckling. He glanced over at the flaps with those pig-eyes of his, then shrugged. "Another raid. What else?"

Mhazem stopped in his work and turned to him. "Go and check, Balza. Make yourself useful."

"Why? Won't change anything."

"Just go."

The boorish guard grunted, heaved his fleshy weight onto his feet, and stamped over to the door. The dead-eyed guard Hiram was on the other side, standing sentry. Balza moved right past him and out into the starless night, leaving them alone.

"I have spoken with Lord Krator," Mhazem told her, pulling another leech off her thigh, inspecting it briefly, and placing it aside. "We both think we may need to consider *other* treatments, child. To hasten your curing."

She didn't like the sound of that. The leeching had sounded horrible at first, but in truth it wasn't so invasive as she'd feared. Now she was used to it. But something new? "What methods?" she asked. "I thought the leeching was working?"

He smiled at her. "No, you have never thought that. But that isn't important. It *is* working, no matter what you think, though slowly, and not fast enough for the sunlord." He pulled off another leech. "I have prepared a tonic, child, which I would like you to drink. It will help to purge you of this poison once and for all." He sniffed at her, nose crinkling. "The infection runs deep, through more than your blood. It is in your meat and muscle too, and your bones. Ever does the Light struggle to fight free of the dark. There will be pain, yes, a great deal of pain, but that cannot be helped. We *must* rid you of this evil, child. Lord Elio Krator demands it."

His bones clicked as he walked, moving to a side counter busy with flasks and vials and containers, some filled with powders, others with liquids, others still containing ingredients both rare and deadly. He picked through his potions, slow and deliberate, before drawing out the appropriate vial. *A great deal of pain,* Saska thought, tugging at her restraints. Mhazem chuckled without turning. "You're well strapped down, child. There is no sense in struggling." He turned and shuffled back over, his small head bobbing sinisterly atop his long wrinkly neck, chin sagging with loose folds of old grey skin. The container in his hand was larger than she'd expected. Black-blue liquid swirled within, fogging.

"What is it?" Her voice was thick with disquiet. She had no notion of what this potion would do to her. Leeching she understood, but this…

"It is a mixture," the old witch-doctor said. "Full of a great many ingredients. Some are easy to come by. The hair of a sunwolf. The whisker of a starcat. Others are much more rare. The tail feather of an Everwood eagle. The crystal fur of a moonbear. And others, yes, many others as well. We *must* awaken the Light in you child, and drive away the dark. I have hope this tonic will achieve the desired result."

Saska shook her head on the table. "No. I won't drink it."

"You have no choice, child." The old man pulled the stopper off the jar, and out swirled a putrid stink. He opened his nostrils and drank it in. "Yes, good. It has distilled as hoped."

Saska tugged at her restraints once more, but she was well tied down and the effort was futile. "What will it do to me?"

"Cleanse you," Mhazem said. "From the inside out. It will spread through your bloodstream, and sink through your muscle and bone. There it will fight the poison, destroying all traces of your Bladeborn side. Now, I must warn you, the process can take some time, and will be excruciating, as I say. You should brace yourself, child, for what is to come. I have hope that one session will suffice, but it may not, I cannot be sure." He clutched her shackled hand, squeezing. "With luck, you will wake a changed woman, free of the curse you have lived with so long."

A more pliable woman, Saska read into that. *Ready to submit.* But no potion or tonic could change who and what she was. Bladeborn, Lightborn, Seaborn. *I'm all,* she thought. *And that won't change.* She looked at the old man with a scowl. "You try to pour that potion down my throat and I'll bite your fingers off," she warned him.

He chuckled. "I see." One of those skeletal fingers rose to the grey jut of bone that was his chin, tapping. "Well, I should prefer to keep my fingers, I think. But no matter. I'm sure Balza will be only too happy to assist me when he returns. Though, I should say…you may pass out, from the pain. And I am awful weary. If I should fall asleep, leaving only Balza to watch over you, well…there's no knowing what he might do to you."

Saska had had about all she could take of these threats. She didn't believe for a second that Balza would be let loose on her. "Let me go, right now, and maybe I won't kill you," she said, thinking it was time to deliver a threat of her own.

The old creature just smiled. "A tempting offer, but no. Now will you drink the tonic, or shall we wait for Balza to return?"

"We'll wait,"

"So be it."

They didn't have to wait too long. A few minutes later, the pig came tramping back through the flaps, breathing heavily. "We're attacking," he said, wiping his brow. "Lord Krator is going himself."

"He is such a brave man," Mhazem said, bowing his head reverently. "How many, Balza?"

"A good host. Sunriders and Starriders. And some of those like *her*. Those Bladeborn sellswords the merchant brought."

Mhazem flinched at the thought. "I do not think Lord Krator should use those men. Them and their *impure* blood. Though of course, who am I to question one so great? I am but a humble servant. He knows best, I'm sure."

"Knows better than you," Balza grunted, shifting his swordbelt around his heavy waist. "He's attacking their western lines tonight, Mar Malaan told me. Might cause them to panic and break, flee back to their ships." He snorted at the thought. "The northmen are weak. I should be out there too. I want my taste of northblood."

Mhazem looked at him curiously. "Balza, do be quiet. You sound such a fool when you speak like that. You are a terrible fighter."

The oaf rounded on him. "And you're a terrible leecher, you sour old crow. You've been working on the whore for weeks and nothing's happened."

"These things take time, Balza," Mhazem told him calmly. He looked like he was about to say something else, but some noise outside distracted him. More men were calling out and more wolves were howling. "Well, it seems they are leaving for their hunt. Let us take a moment to pray for the good sunlord's safe return."

I'd pray for the opposite, Saska thought, *if only I could put my hands together.* There had been plenty of night raids over the last week, both armies probing for weaknesses in the opposing lines. Many hundreds had died on both sides but regrettably none of them was named Krator or Kastor, so far as she knew. It was all brewing up into something much bigger, though. Word was, the following days would see the armies clash proper. As soon as that happened, she'd find one of those Bladeborn sellswords, take whatever godsteel they carried, leap up onto Joy's back and be gone, no matter the consequences.

Mhazem completed his prayers, just as the host outside charged off in a great fog of cries and roars. Saska could feel the ground shaking beneath her. Eventually, it trailed off along with the din of their departure. The old man unclasped his bony spotted hands, reached to the table and picked up the flask containing the fetid potion. "Well now, shall we begin?"

Balza clearly didn't know about this. "What's that in your claws, crow?"

"A tonic that will mend the girl. It must be ingested, all of it. Balza, be a good warthog and hold her mouth open, so I might pour it down her throat. And watch out. She may bite."

Saska glared at the man. "You keep your hands off me, Balza!" she growled at him. "I warned you already. You touch me and I'll have Elio take off your head."

"You won't. You messed all that up when you displeased him the other night. *Whore.*" He liked that word, grinning stupidly as he said it. "All you had to do was open up your legs like a good northern whore, and you couldn't even do *that.* My head'll stay where it is. Be yours that goes tumbling if you keep refusing him." He stepped in and wrapped a set of pudgy fingers around the bottom of her chin, planting the others down on her face, hauling her jaws open. She fought and struggled and tried to fight it, but it was no use. He was too strong. "Go on then, old man, pour it in. What'll it do to her anyway?"

"Send her to a dark place. A *very* dark place. But sometimes you must pass through the darkness to reach the light, yes?"

"She'll pass out?" Saska could hear the hopeful undertone in the oaf's voice.

"Most likely."

Through a gap in his fat fingers Saska saw Balza smile. "Drink up, whore," he whispered to her. "Drink up…and night night."

She stilled, ready to put all her strength into a final attempt to dislodge the flask from Mhazem's grasp, so it might smash on the floor. She could see him nearing, moving the container over her open mouth, only a few inches away, turning it slowly up, up. *Now*, she thought. With a sudden violent jerk, she pressed forward with all the strength in her neck and shoulders, trying to butt the flask from his hands with her forehead. She felt the glass graze her skin, but that was it. Just that. At once Balza thrust her head right back down on the table with a thump.

"Restrain her, you great pig!" Mhazem hissed at him. "Do you have any idea how valuable this tonic is!" He looked at the guard fiercely. "Do you have her?"

"I do. Stop fretting, you old crow. Just pour it in."

Mhazem came again, though kept the flask a little higher this time. He turned it. Saska could see the blue-black liquid reaching for the lip. That rancid fog was already pouring over it, causing Balza to turn his head away. "Don't be so sensitive, Balza," the old man scolded. "It doesn't smell so…"

A short sharp grunt sounded outside the tent door. A light thud followed. There was a shuffle of feet.

Mhazem's hands stilled, the potion teetering on the edge.

"What was that?" Balza mumbled. His grip weakened for just a second, and that was enough. At once Saska wrenched her face free of his fingers and bit down hard on his thumb. She felt hot blood squeeze out between her teeth as the droopy-eyed guard gave out a squealing yelp, trying to pull his hand away. She bit down harder, harder, harder, until she felt a crunch of bone between her jaws. Balza roared. He began swinging at her wildly with his spare hand, screaming, a slap first, then a glancing punch, then a harder one that caught her firm in the jaw and was enough to dislodge her. Her head swam, but she mustered enough energy to spit at him, spraying blood up into his face.

He screamed again. "Bitch! You northern bitch! You'll pay for that! You'll…"

"Balza…" The voice was Mhazem's. He was looking at the tent flaps. There was a figure there, standing at the doorway. Saska blinked through her blurred vision. It was a girl, a small girl, olive-skinned and dark-haired and young. She wore a cloak, but beneath it was armour, red armour. There was a misting shortsword in her grasp, dripping blood.

"Who's next?" she asked.

Mhazem gave out a high pitched wail and that seemed to make the girl's choice. The old man turned and tumbled away, dropping the vial of blue-black liquid, crashing through potions and poisons and a table of instruments as he went. She was on him in a flash, pouncing like a hunting cat, driving that godsteel shortsword through the back of his neck. It exploded out of his throat in a great gushing fountain of red-black blood.

She pulled it free and turned to Balza, eyes narrow, as Mhazem collapsed lifeless to the floor. The oaf had soiled himself, bowels and bladder emptying. "Now you," the girl said.

"No!" Saska roared. "No….he's *mine.*"

The girl grinned approvingly. "I should stop him getting away at least, right?"

Balza was making for the flaps, stumbling and falling over himself as he went. The girl danced right after him, hooking his trailing leg with her foot to trip him up. He collapsed forward, the wind knocked out of him, cutting off whatever screaming bleat he was trying to give out. At once the girl reached down, grabbed his swordbelt, and flung him across the room, her strength enhanced by the godsteel in her grasp. He landed hard against a thick support beam, wheezing.

Saska watched. She had to blink through her blurred vision but… *My gods,* she thought, *My gods, is that….* "Leshie?"

The girl's mouth twirled into a grin. "You recognised me, Sask?" She made a glum face. "And I thought my disguise was good. It's been working well so far."

"Leshie!" Saska cried, scarcely able to believe it. "How…how are you…what…"

"Later," Leshie said, darting over. She slashed through the straps at Saska's legs, arms, waist, releasing her. Then her face was in a frown and she was gesturing to Balza, the oaf spluttering on the floor, bloodied and winded. "This one. What was he doing to you? He didn't…"

Saska shook her head. It hadn't looked great, her strapped down in that tiny linen shift, Balza looming over her. "He never got that far," she said. "Hand me your blade, Lesh."

"Gladly."

Saska had to compose herself, for just a moment. She'd not felt the touch of godsteel since her weapons had been taken when she arrived in Aram months ago. Her fingers curled reverently around the grip, engaging her blood-blond, feeling that intoxicating surge of power and strength. It coursed through her body and blood, heady and primal. A broad smile stretched wide at her lips as she shut her eyes, and breathed out in a long pleasured breath.

"Feels good, doesn't it?" Leshie asked.

Saska opened her eyes. "Better than good." She had so many questions for her friend, but had to push them aside. Balza was stirring, trying to stand. His breeches were stained brown from front to back and the stink was appalling. "Balza."

He turned his droopy eyes up at her, though they were droopy no more. Fear filled them up, right to the brim, and already his face was cringing, pleading. "My…my lady, please, please don't…I didn't mean…"

"Call me whore, Balza." She took a pace toward him. "Go on. Call me whore, one more time."

"No, I….princess, you're a *princess*, not a whore. I didn't mean any of it, none. Lord Elio, he told me to…to treat you like that. To speak to you like that. He thought it would…drive you…into his arms…he thought…he thought…." He went to his knees before her. "I only serve. That's all I do. I serve."

"Like when you murdered my father? Like when you beat him to death, and broke every bone in his body." She drew forward another step. "You remember telling me that, don't you, Balza? That first time I was leeched. You remember telling me you were the one who finished him off."

And she remembered what she'd promised herself too. *I will kill him first.* And she would.

The fool continued to splutter and sob. "I was lying…just trying to scare you. I've only worked for Krator for a few years. I wasn't there, back then. I never met your father."

Leshie spoke from the side. "If you're going to kill him, you should get it done, Saska," she advised. "The others are waiting. We have to go while Krator's out raiding." She wrinkled her nose, disgusted. "And I want rid of his stink. Just put him out of his misery, and be done with it. We need to go."

Saska stepped forward, brandishing her misting blade. "I don't believe a word of what you've just told me, Balza. Not a word."

"But…it's true, all of it. It's true, I swear!" He managed to get to his feet, and even drew out his sword, though his hand was shaking so much he almost dropped it as he pulled it from its sheath. Quivering, he held it forward, tip first. "Please, I don't want to fight…I don't want to…I…I. " He had a sudden thought. "I'll serve *you.* Yes! I'll serve you instead!" He dropped right back down to his knees again, placing the blade before him. He was so piteous and pathetic a small part of Saska even thought of sparing him. "Please, I'll do *anything.* I'll…I'll kill him. Krator." He looked up, nodding. "I'll kill him for you. I will. Just let me live and I'll do it. I will. I promise I will."

"Then you deserve to die twice over," Saska told him, unmoved. "I don't care for oathbreakers, Balza. Killing you will be a mercy."

"No…no…" He moved onto his haunches, holding his palms up. "Please…don't…."

She closed the space between them in a sharp swift step, wrapped fingers around his throat, and lifted him to his feet. She had thought so many times about how she'd kill him. In her fantasies, she would beat him to death as he had her father. She'd take a fistful of hair and smash his head down against some hard surface, a table or trunk or the hard wood floor, driving his round empty skull into that surface again and again and again until there was nothing but pulp in her grasp, blood and bits of soft witless brain. But that was just a fantasy. Seeing his lamentable squirming fear, such a violent death felt hollow now.

So she drove the sword through his gut instead, and out the back of his spine. And that was the end of Balza.

"Nice," Leshie said, pursing her lips. "Quick and clean." She stepped up beside her. "Can I have my sword back now?"

Saska opened her grasp and let Balza's corpse tumble to the ground, blood flooding out of his open gut. She leaned down and wiped the blade clean on the pig's cloak, then handed it over. "Thanks. Nice sword."

"It does the job. What do you think of my armour?" Leshie opened up her cloak to give Saska a better look. "It's leather, not godsteel or anything, but I don't plan on getting stabbed or shot, so that doesn't matter. It looks good, though, right? Goes with my hair and freckles." She thought a second, chewing on her lip. "Well, not now. My hair's darker now, and my skin too, but that's just a lotion, you know, like we were taught by Mistress Tufnell back at the academy. But, before then. When my hair was red. It looked better before then, that's what I mean to say. My armour did. It matched my red hair."

Saska had half-forgotten how much she adored this girl. "It's really nice, Lesh. Where did you get it?"

Leshie gave out a soft little snort. "That merchant, Vincent Rose. You remember, the one me and Ranulf left with back in Thalan? He had it made for me. The bastard." She snorted again.

There was clearly a bigger story there, though Saska didn't think now was the best time to hear it. "You can tell me about it later," she said, mind racing. "So....what now? You have a plan, don't you?"

"Of course. Though...it's not *my* plan, not really. I'll admit that. It's Ranulf's. He's waiting, over in the follower camp. With those sellswords he hired."

Saska was still trying to compose herself. It made sense that Ranulf would be with her, though how either of them were all the way out here, she couldn't possibly say. They were heading for Vincent Rose's estate in Solapia when they left Thalan, she recalled. "You...you came all this way for me, Lesh? You and Ranulf? How did you even know I was here?"

"Luck," Leshie said, gripping tight at her godsteel dagger. Saska could tell she was listening for movement outside. "We were at the palace in Aram when the King's Wall was brought out to be sentenced. We'd heard a rumour he'd left Rasalan, with a girl. Ranulf thought it might be you, so we went to the Red Pits, and Ranulf went down to the Whaleheart's cell. He confirmed it. And we saw you…with Krator on his balcony. You had some black hood covering your face, but we knew it was you. We've been following you since, trying to work out how to get you out." She stopped, listening for something, then relaxed, giving Saska a quick look up and down. "You're half-naked. Where're your clothes?"

Saska was reeling from it all. "I…I came from my pavilion like this. Mhazem likes me sparsely dressed for when I'm leeched." *And Balza even more,* she thought, *the dumb dead lout.*

Leshie scowled down at the old vulture's corpse in revulsion. She only just seemed to notice the bite marks on Saska's skin. "That's what they were doing to you? *Leeching*?"

"Long story. Krator thinks it'll suck out my Bladeborn blood, make me Lightborn only."

"Then he's mad. You can't do that."

"I think he knows that really. He's just trying to break me. He… he wants children from me, Lesh. I suppose Ranulf told you? About who my mother was?"

"Yeah, I know it all." She gave a curtsey. "Princess." Then she grinned that grin Saska missed so much. "Right, enough talking. We can catch up properly when we're free of this place."

Saska agreed wholeheartedly. "I need to go back to my pavilion first…"

"No time," Leshie broke in. "And those maids of yours are there, aren't they? What if they raise the alarm?"

"They won't." She hoped so, anyway. "And what does it matter? Someone's going to find Mhazem and Balza sooner or later."

"Later better than sooner." Leshie looked to a cloak hanging near the door. "That yours?" It was, but the girl didn't wait for an answer. She fetched it, tossed it over. "We have clothes you can wear. Put that cloak on for now. It'll do while we get back to the follower camp."

Saska shook her head. She was thinking of the piece of coral that was so close to her heart, and the necklace of stones and shells little Billy Bowen had given her, and her other trinkets too. All were in her pavilion; all were dear. Yet most of all, she was thinking of Joy. There wasn't a chance in all hell she was going to leave her. "I'm going to my pavilion, Leshie," she said in a voice that brooked no argument. "You can come with me or not. It's not just me now. Joy comes too."

Leshie seemed to know about that. "Right. That's your starcat? You..." A smile played about her lips. "You...called her *Joy*?"

"Don't laugh."

"No, course not." She swallowed down her giggle. "Fine... supposed you might want to bring the cat as well. But if we die for this, after everything I've been through, then damn it, Saska, I'm going to kill you."

"You always had a way with words, Lesh." Saska gave a smirk of her own and moved to the flaps, peeking out. She couldn't see Hiram's body out there, which was most curious. "What did you do with the other guard?" She was certain that sharp grunt she heard was Leshie killing the man.

"He's hidden," Leshie said. "I've got help, some of those sell-swords Ranulf hired. They moved the body to one of the Sunrider's tents. He'll have a fright when he gets back, that's for sure, but he'll be gone a while."

Saska couldn't see any sellswords out there. The heart of the camp was largely deserted with Krator and his Lightborn host gone raiding. "Where are they?"

"Watching," Leshie said. "I told you, Ranulf's thought it all through. He's had people watching for the last week, waiting for the right time. He wanted these sellswords to come and free you, rather than me, but oh no, I wasn't having any of that. I didn't come all the way out here, travelling with that festering horde of a follower army, only to stand by doing nothing. *I'm* saving you, Saska, not anyone else. Now don't go screwing that up for me. Let's get to your tent and get out."

They wasted no time in doing that, slipping quickly out beneath a moonless black sky, turning left, left again, and crossing the yard to Saska's pavilion. A couple of soldiers were standing sentry outside another tent nearby, but Leshie told her not to worry. "They're ours. The Butcher and the Baker have plenty of men around here, watching the Sunriders' stuff when they're gone. Lots of rivalries between them, apparently. Maybe you've noticed that?"

"They squabble a lot," Saska agreed. She stopped before reaching her tent. "No violence, Leshie," she said, voice low. "My maids are sweet and innocent. I don't want them hurt."

"Wouldn't dream of it. So long as you're sure we can trust them."

"We don't have a choice." Saska pushed straight inside, Leshie following. As per her typical daily routine, a bath had been prepared. Yasha, Milla, and Koya were all waiting to wash, oil, massage, and dress her, the room smelling of lavender and lemons. Joy stood at once and prowled straight over, giving Leshie a mistrustful glare.

Yasha was first to speak. "And who is this, my lady?"

"A friend," Saska told her. She slipped straight out of her cloak and went to her dressing stand. She reached for her riding garb, speaking as she dressed. "I'm leaving, Yasha. Leshie's here to rescue me. I don't want any of you hurt by Elio when he finds out I'm gone. It's best you pretend I'm not here."

"No, my lady, that won't do," Yasha said, taking it all in her stride, as though she'd expected this day to come sooner or later. Saska pulled on a shirt, turning to her. "Lord Elio will know you have returned here to dress, after your leeching. And you will take Joy as well, yes? This puts us in danger."

"I don't want that." Saska looked to the other girls, Milla with the gap in her teeth and Koya, such a beauty. "I don't want any of you to be hurt."

"Maybe we could come with you?" Milla said. "We have enjoyed serving you."

Koya nodded. "We have."

Saska smiled at them. "You've been wonderful to me, all of you. But it won't be safe. As soon as Elio finds out I'm gone, he'll send men to hunt me down." She glanced over at Leshie. "I'm sure my friends have planned for that, but...we'll not be safe until we reach Aram and that might take a while. We *are* going to Aram, right Lesh?"

"So Ranulf insists," she grunted. "I wanted to take you home... you know, *proper* home, but Ranulf's obsessed with seeing your grandmother about something. You ask me, we should take one of Denlatis's ships and sail north, but no one seems to listen to what I say."

Denlatis, Saska thought. *So the merchant is involved as well...*

"We would not mind the danger," Milla argued. "All is danger now. The whole world...it is ending."

"Ending," nodded Koya. "We would come and see the end with you, Princess."

"We can't take you," Leshie told them bluntly. "Sorry, but we've planned this for weeks, and can't have you joining or slowing us. It's already taking too long being here." She gave Saska a firm look. "We *have* to go."

"The north-girl is right," old Yasha said. "We cannot interfere with this. But I will not have Milla and Koya interrogated and tortured by Lord Elio to find out where you have gone."

"Tell him Aram," Saska said. "He'll know that anyway."

"Yes, but there are many ways to Aram, by land and sea. He will torture us to find what we know. I could accept this for myself, but not for these girls. They are too young."

"Then what do you propose, Yasha? If we can't take you…"

"You must hurt me," the old woman said. "Milla, Koya, both of you leave. I will say that Saska came here and took her Joy and left. That this friend of hers attacked me when I tried to stop her. This is the only way." She turned to Leshie. "Please, you must do this."

Leshie hesitated. "Do what? Saska told me no violence."

"Knock me unconscious, this at least may put Lord Elio off the scent." Yasha turned. "Milla, Koya, go. I will not tell you again."

The girls looked torn. "But…"

"No buts. Go. If fate is kind, we may yet return to Aram as well. Now go. And no goodbyes." She shooed the two girls away when they hesitated, causing them to scurry from the tent and out into the night.

Saska watched, feeling strangely saddened about it all. For all her desires to escape Lord Krator's care, she'd liked her maids a great deal. It was her favourite time, when they bathed and cleaned her, and told her of all their legends and myths and mysteries. *They took me away from it,* Saska thought. *They made my life here bearable.* "You'll find me, when you get back to Aram?" she said to Yasha.

The old woman smiled a crinkly smile. "I will."

"And if the battle goes ill? If Elio dies? Make sure you get out, Yasha. Get Milla and Koya and get out."

Yasha stepped in and took her hands. "Yes, sweet girl. Now quickly, you must not delay. Get your things and go."

Leshie agreed with that. "She's right, Saska, get on with it. I've seen snails move quicker than you." She turned to the old woman. "Right, so what are you wanting me to do, exactly? Just hit you in the face? I might kill you. You're old. I mean, *really* old."

"I'm tougher than I look. Lord Elio has trusted me many a long year. I should hope that some bruising to my cheeks and eyes will suffice. But a cracked rib might also be useful to sell the lie. Come, strike me, north-girl. And do not hold back."

Saska didn't want to watch this. She gathered her things and set about saddling Joy as Leshie saw to Yasha's request, trying not to listen to the heavy thumps and the groans and the final thudding sound Yasha made as she hit the floor. Once all had gone quiet, she turned and found the old woman lying on the ground, blood dribbling from a broken lip, eye already swelling. "Is she breathing?" she asked, worried.

Leshie knelt and checked. "She'll be fine. I didn't hit her *that* hard. Now for the last time, Saska, let's go or I'm leaving you behind."

Saska took a final look at Yasha, bloodied and bruised on the floor, hoping it would be enough. She had no notion of what Krator would do, in truth, but had to pray his sense would win out. "Fine. I'm ready." She climbed onto Joy's back, sliding into her well-worn saddle

Leshie watched, eyes raised. "Gods. You're a *Starrider*. You've gone full native, Saska."

"I'm half Lightborn, Lesh. What did you expect? Now come over here and hop on. You're so small I'm sure Joy can take your weight as well."

Leshie balked at the notion. "Not with godsteel at my hip. And anyway…hell no am I riding that thing. I mean, she's beautiful and everything, but…no, Saska. I'll stay on my feet, thanks."

"Fine, up to you. So which way?"

"We have a route plotted, down back alleys and lanes. It's all planned out so we can sneak away unnoticed. Garth and Merinius are waiting."

"Sellswords?"

"Bloody Traders. Now follow me, and do exactly what I tell you."

Saska followed, and did exactly what Leshie told her.

46

Cecilia

She looked down at the man on the bed, tucked up beneath the warm woollen covers. Cecilia had rarely seen anyone so ancient and frail. He looked so fragile she wondered how they'd got him here without snapping every bone in his body. *A good gust of wind would blow him over,* she thought.

"Do you recognise him?" Sir Mallister Monsort asked her.

Cecilia shook her head. The man had been brought to the city from Mudport, they'd been told, having spent many long years as a prisoner in some godsforsaken dungeon somewhere in the deserts of Pisek. She turned to the soldier who'd delivered him. "He's a relative, you say?"

The man gave a nod. He was one of Lord Morley's men, wearing the Lord of Mudport's ugly dull colours of brown and black, with that crest of his; a bulky ship sailing on murky brown waters, sewn as a badge on his surcoat. "That's what I was told, m'lady. Lots of long-missing folk were found down in those pits. You must have heard of them by now? Lady Kathryn Merrymarsh. Sir Torvyn Blackshaw. Few others, though none so long missing as them two. And this one here." He gestured to the old man in the bed. "Sir Borrus Kanabar told me he was a relative of the king. Though he said he'd had that from some other source, so couldn't confirm it. A Rasal adventurer, such as I can remember. All gets a bit muddled eventually, when you try to unravel it."

The Morley man looked like the sort who got muddled easily. He had a heavy beetled brow, dull eyes, and something of a slack jaw. Not quite a lackwit, but close enough. "Yes, I've heard these rumours." Cecilia had no doubt of who this Rasal adventurer might be as well. "A man called Emeric Manfrey was travelling with Sir Borrus, is that true?"

"Aye, m'lady. That he was. He seemed much in charge, though there were a few who might lay claim to that. Anyhow, they docked at Mudport with a few of these pit-prisoners they'd saved, and had them shipped back home to their own lands. I was commanded to have the old-timer here sent to you, direct to the palace." He made an unseemly smile. "Was told there might be some reward in it for me." He fell short of opening out his palm in request for coin, though his words were clear enough.

"A reward, for delivering some stranger to my father's palace? Who's to say he's a relative at all?" She gave the shrunken old man another quick study. "Does he not talk? I should think he would be best placed to tell you who he is."

"Ain't said a word all the time on the road," the soldier said. "Just sits there looking vacant, mostly. Though that's when he's not sleeping. Does that a lot too."

"He must make for delightful company, then." She dismissed the soldier with a wave.

"What…that's it? Begging your pardon, m'lady, but I've come a long way."

"Then you've wasted your time. If you have no proof of who this man is then what good is he to me?"

The man grasped for something to give her. "He had a cloak, I was told. A rotted old one, from the Emerald Guards. And he looks a generation older than the king. I was told he was an older cousin, or uncle…something like that."

Cecilia looked at the rumpled old figure in the bed once more, studying him closely. *Hmmm.* She nodded to herself, musing. "Any man can claim a great many relations, if he looks far enough afield. And my family is not short of Emerald Guards." She thought a moment longer. "But even so, I'll keep him here for now, should the answer come to me." She turned. "Sir Mallister, give this man a golden sabre for his trouble. I'll not have it said I'm a miser." *They call me enough names as it is,* she thought.

The soldier seemed happy enough with that, taking the coin and giving a bow before trudging out through the door in that muddy brown-black cloak of his. A pair of palace guards went with him. "I can speak with Master Archibald, if you like, my lady," Sir Mallister said. "He is sure to know if this man is truly a relative of yours."

"That won't be necessary," she said. "This man is Sir Garfield Suffolk, if I'm not mistaken."

Sir Mallister Monsort's criminally handsome face gave a querying look. "You knew all along?"

"No, it has only just come to me. That's why I decided to pay the man. I recall Sir Garfield, though vaguely." She gestured to a small scar on the bridge of the sleeping man's nose. "I recognise that scar. He earned it many long years ago, if my history serves me correctly, fighting off some bandits out in the Stonehills, near the Suffolk lands. An arrow grazed his nose, gouging out that shallow rift. He was wed to one of my father's aunties on his mother's side. Lady Luane Westermont, if memory serves."

"So no blood relation?" Mallister asked.

"No. Only by marriage." Cecilia shifted the covers, tucking the old knight in. "He was a good man, in his day, and a good knight, loyal and proud. My father always liked him. Often kept him around when he went on campaign." She wiped a strand of white hair from his brow. "We'll give him the rest he's earned. See him taken to a bedchamber more befitting him, Sir Mallister. Somewhere with a nice view into the valley. And have nursemaids brought to tend him. I'll visit again when he stirs."

Sir Mallister inclined his head. "As you wish, my lady. I'll see to it right away."

She left the bedchamber to find Hog waiting for her outside. "Who is he, then?" the big moustachioed sellsword asked.

"An old relative, returned from the dead." She began walking down the corridor, footsteps echoing on the stone. The man had been brought to the servant's quarters of the palace, pending Cecilia's verdict. It wasn't a part of the palace she knew especially well, poorly decorated and sparsely furnished, with many long quiet passages and chambers filled with supplies and old odds and ends long forgotten. Torches burned low and sombre in rows along the walls, clutched in iron sconces, though not all were lit. Perhaps only one in ten had been set afire. "Did you check in with Gerret?"

"I did, my lady."

"And?"

"It's done," Hog told her, in that rumbling voice. "They're all dead."

She sighed, relieved, yet feeling in need of a good long scrub as well. She'd not wanted to kill all those workers and stonemasons, but what could she do? That tunnel system leading into the mountains was a secret, as was the stair to Tyrith's forge, and the heir of Ilith himself. She couldn't be having any of those men spreading word about that, no matter how many times they claimed they would never speak of it.

"The blacksmith's waiting to come down, my lady," Hog went on, as they climbed a short twisting stair, then moved down another long hallway. There were windows cut into the stone here, no more than narrow slits. Cecilia could not help but glance out of each and every one of them, expecting to see a dragon out there in the pale misty skies. "Gerret's still too scared to climb the steps, even with the rope I set. Best I head up and bring the lad down myself. I can be back by the time you're finished in council."

Cecilia nodded. "Do that, Hog. But be quick. Tyrith might get restless now that he knows the tunnel's unblocked. The last thing we need is him trying to descend the stair alone and falling to his death."

"Right. You want me to go now, then? You'll be all right getting to the council chambers alone?"

"I can manage. I'll see you after."

Cecilia walked the rest of the way by herself, striding briskly through empty undecorated corridors and uncarpeted hallways where her footsteps echoed and rang. She didn't much like this part of the palace. Though more likely, it was being without her guards that she didn't like. For some days now, Cecilia Blakewood had been under the distinct impression that she was being watched. It was nothing she saw, no, unless the twisted shapes of shadows counted, thrown along the walls and floors by every torch she passed. Those were sinister enough, but only shadows, she knew, nothing to fear. No, it was something else. A sensation, she'd call it, a tingle at the back of her neck. The sense that someone was behind her, watching, following, yet whenever she turned there was never anyone there.

Except that one time. That one time, when she was quite sure she'd seen a bit of blue mist, trailing away through a wall.

She was breathing heavily by the time she marched through the doors of the council chamber to find the rest of the conference assembled. Prince Raynald rose at once to his feet, and all the others followed, barring Gershan, whose back was too enfeebled to warrant the effort. "Auntie, not like you to be late." The prince frowned at her. "You're perspiring. Are you unwell?"

"I got a little turned around, is all," she said, moving to the drinks counter. "I hope you haven't been waiting for me?"

"Turned around?" Lord Emmit Gershan sat crookbacked in his chair, frowning at her through those mean beady eyes of his. "Here in the palace? You're a little young to be losing your wits, aren't you?"

"We've been discussing the latest dragon sightings," Raynald told her, ignoring the old man's remark. "Another was reported just this morning, high above the Marble Steps. It was the same one as before, we think."

"It's always the same one," Gershan said. "That purply black monstrosity. Keeps on coming back, no matter how many times we drive it off."

Cecilia filled a cup of wine and took a sip. Her heart rate began to come down, returning to a slow and steady beat.

"It's looking for my grandfather," Raynald said, unexpectedly. Cecilia turned from the counter, cup in hand. "We've been hearing the bearers are being hunted and targeted. It's the only explanation. He must be here, somewhere. In the palace or the city."

"Might be the beastie is tracking the blade, not the bearer," Gershan suggested. "If Janilah was here, why not show himself? You ask me, he's dead, locked down in the bedrock below Galin's Post. And the Mistblade too. You should get some good strong men down there, and tell them to start digging, my prince. You're king now, half the city's saying. You find the Mistblade, you'd be a bearer too."

Raynald shook his head. "I'm not king, no matter what the people say." He turned to Cecilia. "Auntie, Lord Gershan has news."

"Oh?" She imagined it was from Lord Kastor down at Eagle's Perch. "How goes the siege, Emmit?"

Lord Gershan picked at his ear with his little finger. "Same as last we heard," he said, flicking whatever he'd unearthed away. "Cedrik's been toying with this sunlord of theirs, Elio Krator. Pompous one, that. Thinks a lot of himself. His head will look good on a spit, Cedrik says." He gave a throaty cackle.

"I'm sure this sunlord thinks the same."

"Most likely he does," the lecherous lord agreed. "But these tidings, they're not from Cedrik, no. Had a crow from a man of mine up in the moorlands. He wrote of a skirmish north of Clearwater

Castle, out on the moors a few days gone. Was that lot of rogues, the Barrel Knight and the exile and the rest, he says. They killed almost three dozen good men; mine, Cedrik's, some Swallow men as well. Sir Rupert's ire is right up, I'm told. And Caleb Kastor's furious too, raging about his castle halls, shouting of vengeance."

Cecilia doubted that last. Caleb Kastor did not share his older brother Cedrik's sense of pride, and was not known as a man to be stirred easily to anger. He'd been born with a lame leg, so had never been a fighter, and had developed a more thoughtful and calm disposition off the back of it. "What provoked this bloodshed?" she asked.

Gershan looked ready to answer that, but Raynald held up a hand to speak. "Seems that this foreign host is travelling with some southerners, Auntie," he told her. "Sellswords, apparently, of a company known as the Sunshine Swords. And a few other cutthroats besides with southern ancestry. There was trouble at the docks in Blackhearth. A man was killed by one of these Sunshine Swords and Sir Rupert Swallow saw to mustering men to give hunt and...well, this bloody skirmish ensued." Raynald sighed and sat back in his chair. "This Emeric Manfrey is giving me headaches. He was exiled by my grandfather Modrik a long time ago. To step foot on Tukoran soil puts him under penalty of death, and those with him as well." He gave her a bemused look. "The Ghost of the Shadowfort is among the party, did you know? I can't fathom it, truly. It's such an odd assemblage of men."

"Most odd, I agree." Cecilia had heard a long while ago that her son and the exile had paired up, yet since then had learned little of their fate. This intrigued her greatly. "They're making for the Shadowfort, then?"

Gershan shook his head. "Reinstating this Manfrey to his lands and castle, I'm told. Modrik Kastor gave it to Sir Dudley Reed for good service in the war. But Dudley's a fat old fool now and won't put up much of a fight." He picked at his other ear, digging.

Cecilia looked at him in distaste. "Would you mind your manners, Emmit. I'm sure you wouldn't be doing that if my father were here."

The old man shrugged, flicked away a bit of crust, and settled his hands on his lap.

Cecilia went on. "There would be no sense in Emeric Manfrey ousting Sir Dudley from Osworth Castle," she dismissed. "Kastor will only drive him back out when he returns after the war. The only way for Manfrey to permanently regain his rights, lands, and titles is by royal decree. No, the Shadowfort is their quest." *And my son is the leader, not Manfrey or Kanabar,* she thought.

Raynald nodded thoughtfully. "If they intend to rid the world of that dark order up there, so much the better," he said. "It makes more sense than reinstating Manfrey to his lands and castle, I agree. Why should this host care to do that? But destroying the Shadow Order? Well, that sounds like a more worthy goal, and one that has clearly drawn all these men together." He reached for the table and took a neat sip of wine. Raynald had always preferred to drink ale when at feasts, yet clearly thought wine a more kingly beverage for these councils. "This Shadowknight must be more charismatic than we first thought. I can only assume that he has been the catalyst for the coming together of these men, and this globetrotting adventure they're taking." He had something of a wistful look on his face. "A part of me wishes I could ride up there and join them. Folly, I know, and impossible, but still…"

"All young men yearn for adventure, my prince," Lord Morwood said, with a dignified dip of the chin. "But your calling is a higher one. To rule, in your grandfather's stead, and your brother's. Which you have done exceptionally well thus far, I might add."

"Thank you, my lord. I only hope to make a positive difference, until Robbert returns." It was instructive that he made no mention of Janilah. To Raynald, and most others, Jan the Mad Man, as the smallfolk had taken to calling him, had had his time as king. "And that leads us to this issue…one that has me torn, I will admit. This group, no matter how virtuous their purpose, saw to the killing of soldiers of North Tukor, some of them sworn knights and retired Emerald Guards. I can't just let that pass."

Old Archibald Benton cleared his throat of an accumulation of mucus. It seemed to take an age. "I…I would advise against doing anything, my lord," he said in that annoyingly ponderous way of his. "It does seem that this band is on a righteous course, as you say, and…and had no intention of stirring trouble, lest it come to find them. Which it did, um, regrettably. But it would seem senseless to me to send more men to their deaths. This is something of a formidable host, as we know."

Gershan glared at him. "They killed my men, Benton. You think I'll just let them walk free?"

"You'll do as your liege commands." Cecilia had had about all she could take of Emmit Gershan's insufferable self-importance. "You are a vassal of a northern greathouse, but no greathouse lord yourself. Know your place. Any reprisal here will be by Raynald's command, not yours."

Gershan scowled and thrust out an old black-nailed finger at her. "Don't talk down to me, Cecilia. I know my standing well enough, but you? You prance about this palace as though you're queen. You're not. The Bastard Bitch of Blakewood, that's all you are."

Cecilia narrowed her eyes. "Don't you ever call me that again."

"Or what? You'll have your little princeling string me up, like he did Sir Rottlor?"

"*Princeling*?" Raynald wasn't happy with that. "Now I've told you before not to refer to me as such. Lord Gershan. Your forgetfulness will get you into trouble one day." His words carried enough sting to silence any rebuttal. "But enough, both of you. You are here to counsel me, not waste my time with these petty squabbles." He looked at them, one after another. "Now, I understand your desire for retribution, my lord, but Archibald may have a point. This group did not go seeking violence. If Sir Rupert Swallow had not mustered these men to chase them down, bloodshed would have been avoided." He turned to Lord Morwood. "My lord, what would you do?"

The stout watch commander stood, jowls wobbling. His arm remained in a sling from the wound he took during the riots, though it was no more than a precaution now. "My prince, I would let them pass unhindered. We have too much to deal with here to concern ourselves with this matter. Even if you wished to bring these men to justice, who would you send? Our best are a long way from here, and as we have seen, this host who rode to meet them met a grisly end. Almost all were slain and yet they managed to kill only…how many?" He looked at Gershan for clarification.

"One or two, my man writes."

"Well there you go. Just one or two killed, for the cost of almost three dozen. And no surprise, with the likes of Sir Borrus Kanabar and the Beast of Blackshaw in their party, and this Ghost of the Shadowfort most of all. These are formidable foes, and you'd need to rally an equally formidable group to challenge them, or else attempt to overwhelm them with numbers."

"Two, three hundred should do it," Gershan said to that. "We send word to every petty lord up there in the northwest and I'm sure we can muster enough men to cause them trouble. We kill Manfrey, and these southerners, that'll be enough to make it worthwhile. And that *Shadowknight* too." He scoffed in disgust to even say the word. "Sir Dudley can lead them, I'll give the fat fool something to do."

Cecilia was getting frighteningly close to wringing the man's wrinkly neck right here in these fine chambers. *My son,* she thought. *That is my son you're speaking of, you grotesque little monster.* "You're a thunderous fool, Gershan, if you think there's anyone capable of killing *him,*" she thought better to say. "And just who is this *man* of yours, exactly? I'd love to know where you're getting your information."

"Got my sources."

"And?" She stared at him. "That's it?"

"He's a squire, Auntie," Raynald said. "This man. A youth called Perry, Lord Gershan informed us before you arrived, who was squiring for one of the older knights. He and several of the others laid down their arms and got away, once the fighting was done."

"Got away or were allowed to leave?" Cecilia already knew what the answer to that was and didn't need a response. "If the latter, then mercy was shown," she went on. "This host rode after them, forced them into violence, and yet they let the survivors go once the battle was over." She looked at her nephew. "Raynald, you've heard your council, and I'd add my voice. This is a noble group with a noble purpose, no band of rogues and murderers. Leave this be. If you pursue them, nothing good will come of it."

Raynald was deep in consideration. "I hear you, Auntie. I hear all of you." He nodded, took another small swallow of wine to give himself time to think, and then made up his mind. "I'll let this matter pass for now," he decided, though Cecilia sensed he was going to do that all along. "To stir the ire of Lord Kanabar by going after his son and heir would be folly at this time, and we've other matters to contend with." He looked to Lord Gershan. "Does my ruling satisfy you, my lord?"

"My satisfaction doesn't seem important in this case, young prince," Gershan said, with frosty courtesy. "I'll not pretend I don't understand your reasoning. But as to whether I agree..."

"You don't need to agree. You just need to obey." Raynald paused, staring across the table at him. "If I hear that you've sent any correspondence, against my command..."

Gershan showed his palms. "I'd not dream of it, my lord."

"See that you don't. Now..." Raynald looked around at the others. "Onto other matters..."

The meeting continued. First Archibald told them about some thievery going on down in the kitchens, a trivial matter all agreed, and then Lord Morwood was asked to delineate the latest civil disharmonies being reported around White Shadow - all thrilling stuff - before the freshest and juiciest tidings from the south were discussed. It wasn't anything Cecilia hadn't already heard. They held these councils every single day now, by Raynald's command, and much of the time they simply trod over old ground; the latest news from the Perch, the Trident, and Dragon's Bane, Elyon Daecar's slaying of a dragon and the sundry other sightings of the beasts that had been coming in across the north, troop movements through Tukor, the defence of the realm and the city and all of that military business that Cecilia tired of, and quickly.

Today, she had no time for it. There was nothing new or critical to report, and she had other matters to see to, of a greatly more urgent and interesting nature.

So she absented herself as politely as she could, gave Raynald a small kiss on his smooth wrinkle-less forehead, and told him she was weary and in no great state to contribute. "I shall come to see you a little later," she told the prince. "There was a man who arrived here this morning I'd like you to meet."

He frowned up at her with those warm brown-green eyes. *So like his father's*, she thought. "Not something to discuss now, Auntie?"

She readjusted his golden circlet, smiling. "It suits you, Raynald," she merely said. "I'll come find you later, OK."

With that, she strode from the room, passing Sir Kevyn Bolt at the door. Some of Raynald's personal guard were waiting outside, looking bored. They stood to attention as she bustled right past them too and down the corridor, looking for Hog. *No, he won't have made it back yet*, she realised. She thought for a moment about waiting for him, then decided that she was far too big and old to be frightened of her own shadow. So off she went, marching alone through the palace, down the narrow, quiet corridors that led into the northern wing, then beyond, to the silent spaces no one visited, and further on still, through the gate that led into the mountain, and on and on from there.

She was halfway through the tunnel system when she ran into the big man, clambering through a tight passage, fire flickering from the torch in his grasp. Cecilia held one of her own - there was no other light in these dripping, darkened depths. The torches came together, beating back the gloom. "My lady, thought you were going to wait for me," Hog said.

"The council meeting didn't last long. Is Tyrith safely down?"

"No, dropped him from the stairs. He's dead, my lady." The attempt at humour was ill-judged, he realised. "See you're not in the mood for jesting. Something the matter?"

"Nothing." She paced past him and led the way on.

Ten minutes later, they reached the large rocky cavern that Gerret and Hog had set up for the stonemasons to live in while they worked to clear the tunnel blockage. There were pallet beds strewn about, tables, chairs, flagons of ale and wine. And lots of blood. Blood everywhere, on those beds and tables and chairs, splattered across the flagons of ale and wine. There were still a couple of corpses as well, newly slain, both cleaved open at the neck. One lay face-up on the cold hard rock and the other was crumpled awkwardly against a table, as though he'd tried to hide beneath it when Gerret had massacred them all.

Cecilia felt sick. "Where are the rest of the bodies?"

"Gerret tossed them in some chasm. They'll not be found, my lady."

"And these?" She could barely look at the two dead men. *I killed them, not Gerret,* she thought. *Me.*

"He hasn't gotten around to disposing of them yet."

"See to it. And all this blood. I'll need it washed away. The cavern should be returned to how we found it."

"We'll see it done, my lady. No rush, though. Not like we're expecting visitors, is it?"

"Just…do it, as soon as you can."

She walked on, unable to stomach the place any longer, quickly arriving at the tunnel that had been blocked, not so long ago. Support beams had been built and strong scaffolds too, to prevent the roof from caving in as the blockage was removed. Tyrith had estimated it as being eight or nine metres deep, and hadn't been far wrong. *Ten, maybe eleven,* Cecilia thought, as she passed through the gap they'd excavated through the rocks. Hog followed behind her. "Have you seen what's beyond yet?" she asked him.

"Not yet. Gerret took the blacksmith through once I'd gotten him down the stairs. I was coming back to fetch you, my lady. They've not been here long."

They continued past the blockage, rounding a short bend. Their torch-fire causing shadows to dance upon the glistening rock walls, creating odd shapes and warped, unfriendly figures. *Just shadows,* Cecilia told herself. *Nothing to fear.* A second light bloomed further on, giving shape to Gerret and Tyrith, who stood together at what looked like the end of the tunnel, facing a wall of pristine black rock. *Another blockage?* she wondered. Disappointment sank through her like a stone. *If we just killed all those men for nothing…*

She pressed on, as the whispered voices of the two men rang out softly down the passage. She saw the Hammer of Tukor, held at Tyrith's side, glowing softly. The pair turned as they heard them approach. "My lady, you made it." There was the usual energy in Tyrith's voice. His face was lit by the torch in Gerret's grip, swollen with excitement. "This is it, Cecilia. The portal…we've found it."

Confusion clad her tight. "But it's just a wall…"

"A wall? No, my lady. It's a *door.*"

And then she saw it. It was no black wall at all, but an opening, leading into a great void of utter darkness. It was rectangular, bordered by rough-hewn rock on either side. The darkness seemed to shimmer, ever so slightly, but otherwise there was no light, no sense of depth, no breeze or breath of wind flowing out of it, nothing. Just blackness, an open door of pure, flawless, silent blackness. "I…I thought it would look…different," she admitted. "It looks unfinished."

"It is," Tyrith told her. "If given the time I'm sure Ilith would have had a pretty lintel and doorframe built, but the cruel whims of fate had other ideas."

"But the doorway itself? The…the portal. It works?"

"Yes, I do believe so, Cecilia. I can feel the strength of the sorcery, through the Hammer. And in my very blood as well. It's… *thrilling.* More thrilling than I could have hoped for. Yet the portal door is not operative, not yet. It must first be activated. On both ends."

"*Both* ends?"

He nodded briskly. "Yes. My research has led me to believe so, at least. When the portal gate is operating as intended, the door should give a glimpse of what lies beyond; the great tunnel through the mountains, and the door on the other side. We should have a view, such as I understand it, *into* the Shadowfort. As you would when opening any door, and first seeing what lies beyond, before stepping through."

"So it's not open?"

"On this side, yes. But not on the other. The darkness you're seeing represents a corridor between the doors."

Cecilia stared into that darkness. It wasn't the news she'd hoped to hear. Hog drew a little closer. "So there's a tunnel *through* the mountains?" he asked, that great tusk-like moustache of his twitching sceptically. "All the way to the Shadowfort?"

"That's how it works," Tyrith told him, voice animated. "Ilith first had to tunnel a physical passage between two points, Hog, before his teleportation device could work. Obviously, this sort of magic has its limits, and requires a great amount of work to complete, but…"

"How far is that Shadowfort from here?" Gerret asked. "Must be hundred o' miles."

"Almost three hundred, as the crow flies." Tyrith moved to the side of the lightless door, where it gave way to regular rock. He pressed his ear and palm against the cold hard surface, giving the wall a tap with the Hammer, listening. "Were we to cut a way through, we might be able to break into this physical passage, and then walk the distance to the Shadowfort, if so inclined. But that would take weeks, all of them locked in darkness. Ilith desired a swifter method of travel, and thus did he devise this gate."

Gerret looked a little pale at the mind-boggling nature of it. It was far too much for his little mind to conceive. "Are there…others?"

"Other portals? Not that I've been able to find, no. This magic… powerful as it is…is vastly limited in its applications. He had plans to create others, linking the great cities of Tukor, and even the north, but the practicalities were too onerous. You'd have to tunnel underground, beneath woods and rivers and lakes across hundreds, even thousands of miles. Ultimately, the project was always destined to fail."

"But this one works?" Hog moved a little closer to the door, though all of them were keeping a healthy distance. *And for good reason,* Cecilia thought. There was something greatly disturbing about that empty black space, rippling ever-so-gently. "You sure about that, lad? What if I were to go in?"

"I would not advise that, Hog. I fear you would get drawn into the void, to be lost in darkness, until such a time as both doors were opened. At which point, you would exit on the other side. That is the best-case scenario, anyway."

"Right, and er…what's the *worst* case, then?"

"Death, to put it plainly. The device works to pass matter through space at frightening speeds. I believe there is an acceleration and deceleration effect, so that anyone travelling through the gate slows as they arrive. Yet if the other door is not open, this won't matter. If you were to run through an open doorway, what would happen? You would run straight through, yes, and onto the other side. But what if the door was shut? You'd get knocked back, and hurt yourself. Do this at extreme speeds and your body is obliterated. Even with the deceleration effect, no one would survive." Tyrith gave the big man a smile. "How is that for a worse case, Hog?"

"I'd say the other one's just as bad." Gerret was looking at the black door warily. "Be like falling through the Long Abyss. What if no one ever opens up the other side? You'd get stuck in there forever."

"Perhaps," agreed Tyrith. "Though in truth, I cannot say for certain what would happen. Ilith's research notes are limited, to my great regret. He stored most of his knowledge in his own head."

"Must've had a big head," Gerret quipped, though there was a tight strain of unease in his voice. "I'm not liking this, my lady," he said. "Maybe that's why the tunnel was blocked? It wasn't no accident…. someone did it on purpose to stop people getting sucked in."

Tyrith chuckled, though Cecilia had to admit, it wasn't the worst thought in the world. She had a rather unpleasant image of skeletons rattling around in there, men and women hundreds, even thousands of years dead, who'd got sucked into the abyss and never made it out. "When was the gate last opened?" she asked.

"I have been trying to ascertain that myself, Cecilia. It's quite possible that it has been shut since Ilith's day."

"Well I'm not going through that thing, no matter whether it gets activated or not." Gerret took a further step away from it. "It's evil, you ask me. And I've just slaughtered a dozen men, so I should know."

Tyrith looked at him in bemused dismay. "*What* did you do, Gerret? You killed a dozen men? Why…why would you do that?"

"Had to. Them workers who…" Gerret caught Cecilia's glare, and swallowed the rest of his words, spinning his lips into a grin, giving out an awkward laugh. "A jest, m'lord, that's all, just a jest. Got a wicked sense of humour, me. Right, Hog?"

"He does," rumbled the big man. "It's lost on most of us, lad. Best ignore him."

"Yes…well, I suppose I haven't spent much time in company such as yours. Or…well, or anyone's really. I'm not so well versed on the complexities of humour as the rest of you."

"There's nothing complex about Gerret's humour, Tyrith," Cecilia said dryly. "You'd do well to ignore him, as Hog says." When Tyrith wasn't watching, she gave Gerret another fierce look. "You have *work* to do, don't you?"

The skinny young sellsword darted his tongue between the gap in his teeth, nodding. "Aye, much work. I'll see to it now, m'lady."

"Do that." Cecilia watched the man slink away into the darkness of the tunnel, taking his torch with him. Then she turned back to the lightless void of a door, staring, just staring into that strange, mesmerising nothingness. "It…it has something of a…a bewitching effect, doesn't it?" she said. There was something, some vague hint of whispers somewhere deep at the edge of hearing. "Does anyone else hear that?" She gripped her godsteel dagger, kept ever at her hip for security, to enhance her hearing, but it had no effect. She could hear Gerret's muttering as he moved down the tunnel, and his footsteps, and Hog's heavy breathing, but no whispers. "Must be imagining it," she said. Neither of the others seemed to have heard anything.

"It's…soundless, to my ears." Tyrith drew closer, no more than a couple of short paces away. He leaned forward a little bit. "But otherwise…yes, it is quite beguiling, Cecilia. The emptiness of it, the *purity*."

He was getting alarmingly close now, inching forward, little by little. "*Tyrith*," she said. "Be careful."

"I…yes, my lady. I only mean to…to study it." Yet still, he drew closer, so close she feared he might be drawn in. "The Hammer," he whispered, his voice turning distant. "It…it seems to feel…*something*." He raised it, until the head of the ancient artefact was almost touching the shimmering void. "There is some power beyond this gate. Something old. Very old. The Hammer…it *wants* to pass through."

She did not know what to make of those words, though they disquieted her all the same. "Tyrith…please step away."

Yet he didn't. Something…something drew him yet *closer*.

"Tyrith! Hog, stop him…"

Hog lurched forward at once, grabbing him by the collar, hauling him straight back. Tyrith tumbled to the rear and the two fell together onto the stone floor, the Hammer of Tukor dislodged from

Tyrith's grasp and landing with a great, resounding *thump* that sent loose bits of rock and grit raining from the roof above. Hog was on his feet first, grunting heavily as he stood. He looked down at Tyrith, sprawled beneath him. "Now what on earth has gotten into you? You might have pulled us both in!" Dust fell, motes dancing in the fire-light. "You want this tunnel to cave in again?" He turned to Cecilia. "Maybe Gerret's right…maybe we ought to do just that…bring the ceiling back down, bury this place. It's wrong, all wrong. Not sure why you're so obsessed with it in the first place, my lady. Who cares about the Shadowfort; there's nothing there but death."

Tyrith looked ashen from the fright. He raised a hand and coughed against the falling dust, then scrambled back to his feet, lifting the Hammer of Tukor off the floor. "The Shadowfort was once a refuge," he said, his voice shaky. "This passage could prove essential in protecting the people of this city, Hog. If it should come under siege, we might be able to save…"

"Lady Cecilia doesn't care about the people of this city," Hog broke in angrily. "That's not what this is about. She's got another motive, of that I'm sure."

"Don't ever claim to know of my motives, Hog," Cecilia warned him. "I hire you as a guard, not a mind-reader." She looked to the portal once more. Already, Tyrith's eyes were being drawn back toward it. "Tyrith, go back down the passage."

He turned at her. "What? Why? I need to study…"

"Just go. Right now."

The young man was meek as anything when given a firm word and moved off down the passage without further complaint.

Cecilia turned to Hog once the blacksmith was out of earshot. "Take him back up the stair," she commanded. "And don't let him out of your sight."

The man balked. "What? *Stay*? Up in that forge?" Hog glanced down the tunnel. "I'm no babysitter, my lady."

"And Tyrith's no baby. But he *does* need sitting. I'm not going to have him coming down here to study this portal, only to get drawn into the abyss. It's too dangerous. Take him up, and *stay there*."

"And what about when *I* need to sleep? I can't be watching him day and night."

He wasn't wrong. "I'll send Gerret up as well. Once he's done… cleaning. You can take shifts, share the watch. One of you come down and give me an update in a day or so."

Hog blew through his lips, causing his moustache to flutter. "He won't like that. Gerret's terrified of those stairs."

"I'll give him something to be terrified of if he refuses me." The pair were starting to aggravate her. Gerret was often insolent and troublesome, but Hog was loyal as a hound and unquestioning most of the time. "Just do what I'm asking, Hog. Gerret will meet you up there."

The big sellsword relented. "Fine, as it pleases you, my lady. I'm just worried about your protection, is all. Who'll look out for you without me and Gerret around?"

"I'll be fine. Sir Mallister can chaperone me if needed."

She had nothing else to say on it. Before moving down the tunnel to rejoin Tyrith, she had a final look at the lightless black gate. *Something ancient*, she thought. *Something powerful.* Was it the Shadow Order he was referring to, or something worse? And staring into the void, she imagined her son, striding up to face his demons. Nightblade to grasp, stout men at his side, he strode forward, a leader and champion. The image made her smile. *That's my motive, Hog,* she thought. *My son.*

47

Janilah

He was used to the darkness now. Used to that strange space between thick rock walls where no one else could go. Used to being a shadow, unseen and unheard, even by those only a few feet away.

It was liberating. He had lived his entire life in public, two-faced and torn. One side was the noble king, the other the schemer, working year after year, decade after decade, to fulfil a greater purpose. *I hold the torch,* he thought. *I light the way.* He had been lied to, deceived, failed and forsaken. *It was never meant to be me. My entire life has been a lie.*

He could hear the voices beyond the wall. "....you're saying he was brought only this morning?" Archibald Benton was asking. Loyal old Archibald, with that great red birthmark and long white beard. *Yet like everyone else, he hopes me dead too.* They all did, everyone, smallfolk and large, the common men who drank in taverns and the rich old lords who supped in their keeps. Wenches and warriors, cobblers and commanders, the bowmen on the battlements and the grooms in the stables, knights, drunks, labourers, whores. *All of them want me dead and gone.*

"Yes," answered the woman who wanted him dead most of all. "A Morley man came from Mudport with him. I paid him well enough for his trouble."

A sweeter voice sounded beyond the darkness of the rock. A voice as yet untainted by the heavy weight of years and schemes and murderous plots. "He was one of the prisoners we've heard about? From those pits?"

"Yes, Raynald," the spider said. "He was an Emerald Guard once, like you. A worthy knight called Sir Garfield Suffolk. He went missing a long time ago."

Twenty five years, Janilah thought. *Or...or was it even longer?* He could scarcely remember now.

"He's a relative of ours, Raynald," the spider went on. "An uncle of your grandfather's. So that would make him a great-great uncle to you."

Archibald gave a little cough. He'd been suffering lately from a poor throat, Janilah had observed. "I recall him well," the old man said, clearing his throat of the tickle. "He is no relation of yours by blood, my prince, but through the bonds of marriage. When your great-grandfather King Jeerah died, Sir Garfield was most staunch in his support of Janilah, once he'd succeeded his father to the throne. Your grandfather rewarded him by giving him the hand of his mother's sister, Lady Luane Westermont, who was your great-great auntie. She had been wed once before, to a...a..." He fumbled for a name, and failed. "Well, I forget. Either way, her first husband died and that freed her hand to be given to another. Sir Garfield was that very man."

Raynald gave a soft scoff. "It seems my grandfather used marriage to secure loyalty, even back then." Janilah was not surprised by the harsh tone of his grandson's voice. He had heard him speak like this of him often now, as he had so many others. "Some say that he killed my great-grandfather Jeerah. He pushed him down those steps because he wanted the throne. I heard that once, when I was little. Some squire was japing about it, and we almost killed him when we heard, Robbert and me. But now it makes sense, doesn't it? I thought the monster had only recently grown in him, that it was the Mistblade that made him like that, but no. He was always a monster, even back then. I hope he never comes back."

Silence wrapped up the room like a blanket. Janilah listened from his hiding place amid rock and stone and mortar, humbled and shamed. The Mistblade was in his grasp, shimmering a wondrous luminescent blue, hidden in the rock alongside him. *I wonder what would happen if I just let go?* he thought. *Would my body become crushed within this wall? Or trapped?* He stood there, his arms and legs and torso and trunk incorporeal, melded as one with the wall. But if he lost that power, severed that bond, what then? Sometimes…sometimes, a part of him wanted to find out. To let go, and give the people what they wanted. To die the monster he'd become.

In the bedchamber, Cecilia spoke gently. "Jeerah Lukar was a weak man, Raynald, and a weaker king. I have heard that rumour as well, that your grandfather pushed him, though whatever truly happened that day, the Kingdom of Tukor became stronger the moment that King Jeerah snapped his neck."

Raynald huffed. "So you're saying it was justified? Patricide… regicide? I cannot agree with that, Auntie. Look at Hadrin. He killed his father for the throne, and everyone hates him for it."

"That was different, Raynald. King Godrin was much loved, and Hadrin much-reviled. Jeerah…he was a man who *wanted* to be loved, yet it made him weak. And after what happened to your great uncle, Prince Jaylor…well, let's just say that few shed any tears the day your grandfather took the throne."

"Jaylor…" Raynald seemed to be trying to recall his history. "He was slain in Agarath by bandits."

"So some say," Cecilia told him. "Others say those bandits were no bandits at all, but men hired to kill him by the Agarathi crown. That Prince Jaylor and his honour guard were drugged by their Agarathi guides, so that they did not wake, even as men crept into their tents and opened their throats, one after another. But whether a planned attack or a random act of banditry, no justice was served, nothing was done. King Tellion of Agarath claimed no part in the murder and King Jeerah just nodded meekly and said, 'OK'. But not your grandfather. Janilah called it an act of war and stirred half the greatlords and knights in the realm to muster their men and call their banners. In the end, nothing came of it, but it became clear then what sort of king Janilah Lukar would become."

"A warmonger," Raynald said bitterly. "He's always pushed for war with the Agarathi. Always."

"Not all would blame him for that, or reproach him for seeking vengeance. How would you feel, if Robbert was murdered and the perpetrators never caught or condemned?" There was a pause to let the boy think on that. "I know it's hard for you to see, Raynald, but your grandfather loved his younger brother dearly, and was not always so loveless and cold as some believe. As a young man he was known to smile, and show passion in his riding and swordplay, to come alive during feasts and festivals much as you and Robbert always have. One might say you're not so different from him, take away fifty years. And in that time, much can change. Love can sour, smiles can wither and fade, laughter can turn silent as stone. When you look at your grandfather, it can be hard to reconcile the man he once was, with the man he has become, yet when you understand the things he's been through, everything he has seen and done…when you can step back and look upon the full tapestry of your grandfather's life, then you might just come to understand him."

"Well put, my lady," croaked Archibald. "Our lives are all but a series of chapters, none of which make sense unless you've read the one before. I have had the honour of reading Janilah's chapters as they've been written, observing his writing process, if you will. During that time I have often felt that I was bearing witness to the creation of one of our greatest men. A man who would shape the north, even the world, in a way so few have done."

"But at what cost?" Raynald asked. "At what cost, Archibald?"

"I…I couldn't possibly answer that, my prince. It is far too complicated a puzzle for me to put together. Some things your grandfather has done…well, perhaps they could be justified, in context, as worthwhile for the greater good. Yet others…no, others I cannot understand. Some things cannot be so easily forgiven, or forgotten."

"He started the War of the Continents," Raynald said suddenly. "Lord Gershan told me. He said that my grandfather ordered his men to poison King Horris Reynar while he was in Eldurath. So that the Vandarians would blame that on King Tellion, and then raise their banners in war. Tukor was never strong enough to fight Agarath alone. Not the gods. Not the kingdoms. But Vandar. We needed them. We *always* need them. So my grandfather killed *another* king to get his war with Agarath instead. Murdering his own father wasn't enough. He had to kill the King of Vandar too."

"Raynald…" Cecilia's voice. Then a short pause. "You should not trust that goatish little man."

"Why not? Is he lying?"

"No. You cannot lie when a matter is borne of rumour. By its very nature, rumour is factually fallible and unproven. Only truths can be twisted into lies."

"So it's just a rumour, then? This about the murder of King Horris."

"Yes. A rumour that has persisted for decades. I have asked my father about it myself, in the past, and heard through his very lips that it is false. Now, believe that if you want, or don't. That is your right. But do not put your trust in anything that Emmit Gershan tells you. He is your uncle Cedrik's creature, and for that reason you must remain wary."

The pause suggested Raynald didn't entirely understand. "Why should I be wary of Uncle Cedrik?"

"Because he is next in line to the throne, after Robbert and you. With the kingdom in turmoil, I would not stake against him trying to take the crown."

"He'd never. Mother, she'd..."

"She'd what? Raynald, your mother is a hermit who does not leave her rooms."

"But Uncle Cedrik loves her. He'd never kill her children." Janilah heard him pace the room. "No, this is a nonsense. Don't fill my head with this stuff, Auntie. You'll only make me worry for Robbert's return even more. He has this Elio Krator to concern himself with, and all these wolves and cats he keeps around. He doesn't need to be looking over his shoulder, fearing his own uncle might put a knife in his back as well."

"I'm sure you're right." Cecilia spoke mildly. "My point is to be mistrustful, as a matter of routine and habit, especially with those whose motives you cannot be sure of."

Good, Janilah thought. *Good, teach the boy*. The idea of Cedrik Kastor taking his crown... *No, a Lukar will always sit the throne. Robbert or Raynald, it matters not. A Lukar. Always a Lukar.* He gave out a breath, too loud. Beyond the wall, a silence fell.

Archibald cleared his throat. "Is there...someone staying in the chamber next door, my lady?" he asked.

"Yes." She gave no detail. More silence enrobed the bedchamber. "Well, perhaps...perhaps it's about time we leave Sir Garfield to his rest. I'm sure all this talking is disturbing him."

"He's still sleeping, Auntie," Raynald argued. "I had hoped he might wake up, so I could talk with him."

"We can try tomorrow. Um, Archibald, why don't you tell Raynald a little more of our long-lost knight? You can use my own chambers. I'll come and join you in a moment, once I've tucked him in."

"As you wish, my lady."

There were footsteps, two sets, one shuffling and slow, the other more direct. They reached the door, then faded off as it opened and closed. Then silence, deep and long. Janilah stood still inside the wall, waiting.

And then she spoke. "Are you there, Father?" There was a ripple of fear in her voice, something tremulous and shaky. "Father?" He could hear her getting closer to the wall, mere inches away from him. "There's no one next door, I know that. Please, if you're there, just… just come out. I can't take this anymore. I know you've been following me."

He remained resolutely still, utterly silent. The urge rose to step out and unveil himself, yet he thrust it down, denying it as he had a hundred times before. *Not yet,* he told himself, as he had so often since he'd left the basement of Ethelda Rivers behind. For days he'd remained hidden, creeping, listening, subjecting himself to these humbling rebukes. *My atonement,* he thought. *I must know how they see me. I must know what I have become.*

"Father. Please, come out." Her voice was a whisper, faint and fractured. She sounded close to tears. *Crocodile tears,* a part of Janilah thought. *My daughter, the spider I sired, who isn't so innocent either.* He knew what she was. He knew what she'd done. His grip on the Mistblade tightened. But still, he didn't stir.

A long moment passed, leading into another, and another. Eventually, he heard his bastard daughter titter, a nervous sound, and withdraw. "Look at me, so silly. Seeing ghosts and ghouls around every corner." He could hear her moving to the bed, fluffing the pillows, pottering about, speaking to herself all the while. "Get a grip on yourself, Cecilia," she said. "And enough wine. It's making you see things."

Still muttering, she walked to the door, opened it, and left. Janilah waited. For a minute, two, five he waited. Only once he was certain there was no one there, did he step out through the wall and into the bedchamber, letting his body retake its physical form. He sheathed the Mistblade, steadying himself as its power drained out of him. He was still weaker than he'd like, but growing stronger by the day. Time spent foraging through the castle kitchens had given him ample provisions, which he kept safe in a bag on his back. He was dressed in wool breeches, a leather vest and jerkin, with the large cloak he'd taken from Ethelda's hovel over the top. *The beggar king,* he thought, *scavenging for food in his own kitchens, wearing hand-me-downs from an old woman's dead husband.*

The room was lit by a low-burning hearth, crackling gently. It was a fine chamber, well-appointed, with a four-poster bed and viewing balcony. The bed drapes had been drawn back, and Sir Garfield was in the throes of a dream, it appeared. His lips were twitching, eyes moving behind sallow lids.

"What are you seeing, old friend?" Janilah whispered. Someone had placed a stool beside the bed. He sat, resting his weary legs. "I hear you were imprisoned in Pisek? All these long years…and you've been trapped in some hell." He wrapped his thick callused fingers around the man's withered hand. "I am so sorry, Garfield, for what you've had to endure. If I'd known…if I'd ever known you were there…"

He felt the old man's hand twitch in his grasp. His eyes flickered open. Janilah leaned closer. "Garfield. My friend…" He smiled through his thickening beard, shaded grey and dull brown where some colour still remained. "Garfield, it's me. Janilah." *Your king*, he thought, but he said, "Your friend and nephew. Do you…remember me, Garfield? Do you remember yourself?"

Cognisance came slowly to the old man's eyes, yet it seemed only half-remembered, as a dream upon waking, lacking detail and form. "Janilah?" he croaked. His voice was horribly rusted, his skin the colour of faded parchment. Thin seams spread out from thicker ones, and all across his face were deeper fissures too, wrinkles and folds so numerous a count would prove impossible. There was no fat on his face, nothing but skin layered over bone. His head was spotted in black and brown and grey, with wisps of random white hair trailing haphazardly across his scalp.

How he'd survived this long was astonishing; Sir Garfield Suffolk had been on the wane a quarter-century ago. "Yes, it's me, Garfield. It's Janilah." He blinked through a pair of misty eyes. "My friend…you're in Ilithor. *Home*. You're home." He clutched his hand tighter, hoping to feel a response, but the man had no strength to give.

"Home?" His eyes moved around the room, aimless. "Ilithor?"

"Yes, Uncle. Ilithor. You're home, and safe…safe now. Nothing will happen to you."

A tear crept down the old man's face, trailing through a deep wrinkle to left of a jut of cheekbone. It reached his lips and hung there a moment, before falling as he spoke. "Are you…real?" He tried to lift his hand; Janilah had to help him, drawing it up to his cheek, pressing it through the tangles of beard and against his roughened skin.

"I'm real," he said. "All this is real." He held his hand there. "Tell me…this moonlord, Pal Palek. Tell me where he is, Garfield. I'll have him killed for you, I promise it. I'll have his head shipped here. We can make a cup of his skull, drink to his death. What do you say? You need but tell me, old friend."

That was too much. Sir Garfield Suffolk recoiled, drawing away again, shaking his head. His eyes flickered and turned aside and he began mumbling insensibly, speaking words Janilah couldn't understand.

He can't help me, Janilah realised. But there were others who could tell him, if he should track them down. Sir Borrus Kanabar. The exiled lord, Emeric Manfrey. Jonik… All had been a part of this plot to free Garfield and the rest. Janilah had heard it all as he eavesdropped on the council meetings. He'd missed much, too much. *The world has changed as I slept.*

Eventually, Sir Garfield calmed and blinked, looking around the room again. "Home," he whispered. It seemed to have settled in now. "I'm…I'm home."

Janilah took that up. "Yes, you're home. You'll live in comfort now, Garfield. All your needs will be attended. Anything you want. Anything…"

"Home…" The old man's lips were in a smile, soft, satisfied. He settled down, relaxing, staring up at the ceiling, listening to the crackle of the hearth.

"Garfield…"

The old man closed his eyes. There was something final about that. "Home…" Janilah watched as his chest moved up and down, up and down, up and down, slower, slower, until at last he gave out a long breath, emptying his lungs, and stilled.

He didn't take another.

"*Garfield.*" Janilah took his shoulder, shaking gently. Nothing. He shook again, reached for the man's neck to feel for a pulse. Nothing. "Damn you! You…you come back here only to die! Damn you!" He placed a hand over his chest, thumping, thumping, the old body bouncing up and down on the bed. That little smile clung to Sir Garfield Suffolk's face. *Home,* it said. *I made it home, and now I can rest.*

"No, you can't die." Janilah pounded at his chest again, felt for a pulse. Nothing. Ridiculously, tears were moving down his cheeks.

Tears of rage, he told himself. *The fool comes back to me, only to leave me so quick. How dare he! I'm his king!* He pounded at the back of his hand until he was sore and bruised and panting, yet still the old man just lay there, peaceful, drifting away to the Hall of Green.

Where Rylian awaits, Janilah thought. His eyes burned, hot and salty. He squeezed them shut, stood, knocking the stool aside, backing away. *I was meant to have a Table of my own. That was my duty. That was my purpose. Rylian… my son. My son…*

He stormed out toward the balcony, pushing through the doors, feeling the sting of cold on his cheeks, the slice of wind through his wools. He wanted to scream out in rage and loss, but only planted his hands on the top of the balustrade and squeezed. He looked away into the valley, and the city below, and the swirling mist, and the fall, the long fall to the square below, and wondered whether he might throw himself off.

I shouldn't have killed him. I shouldn't have killed Ellis. Or Godrin. Or Aleron. I shouldn't have crippled Amron Daecar. He shook his head from side to side. *What have I done? How did I get here? A lie,* he answered himself. *I was deceived by a lie. I have never held the torch. I have never lit the way. I stumble now through darkness, darkness and dread and doom. The world hates me, all the world hates me. I have killed my son. My own son. That was my doing. Mine. He died because of me!*

He pressed up off the balcony rail, lifting himself off his feet. *A quick fall, and it's over. Someone else can take the Mistblade. Someone more worthy.* It had led him astray, he knew that now. "A worthy course defends the mind against madness," he whispered. He'd thought himself stronger. He'd thought his purpose righteous. *My path was paved in blood and bone, but the end was meant to justify the means.* He'd believed that, told himself it so much he'd fallen for the lie. But he knew now it wasn't true. *Murder, treachery, treason, deceit. They have led me down the wrong path. And there's no turning back for me now, none. My son… my son…my son is dead because of me…*

He leaned forward, ready to fall. A quick death. And let it be done.

The Mistblade drew him back.

Somehow…somehow it shifted its weight in its sheath, pulling him back down. He landed on the stone balcony. *How? How did…* And then felt that strange rhythm thrum at his hip, and a *thwump* pulsed through the skies. And another. And another. His eyes shot up, and there…there, the dragon, purple and black, circling, watching.

Janilah Lukar set his jaw and looked up. His urge to leap vanished, blown out like a candle in a storm. He watched as the dragon moved above him, high enough to be out of range of the ballistas. Away to the right, somewhere above him, he heard shouting as sentries spotted the beast. "Nock," someone bellowed. There was clanking, as the mechanisms were set on the massive mounted cross-bows about the walls and towers. The rallying cry spread, moving down the nearest battlements. "Dragon! Dragon! Nock! Fire!" Bolts and arrows flew out into the darkness, but the beast was already gone, slicing up and away into the murky black skies.

Janilah stared up into the clouds, unblinking. There was a soft whispering in his head, desirous, eager. *Kill it,* the Mistblade hissed. *Kill it. Kill it.*

He gave a single affirming nod. *Purpose,* he thought, closing a fist around the Mistblade's hilt. *Purpose, and a path.*

48

Elyon

He scythed through the mists in a defensive flight pattern, watching for dragons, keeping lookout for the men below. His armour glistened, droplets of water running down the length of his breastplate, pauldrons, gauntlets, greaves. The blanket of fog was wetter than usual, and above them the skies were weeping. Rain fell in a ceaseless drizzle, filling the ponds and puddles amid the marshes, and down below, the frogs were croaking, croaking that incessant song.

He swept lower, cutting a path ahead of Rikkard and his soldiers, Lord Rammas and his. They were out with crews of men, spreading Rasal oils across earthen bridges, laying traps for the incoming horde. Lord Kanabar had called it a waste of time - "they'll just keep coming anyway," he'd argued. "Burn one man and a thousand more will step up to take his place," - yet all the same, Rikkard had insisted, so here they were. Further back, little hideouts were being constructed, to house the bowmen who'd be tasked with lighting those bridges up. They were made of reeds and mud and twigs, a hundred metres back, within little copses or gnarled old trees.

Elyon came in to land next to his uncle, dismounting from the skies in a whirl of wet wind. "How long do you plan to stay out here?"

"As long as it takes until these paths are doused." Rikkard was a man possessed in his task. Others were happy to sit idle and wait for battle, yet not Rikkard Amadar. Every man slain in a trap to him was one less for them to deal with on the field.

"It'll get dark soon," Elyon told him. The croaking frogs made that clear enough; their song was a song of dusk, a nightly occurrence, and loud. "Perhaps it would be best to continue at dawn."

Rikkard shook his head. "It'll be too late by then, Elyon. Our last sighting had them crossing the Red Rift. That's only ten miles from here, and the sighting was several hours ago. They'll be raising their tents before the sun comes up."

Elyon could hear the tension in his uncle's voice. The Red Rift was a wide channel in the marshes, often used for ships passing between the Bay of Mourning and the Red Sea. Across it spanned a pair of large wooden drawbridges, that Lord Rammas and his men had destroyed some days ago, but to no avail. As feared, the enemy had come with crossing crews of their own, laying down pre-built bridges to pass over chasms and cross between islands, and they had great rafts as well, fixed with wheels and pulled along the dry stretches by horse and soldier both, to be deployed into the water channels and wetlands when needed, and many small boats besides.

Their march was inexorable, inevitable, and nothing they did seemed to slow or impede them. Not the broken bridges, not the raids and sallies they'd made from poleboats and barges and skiffs. *And not this*, Elyon thought, as he watched Rikkard's men move along the earthen crossing, pouring oil from pails and buckets. He had come to agree with Lord Kanabar now. *We are pricking them with needles, drawing droplets of blood, no more. We aren't slowing them. We aren't weakening them. All we're doing is wasting good resources.* "Uncle..."

Rikkard heard the inflection in Elyon's voice. He spoke up at once. "I know. You think this is a waste of time."

"We'd be better served saving the oils for the plains beyond the Bane," Elyon argued. "If we're lucky, and the Agarathi make camp where..."

"We don't have enough oil for that," Rikkard broke in. "They could make camp directly south of the Bane, or some way to the east or west, or they might not make camp at all, and simply come pouring out of the marshes and attack. It's too large a tract of land to cover completely, so we'd be guessing." He gestured brusquely to the earthen bridge on which they stood, a broad stretch some fifty metres wide, with large lakes to left and right, busy with water plants and duckweed and thousands of croaking frogs. "They're much more likely to cross here, given the direction of their march. It gives us a better chance of catching some of them in the blaze."

Some, Elyon thought. *But how many? A few dozen? A few hundred?* Unless it was a few thousand, it would hardly warrant the effort. "We're exposed, and the light's fast fading. If a dragon should spot us, we'd be vulnerable."

Rikkard shook his head. "We're well armoured and protected."

"And the men?" Rikkard and Rammas were garbed all in godsteel as he was, true, but their crews wore mail and leather at best. "We're risking them."

"It's war, Elyon. Every man at the Bane is at risk. Every man in Vandar, and across the north as well. Every man, every woman, every child is at risk. But these men have a duty to attend to, and will do as commanded. If a dragon comes we shall defend them. It's the best we can do."

"Fine." Elyon knew better than to argue with his uncle; he'd grown truculent on this issue and wouldn't yield. "How much longer do you need?"

Rikkard considered. "An hour should be enough to cover most of what I had planned."

"Too long. It'll be full dark by then, and the Agarathi can't be far. I'll give you *half* an hour. But no more." Elyon gave him a stern look. "Since you're so fond of men following commands, how about you follow that one? Half an hour," he repeated. "Then we're leaving."

He took flight before his uncle could respond, cutting down the line to where Lord Rammas was attending another earth bridge two hundred metres across the lake. It was roughly the same size as the other, with the lake to its west and a sprawling fetid bogland on its eastern border, sticky with mud and sinkholes and no place for an army to cross. "We're leaving in half an hour," he told the Lord of the Marshes. "I'll scout ahead until then, make sure we're not in for any surprises. Be done by the time I'm back. I don't want to remain out here once it's fully dark."

Rammas said not a word to that. He seemed to consider them as a form of currency to spend, and was most thrifty with his verbal coffers. A nod was ever-sufficient to show he understood.

"Good." Elyon shot skyward once more, punching up beyond the thick fogs that carpeted the marshes. The skies were a deal brighter above them, eighty or so metres high, though the drizzle was not abating. He continued half a mile south, watching for the blur of torchlight in the haze below, listening for the clank and clamour of a great horde on the march. Nothing. He flew yet further, another half mile, and another, feeling for that distinctive rhythmic thrum in the Windblade that told him the spawn of Agarath were near. Nothing.

He stopped there, hovering, scanning the horizon. The sun was a glaze of red light out west, suffocated by clouds and smog and distance. North, he could see the immense shadow of Dragon's Bane from this vantage, and the great spread of camp outside. Lights began to blink awake as twilight fell, a dozen at a time it seemed, as campfires were lit and the lanterns and torches set ablaze about the great black towers.

It looked peaceful from this far off, though Elyon knew it would be anything but down there. There would be a hundred different noises competing to be heard; horses whinnying, steel clashing, whetstones scraping, men roaring and singing and laughing, filling their bellies with meat and mead. Even now, with the enemy approaching, some would be drinking. Elyon doubted the sense in that, but Lord Kanabar had told him that each man prepared differently for battle, and some liked to brace themselves with a few goblets of ale and wine. It was the way out here, he'd said. "We men of East Vandar fight better with a bit of something warm in the blood," he'd told him. "Rivermen, Lakemen, Marshmen, it makes no matter. I would always take a drink or two to relax before facing a foe, young prince. It can loosen the limbs, free up the mind, douse a little bit of that fear you're feeling. Not too much, of course, no. Just a cup or two or three. Each man knows what's best for him."

Elyon had no personal desire to drink ale or mead or wine himself, yet wasn't going to deny men the custom if that's what it was. Others had their own traditions. "I like to seek solitude," Sir Killian had told him. "Somewhere quiet, where I might sit in prayer, and prepare for my ascension to Varin's Table." Lady Marian had spoken of a need to be seen by her people. She would walk among them, she had said, giving a soothing word here, a reassuring nod there, inspiring them by her presence alone. Elyon had tried to do the same this last week, ever since Killian had spoken so profoundly of his duty to share his men's burden of fear, ever since Lord Kanabar had scolded him for his naysaying. "You're a Daecar, a bloody Daecar," the big river lord had said. "Act like one!" And Elyon had, so much as he could, in emulation of his father, his grandfather, his great-grandfather, First Blades all, and Aleron…he'd thought of how

Aleron would have been. *He'd have worn the mantle of dragonslayer and prince and champion well,* he knew. *I must do the same now. Show no fear. Inspire strength and fortitude. Energise, galvanise, rouse them all for war.*

The rain was coming down harder now, falling thicker as the darkness deepened. Elyon hovered, embraced by the swirling winds, alone among the soaking skies. *I want to see them,* he thought, drifting further south, deeper into the marshes. *I want to look upon my enemy. I want to see what we're to face.* He ran his eyes over the endless spread of smog that hung above the world, peering through the thickening dark for some sight of his quarry. He could hear the frogs below, still giving out their nightly song. The mists here were as dense as ever, yet in places they thinned, just enough for him to see a blurred glimpse of the world below. *And there…there,* he thought, narrowing his focus. *A light, moving…*

He squinted through the dimness and the rain and the fog. The light was from a torch, giving shape to the men around it, moving in a column ten abreast. He saw another light behind, and another, and another. Through that single open pocket in the mists hundreds of men were visible, a great snake of soldiers, slithering through the swamp.

A shiver moved up from the small of his back, climbing his spine with icy cold fingers. The rain pattered against his armour, tinkling, and over those sounds he could hear the rumble below, the great swelling sound of a hundred thousand men on the march.

He held there, high above them, peering through pockets in the fog. More light bloomed, to east and west, and further south, little blurred balls of light stretching away to the edge of sight like stars strewn across a black night sky. He sighted men afoot, and men ahorse, rafts and carts and wagons being drawn. Dragonknights rode past on barded horses, their backs embraced by those rich red cloaks, tall black spears affixed to the flanks of their steeds. Elyon felt a ripple move up his arm and saw the fogs shimmer and move. *Dragon,* he knew at once. It moved eastward along the front of the column, fading from sight. *There are more,* he realised. His eyes picked up those patterns almost instinctively now; the fog parting and swirling strangely, indicating the passing of Agarath's spawn. They appeared as sharks beneath the waters, moving amidst the murky fogs, shadows barely glimpsed. *Three, four, five,* he counted. *Gods…my gods, how many are there?*

He whirled around at once, wary of being spotted, firing himself back in the direction of the Bane. It was almost fully dark now, the last of the light waning out west. Miles to the north, the camp beyond the fortress was twinkling, a vast spread of cookfires and campfires burning across the plains. Torches glowed bright around the towers and walls of the stronghold, peeking out of windows, giving shape to its immensity.

Elyon searched through the fogs below him; through a thinning patch of shifting mist he spotted movement and plunged straight down to find his uncle at the northern edge of the wide earthen bridge. Some of his soldiers were still at work, splashing the last of their oils, though most had emptied their stores and were fixing pails and buckets to the sides of their horses, readying to leave. Elyon surged straight down, landing before Rikkard. By the haste of his return and the strain of worry in his eyes his uncle knew at once he'd seen them. "How far?" he asked, looking south.

Elyon's voice was breathless. "Two miles, at most. They'll be here in less than an hour. We need to go."

Rikkard thought a short time, then said. "I'm staying."

Elyon was perplexed. "No, Uncle, you're not. There are a hundred thousand men marching this way. With gods know how many dragons in support. You're not staying."

"I'm staying with my bowmen," Rikkard spoke calmly. "I'll instruct them when best to light the oil, then retreat. They may panic and fire too early if I leave."

"That's not your job," Elyon reminded him. "Nor your risk to take."

"The hideouts are a hundred metres back. I'll call the order, the arrows will be lit and fired, and we'll retreat. In the smoke and chaos of it, no one will notice a few men fleeing into the darkness." He could see Elyon was about to deny him again, so went on. "Tell me what you saw. Did you see the front of the column?"

Elyon had to think. The frogs weren't helping, with all their damnably loud croaking. "I only saw glimpses, shadows. *Lights*. So many lights, Rikkard. They seemed to go on forever." Another chill climbed the discs of his spine. "And dragons. Moving in the mists, in defensive patterns."

"How many?" Rikkard's voice went dark with tension.

"Four, five, that I saw. But I could only see a fraction of the army. Might be many more."

"They're protecting the vanguard," Rikkard said. "Protecting the advance."

"And soon as you fire on the bridge to light the oil, they'll know," Elyon told him. "It's not worth it, Uncle. None of this is. We have to go, all of us. If you can find a brave man or two to stay, fine, that's their choice, but I'm not going to order anyone to remain here with a hundred thousand men and half a dozen dragons bearing down on them."

Rikkard looked at his wit's end. "It's worth the risk. Why else do you think we're out here?" he stressed. "We leave a man at each shelter. One arrow should be enough to light each bridge, and they'll be gone. Rammas's marshmen will be best; they're used to going unseen in these bogs."

"But you're *not* staying," Elyon was keen to tell him.

Rikkard clenched his jaw. "Is that an order, Elyon?"

"Yes," Elyon said. "If anyone's staying, it's me. The dragons get a sniff of me and they'll be sure to follow." He had a thought, then, and came to a swift decision. "Might be worth the gamble, actually. I can fly over the top of them, try to get one or two to chase me. Distract them, while the bridges burn. Cause a bit of chaos on their ranks."

Rikkard didn't seem to like the sound of that, or the look on his nephew's face. "Elyon..."

"If I can lure them back to the Bane," Elyon went on, not listening, "we might have a chance to strike a few down." He nodded, thinking fast now. "Ride back, Rikkard. Have the ballistas manned, every one, and get your best Bladeborn bowmen on the south-facing walls and towers, around the gatehouse. I'll try to lure a few that way."

"They won't go for it. The Fireborn are cautious creatures."

"Not all dragons are ridden, didn't you hear?" Elyon managed a heady grin. "These riderless dragons...they're different, more reckless. They may not understand the threat of the fortress. I lead them there, and you fill them with godsteel bolts. That'll be more worthwhile than burning a few hundred men on these bridges, Rikkard."

"If it happened, yes." Rikkard was clearly looking for a reason to deny him, yet couldn't see any.

"Uncle..." Elyon put his hand to the man's shoulder, in a clank of steel on steel. "I'm a Daecar, a dragonslayer, a champion. Who are you going to trust if not me?"

"I do trust you, Elyon. But I care for you as well. Your father would string me up if he knew I was permitting such recklessness from his last remaining son."

"You're permitting nothing. You're just following my commands." Elyon smiled. "Ride to the Bane, make sure they're ready. Have Rammas leave two of his best archers and I'll do the rest."

There was no time to further debate this, and Rikkard Amadar knew it. "Fine," he relented. "I suppose it's worth a shot."

The plan was quickly arranged. Within five minutes, Rikkard and Rammas were riding north with their men, leaving two valorous archers behind in their shelters. The hideouts were close enough for Elyon to go between them, speak to each man in turn as they waited. One wasn't so talkative. *Must be a relative of Rammas,* he thought. He sat in his lair of mud and twigs and reeds, staring resolutely south, wanting only to do his duty and go. The other was a man by name of Trevon, a young Bladeborn archer no older than Elyon with rich red curls of hair and freckles covering his cheeks. He had a nonchalant way about him, and buckets of confidence. "You think we got a chance then, my prince?" he asked, with an impish grin, as they crouched down in the shelter. "You and me, against this great big horde? Couple of heroes like us, why not?"

"You count yourself a hero, Trevon?"

"Will be after this." He clutched a godsteel dagger in his right hand, to better enhance his senses. "So, you're gonna lure a few of the beasties away, are you? That the idea?"

"It'll give you a chance to escape, once you light up the bridge. Best case scenario: I lure one or two to the Bane, and we'll have one or two fewer dragons to worry about."

"Got one less already," Trevon said. "Zyndrar the Unnatural. Heard that about your father last night over a couple of ales. Welcome news, welcome indeed. Amron Daecar, back in business! What could be better?" He gave a carefree laugh.

"Not much," Elyon agreed. It had been reported only yesterday that his legendary lord father had seen fit to remind the world of his dragonkilling abilities, by taking down one of the most feared beasts of the last war. *And with the Frostblade, no less,* Elyon thought, still half shocked by that. Rikkard had reported it in council, by way of a letter sent from Lady Crawfield. Apparently, Amron had been travelling down the High Way from Blackfrost, when that oathbreaker Sir Gerald Strand and some Taynar men had accosted him on the road.

They were in the midst of some tense exchange when Zyndrar the Unnatural came swooping down from the skies, leading the titan that was Amron Daecar to pull the Frostblade from its sheath and proceed to call down the beast for a duel. A ferocious battle had ensued, ending in the Unnatural's defeat and another notch of the Crippler's dragonslaying belt.

Trevon gave a whistle through his teeth. "He heading here, d'you think, Prince Elyon? Your father? Could sure use him. Two Daecars. Two champions. The firefolk would have no chance!"

Elyon hated to tell him otherwise, but there was no chance his father was coming all this way. "He's heading for Varinar," he said. That had been reported in Lady Crawfield's letter too; apparently, his father had stayed in her keep the night of the dragonkilling, he and these companions of his who'd ventured with him into the Icewilds, and Sir Gerald and his men as well. Sir Gerald had broken his arm during the confrontation, and several of his men had rushed out to help finish Zyndrar off once the beast had been duly defeated. '*They were singing of the triumph all night,*' the lady had written, '*and singing of Amron's gallantry as well. Sir Gerald just sat aside, looking glum! But the rest... oh, they revere Amron more than ever now. Will be singing of him all the way to Varinar too, I'll bet.*' Elyon had smiled broadly when he'd heard Rikkard read that bit. Only Amron Daecar could so swiftly win around his rivals.

"Varinar?" Trevon said, frowning. "Surely he'd be best off going to fight somewhere? No war in Varinar, that I know of." He thought a moment, then said. "Ah, course. He's king now, leastways he is around here. He'll be planning to shift old Godrik from the throne, I suppose."

Elyon wasn't so sure about that. His father was a man of duty and due process and not likely to remove Godrik Taynar through unlawful means, and especially not now. *No, he'll help mend the rift,* he thought, *and pull this fragmented kingdom back together.* Amara would be part of that bargain too, he hoped. She and Jovyn, and Carly too, who were still being held in the palace dungeons, so far as he knew. He'd sent a fierce letter to Godrik in demand of the trio's release, yet had heard nothing back. *I wanted to fly there,* he thought, *seek to rescue them all on my own.* Well, his council had convinced him against doing that, and now....well, now he didn't have to. *Father will set them free,* he knew. *He'll set these wrongs to right.*

He put that aside for now, though. It was no time to be thinking about it. "Quiet now, Trevon. We need to focus." From the lakes either side of the earthen bridge, the frogs were still croaking among the little islands and reeds, though their eventide song seemed to be ending. It would help them hear for the movement of men and mounts, the *thwump* of wings in the skies. Elyon clutched the Windblade, listening. Distantly, he could perceive the advance of the host, though they remained a way off. "Try to wait until as many are on the bridge as possible," Elyon told the archer. "I'm going to head up there, see if I can cause a distraction. Maybe even spook a few, get them running this way."

"*Running*?" Trevon didn't like the sound of that. "Shouldn't we just wait for them to plod onto the bridge, all thick and packed in tight, shoulder to shoulder? We'd catch more in the blaze that way."

Elyon had his doubts. "The Agarathi are more wily than that. They know the marshes end a few miles north of here, and they know these two bridges are the best way to cross. They'll be wise to our tricks, Trevon."

The archer frowned. "So…you think they'll know we've doused these bridges?"

"They might. And if they do, they'll either send down fire arrows of their own or have one of their dragons make a pass, to make sure the crossings are safe. Surest way for me to stop that from happening is by distracting them, causing havoc in their ranks. I'll make a few passes, stir things up, get men running this way. Then I'll make for the Bane. That'll give you a chance to flee back to camp."

Elyon made sure the archer understood, then turned his eyes back out across the lakes. A hundred metres south, the bridge was impossible to see, so Trevon would have to use his judgement about when to fire. He had to trust in Lord Rammas's choice of men. "Good luck, Trevon," he said, standing. "I'll see you back in camp after."

He left the shelter, walking south toward the crossing. The rains had weakened again, coming down in a fine mizzle, droplets dancing on the surface of the water. Visibility was restricted to some ten or twelve metres here, not so bad as in other parts where you could scarcely see your hand in front of your face. Sometimes a wind came blowing in, moving the mists about a bit, yet that was rare. There was something queerly sluggish and inert about these fogs. Legend said the islands of the Bloodmarshes had once been a great land bridge, a hundred miles wide, linking the continents of north and south. One day the god Vandar had come here and smashed the lands up into a thousand fragments with his great warhammer, stirring the waters in a brume, to stop Agarath's minions crossing over so easily. *This world was their battleground,* Elyon thought. *Reshaped and reworked as they saw fit, to better play their games of war. And here we are, all their little pawns, still playing that game to this day…*

He remained on foot for a short time longer, saving his energy, listening, watching the skies for stirrings. The rumble of the approaching horde grew louder with each passing moment, each step. *Three hundred metres,* he thought, *maybe four.* He stopped there, waiting. The Agarathi might have outriders and scouts, he knew, searching the way ahead for trouble. *Or else they just use their dragons.* Either way, it was better if he was airborne. *Easier to hide up there,* he knew.

The last of the frogs gave out their final croaks and their chorus died away. Now there was just the soft fall of rain, the tinkling on the water, the heavy thunder, growing heavier, closer, of the marching horde. His lift-off was quiet, graceful, serene. Water ran down off his armour, joining the rains. Windblade raised with his right hand, he lifted his left to turn down his visor, reducing his vision to what he could see through the eye slits. His helm and face-plate, like all his armour, had been forged and hammered to his frame, and those eye slits were no different. Some men went into battle barely being able to see, but not Elyon. His sight was scarcely reduced. *And I'll need my eyes now, and my ears. And my wits, those most of all.*

He came to a stop some fifty metres off the ground, reducing the winds around him to a light stir. Beneath him, the glow of fire bloomed now, lights burning in the mist, gloomy gold and amber. The slow distant thunder of movement began to separate into distinct sounds; horses snorting, boots plugging in mud, armour rustling. There was the occasional call of a commander, though Elyon knew no words of Agarathi save a few fruity slurs he'd like to use on his friends at feasts. And how long ago that seemed now. The world had changed so much that the idea of frivolous feasting on the Varinar social circuit seemed so utterly fatuous to him now.

He turned his eyes left and right, watching for dragons. Eastward came a warning, a spike of primal tension, alerting him to one's presence. It was flying a scouting path across the front of the army, low to the ground, searching for threats. Somehow, he hadn't been spotted yet. *Curious,* he thought. Ezukar had chased him all the way out into that storm, and it seemed as though Zyndrar had done the same with his father, tracking him from afar, yet it appeared that not all dragons had access to the same hunter-seeker instinct.

The men were almost directly beneath him now, the dragon passing ahead of them, before banking around and moving the other way. Elyon breathed out, slow and silent. He heard more calls echo out from commanders and captains below, and wondered if they knew the crossing was near. Much of the vanguard was made up of dragonknights, he guessed, though he couldn't be sure. Either way, the shapes in the shroud suggested many mounted men. *Horses are easy to spook*, he thought. *Why not give them a fright?*

By silent mental command, a stirring of wind began to swirl around his blade, slow at first, then faster. Elyon's continued training had granted him a greater control of the Windblade and its functions. Flight had come first, though once mastered he had turned his efforts to other skills. He began to lower himself, metre by slow metre, and all the while the vortex quickened. *Wait*, he thought, *wait.* He was forty metres from the ground now, thirty five, thirty. About him, the brume began to stir, swirling slowly in a wide orb. Twenty five metres, twenty, eighteen…

A shout came from below him, and suddenly men were looking up. Seventeen, sixteen. He could sense panic spreading at the strange shape they saw; a man, floating, the fogs rotating around him, a whirlwind swirling at the end of his arm. Already, horses were whinnying loudly and tramping on the spot, and some men were pulling spears and bows from their backs. Elyon waited. *Faster, faster*, he thought, as he fell to fifteen metres, fourteen, thirteen, twelve. The tornado encircling the blade was roaring now, bellowing out loudly like some wild enraged beast. He heard shouts again, and then several arrows came flying at him, though the force of the winds sucked them up, spinning them away into the shroud. Several black spears of dragonsteel came thrusting as well; those too were turned aside, all but one, which bounced harmlessly off his pauldron in a glancing blow, then went hurtling chaotically away.

Wait, he thought, *wait, wait…*

The roar of the wind was deafening. His sword arm began to shake from the tension. Faster and faster the winds spun, faster, faster, faster. Eleven metres. Ten. Nine. Elyon grimaced against the force of it; it felt like his arm might be ripped from its socket at any second.

*Wait...wait...*He clenched his jaw. More arrows flew and spun. *Wait...wait...wait.*

Now!

He swung his sword arm down in an arc, releasing the tornado. It spread away in the direction of the blade, widening, broadening, parting the mists. The force of the winds hit so hard that soldiers went careening out across the bogs, flung ten metres, twenty, and out of sight into the gloom. Horses were flung sideways too, throwing their riders from the saddles. Some landed awkwardly, breaking bones. Others were knocked unconscious, lying face down in the mud to drown. At once yells rang out, a hundred of them, a thousand, and the chaos Elyon had hoped for ensued as men scattered and ran in all directions.

It begins, he thought, as he dropped straight into a swoop and gave chase, like an eagle hunting prey, swinging the Windblade through his foes. It moved through leather and bone and muscle and mail like the finest godsteel, cleaving through all as he passed. Blood splattered across his armour and spat through the slits in his helm, yet he blinked those away and kept on swinging, flying, swinging, swooping, thrusting and cutting at necks and arms, legs and faces, massacring anything that moved.

The bodies were thick about him, and the panic yet thicker. He lost all his bearings for a moment as he ploughed right through them, gripped by the thrill of battle, the bloodlust. These weren't men to him, but meat to be cut and cleaved. They had no friends, no families, no passions and lives. They were sacks of bone and blood and meat that might kill someone he knew. So he killed them first.

One, two, five he killed. Six, seven, ten went down. *My first kills,* something inside him said. It was a queer thought to have at the time, but he had it all the same. Half the realm thought he'd slain Sir Griffin Kastor, but he hadn't; that was Saska, and she'd done for Borgin too. Others still believed he'd slain Lord Paramor's second son, the mute Sir Brendan, at the parley outside Harrowmoor, but he hadn't; that was Vesryn, punching the Sword of Varinar through the Suncoat's back. It was thought he must have killed someone during that siege, or that he'd killed a guard of two when he'd stolen the Windblade, or when he escaped his cell, but he hadn't, not one. And Melany. He'd never killed her either, despite what his enemies thought.

No, Elyon's first true kill had been Ezukar, as Lancel had japed when he'd returned after that fight. "Trust you to start with a dragon, El. Only way is down from here." But that wasn't the same. *It was a dragon,* he thought, *a beast, and I've killed beasts before on hunts*. This was different. These were men. The first men Elyon Daecar had killed, and kill them he did, in great abundance.

The Windblade swung through another man's legs, then took a second in the gut. Elyon spotted a group nearby; he surged at them at speed, scattering them apart, swinging, slashing. Thirteen, fourteen, he thought. He pushed the tip of his blade through a man's wide, terrified eye, then spun, pulling the Windblade across in a horizontal swipe, taking off another soldier's head. *Just bags of blood and bone,* he thought. *This isn't real. None of it is real.*

Suddenly, away to his left, he saw a great blaze of flame rising up and spreading as the earthen bridge took light. A moment later, the second erupted in an inferno, as two great pillars of smoke reached up to the belly of the sky. Elyon was transfixed for a second. The fire was a great bright glory, burning away the fogs around it, giving shape to hundreds of men, thousands, many caught in the flaming maelstrom on foot and horse both. He saw some rushing for the lakes, wreathed in fire, others charging away in an agonised fury, knocking into their companions, causing them to catch alight too. Horses galloped, trailing smoke. Men lay in charred heaps everywhere, a hundred, two hundred, more than Elyon could count. And everywhere there was screaming.

He had no time to savour it, or be horrified by it, or bask in this bloody, fiery triumph. Around him men were rallying, closing. He stood amid bodies, some groaning, others lost of limb and dying, others already gone to the Eternal Flame of Agarath.

His eyes passed over one dead soldier at his feet, saw the face within the helm. He was just a boy, no older than fifteen or sixteen. His mind went to Del, strangely, a boy he'd never even met. *A boy of sixteen summers,* he thought, *tall, with a mop of messy black hair.* This boy *was* Del, just an Agarathi version, born south of the Red Sea, not north. Saska had told him how the young farmhand had been drafted during the muster of North Tukor, when boys even younger than him were being conscripted as part of Janilah's drive to swell his numbers. And now it came to Elyon that the Agarathi had done the very same. Now this horde made sense, so vast as it was. *How many of this army are boys like this?* he wondered. *How many boys will I have to kill, before this battle is done?*

A bellowing command called away his attention. He looked up from the face of the boy. A host of dragonknights were approaching, in formation, brandishing their tar-black spears. Their red capes hung heavy, sodden from the rains, clasped by dragon claws sprouting from their dark scale-mail armour. Fearlessly, they surged at him, spears forward, thrusting.

Elyon swung the Windblade up and took flight, away into the mists. A few black spears whistled past him, missing. Smoke and ash swirled among the fogs and all about him was a din of shouting and screaming. Then, through it all, pierced a deep thrumming roar, a roar to rattle bones, and Elyon swirled around.

His eyes widened. A dragon was approaching at speed, jaws agape, massive. It was a brute, greatly bigger than Ezukar, short-nosed and heavy, its scales black and gold and scarred, littered with old war wounds. Amid the cries and ringing screams of pain Elyon heard a cheer spread below him, and a word came with it, a name. *Malathar*, he heard. *Malathar, Malathar!*

Vargo Ven, he thought, sighting the Fireborn rider atop the beast's back. *So this is who leads the horde.* The Dragonlord had been promoted ahead of Ulrik Marak, rumour said, as Lord of the Nest, King Tavash's savage right-hand man. Elyon scarcely had time to think. The monstrous dragon was approaching quickly, roaring, a dim orange light beginning to glow in its thick muscled chest. Elyon had no thirst to fight the pair here. *Chase me,* he thought instead. *Chase me home, Ven.*

He shot skyward, straight up and over the beast's approach, trusting his agility. Malathar was no sleek dragon. He barrelled straight beneath him, bellowing, but suddenly Elyon sensed other dragons coming, sizzling through in Malathar's wake, one, two, three of them. They were no match for Malathar in size, yet swift, wild, roaring, and *riderless*. Elyon caught glimpse of manic red eyes in the mists, burning in scaled faces fierce and wanton. He thrust straight upward and out beyond the brume to get his bearings, and *there*...the twinkling lights of Dragon's Bane, a few short miles away.

Delaying not a moment, Elyon swung the point of the Windblade directly for the southern gatehouse, and surged on. From the swirling smokey fogs, the three wild dragons came punching, one, two, three, then Malathar right after, bursting out behind them. Another roar echoed and rang, and to left and right gouts of flame lanced by. *They'll overwhelm me,* Elyon thought. *Faster, faster, must go faster!*

He spent his focus on speed now, ignoring all else. He could sense the dragons chasing, snapping, biting at his heels. He passed straight through the pillar of smoke pouring from the crossing, breaching through to the other side. In that moment he saw carnage below. The second earthen bridge had taken fewer victims, he saw, yet enough. Beyond them, flaming horses were still running amok, and there were many soldiers out there too, broken from the lines. *We should have had men waiting in ambush,* he thought. If they'd had their full-armoured Bladeborn down there, their Varin Knights, they might have wrought havoc on the enemy's forward lines.

Yet the thought was fleeting. He couldn't have known it would work so well. Ahead, the fortress grew larger, and quickly. He spared a glance back, saw the dragons still there, chasing. Yet not Malathar, no, the feared beast had slowed and wheeled away now, returning to his men. *He knows the threat of the Bane,* Elyon realised. *But not these others…*

Hope surged in him. *Be ready,* he prayed. *Please be ready.* He could see men on the battlements now, waiting to fire from the crenels, the mounted crossbows taking aim. *Just don't hit me!* He hadn't thought of that, but a godsteel-tipped bolt from a ballista would punch straight through his armour, and smaller quarrels and arrows could do the same, depending on where they hit. Distantly, he could hear shouting, orders being given. He thought he saw Rikkard but couldn't be sure. It might have been Killian or another armoured knight. The chaos at the marshes was long behind him, the plumes of fire a distant blur, no more. Instead, he could hear the fierce roar of the wind, the snapping jaws behind, the beating wings, the clamour of the camp, and those orders.

"Hold," he could hear someone calling. "Hold." An arm was raised, ready to fall, telling all bowmen to fire. He squinted. It *was* Rikkard, his handsome face and curls of brown hair unmistakable. "Hold!"

Elyon made for his uncle, flying directly at him, standing on the wall walk above the bulky barbican. The twin towers of the gatehouse neared, a hundred metres, ninety, eighty, seventy. When he was just fifty metres from the walls, he swung the Windblade up, arcing skyward. The dragons followed, heedless of the danger. He heard the deep *snap* of bolts firing from the scorpions, the *clank* of the mechanisms in motion, heard Rikkard shout, "Loose!" as the archers released their strings, caught the *thump* of godsteel bolts hitting their mark, and the short sharp shrieks as the dragons were struck, and struck, and struck, and struck.

Elyon slowed to a swift stop as he rose up past the battlements, turning. He let out a breath at what he saw. One dragon was already falling, spinning away to the ground, pierced by a dozen quarrels and arrows. A second was close to following, several thick ballista bolts struck through its neck and chest. It tried to flap its wings, but failed, gave out a shrieking cry, then dropped. The third was swiftest, smallest, most agile. It had taken an arrow to the left wing and had another in the shoulder, but was otherwise unscathed. Screaming and hissing and spitting smoke, it swept into a sharp dive, beat its wings, and fled, just as the second dragon thumped into the ground below, joining the first. At once, the gates opened and men came pouring out like angry black ants, steel to hand, stabbing and thrusting, stabbing and thrusting.

Elyon lowered himself down, breathing heavily, and came in to land on the battlements beside his uncle. His heart was racing, pounding out through his chest. He raised a shaking hand to lift his visor. His armoured fingers came back slick with blood. The men nearby were staring at him. There was cheering elsewhere. The sound of warcries. Elyon heard a few of his names sung out.

"Elyon," Rikkard said, softly. "You're…you're covered in blood."

Elyon didn't want to talk about that, not yet. Already, away from the thrill of it, he was reflecting on what he'd done. The brutality, the carnage, the feel of steel through flesh, again and again and again…

He turned to look out over the burning marshes. There was nothing from here, no sound, no sight of men dead and dying. Just a distant blur of orange light. Far below, he could see two men racing afoot across the plains. Elyon smiled. *Good. They made it.*

"Elyon…"

"Vargo Ven leads the host," he said. "I saw him, atop Malathar. He chased me, for a time, like these others. But gave up. He knew the threat of the fort."

Rikkard looked to the two dead beasts far below them; the walls of Dragon's Bane were so thick and lofty, one had to squint sometimes to see the ground. "These were wild dragons from the Wings," he said. "They had no fear of this place."

"The rest will learn soon enough."

Elyon could hear the Windblade whispering. *Soon all the skies will swarm.* He thought of how Vargo Ven had turned back, not caring should the other dragons give chase. *Not caring should they die*, he thought. It worried him immensely. *How many do they have, to so willingly lose two?*

He took another look out over the marshes, sliding the Windblade back into its sheath, letting go. Those whispers unnerved him; he had no want to hear them now. "We need to prepare for an attack tonight," he said. "Ven might retaliate for this. I fear…I fear we've only prodded at the hornet's nest."

"We're well prepared," Rikkard said.

Below, the sound of hacking and slashing echoed up as the dragons were butchered. *War makes beasts of men,* Elyon thought. His father had told him that once, he remembered. He turned and began walking away.

Rikkard's eyes followed. "Where are you going?"

Elyon did not stop or turn. "To wash, and to rest," he said. *And scrub away the blood of a boy.*

49

Ranulf

The captain of the Bloody Traders had an appetite, to be sure.

Does he ever not eat? Ranulf wondered, as the big scarred man with the tattered crimson cloak ripped off another bite of rabbit. He chewed noisily, wiping grease from the rips and tears on his chin. "I like to eat well, even when travelling," he said. "My men carry good meats in their saddlebags, for when we cannot hunt. And I am never far from a block of cheese; I carry those in my own." He took one of those up now, enjoying an enormous bite, swilling it all down with a swig of wine, half of which spilt out over his lips and down his burly chest.

Ranulf gave the Butcher a polite smile. Their evening camp had been raised in some quiet hills far from any road, but still, he wasn't so sure about the fire. "Is it wise, to have an open flame out here? We're only a few days from Eagle's Perch, Captain. Shouldn't we..."

The man waved him to silence. "I prefer you to call me Butcher," he said. "Or even Sir Buckland, if you like. My father was a knight of that house, did I tell you?"

Yes, Ranulf thought, *but you're no knight yourself, that's clear enough.* "You did, the first time we met. Actually, it was your brother who told me that, I recall."

The sellsword ripped off more meat, speaking as he ate. "Yes, I remember. You made the jape about the candlestick maker. I liked that one, Ersel San Sabar." He gave Ranulf a big grin. "Sorry, I forget. Ranulf Shackton. This is your *real* name, of course."

There had been no hiding all that, not once Cliffario Denlatis had stuck his oar in. In the end, that oar turned out to be rather useful, though. *Gold plated,* Ranulf thought, *and encrusted with jewels.* It was the merchant's coin that had paid for the Butcher's service, and these other sellswords he'd hired to return them safely to Aram. *And now I have to keep to my end of the bargain. The simple matter of seeing Denlatis wed to the Lady Asherah Tamaar…*

"I prefer Ersel, though," the Butcher was going on. "Ranulf Shackton…this name is decent, I suppose, but *Ersel San Sabar*. Oh yes. This one runs very nicely off my tongue."

I can tell, Ranulf thought. The sellsword captain used it every time he said his name. His brother the Baker merely called him Ersel, but no, not the Butcher. It was Ersel San Sabar every time. "Feel free to call me whatever you wish, Butcher," he said. "This fire, though…" he pressed, still wary of someone who might spot it. He was under no illusions that Lord Elio Krator would let his prize go so easily. *No, he'll have sent out men to track us, mounted men on wolves and cats.* "Are you certain we need it? It seems an unnecessary risk."

The sellsword was unconcerned. "There is no one else here, Ersel San Sabar, not in these hills. And we are well-protected. Do not fear." They sat by the fire alone; around the camp, the rest of the men were either on watch or sleeping or sharpening their blades, or doing the sundry other things that sellswords did. Saska and Leshie were asleep in their tent. "So, Ersel San Sabar. Let us talk, you and I. You mentioned risk. Good. I would like to talk about this."

Ranulf gave him a careful look. "Risk? You're talking about Saska. The risk you're taking delivering her to Aram?"

"Very good. Yes, this is what I am talking about. For sellswords such as me, risk and coin are always linked. And I have had time these last days to reconsider the price that Denlatis agreed." He pulled a godsteel dagger from his belt, began cutting bits of chicken from the bone. "I like Cliffario very much, but he has always been a scoundrel, and good at driving down the price. He got us to agree before we knew what we were getting ourselves into. So yes, I have reconsidered. And the price will go up…considerably."

Ranulf had half expected this. "I'm sure Cliffario will be willing to pay you more, once we reach Aram," he said. The merchant had travelled back already on his little armada of ships, some days before Leshie had crept into camp to rescue Saska. He had no intention of being linked to their plotting, should Lord Elio survive the sting of Cedrik Kastor's blade. *Well, I did tell him to play both sides,* Ranulf thought. *I can hardly blame him for hedging his bets.*

The Butcher gave a swift shake of his scarred hairless head. "No, Denlatis cannot be trusted to pay us more. We made an agreement with him, and he will only wriggle free if we try to shake more coin from his pockets. He is good at wriggling, this merchant. I feel *you* will struggle less, Ersel San Sabar."

"Shake away, Butcher. You'll find no coin in my pockets."

The big man laughed. "Perhaps you can pay us in these jokes?"

Ranulf smiled modestly. "If it's coin you want, you'll be well compensated by the Grand Duchess, I assure you. She'll be most pleased with you, for returning her granddaughter to her, healthy and *unharmed*."

He made a point of stressing the word. Ranulf Shackton had not missed the looks some of these sellswords had given Saska, and Leshie as well, these last few days. It was probably nothing - Leshie and Saska were as deadly as any of them, and Saska had her starcat too, ever watchful, always on guard - but all the same, he wasn't going to take any chances.

"Unharmed." The Butcher repeated the word, grinning. His face looked especially grotesque in the firelight, with all those scars, though he'd always seemed amiable enough. "Of course unharmed. We are Bloody Traders, Ersel San Sabar. We do not shirk our contracts, unless somehow compelled. This one…it will be fulfilled, so long as we are *properly* compensated." He picked at his teeth with the knife. "What if the Grand Duchess is not yet in Aram? Rumour says she remains with the Empress, far west in Lumos."

"Then you'll be paid on her return. Or by Lord Hasham in her place."

A rumbling laugh echoed out of the big man's mouth. "You wield a lot of power for an adventurer, Ersel San Sabar, to make such bold claims of royals and moonlords. This is who Ranulf Shackton is, yes? An adventurer?"

"It's one of his many occupations."

"And what are the others?"

"Scholar, teacher, seeker of the arcane." Ranulf shrugged.

"Lately, I've been a rescuer, I suppose, masquerading as a merchant. And before then, a prisoner. I've been lots of things, Butcher. But right now…right now I just want to get Saska to Aram, and into her grandmother's care."

And see her myself, he thought. That was his mission. That was King Godrik's order to him, sent through time in the Book of Thala. Ranulf hadn't come to Aram for Saska - no, he'd not even been certain she was present in the city until that day at the Red Pits - yet had come to believe she was a part of this too. *It cannot be a coincidence,* he thought. *My task was not just to find Safina Nemati. It was to make sure I united Saska with her too.*

A whisper of footsteps sounded to his right, and he turned to find the girl in question emerging from her small tent, stretching like a cat. Her starcat followed, stretching too. They yawned in unison. "Beautiful creatures," the Butcher said, admiring the pair. He had moved on to sweetbreads now, and succulent fruits. He bit into a persimmon. "Come, join us. We were just talking about you."

Saska moved over, pulling a cloak about her slim shoulders. It was chilly at night here in these hills. For that the fire was welcome, at least. "Can't sleep?" Ranulf asked, as she settled down onto the stone seat beside him.

She shook her head. "I wake often most nights." She looked pointedly at the fire. "That wise?"

The Butcher let out a rumbly laugh. "You two are much alike, you know. I could douse the flames, but then we would all go cold. And I would not have the pleasure of looking upon your beautiful face, pretty princess."

"Nice of you to say." Saska neglected to return the compliment. Darkness suited the Butcher better, certainly. "So, what were you saying about me?"

"Oh, nothing to make a pretty princess blush. Ersel San Sabar here was just saying how important it is that we get you to your grandmother. And I was talking about coin. You are precious cargo, pretty princess. Worth your weight in gemstones and jewels."

Saska rolled her eyes. "I've had enough of being precious to people. I thought Denlatis paid you?"

"He did. But not enough."

"Was it a flat rate? Or does he pay you by the day? Or mile, perhaps?" The Butcher looked baffled by those questions. Saska pulled a little rock from her pocket, tossing it hand to hand. "I'm just wondering why we're going so far west. If we'd ridden hard down the Capital Road, we might have been able to find a ship along one of the coastal ports. Or else Denlatis might have let us use one of his."

"Denlatis is a cautious creature. He wants no part of this. And no, the Capital Road would have been too dangerous. The sunlord will send men that way, this is certain. And he will send eagles too, to Cloaklake, and elsewhere, and soon men will be coming the other way as well. That would not be good for us. It is better to go deeper into the hills. We will be harder to track this way."

"But how much longer will it take?"

"The pretty princess is in a rush, is she?"

"Yes, actually. I've been trying to get to my grandmother for what seems like forever. A ship…I just hoped we'd be taking a ship." She tossed that hunk of rock side to side, then caught it in her right hand, squeezing. She gave a sigh and a shake of the head. "Sorry. I sound…ungrateful, I know. I don't mean to be. I'm just…"

"Impatient?" offered the Butcher, smiling.

"Tired," said Saska. "And not for need of sleep. I'm tired of being out of control. I'm tired of being on the move all the time."

"There can be no helping this. Aram is a long way from here. We must move if we wish to get there. And this is the safest road, this way that is no road at all." The Butcher stood from the rock he was sitting on, and took two brisk strides around the campfire. That tattered cloak hung down his back in a hundred shades of red, ripped here, torn there, patched and sewn up like the scars across his body. He thrust out a hand in Saska's direction, offering her his skin of wine. "Here, drink. It will help pass the time. And help you sleep as well."

Saska took the skin, seeming half grateful, half resigned. She drank a long gulp, then coughed. "That's…that's spicy."

"But good, no?" The Butcher stood over her, thick-chested and gruesome. "Kasbar Noy makes it." Ranulf could tell she had no idea who Kasbar Noy was. "Go ahead, have some more. There is always more wine." The man laughed. "Cheese in my saddlebags, wine in my skins. I never travel without them."

Saska's lips moved into the shadow of a smile. "I didn't take you for a cheese and wine sort of man. You have more of a meat and mead look to me."

"Ah, meat and mead. These I like too. You did not see the pavilion that I shared with my brother, the Baker. Lots of meat and mead there, and cheese and wine as well. Lots of men, lots of women, lots of fun. You would have liked it, pretty princess."

Ranulf didn't imagine so. "Be thankful you never visited."

Saska raised a brow. "Well, now I'm just intrigued. What was so bad about it?"

Ranulf thought through the list of offences he'd seen there. He wasn't especially keen on enumerating them, so decided to say, "The singer. He had a terrible voice."

Saska frowned. "A singer?"

"A naked singer," the Butcher came in, moving back to his stone seat. "A naked, dancing, prancing singer, with a greatsword swinging between his legs. Oh yes, he is well endowed. Much nakedness, pretty princess. And fun to be had with it. But perhaps your good friend Ersel San Sabar is right. Not a place for a pretty princess like you."

"His name is Ranulf, you great big oaf," hissed a voice. Now it was Leshie's turn to emerge from the tent, clad in her underclothes, a blanket around her shoulders. And, as ever, a good length of godsteel in her hand. "Why do you keep calling him that? It's Ranulf. *Ranulf.* It's not so hard, is it? *Ra-nulf,*" she said a final time, measuring out every syllable. "Just how stupid are you?"

The big sellsword took no affront to that. In fact, he seemed to find the idea of a small redheaded Bladeborn girl most amusing; lately, Leshie had given up darkening her hair with oil, letting her true person reemerge. "I prefer Ersel San Sabar," the big man said. "And you, *Ersella* San Sabar. Yes, this is better than your real name. *Leshie.*" He grimaced. "No, I don't like that at all."

"Don't you call me Ersella, *scarface*. I'm warning you. You'll wake up with another few scars if you do."

The man was bemused. "You think this is a threat?" Laughter rolled out over the hills. A few of his men glanced over, though most ignored him; it seemed they were used to the captain's roisterous ways. "Most of these scars I did to myself, little red. Here, look at this." He flicked aside his tattered cloak, bearing the open flesh of his upper right arm. The meat there was carved in a series of lines, one after another, moving up his bicep and to the hairy bulge of his shoulder. "Each of these is a kill. Northmen, these. And here..." He swung around the other way, showing his opposite arm. "These are southmen. More of these, yes. I have worked more south than north. They are on my legs too, the kill-scars, and my back. And here, right here..." He reached down and gripped his groin. "I have a *special* place I cut, for little redhead girls like you."

Leshie hissed at him, pointing her blade. "You think that's supposed to scare me? I've killed men before too, you know. I just don't have to maim my flesh to show it off. And I'm half your age at least. I'll kill more men in my lifetime, I'll bet. I'd kill you now if we fought."

The Butcher was thoroughly enjoying himself now. "I would love to have a tussle with you, little red. With blade *and* in the bed."

Leshie recoiled. "With you? You think I'd sleep with *you*?" She made a gagging motion, though the Butcher only laughed louder. "I've never seen anyone so ugly. Not even that old man Benjy, from the boat. That smile of his, those *teeth*." She wretched a little more. "But you might be even worse."

"Well lucky I am a sellsword, and earn much coin. I do not have looks to lure like Denlatis does. I just pay, and they come to me."

"There isn't enough coin in the world to make me want to go to bed with you." Leshie was in one of her moods. Even after saving Saska - which she'd been begging to do herself all along - she'd remained grumpy and querulous and continued to moan about having these 'stupid sellswords' along with them. She said it again now, looking straight at Ranulf. "We should leave this lot behind, go on ourselves. I can't bear to look at him anymore. You remember Benjy, don't you? You remember his *teeth*."

Ranulf had had enough of her complaints. "What I remember, Leshie, is how rudely you spoke to him. Just as you are now. All this time we've spent together and you've still learned nothing of manners."

"Yeah, well...you know my *tricks*, Ranulf." She gave him a look, and he remembered.

Ah, of course. She'd only spoken so harshly to old Benjy because she thought he was hiding something. She believed the old man might crack in front of Jonik and show his true colours if she prodded and abused him enough. Well, he had. He'd bitten back at her, calling her a couple of names of his own, and she'd taken that for some sort of victory. To Ranulf it was a perfectly normal reaction, the way she was behaving. *The girl is deluded,* he thought.

"Saska, what do you think?" Leshie went on. "I heard you, just now. You're fed up the same as me. We don't need to be going all this way into the wilds like this. We need to go to Aram. And once we've done that, we can go home. *Real* home." She kicked a stone, and it rattled away into the darkness. "I'm sick and tired of this dry bloody desert!"

The Butcher gave a softer chuckle. "I think Ersella needs a lie-down.

That comment was ill-advised. Leshie spun at him at once, lunging, and the Butcher was forced to leap back and draw his own blade. It was a bastard sword, the godsteel in need of a clean, but deadly. He retreated from Leshie's advance, stepping around the fire. Ranulf feared Leshie might actually take a swing at him, the mood she was in.

"Enough, Leshie," he shouted at her. "You reap what you sow, for goodness sake. If you can't take the insults, then don't give them."

"I told him not to call me that name. *I told him.*" She snarled at the big sellsword across the fire. Several of his men had approached now, hands on the hilts of their blades, and Joy was moving those keen eyes of hers from one to the next, judging their intent, ever at Saska's side.

"It's just a name," Ranulf said. "Now either sit down and shut up, or go back to your tent and leave us alone. We were having a perfectly nice conversation before you came out."

Leshie snorted at him, picked up a stone, and threw it away into the blackness. "Fine. You're all boring anyway." She stormed straight back into the tent, growling and grumbling as she went.

Saska made to stand. "I…should probably go and talk to her."

"You shouldn't have to." Ranulf was at his wit's end with that girl. "She's been like this for weeks. Just…let her calm down. She blows so hot and cold I don't know what to do sometimes."

"Welcome to parenthood, Ranulf." Saska gave him a wan smile. Through it all, she'd barely moved an inch. Was that confidence? Fatigue? More likely, she just knew Leshie well enough to realise she was never going to follow through. The girl was all bark and no bite most of the time, though that bite was lethal when she wanted it to be.

The Butcher was still smiling, though his pupils had dilated and there was a mild tension in his limbs. "The girl is *wild*," he said. "She would make a good Bloody Trader, I think. But first, a strong man to break her in. Yes, I could take care of that."

Saska didn't like that comment. "Leave her alone, Butcher," she warned. "And don't talk about her like that."

The sellsword considered that, then nodded. "As you wish, pretty princess. Who am I to question the word of the heir of House Nemati?"

Saska studied him calmly as he sat, giving Joy a tickle behind the ear. The starcat seemed to enjoy it immensely, eyes squeezing shut, a great rumbling purr spreading out from her chest. "What you said about those scars…is all that true? They're from men you've killed."

The Butcher nodded. "On my arms and legs, yes. That part about redheaded girls, no. That was just to rile the girl."

"And the rest? Those deeper ones? The jagged cuts? They're battle wounds?"

"Yes. I was a pit-fighter once, before I began selling my sword. I used to compete in the Red Pits in Aram, long ago."

A glaze passed over Saska's eyes. Ranulf knew she was thinking of Sir Ralston, similarly scarred as the Butcher, though much of the damage to his skin and flesh had been wrought of dragonfire, not steel. It had been one of the first things she'd asked him, when Leshie had brought her to their exit point on the western edge of the follower camp; whether the Wall was still alive. He'd not been able to answer as she'd wished. "I don't know, Saska," he'd told her, sadly. "We left Aram the same time as you, following behind the army. I know only as much as you do."

It was always on her mind, he knew, the fate of her giant protector. Over the last few days, they'd ridden alongside one another often, and spoken of their stories. He'd told her of Solapia, Vincent Rose, the Book of Thala, Pal Palek's pits, Jonik and Emeric Manfrey and the rest of their saviours and all else in between. She'd spoken of her time with Lady Marian, her infiltration of the Kastor camp at Harrowmoor, Cecilia Blakewood, Elyon Daecar, the two Varin Knights, Lancel and Barnibus, who Elyon had ordered to take her south to the coast, her fateful meeting with Sir Ralston Whaleheart at the docks of Shellcrest. And the rest. Her voyage on the Steel Sister with Captain Rikki Bowen and his crew. Her journey across the Aramatian plains with the smuggler Mellio and his mute helper Pig, her arrival at Aram, of which she had most regrets. "I thought my grandmother would be there," she'd told him. "I promised Rolly it would be safe. I *promised* him, Ranulf, and he was taken from me." She'd been in chains ever since, shackled to Lord Elio's will, kept in the dark as to the Whaleheart's fate.

But no more, Ranulf thought now. *We'll get you back to Aram, find out what has come of your Wall. Now you can shape your own fate, Saska. Together...together we can help shape the world.*

It was a clear night, the skies strewn with stars. A calm settled between them. Ranulf looked at the girl he'd come all the way out here for; she still held that little rock in her grasp, fiddling with it, turning it around between her fingers, idle movements that she seemed to perform by habit.

For all the tales they'd shared, there remained matters they hadn't yet spoken of. Ranulf had said nothing of his duty as yet, of the secrets he'd unearthed in the Book of Thala. *And there are things she hasn't spoken of yet either*, he knew. *At least, not to me.* One night, he'd heard Leshie gasping and giggling in their tent, and had overheard her exclaim, "Elyon Daecar! Really? My gods, Sask, could you have picked anyone better for your first time!" But that was none of his business, and not something she'd wanted to share with an ageing adventurer like him. *But that rock*, he thought, watching her turn it between her fingers, deep in thought. He'd seen her fiddling with it before. *It means something to her. It means a great deal.* He cleared his throat and broke the silence. "Do you mind if I ask you something, Saska?"

She withdrew from her reverie, turned to look at him. "Yes, Ranulf?" There was such an innocence to her face, sometimes. *She's only eighteen, nineteen at most*, he had to remind himself. She'd always seemed older than that, wiser, more world-weary and mature, yet sometimes he saw the callow youth in her years. "What is it?"

He turned to look at the sellsword captain, giving a gentle cough to get his attention. "Butcher, um, would you mind..."

The big man had returned to his feasting, munching happily on another persimmon, of which he had a particular liking. He looked up, sucking some juice from his fingers. "You want some privacy, yes?" Ranulf nodded, and the big man stood. "Say no more, Ersel San Sabar. I should go and check in with my men anyway. Tell them not to worry, that the little redhead girl is no real threat." He grinned. "Merinius should be returning soon as well. And Slack Stan. I shall await their reports." He inclined his head and paced away in his tattered crimson cloak.

Saska followed him with her eyes. "Something you couldn't ask me in front of him?"

Ranulf looked at the rock. "*That*," he said. "I thought...well, you've not said anything about it yet. I wondered if it might be something personal, that you'd prefer not to discuss in public. Or at all," he added. "Please tell me to mind my own business, if you want."

"No, not at all." She smiled and handed the little piece of rock over. "It's coral," she told him. "I've been meaning to talk to you about it, actually."

He lifted it to the firelight, inspecting the grooves and pits. "Coral? You picked it up on your voyage with Captain Bowen, then?"

"I did. Not so far from here, actually. We stopped for half a day off the northeastern coast, a little south of Eagle's Perch. Did some swimming among the reef, relaxed on the rocks." She smiled as she reminisced. "Rikki was telling me about his family. They liked to stop there on their voyages, and go diving for shells and rare plants down the drop-off. He said that it was a popular place for the Seaborn to explore as well, lots of treasures on the seabed, hundreds of metres down. I went swimming too, with little Billy. They told me to look for a coral that called to me." She nodded to the hunk in his hand. "That's it."

He spun the coral between his fingers. "Sounds like an idyllic day, Saska. Nice to have a physical reminder of it."

He handed the coral back, and she resumed her fiddling. "It's more than that," she said. "I haven't told you much about Old Hob yet, have I? He was Rikki's grandfather, a lifelong seaman, with some old Seaborn blood in him. Any new crew member who came on the ship would be told to look for a piece of coral or rock, or even a shell, at that reef. Old Hob would read it for them. See their future in the pits and grooves. He had a funny way about him, always reading the skies, the birds and clouds and such, foretelling what they meant. It was doom, mostly. He seemed pretty sure a great shadow of war was approaching."

He wasn't wrong there, Ranulf thought. Though it hardly took a prophet to see that. "So this coral…it *called* to you, you said? What do you mean by that?"

"Just that. I was…drawn to it, somehow. This particular one. I found lots of rocks and shells and bits of coral, much more colourful and eye-catching, but this one…" She smiled down at it fondly. "This little grey one called out to me. I knew at once that it was the one. Just by instinct, I knew it."

Ranulf hadn't heard anything like this before. From north to south, unusual men and women claimed clairvoyance in their own ways, and he'd met many of them on his travels. The Elders of the Everwood read the future in the seeds and leaves of the great trees that gave them shelter. Piseki wisemen would stand upon a high dune in the desert, and read the shift of the sands. There were queer folk in the Tidelands who conjured prophecies from the rise and fall of the water. Ranulf had once met a sorcerous dwarf who could blow strange shapes out of pipe smoke, and bird-readers and storm-seers were popular enough in Rasalan. This old man sounded like one of them, though reading corals wasn't something he was aware of. "So…you brought the rock to this old fortune-teller?" he asked, already sceptical. "What did he say?"

She shrugged. "That my future was blurred. He couldn't see much into it, he said."

"Oh…well, fortune-telling is a notoriously unreliable business, Saska. Even the Eye of Rasalan's forecasts can be rather mercurial, as you know. You shouldn't read anything into it. The old man sounds like something of a crackpot to me."

"Sure." Saska gave a faint smile. "He knew I was royal, though. And he spotted me as Seaborn too."

"You…*what?*" Ranulf's brows twisted into a frown. "You're *Seaborn*? How do you…why didn't you…you should have said something, Saska. When did you find out?"

"That day at the reef. I was diving deep, staying down for almost ten minutes at a time by the end."

Ranulf was shocked. "And you never knew this before?"

"You think I wouldn't have told you if I knew? During all that time we spent together in Tukor and Rasalan, and in the university library?" She shook her head. "Before going on the ship, I'd never swum in deep water, not once. Just the river near Willow's Rise, and some other rills and brooks. I'd never been in a situation where I needed to hold my breath for minutes at a time either. That only seemed to activate once I'd dived a few metres down. My body just…reacted. Same as when I first held Marian's dagger. Didn't know I was Bladeborn until she put that length of godsteel in my grasp. You remember. You were there."

Ranulf took a second or two to puzzle through all that. "So…this Seaborn blood…it must be from your father's side," he said, thinking. He'd tried hard back in Thalan to discover who her father might have been, but had kept running into dead ends. An Ilithoran lord or knight was his most likely guess. But this…this meant he had to be part Seaborn as well. Her mother was a pureblood Lightborn of Lumo's descent so it couldn't possibly have been from her. "I had assumed, because of your strong bond to godsteel, that your father was a pureblood Bladeborn," he went on. "So you're Bladeborn, Lightborn, *and* Seaborn." He had to laugh. "Gods, you're even more unique than I thought."

Saska had never much liked that tag, he knew. Unique. Special. Important. She gave a quiet huff. "I'm royal too. On that side. My father's side, Old Hob said."

Ranulf wasn't understanding. "Royal? I thought you'd meant your mother?"

"So did I, when Hob first said it. I told him I was born of royal Lightborn blood, but he just looked at me with this strange little smile, and said, 'I wasn't talking about your mother'." She turned the coral idly between her fingers. "Was my father he was talking about."

Ranulf was thinking hard now, though he was tired and saddle-sore from the road and his brain wasn't working half so well as he'd like. "So your father was Bladeborn, Seaborn, *and* of royal birth?" He thought some more, searching for an answer to that riddle. Saska had a look on her face. "There's more?" he asked her, seeing she had something else to say. "What else haven't you told me yet?"

"Well…Krator…he told me my father was a slave, kept in the palace. He told me he raped my mother and that's how I was born. And he told me…" She sighed heavily. "He told me he beat my father to death for it. And his skull…he kept his skull in his estate, Ranulf. He…he had it put in my room, to keep me company."

Ranulf Shackton was horrified. "What sort of monster…" He closed a fist. "Lies, Saska, all lies. Lord Krator was just trying to control you. Your father…he couldn't have been a slave."

"Why not? I was, wasn't I? Me, the Bladeborn and Lightborn and Seaborn girl, just a slave and a servant, tucked away in the northwestern corner of Tukor. Maybe my father was the same? Mar Malaan told me he was brought to Aram by slavers, when he was a boy. That Safina Nemati kept him in the palace. I…I didn't think she was like that, my grandmother. I've always been told she was opposed to slavery."

"She always has been," Ranulf said. "And that's why it's so hard to believe." He rubbed the bristles on his chin. "Perhaps he was never a slave at all, but a guest. Have you thought of that, Saska? Safina…

she was close with King Godrin. Maybe they knew something…of this boy, and…and who he would sire?"

"*Me*?" She shook her head. Her scoff was so quiet as to be almost inaudible. "You think this is all about me?"

Yes, he thought, with a sudden conviction. *Yes, I do.* But he could tell she didn't want to hear that now. *She still doubts herself, doubts the part she will play*. There had always been much of a mystery around Saska and yet now…now it was starting to unravel. A thought came to him, then, though he didn't voice it. If right, she would not want to hear it now. *And if right,* he thought, *Safina Nemati will know.*

Away across the darkened hills, Ranulf heard the sound of hooves quickly approaching. *Merinius*, he thought, *or Slack Stan, returning*. Both had been sent out to watch their rear, scouting for followers, to north and east. The Butcher stepped in that direction, moving away around a crag and out of sight. Joy's ears pricked up, listening. "Trouble, girl?" Saska asked.

The starcat gave a tense rumble in answer, though if that meant anything, Ranulf couldn't hope to decipher it. Leshie stirred at the noise too, poking her head through the flaps of her tent. Ranulf could see the misty glow of godsteel in her grasp. "What's happening?"

"Scout's returned," Saska told her. "Here, fetch me over my blade, Lesh."

Leshie pushed through the flaps, Saska's shortsword in hand, free of its sheath. It was a fine blade, and a gift from Cliffario Denlatis, to be given to Saska once she was freed. "I will not have her unarmed on the road, my friend," he'd told Ranulf before he sailed off on his ships. "No, if the princess does not return safe, then what will come of our accord?"

Ranulf's accord with the tall smirking merchant was far from his mind right now. He was trying to listen to the voices around the rocks. They sounded strained. "Can you hear what they're saying, Leshie?"

The redhead skipped over, handing Saska her blade. "Something about men closing on us. They've caught our scent, I think."

"How close?" Ranulf asked, suddenly tense.

She shrugged. "Dunno, but Merinius sounds breathless, so he's clearly come riding back swift." Leshie gave Saska and Ranulf a conspiratorial look and lowered her voice. "This'll be a good time for us to go," she whispered. "We grab our things and run. Or ride, whatever. We escape, is what I mean."

"We don't need to escape. These men are working for us. They're not holding us prisoner."

"Don't split hairs, Ranulf, you know what I mean." She wagged her finger at him. Then she pointed it into the darkness beyond the camp. There were no men watching the southern way; they'd been drawn over to the commotion. "We slip away, right now. If we're lucky, whoever's on our tail will track scarface and his men, instead of us."

"*Whoever's* on our tail? You know who's on our tail, Leshie."

"Gods, Ranulf, shut up with that. You nitpick at everything. Saska..." She turned to her. "What do you say? Worth a shot, right? These sellswords are only slowing us down anyway. We'd be so much quicker without...."

"OK, bad news," came the voice of the Butcher, striding back around the rocks and into view. Leshie cursed as if they'd missed their chance; by Saska's face, she was never even considering it.

"We know," Ranulf said, standing. "They've caught our scent. I just hope it wasn't your fire, Butcher."

"It wasn't. They're too far away to see it." Merinius was at his side. He was the man Ranulf had seen outside the Butcher and the Baker's tent the first time he visited, wearing a silken blue scarf around his neck. It was his wife's, Ranulf had since learned. He'd been wearing it ever since the day she died. "Merinius tells me they are an hour behind us, two at most. The fat Sunrider Mar Malaan leads them."

Saska began moving straight for her tent. "We have to go, then, right now. Mar Malaan will not stop until he has me."

"I agree." The Butcher shouted orders and at once the camp was struck. It took a few minutes to have the tents packed and horses readied. The moon was wheeling overhead, stars packed tight around it. *A good night for riding,* Ranulf thought. *And wolves and cats are quick.*

He went to the Butcher. "How many are in this chasing pack?"

"Enough to cause us trouble, if they catch us."

And if they do, will you stand and fight, or hand us over? Ranulf had to wonder. He knew all about the fickle loyalties of sellswords. *They change sides as easily as the wind changes direction,* he thought. *Their only allegiance is to coin.*

Saska strode over, garbed in her travelling leathers, sleek black cloak about her shoulders, Joy at her side. Leshie was at her other, red-armoured and ready. "So," Saska said. "Which way are we going?"

The Butcher jabbed a scarred finger south. "The mountain," he said, pointing into the darkness. "The cats and wolves fear it more than men do. They will be less likely to follow us there."

The mountain, Ranulf Shackton thought. He didn't need to ask which one.

50

Amara

She sat on the edge of her hard wooden bed, looking at her mutilated hand. Torchlight flickered in the corridor beyond her cell; it was the only light down here, burning low and sombre, and always threatening to go out. It had, once, leaving her in total darkness for half a day, before her gaoler had come to deliver her daily dinner and relight it.

He was an uncouth man, that gaoler. Porg was his name, a soft-bellied oaf stuffed into an ill-fitting vest, leather and sleeveless and stained. He had an unpleasant look and an even more unpleasant smell, which never failed to precede his arrival. Half the time Amara got a whiff of him before she heard him coming, lumbering down the steps to deliver her rations and take away her chamberpot. And he was clumsy too, the ham-fisted lug. Twice he'd tripped on the steps, dropping her dinner and forcing her to go hungry, and he'd even dropped her nightly ration of wine once too, unforgivably. It was made up for the next morning, though, when he'd slipped when carrying her chamberpot, spilling its contents all over himself. Amara had laughed so hard at that her sides had almost split, until Porg had threatened to cut off another one of her fingers, and then she'd fallen silent.

She looked at her missing pinky, trying to wiggle the phantom digit. "Who needs a little finger anyway," she said to herself, voice falling flat against the dull rock walls. There wasn't anyone else to talk to, unless she counted the furniture, and that was sparse enough. A bed. A desk. A chair. Nothing more. "See her confined to the dungeons in a cell to befit her station," Godrik Taynar had said. *He doesn't think much of me, does he?* she thought. *Even Porg deserves better than this.*

Her hand didn't hurt anymore, at least. Well, not much, anyway. It had happened the same day she'd arrived in the city, shortly after her confrontation with Godrik. She'd been amenable at first, agreeing to write Elyon a letter, as Godrik requested, but once she'd found out about the trap…about the Taynar men waiting outside Keep Daecar to slay the Flame Manes, take Carly captive, and Jovyn, and even kill her household guards if they got involved…well, that was too much. She'd raged. They'd knocked her out. And she'd awoken down here, with Porg and another guard standing over her. There had been a quill and inkpot and parchment on the table.

"Write the letter, as you said," Porg had demanded in a thick voice, staring down at her through black beady eyes. He'd brandished a cruel-looking knife. "Write it, else you'll lose something you don't want to lose."

She'd spat in his face.

The other guard grabbed her hair, then, and hauled her to her feet, pulling her across the cell, planting her on the chair. "Write the letter," he'd told her. "To your nephew. Tell him King Godrik wants the Windblade. Write it, like you said."

She'd tried to spit in his face too, but the man had seen it coming, twisting her head aside so the spittle sprayed across the parchment instead. Then she'd heard a voice from outside the cell. "My lady, please. Just write the letter. This needn't go ill." Footsteps sounded and the man entered. She looked into the face of Sir Nathaniel Oloran. "I hope I didn't strike you too hard, Lady Amara? Perhaps you're not thinking straight." He smiled as though it might mollify her. "I can dictate for you, if you wish. You need only write."

"Spare me your courtesies, worm. I'm not writing any letter." She swept an arm across the table, scattering its contents to the floor.

"Worm?" The Commander of the Greycloaks stiffened his spine. "You remember what King Godrik said, about your hand? Much pain can be inflicted there, if you…

"Wriggle away, worm. Wriggle away and leave me alone." She didn't think he'd follow through with the threat, not for a moment. Nathaniel Oloran was a coward clad in treason and treachery, and had never had a backbone. "Just leave me," she'd told him fiercely. "Wriggle off to your false corpse of a king, you pathetic little oath-breaking…"

"The right hand," he'd interrupted, in a cold voice. "The little finger. The king will have it."

Empty words, she'd thought. *Empty threats.* She'd been halfway through a mocking laugh, when the guard had grabbed her wrist with one hand, spread her fingers with the other, and Porg had plodded in and started sawing. She was so shocked by the suddenness of it she'd almost forgotten to scream. And then she saw the blood, saw the blade, saw that it was all real. And her throat had never unleashed such a sound.

She'd passed out again, a moment later, from the pain and the shock and the sight of all that blood. And when she'd next awoken, her hand was bound in bandages, her pinky was gone, and she was lying again on the hard wooden bed, a small man seated outside the cell on a stool. She'd squinted at him, through the gloom. He wore the garb of a healer, his chin extending in a long wisp of grey beard, eyes slanted sympathetically. "My lady, how is the hand?"

Her throat was raw when she tried to speak. From the screaming. "My hand…" She took a moment to remember, but everything had happened so fast. Her eyes went back to the bandaging, the red stain, the missing finger. "My…*my hand…*"

"I have seared and sewn it, so you shouldn't suffer any fever," the healer said. "And I rubbed in a good drakeshell ointment, to speed the healing." He gestured aside. "There is water there, on the desk, and some wine as well, with added roseweed for the pain."

He stood, robes trailing to the floor. His sleeves were bunched and tied at the elbow and he had healers hands, callused and worked, yet nimble for all that. "The worst of it is over, my lady. Now, it will be a matter of readjusting. You write with your left hand, I'm told?" He took her silence for an answer. "Good, this is good. Many people wrongly assume that the little finger is mostly useless, but that isn't true. No, it's quite essential in grip strength and fine dextrous movements, as it happens. I'm sure Sir Nathaniel wasn't aware of that when he chose it; the index finger would have been better to remove, in some ways. But…well, you're left-handed, so…" He'd smiled, as though they were discussing nothing more trivial than the weather. "I'll return in a few days, to change the bandaging, and make sure there is no rot. Other than that, I sincerely hope my expertise should not be required again."

There was some threat in there, Amara could see, and later that same day - or perhaps it was the next, it was hard to be sure - pig-eyed Porg had had his turn too. "You best write that letter," he'd told her. "Or I'll be cutting more bits off you." He'd pushed a tray of food under the bars; poor fare, but what did she expect? "King's orders, woman, so don't look at me like that. I just do what I'm told."

"And you think that will save you?"

Those words had unnerved the lout. "What am I supposed to do? Deny King Godrik's orders? He'd have my head on a spike quick as spit."

There was truth in that, though Amara didn't care to hear it. "Poor you. I guess you're doomed either way."

"Then what'll stop me from hurting you some more? You shouldn't talk to me that way, woman. *I* hold the power down here."

"That you do. The lord of gloom and rusted iron bars." She stepped up to them. "If I were you, I'd run. You think you can take my finger like that, and suffer no reprisal?"

He got a defiant look on his face. "Aye, I do. Got the king protecting me. The *king*. And what're you? Some widow stuck in a cell."

She'd taken a sip of that wine the healer had given her, swilled it, and spat it in his face. The fool hadn't learned from the last time, clearly. And ever since then, well, they'd not been on the best of terms.

So followed the nights when Amara went hungry, the slurs and curses, the occasional grab of her throat or pull of her hair when Porg's mood was particularly frightful. He'd threatened to cut her other fingers off a hundred times, and her ears, her nose, her toes as well. He'd threatened to put out her eyes if she looked at him wrong again, or take off her tongue if she was rude, or knock her teeth into the back of her throat if she dared smile at him in a way he misliked. But mostly it was about the fingers. "It'll be your middle finger next, the longest one," he would say. "The king says I'm to flay it first, before cutting it off, strip off the skin and meat and the nail. Says I can burn you too. That right hand's mine, woman. I can do whatever I want to it."

He'd done nothing, though, since that first bit of surgery, except strike her a few times with an open hand, and even those were feeble efforts. And half the time he'd tell her it wasn't his fault. "Just doing what the king says," he liked to reiterate. "But I'm going easy on you, woman, don't forget that. I'm just a tool, that's it. Blame the worker, not the tool. My pa used to tell me that. Don't forget."

He was a tool, that was obvious enough. Amara had tried to get information out of the tool, but he never gave her anything. Not about the war, not about the fighting at the Perch and the Trident and the Bane. Nothing about Carly or Jovyn, who she was sure were somewhere down here too, or which of her guardsmen had died. Once, he'd slipped up and told her that the Flame Manes were all slain - "Those sellswords all had their fires snuffed out," he'd told her, grinning stupidly - but he'd said nothing of Sir Connor or Sir Penrose or Sir Gilmore or her other men, which gave her hope.

That about the Flame Manes had wounded her though, and worse even than the loss of her finger. She'd travelled with Carly's band for many long weeks and had come to like them fondly. Big Sally Scarlet who could drink any man under the table. Lanky Will Red, always looking to learn. Old Crowfoot, with his stories, and Sunset Sam ever-gazing out west. Mad Maroon Murley who spoke such utter gibberish and Renford of the Rust, a small quarrelsome man who wore a rusted halfhelm on his head, and would argue with a stone if he could. And the rest, the half dozen others who'd escorted her from Elmhall Hold to Varinar. All dead now, all gone.

She'd wept for them during those first days in the darkness, wept for what a fool she'd been. She wondered how much Elyon knew of it all. *Godrik will send him a letter himself,* she told herself, *and maybe my finger too.* She imagined that's why Nathaniel had taken it. "The king will have it," he'd said, and Sir Nathaniel Oloran was no man to make that decision himself. *He'll send it to Elyon, with a note*, Amara decided. *He'll use my little pinky to frighten him, get him to hand over the Windblade.* It wouldn't work, though. Much as Elyon loved her - and even that she'd started to doubt, after Rylian, after how he'd been that night at Elmhall - she wasn't so important as that, and Wallis, Rikkard, Killian...all would counsel him against rising to Godrik's demands, she knew.

She spent her days like that, wondering about a great many things. Mostly, they were unpleasant things, past, present, and future, and she often found herself descending into deeply vengeful thoughts. For so long she'd wanted her king cousin Janilah dead, wanted to see him die in some horrible, agonising way, but now two men had stepped ahead of him in that queue. Godrik and his co-conspirator, the duplicitous Lord Brydon, who'd sent her here as bait and stolen her sweet Lillia.

"I'll kill him," she would whisper to herself by night. "If it's the last thing I do, I'll stick a knife in that bastard's cold black heart." She didn't care that he was Lillia's grandfather, and Elyon's, and Amron's father-in-law, and one of the most powerful lords in Vandar, nay the whole bloody north. She didn't care about any of that anymore. "He took Lillia from me, and served me up like a lamb for slaughter." She would not forgive that, no more than she would forget it. Janilah, Godrik, Brydon…it was a formidable list she wanted dead.

She was fantasising about that now, about how she would slip the knife through Brydon Amadar's ribs, and give a good strong twist for good measure, when she got a pungent whiff of Porg approaching. A few moments later, she heard his grunts and footsteps and saw the light of his torch coming down the stairs. He was breathing heavily by the time he came into view.

"What's on the menu tonight, then, Tool?" she asked him. She imagined it was about dinnertime, though could see no tray in his hands. "Oh? Trip on the stairs again, did you? I confess I heard no clatter."

"Always with the smart tongue." He plodded toward the bars, pulling the keychain from his belt, stuffing the key into the lock, turning. He rarely entered unless bringing her something, so she braced for one of those flaccid, fat-fingered slaps of his. He made no move to approach her, though. Instead, he swung a bag from his back and threw it on the floor. "Clothes," he said. "Get changed. You're dining with his kingship tonight."

She'd not expected that. How long had she been down here? Two weeks, three? In all that time she'd had neither sight nor sound nor smell of anyone but this reeking oaf, barring the wispy-bearded healer who'd visited those early days. It made her wary, her mind searching for a trap. *This is some ruse,* she thought. *The tool only wants to see me undress. Or else this is it, they're taking me to the gallows, and there's motley in that bag for me to dress in.*

"Well? What're you waiting for, woman? This ain't no trick. Get changed!"

Tentatively, she drew forward and picked the bag up, digging inside to draw out…huh, a dress, and fine enough. There were fresh underclothes too, a scarf and shoes and a warm fur cloak as well. "I should wash," she said, setting the clothes aside. She'd been wearing the same attire as when imprisoned some weeks ago, and the stink on her was ripe. "I smell almost as bad as you do, Tool."

"Don't push it. King wants you *looking* nice, don't care about the smell. You'll be far enough away." He stepped out of the cell, then turned his back to give her privacy. "Get on with it. He don't like to be kept waiting."

~

THEY FOUND the king seated at the end of a long dining table within his private residence. Amara had dined here before, and often, with King Ellis Reynar and his wife Elitha when Vesryn was Commander of the Greycloaks. She looked around. The dining room was much the same; opulent, grand, as stately as the rest of the palace. *The king has changed a little, though,* she thought. Ellis was a spineless little weasel, but he wasn't half so odious as the corpse king who'd stolen his throne.

"You look well, Amara." Godrik Taynar did not stand. "How is your hand?"

"Well recovered, thank you. I always considered my right hand to be unnecessarily heavy, Godrik. I thank you for lessening its weight."

He smiled an empty smile. "Do sit. We have matters to discuss."

She did as bidden, Porg tramping from the room, leaving them alone save a pair of Greycloaks at the door. There were no servers present; if Amara wanted a drink of wine, she'd have to serve herself. She wanted one well enough, so poured herself a cup and took a good swallow. "Delicious." She smacked her lips for good measure.

Godrik gave that dead smile again. "You do not fear you'll be poisoned?"

"If you wanted me dead, you'd have had Porg throttle me already."

"True," the old man said. "How do you find his company?"

Sickeningly unpleasant, she thought. Instead she continued to play at flippant and said, "Rather enjoyable, actually. There's never a dull moment with Porg. One second he'll be calling me the most unpalatable names, and the next he'll be tripping over his own feet and spilling the contents of my chamberpot all over himself. The Tool does make for wonderful entertainment. I thank you for selecting him to serve me."

Godrik gave that no reply. He put his skeletal fingers together, making a spire beneath his chin. "You've dined here before?"

She looked around, smiling, indulging the old monster these pleasantries. "Many times, with your predecessor and his wife. I hear Queen Elitha has returned to Silverspear?"

"With her daughter, yes," Godrik confirmed. "They wouldn't have had to, if it hadn't been for your meddling. The dowager queen made a fine bargain with Janilah to wed Lyriss to Prince Robbert, but you couldn't have that, could you?"

Well, those pleasantries didn't last long. "If you're referring to Lillia's betrothal to Prince Robbert, I had no hand in that," she told him. "That was arranged by Elyon and Rylian, not me."

"Yes, I'm sure. And look what has happened as a result. Prince Rylian dead, your nephew a traitor and thief, Janilah missing. Much harm has been done on the back of your interferences, Amara."

"I'm aware." She spoke flatly. Time in the dungeons had given her plenty of space to think on that, and she had her regrets, Rylian most of all. "Why am I here, Godrik? If you just want to lay blame at my door, I might as well return to my cell."

"You'll return there soon enough, fear not. I wouldn't want you thinking this is anything more than a short reprieve."

"Good. I was starting to get comfortable down there. Who needs a featherbed when you can sleep on splintery wood? And aren't personal privy chambers so overrated? I much prefer squatting over a bucket."

"Droll as ever." Godrik unlaced his fingers and set them on the arms of his chair. "Your nephew seems unconcerned about your fate, Amara. I had hoped the little gift I sent him would have stirred him to action, but no, he remains less than interested in securing your release."

Amara drank her wine. Her phantom finger gave a throb of pain. "Did you ever really think he would?"

"Call it an old man's foolish hope," the corpse king said. "A folly on my part, I will admit. But as it turns out, the boy has grown quite gifted with the blade during his months in possession of it. Not to say my son would not have as well, but even so…" He let a short silence enwrap the room, then said, "I suppose you don't know, do you? Your nephew slew a dragon, out in some thunderous storm north of Dragon's Bane. Ezukar, they're saying, once ridden by the Fireborn Sa'har Nakaan." He picked a walnut from a bowl on the table and had a nibble. "What do you say to that, Amara?"

"I say I'm not surprised," she said at once. Showing such was never a good idea with Godrik Taynar; he tended to respond better to those who shared his dour disinterest in everything. "I have always known Elyon's worth. He is his father's son; dragon killing is in their blood."

"Ah, how funny you should say that. Amron has returned to his dragonslaying ways as well, I've been informed. Zyndrar the Unnatural, defeated not far from Blackfrost." He nibbled his walnut a while, taking his good time. "Perhaps *that* news is more surprising to you?"

She held her smile. Inside she was *elated. He…he must have returned, then,* she thought. *And not just that…returned whole and one, as I'd hoped, as I'd prayed…* She had so many questions, but bit down every one. When she'd been locked away in the dungeons, she'd feared Amron would never return. It had been so long, *too* long, but…but…

"Well, I can tell by that smile you're trying to hide that this news is most welcome." Godrik set his half-eaten walnut aside - a full meal for such a wasted little man - and picked up his spiced wine. He had a thrifty sip, barely wetting his lips. "Of course, you'll want some more detail, I suppose?"

She inclined her head. "If…you would be so kind."

He placed down his cup and went straight into it. "Your brother-in-law is now bearer of the Frostblade, Amara, and this he used to defeat the dragon." He studied her face. "Shocking, I know, but isn't everything shocking these days? Word has reached me of Amron's fated journey into the Icewilds, of some local clan called the Snowskins, of a tribal prophecy, if you would believe it, that the Frostblade would be found. All very compelling stuff, I'm sure you'll agree."

"Compelling indeed." She took a moment to think it over. The expectation had been for Walter to lead Amron to Vandar's Tomb to be blessed and restored to full health. This was more than she could have hoped for; with the Frostblade, Amron Daecar would be a force of immense power, a great boon in the war. *Father and son, slaying dragons,* she thought. She could not hold her smile now; out it came, full and bright. "This is good news, Godrik. Even you must agree that Amron's return is beneficial to us."

"As a warrior and commander, Lord Daecar has few equals, that I will admit. But we cannot forget his true motives."

"True motives?" She let out a sigh. "If you think Amron's going to come here to try to take your crown…"

Godrik Taynar cut her off. "Lord Daecar travels here as we speak, in the company of my nephew, Sir Gerald. You were there, Amara, when I sent him to seek word of your brother-in-law at Northwatch. Well, he happened to meet him on the way and was present when Zyndrar descended from the skies. Some of my own men shared in the victory, I am told, reddening their blades with the dragon's blood." He paused, running a bony digit down his chin. "Now I wonder why Amron should wish to come here, if not to attempt to remove me from the throne using this long lost weapon of his? He must know that I am king by official decree of my predecessor, granted that power and office by the good laws of this kingdom. Yes, that is onerous for many to hear, but it is a simple and unarguable fact. I will not have him steal my crown."

Amara had much to say to all that, but decided better to bite her tongue. "No Blade of Vandar would be enough to remove you," she said. "You have twenty thousand Taynar swords in the city, Godrik. Unless Amron is coming with an army of his own…"

"He isn't. He comes with a few Crawfield men and this pet ranger of his."

"Then what are you worried about? Doesn't that tell you that he has no intent to overthrow you? He would be foolish to try, and Amron is no fool."

"Even wise men can be drawn to certain follies from time to time, Amara." He wet his lips with a bit more wine. "My son still lacks what he is owed, and Amron's return presents an opportunity. I cannot in all good conscience demand the Windblade off your nephew, not with matters as they stand at the Bane." He set his eyes on her. "A horde marches upon them, I am told, a hundred thousand strong. Think what you will of me, but the security of this kingdom is my highest priority. I shall thus permit Sir Elyon to keep the blade. For now."

Amara didn't say anything to that. Oh, it sounded gracious enough, but she knew better than to think that this was some unselfish concession for the good of the realm. *No, he's had his bluff called, and he's trying to save face*, she thought. *But what did he say there? My son still lacks what he's owed?* She put the pieces together quickly enough. "You intend to take the Frostblade from Amron, in lieu of the Windblade?" she asked him, incredulous. "Godrik, you cannot be serious. Dalton is…"

"Dalton is my son," he cut in, "and both prince and First Blade of this kingdom. Somewhere, people seem to have forgotten all that. By all rights, the Sword of Varinar should be clutched in his grasp, but no, your husband saw fit to deny him by turning his cloak and running. And to rub salt into that wound, you then plotted to steal the Windblade as well, giving it to your nephew. But here, perhaps, we have a final opportunity to set something right on that account. If Amron wishes to mend matters between us, he will hand the Frostblade over willingly, to be taken up by my son, in exchange for the other blades he should already have held. If not, we will have a problem on our hands."

"The problem is *you*, Godrik. It is your inability to see the fault in what you have done. It is this persistent belief that you are owed those blades, and your crown, when your only claim to them is borne of treason and regicide."

The old man yawned. "We have covered this ground already. Your cousin Janilah slew Ellis, not me. You can claim I had a part in it all you like; that doesn't make it true."

"But it *is* true…"

He held up a palm. "Enough. I shall not have us retrace our steps on this. Onwards, Amara. Do you believe Amron will be willing to give up the Frostblade willingly?"

"No," she said at once. "To *you*, no. And if your priority is the security of the kingdom, as you claim, then you would not demand it of him. He will deal more damage with it than *Dalton* ever will. Even you, his father, will admit that. Or are you half blind as well as half mad?"

The old man didn't like that. "Your attempts at wit fall blunt as ever. Even after being lessened a finger, you rant and rave and show this defiance." His eyes were on her, black and empty. "You no longer fear any further mutilation and dismemberment, do you? It's been weeks, you'll be thinking, and nothing else has happened. Well, it will. It will, at any moment of my choosing." He clipped his fingers, and the two men at the door began stepping down the table. Amara didn't recognise them. There was a time when she knew every good

Greycloak under Vesryn's watch, but not these. These were new; Taynar men and loyalists, dedicated to their lord's will. "Choose a finger, Amara," Godrik said. "My men will be kind; only the nail, I think."

She recoiled from their approach. There was something unhinged about the way Godrik was behaving. He'd always been a pragmatist, but his obsession about getting what he saw was rightfully his had made him increasingly unbalanced. "It won't get you anywhere, hurting me," she said. "Godrik, think clearly. Please. I am only trying to help."

"By calling me half mad? By ridiculing the abilities of my son? Not since Rufus Taynar has my house had a First Blade, but Dalton has every chance to emulate him as a warrior and champion if given the chance. Yet you continue to deny him, with your ill-begotten interferences and arrogance. All of you. Your husband, your nephew, your brother-in-law, who comes riding here to claim my crown. The sheer egotism of it, the hubris. It is a trait that all Daecar men possess, this inbred sense of superiority, rooted in every one of them from birth. They're pulled out from between their mother's legs, thinking themselves above the rest of us, and here…here we have *you*, Amara, born a Lukar, but just as accursed by the same pompous affliction. I have grown weary of it, weary to the point of distraction."

The old man stood, pushing himself to his feet. He shuffled down the table, speaking all the while. "When Amron gets here, I will have him met by a strong host who will demand he give up the Frostblade. You will be there with us, Amara. And we shall see whether you have any worth left at all."

The blood was starting to run cold in her veins. "What do you intend to do?"

"Kill you, in front of his very eyes, unless he should submit. Your nephew didn't take me seriously. Perhaps he believed the finger wasn't yours. Or perhaps he just doesn't care. More likely, he has other matters more pressing to distract him, and sage counsel to steer his course. But Amron will come face to face with your fate, and we shall see what he says then."

"You…you *are* mad," she whispered. "You *cannot* think this right, Godrik. And your son…your son is at the Trident, weeks away. What good will you do by denying Amron the Frostblade, only to have it shipped across the Red Sea? He'll take long months to learn to master it, if he ever will…"

"My son will soon sail home," Godrik came back. "There are reports of an Agarathi army marching from Dorath, with dragons in support, and legions of Lumarans as well. His blockade of the Trident has not yielded the result we had hoped."

"He's…*fleeing*? After barely even throwing a punch?" She'd heard the rumours of how Sir Dalton's army had been given strict orders to starve out the fortress, rather than win it by force. A move of utter folly to try to preserve men for any future civil war. "You have permitted the Agarathi a free crossing," she said, horrified. "They'll follow Dalton straight across the sea. King's Point will come under attack within weeks…"

"Are you calling my son a craven?"

She had no words. "I'm…I'm trying to say…"

"You insult me with impunity." The old man stared at her. The two Greycloaks were close at her sides. "You insult me and my son and my house. You condemn my commands as king." His eyes were black pits ringed in wrinkles. The skin was so loose and old it seemed to slough off his bones. "I cannot hear this any longer. Your screams would be better." He turned to the Greycloaks and gave a single nod. Amara heard the scrape of steel as a knife was pulled from a sheath.

"No…please, I'm only trying to…"

"Help? You're not helping. You are aggravating me, and my ears can take it no more. The index fingernail. Rip it off."

She tried to stand and bolt, but the men bundled her right back down. It was as before. A strong hand grabbed her wrist and flattened her fingers against the table. A blade came sliding in, pressing beneath the nail of her right index finger, pivoting up. Blood welled and pain soared and Amara's lips opened in a throat-burning scream.

"The middle finger too," she heard Godrik say over that. "You need to learn, Amara. You have to learn. I'm sorry."

Her middle finger came next, as ordered. She jerked and screamed and tried to pull her hand away, but had nothing, no strength to overpower them. The knife dug underneath the nail, tearing upward. Amara juddered and blinked, her head fuzzing.

"The others as well. All of them. Take them all."

"No…" She could barely speak now. Her voice came out a spluttery mess. She looked at the king through eyes stained wet with tears. "Please…I…"

"You will learn. You *must* learn, Amara. All of you Daecars. You must learn how to submit."

The men went to work on her third finger, digging, pulling, ripping the nail from flesh and skin. She shrieked in utter agony, struggling for all the good it would do, as they turned to her thumb. Her entire hand felt afire, throbbing and pulsing, red and raw. *They'll flay me next,* she thought. *Strip the skin and flesh. Burn my hand until there's nothing left but blackened bone, absent meat and muscle.* Suddenly all Porg's many threats were unfolding before her eyes. She blinked, wept, wailed, and pled mercy. "Enough....please enough...I can't...I can't take..."

The door crashed open at the far end of the hall.

At once the hands of the two Greycloaks were off her. Godrik was turning to face the intruder. "Who dares barge in like..."

Amara caught an unwashed whiff. *Porg*, she thought. She lifted her shivering left hand to clear her vision. Through the blur she could see a man standing in the doorway, cloaked and cowled. Beyond there were sounds of fighting, the clang and clangour of steel echoing out through the halls and corridors of the palace. The man at the door held something in his grasp, something round. He tossed it forward. It landed with a clatter on the table, rolling past plates and cups and candles before coming to a stop.

Amara looked down at Porg's decapitated head, eyes staring blankly, mouth cast open in dimwitted alarm. Blood oozed out of the stump that was his neck. She blinked, wiped her eyes, looked up. Now she saw *gold*. A golden blade, emerging from the cloak of the man, grand and misting. And silver beyond; armour, godsteel.

"*You*," said Godrik Taynar. "How did you..."

"I am sorry, Amara, for taking so long." Vesryn Daecar stepped forward. "You men, I would give you a chance to flee, but seeing what you've done to my wife's hand..." His voice was suppressed rage.

"Come one step closer," Godrik warned. "One more step and..."

An arrow fizzed past Vesryn's shoulder, taking the first Greycloak in the neck. He stumbled backward, gurgling, dying. A second arrow whistled into the room, cracking into the other guard's forehead and punching through into his brain. His head snapped back as his body toppled to the floor.

In the chaos of it, the Greycloak's knife had been left on the table. Godrik made a sudden grab for it, but Amara was quicker. She snatched it up, and plunged it down, straight through the back of Godrik's palm. He screamed horribly, old knees buckling beneath him.

And without thinking, Amara Daecar tore the blade back out, and stabbed again.

Right into the old man's neck.

51

Saska

She could see the dust trail on the northern horizon, a cloud of dirt and grit kicked up by pad and paw. Their pursuers were not ahorse. Every one of them was mounted on a sunwolf or starcat, beasts better suited to this hilly terrain and swifter across the ground as a result.

"Come, we ride on," bellowed out the Butcher, turning about on his charger. They had stopped only for a short break to give their horses a rest, and water them at a trickling rill coming down from the mountain. "We will lose them on the wooded slopes. They will not chase much further."

"How'd you know that?" Leshie demanded, leaping back up into the saddle of her rouncey. "You've been saying that since last night. And they've been chasing us all day."

"The mountain nears." The big scarred sellsword pointed, as though they needed showing where the mountain was. It was hard to miss, in truth; ahead it loomed, a great surging monstrosity that soared imperiously above the many small peaks and hills clustered at its sprawling base. Saska knew mountains well enough from living in the shadow of the Hammersongs, but this one was different. *Lonely*, she could only think. *A great lonely thing, like an island in the ocean.* "The cats and wolves fear it," the Butcher went on. "They will waver, I know this to be true."

Saska was getting that sense as well. Joy had begun to grow

increasingly nervous over the last couple of hours, growling randomly, tensing at every unusual sound. *She knows what lives here,* Saska thought. And so did the horses, and the men as well, half of whom looked like they would prefer to turn back. Already, a few had petitioned the Butcher to that effect, yet their captain had told them no, insisting their hunters would give up the chase eventually.

Leshie wasn't so sure, though. "And if they *don't* waver?" she asked, aggressive as ever. "We should find a good place to make a stand, I say. Somewhere with high ground we can take advantage of, and good places to spring an ambush."

Several of the men murmured assent. "Not so bad an idea, boss," said Stan, a man of mixed Piseki and Vandarian descent, with accents flavoured with both. He'd had his jaw badly broken as a child and it had never healed properly, leaving it all wobbly and slack. "We choose the battlefield and we might have a chance. Plenty of places in these crags we might take advantage of."

"They have twice our number," countered the Butcher. "Sunriders and Starriders all. This is too much, even for us. No, we ride on."

"How'd you get all those kill-scars if you're such a coward?" Leshie wanted to know.

The big sellsword only smiled a toothy smile at her and said, "By being smart, little red, and staying alive." He gave his horse a good firm heel and continued up into the hills.

Ranulf came to ride beside Saska on his brown-spotted horse. "We have to be prepared," he told her quietly. "Mar Malaan will catch us soon, no matter what the Butcher says. He's been gaining on us, and won't give you up easily. And these sellswords…" He glanced at them as they rode past, following the trail up through the hills. "They may choose to hand you over, rather than fight, Saska. If Mar Malaan offers them enough coin…"

Saska shook her head. "The Butcher promised us otherwise," she said, perhaps naively. "I know about sellsword loyalty, Ranulf, but…I don't know, something in me trusts him. If he wanted to turn us in, he'd have stopped already."

"Maybe," Ranulf Shackton conceded. He spoke wearily, posture sinking a little in the saddle. It had been a long night and day of hard riding, and much of that had been through tricky, strength-sapping terrain. "Still, best be prepared. If it comes to it, you may need to run ahead without us, Saska. Joy is much quicker than our horses, particularly over this uneven ground, and we're only slowing you down."

"I wouldn't abandon you. If it comes to a fight…"

"If it comes to a fight, all of us will die, and you'll be taken. The Butcher's right, we cannot hope to defeat that many Star and Sunriders. You'll run. Promise me you'll run?"

She didn't have to think on that long. "I can't make that promise, Ranulf," she told him. "I'm not abandoning you or Leshie, not after you came all this way to rescue me, and that's the end of it." She could tell he was eager to press her on the issue, so decided to race away up the column, Joy leaping over rocks and snarls of old dead trees to outrun him. It wasn't something she wanted to consider, leaving her friends behind only to be hunted down and retaken. *I'd sooner fight and die alongside them*, she thought. Her days of marching to another man's drum were done.

They followed the stream for a time, moving through big craggy boulders and past fields of broken scree. Saska got glimpses up the mountain as they went; further along the northern slopes, broad expanses of scrubby woodland clothed the foothills, thickening in places to a deep impenetrable green, and withering only as the slopes rose much higher. The sky was a hard blue today, though where the peaks of the mountain soared highest, clouds had gathered, blotting the view. Joy pounced among the rocks, greatly more agile than her companions who were forced to pick their way up more slowly. Every so often, Saska would race ahead a bit, if she spotted a thrust of higher ground, to try to get a look below. Every time she did that, she wished she hadn't.

They're closing, she would think, seeing the movement of cats and wolves, clambering up through the hills behind them. It felt inevitable, now, that they'd be caught up with eventually. Ranulf was right on that. She went to ride at the front with the Butcher. "They're right behind us," she told him. "No more than half a mile. Leshie's right, Butcher. We have to stop and make a stand."

The sellsword captain shook his head. "We stop, and we will all die. But up…" He looked that way, where the dense woods garbed the slopes. "We have a better chance up there."

"How?" asked Garth, riding just behind them. He was a fat man, Garth, a glutton with blood from a half dozen different houses running through his veins, if you were to believe him, from both north and south. "We'll be scattered in them woods, Butch. Those wolves and cats will run us down, you know it. We'd be better off fighting as one. An ambush, as the little redhead said."

The Butcher remained unmoved. "There are caves in those woods, Garth. Large caves, gouged into the cliffs deeper in. They may provide refuge if we are able to reach them."

The fat sellsword's eyes went wide. "You're mad. We go in one of them caves, ain't none of us coming back out."

Slack Stan agreed. "Those caves are home to you-know-what, boss. We wake one of those…"

"The risks are great, I agree." Merinius cantered to join them, his blue scarf trailing in the wind. He was more comely than the rest, green-eyed and dusky-skinned, with a good dusting of dark, three-day stubble on his cheeks and chin. "But the risk of fighting these hunters is greater. I saw them myself, when I scouted our rear. The sunwolves ridden are monstrous, and the starcats lethal. If they catch us, we will die."

"Not if we hand over the girl." And there it was, the very thing Ranulf had feared. The proposal came from one of the younger sell-swords, a squat man called Marush Moonface whose lips, nose, and close-set eyes looked absurdly small within that great spherical face of his. "It's her they want, not the rest of us. Why should we all die for some girl?"

"Because she is not just *some* girl, Moonface, but the lost Princess of Aramatia." The Butcher's expression made it clear he'd brook no debate on this. "We were paid to deliver her to Aram, where we shall be more richly rewarded for our toil. Her grandmother will pay us handsomely, I am told." He glanced at Ranulf as the adventurer came up the stony trail.

"Money means nothing if we're dead." Moonface looked around the other men for allies. "And I don't care who she is. We should never have taken this contract."

"*We?*" The Butcher moved closer on his horse. "You took no contract, Marush. I did, me and my brother. You have no say here, no voice. You are paid to swing your sword, to sweat, to bleed. And to die, if needed."

The man's huge round face went side to side. "I joined for plunder. I'm not dying for some…"

"You'll die when you're told to die," the Butcher broke in, giving the man a dark look. "*I* am captain. Another word from you, Marush, and you will wish you'd held your tongue."

The round-faced man didn't heed the warning. He looked at the other men again, searching for support, snorting. "You're fools, every one of you, dumb old fools. I'm not dying, no matter what you say. Not for a princess, not for no one. You can stick your coin where the sun don't…"

The Butcher moved so swiftly Saska scarcely saw it, but within the blink of an eye, his blade was out and Marush Moonface's big round head was rolling off down the trail, bumping from rock to rock. His squat body still sat in the saddle a moment. Then it slid sideways, toppling with a dull thud, blood squirting from his severed neck. "I'll have no more discussion on this," the captain said. "We ride for the woods. Perhaps our pursuers will stop for a snack." He eyed Moonface's bloated body with disdain, then turned his horse and continued up the trail.

A ripple of unease went through some of the other men as they followed. Saska could see it in their eyes. *They think the same as Moonface did,* she thought. *And how quickly his life was snuffed out.* "The captain doesn't like being questioned, does he?" she said to Ranulf.

"A sellsword captain must show strength," the adventurer told her. "If his authority is challenged, he must act quickly, and often brutally, to show the others that dissent will not be tolerated. It's a savage world they live in."

"We might have used him, though," Leshie offered. "If it comes to a fight. It's not like we can spare the men."

"A matter he weighed, I'm sure. One man talking mutiny can soon rouse the others to betray their leader. When spotting a weed, best pull it, or it may spread."

"At least we can count on his loyalty," Saska said. "You can put those fears to rest, Ranulf."

"It would seem so," the man agreed. "Though there are other fears to consider up here."

Saska didn't need to be told what those were. She glanced down the path again, at the headless body of Marush, the trail of blood left by his bouncing head which had disappeared now beyond the rocks. She wondered for a moment if the Butcher had another motive for killing him. *Bait*, she thought. *To lure something more fearsome out…*

The hills became increasingly rugged as they raced upward, and steeper as well. Saska gripped her godsteel shortsword, a welcome gift from Cliffario Denlatis, and could hear the panting behind them, the scrambling claws and paws, the shouts of the men giving chase. *A few hundred metres*, she thought. They had a few minutes, little more, before they were caught.

"Quicker, quicker," she heard the Butcher bellow. "The woods near. Follow me, on me!"

The horses were struggling more and more, though Joy had no such troubles. She weaved through them, up and down the column, bounding so effortlessly over the rocks and roots in their path. A sharp thin trumpeting sound screeched out from one of the mounts as it landed awkwardly upon a loose stone, snapping its leg. Down it went, throwing its rider from the saddle, who happened to be Slack Stan. The man's wobbly jaw crashed into the earth, shattering it yet further. Saska was first to react, leaping straight from Joy's back and pulling him to his feet. He looked dazed, blood dribbling down the side of his mouth. "Butcher!" she roared, and the big sellsword captain wheeled back to join them. "He'll have to ride with you. You have the biggest horse."

The captain gave no complaint. Eyes flickering, Slack Stan was hauled up into the Butcher's saddle and on they rode, one of the other men taking a moment to put Stan's steed out of its misery. A broken leg often spelt the end for a horse, Saska knew all too well. By the time all that was done she could hear the hunters behind them without the enhancing effects of godsteel. She caught glimpse of them, pouncing and leaping over a rise only a hundred or so metres back. Merinius had the rear of the column, Leshie with him, Ranulf a few paces ahead. Saska's heart thundered in her chest. *Do I run?* she asked herself. *Not for myself, but for them?* If she bolted she might be able to pull some of them off, if not all. Give her friends a chance to escape.

She was halfway through deciding what to do when the slope suddenly shallowed and straightened out into a wide plateau, leading to a patch of thick gnarled woodland thirty metres back. The trees grew in harsh tangles there, every bit of space filled in with thorn bushes and dense brambly brush that would not be easy to penetrate. Yet there was a trail, she saw, a path leading in, the bushes and trees smashed and parted. The Butcher saw it too, pointing, shouting as he slowed his horse and wheeled about. "Make for the woods," he yelled out, waving his men past. "Into the trees!"

Ranulf was coming up as quick as he could, shouting, "No, stop…don't go in there!" There was something desperate and ragged in his voice. "It's a game trail! Stop!"

Saska heard something then, something the others didn't seem to hear; a deep and distant rumble, somewhere away in those woods. She stared at the trail as the first of the sellswords sped into the trees, Garth the Glutton leading the charge, with Juri, Umberto, and Marco of the Mistmoors fast on his heels. Ranulf was still shouting, and the Butcher was drawing his blade, counting his men as they went by. Leshie dashed up over the rise and into view, followed by Merinius, who called, "I'm the last, Butcher. There is no one behind."

But there was. *There are twenty of them,* Saska thought, hearing the hunters scrambling up right behind them. A part of her urged Joy to follow the men into the forest, yet another heeded Ranulf's warning. And no matter, Joy was rooted to the rock beneath them, it felt, unwilling to go any closer. She growled at the boles and the branches, those sleek silver eyes narrowing, every inch of her body tensing. And through the ground, Saska felt something. A gentle tremor, and another, and another...

"Saska, Saska…we catch up with you at last." She whirled about, and there was Mar Malaan, all in flowing silk of copper and gold. Sweat ran profusely from his brow as he rode over the rise and onto the plateau. His silver-maned sunwolf Taro looked spent from the hunt, panting heavily. Malaan was breathing heavily too. "A fine chase," he said, wiping his brow with a sleeve. "Commendable, yes, but over now." He hauled a breath into his lungs as several other Starriders and Sunriders prowled up to his left and right. Joy's shoulders pulled in, body going taut and ready to spring. A low threatening growl rumbled out of her chest. "Come, child, enough games," Malaan went on. "You cannot hope to win in a fight. Return with us willingly and perhaps Lord Elio will forgive you."

"She's not going anywhere, oaf," snarled Leshie, dismounting from her horse, moving to Saska's side. Her red armour looked wonderfully rich and radiant under the sun, and her hair as well, bright as blood, godsteel shortsword puffing silver. "Any one of you star or sun people come any closer, you'll get a taste of the *north* in your gut."

A gale of laughter accompanied those words, the Sunriders guffawing in great mocking tones."You'll have to excuse my men," Malaan said, face swollen in a sweaty smile. "They do not think you capable of carrying out this threat, child."

"Send one forward and we'll see, *pigborn*."

The Butcher laughed now, swinging a leg over the neck of his charger and landing with a thump on the ground. Slack Stan remained in the saddle, looking utterly oblivious as to what was going on. "I like this," the scarred sellsword said. "Pigborn. Because you are fat, Sunrider Malaan." He laughed again. "Very good, little red."

"I know who you are." Mar Malaan said to the Butcher. "You are a captain of the Bloody Traders, and are making a grave mistake. But all mistakes can be corrected if the solution is spotted in time. I shall give you one." He gestured to Saska. "Let us have the girl, and we shall let you live. If not you shall all perish here today."

"I'm getting old." The Butcher stretched his back, bending and twisting from side to side. "And life's too long anyway. I've lived a good one, in my years. And where better to die, than upon this special mountain?"

Saska gave the pack a quick study, looking into the eyes of the men, and more than that, the beasts on which they sat. There was an unmistakable tension in them, some clawing restlessly at the ground, others growling at random, eyes darting here and there, ears pricked up and listening. *None of them want to be here*, she thought, *same as Joy*. She gripped her godsteel shortsword, and felt those tremors again, *boom…boom…boom…boom*…nearing.

"Money, then," Malaan said. "Gold, silver, and gemstones await you back at Lord Elio Krator's warcamp. Hand us the girl and it shall be so. Do this not and…"

"We shall all die. You have said that already, Pigborn Malaan."

"Then let me add this…" Mar Malaan paused a moment, eyeing the woods. Taro was looking at them as well, more wary than Saska had ever seen him. "Your brother," the perfumed Sunrider went on. "He will die as well, lest you surrender. The Baker, he is known as, yes? He and all men under your charge will be slain."

The Butcher shrugged. "Then I'll see him in the next life, and we'll get sotted there instead." He brandished his godsteel bastard sword. Merinius drew his blade too, and so did Owen Oat and the man they called Dobbs. They seemed to have held back to face off against their foe while the others had fled. *Though*…Saska could hear the sound of hooves returning now, charging urgently back down the trail toward them, pursued by that distant booming. The Butcher heard it too. He gave a smile. "We will not beat you, this I know, but even Bloody Traders have some honour, Malaan. A good death is a good prize, we like to say. We consider this a special plunder." He turned his eyes over the host. "Can any one of you give me the good death I crave?"

"I wouldn't call it good." Mar Malaan was growing impatient. "Having your stomach ripped open isn't good, *sellsword*. Nor is being eaten alive. This shall be your fate if you resist. Why bother? We'll only take the girl back anyway."

"Enough talk. You are known for it, I have heard. The pretty princess has said how you drone on and on and on, Malaan." The Butcher gave a quick glance back, then stepped before the rest. "Come, then, if it's to be blood, let's have it."

Mar Malaan hesitated, then gave out a grunting sigh and said, "Sesto. Bring me this man's head."

A monstrous sunwolf loped forward, as big as Agarro who prowled Lord Krator's estate. His mane was thick and gold; this was a young wolf, that was clear enough, eager for blood. The man atop him was equally brawny, links of copper discs covering his chest, a silken cape in shining bronze flowing down his back. The Butcher wore armour of his own; mail and a studded leather jerkin beneath his torn red cloak. He stood with his blade pointed forward. "Come, wolf, have a taste of my tattered flesh."

Sunrider Sesto drew a long thin spear from his back. He lowered it suddenly and charged right for the sellsword. The Butcher swivelled at once to the right, slashing, yet the sunwolf was swift as he was large, bounding away. Joy danced back from the action; Leshie and the other sellswords too, giving the pair space to fight. Ranulf was aside, staring the other way. *Into the trees. He looks* into *the trees.*

"Must do better, champion," mocked the Butcher. "I am sired of House Buckland, a powerful Bladeborn line. Bears, they are, these Bucklands. Come face me. Come face the *bear*."

Sesto grunted and his sunwolf lunged, the pair snapping and stabbing with fang and spear. The Butcher dodged again, moving aside, showing good speed and control. Once more the sunwolf pounced forward, and once more the Butcher slipped out of its reach, swatting aside the attentions of that spear with swift parries of his blade. Mar Malaan was growing anxious, Saska could tell, glancing to the woods, back to the fighting, away into the woods again. The wolf came once more, though this time the Butcher turned aggressor, ducking and rolling away from its charge, catching the beast with a good strong lunge to the leg. Blood spewed out from a wound there, weeping through its long golden fur. A roar bellowed, echoing down the hills. Malaan had seen enough. He threw out a hand, shouting, "You fail me, Sesto! Kill them, all of you! Bring me the girl unharmed." And with that the rest rushed in.

What followed was nothing short of chaos. Saska's blade was in her grasp in an instant, and she was pouncing toward the nearest foe, swinging. She caught a glimpse of Leshie rushing in, utterly heedless, stabbing and darting and scuttling underfoot, using her size and speed. Merinius, Dobbs, and Owen Oat were still ahorse, all three of them charging in as one. And from the trees, too, came the rest. Marco of the Mistwood and Umberto and Juri and Garth the Glutton, last of all, already screaming some war cry as they emerged. And behind them all was that pounding…those tremors shaking louder beneath paw and boot and hoof.

Boom, they went, and *boom* again, and *boom* and *boom* and *BOOM*…

Saska could hear crashing now, trees being shattered, bushes trampled. Suddenly, a great flock of birds came bursting from the woods some twenty or thirty metres in. The trees swayed, bending sideways. "Bear," she heard someone call. "Bear! *Bear*!" Garth the Glutton's face was pale, she saw, and the others who'd followed him into the trees looked terrified.

Saska could only catch a glimpse of it all before she had to deal with a sudden assault as a sunwolf leapt at her from a rock, but Joy was quick to it, slinking underneath, just as Saska thrust upward with her shortsword, slicing through its underside. Blood flooded down atop her and by the time the sunwolf had crashed down onto the plateau, the entire world was shaking.

She turned and faced the trees. The battle was ongoing in patches, yet others were turning too. *Boom*, went the world, *boom*, *BOOM*, and crash went the trees and the thorns and the leaves. Wolves and cats were backing away. Some were dead, and Saska saw that Dobbs was dead too, and Owen Oat, and Juri was on the floor, trapped beneath his horse. Marco had leapt from the saddle and was trying to free him. The Butcher was still battling Sesto and his sunwolf, and Mar Malaan just sat atop Taro, staring forward in horror.

And then it came.

In a great bursting crash of bark and branches it came, smashing its way through the trees, charging to a stop upon the plateau, roaring. That roar was unlike anything Saska had ever heard. The primal overwhelming force of it, filling all the world. She could only gape, eyes watering, as the moonbear reared on its hind legs, an immensity in silver and white, the sunlight sparkling off its crystal fur. Its bellow went on, and on and on, and even when it shut its massive jaws, that roar still echoed out and rang, down and away through the hills.

Saska blinked to clear her vision. Away to the sides she could see shapes scrambling away, sunwolves and starcats leaping off down the hillside, their riders barely able to cling to their saddles as they ran. Others were not so lucky. With a savage explosion of speed and aggression, the moonbear charged, snapping up one Sunrider in its jaws, sweeping another one down the mountainside with a ferocious sweep of its paw. A Starrider tried to leap up onto some rocks, but the beast saw it and spun, swinging, and away that cat went too, tumbling out of sight with a piteous cry.

By then every horse had spun and bolted, several tripping as they galloped for the slope. Saska saw one fall forward, crashing away beyond her sight, screaming. A second broke a leg and twisted sideways, rolling off down the rocks. Merinius tumbled out of the saddle as his steed followed in a blind panic, disappearing from sight. Marco of the Mistwood had given up trying to help Juri from beneath his fallen beast. He was gone too, running from the beast, and so was Umberto, dashing away behind some rocks with Garth the Glutton at his side.

Only the Butcher stood his ground, and Leshie too, and Ranulf, who stood aside, crouched by a boulder, staring up at the moonbear with a look on his face, a look of wonder and awe and something more. *Recognition*, Saska realised. *He knows this beast.* And then suddenly she realised it too. *I know him,* she thought. *I know this bear, I know him…*

She climbed from Joy's saddle, feet hitting the hard stone floor. Instinct drove her, something deep down inside. *Calm*, she thought, *calm*, as she ran her hand down her cat's sleek black coat, walking forward, slow and steady, moving toward the beast. Still it raged, swiping aside any cat or wolf who came near. She'd never seen anything like it. The violence. The ferocity. Yet she walked forward all the same into the cauldron of death. *Calm*, she thought to herself once more. *Calm. Calm...*

She heard a hissing voice behind her. "Saska!" It was Leshie. "Saska, what the hell are you doing!"

She ignored her. Through the corner of her eye she could see

Ranulf, staring at her now. His eyes were wide with worry, yet he was nodding. *He understands,* she thought. *He knows.*

She reached out a hand, fingers up, palm forward, in a pacifying gesture. She could hear Joy whimpering at her rear, and Leshie too, still hissing for her to stay back.

The moonbear gave another bellowing roar, standing up onto its hind legs, before smashing its massive front paws back down as the whole world trembled. It spotted her approaching, baring a mouthful of glinting silver teeth. Great curved claws dug into the earth, long as swords, ready to surge, ready to swipe and slay, yet something stopped it, something stayed its wrath.

"I know you," Saska whispered, still moving toward it. "And *you* know *me*."

"Saska…Saska, stop…*please stop*…" Leshie's voice was a faint noise now. She sensed Ranulf moving to join her, urging her to stay silent.

But that was it. It was just her and the bear now, looming above her, staring at her, studying her. Slowly, its teeth retracted behind its jaws, and its claws as well. The crystalline structure of its fur seemed to soften a little, the sharp lines and edges smoothing, where before they had been jagged and raised. *Calm,* Saska thought, and, "I know you," she said. "And *you* know *me*."

She was close, a half dozen metres away. The beast towered over her, eight metres tall at the shoulder even on all fours. She had heard tales of them, these bears, knew of them, read of them, yet seeing one...seeing it so close...

She had to remember to breathe, to stay relaxed, keeping that hand outstretched, whispering, "You know me," as she drew nearer...nearer. "You know my *blood*, and you know my *light*."

The bear was breathing evenly now, the dark veil of rage withdrawing from its eyes. Slowly, it began leaning down, and forward, the black tip of its snout shifting, nostrils flaring, *sniffing*.

Yes, she thought. *Yes, you know me.*

She gazed up into the bear's eyes, a vivid iridescent blue, though only one was working. The other, the *right*, had been cut through by a blade once, a famous golden blade in the north, she knew, held through history by many famous men.

She reached out to touch the bear's cheek, laying a hand on that strange crystal fur. It felt hard at first, then softened to her touch, the crystal points seeming to spread and open into fine hairs of silver and white. She could feel a deep thrum of affection move through the beast, a thrum of old joys and bonds, long since severed. And then came a rumbling noise from its chest, something she could understand. *I know you*, the bear told her. *I know your blood, and I know your light.*

She smiled. Tears welled in her eyes. "Agarosh," she whispered, giving the moonbear its name. "My name is Saska, great-niece to your old rider, Justo Nemati. And I humbly beg for your help."

52

Jonik

Jonik stared down at the sleeping man darkly. Even in slumber he looked smug, those plump lips twisted in a self-satisfied little smile. *I wonder what he dreams of?* he thought. *Enjoy them, merchant, they'll be your last.* He prodded him hard with his boot. "Wake up, Rose. You're needed."

The merchant's eyes broke open, blinking up at him against the gentle glow of dawn, slanting down through the woods. The smug smile on his face slipped away. "Something…something the matter, my lord?" His voice was hoarse. There was some confusion in it.

"Get up. Get dressed. We'll be waiting in the clearing."

The merchant mumbled a few more words, seeking explanation, but Jonik ignored them. He turned, marching through the tents and the trees to where the others were gathered in the glade. Some of the men were striking their shelters for the onward journey; others - Captain Turner's crew, mostly - were to stay, making a semi-permanent residence of this woodland while the rest continued up into the mountains.

It was as good a spot as they had found. Down in the low foothills of the northern Hammersongs, with good access to water sources and ample game for hunting, well away from any roads or mountain tracks, they would be safe, Jonik hoped. Others had suggested they stay somewhere stouter. A nearby town or village, perhaps, with inn-space to accommodate them, had been put forth by several of the men, and Sir Mooton had suggested that Emeric's ancestral holding of Osworth Castle might do as well - "Seeing as we're here, why not run that fat little knight, Sir Dudley Reed, out of your keep, Manfrey?" he'd said. "Win back your castle and give the lads somewhere warm and well-protected to stay?" - but that was folly at this time and nothing more than Blackshaw bluster. So these woods would do.

The clearing beside the campsite was a pretty place, bordered by spruce and pine, blanketed in sparkling snow. As Jonik walked out, the men who'd been striking their shelters stopped in their work. Emeric, Borrus, Mooton, Torvyn, Turner, Jack, and many of the others were already waiting. By the time Vincent Rose appeared, dressed in his outlandish winter garb, all had gone deathly still. There was only the song of waking birds, the whispering of a nearby rill, the more distant crash of a waterfall, somewhere away in the hills.

"Well now…what's this?" The merchant's pudgy face had never looked so awkward. He saw that half the tents had been struck, the horses laden with supplies, the warriors in the party readying to depart. "Oh, you're leaving? Of course. You wanted everyone awake, to say your farewells."

They'd been in this wood two nights now, to give them a chance to rest before moving on. It had been a long ride across the moors and heathlands of Northern Tukor, and not without its troubles. Heavy snows and local soldiers had curtailed them early on, though the last week had been mostly uneventful. *And no dragons,* Jonik thought. For all their early concerns, the skies had augured no such beast as yet, and it was thought that threat had passed. "Those leathery bastards don't like the cold," Borrus had said. "They're birthed in fire and smoke; snow and ice don't suit them." Seemed he might be right, or else their concerns had never been valid in the first place, and this talk of bearers being hunted was nothing but hearsay and rumour.

Emeric Manfrey gave answer to the merchant. "We're leaving, yes," he said. "But before we do, there's a matter that needs clearing up, Vincent."

"Oh?" The merchant played at perplexed. He stood facing them all, smiling uncomfortably. "What is this? Some sort of trial?"

"That's exactly what it is, *merchant.*" Borrus looked at him fiercely. He'd never liked the man any more than Jonik had. "You've grinned your way through these last months, but no bloody more. Time for you to answer for your crimes."

"Crimes? What crimes do you refer to, Sir Borrus?" His laugh was a nervous titter. "If you're still angry about my dealings with the Patriots of Lumara, with Pal Palek and other such men, well…I thought we'd moved past all that? Have I not been helpful, giving you use of my ship? And my nursemaids, who helped steer many of the prisoners back to health?" He gestured to Sansullio and his Sunshine Swords. "I have granted you use of my men as well, free of charge. And Kazil too. And even Harden…"

Harden spoke up then, grim and grunting. "You granted no one the use of *me*, Rose," he spat. "And none of what you've just said came from anywhere good. There's *nowhere* good in you. You've been in this for yourself all along. Go ahead, deny it."

"Deny what? That I consider my own life a precious commodity? Well forgive me if I do. I'll not argue that I saw profit in our alliance for my own sake, but I've also taken great pleasure and succour in seeing the poor prisoners of Palek's pits restored to health, and returned to their lands." He looked at Emeric. "My lord, you gave me your word. I have paid for your protection by our original accord and given you no reason to break it."

"That may be true, Vincent, or it may not," Emeric said. "That is what we're here to decide."

The oily merchant's expression remained resolutely bewildered. "I cannot possibly see what I might have done of late to inspire this…this farce." He looked hurt, then, putting on a new mask. "After all the aid I've given, all the generous support. It pains me to see…"

"Oh spare us, Rose," Borrus broke in. "We know what happened in Blackhearth." He gestured to young Devin, standing aside, a little sheepish. "The lad told us you went missing from that brothel, Freda's Fancy. A private room, he said you went to, but when he went to check on you, there was nothing but a whore in there, sitting on the bed, twiddling her thumbs. Now where'd you sneak away to, I wonder?"

"I…I don't know what you're talking about." Rose looked over at the young crewman. "Devin, goodness, what have you said? You've been…spying on me, all this time? For *them*?"

Devin was quick to shake his head. "No, Vincent, I've not, I promise. I just…Lord Jonik, he asked me a few questions and it wasn't like I couldn't answer them. So…so I told him, about the brothel in Blackhearth."

"And what did you say?"

"That you…you were gone, for a little while. You went to that room, the special one. The *Red Room*. When I knocked and came in to fetch you…you were gone."

"Yes, *gone*," said Borrus. "Gone through a secret exit so you could meet with Sir Rupert Swallow behind our backs. Isn't that true, Rose?"

The merchant balked. "No, it's completely false."

"Then where were you?"

"In the privy. I had to relieve myself. It's perfectly normal."

"For forty minutes?"

"I…my bowels take time to move, sometimes."

Sir Mooton Blackshaw laughed loudly, causing a few birds to go exploding from a nearby bush. "This is ridiculous," he said. "We've got a mountain range to climb and a fortress to siege. This little merchant means nothing. Let's have his head or no, and get bloody on with it either way."

Jonik rather agreed with the sentiment, though knew that Emeric wasn't going to see Rose's head leave his shoulders unless they had good cause. "We'll leave shortly, Sir Mooton, fear not," the exile said. He turned again to Vincent Rose, who was desperately trying to piece together his next lie, Jonik could tell. "You weren't in the privy, Vincent," Emeric told him. "The prostitute you were with - Henrietta - she told Devin that you'd gone 'on some special business'. Her words, not mine or the boy's. And she pointed to a secret exit in the wall. This Red Room is used for such, I am aware. The conducting of illicit affairs, and other matters. In this case, you took the chance to slip away, visiting with Sir Rupert Swallow. When Borrus and Torvyn went to speak with him that very afternoon, they were kept waiting for a short time before being permitted entry, they have said. Sir Rupert was with another guest. *You*, we have reason to believe."

The clear manner in which Emeric laid it all out left the merchant with nowhere to go. *His mask slips, little by little*, Jonik thought, watching him try to puzzle a way out. "I…no, I wasn't visiting Sir Rupert," he said. "I had only gone to visit a merchant friend of mine. To catch up on the latest tidings, and share an ale…"

"Share an ale?" Captain Turner chuckled. "Well now we *know* he's lying, aye! You only drink wine that I've seen."

"An…an expression," Rose said. "Shared a drink, I mean. And the latest news."

"Who was this merchant friend?" asked Sir Torvyn Blackshaw.

"Not anyone you would know, sir. A man by name of Buck Farley. He trades in furs."

"So you were meeting with this man, Buck Farley?" Emeric asked. "And this about you being in the privy? That was a jest, was it?"

"Can I not try to bring a bit of humour to proceedings? You have dragged me out here entirely unawares, ambushing me with these false accusations. I turn to humour, in my defence."

"You turn to lies," Borrus told him. "You met with Swallow in a bid to curtail us. You told him where we were going, what we were doing, and who we were travelling with. Those men…those three dozen men we had to kill, their deaths are on *you*, Rose." Borrus took a pace forward, a frightening look on his face. "I had to slay Sir Boleman myself. He was a good man, just doing his duty. He should have been warm in his bloody keep, waiting out the rest of his years, but no, he's dead, him and the rest of them, because of *you*. And two of Sansullio's men as well. Their blood is on *your* hands."

Vincent Rose looked like a cornered animal, eyes flashing from man to man, searching for a way out. "None…none of that is true," he said, his voice thick with pleading. "Why would I wish that? *Why*? I've always supported this mission of yours, to…to take the Shadowfort. I'm a coward, there, I admit it. A coward who only wants somewhere safe to hide while the war plays out. Where better than Ilith's refuge? Why would I want to interfere with that?"

"Because that's who you are," Harden of the Ironmoors snarled. "You rile and interfere and play your little games, but this one…this is no *game*, Rose." He gave a swift gesture to Jonik. "You've always wanted Jonik dead, and me as well, since I told you what you were in Calmwater, right to that smug face of yours. And others too. Sir Borrus, Lord Manfrey, Sir Toryn, Sir Mooton, Sir Corbray….everyone with a *sir* or *lord* against their name…you hate them all, for their noble blood. You're a bitter little upstart, Rose, always were.

"Damn right," said Borrus, looking like he wanted to give Red Wrath a good wash of the merchant's blood. "And don't give us that shit about wanting to scuttle off somewhere safe. You've got a hundred of your own havens from north to south. You want to hide, go to one of those."

"None are…none are the same as the Shadow…"

"Did you meet with Sir Rupert Swallow?" Emeric's voice cut right down to it once again. "Tell it true, Vincent. Did you meet with him?"

"No…no, I didn't, I swear I didn't…"

"Then why the lies? Why the deceptions? You've walked on the edge of a knife ever since we met you, playing your games, trying to win the affections of the men with your coin and these trips to the brothels. Oh, you have your needs, I don't doubt, and the men as well, but we're not blind to what you've been doing."

"What I've been doing? Generosity is a crime now, is it?" He looked at Devin, Sir Lenard, Cabel, Grim Pete, all men who'd willingly enjoyed that generosity. "None of you complained when I had those whores of yours bought and paid for. Or when I let you use my twins. I didn't do any of that to win support. Oh, why would I bother? You're all so loyal to this Shadowknight, aren't you. I could never change that, nor would I want to."

"Then why?" demanded Emeric. "What was your motive?"

"My motive? What do you think! To enjoy the attentions of a beautiful woman. To share that joy with these men." He glanced at Jonik with an ill-hidden hate. "Not *everyone* is celibate, Lord Manfrey. What, you're going to take my head because I employ whores?"

"No." Emeric Manfrey said nothing else, his next words seeming to falter. He appeared to doubt himself suddenly. "But these other matters…"

"What other matters?" The exile's pause gave the merchant strength. "Hearsay? Guesswork? Some ill-conceived idea that I met with Sir Rupert Swallow? Why should I? Swallow had reason enough to send men to chase us down anyway. I have no intention of seeing anyone hurt, no matter what that bitter old man says," he said, flicking a hand at Harden.

A short silence clad the clearing. Vincent Rose folded his arms, looking across those gathered ahead of him. Something resembling victory glittered in his eyes, Jonik saw. *He knows Emeric will not condemn him on evidence so weak, and without proof…* But Jonik had another to give testimony. He turned his eyes onto his former master, and gave a nod.

Gerrin stepped forward.

"What now?" Rose scoffed, seeing the man move into the open glade. "What does a duplicitous Shadowmaster have to say, then?"

"Nothing you'd want me to reveal." Gerrin stopped between the merchant and the men. "Was watching you, that day on the moors," he said. "That day Sir Boleman of the Bells caught up with us on the road. Watched your eyes when you saw that host coming around the lake. Saw the hope in them, at first…and then the *disappointment*, soon as you realised how few there were." He paused, looking straight into the merchant's eyes. "You were hoping for more, weren't you, Vincent Rose? You thought some hundreds would come, enough to overwhelm us. And when they didn't, oh…you didn't much like that, did you?"

"I honestly don't know what to say to that." Rose gave a stunted laugh. "Nonsense, that's the only word that comes to mind. What total and utter nonsense…"

"Was watching you back in Sutrek too," Gerrin went on. "Back at that manor of yours on Goldwater Row. I was old Benjy back then, though, you remember…the broken teeth, the Rasal accent." He paused again. Rose waited. A gleam of sweat on his forehead caught the sun, shining. There was a vein emerging from his temple, and distantly, at the edge of hearing, Jonik could hear the man's heart-rate beginning to rise, as he clutched at the Nightblade beneath his cloak.

Eventually, Rose broke. "*And*? Yes, I remember you as Benjy. You and those others. The big one and the small one, who turned out to be a Shadowknight and a mage." He looked beyond Gerrin, to Manfrey, and the others. "We're trusting *this* man now, are we? This man who entered your service under false pretences? This man who spent the whole entire voyage locked away in the brig…"

"Let him speak, Vincent," Emeric said calmly. "I'm interested to hear what Sir Gerrin has to say."

"He's got nothing to say. Nothing of worth, anyway." A droplet of sweat was now snaking down Rose's cheek. "Whatever he might tell you, the Shadowknight put him up to it. Harden says *I* want *him* dead? He's got that turned around. He's always wanted to put that black blade through my gut…"

"Quiet, Vincent." Emeric nodded at the former Shadowmaster. "Please, Sir Gerrin, do go on."

Gerrin cleared his throat. "Well, as I was saying. I was Benjy, back then. A harmless old man, who no one took much notice of. But during my time in the merchant's manor, I did a bit of digging." He looked at Rose. "Intercepted a few of your letters, specifically. You probably didn't know that, did you, Vincent? Wanted to see what you were saying, learn a bit more about what sort of man you were. Didn't trust you much, no, you stank of ill deceits to me…so I snuck into the office of that steward of yours, that young man Tizan who dealt with your correspondence. All without his knowing, of course. Had a good long look at *what* you were writing, and *who you were writing to*." He shook his head, tutting. "Incriminating stuff, all that."

Vincent Rose had gone pale. He swallowed. "Whatever you found…whatever you read, I…"

"The man's been plotting our downfall all along," Gerrin went on, turning to face the assembly. "He betrayed Janilah once, you all know…stole the Book of Thala from him, and he was looking to make amends. Wrote to Janilah of leading us into a trap, getting the Nightblade back to 'where it belonged', and seeing Jonik, 'back in chains'. If those letters had gotten out, we might have been in trouble too. Vincent rightly guessed we'd be stopped at Rasalan first, at one of the cities around Whaler's Bay. He even put forward that Calmwater would be most likely, seeing as we had Lady Kathryn with us, and that we'd want to return her first to her lord brother. Clever man, is this Vincent Rose, though not clever enough. If I hadn't switched out those letters, then who knows…Janilah might have actually received them, and had a good strong host to greet us."

"Is that true, Vincent?" Emeric asked.

The man could only gulp and shake his head, mumbling, "No… no of course it isn't."

"It is," Gerrin said, ignoring his denials. "Though your plans changed, I'm sure, once we reached the north and you found out that Janilah had gone missing. After that…well, you tried other means. This secret little meeting with Rupert Swallow, that was the latest of them. But when you saw that little force of three dozen riding around that lake, oh, how disappointed you were. Another failure, you thought. And I wonder…just what would you try *next*?"

Silence fell, then, but only briefly, as sure enough, the open clearing soon exploded into a storm of outrage. As soon as Sir Mooton bellowed, "Off with his head!" Vincent Rose spun and bolted, scuttling away into the woods. He wasn't likely to get far, not here. Swift as a deer, Cabel gave chase, with Big Mo charging by his side, and like a beast smelling blood, Sir Mooton couldn't help but follow, half his burly Blackshaw men going too, drawing weapons as they went.

"Don't harm him," Borrus shouted after them. "Bring him back unbloodied, you hear me!"

"He won't get far," Emeric said. He turned to Gerrin. "All that was true, I hope?"

He'd not been aware of it. Only Jonik had, though he'd hoped Rose might crack earlier. Still, it was nice to have that ace up his sleeve, ready to deploy, and Gerrin hadn't disappointed.

The former Shadowmaster pointed into the woods. "Doesn't that prove it? Innocent men don't run, my lord."

"Not typically, no." Emeric rubbed his beard. "You didn't care to mention this before? Tizan might have sent letters you weren't aware of, or else Vincent could have done so himself. You could have warned us to expect a welcome party when we arrived at Calmwater."

"I might have," Gerrin admitted. "Though in all truth, I wasn't thinking about that then. I was working on those notes for you, about the Shadowmasters and mages, about the best ways to siege the fortress, all that. Didn't think the merchant a threat, to be fair, and you seemed to have all that in hand."

"He was saving it," Jonik said. "This information. Gerrin has been watching Rose all along, Emeric, at least since he was released from the brig. He came to me a few days ago with this, after Devin had told us about what he'd seen at the brothel."

Emeric continued to consider it. "It sounds like you've been watching our backs for a while, Sir Gerrin. In your own way."

"I like to unearth people's secrets," Gerrin said modestly. "That's all. Seemed a good time for this one to come out, before we head on up into the mountains."

Sir Borrus agreed. "The timing couldn't have been better," he said, giving Gerrin a good slap on the back. "Well played, sir. And good riddance to that oily little man. I wasn't so happy about leaving him down here with the men, not while we're gone. Who knows what he might have done."

Brown Mouth Braxton took umbrage with that. "Begging your pardons, my lord, but I think we'd have been able to manage one feeble little wine merchant. Rose ain't no swordsman. Me, Jack, Sid, even Devin'd be able to handle that one. Once the lad pulls his nose out of the man's arse, that is."

Devin heard that from a few paces away. "I never…" he started. "I just…he paid for women, is all. What was I supposed to do, turn him down?"

Brown Mouth gave him a lopsided grin. "Point is, Rose woulda been no trouble for us. We'd have had a good watch on him, night and day. He'd not have been let out of sight."

"A watch only gets you so far," Borrus said. "A man like Rose can do much with his slippery tongue, Braxton. He'd have persuaded you to let him take a walk, and the next thing you know, he's off to the nearest town to buy every sword there, and is marching back to slay you with a good strong host at his back."

Turner chuckled. "You make him sound a monster, Sir Barrel. Not sure the man's got cause to quarrel with us lot. No, it's Lord Jonik he's been after, sounds like."

"Yes, but no longer," Emeric said. He shared a look with Jonik. "You warned me of his ambition the first day we met him in Sutrek. You said even then that he might try to claim the Nightblade off you, use it to bargain clemency with the Warrior King. Well, I suppose you saw through him better than I did. I was blinded by his uses, perhaps, and missed his dark intent. For that I apologise. I'll be happier, too, knowing he cannot stir trouble while we're gone."

Across the clearing, the sound of screaming alerted them to the return of the doomed man, as Big Mo came stamping back through the trees with Vincent Rose thrown over his shoulder, squirming like a fish in a net. His weeping was piteous, and the pleading started as soon as he'd been thrown onto the floor, landing heavily in the snow. "Kazil, you…you're meant to protect me," he whined, looking at his Piseki bodyguard. "And Sansullio, *good* Sansullio…you and your men…all of you…I pay you, *I* pay you. Not these. I demand you kill them. Kill them all. I order it of you. Kill them."

Neither Kazil, Sansullio, nor any of his men made a single move to help.

"Coin could never buy you class, Rose," old Harden mocked. "And look at you now, shitting your breeches in the snow." He spat to the floor. "The world'll be better without you in it."

Vincent Rose's only response was to wail, and put himself into a deep genuflection in the direction of Emeric and Jonik. "Please… please, *I beg you,* don't kill me. I…I admit I wrote letters to Janilah. I admit that, I do. I was scared, so scared of him, you saw me…you saw how I was when we met. I wanted to stop him coming after me, that's all. But that changed, I promise you, it changed." He looked up, tears staining his eyes. "Lord Jonik, *please.* Forgive me, forgive me my greed and my cowardice. I didn't meet with Sir Rupert, I promise it. I never tried to stall us, or have any of you killed. I play my games, that's all. I've always played my games." And he wept, loudly he wept, his moans echoing out through the sun-drenched clearing.

Jonik could scarcely look at him, or listen. He'd thought he'd enjoy the man's downfall, but now he just felt sad. "What shall we do?" he asked Emeric. Ever did he lean on the exiled lord's wisdom, and he needed it again today. "Do you think he might be telling the truth? About Sir Rupert?"

Emeric considered it for a brief moment only. "It's possible, but irrelevant. He admits to his early crimes and deceptions, and that's enough to condemn him. He has already sealed his fate."

Jonik nodded solemnly. "Then I will see it done." He stepped toward the kneeling man. Rose's eyes were bright with fear. "Lean forward, Vincent. I will make it quick, I promise."

"No…no please. *Pleeeease*….you can't!"

"Lean forward. Bend your head down. You'll feel nothing. It will be over before you know it."

"No, I won't. I won't do it. I won't!"

Jonik drew a breath. The Nightblade scraped from its black sheath, smoking. "Don't look, at least. Turn away, Vincent."

The man shivered violently, staring at the blade in horror. The stink of his evacuating bowels was appalling. Jonik took not a jot of joy from it all. "Look away," he whispered. "Be brave. And look away."

Finally, seeing no way out, the merchant came to some shred of acceptance. His hands made fists in the snow, squeezing, and he squeezed his eyes shut too. And as soon as he'd turned his head down, Jonik swung.

And so ended Vincent Rose.

53

Elyon

They watched the rider approach, a white banner of truce raised high in his right hand. "Well that was easier than I thought," quipped Sir Lancel, watching from the front of the lines. "They're surrendering already? It's only been a few days."

"If an Agarathi soldier died for every one of your glib remarks, this war would have been won and done weeks ago." Wallis Kanabar was not in the mood for jesting. "Tie that tongue up, Lancel, and be quiet. Elyon, come, let's ride to meet him."

Elyon nodded and gave Snowmane a kick of his spurs, trotting alongside Lord Kanabar and his big red destrier, Thunderhoof. The Lord of Rivers wore his heavy blue cloak, trimmed with silver and green, over a spectacular suit of godsteel armour. He'd had it scrubbed to a glistening shine, the lobstered plate overlapping in shades of silver and gold, and some jade and sapphire as well, with scrollwork and symbols of import to his house etched into the breastplate and pauldrons. "Never thought I'd have to wear this again," he'd said, when Elyon had first seen him in it, the armour offset by that great red bush of a beard. That was a few days ago, when the Agarathi had first arrived, swarming out of the misty marshes. Elyon had scarcely seen him out of it since.

The rider bearing the white banner was approaching from the heart of the enemy host, camped beyond the range of their defensive artillery upon the grassy plains. They had made no move to attack the night they'd arrived, instead pitching their pavilions and raising their tents and spreading out in a vast endless sprawl that made clear their staggering numbers. That night, their little fires had started to wake, popping up like stars in a black night sky. To east and west they burned, and away into the mists as well. Elyon had stood upon the ramparts, cleaned of the blood of the men he'd slain, listening to the gasps and mutters of the men around them. *They are frightened,* he had thought then. *They look out and see their doom.*

That doom had not yet stirred, though. It was thought they were resting after their march, gathering their strength for the assault to come, and waiting for reinforcements to arrive. That was the most troubling news; more were still coming across the Bloodmarshes, the scout reports had said, and not just Agarathi, but battalions of Lumarans as well. The Empress Valura had bowed to Agarathi demands and sent men in support of their invasion.

And not just here, Elyon thought. They'd had disturbing accounts from the west as well, of some great southern army marching on the Trident. It was widely believed that Dalton Taynar would have little choice now but to sail home and abandon the siege. "And how weak will that make us look!" Lord Kanabar had raged in council upon hearing that. "They'll be smelling blood, and will come surging across the Red Sea, make no mistake. *Here*!" He'd slammed his armoured fist on the table. "We make our stand here, show them how *weak* we really are!"

It was hard to stay strong, though, when facing such a boundless horde. A hundred thousand had been Sir Marland's initial estimate, but those had proven conservative. It was now thought that the Agarathi alone amounted to a force twenty thousand beyond that, and with these soldiers from the Lumaran Empire in support…

A hundred and fifty thousand, Elyon thought, as he spanned his eyes from left to right, surveying the staggering strength of the enemy host. *A hundred and fifty thousand men and mounts.* It was a scarcely conceivable number.

The rider was closing now, fifty metres away, sitting upright and proud in the saddle. He had dusky features common amongst the Agarathi; dark hair, tan skin, almond eyes, a braided black beard. As Elyon drew closer he observed a narrow nose, sharp and hawkish, and a mouth held in a tight line. That mouth opened once their horses had slowed to a trot, calling out, "My lords of Vandar, I have been sent to share word of a parley. The great Dragonlord Vargo

Ven would discuss terms. Accept by sending a rider of your own, bearing a white banner of truce, and the esteemed Lord of the Nest shall come."

"A lackey," Kanabar muttered to Elyon. "That's all he is." He looked at the rider. "It'll be done, messenger. Send word to Ven. Have him flap down here to meet us, under terms of holy parley."

"As you wish." The rider turned and rode back.

Elyon wheeled about on Snowmane as well. "I'll get that white banner-bearer out here," he said. They needed one on each side to satisfy the terms. "What do you think, Wallis? Does this say anything about Ven?"

Kanabar huffed. "He wants to get the measure of us, that's all. If you've any sort of hope this'll lead to a cessation of hostilities, think again, Elyon. Prepare yourself to bite your tongue. Vargo Ven will make some unsavoury demands, I have no doubt. Believe me, I'll have some of my own."

Elyon nodded, riding back toward the encampment. The wall-walks, ramparts, and towers of Dragon's Bane were teeming with bowmen at every crenel, the great mounted crossbows manned and armed, ready to fire. The two dragons that had been shot down four days ago had been slung up on the twin towers of the barbican, either side of the mighty gatehouse, as a further warning to the enemy host. Since that day, few dragons had been sighted, though once or twice the brutish Malathar had been spotted soaring across the front lines of the enemy army, bearing Vargo Ven in the saddle, with a pair of unknown wingriders flying at his flanks. Elsewise their strength was kept hidden, the full account of their Fireborn and riderless dragons concealed by mist and fog. And that unnerved the men as well. *They show their strength in foot and horse, yet not wing,* Elyon thought. It felt intentional, giving them no chance to prepare. *Men fear what they cannot see. And when those beasts are finally unleashed, when they come flooding from the fogs, screeching...*

Elyon rode on, toward the front lines of the army camped outside the Bane. *Almost forty thousand men,* he thought, *and how many of them are sick?* That sickness was fear, a fear that had grown and grown and grown these last long days, a fear that Elyon and the others could no longer fight. *It is a tumour, spreading,* he knew. His father had once taught him that fear was a plague in an army, as dangerous as the enemy's blades. If allowed to take root, men could break and run, shattering formations, destabilising lines. "And once that happens," he'd said, "the battle is as good as lost." Elyon worried for that now. He worried for how the men would react, when the fogs parted, when the skies swarmed.

"That was quick," his Uncle Rikkard called as he approached. "What happened?"

"Ven wants to parley. They need a white banner of truce to meet the terms."

Rikkard turned to one of his men. "A white flag. Bring me one." Within moments a pole was being handed to Rikkard Amadar and he was hoisting it aloft, banner fluttering.

"I didn't expect it to be you, Uncle."

"I want to hear what Ven has to say."

"As do I." Sir Killian rode forward as well on his barded steed, Whispering Wind, giving an order for his stout captain, Sir Soloman Elmtree, to accompany him. "Lord Rammas, Lady Marian, Sir Gereon, you as well," the heir of Oloran said. "And Lancel, Barnibus, come. Let us give them a show of force. Make it clear that *we* have nothing to hide."

Elyon made no move to question the logic in that. Killian knew better than he how to wield these sorts of war games. "Come, then," was all he said. "Lord Kanabar looks awfully lonely out there."

They rode out to join him, cantering two by two across the plains. Behind, the vast assemblage of their own forces were arrayed, banners flapping on the wind, ever-prepared should the command be made to charge. It was wearying, all this waiting, and many weren't sleeping well. Elyon could tell by the shadows around their eyes, the haunted cast to their faces, the smiles that had turned wan and wary.

The longer this waiting goes on, the more they will wilt, he thought. He wondered how many of the enemy were feeling the same. *All those boys out there, marched here under pain of death, barely old enough to have felt a woman's warmth, let alone stand in battle against Bladeborn men. Do they quiver as well, when they look upon the fortress, see its immense black towers, see the dead dragons hanging from the walls?*

They reached Lord Kanabar soon enough. He gave the group a scan. "Hadn't expected so many of you to come."

"We're going to set upon Ven and Malathar," Lancel said. "Cut off the head of the snake."

Kanabar wasn't impressed. "I told you about those tiresome quips, Lancel. And what are *you* doing here anyway?"

"Sir Killian said we should come, show strength."

"Yes, well seeing you is more likely to inspire an attack than a quiver," Kanabar gave a grunting laugh; it seemed his seniority permitted him the occasional jest of his own, much to Lancel's vexation. "You just sit back there on Monty, Lancel, and try not to say a word. Barnibus, keep an eye on him. And both of you try to look mean and menacing, if you can. If this is to be some show of force, I won't have Lancel grinning his way through it and ruining the effect."

The Agarathi banner-bearer was riding back out to them now, with three others with him. Elyon scanned the skies. He could see no sign of Vargo Ven just yet. "We have to be wary of a trap," he said. "The parley isn't so sacred as it once was." He was thinking of Harrowmoor, of the violence that had erupted there.

"I didn't realise Cedrik Kastor had gone over to the Agarathi side," Lord Kanabar remarked dryly. "*He* brought the Harrowmoor parley to bloodshed, Elyon, and he alone."

"Ven's just as bad, I hear."

"He might be worse, but bloodying a parley is a sin against the gods and not done idly. The Agarathi know that better than anyone."

It was the reason the parley was sacred, everyone knew - to prevent a repeat of what had happened at the peace talks following the War of Fire and Steel three and half thousand years ago. There, the treacherous sons of Eldur, Lori and Dor, had slain King Varin in vengeance for their father's defeat at the Battle of Ashmount. It was an act so foul and perfidious that ever since, men from all sides had asserted the parley sacrosanct. To draw blood at such a meeting would befoul the aggressor in the eyes of their gods, condemning them to a savage death, and worse, an eternity in whatever version of hell they believed in. *But not all men seem to care*, Elyon thought. *And this Ven might be more in the Lori and Dor camp.*

He put such thoughts aside as the host drew near. They were all ahorse, barring a single man who came prowling forward on a beastly looking sunwolf, its neck and powerful shoulders embraced by a magnificent golden mane. Elyon had never seen one in person, and for a moment sat in silence admiring its approach. He tried to imagine a great pack of them, charging into battle, barded in their special armour. He had tried to imagine that often, in truth; tried to imagine what it must have been like at the Burning Rock, with dragons in the skies and beasts on the ground, Sunriders and Starriders snapping and swarming, and Moonriders, those most fearsome of foes, bringing chaos wherever they went.

How many times had he daydreamed about that as a boy? How many times had he gotten lost in some book depicting it, read the stories, seen the drawings and tapestries and paintings? *Too many times to count,* he thought, *but this is no daydream, no book or story or scroll. This is real. Real death and chaos and horror and war.* Unbidden, he thought again of that boy, the boy he'd slain out on the marshes days ago, when he'd lost himself to the onslaught, when he'd killed his first host of men. *And how many more of them will I kill,* he thought, as he had then, *before this battle is done…*

"Elyon, look sharp." His uncle was riding beside him upon Twilight, his purply black destrier. His horse was armoured, as all of theirs were, in godsteel-plated barding and mail; chanfron for the head, crinet for the neck, petral for the chest, crupper for the hindquarters, and flanchards to protect the flanks below the saddle. As expected, the armour plate on Thunderhoof was particularly magnificent, given Lord Kanabar's enormous wealth, yet the others were well clad too. Some had draped caparisons over their steeds as well, embroidered cloths stitched with their house sigils and colours. It made for an impressive display, to be sure, though no more so than riding in on a sunwolf, or descending from on high atop a fire-breathing dragon. "You looked lost for a moment there," Rikkard went on. "Where did you go?"

Into the past, Elyon thought, *two decades ago, when I was nought but a babe.* And now here he was, amidst it all, amidst history. "Thinking of father," is all he said. "Trying to remember everything he taught me."

"A good place to go to prepare," Rikkard said, approving. "I would say I wish he was here as well, but after what we heard of the Trident, he might be needed more in the west."

Elyon nodded, saying nothing. He wished his father was here too. He wished that more than he could say, yet it would not serve to admit it. Sometimes he still felt the boy, that daydreaming child, walking through a dream. He longed to see his father's craggy features again, hear his voice, see that reassuring look in his eyes. *Eyes that have seen it all,* he thought. *Eyes that have looked upon a host like this and stood firm, and not once quivered.*

But his father was a thousand miles away, and could not help them. *And we have men enough here.* Killian was a decorated warrior, as was his uncle, and both had fought in the last war too. Elyon only wished Lord Kanabar was twenty or thirty years younger, or that Borrus was here, and hadn't gone off on that misbegotten adventure with his Shadowknight brother. *We could do with him as well*, he admitted. Jonik would be a force out here, a weapon of fear for them to wield. *We could have sent him into their camp, invisible, to slay their senior commanders and spread terror through their ranks. He might have crept up on Vargo Ven himself as he slept, and put the Nightblade through his neck…*

But that only made him think of his father's crippling. *He is used to sneaking into warcamps, my Shadowknight brother. No, we need no help from the likes of him…*

"That is Sunlord Avar Avam riding the wolf," said Killian, as the host neared. "He must be leading the empire's forces here."

"He's a known hawk," Lady Marian added. "With ties to the Patriots of Lumara. We should not find that surprising."

"He'll know that Pal Palek, then." Lord Kanabar was looking at the sunlord dangerously, and no doubt thinking of those poor souls who'd been imprisoned in the Palek's pits. "They're all one big cabal of cruelty, those Patriots. Elyon, when the fighting starts, fly down and take that one's head off quickly. It might cause his men to lose heart and flee."

Others murmured agreement. Lancel's eyes had turned to dark pins of anger. Only recently they'd learned that his own lord grandfather, Leyton Greymont, had been imprisoned in those pits as well. He'd been disembarked in Mudport, they'd heard, and was being escorted back home to his castle in the Heartlands. "I…I always thought he was lost in a shipwreck," Lancel had said, on hearing the news. "That's what my father always told me. He was lost in a shipwreck during the war."

It turned out, he'd survived that shipwreck, only to suffer a fouler fate, and for twenty years had festered in those pits, before Jonik and his crew had freed them. Lancel had been too young to know the man, but still, it had wounded him to think of what his grandsire had been through, as much as it had confused him over how to think of the Shadowknight now too. "He maimed your father, and killed Aleron, and I hate him for that," he'd said. "But…what he's done down there in the south, helping those northerners, freeing them…I…" He'd been unsure of how to express himself. "Well, maybe he's not *all* bad, El. Borrus wouldn't be with him otherwise, or Mooton, and these others who've joined him. He just doesn't seem like the murderous assassin we took him for."

He never was, not really, Elyon had to admit to himself. Jonik had been a tool, used by men for power and profit, and since his own emancipation, had turned to a nobler path. Much as Elyon wanted to hate him, he was struggling with that the more he heard. It vexed him, and greatly. *Why can't he just be a devil and be done with it. It would make it easier to seek vengeance then…*

There were two others riding with the host, aside from the sunlord and the banner-bearer. One was a dragonknight, riding a black horse in red dragonscale barding, one hand clutching the reins, the other holding onto a long black spear. His armour was black as well, in line with his order, though the great dragon-head pauldron on his right shoulder seemed to point him out as a commander. His cloak, a deep blood-red, was a shade darker than the other dragonknights Elyon had seen as well. "That one would make a good target too," Lord Kanabar muttered. "A thousand gold sabres to whoever kills him first."

The last rider wasn't so notable. He looked a common soldier, dressed in regular scale armour and cloak, though had on his back a leathern bag, fastened about his shoulders. Elyon watched him curiously, wondering what might be inside, as the banner-bearing messenger trotted forward and dismounted, planting his flag in the earth. Rikkard did the same, to meet the conditions of the parley. "We have an accord of truce," he said, and the Agarathi nodded, saying, "We do. An accord of truce." And with that, the stage was set.

A short silence followed wherein no one said a word. It was a bitterly cold day, a stiff breeze in the air, the skies a swamp of miserable grey cloud. *A storm,* Elyon thought. *Please, bring me a storm.* Eventually Lord Kanabar gave a grunt of impatience, looking pointedly skyward. "Well, where is he? If Ven thinks we're going to sit here at his pleasure, he's got another thing…."

The first distant thwump of wings interrupted him. A second followed, then a third, and out of the midst of the enemy army rose the massive black-gold form of Malathar the Mighty, conveying Vargo Ven to the meet. He came alone, absent his wingriders, the monstrous dragon landing ahead of them with an earth-shaking tremor. Elyon's spine stiffened to look upon him; on instinct he wrapped his fingers around the hilt of his blade, ready to summon the winds, should he need to. All were on edge at once, he sensed. All but Lord Wallis Kanabar, who looked upon Malathar, fearless.

He trotted forward on Thunderhoof. "Speak, Ven," he called up to him. "You called this parley. State your terms and be done with it."

Lord Vargo Ven ignored him. "The champion," he said, in a pompous Agarathi timbre. "This one who has mastered the winds. Where is he?" He scanned the host through a set of dark prideful eyes. The Lord of the Nest had a cruel face, and rich attire; black dragonscale armour of the most intricate detailing, accompanied by a glittery golden cloak to complement the beast he rode. The Fireborn liked to dress to match their fire breathing mounts, Elyon knew, flying into battle with them, colour for colour.

"You want to get a good look at the man who'll have your head, is it?" Kanabar bristled. "Well look no further.' He swung a steel paw at Elyon. "Prince Elyon Daecar, your doom."

Vargo Ven smiled down from his saddle, as Malathar shifted menacingly, smoke snorting from his nostrils. "You think this boy makes me quiver? Just because he can soar the skies?" His laugh was full of mocking scorn. "We Fireborn have owned the skies for millennia. One steel knight among the clouds does not make us tremble, Lord Kanabar."

"That one knight slew Ezukar, as I'm sure you know." The Lord of Rivers gestured to the fortress in the distance. "Squint and you may see him, chained up on our walls."

"I see him, as I do these two *Unnamed* you shot down, hanging by your gates." Vargo Ven sounded not in the least concerned. He studied Kanabar a moment. "You look much alike to your son, Lord Kanabar. And you share his uncouth manner as well. The same is true of many of you rivermen and mudmen, is it not so? You are close to a barbarian people, drinking and raiding and raping. This has been the way of it for centuries. You cross these lands you call the Bloodmarshes in your droves, pillaging and plundering as you please. But this will soon end, and permanently. My master wills it so."

"Your master is a tyrant king who slew his predecessor for the crown."

Vargo Ven smiled with disquieting confidence. Elyon wasn't liking this. "I suppose you must be referring to King Tavash, and the murder of King Dulian, at the hands of your Knight of the Vale."

"Don't you peddle those lies here," Kanabar warned him. "We know the truth of what happened, Ven."

"Do you? Now I wonder...how *much* truth do you know?"

"Everything."

"Everything?" And the dragonlord laughed, and laughed alone, his voice spreading out across the field. "No, I think not. You are starving men, living off scraps and rumours. Oh, it is so piteous to see." He laughed once more, though this time Elyon saw the dragonknight captain smiling too, and the Sunlord Avar Avam looked to be enjoying himself as well. The simple soldier with them grinned stupidly; he looked a halfwit, now that Elyon had a good look at him.

Vargo Ven remained atop Malathar, surveying them. He spotted Lady Marian and his eyebrows jerked upward. "Well now, a woman. So this is what you have been reduced to, cladding women in your godly steel? Even you of Vandar, so patriarchal as you are. You must be more desperate than I thought."

"I am Rasalanian," Marian told him. "Some women are trained there, in the use of godsteel."

Vargo Ven seemed to like her more than he did the rest. "The Rasal people are better than these Vandarians and Tukorans, I will admit. Yet still...a shame you were not born of the south, my lady. We cherish our women as you northerners do not. You need only ask Sunlord Avam here. There are many women among the ranks of the Starriders, in particular. They are lethal, these cats, and the women who sit astride them."

"Most lethal," agreed the sunlord, in clunky Piseki tones, thick and throaty. He looked upon the northern host with hatred. "You have customs...many customs we despise. You are hunters and butchers who treat your women ill. My Starriders will show you. They will show you how they feel on this."

"Now, sunlord," said Vargo Ven, "don't go spoiling the surprise." He gave a command in Agarathi and Malathar leaned forward, massive scaly shoulders rippling, to deliver the dragonlord to the ground. He slipped easily to the earth and paced toward them, that resplendent golden cloak catching in the wind. All others remained ahorse as Ven paced languidly, side to side. *Too much confidence*, Elyon thought, and not for the first time. *Is it just for show, or something more?*

"You're trying my patience now, Ven," Kanabar rumbled at him, his face turning as red as his beard. "Do you have terms to state or not?"

"Terms? What sort of terms might they be?"

"That's a no, I think," whispered Sir Killian. "We are wasting our time, Wallis. This man is known for his gloating."

"I am known, that is true." Vargo Ven was looking at Killian now. "As are you, Goldmane. You are a close ally of Lord Daecar, your new king. Or…or is another king? I get confused. Godrik Taynar, perhaps? You northerners have seemed more interested in slaying your own sires of late, than offering any threat to us."

"You're one to talk," Lancel blurted out from behind. "Dulian was killed by your own hand, everyone knows. Lythian had nothing to do with it."

Ven frowned at him. "And who is this one? He I do not know."

"I am Sir Lancel of House Greymont, Varin Knight, and…"

"Greymont," Ven interrupted. He ran fingers over his dimpled chin, carpeted in dense black bristle. "A house I do not know. And that makes you irrelevant. Do not speak again while the adults are talking."

Lancel looked close to unsheathing his blade, then, but Barnibus was quick enough to grab his wrist and whisper 'no'. Ven was watching all the while, smiling. *This parley is going ill*, Elyon thought. *Say something*, he told himself. *You are prince and champion of Vandar, are you not? Do not sit back and let him dictate.*

He dismounted, swinging himself to the ground, landing in a crunch of steel. Ven's eyes moved to him immediately, but showed nothing approaching worry, or wariness, that Elyon could see. "A fine suit of armour," was all the dragonlord said. "The silver and blue of the Varin Order has always been a handsome combination. And look at you all, so splendidly garbed and cloaked and barded. You make for a pretty painting, lined up like that. Very colourful."

Elyon moved until he was no more than two paces from the man, causing Malathar to emit a deep and threatening rumble. Ven raised a hand to calm him. "You still have control," Elyon said. "That isn't the same for all of you, is it?"

"All of us? You will have to explain yourself better, boy champion."

"The Fireborn Riders of Agarath. When I slew Ezukar, Sa'har Nakaan was nowhere to be seen. And Zyndrar the Unnatural did not bear Kar Von Karosh in the saddle when he fell." He paused. "He is dead as well, did you know?"

If Elyon hoped that news would cause the man to doubt himself, it didn't. "Oh. He is? Now who slew Zyndrar, I wonder."

"My father."

That *did* cause something, some brief flicker of concern. *His name still has power,* Elyon thought.

"I heard Amron Daecar had become a cripple."

"He is restored. Improved, even. He dealt with the Unnatural without trouble."

Vargo Ven mulled on something for a moment, a little twist to his lips. "Restored and improved," he said, nodding. "Yes, it is much as he said."

"He?" Elyon wasn't sure who the man was referring to.

"Yes, He. Him. The Great One." Ven said nothing more on that. He turned his eyes beyond Elyon, to the fortress he had come to destroy. "You want my terms, boy champion? Well, they are simple. Lay down your arms, and surrender. Give up this grim fortress of yours. Withdraw, and some of you may yet live. Your women, perhaps, and your children. But not you here, no. Your warriors will be purged in the fires, one and all, and all those of Varin's blood will fall. This is how it must be. But others who swear to live in the Glorious Kingdom of Agarath, the Kingdom of the Fire Father, Eldur the Eternal, may be given a chance to live on, once the fires have burned down, and this world of ours made anew." He turned his eyes on Elyon, and Elyon alone. "Do you accept these terms, Prince and Champion of Vandar?"

Elyon didn't have to consider that long. "No, I do not."

Ven inclined his head. "I cannot say I am surprised. So be it, then." He turned and made to walk back to Malathar.

"Wait," Elyon said.

Vargo Ven stopped, turning slowly. "Yes? You have something else to say?"

"I have much to say to you, Lord Ven, though will not bother to waste my breath."

"Wise. You only have so many left. Do not spend them imprudently."

Elyon met his eyes. *Time to fight fire with fire.* "It will be you, my lord, who lacks in that currency, should you make the mistake of attacking us here," he said. "I look upon this dragon of yours, and see nothing but an old slow brute, no match for me up there." He turned his eyes skyward. "These are *Vandarians* skies, *my* skies, and not yours to enter. So turn this horde of yours around and crawl back across the marshes to Blademelt. And you tell that tyrant king you serve that these lands are not for taking."

Vargo Ven's dark eyes twisted into a mock frown. "Tyrant king? Oh, you mean Tavash."

"Yes, I mean Tavash. Tell your master that…"

"Tavash Taan is not my master, not anymore." The dragonlord's smile was deeply unsettling. "We have a new king now, though to call him such would be an insult. The Holy Fire Father needs no such title. All he needs is a name."

He said no more, striding back to Malathar, climbing back up the horns and spikes that protruded from his black-gold scales. Elyon watched as he casually slid into the saddle, before calling in Agarathi for his commanders to depart. The banner-bearer came forward again to pull the white flag from the earth, then mounted up and rode away. The simpleton soldier, too, climbed down from the saddle at Ven's command, swinging the bag from his back, throwing it to the ground.

"What's this?" Lord Kanabar demanded.

"A gift" said Vargo Ven. "Something that belongs here. Call it a gesture of goodwill." He moved his eyes to Elyon. "I shall see you in the skies, boy champion. But whoever should prevail here, you or me, your army or mine, in the end it matters not. The fires shall spread regardless, and the inferno shall cleanse these lands, when the dread rises from his tomb." And with those words, and a final smile, he took flight, soaring away into the slate-grey skies.

The ride back to the camp was quiet. For a few long moments, no one said a word. Eventually, Lord Kanabar gave his thoughts. "He's as mad as that king he serves. This talk of the Fire Father. Of some great dread. He's trying to cripple us with fear. Don't let him. You hear me, all of you. *Don't let him.*"

But Elyon *was* afraid. Afraid for his men, afraid for his brothers-in-arms, and his captains and commanders, his confidants and companions. *And for myself,* he thought, *I'm afraid for myself.* He could not help that now. The riderless dragons, the strange red in their eyes, the reports of queer storms about the Wings, of infighting among the Fireborn, about some meet gone ill at the fortress of the Nest, and the theft or destruction of the Bondstone. Elyon hadn't known what parts of all that to believe. *And now this,* he thought. *This talk of Eldur. Of the Dread. Of ancient terrors rising.*

He shivered in the saddle. How could he not be afraid? He could dismiss it out of hand as Lord Kanabar did, but amidst all these strange happenings of late, something...something inside him believed it. *But I cannot show it,* he told himself. No, that would serve no one. *If I show my fear, what hope do we have?* He sensed the others were thinking the same. *They'll return to their men, brave-faced and defiant. And I must do the same.*

But first they gathered in the forward command pavilion, raised at the front of the encampment in shades of silver and blue. Lord Rammas had been the one to take up the bag the lackwit soldier had thrown down. He placed it onto a table with a gentle thump. "Open it," Elyon said, and he did.

Inside he saw bones, wrapped in a blue Varin cloak.

"Lythian," said Rikkard, stepping forward, peering in. "These are his remains."

Elyon's heart sank.

"It is confirmed, then," said Lord Kanabar. He put a paw on Elyon's shoulder. "There never was much hope, really. At least now we can let him rest."

"It isn't Lythian," whispered Killian. Elyon looked up, as Killian reached in and withdrew a red leather jerkin, folded beneath the cloak. He held it up for the others to see. "This is Sir Tomos's jerkin," he said. "Lythian may yet be alive."

Elyon doubted it. They'd tried to find out from Borrus what had happened to the Knight of the Vale, but had failed to receive word on his fate. Elyon had given up on that hope long ago. And now... now what did it matter anyway? Half the men here would likely be dead before summer.

"I'll have his remains sent to his father at Redhelm," Killian said solemnly, placing the jerkin back inside the bag, closing it tight. "Lord Pentar will wish to bury him."

Lord Kanabar gave a sombre nod. "We'll all be burying our sons and brothers and fathers soon, I fear." He gave a slow shake of the head. "Sir Tomos...he was a brave young knight, gifted and eager, and taken too soon. Who knows what he might have achieved if fate had let him try." He placed his hand reverently atop the bag. "Let us raise a cup to him."

The drinks were passed out, cups lifted, words spoken by those who knew the man in the traditions of Varin's Order. *So he hears us,* Elyon thought. *So Varin might hear of all the good that Sir Tomos has done, and permit him a better place at his Table.*

He took a small sip, and a small sip only, preferring to keep his head clear should the Agarathi mount a charge. He could not help but think of Aleron, and the night of his ascension at the family feast hall of Keep Daecar, when men had spoken of his deeds and victories, hoping that Varin might listen. *It wouldn't have helped.* Aleron was taken too soon, like Sir Tomos was, before he had time to claim any true victories of his own. Elyon sighed, wondering if Aleron and Tomos might be sat beside one another now, perched halfway down that endless table for all time, lost in eternal obscurity, sharing in their regrets.

The thought made him sick as he set down his cup, reflecting on the curse that was this Table. *It drives us all to war, no more. Would that Varin had never written of it in his scriptures. Would that this Table never existed.*

The world, Elyon Daecar felt quite sure, would be a better place without it.

54

Amron

The West Gate was busier than Amron had ever seen it, the smallfolk swarming like flies on a dead horse, begging to be let into the city. "It's been like this for weeks," Sir Gerald Strand told him, as they approached down the final stretch of the High Way. "Though it looks more chaotic than when I left, I will confess. Let me ride ahead, Lord Daecar. I'll have them cleared out so we might pass more easily."

Amron let the man ride on, a pair of his men going with him. "Ought we not fear a trap?" Rogen Whitebeard asked him, glaring at his brother as he cantered away. "Gerald has seemed nervous this morning. He expects Lord Godrik to send out a welcome party, I'm sure of it."

Amron might have feared the same, were it not for the host he'd summoned at Lady Crawfield's keep, and the simple matter of Gerald's own men. Though sworn to House Taynar, they had shown great reverence and obedience toward Amron ever since he'd slain Zyndrar the Unnatural, and those who'd put their blades into the dragon most of all. "We ride under a banner of peace and parley," Amron told the ranger. "Not even Godrik will seek quarrel, not now."

Rogen nodded and gave no complaint, though looked ready for violence all the same. A part of him hoped for it, Amron knew. Rogen Strand would like nothing better than to put a length of steel through his brother's gut, he wagered, for the ills he suffered in his youth.

The carts and wayns were in such numbers that they stretched a quarter mile from the gates. Some were sellers from the local farmlands, coming to hawk their wares. He saw wagons loaded with barrels of apples and pears, casks of cider and ale, great big bales of hay, crates of furs and wools for the winter, and much else besides. Yet those were only one in ten. The rest bore only possessions - clothes, keepsakes, small bits of furniture - and children, often trailing livestock as well, and even household pets. The dogs were in great supply, barking and growling and running amok, though most of the cats, chickens, and fowl were caged.

Amron had spent the last war on campaign, so never saw the city like this, though had heard from Kessia how hectic it had been. His wife had spoken of great throngs, flowing to Varinar in surging rivers, abandoning their homes for the safe harbour of the capital. He didn't imagine it would be so poorly run, though, not back then. Vandar was united at that time, the greathouses all dancing to the same tune after the death of King Horris Reynar in Eldurath. When his son Storris called his father's death murder, and a foul and craven crime by the Agarathi, none had argued. *No, we stood shoulder to shoulder against them, and now look at us, so fractured and broken.* Amron was quite aware that people were privy to his return now, and many would be wondering of his intentions. Will he try to fight? Will he try to take the crown? If anyone cared to ask him, he'd give them a simple answer. *No*, he would tell them. *My purpose is cooperation, not a coup.*

The crowds thickened yet more as they approached the gate, where they found Sir Gerald in privy conversation with its commander. The Greycloak looked anxious about something, that heavy brow twisted into a frown. "What's the problem?" Amron called out to them, hastening forward. He could see why the queue to enter had grown so long now. By the look of it, guards were taking payment from every person arriving, taxing them for the pleasure of seeking safety behind Varinar's walls. Every person, be they man, woman, child, young or old, able-bodied or infirm, were being charged. For a good many large, impoverished families, the cost would be prohibitive. "How much are these people being required to pay?"

The gate commander was not a man he knew. He wore a Taynar badge on his surcoat, rather than that of the crown and kingdom. *Godrik has handpicked loyal men for senior posts,* he knew. When Amron ruled Vandar by proxy during Ellis Reynar's reign, he would never have allowed such. The soldiers who guarded the capital gates and manned its towers and walls were to show no loyalty to any one house. As with the Greycloaks and Varin Knights, they were drawn from a range of houses, great, middling, and small, and sworn to serve the kingdom, not the interests of the man who wore the crown.

The commander gave answer. "One bronze scythe per man, my lord."

Amron pulled up before them. "Some of these families have eight, ten people among them. How are they supposed to afford that?"

"It's taxes, Lord Daecar, for the war."

"Yes, I can see that." Amron looked at Sir Gerald, who appeared to be mulling on whatever they'd been discussing. Evidently, it wasn't this news of the commoners being taxed that had him vexed. "What is the trouble, Sir Gerald? You've gone unusually pale."

"I was just telling Sir Gerald of fighting in the palace, my lord," the gate commander informed him. "It was taken, some days ago, by a host of well armed men. They have it blocked off and barricaded, firing upon anyone who comes near."

Amron hadn't expected that. Nor did he much like the sound of it. "Who are these men?"

"Yours, my lord. Daecar men, we think. Though how they got into the palace in the first place isn't rightly known." He caught the question in Amron's eyes. "There was no bloodshed on the steps," he explained. "It seemed to start from *inside* the palace, somehow. Our soldiers have tried to fight their way in, but it's been blocked off, as I say. And they're worried for King Godrik. Sir Bomfrey fears he's being held hostage, and will be harmed if his men get too close."

Amron liked this less and less. "Have they made any demands?"

"No, my lord, no demands." He frowned. "Well…just one, in actual fact."

"Yes?"

"That *you* be left to pass unhindered, Lord Daecar. To the city, and through this here gate, that is. Seems they knew you were coming this way."

Amron had heard all he needed. He spanned his eyes briefly down the great train of wagons and carts waiting to enter the city, and the many thousands milling among them with their goats and dogs and children. "A bronze scythe is far too dear a price for poor rural families to pay. I'll have you abolish this tax at once. Let all who wish to come to the city enter without charge. This is no time to be trying to fill Godrik Taynar's coffers."

"My lord? It's the crown's coffers the tax is filling."

Amron doubted that sincerely. This was blatant opportunism on Godrik's part, to better increase his wealth for when the war ended, and he had to fight to hold his crown. "Just do it. The crown is rich enough. I'll take this up with Godrik myself."

He rode on, as the guards moved aside and let them through. The inner ward was much quieter than one would expect, given the great numbers bustling about outside. Clearly many had been struggling to pay the charge and given no choice but to return to their homes, or else find some other refuge. Amron couldn't decide whether they were the lucky ones or not. *This city shall come under attack one day soon,* he knew, *and when it does, some of these people might wish they'd stayed away.* Still, he thought everyone should have that choice. "Did you know of this policy?" he asked Sir Gerald. "Was it in force before you left Varinar to find me?"

The man was still a little subdued. "No…no, my lord. It must be a recent policy, to better stem the flow of people through the gates."

"A man's capital city is his last refuge," said Walter Selleck. "Is that not the intention of these capitals of ours? Is that not why they're so heavily reinforced and guarded, why they have so many scorpions and ballistas and towers and soldiers? So that the people of these lands can come here, at their time of need?"

"Well put, Walter. I've always thought the very same." Amron sensed Sir Gerald Strand felt different, though he swallowed whatever response he might have given.

"Gerald never cared for the *little* people," Rogen said, looking darkly at his older brother. "He saw them as beneath him, vermin to be trampled and ignored. Don't believe that empathy you're seeing on his face, my lord. It's false. He isn't capable of it."

Amron was seeing worry, not empathy, and it didn't come from this about the smallfolk either. *He is worried for his uncle, and worried for himself,* Amron thought. *And he has good reason as well.*

He kicked Wolfsbane into a canter, speeding down the Street of the Sun in the direction of the inner wall. It was a bright day, warm for the season, and the waning sun was painting the cobbles in pleasant shades of gold. Ahead, the Ten Hills rose up, crowned in their keeps, within the ancient core of the city. Amron could see the top of the palace, coiled about its hill. A part of him expected to see a smoking ruin, but it looked well intact. He could only see a small part of it, though. *Perhaps the lower levels will be a wreck?*

They weren't. There was little to say that there had been any fighting at all, in fact, except for the barricades that had been erected atop the steps leading toward the entrance. At the foot of those steps, Amron found a great host of Taynar men, some hundreds, keeping guard and watch on the palace. They had the streets well cordoned to prevent any civilians from getting too near, though most looked to have stayed away. Sir Gerald hailed their leader - a stout Taynar knight called Sir Bomfrey Sharp, who had a nephew called Sir Quinn within the Varin Knights. Not Sir Bomfrey, though. He was a long-serving Taynar household man, though looked more like a man of the rivers or marshes than the Ironmoors, with an ample belly and thick, stocky legs, and a big red face made for shouting orders.

"We've been camped out here for three days," he explained to them. "Have considered mounting a charge once or twice, but…the king. We daren't risk it." He gave Amron a cautious look. "They've been waiting for you, Lord Daecar. Shouted that down a few times. Said you're to pass by unharmed, else there'd be trouble."

"I heard." Amron dismounted from Wolfsbane. "Walter, Rogen, you come as well. The rest of you, remain here." Already, he could see some tension between the Crawfield men he'd brought, and these Taynars. "There's to be no trouble," he called out, to all who could hear him. "You've heard of this Agarathi army at Dragon's Bane. You've heard how vast it is. This is a common threat, one that forces us to put aside petty rivalry. Any man who draws blood here, *any* man, from either side, will face the gallows." He drew the Frostblade, to a soft gasp of voices. "I may not be your king, or your First Blade anymore, but I am given authority through this holy sword, that is part of Vandar's Heart." He paused, looking over the assembly, making certain they understood. "*No* violence. We are brothers, all of us. Daecar, Taynar, it makes no matter. We are brothers in arms against the south." He thrust the Frostblade back into its sheath and limped his way up the steps.

Walter and Rogen were a welcome presence at his flanks. The pair's relentless bickering had abated ever since that day near Blackfrost, when Sir Gerald had joined their host, and a dragon plunged from the skies. It seemed they'd found common cause in their loathing for the Greycloak. "Do you think he might be dead?" Whitebeard asked. "My uncle?" His tone of voice made it clear he hoped that would be the case.

Amron hoped for the opposite. Others might lower themselves to killing kings, but he did not want any of his own men to have resorted to such things, no matter the circumstances by which Godrik took the throne. "We'll find out soon," was all he said. They weaved through the barricade of chairs, tables, and other pieces of broken furniture, as several figures appeared from the shadows beyond, bearing blades and looking weary. Amron recognised Sir Penrose Brightwood at once. He was a member of the Daecar Household Guard under the command of Sir Connor Crawfield, a young man of thirty, leal and capable.

"My lord," the knight said, bowing. "You came." He sounded relieved.

The man was bloodied and unwashed. He had stains on his breastplate and cloak, a gash on his cheek, and looked to be carrying an injury to his right leg that forced him into a limp. There were several other men behind him, those Amron didn't recognise. They were not Daecar men, so far as he knew, leastways not men he'd seen about his own keep. "Sir Penrose. You have command here?"

"Sir Connor posted me here, sire."

Amron nodded. A part of him had suspected that Sir Connor Crawfield might try to mount a rescue of Amara, yet for all that the captain was too circumspect. Nor did he have the men for it, or so Amron had thought. His cousin Gereth had told him that he'd been unable to send men in support of Sir Connor, despite the knight's requests, and his own mother had said the same. "I can't be sending men to die for this cause," Lady Crawfield had told Amron the night he'd stayed at her castle. "I have always liked Amara, but it's folly to try to rescue her." She'd put up no fight when he'd asked men from her, though, to join his protective escort to Varinar. "For you? Of course. You're my lord and now my king, Amron. Take as many as you need."

Yet clearly Sir Connor Crawfield had found support from somewhere. "Who are these men?" Amron asked Sir Penrose. He took a closer look at them, then spotted one he knew. "Sir Winslow?" He was an old grey-haired knight, long past his best, who'd once commanded the Lake Gate under Ellis's rule. "What are you doing here? You're no Daecar man."

"I'm a king's man," the old knight came back. "A true king, no matter which house they're from. That's you, Your Majesty. Godrik was never a king of mine."

Amron put the pieces together. Sir Winslow had been ousted from his post and replaced by a Taynar loyalist, just the same as the commander at the West Gate. This was his response. *I'm starting to see where Sir Connor found his support,* he thought. "How many of you are there?"

"Seventy five of us," Sir Penrose said. "Half are long-serving Daecar men, my lord. The rest are like Sir Winslow, or those paid for by Lady Bradbury."

"Lady Bradbury?" Amron shouldn't have sounded so surprised. Lady Jane Bradbury was a close friend of Amara's, a woman without house loyalty whose main mission in life was to help the poor, feed those who couldn't feed themselves, and make the world a better place. She would be one of the first people that Sir Connor Crawfield would have gone to for aid.

Still, there remained many unanswered questions. Amara was chiefly on his mind. "My sister-in-law is safe?"

"Safe, sire, yes," Sir Penrose confirmed. "She is with your brother, in the throne room."

Amron must have misheard. "My brother?" The last he knew, Vesryn had gone missing. For long months no one had seen him. "He's *here*?"

"Yes, sire. He planned the entire thing, he and Sir Connor. It's how we got into the palace unseen. There are few men who know these halls and corridors so well as your brother does, and with the Sword of Varinar, he was able to tunnel us in in secret. Without him we'd have been lost, sire. I shall lead you to them right away."

Amron didn't need to be led - he knew the way to the throne room well enough - but let Sir Penrose escort him all the same. They climbed the grand staircase in the main hall and came to the double doors that led into the throne room. Sir Penrose pushed right in. A great groan of wood gave out, drawing the attention of those gathered within. Amron gave the hall a scan. A table had been set up at its heart where several sat; others were perched upon the steps leading up to the misting godsteel throne, and others still stood at the windows, looking down toward the streets below.

"*Amron...*" It was Amara who was first to speak, and first to move. She pushed straight up from her chair and rushed toward him, throwing her arms around his shoulders, squeezing. "You're here....thank the gods, you're here!" She clutched him tight with her left hand, but not her right, he felt. When she drew back, he saw the reason; her right was covered in bandages, well-inked in blood at the tips.

"Amara...what happened?"

"Oh this...nothing, nothing." She tried to dismiss it. "I fell, Amron, that's all. I fell over."

He had a closer look. It seemed as though she'd had every nail on her hand torn off, but worse... "Your finger, Amara. Your little finger..." He crunched his fingers into a fist. "What did that bastard do to you?"

"I think my hand tells that tale well enough, Amron." She tried to smile. "It's nothing, really. A missing finger is of no concern to me, nor should it be you, and the nails will grow back. Others have suffered a great deal worse."

She gestured to the others assembled in the throne room. Amron recognised many at a glance. Sir Connor, cradling his arm around a wound in his gut. Sir Gilmore Gully, another of his household guard, looked to have been injured as well, bandaging wrapped around his right arm and shoulder. Jovyn was there too, to Amron's great relief, freed from his cell, and there was a teenage girl with fiery red hair who could only have been the leader of these sellswords his cousin Gereth had told him about. Even Lady Bradbury was present, with a tall armoured man at her side; her bodyguard, no doubt. And there were several other men he knew as well, knights who'd once held positions of note in the city, like Sir Winslow, only to be cast out by Godrik Taynar.

And Vesryn. My brother. He sat on the steps, the Sword of Varinar laid down beside him, giving off that glittery gold mist. He looked more slim than Amron had ever seen him, yet there was a steel in his eyes as well, as their gaze met across the hall.

Amara cleared her throat. "We'll have the room," she called out. "All of you, out. We have matters we need to discuss in private."

A procession of men and women moved for the doors, some sharing words with Amron as they passed, others simply bowing. Amron inquired as to the health of those who were injured, thanked Lady Bradbury for her support, asked Jovyn of any ill-treatment he'd suffered in his cell, and told the redheaded girl (her name was Carly, he soon discovered) that he was deeply sorry for the loss of her men, and that she would have a place with them, if she wanted it. In the meanwhile, Amara reunited with Walter, met Rogen Whitebeard, and then ushered them both out. Then it was just the three of them.

Vesryn stood from the steps. "It's good to see you, Brother. I hear you have a new Blade of Vandar now? And well mastered, to hear your tale."

Amron nodded. "Well enough."

"Well enough?" Vesryn gave a short laugh. "Well enough to defeat Zyndrar the Unnatural in single combat. If that is well enough for you, then the Agarathi stand no chance."

"Zyndrar was sent to hunt me, for this blade." Amron looked at the Sword of Varinar, the sword he'd held for twenty years. "Have you not been targeted, Vesryn?"

"I've been here, in Varinar," his younger brother told him. "For some weeks. No dragon would dare come so near."

"Here in Varinar," Amron repeated. "And before then? I was told you went missing long months ago. That you abandoned your post at Harrowmoor?"

"I did." Vesryn looked down at the Sword of Varinar. "It was the night that we learned of King Ellis's death. I got wind that Dalton Taynar was planning to strip me of my title. I could not in good conscience permit it. I chose exile."

"And yet here you are, in our good capital." Amron turned his eyes to the godsteel throne, misting magnificently upon the dais. "Where is Godrik now? Do you have him in the dungeons?"

"We have Nathaniel Oloran in the dungeons," Vesryn said. "And Alyn Porter as well. Gerald Strand will join them in due course. All three were present when Janilah threw Ellis from that balcony, I'm sure you know. All three stood by as their king was slain. And all three will pay the price."

"Where is Godrik, Vesryn?"

"He has paid his price already."

Amron's fears were realised. "Dead?" He saw the answer in his brother's eyes. "You're a fool," he told him. "There are hundreds of Taynar men outside on the steps. Thousands more in the city. They all hope their king lives; it is the only thing that has stopped them from storming this castle and taking all your heads. What now? What will happen when they find out you've killed him?"

"He didn't kill him," Amara whispered. "I did."

Amron whirled on her. "*You*? Amara…"

"I put a knife in his neck, Amron," she said fiercely. She showed him her hand. "He had two of his men ripping my nails off with a knife when Vesryn arrived to rescue me. Both were shot, but that knife…that knife was left on the table. Godrik went for it. I got there first." She clenched her jaw. "I'd do it again too. It was self-defence, not murder, but well-earned either way."

"It was regicide, Amara."

"There can be no regicide against a false king," Vesryn claimed. "He stole your throne, Amron. If Amara had not killed him, I would have. And that's all anyone will ever know. *I* killed Godrik Taynar. Me, the turncloak."

"That isn't the truth, Vesryn."

"It's the truth we'll tell, and who would question it? I can carry that burden, as I can the consequences. I will not see my wife suffer for this."

Amron looked his brother in the eye. "You know what this means. You know they'll want your head."

"Better mine than hers."

"Better neither of yours."

"You don't mean that." Vesryn picked up the Sword of Varinar and paced across the hall, until he was but two short paces away from him. "You don't mean that, Amron," he repeated. "My head. My head is well-deserving of removal, for all the wrongs I've done you."

Amron studied his brother's eyes. *Does madness fester in him? Has he been led astray?* Those were the rumours he'd heard, yet he saw in those eyes only cognisance and clarity. *And shame,* he realised. *Shame, regret, and acceptance for what is to come.* "What wrongs have you done me, Vesryn?"

"Many wrongs, Amron. Many wrongs that stemmed from a single mistake I made in my youth, a mistake borne of envy, greed, and cowardice." He did not remove his eyes from Amron's, even as he confessed his sins. "Your son," he said. "The Shadowknight. I was complicit in that scheme, bought and paid for by the Warrior King. I helped Cecilia Blakewood sneak into your pavilion that night. I helped her poison you so you'd not remember a thing, so you would think it was Kessia with whom you lay. I did that because I was envious of you, Amron. Envious of the power you wielded, the love and respect you drew. And Kessia. I was envious of her love for you most of all. I was young, foolish, *pathetic*. I thought she might turn from you, if she'd learned of what you'd done. But I never told her. I couldn't. Not once did I…"

Amron struck his brother with a closed fist, knocking him bodily to the floor. "You'll not speak of Kessia again. You'll *never* speak of her."

Vesryn looked up from the ground, his lip split open, weeping blood. He nodded. "I deserved that. I deserve more…much more." He stood, a little groggily, to take his place before Amron once again. "Strike me again, Brother. Strike me down for what I've done."

"*What you've done*?" Amron spoke through his teeth. His hand was clutched now at the haft of the Frostblade, knuckles white. "What you've done is kill my son, Vesryn. My firstborn son, your own nephew." He thought back on it, on the night of Aleron's ascension. Vesryn had been drinking heavily that night, blaming Hadrin, swearing vengeance. *But he knew all along. He knew all along who the Shadowknight was.* Even then, Amron had suspected his part in it, yet Vesryn had spoken so sincerely of his mistakes, and his grief had felt so real. *And I believed him. Fool that I was, I gave him the benefit of the doubt.* But now…now here it was, the cold hard truth of it. "You helped the Shadowknight enter the Song of the First Blade under a false identity," he said. "You protected him, as Fitzroy Ludlum, and made sure he reached the final. You, Vesryn, are responsible. You are responsible for the death of my son."

"*No.*" Vesryn stood before him, shaking his head. "I never knew Aleron was to be killed by Jonik, only defeated. I never knew he would die, Amron. I would never have gone through with it if I had. Never."

Amron studied his face. *Jonik*, he thought. It was the first time he'd heard the boy's name. "My son, Vesryn. My firstborn son…"

"He didn't know," blurted Amara from the side. "I swear to you, Amron, he didn't…"

He raised a palm to silence her. "And what of *me*? What of your own brother? Did you know that the Shadowknight…this Jonik…had been sent to kill *me* that night in Rasalan? Did you know I was to be assassinated by my very own blood?"

Vesryn made no attempt to deny it. "Yes," he said, without hesitation. "I knew that, Amron."

Amron drew the Frostblade from its sheath. It took all he had not to swing it. "I should kill you right here and now."

"You should. I agree." Vesryn went down onto his knees, placing the Sword of Varinar at Amron's feet. "I took this blade from you, through treachery. Ever since, I have tried to make things right. I denied Janilah when he demanded I give it to him. I ran and cursed myself as a turncoat when I knew the Taynars had taken power. I came here to remove Godrik from the throne, so you might assume it on your return. I have done as I intended, and have nothing left to do. Except die, by your hand. As it should always have been."

"No…" Amara came suddenly forward, reaching out, teary-eyed. "Amron, please, don't. He paints a ghastly picture, but really…really it isn't so sinful as all that." He turned slowly to look at her. "*Please*, Amron. He was young and foolish and jealous when all this started. And ever since, he's been under Janilah's controls, unable to wrestle free of him. Show clemency, please, I beg you."

"Kill me, Brother," Vesryn said from the floor. "Take up the Sword of Varinar again. Wield them together, the gold and the frost. Win this war. Do what you were born for." He lowered his head to show his neck. "You are returned, and Amara is safe. My part in this is done. Kill me."

Amron stared down at the nape of his brother's neck long and true, wondering. Amara was still bleating in his ear, yet he didn't hear her. His fingers tightened…tightened about the hilt. For a long moment he stared, yet could not bring himself to do it. *I will not become like them. I'll not.* Grunting, he thrust the Frostblade back into his scabbard.

Vesryn looked up. "Brother, please…"

"You are no brother of mine. You gave up that right when you got into bed with Janilah Lukar." The depth of that was still dawning on him. He'd not known that Cecilia Blakewood was Jonik's mother, yet it made sense, given what he'd heard of the woman of late, whispering into her father's ear. He felt sick to be the subject of their schemes, sick down to the pits of his stomach. *And twenty years,* he thought. *For twenty years Vesryn has been hiding this from me.*

He could barely look at him, kneeling there at his toes. He turned to face Amara. "I shall do what I can to clear up this mess," he told her. "What you've done here…" He shook his head, more disappointed than he could say. "I came here to free you, Amara. By diplomacy and negotiation. Now look where we are. Yet another king slain, and the good name of Daecar sullied. And for what? To make me king? Do you believe that this is what I would have wanted? To pay treachery with treachery…to continue turning that wheel?"

"You *are* king, Amron," Amara said, defiant. "Deny it all you like, but you are."

"And do you think that the thousands of Taynar soldiers outside will agree? Do you think they will just accept me on the throne when I walk out there and announce to them that Lord Godrik is dead?"

"Yes, I do. You inspire like Godrik never could. You hold the Frostblade, and the legend of how you got it is already spreading. People look at you as a man fated to lead, Amron. As Varin reborn, returned and restored. Who do you think would deny you? Who would dare tell *you* no."

Amron had no answers. "Dealing with our enemies is all that matters," he said. "It is unimportant who wears the crown."

"You don't truly believe that."

"I do. Call me king all you like, I'll not sit that bloody throne." He thrust a finger at it, too irate to consider the notion. *I should have it melted down,* he thought, *forged into armour and blades.* "It has been a curse ever since King Lorin fell to that kraken," he went on. "The throne was cast for Varin's line. That line is ended, Amara. *Ended.* All who sit it now are but shadows."

"You are no shadow, Amron. Goodness, listen to yourself. You're a greater man than King Lorin ever was, and half of the Varin kings besides. If Varin has an heir, it's you. You were born to rule."

"I was born to rule a house, not a kingdom."

"Yet you ruled for twenty years. Ellis was never king, everyone knows it. You have sat the throne since your twenties. That you've never perched your backside there makes no bloody difference."

"Enough," Amron snapped. He was not going to further this topic right now. "I am *not* king, Amara. Get that through your skull."

"Then you'll leave it for Dalton Taynar, to take up when he returns? You'd let a man like *that* rule instead?"

Amron wasn't understanding. "Why should Dalton return? He is sieging the Trident."

"No longer," Amara said. "The siege has been broken and Dalton is sailing home. Godrik told me himself, before I sawed through his rotten old neck. Dalton sat outside those walls for months and did nothing. That is the man you would let be king ahead of you?"

Amron had to think on that a moment. It was ill news. "Is his army intact?"

She frowned. "I don't know, Amron. Reports are thin on the ground. But it's a defeat whichever way you look at it. The Agarathi will smell weakness here, we can be sure of it."

In that, at least, he agreed. If they scented blood, they could sail for King's Point, and if they took the city with their dragons, they'd have a staging post to strike them here. "We'll have to bolster our defences at the coast. I'll send word to the Twinfort and Green Harbour to send reinforcements at once." He thought on it some more. "A retreat is better than a rout," he went on. "If Dalton believed his army would be crushed, sailing home was the sensible course."

"It was the craven's course."

Amron was tiring of her objections. "And what do you know of war, Amara? What do you know of sieging a fortress, of leading an army in the field? Dalton Taynar is a dour man, yes, and uninspiring, but he's a sound strategic mind, and a good knight. It is easy to judge him from here. I shall reserve that judgement until such a time as I can speak with him myself, and know more of what has happened."

"We know what has happened. He sat outside the Trident for months, twiddling his thumbs, giving the Agarathi a chance to muster a response. That's what happened, Amron."

"By order of his lord father," Amron came back. "Left to his own devices, Dalton might well have commanded differently." He turned away from her and ignored any further complaints. A thought came to mind as he looked down at Vesryn, still kneeling on the floor. "You say I should hold that blade again, Vesryn. You say I should wield both the gold and the frost?" He would never hold the Sword of Varinar again, he knew. He'd made that promise when he set it aside down that quiet old corridor in Keep Daecar, the very night Aleron had died. "I won't. Yet Dalton's return gives us a chance to make something right. He shall take it up, as First Blade of this kingdom. No matter what treacheries the Taynars have colluded in, Dalton Taynar is worthy of that post."

Amara scoffed. "As worthy as a whore who wears a crown. And what about Brontus Oloran. If we're discussing beaten semi-finalists in the Song of the First Blade, why not Sir Brontus? He's a better swordsman than Dalton is."

"Don't play the dolt, Amara, not with me. Giving Dalton that blade might just appease the Taynars and their allies while we sort through all this mess."

"It won't. No one cares about the post of First Blade anymore. It's meaningless, with the Varin Knights so scattered. There is only house loyalty now."

"Yes. And that's why we have a great deal to do to mend the rifts between us. The rot must stop. It starts with handing Dalton that blade, and going from there."

Amara breathed out, yet had run out of ways of denying him. She turned to look down at her husband, silent on his knees. The pain in her eyes was unmistakable. "And…him?" Her voice softened. "He loves you, Amron, you must believe that. Everything he has done…"

Amron didn't want to hear it. "He'll be placed in the dungeons with the other traitors, until such a time as we can consider his fate." He did not look at his brother again. Turning, he began pacing from the room.

"Where are you going?" Amara called after him.

His footsteps echoed as he marched through the hall. "To announce the death of a king."

55

Cecilia

Cecilia paced her bedchamber, swirling a cup of wine between her fingers. *Something has happened,* she thought. *It's been too long. Something has happened.*

It had been three days since she'd had word from Hog or Gerret. Before then, one would come to her every day or two - mostly Hog - climbing down from Tyrith's forge to give her the reports she'd requested. Those reports had been worrying too. "The lad asks constantly about returning to the black door," Hog had told her, more than once. "He's got this look in his eye, my lady. Like he's possessed. He won't stop until he's had a chance to study it."

He wasn't possessed, Cecilia knew, just *obsessed*, but that could be just as dangerous. There *was* something beguiling about that portal door, in the way it shifted and shimmered, in the great abyssal nothingness that lay beyond. Cecilia had often heard people speak of an unexplainable urge to throw themselves from high places, a bizarre sensation that forced many to steer well clear of balconies and bridges for fear they might just follow through. The portal door inspired something similar. *Even I felt that urge when I stood before it*, she reflected. *That urge to step within…*

She took a sip of wine, pacing, worrying. *Three days. Three days and still nothing.* She wondered what might have happened. Could they have lost track of time? Might Hog have wearied of making the trip to report nothing of note? *No*, she thought. *This is something different, something worse*. She'd commanded Hog to come to her every two days at worst, and he wasn't likely to ignore her order. *Something must have happened,* she told herself again. *I need to go up there. I need to find out what...*

She didn't much like the prospect of that, but by now she had little choice. She donned her cloak, girdling her waist in her favourite belt, complete with sheath and dagger, and stepped out into the corridor. For a moment she thought about summoning Sir Mallister to accompany her, but decided against it. He wasn't yet aware of the secret tunnel system, no more than he was what lay beyond it. A select few knew about Tyrith, about Ilith's forge, and fewer still this portal. *And better it stays that way,* she thought.

The shadows were as menacing as ever, painting the walls and floors in sinister demonic shapes. Cecilia tried to ignore them as she paced on, finding solace in the presence of every guardsman she passed, standing at his post, or wandering on his rounds. But those were few and far between and soon enough, gone entirely. When she descended through the secret doors and corridors and reached the entrance to the tunnels, she was all alone. For a moment she hesitated. *Three days,* she thought. *Perhaps I could give them a fourth? Maybe Hog will come to me tomorrow? Or else...or else I could wait until daylight, and travel the tunnels then?*

She walked on. It would make no difference, not here. Day or night, these tunnels were bathed in darkness. *There is no day or night here...*

She held her torch before her, the uneven rock walls giving form to shapes more foul and forbidding than ever. *But shadows,* she told herself. *They're only shadows. There is nothing to fear here...you've travelled these caves a hundred times before.* Yet the fear of her torch going out was ever-present, and more so tonight than ever. For reasons she couldn't fathom, the winds were blowing and whistling more restlessly, causing the flames to flicker and dance more fiercely than she'd like. More than once she had to turn and put her back to the breeze to protect the flames, crouching to shield the light. *Don't go out,* she would pray. *Please, don't go out.*

By the good grace of the gods, the torch remained lit, as she traversed those caves and caverns, clambered through the tunnels, passed over the rickety wooden bridges erected over yawning chasms. Some of the passages here were tight, her shoulders almost touching the walls. Others opened into great wide open chambers, the fire in her grasp nothing but an island of light amidst a sea of black. She reached the chamber where Gerret had slaughtered the labourers and knew that she was close. The bodies had been removed, the furniture too, and the bloodstains had been washed from the floor and walls, yet the stench of death remained. *I killed them,* Cecilia thought, as she had the last time she'd been here. *Gerret swung the blade, but I sealed their fate. I killed those men, me.*

She reached the crossroad, where the tunnels diverged. To the left led the path to the foot of the stair; to the right, the way to the portal door. Cecilia stood for a moment, listening. She could hear nothing but the high distant whispering of the winds through the tunnels, and the gales beyond, as they howled about the mountains. Yet something made the hairs on the back of her neck stand on end. The cold, perhaps, and the quiet and the darkness. Or maybe something else.

She turned left, pacing briskly now, eager to escape the claustrophobia of the caves. To either side of her two cliffs of rock rose up; she marched between them, out into the night, where the face of the mountain soared away into the inky skies, cut with the ancient switchback stair. She peered up through the mists and the darkness, hoping to see a blur of light up there, but there was nothing. *The fogs are too thick,* she thought. *And the forge is set back from the top of the stair.* There was no reason she should see anything from here.

Yet something cold was crawling up her spine all the same. *Tyrith,* she thought about shouting. *Hog. Gerret. Are you up there? Do you hear me?* She looked at the twisting stair, dreading the climb. She was getting a dull feeling in the pit of her stomach. *He has fallen,* she thought, staring up. *That's why no one has come. Tyrith tried to escape, to climb down and study the door, and fell to his doom.* And what would her sellswords have done then? she wondered. Obedient as Hog was, he might just come and confess it to her, but not Gerret. *No, he'd be just as likely to slit Hog's throat and slink straight out of the city, to better avoid my wrath…*

The answers were at the top of the stair. She stepped forward and started the climb.

The rope made it easy enough. Hog had done a good job fixing it, yet all the same, with her nerves so frayed, Cecilia took it slow, pulling at the rope every few steps to make sure the brackets were secure. Halfway up, she thought she heard someone crying out from above her, yet told herself it was only the wind. *The shadows make shapes and the wind makes voices. I'm going mad,* she thought.

She drove herself on through the biting gale, and the heavy thick pall of fog. Visibility was poor, and growing poorer as she climbed. By the time she reached the last couple of switchbacks, she could scarcely see more than a few steps ahead. She hurried on, reaching the final set of stone steps where they turned in to face the plateau. At the top she was faced with great banners of grey fog, moving slowly on the winds. Through them she could glimpse firelight now, within the cave beyond. She listened for the beating of Tyrith's hammer at his anvil but heard nothing.

She paced on, then stopped.

Her eyes fell.

On the ground at her feet were bootprints. They were large, heavy, heading *toward* the forge. Yet others…she could see others going the other way, smaller ones, and in some places there were others still, all churned and mixed together, and…

She saw the blood.

It was sprayed across the snow, gouts of red spotted amidst the white. Her heart rose up in her throat, as the winds pulled away the mists and, *there*, there on the ground ahead, she saw the shape of a body.

Tyrith, she thought in a moment of panic. *No, please…*

She rushed over, drawing her godsteel dagger… and saw the missing front tooth, the skinny frame, the crooked nose. Gerret had not died well. His stomach was open, guts hanging out. In both his hands were daggers, clutched eternally in his cold dead grasp…

"I didn't intend to kill him," said a man.

Cecilia whirled, brandishing her dagger before her. "Who…who said that?" Her voice squeezed out, stricken with fear. "Who's there!"

"Don't tell me you have forgotten my voice, Cecilia."

She peered through the darkness, through the swirling ribbons of mist. "F-father?" For weeks she'd felt hounded by him, haunted by the blue ghost. *And now he reveals himself. Up here, in this ancient place.* "Father, is that you?"

He stepped forward, body blue and shimmering. The Mistblade was sheathed, his fingers clutched about its hilt. One by one he unfurled them and his body took form, hardening to cloak and cowl, flesh and bone and beard, ragged and grey. "Sheathe your blade, Cecilia," he told her. "Put the dagger away."

"*No*." The word tumbled out on a breath. "No…I'll not."

"You don't trust me? Your own father?"

"You're not him. You're changed." She took a step back, her

right boot catching on Gerret's arm. It almost tripped her but she maintained her footing. "Why did you kill him? You said…you said…"

"He attacked me first. Thought me some vagabond, perhaps, who can say?" He looked down at the dead man. "I let the other one go. The bigger one. He and Tyrith, they fled down the stair."

"Where?" Cecilia could only blurt.

"Where do you think? He has followed his obsession. And yours."

The door, she thought. *He went through the door…*Her eyes fell back to Gerret. He was bone white, dead a day or so, she guessed, frosted and frozen. "You…you've been waiting for me?" she asked tremulously. "All…all this time?"

He took a pace backward, fading into the fogs. "The forge is warmer. Come."

She followed, though at a distance, creeping past Gerret's body and toward Tyrith's workshop. Her father went ahead of her, clad in mist, moving with an eerie calm. The mouth of the cave opened before them. A pair of braziers burned inside, setting a sombre orange glow to the forge. Janilah moved toward one, lifting a poker to stir the coals. He glanced outside, into the skies. "It's not you I've been waiting for, Cecilia," he said.

She frowned, not understanding. "Who would come here but me?"

He placed the poker down, had another brief look outside. She saw now that he wore armour beneath his heavy wool cloak, the armour Tyrith had been hammering for him. It caught the light of the fire, a glimmer of green and gold. There was no better godsteel plate in all the world. He saw her looking at it. "Tyrith has made me a suit fit for a god," he told her. "As I asked him." He made a mocking sound. "How do you like it? Do you think it fits?"

"It fits you…perfectly, Father."

"Does it?"

Silence settled. She was trying to figure through things. *Has he come to fetch his armour? Is that it? Why would he let Tyrith go? Why, after holding him captive up here for so long?* She asked none of those questions. "You've been gone so long, Father," she said instead. "Why…why reappear now?"

"Why indeed?" He paced slowly to the rear of the forge. The only part of the armour he wasn't wearing was that helm, wrought with miniature versions of the Five Blades surging from the crest. He picked it up. "I never liked this piece," he said. "Too garish for my tastes. But I understood what Tyrith was trying to do. The Five Blades. Ever did he believe I would gather them."

"And you *will*," she said at once, falling into old habits. "You still…you still may, Father."

He turned to her. "I will. I may." He shook his head. "I won't. It was never my fate, Cecilia. *I* hold the torch. *I* light the way." He shook his head. "Lies. Those were the lies I told myself for decades, lies I let myself believe. But I have come to see the truth now. I have come to accept who I am."

Who you are, she thought. *A tyrant. A monster. A madman.* Those were the slurs being thrown about the city, the kingdom, the north. She wondered if he might admit it. "And who are you, Father?"

He placed down the helm. "A man," he said. "A king. A *dragon-slayer*." He almost smiled at that last, though not quite. "That is all I ever was. Those are the limits through which I was never meant to break. Ever did I believe otherwise. Ever did I believe in King Galin's promise. But no…I was wrong. *Divinity*, Cecilia, was never in reach. Not for me."

Does he mean it? Does he? "What…what happened to you?" she whispered. He *had* changed, she saw. This was not the monster she'd expected. This was not the ghost she'd feared. "After…after the riots. Where did you go, Father?"

"To a place I never expected." He stood in thought, his eyes moving once more to the mouth of the cave, and beyond. He scanned the skies, then said, "I had a second heart attack, Cecilia. I needed rest. I needed time. I was given kindness. Kindness I first took as cruelty, yet it was kindness all the same. What happened that day…" He shook his head. "That is not the man I want to be. This…" He rested his hand on the pommel of his blade. "This blade led me ill, I know that now. And my ambition. But no longer. My vision is clear. I see the truth." And he looked at her. "*All* of it, Cecilia."

She swallowed. Her body was primed to flee. Across the plateau, down the steps, away from him forever. *He knows,* she thought, looking into those eyes. She gulped once more, throat dry, and said. "What are you going to do, Father?"

He didn't answer. His hand brushed over the helm again, fingers tapping on the tips of the blades. "I killed my own father," he said. "You've known that all along. I heard you speaking with Raynald about it, in Sir Garfield's room, denying it, yet it's true. I pushed my father down those steps to take the throne. I did that for the good of the people, the good of the realm. I did it for Jaylor, for the vengeance my brother deserved. But I did it for myself as well. He was weak and craven, and deserved it. Yet kinkilling…patricide… those are crimes more foul than any. The day I threw my father down those steps was the day I cursed my soul. The gods do not reward kinkillers, Cecilia. I think I know that now."

He turned to face her. There was no anger in his eyes, no hate, nothing. He looked upon her calmly. And that unsettled her more. "And Rylian," he said. "My son, and my heir. People say I killed him too, don't they?"

"They…some…They're the mob, Father. It doesn't matter what they think…"

"You killed Rylian," he said.

She wanted to flee, yet her feet felt frozen, stuck to the floor. "I…"

"You provoked him, Cecilia. *You* stirred that violence. And you gave Sir Maxwell the order. 'Kill him', you told him. 'Kill him. Your king commands it'. I remember that now, Cecilia. I remember everything."

"I…" She was starting to panic. *If I run, he'll chase me. I'll never get away.* "For *you*, Father. I did that for you. Rylian…Rylian was a threat. He could not leave that room. He'd have…have taken your throne. I was only trying to protect you."

He smiled at that. "Protect me? Or protect yourself?"

"Father…"

"You are a spider, Cecilia. All these strange and random occurrences. All these disparate little details. Oh, they seem unrelated, yet they're not, not really, they're all part of the same web. And when you look at it, when you look hard, you realise there was a spider behind it all along."

"I don't…I don't…"

"You had Sir Rottlor hanged for setting up those riots. An innocent man, and a good knight. His only crime was not seeing you coming." He set his eyes on her and said, "Those riots were arranged by *you*, weren't they?"

She tried to speak, but couldn't. Only the spluttery beginnings of a denial came out.

"You might have killed me in my bed, while I recovered from my heart attack. But no, you couldn't. Not with Sir Owen and Sir Kevyn and Sir Edwyn watching me, night and day. Not with my physicians swearing to my recovery. It would have looked too suspicious. No, you needed to get rid of me in a different way. Something that could never come back to you. Like a public riot, in which you were present. Who would blame you? Who would ever believe you had a hand in that?"

"I…no, that isn't true, I…"

"You had your spiderlings in the crowd. You had them whispering into the ears of malefactors and disgruntled men. You made sure enough of them were armed. You made sure there would be plenty of people to call out those slurs, to throw fruit, to spark things off. You blew on the embers of a simmering fire and turned it into a blaze. Chaos, Cecilia. You thrive in it. And how you've thrived, grooming Raynald in my place, and Tyrith now too. Perhaps you think he might make a good king instead? Perhaps you think the heir of Ilith is more deserving of the crown that Galin Lukar stole?"

"I'm just…I'm trying to…"

He broke her off. "Perhaps you're right," he said, unexpectedly. "Lies, Cecilia. They started three hundred years ago, when Galin went to Vandar's Tomb. When the *promise* was made. 'Win the War Eternal,' the spirit of Vandar told him, 'and you'll have a Table of your own'. *Lies.* Lies that led him to conquer Tukor, slay King Neyrith, sever Ilith's divine bloodline. And you think, perhaps, it might one day be restored? That Tyrith might be raised to the throne, that ancient line of kings remade?"

She *had* wondered that. But she only said, "No, of course not. I would never…"

"Raynald, then? Perhaps you would like to hear that young Robbert has been killed at Eagle's Perch? A crow would come cawing that news, and I wonder…would you grieve or rejoice to hear of your nephew's death? To see Raynald…Raynald who is *so very fond of you*…ascend in his place, and mine?"

"No. You're back now, Father. *You* are my king. You. Always."

"Am I? Truly?" He shook his head. "I have listened. I have watched. I know what is said about me. No, Cecilia. I am no one's king, not anymore." He gave a shake of the head. "And I have only myself to blame."

Those words shocked her. *He admits it, openly?* She could only look at him, wordless.

"You think I would blame *you?*" he asked her. "That I would condemn you for what you've done?" He thought on that a moment. "You are what I made you, Cecilia. Can I deny that you're all I wanted you to be? A part of me is proud to see what you've become. A part of me knows that you have supported me these long years. That you stood beside me, obedient and loyal, running my schemes, dirtying your hands in place of my own. Yet of late, you have started to see the folly in my designs. You have started to doubt me, fear me, worry for what I might do. You realised I was never going to gather the Five Blades. Long before I did, you saw the truth in that."

A trick. He's trying to trick me into confessing. "You may yet, Father. There is still hope…"

"Hope?" He laughed. "What hope is there? I built a world of shadows and ghosts, a world that thrived in darkness. But the drapes have been opened, Cecilia, and the light let in. Those shadows and ghosts have fled to their corners. Elyon Daecar wields the Windblade, and wields it well. His father has returned. A man more loved than any. A man who is my opposite, in many ways, and will rally the north behind him, I'm sure. Vesryn remains elusive, and your son…" He looked at her. There was something in his eyes she'd never seen. Regret. Shame, even. "I am sorry for what I did to you. Perhaps you have hated me for it, ever since. You will say you gave the boy up willingly, and may even believe it, but it isn't true. There is no free will for those under my wing. You were never given a choice."

I never was, she silently agreed, yet still she said not a word.

Once more, he glanced past her into the skies. For a long time he said nothing. Eventually, he went on. "I almost died," he murmured. "Twice I almost died, my heart ravaged by the things I have done. Where did it start? I have wondered this often of late. Was I always this tyrant? This monster? No. Those who have known me longest know I was a good man once. Yet I let my ambition get the better of me. And this sword." His hand clutched at the pommel of the Mistblade once more. "It has only served to darken my path. *Kill him. Kill her. Kill them all.* Those are the words it whispers to me, whispers that have grown louder and louder these last months. I have fought hard to ignore them, yet that struggle is one no man can win, not after so long, not with so many setbacks and frustrations and doubts. The night Rylian died, it was whispering those words. *Kill him,* it said. *Kill him, kill him.* And that day at Galin's Post as well. *Kill them all,* it told me. *Kill them all. Kill them all.*"

He slid his hand down, wrapping his fingers around the hilt. For a moment he closed his eyes, listening. Then he opened them and said, "No longer, Cecilia. The blade seeks blood, blood and death, yet it is not the blood of men it craves. No. There is a richer ichor it yearns for now. And *this*...this I *will* give it."

He removed his cloak, picked up the five-pointed helm, and placed it onto his head. The armour set was complete. There he stood, majestic, clad in exquisite plate armour, as a great king of old. *As a god,* Cecilia thought.

He took a step toward her. "You should go, Cecilia. It isn't safe up here."

She frowned at those words. "You'll…let me go freely?"

"Why should I not? Do you think I wish to blacken my soul yet further by taking your life?"

She still couldn't believe him. *He'll wait for me to turn, then strike me from behind. He won't want to look into my eyes as he does it.* She backed away, still facing him, feeling the sting of the cold behind her, hearing the great howling of the winds.

"Leave, Cecilia," he told her. "Follow Tyrith. Help him. Go to the son I denied you."

"My…my son…"

"Yes, your son. The Shadowknight. Jonik. He makes for the Shadowfort, I know. Go to him. Meet him. I know you have always wanted to."

"But…the portal…it doesn't…the gate isn't…"

"*Go,*" he said, more firmly. "Go, before I change my mind. "

She drew away from him, from that look in his eyes, the flicker of the man he was. *That man is still in there,* she thought. *He cannot have changed so quickly. He cannot. One day soon, he'll snap, and kill me.* Somehow she knew it. *I must be away from him for good…*

So she turned, rushing out into the cold. At once the fogs gathered around her, cladding her in swirls of mist. She punched through them, toward the top of the stair, slowing only as she reached the first step. She turned back just once as she prepared to make the climb down. Through the mists she saw her father, in gleaming green and gold, stepping out of the forge, looking to the skies. There seemed to be a great sense of purpose etched into his eyes. And distantly, up there above her, she heard a faint deep *thwump* of wings.

It isn't safe up here, he'd said. She knew now who he'd been waiting for. A beast in purple and black.

She sped on down the first switchbacks, clinging to the rope, legs shaking so hard she almost fell. The gaping abyss tumbled away beneath her. Above, she could hear more wing-beats, growing closer. She was halfway down when the first screech echoed out through the world, as the dragon descended for the duel.

The noise sent a deep shiver through her bones. *The Battle Upon the Plateau*, she thought, in a moment of wonderment, stopping, looking up. *The Fight at the Forgotten Forge.* She could see nothing through the swirling mists, but could hear the beast, screaming up there, and in her mind's eye, she could see him…her father, stepping forward, Mistblade to grasp, purpose in his heart, garbed all in godsteel plate. Janilah Lukar was to write more lines to his story up there tonight. *Dragonslayer*, she thought. *That is how he defines himself now.*

She did not stop to listen, nor wait to find out if her father would live or die. Instead she took the advice he'd given her. *Follow Tyrith. Help him….Go to the son I denied you.* Reaching the bottom of the stair, she ran, dashing through the winds and the fogs, surging back into the tunnels, past the opened blockage, and the wooden scaffolds, down the passage, around the bend, until she saw the black door, shimmering.

She stared at the portal, at that great empty abyss, beguiling and frightening at once. *Does death await me within?* she wondered. *Are Tyrith and Hog already gone?*

She did not give herself time to consider the consequences of it. Standing before that strange glistening door, she let herself be drawn forward. *Jonik*, was her last thought, as the cold blackness reached out to take her. *My son…*

And into the void she went.

56

Jonik

"No one," Jonik said, returning to the men. He had scouted ahead up the final passes on the approach to the Shadowfort, searching for sentries who might call the alarm, and finding none.

"You're certain?" Gerrin asked him. "You checked the high perch like I said? The one on that ledge, a little down the path across the bridge?"

"I did. There's no one there."

"What about the gate itself?" Emeric asked.

"A sentry either side, on the wall walk," Jonik told him. "I saw no one else."

Emeric looked to Gerrin. "Is that normal?"

The former Shadowmaster, Emerald Guard, and Sworn Sword of Janilah Lukar gave a craggy grin. "You've read my notes, Lord Manfrey. Perfectly normal, yes. Only men of the Shadow Order pass this way. They have no reason to suspect an attack."

They'd been careful anyway, taking their good time climbing the route over the last week since leaving Turner, Jack, and the rest down in the woods, along with the horses. It had made the going even slower, losing their mounts, forcing them to walk in their armour, or else bear it on their backs, but they had little choice. There had been some grumbling about that during the first couple of days, where the route was easy enough that the horses might have managed it, but those complaints had soon gone silent as they ventured higher. Only Shade could have traversed the route. The rest would have broken a leg or slipped down some ravine, sure as day follows night, Jonik knew.

Sleeping hadn't come easy either. Every night they made camp as far off the path as possible, though that wasn't always easy, not up here. The further up into the mountains they went, the harder it became to find flat places to pitch their tents. Mostly they just slept in their bags and furs, shivering against the cold upon the bare rock floor, though two nights past they'd found a cave in which to rest. They'd not lit a fire though, no, despite the calls to do so. "We give no warning that we're here," Emeric had said. "As Gerrin and Jonik are wont to tell us, we never know who might be watching."

So far no one had seen them, that they knew of anyway. Sentries were placed come nightfall to watch the passes ahead for movement, and Jonik himself had ventured forth many times to scout up the path, Nightblade to hand, unseen. This had been the latest and last scouting, and yielded the same result as before. No lookouts. The path to the Shadowfort was not being watched.

"Two sentries," Emeric mused. He rubbed his short black beard, gold eyes looking up the track as it wended away through the rocks in a sharp ascent. It was deep into the night, and bitter cold, and Jonik could tell the men were restless. *They want to storm the gate, and soon*, he thought. *They want this done by morning*. "Jonik, how shall we proceed?"

They had two options, between which Jonik had gone back and forth. The first was for him to climb the wall in secret, slay the sentries, and open the gate. Then the fun would begin. The second involved Gerrin, and subterfuge. The old Shadowmaster would appear with Jonik as his prisoner and demand the gate be opened. Would it work? Jonik couldn't say. Did he trust him? Well, that was the more troublesome question. *Because I do,* he thought, and that brought him scant joy. Despite his best intentions, the old man had worn him down.

But not enough to choose that option. Call it defiance, call it a need to do this himself, but Jonik was going to see this done alone. "The winds aren't so fierce as they might have been," he said, giving answer to Emeric's question. "That'll make the climb easier. And the mists around the gate are thick. They'll offer good cover for you to approach. I'll scale the ramparts, kill the lookouts, and open the gate. It's the surest way."

Unexpectedly, Gerrin gave no remark to the contrary. All he did was dip his grey-bristled chin as though it was the choice he would have made. It wasn't, Jonik knew well enough, but he'd asked Gerrin not to speak against him in front of the men, and he'd been good to his word on that as well. He'd been so leal and loyal these last long weeks, in fact, that he'd been granted permission to join them, and even given armour and weapons. *He is one of us now,* Jonik thought. If this was some trap, he'd have to give the old man his credit. But for the life of him he couldn't think how.

"We'll be waiting, lad," Sir Borrus Kanabar said. He wore a fine godsteel breastplate, with pauldrons, gauntlets, greaves, gorget, and a few other smaller pieces of plate over a glittery shirt of mail. The others were similarly garbed in the offerings cobbled together from Lord Merrymarsh's armoury, with quilted clothes beneath and cloaks on top, to ward off the worst of the cold. Borrus gave a shiver anyway, despite all those layers. "Let's get this bloody done, shall we? It's freezing. I need to get Red Wrath swinging to warm myself up. And I want to get that blasted life debt off my shoulders too."

"You paid it already, Borrus, at the battle by the road."

"No." The big knight shook his bald head. "Killing Sir Boleman of the Bells was no debt I wanted to pay. His death is on Rose, may he rot. But there…" He pointed up the pass. "Up there there's a mage or Shadowmaster with the name of Borrus Kanabar written all over him. Or maybe I'll kill this Shadow King you've been going on about, and make this trip worthwhile."

Jonik met eyes with Gerrin. The Shadow King had been much on his mind these last days, yet for all that there remained much mystery about the man, mage, or whatever he might be. For all Jonik's questions, Gerrin had few answers. The old man could write out notes on every Shadowknight and master and mage at the fort. He could list their names, their ages, their skill with blade and bow, whether they carried old war wounds or not, fighting stances against which they would be weak or strong. But for all that, details on the Shadow King remained scarce, and elusive.

"Can only tell you what I know," the man had protested, when Big Mo demanded something more certain on the king. "Or I could lie, if you'd prefer? Make something up, just to satisfy you. But I see little point in that." There were up to seven mages left at the fortress, that he knew of, after the deaths of Ghalto and Parsivor, though he couldn't say for certain which might be there. Only two were in permanent residence; the others came and went, he said. "Might be all seven are lurking about. Might be only the two left, but best be wary all the same. Expect the worst, hope for the best. Isn't that the way?"

Those two were the senior pairing. Fhanrir, a shambling old creature with a long nose and empty eyes, who did much sorcery in the occult. "He's the one does the ritual work on the Shadow King," Gerrin said, "the blood magic that keeps him alive." But that was only a guess. A guess based on how grotesque Fhanrir looked. Dark magic stained the soul, and that staining manifested in a rotting outer shell, all knew.

The second was the more concerning. The Steward, Gerrin had called him, for his true name wasn't known. He was in charge at the Shadowfort, running the place for his king. "Looks young," Gerrin explained. "Kinda plain. But you never can know with these folk. He's a master illusionist, most like, and a Whisperer, and a powerful one, that I know for sure. It's how he controls the order for the king, keeps them all in line. Be careful of his *voice*, that in particular. Else he'll take you under his spell."

Even Sir Mooton Blackshaw, great bag full of bluster that he was, had quivered a little at that. For weeks he'd bellowed about wanting to duel a dragon, but the idea of losing his wits to some spell was enough to make him quake. "I don't like all this trickery," he'd declared. "A man should be able to look his enemy in the eye, and face him with axe and blade. A battle of strength and speed and skill, that's what it's about. Not this sorcery."

Few disagreed. Jonik didn't either. He still dreamed sometimes of that night at Russet Ridge, where the Whisperer Ghalto had tried to bewitch him. His voice wasn't one a man would soon forget, nor that face of his, that demonic rotting face, emerging from the mild facade he'd been wearing all along. Gerrin had said the Steward would be greatly more powerful, and that worried him. *It took all my strength to repel the creature's will. What if the Steward should seek to do the same?* Jonik knew what to expect. He'd had dealings with these mages and had a Blade of Vandar in his grasp as well, protecting him. Yet the others? What of the others?

He could not worry about that, not now. If all went to plan, they'd overwhelm the Steward and the Shadow King both. *Take their heads, and their voices won't matter.* It had worked well enough on Ghalto, anyway.

"I should go." Jonik turned his eyes across the group. The senior men were with him; Emeric, Borrus, Sir Torvyn, Sir Mooton, Sansullio, and Gerrin. The rest stood aside, huddled among the rocks, awaiting their commands. *A good group,* Jonik thought. *Committed and loyal. I won't let them down after dragging them all this way.* "Be ready for when I open the gates. Gerrin, you know where to wait until that happens. If you hear nothing from me half an hour from now, assume I'm dead. I'll let you decide what to do then."

He left them with that unpleasant quandary, though had no intention of failing. Cloak furled about him, hood up, he picked his way up through the rocks, following the cliff that rose up to his left. To his right a plunging ravine fell away into blackness, across from which more peaks climbed up into the chill night skies, fading from sight in the fog and clouds. Jonik faded too. Gripping the hilt of the Nightblade, he let its power imbue him. His body vanished from sight.

He still had to be careful, though. Snow was his enemy here, as much as the men of the order. If one of the sentries saw boot prints appearing by magic they might just smell a rat. He kept to the rocks, then, avoiding the drifts, diligent and cautious in his step. Before long he was summiting the narrow track that led up to the ancient stone-paved plateau, beyond which the Shadowfort loomed, nestled amidst high black peaks that encircled it like the points of a crown. Long fingers of icy mist moved eerily about the towers, the wind keening unpleasantly in his ears. Once, not so long ago, he'd felt comfort in those winds and fogs, in the bleak black peaks and clouds, that storm that never ended. Now he just felt dread.

He could see the sentries on the walls, either side of the gate. One was pacing, side to side, spinning a dagger between his fingers. The other was moving up and down on his toes, blowing into his hands to warm them. *They cannot see me.*

Jonik continued forward, stepping silently toward the bridge. It was a simple stone thing, spanning a bottomless gorge to the gate on the other side. A soft cover of snow had settled upon the stones, though the wind had blown it thin in places. Jonik kept to those patches, watching the sentries each time he set down his foot. He could not avoid leaving prints, not here, though they were shallow enough to be missed if he timed it right. Glancing between the lookouts, he made certain their eyes were elsewhere, before taking each step. *Slow,* he thought. *One step at a time.*

The going was glacial, yet this was no time to rush. The winds blew in from his right, thinning the snow on the left side of the bridge. That forced him close to the edge, where the lightless chasm awaited him, a gaping maw of darkness and doom just waiting to gobble him up. Once or twice he looked down and wished he hadn't. The bridge had no parapets. Just an edge, and a fall, and death.

He set his eyes forward and took another step. The winds whistled past him, dragging the mists along with them. A thicker pall came through, momentarily blocking off all sight of the gate, the walls, the towers and peaks. Jonik took that chance to step forward a little quicker, one, two, three. By the time the heavy band of fog had moved on, he was onto the other side, slinking silently toward the walls.

He crept around to the right of the gate. The outer walls of the fortress were twelve metres of ancient black stone, rising sheer and smooth above him. Time and wind had not worn them as he'd like, though in places where the stones were linked together, thin holds had been carved out. *They'll do*, he thought, sliding the Nightblade into its sheath, removing his gloves so he might get a better grip. The sting of the cold hit him at once, but cold he was used to. Still, he'd need to be quick. If he lost sensation in his fingers and fell...well, he didn't want to think about that.

He began the climb, moving up the face of the wall like a lizard. Jonik had forgone armouring himself in heavy plate. He wore a slim breastplate only, and godsteel mail as well, though elsewise it was leathers and furs for the ghost. He thanked himself for that decision now. Making this climb in clunky godsteel gauntlets would not have been possible.

The top neared. The winds howled, though weren't so strong as they might have been. He clung to a narrow hold with his left hand, feet dug into a pair of grooves below. The fingers of his right hand clasped the Nightblade in his sheath, to enhance his strength and senses. He stopped there, near the top, listening.

Footsteps. One of the sentries was nearby, walking his way, his leather boots scuffing on stone. Jonik waited for him to turn back, before taking his chance, pulling himself up and over the parapet, landing silently atop the wall.

He dropped into a crouch, watching the sentry move away. He hadn't heard him, not over the blowing winds, singing their ceaseless song. The man kept on going, back toward the gatehouse, furled in a cloak of thick black wool. Further on, Jonik could see the second sentry standing flush against the wall, peering between the crenels and down toward the bridge. *He's seen my bootprints,* Jonik thought. He needed to move quickly. *Go.*

He drew the Nightblade from its sheath, soundless. Jonik's mastery of the blade was complete. There were no thin tendrils of wispy black smoke curling about him. His shape and form and outline were completed and entirely invisible. *I am the night,* he thought. *The darkness belongs to me.*

The lookout was a half dozen paces ahead of him now, still moving away. Jonik hadn't gotten a good look at their faces, yet sensed this one was old by his plodding gait. *A senior knight,* he thought. *Ripe for killing.* He crept in behind him, closer, closer....

And slid Nightblade through his back.

The old man gave no sound but a low coughing splutter, as the blade slipped through his spine, and out the front of his gut. Jonik pulled the blade out at once, then ran.

The other sentry was twenty yards away down the bulwark, still gazing down toward the bridge. He turned, eyes narrowing in confusion as the old watchman slumped forward in a boneless heap, blood leaking from his belly and into the stone. Then he saw something. The subtle shifting of the air, parting as Jonik came at him, perhaps. Or maybe he heard his footsteps over the wind. Whatever it was, he reached at once to draw his sword, but too late. Jonik was upon him in a flash, slashing with his black blade, severing his windpipe. The man's hands rose at once to his neck, eyes glazing with shock and horror. Blood squeezed out between the black fabric of his gloves. Then he fell to his knees, collapsed, and died.

Jonik turned at once to look over the fort, scanning. The yard below was empty, the stables silent, the towers half-hidden in mist. There were some lights in the windows, burning low and sombre, but not many. To his left, beside the kitchens and dining hall, was the tower where he'd lived in his youth. Inside were twenty stone cells, each just large enough to fit a bed, a desk, and a chair. *And twenty boys,* he thought. *Boys I've come to save.*

He turned his eyes down to the man dying at his feet. He recognised him. *Brock,* he thought. He was a younger knight, no older than five and twenty. *Young enough to save,* he thought. *Not so far gone as to be lost.* He closed a fist, cursing himself. His purpose here was to free those who were enslaved. Spare the young ones. Slay the old ones.

This was an emancipation, not a slaughter, he had told his men many times over. "We are to be liberators, not conquerors. If you can knock a foe unconscious, or otherwise restrain them, do it. Don't kill wantonly, lest you have no other choice."

He needed to take his own advice, though had little time to chastise himself. *Later*, he thought, as he rushed for the steps, descending to the ward. From the corner of his eye, he spotted movement at a window. *Someone's there. They can see the bodies.*

He rushed for the gate, a bulky wooden thing, banded with steel, painted black. It was fastened with a pair of heavy wooden bars, though it only took one strong man to remove them. He heaved the lower bar aside, dropping it to the floor with a *clunk*. The man at the tower window was still there, watching. *He knows,* Jonik could only think. *He knows I'm returned.* There could be no other explanation for a heavy wooden bar moving all by itself. Jonik had hoped to enter unknown, but had never expected so much. *So be it.* He turned again and lifted the second bar from its fixings, tossed it aside, then pushed hard. The doors gave a great groan as they opened outward toward the bridge. He peered through the swirling mists, waiting. *One, two, three, four,* he counted. *Five, six, seven, eight...*

Nothing.

He glanced back. The man at the window was gone. More lights were wakening among the other towers, torches set afire. He could hear shouts now, passing across the yard, and subtle shifts of movement. "The gate," he heard someone shout out more clearly. "The gate is open..."

Then he heard the first bell, ringing clean and crisp in the night. He turned back to the bridge. *Hurry,* he thought. *Hurry...*

The mists were beginning to swirl and part and through the fogs he saw them, running. Emeric at the front, with Borrus, Sir Mooton, Gerrin. Behind he sighted the gargantuan figure of Big Mo lumbering along in his armour, Cabel slinking alongside him. *He'd have made a good Shadowknight himself,* Jonik thought. The dark youth was half shadow himself, in the way he skulked and moved.

The rest came after. Harden. Kazil. Sansullio and his Sunshine Swords. The five Blackshaw men were barreling forward with Sir Torvyn, their lord, armour clanking. And there was Sir Lenard too, paired with the Silent Suncoat, and old gruff Sir Corbray Walsh, bringing up the rear. Jonik whirled to face the yard as his host came in behind him.

More movement caught his eye. *Shadows*, he thought, lurking among the lanes and alleys between buildings, keeping to the darkness they dwelt in. *But none know the dark as I do.*

His men at his back, the Nightblade in his grasp, he stepped forward, to liberate.

57

Elyon

He was dreaming of a girl when the warhorns awoke him. A girl of silver and blue. His eyes ripped open and Saska was gone. Instead he saw Barnibus, red-cheeked and panting, standing at the flaps of the tent. "They're attacking," he breathed out. "It's finally happening, Elyon."

Elyon surged to his feet so fast he nearly keeled over. He steadied himself with a hand on the chair in which he'd been dozing. He'd been sleeping in his armour again, as he often did. Outside, the din of the horns grew louder, spreading through camp, one after another. He could hear men shouting and running. There were a hundred voices competing to be heard.

He marched straight out to join them, turning his eyes around. It was dark still, the eastern horizon showing not the faintest hint of predawn light. Ahead, he could make out movement coming from the Agarathi lines, though scarcely, a great churn of men and mounts approaching from the marshes. Drums sounded distantly, thudding at the edge of hearing. To his left the towering fortress walls went up and away into the misty skies. Soldiers were scrambling to man the ballistas and trebuchets, the parapets teeming with archers and crossbowmen.

From the main encampment, thousands of men were emerging from their tents and pavilions, rubbing their eyes, fixing their sword-belts, moving to their positions. Horses charged among them, hornblowers riding up and down through the ranks, rousing them to the fight. Those who were already awake and armoured were gathering ahead of the lines in formation, their banner-bearers going before them. There were mounted knights and men-at-arms, spearmen from the marshlands and axmen from the rivers. Elyon saw Lord Justin Huxley and his hundred men arriving to take position for the defence, Sir Lutherton Wane and his sons alongside them. Sir Peter Hornmoor had finally pulled his nose out of his books and was stepping forward with his squires, armoured in a mix of godsteel and castle-forged plate and mail.

Elyon spotted his uncle, bellowing orders to his Amadar men. There were five thousand of them here at the Bane and by the looks of it, most of those were already surging forward to take their places, dressed in their pink and pale blue surcoats and links of ringtail beneath. Clustered about among the formations were hosts of shieldmen, bearing great shiny shields on their backs, lacquered in fireproof oils. They were well drilled and well trained and essential in a fight against dragons. All bore swords at their hips and some axes and spears too, but their primary purpose was defensive; to provide shelter against the dragons when they flew over, raining fire.

Elyon marched to join his uncle, pulling the Windblade from its sheath. Men turned to look at him. *Give them strength,* he thought to himself. *Show no fear. Inspire.* He held his chin high and walked with a purposeful gait. "Uncle," he called. "Is it a real attack, this time?"

The Agarathi had feigned as such once or twice over the last few days, banging their drums and mustering their men to charge, but hadn't yet followed through. This felt different, though. Rikkard thought so too. "It's real," he said. "The night is darkest just before the dawn, Elyon. And the clouds are thick. It'll make it harder to see their dragons." He looked to the fort, where the great scorpions were moving on their turntables, watching the skies. Each had Bladeborn men to mount the godsteel-tipped bolts, and others to scout, Bladeborn blessed with good eyesight who would aim and call the commands to fire. "They've been waiting for the right conditions."

And wearing us out, Elyon thought. *Letting us linger in doubt and fear.* It had been long days since the parley with Lord Vargo Ven and still no attack had been called. *Let it be tonight,* he thought. *Let it be done.*

"Did you sleep, Elyon?" Rikkard asked him. His eyes were alight with the fevered heat of approaching battle. "Are you rested?"

"Well enough," Elyon could only say. He might have slept an hour, maybe two. It would have to suffice.

He heard calls down the line, for the defensive artillery to be loaded. They had many catapults and trebuchets lined up ahead of their lines, to fling stones and barrels of flaming pitch into the midst of the enemy charge. Elyon watched as the swinging arms were drawn back, the bays loaded, the mechanisms set to release. Upon the fortress walls and towers, the same would be happening. Men waited with flaming torches to light the barrels, though it wasn't yet time.

"Hold," Rikkard called out. "Wait for them to get nearer."

A groom came rushing out with Twilight, and Rikkard leapt up into the saddle. Lancel followed behind, riding atop Monty, Biter at his side. "Here," he said, handing Barnibus the reins. Barnibus climbed atop his destrier with a little less grace than Rikkard, though no less urgency. All the horses were fearsomely barded in their godsteel-plated armour, wearing caparisons in the colours of their houses. Elyon had no need of Snowmane, not tonight. *My steed is the wind,* he thought. *My battlefield the skies.*

He looked up. Those skies were empty right now, though wouldn't be for long. "Will they stop out of range of our artillery, do you think? Wait for us to engage?"

His uncle shook his head. "We hold the fort. If they want to take it, they'll have to charge us. There's no reason for us to meet them on the open field."

Along the lines the ranks of armoured horse were lining up, clad in barding of steel and beaten leather. Units of archers clustered around the siege weapons, ready to nock and loose when the trebuchets fired, and retreat when the enemy drew near. And when that happened, when they came together and clashed, those arrows and bolts and barrels of pitch would be worthless. *They hope to get past without suffering heavy losses*, Elyon knew. *Rush to close the gap and overwhelm us with their numbers.* And superior numbers they had. *Four to one,* Elyon thought, glancing skyward. *And how many to one, up there?*

More men were still moving out beyond the encampment, joining in formation. Elyon summoned the winds, lifting himself off the ground to get a better look. Through the darkness he could see the battle lines forming, well ordered and neat in places, more chaotic in others. Nerves and the cloak of night had rendered many unable to find their positions. He could see patches where the lines were weak, archers and axmen and mounted men all mingled together, showing colours of different houses. *It begins,* he thought. *Their heads are clouded by fear. Already they panic.*

He flew that way, swooping over the heads of a host of Amadar shieldmen, passing some of Rammas's spearmen, getting a bellowing cheer from a group of brawny Riverlanders who banged their axes against their breastplates as he passed. *Show strength,* he thought. *Inspire.*

He came in to land where the lines were broken. "Who takes charge here?" he called over the tumult.

"Sir Lawrence, my lord," returned a soldier. He pointed to a pavilion nearby. "He's still putting on his armour."

Elyon stepped that way, though didn't need to enter. As he neared, the fleshy form of Sir Lawrence Bollingbrook came stumbling out, bleary-eyed and nervous, a squire following with his shield. "Sir Lawrence," Elyon called to him. The man's arms were a barded unicorn, drinking at a river, though instead of a horn the unicorn had a godsteel spear surging from its forehead. It was one of the stranger sigils that Elyon had seen. "This is your host. Get them in order, and quickly. Don't you hear the horns? The Agarathi are coming."

"Yes...yes, Prince Elyon, I hear them..." Sir Lawrence was a known craven and many had expected him to leave as soon as the Agarathi had appeared from the marshes, but he hadn't. Perhaps he wasn't so craven after all. "Men...form up! Form up!" the man commanded. A second squire came out with his horse and helped him into the saddle. "Garrick. Where's Garrick?"

"Here, Sir Lawrence." Sam Garrick did not sit a horse. As an independent swordsman, and tournament specialist, he probably felt more comfortable fighting on his feet. He noticed Elyon standing there with the Windblade, and dipped his head into a bow. "My prince."

"Garrick. I'm glad you're still here." He was one of the few men who had a full suit of godsteel plate, and would be worth a great deal in the field. "I'll have you at the front of the lines, Sam. Show these men what you can do. Show them you're as fierce on the field as you are on the sand."

"I shall, Prince Elyon." Sam Garrick bowed again, then pulled down his visor, vainly etched into the likeness of his own face. *If that vanity drives him to kill many men tonight, so much the better,* Elyon thought.

He took flight again, surging twenty metres into the air. The enemy were still making their approach, closing in on the range of their artillery. He could hear the calls for 'nock' echoing out beneath him, the trebuchets being loaded to fire.

He flew past the Oloran banners, where Sir Killian rode up and down the lines before his men, mounted on Whispering Wind. He was giving a rousing speech, his whispered voice forgotten, calling out loudly for all his men to hear. "...here, tonight, we make our stand," he was saying. "Here, where we have awaited them these long months, will we show them what it means to be Vandarian. To be born of steel and war. We fight here for our families, for our wives and our mothers and our children back home. We defend this passage as we always have, and tell the enemy, *show* the enemy, that they *may not pass!*" A roar accompanied those words, and a great crashing of swords on shields. "If they breach us here, all of Vandar will be under threat, all the north. *Here*, we make our stand. *Here*, we redden the earth with the blood of Agarath!"

Elyon flew onward down the lines, Killian's voice fading as he continued west. *He inspires them. I must do the same.* Thousands more soldiers stretched away into the dimness, many rows deep. Here at the western flank Lady Marian had command, with Sir Gereon of Greyguard in support. Elyon spotted them both, riding side by side in the saddle, checking their lines. Those lines were immaculate, every man in his place. The trebuchets were loaded and readied, the archers slightly forward to improve their range. If Marian's men - Roark and Quilter and the others - were down there, Elyon couldn't hope to see them. *Fodder for the battle,* Marian had called them. He hoped not, for Saska's sake.

The enemy were still advancing, less than half a mile off and closing. They held no torches, bore no light. Elyon could only get a sense of them, of a great shadow, advancing toward them like a slow-moving wave. *A tidal wave,* he thought, *that they hope will wash right over us.*

He whirled about and made back for the Bane, flying toward the fortress across the front of the lines. Men cheered him as he passed, raising their swords and spears and shields, waving their banners and flags. *Inspire them,* he thought. *Bear their fear.* He spun in the air and closed his fist, bellowing out, "For Vandar!" as he soared by. "For Vandar, for Vandar!"

Men returned the call, roaring it right back at him. The din grew louder as the enemy drew near. Elyon swept on past them, as the chant spread out down the lines. The immensity of the Bane soared up above him, and he rose, surging up toward the southward barbican, where Lord Kanabar stood in command, bellowing orders as he marched up and down the battlements. Elyon could smell the stink of rot rising from the two dragons hanging on the twin towers, and Ezukar on the western wall. The crows had been getting at them, pecking through their armoured scales to feast on their flesh and blood. They exploded from the corpses as he passed, flapping away in a chaos of wings and out into the blackness of the night.

He slowed, dismissing the winds, landing upon the wall walk as the Lord of Rivers marched down toward him. Everything looked well in order here. The ballistas were manned, the catapults loaded, bowmen teeming at the crenels with baskets of arrows between them.

"It's a bloody dark night," Lord Kanabar grunted over the noise. Down below, the army were still roaring out, *for Vandar, for Vandar*, in a great spreading cheer. For a moment Elyon wondered what Marian's men would be shouting. *For Rasalan, perhaps?*. But that might just confuse things. "There might be a hundred dragons just a hundred metres away and we'd never know." Lord Kanabar turned to a nearby scorpion, mounted on its turntable. "You, *you*, crank that bloody thing higher! It's too *low*. The dragons will come from above us, not below!" The soldiers got to the task, raising the front of the ballista. Each was capable of turning a full circle on those turntables, and could be raised and lowered quickly as well. That was critical when battling dragons. "Will you stay here, Elyon?" Kanabar asked. "Help protect the Bane?"

"I'll target their leaders," Elyon said. "Sunlord Avam. That dragonknight commander. Vargo Ven. *Him* most of all."

"Don't be reckless," Kanabar warned him. "Borrus fought Malathar and Ven during the last war, and a dozen other knights tried the same. My son is the only one still living. They're a formidable pair, Elyon, be careful. If we lose you, the men will lose hope."

"And if the Agarathi lose Ven, maybe they will too." Elyon flexed his sword hand and scanned the skies. "I intend to drop Malathar right down on top of them. Let's see what happens then."

The chants of 'for Vandar' were fading now. Elyon could hear calls below, for the trebuchets to prepare to fire. Wallis Kanabar squinted away into the darkness. "How far are they, Elyon? How far?"

Another soldier gave answer. "Five hundred metres, my lord."

"Just out of range," Kanabar muttered. He peered into the gloom. "They're slowing, it looks."

He was right. That great shadow, that slow-moving wave, was grinding to a halt just beyond the range of their artillery. "Might this be another feint?" Elyon wondered.

Kanabar's beard swung side to side. "They're grouping for the charge. They'll come at us fast from here, try to close the gap quickly." He turned and opened his mouth in a bellow. "READY! READY TO FIRE ON MY COMMAND!"

Elyon heard similar calls below. He could see Rikkard riding up and down before his Amadar men. Lord Rammas had command further on, with his captains around him. From there the army bled into shadow and darkness. The camp behind looked almost deserted now, but for a few stragglers rushing to join the ranks. Torches burned, and campfires too, but there were no men sitting around them, joking and drinking, no sentries at their posts. The only souls left were the women in camp, and the scholars and scribes and squires too young to join the battle. But even they would be ready, just in case. *We may need every man,* Elyon thought, looking at the vast shadow of the enemy, five hundred metres away. *Four times our number. They have four times our number. And how many dragons?* He still didn't know.

A silence settled, eerily calm, the breath before the plunge. Distinct voices could be heard, calling 'hold,', and 'ready', and 'nock' as the archers picked up arrows and set them to their bows. In the distance, the drums of the Agarathi had turned slow and sonorous. They rang out across the darkened field, *ba-dum, ba-dum, ba-dum.* Elyon's heart beat along with them. *Be calm,* he thought. *Be fearless. Inspire.*

The drums picked up their pace. *Ba-dum, ba-dum, ba-dum, ba-dum...*

"DRAW!" bellowed Lord Kanabar. That call echoed across the walls and towers. The archers pulled back their strings.

Elyon curled his fingers around the Windblade's hilt. It thrummed in his grasp, excited, afeared. As he was. The drums beat yet faster, *ba-dum, ba-dum, ba-dum, ba-dum*, and his heart followed, quickened by the thrill. Elyon could hear snarls out there, and howls, though could not make out where the wolves and cats were among their vast formations.

He drew a long breath to cleanse his lungs. *Be fearless. Inspire them.* He could not imagine how afraid some of the younger men must be. *On both sides,* he thought, his mind returning to the boy he'd killed in the marshes. How many boys were out there now, looking upon the immense shadow of the Bane? Looking at the tall trebuchets and catapults and ballistas, the thousands of archers, all nocked and ready to loose. It would be hell, that charge. A hell of boulders and stones and flaming barrels of pitch, of thousands upon thousands of arrows, filling all the skies...

And through those skies, came the beating of drums, faster, faster, and the battlecries of the horde, and the snarling of cats and wolves, echoing out across the plains. Slowly at first, then faster, faster, the vast shadow crept forward.

"HOLD!" roared Lord Kanabar. "HOLD!" His eyes were fixed on the approaching army, watching, waiting for them to come into range. "HOLD...HOLD...HOLD..." They crossed the threshold in their thousands. Lord Kanabar's voice bellowed out louder than ever. "FIRE!" he called, "FIRE! FIRE!"

The order spread, a hundred others taking up the call, "FIRE, FIRE, FIRE," and across the fortress and down the lines, the trebuchets and catapults swung, and the bowmen released their strings, and so the skies did fill...with boulders and stones and barrels of flaming pitch, and arrows, thousands of arrows, as they were nocked and drawn and loosed, again and again and again.

So it begins. Elyon stood on the battlements, watching, the winds stirring lightly around him. And through the noise of the trebuchets and catapults, and the thrumming of strings, and the roaring of orders, and the din of the coming horde...he heard the first screech above him.

His eyes went upward, widening, widening.

Soon all the skies will swarm, he heard the Windblade whisper.

And all Elyon could think was, *we're doomed.*

58

Jonik

He kicked through the door and stepped within. The bells were ringing outside, chiming through the blackness of the fort. The clash of steel rang out as well, and there were voices, shouting, as his men moved through the buildings. Each pairing and group had been given their orders. All had learned the layout of the fort from Gerrin's drawings. All knew their targets.

Jonik paced down the corridor, his old master a step behind. They moved up a spiral stair to the floor above. Jonik could hear the scuffling of boots on stone, the rattling of keys, echoing from the far end of the hall. To either side were simple cells, windowless, ten to the left and right. One of them he knew particularly well. *My old home*, he thought.

At the end of the corridor, a cloaked man was thrusting a key into a lock. "Step away from the door," Jonik warned him. "Take your hands off those keys."

The man turned to look at him with an empty smile. Jonik knew the face. Stregor. A long-serving man of the order, he was well past saving. "Jonik," he rasped. "You return." His eyes shifted over Jonik's shoulder as Gerrin came in behind him. "And *you*. Thought you'd bring the boy home eventually, Gerrin. Just not like this."

"Let me kill him, Jonik," Gerrin said, curling fingers around the hilt of his blade. "*Stregor*." He spat out the name like it was a curse.

"You were always one of the worst. How many of your apprentices did you beat to death?"

"Four," the Shadowmaster said, without pause. There was nothing approaching remorse in his voice. "Some boys need pushing. If they fall, that's on them. Strong boys don't die from a few punches and kicks."

"Kill him, Gerrin," Jonik said.

"Gladly."

Jonik stepped aside to let Gerrin pass. They had reached the barracks just in time. Jonik had feared some of the boys might have been let out, but no, all of the doors were still locked by the looks of it.

Good. Hopefully Emeric has the same luck. There were three such barrack towers in the fort, for the habitation of the apprentices in their different age groups, and in all three the boys were locked away at night. Jonik had instructed Emeric to see to one of the others, with Harden in support, and Sir Torvyn the third, along with some of the Blackshaw men. The rest would be hunting the more dangerous of the known knights and masters. If they could strike down the worst of them before they could regroup, the night might just go easy.

The two old men came together at the heart of the hall. Stregor was of an age with Gerrin, or thereabouts, and had been here from a pup. He was a man of the shadows, through and through, spare and gaunt, with hollow eyes and an eagle nose, beneath a head of sparse grey hair, receding into a deep widow's peak. "You want to make this a fair fight, Gerrin, you'll take off that pretty amour you're wearing."

Gerrin looked like he might just answer the goad, though seemed to realise they had no time for it. "You'll not lay a blade on me regardless," he told his peer. "You forget who I was, Stregor. Janilah doesn't choose his Six lightly."

"Aye, Janilah. The mad and missing king. You were always his creature, and this boy too." He spat to the side, spraying spittle on the wall. "This his orders, then? The Warrior King trying to cover up his crimes, is he?"

"We answer only to ourselves now, Stregor. We've decided it's time for you and your order to fall."

Stregor's upper lip pulled back. "Centuries this order's stood, keeping the world in balance. Just who are you to tamper with that?"

"Balance?" Gerrin laughed. "This order is a lie and always was.

You're a brotherhood of cowards and killers, nothing more, bending to the highest bidder." Gerrin drew his blade.

Stregor followed. "Suppose you killed Valtho and Parsivor, did you?"

"With great pleasure, yes. Though I'll say this, Stregor, killing you will be even more satisfying. You always were a bastard."

"Aye," Stregor said, swallowing a chuckle. "Aren't we all."

The fight did not last long. Better armoured and armed, Gerrin quickly overwhelmed him, buoyed by the confidence of plate and mail. Jonik sensed he didn't need it, much as his old master had claimed. Once or twice Stregor got close to striking him, but here in this hall, with no shadows to hide in and firm footing beneath his feet, Gerrin showed his mastery of the forms. From Blockform to Glideform he went, back to Blockform, into Strikeform, before a burst of Rushform had Stregor stumbling back, giving an opening for Gerrin to slash at his belly, unfettering his insides as they came slithering out onto the stone.

Stregor fell to his knees, making a futile attempt to scoop up his innards. He grunted and spat out a mouthful of blood. "Janilah's Six, aye," he croaked. "Forgot how skilled you are."

"Happy to have reminded you." Gerrin put the flat of his blade onto Stregor's shoulder, beside his neck. "I'll ease your passing. This is no way to die."

"Don't need no mercy from the likes of you."

"Even so." Gerrin gave a quick swipe, cutting through the man's throat. Stregor died quickly after that, bundling to a bloody heap on the floor, ichor gushing from stomach and neck, filling the hall with the sharp tangy taste of iron. Gerrin looked down at the dead Shadowmaster and shook his head. "This is what the order is, Jonik. *Lesser* men like this. Trained to lurk and deceive. They're no threat against armoured Bladeborn knights." He turned, wiping down his blade, thrusting it back into its sheath. "What do you want to do about the boys?"

Jonik looked down the corridor. He knew every boy would be awake now, listening on the other side of their doors, ears pressed up against the wood. If released he had little doubt they would join the fight. *I would have,* he thought, *if the fort had come under attack.* "Best keep them locked away, until it's over. I'll have someone watch the door downstairs, make sure no one sneaks in to set them loose." Jonik studied his old master. He had a strange look on his face. "What is it?"

"Memories," Gerrin said. He looked down the corridor, at the door third from the end, on the left. The room where Jonik had lived as a boy. "Hate what I did to you, back then. Hate the person I was. Being here again…makes me reflect…" He shook his head. "Ah, don't listen to me. We've not got time for it, I know."

"I understand, Gerrin," Jonik told him. "You were under coercion as well. The mages…that was their purpose. To subtly coerce and control every aspect of this order, every man and boy, knight and master." He could hear some light banging now, on a couple of the doors, and muted shouts inside. "These boys are slaves, like I was. And you, for a time. Don't blame yourself for what you were. Perhaps it was all for a reason."

Gerrin nodded to that. "I'd like to think so. Not sure it excuses what I did, though."

"It does," Jonik assured him. "You training me. Me mastering this blade. Us reuniting to come here together. There is purpose in that, Gerrin, and providence. We break from the shadows, only to return to drive them off." He set his jaw. "Only there's one shadow darker than the rest."

"Then let's go cast it out," Gerrin said. "Time the king was struck from his throne."

They returned to the main ward, rushing down the corridor and turnpike stair, out into the dark misty night. The bells were still tolling, ringing out across the fort. Jonik spotted Sir Lenard near the gate, standing sentry with the Silent Suncoat. The big mute Rasal looked none too pleased about being left to stand guard while others wetted their blades, yet had no tongue to give complaint.

"My lord," Sir Lenard called out to him. "We spotted some men rushing into that building there, men with black cloaks." He pointed to the armoury, adjacent to the barrack they'd just left. "Half a dozen of them. I thought about giving chase, but…but you told us to stay here. And there are six, to the two of us. Those aren't the best odds, my lord."

The Silent Suncoat huffed to show what he thought of that. He still wore his tattered golden cloak, though beneath it was godsteel plate and mail.

"I'll see to it," Jonik said. "Sir." He met the Silent Suncoat's cold stare. "Care to join me?"

The man nodded, slowly.

"Gerrin, you too. Sir Lenard, hold the gate."

"What? No, me…on my own?"

"You were a Knight of Varin once, Sir Lenard. Or did I get that wrong?"

"My father…I only got through selection because of my father. I was never good enough, my lord. You've seen me. I'm not good enough."

"You are. Now hold the gate." Jonik wasn't going to spend time listening to the man's excuses, not now. He pointed to the barracks they'd just left. "And see that no one enters that building. If someone goes near, you frighten them off." He turned and made for the armoury.

There were sounds coming from inside. Voices and the noises men made when they pulled on their studded leather jerkins and girdled their belts, the scream of metal as blades slid from sheathes. Jonik turned to the others. "If there are any youngsters in there, try to spare them. If you need to cut them, do it where they won't bleed out." He made sure they understood, but knew it wouldn't be that easy, not in the heat of battle. "Follow my lead. I'll go in unseen."

Jonik let his body fade into darkness, then moved forward and put his boot to the door. It swung inward to a crash of wood and hinges, unveiling the men within, armouring up for the fight. Jonik scanned them as quickly as he could but in the gloom it was near impossible to tell one man from another. *This is the Shadow Order,* he thought, *and they are shadows, indistinct.*

He rushed for the nearest enemy, judged his age in an instant, and attacked. The man had no hope of seeing him come. In a heartbeat Jonik had pressed the tip of the Nightblade through his jerkin and into his heart. Gerrin and the Silent Suncoat flew in behind him. The other five men turned to face them, brandishing their godsteel broadswords. Two had pulled on godsteel hauberks, though the rest were in nought but boiled leather. The men in godsteel moved forward to the front. Jonik heard one grunt, "Gerrin", in a growly voice, before he swung forward in attack. The Silent Suncoat moved in with a silken grace you'd not expect from a man his size, cutting him off. The clash of metal sounded. Jonik moved around to the back, in behind the other three in leather. One was glancing into the darkness, prodding with his blade, wary of the ghost.

"Show yourself!" he roared. "Show yourself, coward!"

Jonik showed himself. His body took form from the darkness, and he looked into the eyes of the man before him. *Edvin.* A Shadowknight, well past thirty, and cruel. *Too far gone,* he thought. He might have bled back into the night, but he faced his enemy, man to man, parrying his first attack, slashing aside his second, dismissing his third, then striking. Edvin died the same as the first man, with the Nightblade piercing his heart. When he turned, he found that the Silent Suncoat had taken his own prize, a body lying aside with the top of his head shaved off at the temple, brains spilling out onto the floor. The mute Rasal knight had moved onto his next target already, working out his attack patterns in that cold assured way of his. Gerrin was engaging with the second man in the hauberk. The final foe stood at the rear, unsure.

"You," Jonik called to him. When he turned, Jonik realised he knew him. Friendship was forbidden at the Shadowfort, and the boys were kept separate as often as possible, yet sometimes they trained together, ate together, studied together, and spoke. That was impossible to curtail completely. "You needn't be a slave anymore, Henrik. We come to liberate you. Throw down your arms and be free."

"Liberate?" Henrik looked at the dead men on the floor, their blood soaking into the wood. "This isn't liberation."

"These men are beyond saving. I'm here for the young, not the old. I escaped, Henrik. You can too."

"No. Never." Henrik slinked forward darkly. He did not know the forms. Most of those trained here were never taught them. They were instructed in how to kill from the shadows, not face a man in the open like this. Jonik had never truly appreciated how poorly suited to this sort of combat they were. He'd fought seasoned men in tourney conditions, defeating Varin Knights and famed sellswords in the Song of the First Blade. Young Sir Godfrey Wilmar. Sir Nathaniel Oloran, well fancied to go far. The smirking sellsword Sam Garrick. Dalton Taynar, now prince and First Blade to many, whom he'd taken apart in the semi-final. And Aleron. *Aleron and my father. I have faced them both.*

He looked at Henrik as he stalked forward through the gloom, hesitant and uncertain, the others clashing around him. "You don't want to do this, Henrik. You cannot beat me."

"I know. But I'll try anyway." Henrik rushed forward, jabbing. Jonik drew back, parrying.

I have been trained all of my life by one of Janilah's Six, he thought. *I have seen instruction under Sir Borrus Kanabar, the Barrel Knight, and Emeric of Sir Oswald's line. I have the blood of House Daecar running rich through my veins. I have mastered a Blade of Vandar, mustered great men to my side. I have driven off a kraken, slain sunwolves, killed mages. Henrik, you are nothing to me.*

He said not a word of that, as Henrik came again, slashing, stabbing, swinging. Jonik might have killed him half a dozen times already, yet he watched, waited, spotted his chance, then slipped in behind him, driving the hilt of the Nightblade into the back of his head. Henrik tumbled forward, crashing heavily into the wooden floor, insensate. Behind him, Jonik heard the grunts of men dying. He turned to find his allies standing over their defeated foes.

"Was no helping it, Jonik," Gerrin told him, giving out a pant. "These ones…they needed to die." He looked down. "Who's that on the floor?"

"Henrik."

"You spared him?"

Jonik nodded. "Take him outside, if you would, sir," he said to the Silent Suncoat. "And bind him hand and foot with rope. He'll see the light in time."

They left the armoury, victorious. Across the yard, Jonik spotted Emeric standing with Sir Lenard, Harden alongside them. Sir Lenard was gesturing in their direction as they stepped out. He gave a great sigh of relief to see all three of them emerge unharmed. "Oh gods be good, you're all right. I feared you'd come unstuck. All that noise…"

"We're fine, Sir Lenard." Jonik marched straight across the yard to Emeric. "Are the apprentices safely locked away? Did you get there in time?"

Emeric nodded. "All the cells were locked when we got there. There were a pair of men coming to let them out, but we dealt with them easily enough."

"Did you leave someone on guard?"

"Crasson and Regnar are watching both the barracks. Seems Sir Torvyn had a little more trouble with his. A couple of the lads had been set loose. Far as I know, they were killed, Jonik, by the Blackshaw men."

"Just two?" That was more than Jonik might have hoped for, in truth.

"That I know of. Both were in their mid-teens, maybe fourteen or fifteen, Torvyn said. Almost men grown. They knew what they were doing when they attacked."

Jonik offered no response. *I was once a fourteen year old here*, he might have said, *and I'd have attacked as well.* Every single boy would do the same, no matter their age. This was their home, and all they'd ever known. *They do not truly realise that they're slaves*, he thought. *You have to escape first, and then look back. Only then do you see the darkness you left behind, once you've stepped away into the light.*

Jonik noticed Harden cradling his arm. "You're wounded, Harden."

"Just a scratch," the grim sellsword told him. "Some shadow came from the darkness and poked me in the shoulder, between a gap in my plate. Good shot, I'll give him that." He shrugged, wincing. "Then I killed him."

"Do you know which one it was?" Gerrin asked.

"They all look mighty similar to me. Black cloaks and hoods, all that. He was skilled enough, though. Might have troubled me if I wasn't armoured."

"We have much to thank Lord Merrymarsh for. This armour is proving a great boon, as we'd hoped." Emeric turned his eyes around the yard, peering through the gloom. More men were entering from the eastern side of the fort. "Sansullio," he said.

Jonik saw that he was right, the tall dark captain striding toward them in that lithe smooth step of his, dressed in his fine scalemail armour and golden cloak, his men marching neatly in his wake. They looked to have taken a couple of prisoners, a pair of cloaked men bound and gagged and being drawn along behind him. "My Lord Jonik, we have slain our targets. And found these two as well. I thought them young enough to take captive."

"Thank you, Sansullio. Set them over there." Jonik gestured to where Henrik had been set down, as the Silent Suncoat worked to fetter him in rope. "Gerrin, take a look at them."

Gerrin nodded and stepped over.

"Did you have much trouble?" Jonik asked the captain. He'd made sure to keep all of the Sunshine Swords together, in a single unit, knowing how well they operated in tandem. Yet all the same, their numbers looked further depleted, after two had perished when fighting Sir Boleman's host several weeks ago. There had been ten left after that, though Jonik could see only seven remaining. "Where are the others, Sansullio?"

"Deceased." Sansullio dipped his chin in a gesture of mourning, as his men did the same. "They fell fighting, and did not succumb easily. We shall retrieve their bodies, once the fortress is taken."

Jonik gave a consoling look. "I'm sorry, my friend. I know this is not your cause."

"We are Sunshine Swords, Lord Jonik. Our cause is what our paymaster tells us. Yet this one...this one we do willingly." He looked around with his keen purple eyes, at the towers and peaks, clad in bands of mist. "This is a dark place, full of malice. We are happy to help cleanse it, even if it should mean our lives."

And who else might have fallen? Jonik wondered. The fort had gone more quiet than he would like, the bells falling silent, the air still. Distantly, he could hear the faint echo of battle carrying on the wind, though he couldn't be sure of its source. His orders had been for the men to seek their targets, kill them if they could, and retreat back to the ward. It was a mission of search and destroy to rip the guts out of the order. Once reassembled, they'd be able to strike at the leftovers and seal their victory. *Then the Steward,* he thought, *and the King.*

"I'm going to go out there and help," he said. "Emeric, Gerrin, with me. The rest of you stay here, guard the gate and watch the prisoners. Sansullio, take charge. Harden, Sir Lenard, keep a lookout on the barracks."

Jonik stepped away across the ward, Emeric and Gerrin to his sides. For a moment he recalled his dreams, where he'd stood with Emeric to one side, and Jack to the other, with the rest fanning out alongside him, facing the fort. Well, Gerrin was a little older than Jack, rather less comely, and not so well-liked, but all the same, he'd proven a worthy replacement. *He shows his value, time and again,* Jonik thought. "Did you recognise the two prisoners?" he asked him.

Gerrin nodded. "Youngsters, as Sansullio said. Zacarias and Nils."

Jonik knew them both, though not well. They were younger than him by a couple of years and must only recently have graduated beyond their cells, to take their place as grown men of the order.

They passed beyond the ward, moving down a narrow alley that led deeper into the western side of the fort. Jonik had sent three groups off in this direction. Borrus and Sir Corbray. Sir Mooton, with his leal man, Sir Bulmar Brown. And the trio of sellswords, Big Mo, Cabel, and Kazil. All three groups had taken to different buildings to hunt the senior knights and masters in their beds. With the mages it wasn't so simple, though. They lived in the mountains at the rear of the fortress, where Gerrin had never once stepped foot. He could give no guidance on that, nor insight. *We shall regroup and attack in force,* Jonik thought. *Together we'll overwhelm them.*

They found Sir Mooton first, the beastly Riverlander stepping out of an arched stone doorway with his big fist clinging to a severed head. He lifted it up for their inspection. Strands of sinew dangled from the ruin of the neck, dripping gouts of blood. "This the one you were after, Gerrin?"

Gerrin peered at it. "Shadowmaster Selander," he confirmed, nodding. "You found him in his rooms?"

"In his bed," the Beast of Blackshaw said. "The old man was dressed in nought but his breeks, all knobbly knees and skinny arms. *Shadowmaster*," he scoffed. "Thought he'd be more of a challenge."

"It's going easier than I thought," Sir Bulmar agreed. He was a big man by any normal standard, but next to Mooton, not so much. Rare among the Blackshaw men, he had only stubble in place of a beard, and wasn't so heavy in the gut either. "We killed another three in the building. One was Crevlin, I think. He wore a patch on his left eye."

Gerrin nodded. "That'll be him." His notes gave little details like that, physical quirks for the men to look out for. "Did he put up much of a fight?"

"A bit," Sir Bulmar admitted. "Caught me with a slash or two, but did nothing but scratch my armour. I just needed one clean strike and then he was mine."

"Any word on Borrus or the sellswords?" Emeric asked.

"What word are you expecting?" Mooton said. "It's a bloody rout, that's clear enough. I daresay Borrus could have cleared this fort out all on his own. These men are no match for us, armour or no." He craned that enormously thick neck of his to left and right. "Where's my cousin?"

"Heading back to the ward," Emeric said. "He's unharmed, Sir Mooton. Norwyn and Radcliffe are with him."

"Unharmed?" Sir Mooton Blackshaw laughed. It was such an odd sound, here in the Shadowfort, echoing away into the cold black skies, spreading to the towers and peaks that enclosed them. Jonik wasn't certain if he'd ever heard laughter here. "Of course he's unharmed. Who here could harm a man like Sir Torvyn Blackshaw?"

"A good many men," Gerrin said, "given the right conditions. We've taken them unawares, and it's worked. On another day we'd have faced a much stiffer challenge."

"And it's not over yet," Jonik was keen to remind them. "We've struck a blow, but not a killing blow. There will be men lurking around us as we speak, be sure of it. That's how they're trained here, to strike from the darkness, and disappear. Be on your guard, and take nothing for granted. I'll not rest until every man and mage in the fort is either killed or captured."

"Fine." Sir Mooton reached behind his back and pulled out his enormous godsteel axe. It looked pristine, unbloodied. "I've given my greatsword a swallow of shadow blood. My axe wants a taste. Lead on then, Jonik. Let's go hunting."

They continued around the building, through a short stone tunnel with unlit torches on the walls, past the round stone tower that housed the library, and into an inner yard, used for training. To left was a viewing gallery, to right a stair that bled away into darkness and a higher part of the fort that Jonik didn't know. Ahead lay living quarters for some of the senior men. From inside came the sounds of fighting. Sir Mooton did not waste a moment in delay. Greataxe to hand, he lumbered forward, armour clanking, and barrelled through the door. The rest followed.

The interior was black as night, stinking of blood and bowels. A half dozen men had fought in the common room. Jonik scanned the dead, and saw a gleam of armour among the men in black. He rushed over and bent down, turning the man over. "Kazil," he said. "Kazil, can you hear me?" He pressed fingers to the Piseki's neck and they came back slick with blood and gore. His throat had been cleaved open by a savage cut, almost to the bone. He stood up. "He's dead."

A groan sounded across the room. A huge shape stirred in the shadows. All turned. Emeric was closest. "Maurice?" He moved quickly in and checked on the scarred giant. "Maurice, what happened here?"

The huge sellsword seemed unable to form words. *He's dying,* Jonik thought. Above them, a sudden crashing sounded, as though someone was being thrown across a room. Jonik spun on his heels and sped up the stairs, reaching a corridor. He could hear the others charging behind him. The commotion was coming from inside a bedchamber. He made for the door, but before he could get within ten paces of it, Cabel came staggering out, clutching at the side of his head. He turned to face them, blinking, then collapsed.

*Who...*Jonik thought. *Who could have...*

And then he saw Sir Borrus Kanabar. The big knight stepped out, glassy-eyed, grimacing. *He isn't himself,* Jonik realised at once. "He's hexed," he called back to the others. "Someone's put a spell on him."

"Back," said Emeric immediately. "Step back, everyone, back." As he said those words, he pushed forward, speaking calmly as he went. "Borrus, wake up. You're not yourself, Borrus. *Wake up.*"

"Words won't work," Gerrin warned from behind. "We either put him down or knock him out, let the spell weaken as he sleeps. There's no other way. He's one of them now."

"That's the heir of bloody rivers you're talking about," Sir Mooton blustered. "We're not bloody *putting him down.*" He stepped down the corridor, shoving Emeric to the side. "I'll deal with him. Don't you worry."

"Deal with me?" Sir Borrus Kanabar's voice was odd, thick with contempt and confusion. He held Red Wrath in his fist, its edge dripping blood. There was more blood on his armour, lacquered from breastplate to greaves. "None of you can deal with me."

"Borrus, come now," Mooton said. "Look...look what you've done." He pointed at Cabel, who might be alive or dead, it was hard to say. The right side of his head was sticky with blood, leaking from a severe gash that cut right down to the chin. "The boy's your ally, your brother in arms. Was it you, downstairs? Was it you killed Kazil and Big Mo? And those other men?"

Borrus stared through eyes of black stone, His skin was pale, spattered red.

"I told you, you can't talk him down," Gerrin repeated, more firmly. "He'll kill every one of us if he gets a chance."

Borrus took a step forward, eyes locking on the huge great man in his way. "Borrus, listen to me," Mooton said. "You're Borrus Kanabar, heir to the Riverlands, and a bloody godsdamned terror on the battlefield. There's no hex of spell that can tame you. Now come, enough of this. Snap out of it and let's hunt some mage."

It's not going to work, Jonik knew. Gerrin was right. "Get back," he said. "Everyone, back..."

Mooton snorted. "Don't fret, lad, these sellswords he'll go for, but me? Oh, I think n..."

Borrus surged forward like a bull, closing the gap so fast that Mooton had scant time to defend himself. Red Wrath came down in a slicing arc, right for Mooton's head, as the Beast of Blackshaw stumbled back, heaving his axe up to block it. He managed to, just in time, though Borrus was already swinging again.

No, Jonik thought. *No. Enough.* He shot forward like a bolt, swung up with the Nightblade, and parried the blow with force enough to knock Borrus off balance. "Back," he shouted to the men behind him. "Everyone, outside, into the yard. NOW!"

He heard them retreating, as he took a pace to the rear, and another, and another. Borrus righted himself and followed, snarling, gathering himself for another attack. "Bastard," he growled. "I'll kill you for what you did." He charged again. Jonik knew better than to fight him here in this corridor, where it was tight and dark.

Follow me, Borrus, he thought. *Come on outside.* He could hear the others stamping down the steps, and turned to follow. The Barrel Knight was on his heels, panting wildly, roaring bloody vengeance for the maiming of Amron Daecar, the death of Aleron. Jonik ignored him. *It isn't him,* he told himself. *He doesn't think that, not anymore.*

He reached the common room, as the men sped out into the yard. Jonik chanced a look back, inadvisably. Not looking where he was going, his foot landed on a dead man's hand and he slipped, tumbling forward, the Nightblade dislodged from his grip. He could hear the great bull closing in on him, hear the wild pants growing nearer. He scrambled back to his feet, reaching forward to take the black hilt, and suddenly Gerrin was there, helping, grabbing him by the arm and pulling him out the door.

Jonik stumbled again as he exited into the chill night air, losing his balance, falling to the icy flagstones. He spun onto his back. Gerrin was there, defending him. He had his broadsword in his grasp, swinging it two-handed in a heavy strike. The attack caught Borrus flush on the breastplate in a great clanging blow, hard enough to rock him. It slowed him, but only just. Borrus's rage turned on Gerrin now, hacking hard with his blade, left, right, downcut, up, swinging sideward in a great sweeping arc. Gerrin went on full retreat, stumbling away, parrying where he could. He was well armoured from heel to neck but his head was exposed, and the links of ringtail he wore between his plate were vulnerable to a man of Borrus' strength and skill.

The Barrel Knight drove him hard across the yard, forcing him to the wall beneath the viewing gallery. Jonik was back on his feet, readying to give chase. The others were already closing, Emeric, Mooton, Sir Bulmar all dashing to encircle the man, like wolves around a raging bear. They were shouting at Borrus, telling him to wake, or trying to distract him, Jonik couldn't say. He took a pace toward them, then heard the voice behind him.

"Jonik."

It was said in a soft whisper.

Jonik turned and saw a man, standing at the top of the steps, bordered in darkness. He wore a plain cloak of dark umber, a match for his plain face. *A face I've seen before,* Jonik realised. An unremarkable face, forgettable, expressionless. The face of the Steward.

"Jonik, come with me."

Jonik tried to fight the voice. *No,* he thought, *no, I'll not,* but even as that thought went through his head he found himself moving forward, making for the steps. He frowned down at his feet. *No…no… turn, go back.* They went forward, one after another, left, right, left, right, up the steps, up and up.

"Jonik!" The voice was behind him. Emeric's. It sounded strangely distant, as though heard through water. Jonik wanted to turn around, but couldn't. Up the steps he went, up, up… "Jonik, stop. *You*…you leave him! Leave him alone, sorcerer! Get out of his head!"

"Emeric Manfrey," said the Steward. The voice was as clear a voice as Jonik had ever heard. Suddenly there was no other sound in the world. "Stop. Do not come closer. Stay here with Sir Borrus. In two minutes he will tire, and return to you. You need but dance with him a little longer."

Jonik was reminded of Ghalto, the Whisperer, but there was something profoundly more powerful about this man. "Who are you?" he managed to ask him, staring into that plain, ageless face. "What do you want with me?"

"Who I am is not important. It is whom I serve that matters."

"The Shadow King," Jonik said.

The Steward smiled. "So you call him. Now come, Jonik, and do not fear for your friends. The dying tonight is done."

59

Elyon

He landed, exhausted, buckling to his knees. Blood dripped down his armour. The blood of dragons and men and beasts, reeking of iron. Elyon planted the Windblade into the earth, pushing up. The battlefield was a frenzy of fighting all around him, half-seen through the predawn gloom. Hundreds lay dead and dying. Thousands. He could hear them, hear them all. The battlecries of the living. The bleats and whimpers of the doomed. Amidst the chaos, sunwolves roared and starcats hissed, and dragons screeched through the skies. *So many dragons,* he thought. *Too many…*

"Prince Elyon!"

He looked in the direction of the voice. It was Sam Garrick, the sellsword, as drenched in blood as he was, striding toward him. Elyon righted himself, pulling air into his lungs. *I need to get back up there,* he knew. *Show strength. Inspire.* "Sam. Where is Sir Lawrence?"

"Dead, Prince Elyon. A dragon…it came down and killed him. Half of his men have fled for the hills."

Elyon gave no reaction. He'd known men would desert as soon as the battle began. He had even seen them, the shapes of soldiers escaping north through camp, moving past the torches and campfires. "But not you, Sam," he said.

Sam Garrick shook his head. "I'm no coward, my lord."

"I can see that."

Elyon drew several more breaths. The air was a blend of smoke and morning mist, the eastern horizon beginning to burn with the early glow of a blood-red dawn. The fighting had spread far beyond the boundary of the camp now, descending into a chaos of fire and steel and blood. Everywhere fires were ablaze, the grasses scorched by passing dragonfire and burning barrels of pitch. The immensity of the Bane stood to the east, half shadow and half flame, dragons swarming around it like crows above a corpse. *They smell death,* he thought. The greatest fortress in all the north was about to fall, he knew.

"Have you seen my uncle, Sam?"

"No, my lord. It's hard to see much of anything out here."

Elyon could waste no more time with him. He'd only landed for a brief moment to catch his breath, stopping here in this rare pocket of calm as the fighting raged around him. "Get back into the battle," he ordered the sellsword. "Take charge of Sir Lawrence's men."

He mustered the winds and took flight, bursting up through the smoke and the mists. The fires lit the battlefield to east and west and south. The noise was deafening, a cacophony beyond anything Elyon could have prepared for. *This is what two hundred thousand men, mounts, and monsters sound like, when they come together in battle.*

Away to the south of his position, a dragon had landed upon the field. A small swarm of men were prodding at it with spears, as Bladeborn leapt and stabbed, using their enhanced strength and speed to overwhelm it. All around it smaller battles were raging. There remained a semblance of order in the lines, yet there were several breaches now, the enemy breaking through the ranks and getting in behind them. Some were rampaging through the encampment, Elyon could see, burning tents and pavilions. A host of Sunriders appeared to be surging through to their rear, hunting down every archer they could find.

He bellowed out orders to whoever might listen. "The lines are breached! Close the gaps! Hunt those Sunriders down!"

A mounted host heard him and gave chase. They passed by a catapult, as men worked to load it, releasing the mechanism to send another spray of heavy rocks into the enemy's midst. Most of their siege weapons sat idle now, for fear of hitting their own men, yet occasionally one would groan and throw to where the Agarathi were clumped together. The enemy did not seem so constrained. Many times Elyon had seen the dragons sweep over the battlefield, disgorging great spouts of amber-red fire over the men clustered below, catching their own soldiers in the inferno. Elyon could not tell if this was simply the work of the wild dragons, unable to tell friend from foe, or whether they just didn't care. *Collateral damage,* he thought. *When you have four times as many men as your foe, you can afford to lose a few in the crossfire.*

Dawn was brightening in the east, turning the skies to a deep cobalt blue. The full scope of the battle began to emerge from the pall of darkness, spreading distantly in its devastation. Elyon could see several large heaps dotted across the fields, shadowed mounds that could only have been dragons. He wondered who had killed them, and how many had died to do it. But it was a fleeting thought. In the aftermath the stories could be shared. Now was not the time.

To the west, lit by the rising sun, he sighted men dressed in pink and pale blue, blades flashing in the morning light. He descended toward them, and there he spotted his uncle, amidst the thick of the fighting, scything imperiously through a troop of rank and file Agarathi.

"Uncle!" Elyon came crashing down to land beside him, a knee to the ground. He stood, as Rikkard's men surged forward to continue the fight. "Twilight, where…"

"Dead." Rikkard gestured across the field. "A starcat slashed under his crinet as he reared up, cut his throat." He blew out a sigh, but could not mourn his horse now. "I got the beast and rider both. And others. But it's not enough."

"Uncle." Elyon stepped in, took his arm. "The Bane will fall. The Golden Tower is close to toppling and the Lookout Tower will follow. Half the wall walks are ablaze, and half the scorpions destroyed. I don't know how many are dead. Hundreds. We've killed a dozen wild dragons, but they keep coming. Ven seems happy to sacrifice them to take the fort. This isn't a battle we can win."

"We hold the line, Elyon." Rikkard lifted his visor. His eyes were narrow and intense. "We've killed thousands of them, tens of thousands. We keep killing until they break. We've seen it before…"

"We haven't. The Agarathi have never attacked with this many dragons. Never. Not since the gods were at war."

"We hold the line." Rikkard didn't want to hear it. "We hold the line until there's no other choice. We're not routed yet. Every Agarathi slain, every dragon downed, is one less to continue the fight. We make them pay in blood and death, Elyon. We make them bloody pay."

He doesn't know, Elyon realised. *He doesn't see the battle as I do. None can.* "If I could only fly you up there, you might see…" He stopped, breathed out to clear his lungs. A part of him knew his uncle was right. *Not yet,* he thought. *There is still hope.* "Hold the line, then," he said. "But when I see those lines shattering, we'll have no choice but to retreat. A retreat is better than a rout, Uncle. Already they're getting in behind us."

Rikkard didn't seem aware of that. "Where?"

Elyon pointed. "There, and further west as well. I saw Sunriders breaking through. Others are burning the camp. Sir Lawrence Bollingbrook is dead, half his men fled. It left a hole. It needs to be plugged. But there are others…"

"I'll take care of it." Rikkard looked around, as though wondering where his horse was, then remembered. "A horse!" he shouted. "Someone bring me a strong bloody charger!"

An Amadar man-at-arms came riding in. "My lord, take mine." He dismounted to allow Rikkard to take his place.

"I commanded men to give chase on those Sunriders," Elyon called out, as his uncle mounted up.

"They'll need help." Rikkard settled in the saddle and grabbed the reins, turning the horse back, then shouted orders to his men. Some came to ride beside him; the rest continued the fight. "Have you seen the others, Elyon? Killian, Rammas, Marian…"

"I've been at the fort," Elyon said. He had spared little thought for them, nor Lancel and Barnibus or the rest. He'd not had the time. Before the battle began, he'd told Lord Kanabar that he intended on hunting down the Agarathi leaders, and Vargo Ven in particular, but he'd found himself dragged into the Bane's defence. For hours he'd helped to fight the dragons there, yet its fall felt inevitable now. He looked skyward. The brightening skies would make it easier to track his targets. "I'm going to find Ven," he said, coming to a decision. "If I can kill him, it might break them. At the very least it'll weaken them."

Lord Kanabar had told him to be wary of the pair. Rikkard said the same. "Dragons have incredible stamina for beasts their size," he said. "Malathar will not have tired, not so soon." He judged his nephew. Clearly, he saw the fatigue in his eyes. "Don't try to fight him unless you feel strong enough. If we lose you…"

Kanabar had said that too. "I know," Elyon broke in. "The men may lose hope. I don't intend to lose, Uncle." He steeled his eyes, such as he could, and took flight.

The clouds had lifted and broken up overnight, thinning to slim fingers stretching westward across the skies. As the sun climbed above the horizon, it painted their undersides in shades of rose gold and red. Beneath them the dark shapes of dragons moved in high circling patterns, resting before descending for their next attack. No dragon could breathe fire indefinitely, Elyon knew. Strong though their endurance was, the act of fire creation required great reserves of energy, and between flights they would need to recover.

Many others were flying much lower. Well rested, they dove and engaged, fighting with flame and fang and claw in shapes both large and small, thick-bellied and skinny, wide-winged and short, stubby-snouted and long, some with long lashing tails covered in spikes and horns and others blunt heavy ones tipped with bone-breaking clubs.

And not just here, Elyon thought. Some two hours ago, when the fighting had begun, he was certain he'd seen a flight of dragons heading further north. A dozen, perhaps even more, soaring high above him in the direction of the Lakelands. At their head had been one much larger than the others, the size of Malathar, maybe even bigger. But it was just a glimpse, and nothing more. A fragment of a nightmare, half-hidden in the gloom.

He scanned the skies, in search of his quarry. *Ven, where are you?* He'd not seen Malathar the Mighty once all through the night, nor the cruel dragonlord who sat his saddle. Elyon had not been surprised. Vargo Ven was no fool and would not risk himself or his dragon by venturing too close to the Bane. A single ballista bolt, tipped in godsteel and well-aimed, could kill even a beast of Malathar's size. Instead, he'd sent in the wild ones and the rogues, the dragons he could spare, those who had no fear of man and the deadly weapons they'd forged. *The expendables,* he thought, *but I'm not at the fort now, Vargo.* He scanned the skies again. *Come face me if you dare…*

There.

Elyon squinted against the rising sun, focusing his eyes on a patch of raised brown earth away toward the southwest. He could see a large beast landing, glittering gold on black, with two others circling above. *Ven, and his wingriders.* It had to be.

Ahead of Malathar gathered a host bearing banners of brown and grey, whipping in the wind. Payne colours. These were Marian's men, defending the western flank. The soldiers were making space, though, spreading it looked, and the Agarathi were doing the same. There seemed to be a brief impasse, as if the two groups had come to a short peace, even as the plains around them swelled with battle.

And then the answer came to him. *A duel,* Elyon realised. *Someone has called Ven down for a duel.*

They were some mile or so away, a short distance when in flight. He soared over the heat of the battle, over the thousands clashing beneath him. Some cheers accompanied his passing. *Show strength*, he thought. *Inspire.* He could see a figure now, garbed in godsteel plate, stepping before the great black-gold dragon, standing alone in its shadow as the sun climbed up behind it. His first thought was Marian. Or perhaps Sir Gereon of Greyguard. Yet as he drew nearer, he saw that it was neither of them.

Lancel, he thought. *Lancel, no…*

Elyon could only think of what Lord Kanabar had told him earlier. Of how Borrus had fought Malathar and Ven during the last war two decades ago. Of how a dozen other Bladeborn knights had drawn the pair down for a duel. Of how Borrus was the only one still living. *And Lancel is no Borrus Kanabar.* He was skilled, a fine proponent of Glideform and Strikeform in particular, but against Malathar, against a dragon that size…

The contest was already beginning as he landed at the front of the crowd. There must have been several hundred soldiers watching, cheering out Lancel's name. "Greymont!" they bellowed, as he dashed forward with his blade. "Greymont, Greymont," and all Elyon could think was, *Lancel, you fool. You bloody gallant fool.*

"Elyon…I tried to stop him…but I couldn't….he wouldn't listen…."

Elyon turned. Barnibus was there, riding in atop Biter. Both horse and rider were well spattered in blood and gore. He climbed from the saddle, looking weary and sore. He had to shout to be heard over the racket. "We were fighting…driving men back from the flank with Lady Marian…when we saw Ven and Malathar in the skies. Lancel rode after him, calling them down. I chased, but it was too late…" He looked at his friend, eyes curdled with worry. "It was what Ven said, at the parley. He dismissed him, you remember? Mocked him. Lancel's been muttering about challenging him ever since, for the honour of his house, but I never thought…I didn't think…"

He was interrupted by a loud trumpeting bellow, as Lancel

dashed forward in a silver whirl and swung down hard, slashing through one of the old scars at Malathar's flank. The dragon's scaly armour was weaker there, and the attack was true. Blood oozed from the open gash, red on gold and black.

Barnibus's eyes widened in sudden hope. "Go! Again, Lance! Again! Hit him again!"

He can't win, Elyon thought, even as the men roared out their cheers. He didn't say it. What good would it do? All he could do was stand there and watch. Watch his friend dash around and dance to his doom.

Lancel seemed buoyed by the drawing of blood, though, and the roars of the crowd. He went again, using his speed and size to get around Malathar's back. He looked tiny against the great black monstrosity, an insect circling the toes of a raven. The noise around them was frantic. The soldiers gave out another cheer as Lancel hacked at Malathar's thick muscular tail, though he did little but chip at his armour. The beast swung around, Vargo Ven craning his neck in the saddle, searching.

Kill him, Elyon thought. *The man, not the beast.* "He should target Ven if he can," he called to Barnibus. "Draw Malathar down, then leap and attack Ven. One good strike and he'll kill him."

"Ven's no threat," Barnibus shouted. "It's Malathar needs to die."

Elyon didn't disagree, but that wasn't what he meant. "If he kills Ven the duel is over, Barn."

Barnibus frowned at him. "You don't think Lance can win."

Elyon was done holding his tongue. "He'll die, Barnibus. He'll die and we can do nothing but watch." He hated that. These duels of honour. Like the parley, they were sacrosanct, and none could interfere. Once the challenge was given and accepted, it was dragon against man, Fireborn against Bladeborn, and anyone who might seek to intrude would be cursed as craven and condemned forever. *By the gods,* Elyon thought. *The gods, who are to blame.* He took a step forward. "I'm not going to let him die."

Barnibus reached out, grabbing his arm. "You can't, Elyon. You can't get involved."

Elyon whirled. "Why not? For my honour? For the *gods*." He spat the word out. "They want their show, that's all this is. They want to sit and watch from their high golden thrones as their game of war goes on and on." Elyon snorted, as Lancel slinked around Malathar's back once more, prodding futilely at his hindquarters.

He was having no effect. *You kill a dragon at the head,* he thought. *Through the eye and into the brain. Or if you're strong enough you might be able to cut its throat.* Some of the scars on the beast were there, at the neck and shoulders, and inflicted by Borrus Kanabar long years ago. *A huge great man of the rivers, splitting six and seven feet, and strong as an ox. And still he failed to cut through.* What chance did Lancel Greymont have?

Elyon grimaced as he watched, frustrated. Death by a thousand slashes and cuts was only good when dragons were outnumbered, when men fought them in force and wore them down. In the duel, in the one-on-one contest, Lancel would tire much sooner than the dragon.

The head, he thought again. *Take a chance and go for the head, or try to target the heart.* That was another way, though not easy. A dragon's heart was big, yes, to pump all that blood around its body, but it was deeply set behind scales and muscle and cradled in a basket of bone that was extremely difficult to pierce. *But Malathar...he only needs one chance,* Elyon knew. *If he gets Lancel in his jaws...or his claws...*A beast that size could crush godsteel, he did not doubt. Vallath could, and so could Garlath the Grand, and Malathar was of their breed, immense and extremely powerful. He could scarcely watch. *And damn the gods,* he thought. He took another step forward. "I'm stopping this. Ven's mine."

"NO!" Barnibus shouted, so loud Elyon was forced to turn. "You sully your honour, you sully us all. You're our prince and champion. You can't..."

"So you'd let him die! Your best friend. Your brother."

"I have no choice. And he's made his."

"No." Elyon shook his head violently. He cursed himself for not getting here sooner. *I shouldn't have wasted time. I might have called him to duel myself. Slain him before his own men.* What would that have done for their morale? To see their great dragonlord fall. *I could have turned the tide, right here. I might have taken their hope and raised our own. I might have won this battle as Father did his, when he stood high upon the Burning Rock...*

But deep down he knew Barnibus was right. It was too late. If he joined the fight, the Agarathi would take it for a slight, and fight doubly hard. *And those bastards up there will curse me,* Elyon thought, sneering at the skies. He hated the gods, he had come to see. He hated their rules and their games.

"Fine," he relented, looking up to the skies. *There might be another way,* he thought. "I'll not interfere. Not in the duel. But *them*….them I *can* fight."

Barnibus followed Elyon's eyes up, to the pair of wingriders circling above them. He nodded, seeing Elyon's intent. "They're not part of the duel. Yes, you can fight them."

Elyon closed his fist around the grip on the Windblade's hilt. He had a final look at Malathar as the beast spun wildly, trying to catch the fly beneath his wings. Lancel was doing well, but wouldn't last. *He'll die*, Elyon knew. *Unless I can draw Lord Vargo Ven away.*

His wingriders were his hope. Attack them, and Ven might give chase, abandoning the contest. The northerners would mock him for a coward, but a man like Ven mightn't care. *Chase me, Vargo,* he thought. *It's me you want really. Who is Lancel Greymont to you?*

Elyon surged up into the sky as quickly and loudly as he could, hoping to get the dragonlord's attention. The two beasts above him were both ridden, unlike most. They had become a rare breed, these Fireborn riders, and these two were young and newly bonded, he guessed. If they were older or had fought in the last war, someone would have recognised them by now, but they hadn't. *Young, callow, and not nearly so large as Malathar,* Elyon thought. *And greatly easier to kill.*

The dragons screeched when they saw him coming, fizzing through the air like a thunderbolt. Both had classic forms, their wings, chests, snouts and tails in good proportion. One was a deep blue, with sparkling scales in pink and purple on its underbelly, the other a rich umber brown with a tail and wingtips that bled to grey. Their riders wore cloaks to match them, as ever.

They circled around to face him, the blue one shrieking as it folded its wings and plunged in his direction, the brown taking a wider arc, trying to get in behind him. *Try, just try,* Elyon thought. He shot straight for the blue, abandoning all sense of caution. Elyon was done with it. *These are my skies, mine. You do not belong here.*

He sped up as he neared the beast, flying faster, faster, faster. Out came those deadly claws, reaching, grasping, yet at the last second, Elyon flew up and over the creature's back, and swung. The Windblade raked along the top of its neck, severing scales, slicing through horns, and met the man sitting the saddle. Elyon had time to see the rider's eyes widen in sudden alarm as he jerked sideways, trying to avoid the steel, yet it caught him regardless, cleaving through his right shoulder and down the length of his arm, parting limb from torso.

Blood burst from the breach, and the Windblade sang in glee as it heard the dragon shriek.

Elyon swung about on a sharp turn, giving chase. He could hear the Fireborn shrieking in agony, though only thinly beneath the bellows of his beast. *Their pain is shared,* Elyon thought. Blood splattered into his face and armour as it poured from the rider's severed arm. The flow was fierce, and the man would soon be dead. *Let's end him a little sooner.*

He thrust forward in a blistering burst, pushing the Windblade through the man's back. The dragon emitted an ear-splitting scream. Elyon took a grip of the dead man's purply-blue cloak with his spare hand, holding on as the beast spun and whirled in grief and agony, trying to dislodge him. He held on tight, hauling himself down so he was seated in the saddle behind the dead rider. He slashed through the buckles, tossing the Fireborn to the wind. He went tumbling away into the sunlit skies, sparkles of bright red blood glittering in his wake. The dragon spun again, twisting and turning, yet Elyon held onto the handle at the front of the saddle, used for stability in flight, and thrust his feet into the stirrups.

He clung on tight, waiting for the beast to level out, before raising the Windblade high above his head and driving down with both hands in a savage thrust. He felt the point dig between the thick scale armour at the back of its neck, down through meat and muscle, cutting deep and deeper still until it jarred hard against the bony discs of its spine. He pushed harder, harder, summoning the winds to help him, and through the bone the blade went, cutting into the cord. The dragon's body juddered, its twisting and turning halting at once, body going immediately limp. And suddenly it was falling.

Elyon held on as it tumbled down in a vertical descent, tail and wings fluttering. He searched above him, behind him, to left and right, and saw the second wingrider away to the south, keeping its distance. He wondered why he wasn't engaging. *Fear? Does he fear me?* Then he saw the black-gold blur coming right at him. Malathar and Ven had disengaged from their duel, as he'd hoped. He spared a quick look down, to where the duel with Lancel had been taking place, but could see nothing but the chaos of battle below him.

Elyon withdrew his feet from the stirrups, unclasped his fingers from the handle, and let the dragon fall away. He waited in a cushion of air, hovering, as Malathar neared. *Not a mobile beast,* he thought. *Slow on the turn. Too bulky to be agile.* He narrowed his eyes on Vargo

Ven. There was something victorious in that cruel swarthy face. "Ven!" he shouted out. "You finally find the nerve to face me!"

He did not wait for an answer. *I'll kill you as I did your wingrider,* he thought, thrusting up and over Malathar's back, swinging. The dragon was wise to the threat, spinning into a barrel roll, blocking off Elyon's strike. Elyon spun about to give chase. Over the roar of the wind he could hear Vargo Ven laughing. "You're next, boy champion…oh, you're next…"

Next? Elyon felt his chest tighten. He slowed a little, as Malathar swung around to come at him again, momentarily blotting the rising sun as he passed. Then the light of dawn lit the beast once more, causing the gold on his scales to glitter. *And the red on his jaws,* Elyon thought. The beast gave out a thunderous roar, and Elyon saw blood on the tips of its teeth. *Lancel's blood,* he knew at once. *I…I was too late.*

Laughter cackled through the skies. Somehow Ven's voice sounded amplified up here, ringing out cleanly above the dull din of battle below. "Your friend was the fool to challenge me. Fear not, you'll join him soon…"

Elyon's lips broke open into a snarl. He went again, striking for the man atop the beast's back, but Malathar spun and dipped, and the chance was gone. Elyon went after him, getting in behind, following. Malathar had no hope of outmanoeuvring him, not so large as he was. "I'll kill you for this, Ven!" he roared, avoiding the whipping movements of Malathar's tail. "I'll kill you!"

Through the morning mists, the dragonlord looked back, grinning. "You are a coward to target the rider, boy champion. That is not how the duel is done."

The comment enraged him. "This is no duel! I don't play for the pleasure of the gods!"

He flew faster, closing, ducking past the swishing tail. *A little more…a little more.* Vargo Ven watched him come. Elyon saw him glance aside, and smile. Elyon glanced that way too, saw the second wingrider swooping down toward him. The brown-grey dragon was half Malathar's size, but swifter. His taloned feet came grasping, forcing Elyon to roll aside and dive away. Suddenly he was the hunted, as the beast drew in behind him. Light bloomed at the edges of his vision, a scorching orange-white. Elyon felt the heat and ducked, plunging, as the gush of fire flooded past, then spun in a sharp turn and shot upward. The brown beast was agile, but not agile enough. Away it went, climbing once more, circling. *Watching*, Elyon thought. *It will wait for another chance, and…*

Turn, whispered the Windblade.

Elyon whirled. Malathar was closing behind him. At once Elyon fell to habit and shot up, but the dragon anticipated it, going with him, snapping down hard with his massive jaws. Elyon felt the air shatter and tremble as those huge bloodied teeth smashed together, missing his feet by inches. "Close, boy champion. Oh…so close."

Elyon shot away, out of reach and range, spinning. Malathar flew by, a monstrous back form, moving into a wide smooth orbit around him. Above, Elyon could see the wingrider circling, watching. He remained where he was, turning slowly to follow Malathar's path. Vargo Ven's eyes were on him. There was a cruel smile cast onto his lips. "You tire, boy champion," he called out. "I can see it in the way you move."

"I'm just getting warmed up, Ven."

Vargo Ven laughed. A broil of black fume came puffing from Malathar's mouth, squeezing out from between his teeth, swirling. "Your army is tiring as you are, Prince of Vandar. Look…look how they break."

Elyon glanced down. They were hovering high above the battlefield, a mile up, near the border of the Bloodmarshes. From here, he could see the fighting in its entirety. See the fortress in flame. See the camp beyond it burning. See the lines of his army, punctured and broken. See the scattered carcasses of dragons and wolves, cats and mounts and men. See the skeletons of the siege weapons, and the black and broken barrels of pitch, and the thousand scorch lines that crisscrossed the fields where the dragons had blown their flame.

"This isn't a fight that you can win, boy champion…" Malathar continued to circle him, the wingrider doing the same above. "You have done well, better than I thought. I believed you would break when I sent the dragons in. But it was only ever a matter of time."

Elyon had no response. *He's right. We're breaking.* He remembered then what Vargo Ven had told them at the parley. About Eldur. "What you said…about the Fire Father…"

"It is true." Vargo Ven smiled cruelly. "Eldur the Eternal is arisen, as prophesied. Even now, as we do our dance up here, he seeks to strip away your one advantage. Even now he moves against you."

"*Where*?" Elyon's voice tore free, desperate. He thought of that flight of dragons he'd seen earlier, heading north. *It was him,* he realised. *Eldur*… "Where does he go, Ven! Tell me!"

Vargo Ven only laughed. "Why? So you can fly there to defeat him?" He threw back his head, roaring in joy at the notion, as Malathar rumbled, circling. "There can be no defeating him, boy champion. All shall be cleansed by Agarath's Eternal Flame."

Elyon didn't want to hear it. *Kill him, just kill him,* he told himself. *Cut that smirk off his smug face.* He narrowed his eyes as the dragon wheeled around him. Above, the wingrider was circling the other way, constantly vanishing from sight, before appearing again. Elyon had to keep glancing up and behind him to make sure it wasn't descending in attack.

"You cannot defeat us both, boy champion," Vargo Ven chuckled. "Not so weary as you are…"

"I call a duel, then," Elyon said. *I'll play your games,* he thought, snarling at the heavens. *If that's the only way to face him one-on-one, so be it.* "We'll fight on the ground, flightless. You against me, Ven, a battle of champions." He looked the dragonlord in the eye. "Do you accept?"

"No," Vargo Ven said at once.

Elyon snorted at him. "And *you* call *me* a coward?"

"Your army is defeated, the battle lost. Why should I risk myself against a man so *mighty* as you?" He grinned through the flattery, as he looked over Elyon's shoulder. His eyes lit up in joy at what he saw. "See," he said. "Your fortress falls."

Elyon glanced back, just in time to see the Golden Tower finally crumble and topple, breaking under its own immense weight. Huge blocks of ancient black stone, welded together by Ilith's magic, came undone, tumbling. The tower fell forward, southward, toward the walls, crushing men atop the bulwarks, sending up great surging plumes of smoke and dust as fire swelled all around it. A moment later, the sound reached them, a heavy distant rumbling shattering the air.

"A bane of dragons, no more," Elyon heard Vargo Ven laugh, and even as he did so, the Lookout Tower followed, collapsing as well. They were the only original towers of Ilith's creation still standing. And no longer. "Your fortress is fallen, boy champion," Ven called giddily. "The Bloodmarshes are mine. Death's Passage is mine. Won in the name of our Fire Father, the great and undying Eldur the Eternal."

Elyon was not listening. *Wallis,* he thought. *Get out, Wallis...get out...* He knew Lord Kanabar too well. He would stay to the bitter end, even as the fortress fell around him. Elyon felt a sudden urge to fly back, to help, to call the retreat. *It's over,* he thought. *We've lost, it's over...*

"Go," said Vargo Ven, as Malathar beat those huge black wings, circling. "You would be wise to go now, boy champion. I will grant you this clemency..."

"Clemency?" Elyon hissed, spinning to face him. He pointed the Windblade, gathered a vortex of roaring air about its length. "I've been hunted for this blade by others, yet you...you would let me leave?" He snorted at him. "You know you cannot beat me, Ven. You fear me, as you fear my father. Believe me, my lord, this is *not* done."

Vargo Ven only smiled that cruel smile. "It is done," he said, lifting a hand, gesturing below. "Oh, you didn't think this was our *full* strength, did you?"

Elyon turned his eyes straight down. He saw more men pouring from the marshes. There were thousands of them, swarming from the fogs like flies. *A second wave,* he thought, in dismay. *He sent out only a part of his strength. The rest...the rest he kept in reserve...*The rising of the sun was their call to enter, their call to join the fight. *It is done,* he knew. *We are lost.* His only task now was to save those he could.

So he spun, and fell, plunging down through the skies, leaving Vargo Ven behind him, with his dragon and his laughter. Over the dead and the dying, those fighting and already fleeing Elyon soared, screaming at the top of his lungs, "RETREAT, RETREAT, THE BATTLE IS LOST....RETREAT!"

He flew to the flank, where Marian's men fought on, and shouted. He flew down the shattering lines and shouted. Over Olorans he flew, bellowing those words, and over men of the marshes and lakes and rivers too. Over simple soldiers and highborn commanders, over men born in hovels and men born in castles, over men bearing spears and men bearing shields, men ahorse and men afoot, over Varin Knights and households knights and hedge knights and sellswords, over one and all he flew, shouting."RETREAT, RETREAT, THE BATTLE IS LOST...RETREAT!"

By the time he reached the wreckage of the Bane his voice was hoarse from the word 'retreat', yet he kept bellowing it all the same. He flew down through the tumbled towers and broken walls, calling for the survivors to flee north, for the hills and woods, for what havens they could find. Smoke poured up from the fires, billowing, and still the dragons came diving, picking off men as they ran.

Elyon saw blackened corpses, saw the dead trapped beneath the rubble, saw the skeletons of scorpions and ballistas tangled amidst the stone. The southward barbican and gatehouse had been decimated as the Lookout Tower fell, coming down atop it. The triple walls at the front of the fort were breached, and Agarathi soldiers were flooding in like water through a break in a dam.

Elyon swept through it all and landed at the enormous ward inside the northern gates. The thousand-horse stables were chaotic with men leaping upon their mounts, charging for the gates and hills beyond. Others looked intent on continuing the fight until Elyon bellowed out that the fortress was lost, and the battle too. *And the war,* he thought, though didn't say. *How can we fight Eldur? How?*

He grabbed a passing Marshman by the arm, his cloak showing Lord Rammas's crest. "Where is Lord Kanabar?" he shouted at him.

The man recoiled such was the intensity in Elyon's eyes. "I…I don't know, my lord." He pointed back. "He was still defending the barbican when it fell. On the walls, my lord. He…he…"

Is dead. Elyon let him go. "Get out of here," he said. His voice was suddenly dull. "The fortress is lost."

More men flooded past him, but for a moment he could only stare at the tangled wreck of stone and flame that filled the world before him. *Focus*, he told himself. *Focus, they still need you*. He uprooted, turned, and headed for the stables. "Snowmane," he shouted at a groom. "Where's my horse?"

The man had no answer for him. Nor did the next he asked, nor the next. In the chaos of it, anyone might have taken him. Horses were riding past, many of them without riders it seemed, bolting for the northern gates. Elyon scanned for any white ones amidst the frenzy but saw few. So long as Snowmane got free, that's all that mattered. He had no intention of riding him. *But I'll not lose him too…*

He was halfway through another scan when he sighted Rikkard riding through the northern gate on the charger he'd appropriated earlier, moving against the great tide of men and mounts in flight. "Elyon! I saw you flying this way…" His uncle galloped over and pulled the reins, coming to a swift stop. He turned his eyes to the devastation at the south of the fort. "My gods…I hadn't realised from outside…" He looked back down at him. "Wallis…"

Elyon shook his head. "He…he was in there, when it came down."

"Dead?"

"I don't know, Uncle." He could see little in the tumult of swirling smoke and fire. A part of him wanted to pick through the rubble, search for Lord Kanabar, but the chances of finding him, with the Agarathi swarming…

Another loud crashing echoed from the southern side, as a part of the Golden Tower still standing came tumbling down, shaking the ground as the great black blocks of stone plummeted into the earth. *Dragonfire undoes magic,* Elyon thought. They had worked relentlessly to undo the spells that bound the towers together, and succeeded. Any hope of finding Wallis Kanabar was gone.

Rikkard seemed to know that too. "There's nothing we can do, Elyon. The fortress is taken. We have to go." Men were still on the battlements on the northern side, and some of the ballistas were still firing. Through the pouring smoke, dragons flew past, sometimes diving in attack, always screeching. The noise was deafening, the tumult overwhelming. "I passed Killian on the way here," Rikkard went on. "He's mustering men for a rearguard, to defend the retreat." He turned in a circle on his borrowed horse, bellowing orders to flee. The men on the battlements were beginning to rush for the steps, though a few stout fellows were refusing to budge. Rikkard looked at him again. "Go, Elyon, you're not doing any good here. I'll get them out."

Elyon felt suddenly lost. Lost, stricken, and exhausted. "Where?" he could only ask. He felt helpless. How many of his countrymen were dead? How many couldn't he save? *I was meant to show strength, to inspire.* And what had he done? Not enough. Not nearly enough.

"Join Killian. Protect the rear." Rikkard took a moment to swing from the saddle, stepping toward him. He clasped his armoured hands to Elyon's armoured shoulders in a clang of steel. "We fight another day, Elyon. Not all of us, but those who remain. We fight another day, for those we've lost. It's not over. *It's not.*" He gave him a shake. "Do you have strength left in you, Nephew? Tell me true."

Elyon found it. "Yes, Uncle."

Rikkard studied his eyes. "Then use it," he said. "Join Killian. Help the men escape. There will be a time to mourn those we've lost here, but it isn't now. It's *not now,* Elyon. Do *not* lose hope."

Elyon swallowed. *Do not lose hope.* He filled his lungs, nodded, and summoned the winds once more. And out of the fortress he flew, to help defend the retreat.

60

Amilia

The room still stank of death, long after they had taken him away. *Sir Jeremy,* she thought, *my sweet handsome knight.* She touched the chains on the wall where he'd been fettered, softly, just to hear them rattle.

For two days he'd been suspended here, in this cold stone bedchamber, before the poison had killed him, bursting his heart in his chest. The poison that had been meant for Hadrin, the poison that should have set her free. But it hadn't. It had doomed her. Doomed her to this cell, and this curse. Doomed her to sit here and watch, tied up to the end of the bed, so that she might bear witness to her lover's death.

Those two days had been the worst of her life. Sir Jeremy had been beaten beyond recognition, his jaw shattered, teeth a red ruin, eyes so swollen he could scarcely see out of them. For the first day, he'd hung there unconscious, breathing in a slow painful rattle as blood and saliva dribbled down his chin. But that wouldn't do, no, not for Hadrin. A man had come to revive him, thrusting some putrid potion down his throat so he might wake. "You'll be conscious for your death, scum," he'd said, spitting in his face for good measure. "By order of the King of Rasalan."

Amilia had wept more than she thought possible that day, as she sat there, bound in rope against the bedframe, unable to reach out to comfort him as his final hours and minutes ebbed by. "Don't cry, Amilia," Jeremy had told her, in a spluttery slur of a voice, blood dripping from the wreckage of his mouth. "Don't cry, it'll all be OK soon."

That had only made her cry all the more. *He's the one who's about to die,* she'd thought. *It should be me giving him solace, not the other way around.*

But that wasn't true, not really. *He's the lucky one*, she realised, as his final moments neared. *He'll ascend to the Hall of Green, to a place of peace and plenty. He'll leave me alone, all alone, in here. In this room, where Hadrin will take me, again and again and again. Where I'll be trapped until I bear his child, until the foul fruit of his loins comes crawling through my legs...*

Her tears had run hot as fire down her cheeks. She'd pulled at her fetters, raging, but it was no use. "Be calm, my queen, my beautiful queen," Jeremy whispered. "It's OK. I feel blessed, to have loved you. You have given me more than I could have ever hoped for." He had even smiled, showing a mouthful of ragged gums and splintered teeth. "Find the happiness you deserve, Amilia. Be happy...my queen..."

Those were his final words. Even as he spoke them, he'd convulsed suddenly and horribly, opening his bloated, broken lips into a silent, muted scream as his heart exploded within him. It was terrible to behold, the way his swollen eyes opened so wide, bloodshot and blaring, the way his chest pumped outward, one, two, three, before his body fell limp and still. And in that moment, her tears had streamed harder than ever. *Alone*, she'd thought, watching his final breath give out. *I'm alone, all alone...*

The body was not removed for a further day or two, by which time the reek was ripe. The men who came to take him had to shield their mouths and noses with their sleeves, and one of them even dashed back outside to retch, his gags echoing loudly down the hall. When they'd managed to get him unfettered from his chains, Sir Jeremy's body had collapsed to the floor in a boneless heap. The way he fell forward brought his face close to hers, those empty eyes, that beautiful brutalised face, those tousles of rich brown hair she'd loved to play with when they lay abed, slick with grime and blood.

My handsome knight, she'd thought, staring at him vacantly, as one of the guards stepped over to untie her from the bed. He'd looked down at her, staring at him like that, and gave a huff. "What, no tears? Thought you cared about the boy."

Amilia just kept staring, saying nothing. *I loved him,* she thought. *And I've no more tears to give.*

She was given little comfort in the days and weeks that followed.

Maids attended her, ugly old things, bringing her food and clothes to change into, taking away her chamberpot for washing. They looked at her sinisterly and said nothing when she asked for tidings. "We're not at liberty to say," one told her once, in a sharp angry voice. "Don't ask again, else you'll feel the back o' my hand."

She hadn't asked since.

It was five days before Hadrin visited her, arriving with the same guards who'd dragged out Jeremy's corpse. He looked more drawn out and crazed than ever, a manic look etched into his eyes. There was something jittery about him, in the way he blinked and moved. "You'll give me a child, Amilia," he'd said. The cloying adoration in his voice was no more. In that at least she was thankful. "No more potions for you, to slay my seed. No more kindness, no more courtesies. I will tie you down and take you, as often as I see fit. Men." He waved to the bedposts. "Get her ready."

She fought, though it was of little use. Perhaps it was for Jeremy that she did it, or perhaps herself, but she managed to rake her fingernails down the side of one of the guard's faces, digging bloody gouges into his cheek. He'd roared and gone to strike her, but Hadrin had told him no. "I like her pretty," he'd said. "Thank you for proving to me why you need to be bound, Amilia. I had considered letting you out soon, to rejoin me in our marital bed, but no, I can see you need more time."

The curses had boiled off her tongue then, foul words she'd never once spoken. By the time the guards had her tied to the bed, her voice was raw and hurting, yet she screamed on all the same. "She'll need to be gagged as well," Hadrin said, as he disrobed, and it was done.

It was nothing she hadn't endured before, and as ever her husband did not last long. He instructed his men to release her once he was done, before telling her that he would return soon. And he'd been good to his rotten word too, creeping back into her cell every two days or so, sometimes eerily calm, sometimes jumpy and unsettled, his demeanour growing increasingly disturbed all the while.

After two weeks Amilia thought about ending it. She could try to dash her head against a wall, or break a leg off the bed, and impale herself. She could wrap her neck up in the chains that her Jeremy had died in, and hang herself, or pounce on one of those old winkled crones when they came to bring her food and see if they had a knife with which she might carve open her own neck. She had a hundred thoughts like that, but none went any further than her head. *I'll not take my own life on his account,* she thought defiantly. No, Amilia Lukar still wanted to live.

Her cell was somewhere at the rear of the royal residence, itself tucked away into the back of the palace under the shadow of the Snowmelt Mountains. Most days she could hear nothing from in here, nothing but her own breathing, her own footsteps, her own voice. When the silence got too desperate, she would speak to the ghost of Sir Jeremy to stay sane. But elsewise the only sounds she heard were those made by her guests. The old crone maids and the guards and Hadrin, when they ventured here for their visits.

Until today.

Today, she *could* hear something. A dull din, hanging in the air, as though hundreds or even thousands of people were all shouting out at once. *A festival?* she wondered. *Somewhere down in the city?* She did not know the Rasal events calendar like she did that of Tukor, though with all their ludicrous sea gods and nymphs and sprites, all their temples and holy sites, she could quite imagine that every day here could be filled with zealots and worshipers praising one deity or another.

But then, she'd not heard anything like this before. And it didn't seem the time for festivals, with war in the south. *A riot?* she thought, and that gave her a little more hope. Maybe Prince Sevrin had stirred his followers to attack the palace? They would surely have heard by now of her failure to kill the king, and if they wanted Hadrin gone, what choice did they have but to march on the palace in force?

The notion inspired her. She stepped to the wall and pressed her ear against the stone, listening. There was a faint humming, though so far back to the rear of the palace she couldn't hear much else.

But…was that screaming? Something thin and high reached through the stone to claw at her ear. She listened some more, and heard it again, though oddly, it seemed to be coming almost from *above* her. She drew back, moving to Jeremy's chains. Her fingers curled about the cold iron for comfort. "What is it, Jeremy? Do you think they're coming to save me?"

She had wondered what had happened to her other Emerald Guards, the knights she'd not entrusted to know of her plots and plans. Most likely, Hadrin would have had them rounded up and killed, or imprisoned at best. But…maybe not. *Maybe some of them got away, joined with Prince Sevrin's forces. Maybe they're coming here now, cutting their way through Hadrin's Suncoats and palace guards.* She had an image of Sir Munroe Moore being cornered by her men and chopped to bloody pieces. That made her smile. Or maybe that knight standing guard for Sevrin could do it? *Sir Karsten,* she remembered. He had a strong look to him, that knight. *They could all take turns, hacking Sir Munroe up, then come down here and whisk me away back to Ilithor. Back home.*

It was a childish fancy, probably, but maybe not. She pressed her ear against the wall again. The noise was getting louder now, she was sure of it. *Something's happening out there.* There was panic. She could feel it, humming in the air.

She paced away again, moving side to side, thinking. If this was Sevrin attacking the palace, Hadrin's men might get to her first. *I have to arm myself,* she thought. *But with what?* There was nothing in the room save that bed and a chamberpot.

She marched to the bed, bent down, and tried to turn it over so she might break off a leg or support slat, use it as a spear or club. But the bed was far too heavy, a massive bulky thing that she had no hope of shifting. The chamberpot would have to do.

She moved to pick it up. Once, Amilia Lukar, the Jewel of Tukor, would have balked at the idea of handling her own filth. Yet that girl was dead. *Hadrin's killed her.* She picked the pot up, threw aside its fetid contents, and moved to the door. She thought about what she might do. If Hadrin's man, she'd bring this pot down on his head, take his blade, and run. If Sevrin's…

She paused, unsure. *I failed to kill Hadrin,* she thought. *I failed my side of the bargain.* Sevrin had every right to let her rot down here for that, yet something told her he wouldn't. She looked to the chains where Sir Jeremy had been bound. "He was a good man, wasn't he, Jeremy? Sevrin. He'll send me home, like he promised. He'll take pity on me, and mercy, don't you think?"

As ever, the ghost of Sir Jeremy Gullimer gave no answer.

She turned again to face the door, waiting. The wait went on too long, so long she grew weary of holding that heavy chamberpot in her hands, and put it back on the ground. She pressed her ear up against the thick oak. *I'll hear it when they come,* she thought. *I'll pick the pot back up then.*

She heard no one coming, though, not for three minutes, five, ten at least. There were other sounds, though. The distant clank of steel on stone, of armoured men running and shouting. A buzz of panic, in the palace and beyond, as though the great hive that was Thalan had been prodded at with a giant stick, and every resident in the city had come swarming from the nest.

"It has to be Sevrin," Amilia told herself. She glanced back at the chains. "It has to, Jeremy. What's the alternative? No enemy army could march this far, could they?"

She moved away from the door again, pacing at the foot of her bed. She needed to get her legs moving. *No*, she thought. *There's no chance*. The Agarathi and their allies would never try to attack Thalan, not before subduing the other northern powers. And even then, how would they get here? Overland would take too long, and by sea was hardly simple. They'd have to sail to Bleakrock, and attack from the east, but sailing the Stormy Sea was notoriously difficult in this season. The other route would be up the Sibling Strait, then the Izzun River, right into the harbour. But there was no sea power greater than Rasalan, and they'd make them pay dearly if they dared approach that way.

She continued pacing. "This is Sevrin, for certain," she said, to the chains. "This is Sevrin and he's going to free me. Nothing else makes sense."

She pressed her ear back against the door. Still nothing. The not knowing was setting her on edge. She spoke some more to the Ghost of Gullimer to try to calm herself, pacing every once in a while, returning to the door to listen. There were other sounds out there now. Destructive sounds, as though the palace was being besieged, shaking the walls. She sniffed the air, and frowned, alarmed.

Smoke. It was smoke, she was certain. The palace was burning. *I'll be trapped in here*, she thought, suddenly afraid. *If they don't find me, I'll be roasted alive…*

There was nothing for it. She picked up the chamberpot and slammed it against the door. "Help!" she called out. "Help! Let me out!" She smashed the copper pot against the wood again and heard the thuds echo away down the corridor. "Help, help!" The smell of smoke was getting stronger. She could see wisps of it now, curling under the door, thin grey fingers reaching for her toes. "HELP! HELP! I'M IN HERE! HELP!"

She smashed at the door some more, screamed some more, and made such a racket that she barely even heard it when the key was thrust into the lock. But she did, just. She perceived that scraping sound, over her shouting, and stepped back abruptly, so startled she dropped the pot.

It clanged on the floor, as the door pushed open. At the threshold stood a young maid with a thin face, narrow jaw, and sharp eyes. Amilia had expected some soldier or guard. She frowned, recognising her. "Astrid?"

"Queen Amilia." The girl stepped inside, leaving the key in the lock. She was about Amilia's own age, perhaps a year or two older. "We have to go."

"Yes, I..." Amilia looked down the corridor. Smoke drifted about, eddying on the air, though wasn't as thick as she'd feared. "What's happening out there?"

"The city's under siege." Astrid looked around the chamber. She'd come to Amilia once before, giving her a message from Elyon Daecar, to see that she was OK. Amilia had told her yes, that she was fine, but that was before everything had gone so wrong. *So horribly wrong*. But she had the sense that the girl had been looking out for her all along.

"Who are you?" she asked her. "You're no normal maid."

"I work for Lady Marian Payne, Your Majesty."

Amilia had heard of this Lady Payne. "The spymaster?" It fit. "You're a spy?"

"I was placed here to report on matters in the palace," the girl said. "But that was before. I haven't heard from her, not for a while. But the message I gave you, from Elyon Daecar. I was told by Lady Marian to help you, if you needed it..."

Too late, Amilia thought. She might have come sooner, once Amilia was locked away, but truly, what could she do? It seemed like she was just one girl. No match for Sir Munroe and his men. "You're Bladeborn, then? Trained?"

Astrid nodded. "I trained here at the university, for a time. I'm no great warrior, Your Majesty, but..."

"Amilia. My name's Amilia."

"Yes, A...Amilia." Astrid opened her maidservant robes. "I have a godsteel dagger with me. And I know the palace well enough now. I've learned its secrets these last months. I can help get you out of here."

"For Elyon? Why would *he* care to help me? He killed Melany." Even as Amilia said the words, she doubted they were true. She sensed her grandfather's foul prints all over that. And Elyon had been a great admirer of her father. *And...and Aleron,* she thought. *Perhaps he's helping me for his brother's sake?*

"I…I don't know about any Melany, my lady," Astrid said. "But either way, I'd help you. I'm Tukoran by blood and birth, and you're my princess. I won't leave you here to die."

Die. It was bad, then, out there. "You said the city's being besieged? If this is Prince Sevrin, it's OK. I was working with him. Get me to his forces, and I'll…" She broke off, seeing the look in the girl's eyes, that fixed look of fear. "This isn't Sevrin, is it?" she asked.

Astrid shook her head, swallowing. "No, my lady. It's…it's dragons."

Dragons… Amilia's eyes shot up to the ceiling on instinct. *That screaming, above…*

Astrid took a hurried pace into the room, glancing around. "Your things…"

"I have no things," Amilia said. "Just this chamberpot." She gave it a kick. "And I'm happy enough to leave it behind."

"Yes, my lady." The girl sounded contrite. She blinked at her guiltily. "I…I'm sorry I couldn't have come sooner. I heard you tried to kill the king, and feared what would happen to you, but…"

"But it was too dangerous, and too risky. I understand, Astrid. No regrets." More smoke was puffing in from down the corridor. That made sense as well now. *Dragons.* She shivered in her skin. She'd heard that they were ranging far, yet all the way up here? And more than one. "Do you have a second blade on you?"

"I'm afraid not, my lady. Can…can you bear godsteel?"

"I'm a Lukar. Of course I can." She wasn't trained, but the strength of her blood meant she'd be able to wield the metal well enough. "How hard can it be? Point and poke."

Astrid smiled. "Point and poke. Yes, that's all I can do. Saska was always the best."

"Saska? A girl you trained with?" Amilia realised this was no time for chitchat. "Later," she said. "You can tell me all about yourself once we get out of here." She had a final look at the chains on the wall. *Goodbye, sweet knight,* she thought. *Maybe I'll see you again soon…*

The odds of that were strong, she wagered, as she followed Astrid down the smoky corridor. *Dragons…how can there be dragons so far north?* She tried to put it from her mind, though the implications were bleak. *If they're striking here, where else are they attacking? Varinar? Ilithor?* That last thought set her teeth on edge. *My home. Will I return to find it in ashes?* "Do you know how many there are, Astrid? Dragons?"

"No, my lady." Astrid walked briskly, clinging to her dagger in its sheath. She looked nervous and unpracticed, yet diligent enough, stopping at every turn to check the way ahead. Amilia wished someone less callow had come, but wasn't going to quibble. *Better her than one of Hadrin's men…* "I think there are several, though. I could hear them screeching, above the palace walls. They seemed to fly in from over the mountains to the south, taking the city soldiers unawares. They're at their ballistas now, trying to drive them off. It's the best chance we'll have to get you out."

The smoke thickened yet further as they came to a circular stone hallway with a frescoed domed ceiling, branching into other parts of the residence. Ahead, the central chamber that gave access between the residence and the palace proper lay undefended, the doors wide open. *They've all been drawn out to fight,* Amilia thought. She stopped for a moment. Smoke was pouring from several different corridors and she could feel heat burning there too, sense the licking tongues of fire slavering upon the palace. There were booming sounds as well, and shaking, as walls and buildings were blasted by dragonfire.

The city is being destroyed, she thought. *Is this it? Is this the doom Hadrin muttered of in his sleep? Is this what he's been seeing in the Eye?*

"My lady, we *must* go." Astrid gripped her arm and led her on. They hurried down a fuggy corridor and up a set of stairs.

"Where are we going?" Amilia called out over the din. There was shouting not so far away, up above them. Men would be firing their scorpions upon the parapets, and archers would be sending flights of arrows at the dragons as well.

"To the north, my lady," Astrid called over the noise. "There's a way, that leads up into the Highplains from the palace. We can make for the coast from there. Find a boat, maybe. Get you back to Tukor."

She sounded uncertain. Was anything certain now?

They passed down a broad hallway with paintings on the walls, more frescoes on the ceiling depicting Rasal heroes and battles of old. Amilia had enjoyed looking at them as she wandered the palace halls and corridors, before she was imprisoned in that cell. That and gazing from the balconies was her only solace. *And Sir Jeremy,* she thought. *He and his bed, and the whispered dreams we shared…*

A cold wind came blowing in from the left, where a broad garden terrace opened out, scattering the smoky air. The sounds of battle roared from without, the shouts of men and screeching of dragons. *I have to see,* Amilia thought. *I have to…*

Before Astrid might grab her arm again, she rushed outside and onto the open balcony, one she'd visited often to gaze out over the city and harbour, watch the boats come in, listen to the hum of the markets and city life down on the streets, the chants and murmured songs of prayer as worshippers gathered at the temple steps.

Yet all that was gone now. The boats in the harbour were afire. The city was burning. The streets were filled with panic and screams. It was nighttime, the skies dark and curdled with smoke and cloud, the moon and stars blotted and hidden. She had thought it was day, but time was hard to judge in her cell. Above, shadows flew past, stirring the smoggy air. She saw rivers of fire pouring from the darkness, saw thick ballista bolts flying, sighted the shadows of men on the walls and towers, desperate in their defence of the city.

"My lady…Amilia! We *have* to go!" Astrid came in behind her, taking her arm again. "Please, Princess…it's not safe here…"

Is it safe anywhere, Astrid? Amilia thought. She was seeing it, the doom. *Hadrin was right. The end is upon us.*

A shadow bigger than the rest flew overhead, pulling at her clothes as it passed. Amilia's heart rose up into her throat as she watched it soar above her. In its saddle was a white-haired man in a rich red cloak, lit by the light of an orb, glowing atop a black wooden staff. She followed the dragon's flight path, as it swept toward a high tower at the northern edge of the palace, near the rugged mountain cliffs.

Hadrin's tower, she thought. *The Tower of the Eye.*

She squinted that way. The top of the tower was crowned in a magnificent steepled dome, accessed by a steep switchback stair with thick stone walls and lanterns hanging at every turn. Amilia had been up there but once, when Hadrin showed her his prize. "The Eye of Rasalan," he had said, so proudly, showing it positioned at the heart of the rotunda atop the tower. It was on an ornate yellow stone pedestal, decorated in squares and diamonds in shades of blue and gold, before which Hadrin would stand for hours on end, gazing into the Eye, trying to divine sense from the shadows and shapes and swirls of colour he saw.

Amilia had never wanted to go up there again, not after that first time. That Eye had turned him into a monster, driven him mad. He was haunted by his father's brilliance, by the heckles of the commons who dismissed him as a pale shadow of his sire, lacking in foresight, deficient in the wisdom with which his forebears were so famed. In response he'd fallen into a dark obsession, watching the shadows of doom approach. And even now…even as the city fell, Amilia could see him up there, see his figure through the windows, standing at the plinth.

She closed a fist. The entrance to the tower wasn't far. Her mind waded through the hurts and cruelties he'd made her endure. She thought of all the times he'd wriggled between her legs. She thought of that night at dinner, when he'd seen through her plot to poison him, when he'd screamed and raved and had Sir Jeremy so brutally beaten. And the days that followed. Tied to that bed, watching her sweet noble knight die before her eyes. And after…the rapes, the abuses, the despair he'd wrought.

It all bubbled up inside her, fierce and hot, as that great dragon circled the tower. *It will kill him,* she thought. *It has come to kill him, destroy the Eye.* The thought did not give her the pleasure she'd expected. *No. It should be me. I want to kill him, like I was supposed to…*

Without thinking, she turned, reached into Astrid's robes, and pulled her godsteel blade from its sheath. The girl stumbled back, stunned, though Amilia did not stop to hear her calls and objections as she sped away, rushing down the corridor.

The godsteel felt *right* in her grasp. She had held the metal but rarely, though had never had trouble wielding it. *I'm a Lukar and a Kastor both,* she thought, feeling that heady sensation as the power of the divine metal infused her. *I was born to bear godsteel. Born, if not bred…*

The dagger gave her strength. She ran clumsily, though quickly, quicker than she ever had, almost tripping such was her haste. Her eyes blurred at first, yet after several rapid blinks, they cleared, keener and sharper than ever. *I am daughter to Rylian the Brave, granddaughter to the Warrior King, niece to Cedrik Kastor, born to kill, they say. Godsteel is in my blood and bones.*

The sensation was intoxicating. She had always known that, of course, but had never used godsteel in anger, never held it with intent. *I would sneak Rob and Ray's daggers from their belts when they were younger*, she remembered. She did that just to toy with them, though always gave them back quickly enough. *I liked to prove how strong I could be, if I'd been born a man.* Sometimes, she wished she had. To be a warrior, not a woman born to wed. *That's all I ever was. A pawn in my grandfather's games.* She narrowed her eyes and ran yet quicker, reaching the door to the tower, pushing in, speeding up the first switchback stair. *No longer…*

Behind, she could hear Astrid screaming at her, her voice echoing through the halls. She ignored the girl, moving up the steps, up and up, back and forward, up and up…

Halfway to the top she slowed. The dagger started to feel heavy in her grasp. Her potential was strong, but her blood-bond weak. *I haven't had a chance to develop it,* she cursed. *But I will, if I get out of here alive. I'll learn to bear this metal. I'll learn to fend for myself…*

A sudden rumble shook through the stone at her feet. She stopped, looking up. Dust motes swirled in the air, and bits of grit came raining down, clattering through the hollow of the tower. The world shook again, harder, so violently she needed to steady herself against the wall. Then there was a crashing, right there at the top, and a loud rending of stone. *It's landed,* she realised. *The dragon, it's here…*

She might have turned back then, fled away, given up, but something drove her on. Hatred. A deep and implacable hatred for her husband that bulled her own sense of self-preservation out of the way. She was near the top, so close. *I can't turn back, not now. I need but a chance,* she thought. Maybe Hadrin would come running down after her in a bid to escape, or she'd catch him near the top of the stair. *One stab, through that dark heart of his*, she told herself, *and it'll be done. And one in the groin for good measure…*

On she went, panting hard now, the blade beginning to weigh like an anchor, but she held on tight. Astrid was coming up from below, closing. "Amilia…my lady…Amilia…stop…" she could hear the girl pleading.

She saw the top of the stair, where it opened into the rotunda. A hot smoking wind came swirling down from above, through the breach the dragon had made. She could hear a shrill bleating, high pitched and terrified, over the din of the city under siege. "….you… you've come for me…" Hadrin was whimpering. "Oh gods…you've come for me…"

"I come for the Eye." The voice was a restrained whisper, yet sounded like it was right there, in her ear.

Amilia recoiled at the sound, stumbling as she neared the top. A deep thrumming fear crawled up her spine, yet she didn't stop, she couldn't. Surging up and over the final steps, she burst into the open chamber, godsteel to grasp.

Her eyes took in the scene. Hadrin stood with his back to her, cowering from the man in the fiery red robes. Between them was the plinth, and the Eye, glowing in shades of gold and blue. Behind the old man, the stone wall of the dome had been torn apart where the dragon had gouged a door for him to enter. Amilia sighted the beast outside, perched on the mountainside just beyond the tower. *Blue and silver*, she thought, seeing the scales catch in the firelight, spreading through the city below. *And eyes as red as blood.*

She took it all in with a glance. "Hadrin!" she shouted. He was close, only a half dozen paces away. "Hadrin, look at me!" He turned, face a mask of utter terror, pale as milk, lips quivering. "Bastard!" she screamed at him, as she rushed forward, stabbing.

"No." The word filled the chamber. "He is mine."

The white-haired dragonrider tapped the bottom of his black staff into the stone. A tremor ran through the floor and a pulse spread through the air. It hit Amilia hard, knocking her backward against the wall, the godsteel blade tumbling from her grasp. Her head hit against the stone, fogging. She wheezed, trying to pull air into her lungs. Through her blurred vision, she could see the wizard step forward.

"Stand," he said to Hadrin. "Pick it up."

Hadrin shivered to his feet, back bent in terror. He reached out with tremulous hands to lift the Eye of Rasalan from its sacred plinth. The old man looked at it, red eyes in a bone-white face. "You are the Blood of Thala," he said to Hadrin.

"I…I…"

"You. Yes you." The man considered him, nodding. "Come," he said, in that spreading whisper. He turned, and said a little louder. "*Garlath*, come."

The dragon stirred from the mountainside, opening out its great wings. *Garlath*. Amilia knew the name. It glided over and landed with a crash on the side of the tower, claws grasping at the stone, lowering its massive bulk for them to climb atop its back. Amilia stared in horror and wonder, paralysed. She could feel her bladder emptying into her dress, warm and wet. Thinly, Astrid's voice could be heard screaming somewhere. "Princess…princess…Amilia…we must go…"

She turned her eyes up. The girl was right there, right there beside her, trying to lift her to her feet. The world seemed hazy and indistinct, as though this was all a dream. Everything moved slowly, shapes and colours shifting. "Amilia…stand…stand up… stand up!"

Drunkenly, she obeyed, pushing to her feet. Astrid dashed to fetch the dagger, thrust it into its sheath, grabbed Amilia by the arms and pulled her to the steps. She could scarcely walk she was shivering so hard, her legs wobbly and wet, head pounding. She tripped at the top step and went tumbling forward, slipping from Astrid's grasp. Half a turn down the stair she went, before she came to a stop at a landing, battered and bruised. Astrid plunged after her. "My lady…my lady, are you OK?"

Amilia gave a ragged nod. She could not summon words. Astrid pulled her back to her feet. Above was a crashing, the beating of wings, a swirl of air, as the dragon took flight. "My lady…please, if you can walk…we have to go…"

Amilia drew on her reserves of strength. Muddy-headed, foggy-eyed, she fumbled her way down the steps, one after another, Astrid at her side.

When they eventually reached the bottom, she collapsed out into the hall in a sprawl of limbs, panting and shivering. Astrid was shivering too, curling her arms about herself. "Who…who *was* that?" Her eyes were wide. She sounded deeply shaken. "He had…he had a staff. And that orb, that stone. What…what was that, my lady? He was not like the Fireborn I've ever heard…"

"He wasn't a Fireborn," Amilia said, in a hoarse whisper. Her lungs were still burning, smoke swirling in the air. She started to get to her feet, stumbling over to a nearby window. Outside she could see the city burning, the dragons swarming, hear the screams and wails and shouts.

"Not a Fireborn, my lady? But…but, he was riding a…a…"

"That was Eldur, Astrid, arisen," Amilia said, looking out. Her husband had been right all along.

And this is the doom of our days.

61

Jonik

They walked down a wide ancient hallway of polished black stone, black iron sconces holding torches along the walls. It was a part of the Shadowfort Jonik did not know, a part that no man did tread. *Only the mages*, he thought, as he followed the most powerful of them. *Only the true masters of the order.* "Was that you, with Sir Borrus?" he asked the Steward. "You put him under that spell?"

"I did." The Steward had a smooth voice, smooth gait, smooth manner. Everything about him was effortless and ageless. "I needed the distraction, Jonik. But do not fear, he will have calmed by now, and retained his rightful mind. No more of your friends will perish tonight. This I promise."

Jonik walked a step behind him, and to the side, powerless to do anything but follow. The Nightblade sat at his hip, resting silently in its black scabbard. There were no whispers, no urgent warnings. Much as Jonik might want to reach for it, and thrust it through the Steward's back, he couldn't. "It trusts you," he found himself whispering. He could feel it, somehow. He could *feel* that in the blade. "It…it *knows* you."

"It should," the Steward said. "I was there when it was forged."

It took a moment or two for that comment to sink in. Then Jonik shook his head. *No…no, that makes no sense,* he thought. The Nightblade had been forged three and a half thousand years ago, along with the other four Blades of Vandar, hammered by Ilith in his ancient workshop high in the mountains above Ilithor. "You...you can't have been," he finally said.

"Why not?" The Steward slowed, then stopped, turning to face him. His eyes were a burnished brown, deep and rich, his skin no more aged than a man of thirty five. "Do I not look old enough?" Something approaching a smile curled in the corners of his mouth. "There is much you do not know, Jonik. Much that has been kept from you, as it has from all others. This...*Shadow King*. You think him evil, yes? You think him some malicious spirit, or mage, some demon sorcerer, living off the blood of Bladeborn boys." He gave a short chuckle, then his smile was gone. "There is some truth in this, perhaps, and matters that one might find sinister. But however sinister, they are essential. As are the things that *you* have done. The burden you have been forced to bear has always been part of something bigger."

The mage turned, and walked on, giving Jonik a moment to ponder that. He followed, as though drawn on a string. "You're talking about my orders," he said, after a few seconds had passed. "To assassinate my father? Kill my brother?"

"I am."

Jonik didn't understand. "But those were by order of Janilah Lukar. I thought...I was told..."

"You thought wrong, Jonik." The Steward's slippers made little sound as he walked, whispering faintly on the stone. "Janilah Lukar has only ever had the illusion of power. He has been a king, yes, and a man of great influence in his time, but his true desire of divinity was never meant to be. He is realising this only now. And in doing so becomes a better man. A man walking a more righteous path, as he must."

They continued through the hall, moving between pools of shadow created by the torches on the walls, taking him deeper into the mountains. A thousand questions were bubbling up inside Jonik's head, though when each bubble burst it frothed into a dozen more.

"So...it was you?" he asked eventually, staying a careful step behind him. "*You* gave the command? You set me on this path?"

"I gave nothing. The path you walk was not of my design."

"The Shadow King, then?"

The Steward kept on walking, giving no answer. He led him toward a wide arched doorway and into another chamber, square in shape and empty except for the armoured men, standing at the corners of the room. None moved or stirred. Jonik peered at the one nearest and saw that it was stone.

Statues, he realised. Statues depicting great heroes long gone. He recognised Varin, in all his might, great-bearded and broad-shouldered, with a cloak flowing at his back, armoured from heel to neck in lobstered steel. In his grasp was the Sword of Varinar, planted into the earth before him.

The Steward saw Jonik looking. "A fine depiction," he said. "Varin was always as loud as he was large. A little *too* loud, for my tastes, though my master was ever-so-fond of him." He gestured to the other statues, one by one. "Varin's children," he said. "Elin, Iliva, Ayrin. Elin was much like his father, powerful, tall, heroic. And Iliva, my…she was as fierce as she was beautiful. They hold the Frostblade, and the Windblade, as you can see. These are the Blades of Vandar they died with, in the famed fight with Drulgar the Dread."

The Steward stepped over to the final statue, that of Ayrin. He shared in the likeness of his father and brother, yet was notably smaller, strong if not so grand, armoured if less spectacularly. He bore a blade, though it was sheathed, his sword hand only resting lightly on the pommel. Between his other fingers was a book, opened out, as though he was reading. It was in keeping with what Jonik knew of the ancient king. "You knew them," Jonik could only say, finally finding his voice.

"I did. Though none so well as Ayrin." The Steward stood before the statue, looking up into his face. "Ayrin understood the value of temperance and learning. He was an erudite man, with a strong inner authority. Oh, he could fight, yes, but that was never his first instinct."

"The wise man and the warrior in one," Jonik whispered. He'd thought the same of Emeric. But where Jonik rubbed shoulders with modern men of renown, this man, this Steward, had lived in the time of Varin and Ilith and Ayrin. He could not get his head around that. "Who are you?"

"A servant." The Steward did not turn. He stood as still as the statue before him, staring up into Ayrin's wise eyes. "This order was built to fulfil a function, to carry out a specific purpose. I was given that task, to build it, guide it, follow the instructions she did give me. *Balance…*" He let the word hang in the air a moment. "You have heard that preached many times before. We keep the world in balance, we help steer its course. Oh, you have come to believe otherwise, but in truth there is no lie in those words." He turned, finally, to face him. "Ayrin's teacher is our own, Jonik. She who took the youngest son of Varin under her wing and taught him wisdom and restraint. She who looked through the eye of a god, and saw the future shape out before her. Thala, the Prophet Queen, has always been the patron of our cause."

Jonik stood there in mute astonishment. "Thala..." Everything he knew of the founder of Rasalan was of goodness and light, righteousness and wisdom. *How could she be associated with such a place as this?*

"I understand your confusion," the Steward said, smiling at him. "Come. There is more to show you."

He continued on in that effortless stride, moving through into the next chamber. This one had a statue as well, but just the one, a great gargantuan figure of the Prophet Queen herself. Thala, wisest of them all, carved in a flowing silken gown, hair tumbling in a wavy waterfall down her shoulders and neck, all the way to the small of her back. She faced into the hall, hands placed upon a great stone plinth accessed up a short stair. A light seemed to shine upon it, though Jonik could not see its source.

Atop the plinth a book was illuminated.

"Climb the steps, Jonik. Have a look."

Jonik walked to the stair, and up onto the raised platform. The statue of Thala smiled down at him, her eyes seeming to follow as he moved. The book was leather-bound and ancient, its clasps of simple silver styling. It lay open toward the end of its many pages, the parchment etched in a beautifully graceful script that Jonik could not understand. "This language," he said, voice echoing softly into the room. "I...I don't know it."

"There are few who do. It is an old Rasalanian dialect, long since fallen into disuse. Before the northern kingdoms adopted the common tongue there were many languages spoken across this continent, as there are in the south. This is one, a very old one, known only to rare scholars and men of esoteric study. But as you can see, the writing is singularly beautiful. I have often wondered if that is the reason Thala chose it. Simply because she liked to scribe in those long flowing arcs and curls."

Jonik had to pinch himself. *Thala.* The demigoddess was universally accepted as benevolent. He was struggling to reconcile what he was hearing, with what he knew of the order. The abuses of the boys, raising them in pain and darkness, the bondage and brainwashing and corrupt contracts. It all flooded through his head, yet he could not find himself angered. Perhaps the Steward was somehow suppressing it. Or perhaps there was more to this than Jonik realised.

He looked down at the book again. He could guess at what was written within. "This book instructs on the contracts," he said. "It lists those to be slain, through history and time."

The thought of that was almost overwhelming, yet he steadied himself all the same, and waited for the Steward's response.

It came swiftly. "Just that, yes. Long ago, Thala brought this book to me, and told me of my task. I am but part a piece of a puzzle, Jonik, as you are, but there are others, many others, spread through space and time. Your task was to master the Nightblade, to ride forth and cripple Amron Daecar. This was an order given by Janilah Lukar, yes, but one seen by Thala, long millennia ago. She wrote that it must be accepted."

"But..." Jonik thought on that a moment. *Cripple*, he thought. *Ride forth and cripple him.* "You're saying I was never meant to kill him? Only cripple him?"

"What happened, happened, and it happened for a reason. You were sent out to slay your father. That he was merely crippled and not killed is critical, for he had a journey of his own to take. All is connected in the great tapestry of time. Thala told me that once." He smiled at the memory.

Jonik wasn't smiling. He was struggling to compose himself, struggling to comprehend the implications of it all. He looked down at the book once more, wondering if Aleron's name was written in there somewhere, if his death in the final of the Song of the First Blade had been foreseen as well. It might have absolved him of some guilt, but didn't. He felt like nothing but an instrument, just a tiny cog in a vast machine, clicking and clanking and turning through time...

He steadied himself against the stone plinth. He felt lightheaded all of a sudden. "Why?" he whispered, swallowing. "All this killing... all this death...why? What is its purpose?"

"War," said the Steward at once. "All that has happened these last months and years are but small individual events that have accumulated to instigate war. The conditions must be met, for the favoured outcome to present itself. That you had to strike at your own father, and brother, is of great regret to you personally. Yet in the tapestry of time, a single life is irrelevant. To achieve a great end takes great sacrifice, Jonik."

Jonik gave that no response. He understood the logic, though it tasted bitter on his tongue. His eyes moved from the book before him, to the blade at his hip. Still it rested there, silent. "Is my purpose complete?" he asked. The Nightblade had whispered of him becoming a leader, and a champion, but perhaps that was just a lie. *And Ranulf...he spoke to me about giving it up,* he remembered. Hearing all this...it made much more sense now. Yet all the same, the idea of being parted from it...

"That I cannot say," the Steward told him. "Thala only saw so far herself, and beyond a certain point, all is blackness, Jonik. The blank pages in the book before you demonstrate this. The board has been set, and the pieces placed, yet from here...from here the final outcome is unknown."

Jonik turned and climbed back down from the high plinth. There was nothing else in the chamber but the stage and statue and book, as there was nothing in the one before save those statues. He could see more passages leading away, more chambers unfilled and unfinished. Ilith had built this refuge, he knew, but its vastness had never been needed, save for the few who lurked these halls. He thought of the Shadow Order, of the battle just gone. There were so many more questions fighting to be spoken, so much that didn't make sense.

The Steward seemed to sense it. "You have questions, I know. You wonder now, having heard all you have, why I did not greet you at the gate, explain to you all the truth right there."

"It might have spared bloodshed," Jonik said. "Men have died out there tonight." He cleared his lungs. "Do they know? Do the masters know of any of this?" *And did Gerrin?* he wondered. *Was this a part of his purpose, to bring me back, and the Nightblade too?*

But the Steward shook his head. "The men knew nothing. Only the mages have knowledge of these halls, though even they can be kept in the dark. I have selected wisely for the jobs I have needed filled. Trust is a commodity not given freely here, Jonik. I learned that from Queen Thala. She herself had a particular interest in keeping the pieces of the puzzle separate, as was necessary."

"So the rest? The masters and knights? What are they to you, but hired killers, living a lie?"

"They are tools sharpened for a purpose. They are men raised to fulfil a function." He gestured to the book. "Every instruction therein needed to be carried out, every vision seen in the Eye of Rasalan brought to completion. This is our duty, Jonik. This is our task."

Duty. Task. Violence. Darkness. "You could have done it another way," he said bitterly. "You didn't need to raise these boys as slaves and weapons. You didn't need to make us suffer such cruelty."

"In the span of time the lives of those here mean little. Men have died here tonight, dozens of them. Do you know how many have died further to the south? How many hundreds. How many thousands. War rages, Jonik, and hundreds of thousands will die before it is done. It is our task to ensure that their sacrifice leads to a brighter dawn. If we fail, all will be shadow and war, a battleground of eternal conflict not seen since the age of the gods. Already it begins. The skies swarm and the monsters rise, yet in this darkness, so light fights back. You are a part of that light, you and others. That this order has become known as the *Shadow* Order is a matter of irony that has never been lost on me, but in its founding, secrecy was ever essential, and secrecy lives in shadows, Jonik. We have built the order to operate in a specific way, for reasons you may never fully understand. The trauma you have experienced growing up here compromises your judgment. You may never be able to look upon what we have done with dispassion."

Dispassion. This ancient mage had it in spades, clearly. "It's a lot," was all Jonik said, grunting the words out. "I came here to kill you, you and your king. Now I learn all this. What do you expect?"

"Just this. You are only human, Jonik. It may sound trite, but all of us have a fate, and yours has brought you here. Trust that, if nothing else. And follow me. It is time you met him."

Him. The Shadow King.

He followed, unable to resist even if wanted to, moving nervously behind the Steward as he stepped down another corridor, through a great cavernous hall filled with tables gathering dust, past an ancient armoury and library and lounge, down a passage with bedchambers to left and right, dozens of them, dozens upon dozens, sitting idle and unused for millennia.

He saw many statues and busts along the way, though this time his host did not stop to discuss them. It seemed that half of history's famed men and women were exalted here, kings and queens, warriors and champions, great thinkers and scholars and singers and scribes. Jonik was looking upon the true refuge that Ilith had built, a haven full of treasures, for the people of his kingdom to flee. He had wondered how the Shadowfort could possibly accommodate so many, but he wondered no more. The place was immense, vast, seemingly never-ending. And empty. Completely and utterly empty.

Until Jonik caught sight of a hunched old figure, waiting at a door. A long nose poked out from beneath his hood and he wondered, for a moment, if this was the king he'd come to kill. Then the Steward spoke his name. "Fhanrir. Fear not, all is well."

Fhanrir. The creature Gerrin has described as performing the blood rituals on the king, keeping him living. Was any of that true?

"Hamlyn," the old mage said. "You got the boy alone."

"With a distraction," the Steward told him. *Hamlyn*. Something in the name rang a bell. "The violence is over, Fhanrir. The purge is complete."

The creature Fhanrir looked at Jonik from beneath the folds of his cowl. His face was mostly shadowed, but what Jonik could see was visibly rotting, his flesh and skin accursed. Blood magic. Dark magic. But performed on whom? Jonik wondered now if it was in fact the Steward who the likes of Fhanrir were keeping alive. Was that the reason he looked so youthful after all these years? Or was it merely illusion that clothed him, as it had the creature Parsivor?

Jonik pondered that as the two mages met eyes. "You have him well controlled, Hamlyn?" Fhanrir asked. He glanced at Jonik suspiciously, though Hamlyn only laughed.

"I *had* him, at first," he said. "But now Jonik and I have spoken, and he understands what we are here to do. I need not take him under my spell again." He gave Jonik a brief, questioning glance. "The boy will bring no bloodshed here."

Fhanrir remained unsure. "That the truth of it?" he asked, in a rattling voice. "I'll not let you near him until you give your word, on your honour. No blood. No violence. Swear it, boy."

Hamlyn chuckled once more. "Fhanrir is a worrier, always has been, Jonik. We have been working toward this for so long, you see. He fears something foul will befall us, at the end."

"If it does, it won't be from me." Jonik reached to take a grip of the Nightblade, though made no move to draw it. In truth the Steward's magic was so subtle that he could not say whether he was under his spell or not. All the same, he gave his oath. "I'll bring no blood or violence here," he said. "On my honour, and this blade."

Fhanrir snorted softly, though seemed a little happier with that. "Fine. He may pass, then."

Hamlyn smiled and placed a hand on Jonik's shoulder. "Come. He is right through here."

He led him into the chamber, a large open space, circular in shape, with a single item of furniture; a marble bed, sitting at its heart, with a figure sleeping atop it. Jonik peered at him as he neared, his heart hammering softly in his chest. The old man on the marble table was small, slim in the body and face, his arms neatly laid out by his sides, his head cushioned on a satin pillow. A soft blur of light filtered down from above, though as before, Jonik could not see its source. Dust motes danced and capered in the glow, giving off an ethereal air. He looked dead. Jonik could see no rise and fall of the chest, nothing to suggest he was breathing.

"Who is he?" he whispered. Speaking any more loudly felt wrong here. He gazed at the man, studying the mild features of his aged face, the golden hair going grey, the hint of a brown tunic beneath the single green sheet atop him. *Brown and green. The colours of Tukor.* As with the name Hamlyn, he was certain he knew the face. *I've seen him before,* he realised. *But where?*

He looked up into the Steward's eyes as he gave answer. "This is the man you know as the Shadow King, Jonik," he said. "But in truth there is nothing of the shadow about him. King...yes, he was once a great king, long years ago, the greatest who ever lived. But never did the shadow touch him. Not one so loved as he."

He stepped forward and reached out to the sleeping king's head, tenderly moving aside a curl of hair. "He has lain here for millennia, sustained by my magic for a single purpose, by order of the Far-Seeing Queen." His eyes dipped at that, deeply saddened. When he lifted them again, he turned to look across the hall; through another open archway, Jonik saw a curious void of light, rectangular in shape, shimmering. "The pieces of the puzzle are coming together, Jonik, as Thala did foresee. What you are looking at is a portal door, through which another critical piece has come. A young man who shares blood with the king who lies before you, a man who is his last living heir."

Jonik looked at the face again. Realisation dawned. He knew the face now. He'd seen it a thousand times before, on statues and busts, in paintings and parchments, etched and illustrated into innumerable works of art. But even so, he could scarcely say it. He opened his mouth to speak, and out came the name, so softly, so quiet. "Ilith," he whispered. "This...this is Ilith."

"Yes," Hamlyn said solemnly. "Ilith, who forged the blade at your hip, who was my friend and my master and my king. Ilith, who built the world in which we live. Ilith, never to rise again." He reached out and touched a finger to the king's cold cheek, as a tear drifted down his own.

"But...he died. How…how can he still be here?"

"To fulfil a purpose. And a function. To pass on the last of his power, so he might rest, freed forever from this form." Hamlyn looked up into Jonik's eyes. "The heir's name is Tyrith, Jonik, and he didn't come here alone. There were two others who came through the door with him. One…one will be of particular interest to you."

Jonik could take little more of this. He'd stepped into a world of gods and myths, a world of portals and purpose and instructions written through time. He let out a breath, still reeling from the reveal that Ilith, the founder of Tukor, was lying in stasis before him. *This is impossible. I am dreaming, I am dead. Someone slew me out there in the fortress and this is all happening in my head.* Eventually he found his voice. "Who?" he asked

And for once the Steward did not drag it out. "Your mother," he said.

62

Ranulf

Ranulf Shackton set the parchment to the flame and watched it blacken and burn.

For the last time, he hoped. It was his ritual, his duty, the weighty burden he'd borne on his back. Long months he'd kept the formula secret, kept it safe, but that trial was at an end. Things going well, they'd reach Aram by nightfall, and when they did, he had every intention of passing it on.

"Doing that little burning thing again, are you?" Leshie emerged from her tent, stretching, catching him as she had several times before. She yawned and walked over to the fire where he sat. "So? You going to tell me what that's about yet?"

"I'm going to tell you what I've told you half a dozen times before, Leshie."

"To mind my own business?" she ventured.

"Just so. In time it will all be revealed, and you'll likely find it terribly dull. But for the time being, grant me this secret. At least for a little longer."

She shrugged insouciantly. "You the only one up?"

Ranulf looked over to the monstrous silhouette of Agarosh, sitting a hundred or so yards away upon a shallow hill, watching the sunrise. "Just us," he said. Sentries weren't so important anymore, not with the mighty moonbear in the company, so most of the time the Butcher just let his men sleep.

"He likes doing that, doesn't he?" Leshie said. "Watching the sun come up."

Ranulf had noticed that too. Every morning, Agarosh could be seen somewhere nearby, gazing east at dawn. Even in the rugged hills he would find somewhere high to climb so he might observe without rocks or trees to obstruct his view. "Perhaps it reminds him of his home," Ranulf said. "The plateau where we first met him faced east, and moonbears are very thoughtful creatures, Leshie. I wonder what he thinks of when he watches the new day dawn."

"That it's very pretty, probably," Leshie offered. "Isn't that why anyone likes to watch the sun rise and set? For the colours and the beauty?"

"It reminds him of my great uncle," Saska said behind them. She stepped over from the tent she shared with Leshie. Joy came with her, loping at her side. "He and Justo used to watch the dawn together, every morning. It strengthened their bond, seeing the moon fall and sun rise, the changing of the celestial bodies. Agarosh kept doing so after Justo died. It's why he'll never bond me, even if I wanted him to."

She turned and stepped away from them, stroking Joy as she went, and began packing up her tent. The other men were beginning to emerge from their tents as well, stretching, yawning, moving off around the rocks to empty their bladders of the wine drunk the night before. They had enjoyed a few more cups than normal, owing to their proximity to Aram. *One more ride*, Ranulf thought. *One more ride, and I'll finally get to see her…*

Leshie lingered with him a moment. "It's…kinda sad, what Sask said, don't you think? Who knew something so big could be so sensitive." She looked at the monstrous bear forlornly. "Poor thing. It makes me want to cry."

Ranulf raised an eye.

"Don't look at me like that," Leshie scolded. "I *can* cry, you know. I'm not completely heartless." She strained to shed a tear, as though to make a point, her face going as red as her hair. After much effort, her eyes glimmered wet and a single tear gathered, grew, and slipped down the side of her cheek, snaking lazily toward her jaw. She pointed at it in victory. "Aha! You see! I told you, didn't I say!" She grinned at him, wiped the tear away, then marched off to help Saska pack.

The camp was quickly struck, Umberto, Slack Stan, Garth the

Glutton, and Marco of the Mistmoors seeing to most of the work. The rest were either dead or too badly injured to help. Dobbs and Owen Oat had been killed during the fight with Mar Malaan's men, Marush Moonface was beheaded by the Butcher himself for dissent, Juri had broken his leg when his horse fell on him, and the dusky, green-eyed Merinius fractured an arm falling from the saddle.

The Butcher was neither dead nor injured, but considered himself too important for such work. He stood aside looking south, munching on a ripe persimmon as his men made preparations to leave. Ranulf stepped to join him. "All set to go?"

"The Butcher is set for everything, always," the sellsword captain said. He took another bite of fruit, the juice glistening on his lips and chin. "But is the little Rasal adventurer set to keep his end of the bargain? This is the real question, Ersel San Sabar."

"He is," Ranulf said. "I'll speak to the Grand Duchess when we reach the city. She will see you well paid."

"I hope so, I do. It would be a great shame for me to have to hurt you, my friend, for lying to me." He delivered the threat with a customary smile, but a threat it was, Ranulf was sure.

"Hurt him and you'll have *us* to answer to." Leshie was clearly listening to their conversation, even as she and Saska packed their things. "Oh, and him." She pointed to Agarosh, the bear's silver-white crystal fur bathed in a glorious gold dawn glow. "He's on *our* side, Scarface. Mess with one of us, you mess with us all."

The Butcher laughed. "I think me and the great bear get along quite well. I am part bear myself, haven't you heard?"

"The Bucklands *aren't* bears," Leshie snapped back. "They're just hairy men. And who says you're related to them anyway?"

"I do. And that has always been good enough for me." The Butcher looked at Ranulf again. "Well, Ersel San Sabar, I shall trust you to make this a priority, when we reach Aram. I have lost three men, let us not forget. For this the price goes up."

"You didn't *lose* three men," Leshie called over, irritated. "You lost two. The other one you killed yourself. We all watched his big fat face go bouncing down the rocks."

"An insignificant detail. Death is death. These men were killed in the service of protecting the pretty princess and for this, I expect to be..."

"You'll be paid." Saska spoke stiffly, as she stuffed a blanket into the saddlebag of Leshie's rouncey. "You have my word. Just stop talking about it." She gave him a hard look, then strode away across the rocks to spend some time with Agarosh.

The Butcher pursed his lips. "She is curt today, the pretty princess. Why is this, when we are so close to home?"

"Nerves," Ranulf said, watching Saska walk away. "She's never met her grandmother before, Butcher. And she's been trying to get to her for half a year. Part of her is worried something will go wrong, and the rest is worried by how she'll be received."

The sellsword frowned, scars twisting in the morning light. "She is the lost heir of House Nemati, the lost Princess of Aramatia. How else could she be received, but in joy and celebration?"

Ranulf didn't want to get into the deeper details of it, not now, not with this man. "Just go easy on her today. And enough of this talk of money. It's classless, Butcher, even for you. Safina Nemati is back in the city now. She'll pay you. Just stop yapping about it."

The big sellsword lifted his shredded chin. "The Butcher does not yap. This is for little dogs. Bears like Agarosh and me…we roar." He smiled over at Leshie, knowing she could hear him.

They were on the road soon after, riding along a dusty old goat track that wended through the parched Aramatian Plains. The weeks since that day on the mountain had been smooth sailing, their party unmolested by Mar Malaan or anyone else. Having a moonbear in the company tended to have that effect. The plains were noted for being good hunting grounds for bandits, yet if there were any such groups hiding about these hills, Ranulf had seen no sign of them.

The bear had often felt a reluctant member of their company to him, though. He walked alone most of the time, staying off the road or following some distance behind, and at night would sleep well beyond the bounds of their camp. Leshie had found that curious. "Aren't you going to bond him?" she'd asked Saska that first day, as they descended down the south face of the mountain. "I mean, Joy's awesome and all, but she's *just* a starcat. You could ride a moonbear, Sask. A moonbear. Imagine that. A *moonbear*."

"Saying it over and over won't make a difference," Saska had told her. "Agarosh was bonded to my great uncle Justo. That's why he's with us. To protect us and make sure we're safe, as I asked him. But he won't let me bond him. Nor would I ever want to."

Leshie chewed on her lower lip in thought. "I guess I understand. It's like…if you're married to someone. And you jump into bed with someone else. That's being unfaithful. It's the same thing."

"Sort of," Saska allowed. "I'm bonded to Joy now, and I'd not have it any other way. Agarosh is just with us for a while. He's doing it for Justo. Their bond…it was special, Lesh. I would never want to try to compete with that."

She did spend time with Agarosh, though, often moving off atop Joy's back to ride alongside him. When that happened, Ranulf would hear a deep rumbling sound echoing out of the bear's massive chest, and he knew that they were communicating. Saska could understand those rumbles, she'd said, and would speak back at him, learning of her great uncle Justo and the experiences the two had shared. Sometimes they would sit together at night as well, and Ranulf would watch them from afar, listening to the rumbles and the whispers, marvelling at the beast and the girl, yes, her most of all. *She is special,* he would think at those times. *Truly special, and more than she knows.*

He was thinking the same thing now, as he rode at Saska's side down that old goat track, studying the strain in her eyes as they inched closer to the city. Ahead, Leshie was riding with the Butcher, being wound up by him, or winding him up, it was hard to say. "I wonder who'll be the happier of the two of them when we reach Aram," Ranulf said, breaking the silence. "Leshie to be free of the Butcher, or the Butcher to be free of Leshie." He chuckled and looked over, but Saska hardly seemed to be listening. "Saska?"

She blinked and turned to him. "Oh…sorry, Ranulf. I was…in another world. What were you saying?"

"Nothing important." He saw that she was holding the little piece of coral she'd picked up at that reef. *For comfort,* he knew. *Her totem.* "She's going to be over the moon to see you, you know," he said softly. "Your grandmother."

Saska nodded, smilingly uncomfortably. "I know. I just…I hope I'm not a disappointment. Everyone seems to talk about my mother with such fondness, for her beauty and spirit. And she was pure…a pure Lightborn, pure Aramatian. I'm…" She shrugged, fiddling with the rock. "Well, I'm a mutt. A bit of everything. What if everyone looks at me like Elio did. Half the time I felt like he wanted to kiss me, and the rest…"

"To kill you?" When Saska nodded, Ranulf said, "Elio Krator thinks your father raped your mother. He thinks she died as a direct result of that, giving you life on the birthing table. And he has always hated the northerners besides, and Bladeborn most of all." He paused. "Not everyone is like Elio Krator, Saska," he told her, with all the comfort and reassurance he could muster. "The great and good of Aram will be overjoyed to see you. And your grandmother most of all."

She still doesn't believe it, he thought, seeing her give that awkward smile again and look forward down the road. Nothing he said would change that, he knew. *She need but wait, and see. Soon she'll know the truth.*

They laboured on through morning as the sun rose high in the sky, scorching hot and merciless. It had been as such for days, not a wisp of cloud in the air, barely a breath of wind to cool them. The trail led them past a dusty desert village, no more than a cluster of baked stone huts spread out among the rocks. The residents stared open-eyed to see Agarosh pass by, some falling to their knees in holy veneration, others fleeing in fright, disappearing into their reddish-brown hovels, dragging their naked children with them. Goats scattered, dogs barked, and cats hissed, slinking into the shadows. Agarosh ignored them, one and all. *He is above them,* Ranulf thought. *This bear is born of magic; he exists on a higher plane.*

They stopped briefly so they might water the horses at a little stream that ran down from the hills. Ranulf thought it best to speak with the villagers and see if they had news to share. He ventured forth on foot, leaving his horse in Leshie's care, and found a wizened elder still on his knees, humming some prayer in the direction of Agarosh, who stood a good distance away, utterly aloof and disinterested.

"Good morning to you," Ranulf said, in Aramatian. He had returned now to Ranulf Shackton in appearance, letting his hair and skin resume their original colour, as Leshie had long weeks ago. *I am Ersel San Sabar no more,* he thought, *no matter how much the Butcher calls me that.* "We make for Aram. I wonder if you have new tidings from the city?"

The village elder completed his prayer and rose. He was as thin as a bolt, all gristle and deeply tanned skin, wearing no more than a linen sash across his torso. "Stranger," he said. "Who among you rides the divine bear?"

"None," Ranulf said. "His rider is long lost."

The old man looked most surprised by that. He pulled at a brittle white beard. "I am soon to arrive at my eighth decade upon this good earth. Never have I heard of a moonbear that is not ridden, not here. All such reside at the mountain to the distant north, beyond the Everwood."

Ranulf didn't want to tell the man he was wrong, but there had in fact been occasions through history where moonbears had lost their riders, only to continue in some sort of service to another. Usually it involved close members of the rider's family, as was the case here with Saska and her great uncle Justo. Though, to be fair to the elder, such hadn't happened for long centuries, that Ranulf could recall. "Indeed," was all he said. "The bear will be known to you, I'm sure. Agarosh, the One-Eye, most exalted of all living bears."

"*Agarosh.*" The man's voice lifted and he collapsed straight back down to his knees, bending his back in praise. Ranulf waited. The elder rose again, eventually. "Holy Agarosh, the Magnificent. Can it be true?"

"It can." Ranulf looked around. Others had heard and were gathering, staring at the bear in wide-eyed awe. Even those who'd scuttled to their homes were re-emerging into the daylight, clasping the hands of their children, drawing them out to see. Soon enough almost everyone in the village had assembled. "I was asking about tidings," Ranulf pressed the old man, over the noise of voices and prayer. "From Aram."

I should just go, he thought. They had passed other villages and this was a common reaction. Ranulf had always known the legend of Agarosh, a bear of great age and eminence whom many noted Light-born from pure-blooded families had tried to bond in years gone by. All had perished in the trying, as was common, until a young Justo Nemati came along, proud in his confidence, declaring he would return to Aram a Moonrider, with Agarosh himself beneath him. And he had.

Until that point, many believed Agarosh would never be tamed or bonded. He was said to be centuries old, deeply intelligent, richly connected to the magical world. That Gideon Daecar had fought him to a draw was probably the famed First Blade's greatest feat. Which said a lot for a people so enamoured with the glory of triumph. *And now he returns,* Ranulf thought, *after twenty long years in isolation. For her…*He looked across at Saska, standing by the stream with the others, waiting. *He steps out of the wilderness to protect her. For she must be protected. She must.*

Finally, the village elder pulled his eyes away from the great bear, and put them on Ranulf instead. "You're heading for Aram, you say?"

"Yes, Aram. We heard two days ago from a traveller that Safina

Nemati had returned from Lumos. Perhaps you've heard that as well? It would be nice to have confirmation." *Because so much rides on it,* he thought. And that traveller hadn't seemed as reliable as he would like.

"Freely given," the elder said, smiling through dry wrinkly lips. "I have been told the same, friend." He looked at Agarosh, eyes glassy with awe. "She will be overwhelmed to see her brother's bonded bear again, after so long. I only wish I could come with you, to witness her face."

Ranulf decided best not to extend the invite. He had what he hoped for, though. "Well, I should go, then." He made to step away.

"Truly? Must you?" The elder gestured to the villagers. "We would sorely love to look upon him, a little longer. Perhaps...perhaps you could even get him to turn to face us?" True enough, the bear had faced resolutely away from them the entire time.

Ranulf smiled politely. "I have no power to get Agarosh to do anything, I'm afraid. And we have not the time. Once the horses are watered, we'll be on our way..."

"Then we will follow. Yes we will." The old man turned to the villagers, and shouted words to that effect. A cheer greeted them and Ranulf let out a sigh. *I should never have stopped,* he thought.

When they continued down the track, then, their retinue had swollen by some dozens, the villagers trailing along behind with children at their skirts and a host of bleating goats and barking dogs accompanying them as well. Ranulf gave his apologies, though Saska didn't seem to mind. "I think Agarosh is less pleased than I am," she said, with the first grin she'd shown in two days. "Maybe I should ride with him, keep him company. And make sure he doesn't do anything...violent."

"*Would* he?" Leshie was even less pleased than the bear to have the extra company, by that look on her face. There was some hope in the question. "At least he could drive them off," she grunted, looking back at the villagers. "This reminds me *far* too much of that stinking horde we rode with. Gods I hated that."

"You hate almost everything," Ranulf said to her. "And no, Agarosh won't attack anyone unless he's provoked."

"He attacked us on the mountain without provocation," Leshie argued.

"We gave him plenty of provocation by entering his territory. He was only defending it. But here? No. You've seen how placid he is,

Leshie. He is above all this. I doubt he even realises these people are following."

"Yeah, well I *do* realise. And I don't like it." She looked back once more, snorted, then cantered on up the road, to ride alone at the front.

Several hours later, their trail of men, women, children and livestock had grown into the hundreds. At each village they passed, more came pouring forth to accompany them on the final leg to Aram. The murmuring grew into a steady and constant din, of shouting and praying and barking and bleating. Leshie hated it, of course, though the Butcher just found the whole thing wildly amusing. "You think it is the great bear that causes this stir, Ersel San Sabar?" he said, "No, you are wrong. In truth it is me, the *greater* bear, who these people come to see." He pounded his scarred chest with his fist and beamed. As expected, Leshie gave the reaction he wanted.

"You're *not* a bear!" she shouted at him. "You're just some big stupid ugly sellsword who scars his own flesh to make himself look scary. And *stop* calling him Ersel San Sabar! His name is Ranulf. Ranulf Shackton. When we get to the city, you go one way and I'll go the other. If I see you again I'm going to give you a sharp red kiss with my blade, from here to here." She ran a finger across her throat. "I promise you I am."

"I could do with a kiss from you, little red. Just not the sort you're talking about." The Butcher laughed loudly and had a swig from his wineskin. "*Ersel,*" he said to Ranulf, just to rile Leshie a little more. "The city is not so far, just a few miles beyond those hills. It would be wise, I think, to ride ahead and give warning of our coming."

Ranulf agreed. There was a risk that Elio Krator would have sent word ahead to have men on the lookout for them, and he still had a great deal of support from a good many houses, great, middling, and small across the duchy. "I'll go," he said. "Though perhaps you might come with me, Butcher. You and a couple of others, for protection."

"You should not have let your pale skin come out, Ersel San Sabar," the Butcher said. "You make yourself a target."

"I've had enough of pretending to be someone else."

"Yeah, you hear that," said Leshie. "So *stop* calling him Ersel."

"*Ersel,*" said the Butcher, ignoring her. "I will come with you, as you ask. Perhaps little Ersella will come too?"

That was almost too much. Leshie looked like she was about to pounce right out of her saddle at him, but then a dog barked behind them, some children screamed out at play, and she remembered the following horde. "I'll come too," she said. "Anything to be away from this noise."

Ranulf went to Saska, riding with Agarosh some forty or so metres off the road. The enormous bear turned to look at him as he approached, contemplating the intrusion. Ranulf still felt awestruck whenever he was allowed to get so near. "Saska…" His voice came out a little squeaky, under that deep blue penetrating gaze. "I'm going to ride ahead, to the city. Announce your coming. Make sure there are no surprises in store."

Her face got nervous again at that. "You're leaving?"

"Just for a little bit. We're only an hour or so ride away. I'll see you soon."

"Fine…OK." She nodded and drew a breath. "I'll stay with Agarosh." She looked back. "There're a lot of people now, Ranulf."

And looking at her as much as the bear, Ranulf realised. It was clear enough who Agarosh was here for. No doubt a great deal of that murmuring back there was the crowds trying to work out just who Saska was. "You're going to need to get used to crowds, Saska," he told her.

She nodded, knowing there was no way around that. "Agarosh tells me he won't enter the city. Too many people. He'll stay outside the walls for now."

For now? "So…he's intending on staying?" Ranulf had wondered if the bear would simply wander back to his mountain after delivering her safely to Aram.

Saska glanced up. "He's…unsure. We're negotiating, Ranulf." She gave him another grin, though the shadow of nerves remained. "Find out about Rolly for me, will you. Whether he's still alive."

"I will. It'll be the first thing I ask. I'll come tell you when you arrive."

"OK." She nodded again, took another breath, and built a more confident smile about her lips. "You'd best go, then. I'll see you in a little while."

A part of him misliked the idea of leaving her for the final stretch, after going so far away to fetch her. But he put that aside, joined the Butcher, Leshie, and Marco of the Mistwood, and rode on, leaving Merinius in charge. They rode swift, passing over the hills ahead at a strong canter, enjoying the feel of the wind in their faces as the sun began to wheel away to the west, cooling the skies. When they crested the final hill and saw the shadow of Aram clothing the coast in the distance, the sea sparkling so splendidly beyond, Leshie gave out a *whoop* of joy, the Butcher smiled a broad toothy smile, and Ranulf Shackton breathed a great sigh of relief. Then he told himself it wasn't over yet, kicked his spurs, and kept on riding.

The northern gate was growing quiet when they arrived some time later, the immense city walls and great curved bastions rising high up above them, a deep gold in the fading light. Ranulf felt at once wary to look upon the soldiers up there on the battlements, and for a moment he wished he'd taken the Butcher's advice and continued as Ersel San Sabar after all.

They see I'm northern, and Leshie too, he fretted, as a pair of city soldiers came forward with their shirts of copper scale mail, feathered bronze cloaks, and eagle-crested halfhelms. Then he remembered that Lord Elio Krator no longer ruled the city. *She is back,* he told himself. *Safina Nemati is back.* And even if she wasn't, and he'd been sold a rotten lie, he knew for certain that Lord Hasham was here. *Calm,* he thought. *You're growing as nervous as Saska.*

"What business have you in Aram," one of the guards demanded. He peered at them as they passed the last few carts and wagons trundling through the open gates. "How many of you are there? Four, I see. And armed, yes. And…" He looked at Leshie, seeing her red hair and freckly cheeks. "Northern."

"*These* are northern," said the Butcher, giving Leshie and Ranulf a quick wave. "I am only *half* northern. And Marco of the Mistwood is as well. Marco is a name common in the south, and the Mistwood is a forest in the north. He covers both bases with his name." He laughed, as casual as anything, and swung to the ground. "My name is the Butcher. You may know me."

The guard behind nodded. "You're a sellsword. A Bloody Trader."

"A captain of such, yes. I am probably the best sellsword in all the world. Though my brother the Baker will not like to hear me say it. But he is not here." He shrugged, laughed again, and said, "Is the Grand Duchess returned?"

The men exchanged a look. "She is."

"You serve her?"

"Always."

"Then you serve us as well." The Butcher opened an arm. "I present an important man, who the Grand Duchess will wish to meet. Ranulf Shackton. Known to his *closest* friends as Ersel San Sabar." He gave Leshie a grin. The man just couldn't help himself. "But that is not important. Please run to the palace and tell Her Serenity of our coming. Oh, and add that her granddaughter is on the way, in the safe company of Agarosh the Magnificent, the One-Eye, greatest of all bears. Except me," he added, under his breath, once more for Leshie's benefit.

The two guards gaped at him. "We heard a rumour about this lost granddaughter," one said. "People say she was killed, near Cloaklake."

"A set up and a lie, of Lord Krator's making. She comes, in all her pretty glory. She really is *very* pretty, this princess." The men continued to stare, dumbfounded. "Well come on, go, go…" The Butcher clapped his meaty hands together. "They will be here soon. Rush to the palace. Go…go…"

He smiled and turned once the guards had dashed off, a great victorious grin on his face. He gave his tattered red cloak a dramatic swish. "Well, Ersel San Sabar, how did I do?"

"Very well," Ranulf had to admit.

"And you, Ersella, are you impressed?"

Leshie's eyebrows were twisted into a frown. "I can't speak Aramatian, you idiot. I have no idea what you were talking about."

"Ah. Well let me repeat it in the common tongue of the north. I had good japes in there, just for you."

"Please don't. I got the gist."

"Enough of a gist to get a kiss?"

"No." She folded her arms. "Never."

Ranulf looked up to the battlements. There was some shouting up there now, and beyond the gates as well. *The news is spreading.* Among the city guard in their garb of copper and bronze and gold, he saw several men wearing the white cloaks and dual-moons of Hasham, wandering along the wall walks. If he had any further fears, the sight of those men banished them. *Rest easy, Ranulf. You can rest easy now.*

It didn't take long for soldiers to arrive, a unit of city guards several score strong arriving to create a cordon outside the gates. After that, a mounted host appeared, paladins on their heavy horse, then came some Sunriders and Starriders as well, all adding to the royal cordon. Some wore white and grey, bearing the crest of House Hasham. Others had feathered cloaks of silver over mail shirts in shining black, with badges showing a black eagle silhouetted against a silver moon, its wings outstretched.

"Which sigil is that?" Leshie asked.

"Nemati," Ranulf told her. "That is the crest of the Grand Duchess."

As all that was going on, a senior man rode up on a sunwolf with long streaks of grey in its faded golden mane. "I am Sunrider Tallar Munsoor," he said. "Leal man of House Nemati. I am told you have a man named Ranulf Shackton among you?"

Ranulf rode forward.

"Master Shackton." Sunrider Munsoor gave him a long look up and down. "Yes, you are he. We met before, once. Do you remember?"

It came to Ranulf only as he said it. "I do. During a visit, some years ago. You kindly spoke to me of the latest security measures I ought to be aware of in the duchy."

"You were planning an expedition to study the holy people of the Everwood, if I recall correctly."

"Yes." Ranulf smiled. Seeing a man he knew was oddly comforting. "Just that. It wasn't the most successful trip in the end, but you were most helpful, Sunrider Munsoor."

"I was happy to assist." The man bowed, the model of courtesy. His sunwolf dipped its head as well. "Times are different now, of course. We are at war, north and south. But that is not to say all agree with such. Her Serenity is, as I'm sure you know, opposed to this conflict."

"I understand her to be a proponent of peace," Ranulf agreed. "Loyal to the tenets upon which the empire was built."

Tallar Munsoor gave a sigh, nodding. He had long brown whiskers growing down the sides of his face, going grey, though his chin and lips were shaven. His hair atop retained more of its colour, thinning at the temples and crown. He had a mild face otherwise, smart and kind, with wise grey eyes and a scholarly air. "Perhaps this would be best discussed later," he said after a while. "Her Serenity is approaching from the palace, and would like to speak with you alone, before her granddaughter arrives." He turned on his wolf. "Please, come with me."

Ranulf left the others beyond the gate, as he rode side by side with the Sunrider through the cordon. He remembered then what Saska had requested. "Can you tell me, Sunrider Munsoor, what has become of Sir Ralston Whaleheart? I have heard nothing of his fate since leaving the city long weeks ago. Is he…still alive?"

"The King's Wall lives, yes. Lord Hasham took him straight into his custody, after he had been wounded in the Red Pits. There was an incident…some assassin came to finish him off, but Hasham's guards managed to kill him before he could cut the Whaleheart's throat. He had his knife there, at his neck, when they came. It was very close, yes, very close."

"Elio Krator sent the assassin," Ranulf said. "He wanted to silence him, so he couldn't speak of Saska."

"Yes. But the Whaleheart is not built like normal men. I have never seen such size and strength. Any other man would have died from his wounds."

Ranulf nodded, allowing himself a smile. "Saska will be overjoyed," he said, more delighted for her than he could say. *She deserves this,* he thought. *Gods does she deserve it.* "She felt guilty," he explained, "for bringing Sir Ralston here. And subjecting him to Krator's tortures. This will be a great weight off her shoulders."

Tallar Munsoor smiled pleasantly, as his sunwolf loped along, matching his welcoming air. They passed the cordon and gate, moving into the yard beyond, where they stopped to wait. "Another man came to tell us of Saska," the Sunrider said. "Your friend Sallor Sanara, the shipwright. He begged audience with Lord Hasham and told him he had been sent by your request."

"That's true. I asked him to go to Lord Hasham on my behalf."

"Why did you not do this yourself?"

"I couldn't spare the time waiting. I had to follow the army, watch over Saska such as I could, and hope that word reached Lord Hasham so he might send men to bring her back."

"Which he did," Tallar said. "Yet when they returned, they reported that the girl was slain in a riot. This was a ploy by Elio Krator, was it? Or were some of Lord Hasham's men in on it?" He looked at him closely. "Tell me true, Master Shackton. If there has been some deceit…"

"They didn't know," Ranulf assured him. "Lord Krator brought out a lookalike. Even I had trouble recognising her as a double at first. After that…well, we had no choice but to rescue her ourselves."

"A wonderful tale, it sounds," the Sunrider said. "A tale of sacrifice and bravery. You have done a great thing here, Master Shackton, you and your friends. When Her Serenity was informed of her granddaughter's return, and supposed death, she sailed home from Lumos at once. Not once did she believe it true. She said to me, 'Tallar, there are lies here, and falsehoods, but soon the truth shall be unveiled. My granddaughter is not dead. She cannot be dead. We sail for Aram and await her. Fate will bring her home.'." He smiled. "And so it does appear."

Ranulf could hear the soft clopping of horse hooves on stone approaching from down the street, the groan of turning wheels. *She comes,* he thought, as the honour guard approached, bearing the Grand Duchess in her litter. "Age has blunted her strength," Tallar Munsoor confided as they neared. "No longer does she ride a saddle, as she once did, but rest assured, her wits are as sharp as ever."

He was glad to hear it. There had been rumours of senility of late, but he'd never given them much credence. "Are there customs I should observe when meeting her?" he asked.

"A man like you knows them already, I'm sure."

"I forget, I confess. Etiquettes can be hard to keep track of when you travel as much as I do."

"Understandable. In this case, a bow will serve. Let her speak first. And do not worry so. Her Serenity has little time for customs and etiquettes these days."

Still, Ranulf could not stop his heart from hammering as the carriage neared, a great wooden thing styled with gold and silver and bronze ornamentation, and a large figure of Calacan, the Eagle of Aramatia, surging from above the driver's seat in magnificent dramatic detail. He dismounted from his horse, wiping down his sweaty palms, attempting to make himself look presentable. After the heat and dust and grit of the desert, that wasn't so easy. *I wish I had time to wash,* he thought. But even as he had that thought, the carriage rolled to a stop, the heavy gold drapes opened before him, and the Grand Duchess of Aramatia, Safina Nemati, climbed out.

"Ranulf Shackton," she said, smiling at him. She wore a cloth-of-silver gown, flaring at the sleeves, the neck and breast decorated with strings of gleaming black pearls. Her hair was a shimmering grey, tied up in a hairnet of black gold, studded with tiny sparkling silver diamonds. She tottered over, her dress dragging along the stone behind her, her beauty still apparent despite her years. *She looks like her,* Ranulf thought. He could see Saska in the shape of the jaw, the cheekbones, the effortless regal charm.

He bowed, neat and low. "Your Serenity. It is such a profound pleasure to finally meet you."

"Rise," she told him, moving so close he could see every line in her face, every little twinkle in her honey-coloured eyes. She was taller than he'd expected, only a little shorter than he was. Ranulf Shackton was not vertically gifted, but he'd expected her to be smaller, more fragile and frail. "I'm told you've brought my granddaughter home?"

He swallowed in a dry throat. He could feel everyone looking at them, in the yard and at the gate, on the battlements above. "Yes, Your Serenity. And we have Agarosh with us as well."

"I heard that too." She took his hand, lifted it, and kissed the back of his palm. Ranulf was taken aback. He knew much of custom and etiquette, yes, and that was a startling honour. "Well deserved," she said, as though reading his mind. She glanced up and around them. "Look at all these eagles, perched upon my walls, listening. Now may not be the best time to discuss what you have come to tell me, Ranulf. And you do seem terribly nervous. I did not think you a man inclined to such."

"I'm not….as a rule. But…"

"But you have matters of great significance to share?" She moved closer, her voice a whisper. "Tell me. Are you here on the orders of a king, recently departed?"

His eyes widened. Yet he kept his calm. "I am. Orders sent through time, my lady. Orders that come with a secret."

"Ah. A secret. We all have those, I'm sure. But yours…it is of some import, I know."

"*Great* import. I have memorised it, my lady, as Godrin did instruct." He tapped his head. "It lives only in here now."

"Could there be a safer place?" She smiled. "That head of yours will need protecting, then. As will my granddaughter. What do you know of her?"

"I know that she is a lost Aramatian princess. I know that she is part Seaborn. I know that she is born to royalty, on her father's side."

"Oh you do?" Something sparkled in her eyes, and they went over his shoulder, to the hills beyond the city. Shadows and shapes were moving back there now, flowing down from the hills. One was greatly bigger than the rest. "How much does she know of herself, then? Perhaps that's the better question."

"Everything I've said."

"And less than what you're *not* saying?" She smiled again. *Sharp witted indeed.* "Well, we can speak later, Ranulf. Once I've had some time with my granddaughter. I'm sure we have a great deal to discuss."

A great deal, Ranulf thought, though already he felt more at ease. "Will you speak with her tonight?"

"Oh yes. Unless you think it should wait?"

Ranulf looked through the gate. "She's…sensitive, to this issue, of who she is. She's been lied to her entire life, my lady. I would tread carefully, if I could."

She considered that. "I will judge her, then, and decide." She frowned to the distance. "Did you bring half of Lord Krator's army back with you?"

He chuckled at that comment. "Alas no, only a few sellswords, a famous moonbear, and several hundred local villagers. Those last have only joined us this afternoon. They find fascination in Agarosh. And in Saska too."

The old woman smiled. "Oh, if only they knew."

She stepped away at that, though gestured for Ranulf to come with her, shuffling out through the gate and down the cordon of guards. The moon was climbing now, rising through a vermillion sky. She saw the Butcher, Leshie, and Marco of the Mistwood upon their horses nearby. "Your friends?"

"Friends would be a loose term. One, yes, the girl. She has been instrumental in your granddaughter's rescue. Her name is Leshie."

"She's very small," Safina noted. "Sometimes the finest souls can be stuffed into the smallest packages, don't you think?"

"Is that your way of calling me small, my lady?"

"Only if you think you're a fine soul, Ranulf Shackton." She considered the others. "Bloody Traders, I'm told. One is a captain. Let me guess. The big one with the red cloak and scars."

"He calls himself the Butcher," Ranulf told her, nodding. "As frightening as he looks, I've met few men so unashamedly jovial." He thought now might be a good time to tell her of his demands. Still, he felt a little seedy going straight into it. "He…he expects payment, my lady, for helping escort us here. We had an agreement, with a merchant, but…"

"He'll be paid," she said, sensing his discomfort. "I know how much these sellswords love their coin. I'll give him so much he need never sell his sword again, if he doesn't wish it."

Ranulf sighed. *Another matter sorted.* "He'll be most pleased to hear it. Thank you, my lady."

She waved that off, watching the shadows near. Ranulf wondered if he might bring up the small matter of Cliffario Denlatis and the hand of Lady Asherah Tamaar, but imagined that might be one battle too many. *And she grows nervous herself,* he could see. A woman who'd spent all her life in the public eye knew well enough how to hide her discomfort, yet all the same, he could see the tension in her eyes. "My lady, I wonder if you have tidings from the north," he said. "And the east. We've heard nothing of the siege at Eagle's Perch since we left the warcamp."

"And you want to know what will become of the treacherous Lord Elio Krator?" She didn't turn to him; her eyes were fixed on the form of Agarosh, easily visible now, and more so the starcat slinking alongside him, and the girl sitting in her saddle. "From what I have heard, Ranulf, Lord Krator's army have faltered. I cannot speak for the sunlord himself, but the Tukorans have driven his army back and won the fortress. As to the north, I will have to speak to you later." She drew a shaky breath and freshened her lungs. "My granddaughter nears, and I would like to be alone when I meet her. Tallar, lend me an arm. The ground looks uneven and the last thing I want is to fall flat on my face in front of her."

Tallar Munsoor stepped in, smiling. "I'll keep you steady, my lady, never fear."

He led her out to the front of the cordon, to await the return of her long lost granddaughter.

63

Saska

She stood at the summit of the three-tier pyramid palace of Aram, the cool night air tugging at her cloak, stained red and brown by the dust of the desert. Her hair hung down in unwashed waves, skin filthy from the ride through the plains.

What would Elio think of me now, she thought, staring out toward the hills across the restless Amedda River, where Lord Krator's residence was perched. Every day in the sunlord's company, she'd been scrubbed and scoured and polished to perfection. *I was his prize, his bright shiny prize.* Now here she was, at the top of the palace Krator had craved, filthy and unwashed. The thought made her smile.

Footsteps whispered on the smooth stone behind her, and her grandmother appeared at her side on the high garden terrace. *My grandmother, the Grand Duchess of Aramatia.* "Wine, child," she said, setting a silver cup on the broad sandstone balustrade. "Or would you prefer something else? Tea, perhaps, I have many varieties of tea."

"Wine is perfect...my lady," Saska said.

"*Grandmother*, Saska. I am your grandmother."

"Yes…Grandmother."

It felt so odd to say it, so very, very odd. Saska had never had a father, nor a mother, nor brothers or sisters or uncles or aunts. No cousins. No nieces and nephews. No grandfathers or grandmothers, until today. It was much to take in, and the last hour had been a blur;

meeting her outside the gates with all those soldiers watching, and the villagers who'd followed them too, and the men on the battlements and above the gate, and everyone else who'd stood gawping as she joined the Grand Duchess in her carriage, and rode through the streets to the palace.

They had spoken a little, then, but only simple things, small things. The weather, they had talked about the weather a bit, she remembered, and how Saska had met Joy that day on the plains. They'd spoken of Ranulf, who had been such a mentor to her, and Leshie, such a spirited friend, and Sir Ralston, her gallant protector, who was still alive, to her eternal relief, and fast recovering from his wounds. Saska had said how beautiful the city was at dusk, and had commented on her grandmother's dress, and the diamond encrusted black hairnet she wore. But half of what they'd spoken about she could scarcely even recall. The bigger questions would be left for later, for when they were alone, and those had been simmering in the back of Saska's head all the while. *What happened back then? Why did you send me away? Did you ever want me? Is it true what Elio said of my father?*

But still she couldn't ask them. She took the cup and had a sip to steady herself. "The view is so lovely up here." More small talk, but she didn't care. "I would look at the palace every day from Elio's residence. It's strange to be up here, after all that." *So very, very strange...*

"This is where you were born, Saska." Her grandmother turned to look back through the residence, gesturing to a corridor that bled away into the gloom. "Just through there. That is where you came into the world, pink and perfect. I have seen many births before, but never one like yours. You were silent, you know, when you arrived. *Silent*. You never made a sound."

For some reason that disquieted her, for her mother had died the same day. "Were you worried?" she asked. Most babies came out bawling, she knew. "That I was so quiet."

"No. I was not worried, not for you. Silent you may have been, but there was a determination in your eyes." She reached out and cupped an old wrinkled palm to Saska's cheek. "You have your father's eyes, you know. Not just the colour, that radiant blue, but the shape, the strength. Oh, he was strong. So much stronger than he ever knew. As you are."

She swallowed, suddenly so nervous. *This is it,* she thought. *The truth.* "Who was he? Elio...he said...he said he was a slave. He said he…" She couldn't even say it, not in front of her grandmother. Not about her own daughter. Not to her.

But Safina Nemati said it anyway. "He said he raped her, didn't he?"

Saska nodded. Her chin was low. She looked up through her glimmering blue eyes. *My father's eyes.* "Is it…true?"

"That he forced himself upon her?" Safina Nemati shook her head. "No, it isn't true, Saska. Your parents loved one another, for the brief time they had. You are the fruit of a loving union, never believe otherwise."

She could breathe again. "I never did. Not really." Her hand was shaking when she raised her cup again to drink. "But…he *was* a slave? That part's true? Mar Malaan told me he had been brought here on a slaving ship, when he was only young."

"He was still a teen," Safina said, turning her eyes south, away to the bustling harbour, swaying with a forest of masts and hulls. "A young man with a great head of rich black hair, and piercing blue eyes that had all the ladies in the palace swooning." She smiled. "Oh yes, your father was a handsome young man, child. But a slave? Never. He served here, yes, under my watchful eye, but only ever under the illusion of bondage. That was my task, to take him in, and watch over him. A task given to me by a king."

"Godrin," Saska whispered at once. She remembered his words. *You're exactly where you're meant to be.* "He *sent* my father to you?"

"No. Your father was brought here by happenstance, and by his own untamed spirit of adventure. King Godrin had only glimpsed his coming in the Eye of Rasalan and asked that I look out for him. He was not hard to spot, with that hair and those eyes. Even at sixteen, he was strong and muscled, singleminded and daring as his own father was. You have inherited that, such as I've heard. I'm told you bear godsteel as naturally as anyone?"

Saska recalled the day she'd first grasped the metal, when Lady Marian had rescued her from that wagon, along with Ranulf, and put her godsteel dagger in her hand. It had felt *right*, more right than anything had before, just as bonding Joy had later. *And when I dove beneath those waves and fished about that reef*, she thought. *When I stayed down there for long minutes at a time. That had felt right too.*

"I took to it well," she said eventually. "I missed it. Being without its touch when I first came here. Until I was given this." She tapped the shortsword at her hip.

The Grand Duchess studied it. "A nice blade. Did these sell-swords give it to you?"

She shook her head. "A merchant called Cliffario Denlatis. He gave it to Ranulf, who gave it to me."

"The same thing happened once before, did it not?" Her grandmother smiled at her. "Sir Ralston gave you a blade, a gift from King Godrin." She saw the question in Saska's eyes and said, "He told us, the King's Wall. He said your weapons were taken from you, this dagger included, when Lord Krator took you prisoner."

She nodded, half forgetting about that wondrous blade. "He stored it in his armoury, I think. He let that slip at dinner, once. Perhaps…perhaps you could have it retrieved?"

"Oh, child, I already have." The old woman turned in her cloth-of-silver gown and shuffled back into the residence. Saska followed. Beyond the terrace was a large audience chamber, with comfortable chairs and recliners, cushions and drapes. There was a table, with talon-legs and eagle-heads at the corners, wrought in silver. Atop it was a box. "Go ahead, child, open it up."

Saska stepped in and opened the box. Within was the dagger, six inches of misting godsteel in a shimmering pale blue, gently curved along its edges to a point as sharp as a pin. The hilt and pommel were marked with ornate silver symbols that she had never been able to translate.

"Pick it up, Saska. I would see you bear it."

So she did, reaching in, folding her fingers around the haft. She turned the blade over in her hand, looking at those strange symbols. Her grandmother was watching her closely, some deep fervent look in her eyes. Saska frowned to see that look. "Do you…know what they mean?" she asked. "I was never able to understand them."

"They mean you are the heir of Varin, Saska."

The words didn't settle in her, not at first. When they did, she looked up with a frown. "I'm…"

"Your father's father was King Lorin, the last of the Varin Kings. You know the story of him. How he died fighting a kraken with the Nightblade in his hand." She gestured to the dagger. "This was *his* dagger, and his father's before him, and his before him, going back millennia. King Lorin left it in the City of Thalan when he went on his final hunt. He left it there with the woman he had fallen in love with, the woman he had secretly wed. Princess Atia, the fourth child of King Astan of Rasalan and Godrin's younger sister, who died bringing a child into this world. That child was your father, the boy who lived in this palace. A child raised in secret on the Lonely Isle, for his grandfather King Astan had glimpsed in the Eye of Rasalan his purpose. He had seen the dangers the boy would face. So he hid him there, to be raised under guard, but ever was your father his own father's son. Ever was he adventurous and audacious as King Lorin was.

"So he escaped, one day, when he was sixteen years old. Tired of living his life in secret, not knowing the truth of who he was, he crept down to the coast, found a small sailing boat, and escaped through the raging seas. Half Seaborn on his mother's side, with Atia's rich blood flowing through his veins, he made it beyond the snags and rocks and mists that most sailors fear. He sailed east, for the coast of Rasalan, but could find no place to land. So around the cliffs and shores he went, searching, until eventually the seas got the better of him, and a great storm swelled in the skies, and he and his small boat foundered, dragged down to Daarl's Domain.

"He awoke on a slave ship, bearing south under a summer sky, forced to row and forced to work, until he made berth here in Aram. My men were waiting, watching at the docks, as instructed. They saw him, bought him, and brought him here to the palace, to be kept in secret, to live and to work and to fall in love with my daughter, so that they might have a child of their own. *You*, Saska. You are that child."

She stepped in. "Your father's name was Thalavar, the secret child of King Lorin of Vandar, and Princess Atia of Rasalan. King Godrin is your great uncle, he who did watch over you when he took his father's throne. You are the blood of the *blade*, Saksa, and the *sea*, and the *light*. You are the blood of royalty, born of Thala's line, and Lumo's, and direct descendent of Varin himself..."

Saska stared, shivering. The silver-blue blade was barely clutched in her hand, slipping, slipping from her grasp. *Silver and blue*, she thought. Her mind went to Elyon Daecar, and the dream he'd had of her. *He told me I turned into a light of silver and blue. He thought that meant my father was from Vandar. And he was right...he was right. Lorin. King Lorin is my grandfather...*

She stumbled back, the knife falling from her grasp, hitting the floor with a heavy dull thud. Her eyes blurred momentarily. She heard her grandmother talking. "Breathe, child, take a breath, just breathe."

My grandmother, the Grand Duchess. My grandfather, the Vandarian King.

Faces swirled before her eyes. She saw King Lorin battling that kraken out on the raging seas, Nightblade to grasp. She saw a boy in a boat with rich black hair, fighting the waves and failing, his skiff turning over as he drowned. She saw him being dragged out by slavers, thrown onto deck under the baking sun. She recalled her grandmother, her *other* grandmother, and what she knew of her. *Tuberculosis*, she thought. *Princess Atia died of tuberculosis.* But that was a lie. Another lie. *How many have I been told?*

She put her hands to her knees, struggling for breath. *Godrin knew,* she thought. *He sent Sir Ralston to protect me. To give me that blade. He knew who I was…he knew, and he let me suffer anyway.*

She needed air. Standing, she rushed for the balcony, striding across the garden terrace and to the wide stone balustrade. The city opened out before her. The river, the harbour, the hills, the walls. All was a blur of colour and movement. She took several deep breaths. *Thala, Lumo, Varin,* she thought. *But I'm a mutt, just a mutt, a servant and a slave and a farmhand and a maid…*

"Saska…"

She spun. "How long have you known?" she blurted, seeing her grandmother there before her. "Did you know where I was? Did Godrin? Did you know what I *went through*, living under Modrik Kastor's roof? And everything else…" She thought of Lord Quintan, and his soft fleshy body, and his fumbling hands, and the sounds he made when she stuck his own blade in his gut. She wondered what had come of Master Orryn and Llana for that, murdering a noble in their house. She thought of Griffin Kastor, and that oafish soldier Borgin, who she'd killed as well. She remembered the days under Cecilia Blakewood's wing, and Elio Krator's. There had been patches of freedom in there, but so much of it was suffering and servitude, control and abuse. She looked her grandmother in the eye again. "*Did you know*?" she demanded.

The old woman shook her head. "I was never told where you were, child. When I sent you away as an infant, I hoped to put you into a caring home, a good home, to be raised in peace and secrecy, away from Elio Krator's wrath. But it was wartime. The handmaid who took you north was killed, and you were taken into bondage. I asked Godrin many times if he had glimpsed you in the Eye, but he did not say. He only told me you were on the right path. The path that would make you into who you are today. He told me that to interfere would be to interfere with the future, and with fate. The steps you have taken to be here have all been necessary, however tragic."

Saska turned away again, looking out on the world. Her mind went back to her one and only meeting with King Godrin, the day the Book of Thala was stolen from the palace. The day he told her those immortal words. *You're exactly where you're meant to be.* He had been so melancholic, apologising for all she'd been through. *He said he hoped I'd understand, one day,* she remembered. *He knew I'd come here, and learn all this. He knew how angry I'd be…*

She filled her lungs and cleared them, as Joy came out to nuzzle at her side. The cat was a calming presence, always. *What would I do without her?* She thought some more, trying to piece it all together in her head, trying to understand. She could see Agarosh out there, beyond the walls, his great shadow sitting upon a hill. Many people crowded around nearby, humming in prayer. *He agreed to protect me,* she thought, *as Sir Ralston did.* The biggest man in all the world, and this most fabled of bears. *Why? Why am I so important?*

She turned to face her grandmother again. "What is your purpose for me?" she asked her, unable to restrain the accusation in her voice. "I'm born of north and south, of the blade and sea and light, you said. I'm royal, from Lumo's line, and Thala's line, and… and even Varin's." She still could scarcely believe that. *My grandfather, the swashbuckling King Lorin, who fought krakens for fun.* She had to laugh at the madness of it. "So…I'm to help unite the world, is that it? Help bridge the gap between north and south?"

Safina Nemati judged her words. "You are unique, Saska. In your bloodline. Who better to bring the peoples of the world together than you?"

"So that's it?" Saska snorted softly. "I'm a puppet? A pawn?" Somehow that disappointed her. "Elio was right, then. He said the same. He said you and Godrin were only using me."

Safina shook her head. "You're not *just* a puppet, Saska." She stepped forward, moving to a chair to sit. "Come, sit here with me."

"I'd rather stand."

"I know. But do me this favour, child. Please, come sit."

She wants me off my feet for this. Saska moved over and took a seat opposite her grandmother, across a small terrace table. She sat uneasily, waiting.

Her grandmother looked deep into her eyes. "There is a prophecy, Saska, that foretells of the rise of Eldur. This is commonly known in Agarath, if not so commonly believed. Those who have long adhered to it have done so under the faith that Eldur would rise by the hand of his own blood, and that he would rise benevolent. Certain of these Agarathi scholastic factions think this is the key to ending the War Eternal, once and for all. They think Eldur will rise to master the Soul of Agarath, and that the heir of Varin will rise to master the Heart of Vandar. These artefacts are the last burning embers of the gods themselves, and thus are the very essence of war. If figures of sufficient power come forward to master and command them, thus will the fires of war go out. And thus will our world come to peace."

Saska listened quietly. "So you believe I am this heir of Varin, to master the Heart of Vandar?" She wasn't understanding much of that, in all truth, or believing it. The Heart of Vandar required that the Five Blades be combined, she remembered Ranulf telling her, though in all history that had never happened.

"It is not a matter of belief, but knowledge," her grandmother said. "You are the last of Varin's direct blood. You are his last living heir."

Saska shook her head. It was an instinctive reaction. "I can't be his heir. Vandar is a patriarchy. If you think they would accept me as their queen…"

"This has nothing to do with the crown, or ruling. This is about ridding the world of these cycles we call Renewals, cycles that have brought untold suffering to our world twenty five times over the last three and a half thousand years. This is the last of them, as foretold by Thala. But what lies beyond from here, we cannot yet know."

Saska thought of her maids, Yasha and Milla and Koya. She thought of their discussions on the oiling table as she was rubbed and massaged and cleaned. The two young girls seemed convinced that this was the ending of the world, that a battleground of fire and ash and death was coming. *They called it the Ever-War*, she remembered. *They said that the Wings had broken open like an egg, and a thousand dragons had flown out…*She had never given that too much mind, even with these reports of wild dragon attacks, but now…now it all felt more real. "Some people think this Last Renewal will end, not in peace, but in a world of endless war," she said. "That monsters will rise, and kingdoms will fall, and that…that it will be every man and woman for themselves." She looked into her grandmother's deep honey-coloured eyes. "Could that be true?"

"This is a possible outcome, yes, should we fail."

Saska balked at that. She'd expected her to dismiss it out of turn, as Yasha so often did. "But…these prophecies, they're…they're not real, are they? There are so many, and they all seem to contrast. How can you be sure? Maybe Eldur won't rise at all, like they…"

"Eldur is arisen, child."

Saska blinked at her. "He's…"

"Arisen, as foretold, by the hand of his blood. And in command of the Bondstone. Already the shadow spreads across the north, but it will only grow longer, and darker in the days ahead."

Saska was having some trouble coming to terms with that. "He's alive? After…after all this time? How…how can that…"

"He was sustained by the same power that gives life and strength to the dragons. The Breath of Agarath, the fires that burn eternal beneath the Wings. They kept him living, for this day to come, yet it took the Soul of Agarath to finally raise him. Now Agarath's vengeful spirit resides within him, driving him toward a dark purpose that will bring about these conditions you have just said. Kingdoms falling. Monsters rising. People fighting for survival in a battleground of fire, ash, and doom." She stopped, seeing the horror in Saska's eyes. "Unless he can be stopped."

Stopped. Saska inched away from her, in her chair. "By…you think by me?"

Her grandmother reached out to take her hand, squeezing. "None of us can win a war alone, Saska. It takes many to accomplish that. Yet some individuals are more important than others. The Agarathi prophecy that Eldur would rise benevolent is false, a fabrication created by Rasal manipulators, under the guidance of Queen Thala herself. This was a part of her puzzle…"

"*Why*?" Saska broke in. "Why would…why would she lead the Agarathi to wake *him*?"

"Because he must be killed. Eldur *must* be killed, Saska, and the Soul of Agarath destroyed. These artefacts, these embers of the gods…they must *all* be destroyed. Only in a world ridden of their spirits can this cycle of Renewals be ended for good. And so here we are, at the precipice now, staring into the void. It will be the end, one way or another. Peace or doom…those are the outcomes that lie beyond."

Saska drew her hand away, stood, turned, and went right back to the balcony. Her grandmother gave her time. *She thinks I'm Varin's heir.*

*She thinks I'm the only one who can wield the Heart of Vandar. But I'm a mutt, just a mutt...*It was ludicrous, and overwhelming, and inexplicable to her still. "Might it not be someone else?" she asked after a while. She sounded like a little girl in her head, some scared little girl, hiding from the monsters under her bed. "This heir?"

She wants to tell me so, she thought, seeing that look in her grandmother's eyes. *She wants to comfort me and reassure me, but she can't, not in this.* "By blood, there is no one else...at least not that I am aware of, child. Yet I am but a tool, and a guide. It might be that information has been kept from me, regarding you, and others. Or it might be that this prophecy itself is less literal, and more symbolic..."

Saska seized on that. "A *symbol,*" she said, nodding. "The Vandarians admire strength. This is how they choose their First Blades, their champions, their greatest warriors. They're the strongest, the mightiest of them. Maybe...maybe this heir of Varin is the same. The *greatest* of them. The man most *worthy* to lead."

Safina Nemati smiled softly. "Maybe," she said, quietly. "It is wise to consider all ends, Saska, yet not to *rely* on them. For here we stand, facing the unknown, and none can say what will happen from here. Not for certain. We can only wonder, and guess, and stand by what we believe. And I believe in *you*, Saska. After everything you've been through, after all the darkness through which you've passed, I do not think there could be anyone better to help lead us into the light."

Saska nodded quietly. She could not even begin to imagine what she was being asked. *Even if I am the blood of Varin*, she thought, *I'm still not pure. Only a quarter of me is from King Lorin. Only a quarter. I'm as much a Seaborn as I am a Bladeborn, and I'm more Lightborn than either, by blood.* She looked at Joy again, and felt like she wanted nothing more than to ride away with her into the hills and let this future play out without her. *But I can't,* she knew. *I have to help, however I can.* She scratched under Joy's chin, and the cat emitted a strong rumbling purr. Suddenly, strangely, the world felt more simple again.

Her grandmother stood and came to join her. "She really is such a beautiful starcat, Saska. Do you mind if I..."

"Of course...please..."

Safina reached out and gave the cat a stroke. She responded by purring yet louder. *I can trust her,* Saska knew then. *She is my grandmother, and I can trust her to help protect me and guide me.* "Joy," the woman said, smiling. "You gave her this name, because that is what she symbolises for you. Joy. Happiness. All that is goodness and light." She looked up. "I would hear more of this, sweet child. Of what joy you have had in your life. Of the people you have loved, the friends you have held dear. I would see you smile, and hear you laugh. I would see the granddaughter I have so longed to know." She flicked a hand. "Enough of this doom and gloom. We can leave that for another time; it will keep, of that I'm quite sure." A smile teased her lips. "So let us eat, and drink, and get to know one another, just you and I. Gods and prophecies can wait, child." She cupped her cheek. "*You* are much more important."

So they took their seats again, out on that tranquil garden terrace, as the sounds of the city set a distant din beneath them. They drank wine, and ate sweetbreads and fruits and laughed, oh they laughed, as Saska put her fears and frailties aside, for a time, determined not to think on them.

Yet that night, once they had parted, and Saska slept alone in her bedchamber in the palace residence, a dark figure came to her in her dreams. A figure cloaked and cowled, with a voice like whispered thunder, pulsing and flickering with flame as he moved.

"Stay back," she said to it, swatting out with her silver-blue knife. "Don't come any closer. Or I *will* kill you." Yet forward it came, and backward Saska went, until suddenly the knife in her grasp came alive with light, growing into a great glowing blade, brighter than a newborn star, so bright she could scarcely look upon it. She held it forward, standing tall, filled with strength and courage. "Go back!" she roared, as loud and fierce as she could. "Go back to your shadows, demon. You are not welcome here!"

The cloaked creature stood still, waiting, making not a sound. Then in a sudden burst of fire and shadow, the world erupted into chaos around him. Saska drew back in shock, turning her eyes around, and in that moment saw that all the world was burning. Castles, forts, cities, strongholds, woods and mountains all. Across the lands she heard screaming, and across the skies she saw them, swarming. A hundred of them, a thousand.

And all of them dwarfed by *one*…

She woke in a cold sweat, sitting bolt upright, panting. It was a dream she'd had before, once, when she'd been travelling the Lowplains with Lancel and Barnibus. A dream she hadn't understood back then. But now she did. *Eldur*, she thought, shivering. *And the doom he will bring*. And that blade. That great glowing blade, bright as the heart of a star. *No, not a star,* she thought. *That was the heart of a god…*

She would not sleep again that night, she knew. Rising from her bed, she returned to the cool of the balcony to look down upon the city as it slept. And there she stood, until dawn shimmered pink and gold on the eastern seas, musing on the possibilities of her future, and her fate.

EPILOGUE

The storm was strange today, and that was saying much. For long months Kai Juren had stood watching those queer crimson storms, yet this one seemed different. *Darker*, he thought. *And the red lightning is more fierce.*

He drew back from the telescope and frowned. Even from here, dozens of miles from the northern coast of the islands, he could see the storm fizzing and swirling, see the distant flashes of blood-red lightning cracking down from the cloud-curdled skies. "Odd," he said, to Tavin, who was stationed with him at the very top of the watchtower, hundreds of metres above the high headland. "Take a look. The skies stir strangely, Tavin."

Tavin was younger than him, and his subordinate, but had a wise head on youthful shoulders. He took Kai's place at the large telescope, closed his left eye, and looked through the eyeglass with his right. For a moment he turned the instrument around on its swivel-stand, searching the distance, before drawing back. "Strange, I agree," he said. "But everything is strange now, Kai."

And wasn't that the truth. For months the men of Dragonwatch had stood witness to the bizarre, seeing the Ire of Agarath bubble and boil in the skies, seeing the dragons screeching and flying overhead, leaving the Wings in numbers never known before. Their duty was to observe, record, and report what they were seeing, a holy duty that had gone back long millennia.

And a duty that no longer has merit, Kai Juren thought dismally. The essence of their purpose was to watch for the *special* dragons, the ones that would fly to the Nest, to be bonded to the Fireborn. But to be bonded required the Bondstone. *And that is at the Nest no longer,* Kai knew.

He gazed into the distance, musing on what the world had become. There had been much talk of late that the arcane prophecy of Eldur's return had come true. The Fire Father was risen, people were proclaiming, and the command of the Bondstone was his. Some of the men here at Dragonwatch had even reported *seeing* Eldur themselves. Not Kai or Tavin, no, but others who'd been on watch one day, months ago, when they'd sighted a group of dragons down on a distant beach, to the east. It was a beach frequented by a known corpse-robber and thief who would climb down there from the cliffs, sometimes, and look for valuables amidst the refuse washed up on shore.

That day, the old thief had been down there again, picking through the rocks, when another man had appeared, a white-haired man in a rich red robe with a black staff in his grasp, topped with a glowing orb. They had spoken for a short time, the men on watch reported, before a dragon had come in behind the thief and bathed him all in fire. On hearing that, Kai had smiled. It was just, he thought. That old thief was a parasite, and no one at Dragonwatch liked him. That he was killed by a dragon was fair reward for all the dead he'd picked at and pillaged.

All that had been the talk of Dragonwatch for long weeks after, yet at first Kai hadn't believed it. *They must be lying, or seeing things,* he'd thought. *Eldur cannot be risen.* But then he heard about the theft of the Bondstone at the Nest, and he heard that Tethian, son of Dulian, the long-missing prince, had been working to revive Eldur all along. And he learned other things too, things that would not have made sense on their own, but together...together with the rest...they joined to form a picture that Kai Juren did not like.

The Ever-War, he thought now, looking out at the crackling red storm. *The return to the Days of Dread.* He had grown up in a simple rural community not far from the Bloodgate at the border with Lumara, and those sorts of stories were always in his ear. His mother had been half-Lumaran, on her own mother's side, and so spoke often of the Ever-War and how the Wings would one day crack open like an egg and a thousand dragons would swarm out. That image had stuck with Kai as a boy, and he'd decided then that he'd become a man of Dragonwatch, standing sentry at that famous high watchtower, the highest in all the world, watching for the day the dragons would come.

The long years since then had made him see that life at Dragonwatch was not as he'd expected. It was mostly dull, in truth. So far from the islands, the dragons were only ever seen in glimpses, moving through the clouds or hunting in the seas, and counting them was impossible. Still, they noted down each they spotted, wrote of their appearance and colours and physical quirks, and tried to figure out how many there might be living there.

Not a thousand, he had always thought, *not nearly so many as that.* Yet recent events had made him wonder if he was wrong. Perhaps there were more *inside* the islands, down in the network of tunnels and passages and chambers beneath the surface. Maybe...maybe if the island *did* break open, they'd come flying out, as his mother and his grandmother always said. Maybe then the stories of the Ever-War would come true, and every foul creature in the earth would crawl from their tunnels and caves, and the beasts would creep out of their woods, and the monsters of the ocean depths would come up to the surface, to pull ships and sailors to the bottom of the sea.

He shuddered to think of what a world like that would be like. Already, he'd seen dozens of dragons coming from the Wings, yet that was only dozens. What if there *were* hundreds? What if there *was* a thousand? If that happened, no one would be safe. Not even Eldur could control a *thousand* dragons, he knew. And the rest? The creatures of the deep, and the woods, and the mountains and caves, and all the dark places of the world? What if they all sensed the doom approaching and came crawling and slithering and prowling out at once? What then? What would happen *then*?

He felt Tavin nudge at his arm, disturbing him from his thoughts. He looked over. "What?"

The younger watchman was pointing to the distance. "Something's happening out there. I think...I think one of the mountains is erupting, Kai."

"*Erupting*?" Kai set his right eye to the glass, closing his left. He peered out to the distance, and saw that Tavin was right. A thick pillar of bulging black smoke was pouring into the skies, away on the southern island. He drew back again, rubbed his eye, and had another look. He could see fire now, bubbling from the top of one of the mountains. It was west of the southern isle, near the northern shore, so far as he could see. *Eldur's Shame*. That's what some men called it. The mountain where Eldur had made his tomb. Where he had been kept alive, rumour said, by the Breath of Agarath beneath him…

And Agarath breathes harder than ever, Kai thought, disquieted. Those rivers of molten flame that ran beneath the mountain had never once boiled up to the top, that he knew. He pulled away and looked at Tavin in confusion. "It is Eldur's Shame, Tavin. Agarath's Breath rises to the top."

"Let me see." Tavin moved in to look. A moment later, he exhaled softly. "By the Fire Father," he whispered. "I…I see more smoke rising, more fire. It is coming up fast, Kai. It looks…it looks like the top of the mountain is *shaking*. Like it's about to…"

Explode, Kai thought, watching. He did not need to look through the telescope to see what happened next. Even from so far away he could see it with the naked eye, the top of the mountain opening out into a great cloud of ash and fire and smoke. Tavin pulled away in shock, though Kai did not take his place. He stared at the red storm, and the lightning, and the high heavy clouds, and the lower one, that one of ash and flame and molten rock, the pyroclastic cloud that came surging out down the slopes of the mountain and spread out across the islands in a vast, black shadow, killing all before it.

The two men observed in stunned silence for a time, until finally, after long minutes had passed, the sound arrived to greet them. It came as a juddering *boom*, shaking all through the air, and above them, the bells that were sounded when dragons were sighted began tolling as they trembled.

There was no need to silence them.

Kai moved back to the telescope, to get a better look. His heart was pounding, beating hard against his chest. From the top of the mountain, through the choking cloud of fire and smoke and ash, he saw one, two, ten of them coming, twenty, fifty, a hundred, more…

Holy gods…

Each was no more than a little black shape, speeding away into the skies, scattering. Kai tried to keep count, but couldn't keep up. He watched in silent awe as the fables he'd heard in his youth came true. *It cannot be*, he thought. *A thousand? Are there truly a thousand locked down inside?*

But suddenly it wasn't the numbers that mattered to him. Among the little black shapes, zipping out through the smog, he saw one that dwarfed all the rest. He could not conceive of its size, not entirely, not from here, but it was the largest he had ever seen. *The largest there had ever been.* Through the top of the mountain it came, beating up and away into the storm, moving fearlessly through the tangles of red lightning, bellowing out in a terrifying roar that Kai could only think meant 'freedom'.

"Kai…what are you seeing, Kai?" he heard Tavin ask beside him. "Are there dragons? Should I be recording them?"

Kai Juren, long-serving sentry of Dragonwatch, could not summon the words to answer.

He could only stare, in horror, at the calamity in the skies.

At the titan from an ancient time.

At the dread in red and black.

THE END

The Bladeborn Saga will continue in Book Five - ***The Fetters of Fate***

ALSO BY T. C. EDGE

THE ENHANCED SERIES (MAIN SERIES):

The Enhanced (Book One)

Hybrid (Book Two)

Nameless (Book Three)

Assassin (Book Four)

Captive (Book Five)

Renegade (Book Six)

Invader (Book Seven)

Avenger (Book Eight)

Defender (Book Nine)

Nemesis (Book Ten)

Sequel (to main Enhanced series, and Warrior Race series):

The Enhanced: Awakening

The Enhanced: Conquest

The Enhanced: Fractured

The Enhanced: Invasion

THE WARRIOR RACE SERIES (ENHANCED UNIVERSE):

The Warrior Race (Book One)

The Red Warrior (Book Two)

Angel of War (Book Three)

CHILDREN OF THE PRIME SERIES (ENHANCED UNIVERSE):

The Chosen (Book One)

Trial of the Chosen (Book 2)

Blood of the Chosen (Book 3)

March of the Chosen (Book 4)

War of the Chosen (Book 5)

Fall of the Chosen (Book 6)

Rise of the Chosen (Book 7)

Fate of the Chosen (Book 8)

VARIANT SERIES (ENHANCED UNIVERSE)

Variant (Book One)

Initiate (Book Two)

Survivor (Book Three)

Pathfinder (Book Four)

Legend (Book Five)

Prodigy (Book Six)

Worldkiller (Book Seven)

OTHER BOOKS BY THE AUTHOR:

THE WATCHERS SERIES:

The Watchers Trilogy:

The Watchers of Eden (Book One)

City of Stone (Book Two)

War at the Wall (Book Three)

The Watchers Trilogy Box Set

The Seekers Trilogy

The Watcher Wars (Book One)

The Seekers of Knight (Book Two)

The Endless Knight

The Seekers Trilogy Box Set

THE PHANTOM CHRONICLES:

The Last Phantom (Book 1)

Phantom Hunter (Book 2)

Phantom Legacy (Book 3)

Phantom Unleashed (Book 4)

www.ingramcontent.com/pod-product-compliance
Lightning Source LLC
Chambersburg PA
CBHW020720310726
48979CB00004B/1001

* 9 7 8 1 0 6 8 5 1 8 2 3 2 *